WUHAN

WUHAN

JOHN FLETCHER

An Apollo Book

First published in the UK in 2021 by Head of Zeus Ltd
This paperback edition first published in 2022 by Head of Zeus Ltd,
part of Bloomsbury Publishing Plc

9 7 5 3 1 2 4 6 8

A catalogue record for this book is available from
the British Library.

ISBN (PB): 9781800249899
ISBN (E): 9781800249851

Typeset by Divaddict Publishing Solutions Ltd.

Printed and bound in Great Britain by
CPI Group (UK) Ltd, Croydon CR0 4YY

Head of Zeus Ltd
First Floor East
5–8 Hardwick Street
London EC1R 4RG

WWW.HEADOFZEUS.COM

CONTENTS

BOOK ONE

THE ROAD TO WUHAN

To Paula.

Nations stumble upon establishments, which are indeed the result of human action, but not the execution of any human design. If Cromwell said, that a man never mounts higher, than when he knows not whither he is going, it may with more reason be affirmed of communities, that they admit of the greatest revolutions where no change is intended, and that the most refined politicians do not always know whither they are leading the state by their projects.

Adam Ferguson, 1767

1

The North China Plain. Autumn 1937.

Wei was a short, stocky man with a strong athletic body and sharp, observant eyes. Like all farmers he had a slight gait, as though his feet were trying to pin down the earth, his earth, as he walked across it.

It was just before dawn. While most of his family still slept, he was doing his first round of inspection. His farm consisted of six acres of thin interlocked plots and strips, set among a kaleidoscope of other farmers' strips and small fields and paddocks. They stretched off – north, south, east and west – seemingly into infinity.

His crops were laid out in immaculate east–west rows, exact as any military parade. On one plot grew cabbage, on the next gaoliang, then the burdock which was almost ready to harvest, then soya beans. All his crops were entirely without weeds. His eagle eyes noted three sturdy cabbage stems which had been bruised by his eldest son's clumsy hoeing. He would reprimand him for this, but Eldest Son worked with a willing heart.

Wei reached the strip where his wheat stood. Most of the crop had already been cut, gathered and threshed. The stalks stood against his courtyard's south-facing wall, drying completely before being used for thatching. The hulled grain was stored safe indoors in huge earthenware jars.

The rest of the crop, already cut, was stooked on the open strip ready for gathering. Wei had already stored sufficient grain for the family's winter needs and for sowing next spring. Which meant what stood before him now could be threshed, stored, then sold at market for a tidy profit when prices started to rise in late winter. He felt the ears. Still damp from the morning dew, but fat and ripe to his fingers. Farmers never feel more comfortable than when they have surplus grain in their storeroom.

He turned north to view his farmhouse, built within its surrounding courtyard wall. Already smoke was wisping out of the chimney which meant his second daughter, Cherry Blossom, was up and about her household duties. But then Wei saw something strange. Far, far beyond his farmhouse, on the very edge of the northern horizon, he caught sight of a dark sinister cloud. Lying low, crouching like a black serpent. What could it be? Farmers burning their stubble? Too early in the year. A thundercloud? He had never seen such a cloud in his life.

Puzzled, slightly apprehensive, he shook his head and continued his inspection. He passed a strip of millet, then rows of potatoes ready for lifting. As head of the family Wei bore sole responsibility for its well-being. His family consisted of his ageing father, his wife and six young children. It was his duty alone to protect them, to feed them, to secure their futures. If the farm failed, they would all starve.

But in some ways they were the least of his problems. Buried in the ground lay his ancestors, those who had farmed this land for countless generations before him. The Wei ancestors were never short of an opinion on when a crop should be planted, when harvested, whether a wedding was wise, should he buy another strip of land. In his prayers, Wei had to negotiate very carefully with them. They wielded great power in the afterlife, deciding who would be allowed to join them after death and who would be cast aside.

At night Wei worked while his family slept – repairing farm implements, mending furniture. Each morning he and his eldest child, a daughter, rose before dawn – he for his inspection, she to run errands in the village.

As he inspected his land he worked out mentally what work each family member would do that day. He and Eldest Son would transport the remaining stooks in for threshing. His son, aged thirteen, could only carry one at a time but he, Wei, would carry two under his arms and one strapped across his shoulders. He did not want to use the cart as two of the spokes on one of its wheels were rotting and could break if overloaded. He hoped to hold off repairs til he got money for his surplus wheat in the winter.

On the strip for family vegetables, most of them were past their prime and dying. The onions' spiky green leaves had long since died and been laid to one side, ready to lift. His second daughter Cherry Blossom would carry them back to the courtyard and plait them. Meanwhile his second son would strip the older leaves from the burdock patch and, having carried them back to the courtyard, climb onto the shed roof. Second Son was only five years old but more responsible than his elder sister Cherry Blossom, aged eight. She could pass the onions and burdock leaves up to him so he could lay them on the thatch to dry. The fennel and garlic up there were dry by now, so they could pass them down, tie them in bunches, and hang them in the storeroom. He passed the family's three walnut trees. Already their green-husked fruits were falling. Grandfather, while he was minding the two youngest children, could potter out with them and gather them up. Meanwhile Wei himself would get the long thin poles out of storage so the rest could be beaten down.

A family that is not working is dying.

He looked up at that cloud again. It still squatted there on the far northern horizon. He wondered if the rumours in the village were true.

Wei's eldest daughter stood in the village street. It was empty. A lesser being than this sixteen-year-old girl would have panicked. Not Eldest Daughter. She stared ahead of her, calculating. The news needed to be told. But how? How could she say to her family what had to be said so that they would believe her and act on it?

In front of her, as the first rays of sunlight started to strike out from the eastern horizon, Old Man Chen sat in the street with his back against a wall, smoking on his opium pipe, shivering in the early morning cold. Behind him, on the wall, he had pasted the pages of a recent newspaper.

He and Eldest Daughter – known to everyone as Spider Girl – were the only two people in their whole community who could read. Chen had taught her. Old Man Chen claimed to be indifferent to what he had just read in the newspaper. But Spider Girl knew she must act.

Wei was approaching the most difficult part of his daily journey. Some green, grass-covered mounds which stood just above the earth. In their midst grew an ancient wild pear tree, its branches pointing arthritically towards the sky. It had already shed all of its leaves. Its tiny fruits had been pressed into the sweetest of juices.

Among the mounds, as he approached, he could feel disquiet, turmoil. Beneath the soil which held their bodies he could sense the spirits of his ancestors, demanding – some of them quite rudely – to be told what was happening, what was causing such great upset in the world above?

Wei hastily lit two joss sticks to calm their nerves but it had no effect. Perhaps they were trying to warn him of floods, a new plague, maybe even of troops? A civil war had been going on for almost as long as Wei had been alive – but always when the rowdy soldiers had turned up demanding food and wine and his women, he'd been able to slip them enough money to keep them going down the road. Perhaps his ancestors' fears were connected to the rumours he'd heard in the village, to what Spider Girl had been trying to explain to him over the last few days but which he could not understand.

What was that black cloud?

Of all Wei's many duties – to his land, to his family, to his gods – his greatest was to his ancestors. To keep open the communication, the good feeling between those alive in his family and those who had died within it. But for some reason now they were angry and perturbed. Why? Suddenly the strangest of all sounds rolled through the vast landscape. He'd never heard such a noise before. It wasn't the shotgun his neighbour fired to scare away the crows. It wasn't thunder. Then again he saw that mysterious black cloud moving, unwinding across the northern horizon.

Wei started to panic. He felt he must be with his living family. But before he left he stopped before a tiny mound at a distance from the others, close to the roots of the wild pear tree. The grave of his elder sister. She who had loved him, protected him from all things, who had died in a famine when she was only seven years old. His parents had decided to abandon her so that he, their eldest son, might survive. She haunted the land outside the farmhouse for several days, her plaintive cries pleading for help, but Wei had been forbidden to take food out to her. He did once but was severely beaten. She died and her body was left for the wild dogs to devour before he himself managed to recover parts of her and secretly bury them close to her ancestors. Now it was always to her that he revealed his greatest fears, his deepest feelings. Today she stood at a great, great distance from him. She smiled sadly. She waved to him. As though wishing him farewell.

Wei had never known such a thing before. He turned and hurried back towards his farmhouse. The land of the living.

Spider Girl was hurrying along the rough trackway from the village to their farm. It was imperative that she reached her father and spoke to him before he entered the gate to the family courtyard.

She hurried with all her young might, but she wasn't very fast. Her gait was more like a waddle, a sort of slow roll. When she was only three years old a drought had occurred, leading to a terrible famine. Her mother was breastfeeding her newborn son, the family's first son, Eldest Son, and her mother decided – quite correctly, as Spider Girl now understood – to withhold food from her daughter so that her father – who fed the family – and her mother – who fed Eldest Son – and Eldest Son himself would survive. Her father found out about this. There were terrible rows between her father and her mother. Her mother would not feed her so instead her father would drop food to her from his bowl at the table, slip her raw vegetables as he returned from the field. Spider Girl would not die as his elder sister had died.

She survived. But because of her near starvation she developed rickets – in her hips, in her legs. Hence her hobbling gait, hence her universal name – Spider Girl. She wobbled and shuffled just like a giant spider.

She saw her father, close to the courtyard gate, hurrying towards it. She redoubled her pace, pains shooting through her legs and hips. He was about to go through the gate. She cried 'Father!' He stopped, was obviously in two minds, but then decided to wait for her. Usually when he saw her he smiled. Not this time. He looked worried, drawn. Good, she thought, I can get through to him. She hobbled up the last few yards.

'Father…'

'What is it?'

'Father, we must leave.'

'What do you mean, "leave"?'

'Father, the whole family must leave. Must pack food and shelter and our valuables and flee. The Japanese are coming.'

'Not this again. We can't flee. We can't leave our land. The Wei family have never left their land.'

'The Japanese Army are marching down from the north – their guns are firing, they are murdering all the people, every one of us, in all the towns and farms they come across.'

'How do you know this? It sounds to me like rumours.'

'Father, we must gather together all our belongings – enough food, clothing and money – and flee. They are marching from the north. They have flying machines, they have huge guns that can kill ten men with one bullet, they have great armoured machines. They kill all the Chinese they find, or they turn us into slaves and drive us til we die.'

'Where have you heard this?'

'I read it in the newspaper. The newspaper Old Man Chen posts on the village wall. Japanese soldiers compete with each other to see how many Chinese they can behead with their swords.'

'But they tell these stories about every war. When the warlord marched towards us twenty years ago with his army everyone thought it would be the end, he would kill everyone, but we managed to do deals with his men – they took our money but not our land.'

'They *will* kill us. The Japanese do not believe in heaven or morality any longer, Father. They believe in some European filth which is taught in their schools. That all human beings are descended from monkeys.'

Wei laughed. 'From monkeys?'

'Yes, Father,' said Spider Girl, getting desperate. 'The Japanese believe they have superior breeding to us, have become superior men, a master race, that we Chinese are only monkeys and rats they can kill or enslave as they wish. That's what their filthy European science teaches them. They believe all men are animals. Therefore they can treat us like animals.'

She fumbled beneath her jacket, drew out a scrap of paper.

'I tore this from Old Man Chen's newspaper. Listen, Father. This is what a German man witnessed in Nanking. Our capital city.

"Two days ago about thirty Japanese soldiers came to a Chinese house at #5 Hsing Lu Koo in the south-eastern part of Nanking, and demanded entrance. The door was open by the landlord, a Mohammedan named Ha. They killed him immediately with a revolver and also Mrs Ha, who knelt before them after Ha's death, begging them not to kill anyone else. Mrs Ha asked them why they killed her husband and they shot her. Mrs Hsia was dragged out from under a table in the guest hall where she had tried to hide with her one-year-old baby. After being stripped and raped by one or more men, she was bayoneted in the chest, and then had a broken bottle thrust into her vagina. The baby was killed with a bayonet. Some soldiers then went to the next room, where Mrs Hsia's parents, aged seventy-six and seventy-four, and her two daughters, aged sixteen and fourteen. They were about to rape the girls when the grandmother tried to protect them. The soldiers killed her with a revolver. The grandfather grasped the body of his wife and was killed. The two girls were then stripped, the elder being raped by two to three men, and the younger by three. The older girl was stabbed afterwards and a cane was rammed in her vagina. The younger girl was bayoneted also but was spared the horrible treatment that had been meted out to her sister and mother. The soldiers then bayoneted another sister of between seven and eight, who was also in the room. The last murders in the house were of Ha's two children, aged four and two respectively. The older was bayoneted and the younger split down through the head with a sword."'

Wei shrugged. 'Nanking? Where is Nanking? I have never heard of it. Listen, my dear child, these foreigners, these Europeans and Americans, are all liars. They will write anything to trick us, steal from us. You should not believe them.'

'Father – why do you deny you've heard these rumours, talked to people in the village about them…?'

'Who I talk to and what I talk about is my business.'

Spider Girl looked directly at him. Wei looked downwards. Hanging his head. 'I cannot leave. I am head of the family. If we leave we could lose all our lands.'

'If we do not leave we will lose all our lives. After the war we can return.'

'But our neighbours may have taken our land.'

'If they do not leave now, none of them will survive.'

'But who will tend the land, produce the food?'

'The Japanese will seize the land and farm it. They will fertilize it with our dead. Our kind will be known no longer.'

'They will need someone to till the land, gather the crops.'

'They and their great machines will do that.'

Wei still stood there with his head hanging. Spider Girl looked at him. She loved him so much.

'Father,' she said, pointing to the north, pointing to the long black cloud hanging and billowing on the horizon, 'what is that? You must have seen it.'

He still stared at the ground. He shuffled his feet.

Just at that moment another strange boom rang across the landscape.

'What is that sound, child?' he asked softly.

'The sound of the Japanese guns. The great big ones they possess which can kill ten, twenty people with one bullet. And they possess many of them. Look at the horizon, Father. That cloud is the smoke, the dust the Japanese soldiers throw up into the air as they burn and pillage all the buildings and kill all the people in their way. Those devils will be here in this village, in our farmhouse, by this evening, murdering and raping us.'

'But where will we go?'

'In the newspaper they say people should go south. They are gathering at a place called Wuhan.'

Still he looked downwards. Almost stamped the ground as he fought desperately to keep it under his feet. All the land he had toiled unendingly on since childhood to keep immaculate and fruitful to feed his family. It was slipping away.

'When you spoke to them just now, Father, how were our ancestors? Were they calm?'

A look of sheer agony split his face. His whole body fought convulsively for its next breath. Finally it came. 'If we desert them now, if we cease to worship and pray for them, they will cut themselves off from us for all eternity. We will be like lost ghosts.'

'And what did the spirit of your elder sister have to say? Because I know you love her more than all the others.'

He paused. 'She waved me farewell.'

He reflected a moment, then looked up at Spider Girl. He spoke to her quite calmly and with affection.

'Why do you insist we leave, daughter? You must know that if we flee a great distance, your legs will not be able to carry you and neither will we. We will have to abandon you. Just as our family abandoned my elder sister.'

'I know that, Father. I say it because I love you and my family above all else. I want you to survive.' Then she smiled. 'Besides, I have no intention of dying.'

There was a pause.

'Firstly,' stated her father, 'I have some family matters I must deal with in our farmhouse. I'll want you to keep away from there but work out in your head what we shall need for our journey, and who in the family should gather what. I will also think about such matters as I talk.'

He turned towards the farmhouse and 'family matters'. The first 'family matter' he'd have to deal with was the fact that his wife was about to give birth to their seventh child.

2

Wei walked through the flimsy canvas ghost gate, hung in front of the courtyard's main gate to confuse and keep out all evil spirits and ghosts. He walked through the main wooden gate itself and, stepping to the left, aligned himself on the exact north–south axis which precisely bisected his courtyard and farmhouse into eastern and western halves. He walked determinedly north towards his farmhouse.

Beneath his feet it was as though the whole earth was in revolt. It felt as though it was buckling and shaking, as though some great northern dragon was writhing and convulsing and jerking the lines which run southwards all across the earth. What was happening up there in the Heavenly North where all the gods abide? What chaos and dissension was breaking out among them to cause this upset? None of it stopped him, though. He kept doggedly to his course.

He passed the sheds and stable where the farm implements and livestock were kept, where the firewood was stored and the straw stacked. They would not take firewood with them on their journey – they could gather that on the way. The same with water. At the dead centre of the courtyard he passed the shrine to his ancestors on which their names were inscribed on tablets. They ignored him. He continued on his straight north course, passing the room on the left where his father still lived, the room on the right reserved for his eldest son when he came of age and started a family – the room he himself and his wife had first lived in when they were married. All the time he was running through in his head precisely what would be needed for their journey, who in the family he would choose to carry out each separate responsibility of gathering and packing all the many things they would need.

He came to the main entrance to the farmhouse. A double door opened into the large space of the kitchen. There was a smell of cooking so Cherry Blossom, his second daughter, was preparing food. Something nourishing for his wife. He could hear his eldest and second sons sawing planks in a nearby shed. His father, now elderly and not very strong, was sitting by the fire and telling Wei's two youngest children a story about the legendary courage of Zhuge Liang and the wickedness of Cao Cao. Their two tiny mouths hung open in wonderment.

Wei turned to the right. Before him the double doors to his and his wife's bedroom. He opened them. Cherry Blossom was gently feeding her mother some gruel from a bowl with a duck spoon, leaning over her as she lay on the bed. Seeing him she put the bowl and spoon down and hurried from the room, shutting the doors. Wei stared at his wife as she lay on the bed he himself had been born in. Beneath it lay his birth caul, buried by his father to celebrate his birth. Beside it the caul of his eldest son, buried by himself, and the cauls of his father, grandfather and all the Wei family's firstborn ancestors back til...

Wei shook himself and looked at his wife. She was on her back, her legs moving slowly back and forth to relieve the pains in her back. Very pregnant, she was staring directly at him. He saw she knew something was about to happen. She was already marshalling her arguments.

'Good morning, wife. How are you?'

'I am not too bad. As always my back has started aching. What are those strange sounds from the north?'

'Wife, you and I must talk. Now. On grave matters. The sounds you hear are explosions from the guns of the Japanese Army that is marching directly towards our village.'

'I see you've been listening to our eldest daughter with her mindless gossip.'

'I can see the dust clouds of their army on the northern horizon. See the flashes and explosions of their guns. My dear wife, with a heavy, heavy heart, I have decided – awful as the time is, especially for you – that for our safety we, the whole family, must leave immediately.'

She sat straight up, her arms behind her, supporting her.

'What? Leave this land? Our land? Which your family has farmed for a thousand years?'

'Yes. There are many terrible and true stories of these devils' savagery towards our people. I have heard this not only from our eldest daughter and her newspapers but from people in the village.'

'They always speak nonsense when armies approach us. They said the same when the warlord came twenty years ago. According to my great grandmother there was the same talk when the mad Taipings invaded us seventy years ago. A few men killed, some women raped, we shall endure them. People only spread these rumours because they hope gullible people will desert their lands and they can take them over.'

'I have been thinking about all this for several days. Yesterday I spoke secretly to my cousin over the hill.'

'Has he decided to leave?'

'No.'

'Has anyone else in the village decided to leave?'

'No – but that is unimportant. This is my decision. As I was saying, I spoke to my cousin and he said that if we left – I had not decided then – he would tend and protect my land, and if we had not returned after twelve months he would take our land as his own.'

'Your land! The land you love! The land you put every second of your life into caring for and nurturing. You are the most revered farmer in this village. Every year at our festival the village honours your merit by giving you senior duties in its rituals and dances and speeches. It is said you have a wise heart. Villagers come to you to settle their disputes. You are deserting what you, your ancestors have built up over a thousand years? What will be their judgement on your desertion of their sacred, living land? Who will kneel at their graves and tell them the latest news? Have you told them of your decision yet?'

Wei didn't know how to answer this. But suddenly there were two of those loud, ominous explosions from the north. A silence fell between them.

Wei sympathized with his wife. He understood why she argued this way. At the moment she had no standing among his family's ancestors. They viewed her as an outsider, some sort of interloper, and largely ignored her. It was only when her and Wei's eldest son inherited and farmed the land that they would recognize her and hold her in esteem as his mother, that she would become seen by the family, both living and dead, as honoured mother and grandmother of the ensuing generations of Weis. If they left now and never came back, the door of the ancestors would be shut for ever on her; she would be doomed to become just another abandoned soul, hovering pitifully outside the ghost gate of the farmhouse. Just as his eldest sister would have been had he not secretly buried her remains.

His wife's face twisted in fury.

'It's that she-witch our eldest daughter who's been poisoning your mind isn't it, with all her lies about newspaper stories? She does it because she hates me.'

'She does not hate you, and she is not lying. She read to me from the pages of newspapers.'

'She could be saying anything she wanted, just making it up, because you can't read, can you? She is a witch. It all goes back to your mistake during the famine when she was an infant. You should not have fed her. You should have left her to die. A woman has no value and is easily replaced.'

'Enough!' Wei shouted. 'I have made my decision. You will obey.'

For a second she looked at him, then bowed her head in wifely submission.

In a gentle voice he said, backing slowly out of the room, 'Stay in your bed and rest, dear wife. We will carry you out when we are ready to leave and you will, of course, have the place of honour in the cart.'

Spider Girl was lurking in the courtyard behind the door waiting for him to finish. He joined her. They spoke quietly so his wife would not hear them.

'We must get the cart up here at once to start loading,' he said.

'You're going to risk its rotten spokes?'

'I'll do the best job I can repairing them. We're lost without the cart.'

His eldest son was passing with a whetstone to sharpen his saw.

'Eldest Son, you and Second Son get the cart up here immediately.'

'Yes, Father.'

'I'll clean the cart all through,' continued Spider Girl, 'then I, with Cherry Blossom, will start cooking enough food – buns and dumplings – to keep us going for the first few days. I've already got her stoking the fire and filling the cauldron to the top with water.'

'Good. How long do you think your food will last – before we have to start using dried food?'

'About five days or so. But I'll go into the pantry, sort out what grain and beans and seasoning and dried food we'll need.'

With that, Spider Girl went off into the kitchen to start preparing the dough for steaming.

Eldest and Second sons were pushing the cart up the courtyard, shouting and competing with each other about who could push hardest. Wei did not reprimand them for endangering the wheel. Now was not the time. And besides, they had not damaged it.

He thanked them, then drew them away from the house and down towards where the ancestors' shrine was. Rather than further upset his wife or have his father overhear what was about to happen it would have to be his ancestors who received the shock. Spider Girl had gone into the kitchen to start preparing the dough for steaming.

In a quiet authoritative voice Wei told his sons what was to happen. Eldest Son stared ahead, not fully comprehending what Wei was saying, trying to work it out in his head. Second Son stared at his father white-faced.

'We are going to leave the farm, Father?' asked his eldest.

'Yes. Immediately. These soldiers are going to kill us.'

'Leave our home?'

'Yes. It is vital, so that we can live, that you must now do exactly what I tell you.'

Second Son was horror-struck too, but already behind his staring eyes Wei could discern flickers and frowns of thought.

'I need you to go down to the stable, groom the donkey and water and feed him and the goat well with their best feed – I'll want you to do that again before we leave… And press all the goat's cheese so we can take it with us.'

'Feed them twice in a day?'

'Yes, and put the rest of their best feed into small sacks. Then get the old canvas from out of the small shed, brush it, then with the poles that slot into the cart for the roof and the ridgepole, bring them and the feed sacks up here. After that I'll want you to go out into the fields to gather fresh fodder.'

His two sons still stared at him.

'Do you understand me?' asked Wei gently.

'Yes, Father,' replied his second son, leading away his still puzzled elder brother and explaining things to him as they went.

Wei rejoined Spider Girl outside the kitchen doorway.

'After I've cleaned the cart, Father, I'll line the floor with cloth, then get two cushions for mother, one for Grandfather, and one for the two tots.'

'Yes.'

'What are we going to do about Grandfather and the tots? He'll catch on pretty soon that something is up, and when we have to tell him we are going to leave his home…'

'I know. I'll ask him and the children that while they are playing to kindly go down to the walnut trees and gather the fallen fruit…'

'I'll give them the noodles we didn't eat last night.'

'…and then gather some fresh spinach and sorghum leaves in the fields. I don't want to tell him what we're doing until the last minute. It will be a terrible shock.'

'And ask him while he's down there to say some prayers for us to the ancestors,' added Spider Girl. 'We'll need his intercession for us with them.'

'You're right.'

They both turned together into the kitchen, Spider Girl to start kneading the dough with Cherry Blossom, Wei to gently persuade his father to take the children out to the walnut trees.

Three more heavy crumps came from outside, the third so heavy that they felt the ground lift beneath their feet.

Suddenly the doors to Wei's bedroom flew open with a crash. From them – back straight as a ramrod, arms akimbo – issued Wei's wife, looking imperiously from side to side, her pregnancy seemingly miraculously swallowed back into her body. Gone was her weakness, her sickness, her unwieldy bulk.

Lying on her bed and hearing the whispered conversations outside her window, the arrival of her two sons with the cart, the sounds and smells of extensive cooking from the kitchen had told her that her household was starting to run in an unusual way. The shaking of the ground from a shell landing some ten miles away had propelled her from her bed. If the family was in crisis, if this crazy plan of her husband's to leave (instigated by the malignancy of her eldest daughter) was actually happening, then she – head of the household, who alone knew where everything was stored and how all things interlaced – must arise and organize such a complex task or everything would go widdershins. So she arose from her bed and advanced. The jolt of adrenalin within her body was so strong that all the normal operations of giving birth seemed to be put on hold.

At the sight of her Wei flinched, momentarily, but almost as soon managed a smile of welcome while simultaneously signalling her not to start making a scene in front of his father and the two tots. She was aware enough to read his signal and gestured the three of them should move outside.

'Dear wife,' said Wei, once they stood by the cart, 'I did not expect you to get up from your bed. You are looking remarkably well.'

His wife stared beadily at Spider Girl.

'I know exactly what game that evil daughter of ours has been playing,' she said, pointing at her daughter. 'Scheming to take over my role in the family. Running my household for you. Send her away now.'

Spider Girl knew immediately that she must withdraw, show her humility. Her mother ran the household. Had she been in her mother's place she would have acted in exactly the same way. She and her father could still quietly liaise with each other to ensure that things were running effectively.

'I apologize to you,' Spider Girl said, bowing obediently to her parents, and then waddled off to the shed where the fabrics were stored, so she could brush the cloth she was to line the cart with and comb out all its lice eggs. While she was there she would stuff some dried hops into Grandpa's cushion so he would sleep better.

'What are you doing, husband?' his wife asked bluntly.

As quickly as he could without irritating her, Wei explained most of the plans the family was carrying out, emphasizing again and again that the Japanese could be expected to arrive within a few hours and they must hurry. To his relief she agreed with most of their arrangements, only drawing the line when it came to Spider Girl's role. She would take over control of the kitchen and the cooking, Spider Girl would be demoted. After she'd finished cleaning the cart and furnishing it, Spider Girl could prepare the dried food in the pantry and bring in herbs and condiments to her whenever she ordered them.

There was only one other matter his wife insisted on. That, before they left, all the family should go down to their ancestors' graves and Wei should explain to them why they were leaving. Wei had been in two minds about whether they had time to do this. She was quite emphatic. She wanted to be certain the ancestors knew the decision to leave had nothing to do with her. Wei was glad she had made the decision for him.

She marched into the kitchen then into the pantry, shut the door, looked at all the family's food laid out so immaculately, ordered in strict rows and stacks of which should be eaten at once, which would keep three months, six months, a year. All her own work. Now to be torn apart, plundered, destroyed in a moment of madness. For thirty seconds she wept. Then, with a grim, mean look in her eye, she marched out into the kitchen, sharply ordered Cherry Blossom to bring fresh herbs from the courtyard, and started using her strong forearms to knead the dough.

As Wei went to get his tools to patch up the cartwheel, he reflected that in fact it was better if his wife was in control there.

Spider Girl had plenty of other things to do, and if little Cherry Blossom started to play up his wife would solve it with a swift smack round the head. Spider Girl could never run fast enough to catch her.

In the stable at the southern end of the courtyard Eldest Son slowly brushed the donkey's hide. He loved this donkey – his gentleness, his patience. The donkey and the goat stood chewing their fodder, the donkey his dried sorghum, the goat her hay. Second Son was using a scoop to fill small sacks with the special feeds for the donkey and goat. The donkey's feed was a mixture of leaves, herbs, some bark and a handful of thistles and blackberry leaves; the goat liked dried hay and clover, with a handful of hawthorn leaves. Second Son deftly looped and knotted the necks of the sacks with cord and stacked them by the doorway.

'We must be quicker, elder brother, we'll be leaving soon.'

Second Son was still trying to explain to his elder brother exactly why they were leaving and why the Japanese were so terrible. Neither of them had any idea who the Japanese were, but Second Son, always keeping an ear out for what his elders were saying, had worked out that they were evil and bloodthirsty murderers. He had heard the fear in their voices. As he worked he explained this patiently to his brother.

'But,' said his brother, 'if an evil man kills another man, an executioner comes around and chops his head off with an axe or a sword. I saw it once in the village. There was a lot of blood. Why doesn't an executioner do that to the Japanese?'

Younger brother wasn't certain how to answer that at first – he was mainly wishing he had seen all that blood – but thinking about it he said that he thought that the Japanese were too strong and evil to allow any executioner to behead them.

Elder brother wasn't listening. He stood lost in a dream, a shaft of sunlight streaming down from a hole in the thatch on to his head. Who knew where his brains were?

Younger brother watched him, then reached up and lifted down a tray of goat's cheese maturing in the rafters. He started patting them into shape and wrapping them in basil leaves. The family would take them all.

Looking at his elder brother he suddenly thought that perhaps, with all this happening, this might be the last time the two of them would ever stand together in this stable, their favourite place, and do their tasks with their beloved animals. Perhaps they were all going to be murdered. He shivered.

'Come on, elder brother, we've got to get the canvas and poles ready for the cart.'

When Spider Girl had finished cleaning the cart and lining it and the two boys had started spreading its canvas hood over it, Spider Girl went into the pantry to supply her mother with what she needed in the kitchen and start packing dried foods for their journey – soya (last year's, because this year's was still in the fields), green beans, lentils and peas. Jars of bean curd and pickled turnip. She took down the three dried and salted hens – they could hang from the side of the wagon along with the dried sorghum and spinach and strings of onions and cabbages. They'd need two bags of freshly picked potatoes and three earthenware jars of wheat. They would add to the weight of the cart she worried, especially with the jar of water.

While she was doing this – and hurrying back and forth keeping her impatient mother supplied with salt and pepper and herbs – her mother was kneading out dumplings of dough and then thumping them to stick on the inner rim of the cauldron so they would steam. Those that were ready she piled on a sideboard. They'd probably have enough, she calculated, to trade some on the road.

She looked around her kitchen as a general inspects his troops deployed for battle. They would be able to pick dandelion and sorrel leaves on the road for their salads. She'd chopped the heads off five chickens and, with a few deft slices from a large knife, skinned, gutted and de-feathered them. They were now boiling happily in the water strung from a wooden pole. She shouted at Spider Girl to bring in potatoes to boil – and pack some senna pods to help Grandfather with his constipation.

With Mother and Spider Girl so intensely preoccupied, Cherry Blossom chose this moment to slip off unnoticed and visit and enjoy her great secret. A secret known only to herself. No one else in the entire world knew anything about it. She slipped out of the back door of the pantry and ran down the narrow passage between the courtyard wall and the farmhouse. She'd hidden it under a pile of half-rotted timbers. She lifted them up and there beneath was, in an old wooden birdcage, her beautiful, her magical baby hedgehog. It was always pleased to see her, especially the piece of dumpling dough she held out on her finger, and the tiny bowl of goat's milk she'd smuggled out.

For a moment she gazed raptly at it, then she heard Spider Girl call her. She carefully put the cage back in the woodpile, replaced the timbers. This was Cherry Blossom's secret – no one else would ever know about it.

She went back through the pantry where Spider Girl was packing roast melon and pumpkin seeds.

'Where've you been?' asked Spider Girl.

'Out for a shit,' replied Cherry Blossom.

The boys had finished stretching the tarpaulin roof over the cart and had set off with a hand-drawn wooden raft to gather fresh sorghum from the fields for the donkey and fresh spinach, potatoes, carrots and cabbages for the family. The sorghum and spinach should be bundled for easier carrying, the carrots and potatoes washed and put in a sack with the cabbages.

'And hurry,' Wei said, 'we have little time.'

Spider Girl was passing and he told her to kill the bees but keep the honey in the combs. 'We can drain the honey on the road and trade the wax with a pedlar.'

He got himself under the cart and started to work on the two rotten spokes. No time to take apart the wheels and insert new spokes. Reassembling such a complex thing as a wooden wheel was the work of an expert and could take hours. He took four iron splints to act as braces on each spoke, and then tightly bound each splint where the wood was sound with strong wire, finally stapling the splint at one end into the axle and at the other into the wooden felloe of the outer wheel. He pushed the cart back and forth a couple of times. It seemed to hold, but he mustn't allow the cart to be overloaded.

He hung a pot of pig lard under the wagon to keep the axle greased and a spare brace for the wheel. He went into the side shed and looked at all his tools and implements. Which must they take? Something for digging – a large trowel for shitting? But what if he had to dig a larger hole for…? He didn't allow his mind to go there. So they'd need a spade – with a sharpened end which would be good if they met any bandits on the road. A short sharp dig with a sharpened spade would take their guts out. What had Eldest Son done with that whetstone? He fetched it from the sawing shed and slotted both it and the spade into a leather collar on the side of the wagon, then he hurried into the kitchen to see how his wife wanted the food packed in the cart.

Singing her song to soothe her bees, Spider Girl lifted the first skip gently and looked inside. With a drowsy hum, the bees slowly and surely went about their business around the combs. They liked Spider Girl and trusted her. Yet she was to kill them. She did not want to. All she had to do was hold the skip over a sharp fire, swiftly sear and kill the bees with the flames, then cut out the combs.

The family needed the honey for the strength its sweetness would give them and for its medicinal and antiseptic qualities, but she would not do it. Bees were not only good and fruitful, they were also powerful in the spiritual world. If they were killed outright – especially the Emperor Bee at the heart of the hive – bees would take their revenge on the family, they would bring bad luck on them. To avoid this would mean being stung quite badly, but if she just cut out some of the combs and replaced the skips, they could resume their lives and still feel generous to her family.

She stopped crooning her lullaby for them and instead gently hummed it – so that no angry bees could fly into her mouth. Then she started cutting the combs and it hurt a lot, but in a short while she had wrapped the dripping combs in wax paper and was gone.

The bees resumed their unending toil. She prayed for their future prosperity and happiness. They prayed for hers.

Three large jars filled with wheat and one with drinking water had already been placed in the front of the cart. Wei intended to have two buckets of water slung beneath the cart. They would be dirty from the dust and dirt thrown up, but good enough for the donkey and goat. Besides, Wei was expecting to be able to get plenty of fresh water on the road.

Between the heavy jars he tightly packed the bags of dried beans and peas, corn and flour that Spider Girl had prepared, together with a small sack of roast melon and pumpkin and fennel seeds. Also one of last year's hazel and sweet chestnuts and walnuts. On top he piled their bedding and spare clothing, and the knives and chopsticks and bowls and small iron cauldron they would need for their cooking and eating. The fresh food that the boys would be bringing in from the fields and his wife cooking would be stored at the back of the cart amid the family. The cart groaned a bit. He looked sharply at the spokes – they were holding tight.

His wife shouted from the kitchen to get the garlic and fennel leaves off the roof. He shouted to Cherry Blossom so he could pass the food down to her and she could plait the garlic and tie the fennel leaves in bundles.

She came out and he climbed onto the roof to collect the food. He saw Grandfather and the two tots returning to the farmhouse and almost at its gates. He started to hand down the garlic when he saw something else, something to the north. The dark cloud that had turned into a dust cloud, made by the Japanese troops, was not only huge but now no more than three miles from their village. Apart from the crump of artillery shells, now he could hear the snap and crack of rifle fire and a strange high-pitched chatter of guns firing he had never heard before. The worst thing he saw, though, was at the very centre of the black cloud. As though glowering from the belly of some vast dragon, he caught glimpses of strange flashes and glints of bayonet and fire issuing from the fighting. He knew they must move very soon. As he threw down the remaining garlic and fennel to Cherry Blossom, he screamed at his two eldest sons – who were some distance off – to bring back the food they had gathered and lead the donkey and goat up immediately from the lower courtyard.

He vaulted down from the roof and ran into the farmhouse. There was something strange and very important he had to do.

Their bedroom door was bolted behind them. His wife, not pleased with what they were doing, angrily worked to loosen a brick from the wall above their bed with a hammer and chisel. He was using a crowbar to lift a flagstone.

Farmers had little wealth, but what they did have they tended to hide in their own buildings and lands, rather than risk entrusting it to the hands of slippery merchants or, even worse, banks. But it did make them vulnerable to bandits – soulless, evil men who could come at night and torture farmers and families to try and extract from them where they hid their money. Wei knew farmers who had suffered this. Some had given away their secret places, some had died refusing. Fortunately it had never happened to him.

Wei could feel his wife's anger. Indeed, it had been growing all day.

He took a bag of coins from under the flagstone as she pulled some cheap silver jewellery and a gold brooch from behind the brick. They were keepsakes given to her by her own family on the day she had been sent far away to marry Wei. She had never seen her own family again. He took them, stuffed them in with the coins and fixed the bag firmly inside his smock. He turned to go.

'Husband – we must replace the brick with plaster – re-lay the flagstone,' his wife said with contempt in her voice. 'Anyone who comes into our house after we've left will know our hiding places? Can rob us easily in the future?'

'We don't have time,' he said, reopening the doors. 'If we return we'll have to find new places.'

His wife would just have to swallow her anger. The situation was too dangerous.

He came out into the sunlight as Grandfather and the two infants came up the courtyard. His father was looking upset and disorientated. Wei knew that very soon he would have to tell his father – and those family members who did not know, including their ancestors – that the family was leaving.

'Son, son,' cried his father, coming up to him, the two toddlers rushing into the kitchen for food. 'I have just seen a strange thing. It scared me.'

'What was it, honoured father?' replied his son.

'This strange man. He passed us on the track while we were by the walnut trees. His hair was all awry and he stared ahead of him with this awful, stricken look. His clothing was torn and burnt. I asked him if he was all right, if he needed help? If he wanted he could come into our home and eat and rest? He ignored me. He brushed past me and walked on southward, as though I was not there. Then came two families I had never seen before, one with a cart and one all on foot, all carrying heavy loads, all hurrying past me with terrified looks, ignoring me. What is going on?'

Wei knew that the time had come. Now he must explain to his father, his ancestors, all the members of his family who did not yet know – the shocking thing that was about to happen to them.

'Come and listen to me,' he told his father and toddlers and Cherry Blossom.

As they gathered round him he stood himself deliberately in the very centre of his house, his farm, his world. Where the precise north–south axis of his farm and courtyard bisected the precise west/east axis on which his farmhouse had been built, 2,000 years ago. The most sacred spot in the farmhouse – where the coffins of the dead always rested before burial – where the head of the family stood to pass judgement and speak on the most important of occasions. He knew it would give what he had to say immediate authority. And as he stood he could feel the unrest running through his feet up from the south – from the shrine of his ancestors – and down from the north – from whence the Japanese came, and beyond them, from the abode of the gods themselves. There pandemonium and tumult reigned. It filled him with more dread than anything else. At such a time as this? All the gods fighting each other in Heaven. Abandoning all responsibility for their people.

Without letting his voice break, but firmly, he explained they were leaving. His mind was made up. His father howled. His ancestors howled. His infants howled til they remembered their food and recommenced chewing on it. Cherry Blossom turned sheet-white, stopped plaiting her garlic cloves, and rushed through the pantry.

'Where are you going?' asked Spider Girl.

'Got to shit,' said Cherry Blossom, disappearing into the back alley.

Now rural families, of necessity, because they all shat together haunch by haunch on a plank hung precariously above a communal dung pit, tended to be well acquainted with the vicissitudes of each others' bowels. Cherry Blossom, Spider Girl reflected, had shown no unusual signs of any recent looseness, but this was the second time she'd been out to shit in half an hour. She followed Cherry Blossom into the back alley.

Meanwhile in the courtyard Grandfather was invoking their ancestors. The beauty of the farm. The untold centuries and ages that all the generations of their family had poured into their soil, its fruitfulness, its beauty. How he himself had taught Wei step by step to run their farm. His description was so beautiful, so heartfelt, it made Wei weep, but not change his mind.

'We are leaving,' his said simply, wiping his tears away, and lifted his father into the cart. 'See, we have put down a cushion for you.'

'But what of your wife, she is about to give birth?'

'We have two cushions for her.'

In the distance the sounds of rifle fire and explosions were increasing. Eldest and Second sons were hurrying up the courtyard, Eldest Son drawing the goat and the harnessed donkey, Second pulling the wooden raft carrying the vegetables they'd picked.

'Eldest Son, hitch up the donkey at once,' shouted Wei, 'then tether the goat to the rear of the cart. Water them both from the well. Everyone drink as much water as you can. Second Son – put those vegetables into the back of the cart without washing them. We do not have time. And tie those bundles of sorghum and hay onto the shafts. Eldest Son – make sure you harness the donkey tightly enough so he can't bend his neck and eat it.'

He checked his wife had packed the fresh food, then suddenly a most bloodcurdling scream cut through the whole courtyard. Cherry Blossom's scream. Followed by some very strong language from an older voice – Spider Girl's. Both coming from the pantry. Wei hurried towards it. Cherry Blossom's scream was nothing – she was always screaming. But Spider Girl speaking in a voice that was angry? That rarely happened.

He burst in on them. The two were standing in the middle of the floor, each tugging on the two ends of an old wooden birdcage.

'I'm taking it,' screamed Cherry Blossom.

'You can't,' shouted back Spider Girl. 'Give it to me, you little bitch. We don't have enough room to carry it..'

'What is this,' demanded Wei, 'what is going on?' He looked in the old birdcage. To his amazement he saw a small hedgehog nonchalantly chewing on a melon seed.

'He's mine,' shrieked Cherry Blossom, 'he's the most precious thing I have in the whole world, I am not leaving him to die.' She started to wail. Wei did not have time for her dramatics.

'I told her it was too heavy and too big to put in the cart,' said Spider Girl.

Wei was about to intervene just as his wife marched in, a look of cold fury on her face. Wei had been expecting her frustration to boil over all day – but now!!! She marched straight up to her hated eldest daughter Spider Girl.

'You ugly cripple,' she spat, 'you fat, lazy waddling bitch. What are you doing to my poor little Cherry Blossom?'

'I was doing what my father ordered me to do. Keep down the weight of the cart.'

The tiny hedgehog continued chewing its melon seed, indifferent to all this human blethering around it.

'It's all your fault,' shrieked Wei's wife. 'Your devil lies and schemes which fooled your father and got us to undertake this crazy journey. Cherry Blossom's taking her pet!'

'Silence!' Wei thundered.

Silence fell immediately.

Wei breathed in to give his judgement, which was that the hedgehog was to be freed to face the invading Japanese as best it could. Meanwhile, they all had to get in the cart and on the road NOW – but he suddenly became aware his wife was looking at him, moving her eyes meaningfully. He sighed and ordered the two girls out of the room, Cherry Blossom looking triumphantly at Spider Girl because she was still carrying the cage.

His wife spoke gently. 'If she takes it, it will force her to behave well. No hysterics. Otherwise she loses it. When we run out of fresh food I can kill it, we can eat it, and I'll tell her it ran off.'

Wei almost smiled. 'We must leave,' he said curtly, marching towards the door.

Cherry Blossom's hedgehog was coming with them.

Outside the cart was ready to go. The sound of explosions and rifle fire was crowding in on them. The first shades of evening were starting to fall.

Eldest Son stood by the donkey ready to lead it on. Second Son was tying leather straps to either side of the cart so members of the family could help pull it. The cage of the hedgehog was hung under the cart between rattling pots and pans and ladles and buckets of water. The two young ones were already in the cart playing a game. His wife was coming out of the kitchen with a last bag of boiled potatoes. But his father, sitting on the back of the cart, his legs hanging down, was looking at him. He was not looking in his usual random, unfocused way, he was staring right at him with authority in his eyes.

'Father?' he said.

'So we are going away?'

'Yes.'

'I have been speaking to our ancestors. Especially to one

32

ancestor, one held in great esteem, my grandfather, your great grandfather.'

'My great grandfather was a very wise man.'

'When he was young the family then was forced to go on a similar journey when there was a terrible plague. And many, many other families and villages had to do the same. And he said that what everyone lacked on the march, everyone cried out for, was not food, it was water. Because the streams and ponds all ran dry and were muddied and befouled by the travellers and many people died of thirst. I have been looking. You need more water. And there is something else he told me, but I can't remember now. I'll try to remember it.'

Wei looked at him. Suddenly he remembered he too had once heard this story of the water. And his father was right. The water would only last a few short days.

'Three large jars of water are needed at least, two of wheat...'

'But...'

Despite the extra weight, Wei knew he was right.

'But we only have four large jars. Three for water only leaves one for wheat.'

'I know what to do,' said his wife, easing off the cart. 'Cherry Blossom, Spider Girl,' she shrieked, 'get in the cloth hut. Spider Girl, fetch a big straw mat, Cherry Blossom, my biggest needle and strongest sewing twine.' They vanished inside. She turned to the men. 'You empty one of the jars, put it in the cart, and fill it with water. Leave a jar-sized space between the jars in the cart.'

She scurried into the hut. Spider Girl was holding the large mat, Cherry Blossom the threaded needle and twine.

'It's a question of twisting it correctly,' she said, taking hold of two corners of the mat so Spider Girl held the other two. 'Twist hard,' she said, twisting her own end and signalling Spider Girl should twist in the opposite direction. Both ends crossed each other and came to rest against the opposite middles. 'Grab it there,' she shouted at Spider Girl, grasping her own crossed middle firmly in her hand. 'Hand me the needle,' she ordered Cherry Blossom. 'Now hold where I'm holding,' she told Cherry Blossom, who did so. She went to the bottom where one end overlapped the other and started sewing with fast, powerful stabs. Cherry Blossom was having difficulty holding on. Spider Girl held her own ends together in one hand while with the other she held Cherry Blossom's ends while Cherry Blossom rearranged her grip.

Outside Wei and Eldest and Second Sons had lifted the canvas and manhandled one of the jars firmly on to the flagstones. Second Son took the wooden lid off. Inside lay the golden wheat. All of them looked at each other. All their wealth. All their security.

A voice came from the back of the cart. Grandfather's. 'Throw it over. Throw it away. It has no value.' So they did. Their wealth spilled golden over the courtyard. The chickens went crazy.

They lifted the jar back into the cart, and, forming a line from the well, as fast as possible started filling it with buckets.

Inside Wei's wife had already sewn up the bottom half of the sides so that it swelled out like a jar. As the two sides crossed over she started to stitch again, which drew the shape narrower, also like a jar. Only Spider Girl was needed now to hold the top open, so Cherry Blossom was sent out to help with the water.

In the courtyard Wei was increasingly worried by the weight being put on the cart, not only by the extra jar, but by the weight of him and the boys loading it. He constructed a crude platform of a plank on two stools which ran beneath the shafts, finishing just as his wife issued proudly from the cloth shed carrying her finished mat jar. Everyone applauded. It was placed in the cart and Wei and Eldest Son, their weight on the plank, picked up one of the two wheat jars and started, guided by Second Son on the cart, pouring it into the mat jar. Jammed between two stone jars it held. The empty jar was placed where it had been and immediately started being filled with water. The whole family taking part it took only a few seconds. As they retook their positions around the cart, feet crunching over the abandoned grain, Wei touched his wife's arm to express his gratitude.

They stood. Wei did not want to look around. He wanted no one else to look around. 'Push.' he commanded, and the family pushed the cart. It creaked, it groaned, and then it started to move, wood straining, pots and pans clanking, canvas waving above, like some stately old junk setting sail onto a vast ocean. Soon, as it started to roll down the slope of the courtyard, they had to hold it back rather than push it on. Wei, worried about the wheel, positioned himself behind it to watch it. They came to the courtyard gate, creaked through it, Second Son drawing aside the canvas of the ghost gate so they could pass under it. Now any ghost that wished could enter and roam the deserted buildings.

The cart stopped and the family started to hurry towards the graves. Wei's wife was handing out paper money to burn on the graves so their ancestors could have money to spend in the afterlife and paper flags to assure them there would always be descendants there to serve them. Not that there probably would. She had freshly cooked food for their table. She wanted to be certain she would carry no blame for their departure.

Wei noticed Spider Girl remained by the cart.

'Aren't you coming?'

'Father, I do not wish to be a burden to the family. If I walk to the graves and back and then follow the cart, my slowness will slow down the family. I will set off now along the track and you can catch me up. Please remember me to my ancestors.'

With that she set off stolidly on the trackway south. He hurried to catch the rest of the family. He didn't want this ceremony to last any longer than it had to.

Beneath the skeleton branches of the wild pear tree, the money had been ritually burnt, incense lit, the flags planted, a prayer been said, and Wei was about to (briefly) inform his ancestors on why they were to be abandoned, when it happened. There were three sudden sharp cracks followed by explosions from their village about half a mile to the north. Over the low hill to the north of the village suddenly poured ranks of khaki-clad Japanese soldiers, bayonets and helmets gleaming in the last rays of sunlight. The family could see it all quite clearly. Chanting and shouting the Japanese charged into the defenceless village. Confused cries, rifle shots, the screams of women and children and men as they were butchered.

For a second the entire family stood frozen. Then Wei grabbed up his father, Eldest Son grabbed the tots, and the whole family hared towards the cart. They piled Grandfather and the two toddlers into the cart, Eldest Son applied the whip to the donkey and everyone else pushed. Wei didn't even look at his wheel. Cherry Blossom thought nothing of her hedgehog. They just wanted desperately to get the cart over the brow of the nearby hill and out of the sight of the Japanese devils they had at last seen so close.

Only one person looked back as the cart tumbled over the horizon and out of the sight of their Japanese pursuers. Grandfather – face desolate and vacant, hair awry, mouth mumbling – stared back at what had been his home, his farm, his village for all his life. His soul ate bitterness.

One other member of the family was thinking of what they had left behind them. Wei remembered as he ran from the graveyard carrying his father, as he passed the wild pear tree he had glanced at his elder sister's grave amid its roots and there he had seen her standing. Unsmiling, sombre, but with ineffable love shining from her eyes.

He remembered one other thing. That during the madness of their departure he had not forgotten to secrete two small stone bottles of the tree's wild pear juice. The sweetest, most nourishing, most life-giving juice he knew. One he stored in the cart, one he hid in his clothing.

Tumbling down the south-facing slope in their cart, darkness swallowed the family.

3

Spider Girl walked in the dark. If she rolled enough from side to side as she walked it lessened some of the weight on her hip joints and upper legs so it did not hurt so much. She was glad she'd had the foresight, a week earlier, to buy some ointment from the village apothecary. A mixture of horny goat weed, teasel root and scurf pea fruit, it strengthened her bones and lessened their inflammation. She had it hidden among her clothing.

She did not think the Japanese would pursue them tonight. They'd be too busy eating, drinking, torturing and sleeping in the village. She looked back. She could see a garish light on the northern horizon where, presumably, they were burning the village. She shivered. She wondered what had happened to Old Chen, the many others she knew.

She forced herself to think of positive things. She was glad that the whole family had managed to escape, just in time. She was glad that her mother had helped her father in dealing with Cherry Blossom and the hedgehog and, despite her condition, had made up her mat jar so swiftly and expertly. Her father had been so moved by her skill and coolness he had touched her arm. Their parents united could bring good fortune to the family. But their journey would have to be swift or the Japanese would catch them.

She waddled on. Then she heard something behind. Voices. She slowed. They spoke in Chinese but as they approached they were not the voices of her family. Harsh and masculine. Crude in their language and foul in their jokes. She quietly, carefully felt her way off the side of the trackway, ending up crouching in a dry drainage ditch.

The voices came closer. Then they stopped. Just by Spider Girl. She silently drew her knife from her clothing.

'Where are all these fucking families you told me would be on this road – with all their fucking belongings and wealth ripe for stealing? Soft-breasted fucking women and girls?'

'Fat Wang told me he'd seen lots of them coming south, fleeing the Japanese devils.'

Other members of the gang tried to enter the argument but were abruptly shut up by the two protagonists.

'You fucking twat, Chao. Fat Wang must have been talking about the main road heading south, not this back track. That's where the fat ones will be. We've lost a whole night's loot.'

'Don't hit me, Zhong,' pleaded Chao. But Zhong hit him. Spider Girl could almost feel the blow. 'Where's that wine?'

Boss Zhong drank the wine an underling passed him. 'Come on,' he said, 'let's head for the main road.'

They marched on briskly down the track, Zhong cussing out each of his gang members in turn.

Spider Girl emerged from the ditch. She started to follow them down the road. Not fast enough to catch them up, but fast enough to keep ahead of her family.

The family caught up with her about two hours before dawn. She told her father about the men she'd heard last night. She thought they were either bandits or deserters from the army. He immediately stopped the cart. Went forwards a hundred yards or so, listened intently but could hear nothing. He returned to the family.

Grandfather and the two infants were still sleeping in the cart. Cherry Blossom sat on the back of it playing with her hedgehog, who'd become quite active in the night. The rest of the family gathered round Wei. Wei's wife handed out dumplings.

'We must all keep quiet. No noise, no chattering.' Wei looked especially at Cherry Blossom when he said this. 'I need someone to walk three or four hundred yards ahead of the cart. Very quietly. All the time listening and watching ahead of them and to each side of them. If they hear or see anything, they are to quietly run back at once and tell me.'

Eldest Son volunteered immediately.

'No, Eldest Son, and thank you for volunteering, but we need you by the cart. We need our strongest people by the cart, to defend it, because if we lose our cart we lose everything.'

'I want to do it,' said Second Son.

Wei looked at him. Five years old – but so quick, so alert. So able to think for himself. He felt a deep emotion. He felt so ashamed of giving so young and dear a child such a dangerous task, but he was obviously the best person to do it.

He touched his son. 'Thank you, son, for doing this.' Second Son hurried forwards into the dark, quickly disappearing.

'Father,' asked Spider Girl, 'do you think the Japanese are following us?'

'They will. But I do not think they will follow us tonight.' He indicated the glow in the sky behind them. 'They will tomorrow morning. We must press on.'

'What if they do follow us tonight? Just a few? There should be someone behind us, to warn us.'

Wei pondered this.

'I'll go,' said his wife, who'd been clutching a cleaver ever since Spider Girl had told them of the bandits.

'You will not,' said Wei, 'not in your condition. You stay with the cart.'

'I'll go,' said Spider Girl.

'And how will you keep up?'

'I will. I will walk faster. If I hear them and cannot catch you up I will shout and scream and lead them off the track. If they follow me I will fight them with my knife. I just have to wound one of them to slow them down.'

Once again Wei felt deeply moved. He did not have any alternative but to accept her offer. Spider Girl sat down to rest as the cart lurched forwards into the darkness. Once they had gone she started to rub ointment into her hips and thighs.

Eldest Son led the donkey with his right hand and carried an axe in his left. Wei walked on the right-hand side of the donkey with his sharpened spade in his right hand. He kept a sharp ear out for the wheel behind him. Behind the cart walked Wei's wife with her cleaver in her hand. Beside her Cherry Blossom carrying her hedgehog in its cage. There would be no free rides for her or her hedgehog.

Next morning the sun rose on a wide grass plain. There was no sign of any bandits or renegade soldiers. In the distance stock was being grazed – flocks of sheep with their shepherds, goose girls with white rings of geese feeding around them.

Second Son rejoined them, after great effort Spider Girl did too. Speed picked up. Every ten minutes Wei would climb on the front of the cart and survey the ocean of grass around them like a sailor in his crow's nest. From his sightings of the Japanese from morning to evening yesterday he calculated they marched about twenty miles a day. He thought the family had already covered about fifteen miles during the night but wanted to press on. The cartwheel seemed strong.

Grandfather and the two tots were woken. They got down, each given a bun and water, and Grandfather led them along, telling them the heroic story of how during the wars of the Three Kingdoms, Liu Bei, himself in retreat from the evil Cao Cao, had refused to abandon the defenceless civilians fleeing with him, even putting his own soldiers at risk to defend them. 'He was a good father to the people,' said Grandfather. Wei's wife was lifted up on to the cart to rest. Spider Girl was amazed when she invited her to join her. Both fell asleep instantly. When Grandfather tired of leading the young ones and telling them stories, Wei carried one and Eldest Son the other. Grandpa himself continued ambling along happily enough, singing some songs to soothe and amuse the children, himself, and the rest of the family. After about an hour Grandfather started to wander about and become confused so he replaced Spider Girl on the cart.

Cherry Blossom and Second Son were sent out onto the grasslands to gather fresh salad leaves – dandelion and sorrel and shepherd's purse. Second Son found some field mushrooms, shaved the soil off their stems with his knife, and placed them carefully in his bag with the leaves.

About noon they came to a stream, the track crossing the stream at a ford. Before they'd arrived Wei decided they would stop at the ford for a brief rest, while the donkey and the goat were watered and the water in the buckets below the cart replenished. But as he approached he saw something, more than one thing down on the banks of the stream. He stopped the cart, gave the tot he was carrying to Spider Girl, and walked forwards alone armed with his shovel.

In the gully in which the stream flowed, to the left of the ford, he saw bodies. Ten or fifteen. A family. Men, women, children, grandparents. Cut down mercilessly. Signalling back for his family not to follow him he went down among them. They'd been stripped of all their valuables, gold teeth too. Quite a lot of their clothing and family belongings had gone. Their bodies lay at grotesque angles, frozen in the agonies of rape and death. The bandits! He made a quick decision. Having checked all the bodies for valuable or useful things – there were none, the bandits had done a thorough job – he walked back to the cart, again checking the horizons.

The stream flowed from right to left across the track. If he ordered his family to look only to the right at the ford, they could do the watering quickly in the stream and move on to rest and feed later. Wei especially did not want his young ones or his father seeing the slaughter. They moved forwards, Wei telling Cherry Blossom if she looked to the left he'd have her mother whip her. The donkey and the goat lowered their heads to the water and drank. Wei emptied what remained of the water in the buckets beneath the cart and refilled them. A thirsty family ladled water into their mouths with cupped hands. As they started to move again Second Son caught sight of some watercress upstream to the right of the track. He asked his father if he could gather it. Wei said yes, but told him not to return to the ford but cut across the grassland to rejoin the family.

Second Son ran up the stream bank and started to pick the fat leaves and stems of water cress. Suddenly he saw something.

Among the rich banks of watercress the body of a young boy, a young boy about the same age as him. He lay face down in the watercress, his body twisted, his throat cut. Back at the ford, while father was watering the donkey, he'd already snatched a peek at what they were forbidden to look at. He also noted Spider Girl doing the same. This young boy had obviously made a run for it from his family and got to here before the killers ran him down. The boy lay there, his throat still bleeding. At the ford, he realized, as they drank, the whole family had been drinking the boy's blood. He shook himself. Even quicker he started gathering the watercress, ripping out the green stalks and white roots til he had an armful. Holding all he had gathered he leant down and washed it quickly in the stream above where the boy was bleeding, then hared off across the meadows to catch the receding cart.

A mile further along the track the family halted for their delayed meal. Wei had one last gaze around from the top of the cart and saw nothing dangerous. The animals were given nosebags. Wei's wife was eased down from the cart and allotted to everyone their portion of dumplings, salad leaves, bean curd and pickled turnips. Second Son did not drink any of the fresh water out of the buckets because he did not want to drink blood. But he did not tell anyone else of what he had seen.

The family ate hard with a lot of 'aahs' and sighs and appreciative burps, and then, for a few precious minutes, lapsed into semi-drowses. The sun beat down, flies buzzed, kites and buzzards circled high in the upper airs, stillness everywhere. It was Cherry Blossom who heard it first.

'What's that funny noise?' she asked.

They all listened. Yes, a strange droning sound. A sort of giant mosquito. It was Second Son who spotted it. High in the sky, this black thing, flying slowly, in a straight line, towards them. What was it? No bird ever flew that far in a straight line. Some great black insect would fly faster.

A tot asked, 'Is it a dragon, Grandpa?'

'I don't know.'

Staring fearfully at it, they all clambered to their feet. That strange, unchanging, grinding drone.

It was Spider Girl who realized what it was.

'It's an aeroplane.'

'An aeroplane? What's an aeroplane?'

'A machine that flies. I've seen photographs of them in a newspaper.'

'Someone who came to the village was talking about them,' added her father.

No one had ever seen an aeroplane before. It flew steadily towards them from the north, a light single-engined Japanese reconnaissance aircraft.

'They can fire guns and drop bombs on people below them,' whispered Spider Girl.

They all stared. For a few seconds it dipped towards them, but then, disinterested in such slim pickings, turned and set off on another of its straight lines towards the south-west.

'It's flying towards the large road we're heading for,' observed Wei.

The plane disappeared. They all felt very grateful that it had not fired its guns or dropped its bombs. Each one of them silently thanked whichever god they thought appropriate for their deliverance. Suddenly everyone was reloading the cart and getting underway again.

In late afternoon they joined the large road going south. There were a few carts like theirs, some families on foot, the occasional wealthier passenger in a rickshaw or bathchair, the coolies sweating away. In the opposite direction came the occasional lorry, soldiers sitting blank-faced in the back, staring stoically into nothingness as they were driven towards the front. One sipped water from his upturned helmet. Agricultural traffic also passed them heading north – dung putts, large four-wheeled carts groaning with grain or potatoes, hay and straw wagons. The occasional herdsmen drove livestock for grazing or slaughter.

Wei tried to speak to a goatherd they passed with his flock. They hardly understood what he was saying, so thick was his accent. Occasionally in the far distance behind them they heard distant thumps and explosions.

Wei decided they would stop for the night. He calculated they were at least thirty miles south of the Japanese. Everyone desperately needed some rest. To tire everyone out at the very start of what could be a long and arduous journey was not wise.

They drove off the road a hundred yards. Hills were starting on either side of them, funnelling the road into a shallow valley, but there was abundant grass on the slopes and signs of some firewood. The animals were tethered a few yards from the cart. First Eldest and Second Sons returned with enough firewood for a fire. Wei's wife decided she had sufficient prepared food that they did not need a fire and could store the wood in the cart. She cut up and handed out a boiled chicken and some boiled potatoes. They could enjoy the fresh salad with some salt and gnaw on raw carrots. By this time Second Son was so tired and so thirsty he did not care whether he drank the poor dead boy's blood or not and had three ladles of it from the bucket. Cherry Blossom complained that she had to share her food with the hedgehog but a look from her mother shut her up.

They finished eating quickly and everyone pissed or shat into a hole Wei had dug in the earth a few yards downwind. After everyone had finished he filled it in. He expected other farmers to respect his land, so he would respect theirs. The family all settled down on the ground to sleep. The cart was to be given a night's rest. Wei would take the first watch til two o'clock. At two o'clock – or after the Plough was almost under the horizon – he woke Eldest Son to take over the watch from him and immediately fell into a deep sleep.

Eldest Son managed to stay awake for half an hour before himself falling back into a deep sleep.

It was a very dark and a very silent night.

It started about twenty minutes after Eldest Son had fallen asleep. A low, distant thrum which gradually turned into a soft, distant roar, like water or wind on the move. All the family stayed deep in their different dream worlds. Then, from the bottom of the valley, the whisper of a quiet voice, as if in prayer, then more, a quiet babble of voices flowing through the valley, the creak of wheels, the clop of footsteps and hooves, the thunder of many footsteps spreading from the valley bottom up its two sides, shouts and screams and the bellowing of animals...

Wei sat bolt upright. What on earth was happening? A carriage drawn by two great black horses was driving straight at him, looming out of the darkness, the driver swearing at him to get out of the way, swerving only at the last moment. Already Wei was scooping up his other family members, screaming at them to reach the shelter of their cart. Blurred figures were rushing past on either side, donkeys trotting past with their riders frenziedly whipping them to go faster. Wei kicked Eldest Son to wake up and fetch their donkey, harness him to the wagon, Second Son to get the goat and tether him behind the cart. Meanwhile Wei's wife and Spider Girl were ladling Grandfather and Cherry Blossom and one of the tots into the cart and at the last moment Mrs Wei, seeing her other tot, Baby Girl Wei, about to be devoured by the wheels of an ox cart shuddering past, snatched her from death's jaws at the very last second.

And all the time from the roadway below arose a pandemonium of sound – people screaming, cattle bellowing, terrified horses neighing, wheels creaking and wagons colliding. It was as though a mighty dam had burst and its pent-up waters were roaring chaotically and manically through the valley.

Wei and Eldest Son were trying to back the donkey into the shafts, frantic as they fumbled to fit his harness and thread its traces, Wei cursing Eldest Son for falling asleep. Mother was arranging Grandfather and the two tots in the back of the wagon and trying to calm them while Spider Girl and Second Son were dodging running figures and animals in the nightmare darkness as they gathered their sleeping rolls and belongings from the ground and threw them higgledy-piggledy into the cart.

The donkey was finally harnessed. Wei apologized to Eldest Son for shouting at him, and started for the rear of the cart, explaining they needed to move at once or they would be run down, and that

Eldest Son should lead off the donkey the second he heard him shout from behind. Suddenly alone, Eldest Son burst into tears.

Wei briefly checked everything was in place at the back, lifted his wife onto the cart, avoided a bolting steer, roared to Eldest Son to start, and he, Second Son and Spider Girl all put their shoulders to the cart to get it underway. Their tiny rickety cart jolted off into the night. Not daring to look at the wheel with rotten spokes and wincing at the shrieking of the ungreased axle, Wei joined his son at the front, skinning his eyes for obstacles, wielding his spade in his hand in case there was trouble. At the back Mrs Wei wriggled off the rear of the cart, wielding her cleaver, and with Spider Girl and her knife guarded the back of the cart.

The Wei family was a tiny leaf being sucked down an enormous drain.

Gradually the dawn broke. All around them they started to see a vast aggregation of people and animals and vehicles – running, riding, walking. stumbling – each one making their terrified way southward. Wei steered around families lying exhausted on the ground, loose cattle, people crouching to shit, dead bodies lying unexplained and abandoned on the ground, horses with broken legs screaming in pain.

The valley through which they had travelled was widening out into a plain. With more space people started to spread out and move at their own pace. Farmers perching pots, sacks of grain and household goods on their backs. Old women carrying sacks, baskets on their heads. Blind people being hurried bewildered along by a held hand. A single woman dragging along three infants, all clinging hysterically to different parts of her. Ancient grandmothers with sticks hobbling along on bound feet tiny and delicate as pigs' trotters. Women wearing black and striped trousers and faded green or blue jackets and women decked out in long gowns. Old women with buns, young women with braids or short bobbed hair. One brave young lady with a suitcase sported a permanent wave hairdo, just like a Shanghai film star, but was walking barefoot because she'd had to abandon her high heels.

Coarse dirty country girls cursing and laughing to each other in unfathomable accents, happily shouting obscenities at young men who darted swiftly through the toiling crowds.

Blue-coated farmers with wheelbarrows, sturdy barefoot wives carrying on either end of shoulder poles great round baskets, their children obediently lined behind them like ducklings. Monks. A fat man sat astride a tiny donkey, whipping it furiously to get more speed from it. An old man carried a birdcage on his outstretched arm, trying to persuade his beloved bird to sing. Madmen and lunatics on the loose wandering about. Long lines of neatly dressed schoolchildren in their uniforms chattering and following their teacher. Blind beggars roped together by their owners, still singing their chants and rattling their bowls. Fortune tellers and pipe and glove and glass makers and electrical technicians. Stump-legged pedlars. Thousands of handcarts and wheelbarrows stuffed with goods and keepsakes and food and people. An enormous and luxurious roadster – a Studebaker – its roof rolled back so its passengers – a clique of Tientsin bankers – could all continue wearing their top hats. Their chauffeur with his palm jammed permanently on the horn. An astrologer with all his charts and books and astrolabes stuck in a handcart. Dung carriers. Craftsmen of all sorts with their tools. All classes jammed together, fleeing from the Japanese. People who'd never even acknowledge, let alone speak to each other, jammed elbow to elbow. All shifting with the same urgency, the same fear drawn on their faces, knotted brows, panting mouths.

And as the horde spread out across the plain, three or four miles in width, all still travelling exactly south, they toiled and trampled across agricultural lands, driving the crops into the ground, turning the dried yellow earth into dust which started to swirl up into the air, setting them coughing and spluttering, drying their throats and inflaming their eyes. Through the clouds, amid the people, travelled herds of pigs and sheep and cattle. On all lips there was one word. 'Wuhan.' All were hurrying south to a place no one knew called Wuhan, where there would be food and water and shelter and, reportedly, life.

As always in times of calamity, some quick-witted folk were

making killings. The animals, driven by young girls and boys, were being slaughtered one by one on the hoof, their blood being boiled for black pudding, their bodies hoisted onto large carts where they were butchered and then their remains lowered into portable cauldrons and their sweet tasty meats and soups sold to a ravenous public.

By the sides of the march local farmers had set up stalls where, smiles on their faces, they were selling their farm produce, raw or cooked, to anyone with money. After their carts were emptied of produce they loaded them up with their household possessions and families and, with full purses, joined everyone else in their flight.

Another group of relatively poor individuals doing well from this calamity were coolies. Normally coolies only found work hauling rubble or bricks or dung, but suddenly everyone was demanding their services. Their spot hire price shot up. Coolies were everywhere carrying every sort of furniture and utensil and machine on their bare backs. One even carried a potted plant on his head. Often only in loincloths – they were not the wealthiest of men – in two panniers slung from a bamboo pole over their shoulders they carried grain, babies, pets or family heirlooms. Some coolies worked in unison, a long pole, each end on their granite-hard shoulders, from which was suspended a hammock containing old people, fat people, pregnant people, books, or, again, just family valuables. They were in a good mood as they trudged through the dust and traffic, slowly intoning their universal work chant, 'Hey yah, Hai-yah,' and proudly boasting to each other exactly what rates they were on. Some coolies, suddenly realizing what low rates they'd agreed on, stopped dead and would not budge an inch before their patrons paid the new rate.

But the greatest commodity of all, the one that commanded the highest price and was most scarce and desperately sought for, was water. The streams they passed over were all trampled into mud and mire and piss and shit by the thousands who had passed already. There were no rivers across that unending plain. Entrepreneurs vending water were always accompanied by large sour-faced guards.

The rich travelled by and large with each other. Moderately

prosperous people were in sedan chairs and rickshaws. They could afford to buy water, but when they bought it, if they wished to progress further, they were forced to buy it for their coolies too. Which they did with ill grace.

A once beautiful but now ageing woman, obviously lost, wandered in a confused state through the crowds in a long and beautiful silk gown, smoking an ebony pipe of orchid-scented opium, her wilting hair elaborately structured and glossy with elephant-dung lacquer, but slowly collapsing around her ears. She was knifed that night by a desperate father who found no money but stole and traded her gown, her pipe and her opium.

In all this swirling and confusion the wealthiest of them all was an ageing prince from Beijing. He had hired troops from a friendly warlord to protect him and his family on his journey. The soldiers marched aggressively on either side of his column. He himself travelled first, alone in an open carriage with a servant holding a parasol over his head to protect him from the rays of the sun. His perfume was so exquisite it easily kept at bay anything so vulgar as sweat. His plump little hands were like flowers of softness, their nails growing at least six inches beyond his fingers. Unbefitting as it was, he held a silk cloth to his nose and mouth to keep out the dust.

Behind him toiled a black horse-drawn carriage, silk curtains tightly drawn to hide his exotically dressed wives and children and parents and favourite concubines all sweating and moaning and arguing and lamenting in the heat. Jammed in with them was the family safe.

Behind them, heavily guarded, rolled a steel wagon into which had been welded an enormous tank of water.

Behind that came a train of his wagons piled high with food, with clothing and fineries, a kitchen range from which the sweating cooks regularly despatched exquisite morsels of food run forwards in a silver bowl by a favourite servant to the prince who almost invariably refused them. In the next cart, the valuable furniture from his palace, his family papers, plants, and the memorial tablets and portraits of all his most influential ancestors.

On either side of these wagons trotted lines of donkeys tethered head to tail, carrying huge burdens of clothing and bedding piled on their backs. So heavy was their weight their nostrils had been slit open so they could pant more rapidly under their enormous loads.

Behind them, on foot, followed the household servants and astrologers and cooks and gardeners and slaves and doctors and sing-song and taxi girls.

Behind them followed a train of beggars and the starving, desperate to pick up any scrap which had fallen from his vast train, all the time crying out for water and alms.

At the front, in his carriage, rode the prince, his face a study of exquisite blankness. As blank as the vast plain across which they now all toiled.

Floods of humanity flowed relentlessly southward across the great yellow plain. In the centre, on the road, travelled the rich and strong. Further out the common people spread out and moved more slowly. Finally, on the fringes, hovered clouds of bandits and criminals watching always for signs of weakness or exhaustion on which to pounce. Above them wheeled vultures and kites and crows. And above them all flew the fragile, one-engined Japanese reconnaissance plane, all the time sending back radio reports on what it saw.

Wei and his family watched this vast armada stream past them as they rested and fed themselves.

He and his wife stood at the front of the cart while the donkey fed from its nosebag. They ate a dumpling each stuffed with goat's cheese. Each sipped a tiny amount of water from a bowl they shared.

'There will be no water,' said Wei's wife, 'except when we get to a river. And even then we will have to boil it. And there will be no wood for fires.'

'We will have to eat all our prepared food and what vegetables we can raw,' replied Wei. 'Then with the firewood Eldest and Second Sons gathered, we will have to cook as much of the dried food as possible.'

'How is the wheel?'

'After last night the splints are still good, but the nails which hold them are starting to move in the wood. More people must walk. There's still a bit of water in the buckets beneath the cart, but most of it was spilled last night. From now on I'm only going to water the donkey.'

'We can keep the goat til it stops milking,' said his wife, 'then you can slaughter it and I'll sell it to a family with some firewood – so we can have some of it cooked in return.'

Suddenly his wife groaned.

'Wife?'

She looked back at him. Her face wrenched in pain. She sank to the ground. For two days her willpower had held the child back. Now she was going into labour.

'Get me into the cart,' she ordered. 'And get underway.'

Once again the cart started to roll across the Great Plains of Central China.

4

THE UNIVERSITY CAMPUS OF THE CITY OF JINAN. AUTUMN 1937.

I am, I think, what you would call stupid. Or, to put it another way, an intellectual. I, a stupid man, look at the dungheap that is China and for some reason am attracted. A normal intelligent man simply walks straight past a dungheap. And if he is a super intelligent man he walks straight past while averting his eyes and holding his nose. But I, a stupid man, an intellectual, an intellectual so brainless he even loves his country, tarries by the dungheap that is China. I even approach the dungheap and attempt to engage the flies, crawling all over the turds, in uplifting conversation. I cheerily put forward grand ideas and theories for improving, rebuilding, even totally cleansing and disinfecting this shithole and building a brand new and wonderful city in its place. Do the flies, sucking greedily on their turds, even grace me with a reply?

Someone – another intellectual – once said China was like this emaciated, worn-out old nag, whose master harnesses her to this incredibly heavy wagon, just at the foot of this dangerously steep hill. And then he whips her and curses her and kicks her til the terrified beast lumbers forwards in her traces and slowly starts to climb her way up this amazingly steep hill, straining every muscle and sinew of her broken-backed old body. Her owner screams obscenities and threats, laying into her with whips and sticks, so she gradually wheezes and totters upward yard by yard, straining on inch by inch, til, eventually, halfway up, the creature reaches this point where she cannot pull it another step but is too terrified, with the weight of that great wagon behind her, to let it slip even an inch backwards. So she is stuck, teetering back and forth on the edge of disaster.

In the darkness I lie in my warm, warm bed, next to my soft, soft wife, who in her sleep pushes her arse so intimately into my crotch, but all I can do in response is sweat. Not sweat with lust, sweat with fear.

I'm in despair over my beloved China. I mean, our last tyrants, the Manchu emperors, collapsed, thank God, but did the Glorious Revolution of 1911 follow them with enlightenment and socialism and justice and the emancipation of women? No, it followed them with thirty years of civil war and famine and warlords and bankers and landlords sucking every last drop of blood out of the corpse. To say nothing of all the foreign invaders. Take the English, pushing into all our rivers and ports with their gunboats, controlling our trade, force feeding us opium. Not that I have anything against the English. I quite like them, in fact – even though they killed my father. I spent a few years living in the rougher end of Bloomsbury in a freezing cold lodging house eking out a living teaching at the School of Oriental Studies. (One of my pupils was a young man called Graham Greene who these days, I'm told, is making quite a name for himself.). Anyhow I fell in love with English writers – Dickens, Conrad, H. G. Wells, Joyce – even their modernists who have influenced me considerably in my own work. I once saw Virginia Woolf walking down the street in Bloomsbury. She hailed a taxi and it stopped right by me so I opened the door for her and she stepped inside without even a glance in my direction. But it's more the ordinary English I really like and admire. The landlady in my lodgings read the *Daily Mail* and was greatly exercised by their continual claims that the country was about to be overrun by a great 'Yellow Peril' – of which I, apparently, was the vanguard. But once she had ceased belabouring me for my oriental infamy, she would pass on to belabouring hundreds of her fellow countrymen, all of whom were apparently even more infamous than me. What I liked best was if I went into pubs or cafes or anywhere, they would all be full of Englishmen telling each other precisely what they thought about everything and precisely what they were going to do about it. And the people they insulted the most were their own government. Imagine a Chinese person doing that! Most Chinese people don't even know they have a government. So the Englishmen and the Englishwomen would insult and vilify and excoriate every politician alive and then promptly rush out and vote for them. English people know their minds and speak them.

There are lots of other foreigners – French, Portuguese, German, Italian, Americans – who have invaded us and posted their soldiers and gunboats throughout our country – but I don't know so much about them.

But the foreigners who have caused the greatest humiliation, the greatest terror are, without doubt, the Japanese.

My wife turns in her sleep. I feel her soft breath on my cheek. In the next room sleep my three young children. In the room beyond my beloved – if difficult – mother. She talks continuously – even when asleep.

The Japanese are barbarians. They believe in and practise the disgraceful scientific theories of Social Darwinism. Eugenics, they believe, scientifically proves that they are superior to all other races on earth and that therefore it is natural and right for them to butcher and enslave all inferior races, especially us Chinese.

Don't get me wrong. I consider myself to be a progressive man. I believe in all human beings, men and women, working together to build a better world. I believe in the compassionate and loving teachings of Our Lord Jesus Christ. The writings of Count Tolstoy and Rabindranath Tagore, of H.G. Wells and Mr George Bernard Shaw. But do I believe in Science? The great God which all the Western world bows down before? Science gives us medicine, fine buildings, swift transport, good food – but only the rich can afford them. Science also gives the Japanese the flying machines and tanks and shiny weaponry and poison gas to massacre us. And worst of all, Social Darwinism, taught in universities all around the world, gives madmen the just cause to exterminate the rest of us.

I can bear this no longer. With all my churning and sweating I will awaken my gentle wife. I slip softly as I can out of our bed, pass the room my children sleep in, pass the room my mother chatters in. We live in a modern westernized apartment block on the university campus where I teach and write. In the sitting room, in the ghostly light of first dawn, I dress, hopping about beside the drawing board my wife sketches out her graphic designs and paints her paintings on. I slip out onto the streets.

In the cold dawn air I pass traders carrying fresh vegetables and fruit to market, food stalls starting to steam their sweet-smelling dumplings, a beggar out early to catch the early bird. I give him a few pennies. I climb the stone stairway onto our city walls and look outwards. Drink in Thousand Buddha Mountain stood immense and eternal to the south, its snow peak blazing in the first yellow shafts of sunlight. Further down its slopes the refractions of light purples and mauves and oranges and lemon yellows and pinks – a kaleidoscope of mists and hazes and tiny hide-and-seek rainbows. Around its dark base solid crags and sombre pine forests.

I relax a little.

To the north the silent mist-shrouded waters of Daming Lake – lost in a dream of itself. In summer it's matted in a vivid green tapestry of lotus leaves, each with its white spiked flower spearing into the sky. Now in autumn the lotuses have all rotted and the usually clear waters lie brown and rank. Swallows swoop above, feeding on its fat flies, daggering up and down again like black lightning. It warms me that they are still loyally staying with us, not yet starting their long flight south. In the distance, on the far side of the lake, runs a line of willow trees which marks the southern bank of our Great Yellow River. Our Mighty Protector. On its bank looms the black hulk of the Great Iron Bridge spanning the river. From several miles further north of the bridge comes the occasional crump of artillery – our artillery – firmly keeping the Japanese away from us. Unlike in Beijing or Tientsin or Taiyuan or Shanghai or Nanking, our Jinan troops have not turned and fled. Our general, General Han Fuju, has stood and fought. He has successfully fought off Japan's most feared, most arrogant soldier, General Rensuke Isogai, commander of the Imperial Japanese Army's notorious 10th Division. The Great Iron Bridge resupplies General Han's troops on the north bank with food and ammunition and reserves. In our city of Jinan we feel safe.

But it's not just the Japanese who keep me awake at night. I recently received a telegram. Before I relate its contents I think it only courteous that I should explain who I am – otherwise you will not understand the import of the telegram. I say this in all modesty but I, Lao She, am actually a quite well-known writer – well, as well known as any writer can be in a country where 97 per cent of the people can't read. I have written novels and short stories. Last year I wrote a novel, *Rickshaw Boy*, about a rickshaw boy, a sort of social realist State-of-China type novel, which gathered some quite positive reviews and has since been translated into several languages. Hollywood is apparently talking about making it into a film.

So I, a writer, receive this telegram. From a firm friend, General Feng Yuxiang. He, like me, is a Christian. He used to baptize his troops by lining them up in a field and drenching them all with a fire hose. He was an extremely successful and humane general, and whatever lands he gained control of he always governed justly and with an eye to improving the lot of the ordinary people. He dresses like a peasant because he says he was born a peasant and will die a peasant.

We met six or seven years ago when our great and wise leader, Generalissimo Chiang Kai-shek, saw fit to send us both, separately, into exile here in far-off Jinan – myself for my critical writings, Feng for being too successful a soldier. We met at our chapel social, over tea and biscuits. He told me that, in order to educate his troops, he had regularly read them some of my short stories. Our families immediately took to each other. Feng's wife, Li Dequan, had set up fifteen schools for poor rural children in the Mount Tai area and myself and my wife would sometimes go and teach at them.

After chapel we frequently took picnics together on the slopes of the majestic Thousand Buddha Mountain. Since the Japanese invasion three months ago, though, our beloved leader, not trusting General Feng to be so close to actual fighting, had ordered him to attend him at his new capital, Wuhan, where he could keep a closer eye on him. However Chiang, being widely criticized for losing Beijing and Shanghai and Nanking, was not in as strong a position as he had once been and was forced to grant Feng a more powerful position. That would not involve – perish the thought – actually fighting the Japanese, but two areas where Feng Yuxiang also had a reputation for expertise – social reform and propaganda.

Feng sent me this telegram offering me a job as a propagandist in Wuhan. He was vague about the details. I thought about it and came to this conclusion. I am not a propagandist, I am a novelist. My latest novel, half finished, is all about the invasion – the horrors of the Japanese, the heroism of the Chinese. I feel my novel will be more effective in stirring people up to fight than any propaganda I might attempt. Moreover my family are happily settled here in Jinan and we seem relatively safe. And I am certain my mother would find the long journey south extremely arduous. I sent my friend a telegram last night thanking him but turning down his offer. Though I still felt sufficiently guilty about turning him down to toss and turn all night.

While I am thus pacing the battlements bewailing my indecision like Hamlet on the walls of Elsinore, a huge explosion occurs. Even though it is a long way off it knocks me on the hard stone walkway. As, bewildered, I am still trying to recover my senses, I become aware of these dead leaves from the willow trees above all descending upon my head and the sound of breaking glass and screams from within the city. I stand up and look immediately in the direction of the university campus – no smoke or flames there. I look round the city – nothing there. I look at Thousand Buddha Mountain. It's still there. Only then do I turn and look north at Daming Lake. There are waves and disturbance on its surface, shrieking waterfowl rising all over it in panic as behind me jackdaws and crows and kites scream above the city – but nowhere on the lake is there any sign of an explosion. Only then do I look even further north. And that is where the explosion has occurred. The Great Iron Bridge over the Yellow River is belching fire and smoke. Some of its spans have been hit as well as the piers beneath them so its central section appears to have collapsed into the water. Parts of it are still creaking and crashing. Our bridge! Our defence! We will no longer be able to resupply our troops and hold the Japanese back, they will be able to advance and shell our city at will.

I know I should be with my family. I start running home. The explosion has broken windows everywhere and they might have been caught by the flying glass. All the time as I run I see people who have been cut and wounded by glass, others just milling about in confusion.

I finally get home. Fortunately our apartment faces away from the direction of the explosion. I rush into it and see my young son Little Yi. He says no one has been hurt by the glass but then he points towards my old mother's room. The look on his face indicates something grave has happened. The door is shut. I knock on the door saying it is me. My wife's voice says 'You can come in.' I go in and shut the door behind me, all three children having gathered on the other side of it. On the floor lies my mother. She is moaning and obviously in pain.

'What happened?' I softly ask my wife.

'She was just getting out of bed,' she says, 'just as it happened. The bang. It knocked her sideways. Her leg fell across this stool. I think it's broken.'

'Have you called a doctor?'

'Little Yi ran down to the medical facility on the campus. A doctor is on his way.'

'Get her something to soothe her,' I say.

'I'll infuse some corydalis root. I should have bought those aspirin pills I saw in town yesterday.'

'Don't worry about it,' I say, sitting beside her on the floor with my back against the bed. Very slowly we transfer my mother's head from my wife's lap to mine. She gives out little sharp cries as we do so. Her fractured upper leg lies at two angles from where it has been broken. My wife scurries away.

I sit there with my mother's head cradled in my lap, soothing her with words and the odd crooning, keening noises I remember from childhood. My three children creep slowly into the room and stare at us in wonder.

The doctor comes. He confirms that her leg has been broken and that it will take several weeks to mend. He says in the meantime she cannot be moved.

5

The shells from over the river have started landing in our city. Not too many of them at the moment. We have hunkered down in our apartment – I go out to do the shopping and I still do a bit of teaching on campus. Some of the students have left for the south from the railway station, but many have stayed. They still come to my classes, but they spend most of their time in the city – digging out and nursing the wounded, putting out fires, feeding the poor, helping to house the many refugees who have poured into our city. They constantly hold meetings to stir the people up by explaining why we have been invaded and how we can fight back against the invaders. They issue pamphlets. They improvise theatre and drum singing shows – some showing stirring moments from our history, others set today – to raise morale and rouse peoples' fighting spirit. Some have joined the armed forces. I am immensely proud of them.

I spend some of my time at home writing my patriotic novel, but a lot of it talking with my bed-bound mother. She talks only about the past – when we lived in Beijing. It brings her comfort, but there is little comfort in our family history.

I should explain that I was born a Manchu. That means that I belong to the racial minority which arrived in China in the seventeenth century as the horse and foot soldiers of the invading Manchurian warrior, Prince Dorgon. Prince Dorgon became the first Manchu emperor; his soldiers were garrisoned throughout China to impose his rule. My ancestors were posted in Beijing, and as the years went past their duties became less and less onerous and more and more ceremonial. And as the Manchu Dynasty was weakened in the nineteenth century by rebellions, invasions and loss of revenue, their pay became less and less. But they always considered themselves a cut above the native Han population, and even though they were virtually penniless, living in their compounds, they still cultivated an air of languid refinement, specializing in breeding exquisite songbirds and ferocious fighting crickets.

Which is how my father came to his grisly and non-heroic end. He still held the honorary post of a Red Bannerman in the Imperial Guard of the Emperor. In fact he was a corpulent and unhealthy middle-aged man living a life of ease. The nearest foreign equivalent I can think of is the English Beefeater, whose portly figures and red uniforms I occasionally glimpsed in London. Anyhow, when I was one year old the Boxer Rebellion broke out. This internal Chinese affray apparently incensed all the foreign imperialists who promptly sent their young and virile soldiery to quash this outrage. My father, who had hardly ever had any military training, was stuffed into his Red Bannerman uniform, had a seventeenth-century pike and an eighteenth-century musket thrust into his hand, and was ordered to rid his country of the foreign devils. He waddled to the end of our street, waddled round the corner, and was promptly shot dead by a keen and youthful British soldier.

(There is another family version of my father's unfortunate end. Namely that, never having fired a musket in his life, he practised in our backyard. In a state of some inebriation he experimented with connecting the burning saltpetre fuse to the gunpowder in the firing pan, but while trying to set the fuse alight with matches from his pocket, he instead set alight the voluminous Red Banner robes he was accoutered and enfolded within and promptly burnt himself to death. Our uncle allegedly found his smouldering body in our wood shed. But there must be some doubt as to the truth of this account as my uncle only told it when he himself was drunk.)

Anyhow, the fact was that my mother suddenly found herself in a terrible situation. With all the vicious sanctions and levies imposed upon the Chinese government by the victorious foreigners, all pensions ceased immediately. My mother, without a husband, suddenly had to support herself, myself, and my elder brothers and sisters. Feed us and find us shelter. She at once took in washing. My earliest memories were of sheets and clothing of all colours and hues hanging from the rafters and in the courtyard and me having to make my precarious way among them, sometimes pulling them down and immediately enduring a barrage of slaps and scolds. I remember once burning myself on the side of the huge laundry cauldron. From the earliest age my elder siblings went out on the streets to deliver and collect washing or run errands for neighbours or to shop or even beg. I think one or two of them were caught stealing and my mother had to go down to the police station and persuade them her children were poor but honest and from a poor but honest family.

I, an urchin, grew up on the streets of Beijing and I loved it. All I have to do is close my eyes, and immediately the city appears before me like a vivid, richly coloured tapestry. I hear the different cries of the market sellers, hucksters, hawkers, touts, barkers and balladeers, pedlars selling plum juice and almond tea, tinkers their wares, each trade with a different cry and chant and patter. Some were so funny, so sharp, some so sad and moving. I knew which street I was in simply by their different calls and songs. And there were the street entertainers and storytellers – sometimes even bigger shows like the puppeteers or drum singers with their musical instruments and chanteuses – warbling their songs and telling their tales of ancient heroes and villains, beautiful princesses and dragons and magical horses. Far too often I tarried and stared, sucked into imaginary landscapes and fantastical events, and far too often my mother found me and beat me.

My mother was the centre of all things. She kept us all revolving around her, doing her wishes, earning her money, delivering letters and notes and bills for shopkeepers to other shopkeepers, carrying water from the wells and coal from the merchants' yard, haggling and arguing with stall holders at the end of the day that their unsold vegetables and meats and dumplings had gone rotten and should be sold to us at a quarter their price. Each evening the laundry cauldron would be emptied of its water and we would wash in it, then replace it on the fire with a cooking pot round which we all gathered to inhale the wondrous smells of cooking food.

And when the woman who lived down the street and read books and saw my interest in stories started teaching me how to write and read, it was my mother who encouraged me and said it was a good and a proper thing for me to do. For a while, God knows how, she found the money to send me to the Beijing Normal Third High School, but then she ran out of money and couldn't afford it anymore so I had to leave. But by then I had a thirst for learning, so, by beating on important men's doors and making a nuisance of herself – all the time running a household and a laundry and all my other brothers and sisters – she leveraged me, a poor street Manchu, into the free Beijing Normal University.

So now you understand why I cannot leave her. It is not only my Confucian duty as a son, it is because I owe her everything. So I sit and listen to her memories of Old Beijing and join her in them. The man from over the courtyard with snaggle teeth, the knife grinder that kept cutting himself, the barber with the hiccups, the criminal being led down the street to execution scattering pennies to all the children so they would speak well of him when they arrived in the afterlife, the whores who lived in the hovel in the next street and sang such sad beautiful songs.

I was her son. I am now her mother, nursing her. I feel all the tenderness and anguish for her a mother feels for her child. And all the time the shells land closer.

With all their mad scientific ideas about master races and Social Darwinism, the Japanese must believe that they are superior to us in every way. That we are mere sub-animals and inferior apes. After all they've measured our skulls with calipers and tape measures and proved it! So since they possess in every way superior brains and skulls and IQs, it must follow that we Chinese have no brains at all and the IQ of a head louse. The fact that we have superb scholars at first-rate universities and a 3,000-year history of brilliant civilization and poets and painters and philosophers is, to say the least, problematic to them. In fact, it demolishes all their crazy European theories. So it can be no surprise that from the start of their war against us they have adopted a deliberate policy of always bombing and destroying universities first in any city, of deliberately killing as many high IQed students as possible. Whenever they come across a household which owns books they butcher everyone in it and burn their books. All to drive down our IQ statistics!

Which is why our home, within the university, comes under pretty continuous fire from Japanese artillery and their air force. My children are terrified, my wife is terrified, I am terrified. My mother is too sick to understand what is going on. I have to choose between the life of my mother or the lives of my children and my wife and myself. If we stay here we are all going to be butchered by the Japanese. If my wife and my children and myself leave, then my mother remains here alone to be butchered by the Japanese – provided she lives that long. But confronted by this seemingly simple conundrum my dyed-in-the-wool Confucian blood immediately kicks in and decides we must all perish. It is our fate. And what is worse, my wife and all my children not only immediately assent to my decision, but agree 100 per cent with the sentiments behind it. As a halfway house I suggest to my wife and children they should leave from the railway station and I should remain here in Jinan with my mother and my books. They reject this even more vehemently.

Finally the part of our apartment block facing the Japanese is destroyed and our apartment becomes structurally unsound. We have to move. The doctor is summoned. He says that my mother should be able to withstand about ten minutes of gentle movement. I go into the town and rent a solid stone single-storey home in a solid stone courtyard about ten minutes from our present apartment. I choose it mainly because, as well as being extremely solid and facing south, it contains in its courtyard a red persimmon tree. I love the red persimmon's spring blossoms more than any other – not that we're likely to still be alive by spring. I also hire coolies to move our furniture and belongings. The doctor doses my mother with four tablets of opium. When she is almost comatose a coolie and I lift her up and carry her out. Carry her down a stairwell whose walls have been blown away so we look straight out over Daming Lake, its silent waters coldly, beautifully reflecting the hills to the east. All the time she gives out a high-pitched keen, writhing slowly as though she is far underwater.

We carefully put her down to rest in our new home.

In order to keep up with what is happening in the world and the latest war news, rather than take a paper home and risk my family reading the latest Japanese atrocities, I visit the partly demolished staff room on campus. I'm told by a surviving academic that the Japanese have crossed the river and there is now heavy fighting in the north-eastern industrial suburbs of the city. But he also assures me that the rock-solid General Han Fuju has everything in hand.

I pick up a copy of the *Shanghai Evening Post & Mercury* and read an article by some fat-necked upper-class Englishman called Mr T. O. Thackery:

The entrance to my favorite stand at the Shanghai Racecourse is blocked with corpses, fresh corpses newly made before my eyes. There are women and children among them; women shot through the back, their padded coats run through with military sabres, children whose bodies are riddled with bullets; men garbed as peasant farmers heaped grotesquely about, their wounds soaking the ground.

Later in the article T. O. Thackery travels out into the countryside:

The houses are burned. I saw them burn, with neat precision – not a wasted match, nor an extra piece of kindling. I witness a Japanese officer killing farmers fleeing from their burning huts. His shining sabre flashes up to its hilt in the human sheath; the body falls. A second takes its place and once again the sabre finds its pulsing scabbard. The next, a tall and likely lad, is flung unbound face down upon the two who clutch the earth in death; and as he falls a volley from six officers' revolvers make an outline on his back and up his spine.

I digest this while I go into the city to do the family shopping. The streets are fuller – with civilians fleeing from the north-eastern suburbs. I also hear an ugly rumour. That the Great Iron Bridge across the Yellow River was blown up not by the enemy but on the direct orders of a panicking General Han Fuju. Not only that, but he blew it up while hundreds of refugees were crossing it, and before some thousands of our finest troops to the north of the river could be withdrawn, thus causing them to be massacred by the Japanese.

When I get home there is a knock on the courtyard door. Little Yi goes to see who it is. He comes back with a soldier in an immaculate uniform. He salutes me and then presents me with a rather ornate envelope.

'Thank you,' I say. 'My son will see you back to the gate.'

'I am under orders,' says the soldier, 'not to leave until you have written a response, which I will take with me.'

'Oh.'

I retire to the cubbyhole where I work on my patriotic novel, sit down, and read the letter. It is from my friend General Feng Yuxiang. That soldier must have had a long journey from Wuhan. I slip out to ask my wife to prepare some food for him and find she already has. I return to the letter.

Lao She, my dear friend,

I apologize to you for the brevity of my telegram last week, and for not explaining to you properly what exactly it is that we need of you. I understand completely why you turned me down. The fact is that here in Wuhan matters are moving at great speed as we set up our new government, and what we, and I, intend to do has been evolving and changing day by day. I now know precisely what I want of you, but, as ever, the decision is with you.

I will explain to you why I think you are the only person in our country who can do what I want you to do for us.

I like you, Lao She. You are a person I trust. And trust is a quality very rare in government. I like and trust you not just because we are both Christians, but because of the sort of man you are. You have integrity. You have humour. You honour the truth. You are intelligent – not arrogant-intelligent but humble-intelligent. Unlike most artistic people you are not self-centred and narcissistic and melodramatic, instantly antagonistic to and jealous of all other creative persons – you appreciate and praise the work of your fellow writers. Well, almost all your fellow writers. I know you have especial difficulties with the work of one Guo Morou and some other holier-than-thou upper-class East Coast intellectuals with their impenetrable jargon-filled Marxist diatribes. But Christians from poor backgrounds such as ourselves are well used to politely and effectively dealing with such grotesques.

At this time of catastrophic crisis for our country, what we need above all is communication. Most Chinese – of whatever class, whatever region or village – are not even capable of speaking to each other in a common dialect. Ninety-seven per cent of our nation cannot read. We, very quickly, obscenely quickly, must develop a common language, a common understanding through which we can communicate directly and powerfully to each other. So that we can organize and rally ourselves into some sort of effective defence, and, given time, offence. It can only be done through language. And you are our master of language.

Through our many conversations I know your love of street theatre, folk art, the legends and stories that our common people adore and know by heart. I know there is a group of you who specialize in this, who have worked to promote your socialist views through writing and performing plays and drum singing, who know and love and can speak strikingly in the common tongue.

But the problem is that, vital as you are, you are few. We live in a nation of hundreds of millions who must be brought to think of themselves as one nation. There are many other writers in this country, but, as I have already mentioned, they tend to be well-off intellectuals, writers used to expressing their agonies and sufferings and Marxist ecstasies in a high Mandarin style totally incomprehensible to 99 % of our population.

We need someone who can teach them to speak and think and write in ways which will immediately enter the hearts and souls of us rude untutored common folk.'

I sigh deeply.

My dear Comrade Lao, of old I know that in an argument you can see and understand and respect both sides, and while not compromising your principles can usually with the greatest subtlety and grace finesse both sides so that each can recognize the good points the other side is offering. I don't know how you do it. But you do. And this country needs that beautiful quality of yours in order to bring together our writers and artists and get them to inspire and instruct the Chinese people in what we have to do.

That, my friend, is what I require of you. Come to Wuhan. We will set up the facilities so you can work with all these different people and help save the country we both love so much.

I can feel your pain at my request even from this distance.

Your friend,
Feng Yuxiang

Well, thank you very much, bloody Mister bloody Feng Yuxiang. Thanks for skewering me right through the gut with your bloody bayonet pen and then twisting it around and around. I slam the letter down on my desk and exit my cubbyhole, banging my head on a beam. I inform the soldier that he will have to wait for my decision and tell my wife that I am going out for a constitutional.

The streets are full of refugees from the north of the city. There are few street hawkers or stall holders and many of the shops have put up their shutters and closed. I see soldiers – individuals, small groups – who've obviously deserted their units. The crump of artillery shells and the distant sounds of rifle shots and machine gun fire play continuously on my ears but I hardly notice this. My whole being is in chaos.

Again I am on the ancient walls of Jinan. The skies, the lake, the landscape are all cold and bleak. The fighting in the north of the city fills the air with smoke. I pace melodramatically back and forth.

I am a progressive. A socialist. As I have said before, I believe with all my heart and all my soul in all human beings, men and women, working together to build a better world. A better China. It has been what all my work, all my writings have been about. And I believe there is nothing more reactionary, more responsible for keeping China in its feudal dungeon, its fetid shithole, than the teachings of bloody Confucius. I have made a career, an increasingly successful career, out of ridiculing his teachings on society and the family. How they tie down individuals, and the whole country, into a vicious web of obligation and service. How eldest sons have to sacrifice their whole lives to serve their almighty families. How second, third and fourth sons can have no individual careers or lives because they must always be subservient to and dependent upon their eldest brother. How women are reduced to powerless helots and married off to complete strangers. How all are ruled by their omnipotent parents who are themselves ruled by their even more omnipotent ancestors. It is ludicrous, unbelievable, fascistic, Jurassic. But yet, at this, my moment of crisis and supreme test of being, what is the ridiculous mode of thought and harness of behaviour I immediately, willingly, rejoicingly climb back into – bloody Confucianism! Honour thy mother! Honour thy parents! Honour thy ancestors! They come before all! Sacrifice your children, sacrifice your wife, sacrifice your country! I wish for just a moment that perhaps I was one of those bloody – I really must think up a better swear word – Westerners – you know, the atheists, the Social Darwinists – they wouldn't hesitate for a second. 'Desert your dear old mum, dear boy. Survival of the fittest, dontcha know? Is it your fault she can't run as fast as you?'

Here it is. China at last has a chance of change. Something I had despaired of ever happening. And I could actually play a useful role in bringing about that change. It is my duty. My sacred duty. But I can't, because... because... because I love my old mum. I love her beyond all reason. I love her because, from nothing, she created me. My whole family and I have already been through all this once, and have reached the same conclusion. We stay.

I start to walk back. In the streets rubble is piling up where shells have hit buildings. There are fewer refugees and more soldiers, some of them obviously drunk. I avoid them. The Japanese can only be a few hours away. I spend my time pondering on what will happen when they arrive. They'll break into my home, and I'll, I suppose, be standing in front of my family to protect them, and I'll walk forwards to try and explain that they should not kill us, and they'll bayonet me. I'll fall to the ground in such a way that I can see them as they bayonet and shoot my wife and children, and finally, just before I die, I'll see my mother being macheted to bits on her bed.

I walk through our courtyard door and see the soldier sitting on the ground under the red persimmon tree. He is eating one of its fruits as he plays games with my two young daughters and tells Little Yi about what it's like to be a soldier. I start to tell him that he should tell his general that I will not be coming, but as I do I see my wife walking down the steps from our home. She is walking in a rather decisive manner. She is speaking to me in a tone of voice which she has never used before. She is speaking to me with authority.

'Husband, I want to talk to you. Come inside. Tell the soldier to wait.'

She walks back up the steps. I automatically follow her. We go into the cubbyhole. 'Mind your head,' she warns me. We sit down. She at my desk, me sort of crouching on the other side.

'Husband, while you were away, I have been reading the letter from Feng.'

'I have decided I am not going. We are staying.'

'That is not what will happen,' she says with authority.

'But...'

'Listen to me.'

I listen to her.

'All our lives we have been progressives. Every day we have worked, we have spoken, we have dedicated our lives to bringing reform, to bringing justice and equality, to this terrible, backwards, crumbling country of ours. It has been what all my painting has been about, your writing. Yet what happens when we reach the crunch, this moment of change? When we can actually do something to help change our beloved China? We give in. We run away.'

I do not know in which direction to look. She holds me with this terrifying basilisk stare.

'I am not going to allow this to happen. You are going to go to Wuhan. You are going to work for the new China. I will stay here and I will do my best to protect our children and your mother. As is my duty as a wife and dutiful daughter-in-law.'

(She is actually out-Confucianizing me with that point!)

'But the Japanese will be here at any moment, they'll slaughter...'

'This is a war,' she grinds at me. 'It is a war for the future of our country. In wars terrible sacrifices must be made. People, beloved ones, die. For the good of our country you must go to Wuhan and do work only you can do. I will do my very best to survive the Japanese. If they let us live I will find the money – I can sell my graphic designs as I already do, I can do secretarial work, I can teach – to support the family. And then, through God's grace, let us survive until you and the forces of change return to free us. That is what you will do, husband, you will go to Wuhan. Go and tell the soldier our decision. Then we will pack your bags, you can say farewell to us, and you must go to the train station immediately.'

My wife always wore a beautiful Indian silk scarf around her slender neck. It was a gift from Rabindranath Tagore, the illustrious Indian poet and anti-colonialist. When we were first married we had met him and some fellow Indians when they were doing a lecture tour of China. They spoke of socialism, freedom, and the solidarity of all peoples around the earth, especially China and India. He handed us this beautiful silk scarf as an example of exquisite Indian craftsmanship. We have treasured it ever since.

Now she unwinds it from around her delicate neck and hands it to me.

'Take this with you,' she says. 'I will pack it in your case. And when you think of me, take it out and hold it.'

I write a brief note to Feng saying I will come. I hand it to the soldier who thanks me and departs.

To say farewell to everything you are is very difficult. It is as though I am among ghosts. I wander around the home. There are my wife's paintings, paintings powerful and serene, paintings which have sold so well in Beijing and Shanghai. On the walls, attached with drawing pins, are my children's imitations of their mother's work, garish crayon gashes and vivid splodges of paint. Tiny stick figures seemingly trying to avoid enormous explosions.

I start to feel horribly emotional, but I must calm myself down. The whole family sort of walks around each other, detached yet attached, avoiding each other, it is the only way to deal with such moments. But for one second I let myself go. And I have never forgiven myself for this. I am about to desert my family, I am probably never going to see them again. We are packing my suitcase, my wife folding each garment as she puts it inside, silk scarf and all. And there is this moment when she cannot quite press them in, and so Little Yi, my son, in his keenness to help, pushes in to press it and knocks an ornament off the table and I snap at him. Harshly. He bites his lip, desperate not to cry. I apologize to him, I apologize again, aghast. That at this moment...!

My wife cuts across it all. 'You must go. The last train is leaving Jinan Station at seven o'clock. Go.'

We stumble outside. All except my mother, who is fast asleep. From the street outside come confused shouts and the sound of rifle shots. I look at them all.

'How are we going to communicate? So I know you are all right?'

'We probably won't.'

'You could write to me *poste restante* at the Wuhan Post Office – I'll check every day.'

'That would be too dangerous. You are a famous person. If I think it is safe to send a letter there I'll address it to Wu Lei.'

'Wu Lei?'

'Wu Lei.'

My wife picks a red persimmon fruit off the tree and hands it to me, I put it in an inside pocket. She opens the gate. I touch her arm. With my suitcase in one hand and my typewriter and the script of my patriotic novel under the other arm, I stumble out onto the streets of Jinan.

6

Millions of people, like a giant column of ants, slowly, painstakingly crawled their way across the face of a great unending yellow plain. Clouds of dust swirled about them. The autumn sun shone down relentless. Similar scenes were occurring all over China as Japanese armies advanced into Central China from the north and the east.

Above the floods of fleeing civilians flew the Japanese air force, bombing and strafing and machine-gunning the refugees. From the rear of these hordes came the sounds of Japanese artillery and rifle fire driving them on, slaughtering or enslaving those they overtook.

Within the wagon Wei's wife groaned and convulsed in labour. Her husband slept beside her. Second Son lead the donkey and in his tiny head tried to work out what had been happening to him in the last day – the flight, the bodies in the stream, the madness of the midnight panic. And what strange thing was now happening to his mother? She was in pain. Was she dying? But not for one second did his eyes stop from looking all around him for more danger. His grandfather, with a conical straw hat on his head and a cloth tied across his mouth and nose to keep out the dust, walked on the other side of the donkey's head. Worried and preoccupied, hunched like a dried-up old shrimp, he was trying to remember something. He had taken to wandering in random directions. Second Son kept an eye on him too.

Behind the cart, sharpened spade in one hand, a two-year-old sleeping Baby Boy Wei in the other, walked Eldest Son. He'd not forgotten his shame of falling asleep on the night of the great stampede. He was looking all about him diligently, constantly. Twenty yards to his right plodded on foot a farming family all in red clothing. Eldest Son had never seen this before. Everyone in his village always wore blue. They spoke to each other in strange accents and were always arguing. Eldest Son smiled a lot to them. To his left were mostly small groups or individuals, continually overtaking or falling behind the Weis. A drunken man staggered towards him, but on seeing Eldest Son raising his spade, headed back into the horde.

Since her father was asleep and her mother for some reason was ignoring her, little Cherry Blossom had climbed onto the rear tailgate of the cart and she and Baby Girl Wei were playing with her pet hedgehog. Baby Girl Wei, three years old, was less interested in the hedgehog and more in the delight she felt that Cherry Blossom was for once taking notice of her. She smiled beatifically at her sister.

Over their heads flew a flight of Japanese bombers. They had dropped their bombs on the fleeing civilians further south and were now returning north to their airfield, machine-gunning the Chinese hordes in a random fashion. Quite close to the cart a random university professor, clutching valuable papers, was felled to the ground. His papers fluttered away in the wind.

Spider Girl waddled behind the cart's tailgate. Before he fell fast asleep her father had instructed her to prepare a honey concoction to strengthen her mother's constitution and protect her against infection. He'd poured some of the wild pear juice from his bottle into a bowl, and now Spider Girl, ignoring her own pain as she walked, carefully held a honeycomb above the bowl and, having sliced the caps off some of the cells with her knife, bled the honey slowly into the bowl. When she had finished she broke off the corner of emptied cells and handed them to Baby Girl Wei and Cherry Blossom to suck. She had to police them to ensure Cherry Blossom didn't take it all. She stirred the honey and the wild pear juice together. The honey taken from all the flowers and blossoms growing on their farm. The wild pear juice from the tiny pears that grew on the wild pear tree whose roots went first into the bones of the sister her father loved so much, then, further off, into the bones of all the generations of ancestors who had lived on and worked on the farm before them. All the love, all the strength of their entire family, as her father had intended, was present in this medicine for his wife. The family must survive. That was why Spider Girl loved her father so much. All the thought he put into everything, and all for the sake of the family.

She fed it to her mother. Her mother took sips between contractions, all the time staring at Spider Girl with this black, bleak look, as though Spider Girl was a monster from hell.

Spider Girl knew that her time with the family was not long. But she would serve them whole-heartedly until they cast her off.

A few hours later, as evening came on, Wei's wife's waters broke. She went into the second stage of labour, her body starting to push her unborn child out.

Wei stopped the wagon. His wife's breathing was complicated by all the dust in her lungs. Every time she breathed in hard to help her push, she coughed and spluttered pitifully. As Wei tied a cloth over her nose and mouth to ease her breathing – inwardly cursing himself for not having thought of this earlier – he ordered Second Son and Cherry Blossom to remove all the utensils and tools hanging under the cart and stacked them in the cart – in case they had to make a sudden getaway. He took the three wooden buckets – all empty – knocked the hoops off two of them and piled the staves for firewood in the cart. He put the iron hoops in as well for later barter. The third bucket he kept for the donkey to be watered from – provided they could spare the water.

Meanwhile, Spider Girl had taken out some of the fabrics and was draping them around the outside of the wagon so the space beneath the wagon became a private area, hidden from the outside world. Wei's wife, as emphatically as her raw lungs would allow her, told her husband she did not need any help at any time, she must be utterly by herself. She then crawled under the back of the wagon and her husband closed the curtain. She removed her clothes, piled them neatly in a corner, and squatted on her haunches. She was very thirsty but did not let it bother her. She spat out what phlegm she could. Rocking back and forth she started to moan and shudder.

Wei stood on guard by the curtain. He prayed to the earth god Tudeh for his wife and his unborn child.

Outside the first of their three water jars was unsealed. The family was fed by Spider Girl, who did it as quietly as possible so their mother, under the cart, did not hear and grow jealous and fractious that her daughter was usurping her role. And all the time the family eavesdropped for even the slightest sound coming from beneath the cart.

Spider Girl handed out the remains of their salad leaves – wilted and dry but still nutritious – two cold dumplings, two raw carrots, three dried apricots and the carcases of the remaining two chickens which would go rotten if kept any longer. Spider Girl was scrupulously fair in every portion she handed out – and with the sips from the bowl of water – but when she was distracted by Baby Boy Wei falling over and having to be comforted, she handed Grandpa two senna pods instead of one.

It was at this moment that Grandfather – who had been fretting about it ever since they left the farm – suddenly remembered the second piece of wisdom his grandfather had passed down to him so many years ago about how to survive a mass flight such as this. The first piece had been that water is always more vital to survival than food. This had been most useful and the extra water they had brought was already helping them. But the second piece of advice – which he had remembered the moment Spider Girl passed him the senna pods – was even stranger. 'What my grandfather said,' he announced to the family, 'was to drink your own piss.'

This suggestion was met with almost universal disgust. Cherry Blossom was loud in her horror. Baby Girl Wei also expressed her horror, because that was what Cherry Blossom was doing. Baby Boy Wei didn't really have an opinion either way. Eldest Son giggled and looked embarrassed. And for Second Son this was yet another sign that the world he lived had gone terrifyingly crazy. Wei, however, noted the advice, saw its virtue, and started immediately practising it. So, of course, did Grandfather, who, following every future urination, loudly declared himself mightily refreshed. Spider Girl did it too, calculating, from the pure water she would save, that it would marginally increase her time with the family.

Wei, seeing that a lot of urine would be going to waste, ordered everybody who wouldn't drink their own to piss into the remaining bucket. Perhaps the donkey would drink it. If the donkey didn't, maybe the goat would. Everyone knows goats are more intelligent than donkeys. But the canny little donkey drank it without a moment's hesitation.

Grandfather and Baby Boy and Baby Girl Wei lay asleep in the cart. Eldest Son and Spider Girl lay asleep on the ground. Second Son lay beside them, desperately trying to understand this new world into which he had so suddenly been cast. Wei kept guard, pacing round and round the tiny circumference of his family. He checked the donkey had eaten the feed in his nosebag. He chased off a shadowy man trying to steal a pot tied to the side of the cart. He fed the goat. It was still producing some milk, which he fed to his wife and Baby Boy Wei, so he would wait til it dried up entirely before slaughtering it. He'd cut its throat into a bowl so they could make blood cakes from it, then barter some of its meat and the wax from the used honeycombs with a family that already had a fire lit. That way he would waste no firewood. In exchange the Weis would boil the rest of the goat's meat and some beans on their fire and make blood cakes. If it could be arranged, both sides would gain.

He looked around him constantly while concentrating his mind on the dark tent beneath the cart. The groans and mutterings were increasing. He woke Spider Girl to mix another concoction of honey and wild pear juice. When she had made it she passed it to him and he told her to go back to sleep. He squatted by the curtain, opened it, and passed his wife the bowl.

'How is it, dear wife?'

'It is coming.'

'Do you know how long it will be before you give birth?'

She grimaced as her body tensed and convulsed again. She gave out a cry. When the contraction was over she asked:

'Who made this restorative for me to drink?'

'Your eldest daughter.'

Her soul flooded with black anger. That she should dare to take over her duties in the family and usurp her. But she knew she could not speak out to her husband, who disapproved of such thoughts. She let out another cry as the next contraction came. When it was over Wei gently addressed her.

'Dear wife. Please try to make less noise, if it is possible. I know you are in great pain but you are drawing attention to us among all the people around. They will realize our weakness, our vulnerability.'

She agreed with him and nodded her understanding, then indicated he should leave. He carefully put the curtain back in place and stood up.

Inside she held the bowl. Should she drink it or throw it away? Her body was wracked in pain from her contractions, her lungs ached from the dust, and she had to hold within herself all these pains and agonies without releasing them in cries and screams. All this she could manage and control. But the pain she could not control was her rage against her eldest daughter. What should she do? Should she smash the bowl as if it contained poison? Which it did. The poison of treachery and power. Who had persuaded her husband to leave their home, their land? To take part in this nightmarish journey which must surely end in their total extinction? She whose over-loving, foolish father had allowed to live when it was best she had been put out to die. She who had grown into a cripple, a constant drain on the family, and now whose waddling was slowing them down.

Five miles ahead of the Wei family the Japanese air force started to attack the refugee column. Bombs dropped, machine guns crackled and chattered like demented magpies. The horizon was lit with sudden flashes and flares and balls of flame rising into the sky where petrol-driven vehicles were hit. The ground shook. Wei stood watching it. Then, as suddenly as it started, it stopped.

Wei looked round. All of the family still slept. He looked at the blackness beneath the cart.

Beneath the cart, so intense were her thoughts, Wei's wife had not even noticed the raid. Should she throw away the wild pear and honey juice or drink it? It would strengthen her, bring another baby into the family. But she knew that the juice was formed among the bones of her husband's elder sister, she who was the cause of all her husband's foolish soft-heartedness and indulgence when it came to his dealings with his children. So she should throw it away? But the root of the wild pear tree also passed among the bones of her family's ancestors. How would they feel that she had rejected their fruit? They were the important ones. They were the ones who decided whether she, an ignored outsider, was granted full recognition and honour within the family when her eldest son became the farmer of their land.

She breathed in, controlling her breath. Then breathed out, allowing no cries or moans. She could feel her baby's head lowering into the birth canal.

In the darkness beneath the cart her thoughts turned even blacker. Her eldest son above all others had to survive this madness, had to return to farm their land. Nothing was of importance but that. That the land would continue having a Wei farming it. That was what the ancestors, on and on through endless generations, would praise her for. Would welcome her into their midst for, give her a seat of honour. Would rescue her from becoming forever a lonely, wandering ghost.

Her birth canal was on fire. The baby's shoulders were now pushing their way into it. She knew birth was not far off. She gave half a groan before realizing it and suppressing it. This thing must be done. She lifted the bowl and its precious contents and drank them down – poison and all. Whatever the consequences the family must survive.

The head of the baby started to emerge from the lips of her vagina, it emerged fully from her vagina and she wrapped her hands around the baby's head and pulled it out, first the head and then the body, her whole body screaming in pain. She looked at it. Then she strangled it.

She slumped, for a few moments she panted, then she hardened herself and summoned her foolish husband. He drew the curtain, asked her quietly what had happened.?

'It is dead,' she said, handing it to him, holding it by its ankles as a hunter would carry a dead rabbit.

'It was a girl. So I did the right thing. I killed it.'

Wei, holding it, let the curtain fall back. For a few moments he could not stand up. Then he managed to. His dead child rested against his leg. Now it was his turn to be filled with black emotions, anger and dread. He glanced round his family, saw they were all still asleep. He took his spade and walked a few yards off. He knew what his wife had been thinking. That this baby would hinder his family and that his family's survival was all. Because she loved his family and because that was her only way of gaining recognition from the dead. But...

He realized that he could not afford his emotion. He must eat his bitterness. His family must be protected.

He dug a small oblivious hole in the ground. He took his dead baby girl to lower her gently into it, but as he does did so, in the earliest light of dawn, he saw something. The baby was not a girl, it was a boy. That was how desperate his wife was to gain admiration among the ancestors by ensuring the family survived. Even if it meant murdering a son. She had probably calculated that they already had three sons – healthy and hard-working. Another boy could be lost. And she still had plenty of time to carry more sons. His heart choked with shame and despair that he had allowed his family to get to these straits. Then he stopped himself. In his deepest heart, ruthless as she was, he knew his wife had done the right thing.

He turned and walked back towards the cart.

From this moment, from the time when she killed their newborn son, power in the family started to shift away from Wei and towards his wife. But it would be a power which would kill her, poor bewildered woman.

7

By the time Wei got back to the cart his wife had buried her afterbirth, wiped her hands and body of the blood and gore, and put on her clothes.

She and Spider Girl were tidying up, Cherry Blossom and Second Son were rehanging the utensils and bucket beneath the cart, Eldest Son was preparing the donkey for the journey, and Grandfather and the two tots continued their sleep in the cart.

The children were informed that the baby had died in childbirth. Wei told Eldest Son to fall back and guard the cart from the rear with the spade and Second Son to go forward and lead the donkey on. A random bomb fell on the column a few hundred yards away. No one took any notice. The cart swayed and started.

Two others knew what had really occurred last night:. Spider Girl, who had overheard it and agreed completely with her mother's actions, and Second Son, who was already desperately struggling to work out what was happening in this strange new world.

Wei, his mind still filled with last night's events, suddenly realized his wife was walking beside him rather than riding in the cart and immediately lifted her onto it so she could rest, gave Baby Girl Wei to Eldest Son to carry and took Baby Boy Wei himself. She as quickly wriggled off and started walking again.

'Why did you do that, wife? You need rest.'

'I do not need rest. I do not wish Eldest Son and you to grow even wearier having to carry the tots. Put them back on the cart.'

They had a brief argument. His wife refused to get back on the cart. Wei hit her. She muttered curses but climbed back onto the cart with some alacrity. Wei had to smile at his wife's artfulness. She wanted a rest in the cart but had to show herself willing to sacrifice her comfort for the good of the family. Her slyness was one of the reasons he liked her so much. Spider Girl also saw her mother's cleverness and grinned too. Her mother saw this.

'Why do we allow this monster to stay in the family one more second?' she asked Wei, indicating she was talking about Spider Girl. 'Look at her waddling along like some fat duck, grinning her evil grins. If it hadn't been for her we'd still be safely at home, with our land all around us.'

'Stop showing your ignorance,' replied Wei, 'if we'd stayed we'd all be dead by now. It's because of Spider Girl we're still alive.'

'She made up all that stuff about her newspapers, just to scare us away. She's a malcontent. She works to destroy her own family. Look at that hair on her lip. She's the child of some devil.'

'Are you saying you slept with a devil?'

'I'm saying a good child listens to her elders' words and obeys them. She has never obeyed them. She has made up her own words and got us to obey her.'

While this bad-mouthing was going on, Wei's wife suddenly realized she had two tits full of milk going to waste and, without breaking off her verbal bombardment for one second, took Baby Boy Wei from the arms of her husband and attached him to one of them. Since it was at least a year since he had last been on her breast, Baby Boy Wei had forgotten some of the etiquettes of breastfeeding. His sharp little teeth bit into her tit. She cuffed him and cursed him. She also ordered Eldest Son to stop tiring himself and to place Baby Girl Wei on the cart too. Wei, worried by the extra weight on the weak wheel, checked it, and seeing the splints still firmly in place, permitted this.

While this was going on Wei quietly told Spider Girl to prepare another honey concoction for her mother with some added milkwort root to get her to sleep. Spider Girl moved to do this.

Wei's wife, breastfeeding etiquette agreed with Baby Boy Wei, resumed her barrage.

'Why's she doing that?' she asked, pointing at Spider Girl who was preparing to cut a honeycomb.

'Because I told her to prepare a concoction for you.'

'She's trying to take my place in the family.'

'I would never allow her to do that.'

'She's cleverer than you think.'

With that riposte, satisfied that she'd restored her position in the family hierarchy, Wei's wife fell immediately into a deep sleep. Spider Girl hadn't yet stirred in the milkwort root so instead offered the honey to her father.

'Take it yourself, daughter,' he told her. 'How are you?'

'I am alive, Father. And how are you?'

A grin twisted Wei's lips. 'I am alive also.'

On the cart Baby Boy Wei had finished his feeding and fallen asleep on his mother's breast. Baby Girl Wei had also managed to worm her way into her mother's rich warm body and was sucking, without biting, on the other tit.

Over and over as he lead the donkey, Second Son tried to work out in his small little head how parents could kill children. When they'd first left home, when he'd volunteered to go ahead in the darkness towards the bandits, he had seen this as a sort of game, like those he played with other children. He had heard at home stories of bandits killing people, so when he came across dead people killed by bandits it was horrible but no big surprise. But now, his mother killing a baby, his father accepting it, then them lying? Did parents have children in order to kill them? Would they kill him? Was this what this whole strange journey was about?

As he trudged on, trying to work all this out, he scarcely noticed the ground he was travelling across. It was littered with the ephemera and paraphernalia of everyday life – household objects, farm implements, articles of clothing – abandoned by the weary, desperate multitudes. He just steered his cart between them.

He passed amid rakes and hoes and pruning forks and crowbars and shears. Wind-up gramophones, bicycles without wheels, wheels without bicycles, spanners, hammers, sickles, neatly folded newspapers, tables, chairs, pots and jars, an axe, reels of unspooled film from some cinema, umbrellas, parasols (Cherry Blossom purloined one), hats, houseplants, dead pets, live pets, books, broken jars, flutes, abaci, drums of all shapes and sizes, votive tablets, dried flowers, mirrors reflecting nothing, cheap paste jewellery, knick-knacks, chamberpots, spittoons, a bust of Sun Yat-sen, tambourines, dragons' heads, an immaculate mahogany calligraphy table, its raised board awaiting the scholar's perfect brush stroke. All too heavy to carry by exhausted, dehydrating people, all discarded left right and centre.

And there were dearer, more intimate, more heart-wrenching objects left lying. Those objects sacred to family memory that people snatch up in their final moments before abandoning a lifelong home. Family photographs, locks of hair – sometimes from the most intimate places – grandfather's old pipe, pieces of wood carved especially for a lover, statues of hearth and household gods who had shared every family meal for generations, letters, articles of intimate clothing.

Second Son wended the family's way past dead men, women and children, dead cows and goats and dogs and dismembered pigs, favourite singing birds dead in their cage – all rank and stinking.

He came into the area which had been bombed and heavily machine gunned the night before by the Japanese air force while his mother was giving birth.

Burnt twisted bodies, wounded horses screaming, flames pouring out of blackened machinery and wagons, a bacchanalia of flies on every blood-drenched corpse.

And as he led the donkey through this he accidentally trod in a dead woman's stomach. And stopped.

His father came forward to see why they had stopped. He saw what had happened and took the rein from his son. He looked into his son's eyes and saw the suffering and bewilderment.

'I am sorry I made you do this, son,' he said. 'Go to the back of the cart and sleep. Do not worry.'

'Yes, Father.'

And as Second Son turned Wei gently touched his arm.

In the back of the cart Second Son covered his face and wept. And then he fell into a deep, deep sleep.

Wei walked on, in a sort of daze. He knew his body was very tired – but not much more tired than he would be at the height of harvest – and he knew his mind was exhausted by the constant need for vigilance, both in monitoring the difficulties within his own family and protecting them from the dangers from outside. He chastised himself for not noticing Second Son's distress and bewilderment. He would speak to him and cheer him as soon as he had time. And he was worried by his father's growing confusion and babbling and his habit of wandering off. His wife wanted to tether him – when he was inside the cart and when he walked beside it – but Wei vetoed this. His father was a dignified man.

What grieved and agonized Wei most was the killing of his newborn baby. It was his duty above all to serve and protect his family, every single one of them, whether alive or among his dead ancestors. His wife accused him of being soft because of the death of his elder sister, because he had ruled that Spider Girl, as an infant, should live and not die in a famine. But the killing of this latest baby, a boy, had happened and he had not foreseen it, and when it had happened he had accepted it. He had even agreed with the deed. He still agreed with the deed. This is what ate through his bowels like a snake.

Of course, all the time he was thinking this, he was also looking from side to side – at all the people and individuals and groups they were travelling among and through. He was checking on his family. Grandfather was demanding he had a shit and he stopped the cart briefly so he could. Cherry Blossom was proudly holding her blue parasol – her hedgehog asleep in its cage – and trudging along with Baby Girl Wei who was happy to be anywhere close to Cherry Blossom and laughing happily as Cherry Blossom twirled the parasol. His wife was walking behind the cart preparing a family meal on its tailgate. Eldest Son walked behind, looking around, carrying the spade. Second Son and Spider Girl slept. A Japanese reconnaissance aircraft whined far above them like a mosquito.

They were approaching a farming family with a cart that had stopped and lit a fire to prepare food, perhaps to boil water. Wei studied them. They looked respectable – or as respectable as any family could be in circumstances like this – and spoke respectfully to each other. Perhaps they would be prepared to share the fire in exchange for some of the goat, some fresh water, and the wax from the drained honeycombs. Maybe throw in the four iron hoops from the two buckets.

He stopped the cart. He woke Second Son saying he needed him to hold the donkey's rein – to give her some feed and any piss there was in the bucket – while keeping his eye on what was happening in front of the cart. Spider Girl he left sleeping in the cart. He told Eldest Son and his wife to be extra vigilant.

Then, without carrying anything, he walked slowly towards the other family. The family turned round from the fire they were sitting around as he approached and stopped talking. A young man – he assumed their eldest son – had been standing guard holding an ancient blunderbuss. As Wei approached it he raised it and pointed it at Wei. Wei stopped some ten yards from them.

'Good day,' he said.

Silence.

'I am a respectable man and father. I want to suggest a trade. You have a fire. I have a goat I should slaughter. In the exchange for a hind and a front leg of the goat, a gallon of water,' the father of the family's eyes flickered at this, 'and some beeswax, you should allow us to boil a pot of water to cook the other parts of the goat and some vegetables. I repeat, we are honourable people. What do you say?'

The haggling commenced. Fortunately each family spoke a dialect recognizable to the other. Wei finally agreed to the whole of the hindquarters of the goat minus a leg, the beeswax, two gallons of water and two iron hoops in exchange for use of the fire.

Wei bowed to them. 'I will kill the goat and return,' he said.

He walked back to his family's cart.

'Get the large bowl, please,' he asked Second Son, 'and help me.'

As Second Son came back from the donkey he sent Spider Girl

forwards to take the rein. Second Son was delighted to help his father. Ever since his father had told him to go and rest and had touched his arm so gently, Second Son had known that whatever insanity was happening in the world, his father would not harm him and that he would do his best to save him from all trouble

His father took out and sharpened his knife, then, upturning the goat, which kicked feebly, he rested the back of the goat against the cart's tailgate, took the goat's weight on his left knee and held down the head with the throat exposed. Second Son slipped the bowl beneath the head. Cherry Blossom and Baby Girl gathered to watch.

'Hand me the knife,' Wei ordered Cherry Blossom. She did this and came even closer.

Wei cut the throat precisely. The goat struggled weakly and feebly, its anaemic blood flowed out.

Second Son, holding the bowl and catching the blood, looked up at his father. His father's face seemed so tired, dusty and lined. He was so proud to be his son. The blood fully drained and the goat was dead, Second Son carefully placed the full bowl onto the cart so his mother could make blood cakes. He covered it with a cloth to keep out the attacking flies.

A few deft cuts to the skin of the lower hind legs and Wei's wife was able to quickly strip the skin off the goat. Hearty blows from her cleaver divided it into manageable chunks. The edible organs were cut out from the intestines which were slopped into a pre-dug pit and covered. The offal was packed into the bottom of the cooking pot on top of the dried beans and vegetables. Then the chunks of the body and the head were expertly packed in above them, the hindquarters last. Extra beans were expertly stuffed into all the openings between the joints. Salt and herbs were spread on top and finally Wei carefully poured water from the opened jar into the pot til it was full.

With the two gallons to be traded with the other family, their third water jar would be empty. The family had two jars of water left.

Wei ordered Cherry Blossom to hold some tongs and to pay attention. Otherwise he'd get his wife to whip her.

Just as they were about to leave Grandfather announced that he needed a shit and asked to be lifted down from the cart.

'You had one only a few hours ago,' said Wei. 'Please wait til this is over.'

He picked up the heavy cooking pot and started to carry it over to the family with the fire followed by his wife carrying the emptied honeycombs and the two iron bands. She also carried a ladle. Wei did not want the blood cakes cooked yet, as he wanted time for the two families to get to trust each other. He also decided not to leave his wife alone with the other family's wife. In such close quarters, both wives would consider themselves to be on their mettle, and arguments and territorial disputes might easily flare.

They stopped ten yards from the fire. The father of the other family indicated that Wei's wife should bring the water and honeycombs and iron bands closer. She put them on the ground five yards from the fire. The farmer examined them. Leaving them on the ground he indicated Wei could come forwards. Wei placed the pot on the fire. The water, honeycombs and iron bands continued to lie on the ground. Wei retreated to them and the farmer indicated Wei's wife could come forwards to tend the pot. 'Keep your dignity,' Wei whispered to her as she passed with her ladle.

The pot started to bubble. Sweet smells arose. Wei's wife began cooking the blood cakes.

Each side watched the other. Wei's wife and the other farmer's wife cast swift furtive glances at each other. Their eldest son with the blunderbuss watched Wei's eldest son with the spade.

It was when the cooking was over and the hindquarters of the goat started to be lifted out of the pot for the other family that the trouble started. Wei's wife was taking them out and laying them on the wooden board when the other farmer's wife suddenly started to demand that they should not only get the meat but the beans which were wedged between those joints and some of the gravy. If you can see starvation ahead of you such fractions loom large.

At first Wei's wife did not respond – but did not add beans or gravy in a proffered bowl. The rest of the family, except the farmer, became animated, and the two eldest sons exchanged threats. Wei continued silent but stepped closer to the water, honeycombs and pots. The other wife saw this and started screaming insults. Wei's eldest son started to shout, the other farmer's eldest son raised the blunderbuss to his shoulder and fired. There was an enormous explosion which threw the other eldest son several yards backwards onto his back while a shower of nails and bolts – the only ammunition they had been able to find – ascended a hundred metres into the air before showering harmlessly on his body.

Wei's wife suddenly screamed 'Stop!' Everyone stopped. She put a ladle of beans on the board and a ladle of gravy in the bowl.

'Thank you,' said the other farmer's wife.

'I hope you enjoy my excellent food,' said Wei's wife, turning and calling Cherry Blossom forwards. A frightened Cherry Blossom ran forwards with the pair of tongs for Wei and returned immediately to the cart. Wei's wife retreated from the pot and Wei advanced to the pot and, on a nod from his fellow farmer, lifted the pot with the tongs and started back to his cart, avoiding the water, honeycombs and iron bands which lay on the ground. His wife walked beside him with the ladle and the boiled blood cakes.

'Thank you, wife, for your proper and quick-witted behaviour.'

'You are welcome, husband,' replied his wife, already calculating ways the capital her good behaviour had accrued could be used to her – and the family's – advantage.

When they returned to the cart, everyone hungry for the sweet taste of goat's meat, they discovered yet another crisis. During the drama of the stand-off between the two families, while Eldest Son had been squaring up to his opposite number, Cherry Blossom and Second Son and Spider Girl all staring at the spectacle, Grandfather Wei had disappeared. Gone.

'Where is he?'

'Can't see him anywhere?'

'He might have been robbed. Bandits might have snatched him.'

'He didn't have any money.'

Wei was filled with dread. His dearest father. Who he owed

everything to. His inattentiveness had put him in danger. He climbed onto the cart, waking a sleeping Baby Boy Wei, and looked all around him. His father must have gone in the opposite direction to where all the family's attentions had been focused – on the cooking and the argument. He desperately scanned the hundreds of refugees he could see in the other direction, trudging on through the billows of sand. Where was he? The figure he so loved. He saw some wispy hair. Hair he recognized. He ran towards his father, caught him in his arms, brought him back.

His wife was ready to spend her capital.

'That old man is a liability to the family. A burden to us on this awful, stupid journey,' she announced to everyone. Then she addressed her husband. 'He is old. He is foolish. We have to keep our eyes on him all the time just as we do with the children. He should be tethered to the cart – when he is inside it, when he is outside it.'

'He is my father,' Wei shouted angrily at his wife. 'He must have his dignity. You, a wife, should not speak to your father-in-law in such a way. Do not speak again.'

He stared at her. But where she would once have looked down in respect to him, today she stared straight back at him.

'I know, and you know,' and how she emphasized that 'you', 'that he should be tethered to the cart. We have too many other things to look out for without having to constantly wear out our eyes watching him. You know I am right.'

So Grandfather was tethered to the cart. He complained bitterly at the humiliation. Wei avoided his eyes. By way of explanation Grandfather explained he had wandered off because he had needed another shit.

'I haven't been normal since Spider Girl gave me two senna pods instead of one.'

This further revelation of Spider Girl's iniquity gave Wei's wife another opportunity to rail against her, accusing her of all manner of crimes against the family.

'If we do not cast them off, that old man and this witch will kill the whole family. We cannot afford them eating our food, drinking our water.'

Wei stood up. He advanced on his wife. She had already won one confrontation and his father was tethered like a beast to the cart. Now she wanted him – the old, old argument – to cast off his beloved Eldest Daughter. Abandon her to die.

'Do you want me to gag you? Do you want the public shame of that? As if you were some madwoman? Stop your mouth or I will.'

A meal, whose wonderful smells and aromas had once had all their stomach juices dancing and gurgling in anticipation, now tasted like acid. It was eaten in sullen silence.

Afterwards, to escape the animosity, Spider Girl volunteered to lead the donkey.

As she drudged through the night she realized her time with the family was almost up. What her blunt-speaking mother had said was true – she was a burden on them all. Despite drinking her own urine she also drank some of their vital water, ate some of their scarce food, and on occasion held them up with her slow walking. If she was her mother she would say the same thing.

The ointment she had purchased from the village apothecary had almost run out and her joints, now inflamed and swollen, caused her intense pain as she walked.

'Look around you, girl,' she told herself, 'keep your eyes open.'

8

The next morning, in the grey of early dawn, Wei looked round at his family. Their faces were uniformly grimy, their eyes were caked with dust, and every so often they emitted short, gruff coughs as they tried to dislodge the dirt and phlegm from their lungs. Exhausted, sunk in upon themselves, but still walking.

Grandfather and the two tots slept on the cart beside Second Son, who Wei still had not talked with. Spider Girl was trudging along at the rear of the cart, vigilantly looking around for danger, but she walked with the utmost difficulty and her face was distorted with pain. Wei could only glance at her. She was flagging, increasingly unable to keep up, so he was having to slow the cart.

Not that the cart was going that fast. During the night the donkey had also visibly flagged. At first Wei had whacked him hard on his rump with his stick but after a while not even that hurried him on. He needed water. As the humans dehydrated they peed less and less and the little donkey dehydrated even faster.

What should he do? They were now down to less than two jars of drinking water. Give some to the donkey? On the dusty plain there were no signs of rivers or lakes. They did cross streams, but, because of the hordes which had already passed through them they were trodden-down mires, filled with mud and faeces and piss. Not even the donkey would drink that. After every stream they passed desperate people who had attempted to drink the water, now rolling around vomiting and shitting diarrhoea, or at last in the wrap of death.

Wei thought they could gather some of the water and boil it

before trying to drink it – or at least give it to the donkey – but that would cost them valuable firewood.

The solution they arrived at was to help the donkey with her load. On each side of the cart, before they left home, Second Son had attached leather straps. Now Wei and Eldest Son pulled hard at them and took some of the weight. This hurried up the cart and cheered the donkey, which was being led by his wife, but it added to the difficulties of Spider Girl.

Eldest Son, pulling on the other side of the cart, brought Wei some comfort. He was strong, like an ox, but with a face so gentle and unperturbed. He never made any fuss. Just accepted a task, however difficult, and got on with it. Wei was so proud of his son. Of course, he was not the sharpest, most quick-witted of people. To be a farmer you not only needed strength, you also had to have your wits about you, to be aware of everything that was happening on your farm. If, pray to the gods, Eldest Son ever became the farmer of the family's lands, he would have difficulties, but for now he was everything a father, a family, needed.

On they slogged. His wife had fallen back slightly, letting the rein lengthen out, and she and her beloved Eldest Son were talking softly. Wei was half listening. She was speaking to him in a low soothing voice, almost crooning as she had when she was lullabying him in his wooden cot. She was telling him about how their life would be when this madness, this evil was over, when they were all once more safely returned home, living on their land. How, when she was in old age, he would be the owner and farmer of the land, she and his father, the grandparents, looking after the youngest grandchildren while he and his wife and his older children farmed the land and ran the household.

But while he listened, suddenly Wei was gripped with horror. With a jolt he understood what was actually going on right before his eyes. As she spoke his wife was quietly, surreptitiously, slipping her son something. He would take it and then quietly, calmly, place it in his mouth. No wonder she had recently started to look so thin, so worn, so manic. It was not just because she had just given birth. She was secretly feeding her beloved eldest son. She was deliberately, repeatedly starving herself that he might live.

Wei always checked portions of the food as it was handed out so there would be no arguments. Last night she had given fair shares to all. So what she was now feeding Eldest Son was certainly out of her own bowl.

He turned his face away in agony. What should he do? He could remonstrate with her, demand she ate more food, but he could not force her to. She would just point out that in doing what she did she was doing what he himself should be doing – preserving the life of their eldest son. She was being forced to starve herself by his refusal to do the necessary, moral thing in defence of his family and casting out its weaklings. She would say it was her iron will that was standing between the family and extinction. It wasn't that she didn't love all her children – except Spider Girl. It wasn't that she didn't love and normally show full respect to her father-in-law. It was just that she loved her eldest son most.

Awful decisions were facing Wei. He was not unobservant. Families were reaching these impossible decisions all about him. Casting off the oldest, the youngest, the weakest. Again and again abandoned little toddlers and children came running towards them crying out for food and water, holding out their arms for warmth, but they had to walk right past them as though they did not exist. Old people stumbled and zigzagged towards them, pleading for help, a ride on their cart. They ignored them. These deserted old folk formed groups where they embraced each other for comfort. Round their feet and legs clung the young who had also been abandoned. The living had to navigate their way around these islands of the dying.

I am becoming a murderer, he thought. Do I, against all my sacred and familial obligations, cast off and condemn to death members of my own family? Do I, whose sole purpose in life is to protect, cherish, keep my family together, now plan how to murder them? So I choose Spider Girl – who then – my father? And then, as conditions worsen, one by one Baby Girl Wei, Cherry Blossom, Baby Boy Wei, Second Son, followed by…?

My wife would insist it was her. She would kill herself to put it beyond all argument. Just let my ancestors try to keep her out of their afterlife after she'd done that!!!

On their journey different people, different groups, talked to each other, exchanged news and information. Always, of course, from a safe distance. Wei had heard rumours of mass suicides. Of men who'd dug a hole, killed their family and laid them in the hole, then laid down on top of them and killed themselves. All so that, even though they could not be buried among their ancestors, they would not die and lie individually, doomed to be lonely, perpetually wandering ghosts. But instead they would all still be one family together in the afterlife.

Then things got worse. At a brief stop for a midday meal – a Japanese reconnaissance aircraft droning lazily above them – Spider Girl had passed Grandfather a bowl of water and Grandfather had fumbled and dropped it. Precious family water. Wei's wife, with a righteous tremble in her voice that was not to be contradicted, blamed both at once and demanded that, forthwith, these two wasters and malignants were a threat to the survival of the family and should be cast out from it immediately.

Cherry Blossom and the two tots just stared. So did Grandfather, too bewildered to fathom what was going on. Eldest Son was very embarrassed and went to the front of the cart to feed and guard the donkey. Second Son went to stand beside his father to show he supported him. Spider Girl looked at the ground.

Their journey resumed. But Mrs Wei's rage did not lessen, it grew. The folly of it all. The wickedness. And as she shouted and denounced him, Wei did not have the strength to gag or silence her, his dear wife, because, in his deepest heart, he knew she was right. He would have to expel from the family either his father or his eldest daughter. If he expelled one he would have enough power over his wife to insist the other stay. Which one? He could not throw out his beloved father for the reason of filial piety. There was no more foul or loathed crime than a son murdering his father. Quite rightly. He owed everything, everything to his father. Which left only his most beloved child, his eldest daughter. Wei could feel his own elder sister, who had been cast out and died in similar circumstances, moving inside him, writhing with the pain. But there was no choice. The family must survive. As though he had heavy lead in every bone in his body weighing him down, he turned slowly, with great difficulty, towards where Spider Girl had been walking. 'My dearest Spider Girl,' he said, and looked up at her. But she was not there. He could not see her. Everyone in the family looked around. No one could see her. From the rear of the cart where she had been walking she had disappeared. In the midst of their murderous argument, unnoticed, she had simply vanished.

Wei stopped the cart and jumped on top of it. He had last seen her feeding Grandfather, who sat on the right-hand side of the cart. So that was the direction in which she had probably headed. Wei looked back and forth for her. He couldn't see her anywhere. How could Spider Girl, with all her walking difficulties, disappear so utterly?

'Hah,' said his wife triumphantly, 'so she *is* an evil spirit. She can disappear at will!'

Wei could not afford to leave the cart himself to find her. He must send someone else. And out to the right of the cart, where the crowds thinned and the bandits and criminals ranged, was not a safe place to send anyone.

'Father,' said Second Son, 'I will go and look for her.'

'You will not.'

'There is no one else to do it, Father. I can do it just as when we first left home and I went ahead in the night to see if there were bandits.'

Wei's wife, the realist, pointed out drily that as Spider Girl had done what he was just about to do – throw her out of the family – what was the point of risking Second Son's life going out to look for her when all he was going to do was throw her out again?

Wei gagged his wife, tied her hands behind her back, and sat her on the cart. People passing them mocked her for this.

'Father,' said Second Son, 'I want to go and find her. I love my eldest sister more than anyone.'

Before his father could stop him Second Son ran off to the right of the cart. At least, he trotted off. No one in these conditions – being short of food and crucially water – could manage more than a quiet trot. But that applied as much to the bandits as to the honest folk – though the line between the two of them was rapidly eroding.

Indeed, among the crowds, in addition to the rumours of mass suicides, stories were spreading of blood drinking and cannibalism. Of women exchanging their babies and saying 'Your family can eat mine. My family will eat yours.' And some of them weren't just rumours.

Second Son, keeping a sharp eye out all the time, avoiding any person or groups looking in any way hostile, hurried among the crowds, shouting Spider Girl's name, calling out to people whether they'd anywhere seen a fat girl with a bad limp and hair on her upper lip? Uniformly they said no. He asked a group of monks – they hadn't seen her. A group of university students – no. But Second Son did not lose hope. He felt useful and because he felt useful he felt happy. He was serving his father. He was looking to try and rescue his eldest sister, whom he loved more than anyone else. She always was the one who had talked to him most and with whom he had the most fun. She made him laugh. But he could see her nowhere.

With a sensible head on his young shoulders, Second Son returned to the cart after half an hour. Wei thanked him profoundly for trying to find her and reminded himself he must still speak to Second Son and try to soothe him when they were alone. But he was in agony about the loss of his daughter.

For five minutes, so that no one would see him cry, he crawled under the cart and wept. Then he came out. He untied his wife's hands and gag and lifted her down off the cart and their journey resumed.

The next morning the landscape they were crossing started to change. Low hills hemmed them in on either side, so the people on the march became more herded together, started to walk in closer proximity to each other.

Wei was as usual pulling the right-hand side of the cart. His father, tressed to the cart, was sitting beside him, ignoring him, lost in his thoughts. His face and jaw were wriggling and grimacing. Suddenly he turned and looked straight at his son.

'Explain this,' he said in quite a hostile tone of voice.

'Explain what, Father?'

'Explain to me why the Mandate of Heaven has been revoked?'

'I did not know it had been revoked, Father. Why do you say it has?'

'It must have been. It is the only reason why all this can be happening. All this madness and confusion and suffering. It is the emperor.'

'We do not have an emperor any longer, Father.'

'We always have an emperor. And he is not ruling with justice or compassion. Instead there is anarchy. So, according to divine law and custom, the gods would have let the people overthrow him and put in his place an emperor who would rule with justice and compassion. That is what should have happened. Do you follow me?'

'No, Father.'

'Fool. It is the gods. Always in the past the gods have loved us human beings – rightly. The gods up there in the skies have watched out for evildoers and punished them, the gods in Heaven have loved all people equally so that we in turn would love all other human beings and treat them as our own brothers and sisters...'

'Father...'

His father continued, his voice rising shrilly. 'The gods loved us. They ordered the sun and moon and stars to bring us light, guide us day and night. They gave us the four seasons and the snow and the frost and the rain and the dew so that the five grains and the flax and the silk would grow in the ground and on the trees so that we could use and enjoy them. But...'

'Father,' Wei broke in, becoming increasingly alarmed. 'I do not understand. what are you saying?'

'Fool! Halfwit! What I am saying is that the gods, up there in Heaven, who are meant to be grateful for our gifts and offerings, who are meant to listen to our prayers and protect us, have grown malicious and greedy and concerned only with their own pleasures. They have turned Heaven into a brothel, a place of lust and drink and murder. A pigsty. A stinking shithole!'

'Father, I cannot listen to you any longer.'

Straining at his bonds, his face rigid and livid, his father gazed right into his son's helpless soul.

'The gods are drunk! They are killing each other! They have deserted us, their people, abandoned us to the mercies of wild dogs and wolves!'

Wei could not listen to his father's thoughts any longer. They corresponded too closely to dark thoughts he himself had been harbouring over the last few days. He shouted out to Eldest Son on the other side of cart to change places with him so each could rest the arms and shoulders they had been pulling on. Eldest Son would not understand a word his grandfather was saying and just grin at him in his usual embarrassed way.

His wife stopped the donkey. The two men exchanged places. They continued.

Wei didn't know where to look, what to think. It was as though his father had laid his soul bare. All the thoughts, all the anger he had been suppressing for days came welling up. All the lines which had once run directly from him, his family, directly north to the gods in Heaven, seemed to be twisting and jangling and splintering in disarray. Where there had once been calm and loving voices, now there was only screaming and obscenities and lunacy. And he suspected that the ancestors were themselves suffering a similar pandemonium and bewilderment.

The hills on either side of them had come narrowed, squeezing all the refugees close up together as they passed though the gap. The Japanese spotter plane flew over them, dully, slowly.

Wei stirred himself. He had to pay attention. Keep watch. He looked around his family. All except one were still there. Still trying to survive. Families lost members all the time but the family endures. It was his duty to make sure that it endured. Wei ate bitterness and endured.

In the cart Grandfather's mood changed. In his quickly fragmenting consciousness he suddenly saw his grandchildren and he loved them. These were difficult times. He would tell them a story that would soothe them, bring them cheer.

'Do you want a story?' he asked.

'Yes,' Baby Girl Wei and Baby Boy Wei chorused. Cherry Blossom clambered on board to listen. Second Son, who was walking behind the cart to keep guard, would have listened but was called forwards by Wei so he could lead the donkey while his wife fell back to keep guard.

'The story I'm going to tell you is a very special one,' said Grandfather. 'It's called "The Dragon's Pearl".'

'Ooh,' said everyone.

'Once upon a time,' said Grandfather, 'there was a boy and his mother who lived close to the River Min. They were good people but very poor. The boy used to go out every day into the countryside and cut grass to sell at market, and by doing that they just managed to make a living.'

Wei started to relax. A grandfather telling stories to his grandchildren, what could be more right.

'But one year,' Grandfather continued, 'a terrible drought came on the land. Nothing anywhere would grow. The river dried up. And however far the boy would wander into the countryside, everywhere the plants and the grass had died. And every day the mother and her son grew thirstier and more hungry.'

Baby Girl Wei was looking straight at her grandfather and sucking hard on her thumb.

'But,' continued Grandfather, 'nothing would stop the little boy from walking out, further and further into the countryside, to try and find grass. And one day he was rewarded for all his effort. Because he came across a patch of the greenest, brightest grass he had ever seen, shining in the sunlight. He was so pleased. The little boy cut it immediately and took it back to the market and sold it for a great price and he and his mother were able to buy more than enough food and water.

'The little boy kept on going back to the grass. Each day it was as green and plentiful as it had been the previous day.'

Elder Son and Wei both listened to this story they knew so

well. Second Son couldn't hear because he was too far ahead. Cherry Blossom slipped off the cart to walk next to her mother, still listening hard. Even Wei's wife, hostile as she might feel to Grandfather staying in the family, softened and listened to a story that had delighted her in childhood.

The crowds were starting to thicken as they pressed through the narrow valley between the hills. Grandfather continued with his story.

'The little boy wondered how the green grass could keep growing every day. And then he had a thought. Dragons were said to be very kind-hearted and great givers of food and life. Perhaps they were causing the grass to grow.

'And so that night the little boy stayed behind to see if a dragon would come. And sure enough, in the evening, over the horizon flew this beautiful dragon, all glowing with lights and glistening with colours.'

'I love dragons,' said Baby Girl Wei.

'And,' continued Grandfather, 'The dragon flew down and landed just where all the grass was growing, and the little boy knew...'

'Look, Grandfather.' said Baby Boy Wei, pointing, 'there's a dragon?'

He was pointing backwards, behind the cart, into the sky. There was indeed an object there, wobbling slightly up and down, quite close to the horizon. The sunlight flashed and reflected off it. Grandfather Wei looked but could see anything because his eyesight was so poor.

'Yes,' said Baby Girl Wei, 'it could be a dragon. It has lovely colours and is making a dragon sort of roar.'

The Japanese reconnaissance plane had waited until sufficient numbers of refugees had pushed into the narrow funnel of the valley before radioing. The pilot at the controls of the Nakajima Ki-27b fighter bomber he had vectored in jockeyed his plane into the best attack line on the crowds. He carried a single Type 94 fifty-kilo high-explosive bomb slung beneath his plane. He locked into his final line of attack, sped in on the starting-to-panic civilians, dipped his nose, and as the plane's speed increased took aim at the centre of the target, releasing his bomb and simultaneously starting to fire his two machine guns. As the weight of the bomb fell away the nose of the plane rose too. Thus, although the machine gun bullets arrived first among the refugees, they went over the heads of the Wei family and sprayed and shattered the limbs and bodies and lives of people three or four hundred yards ahead of them. But the bomb, falling straight and true on the fighter bomber's original trajectory, was making precisely for the Weis' cart.

Produced at the Tachikawa Hikoki K. K. factory at Tachikawa near Tokyo, the bomb sped through Cherry Blossom's blue parasol, sliced straight through Grandfather and Baby Boy Wei – leaving Baby Girl Wei totally untouched – before passing through and smashing the wheat jars and the full water jar – the wood of the cart igniting through friction – then obliterating the donkey and decapitating a ducking Second Son, and continuing through the air for a further fifty yards, killing three adults, two children and a horse, before embedding itself finally and fatally into a cart full of young men which it slaughtered en masse. It had not exploded. The detonator, made by Korean slave Son Joon-Ho in the Mitsubishi Heavy Industries factory in Nagasaki, had failed to detonate.

In the eighth month autumn's high winds angrily howl,
And sweep three layers of thatch from off my house.
The straw flies over the river, where it scatters,
Some is caught and hangs high up in the treetops,
Some floats down and sinks into the ditch.
The urchins from the southern village bully me, weak as I am;
They're cruel enough to rob me to my face,
Openly, they carry the straw into the bamboo.
My mouth and lips are dry from pointless calling,
I lean again on my cane and heave a sigh.
The wind soon calms, and the clouds turn the colour of ink;
The autumn sky has turned completely black.
My ancient cotton quilt is cold as iron,
My darling children sleep badly, and kick it apart.
The roof leaks over the bed- there's nowhere dry,
The rain falls thick as hemp, and without end.
Lost amid disorder, I hardly sleep,
Wet through, how can I last the long nights!
If I could get a mansion with a thousand, ten thousand rooms,
A great shelter for all the world's scholars, together in joy,
Solid as a mountain, the elements could not move it.
Oh! If I could see this house before me,
I'd happily freeze to death in my broken hut!

Du Fu, eighth-century Chinese poet,
'Song of My Cottage Unroofed by Autumn Gales'

29 Brothers and sisters, this is what I mean. Our time is short. From this day on those who have wives should live as if they do not;

30 Those who mourn should be happy, those who are happy should mourn. those who buy things should treat them as though they belong to all people;

31 those who make use of material objects should not become them; for all around us this world in which we live is dying.

1 Corinthians 7:29-31

9

The family gate slams shut behind me. 'Lock it,' I scream back over the gate, 'pile everything you can find against it.'

I turn towards the street. A drunken man lurches towards me, but he is so slow even I, with my case, typewriter and manuscript, can escape him, hobbling across the rubble and broken tiles. Hell and pandemonium. Everywhere the roar of flames, thick black oily coils of smoke belching like angry dragons. Telephone poles burn like fiery Ku Klux Klan crosses, fall across the streets, their wires lassoing wildly back and forth. Dear God. The Japanese are probably no more than half a mile behind me. Hushed stunned people stand quiescent in the streets and at corners, some holding their heads in their hands, eyes dead as fish on a market stall, some stare upward at the sky.

God help my poor defenceless family.

I make my way, ever so slowly, towards the railway station at the south end of the city.

Meet my first Chinese soldiers. Drunk, so not very fast. They're looting a shop that sells jewellery and watches. Its plate glass window is smashed, they're helping themselves to its clocks and bracelets displayed in its showcases, laughing and singing and fighting among each other. Out of it staggers one soldier carrying an enormous grandfather clock. As he reels down the street its coiled steel innards gush out and catch and drag on the rubble like the bowels of a half-eviscerated man. The clock continues chiming like bells in a mad belfry. Explosions all around from exploding Japanese artillery shells and aerial bombs. Dust everywhere. Soldiers firing blindly into the skies. A shoe shop, all its shutters smashed, without a single shoe left in it, not even a child's. A wealthy woman shrieking with all her fingers hacked off because the bandits could not pull off her many rings. Soldiers in uniform, some semi-naked, one totally naked playing a flute and dancing.

Our glorious 3rd Route Army under the inspiring command of General Han Fuju.

For some reason I seem to be, at least temporarily, invisible, as I slip through the streets. Perhaps I look too stringy or poor to rob. One of the few advantages of being a writer is that no one thinks you're worth robbing!

Expensively dressed women being raped against walls, many dead bodies, wealthy men with their throats cut, soldiers staggering along with enormous piles of loot perched on their shoulders.

It's not just our soldiers who are pillaging and stealing and murdering. Down narrow alleys and in dark gateways lurk the criminals and cut-throats of the city, not daring to come out openly onto the streets while the soldiers are still there, waiting patiently like crows round an eagle devouring its prey. It's one of them who first spots me. There aren't many soldiers around this area as three or four of the footpads emerge and start to lope after me. I start to run – or rather hobble over the rubble and debris. They pursue me, eyes hungry as wolves, gaining on me. I start to think about what I can throw away to distract them. I can't discard my patriotic anti-Japanese novel, nor my case with my wife's silk scarf in it. It must be my beloved Wanneng typewriter. I throw it callously aside. For a second they stop.

'What is it?'

'Junk.'

'Just fit for scrap.'

'Come on, we're losing him.'

One stays on – for the scrap – the other three start to chase me again, one with a sabre, one with a knife. What else can I throw overboard? Not my manuscript, not my case, perhaps they like red persimmon fruit? Then I realize – what about my overcoat? It has a wool lining. Good in winter. I stop a second, put down my case, hold my manuscript between my knees, strip off the coat, pick up my manuscript and case, and I'm away.

This time two stop and start to fight over the coat. Winter is coming. I continue to hare, or at least hare as well as one can over sharp stones while wearing a thin pair of leather shoes. But the man with the knife continues to gain on me, obviously intent on my case and all valuables about my person. (My wife had sewn a few silver dollars into my trouser turn ups). Matters get worse. Three loafers by a looted vegetable stall – the owner sprawled dead over his produce – join in. My lungs are starting to collapse. Never ever smoke again, I shout at myself.

They're about to drag me down when I round a corner and come face to face with a police checkpoint. Official-looking policemen in smart uniforms under the command of an inspector in an immaculate uniform. Beside it a brazier glows to keep the late-autumn chill off. What could look more – normal? I skid to a halt. My wolves come round the corner, take one look, and evaporate. I breathe in. I breathe out. You cannot imagine my relief. I walk up to the checkpoint, trying to look intensely respectable.

'Good afternoon, officer,' I say, in an accent I hope comes across as High Mandarin. 'I've been having a bit of trouble in the streets. Rough fellows. I just wonder if you could spare one of your men to accompany me to the railway station.'

'Who the fuck are you?' asks the inspector in a far from friendly tone.

I swallow.

'My name is Lao She. I am a writer,' I tell him. 'It is quite important. I have to catch a train at seven o'clock.'

He is standing behind a trestle table, a bit like a customs officer.

'Put your stuff on the table, sunshine,' he tells me, 'and no funny business.'

At this the other policemen suddenly become interested in me and give a hard stare.

'My stuff?' I query.

'What you're carrying. We'll body search you later.'

Staring at him I place my manuscript and case upon the table.

'What's this?' he asks, picking up my valuable manuscript.

'That's my new novel. It is very patriotic and anti-Japanese and I'm taking it to my publisher.'

'The fire's getting a bit low,' the inspector says to one of his officers, handing the manuscript to him.

The officer takes the manuscript and drops it into the brazier. I stare at it. It flares up in flames. My manuscript. My beautiful manuscript! Which I have laboured so many painstaking hours over, trying to get it precisely right! It was a bit wooden, admittedly, clunky even, propaganda's not exactly my…

I look at the official.

'That was my manuscript you have just burnt. I am a quite well-known author, and…'

'And we're getting cold,' says the inspector matter-of-factly, rubbing his hands over the flames. 'Now let's see what we've got in here?'

He opens my suitcase. I groan.

'Something the matter, sir?' he asks.

'It's just personal things.'

'Personal things, eh? Well, let's have a look.'

He flicks through the contents.

'Very nice,' he says, 'yes, very nice,' re-clicking the lid and placing it on the ground well behind the table.

I can't believe this is happening to me. In the middle of my own city. Just across the road is the bank I use to cash the occasional cheques I get from my publisher.

A shell lands quite close to us.

'That's my case,' I shout at him, 'containing objects of deep personal value. You've stolen it!'

'Stolen it? I am merely impounding articles I believe to have been stolen by you. We've got a troublemaker here, lads. Grab him.'

I am grabbed. Pinioned flat on my face on the table. They are frisking me. They find the silver dollars my wife sewed into my turn-ups. I calculate feverishly. Can I survive without money? Yes, I conclude, the soldier who came to me from General Feng said he was booking me a place on the seven o'clock train – if I manage to ever catch it. The ticket will cover my restaurant car expenses.

I can survive til I get to Wuhan. The policeman hands over the silver dollars to the inspector.

'Right,' says the inspector, coming round the table on which I am spreadeagled, 'let's see what else he's got.'

Suddenly I feel my trousers being ripped off, then my pants.

'What the hell are you doing?' I cry.

'Think you can fool us? We know where all you rich fuckers hide your really valuable loot.'

And with that he sticks a rough, blunt finger straight up my bum.

I see white light. I scream. I am filled with scalding, inescapable pain. It ricochets up and down my spine. I don't think I can bear this... I can't bear... But then I think, yes, I can bear it. Only a mile away, possibly at this very moment – if they've survived our own Chinese troops – my own dearest wife and beloved children and mother may be huddled up in a corner screaming not as some corrupt police officer's finger jams its way up their back passages – but as a cold steel Japanese bayonet knifes into their sweet, frail, defenceless bodies. If this, as my wife said, is war – then she's got the worst of it. I stop screaming.

He finishes, wipes his finger on a cloth. I stand up, pull on my pants and trousers.

'Looks like you ain't some rich fucker after all,' he says.

'Then would you mind if I had my belongings back?' I respond.

'Hold on there, hold on. It's not that simple. You said your name was Mr Lao She, the author?'

'Yes.'

'Matter of fact I've read your book – *Rickshaw Boy*. Quite enjoyed it. But that's beside the point. The point is you are an author. When the Japanese come you can skip off somewhere else and start a new life without a second's thought.'

'Well, that's not...'

'The point is,' he says, grinding over the top of me, 'We policemen can't just run away. This is our livelihood here. Where we earn our wages and keep our families fed. And now we've got the Japanese arriving. They might just run us straight through with their long steel bayonets – like they do the soldiers and civilians. But maybe they won't. After all, you need policemen to keep order, lock up thieves, listen in on troublemakers. And while they're making their minds up – stab or spare – a nice little tinkle of money can often push them towards "spare". So we, I'm afraid, need your money much more than you do.'

I am prepared to let them keep everything they've taken – I can survive without it – except one thing. The Indian silk scarf my wife gave me. I explain this to him. How I have just had to leave her and my children and I don't know whether I shall ever see them again. He looks at me. Then he goes round the table, picks up the case and opens it on the table. Looks at the scarf.

'Bloody awful pattern,' he opines.

'It's Indian.'

'Doesn't surprise me,' he says, and passes it over to me.

I stuff it down my shirt and hobble off down the street. Writing and dignity so rarely coincide.

There seems to be a lull in the fighting. Less artillery, bombing raids, small arms fire. Every shop and house door is closed and there are only a few coolies carrying goods and produce. There are fewer bandits and 'soldiers' on the streets and quite a few civilians hurrying like me towards the station.

Jinan is the capital of Shandong Province and until the First World War was run as a German concession. In its central square it thus boasts a vast German-Victorian Gothic railway station of crushing ugliness, constructed to celebrate the glories of Kaiser Bill and the German Imperium. One glance at it is enough to drive any true German aesthete to a Goethe-esque suicide. Mercifully it has only partly been destroyed by Japanese bombs.

There is a difficulty about entering the railway station. The large cobbled square in front of it is packed with would-be passengers who are being held back by a line of General Han Fuju's valiant lads who demand a large contribution from every passenger who wishes to enter the railway station. It is all pretty anarchic, with crowds of near hysterical people milling about.

Across the square from the station stands an equally imposing

German monolith, the immaculate Stein Hotel, run with Teutonic efficiency by its proprietor, Herr Stein. General Feng's young adjutant told me he'd leave my ticket at the Stein's front desk, so I enter the crowded vestibule in order to collect it. Almost immediately I am seen by Herr Stein.

'Herr Lao. You look terrible. What has happened to you?' His voice is concerned. 'Do you want a bath?'

For two years now I have been teaching his son Fritz to speak and write Chinese and we have become friends.

'That is very kind of you, Herr Stein, but I am afraid that on the way here I was robbed and have no money. I've come here to pick up my train ticket from your front desk.'

'You were robbed? That is terrible. What is this country coming to? If this province had stayed under Kaiser Wilhelm's rule we'd never have had any of this nonsense – troops out of control, being invaded by these yellow dwarves.'

Herr Stein is an old-fashioned German who looks back nostalgically on the reign of Kaiser Wilhelm II as a golden age. He has no time for Herr Hitler, who he considers as vulgar, but this has not stopped him from painting a large swastika on the roof of his hotel to try and dissuade Japanese bombers – Japan and Germany being warm friends – from bombing his hotel.

'Of course you shall have a bath, Herr Lao, and I'll get your clothes valeted.'

'That is most kind of you, Herr Stein, but I do have a train to catch.'

'Your train will not leave for several hours. I have that on the personal authority of the station master, who is a good friend of mine.'

'Oh, well, that is most generous of you. I could really do with a nice clean bath.'

'These are difficult times, Herr Lao, and men of civilization must stick together.'

He summons a boy to show me to my room. I ask if I could have some soothing ointment without specifying why I want it.

'Of course, dear Lao, and oh,' he adds, just as I am departing, 'I forgot, there's a telegram for you.'

'A telegram?'

That is a surprise.

'Yes. Arrived about an hour ago. I'll have the boy bring it up to you when you're in the bath.'

I climb the hotel stairs painfully. The boy runs my bath and helps undress me. He takes away my clothes – except for the persimmon and my wife's scarf, I wish it to retain her smell – to have them cleaned.

With great delicacy I apply some of the cream to my anus. It is terribly painful. Then I start to lower myself into the bath. Despite being Chinese, while I lived in London I developed a real taste for Western baths. The tight, intimate embrace of the hot water. My body, my mind are just starting to relax from their shocks when the boy comes in and hands me the telegram. It is from Zhang Jiluan, the editor of *Dagong Bao*, our most prestigious newspaper, publisher of such great journalists as Fan Changjiang, Hu Yuzhi and Du Zhongyuan. He wishes me to write an article about my experiences in Jinan – a city under siege – with especial reference to and celebration of the heroism of the Chinese soldier. In far-off Wuhan General Feng has obviously already been at work.

My relaxation in the hot waters of the bath cease abruptly. My body and mind tense. He wants me to write a paean to the thugs and psychopaths of the Chinese Army who have just been running away in the face of the enemy and holding to ransom and murdering every honest citizen of China they can lay hands on? NO, I will NOT write such a lie. 'When falsehood stands for truth, truth becomes a lie.' In addition, will my writing such an article in *Dagong Bao* not immediately make my wife and family special targets of the Japanese, if the Japanese have not already murdered them?

But then these thoughts of outrage melt away as I sink into the darkness of thinking of my wife and children and mother, maybe at this very moment being bayoneted, crushed beneath falling walls, consumed in the flames of our burning home. I am a louse of a man! It is perhaps only an hour since I last saw my living wife, and here I am in a luxuriant bath, sticking exotic unguents up my bum, and refusing to sully my pristine conscience by writing anything so crude and gross as propaganda. For what reason is it my wife is offering her and my children's and my mother's lives in sacrifice for but that I might help save my country by writing ruthless and brilliant propaganda? And if my writing that propaganda adds to their danger then, as my wife so sternly said, so be it! I sit upright, in a patriotic way, in my bath. The Chinese Army consists of the finest, most moral, most heroic fighting men in the entire world bar none!

I leap from the bath – or rather lever myself out of it – stick some more unguent up my anus for luck, wash my hands, and start constructing a viable article. *Dagong Bao* are not employing me to produce crude propaganda but subtle propaganda. The sort of propaganda which is read in foreign capitals and might persuade the mighty of this world that China is still in with a chance. I must emphasize the heroism and stoicism of our average Chinese soldier, but underline the fact that natural heroism and a willingness for self-sacrifice means little when the enemy so clearly has better arms. Were foreign governments, understandably worried by the advance of Japan, perhaps to consider arming us with similarly advanced weapons and the training necessary to put them into use, then maybe Japan could become much less fearsome in the eyes of the said foreign governments... I need a pen and paper.

As I go over to the desk in my room, which has a pen and paper, the boy comes in with my clothes and another thought strikes me. At the best of times Chinese trains are not renowned for their punctuality. Trains can leave far ahead of their scheduled time or equally hours after it. I need to be on the train in case it suddenly decides to leave. I can write the article while waiting on the train and give a finished copy to a messenger boy who can get it sent from the telegraph office in the hotel.

Down in the lobby I tell Herr Stein what I intend to do, and tell him I will add a footnote to my article asking *Dagong Bao* to reimburse the hotel for my bath, valeting, stationary (which I have purloined), and the cost of my telegram. Herr Stein bluntly tells me he will accept no payment and hands me a bag of clothes, soap, toothbrushes etc. which he has gathered from his lost property room and some food from his kitchens. In addition, due to the unpleasantnesses, not to say daylight robberies, which are now taking place in the square between the hotel and station, he has told his young son Fritz to accompany me and make sure I make it safely to the station.

I thank him. He thanks me. We wish each other luck.

10

Fritz Stein is six feet tall, has hair so blond it is white, and piercing blue eyes. Every inch of him screams Perfect Aryan. Indeed Fritz has little time for his old man's nostalgia for Kaiser Bill and his Gothic architecture and is an open admirer of Herr Hitler. He is carrying a sub-machine gun.

Normally, I admit, I have few sympathies for fascism and its overdressed mummeries. But, in a situation like this, walking in lock-step with a budding young Obersturmbannführer has its advantages. We cross the square and the crowds open like the Red Sea for Moses. We approach the line of Chinese soldiers. It is inbred into all Chinese, especially Chinese soldiers, that in no or any way does one ever harm a foreigner. Let alone kill one. Do that and the foreigners are apt to send military expeditions or gunboats to punish you. So the soldiers simply stand aside and we sweep through. Two quick-witted civilians pretend they are with us and get through as well.

Fritz accompanies me to the top of the station steps, clicks his heel in reply to my thanks, and marches straight back across the square. I check my bag and see that Herr Stein has most generously left me some money in the bottom.

I walk into the station. It is a chaotic. Thousands of people are fighting to get on to the one train – my train. Tickets seem of little relevance. People with or without tickets – mainly without – are entering through the doors, they are entering through the windows, children and old people are being passed through the windows by their families, baggage and belongings are being stuffed into it, the roofs of the carriages are packed with people,

people are starting to hang to the side of the carriages where there are rails, where there are no rails with just their fingertips. Underneath the carriages brave – or desperate – people are lashing themselves with ropes to the bracing rods hanging beneath the carriages, only inches above the rails. And outside the train is besieged by a sea of thousands of desperate humans. The whole roofed station is filled with a dull roar of despair and rage and animal fear.

I do not stand a chance of getting on the last train.

General Feng's adjutant, being a very smart young man, has attached to my ticket a military document commanding any relevant railway or military official to ensure I take my seat on the train. It has lots of stamps on it. I push my way towards the station master's office but it is besieged like a medieval fortress. I look round the concourse and see a quite senior military officer standing and staring disinterestedly at the civilian horde. I approach him with my document. He waves me away to some junior officer. The junior officer unfolds and peruses my document. General Feng's adjutant obviously has some pull. The junior officer commands two immaculately uniformed privates with polished boots and gleaming bayonets to accompany us and we saunter down the platform towards my carriage. We get to my window. (I couldn't possibly hope to get through the jam-packed door). The junior officer, with a lazy drawl, orders the crowds in front of my window to make way. His request is accompanied by his privates snapping to attention and brandishing their rifles. A path once more opens. (The power of the written word.) Now all I have to do is climb in through the window. The two privates rest their rifles against the side of the carriages. They seize my bag and throw it through the window. They seize my person and throw it through the window.

I sprawl on the carriage floor. Except I don't sprawl on the carriage floor. The carriage has no floor. It is submerged beneath a sea of belongings and luggage and children almost as high as the seats on which many passengers are crammed. I land on someone's Pekinese but fortunately I am not fatal. Instead it gives me a swift, vicious bite and jumps into its mistress's arms. I pick up my bag.

Passengers without seats sprawl higgledy-piggledy across the mountains of boxes and clothing and bedding and all the other odds and ends terrified people snatch up in the last seconds of leaving home. Bawling babies hang in swaddling clothes from hooks. Pets, birds in cages, some of them even singing. Grannies. People who have been able to wedge themselves between the packages and suitcases on the luggage racks snoring contentedly, at any moment likely to plunge down on the heads of those beneath them. Everyone is sweating, everyone is stinking.

I ask the officer who is still waiting outside if he could arrange for a messenger boy to wait close to my window as I will have a letter for the Stein Hotel before the train leaves. He nods and walks off.

I smile vaguely at my fellow passengers, who are all staring at me, and decide I must get writing as the train could leave any minute. I crouch on the ground, take paper and a pencil from my bag and rest the paper uncomfortably on my knee. I look around. The passengers are still staring at me. I'm used to usually writing in a small room without any company. I ignore them. But what I can't get out of my head is the lunatic concatenation of events I've passed through in the last two or three hours. I must remain calm. Think of my wife. DON'T think of my wife. I shift uncomfortably upon my buttocks, try to unravel what my thoughts were in the hotel room, but all that high-flown international diplomacy cleverness doesn't seem appropriate just now. *Dagong Bao* has its own diplomatic correspondent. The train gives a sudden lurch.

God, I think, the train's leaving.

But that's not it at all. Everyone who can get to it is leaning out of the window, but rather than seeing the locomotive pulling us away towards safety, instead they see that our locomotive has been detached from the train and is steaming away by itself.

Pandemonium. 'We're being abandoned!' Panic all around me. Don't panic, I think! At least I have some time to finish my article. I take a vacated seat and start to think. The passenger returning from the window sees I have stolen his seat and scowls at me, but he's not going to do anything because of the military escort I arrived with. I put my bag on my knee and rest the paper on it. I think of stirring images, daring events, heroic stands, blood spilling. But somehow it doesn't feel right.

This nation is in collapse, panic, despair. Writing cheap heroics like in a Hollywood film won't fool anyone. But calmness, reason, and reassurance will hardly fool them either. And it's my job as a propagandist to fool people. How?!?

Shells are landing quite close to the station now. I can hear planes overhead.

Then something else happens. The locomotive that left our train suddenly backs another train down the rails on the opposite side of our platform. A train completely different to ours. Our train is rough and shabby. It's carried too many people on too many journeys over the last few months. This new train is immaculate. Every carriage has been highly polished. The interiors of every coach are luxurious. Right opposite us stops an armoured baggage coach. Immediately smartly uniformed soldiers form a line in front of it, and also line the platform facing our train, bayonets pointing at us. Under no circumstances are we to attempt to board the train opposite us with 'our' locomotive attached to the front of it.

Well-dressed officers start to parade down the platform, talking languidly to each other. Following them are their wives and concubines and taxi girls in exotic, colourful clothing, chattering and giggling, twirling their parasols. The officers step into the various carriages, then their women. Then, with heavily armed guards, a large cart drawn by heavy draft horses comes down the platform and stops by the armoured coach. A steel door on the coach shoots up and coolies start loading heavy sacks into the carriage. One splits slightly and silver coins spill out.

A sigh goes through our train. So this is where so much of our looted money has gone. The soldiers facing us tighten their grips on their rifles. Poltroons and thieves!

A Japanese bomb hits the far end of the station and broken glass rains down on some empty track.

And then, finally, walking very slowly, grandly down the platform, comes the Hero of Jinan. The man we have put so much trust in to defend us from the Japanese – General Han Fuju. As a grand and a mighty man, before him is borne his coffin, to bring him comfort in this his hour of tribulation. It is huge. Incredibly ornate. Made entirely of silver. Exactly the sort of vehicle you would require to make the grandest of entrances into the afterlife. General Fuju stands solemnly while it is loaded into the armoured coach.

Forgive me for this. I am a literary person and therefore, like all literary people, susceptible to moments of wild and frenzied hatred, usually towards our fellow writers, but also on occasion to our fellow human beings. Well, now I am going to indulge this tendency just a little.

The fact is the wretched Han Fuju is famous for only two things in China. First, until today, he was famous for being a brave and courageous general. A defender of the realm. Well, that's fucked off pretty quickly. The second thing he is famed for – throughout China – is his appalling verse. His poems are renowned and reported around the country even more widely than his military heroics.

In my extreme fury I will repeat only one to you. He wrote it while he was living in our midst in Jinan, defending us. He wrote it about one of my own deepest and most beloved literary inspirations. Daming Lake. The exquisite Bright Lake. Here it is:

Daming Lake, great and bright,
Covered with floating lotuses.
On the lotuses sit toads.
Prod them once and away they leap.

That's it.

His coffin is finally fitted inside the armoured carriage. Han Fuju wipes a sentimental tear from his eye and steps into the next carriage. The soldiers quickly leap upon the train. There is a whistle and it slides swiftly out.

I reflect. Is it any wonder that led by such a man, deserted by such a man, so many of his soldiers, in despair, in disgust, have descended into barbarism and nihilism and turned against the very people, us, they have sworn to protect?

I am a propagandist. I have to write. I have to write in such a way that I do not tell the truth – because that would be censored – but I lie in such a way that readers can still draw the truth, can draw sustenance and hope, from my lies. I will not mention General Han Fuju. I will not mention the cowardice and the murderous behaviour of his troops.

His troops were quartered for many months in our city. In that time, except at the end, they were well disciplined, cheerful and courteous. I spoke to them on many occasions when I was in town. And what did they say? They said they were totally confident that in hand-to-hand, close-quarter fighting with the Japanese – which the Japanese were not very fond of – they were their superiors. What they lacked were adequate weapons – modern tanks, artillery, aircraft, machine guns, gas masks. I can put that in. Because it is hardly a state secret. And, as I noted in the hotel, it's exactly the sort of things that possible allies in the West should be reading.

I write this. What should I say about the generals, about General Han Fuju? Nothing – I would be censored – but with most of our armies falling back people will already have reached their own conclusions about the mediocre generals put in charge of them. Where are our great heroic generals, like Feng Yuxiang, Bai Chongxi and Li Zongren?

The truth is that our leader General Chiang Kai-shek will not allow one of them to lead, because our great leader is not fighting a war against the Japanese, he is still fighting a civil war, and is terrified that such gifted generals will take control from him. Of course I cannot write this. (I've already spent too much of my life enjoying the hospitality of his secret police.) And in war you cannot openly question your leader. The people must be united. So I do it this way. In my article I heap praise on our great leader Chiang Kai-shek. I report the soldiers I have spoken to praising him too – which quite a few of them actually did. But I do not mention by name any of the generals who are presently precipitously retreating in the face of the enemy. Astute people will, I hope, notice my silence.

A bomb drops on a nearby platform. Some people are injured.

With reference to Jinan I describe the brave patriotic students who worked with the fire brigades, who dug people out of rubble, who acted as stretcher bearers or treated the wounded in hospital, who published pamphlets and put on street plays attacking the Japanese, who volunteered directly to serve in the army.

Above all I emphasize that this fight against the Japanese must be fought by the whole nation, a whole nation united.

The train suddenly jolts. Again people rush to the window. Apparently a new locomotive has backed onto our train but people are outraged that, unlike the modern and powerful locomotive purloined by General Han, this one is ancient and decrepit.

I finish writing. I start rereading it to edit. The train starts. Outside the window the messenger boy shouts to me. I finish correcting the final page – it will have to do. I dash to the window. He's running, holding out a stick with a cleft in it. I stuff the article into the cleft, reach into my pocket, haul out a silver coin and toss it to him. He deftly catches it, gives me a grateful grin, and starts to make his way back towards the hotel. If anyone can make it to the Stein Hotel in the midst of this chaos it is a street urchin. I should know. I was once a street urchin.

I turn from the window to see my seat has been retaken by the passenger I took it from. He scowls at me. I smile at him. For the first time today, and for many days, I am happy. I squat back on the floor, take out my wife's scarf, smell it, and start to cry.

The solitary goose does not drink or eat,
It flies about and calls, missing the flock.
No one now remembers this one shadow,
They've lost each other in the myriad layers of cloud.
It looks into the distance: seems to see,
It's so distressed, it thinks that it can hear.
Unconsciously, the wild ducks start to call,
Cries of birds are everywhere confused.

Du Fu, 'The Solitary Goose'

11

Wei lay on his back, spreadeagled. He couldn't move, his brain was blind and black, his body ancient. With great effort he shifted himself, he started to force himself upright, slow as a man climbing out of his grave. He stood, looked around. He saw the corpse of his headless Second Son lying on the ground, his body soaked in the blood of the dead donkey. Then the flames of the cart caught his attention. He turned to see it burning. His family's cart. With all his family's wealth, his family's worth burning in it. He saw the pulp of blood and bone and bowel which had once been his father, the body of his youngest son, Baby Boy Wei, and then suddenly, in their midst, sitting astounded, bewildered, his youngest daughter Baby Girl Wei, her mouth open, her hair starting to flame. Something primaeval, something deep inside him lifted his body up, propelled it over the side of the cart, hoisted her up, and clambered back over the side of the cart, dousing her hair, depositing her on the safe ground, before his strength again deserted him and he collapsed back on the ground, an old man, exhaustion and despair eating every bone and fibre of his body.

His wife by now had run forwards from behind the cart where she and Cherry Blossom had been walking. Cherry Blossom and Baby Girl Wei started screaming – Cherry Blossom because her pet hedgehog was in the cart and Baby Girl Wei because Cherry Blossom was screaming. Wei's wife hit them both. As Eldest Son ran up with a bewildered look on his face she leapt into the cart and started picking water and food from the flames. Honey was bleeding everywhere. The large full jar of water had been shattered but the half empty one was still miraculously intact so she handed it carefully down to Eldest Son – then started throwing all the potatoes, carrots, and other unburning food down to him. Finally, as she jumped clear, she pulled off the two pieces of blue canvas they used as a roof for the cart and which had not yet caught fire.

'Pile all the food we have on that canvas,' she shouted at Eldest Son laying it out, 'and guard it. Get Cherry Blossom and Baby Girl Wei to pick up any more they can find.' Already people were flocking round to pick up fragments that the impact of the unexploded bomb had strewn around the cart.

She herself, thin and strained, stalked forwards to the front of the cart, noted her dead second son and the donkey, then walked round the cart and saw her husband helpless on his back like an upended turtle. For a few moments she looked down at him, thinking intensely. Wei's wife had been denying herself food and water for days now, giving it to Eldest Son. She gave what little urine she produced to him, too. Her body was dehydrated, exhausted, but the fanaticism in her mind to preserve above all her eldest son drove her and focused her with ferocious intensity.

'If my husband is to do what must be done,' she thought, 'I must show him that I respect him – which I do. That I care for him – which I do. That I always have his and the family's best interests at heart – which I do.'

She leant down and gently spoke to him, as though she was addressing a child.

'Dear husband, the remains of your beloved father and beloved sons are burning or are lying on the ground, carrion for the crows. You must get up, you must rescue their bodies, you must give them a proper and respectful burial in the earth. Get up from the ground.'

And he rose. Like a dead man.

'Get your father and Baby Boy Wei out of the cart, put their remains on this canvas. Put the body of our Second Son on it too. Then you and I will drag them on this canvas to a place where they can be respectfully buried. Do it.'

And he did. Again what was automatic, what was instinctive in him took over. He pulled out the starting-to-burn body of his youngest son, placed it on the canvas, then stepped right into the flames and stooping managed to embrace then cradle the pulp of bones and flesh and viscera which had been his father and, stepping out, clothes smouldering, let them slop upon the canvas. Then he pulled out Cherry Blossom who was screaming about her hedgehog and trying to find it in the wreckage. Then he took the decapitated body of his Second Son drenched in the blood of the donkey and placed it gently on the canvas.

His wife touched him quietly on the arm after he had done this and walked back to Eldest Son, Cherry Blossom and Baby Girl Wei, ordering them to follow her and Wei, dragging the canvas with the food and water on it behind them. They were to watch out for thieves. She walked back to her husband and they each took hold of one end of their canvas and started to drag it forwards, the remains of their family upon it.

The family drew slowly away from their flaming wagon. Since she had lost her hedgehog, Cherry Blossom had decided to transfer all her affections and attentions to Baby Girl Wei. Baby Girl Wei was ecstatic. (A peasant from Shanxi Province later found the body of Cherry Blossom's pet hedgehog and ate it. It saved his life.)

As they slowly moved away they passed along the path of the bomb, the bodies and parts of bodies lying scattered on either side until they came to the cart where it had finally come to rest, slaughtering all the young men travelling in it. In the midst of the carnage stood a strange-looking man with a Western hairstyle, orange jacket and pencil moustache. He was looking upwards and cursing the heavens.

They ignored him.

Wei knew only one thing, that his wife was looking after him. That she was looking after the whole family. And he felt profoundly grateful and moved by this.

After a mile the valley widened and the stumbling crowds started to spread out. Wei's wife steered them away from the main stream, but not far enough to be threatened by bandits. Wei just plodded on with his ghastly burden, doing what his wife instructed him to do. They came across a relatively quiet place, on a pleasant slope with a fine view. The dead would appreciate it. She stopped. They all stopped.

'Dear husband,' she addressed him, 'I think it would be better, more reverent, if you dug the family grave, not Eldest Son, since you are head of our family.'

'Yes,' thought Wei, 'she is right.'

Eldest Son passed him the spade and he started to dig. Into the embrace of the earth. As he dug deeper he felt the earth calling him, wanting him. He remembered the stories of whole families of refugees committing suicide so they could stay together in the afterlife.

'Get out of the earth, husband,' his wife told him. 'For you have dug deep enough.'

He climbed out, walked over to the canvas. With care, with reverence, he placed the remains of half his family in the earth and looked down on them. His father, his second son, his baby boy.

He stood alone, staring at them. Then a voice within him spoke.

'Why have you gone against all decent behaviour, Wei, all fatherly duty? What happens when a father does not show paternal piety and duty towards his eldest son? The whole family falls to pieces. Like ours. A whole world falls to pieces. As ours is doing.'

'With your unnatural love for your daughter rather than your eldest son. With your deliberate flouting of the laws of burial by putting your dead sister in a grave beside the bones of those who had rightly rejected her. In your keeping alive a daughter who was for so many years, and especially now, a great drain and burden upon her family. Who told us wicked lies which have led us into this destruction. Who malignly thrust herself between your eldest son and you. This is what has brought us to this.

'You have acted directly against the wishes of all your ancestors, all your forefathers, you have directly killed your father, your second son, you baby son – every one a man. Because of your favouring your daughters you have directly endangered your eldest son. You must act to right the evil you have caused.'

His wife had been watching him intently all this time.

'Fill in the grave, husband,' she gently prompted him, 'so we can be on our way.'

Wei started to do so and then he had a sudden thought. The juice from the wild pear tree whose roots passed through the graves of all his ancestors was still in a small stone bottle he carried in his inner clothing. The other bottle he'd stored in the cart when they left home must have been destroyed in the fire. It would be fitting to pour some of it as a libation upon the grave, so that these family members who'd just died could be comforted by the spirits of their long-dead ancestors.

He did this and then filled in the rest of the grave. Then they were on their way again. Eldest Son, Cherry Blossom and Baby Girl Wei out front, Eldest Son pulling the canvas, Wei and his wife behind them, Wei carrying the shovel.

Three or four miles further on the route passed through a large wood. There were bodies everywhere, but these were so commonplace now that no one noticed them. But what everyone stared at were the trees. The leaves which normally lie on the ground in autumn had all been removed, eaten by desperate travellers. What was even stranger were the trees. All their bark had been ripped off them by people ravenous to eat anything. Even the sacred trees with red rags tied about them were bare and stripped. Without bark, the wood resembled a ghostly white assembly of naked human beings, arms raised high in the air.

It was Baby Girl Wei who first spotted them. Beyond the wood the route of the march crossed the bed of another stream, pulped by thousands of weary feet into a poisonous mash of mud and human faeces. As they trekked south the thousands had not noticed a patch of green-leaved dandelions sprouting under the northern bank. Baby Girl Wei did. She had always picked them when out for walks with Grandpa and she loved them. She pointed and waded towards them. Cherry Blossom snatched them out of her grasp and presented them to their mother.

Her discovery presented the family with a dilemma. Should they eat them? They were naturally nutritious and pleasant to eat in an astringent sort of way. And they contained a goodly amount of water. But, of course, dandelion leaves, since the beginning of time, have been notorious for being diuretic. The odd pissed bed does not present any problems to a hungry family with abundant water supplies. But with only a quarter of a jar of water left no one wanted to lose any more water from their bodies. On the other hand, everyone now was drinking piss. Wei was drinking his own, Eldest Son was drinking his own (and, secretly, his mother's), Cherry Blossom was drinking her own (and, secretly, Baby Girl Wei's). So, being a pragmatic family, it was agreed they would all feast on the luscious and flavourful dandelion leaves.

Afterwards, walking along in front of her parents, Baby Girl Wei had never felt happier. Everyone except her father had congratulated her and thanked her – especially her elder sister. She positively bobbed along.

For people in this awful situation – weary to death, short of both food and, much more importantly, water, their souls eaten by fear and bewilderment – hallucination is not uncommon. Wei was lost in a world of dark thoughts and anger, his wife (starving herself completely of all food and water for her first son's sake) fanatically focused her half-crazy mind on one end. Eldest Son was in a permanent state of bewilderment. For comfort he endlessly remembered the times when Second Son was still alive and the two of them had spent so many hours together in the stable with the clever donkey and funny goat and the sunlight pouring through the rafters. Cherry Blossom and Baby Girl Wei moved in a cloud of new-found intimacy.

Sunk in their individual worlds, none of them noticed that the actual world through which they passed had itself – in an act of natural empathy – started to present itself in ever more strange and surreal ways.

On the skyline of a range of hills which ran parallel with them to the west, as if in a dream, a camel train suddenly appeared loping along, heads to tails. Seventy or eighty of them floating in a line. They carried wealthy coal merchants, their families and possessions. The camels had originally been employed in the coal trade, carrying coal from the pits of Mentougou to the city of Beijing. The Beijing coal merchants had simply commandeered the camels and now swung along in their caravan like grand Arabian viziers, flanked by armed guards riding on mules.

Across the flat yellow plain raced strange single-wheeled apparitions with sails. Chinese wheelbarrows were unlike Western ones. They were much larger and their single wheel was in the centre of the barrow, not at one end, so the wheel, a large one, stuck up through the centre of it, with a platform on either side to carry goods or passengers. Up to six passengers, three on each side, could be carried. Because the central wheel carried the whole weight of the barrow – unlike a Western one, where wheel and man shared the load – the Chinese coolie, at the back of a long shaft, could concentrate his efforts on balancing the barrow and pushing it forwards. Substantial speeds could be achieved. And that was before you added a mast and sail. With the sail providing the pull, the skilled coolie just had to keep the craft's balance and run to keep up with it. If the wind was fair he had a lot of running to do. Thus the passengers, grudgingly, had to give far more water to their coolie than to themselves, and these delicate, fantastical creations curved and spun across the flat landscape elegant as swallows above a spring meadow.

Through the light and sand haze suddenly appeared the burnt-out hulk of the giant Studebaker Roadster which had rolled past them so effortlessly days ago. It had not run out of petrol but out of water, radiator water. The engine had overheated, its oil had caught fire, from which the petrol ignited. A hundred yards beyond the wreck the ground was littered with top hats, where the pedestrianized bankers had suddenly all realized how useless top hats really were. Every so often after that the Wei family passed dead bankers with sunburnt heads – fat blowflies who thrived in the hothouse of financial Darwinism but were rendered toothless on a genuine tooth-and-claw death march. Of the wily chauffeur, who'd probably drunk the radiator water in the first place, there was no sign.

Cherry Blossom tried on a top hat but it was far too large. She tried it on Baby Girl Wei who almost disappeared within it and had to be rescued by her mother. They all thought it incredibly funny. Wei stared at them.

Evening drew on. The sun started to set behind the line of hills to their west, with the result that the bodies and long, long legs of the hurrying camels threw gigantic, elongated shadows across the whole plain, as though huge spiders and monsters fought all around them and slashed across their bodies and faces.

It was with these daggering flashes of light and darkness playing bewilderingly into his face and eyes that Wei suddenly attacked his youngest daughter, Baby Girl Wei. A few seconds before it happened Cherry Blossom, always graced with an uncanny instinct for inner family dynamics, suddenly deserted her newly intimate sister and ran straight to the outstretched hand of her mother. Wei's wife and the rest of the family moved quickly forwards, leaving Baby Girl Wei alone with her father.

Wei did not actually attack his daughter – his own flesh, a being he loved more than he loved himself. Despite the schism and darkness and demons which the Japanese bomb had exploded within him, he still retained enough humanity and grace to not actually strike her with the spade he was carrying. Instead he used it to herd her off, push her away, backwards. At first she thought he was playing with her.

'Why are you doing this, Father?' she asked giggling. 'Is this some sort of game?'

Wei grunted in guilt and terror. He had to do this. For the family. For the water they could no longer afford to give her.

'Why are Cherry Blossom and Mummy going away so quickly? Let's join them.'

With pain he again used the spade to push her away.

A note of fear entered her voice. So many strange, unexplained things had been happening recently in her tiny world. She wanted to be listening again to Cherry Blossom's unending chatter.

'Why are you doing this, Daddy? Let's catch up Mummy and Cherry Blossom.'

He pushed again at her with a grunt. Though it came out more like a whimper. He had to tell her. The two words formed on his lips. He had to force them out.

'Daddy…'

'Go,' he gasped out. He tried again with his treacherous rubbery lips. 'Go away.'

'Where shall I go, Daddy?'

'Go. Go away.'

She tried again, pushing him. He pushed her back hard with the shovel and she fell over. He started to walk fast away from her. She stood up and started to run after him. She grabbed him hard around one leg and curled her tiny arms and legs around it, holding on tight as a clamp. Just like the game they had played so many times before where he walked along with her clamped to his leg, laughing and shrieking. He peeled her off and shouted at her. 'Get off.'

Again she got up and as she followed him, breathless now, she cried, 'What is it, Father? What have I done wrong? Do I complain too much so you have to carry me? I'll walk everywhere by myself, on my two legs, I swear it. I'll be a good girl. I won't cry and whine any more, Daddy,' she cried in her fear.

Again and again she ran up to him as he walked and he pushed her away. His own flesh, his own blood. It was as though he was tearing a part of his own body out of himself. 'This is evil,' he thought to himself. 'This is the work of a demon. But I must do it.'

He did not flinch. For an hour it lasted, her running to him, she growing weaker, til, exhausted, she was following him on hands and knees, her arms and legs pumping round and round like a mechanical toy or some crazed grasshopper. 'Do not leave me, Papa, please do not leave me. I will not do anything wrong ever again!'

It stirred awful memories in him of his elder sister, banished outside the farmhouse and courtyard during the famine, her ignored cries and wails for help coming to him as he lay in his bed as a child. And now he was doing the same thing. But it had to be done. His wife's logic was irrefutable.

Eventually her lamentations, her pleas receded into the darkness. Occasional bewildered cries and moans. Then there was silence. Who knows what her last hours, her last moments were like? Wondering what was happening, what she had done wrong? Running to indifferent strangers, running from wild dogs or murderous crows.

Never would Wei ever use a spade again without remembering exactly to what purpose he had once put it.

He walked til he found his 'family' – his wife, his eldest son, Cherry Blossom. They had stopped and made a tiny encampment. His wife gave him a strange smile and handed him a bowl with a few mouthfuls of water in it and some dried beans floating on it. Eldest Son would not look at him. Cherry Blossom chattered away happily to herself. Wei passed Eldest Son his spade, threw himself on the earth, and fell into a deep, deep sleep.

Where do the lost go? Where do their spirits wander? Will they ever know justice, experience love and joy again? Yes, justice and joy will be seen upon this earth again. In the darkest of dark places there shall be light. Light perpetual. Hallelujah!

12

The next morning Wei awoke and he knew what he had done. The long sleep had healed the rift within his mind caused by the bomb, by the awful onset of grief and shock in him at the deaths of so many so close to him. He understood he had murdered his own daughter. But he also realized that, by his wife's cold-eyed logic, she had had to die so the family might survive. Until the shock of the bomb his old mind had reacted to any thought of killing members of his family with revulsion. After the bomb his new mind had seen the perfect logic and morality of killing one so the others might live. Now his two minds rested in harmony with each other. Became one again.

His one duty was to see to the survival of his eldest son, so that the family would continue. He himself, after his foul murder, would never wish to shame and shock the family by daring to ask that he sat at their table in the afterlife. But his eldest son must have a seat of honour there, as would – and he smiled at this – his wife. Her single-mindedness in service of the family deserved it.

His wife was sitting beside him, watching him, smiling with that gentle smile he had always so much loved throughout their marriage.

'What you did last night was right, husband. I know how much you love your daughters. All the women in the family. What sort of justice do the gods give us,' she asked, 'that we must choose between which of our children we must kill?'

Wei looked around. Eldest Son was standing guard with the spade, avoiding all eye contact with them. Wei looked for Cherry Blossom but could see her nowhere. It was as though she had disappeared. Wei decided to let this pass. He now had no daughters.

'I admire you so much for doing the terrible deed which you were called upon to do. You did what the head of the family has to do – ensure the preservation of the family. The family will immortalize you for this.'

'The family will not immortalize me for this, dear wife.'

'But what choice did you have, dear husband? We could, I suppose, have sold her as a slave to some of the bandits. But they would have hideously mutilated her, blinded her, cut off parts of her body so that she could beg successfully on the pavements and earn good money for them. A lifetime of that? No, that would be too cruel!'

'But perhaps that would have been Baby Girl Wei's choice,' thought Wei, but he did not say it.

He looked at his wife. Her face and body were gaunt and shrunken, her movements slow. Lack of water had reduced her voice to a whispering, emotionless monotone, but above her mouth her hollowed-out eyes still crackled with fire and resolution.

She took his hand.

'Husband, when I die – which will not be long now – go through my clothes. You will find food for Eldest Son there. I have sewn beans and nuts into my seams for him, as well as the money we still possess. And do not waste your strength in burying me. Leave me out for the wild animals and birds. You must press on.'

'Of course I will bury you,' said Wei. 'The earth is gentle. The earth is forgiving. How else will you manage to enter the afterlife?'

What he said caused her great emotion and pain. She turned away from him. When she turned back she had picked up a bowl with a small amount of water in it and a sliced potato.

'We have only a small amount of water left, husband. But I hope it will be enough so that you and Eldest Son, or at least Eldest Son, can make it to somewhere where there is food and water. So that one day you can return to our home and rejoin all our ancestors.'

'I'm sure that will happen, dear wife,' he replied, rising with difficulty to his feet and then pulling her to hers.

They started on their trek again. The men could have walked

faster – a slow plod – but they were slowed by the wander of Wei's wife. They tried to steer her with gentle touches but she angrily brushed them aside.

'Do not waste your energy on me,' she said. 'Keep walking. Leave me. I am finished.'

But they didn't. They continued to guide her slowly across the plain.

Wei thought of when he had first met her. On the day of their marriage. How she had arrived at the gates to their courtyard in a red rickshaw, dressed all in red – sticking her head out from under the canopy to see everything that was happening, drink in every detail. The piety and fear and sincerity she had shown, the procession halfway up the courtyard, when she had been introduced to the ancestors. Reacting brightly, but with reverence, to each one of them, never having to be taught their names again. Then the marriage feast. So interested in everything that was happening. Remembering the names of all her relatives as soon as she was introduced to them. All the time casting a wifely eye around the house, calculating how things worked, deciding what went where, how she would organize everything. And then their marriage bed. Showing complete modesty, of course, but also expressing delight, appreciation, gladness with her soft strong body as they became one. He had never tired of her body, of her presence, of her endless service and bright energy within the growing family.

And now, beside him shuffling and snuffling, like an eighty-year-old crone, except she was only two years over thirty.

It only lasted three hours, then she collapsed upon the earth.

They tried to get her upright. She refused. 'Leave me. Do not waste your strength upon me. You must survive.'

They laid her on her back. Wrapped a coat and put it behind her head. Eldest Son uncorked the water jar to pour her some water. She forbade it.

'Please, Mother,' pleaded Eldest Son, 'please take some water.'

'No,' she ordered.

Eldest Son started weeping.

'Stop that,' she ordered.

He shook his head in disbelief. After a few moments he stopped. She turned her head and looked directly at him.

'You, my son, must live. You, above all, must survive. Through all this "nonsense".' However quiet her voice had become, anger still crackled in it as she said the word 'nonsense' and indicated, with a twist of her shoulders, that she meant all this unnecessary chaos and flight and violence all around them. 'Because when it is over, you, above all, must return to our farm. You must explain to our ancestors what has happened, how this catastrophe of us leaving them occurred. Tell them everything, Son.'

Wei hung his head at this. He ate bitterness.

She continued to her eldest son. 'You are a strong, an able young man, and you must work on the farm again, tirelessly, until the crops grow every spring and are harvested every autumn, and when that is done, because you are a handsome, loving young man, you must find yourself a suitable bride and marry her and the two of you will once again bring children back to the farm, running around and singing songs, and in time a young eldest son who will succeed you, and when it comes time for you to die, sweet son, in ripe old age I pray, then when you meet your ancestors, are welcomed into their midst, I pray,' she sobbed here, 'I pray that you speak for me, that you explain I always remained faithful to them and ask that I might be allowed to join them at their table and might be honoured. Do you understand me, sweet Eldest Son?'

Eldest Son had started crying again. Through his tears he said, 'Yes, Mother, I understand you. I will do what you want.'

'And then I want your son to hold a memorial for me, a funeral feast. Good food, from the farm. Fine wine, from the profits he will have made from his farming. But tell him not to spend too much. He'll always need money in his purse. But if he could afford just a few musicians, a few dancers. Young girls, beautiful bodies. Who will dance around the graves and then slowly take their clothes off, so that the dead and the living might dance together, and his lands and his wife's womb and the wombs of all the wives of your eldest sons following you shall be fertile and unending.'

And as she spoke, it seemed to Wei as though her frail, wracked body wrecked upon the ground started dissolving and melting and she became as he remembered her on their marriage bed, writhing and turning and dancing in the act of love.

She died. Her body stiff and silent on the earth. Wei stood up and started to dig her grave. He would not leave her body out to the mercy of the wild animals and crows. She would lie in the good earth and maybe, somehow, her spirit would be able to find its way back through the earth safe to the graves of his ancestors. He would not follow her. He now considered himself an outcast from his family. He had murdered his daughter.

While he dug her grave, his eldest son had continued to sit on the ground staring at his mother. Wei raised him to his feet. Together they placed her in the grave. Wei poured some of the wild pear juice gently upon her to soothe her and then filled in the grave. As he did this Eldest Son looked away. He could not watch. There was no incense to soothe her spirit, no paper money for her to spend in the afterlife.

After Wei had buried her, he and Eldest Son drank the last of the family's water they had carried all the way from the farm. At least it meant one of them would no longer have to carry the heavy jar. They continued to carry the spade. Not because they intended to fight off an attacker with it – neither of them had the strength to do that – but because implicitly, without discussing it, either of them might have to use it to bury the other.

They went slowly on their way.

As they walked Wei understood that all of his energy must now be concentrated on protecting and defending Eldest Son. He had no other function in life. It was his only reason for staying alive. His wife had been exactly right, Eldest Son would not now be in this terrible situation had not he, Wei, made mistake after mistake in his life. Feeding his elder sister when she should have starved, burying her close to the ancestors, allowing Spider Girl to live, showing affection to her and interest in her which had far exceeded the attention he had paid to his Eldest Son. Listening to her advice and coming on this disastrous journey. Everything now must be about protecting Eldest Son and returning him to his farm.

Eldest Son felt no such resolution. He was bewildered. He no longer had any idea of how to see his father. He of course owed him filial piety and his word and deeds were law, but all through life, being closest to his mother, he had seen things as she saw them. This had not meant that he hated his elder sister Spider Girl as his mother had. Eldest Son was not capable of hatred, he was affectionate with all people. But his deep love was for his mother. He knew his father loved him, but he also knew his father had murdered his younger sister Baby Girl Wei. But his mother, whose will he always followed and who he knew loved him, had murdered not just a newborn baby but had also driven away Spider Girl and murdered his sister Cherry Blossom. If his father loved him – which he did – was he now likely to murder him? Was murdering people part of loving them?

Rather than think about this any longer, Eldest Son's mind escaped once again – as it had ever more frequently during the journey. He remembered back to the stable on the farm. He remembered how he loved grooming and brushing the gentle donkey's soft black coat, again and again, as Second Son fed the donkey his dried sorghum and the goat his hay. The smell of the feed and the cheese. He especially loved the smell of hay, when it was fresh cut in the field with the aroma of every wild flower in it, but even more when it had dried and was in the barn and you stuck your face amid its prickly stalks and drank in its warm smell like new made bread or warm cow's milk. He and Second Son had had such fun. Second Son telling jokes – which Eldest Son often didn't understand – or competing to see who could pee highest up a wall. And that warm sunlight shafting down through the dust, yellow as the hay, as the animals lowed and shifted in the straw.

Wei was watching his beloved Eldest Son. He saw him, lost in some vision, smiling to himself, happy in these awful circumstances. These tragedies which had occurred to the family – through his fault – had resulted in perhaps one positive outcome: the problem between Eldest Son and Second Son had been solved. Eldest Son was gentle and generous and happy. But he was not a natural farmer. Second Son was quick-witted, observant, hard working. He could adapt and think and haggle. The very qualities needed to be a farmer. Always on the lookout, aware of what was happening, moving swiftly to deal with problems. Eldest Son possessed none of these qualities. The slow-moving, easy-going Eldest Son would have become, as they became adults, a constant irritant to Second Son. His lassitude, his basic disinterest in farming, would have provoked constant friction between the two every time a decision had to be made – which in farming is frequent. But Eldest Son's opinion would always have held sway since, simply, he was the eldest son, the revered one to whom all other family members must defer, the future head of the family. Second Son's death, awful as it had been, partly removed this problem. The family would not in the future be torn apart by rows and ill-feeling.

But it did not solve the rest of the problem. That the sweet and loving Eldest Son would make a poor farmer. Under his stewardship the family would suffer and could even lose its land. If his wife's fervent wish that they should return to the farm should ever come true – and Wei had grave doubts about it – then it would be important that he returned as well as his son, for his son would need encouragement and guidance from him. It would be best to marry him off quickly to a fertile wife with not too strong a character, so that Wei himself, as he grew older, could have influence over their sons – especially the eldest – and train him to become a skilful and watchful and quick-witted farmer. (Families go forwards in time as well as backwards.)

After several hours of walking Eldest Son started to grow thirsty. At first he did not complain – but Wei saw his mouth working, his frequent rubbing of his throat, his rasping coughing. Young people have tenderer mouths than old ones. Their taste buds are more sensitive, closer to the surface of the inner skin of the mouth. So when the whole mouth and throat start to dry and parch and pull, the pain inside their delicate mouths comes more quickly, more grievously than with older folk. The sand in the air aggravated it.

Eldest Son complained about it. Wei gave him a dried bean to suck, hoping it would act like a sucked pebble that can moisten a mouth. It helped a bit.

'Cheer up, son. If you suck it long enough it will soften up so you can swallow it.'

Eldest Son gave him a nervous smile.

Still around them ghostly figures continued to trudge relentlessly on, not giving up, leaning forwards into the dust, determined to find some shelter where there was water, food, rest. They were living testament to the strength and endurance of the poor, their bodies whipped and hardened by a lifetime of privation and labour. With little body weight to weigh them down, they did what they had always done, kept going.

As evening drew on Eldest Son was tiring and faltering. The dried beans had not lessened his raging thirst though he'd swallowed several. He was starting to totter and his concerned father helped him as they walked. Wei did not think of his own tiredness. He was doing what he should do, supporting his eldest son.

Wei decided to stop for the night. Eldest Son collapsed groaning on the ground. What could he do for his eldest son apart from cover him? He offered him the only thing of value that he possessed – his own urine. He peed into the crude earthenware bowl which had somehow survived the endless journey and held the small amount of liquid gently, cradling his son's head with his other arm, so his son could drink from it. His son liked it. The heat and stone-like dryness of his mouth moistened and started to soften again. He declared himself profoundly grateful for it.

They both relaxed a bit, sucking on dried beans.

'Father,' Eldest Son asked tentatively, 'I know we had to come on this journey, you told us this and Second Son' – his voice cracked a moment as he mentioned his dead younger brother – 'explained to me what you had said and why we must come…?'

'Yes, Eldest Son?' asked Wei.

'Well, Father,' and there was apprehension in his voice because he knew it was a cause of grievous divisions within the family, 'what I'd like to know is, we set off on this journey, but when is it going to end?'

'I do not know for certain when it will end, dear son, but somewhere there must be water and food and shelter for us.'

'I have heard people on this journey – people walking close to us – saying they are going to a place called Wuhan, where there is water and food and shelter. And someday we will get there.'

'Yes, beloved son, there is a place called Wuhan, and there we will find water and food and shelter. And we will rest there.'

He said this to calm his son, though he had no idea what or where Wuhan was. He had never heard of the place.

His son fell asleep. But he did not sleep long. He tossed and turned throughout the night, his dehydrating body cramping and arching in pain. His worried father lay beside him, giving him what comfort he could. Towards dawn Wei, exhausted and weary himself, fell asleep.

He awoke to find Eldest Son gone. Disappeared.

Tottering slightly, he got to his feet. Looked around him. Nothing. Gathering together their few meagre possessions he walked forwards in the direction they had been walking, looking from side to side, asking fellow travellers if they had seen anything. None of them had.

He did not have far to go.

He came across another stream bed, fetid with trodden mud and sewage, little puddles and pools of foul water lying across it. And then he saw Eldest Son, sitting on the opposite bank. And then he saw that from his mouth came brown froth, that all the front of his clothes were stained and caked with brown faeces and mud.

Eldest Son saw him and waved happily.

'Father, Father, look, I have found Wuhan. Water. Look at all the water.'

Wei waded horrified across the foul stream.

'Eldest Son, Eldest Son, what have you done?'

'I have found Wuhan, Father. And as they said there is water. Drink of it yourself. We will live.'

'How many times,' shouted Wei, almost across the stream, 'how many times have I told you not to drink from these streams?'

'But it is water, Father, it saves our lives. Lean down and drink of it.'

'It is not water, it is poison.'

Scarcely had he said this when, just as he came up to his son, Eldest Son's face and body suddenly contorted and convulsed and out of his mouth shot a stream of brown bile and he started squirming in agony upon the ground, spontaneously evacuating his bowels and what little liquid there was in his bladder. Wei grabbed him, shit and blood and all, embracing him.

'Oh my son. My son,' he cried out.

'What is it, Father, what is happening?' asked his terrified, baffled son.

What precious little fluids that were still in Eldest Son's dried-up body were rapidly evacuating through mouth and anus. His heart, his lungs, both robbed of the vital fluid they needed to function, catastrophically failed, his whole body shaking and cavorting in agony.

'What is happening, Father, what is happening?'

He died in his father's arms, baffled by life until its very end.

Wei buried his eldest son, his last son, his last child. Over him, to soothe him, he poured the last of the wild pear juice and then threw the bottle away. He would keep none of it for himself. He deserved only to die. Anonymous, abandoned, accursed. No link back to the family for him. Then he threw the spade away. If anyone attacked him he would not defend himself. He had destroyed the whole Wei family. Not only the living, but, because they would no longer receive prayers and incense and money from the living, his forefathers and ancestors also.

The last living member of the Wei family set off across the endless, unremitting plain, slowly, a few steps at a time, the dehydration in his body shrinking it so his shoulders bunched inwards and his neck hunched his head downwards. When he remembered he looked up just to check his direction was correct, as ghostly travellers continued to walk ever south. Soon he would be a real ghost himself, wandering. Perhaps he would meet Baby Girl Wei's ghost. She would only spit at him and curse him, her teeth chattering with fear and rage.

Gradually he slipped into a world of fear and hallucination, inhabited only by monsters and demons and half-people. A land of screaming and flame and devouring pains. But as he passed through this land of fear and terror, he came across a most upsetting scene. There was his whole family – his father, his wife, Spider Girl, Eldest Son, Cherry Blossom, Second Son, Baby Girl Wei, Baby Boy Wei, even his just born son, it was a beautiful spring day and they were all sitting on the lush green grass that grows over the graves of his ancestors, the ancient wild pear tree above them having just burst into a cloud of white and cream blossoms waving high among the cold blue skies and around his family lay food – what splendid, mouth-watering food – and drink, rich wines and beers and sweet juices, and upon the small stone altar they burnt incense and poured libations and burnt paper money and all were chattering and talking with great animation and joy to all their ancestors who had joined them from below the earth – even his elder sister who waved to him.– but he could not join them, because a demon with slavering jaws was dragging him away into...

With a start he regained his senses. He was standing still, staring at the ground. Once more he started to plod and waver onward across the plain.

It is not a pleasant thing to die of thirst. While the physiological processes within the body that actually cause death are centred in the increasing malfunctioning and collapse of the heart and lungs through lack of fluids, the pain itself is centred horrendously in the throat and mouth as it dries and shrinks and cements slowly into stone. A traveller can deal with extreme hunger or fatigue – there is always the hope of finally arriving somewhere where he can eat and rest. He can be totally deprived of sleep for days on end and survive, somehow, pressing on and on. But one horror cannot be borne. The parching and drying of one's throat and mouth so that breathing becomes ever more blocked and laboured – one's nose and throat already clogged by sand and dried phlegm – so you must cough and splutter just to avoid choking. But then it is your swelling, ever=growing tongue which proves most deadly, for it expands into an already cramped mouth, monstrous swells up, barging back and forth, blocking the throat. As he walked it increased the rolling of his tongue, the choking, so that he had to sink to his knees, lie on his side on the sand so his fat dry tongue lolled to one side of his mouth and still left enough passage for air to creep through his parched, swollen throat and mouth. All his world became his mouth, the battle between tongue and air.

It was at this time that he was robbed of the last of his money and his few beans and much of his clothing. But he noticed nothing, so great had become the struggle within his mouth and throat. Finally he gave up moving. There was one tiny passage left between air and lungs. He relaxed, awaiting the end. There was quietness. Peace. He started to drift off, into another world. The afterlife? Then there was this voice, coming to him. From a distance. There was something strange about it. It was almost as though he recognized it. It was quite distinct. Crying something. And suddenly, with a jolt, he knew that voice. He forced his eyes open, stared about him, trying not to choke. A woman was coming towards him. She was walking in a way he knew from somewhere. It was so familiar, the roll, the sway. She came right up to him, leant over him, looked down into his face.

'Oh Father,' she said, 'dear Father.'

It was his eldest daughter. Spider Girl.

13

The old train creaks through the night. I try to sleep but the carriage is too packed with people and belongings and Pekinese dogs and my mind is too packed with terrible images and wild imaginings of what has happened to my family. I lie atop a mountain of baggage as the young boy beside me kicks me as he has a bad dream. We are all probably having bad dreams. A baby sucks greedily on its mother's tit. Just down the carriage some men play a raucous game of cards, slapping them down on the lid of a suitcase. Somewhere someone recites poetry. The smell of humanity is close and rank and accompanied by the intimate crawling of lice and fleas.

After about an hour I abandon any attempt to sleep, carefully rise so I do not disturb anyone, then, gingerly stepping atwixt sleeping infants and birds in cages and squeezing around people sleeping standing up and between piled and swaying luggage, I make it, by way of an overused urinal, to the dining car. It is for customers only, which means quite a lot of people are sleeping there and have to be woken every hour by the waiter so he can pour some lukewarm tea into their bowls and collect their payment. Every table has a close-to-death potted plant, and spittoons litter the floor.

I sit at a table. The waiter, at a nearby table, comes over and I order some tea. When it arrives it is so cold you could freeze an ice cube in it. I pay him an exorbitant fee and then rest my head against the cool and dirty glass of the window, staring into the darkness outside. The old locomotive is wrestling with its heavy load, wheezing and snorting, great clouds of yellow smoke billowing past the window. And beyond is engulfing darkness. Black as the hobs of hell. I see the red persimmon tree in our courtyard. I see my wife sitting beneath it. My wife immediately frowns at me and reminds me I must not afford myself the luxury of thinking about her. I shake my head and look around the carriage. I notice that the waiter, when he is wakening and serving a customer with their hourly tea, will often surreptitiously remove any newspaper they appear to have finished with. He has quite a large pile of them on his table and is reading them avidly.

I order another 'tea' and when he brings it ask him if he's read any news about Jinan.

'Ah, Jinan,' he says, charging me heavily, 'you have family there?'

'Yes.'

'So do I. No, there is no news from Jinan in the papers. We'll have to wait til we get to Xuzhou and read their papers. But I did speak to the railway telegraphist at our last stop,' he continued, sitting down opposite me. 'He's a friend.'

'Yes?'

'No reports of anything serious or terrible. Not like Nanking.'

'Thank goodness.'

'Yes,' he agrees. 'I live there with my old mother.'

We both sit there for a while with our own thoughts. Are the Japanese troops there behaving better or worse than the Chinese ones?

'Any news in the papers about the war?'

The waiter brushes aside a frond of the withered potted plant and lights a cigarette.

'The usual Japanese advances, I'm afraid, all across the country, but there is a disturbing report in *The Great Evening News*, which I normally find reliable...'

'What?' I ask.

'...from the far north-west, the Nankou Pass...'

'Ah...'

'It is, as you'd know, a vital pass which we cannot allow the Japanese to seize. General Tang Enbo with his Second Army Corps had the pass well guarded and there was no possibility of the Japanese breaking through it. They attacked and they attacked. It was one of the bloodiest battles yet. But General Tang held on. But then suddenly his underling, the cowardly General Liu, chose to withdraw his troops with the result that General Tang could be attacked from the rear by the Japanese, and he was forced to retreat immediately thus giving up possession of the pass. I read a report of the battle in the *Dagong Bao*. It was written by Fan Changjiang, in my opinion the finest war correspondent we have, so I trust it.'

'I agree with you.'

'At the end of his article Fan demanded the execution of General Liu for cowardice.' The waiter looks straight at me. 'Do you think he should be executed?'

There is something not quite right about the waiter's story. The battle had indeed been a terrible disaster. And General Liu thoroughly deserved to be shot – though, of course, he wasn't. But I'd asked the waiter for any news of recent events in the war and he'd answered me by describing a battle which took place over three months ago. Then I understand why. I'm obviously talking to a far more intelligent man than I realized. He's not talking about events in the far north-west three months ago, he's subtly alluding to an event we'd all just witnessed in Jinan. The flight of General Han Fuju. Waiters must be careful what they say – especially in wartime.

I look him back straight in his face. 'Yes, I agree, General Liu should have been executed immediately for cowardice.'

'He dishonours the name of Liu.'

I offer him a cigarette. He accepts and goes and gets me another tea – this time piping hot and sweetly fragrant, for which he charges me not a penny.

'What is the recent war news?' I ask.

'They've finally withdrawn from Shanghai.'

'Sad but inevitable.'

'At least we stood face to face with them at Sihang Warehouse and fought them back time after time. Showed them what Chinese men can do.'

'Yes.'

I find out his name is Chao. Chao walks over and liberates

a nearly full bottle of French wine from the table of a snoring European – he's already had two bottles so is unlikely to remember this one – and fills two immaculately polished glasses. Our conversation broadens. As the train hobbles through the night – the tracks are terrible – we discuss the various fronts in the war, the terrifying speed of the Japanese advance. Chao is an aficionado of newspapers, knowing which are pro or anti the war, which editors and journalists receive bribes and from whom, which reporters actually report from the front as opposed to writing what some general or politician tells them to write a hundred miles behind the lines. He trusts only *Dagong Bao*. I agree with him.

We discuss the qualities needed to make a proper war correspondent – courage, some military training so he can analyze what is happening, the ability to write vivid, exact prose and pick small details to illustrate wider, more general truths. Above all, he must avoid the slop and emotional mendacity of propaganda. When things go badly he must have the integrity to let his readers know, however indirectly. All the time he talks I make mental notes. This man should be teaching my students in Wuhan.

'Excuse me,' I say, 'but you are a waiter on a train. How on earth are you so well informed?'

He looks at me. He starts to crumble.

'I'm sorry,' I apologize hurriedly, 'I do not wish in any way to offend you. I have been so rude...'

He looks at me. He decides something.

'I will tell you my story. My downfall is gambling.' He looks at me some more. 'Since I was a boy I've bet on things – which fly will crawl up the wall fastest, will a fat man or a thin man come through that gate next? It was only tiny sums but it caused my mother deep grief. My father was a gambler and ran away after he'd ruined us. But I took no notice of her. I got a job on this train. Suddenly I was serving all these important, beautifully dressed men. Rich men. And I noticed they all read newspapers. And that almost all of them read only two things in the newspapers: horse racing – at Shanghai, at Wuhan, at Hong Kong – and stock exchange prices. So that was two types of gambling right there – and they'd all obviously done really well out of it. So I thought, I can do this. But

I couldn't read. So on these long nights on the train I got the guard to teach me. I started to read their newspapers. Well, I couldn't make head nor tail of all that stock market stuff. Far too difficult for my head. But horse racing? Love at first sight. When the train was in Shanghai or Wuhan I'd go to the races – all the colours of the jockey's Shandong shirts and the ladies' dresses and the shouting and screaming and gambling. I thought I was in heaven. And I spent all my money. Then I got into debt, deep debt, gangster debt. So I couldn't eat. My mother couldn't eat. For a week we couldn't eat. I was so ashamed. Then I got enough money to bring her home some food. She wouldn't touch it. "Mother, dear Mother, you'll starve to death, please eat. I've brought you nice food. Good food. I've still got my job on the railways." She was dying but she wouldn't eat a crumb til I swore, hand on the stone tablets of my ancestors, that I would never ever gamble again. Which I haven't. But now I can read and I am stuck with all these newspapers every night. So I started to read other things. In a newspaper you can travel to foreign countries. Through the pictures and photographs in newspapers I have travelled to Chicago, the home of Al Capone, to Paris, to exotic islands like Tahiti and the Bahamas, I have seen the strange rituals of Buckingham Palace. And then I started to read the news. Not only here but in the rest of the world. Should Mr Chamberlain appease Herr Hitler? What is the effect of Mr Roosevelt's economic policies on America and on Japan and on us in China? Is Moscow a good or a bad thing? And all the time the Japanese are threatening. Then suddenly they invade us, full tilt. I feel all sorts of emotions. Most Chinese people do not feel any emotions because they do not know who the Japanese are. They do not know what China is. But I do, because I have read my newspapers and taught myself to think, so I have very definite ideas on why the Japanese have invaded and whether we can fight back or not...'

Suddenly three rich families invade the dining car. They've got on at an intermediate station and are famished and shouting for food.

'I must go, Mr Lao,' says Chao getting up and hiding the wine bottle. 'I look forward to reading your article in *Dagong Bao*.'

'How do you know my name, that I have written for them?'

'There are no secrets on a train, Mr Lao. I hope we can talk again before the end of our journey?'

I make my way back down the train, saying my prayers, asking God to protect my sweet family and country, delicately treading amid snoring bodies and tangled limbs and drooling babies and stacked packing cases. As I do so first light seeps through the windows. The young boy who'd been kicking me now lies arms flung out across my smidgeon of space. I softly move them before assuming once more my fetal curl. I fall asleep to the sweet sound of birds singing as every caged bird in the carriage greets the dawn.

I awake to great excitement. We are arriving at a station. Only a small rural station but suddenly whole bookfuls of things are happening. Even before the train stops it's assaulted by solid waves of desperate would-be passengers from the platform, trying to propel large bundles through the windows and doors followed by their desperate selves. Most are repelled by the stalwarts already in the train with shouts and punches and curses. Eventually, some are allowed in sans baggage, but the rest have to clamber up the ladder at the end of each carriage onto the roof, already covered by passengers stewing in the fierce midday sun and frying on the red-hot metal. Lots of muffled stamping and shuffling and shouts above us.

Simultaneously on the side away from the platform local farmers have already arrived with a whole lot of succulent and less succulent-looking produce and set up their stalls and cooking pots in order to make a killing. As the water tower's hose is manhandled into the locomotive's tank, water gushes everywhere, causing canny parents to dangle their infants out of the windows to encourage them to gush in sympathy. Young children demanding the full works are lowered on ropes tied round their waists and squat by the side of the track. Food is passed up from the track to us inside – I have a very nice rice congee. Strings and ropes from the roof are lowered with money and containers tied to them and rise up with food and water attached. Much shouting and haggling takes place.

Just beyond the spontaneous market something quite surreal is happening. The village where we have stopped is some sort of administrative centre for the area, so it has a courthouse. The courthouse has presumably just condemned several bandits to death, as a gallows has been erected just beyond the market. Since the whole point of official justice is to impress upon the rest of us the importance of not being lured into a life of crime, murder and mayhem, and justice must be seen to be done, it is obviously most efficacious to carry out its sentences in front of as many citizens as possible, and the court official in charge has held back til the market is in full swing and the train has arrived.

As I eat my rice congee I watch the condemned as they're led to the scaffold, climb it, and have the ropes tied around their necks. They chat philosophically, resignedly among each other as though nothing unusual is about to occur. One even makes jokes. The others smile – sadly. But the whole frenzy of activity onboard the train and in the market carries on, everyone completely indifferent to what is happening behind them. People are too busy surviving and eating and making a profit to even glance at the prisoners. I alone, it seems, stare at their melancholy prospect. They are launched into eternity as strings and ropes continued to pass up and down laden with goods and children and money. The bandits struggle and choke.

The train, having taken on sufficient water and coal, suddenly jerks and starts off without warning. Infants are hastily roped in through windows, relieved or unrelieved, last-minute food purchases are hurled through the windows and onto the roof. We steam off round a corner with one bandit still forlornly dancing. Within our carriage the frenzy slowly subsides. Hot food is digested, drinks drunk, experiences related.

The train steams on.

By afternoon it is hot and close. Despite the windows being open the smells penetrate everywhere – viscous and foul. I start to recognize everyone by their distinctive stink. I finger the red persimmon fruit in my pocket. Already, like a prune, it is drying out in the heat. But I keep it close to me, as I do my wife's scarf. They are my sacred lifelines back to my family. Around me families play rock, paper, scissors, groups of men play cards, several women sew. Vicious family quarrels ignite spontaneously. Birds and children sing.

I practise to be a grandfather by telling the children near me traditional tales from the shadow puppet shows I saw on the streets of Beijing when I was a child. Noble princes, beautiful princesses, avaricious merchants, friendly dragons, horrible demons. They love it all. Then I decide to get epic. To tell the wonderful story of Zhuge Liang at the start of the Battle of Red Cliffs – oh that we had Zhuge Liang leading our armies now! – who, being short of arrows, craftily managed to steal all his enemy Cao Cao's arrows and then fire them back at him. How he adapted all of his boats to carry straw decks and superstructures, which he then sailed at Cao Cao's great fleet, so Cao Cao fired all of his arrows at them and all the arrows stuck in the tightly packed straw which Zhuge Liang's soldiers hid behind so, when Cao Cao had fired all his arrows, Zhuge Liang simply turned his boats around and returned to his base with a huge number of brand new arrows. Zhuge Liang then used all these arrows to fight the great Battle of Red Cliffs, which sent the evil Cao Cao reeling far back into Northern China. When I saw it as a child in the puppet theatre I thought it was a huge battle. All those straw ships, all the horses and soldiers fighting by the Red Cliffs. Hundreds of puppets and backdrops. I remember it as an enormous spine-tingling spectacle. There's only one problem with retelling this epic story on this train. I am crouched on the floor jammed between two packing cases so that all I have to tell it with are my two hands, which I can scarcely move, and my face. So I use powerful, vivid words, fierce emotions and expressions on my face, a few sharp gestures from my hands, to paint within their minds the same scenes which I had once seen on such a huge scale. An excellent rehearsal for what I must teach my students in Wuhan. That they must do almost everything with virtually nothing.

My audience cry out for joy when Zhuge Liang does his acts of derring-do, hiss lustily when Cao Cao appears. And the adults start to join in too, correcting me when my version of the Battle of Red Cliffs differs from theirs – every Chinaman possessing his own unique version of the battle. At some point in my performance, I must confess, almost subconsciously, I start to substitute the name Cao Cao with that of the evil Emperor Hirohito, his evil troops for the evil Japanese troops, the wise leader Zhuge Liang becomes our wise leader Chiang Kai-shek and Zhuge Laing's heroic soldiers become our own heroic troops.

I must say, in all modesty, that I do a particularly fine Emperor Hirohito, basing him largely on the Fu Manchu films I used to watch in London. So popular is my cramped, crouching thespianism that I am asked to do another performance about every three hours, with the result that I have to wrack my brains for epic events in Chinese history which can star the Emperor Hirohito and General Chiang Kai-shek.

When I am not doing this historical propaganda I twist myself round to catch a glimpse out of the window of contemporary China. It is terrifying. Beside the railway runs a highway. Men and women and children walk along it in rags, their hair matted and coloured white by the dust, the children's stalk legs attached to stalk bodies. Families shelter from the sun and wind by digging holes and crouching in them, covering themselves with canvas or straw. Other families sit by the side of the road at the end of their wits, too weary to move another foot. A wounded soldier, like a frog run over by an ox cart, pulls himself along. Half of his left thigh has been blown away by a shell. Another, his left hand severed, huddles like a hedgehog. Dead humans, horses and other animals litter the road. It was probably the same in Zhuge Liang's time. I turn away in despair.

Three days into our journey our train approaches a line of mountains which we will have to cross if we are to join the river valley which run down to Wuhan. At the final halt before the climb starts several open wagons are attached to our rear. As they are shunted past us we see them packed with wounded soldiers, groaning and crying in pain, some of their wounds bandaged, many not. There are no medical staff attending them. The stink from their wounds is foul.

As we start from the halt our ancient locomotive appears to have gained a new lease of life. Perhaps a higher quality of coal is mined in this area, but the chimney blasts out sharp stentorian blasts of energy and the boiler, built in 1871 by the Dübs & Co. works of Polmadie, Glasgow (I checked at the halt), must be at full pressure as we hurtle along.

As evening closes in we start to climb into the foothills of the mountains, the wheels hammering on the track.

Each night I have had my learned conversation in the dining car with my waiter friend Chao, freshly briefed from the day's papers. Each night more and more join our discussion, eager to discuss the war. They in turn have told their friends, with the result we've almost become a debating society, everyone giving their opinion at three o'clock in the morning. On this final night Chao draws me aside. He has a rather anxious look on his face.

He sucks sharply on his cigarette.

'Forgive me for this, and for not telling you earlier,' he says.

'Yes?'

'The fact is, I did not tell you the truth when I said I left my mother in Jinan. The fact is I could not bring myself to abandon her, so I smuggled her aboard this train. It is illegal for railway staff to give relatives free journeys on company trains so I hid her on the roof. She is a very hardy lady and I gave her plenty of blankets. When business is slow in the dining car a colleague covers for me and I smuggle her up food. The thing is, she is a very intelligent woman and wants to know from me everything that is happening in the world, so I've been having similar discussions with her on the roof as we've been having down here. And she's been telling everyone on the roof what I've been telling her and they've all become very interested in the war and being informed about it. The people on the roof are far poorer than the people here in the train, but from my conversations with them it seems to me they ask far more intelligent questions than the people below.

'Anyhow, the thing is, I have agreed tonight to give the people on the roof a talk on the war, on how I believe it will turn out, and the military means by which China will defeat Japan.'

This I *must* hear!

'The reason I'm being so secretive,' he whispers, 'is because, of course, organizing meetings on trains and addressing them is illegal for members of staff. I will be sacked if I am found out. And if, by some bad luck, a member of the secret police should happen to be on this train and hears of this talk, attends it and then reports me because I have not spoken particularly highly of General Chiang Kai-shek's military abilities...'

'I understand,' I say. 'Secrecy is vital.'

'The meeting will be on the train roof at one o'clock tonight.' He looks at me directly. 'I have one more favour to ask of you,' he says. 'I would like you to address it.'

'Me?'

'I will give the main talk, of course. But I, we, would be highly honoured if you perhaps would give an introductory talk, perhaps making the points you made in your *Dagong Bao* article?'

'You've read it?'

'When we got to Xuzhou. You understand very well how to tell the truth to people while telling them lies. You write in such a way that people understand they must read between the lines. If we are ever to be free, such is the repression around us, we must all learn to be able to talk in such a way while inside of ourselves knowing the truth.'

Oh China, I think, you are so full of wonderful surprises!

At one o'clock Chao and I climb the outside ladder on to the restaurant car roof. We are greeted with wild applause. It is an extraordinary scene. All around us are snow-covered mountains, glaring white in the light of a full moon, blasts from the Glasgow boiler echoing hard around them. The locomotive climbs steadily, with a river below us. We walk forwards to the front of the carriage, our audience parting before us, holding up hands when we seem unsteady. When a tunnel approaches a warning shout goes up and we crouch. This is the most unusual public meeting I have ever attended!

We turn to face them so the wind carries our voices back

to our listeners. Chao flatteringly introduces me as an honest newspaperman. I blush slightly. He says that I have written a famous novel called *Rickshaw Boy*, a story about the sufferings of the working classes and the necessity for united action. This gets a rousing cheer. He says he hasn't read it yet but will buy a copy as soon as we reach Wuhan. He urges everyone else to do this. (Authors always like to hear things like this.) All those individuals who don't have enough money to buy one he urges to come to the station to borrow his copy.

He sits down. I am to speak. I stare at my windswept, expectant audience. The thunderous blasts issuing powerfully from the locomotive at first disrupt me, but I soon learn to speak between them, giving my speech a staccato and powerful rhythm. I cover the points I made in my article – the bravery and optimism of our troops, the shortage of modern weaponry and equipment (a clear encouragement to industrial workers to produce more and for their employers to take smaller profits), and the courage and wisdom of our great leader Chiang Kai-shek. (The cheer for our leader is considerably weaker than the cheer for our troops.) As in my article, I make no mention of our generals. I end up with a brief appeal for Chinese patriotism, of people starting to think of themselves as Chinese, one people, not so that we can go out and conquer other people, but so that we can defend ourselves against and defeat the foreign invaders and then build for ourselves a nation that is just, compassionate, uncorrupt and equal.

Fantastic cheers. I sit down, Chao stands up. At last the speech we've all come to hear.

He smiles. 'You are not going to like my talk,' he says. 'Because, if we are going to defeat the Japanese, it involves us Chinese people enduring a terrible amount of suffering, a lot of dying. We will have to endure worse things than any other people in history. It will kill many of us, perhaps even most of us. But if we are to survive, not just as individuals, but as a nation, we have no alternative.'

Always start on a positive note, I reflect.

'It is not the first time in our history we have suffered terribly. There were the Zhou dynasties, which collapsed into the chaos and slaughter of the Warring States til the emergence of our first emperor. The Great Emperor seized control and ruled. Then he died and was followed by terrible civil wars til the Han Dynasty brought peace and ruled for four hundred years, til it too collapsed into the Three Kingdoms, and so these cycles went on til our own times with the collapse of the Manchu Dynasty and our unending civil wars. Why is the Mandate of Heaven given, why is it taken away? Why is order always followed by chaos, chaos by order? Because when life is good, life is easy, people forget how to work together, look out for each other, cooperate. Things fall apart. People fall apart. Communities fall apart. But then things become so terrible that people suddenly remember the bonds between each other, the necessity of looking out for each other. People remember they are not just individuals but a people. The Chinese people remember they are China. The Mandate of Heaven is restored.'

I shouldn't have criticized him for starting on such a negative note. People understand, appreciate him for telling the truth. He is listened to in total silence. The deep, deep silence of people digesting, understanding, empathizing.

The train thunders through gorges, and suddenly spans out across ravines on the slenderest of viaducts with dizzying falls on either side of us and rivers far below. All the time above us the mountains are silent and white in the moonlight. We are among the gods.

'I shall tell you why we are going to win this war. Because the Chinese are ceasing to be divided into provinces and minorities and regions. Because the Japanese invasion is jamming us up against each other so that once more, after such a long time of being divided and estranged, this catastrophe is reminding us we can only survive if we are together, as one.'

A cheer goes up. The Glasgow-built locomotive thunders on ahead.

'We are having to unite, whether we like it or not, under the banner of central government. For good or bad, regionalism is dead. Unite or die.'

More cheers.

'Why will we win this war? I will give you the brutal truth.

Because united we are a massive nation. And the Japanese are a tiny one. We have hundreds of millions of people, they have only millions. They are far ahead of us in technology. They can invent machines that slaughter millions of poorly armed Chinese, but there are still tens of millions of us, hundreds of millions of us. If they kill four, five Chinese for every Japanese we kill, by that count, when we have killed every Japanese there will still be hundreds of millions of Chinese alive. They are terribly short of raw materials to build all their technology, their weapons. Believe me, I study the newspapers. And while they are fighting us, as they are drawn further and further into the interior of our land because they need our raw materials, up our roads and valleys and railway lines, into our mountains, so they will become more and more thinned out, isolated, vulnerable – so it is we, who are many, who are united, that will become strong, they weaker and weaker. In our vast country they will become cut off and surrounded by us. So many of them will die that to replace them their factories will have to be stripped of workers, their machines will start to fail. The Japanese rely on their machines. Without them they will die. We Chinese rely on our farming. No matter how much of our land is occupied by them, no matter how many battles we lose as they stumble ever deeper into our grasp, there will still be land to farm, to feed us. The Japanese will perish, we will survive.'

Cheers.

'One more brutal truth before I stop. This terrible war must not finish quickly. It has to last a long time. Many must die. So that at the end of it we are truly one people. That we do not immediately revert to factionalism and infighting. Because if we do, we will immediately be faced by another war. Ladies and gentlemen, I say this. Educate yourselves. Like me. Learn to read. Understand how the world works. So that never again will the world be able to creep up on us and take us hostage. We will suffer. Our children will suffer. But maybe our grandchildren need not suffer.'

He finishes. The audience is silent. So are the mountains.

14

SPIDER GIRL – THE BACKSTORY 1

Spider Girl realized immediately, as she read Old Man Chen's newspapers about the Japanese invasion, of their terrifying advance across China, that it would be necessary for her family to flee their home. It would also be necessary for her family to abandon her in their flight. There could be no way she could keep up with their pace. And her mother would not allow her to consume precious food and drink.

From the very start Spider Girl planned to survive on her own. She bought the ointment from her village apothecary to soothe her hips and joints. She sewed what little money she had into her garments. She kept her knife close to her at all times, sharpening it frequently on her whetstone.

And she took something even more strange. In the narrow passageway between their farmhouse and the outside courtyard wall on the north side of their compound, close to where Cherry Blossom hid her baby hedgehog, Spider Girl too kept a secret pet. A friendly, dozy old black snake. She just liked it. She kept it in a pot. When they were digging up the ground in the spring she fed it worms and centipedes. If there was a sudden glut of spiders, caterpillars, frogs or mice, she fed them to it. She and the snake were quite good friends. Sometimes, when she felt like it, especially when the sun shone, she took it out and played with it in her hands, letting it wind itself lazily around her arms. She always did this when she was by herself because she did not wish rumours to spread that she was a witch.

On the day they left she decided the old snake could be useful to her. So, feeding it a live mouse, she sealed the small jar it was in and buried it in the wheat of the large jar which she calculated would be the last jar her father would open. Her concealment went unnoticed. No one else in the family realized they were accompanied by a black snake on their journey.

But above all she planned to survive by keeping her eyes and ears wide open. Spider Girl had the eye of a practised thief. Not so much because she was dishonest – though she was – but because to survive with her disability and move successfully through the world she had had to develop from the earliest age an eye for the unusual, the unexplained, that which did not add up. And she had the curiosity and acumen to follow these sightings up and find out why certain things behaved in certain ways.

So as soon as her family joined the great refugee columns across the plains of Central China, Spider Girl looked about her continuously. Noticed how different people walked in different ways, judged their wealth by their clothing and possessions, their moods by the way they held their heads and shoulders. But above all she sought for the unusual. Those who were not as they appeared. People who seemed poor and ragged with few belongings but were also plump of belly and calf and moved without weariness or despair. Individuals who followed other people or groups of people, always at a set distance, watching them intently. People who came up to you in a friendly fashion and talked to you in a friendly voice while all the time their eyes wandered over your possessions, your clothing. She had to warn the generous-minded Eldest Son twice when such people tried to engage him in friendly banter. Pretty soon she divided people strictly into those who were watched and those who watched. She watched the watchers.

Simultaneously she observed the deterioration of her own standing within her family. Her mother's increasingly open hostility and criticism of her, her father's defensiveness and indecision. She saw the sudden horror on his face when he at last realized his wife had been deliberately starving herself to feed Eldest Son. She knew that as a man of honour he would soon and rightly decide he must put his family's survival before her own.

She also knew that, having run out of the village apothecary's ointment, with her hips and thighs inflamed with pain, there was only so much more walking she could do.

She must act.

Her eyes scanned the ranks of her fellow refugees, seeking any sign of weakness, vulnerability. Her eyes alighted on one group. She'd noticed them several times before as their cart drew ahead of the Weis' or fell behind it. Their large handcart sported an ostentatious yellow hood and was drawn by a giant of a young man, whose very power and size kept any would-be robbers or bandits well clear of them. But this time Spider Girl noticed the contemptuous way in which this huge fellow was treated by the three young men he was travelling with. They gathered round him, openly mocking and insulting him before parading off as a group into the crowds. One even kicked him. But all the giant did in reply was smile gently back. Spider Girl was interested in him. The giant was obviously a simpleton.

His three companions were equally obviously thieves. They dressed in loud (stolen) clothes, their necks and hands flashed with gaudy jewellery, they walked openly with knives and weapons on their belts. They were clearly highly incompetent thieves. Competent thieves do not swagger around announcing themselves to all and sundry. The ease with which they could attack their enfeebled and starving fellow refugees had obviously emboldened them and made them lose any fear of retribution. Which made them in turn vulnerable.

The final crisis came within her family. Grandfather fumbled the bowl she had passed him; a tiny amount of water was spilt. It was enough. Her mother immediately blamed her and demanded her expulsion. As the cart trundled on an immense row burst out between her mother and father at the front of the cart. Everyone's attention was focused on this. Which gave Spider Girl a brief window of opportunity. Her hips flaming with pain, she wriggled on to the back of the cart, poured a small amount of water into the dropped bowl and handed it back to Grandfather so he would not thirst, then dived beneath the blue canvas and removed the seal to the wheat jar where she'd hidden her snake. She pulled its jar out, but as she did so she felt something else buried beside it. She drew it out. It was the other stone bottle of wild pear juice which her father had hidden before he'd left the farm. She held it in her hand, calculating. She would not take it – but not because, with her departure, the family would now be split in two, so this link to her family's ancestors would continue in both branches in case one did not survive. No, Spider Girl did not rate herself as that important. She was going to take it because at this stage she was not planning to permanently separate from her family but rather to shadow them, to help in any emergency, to protect them. In such circumstances it was better the precious juice was preserved in two places rather than one. This decided, she slipped it beneath her clothing beside the snake jar and, grabbing a handful of mouldy dumplings, wriggled off the cart.

She stood still as the cart and the furious argument continued on its way. Cherry Blossom and Baby Girl Wei walked past her hand in hand, far too agog at the shouting to even notice her. Never before had they witnessed such anger and dissension within the family. Spider Girl stared after her receding family. Her beloved grandfather, her honourable father, her truthful mother, bewildered Eldest Son, sly Cherry Blossom, courageous Second Son, entertaining Baby Girl Wei, unformed Baby Boy Wei. Terrible emotion swept through her, revolt and anger almost overwhelmed her, but then, setting herself, she turned away and, her rickety legs shooting terrible pains, hobbled towards the giant hauling his cart.

You must appear relaxed, she told herself, speak to him politely, in a friendly manner, but with quiet authority. She straightened her back, despite the pains walked more correctly, normally. Approached him.

'Hello.'

'Hello.'

He was enormous.

'How are you?'

He grunted in response.

'I thought you might like something to eat. You look hungry.'

The giant smiled. She handed him a mouldy dumpling. He ate

it with relish. Spider Girl calculated from this that any sort of food – even mouldy dumplings – were welcomed by him because he was probably last in line for food when his 'companions' ate. In fact they probably didn't feed him at all, relying on his enormous bulk to keep him going. She gave him another dumpling.

'Thank you,' he said. 'I was hungry.'

She gave him her two last mouldy dumplings.

As he munched contentedly they walked along.

'I happened to meet your three friends,' she said. 'We had a chat and they said I must cook a meal for you all – especially you.'

This obviously pleased the giant a lot.

'I am a very good cook. I wonder if you could lift me into the back of the cart so that I can prepare the food so that when your companions get back you can stop the cart and all of you can eat a really good meal?'

With a broad grin on his face the giant picked her up and placed her gently in the back of the canvas-roofed cart. Then he walked round to the front and resumed the journey.

The cart was filled with what Spider Girl expected – gaudy stolen clothes, cheap jewellery and knick-knacks, uneaten food and dirty bowls. A thieves' den. She wormed her way to the front of the cart, turned, set her back firm against its front board so she faced backwards, towards the entrance, placed her knife beneath her right leg, took out the jar which contained her black snake and placed it on her left side. She awaited the return of the three thieves.

They returned very soon. Spider Girl heard them approach. They were very happy, loudly boasting about how they'd killed a young girl and stolen her silk scarves. The one Spider Girl took to be their leader – he had a deeper, harder voice and the other two deferred to him – boasted about raping her first.

'She was lush. So soft. I just gave it to her and gave it to her.'

'You did, Wolf Man, you did.'

'First I knifed her,' said their leader, 'then I knifed her,' he chortled.

Spider Girl's jaw set.

'Wolf Man,' said a third voice, 'before you knife her next time – with your knife – can I fuck her after you?'

'Yeah,' said the other one, 'and me.'

'We'll see,' said Wolf Man, 'we'll see.'

They'd reached the giant and started clowning about with him, obviously trying some of the silk scarves on him and complimenting him on his feminine beauty. He took it all in good heart.

'Give these to the new cook,' he told them. 'She would look good in them.'

'What new cook, Ox?' asked Wolf Man.

'Yeah,' said another.

'The new cook you sent, to cook for us all.'

'I never sent no one to cook for us, Ox. What you talking about, you melt?'

'The lady. She was very nice. She said she'd come to cook us all meals. I put her in the back so she could start cooking.'

'What?!? You put her in the back? Where all our gear's to?'

'She was very nice.'

'She'll have nicked the fucking lot, Ox, and hopped it miles ago.' Wolf Man then hit Ox the giant, and all the others joined in, without any seeming effect on him. The cart stopped.

'She didn't jump out the back,' explained a patient Ox. 'I'd have felt it if she had. She's still in there.'

'Whaaat?!?'

Footsteps, cries were heard coming round the side of the cart. Spider Girl loosened the lid of her snake jar. They lifted the hood, stared in, the three of them started to clamber into the back, led, she judged, by Wolf Man, a hard, vicious-looking thug. The Ox, rather confused, was behind them.

'Who the fuck are you, coming into our crib, stealing our loot?'

Crouching beneath the bright yellow canvas, Wolf Man crept towards her, his two fellow thieves on either side. He drew his knife.

'You're dead, you fat bitch.'

At this second Spider Girl jerked the snake-filled jar forwards so the lid flew off and the black snake flew through the air and hit Wolf Man smack in his face. It bit him. Wolf Man tried to wipe it off with his hand and the panicked snake bit hard and deep into his hand. Wolf Man screamed, 'Get it off me. Get it off me!', waving his hand back and forth as the snake bit ever deeper.

Spider Girl leant forwards and spoke directly into his face.

'This snake was in this jar, and into this jar I put scorpions and hornets and poisonous spiders and caterpillars, and this snake ate them all. So all the deadly poison that was in those creatures were eaten by this snake – who is already deadly poisonous – and now all these poisons shoot through his fangs into your hand.' She paused for effect. 'You are dead, Wolf Man.'

Wolf Man let out a terrible scream. His lieutenants were already crawling frantically backwards. Suddenly Wolf Man's fear turned into rage. Dead he might be, but this evil witch would die with him. So, snake still waving, he advanced under the canvas, knife in hand, towards Spider Girl. Which was exactly what she wanted him to do. She blocked his first slash with the snake's jar, then, with her hands and arms, powerful after years of kneading dough and threshing corn, she grabbed him by his collar and with her strong midriff muscles yanked him around, reached beneath her right leg, pulled out her knife and cut his throat from ear to ear in one hard keen slice – just as she'd watched her father slaughter the pig. Then with her other hand she jerked back his head and waved it from side to side so his arterial blood fountained all over the staring, paralyzed faces of his companions and The Ox. And as they choked on the blood they swallowed and wiped it out of their eyes she stopped and thought.

I am a cripple. I need servants. These two are beef-witted village lads. If I terrify them enough they'll serve me faithfully.

She stared into their eyes, and then, with the blood still dribbling from their dead leader's neck, she pronounced these words.

'I am a witch! The most powerful witch you shall ever meet. If you dare cross me in any way, your pubic hair will twist into sharp-toothed worms and eat into your flesh so your balls and pricks and noses fall off and your eyes are sucked into your skull and in the pain your hands will rip out your hair and strangle you. Your arseholes will grow teeth and eat your balls. If you do not do exactly what I order you, all this will happen to you, and worse, far worse.'

(Spider Girl had taught herself this witch-cursing when, as a youngster, she'd sat behind the pigsty with a friend from the village and the two of them had spent many happy hours pretending to be witches and inventing the most bloodcurdling curses they could think of. She'd merely repeated these, and thrown in an improvised one for the hell of it.)

The three young men suddenly realized they faced a Queen Witch, in all her majesty and wrath. They goggled at her like rabbits before a weasel. Ox soiled himself – which led, due to his size, to the air quickly turning rank.

She drew the pistol from their dead leader's belt and pointed it at his two lieutenants.

'Take all your weapons out of your belts and pockets and put them in front of you.'

They obeyed.

'Now take all the money out of your pockets and put it there.'

Again, they obeyed.

'Take him away,' she ordered one of them, indicating the dead Wolf Man. 'Drop him off after dark. And clean this place up,' she ordered the other. She advised Ox to empty his pants and resume pulling the cart. She'd have some supper ready for him soon.

They left. The journey resumed.

Spider Girl looked around her. Suddenly she saw that her dear black snake had been killed in the melee. She felt deep pity.

As Spider Girl was preparing the meal – there were a few dried-out vegetables and fruits and almost no water – she heard Second Son Wei run past the cart crying out her name. The jerk of fear and emotion in his voice as he shouted it moved her but she bit her lip and did not cry. What must be must be.

After he had gone she lifted the front canvas and pointed out to The Ox the blue tarpaulin of the Wei family cart which he must follow, but always at a distance. If anything unusual happened there, he was to tell her. It took a bit of explaining, which she undertook calmly and gently, but in the end he understood.

She sent one of her two thieves off to a nearby travelling apothecary to buy some ointment with some of the money she had stolen from them.

When he returned she reminded the two of them of her curse and ordered them to pull the cart while The Ox came round to the back to share the meal with her – he walking by the tailgate, she sitting with her (newly soothed) legs swinging over the end. After herself she gave The Ox the best of the food – to deepen the rift between himself and the thieves. She also did it because she liked him. But he was not a great talker. After he'd explained he'd lost touch with his family on the march and had been picked up by the thieves there wasn't much more to say. So they ate on in happy silence. Spider Girl shared the rest of the water with him.

She let him walk for another half hour beside the thieves pulling the cart before they were permitted to hand the shafts over to him and come back for food. The stronger, more assertive of the two – Spider Girl discovered his name was Tiger Eyes – she served last, with the least food. Before him she served his younger, more gentle associate – White Devil – with more food. Tiger Eyes gave White Devil filthy looks. There was no water. After a while Tiger Eyes, with great deference, asked her for some. His voice croaked. She looked scornfully at them both.

'Some thieves you are,' she said derisively. 'Not thieves, halfwits and fuckups. Parading around here in all your finery, letting everyone know what your trade is and putting them on guard. Proper thieves hide what they are. Look ordinary, everyday. No wonder I caught on to you.'

They looked downwards. She continued.

'You're so stupid you can't even work out what is the most valuable thing, the *only* valuable thing, on this march.'

'Gold,' pronounced Tiger Eyes affirmatively. 'Everyone knows that.'

'Retard. You make The Ox look smart.'

White Devil giggled and Tiger Eyes gave him a savage kick.

She looked at both of them.

'How's your throat?'

'Aching. Aching with pain.'

'And yours?' she asked White Devil.

'The same. Bloody hurts. I'm fucking thirsty.'

'We have no water. You saved no water. You just fucked around stealing baubles and jewellery. Like brainless magpies. And all the time you missed the real gold.'

'What real gold?' asked White Devil.

'Without water, you die. You die in two or three days. We have no water. We die in two or three days' time. Look at all the people around us dying, all those dead bodies you ransack – dead of thirst. Lack of water. Water is the only gold on this march. Those who have it live – those who don't, die.'

'People still respect a man with gold, with money,' mumbled Tiger Eyes rebelliously.

Spider Girl stared at him.

'No one respects a dead man with gold. They simply steal it.'

She could see that Tiger Eyes could be trouble. He had still not learnt a complete fear of her. White Devil was starting to side with her, but in a confrontation she could see he'd well slide back to Tiger Eyes.

Spider Girl eyed them both. White Devil immediately looked downward, but Tiger Eyes' eyelashes gave a rebellious little flutter before he looked down. Spider Girl decided she had to play the card she'd held closest to her chest.

'You have seen what a strong witch I am. The power of my magic. Your leader thought he could take me, defeat me. Crows eat his eyes. You know that I can tear off your genitals, burn out your eyes.' She paused. 'Tiger Eyes, I can see what you are thinking. You are thinking that all you have to do is hit me with a stone when I am not looking and I will be dead and so will my powers.'

Tiger Eyes shifted uneasily. That was exactly what he'd been thinking. She had not placed her pistol beneath her right leg for nothing. But she had to crush these two mentally, not physically. She still needed them.

She smiled and pointed to the two empty bowls they'd just been eating from.

'That food you have just eaten...'

'Yes?'

'It was poisoned. And you know how all-powerful my poisons are.'

They made strangled noises. One held his stomach, the other tried to clear his croaking throat. They looked at her terrified.

'I am such a powerful witch, my magic is so strong, that now that poison lives in your bodies awaiting my command to kill you. I can kill you any second I choose. I just have to command it. To flow into your blood and veins. Understand me?'

They did. They cringed before her.

'And,' she continued, 'if either of you are stupid enough to think that by killing me you suddenly might stop me sending that command...'

She looked at both of them. This time not just White Devil lowered his head in submission, but so did Tiger Eyes.

'...do not even try. To stop that poison killing you I have to continually order it not to. If, after forty hours, it receives no order from me, it will murder you immediately. From now on you will do everything I say, or you will die.'

She let that sink in, then told them that tomorrow she would find some water. She then sent them up front to pull the cart through the night. They were at all times to keep a watch on her father's blue canvassed cart and if there was any unusual activity they were to wake her immediately. The Ox came to guard the rear of the cart. Spider Girl slept soundly though the night.

15

SPIDER GIRL – THE BACKSTORY 2

Spider Girl had greatly admired a man who lived in her village. His name was Fang. He was a builder. He built walls, farm buildings, small sheds. She did not admire him for who he was but for what he did. Over the years he had accumulated quite a lot of money – not because he coveted money but because he was uninterested in spending it. The only thing which interested him was building.

He did not build as other men build. Before he even started a building he would stare hard at the ground it was to be built on. How it lay, how it was shaped, its texture and consistency. He would prod it with his toe. Dig with his spade to find where the rock lay. Dig in several places because he was as much interested in what happened beneath the soil as what would happen above it.

Then the stones for his building would arrive from the quarry. Be dumped in a pile. He'd look at them. Then one by one he'd pick up every rock, stare at it, weigh it in his hand, observe its precise colour, texture and weight, then place it carefully in another pile, so he knew exactly where it was. Then he'd just stand there. Spider Girl loved this bit. In his mind, in his imagination, he'd be working out precisely where each stone he'd handled would go in his building, what particular place it would have in a wall, how its colours and textures would relate to and blend in with and contrast with the colours and textures of all the other stones he would lay around it. And only when he had completed this process in his head, so he knew exactly where each stone would lie, did he move a single stone on the ground. In every wall and building he built there was this subtle rhythm of delicacy and life and colour.

Most people in the village didn't even notice this. Just walked straight past every day without a glance. But for the few who did, Fang's buildings grew like oak trees in their souls.

Watching Fang taught Spider Girl how to think. You assembled all the facts, the rumours, the circumstances of a matter one by one in your mind, you tested every single one in relation to itself and to all the others – as Fang did with his stones – and only then did you decide what had or was occurring and how you would respond. You only acted when you knew exactly what you were going to do.

Spider Girl understood from her observations on the march that some people still possessed water, but that very few of them were honest. Honest people had been relieved of it by dishonest people. Honest people were now dying and collapsing by their thousands. It was those who had robbed them of their water who survived. And to survive, such people had learnt that you did not flaunt or advertise your water – you craftily hid it behind a facade of rags and despair. If she was to help her family and provide them with the water they would need – and they would need it, desperately, very soon – then she was going to have to track down these clever, violent people and take from them what they had taken from others.

In the morning Spider Girl immediately checked that her family's blue-canvassed cart was still safely ahead of her, then fed herself and The Ox. She ordered Tiger Eyes and White Devil to stop pulling the cart and come to its rear. She looked at them both intently. Both stared rigidly at the ground. She asked if they were thirsty? 'Yes,' they replied. She told them she and The Ox were going off to find water. She reminded them of her magical power and said if either of them left their task of hauling the cart she would immediately know and strike them down dead. Her evil eye would be upon them. At all times they were to follow the blue canvassed cart, but not too close. She sent them off for a shit and then, without complaint, they resumed their haulage.

She told The Ox to lift her onto his shoulders which he did, effortlessly. From this sudden vantage point she could easily see her beloved family's cart. Her father, strong as ever, pulling the cart with Eldest Son on the other side. Her mother stalking along behind holding hands with Cherry Blossom, who was twirling her colourful blue parasol. Second Son was presumably at the front leading the donkey. In the cart sat Grandfather, with his wild wisps of white hair, talking to Baby Girl Wei. Baby Boy Wei was asleep. A stab of deep love ran through her body. She told The Ox to start walking.

A giant with a plump girl astride his shoulders passing through the crowds. Some stared but most just kept trudging doggedly on, heads down. To avoid being seen by her family she got The Ox to walk diagonally to the east, Spider Girl minutely inspecting everyone and everything they passed. Farming families by the hundreds, though with fewer members now than they would have had when they left home. Exhausted, frail, clothing hanging baggy where once it would have been filled out. Some well-to-do people, mostly having abandoned their belongings, now clutched their water which they had to share with their hard-faced guards, marching on. Lost children. Dead children. Dead people. Her eyes would rest on them all for a second, then pass on. She didn't know what she was looking for, but she knew she would recognize it the moment she saw it – however unimportant or unlikely it might be. Some slight crack in the facade of the normal, a hint of the strange.

She saw something. She was immediately interested. A toenail. Two toenails, to be precise. On the end of a foot thin as the cloven hoof of a roe deer, pink as a pig's trotter. Both toenails were painted a brilliant blue with gold dust sparkling on them. Almost as soon as they appeared they disappeared, drawn back swiftly behind a dirty old curtain on a rickety cart drawn by an ox led by a rough-looking peasant. Almost as soon as the foot had disappeared the top of the curtain twitched open and an exquisite, heavily made-up face peeked out, swiftly followed by another and then another. Being a fat girl astride a giant certainly attracts attention. Much giggling from behind the curtain followed by an angry male voice from within and the curtain being abruptly twitched shut. Spider

Girl immediately told The Ox to turn away so that her interest in the cart was not noted.

As they turned she told him to return to her cart. She knew she'd found what she was looking for, but she hadn't yet worked out precisely what it was. She thought deeply on what she had just witnessed. The tiny foot with two big blue gold-sprinkled toenails which had been so swiftly withdrawn obviously belonged to a woman whose feet had been bound since childhood. Feet which wealthy men pay a fortune to fondle, drool over and then fuck. Followed by exquisitely made-up faces peering momentarily through the curtain. What she had glimpsed – hidden behind a facade of squalor and poverty – were almost certainly the members of a very rich man's harem or a very expensive brothel. But it couldn't be a harem. No really rich man would risk committing himself or his girls to a death march like this. He would have purchased a suite in a steamer or hired a private aeroplane to transport himself and his precious cargo. What she had seen were high-class whores – the angry male voice almost certainly belonging to their pimp. He presumably had calculated that this extremely dangerous journey was worth the risk. That lots of China's wealthiest men were descending on Wuhan – China's new capital. And he had to have his finest girls there ready and waiting to service them when they arrived. Spider Girl's opponent was a man of guile and daring. She felt a moment's admiration for him.

He was certainly well financed and his undertaking scrupulously organized. With several whores and the Angry Male Voice in the cart – the whores looking in first-class condition – there would not be enough room in that run-down old cart for all the water and food they and the peasant leading the ox and the ox itself would need to get them to Wuhan. Which meant there had to be at least one more cart to carry the food and water, and, because this was such a complicated, concealed enterprise, there would also have to be strong security. Several men. That meant three carts. Spider Girl looked over her shoulder. There was no sign of any likely-looking carts travelling anywhere close to the whores. But such an obvious convoy – however run down – would have attracted immediate attention. And, as a crafty man, The Pimp would keep as much distance as he could between the young men and the whores. He didn't want them getting close to each other. Young whores are for old men. Young men ruin young whores. So the three carts had been spread out. Therein lay his security. And her opportunity.

Drawing close to her own yellow-canvassed cart, Spider Girl checked again the blue canvas of her parents' cart. Also in the distance she noted lines of low hills converging on their route from east and west. Which meant another valley would be approaching, like the valley they'd travelled through when they first joined the convoy, with everyone pressed close together and rushing on to reach the other side. Just the conditions Spider Girl needed.

Arriving at her own cart Spider Girl ordered Tiger Eyes and White Devil to stop and attend her at the rear of the cart. She inspected them carefully. Both still stared at the ground, not a single sulky look from Tiger Eyes. She rewarded them with two mouldy potatoes. They were famished and their throats cracked with lack of water, but it took them some time before their fear the potatoes might be poisoned were overcome by their famine. They swallowed them down.

She briefed them precisely on what they were to do. Together they were to find the run-down cart containing the whores. She gave them an exact description of what position it was in and what it looked like. They were to follow it from a distance in the crowds without drawing attention to themselves. As soon as someone approached the cart they were to note exactly what that person did and then White Devil (who she trusted more) was to follow that person when they returned to where they had come from. He was then to observe what it was – probably a cart – try to glimpse what its cargo was and then return here. Tiger Eyes was to stay watching the whores' cart and see if anyone else approached it. If they did, he was to observe what happened at the cart and then, like White Devil, follow that person, or whoever they relieved, back to where they had come from. Then report back to her immediately.

Before they went she ordered them to take off the loud, flashy clothes they were wearing and put on some peasant rags she'd found in the back of the cart – probably their original clothing. This caused a considerable amount of whining. Spider Girl reminded them of her powers and, dressed as peasants, they trotted off on their mission meek as lambs.

While they were gone Spider Girl sat silently. She did not allow her mind to become clouded by emotion or worry about her parents' situation or her own. She just concentrated on what had to be done.

For several hours now their cart had been travelling near to a large cart in which a group of stonemasons travelled with their work tools – ready to restart their trade in Wuhan. Spider Girl waddled over to them. Using the money she'd 'inherited' from the thieves and some of her own that she'd sewn into her clothing, she haggled with the masons for two of their hammers. Because time was now short she had to pay all they asked her for, but it would be worth it. Through the thickening crowd she returned to her cart.

She placed the hammers in the cart then loosened its yellow canopy so it could be easily removed when the time came and tore a strip off it. This she tied to a pole which she then raised and secured as a pennant above the cart so everyone would know where she was when the action started.

White Devil returned first. They'd found the whores' cart without difficulty. After about half an hour a scruffy-looking man carrying a large gourd had walked up to the cart and shouted out. The curtain was drawn back quickly and a man with a greasy Western haircut and pencil moustache pulled in the gourd and at once closed the curtain. The peasant, looking round to see if anyone was watching – White Devil and Tiger Eyes were too far off for him to notice – then walked back through the refugees in the easterly direction he had come from. White Devil left Tiger Eyes and followed. The man went about a quarter of a mile til he came to an equally scruffy and quite large cart being drawn by an ox, with a woman leading the ox. The man spoke to the woman and then climbed back inside the cart. White Devil was able to spot inside more gourds and some food sacks before the curtain was drawn. He returned immediately to Spider Girl.

Spider Girl thought about this. They were using the gourds to carry water – which meant that when they got it the water would be sweet and tasty. The man with the greasy Western hair and pencil moustache was almost certainly the angry male voice she'd heard earlier. The Pimp. She was surprised at how little security he'd given the cart carrying his supplies. He was obviously gambling that the less security it had the less attention it would draw. Spider Girl admired his bravado.

The low hills were now crowding in from east and west and the refugees were starting to bunch together, their speed increasing.

Tiger Eyes arrived back ten minutes later. Whereas White Devil had given his report in a quiet and factual way, Tiger Eyes' eyes were flashing and he spoke in an excited, dramatic fashion. After White Devil had left to follow the gourd man he'd continued to watch the whores' cart 'like an eagle'. Pretty soon a tough-looking young man approached from a westerly direction and shouted up to the curtain which opened and a man dressed like a European, with a bright orange jacket and correspondent shoes, gave instructions to this new man. Tiger Eyes glimpsed a very sexy-looking young girl standing behind the man in the cart. Instructions given, the curtain then snapped shut and the tough-looking young man walked round to the front where he relieved the man leading the ox. The man who'd been relieved, also young and tough, walked back towards the west, in the same direction the man he'd been relieved by had arrived from. Tiger Eyes followed him, never letting him out of his sight. After about a quarter of a mile he arrived at another cart. He climbed into the back and immediately fell asleep on the floor. On both sides of him sat two rows of tough looking young guys – seven in number. They were pretty cool. They carried knives and clubs. Most were heavily marked with gangster tattoos – Tiger Eyes was really impressed with this – and all the refugees kept a safe distance from them. He watched them for a while, then returned.

Spider Girl knew she could trust The Ox. She thought that she had instilled enough fear into White Devil with her talk of deadly poisons to enforce his loyalty. But she didn't trust Tiger Eyes an inch. He was far too excitable and as likely to betray her or run away as he was to fight for her. She had to be certain he would do what she wanted him to do – exactly, precisely. Otherwise her plan would not work.

She drew him aside. Spoke softly to him.

'Do not forget how I can poison and twist and shred your body in a second if you disobey my wishes. I'll start with your balls.'

He gave her a quick glance. Behind his eyelashes she detected a flash of rebellion. No, not to be trusted. She thought, then remembered that he was the one who, when Wolf Man his boss had returned from raping and killing the girl, had asked him if he could join in his next rape.

He fancied himself a swordsman.

'I bet you've never fucked a woman in your life.'

'I've fucked plenty of women in my life,' boasted Tiger Eyes, not entirely convincingly.

'Do you want to fuck that whore you glimpsed in their cart?'

'Yes.'

She moved really close to him.

'This is my deal. You do everything, everything I tell you, without hesitation, over the next two days, and if you obey me, precisely, I will let you pick one of those whores in the cart. But never forget my poison is alive, stirring, deadly within you. I hold your balls in my hand.'

His face was half fear, half lust.

'Yes,' he croaked.

Spider Girl then briefed them exactly on what she wanted each to do. She handed White Devil one masons' hammer, Tiger Eyes the other. She then sent each of them off in their separate directions.

She herself wriggled onto the back of the cart, grabbed one of the iron hoops supporting the yellow canvas, and stood up. A full female warrior upon her chariot, pennant flying. For one last time she checked her family's cart. Grandfather, in the back, was obviously telling a story to Baby Girl and Baby Boy Wei, who watched him mouths agape. Close behind walked her Mother and Cherry Blossom carrying her hedgehog in its cage. Both were engrossed in Grandfather's story. Father and Eldest Son on either side of the cart also listened in affectionately to the ancient tale.

Spider Girl felt sorry for Second Son, up there all alone leading the donkey, unable to hear it. She turned and told The Ox to pull their cart diagonally across the ever-quickening crowds in the direction of The Pimp's cart. He did. Normally such an action would have caused much shouting and swearing, but one glance at The Ox and all fell silent.

White Devil, gripping his masons hammer, reached his target first – the cart carrying the supplies. The woman was still leading the ox, the man was behind the cart, threatening all those in the tightening crowds to keep their distance. But, with the valley pressing everyone closer, he was fighting a losing battle. White Devil got quite close to the cart, and while the guard was trying to drive away people from the other side he darted in, raised his masons' hammer and smashed it down twice, each time breaking a spoke on the cart's wheel. The cart crumpled over and ground to a halt. White Devil ran off back towards where the whores' cart would be. Behind him he left the guard shouting and cursing and desperately trying to work out whether he should run and tell The Pimp what had happened or stay guarding the supplies. The Pimp had always told him that guarding the food and water came first, so he stayed. As Spider Girl had calculated he would.

In a few minutes The Ox and Spider Girl reached the whores' cart. The Ox jammed his cart smack in front of it, the young man leading it cursed him and The Ox broke his neck. Simultaneously Spider Girl wriggled off the back of her cart, waddled round to the back of the whores' cart, drew her pistol and ripped open the curtain. She meant to shoot The Pimp but it was gloomy inside, thick with incense and lit by only a single candle. What was worse it was filled with screaming, hysterical girls panicking at the sight of a wild woman waving a pistol at them. Where was The Pimp? Then she saw him lurking at the back and fired, fired again at him, missing him both times. Cursing, she aimed more carefully, but in that second he slipped beneath the canvas in the front of the cart and hared off through the crowds in his loud orange jacket and correspondent shoes. He was running straight in the direction of the cart carrying his thugs.

She shouted to The Ox to pull the yellow canvas off their cart and throw it over the whores' one as a makeshift camouflage and to fly the yellow pennant. She herself was clearing the cart of hysterical whores, waving her gun at them. They came out, screaming. The crowds were still pouring past but giving such violent maniacs a wide berth. The Ox grabbed the ox's rein and began turning the cart. 'Faster!' shouted Spider Girl. The cart started lumbering back through the crowds to where the supply cart should be – provided White Devil had stopped it. And where in hell was that idiot Tiger Eyes?

Tiger Eyes was sweating profusely. The hand grasping his masons' hammer was so slippery that he could hardly hold it. There, only a few yards off, was the security guards' cart, but the more he looked at them, violent, aggressive killers, the more he doubted. It was their glistening tattoos he saw most. Lions' heads, snakes' fangs, curved daggers, flaming pistols. And above all it was the human skulls that terrified him. Staring at him. He imagined the beautiful whore he could sleep with, but simultaneously imagined all of Spider Girl's poisons writhing within his body. The cartwheel was right before his goggling eyes. All he had to do was dart in, smash two spokes, and run off. But these cut-throats would then be after him. Run him down. Slaughter him. Tiger Eyes, his sweaty hands slipping on his hammer, remained paralyzed.

White Devil sighted Spider Girl's pennant and ran up to her, excitedly jabbering about how he'd smashed the cartwheel. Spider Girl told him to lead their cart fast towards the cart he'd crippled while she and The Ox guarded its rear against the attack she expected any second from The Pimp and his gang.

What Spider Girl had totally failed to foresee, and which added greatly to their difficulties, were the whores. She'd assumed they'd just sort of fade away into the crowds, disappear. Instead they were loudly pursuing the cart – their only home, their only source of food and comfort – and robustly and angrily, in all their eye-catching lack of clothing, demanding they be allowed back into it. People stared. Two of the girls, unable to walk because of their bound feet, were being carried by their sisters-in-arms. Spider Girl cursed them, aimed her pistol at them. To no effect. The Pimp would only have to catch sight of one garishly clad whore to see precisely where his cart was.

They arrived at the stranded supply cart. Spider Girl's hips and legs were on fire but she ignored them. She, The Ox and White Devil advanced on the guard, knives and guns drawn. He looked at them, they looked at him. Mercenaries are paid to fight, not to die. He ran. The woman leading the ox also ran. Spider Girl immediately ordered their cart to the back of the stricken cart and for everyone to pile all its supplies into theirs at once. She herself waddled in the direction The Pimp and his men would most likely arrive from and stood her ground, pistol in hand. The whores would not go away. Well, she thought, in that case at least turn them to use. She made a vague promise or two and the three beefiest girls immediately started helping in transferring the goods. Spider Girl looked back towards the crowds. Where the hell was Tiger Eyes?

The war within Tiger Eyes over who he feared most was at last being won. By Spider Girl. Tattoos might be awesome, but were as nothing compared to Spider Girl's horrific powers of witchhood, or the kind embrace of whores. The cartwheel was still just before him, the thugs preoccupied by a noisy game of cards. So dense had the crowds now grown that only three or so yards separated the people from the thugs. All he had to do was dodge in, two hard blows, and he'd have disappeared back into the crowds before the thugs even looked round. His hand was sweaty; he wiped it on his dirty peasant smock, then gripped the hammer's handle and was about to... when he heard this sort of humming, whining sound. For a second he stopped, but then refocused, stepped forwards to deliver his blow, when suddenly the air above him seemed to be ripped and sliced through by slivers of silver steel and he heard people screaming and looking upwards as an aircraft roared overhead. Suddenly there was this awful crumping, groaning sound behind him followed by this roaring as through the crowds came an enormous iron tube scything and scimitaring people left and right before, with an enormous bang, it collided full-on with the cart just inches in front of him. And the cart seemed to implode and disintegrate with all the gangsters inside, butchering and ribboning and slicing them like some awful, unleashed sea monster. In front of his eyes! The huge bomb came to a rest in their midst. Unexploded. The playing cards, which had been blown into the air by its impact, now fluttered down on the carnage like snow. Tiger Eyes stared. The thugs were cut in half and cut in quarters, wholly eviscerated. Blood and guts and tattoos everywhere. Everyone else had run away but he still stood there, hammer in hand. Slowly he started to realize that perhaps something good had happened. Something to his advantage that he could make use of. He dropped his hammer. He picked up a knife that had fallen from an ex-young thug and dipped it in his blood. He was already leaving when through the crowd pushed this screaming, extraordinarily dressed young man. Tiger Eyes watched him, dressed in orange jacket and correspondent shoes, as he stared down on the bloodbath of his young thugs. As he slowly started to realize the death of all his dreams. One of his lads was still flapping about, his legs half sawn off at the hips. The Pimp grabbed him by his lapels, demanding he got fucking shifting to rescue The Pimp's stolen whores. The young lad's legs fell off and he died. The Pimp cursed him. He raised his eyes to heaven and cursed the heavens. Tiger Eyes left him, standing there, shouting, the blood slowly soaking into his immaculate correspondent shoes.

(Thus did the bomb which failed to explode due to a young Korean slave daydreaming about having sex with an imaginary girlfriend – slaves were forbidden to have sex – both cause the annihilation of half the Wei family and almost simultaneously safeguard its survival. Such is war.)

The fatal bombing raid was not noticed by Spider Girl, who had her back turned to the mayhem and was fully preoccupied in trying to get their cart loaded while warding off the whores and watching out for the arrival of The Pimp.

It was nearly loaded when Tiger Eyes finally saw fit to arrive. He was walking, rather than running. In fact he was swaggering. Covered in blood, with a playing card stuck in his hair, carrying a bloody knife.

'Where the hell have you been?'

He answered with some nonsense about an air raid and the thugs being hit by a bomb.

'The bomb killed most of them but I killed the rest with this knife. Two or three,' he boasted.

She snatched the knife from his hand and told him to get the fuck into the cart and finish loading it. Tiger Eyes had obviously chickened out of smashing their cartwheels and invented some ludicrous story to cover it. She continued to hold her ground, expecting The Pimp with his gang at any second.

The cart loaded she immediately ordered White Devil to turn the ox and head as fast as possible south-east through the crowds to take them in the opposite direction to that The Pimp would probably expect them to go. They all, whores included, heaved and shoved on the heavily laden cart to get it moving and then keep it moving at speed while Spider Girl, The Ox and Tiger Eyes took a rearguard position to shield it from any attacks. The crowds swallowed them up, Spider Girl nervously scanning them for any sign of pursuit. There was no sign. She concluded that The Pimp must be watching them from within the crowds and marshalling his men to attack them at their weakest moment. She understood what a ruthless, resourceful man he was.

They continued pushing through the crowds. Spider Girl's legs were on fire – she hadn't had a chance to apply any ointment since last night – but she ignored them and pushed harder at the rear of the cart. At one point she found herself actually punching it to make it move faster. And she had to listen to Tiger Eyes boasting to The Ox of how he'd killed five of The Pimp's men. The Ox smiled patiently back at him. Spider Girl told Tiger Eyes to shut up and strip off his bloody smock because everyone was staring at it. The whores were fanned out behind them, bitterly cursing and telling anyone who'd listen of how terribly they'd been treated by these gangsters. Spider Girl couldn't think of any way of dealing with them which would not draw even more attention to them, so she ignored them.

Five minutes at least had passed since they'd started the cart. No sign of The Pimp. The hills were now starting to recede, which meant that the valley was getting wider and the crowds thinning out. This made them both more visible and more vulnerable, but also gave them warning of any attack. Spider Girl glanced through the canvas at their load. Lots of gourds. Lots of water. Everyone was complaining about parched throats. Give it another five minutes and if they were still safe she'd hand some out. She desperately wanted to sit down on her cart but knew she couldn't. A true leader marches with her troops.

Five minutes past. The crowds were still spreading out. Still no sign of attack. Spider Girl never allowed herself the luxury of optimism. But there did seem a chance that they might have escaped their pursuers. That she, a despised, crippled country girl, had actually managed, by her guile and boldness, to steal a huge amount of water and food from some city thugs with which she might help and save her family. At the moment she had no intention of seeking her family out. Were The Pimp and his killers suddenly to fall on them while they were with her family, out of vengeance they'd kill not only her but all her family. At the moment caution must prevail. But she allowed herself a sliver of hope.

Tiger Eyes moaned that his throat was killing him. Spider Girl allowed her party to march on another quarter of an hour despite her aching legs – just to show who was boss – but then told The Ox to lift her onto the tailgate, which he did. She pulled down a gourd and poured some of its sweet waters into a bowl, which she drank down. The concrete hardness in her mouth started to moisten and soften as the precious liquid loosed and freed her mouth and throat. Then she gave a bowlful to The Ox, then sent him forwards with a bowl to refresh White Devil. She gave half a bowl to Tiger Eyes last. She ignored the lamentations of the whores.

Spider Girl pulled herself upright to stand on the tailgate, grasping a wooden slat supporting the yellow canvas. By now the refugees were leaving the valley and spreading themselves out as once more they resumed their endless trek across the plain. She looked around and around. All the way round, twice, three times, her eyes searching for the least sign of The Pimp and his men and the blue canvas of her family's cart. She assumed her enemy would by now have had the sense to have removed his orange jacket, but her eyes saw nothing. Perhaps the yellow canvas camouflage had worked and they'd attacked a cart with a dirty black tarpaulin like their own and received a tough response. Perhaps Tiger Eyes was telling the truth and there had been an air raid and they'd been killed. She thought that highly unlikely. Once more she swept her eyes all about, but she saw nothing.

For a moment she allowed her mind to feast on the thought of her reunion with her family. How she would ride in her cart up to them, hail them. The joy and pride on the face of her father. The jokes and laughter of Second Son. Eldest Son's slow and happy smile. Cherry Blossom's likely strop when she realized she was no longer eldest daughter. The stories she'd be able to tell Baby Girl Wei about her adventures. Baby Boy Wei's puzzled grin. She hoped and prayed that Grandfather would not be too confused to recognize her. And above all her mother. Spider Girl would have to do it with the utmost humility, showing submission throughout as she presented the water to her mother. Her mother would of course chide and denounce her but the water, the food, would be water and food, and Spider Girl knew that her mother, deep inside, would acknowledge to herself that Spider Girl did serve and love her family, even though she would never ever admit it. And that was all Spider Girl required. Because she admired and respected her truth-speaking mother. Maybe her mother, after she had been accepted into the hall of the ancestors, might even put in the word that her eldest daughter might join them? Not that the ancestors would ever accept such a crippled, ugly girl.

Her daydreams returned to real life with a jolt. Suddenly she was surrounded by a cloud of whores, angry as wasps, demanding water. She said they had no water or food to spare. The tumult increased. 'That's our water you've stolen!' She snapped back that just like everyone else on this march they'd have to fend for themselves. They were whores. Why not go off and fuck in exchange for water? The girls angrily responded that sex was the last thing anyone wanted on a death march. This didn't seem to work. They tried a new course. Didn't she understand what it was like to be a whore? You never leave the brothel. You are warm and secure and fed within it. You are likely born in it and brought up in it being taught from childhood all the techniques and tricks of pleasing a man so that you know no other world but the brothel. It was their home! Their pimp, just to lure them out of it, had had to furnish their cart with silks and cushions and all sorts of luxuries – the finest incenses and perfumes – and they were just about surviving when this monstrous waddling woman had turned up and tried to shoot their pimp and turfed them all out. They were made to walk! They'd hardly ever walked in their lives. They'd mostly just lain on beds and got fucked. And now they'd suddenly been thrown out of their familiar world of tiny little rooms and beds into this huge confusing terrifying world. No curtains and walls, but horizons which just went on and on forever, and this huge sky above them with this evil yellow sun burning their skin and bodies. All these scary swearing crowds all around them.

Spider Girl was not someone much moved by fellow-feeling or pity (unless it was within her family), but she was pragmatic. These girls were not going to go away. She could shoot them, but she didn't want to waste bullets, and besides, she was not the sort of person who shot defenceless people. So an understanding had to be reached. There was ample water in the cart – at least until they joined up with her family – so for the time being she'd allow them a tiny ration of water on condition they walked twenty yards behind the cart and remained totally silent. She reserved the right to cancel the understanding. That did nothing to solve the problem or hush the barrage of outrage. (Spider Girl was starting to realize the job of being a pimp was not an as easy as it might appear.) Two of them could not even walk because of their bound feet. The rest had to carry them because they were family, but they could not carry them any further. They should ride in the cart. No chance, stated Spider Girl. They were very light, the whores argued, holding them up. On their pig's trotter feet they could only hobble a few yards, and having spent almost their entire lives on beds getting fucked their leg and body muscles had never developed. They were like consumptive children. They would hardly weigh down the cart at all. Each side stared at the other.

As a partly crippled person herself Spider Girl had a slight sympathy for these two girls. But she had used her brains to overcome her physical difficulties. These girls hadn't. But then her family had not used their brains – at least enough – to understand and overcome their own difficulties. But these girls were not her family. What would her father have done in this situation? He would have taken them and helped them. But then her family was in this situation at least in part because her father was too kind-hearted. But then she saw that The Ox – without whose help she would by now probably be dead – was looking with great concern and sympathy at the two girls. They were indeed remarkably light.

'All right,' she said, 'but mutter even one word you'll be off the cart and walking.'

The girls were lifted onto the cart, the rest of the whores fell back twenty paces. There was peace.

After an hour, with the crowds widely dispersed across the plain, Spider Girl, standing on the back of the cart, took one last, careful look all around her, studying minutely all the groups and individuals she could see, and came to the conclusion that they were not being pursued by The Pimp or his men. Who knows – perhaps what Tiger Eyes had seen of them being killed by a bomb was true – though as he was now boasting he by himself had killed at least nine of them, she doubted him. Perhaps they'd just been fooled by the yellow canvas and gone off and attacked another cart that looked like theirs. She must continue to keep a vigilant watch for them, but it seemed they might just be safe.

She now felt secure enough to start searching for her family. Her heart lightened. Since she'd travelled fast in her cart to escape from her enemies, she calculated she was now ahead of her parents. Her parents had been travelling on the western side of the march and Spider Girl had deliberately gone to the east to avoid her family becoming entangled in any violence. Now, if she travelled diagonally towards the west, there was a fair chance their paths would cross.

She ordered White Devil to change course.

They travelled on for an hour, reaching the area where Spider Girl had calculated her family would be. No blue canvas roof.

Nothing. For an hour she stopped – they might have fallen back, been delayed. Nothing. No blue canvas roof. She speeded up. Tiger Eyes started to complain but she gave him a look. At the end of two hours she'd seen nothing. Then, suddenly, she spotted a blue canvas roof. She ordered Tiger Eyes – she'd replaced White Devil with Tiger Eyes to keep him away from the girls – to hurry the ox on. They started to catch up with the cart. It was being pulled by a donkey. There was a family travelling in it. It could be hers. No sign of Cherry Blossom's parasol, but that gaunt woman climbing out of the back looked distinctly like her mother. Spider Girl was almost about to shout when around the side of the cart rolled a short, fat man, obviously the woman's husband, followed by a short fat son. Spider Girl's heart sank. She ordered Tiger Eyes to stop. She stared after the receding family. Where should she look now?

A thought which she'd been deliberately suppressing, which she'd been forbidding herself to even think about, now forced its way before her. What if, in all the pushing and rushing and turmoil in the valley, the cart itself had been damaged? At long last the rotten spokes had given way? It would mean her family would now be on foot, clinging on to their last supplies of water and foot, traipsing like so many others across this parched, unending plain. They'd now be well behind her and difficult to spot. And what, worst of all, if there had been an air raid, as Tiger Eyes was constantly going on about, and they had been caught in it? But she had to know.

She got off the cart and walked forwards to Tiger Eyes.

'That air raid you claim took place?'

'It did take place.'

'Describe it to me again. Exactly. And this time no bullshit about all the men you claim to have killed. What did that bomb do?'

'It hit the cart.'

'But I heard no explosion.'

'As I said, it came speeding through the grass, hitting people. It didn't explode.'

'How many people did it hit before it hit the cart?'

He paused. 'Five or six that I saw.'

'And did you see it hit any other cart before it hit The Pimp's cart?'

'No. Just people.'

'Could it have hit a cart before it hit these people?'

'Don't think so. It'd have stopped in it, like it stuck in my cart.'

'You're certain about that?'

'Yes,' he said, but he wavered. Spider Girl correctly saw that his hesitation was not because he was lying, but because, as someone who always told people what he thought they wanted to hear, he was worried he was not telling her what she wanted to hear. So he was telling the truth. He had not seen the bomb hit any other cart. It might have hit a cart before he saw it, she decided, but the chances of it hitting her single family amid the tens of thousands of other refugees crowding into that valley were virtually nil. They were far more likely to be somewhere out here – with or without their cart.

She stood and thought. Something must have happened in that valley, some current in the crowds could have swept them onto a different course so that they had emerged on the eastern side of the multitude rather than the western. She was going to have to sweep slowly across from west to east and back again, making allowances that they might be either swifter with the cart or slower on foot. She knew that they must already be almost out of water, so they would be slowing down, but simultaneously – and she had to fight with herself to even think of this – she knew that her mother, in order to preserve Eldest Son, would be cutting down on the number of lips drinking the family water. She would do the same if she were in her mother's awful position. So she must show all haste in finding them, in giving the whole family her precious water.

She ordered Tiger Eyes to start leading the cart again.

'But you promised me this whore.'

'I said in two days. Not ten hours have yet passed.'

She drew her knife, held out her other hand as though she was fondling his balls, then slashed her knife brutally above it.

He hastily picked up the lead, she indicated they should go

eastwards, and the cart and its attendant group set slowly off. Spider Girl, standing on the cart, continuously scanning the horizon, looking not only for carts but groups on foot, even individuals. Nothing. After an hour or so they reached the western side of the march where refugees started to become bandits – though that line of distinction was fast blurring. But the figure of The Ox always deterred any would-be attackers. She turned back again on the eastward diagonal of her sweep. Again nothing. They completed two or three more sweeps – nothing – before night drew on. What to do? Stop for the night, or continue their sweeps? There was a moon. She was undecided until she noticed, at their water break, Tiger Eyes starting to flirt with the whores. There were whispers back and forth. Giggles. He started to strike poses. Was there anyone ever more beef-brained than Tiger Eyes? He knew that she not only had the power to destroy him through her magic – he was stupid enough to actually believe that – but that she had no compunction about shooting people dead. And still his boasting about those he'd killed – now up to twelve – and his hackneyed flirtings with the whores, one in particular, continued.

She ordered him up front to lead the ox. Their slow sweep resumed.

In the blackness of the night, with the moon setting, she steered her course by the Plough, keeping it roughly to her right and then her left. Through the night she called out her family name – 'Wei, Wei' – then sometimes individual family names. They disappeared into the darkness and there was no response.

During this night Spider Girl passed close by a dying Baby Girl Wei. Baby Girl's throat was so dried out that all her voice could do was croak. She heard Spider Girl's voice and tried to respond but, so tight was her throat, she could make no sound and her tiny mind, already filled with terror and bewilderment, spiralled into blackness.

Spider Girl, unaware of anything, carried on her weary quest.

The search continued through the night and for much of the following day., Spider Girl never ceased standing in the cart, her eyes searching incessantly left and right and all around her. Nothing. The others were given water, food (Spider Girl even allowed the whores to have some), and slept by turns on the cart next to the two whores with bound feet, but Spider Girl, steadfast, never stepped down nor rested.

But as the second evening drew on she knew they were going to have to rest during the night. Even The Ox was starting to flag, and he was too heavy to sleep in the cart. The whores who were walking could go no further. Spider Girl reasoned that her family too – by now very low on water – would be slowing and probably sleeping through the night. They halted. Spider Girl passed out the food and a meagre ration of water. Spider Girl and The Ox would take it in turns to keep watch. But there was a problem. The flirting between Tiger Eyes and the whores was starting to get out of hand. Tiger Eyes especially was flashing his eyes at her while he was doing it, showing her he wasn't scared of her, that he would have his revenge. What a moron! And White Devil was starting to regain his courage and side with his old friend. Even the whores had forgotten their vow of silence and were happily responding. Flirting, foreplay, however crude, was entirely novel and exciting for them. All they'd ever known was fat old men falling on top of them. Spider Girl could see it was getting out of hand. It could lead to feuds, fighting, confrontations – the last thing she needed at this moment. Did they require the two young bandits any longer? She calculated that with The Ox still there, he would give them all the strength and security they needed. Tiger Eyes and White Devil were a threat and a drain on their resources. Superfluous. She waddled up to them – Tiger Eyes mocked her walk – pulled out her pistol and shot them between their eyes. Swiftly and humanely, as her father killed livestock on the farm.

The whores were horror-struck. She was not going to have any more problem with their boring chatter. The Ox was unconcerned. He knew that Spider Girl trusted him and needed him. He carried the bodies a short way and dumped them. They settled down for the night. It was a very quiet one. Spider Girl hardly slept a wink, worrying about her family. Then she took over the watch from The Ox, who slept like a baby. Tomorrow she must find them. They would have run out of water. Unless she found them they would all be dead.

Before they had travelled much further in the morning they reached one of those stream beds, rank and stinking with mud and faeces. They picked their way across it, The Ox pulling on the cart to help the cart cross the stream, the whores following miserably behind. A few hundred yards further on Spider Girl saw a grave. It was not so much the grave which caught her attention as what was lying beside it. She called for the convoy to stop, for everyone to keep well clear of the grave. She walked carefully towards it. It was just an ordinary grave. They had passed enough of them earlier in their march, but by now they were becoming a rarity as people no longer had the strength or the tools to give their dear ones a proper and pious burial. They just left their bodies as they died upon the plain, left their dear bodies to the buzzards.

She walked to the object that was lying close to the grave. A spade. Its shaft was new because the wood was still white. This filled her with dread. She looked closely at the handle. On it was etched with a knife a small square with two lines below it, the sign in the village, if a dispute arose, that this spade belonged to her family. The Wei family. A member of her family was buried in that grave. She started to feel dizzy. She fought for and regained control. The grave was large. It could be Grandpa, her mother, Eldest Son or, worst, her father. She did not want to go close to the grave, to disturb it. Like a dog will not go near the grave of its master, she could not bring herself to approach it for fear of sensing the spirit of the loved one who lay there, who she had let down.

She turned away, searching on the ground among the different wheelmarks for the wheelmarks of her family cart. If they'd stopped here, there would be a sunken dent in the track. There'd be footprints in the ground where the family had climbed down and walked around. The few tracks where carts had passed were continuous and showed no signs of stopping. Did the family still have the cart? Had they lost it? Then she caught sight of another object further off, waddled fast towards it, leant over, picked it up. She was overcome with emotion. The small stone bottle in which her father carried his precious, precious wild pear juice. Empty. The juice that linked the whole family back to their ancestors, that linked her father directly to his beloved eldest sister. What had happened? Her father would never have used up all the juice and then just thrown its bottle away. Neither would her mother – that juice was her one route back to the family's ancestors. Neither would anyone else in the family. And yet here it lay. Empty. Thank the gods she had preserved some of it. She felt the bottle beneath her clothing. She thought for a moment that this could be the work of bandits, cut-throats. But why would they bury the body of their victim? Surely they'd just leave it to the wild animals.

Somewhere ahead of her, she knew, there were members or a member of her family. They pressed on.

Spider Girl was a person of great self-reliance, self-belief, yet as they trudged on and on – she searching ever more desperately to the left and the right – even she started to doubt herself. Condemn herself. She had known long before anyone else in the family they must flee their farmhouse. But she had failed to get them, her father, to move until the very last moment. Had she only used her skills of persuasion properly they could have been on the road before all this chaos and carnage. Could have made their way south in relative safety and calm. It had been her duty to persuade them – she was the only person to understand the true situation – and she had failed to do so. Perhaps her mother had been right. Perhaps the Japanese just killed people in the cities they wanted to live in. In the countryside they would allow Chinese people to stay because they needed them to work the land. Even slavery would be preferable to what she had forced her family to endure.

As they dragged on, yard after yard, mile after mile, it haunted her that it could be that every single member of her family was dead. That she with her cart full of water and food alone was alive. That to be alive without your family was to be dead. A person by themselves is not alive. Only in the warm, constant fractiousness and love and service and certainty of a family can one live. All else is death. She felt the bottle holding the family's wild pear juice against her body. It brought her no comfort. Still alive, she had already become the desolate spirit stranded outside the ghost gate to the family courtyard, hated, rightly excluded by her ancestors. But all the time this went through her mind she never for one second stopped looking for her family.

She saw something. Only a glimpse. A body lying on the ground. But something familiar about it. Lying on its side, face in the soil, unmoving. Probably dead. But something about the way it lay, the curve of the arm, the straightness of the leg? She told The Ox to stop, wriggled down off the cart, started with effort to waddle and heave herself towards the apparent corpse, lying just as her father would.

'Father,' she cried, 'Father.'

It did not move.

She sobbed. It seemed her father was dead. But she kept approaching.

'Father,' she cried. 'Is that you? Is that you?

The body stirred. The body stirred!

The face started to turn, looked up at her, eyes half closed. The face of her father.

From within her clothing she took the bottle of wild pear juice, cradled his head and pressed it to his lips. 'Oh Father,' she said, 'dear Father.'

16

Spider Girl cradled her father's head in her arm. She fed him a few more sips of wild pear juice but not more in case he vomited. But by the grunts and rasps coming from his mouth and throat, she could tell it was making its way – moistening his mouth, loosening his throat – down into his body.

She looked up. Called for The Ox to bring the cart over to her. He did so and stopped so it would be easy to raise her father onto the back.

'Help me lift him,' she said. The Ox, gentle as a lamb, slid his arms softly under her father's shoulders and hips. Spider Girl held his head. Some of the whores helped also. They lifted him up and placed him softly on the back of the cart. And all the whores went 'Ooh' and 'Aah', just as though he had been a newborn baby. Which in a way he was.

Spider Girl wriggled up beside him and reached back for a gourd, feeding him some of its sweet water. He coughed and spluttered quite a bit. Good! It was making its way into his dried-up body. She passed the gourd on to all the rest of them. They could drink as much as they wanted. All the time she stroked his face, his hair, made cooing noises, smelling him. His familiar loving smell.

'Eldest Daughter,' he managed, 'Eldest Daughter.'

He croaked a few more indistinguishable words. She fed him a bit more water. She was totally focused on him except for one worry. One thing she had to know. Were there any other members of the family out there still alive? If so they would have to move immediately to find them.

She looked straight at him. His face was now responding to hers. She needed to know.

'Father,' she asked, 'are there any other members of the family out there still to be found?'

He gave her one look and she knew she would never ask that question again. Except for her and him, every single one of her family was dead. One tiny drop came to his eye – his body couldn't afford any more – then his face fell away in chaos and despair.

For a few seconds she mourned her family. She'd already realized, when she found him alone, that the chances of anyone else being alive were tiny. He might have been forced into abandoning the younger ones, but he'd never have deserted his wife or Eldest Son.

She must be practical. She must get on with things. She instructed The Ox to start the cart again but to proceed as gently as possible. He did. The whores followed along, quiet as mice. She thanked her lucky gods she'd killed Tiger Eyes and White Devil when she had. If they were here now there would be absolute bedlam.

Her father continued to lie on his side and stare down at the floor, unmoving, locked in his own private despair. Every so often she raised his head to feed him water but he would not look at her. She knew precisely why. His shame. He, the head of the family, the man who carried all responsibility for them all on his lonely shoulders, had been the one so foolishly to listen to her counsel to flee the farm, and in their flight had allowed all of his family except her to die. He would not blame her for her counsel, he would blame himself for having followed it. He simply wanted to die. But his eldest daughter, yet again, had turned up and dragged him back into hell.

Spider Girl stared bleakly ahead. She had been right to argue they left. She knew this, but now she had no way of proving it. But it was not all failure. She had saved her father from death. Just as he had once saved her. Each had given the other the chance of life. She was going to nurse him back to health – whether he wanted it or not.

As she thought she chewed on a raw potato, grinding it with

her teeth down to a soft mush in her mouth. With her fingers she picked it from her mouth and delicately dropped it into her father's mouth, stroking his cheeks and throat to make him swallow it, cawing gently all the time like a mother crow feeding her chicks.

As they walked on something strange happened. By now everyone on this vast exodus had become used to the drone of Japanese reconnaissance aircraft flying far overhead, of being strafed or machine gunned by Japanese fighters or bombers. And with so many of the travellers now staring death from dehydration and starvation in the face, few had time to worry about such a rare and random form of death. But suddenly in the sky above flew, or rather wobbled, an ancient, blue-coloured aircraft with the roundels of a yellow sun on its wings and a blue and white striped flag painted on its tail. Japanese aircraft were always painted in dark green camouflage. And even stranger, the aircraft was not dropping bombs or firing guns, but instead falling from it were thousands upon thousands of sheets of paper, floating down. One or two people in the distance were shouting something, gesticulating. People were waving. Some people close to them were trying to cheer, with cracked and wheezy voices. What was going on?

A piece of paper fluttered down and landed on their cart. They didn't know what to do. Until now everything that had dropped from the skies had been deadly. Perhaps this paper contained some sort of poison or gas to kill anyone who touched it. But then a man walking close by told them that the plane was a Chinese one, not a Japanese one, and it was dropping a message for them all to read. It was safe.

Spider Girl picked it up. Everyone gathered round. She started reading it

'A proclamation from the Supreme Council of the Government of the Republic of China,' she announced.

'What's that?' everyone asked.

'It is a message from their supreme leader, General Chiang Kai-shek...'

'Who's he?'

'...It is addressed to all the citizens, residents, peoples and subjects of China.'

'Who are they...?'

Due to the jargon-ridden nature of the text, Spider Girl decided to paraphrase it.

'You are not to worry... Help is on the way... Supplies of water and food are being brought forward to cure everyone's thirst and hunger. Our valiant army is even now starting a counter-attack to drive the yellow dwarves forever out of our beloved land. You are now approaching the great and ancient city of Wuhan where all will be welcomed. Show good behaviour and consideration towards all other citizens when you meet them, as disorder will not be tolerated.'

Everyone looked at each other. Should they trust these fine words? Or not? Around them a lot of people were cheering. They decided to trust them and started cheering too – whatever the message meant.

Once again they set off.

And as they travelled, for the first time, traffic started to come towards them from the south, travelling north from the direction of Wuhan. Soldiers, at first only sections and platoons of them, but then whole ranks and ranks marching, rifles slung over shoulders, shod in straw sandals, carrying parasols to keep off sun and rain. Then lorries, large army lorries, bearing supplies for the soldiers, towing large guns to fight the enemy with. There were more civilian cars scurrying about, honking their horns officiously, rickshaws bearing senior army staff officers. But still no sign of water, of food, of relief.

By this time Spider Girl's father, his strength gradually returning as his daughter fed and nurtured him, had managed to raise himself on one elbow, then lever himself so he sat with his back to the side of the cart. But he said nothing. He met no one's eye. All the time he stared into the far distance.

Then a wonderful thing came into view. A large pavilion or tent, standing to one side of the march, with red flags and streamers flying from it, and a large banner reading 'World Red Swastika Society (Buddhist) Chinese Society of Morality and Charity'.

People were queueing up before tables which had been set up before the pavilion, and small amounts of water and food were being handed out, the people assuring those that were asking for more that more would be available just a short way further along the road to Wuhan. If they gave them more now they would be ill and there would be no more food and water for those following them.

By and large the people receiving the vital food and water were very grateful, some even falling on their knees in profuse thanks. Some demanded more and there could have been violence but the other travellers all pleaded with them not to hurt those who had brought them such gifts.

And as they travelled, other pavilions and large tents did appear, each dispensing food and water and even medical help. The Red Cross, the Buddhist Way of Pervasive Unity, a Daoist charity, a Moslem charity, the Roman Catholic Mission, the Emergency Relief Committee of Chinese Churches, the Young Men's Christian Association and the Young Women's Christian Association.

Spider Girl's cart did not stop because they had sufficient water and food, but their spirits rose. The whores started singing, some of them quite saucy songs which got Spider Girl and close-by travellers smiling broadly. But all the time her father remained in his silent grave. With his strength returning he had managed to work his way off the cart and was slowly hobbling beside it. He had insisted two of the girls took his place but said nothing else.

Spider Girl and her father might walk quite close to each other – she slipping him food and water now and then – but between them remained infinite distance. They were like two separate islands in a sea of ghosts, two houses standing apart where once there'd been an entire village between.

In a family, it is said, when one person stops talking, another starts. There is never silence. But now, when Spider Girl stopped speaking, no one answered. Silence. Their dead family surrounded them, isolated them.

Spider Girl watched her father very closely. Stuck, frozen. What do I do? She wondered. How do I free him from this? He responds to nothing. But I must have patience. He will turn. My father will turn.

And then Spider Girl saw something. It came like an electric jolt to her. She saw a familiar face, a face from her village. The man was standing in a queue at a small booth waiting to be handed some food. Her mouth fell open. A survivor from their village! A whole set of contradictory emotions washed through her. Should she feel elated that it appeared the whole village had not been massacred, or should she feel guilt that her false prophecy had driven her family to its death? There was only one way to find out. She ordered The Ox to stop the cart, told him to keep an eye on her father, and waddled quickly over to the man.

'Xu,' she said, 'Xu – is that you?'

Xu looked at her. 'Spider Girl,' he said, 'it is you.'

Spider Girl stared at him. Xu and his family farmed a strip of land on the other side of the village. They and the Wei family hardly knew each other but they spoke when they met.

'Are there other villagers here? Did the village survive?'

He looked at her, then sighed.

'Ah, dear Spider Girl, I have a story I must tell you.'

And he told it to her.

After he had finished she asked him if he would come over to the cart to tell her father his story. She said they had food and water for him to drink but he said he would not want to eat food or drink water while he was telling his story. Spider Girl led him over to her father.

'Ah, Wei,' said Xu, 'You are still alive. I am so glad.'

Her father just stared back at him.

'Your eldest daughter has asked me to tell you the story of what happened in our village. I will. The Japanese killed everyone. You were wise to leave, Wei. Wise to leave.'

Her father did not respond.

'First they entered different houses at random, just killing people.'

'What happened to Old Man Chen?' asked Spider Girl.

'He ran at a soldier with a rock and wounded him before they bayoneted him.'

'And Fang the Builder?'

'They shot him dead. Against one of his walls.'

'After they had done these random killings they gathered all the remaining villagers in the village square, dividing them into their different families – your two cousins were in one group. They shot or bayoneted or beheaded every family in the village except ours, the Xu. We they left. By now they had broken into the innkeeper's stores and were drinking his wine and setting light to buildings and laughing and shouting. They forced our family to march to our farm. They gave me a spade and told me to start digging this great hole in the ground. My family stood to one side. When it was finished they congratulated me. Slapped me on the back. There was one soldier, an officer, who spoke bad Chinese. Then they ordered all my family into the hole except me. The hole was five feet deep. My whole family stood in the hole. My parents, my wife, my children. Only I stood outside it, above it. Then they told me to start filling in the hole. Jabbed me with a bayonet so I obeyed. I started to do it. When I had filled in enough so it covered up their feet and it started to come up their legs all my family started singing. The anthem we sing each year at our village festival. This annoyed the Japanese so they all seized spades and started filling it in, my children crying, swallowing earth, their heads disappearing below the surface, so that at the end there were only the heads of the adults still above the surface, still singing our anthem. But gradually my wife, my parents, my eldest son stopped, fell silent, then started choking, seizing as the earth gripped them and squeezed them until they could not breathe. Their eyes started popping out, popping out large as hens' eggs and blood pouring out of their seven organs and out from their mouths and noses and eye sockets. All the time the Japanese screaming and dancing and mocking them.'

Spider Girl watched her father very carefully all the time Xu spoke. Every so often his face flickered.

'Then, when they were all dead,' Xu continued, 'the Japanese used their spades to beat my family's heads into the ground. "'Let the dogs eat them,'" said the officer who spoke Chinese. Then they all turned and looked at me, pointed their guns at me. I fell to the ground. They all laughed at me. The one who spoke Chinese said they always spared one in a village, so they could run off and tell everyone they met what the Japanese had done to their village. So everyone flees from their villages before the Japanese even come. So many people flee that they choke up all the roads so that our army cannot get through to face and fight the Japanese Army and there are so many civilians that there is no water nor food so they all die of thirst and hunger and the Japanese do not have to bother doing the work of killing us themselves. So I fled. But I did not tell one single person what I had seen until I met you and you asked me.'

'When you ran away, when you passed our farm,' Wei asked in a voice that sounded as if his mouth was already full of the earth of his grave, 'did you see if they had destroyed our farmhouse?'

'I'm afraid,' said Xu, 'they had burnt it to the ground.'

Wei's face contorted.

'But you were right to flee, Wei,' continued Xu, trying to cheer him, 'yours is the only family in the village to survive. Someday you can return. At the moment the land lies fallow. There is no one to tend it. Only wild grass and hawthorns will grow. But you can return with your family and again start farming your land.' He paused. 'And lots of other peoples' land,' he added.

Wei looked at him.

'Xu, I will never return. There is no one there for me. No one. Every single member of my family, except for myself and dear Spider Girl, lie dead at the roadside, many without proper burial, without me to pray for their souls, pour their libations, burn their paper money, burn their incense, lead the prayers as head of the family at their funerals. I could not look after them in this world, I cannot even look after them in the next.'

'You could marry again, Wei, a new young girl, still have many children, a family to farm your lands, speak once more to your ancestors.'

'I am not going back there again ever,' said Wei.

There was a pause. 'No,' said Xu, 'and no more will I.'

Just as they spoke a most miraculous thing occurred. A couple of miles further back on their route, though they had been too engrossed in their own conversations to notice, two silver lines had swooped in from the west and had run parallel with them, about two hundred yards off. And suddenly – glistening black in appearance, gently hissing steam and flame, pistons and wheels and rods silkily easing in and out of each other – slid like a vast vision this enormous locomotive. Came clanking to a halt. Sat there, simmering, shimmering, silent.

Spider Girl, Wei, Xu, The Ox, the whores all just stared. They had never seen anything like it before in their lives. What was it?

Wei had no doubts. He spoke in awe. 'It is the Dark Dragon, the Mysterious Dragon, the Black Dragon God of the North and of Winter.' He fell on his knees.

'Yes,' whispered Xu, 'Heaven's Highest Deity,' following him on his knees.

As did The Ox and the whores, whispering nervously among themselves. Spider Girl was momentarily uncertain but decided to kowtow too.

Thousands of years ago, when the Shang Dynasty fell and the Demon King ravaged the world, Yuanshi Tianzun, Primordial Lord of Heaven, ordered the Jade Emperor to put Heishen the Dark Dragon in command of the Twelve Heavenly Legions to wipe out the evil invader. Heishen did so, and ever afterwards was worshipped as Mysterious Heaven's Highest Deity. And in all the temples thereafter dedicated to him, his statue stood with one foot above a tortoise and one above a serpent, signifying that good shall always prevail over evil.

The black engine gave a whistle and then, with a stentorian blast from its smokestack which made them all flinch, the vision smoothly glided off southwards and disappeared.

'It was the Dark Dragon of the North,' said Wei.

'Heishen,' Xu agreed.

'I know what I am going to do now,' said Wei.

'I do too,' said Xu.

They said their farewells and Xu returned to his place in the queue. Wei and Spider Girl resumed their journey with their wagon.

Spider Girl had been racking her brains about that strange

apparition. What was it? Then she remembered this photo she had seen in one of Old Man Chen's newspapers.

'Father,' she said, 'I do not think we saw a dragon. I once saw a picture of a thing just like that. They call it a fire wagon. It is a machine that can carry thousands of people for thousands of miles.'

Wei burst into sudden, wonderful laughter. 'Daughter,' he cried, 'daughter, you do amuse me. You and your newspapers.' And he touched her lightly on her arm.

'But father,' she said, 'it is a machine. It is made by the British and Americans to transport goods.'

Again her father roared with laughter. 'Eldest Daughter,' he said, 'Eldest Daughter, who cares what form a god appears in – but that whatever you call it, that fire wagon, that power, that grace, that beauty could have belonged to no one else except Heishen, our Great Battle Dragon of the North.'

Spider Girl momentarily felt miffed as her knowledge was so lightly dismissed, but this irritation was immediately swept away by the joy of hearing her father laugh, of seeing the return of the twinkle in his eye and the animation in his face as he talked to her.

'Father,' she said.

'Eldest Daughter,' he said.

They walked for a while in friendly silence. Then her father turned to her. He had reverted to his sombre mood.

'Eldest Daughter, terrible things have happened to our family. We know now, thanks to Xu, that your advice to leave the village was correct. But such terrible things happened on the... I was responsible...'

'Father,' Spider Girl interrupted him, 'The Japanese barbarians were and are responsible for everything that...'

'I,' said Wei emphatically, 'I am the father. I am responsible for everything that happens in my family. And I failed to prevent death after death.' There was a pause. 'I want to tell you everything that happened in our family after you – disappeared.'

And slowly, with great pain, he did. Slowing even more when he came to the terrible event of the bombing and the slaughter of his father, his second son and his youngest son. Spider Girl's brain flickeringly recognized the tragic ironies and accidents of that bomb – so Tiger Eyes had been telling the truth – but immediately returned to listening to and supporting her father in his agony. As they approached the death of Baby Girl Wei his telling and walking became ever slower so she had to stop the cart and just let him mutter and talk to her.

'This was the thing. The terrible thing. What I should have done – if I had any mercy or compassion – was simply smash out her brains with my shovel. Like that. In a moment. But I couldn't. My feelings, my selfish feelings, kept stopping me – so with my spade I just kept pushing her away, pushing her away, as her terror grew and her tiny voice – my baby's voice, my flesh's voice – got shriller and more terrified.'

Spider Girl listened to him. Her poor father. She hated to hear of lovely Baby Girl Wei's suffering but she hated to listen to her father's suffering even more. Of course the practical side of her agreed with her mother – that girls and women are expendable, and after that grandparents and younger sons. The survival of the eldest son means the survival of the family. But then it is the role of a woman to be practical and the role of a man to be just and merciful. Which was why she loved her father so much.

He finished describing the death of Baby Girl Wei and again the cart started moving. He described the heroic death of her mother and the awful mistakes which led to the death of Eldest Son.

'It was not your fault you fell asleep, Father. You were exhausted.'

'It was my fault! It will always be my fault!'

Then he told her of his own final journey, when he despaired and wished only for death.

'But I was wrong to wish for death,' said Wei. 'I am ashamed of it now. Because you, Eldest Daughter, are still here.'

She smiled. It was a beautiful compliment.

'Besides,' he continued, 'I have yet to hear the story of how you survived, how you suddenly turn up with a giant, a whole pack of whores, and a wagon stuffed with food and water. And I want the truth,' he said, with a twinkle in his eye.

Well, it was easy enough to tell her story when it came to pretending to be a witch, of riding around the crowds perched on a giant's shoulders, of how they inherited the whores with the cart – they both roared with laughter about that. But when it came to the parts which involved murdering bandits, killing a thug or shooting a pistol at a pimp, she glossed all this over, and every time she did so she saw Wei's eyes glisten and his mouth smile, but he was far too wise and loving to demand his eldest daughter told him the truth. Which was why she loved him.

They continued on their journey.

One thing still caused Spider Girl grief. When her father had said to Xu, at the end of their meeting, that he knew now what he was going to do, and Xu had said he too knew what he was going to do, she wasn't certain what they meant, but now she was pretty sure she knew. And it filled her with dread – and great pride.

And so they came to Wuhan.

17

Wuhan, a dark, dirty, industrialized city, lay at the heart of China, situated at the junction of the Yangtze and Han rivers.

It was in fact a tri-city. Three cities. The mile-wide Yangtze flowed from west to east and the Han flowed in from the north. On the southern bank of the Yangtze was the city of Wuchang, seat of government for Hubei Province and now the capital of the whole Chinese nation. There was a large university and a large barracks in Wuchang. In 1911 the Chinese Revolution had started there with a mutiny in the barracks. To the south of Wuchang, on the slopes of the Serpent Mount, rested the great Changchun Daoist Temple.

The city of Hanyang lay between the north bank of the Yangtze River and the west bank of the Han River. It was the heart of China's heavy industry – steel mills, weapons arsenals, aluminium smelters, and large manufacturing factories. The shanty towns and the hovels of the workers clustered all around them. River freighters and junks and railway trains constantly delivered its coal and iron ore and raw materials and took away its steel and weapons and finished products. It was a constant hive of activity.

Between the east bank of the Han River and the north bank of the Yangtze River lay the city of Hankou, the tri-city's financial and trading centre. Like Hong Kong and Shanghai it was a treaty port, with a line of foreign warships anchored in the river to defend their governments' interests. Along its riverfront ran a long promenade, the Bund. The Europeans and Americans lived and worked at the eastern end of the Bund, the Chinese at the western end. Hankou boasted two separate racetracks – one for the Chinese, one for the Europeans.

Wuhan was the collective name for the three cities. They were bound fast to each other by a frenzied web of fast-moving ferries, junks and high-speed motorboats. Wuhan was the Chicago of China. It was the centre of China's heavy industry and manufacturing. To and from it ran most of China's internal rivers, roads, railways and airways. And into it were pouring millions of destitute, homeless refugees. On whose heels were the ravenous Japanese.

Wei and Spider Girl and their fellow travellers entered the city from the north, down the eastern bank of the Han River. On the opposite side of the Han were the steel mills and arsenals and manufacturing mills of Hanyang, a thousand chimneys belching smoke, factory sirens wailing, tugs and freighters' hooters piping. Wei and Spider Girl had never even been to a town before, let alone a city. Let alone a modern, industrialized city. This city just went on and on. People just went on and on. Not just themselves, the refugees, not just the wounded and dying and dead soldiers lying all over the place, but amid them, dipping and swerving and carrying all manner of goods, were coolies, shopkeepers, children, rickshaw men, sailors, carters, porters, pickpockets. All shouting and screaming and cursing them to get out of the way. Wei and Spider Girl had been brought up in a place where they knew everyone – those peoples' parents and grandparents, those peoples' children and grandchildren. Here they knew no one. No one knew anyone.

Wuhan was growing cold in the first clutches of winter. Extra clothing was one of the first things the refugees had abandoned.

The whores disappeared almost immediately – off to find the warmth and security and predictability of a brothel. Wei and Spider Girl and The Ox continued south along the eastern bank of the Han. Gradually the frenzy of the markets and slums and the maze of back alleys and open sewers they passed through gave way to a broader promenade. They passed amid shops of all descriptions – haberdashers, fishmongers, butchers, magicians, geomancers, candle makers, shoe makers, incense makers, shops that specialized in selling certain sorts of ducks and chickens and eggs, displays of medicines in huge jars of oil containing dead snakes, dead animals, herbs and scrolls of paper, stationers. These in turn gave way to large, impressive buildings – three, even four storeys high. They stared at them. Spider Girl read their names – the Wing On and Sincere department stores, the Big World Amusement Park, the Good Fortune Roller Skating Dance Hall, and the All Star and Beneficial Cinema House, covered in garish posters of foreigners who might be called – Spider Girl had difficulty in pronouncing their names – Fred and Ginger. Why would a woman want to be called Ginger?

Everywhere around lay the exhausted, the dying, the dead. Despite the cold the flies still gorged. Crows and kites and buzzards that had pursued the refugees for hundreds of miles, feasting on their dead, had followed them here. The skies above Wuhan were now shadowed by these great birds gliding and floating and crying out in the black clouds.

Wei and Spider Girl and The Ox came out onto the Chinese Bund. They saw the Yangtze. A mile wide, a violent, turbulent force of water. Amid a chaos of people the three just stood and stared at the river. A mile of water. All around them markets and stalls and tables were being set up and hauled down, the surviving refugees spontaneously selling anything they still possessed and buying with that money food and water, and, if they could afford it, warm clothing. Wei decided he'd sell the cart as they had no more use for it. There was a glut of carts for sale and they received little for it. The remaining surplus food in the cart they got even more for, and were surprised by the price they could sell the water in the gourds for. Sweet-tasting water was rare in Wuhan.

Wei looked at Spider Girl. He handed her the money which he'd made at the market. He said he had to go away for a short while. They should stay here and await his return. Spider Girl knew that what was about to happen but she did not let her feelings show.

'Be safe, Father,' she wished him, 'and return soon.'

Wei went. Spider Girl decided that something had to be done about The Ox, who was standing patiently beside her. She looked around. She noticed that the happiest-looking people in this bedlam were the coolies. Even the ones bent double under the heaviest loads had broad grins on their faces. Why? Then she realized. Everyone who had something to sell at the markets employed a coolie to carry it there. Anyone who bought something employed a coolie to take it away. On the pontoons which floated out from the Bund steamers were constantly coming in, dropping their passengers, picking up new passengers, sailing away. Passengers and families who were arriving or leaving needed coolies to carry all their baggage and belongings and household goods from or to the docks. And further down the Bund freighters were continually steaming and sailing in, bringing all sorts of cargoes and loads that had to be transported away, especially food. Wuhan was surrounded by some of the finest, most fertile earth in China. So the huge increase in its population brought no difficulties for the local farmers, just increased profits. And more, much more, work for the coolies. Their rates were astronomical.

Spider Girl walked up to an older, friendly-looking coolie eating at a food kitchen.

'You look happy with your work.'

'Never been better.'

'Your rates are high?'

'Look at my food. I'm eating meat! When was the last time that happened? All you people coming in just create more and more work. And you know what the best is?'

'No?'

'The army coming in. Suddenly they're wanting stuff carried everywhere. All over the country. And they're desperate, so they'll pay anything. That's what's sent the rates so high. Our bosses can charge what they want.'

Spider Girl explained that she was hoping to fix up The Ox, still standing placidly beside her, with a good boss, an honest boss, who'd keep an eye out for him. Wouldn't cheat him.

'You want to go down to the dockside and ask my boss. I've been with him ten years now and he's never cheated me. With all this work around there's a whole lot of fly-by-night men who've just appeared who will cheat and gyp you. You try my boss. He's down by the dockside under the green and white pennant.'

Spider Girl thanked the man and she and The Ox walked down to the dockside, she patiently explaining to him what she was going to do, what was going to happen to him. He was quite upset by this but she said she would look at the boss first, speak to him, and only let The Ox work for him if she thought him honest. 'Besides,' she said, 'with a man of your strength, he is sure to look after you because you will be able to do so much work for him. And other bosses will be constantly asking you to work for them, so he will have to pay you more.'

They walked up to the boss. Spider Girl looked shrewdly at him, he looked shrewdly at her. A deal was struck. Spider Girl and The Ox said a sad farewell to each other, but The Ox wasn't that sad, because he'd just caught sight of the large wooden antique chest the boss wanted him to carry and he was working out how to carry it.

Feeling sad, Spider Girl returned to the spot where she would meet her father. She looked around her. There were so many people, all crammed in on top of each other, all striving and pushing against each other, each trying to walk in a different direction. This is what cities are like. But why? What is the use of it? What is the point of all this random frenzy? Where do they come from, go to? How can you achieve anything with all this crazy movement?

For a moment she felt dispirited but then shook her head, reminding herself she had practical things she must do. She looked around her. She saw something.

About half an hour later Wei returned and they greeted each other. He asked what had happened to The Ox. Spider Girl explained what she had done and he approved. Then he looked at her and explained what he had done.

'When we were on the march I met a man, and he told me that the great god Heishen, the Great Black Dragon, that his power and influence is particularly strong here in Wuhan. You know how in a statue of mighty Heishen his one foot is placed on a great tortoise and his other on a great serpent...'

'Yes, Father.'

'...Well, on this side of the Yangtze there is a Tortoise Mountain on the north bank and a Serpent Mountain on the south bank, and this man said that Heishen, the Great Black Dragon of War, stands astride the great river, one foot on the Tortoise and the other on the Serpent, as a sign to show that he will make certain that good shall always prevail over evil and Wuhan will survive. And this man also told me that on the Serpent Mount there is this old and powerful temple – the Changchun Daoist Temple – so I decided to go there and pray.

'I crossed the great river in a boat – it was terrifying – then I walked to the temple and I burnt incense and paper money and prayed. First I prayed at the altar to my own personal god, Tudeh, the god of the earth, who I was very angry with. All our family's land in ruins, growing nothing, barren. And he had done nothing to protect us. Then...'

'Then, Father,' said Spider Girl, gently speaking over him, 'then you prayed at the altar to Heishen. I know. I admire you for it. And he told you, as he should, that you must become a soldier and fight the awful enemy that has invaded our land. Which is the only honourable thing you can do. If you did not do it I would be ashamed of you. But at the same time it tears my heart out of my body. My heart lies on the ground between us.'

Wei was silent. She had read his intentions.

'You will be worried about me and my future, Father, because you are a good father, so you will sell me to the best and most honourable owner you can find.'

Wei looked at the ground.

'I have been looking around, Father, while you were away. I think I might have found the right owners.'

After she had returned from helping The Ox she had seen this whole long line of badly wounded Chinese soldiers lying on the cobbles of the Bund. They were in terrible condition. Whole limbs blown away, gaping holes in their chests and abdomens, their wounds suppurating and bleeding, flies feeding. The Chinese Army had virtually no first aid facilities or services, and badly wounded soldiers were usually left to die. But here on the Bund at the head of this line of abandoned and dying soldiers someone had erected a small dressing station. At it these two women were swiftly and expertly cleansing the wounds of soldiers and putting on new clean bandages. The two women chatted to each other and to the soldiers as they bandaged them, smiling and laughing. One of the women interested Spider Girl especially. She took her to be a foreign woman. A heap of clumsily bunched curly black hair falling down over her face, and her round eyes were set hard on her task but with a softness and a gentleness to them. Spider Girl had hobbled over and started chatting to them.

The two women were the American Agnes Smedley – a revolutionary from the glory days of the Western Federation of Miners and the IWW (the Industrial Workers of the World) – and now a newspaper correspondent for the *Manchester Guardian*, and the vivacious and talkative Hu Lan-shih, a mill girl from Shanghai. After her mill had been bombed by the Japanese she and many other girls had patriotically volunteered to help Chinese soldiers retreating from Shanghai. They provided entertainment, food, pep talks when the soldiers were thinking of deserting, and hand jobs when sexual tensions needed releasing. On the road, amid the fighting, she had picked up the basics of first aid.

Now Spider Girl led her father over and introduced him to them.

'My father has a proposal for you,' she said. 'He wishes to sell me to you.'

Hu Lan-shih stared at her. As Wei spoke both Agnes and Hu continued their bathing and bandaging, Spider Girl starting to pass Agnes her dressings.

'Good day,' said Wei, 'my daughter has spoken to me about you and she considers you to be people of high integrity and compassion. You must understand that I do not want to sell my daughter. She is a person who I hold in the very highest esteem. She is closer to my heart than my lungs or my liver. But we have just been driven from our lands by the foreign barbarians. My whole family except for my dear daughter have died or been killed upon our journey. I am responsible for that. Their deaths. So I feel that there is only one thing I can properly do. Join our army and fight the Japanese. Thus I must abandon my daughter. And I want to ensure she goes to humane and honourable owners.'

'Excuse me,' said Hu Lan-shih icily, 'but we do not buy people.' Agnes didn't say anything.

Wei, as a farmer, thought she was just haggling. Farmers haggle as naturally as cows chew cud. He continued.

'I want this to be an honest transaction. I will be open with you. Her legs are none too strong. She had an illness when she was young. But at the same time she has just walked a thousand miles on her legs. She is a person of great inner strength and resource, but I would say she is not fit for heavy labour. But my daughter heard you say that, because of your work, you do not have time to cook, and she is an excellent and skilled cook.'

'As my friend said,' said Agnes, 'we do not buy people. I would however pay her an honest wage to be my cook.'

'That is not good enough,' said Wei. 'I want you to buy her because then you will have a lifetime obligation to her, an obligation of honour to always feed and house and protect her. Wages are no good. You could pay her for two weeks and then say "I do not wish you to work for me any longer" and sack her. My daughter will be on the street, penniless, defenceless. She will die horribly.'

'We do not pay a father money for his daughter,' repeated Hu.

'I do not want the money for myself. What use would I have for it? I am going into the army and will probably die.'

'Do not say that, Father,' said Spider Girl sharply.

'If you pay me for her,' continued Wei, 'I will immediately give her that money in case difficulties arise for her in the future.'

'This is what we will do,' said Agnes. 'I will pay you a fair price for your daughter, but I will also pay her wages.'

And so it was decided. Money and the body were traded. Wei handed the money to his daughter. Agnes then told Wei that she knew an army medical officer who could help get him into the army. She handed him a slip of paper with her name and the address of the Wuhan Press Club on it so that were he to return he could contact his daughter through her. If they wished to reunite she would give his daughter back for free. She wished Wei luck in fighting the Japanese. Wei bowed to her and Hu.

Agnes and Hu carried on working on the wounded, Hu still objecting to the principle of a father selling his daughter.

'You,' said Agnes to Hu, 'are from a place where women look after themselves. These people come from a place where women have no such ability. Her father is doing his very best to protect her; she obviously trusts him implicitly. Are you saying he should not fight the Japanese? In war you cannot be right, you can only be pragmatic.'

Hu had never thought she – a socialist, a Christian, a trade unionist – would live in a world where she owned a slave. But here she was. Such is war.

It became time, in the midst of the chaos of crowds, for father to bid farewell to daughter.

'Dearest Wild Pear Blossom,' said Wei.

Wei rarely used Spider Girl's formal name to her. They both knew it was filled with deep meaning and emotion.

'You have been in my life like a wild pear tree. Standing alone in a barren winter landscape, all other plants and trees around you dead, leafless. But always in the midst of darkness and frost you have thrown up brave white and pink blossoms of laughter and wisdom and light. Your jokes, your thoughts, your spirit. You have kept me living.'

Spider Girl was silent. Then she remembered something and searched under her clothing. She brought out the small bottle of wild pear juice.

'Father, as head of the family, you must take this wild pear juice with you. So the family will always be with you.'

'No, daughter,' said Wei, pushing it back, 'you have it now. You are now head of our family, and I am proud of you.'

Spider Girl touched his arm. She had never dared do this in the past. He smiled, touched her arm, then turned and walked away. She watched for a while and then turned and resumed helping her new owners Agnes and Hu at the dressing station.

18

Late one night in December, amid slush and snow, my train finally arrives at Hankou Railway Station. Outside the usual mob of rickshaw drivers fight each other for who will carry the wealthiest patrons. Bloodcurdling oaths splatter the skies. Just like Beijing, I reflect, and feel oddly at home.

I have little money and virtually no baggage so I walk down the packed streets and across the Bund – crowds everywhere and wounded and soaking wet soldiers lying in rows on the cobbles.

I catch a junk to ferry me across to Wuchang. The passengers board and we edge out into the Yangtze, through the other shipping, past the line of foreign gunboats, then the current snatches us and we whirl downstream past the foreign banks, treacherous undercurrents in the water boiling to the surface and swirling out in huge black circles. I look down, I think of my wife, plunge into its depths. I can smell her, she is so close to me, lost to me. Without even taking out her Indian scarf I can smell her body, her whole body, pungent, in love. I shake myself, fight it off, look around me. The rowers are doubling their stroke, standing to their oars facing forwards, stamping on the wooden deck and chanting 'Hey Yah, Hai-yah.' We gain a favourable cross-current and they rest on their oars as the boat drifts diagonally towards the lighted other shore. As we glide between the moored boats towards the quay they ship their oars and light their cigarettes. A gangway is run ashore and we are immediately invaded by piratical-looking coolies clamouring for our baggage. Mercifully I don't have any but get roundly cursed for it all the same. Most of the curses I do not understand. A mental note – I must learn the local dialects as soon as possible, so I can curse back and so I can give my students a new world to discover.

On land I ask for directions and walk to the campus. One of Feng Yuxiang's aides shows me to my room. It is very neat, very tidy. Almost immediately I fall asleep.

The next morning I awake to a room full of light. I hurry to the window, look outside. I see a quiet courtyard. In its centre grow the unmistakable boughs of a red persimmon tree. Snow hangs from its branches like spring blossom. The first thing I must do in the morning is hurry to the central post office and see if there are any letters for Wu Lei.

BOOK TWO

WUHAN

To Joe, Niki and, of course, Yma.

The wagons rumble and roll,
The horses whinny and neigh,
The conscripts each have bows and arrows at their waists.
Their parents, wives and children run to see them off,
So much dust's stirred up, it hides the Xianyang bridge.
They pull clothes, stamp their feet and, weeping, bar the way,
The weeping voices rise straight up and strike the clouds.
A passer-by at the roadside asks a conscript why,
The conscript answers only that drafting happens often.
'At fifteen, many were sent north to guard the river,
Even at forty, they had to till fields in the west.
When we went away, the elders bound our heads,
Returning with heads white, we're sent back off to the frontier.
At the border posts, shed blood becomes a sea,
The martial emperor's dream of expansion has no end.
Have you not seen the two hundred districts east of the
    mountains,
Where thorns and brambles grow in countless villages and
    hamlets?
Although there are strong women to grasp the hoe and the
    plough,
They grow some crops, but there's no order in the fields.
What's more, we soldiers of Qin withstand the bitterest
    fighting,
We're always driven onwards just like dogs and chickens.
Although an elder can ask me this,
How can a soldier dare to complain?
Even in this winter time,
Soldiers from west of the pass keep moving.
The magistrate is eager for taxes,

But how can we afford to pay?
We know now having boys is bad,
While having girls is for the best;
Our girls can still be married to the neighbours,
Our sons are merely buried amid the grass.
Have you not seen on the border of Qinghai,
The ancient bleached bones no man's gathered in?
The new ghosts are angered by injustice, the old ghosts weep,
Moistening rain falls from dark heaven on the voices'
    screeching.

Du Fu, 'Song of the Wagons'

*

Like white featherless broken crippled abandoned chickens
Beneath a blazing sun common people suffer, wracked with
    pain.
In a stream of blood and tears the drums summon the troops.

General Li Pinxian

*

God chose what is foolish in the world to shame the wise; God
chose what is weak in the world to shame the strong; God
chose what is low and despised in the world, things that are
not, to reduce to nothing things that are.

1 Corinthians 1:27–28

1

Marriages and executions have a lot in common. Especially if they involve a famous person. They must be planned meticulously. Their symbolism and pageantry and ritual have to be pre-rehearsed to perfection and then, well, flawlessly executed. Especially if they involve an important person.

For six months now Japanese troops had been pouring into China, annihilating her armed forces, butchering her civilians. Millions had died. Millions had been enslaved.

Japan was advancing from the north and from the east into the very heart of China, her new capital of Wuhan. They must be stopped. The country needed time to transport its heavy industry, its arms factories, its soldiers and civilians all the way up the Yangtze River, through the natural barriers of the Three Gorges, so it could find a safe haven in its south-western provinces and there organize itself so it could continue the war. But how could the Japanese be held back for six months to give them time for this retreat? How?

Although a full general, the President of China, General Chiang Kai-shek, had never been a fighting soldier. He was a politician. A very clever politician. In a civil war many generals fight each other. Civil wars tend to be won not by the most brilliant generals but by those who can most effectively broker deals and build up alliances between all these fighting generals. Civil wars are not won on the battlefield but over the negotiating table. And a negotiator as brilliant and subtle as Chiang Kai-shek, having finally won supreme power, out of self-preservation does not then surround himself with brilliant and fiery generals who are only too likely

225

to overthrow him, but with generals even more mediocre and timid than himself. Such generals had been in charge of China's armies and had just lost disastrous battle after disastrous battle against the Japanese. Chiang Kai-shek had to be seen to be doing something! Immediately!

On 11 January 1938, he summoned a grand meeting of all the senior generals of his Supreme Military Command. It was held in the conference room of his presidential palace in Wuchang, the part of Wuhan which lies on the southern bank of the Yangtze River. The generals who had just lost all these battles sat before him in resplendent uniforms, lining either side of the long table he stood at the head of.

Chiang had decided he needed to make an example of someone. That he must pick on one particularly incompetent general and, after fierily denouncing him, publicly strip him of his rank and all his decorations and then cast this disgraced dog out into the wilderness. This would show his people that he was firmly in control of matters and demonstrate to the rest of his generals that they needed to up their game.

But there was one fly in this ointment. At the bottom of this great long table sat three extremely angry generals. These three extremely angry generals also happened to be, by far, China's most competent generals. Brave, patriotic, brilliant. The very generals who, because of their competence and ferocity, had been kept furthest away from the fighting. They were at this meeting because popular disgust and anger demanded they be there. And these three extremely angry generals were loudly demanding, from the bottom of the table, that one of Chiang's favourite generals – they didn't mind which – should be immediately court martialled, stripped of all rank and decorations, and, for total incompetence and cowardice, executed.

Chiang thought he could fairly easily deal with this. He asked for opinions from his tame generals, assuming they would automatically be against it. But he was taken aback by how little support he received. Such was the immensity of the crisis that his generals did not seem too averse to an execution – provided, of course, it was not they themselves who were executed. Pretty soon the meeting descended into a hunt for the most incompetent general with the fewest friends.

The most incompetent general with the fewest friends sat there with a ramrod-straight back and a face of iron. General Han Fuju, 'hero' of Jinan and shameless looter of the city's citizens. General Chiang Kai-shek, consummate politician that he was, quickly sensed the mood of the meeting and proceeded to denounce the cowardly Han. (It would be possible to later reduce a properly contrite Han's sentence to imprisonment as the execution of one cowardly general might swiftly lead to the execution of a whole lot more cowardly generals!) But the obstinate and deeply stupid Han resolutely refused to play along with Chiang's game. As Chiang's denunciations increased, instead of hanging his head in shame, the culprit stared ever more defiantly and contemptuously back at Chiang. Chiang finished his excoriation with a full-hearted condemnation of Han's cowardice and avarice in Jinan. 'Such a traitor deserves only death,' he roared. And sat down. Han stared directly back at Chiang. 'If I lost Jinan,' he growled, 'who lost Beijing and Tianjin and Shanghai and Taiyuan and Nanking?'

After that there wasn't anything Chiang could do. He sentenced Han to immediate execution.

But the theatrics of Han's execution – its form, its symbolism, its precise mechanics – still had to be worked out.

Chiang pondered the various options.

It could be done with a firing squad in the military barracks next door to Chiang's government offices. But that would be too – military. The people would want a people's execution! Preferably on a scaffold on the Bund surrounded with millions of cheering citizens watching a huge executioner taking off his head with an enormous axe. They'd love that! But the other generals would hate it.

He had an idea.

Wuhan had always been protected by the god Heishen – the Great Black Dragon of War. It is said, in Wuhan, that one of Heishen's clawed feet rests north of the Yangtze on Tortoise

Mountain and the other on its south bank at Serpent Mount. And thus he protects Wuhan.

In the folds of Serpent Mount lies the ancient and deeply venerable Changchun Daoist Temple. If Han was executed there his execution would both please the generals with its piety and deeply reassure the populace that Heishan's foot still lay firmly on all serpents of evil.

Changchun Daoist Temple it was.

Han Fuju's carefully choreographed execution was enacted at first light the next morning. Han chose to wear the traditional long dark gown and black skull cap of a Chinese gentleman. He was preceded at all times during the procession by his magnificent, silver-plated coffin at which he continuously stared and in which he obviously found deep consolation.

The cortège, consisting of himself followed by his fellow generals, wound its way slowly up two flights of stairs in the temple to its sanctuary on the third floor. A cushioned stool had been set in the middle of the room; the coffin was gently placed just before it. Han knelt on the stool. He looked at his coffin and then looked upwards. General Hu Zongman, a young and rising protégé of Chiang Kai-shek, stepped forwards, raised his pistol, and fired a single shot into the back of Han's head. Han slumped lifeless headlong into his waiting and welcoming coffin. A coffin so magnificent it guaranteed his sure and stately procession through all the halls of the afterlife.

During this execution the three extremely angry generals stood impatiently to the rear of the other generals. The three were Bai Chongxi, Li Zongren and Feng Yuxiang (the friend of Lao She). After the previous day's meeting they had gone discreetly to the Generalissimo's private office and there demanded even greater concessions. That in exchange for showing him public fealty, they would take over effective command of the war. Chiang knew his position was weak but on one point he would not yield. While he would allow Generals Bai Chongxi and Li Zongren to have command in fighting the war, he would not allow the socialist Feng Yuxiang anywhere near the fighting. Feng would have to stay here in Wuhan.

The three generals looked at each other. The most senior general, Bai Chongxi, now Deputy Chief of the Chinese General Staff, spoke for them.

'Very well,' he told Chiang, 'but in exchange we demand that here in Wuhan General Feng is put in charge of reconstruction and propaganda. That you keep your secret police away from his writers and journalists.'

Chiang bit his lip.

In addition, Bai Chongxi said it would be necessary that Feng leave Wuhan for two days so that he could inspect the site General Li had chosen for the battle and advise him on techniques of close combat and night fighting in which Feng excelled. Chiang agreed to this.

As they left the three generals agreed to meet in Taierzhuang in three days' time.

2

We are half asleep. In the darkness my wife moves closer to me. Her warm body starts to fit into, cozy up to me. It is as though we are in a warm sea. I become aroused, I start to— suddenly a child wriggles into our bed. Demands it joins our warmth. Then another burrows insistently between us, demanding territory, then a third. What was going to be pleasurable in one way becomes pleasurable in a very different way. An entire family lying and sleeping as one.

I wake up. I am not in my bed with my wife and my family. Instead I lie all alone in a very cold bed in Wuhan. Which is good. Because it means I cannot hang around in my bed indulging myself in untruthful fantasies. Instead I must be up and about my work. When my wife ordered me to abandon her, my children and my mother, so I could work for the good of our country, fight for socialism and feminism and the Lord Jesus Christ, she did the right thing.

The first light of a cold winter dawn is creeping into my room. I get up, look out of my window. In the distance I make out the dark silhouette of the Serpent Mount with the peaceful Changchun Daoist Temple nestling in its folds. I light a cigarette. I glance quickly at the bare-branched red persimmon tree which grows in the courtyard below, then I move across to the water bowl on the side table and splash my face with its ice-cold waters. Too late I realize I still have my cigarette on my lower lip. A fizzle. Carefully I detach the soaked tobacco stuck to my lip, dry my face on a cloth, and relight another one. I pour the heaped contents of last night's ashtray into the wastepaper basket, place the ashtray again on my desk, and sit.

Last night til three in the morning I was working on a propaganda play – a street theatre drum song piece named 'Wang Xiao Drives a Donkey'. I now read the results. Wang Xiao, a peaceful industrious young peasant who breeds donkeys to sell at market, is shocked to witness at first hand the appalling barbarities of the Japanese invaders and decides immediately to volunteer for the army in order to fight the barbarians.

> I shall go enlist in the army.
> I am a man of indomitable spirit,
> To die for my country I feel no regret,
> It is better than living as a slave under the bayonets of the
>   enemy.

To do this he bids farewell to his invalid mother – I think I've managed to get some genuine emotion into this bit – then sets off to fight.

> As I turn around and look at my home again,
> I see my mother standing stiffly at the doorstep.
> Choosing between being a loyal citizen and a filial son is hard,
> But at last I stamp my feet and leave my home.

Frankly it is awful. Terrible – as writing, as propaganda. To write good propaganda, I've discovered, you must destroy any vestige of subtlety, suppress any literary instinct you might possess, and simply hammer your audience with blows of emotion and melodrama. Hammer, hammer, hammer! But this is awful hammering. Its barely tapping. And in only three days' time I'm meant to be teaching a gang of young upper-class Marxist toffs how to write powerful and effective propaganda in language understandable and inspiring to every peasant and factory worker in China. So that, duly inspired, the millions will rise up, seize upon their weapons, and march out singing triumphantly to defeat the barbarian invader.

My dark night of the soul lasts only a second. The door to my room flies open and a human dynamo bursts in – small and wiry in frame, pugnacious in stance and expression.

'Fuck,' it says.

'Xiang,' I reply.

'You look like a dog that's about to be fucking hung.' A moment. 'No, you look like a dog that's already been fucking hung.'

I explain to him my fears about my upcoming teaching assignment.

'Fuck 'em. Kick 'em in the balls. And if these upper-class twats try any nonsense call 'em fuckwits, more-dead-then-alive abortions. Piss on their accents. Blind them with insults.'

'For some reason General Feng Yuxiang thinks I'm just the man to teach them.'

'That fucking peasant.'

Lao Xiang (absolutely no relation) is a free-spirited foul-mouthed south Hebei peasant who miraculously ended up as a writer. A very good writer who speaks several dialects and writes powerful and hilarious plays and squibs. Strangely he also writes beautiful and delicate poetry for children to recite and sing. Exactly the sort of writer we need. After we finally arrived in Wuhan a group of us – folk artists like He Rong, cartoonists like Zhao Wangyun, writers like Lao Xiang and myself – formed a group known as the All-China Resistance Association of Writers and Artists. We write and produce popular drama for the masses. There aren't enough of us. Four hundred and sixty million fellow citizens – 97 per cent illiterate – speaking in hundreds of different dialects and accents, must all be reached. Transformed by my upper-class Han-accented Marxist shock troops.

As I lament the impossibility of my mission Lao Xiang is reading my 'Wang Xiao Drives a Donkey'.

'Fuck,' he says, 'this is awful.'

'I know,' I say.

'I'll rewrite it,' he says. 'You copy as I dictate.' He dictates.

I am a man of fiercest feeling.
I will volunteer now. Fight for my country.
To defeat these demons I will have no fear of dying.
It is better to die under the bayonets of our enemy
than live as a slave and grovel as a worm.

A pause.

I turn and see my dearest mother,
her body stiff with age and sickness,
stand in the doorway of our hovel.
She holds out her hands in supplication to me.
'Do not desert me, my son,' she cries.
Do I stay a pious son or serve my country?
I stamp my feet and march to serve my country.

'That's so much better than mine,' I say.

'It is,' he agrees. 'But I'm having a great deal of trouble with one of mine. "Women at the Front". It's a kuaibanr with bamboo clappers.'

'Let me read it,' I say, holding out my hand.

'Thing is,' says Xiang, 'I've got this rehearsal for it over the river. Could we work on it in a rickshaw as I go down to catch the ferry?'

I agree.

We both pile into a rickshaw and set off down the hill, Lao Xiang's voice resounding round the streets. This is what we arrive at on our journey.

They are women, but fierce as men.
Lovers of China who will not permit a traitors' peace.
Endlessly toiling, they never dress up,
Give all their meagre pennies to the nation
endlessly sewing winter clothing for the troops…
Full of courage, the sisters take up their guns,
Inspired by the heroic Hua Mulan…
Women of a new age, their arms holding up the sky.
These heroines become famous throughout the nation.

The rickshaw driver likes it so much he only moderately overcharges us.

I walk slowly back up the hill to my desk.

★ ★ ★

By the time Hu Lan-shih and Agnes Smedley left their apartment the early morning fog had cleared and a bleak winter sun was shining down on Wuhan. Hu naturally smiled at the sun, as she smiled at all things, because she had an optimistic nature. Agnes naturally scowled at it. She always scowled at everything when she was thinking. They walked along the crowded, frenetic Bund – packed with market stalls and acrobats and astrologers and abandoned orphans begging and picking pockets. Hu asked Agnes about her childhood in America.

'I suppose you were born in some great city somewhere.'

'I'm a country girl,' replied Agnes.

'Oh,' Hu laughed, 'just like me.'

'Osgood, Missouri. End of nowhere. I've Scotch/English blood and my great grandmother was a Cherokee Indian.'

'Really?'

'Raised in a two-room cabin in the middle of nowhere. We had a clock, a sewing machine, chickens but no cows. My father liked singing songs and telling stories. He was never interested in work. Talked endlessly about getting rich quick but never did nothing about it. I caught sight of my parents having sex and it was the most disgusting thing I ever saw.'

'Were there many of your relatives in the village?' asked Hu. 'Aunts, uncles, cousins?'

'Not one of 'em. We Americans ain't like you Chinese. We spend our lives getting away from our relatives, not getting' closer to 'em.'

Hu couldn't understand this so she smiled. She stepped aside as a herd of desperate pigs were driven past.

'When I was seven,' Agnes continued, 'a flash flood washed down our valley and took our cabin and clock with it. But not the sewing machine. We lived in a tent and Pa left us pretty soon after that and took to gambling and drinking full time. Ma rented a room and we took in washing and sewing and patching other folks' clothing.'

'Did you plant any crops?'

'No. Hardscrabble land. A few potatoes.'

'What did you eat?'

'Mostly we didn't. My dad had shifted to a mining camp in Ludlow, Colorado, where he took up with another woman, but she left him and he told my mother to join him.'

'Your father did not seem to have a sense of duty.'

'He stole from his own children. Ma said no for a while, even wanted a divorce, but we had no money, we was starving. He sent us railroad tickets and we went.'

They passed a witch trying to sell them a spell guaranteed to win them husbands, then two keen young medical students offering free injections to inoculate you against typhoid. (The disease was rampant in Wuhan since the huge influx of refugees.) Hu and Agnes had already had injections but congratulated the two students on their public service.

'It's strange,' Hu said, then giggled, 'but we always think of America as such a rich place.'

'Ever been to a mining town?' Agnes asked.

'No.'

'Hell and smoke and dust. You live in shacks or tents.'

'Sounds like us workers in Shanghai.'

'You bought your marked-up food and supplies in company stores. There weren't no schools nor doctors nor hospitals. There weren't no law. The company goons ran the town. If you objected to anything they beat up on you and ran you out of town. That's why I hate seeing all this same stuff in China.'

'In my village,' said Hu, 'if men behaved like those company thugs all the village would meet together. We would try to reconcile with the men, but if they refused the whole village would turn on them and throw them out.'

'In Ludlow we tried go-slows, we tried strikes to get better conditions, but they brought in Pinkertons and the state militia. There was gun fights taking place in the hills around and once on Main Street. Buildings and the railroad station were dynamited. Then we formed the Western Federation of Miners, all across the mines in Colorado. I went to see Big Bill Haywood himself address a meeting. I was only a kid. There were thousands of us there and

Pinkertons and the state militia opened fire on us. Blood and bodies everywhere. It was on that afternoon that I decided I was a socialist, that I was going to start a revolution.'

Agnes, involved in telling her story, walked into a juggler. His balls flew everywhere. He cursed her in fluent Hubei Chinese. She cursed him in fluent Missourian American, gave him some money and walked on.

'What about *your* childhood, Hu?' asked Agnes.

Hu laughed.

'You always laugh when you're embarrassed,' noted Agnes. Hu giggled.

'Well, there's not much to tell. I come from Jiangsu Province. Kaixiangong is my village. When I was very young it was very prosperous. There was lots of farming, but also almost all the women spun silk at home. The silk we spun was sold on to the Chinese silk mills in Shanghai. They sold their woven silk on all over the world. It was famous. But suddenly the whole market collapsed because of cheap Japanese imports.'

'Hurrah for capitalism!'

Hu didn't laugh. 'Yes – hurrah for capitalism. There was no work in the village. Times were very hard. So my mother sold me to a Shanghai cotton mill. It was the right decision. The family needed my wages. Only six years old, I was taken into the Shen Xin Number Nine Cotton Mill. The heat, the noise, the machinery was terrifying. Forty thousand spindles all spinning at once. It was huge. I was put in the slubber room. Bigger girls and women were feeding these huge slivers of raw cotton into the machines, lint and smoke and dust was flying everywhere so you could hardly draw breath, but every time the sliver broke, which was often, that was when we tiny children were used. The machinery was packed tight – all wheels and gears and cranks flying and revolving – and it was only the smallest of children who could worm and wind their way amid all this snatching and hammering and spinning machinery to catch hold of the two ends of the broken sliver and band them together. They particularly valued my work because I had deft fingers from the silk spinning.'

'Bet they didn't pay you nothing more for it though,' observed Agnes.

Hu giggled.

'Carry on,' said Agnes.

'The worst time was my best friend Kaija. She was a year older than me. You have to make friends fast in a place like that so people look out for you or you don't last long. I didn't look out for her.'

Hu Lan-shih stopped dead at this. The memory of it.

'Carry on,' prompted Agnes.

'I was fixing a sliver elsewhere, so when one broke close to the strapping belt she had to crawl in. We'd already been working twelve hours that day. She must have been tired. The strapping belt had buckles on it, loops of leather. It flies round at an enormous rate, takes power from the main spindle up above us to drive all the machines below. The attached buckles fly all around and it must have been that Kaija, already tired, as she was trying to bind the sliver together, moved her arm too far to one side so that the buckle on the belt snatched hold of her and in a second she was whirled dangling upwards, screaming and shouting, and smashed against a beam in the ceiling and then crashed back down again and hit the floor and in a few short seconds, before the strap could be stopped, was pummeled and crashed to nothing, a pulp. Not a whole bone in her body. Blood. She was cut down, carried away. Work continued. That was the day I became a socialist.'

There was a pause. Hu giggled for having spoken so long and greedily.

'But Hu,' continued Agnes, 'you can read and write. You are an educated person. How did that happen?'

'There were good people about. Very good people. You've heard of the YWCA?'

'The Young Women's Christian Association? Sure. They're good folk.'

'In Shanghai they were set up about forty years ago. By American Christian women. Christian Socialists. They believed that Jesus Christ was a revolutionary. Their message was taken up eagerly by many eager young Chinese girls. Within a few years the

Association in Shanghai was run by Chinese women. To bring on the revolution they provided health services and educational and technical classes for working people. Legal support for those with cases against the mill companies. They helped the workers form trade unions to fight for better wages and conditions.'

'And they succeeded?'

'Well, ten years ago they were doing well. But then came the repression. Socialists and communists being shot down, arrested, executed. Just like you in America.'

'Yup.'

'So that in the end the YWCA and the YMCA were really the only organizations left that could fight for working people in Shanghai. After all, Chiang Kai-shek is a Christian himself. So there's a limit to how much he can stop the work of his fellow Christians. The YWCA educated me. Taught me to think for myself.'

They'd reached a part of the Bund which people tended to avoid, where the crowds thinned. It was heralded by the stink of dried blood, unwashed bodies, of gangrene and excrement. Everywhere there were swarms of flies, even in January, feasting on congealed blood, dirty bandages, near-naked bodies. There were groans and screams and curses of pain. Agnes and Hu had reached their destination. The section of the Bund where the authorities – overwhelmed by the tens of thousands of wounded, dying, and dead soldiers, delivered hourly by ferries, by railways, by the cartload, on foot – simply dumped them to die on the bare cobbles.

Hu smiled at Agnes without giggling. Agnes for once smiled back.

As they stepped delicately and carefully over and between the packed bodies, hands grabbed their skirts – 'Water ladies, please. For God's sake, water.' They stepped over the dead, over men who lay dull-eyed with hands clutching their bellies where dried blood glued torn uniforms to wounds, over men from whose broken jaws came inhuman noises and gurglings. Everywhere flies crawled over faces. They reached the dressing station and relieved the dog-tired volunteers who had been working there continuously – cleaning wounds, disinfecting them, rebandaging them, resetting broken limbs – since they had relieved Hu and Agnes the previous night.

The next bloody body was hauled onto the table.

Hu smiled. Has the world always been this insane, she thought?

General Feng Yuxiang, forbidden by Chiang Kai-shek from fighting any battles, stood in front of a vast, very busy building site. On a great grass plain west of Wuhan row after row of cheap wooden homes and shacks were being constructed, all on a precise north–south axis so that the farming families and refugees, on entering them, would immediately feel reassuringly aligned with the gods and the heavens and their ancestors to the north.

It's always so much more satisfying to build houses rather than destroy them, he reflected.

Large army trucks roared continuously on and off site, hauling logs and roofing straw and door frames and stone and light machinery. Carts arrived piled high with iron cooking pots, large sacks of vegetables, wheat and rice. Some carried bricks so that kilns and baking ovens could be built, others firewood and poor-quality coal. Civilian handcarts were laden with yarn and looms for weaving, spades and hoes so that vegetables could be grown in the fields nearby. Endless streams of coolies carried anything and everything in their panniers. Cattle and sheep and geese and ducks were being herded on site by girls and children to be slaughtered and fill the cooking pots of the starving and hungry. A sawmill, powered by a diesel generator, was already at work, its great iron base holding the madly revolving blade steady as it screeched and bit and sliced its way into logs to make floorboards and planks for the floors and walls for the houses in the cold winter weather. The offcuts and sawdust were being distributed for firewood.

As they arrived on foot the country people were being divided into the different provinces they had come from and sent to individual streets, so that everyone in the same neighbourhood spoke the same dialect and felt at home with neighbours who knew the districts they were familiar with. Some happy reunions took place. Some reunions, when only one or two members of a family survived, were tragic. But all the citizens of these new communities had experienced similar grief, and support and comfort were immediately offered by their new neighbours.

Several plots of ground in each row of houses were left vacant for businesses and cooperatives to set themselves up. Some of the refugees who'd already been here several weeks, their homes built and families organized, had opened kitchens and dining rooms that specialized in the foods and dishes of their local areas – familiar tastes and smells again providing reassurance for those so far from home. Others immediately set up as builders and labourers and, paid by the government, started constructing the new homes for all the new refugees pouring in. Central government also provided loans for cooperatives so that the many skills that the refugees came with could be immediately turned to their use and profit. Skilled weavers were making cloth, and women sewed, knitted and made clothes which could be given to the families of their members, sold on to other refugees, or hawked on the markets of the Bund.

A large group of Chinese Christians who'd wished even in peacetime to set up a utopian community imitating the life of Jesus and his disciples had brought with them from Shanghai knitting and sewing machines and set themselves up in a street of their own. They were already exporting their clothes inland to Changsha and up the Yangtze to Chungking. Every third product they made was given away free to their fellow refugees. With great skill and delicacy they weaved in decorations and beautiful patterns because, as they said, they wished to bring colour and delight to all who had suffered so much.

In different streets cooperatives which specialized in skills and crafts native to a particular region in China were being set up. Printing shops from the big cities, paper makers, ink makers, carpenters and furniture makers from forest areas. Skinners stripped the hides of slaughtered cattle, tanners stank the place out as they cured the skins, leather-workers took the cured skins and cut and sewed clothes and bags and suitcases and shoes and a thousand other useful objects. Basket weavers wove (the banks of the Yangtze providing copious reeds and withies), skilled workers turned medicated cotton and gauze into bandages and slings both for the army and wounded civilians. Small foundries belched smoke, puffed rice specialists puffed rice, and workshops for brewing beer and canning food proliferated.

In each street a larger building was put up that it could be used simultaneously as a temple for prayer, a meeting house for the community to debate and decide its future in, and a place where children and adults could be educated. A cacophony of prayers, heated arguments, and determined rote learning rang from the building.

All this might seem a bit impractical to a cynical Western reader, used to having their every need supplied by anonymous supranational corporations. All this getting together and producing things cooperatively is all very well in theory, but when you get down to practicalities a few people end up doing all the work while the rest lounge around and sponge off them.

This misunderstands profoundly the character of the Chinese people in the 1930s. A farming family was almost invariably large – having ten, twelve, or even more members. Unless everyone worked almost all the time they would starve. So from the age children could walk they were given tasks and jobs. Everyone worked for the good of everyone else – it's how they kept alive. Jobs and duties were divided up. Men decided among themselves who was best at particular jobs and each did the one they were best at. The same with women. And when big tasks – constructing temples or dams, or fighting off floods or fires – had to be undertaken, the whole village, after discussion, would set themselves to it as one, united. They regarded their togetherness and industry with great pride.

So when these broken and torn apart families, their lives in pieces, came together – to work as one, to cooperate, to share – this renewed commingling and cooperation felt good, very good. It warmed them. It reassured them. It was a new family, a new community building itself together again, healing its wounds. Working amid people, giving of yourself for others, felt natural, gave you security, pointed a way towards a new life.

General Feng, in his usual peasant dress, stood at the entrance to the site through which all the lorries and carts and refugees came pouring in. Having fought in China's civil wars in almost every northern province, he was fluent in most of their dialects. Smiling broadly, he spoke to every refugee who arrived.

'My back is aching. So are my legs.'

'Don't worry, grandma, there is a warm bed where you are going to.'

'I have lost three of my children. Three.'

'That is a great sorrow, mother. A great sorrow. But here your remaining children will be safe.'

'I have no money to provide for my family. They have had no food or drink.'

'Don't worry, husband. There is work here and you will be paid fairly and your family will eat.'

Feng squatted down.

'Why are you so silent, little one? No need for you to worry. There will be lots of children here for you to play with.'

'We are from Jinzhou in Liaoning Province. We do not know where to go.'

'You've come a long way. You go right here, along to the eighth row of houses. You will find plenty of people from Liaoning there.'

All the time he watched them. He listened to everyone. To refugees who had just arrived and residents who'd been here for several weeks. Listened intently to their comments, complaints, suggestions, his sharp mind cataloguing and analyzing what they said. He would do what he could to ease their problems, but mainly he knew it would be the people themselves who would together deliberate and debate and solve their own problems. As they had always done. Every so often he turned to his aide to note a particular difficulty or to order a soldier to go to a specific street to settle a dispute or affray.

A large column of refugees contains more than its fair share of ne'er-do-wells and bandits, some of them lifelong criminals, others simply adapting to the desperate needs of a death march. Feng had a shrewd eye and winnowed out the likely suspects. After a sufficient number had been collected he gave them a brief talk on what would happen if they broke the laws of the camp. Those he judged harmless he allocated a dwelling, warning them that one of his soldiers would visit them and their neighbours every day to see if there were any problems. If there were, that person would be removed to a row of dwellings next to the military barracks, where those he adjudged serious criminals were already being sent. Anyone breaking the law, depending on the severity of the crime, would either be expelled from the camp or hung.

As he spoke to a group of refugees from Hebei a woman in a peasant smock walked up and smiled at the general.

'Husband.'

'Wife. What have you been up to?'

'A meeting of teachers.'

'Hope you learnt something.'

As Feng had educated himself as he rose through the ranks of the army so had his wife. While Feng learnt and experimented within soldiering and social engineering, Li Dequan specialized in education and children.

'We've got teachers for almost every school except the Shanxi one. We can't find anyone who can speak Shanxi dialect.'

Feng clicked his fingers, thinking for a moment. He summoned his adjutant.

'Who speaks Shanxi in the regiment? There's someone.'

The adjutant thought for a moment. 'That private in the catering corps.'

'Right,' said Feng. 'Cuts up the vegetables. Why isn't he a cook by now? Bright enough. I think he can read.'

'His family's from Jincheng.'

Feng turned to his wife.

'If you send a teacher to the Shanxi school this cook can translate for them until they pick up the dialect. Never know – that private's clever enough to become a teacher himself.'

He indicated the adjutant should arrange this.

Li Dequan looked at her husband. 'We should both be in Wuhan.'

'Indeed. You have that meeting about orphans, I'm meant to be getting on that train to Taierzhuang.'

They hitched a ride on a passing lorry. It was packed with camp carpenters going down to the ferry to work on a similar refugee camp starting on the other side of the river.

Feng hung on one side of the cab, Li on the other.

His adjutant took over his role of welcoming the new arrivals.

3

Standing alone in his private railway carriage General Bai Chongxi, newly appointed Deputy Chief of the Chinese General Staff, ritually washed his hands, his arms, his feet, his legs. A tall, thin man with a clean-shaven head, he had a high-bridged, strong nose and a prominent chin.

In the early morning light he started to recite his prayers. Standing on his prayer mat facing Mecca, he stated Allahu Akbar ('God is great'), and then proceeded with his Rak'ha. Having finished he robustly declared his personal Jihad against all Japanese soldiers who had invaded his country. As did all China's Muslims. He then dressed himself, ate his breakfast, washed his mouth and hands, and stepped down from the special train which had brought him to Taierzhuang overnight from Wuhan.

Generals Li Zongren and Feng Yuxiang awaited him on the platform. He grinned at them. Li Zongren was a small, wiry individual with sharp deep-set eyes and an emotional temperament. As soon as Bai was appointed Deputy Chief of the General Staff he put Li in charge of the Chinese Army's Fifth Battle Zone, an area covering much of Central China and the stretch of its East Coast not yet seized by the Japanese. Li now commanded the very areas, centred on Wuhan, which Japan was intent on seizing.

Beside him stood General Feng, fat and muscular with, as always, a beatific smile on his face and dressed in peasant clothes. As he put it – 'I was born a peasant. I will die a peasant.' Bai noted Feng had wet mud on his knees and concluded he'd been praying to his Christian god. The railway station was outside the city of Taierzhuang so the three men climbed into the back of a large open-topped Mercedes sedan, their adjutants and aides piling into a couple of following vehicles and they set off towards the city.

A branch of the Grand Canal runs along the southern edge of Taierzhuang. It is fifty yards wide and unfordable, pinioning the town as a line of defence. Long a strategic fortress, Taierzhuang's wide walls had been rebuilt in the 1860s with a robust outer casing of fired brick and an inner core of mudbricks to absorb the impact of high-explosive shells. Within the walls the town is oblong-shaped and measures roughly a mile north to south and half a mile east to west. The waters of the Grand Canal feed a moat outside the walls which runs all the way around the city.

The convoy carrying the generals approached from the south. They bumped over a pontoon bridge and entered the city by its south-eastern gate. Inside it was immediately dark and shaded, a dense labyrinth of tiny streets and alleyways, the dwellings crowding together and overhanging every street. An excellent location for a defensive, attritional battle. The enemy would have to fight for every house, house by house, room by room. But it was not this that made Bai and Feng smile at Li's cleverness in choosing Taierzhuang for his battlefield. It was the nature of the dark blackish stone from which these buildings had been constructed.

The convoy passed through the city's narrow streets and emerged through the two large guard towers at its north gate. They motored on, passing farms and outbuildings all made from the same dark stone. After about a mile natural outcrops of this same rock, from which the city had been built, shot up on either side of them. Feng Yuxiang laughed, the convoy stopped, Feng jumped out and bounded over to one of the outcrops. This bull of a man drove his shoulder hard into the rock, grabbed the rock, pulled the rock, kicked it, did everything in his power to shift it short of biting it. Then he bit it. It did not yield an inch.

'Congratulations, Li, you old fox,' chortled Feng. 'Black granite. The hardest rock on earth. Each building, each natural outcrop like this makes a perfect fortress. Bullets, bombs, artillery shells will all bounce off it without harming it a speck. Build a maze of tunnels and trenches between them and under them, then draw in their tanks and infantry and...'

The three men stood beneath the rock, Feng contemplating the beauty of the idea, then Bai Chongxi, the senior officer, coughed and brought the meeting to order.

'Gentlemen, thank you for attending today. I will first lay out for you how I interpret the current world situation – nations' relationships with each other, who might fight who, our own position within this framework – then I'll suggest how this situation might evolve in the future. This will give us some idea of what we can hope to achieve in this war and how we might fight it. General Li will then describe to us his proposed strategy for halting the Japanese advance here at Taierzhuang and thus stopping their advance on Wuhan – a city it is vital we hold for at least six months. Finally I hope that General Feng, irritating socialist and unshaven peasant that he might be, will educate us on the tactics of close-quarter and night fighting, techniques it is vital our soldiers adopt in these surroundings to defeat the Japanese.'

Feng beamed at this description of himself. Bai looked at the ground for a moment, martialing his thoughts, then spoke. As he spoke he did not look at his two comrades but over their shoulders, as though he was addressing the outcrop of rock.

'The whole world is interlocked. Let me begin with Europe. Our leader believes with great faith that England and France, seeing Japan's aggression and fearing it threatens their own commercial and economic interests in China, will come to our aid. I'm afraid I see little chance of this. The British Prime Minister Neville Chamberlain's thoughts are mainly dominated by his fear of Russian communism and he is thus likely to continue to appease the European fascists and influence the French prime minister to support him in this. He hopes that Hitler will turn east, as he has often sworn to do, and invade and destroy Soviet communism. Chamberlain has little interest in the Far East. The only other country with a large economic interest in China is the United States. Following the First World War its people are firmly isolationist in outlook and would show great hostility to starting a war in defence of China. And, of course, American industrialists are making large profits from selling oil and high-quality steel to Japan.

'The only country we share a common geopolitical interest with is Russia. Russia has no interest in being invaded simultaneously from the west by European fascists and the east by Japanese fascists, both hungry for its raw materials. In the last two years there have been numerous aggressive attacks by Japanese troops across the border between Manchukuo and Russia. It is in Russia's interest that we Chinese continue to fight Japan for as long as possible in order to absorb her military forces. Which is, of course, why the Soviet Union has for many months now been supplying us with advanced weaponry and pilots to fly our combat aircraft. We are profoundly grateful to them.

'That is the past. What is the present situation? Japan as a nation is extremely short of raw materials to feed its growing population and industries. Its long-term aim is to invade Siberia to gain these raw materials in abundance. But they do not yet have the military strength to defeat Russia. So instead they invaded us because we have a certain amount of raw materials. They calculated, I believe, that if they invaded they would force us to surrender within three months. They have miscalculated. This war has already lasted six months. And, following the morale-boost of General Han's execution, it is not likely to end anytime soon. What will happen as this war deepens? I believe the Japanese war machine will be sucked further and further into the interior of our country. The Japanese do not have a large population. We have a huge one. We have five times as many soldiers as they do – albeit poorly armed and poorly trained. In battles and skirmishes they only have to lose one soldier for every three soldiers we lose for them to run out of men far quicker than we do. As they are drawn further and further into our vast country, their supply lines will stretch more and more, and they will become increasingly vulnerable to counter-attack from local guerrillas and patriots. Like the Communists recently did when they trapped them in the Pinghsing Pass. Wiped them out. As all their high-technology weapons on which they rely get further and further from their maintenance and supply bases, the Japanese war machine will increasingly grind to a halt.

'This is going to be a long and a terrible war. Of attrition, of slaughter, of massacre, of inhumanity. I know we all realize this. But what will be its outcome?

'This is my calculation. Japan has started all these wars because it is desperate for raw materials. Bogged down in this hasty, unthought-out war in China, it is now even shorter of, more desperate for, these same raw materials. Where can they get them? There are only two sources. They could go north, to the Soviet Union, but the Russians are too strong for them. Which only leaves one alternative. The south. The oil fields of the Dutch East Indies, the rubber plantations of British Malaya, the rice fields of French Vietnam. I believe they will be forced to attack to the south. I doubt if those European powers have either the courage or the resources to defend their colonies. Appeasement is in their blood.'

'So we're screwed,' stated Feng. 'They'll come at us from both ends.'

'No,' replied Bai decisively, and for once looked directly at his two companions. 'In order to go south they will have to go through the Philippines. The American Philippines. The Europeans will not be interested in defending their colonies – they're far too involved in what is happening in Europe – but the Americans will defend their colony. I am certain.'

'So we will have the Russians and the Americans as our allies, the Japanese as our enemies?'

'The European fascists will probably join with the Japanese,' said Bai, 'though that will be of no interest to us.'

He smiled.

'Of course, all this is contingent on General Li here winning the Battle of Taierzhuang.'

Bai having finished his analysis, the three men moved away from the rock outcrop and over an open meadow. Each was followed by his own aide who had been noting down every word General Bai had spoken. They were in turn followed by a fourth aide who was noting every word spoken by everyone. This was for the benefit of Chiang Kai-shek, who wished to keep a very close eye on what all three of his generals were saying. The group approached a large table at which tea was being served and on which several maps had been laid out.

General Li Zongren stopped at the table and Bai Chongxi and Feng Yuxiang stood one on each side of him. There was a large map which covered the province of Shandong in the north – including at the top the Yellow River and the city of Jinan – and stretching all the way south to the province of Jiangsu with Shanghai and Nanking at the very bottom of it. Taierzhuang and Xuzhou rested in about the centre of the map. From the top to the bottom of the map, from Jinan down to Nanking, ran the strategic Tianjin to Nanking railway line, with Taierzhuang at its very centre. Beside this map lay a smaller one of the countryside for fifty miles around Taierzhuang and then a smaller one of the city itself and its complex of streets.

Li opened a fresh tin of Craven A's and laid it on the table. He took one, lit it, drew deep and reassuringly from it, then started waving it at the large map on the table. He spoke in a sharp, emotional voice.

'I expect the main Japanese attack to come down the railway line from Jinan, heading straight south to us here in Taierzhuang. I expect two simultaneous flanking attacks – one from the north-east coming down through Linyi, the second from the south, starting from Nanking and travelling north up the railway to Bengbu. I intend to halt these two pincer movements at Linyi and Bengbu. On no account must they be allowed to join up with the main Japanese attack, the Japanese 10th Division, coming south down the railway line. After delaying the 10th at Tengxian – let's hope it raises their blood pressure – we will let the 10th, the 10th alone, through our preliminary defences so they can fall on our main force embedded here among the prepared rocks and fortresses of Taierzhuang. Then let them enter the city of Taierzhuang. It will be a horrible battle. Long and bloody and terrifying. Anyone deserting will be shot. And that includes my senior officers. I have told them this. They all know about the fate of Han Fuju.'

'Do you believe you will win this battle?' asked Bai Chongxi gently.

Li thought. 'Yes,' he said, looking straight at Bai. 'But it will be very close. The result might go down to the last five minutes. If we do not win, the gates to Wuhan, the gates to China, are open.'

Again he fell into deep thought. Then he fumbled in his breast pocket and pulled out a small photo that he threw on the table. It was of a short unimpressive individual. He looked at it intently. The other two looked at it intently.

'Who is it?' asked Feng.

Li lit another cigarette. 'Rensuke Isogai. Commander in Chief of the General Staff of the Imperial Japanese Army's 10th Division. My opponent. The man climbing into his train and heading south. I have been studying him.'

Li thought.

'A horribly ambitious man. Of course he's an emperor-worshipper. You don't get anywhere in the Imperial Japanese Army without believing that Hirohito is God. But Rensuke Isogai is also a believer in that disgusting English faith – Social Darwinism. The science of racial superiority. Eugenics. The horror of believing all men are descended from apes and animals and that just as with animals, where it is natural for superior species to prey on inferior ones, so it is equally natural, moral even, for a strong race of men to treat all other races as inferior, to be exploited as animals and slaves, killing or sparing them as is convenient.

'General Rensuke Isogai sees us Chinese as animals – to be disposed of like animals. His troops believe similarly. Seven years ago he and they were blooded in the butcheries of Manchuria. They have not stopped since.

'You can of course excuse all this for military reasons. As General Bai just said, Japan has a very small population, so in fighting they must arm themselves with high-technology weapons – tanks, aircraft, poison gas – so that a few men can kill a lot of enemies. The Germans refer to this warfare as "blitzkrieg". Using "blitzkrieg" tactics you can advance very fast, but then, because you have so few men, it is very difficult to hold the ground you have conquered. You need many troops to suppress a large population of armed civilians.

'So you deliberately use the techniques of mass terror to panic the civilian population so everyone flees and chokes up the roads, disrupting your opponent's counter-moves, while all his civilians run out of food and water and famines and diseases break out and millions of people die without you having to kill them. There is indeed some military logic to this. But I do not think, at bottom, that it is for military reasons that General Rensuke Isogai deploys such tactics. I think it is because, at bottom, he enjoys them. Enjoys the killing and the slaughter and the blood. And as such he is an inferior human being. He is, indeed, an animal. Far more an animal than all the Chinese animals he has so carelessly slaughtered. And he is even arrogant enough to believe he is superior to everyone in his own race, the Japanese – except of course his beloved emperor. Because at heart he is an intensely ambitious man. Aren't you?' said Li, leaning forwards and stubbing the photo with his forefinger. 'You are so ambitious.'

And with that Li relaxed and smiled. The other two generals were slightly puzzled at this sudden cheerfulness and peered down at the photograph to see if there was some clue they'd missed. Even the aides ruffled with curiosity.

Li resumed. 'Because it is through your ambition, your arrogance, that we will defeat you, isn't it?'

Li drew lovingly on his latest Craven A, waited a moment, then continued.

'We will win because Rensuke needs so desperately to be the first to break through to Taierzhuang, the first one to win the race to Wuhan, the one to conquer China so he can present it personally to his beloved emperor. He will not wait for his flankers from Linyi and Bengbu to pin us down, surround us to ensure his victory. That would mean he'd have to share the glory. He will rush straight into Taierzhuang because he believes he and his troops are the masters of the master race. And in Taierzhuang we will grip hold of him. And our battle, among these rocks and ruins and tunnels and cellars and trenches, will be terrible. But we will grip him and grip him. And the more we grip that great charging beast the harder he will push in, because he believes he and his men are insuperable, and as we grip him ever harder and our pincer attacks from either flank are cutting off his supply lines and cutting off his escape route and as his troops are dying all around him in terrible, shameful numbers, then perhaps even he will start to think that maybe he should retreat and regroup.

But then he of little intelligence but great ambition will think he cannot give up his battle, he cannot retreat, because for a Japanese general to retreat in the face of Darwinian apes and Chinamen is the ultimate shame and can only lead to his disgrace before the entire Japanese Army and an order to commit hara-kiri. So he will press on against all odds and all hopes and be ground and chewed between these great stone jaws of black granite until he dies.' Li paused. 'Or so I hope. It is our best chance.'

'It is our only chance,' said Feng emphatically.

'Indeed,' agreed Bai.

Tea was served. Li continued to nervously look at his maps. Bai consulted quietly with his aide. Chiang Kai-shek's aide tried to overhear what they were mumbling. Feng beamed tremendously at all about him and congratulated the waiters on the quality of their tea.

His consultation over, Bai clapped his hands and the meeting reconvened.

'Friends,' said Feng, 'thank you so much for inviting me to this extremely instructive meeting. I feel deeply honoured to be here. And I feel heartened by what I have heard. Unfortunately, as you both know, our esteemed leader has ruled that, unlike you, I, wicked socialist that I am, am not to be allowed anywhere near a battlefield. So, while you fight for the very survival of our country, the supreme battle, I must be safely in Wuhan organizing our poor homeless starving people, trying to educate them to fight the Japanese. But be sure, all through this terrible conflict, my heart and my thoughts will be entirely with you.

'Now, I've been allowed here for today only to advise you on urban warfare, close-quarter and night-time fighting. It's very difficult for an under-armed, non-mechanized, poorly organized army such as ours to fight the highly developed weapons and technologies of the Japanese. No one doubts the courage and endurance of our troops. But ageing rifles cannot fight armoured tanks, straw hats are no defence against dive bombers, sandals cannot match boots. What defence is a handkerchief against poison gas? How do we fight back? Bring these bastards to their knees?

'We don't do it the way we've been doing it so far. Our great massed armies standing in ranks awaiting the enemy as Kutuzov awaited Napoleon at Borodino. All they have had to do is soften us up with their long-range artillery and poison gas then bomb us with their dive bombers and finally send their tanks and shock troops hurtling through our shattered, bewildered ranks. Time after time after time they've done that.

'A modern war, a blitzkrieg war, is always fought at a distance. Our troops are defeated before their troops have even arrived on the scene. They rely on speed and shock. We have to nullify both their speed and their shock. Instead of allowing them to defeat us from a distance, we have to at all times be close up to them, as close as possible, to give them no time to build momentum or shock. We must embrace them.

'And that, I see, is exactly what you are preparing in Taierzhuang. As we drove here I saw the trenches being dug, tunnels excavated, each building being fortified, all the tunnels and trenches linking up every building so that you can retreat with speed as the enemy advances and then emerge behind the enemy so he is surrounded. Tanks hate rubble – it breaks their tracks. The more rubble the better. Blow things up. Make use of whatever sewers there are. Take the wooden doors from houses and place them over the top of the trenches so the enemy can't see you moving and you can observe him just by lifting up the door an inch. Tank drivers will not see them and will drive over them –and as they do so, blow them up from underneath. All the time be close to your enemy. Hug him as a friend. If you are within twenty feet of the Japanese then General Rensuke Isogai will not dare bomb you or shell you or gas you because he'll fear he'll hit his own troops as often as he'll hit yours. He cannot afford to lose as many men as we do. Terrible as that calculation is.

'And cuddling close to your enemy, twenty feet between trenches if you can, always remind him of how close you are, of how much you are thinking of him. Sing him merry, happy songs, repeatedly, get a wind-up gramophone and play him endless dance hall numbers, especially at night when he's trying to sleep. Croon along with them. If you have a Japanese speaker listen in on their conversations, then commiserate with them about what a bastard their sergeant is and how they haven't had any food for four days. Eat away at their morale, eat away at their discipline.

'With trenches so close your most effective weapon is the hand grenade. Wait til you hear a lot of voices, then throw several. A good sniper can terrify a whole company of troops. Our troops are already good at hand-to-hand fighting, their natural courage shines through. The Japanese dislike it, they have been trained to fight from a distance. In hand-to-hand trench fighting bayonets are not much use. You need a lot of space to wield them in and you have to pull them back before you can thrust again. I taught my troops how to use broad-bladed sabres. One swing to divert his bayonet thrust, the back swing through his face and neck. And don't forget the hilt. Crown him with it if he's being a nuisance. Or if you're not trained in broad-bladed sabres a sharpened shovel or entrenching tool is just as good. Gouge out an enemy's guts with one dig, then smash the next man's brains out with the next. They become like extensions of your arms. In night fighting you sense your opponent rather than see him.'

The aides were writing fast and wincing occasionally at this information.

Feng stopped and looked around him.

'I could go on and on with this stuff, but it's all largely common sense. Our men will work it out for themselves pretty soon. Just look at what they achieved at the Sihang Warehouse in Shanghai – a few men staving off wave after wave of Japanese for weeks. But if they know this stuff before they go in it will save some of them.'

Feng suddenly looked a bit downcast, but then cheered up.

'I will not be here, but my troops will. My old North-West Army which Chiang took from me in '27, they'll be here, won't they?'

General Li nodded. 'Your old North-West Army, now the Second Army Group. I have ordered them here.'

'And they're still under Sun Lianzhong,' Feng said, 'my number two. I know he has kept them sharp in all these techniques.'

He stopped again. Then resumed.

'This is going to be bloody. Very bloody. As General Li just said, it could come down to the last five minutes, the last five men. My poor men.'

Neither generals nor peasants are ever meant to weep. But General Feng Yuxiang did. But only for a moment.

'Right,' he said. 'I'm finished.'

General Bai thanked them both for attending and stated that he felt this meeting had been extremely useful and had given them a lot to think about. Chairmen of meetings always say this sort of thing at the end of meetings.

Then they walked over to where a table had been laid and where cooks had been preparing a suitably voluptuous banquet.

Before he sat down General Bai laid down his prayer mat facing Mecca and conscientiously performed his midday prayers. He then repeated his personal jihad against the Japanese.

'When the forbidden months are over, kill the polytheists wherever you find them: take them, surround them, and lie in wait everywhere for them. If they repent, perform the prayer, and pay the alms-tax, then let them go their way: for Allah is forgiving, merciful.

'And strive for Allah as you ought to strive. He chose you and made no difficulties for you in religion, it being the religion of your father Abraham. He called you Muslims, both before and in this [book], so that the Messenger might be a witness for you, and so that you might be witnesses to mankind. So perform the prayer, pay the alms-tax, and hold fast to Allah. He is your master, an excellent master, an excellent helper.'

His pieties complete, he and the other two sat down at the table and cheerfully feasted on a sumptuous banquet of pork with many bowls of wine.

As it ended General Feng rose unsteadily to his feet and announced he must be on his way back to Wuhan. 'I have a writer to meet.'

4

As my ferry crosses the river to unload us on the Bund, a cloud of corpses float downstream – there's been a mass execution of pirates upriver. They cluster round our hull like goldfish being fed with bread. We edge through them, the corpses bobbing and rolling against our sides. Their trousers have shamefully been washed away. Bloated, their buttocks stick out from the water, their long hair swirls around them. The stink is awful. Black streams of excrement and corruption flow from both ends of them. We hold our noses as we disembark.

Conditions do not improve!

We've been landed on the section of the Bund which specializes in the coffin and burial trades. Business is booming!

When I first arrived a few weeks ago only a few coffins sat here as their makers hawked for business, singing the praises of their products, banging their sides with their fists to emphasize their robustness and longevity when buried in the earth. But now ahead of us lies a positive mountain range of coffins. Piled ten or twelve high, they tower above us arriving passengers. Death is big business in Wuhan. The dead are laid out on mats before us – we step delicately over them – each one in turn being lifted onto a table to be ritually washed and then dried off and dressed in the garments – expensive or cheap depending on the income or generosity of their relatives – before being placed in their coffins and transported, with their mourners, on funeral barges to the large new cemeteries which have been hastily opened downstream from the city.

Lots of people are making a lot of money out of all this death.

Grave diggers, bargees, professional mourners, entertainers and dancing girls who perform in order to attract large crowds to the funerals, priests, monks, coffin bearers. Side stalls have opened up to sell paper money, funeral food, joss sticks and white banners and clothes for the mourners.

But, of course, the vast majority of people dying in Wuhan do not have the money to afford any such luxuries. Every night the frozen corpses of thousands of nameless refugees and soldiers who died during the day are dragged to the quayside and dropped over the edge to mingle with the bodies of the pirates. May God be with the souls of all the dead.

At last I arrive in the land of the living – I push through solid masses thronging the market stalls: child beggars, some of them hideously mutilated, singing their anthems, hawkers pattering song sheets, newsletters and saucy stories. Witches sell spells – for good or ill – astrologers eternal symmetries amid the material chaos. There are street entertainers and jugglers. But I am looking for one thing in particular. After much searching I finally locate an outdoor puppet show. I cannot resist. My soul needs soothing, just as it needed soothing all those years ago when I was a hungry urchin on the streets of Beijing. I draw close, join the crowd standing silent and rapt in the performance. The final part of China's great legendary epic – the *Romance of the Three Kingdoms*.

The heroic Zhuge Liang, though old and wracked with consumption, is still China's greatest soldier. Passionate about defending civilians from harm and always concerned with the prosperity of his people, he has gradually beaten back his enemy Cao Pi, son of the evil Cao Cao, to the gates of Cao Pi's capital Luoyang. The two armies are drawn up. A desperate Cao Pi has appointed Young Sima as his general. Sima had previously been banished from the kingdom for speaking out against the cruelties of Cao Cao.

Suddenly Zhuge Liang, an old man, spitting blood but still dressed as a dandy, a flamboyant red feather waving from his hat, hobbles forwards and stands alone between the two armies. The audience's breath draws in as one. Then Young Sima picks up a chair and, carrying it, comes forwards alone and offers it to the ancient Zhuge. An adjutant brings forwards a chair for Sima and then returns to the ranks. Between the two armies the two generals sit down on their chairs.

I must admit by this time tears are rolling down my face.

Sima speaks. 'Honoured Zhuge Liang, since I was a boy I have studied all your battles. I know you as a son knows his father. If I were ever to rule a kingdom I would adopt the constitution you wrote for the Kingdom of Chengdu. You are my hero.'

Staunching the blood flowing from his mouth, Zhuge looks full at Sima. 'I serve my emperor. The great emperor of Han. The emperor that your employer Cao Pi overthrew.'

Sima looks at him fully. 'I too serve my emperor,' he replies. 'Cao Pi has inherited the Mandate of Heaven. But before I serve any emperor I serve the people.'

It is of course at this moment, as the two generals stare at each other across the battlefield-to-be, the moment of maximum emotion in the drama, that the puppeteer's children thrust their collection boxes into my face and those of all the rest of the rapt audience. We all swiftly and generously contribute so we can continue with the play.

Zhuge Liang announces the battle will be fought the next day. 'It will be the Battle of Heaven.'

That night, as was his wont, Zhuge Liang stares up at the heavens, trying to discern in their movement what the future holds. Suddenly he realizes that in his passion to guard the Mandate of Heaven, to preserve the Han Dynasty and its justice and prosperity and peacefulness, through his wars he has brought his people to penury and suffering and discord. And at this very second in the heavens he discerns the slightest movement, one tiny star moves one tiny fraction, and in that moment, in that movement, all the alignments of heaven alter, all turns on its head, all is changed.

I suddenly realize I am standing beside a rock. And the rock is speaking. Softly repeating with the puppeteer the tragic lines which Zhuge Liang now speaks.

'I've spent too long studying Heaven. I should have studied the people. I have lost the Mandate of Heaven.'

'Feng,' I say.

The general wipes tears from his eyes. 'I love that bit. I've always loved it. Since I was a kid standing before the stage in our village.'

Zhuge, in excruciating agony, leads his troops into battle the next morning. So great is his brilliance that Young Sima, his opponent, is easily defeated. But at the very moment of his victory Zhuge Liang dies. All the combatants on either side immediately stop fighting in honour of him, China's greatest warrior. The battle is over. But it is the victors, now without their great leader, who withdraw, who disappear from the pages of history. It is the loser, Young Sima, who inherits the earth, the Mandate of Heaven.

As we walk away through the dense crowds we reminisce on our childhood love of street theatre, drum singers – myself on the streets of Beijing, Feng in the fields of Anhui.

'That is what you have to achieve, Lao. That is what you have to get your clever young men from the east producing. Drama and song and propaganda that nails the audience to the floor as they watch it – overwhelms their emotions, sends their minds flying open, rallies them to the cause of China.'

I look at him.

'What's the matter?'

I look at him some more, then confess my doubts about trying to teach people better educated than myself, more lucid, youngsters who are fluent in the complexities and mazes of Marxism.

'Bugger Marxism. You and I have read the Gospels. We know what socialism is about. Keep it simple.'

He pauses.

'Don't let them intimidate you, Lao. Listen, why is our country in this mess? Why have our armies collapsed? Why have we abandoned 90 million of our fellow Chinese north of the Yellow River? Why the callous attitudes of the intellectuals, the wealthy and the middle classes to the deaths of millions and millions of ordinary Chinese yeomen and soldiers? Because of our Confucian culture of class, hierarchy, of deference, of always reaching settlements through discussion, compromise. Talking, talking, talking. Talking ourselves to death – whether it's Marxism or Confucianism – while the wolves surround us and rip our people to shreds. I mean, most Chinese don't even know what China is. They have no sense of us as a country. No patriotism. As you define so concisely in your novels, a Chinaman's only loyalty is to his family.'

'It's not even to that,' I correct him. 'It's to himself. Himself alone.'

'There you are,' responds Feng. 'That is the problem. You must alter that attitude. You must persuade intellectuals and playwrights, journalists and artists, to forget all their fey East Coast theories and pretensions, teach them to know their audiences so they can dig into them, seize them as that puppeteer used a 2,000-year-old story to seize us. Use the plays you and your writers produce to irupt peoples' emotions, wrestle their minds. Show them they actually have minds. Portray for them the future of China and set their souls on fire to reach it.'

I am still looking somewhat sceptical.

'Lao, do not be awed by these upper-class halfwits. It is because of our betters we are in this mess. It is because of their plumb ignorance and arrogance that China is now falling to pieces. I chose you because of your humility, your self-criticism, your humour, your love of simple things and simple people. Your thirst for the truth. You are worth ten of any of them. You have the guile and the patience and the knowledge to wheedle worthwhile things out of them, to lead them, unsuspecting as they might be, to starting to see the world as we see it. To respect and learn from ordinary folk.

'For all your weakness you are a strong man, Lao She. For all their bullshit, they are men of straw.'

A 'strong man' who leaves his family to the mercies of the Japanese? We push on through the crowds.

'I'm meeting a staff officer of mine further up the Bund,' says Feng. 'He's got the list of the names of those East Coasters you are going to teach.'

I fervently pray that a certain Guo Morou is not among their number.

★ ★ ★

Hu Lan-shih, Agnes and a few other volunteers were all working at the dressing station on the Bund. Li Dequan, General Feng's wife, had gone off to get more clean bandages from a warehouse. One soldier after another was lifted onto the tables, treated as best they could, then helped or lifted off.

A fresh one was lifted onto Hu and Agnes's table.

'My name is Chu,' said the soldier. He said it over and over again as he lay on the rough wooden table. 'My name is Chu, my name is Chu.' He'd withdrawn within himself and would not come out. While Agnes disinfected the deep wound in his thigh caused by a shell fragment, the ever-positive Hu tried to divert him with banter – chirruping like a bird, enquiring about his girl, his favourite drink, his home? But even questions about his mother got no response.

'My name is Chu.'

There was nothing they could do for him. Gangrene had set into his wound and his leg. It stank. A thick layer of flies poulticed the wound. Agnes slipped him some spirits to douse the pain and they lifted him gently onto the ground in a space reserved for the dying. He would be dead by nightfall and his body rolled into the Yangtze.

Next on the table was a young soldier with superficial body wounds and a fractured upper arm. Bits of splintered bone stuck out from his arm's punctured flesh. While Hu dressed his body wounds Agnes carefully disinfected the bone punctures in his arm and gently withdrew detached slivers of the bone.

'So who's your girl?' asked Hu.

'How about you?' said the soldier.

'That's my father over there,' said Hu, indicating a large policeman strolling past. 'He wouldn't like you asking questions like that.'

They both laughed.

'I got a girl in Kaifeng,' said the soldier. 'But she's probably forgotten me by now.'

'Easy come, easy go.'

'She had a lovely voice,' said the soldier. 'Like you.'

'Careful,' said Hu merrily, 'or I'll start singing.' They laughed.

Agnes looked up.

'This lad needs the hospital. So they can set his arm properly and ensure infection doesn't get into the wound.'

'Yes,' says Hu, feeling in her pocket. 'I haven't enough for a rickshaw.'

'Same here,' said Agnes. 'Where's Li Dequan?'

'She went off to pick up some sterilized bandages.'

Agnes looked around and saw a rickshaw man resting between rides. She approached him.

'This soldier needs a ride to the hospital.'

'Three coins,' said the man.

'We don't have any money,' said Agnes.

The rickshaw man shrugged. 'No money, no ride.'

'He is a brave soldier,' said Agnes. 'He has been defending all of us, he has been defending you against the Japanese devils.'

The man shrugged again.

Agnes Smedley was a short stuggy American. A childhood spent in poverty in the copper mines of Colorado and a lifetime spent fighting for the underdog had prematurely aged her. Deep lines of fatigue ran across her face but tenacity glowed in her eyes. She believed all poor people were of necessity good people, so, blood all up her arms, bandages in her hand, she set to work on the luckless rickshaw driver. He lasted three minutes. 'All right,' he said, 'all right. I have a few minutes off so I'll take the poor fellow to the hospital. Oh, and by the way, I'll tell my friends about this. If they have a few minutes off they'll probably do the same. Must help our great Chinese heroes!'

Meanwhile Feng's wife Li Dequan had arrived back, put the disinfected bandages on a side table and, fag in mouth, threw a bucket of disinfectant over the bloody table. Hu scrubbed it down. The next patient lifted himself on. While treating the soldier's affliction – venereal disease – Li and Hu started chatting, and Li asked Hu about how she'd got to Wuhan. Hu explained she'd worked in the Shen Xin Number 9 Cotton Mill in Shanghai until the Japanese bombed it. This was at the time of the famous Defence of the Sihang Warehouse in Shanghai, where a few heroic Chinese soldiers had held off the all-conquering Japanese for several weeks. A lone Girl Guide, Yang Huimin, by her own initiative, had smuggled food and ammunition in to them. Patriotic feelings were running high in Shanghai. So, as their mill blazed behind them, the surviving girls held a meeting in the street. This, explained Hu, was the first time she had ever been part of an open democratic meeting. There they were, standing in the middle of the street, talking about whatever they wanted to talk about, with no fear of the secret police, gangsters, or the company's goons. It was *so* enjoyable. Released such powerful feelings within her. The girls decided it was their patriotic duty to do all they could to help the retreating soldiers.

Different groups of girls attached themselves to different regiments. They cooked for them, they learnt first aid to treat the wounded – the Chinese Army provided no medical facilities for their troops – and in the evenings they sang and danced to cheer the men up. Often, when disputes broke out between soldiers and civilians over the army requisitioning food and supplies, the girls intervened and would act as conciliators so that a deal could be arrived at before violence became necessary. They became robust and jolly and their pale skin blossomed.

Li Dequan became fascinated by Hu as they worked on their patients. Her spirit, her enthusiasm. How the girls worked with each other and with the soldiers. She heard Hu's awed descriptions of the beauty of the countryside (which she had not seen since she was a little girl), the solemn wonder of the guardian mountains they marched amid, all the different peoples and cultures they'd met – things she, working in her mill fourteen hours a day, seven days a week, had never known even existed.

'It was as though,' said Hu, 'I suddenly understood what my country was.'

Li Dequan was about to respond when Agnes returned triumphant from the converted rickshaw driver and General Feng and Lao She arrived. Feng gently carried the soldier with the shattered arm to the rickshaw, clapped the rickshaw driver on the back in a comradely fashion, and, with Lao She's struggling help, lifted the next patient, a huge sergeant with a badly burnt leg, onto the table.

Meanwhile Li Dequan had drawn Agnes to one side and was talking in an animated fashion to her. As they talked they frequently looked over their shoulders at young Hu, who was busy examining the sergeant's painful burns. Seeing his wife and Agnes might be some time, Feng joined Hu at the table to examine the patient. Feng, from his years on the battlefield, knew a lot about tending and binding wounds. They decided to smear the sergeant's burns with ointment, then apply a poultice held firmly in place with bandages.

Amid all this earnest busyness Lao She was at a bit of a loose end. It had started to snow, so he helped erect an awning over the dressing tables to give patients and those helping them some shelter, but then he just stood there. Beside him stood a large stern-looking country girl with a shopping basket. He'd noticed that as she approached she walked with a peculiar gait. The two of them stood there watching all this rather morbid activity, the country girl with some relish. Lao wondered if he should talk to her but her manner put him off. Feng, noticing Lao's inactivity, told him to start rolling up the disinfected bandages Li had brought. Lao did this and pretty soon also found himself helping Feng to heave the wounded on and off the table and hold them down, writhing and screaming, as Hu's deft fingers removed shards of shrapnel or bullets from their bodies.

Lao She found all this gruesomeness strangely relieving. It took his mind off what he was really dreading – reading the names of the East Coast writers and playwrights he'd be teaching tomorrow. He knew that Feng's staff officer was due to arrive any moment, carrying their names. He'd decided that he could endure anyone except one individual: China's most feted intellectual, most Han-accented Marxist – Guo Morou. He threw himself with enthusiasm into dabbing a gangrened stomach with disinfectant.

Agnes and Li's private conference broke up. They returned to the table. As they did the country girl waddled up to Agnes.

'Change of plan,' said Agnes to her. 'We're going to have guests tonight. Two special guests.' Li Dequan passed Agnes some money, which Agnes handed to the girl. 'So you'll have to buy some quality food and cook it well.'

'I will,' replied the girl.

Spider Girl waddled off through the snow – it was only a shower – to do her shopping.

Almost immediately Feng's adjutant arrived accompanied by two medical orderlies who were to relieve Agnes and Hu. The adjutant handed an envelope to Feng. Lao washed and dried his hands and Feng handed him the envelope and winked. 'Give them hell.' Lao looked at it gingerly and tucked it swiftly into his jacket pocket. He wished everyone a quick farewell and trudged off through the snow.

Having made my escape I walk along the Bund towards my ferry. It is the Chinese New Year. A very peculiar New Year, in fact, especially in Wuhan. Probably through most of China.

Central to our New Year celebrations are visits to the graves of our ancestors. Feasting, toasting their lives, thanking them for their achievements, filling them in with the latest events in our own lives (about which they are invariably curious), showing them reverence. The only problem this year is that large numbers, perhaps a majority of us Chinese, cannot visit and honour our ancestors' graves. Due to the Japanese invasion many, many of us can no longer access them. Frequently they are hundreds, if not thousands of miles away. Like myself.

The native inhabitants of Wuhan can still visit their family graves and pay them reverence, raucously celebrate their lives with fireworks and drinking and feasting – and that is going on all around us – but many of us here, have no graves we can visit, no ancestors we can chat with and ask advice from. We are adrift and lost from them. We feel that we should celebrate, but the more we feel that emotion the more we realize how and why we cannot.

Suddenly I am hit full in the face by a snowball.! A group of young children, celebrating the New Year in their own particular way, have decided to pelt me with snowballs. Outrageous! I lean down and, fashioning a snowball of my own, pelt it in their direction. This somewhat one-sided fight lasts for a short while, til their attention diverts to a Mongol on a camel and I slip away, wiping the snow from my glasses.

This has greatly raised my spirits. A bit of New Year's cheer. In fact, I decide, I am actually up enough to reading this list of my students to be. I stop, remove the envelope from my pocket, breathe in, open the envelope, hesitate, then unfold the paper, read it, breathe out. Well, at least Guo Morou isn't on it!!! But the others! Tian Boqi – fanatic Han-Marxist playwright, from the very finest American schools and universities, whose plays and diatribes are lionized by intellectuals from Shanghai to Nanking to New York. One of his plays, I am told, was even performed before soldiers of the Communist Eighth Route Army in Yan'an. Apparently it only survived one performance. Then there's Comrades Zou Feng and Chu Taofen, Moscow-trained theorists famed for the length and impenetrability of their writings. A wild anarchist called Yu Yong. A woman poet, Shan Shuang – again a doyenne of Beijing's intellectual coteries. Some I've never heard of. And Chang Lee – who I've heard of somewhere or other, but I can't remember where.

I stand on the Bund. I wipe the snow off my cap. I look up to see I'm standing right next to a long line of floating brothels – converted from barges and moored to the quay. Foreign sailors, Chinese sailors, foreign businessmen, Chinese businessmen line up in the snow (which is already starting to melt), patiently awaiting their turn. The brothels rock gently in the water. Against their steel hulls roll and rub the corpses of the executed pirates while, a few inches of steel away, live bodies writhe and frenzy in the joys of procreation. Such is war.

Suddenly, crashing his way up one of the gangways, pushing clients and security guards into the water, comes a colossal Scottish seaman, roaring drunk and red hair flying, screaming obscenities to all and sundry through his few remaining teeth. He is finally suppressed by seven Chinese mountains and several of his own shipmates. After a certain amount of slipping and sliding on the snow everyone sits on top of him and cheers – including the sailor. What a fellow! I find him deeply inspiring. What I need to do with all my posh-boy Marxists is not to retreat, apologize, but attack, attack. Just like him. And I have just the person to help me.

A man who loves intellectual punch-ups and salty language. The Hebei peasant and noted playwright, Lao Xiang. I must invite him to our classes. He'll relish it. Then, after half an hour of intellectual brawling between peasant and toffs, I'll step in between the two as the voice of moderation...

Allowing myself some modest skips (and slips), I hurry back to the ferry.

Agnes and Hu and Li Dequan were walking in the opposite direction, towards Agnes and Hu's apartment. Feng had disappeared off on some errand – probably to haggle with timber merchants to provide cheaper wood for all the homes he was building.

Li was explaining to Hu this idea she'd had. She'd been greatly impressed by what Hu had told her about her long trek with the soldiers from Shanghai. About what she and the other girls had done. There was someone she really wanted Hu to meet as she thought she would be really interested to hear Hu's story. Would Hu mind if she and this person came to supper this evening at her and Agnes's apartment and Hu told her her story?

Hu stared at her. Then laughed.

'Of course I don't mind,' she said. Then she shrugged.

'Why do you shrug?' asked Agnes.

'It's just I don't like talking about myself,' replied Hu, blushing.

Spider Girl was walking behind them. Spider Girl was finding it quite hard to live in a city. It wasn't that she was unhappy with her employers – Agnes and Hu were good people and they turned a blind eye provided she didn't steal anything too outrageous.

It was the city itself which made her feel uneasy. She didn't understand it. In her village there wasn't anyone she didn't know. In Wuhan there wasn't anyone she *did* know. When she passed someone in her village she knew all their past story, and pretty much all their future story. You just had to look at their faces to see which particular part of their story they were presently in. But here in a city every face was blank. It had no past, it had no future. Where did all these strange people come from? Endless streams of them? What did they all do? You walked down a street and all these people you'd never seen before and would never see again kept coming straight at you, streaming past you, never looking you once in the face. Where did they come from? How did they make a living? In her village everyone did something – all the time! It's how people stayed alive. But In Wuhan no one except for the stall holders and coolies ever seemed to be doing anything. Just walking round and round in circles.

Spider Girl was of course suffering from that fashionable modern urban condition – alienation. Not that she would have the least idea what such a concept either meant or involved. As far as she was concerned, she was just out of sorts.

The three of them, all lost in their own thoughts, walked through a squirl of screaming children ferociously hunting down an even smaller child who'd somehow managed to steal a rice cake. He was desperately trying to stuff it down his throat before they caught him and robbed him of it.

5

Spider Girl was in a bit of a bait. She cooked what she cooked, which was what she and her family had always cooked. And Agnes and Hu had never made any complaint. But now Agnes had told her to cook what she and her family would eat on a feast day, on the day of the village festival. Well, that would be pork. But the pig which the butcher was slaughtering as she approached his stall looked all wrong. It was pink and naked; their pigs had always been brown and hairy. What was more, the meat smelt different to the pork of their family pig. The butcher said rudely that his pork was the finest in Wuhan. She'd been round all the other meat stalls and his meat was definitely the most expensive. Which meant that people were prepared to pay more for his meat – after haggling – than for anyone else's. Which meant, she reasoned, his really must be best.

So she brought streaky pork from him with a wedge of fat – my how her family had ladled in the fat when it came to a feast! – then went on to buy greens for the pork soup and rice and vegetables for the other dishes.

Not only was the strange pork a problem, but the Wei family had rarely eaten rice. Wheat and dumplings were their staple, but they had occasionally had rice on feast days. Like today, the final day of the Chinese New Year. Spider Girl knew rice was considered more 'refined', but had little experience in cooking it. To show her frustration she loudly banged her pots and pans as she cooked and cussed out The Drab she'd hired to help her about the house. The Drab was cutting the vegetables.

Agnes ignored all this pantomime and withdrew to her

bedroom to write her weekly article for the *Manchester Guardian*. She was writing eloquently and bluntly about the medical and refugee crisis facing China and the desperate need for charities and the British government to send aid to Wuhan. Hu sat in her room praying and composing herself for the ordeal of having to talk about herself. Li Dequan had walked to the wealthier Chinese section of Wuhan to escort their guest, Shi Liang, to the apartment.

Shi Liang was noted for her ferocity. From a wealthy background, she'd been the first women ever to graduate from China's most prestigious law school. By the mid 1930s she had fought her way to the top of the Shanghai legal profession. In 1936 she was sent to jail with six male colleagues for publicly criticizing Chiang Kai-shek's craven policy of appeasement towards the Japanese. The government, embarrassed to admit that a woman dared to behave in such an aggressive fashion, dismissed the whole event as the 'Seven Gentlemen Incident'. It was even more embarrassing because Shi was close friends with Chiang Kai-shek's formidable wife Soong Meiling, with Soong Meiling's formidable sister Soong Chingling (the widow of Sun Yatsen, the leader of the 1911 Revolution), and with Soong Meiling's other formidable sister, Soong Ailing, who had married China's richest banker. The three Soong sisters were the most powerful women in China. Shi Liang knew all about networking!

Shi and Li Dequan entered the run-down apartment. Shi immediately looked round the room and then toured it, viewing the furniture and decorations with the concentration of a general inspecting the cleanliness of a barracks. Petite, square-jawed and with glasses, Shi radiated intellectual power and determination. She stared at Spider Girl, Spider Girl stared back at her.

Spider Girl vowed that she would spit in her soup.

Shi and Li Dequan sat down at the table and continued the conversation they'd been having in the street.

'The problem,' said Li, 'is that while Feng and I have successfully set up one large reception camp in Wuhan for the refugees and are busy building two more, upriver in Chungking, where all the refugees are eventually going to end up, the whole process of preparation is taking far too long. Here in Wuhan we're allowing the different groups on their different streets three or four weeks to get to know each other, learn to cohere and cooperate as a community, before ferrying them upstream to Chungking. With the fertile soil of Sichuan and Yunnan the groups from farming backgrounds should be able to produce crops within months. Those used to manufacturing and cities should have their new housing and factories ready so they can immediately start work. We should have been sending groups upstream already – so their houses here in Wuhan can be taken by fresh refugees – but we can't, because no preparation is being undertaken upstream. Feng and I have no influence over the officials and businessmen in Chungking.'

'You need political muscle and finance,' said Shi the fixer. 'Tomorrow morning I'll speak to Soong Meiling about the politics and Soong Ailing about the finance – put a bit of snap into the process.'

Li Dequan smiled gratefully.

At this moment Hu made a somewhat tenuous appearance. Li introduced her to Shi, who gave her a matter-of-fact once-over, turned her back on her and sat down. Li sat down. Hu, as a Shanghai mill girl unused to the more advanced theologies of table manners, hesitated, then sat down too. Li Dequan explained to Hu that Li was a lawyer from Shanghai. Hu glanced at Li sharply. On the few occasions the workers had managed to organize a strike in their mill to improve their appalling working conditions, the bosses had first sent in lawyers to intimidate them with threats of long prison terms, and then, if that failed, gangsters and goons. But only for a second did the polite and exquisite Hu allow her frown to linger before resuming her modest smile.

Agnes, article finished and despatched by a runner, brought in some wine and sat down with them. The conversation became general – the war, the political situation in Wuhan and events abroad. Spider Girl served the food. Shi Liang seemed unaware that Spider Girl had spat in her soup. None of them seemed to find the pork offensive. But Spider Girl did detect one flicker of disapproval from Shi as she tasted her rice. As was usual for a girl from her province Spider Girl had stirred the cooked rice into the lard she had rendered down from the pork fat. It gave a lovely greasy feel to it. Just right after a freezing day's work in the fields! Li Dequan, herself a peasant, ate it with much smacking of lips and appreciative burps. Agnes was indifferent to all food. But Shi Liang, from a refined East Coast family, had only ever tasted rice whisked briefly in the subtlest of oils. For one second her lips moued in distaste. Spider Girl noted this and stored it up for future bile.

The meal over conversation turned to the matter of the evening. Li Dequan briefly explained to Shi the story of Hu's journey from Shanghai to Wuhan. How it might give Shi some solutions to the problems they were wrestling with in high government committees. Hu wondered aloud how her journey from Shanghai to Wuhan could in any way interest or be of use to 'high government committees'.

Li Dequan turned to her.

'Dear Hu, let me explain. Our country is in a very difficult position. Not only because of the Japanese invasion, but because our ruling class, our ruling elite, know nothing whatsoever about the people they rule. Isn't that true, Shi Liang?'

'It is.'

'Until now they've totally and cruelly ignored us. Suddenly, in order to unite us all against the Japanese barbarians and organize us to fight them, they are forced to discover who we are, how we think, how we behave, how they should speak to us. The story you told me shows how well us ordinary Chinese can improvise, organize ourselves, how we are shrewd, resourceful, responsible, moral people. How, if we are to survive, our government must come to trust us rather than fear us, free us, give us control rather than repress us. Shi Liang has an important role in government. She wants to hear your story.'

Hu blushed.

'Your story,' stated Shi bluntly, as if she was addressing the High Court in Shanghai.

'Well,' said Hu, and started slowly and awkwardly. She told of the burning mill – but didn't tell of the misery its owners had inflicted on its workforce. She spoke of the defence of the Sihang

Warehouse and the little Girl Guide Yang Huimin. Then she told of the meeting in the street as their place of work burnt behind them, the girls' common decision to dedicate themselves to supporting their soldiers, and gradually, as she spoke, as she remembered her fellow workers, the taxi girls and common prostitutes and mothers who had lost all their families gathering in the street, starting to march with the soldiers and speak to them and help them, it was as though she was again surrounded by them, all their familiar faces and old jokes and common resolutions, and they started to lift her, her spirits, and her face lit up and she started to enjoy her storytelling.

'Once,' she said, giggling at the others in the room (being a pious Methodist, she hadn't drunk a drop of wine), 'we were all running short of food and supplies, and the enemy were close behind us. It was so funny. We had stopped in this village for the night but had no money. The soldiers said we didn't have time to explain to the villagers that they should share their food and supplies – the enemy was too close. We'd just have to seize it, violently if they fought back. We saw that the soldiers and the village elders were just shouting at each other. So we girls had an idea. It was so funny.

'The enemy was on the other side of the valley – where all the village's fields were. It was autumn, so all the crops were in the field ready to harvest. Potatoes, onions, beetroot. If we wanted to get sufficient food to feed us and the villagers that night, silent as ghosts we'd have to sneak through the enemy's lines – girls, soldiers, farmers – and gather the crops. It was an ordinary woman, an intelligent whore, who came up with this idea. Whoever would have thought a whore could be so intelligent? Anyhow, we did it. I've never been so terrified in my life.' Hu suddenly giggled. 'Creeping through the grass, passing the hut in which all the Japanese were drinking, then, in the moonlight, hugging the ground, all of us stuffing the food into our sacks, our rucksacks, our mouths and bags and pockets. On the way back we were passing through the stream again and suddenly this fat farmer loshed face first into the water. A gurt splash. We froze. The door to the hut crashed open. All these drunken soldiers poured out. I peed myself. They shook their fists and shot into the dark – they couldn't see us – then they started singing this nasty song and, laughing, falling back into the hut. It was terrifying. One of our soldiers said if they'd still had any grenades he'd have thrown one into the hut. We returned to the village alive, divided up the food. We warned the villagers they should leave, and some of them did. Eating our food, we continued our march. And all that was the result of an intelligent whore having an idea and people listening to it.'

Hu paused, thinking. There was a glow to her.

'And the wonder of nature, which I had never seen before. The hum of the bees on the flowers, the chatter of the birds in the branches, the cows yielding milk, the raw beauty of the mountains. And everywhere the children singing like bells.'

Spider Girl stared at her, her face, as Hu relived all the moments of her march. And Spider Girl could not help but compare it with the nightmare and annihilation of her own family's march.

Hu looked about her. Were they even listening to her? Shi Liang was staring ahead impassively. Agnes had sloped off to write an article for *The Nation*. But Li was watching Hu intently. She smiled reassuringly to her. Hu continued.

'We reached this place where the Chinese had prepared lines, trenches, emplacements, to stop the Japanese advancing any further. Lots of troops were manning this front across several miles. Our group of soldiers were ordered to deploy in the centre of the line – which they did. We girls retreated a few miles to a village. We put on some small plays for the children. We dressed some wounds. The villagers were very friendly. Then suddenly this soldier of ours came running back. He told us all the soldiers we'd been with were deserting. Said they far preferred being with us than fighting. That their desertion had immediately put all the other Chinese troops in danger because the Japanese could break through where they had run away. We at once held a meeting about this. We could shame them and shout at them, call them chickens and cowards. But instead we decided to use our feminine wiles and charms to get them back to the front.

'The troops started to arrive. We were ready for them. We'd

laid out tables in the village street. Banners. "Welcome to our victorious troops!" Two of us were playing instruments. Some of the taxi girls danced. We even had some weak wine. We invited them to sit down, congratulated them on their great victory, their courage. Said how proud we were of them. They were a bit awkward. How proud their mothers at home would be of their brave sons. We pointed out some children playing in the street. Said how safe they would be now. They started to get very nervous. Then one of them blurted it out. "We ran away," he said. "We left all those other troops there." A few voices among the soldiers cried it was the right thing to do, being with girls was much more fun. But most of them were silent.

'"Do you want some food?" asked the intelligent whore. "We've cooked some chicken and noodles." Suddenly the soldiers weren't hungry. Soldiers are always hungry! A taxi girl asked one to dance. He wouldn't.

'"Look," Intelligent Whore said, "we like you very much, you are our friends and some of us are your lovers. We will be here supporting you wherever you are. But if you feel you should be back at the front, fighting beside your fellow soldiers against the Japanese, then that is your decision and your decision alone, and we will completely support you, because we admire you and we will always be here to help you."

'With that there was no stopping our brave lads. We all drank a toast with the weak wine to a new China and then they all marched back to the front with us cheering them.

'Then we had a good cry – because we realized many of them would not return. Which they didn't.'

There was silence.

Ignoring Hu, Shi Liang looked directly at Li Dequan.

'I can see your point. This girl's stories demonstrate the intelligence and resilience of the Chinese lower classes. How they should be trusted. And if the poor show patriotism, maybe the rich will be shamed into it too. It's a clever tactic. One we must utilize if we are ever to produce a united front against the Japanese.

'Tomorrow I have this large fundraiser at Wuhan's city hall. Many important wives of influential men will be there who I must persuade to donate large sums of money. Mainly for your work with children, Li – especially orphans – but also to start feeding large sums to charities promoting co-ops, farms, manufacturing. It is progressive. Wives must be got to work on their husbands. The money must flow. I want this girl to speak to these women. Tell them her stories so the women can get an inspiring glimpse into the lives of people they don't know. People they don't trust. It will loosen their purse strings. Maybe even get them working in charities.'

Hu sharply drew in her breath. Shi Liang turned to her and matter-of-factly continued, 'I couldn't help noticing that when Li introduced me as a "Shanghai lawyer", you seemed momentarily ill at ease.'

Hu blushed at her own bad manners.

'It is doubtless very difficult for you to be in the company of people who you think, rightly or wrongly, have caused you so much pain and suffering at your workplace and in your life. But it is your duty, as a Chinese citizen, as a patriot, to put all this to one side and persuade influential people – people who are quite possibly responsible for your own personal suffering – to join the common fight.'

Hu, through good manners, fought the rising anger within herself at the insufferable arrogance of this woman. She must not behave badly! But her anger would not let her respond to Shi's brute request.

'I am a patriot,' Li told Hu. 'So are you.'

Again, a silence.

'Hu,' said Li Dequan gently, 'your story is inspiring. You must retell it tomorrow to these women.'

'I agree,' added Agnes, who'd been listening in from the next room.

There was a long silence.

'You've got to do it, Hu,' said Spider Girl, always the sad realist, 'you have to do it on behalf of all of us who have died.'

Hu assented.

Spider Girl cuffed The Drab just to relieve her feelings then swore to herself that if Li Shiang ever came again she'd spit into her soup three times and hire a proper witch to cast some evil spells on her too.

After the rest had left or gone to bed Spider Girl stayed up with Hu to soothe her feelings. They said some pretty rude things about Shi and rich people in general, but then they started to tell each other stories about their native villages, and Hu laughed a lot. She finally went to bed. Spider Girl alone stayed up.

As the fireworks and laughter filtered upwards from the streets below, where the citizens of Wuhan celebrated their ancestors and the New Year, Spider Girl stood alone in the silent kitchen, memorializing the events of the past year, thinking of her own family. Only two were still alive. Even if she could talk to her ancestors in their graves – she could not, because she was a thousand miles from them – she reflected sadly that they would not want to speak to either her father or her – the two family members who had destroyed the family. She shook with grief. She prayed for her father and his safety. And as she prayed she clung tightly to the small stone bottle which contained the last of her family's wild pear juice.

6

It is a truth rarely acknowledged that writers, all in all, hate each other. A writer only has to hear the most ghostly of rumours of the possible success of another writer for him or her to instinctively and deeply loathe them. This is the plain truth. And yet I, a novelist, am about to proceed into a room full of other writers, mostly playwrights, in order to instruct them on how they must write plays. Am I suicidal?

Myself and my script-writing comrade Lao Xiang walk down the corridor towards the classroom. My legs feel as if they're made of India rubber, I walk like Olive Oyl. Lao Xiang, arms akimbo, is spoiling for a fight.

All through last night my wife's spirit was stalking me. Relentlessly. Again and again she questioned, doubted my motives, rehearsed to me my moral, my human duties as a teacher. 'What is the purpose of teaching, husband? How do you teach your pupils, husband? Is the purpose of teaching to start an argument so you can end up punching each other? Is that good? Is that progressive? Or do you run away from them and cry? No! You do neither! What you do is watch them. Not because you wish to study how to overthrow them, teaching is not war, you watch them because you wish to understand them so you can help them, and in helping them you can steer them towards what is best in them, towards doing good things. It is your function to foster, not annihilate. What other possible motive could you have for teaching?'

With that question from my ever-powerful wife, I grind to a halt. The door to my classroom is right in front of me. I reflect for a few seconds. I turn to Lao Xiang.

'Dear friend,' I state, 'I have reached a decision. I am grateful for all your support and your goodness and agreement to accompany me into this lion's den. But I have decided that I alone must enter, I alone must teach my class.'

My friend disagrees with me.

'Not fucking likely. I'm with you all the way. Fighting those upper-class cunts.'

'Lao Xiang,' I say, 'thank you, but I have decided I must fight my own battles.'

'I could stay outside, in the corridor, just in case there's a barney.'

'There will be no barney, dear friend. I will find a way through. That is what I am being employed to do.'

'Good luck, brother,' he says. 'Fry them in hell.'

With that he turns and marches back down the corridor. Probably secretly relieved, I think, because he's on a deadline with at least two scripts.

I face the door. I walk through the door. I am greeted with a wall of indifference.

I march to my desk.

'Good morning,' I say, 'welcome to the Playwright's Workshop.'

I smile and place my papers on the table. I look at my class.

'And how are you today?'

Some stare out of the window. Others talk languidly among themselves, slouched in their chairs. One individual, large and muscular, sits alone in the front row, glaring up at me, his arms folded in a most aggressive manner. I believe that I am staring at Tian Boqi, the East Coast's most lauded Marxist-Leninist playwright. He wrote a venomous review of my recent novel *Rickshaw Boy*. I give him a quick, nervous smile, turn to my notes, start to speak.

I give them my usual talk. That 97 per cent of our people are illiterate. That therefore speech has to be the medium through which we communicate with them. That there are thousands of different dialects across China, most of which are mutually incomprehensible to each other. That our drama must therefore speak to them through simple actions and universal emotions and images to which they will all instinctively respond. That the natural and practical way of doing this is to adopt the traditional forms of drama and storytelling with which they are all familiar and which they all love – puppet theatre, drum singing, festival plays. New wine in old bottles.

'Of course,' I add, 'we must adapt these legends and characters to contemporary events. Liu Bei needs to become our leader General Chiang Kai-shek' – this is greeted with a few derisory snorts which I ignore (though I agree with them) – 'and the evil Cao Cao could be easily mutated into the Emperor Hirohito.'

Tian Boqi continues his basilisk stare at me. I breathe in. As I do a rather ferrety young man, Chu Taofen, slides into the conversation.

'What you say, Comrade Lao, is indeed most interesting. But erroneous. The Chinese proletariat have been deliberately chained for centuries in feudal repression and ignorance, their minds corrupted by precisely these ancient and reactionary fairy tales of handsome princes and beautiful princesses. The Chinese ruling classes have deliberately imposed these superstitious fantasies upon the masses. They must be abolished, swept away so the masses can break their chains and march forwards into the daylight using the clean, logical language and thought processes of Marxist dialectics.'

I'm about to counter that many of these stories and folk tales, far from being fantastical and escapist, speak directly and powerfully to the reality of everyday life – but before I can another bespectacled young man, Zou Feng, glides into the conversation. Tian Boqi gives me a malicious grin.

'Comrade Chu,' Zou says, addressing the young man who has just spoken, 'I think there are certain revisionist errors in what you have been stating about language. Was it not Chairman Stalin himself who recently stated categorically that language has no part in either the base or the superstructure of dialectical materialism? The base of factories and fields and railway engines: the means of production. The superstructure upon it, of people and beliefs and the arts and newspapers and the law. Neither, the Chairman states, bears any relation to the phenomenon of language. Therefore, he states, language inhabits a sort of meta-totemic vacuum entirely outside the whole base/superstructure continuum. It neither of itself produces nor consumes anything. He states irrefutably it is an intermediate phenomenon.'

He turns to face me directly.

'Do you agree with me, Comrade Lao?'

Comrade Lao has not understood a word he has spoken. Before I can think of any words to fill my vacuum his fellow tag-wrestler, Chu Taofen, leaps back into the ring.

'But, Comrade Zou, if within the revolutionary dialectic one goes back even further than Chairman Stalin, to 1918, one discovers Chairman Lenin himself stating unequivocally, when challenged by Comrade Klara Zetkin, that all cultural forms and artistic expressions and language within a socialist state must never be allowed to develop in a chaotic or anarchistic fashion. An individual can never become spontaneously liberated by art. Art, he states, is petit bourgeois deviationism – no more, no less. Therefore a truly revolutionary consciousness can only be forged within the norms and disciplines of strictly controlled Marxist-Leninist structure. Only through such a dialectic can individuals and cultural institutions come to fulfill their true revolutionary potential in the construction among the masses of a true socialist consciousness.'

Before I can intervene Comrade Zou leaps back in.

'Of course, Comrade Chu, but is not your emphasis upon the individual artist in itself a petit bourgeois deviation? It is a fundamental flaw in bourgeois reasoning to constantly present dialectical materialism as an inflexible, impenetrable dogma when in fact it constantly reacts to and readjusts itself within the purposive, ever-changing modalities of materialist existence. Is that not so?'

What are they rabbiting on about? I feel as though I am drowning in a vat of overcooked noodles. Where do I even start to find a handhold on this conversation?

'On the contrary, Comrade Zou,' purrs Comrade Chu, 'in Marxist dialectic are there in fact any insurmountable historical tendencies which serve as starting points as well as obligatory limits to the purposive activity of individuals and social groups within cultural and artistic matrices while those constructs are outside the rational discipline of revolutionary modalities?'

Before anything more can be said on this subject – whatever this subject is – I hastily move in to quell it, using the language of baffled chairmen throughout the ages.

'Thank you,' I say, 'thank you both very much for your really interesting contributions. You've given us all, I'm sure, a lot of food for thought, but I think it's time for us to move on and hear from some other voices in the room.'

Several Marxists speak in varying degrees of comprehensibility. Then an agitated young anarchist speaks his ideas. They are unusual.

'On the question of languages, I believe we should abolish them all. Yes. Every single language all around the world should be abolished. And they should all be superseded by one mathematically based utilitarian system of communication in which every single written word is replaced by a number and every spoken word replaced by electronic squeaks and grunts. True revolutionary consciousness, yes, can only be synthesized when all traditional modes of discourse and communication have been abolished and replaced by cacophony which in turn, yes, will shock the sensibilities of the whole world population into revolutionary new modes of discourse as yet unthought of.'

I must say, as I listen to him, I'm greatly drawn to the comic potential of his idea. I could use it as the basis for a short story – not, of course, that I still write short stories. As he goes on I manage to keep a straight face. As my wife says, I must first understand my pupils before I can teach them.

'Have you written anything in this new language?' I ask.

'No, er, it's all theoretical at the moment.'

'Complete and utter bollocks,' pronounces Tian Boqi in the front row. A chorus of Marxists echo 'Hear hear'.

Throughout this class there's one young face that has not been scowling or ignoring me. He's smiled steadily. Delicate featured with lively eyes, he's followed all the various discussions. I ask him to contribute.

'Hello,' he says, 'my name is Chang Lee. I'm from Nanking. I've been listening to everyone with great interest. I hope you'll all forgive me for not adding to the theoretical debate, but I wish to explain to you what I intend to write about, and why I want to write it.' He blushes briefly. 'I had a very sheltered upbringing in Nanking. As a boy I was very sickly, so I had to stay indoors with my mother and nurses. I had tutors brought in for my education. I wrote some poems and little plays which people were kind enough to publish and I did attend the performance of one of my plays.' He blushed again. 'Anyhow, enough about me.

When this present war broke out and the Japanese invaded, I like everyone was greatly perturbed. Out of the window I saw all these soldiers and civilians pouring past, fleeing, and I saw how poor and ragged most of them were. So when it came time for us to leave – my mother had booked a suite for our household on a steamer coming upriver to Wuhan – I, for the first time, stood out against her. "No," I said, "I will not go with you, I am going to walk to Wuhan with all the poor people. I want to be with them. Experience what they experience." Mummy was really angry. She pointed out that I was far too ill to walk all that way. But I insisted. So I joined the march, with a servant to accompany me.'

This provokes a ripple of guffaws – which he ignores.

'It was very difficult to start with. I was not used to walking any distance. The people were strange. The food was strange. My slippers soon wore out and my servant had to buy me some boots. Which hurt my feet for a while. But soon I got used to the boots and the food. I learnt how to talk with all the different people on the march. I must say I started to really enjoy myself. And the country people's clothes were so colourful. I had never experienced the beautiful sights of the countryside, the smells of flowers, the sounds of country birds, the clouds in the skies.'

Smothered laughs break out around the class. He remains totally indifferent to them.

'I had never seen anything so beautiful. So inspiring. People were so friendly. I got to know quite a few of them. I must have been quite strange to most ordinary people, but they did not hold it against me. Due to them I even developed a sense of humour. And then we got into those mountains. Those ice-cold, unmoving, almighty mountains – their sublimity, their magnificence...

'The thing is,' he said, 'I am bursting with poetry. I want to go out to all of China, to every village and hamlet and railway station and wayside inn, and I wish to recite all my poetry to them, about the beauty of their country, my country, and by doing this so fill them with inspiration and joy that they rush out and pick up arms and go off to fight the Japanese. That is what I intend to do,' he ended triumphantly.

I blink, desperately trying to suppress all images of what would happen to this youthful Shelley if he ever dared stand on a village stage to recite his poetry. But I am here to listen, not criticize. I am here to make bricks – even if I have no straw.

There is only one woman in the class. She is dressed in severe clothing with a severe haircut and severe glasses. She's been staring fixedly out of the window. In the spirit of feminist fraternity I ask her to speak next.

She turns from her window, stands up, matter-of-factly marches up to the front of the class and faces us.

'Shan Shuang. Poet. Revolutionary poet. Write revolutionary poems. Will recite two to you.'

She does.

'Poem One. "To a Lady who Rejects a Poem about Spring as a Petit Bourgeois Deviation".'

Having announced the title she scowls at Chang Lee. He smiles obliviously back at her.

'So here's my hat into the air.
Three cheers for your amazing hair,
For coal mines, and for turbines too,
For steel, the Comintern, and you!'

This causes riotous applause, led by a beaming Chang Lee.
She sets herself for Poem Two.

'Lines Disassociating Myself from Yesenin and Opposing the
    Unfounded Legend that I am a Foremost Proletarian Writer.
Goodbye verses of Yesenin
Goodbye literary slop –
You are not the line of Lenin
You are not the line of WAPP.
Never shall I moan a
simple lyric from the heart
I'll devote my new corona
to the proletarian art!'[1]

Once again Chang Lee leads the riotous applause. Shan Shuang glares at him and returns to her seat.

Which leaves only one person in the room who has not spoken. The young, muscular Tian Boqi, with the basilisk stare. With some trepidation I ask him to speak. He stands up. He looks down on me.

'You are Lao She,' he announces in an immaculate, cut-glass Han accent.

'I am,' I admit.

'A Manchu. A Manchu traitor,' he shouts, lines of anger writhing across his face. 'For four centuries you foreign dogs with your tyrannical emperors have held down us freedom-loving Han Chinese. Polluted our nation. Exploited and repressed us in feudal servitude. In exchange for bribes you have allowed foreign barbarians and imperialists into our country to ransack it and corrupt it with capitalism and opium and Christianity. Kowtowed unblushingly towards the fascist Japanese bandits. And now we have to sit here and subserviently listen to you?'

There are emotional murmurs of agreement around the class. He is correct that the Manchu emperors for many centuries repressed all Chinese of all ethnicities, not just the Han. But the racism was not entirely one-sided. Following the overthrow of the last Manchu emperor in 1911 the rest of the Chinese, led by the Han, happily massacred hundreds of thousands of us Manchus.

'Excuse me,' I say, resisting the temptation to out-victim him in the persecution stakes and desperately trying to sound as Han as possible, 'but we are all meant to be Chinese in this room, united together as one force to defeat the barbaric Japanese. I certainly consider myself Chinese rather than Manchu. And we are here to, together, cooperate in writing drama and propaganda which will inspire all of us Chinese, whatever our ethnicity, to unite and drive out the Japanese invaders. That is our patriotic duty.'

'I know you, Lao She,' he says, dripping with contempt, 'with your corrupting bourgeois novels presenting honest Chinese working men and women as fools and lackeys. Promoting individualism, making comedy out of the exploitation and destruction of the proletariat, dividing the masses, setting them against each other...'

'I think you are referring to my novel *Rickshaw Boy*,' I say, 'in which I do indeed make my hero, a working-class rickshaw driver, a self-centred and ultimately foolish character. But I do this because I wish to make him a symbol of all of China – all classes, all ethnicities. Because as a nation we think only of ourselves, show no solidarity or unity in the face of repression and exploitation – whether it comes from foreigners or from our own bosses and landlords.'

'Really? Then if you want to truthfully expose the vicious exploitation that working-class people daily endure in this country, why choose a working-class villain to illustrate it – why not portray a wealthy bourgeois as the villain, a member of the exploited, not the exploiting, class? You show nothing but contempt for the innocent working classes. You're nothing more than a grovelling capitalist lackey.'

'Excuse me,' I say, not managing totally to control my anger, 'but I am myself a member of the Chinese working classes, brought up in poverty on the streets of Beijing...'

I manage to restrain myself from pointing out his own obvious upper-class background.

'You are a Manchu,' he reiterates. 'A Manchu traitor.'

I watch him with great care as he flings these insults at me. His face is contorting with rage, his body giving rictus jerks. Somewhere inside Tian Boqi there is great pain, great torment, great guilt even. As my wife says, before you can teach a pupil first you must know him. He is undoubtedly the most famous writer in the room – he has written more plays and received more East Coast plaudits than anyone else here, including me – but that won't impress or inspire a single peasant. If I manage to win him over, so that he understands the truth of our situation, all the rest will follow.

'Counter-revolutionary, collaborator, treacherous fascist!'

Thank God Lao Xiang did not come to this class. We'd be throwing each other out of the windows by now!

Tian Boqi continues like an implacable steamroller.

'The Chinese masses are going to arise. We are going to overthrow all you imperialist stooges. Language, you say. You keep on saying, in our plays, in our propaganda, we have to speak the language of the peasants. The medieval language and culture you so assiduously promote corrupts the proletariat's mind, destroys any prospect of a high culture that will inspire and exalt them so their struggle will overthrow all oppressors – Japanese, Manchu, British, Chinese – and allow them to reach a true revolutionary praxis.'

Speaking as simply and gently as I can I ask, 'How do you intend to get your ideas across to the peasantry?'

'All they have to do is know their Marx.'

'But only three per cent of them can read.'

'Then what we will do,' he replies, 'is stand on our stage and on our street corners and speak the truth of Marxist revolution, the overthrow of the bourgeoisie and landlord classes, the liberation of the working classes, their inevitable and unstoppable advance to seize control of the means of production. Our people have been kept in darkness and ignorance long enough. We shall speak in a clean language. A pure language. The language of Marxism–Leninism, the light of whose logic and truth will strike like lightning in their hearts. Fill them with fire. They will rise up, seize power.'

The room bursts out into spontaneous applause.

After this Tian Boqi seems to calm down. He's relieved both his intellectual wrath and his, unconscious I am sure, desire to prove himself the greatest writer in the room. As I pointed out earlier, we writers are incredibly insecure.

I decide we have done all we can today. We've had enough theorizing. Only practise can resolve our various problems. I tell them that in the next twenty-four hours each of them must write a short propaganda play suitable for performance on a village stage. It must inspire its rural audience to rally to the flag of China and fight the Japanese invader. If they have never visited a village I suggest they do so before writing their play. Ninety-five per cent of Chinese people live in villages. They depart.

I am left asking one question. Why is Tian Boqi so apocalyptically angry with everything?

7

As she walked through the crowds on the Bund, smiles and frowns fought for precedence on Hu Lan-shih's face. Rarely was there any contention. Her face was usually wreathed continuously in smiles. But this morning Hu was in turmoil. Last night she'd agreed, after great resistance, to appear before a group of wealthy women and tell them the story of her journey from Shanghai to Wuhan. The fierce Shi Liang had pushed her into it. Her job was to beg these rich women for money. It was not Hu's pride which bridled at begging – Hu had no pride – it was the rich women themselves. Just before she left Shi Laing had handed her a list of the names of the ladies she was to address. As soon as she saw it hatred momentarily flooded through her body. She almost collapsed. Horrified with herself at allowing such an awful emotion loose in her body, she forced it out and stood there shaking.

On the list were three names – Nie, Rong and Guo. The family names of the three most prominent cotton mill-owning families in Shanghai. And there at the top of that list was the name of the wife of Nie Zhiku, founder of the New Cotton Spinning and Weaving Bureau, which owned the very mill, the Shen Xin Number 9 Cotton Mill, where she herself had slaved and faced death daily. She remembered the death of her best friend Kaija there, how her arm had got caught in a strapping belt and within seconds she had been bludgeoned and smashed to a bloody pulp in the machinery. She would be begging money from the wife of such a person. Have to meet Mrs Nie face to face – smile at her.

Hu was walking from west to east along the Bund. The crowds

were already starting to thin as she approached the more affluent eastern end. Here the wealthy Chinese bankers and merchants had their large mansions. And beyond them lay the even more wealthy banks and embassies and mansions of the various Western treaty nations. Gentle sprays watering immaculately kept lawns, gardens overflowing with rare and exotic floribunda, shaded walkways and quiet bowers.

With the arrival of so many refugees many had taken to sleeping and camping the length of the Bund. In response the Western nations had erected a barbed wire barricade between the Chinese section and theirs, manned by enormous British Sikh police officers armed with rifles and bayonets. A couple of hundred yards out on the river were anchored a line of Western gunboats. Just to remind all and anyone what was what.

Hu Lan-shih turned down a side road before she reached the checkpoint. Before her was a large Chinese mansion behind an imposing set of iron gates. Before it stood a smartly uniformed Chinese guard.

'Good morning,' said Hu.

The guard didn't say anything.

'Hello,' said Hu again. 'Can I go in, please?'

'Fuck off,' said the guard. His bayonet glistened in the morning sun.

'Excuse me,' said Hu, 'but I've been invited to a meeting at this house?'

No response.

Hu suddenly realized she was just wearing an ordinary blouse and some workaday trousers. She looked like anyone else on the Bund – at least those who could afford clothes. Then she remembered Shi had given her an invitation. She reached into her pocket.

'This is my invitation,' she said, handing it to the guard, 'please let me in.'

At first the guard refused to look at it. Hu smiled at him encouragingly. For a second he glanced. A flicker of surprise crossed his face followed by a grimace when he realized he had to let her in.

He turned, opened the gate, let Hu through, then, without saying a word, slammed it shut behind her back.

Hu walked up a long driveway. The mansion came into view. She had never seen such a massive building before except the Shen Xin Number 9 Cotton Mill. Remember, she told herself, you must control yourself at all times. Up the workers!

She was halfway through her speech – pretty much the same talk she'd given to Shi and Li last night in the apartment. But no one seemed to be in the least bit interested. Shi Liang, the woman who'd invited her, was least interested of all. Immediately after Shi Liang arrived, she dived headlong into a maelstrom of exotic femininity. Ladies in the most spectacular Parisian and Hong Kong couture, sporting the most daring hairstyles, embossed with dazzling jewels, were loudly talking at each other, scrumming together, parading around, deciding to sit down beside dearest friends and then immediately moving when they saw even dearer dearest friends. One rather large woman, who didn't fit particularly well into her very expensive designer dress, seemed with her booming voice to dominate the entire room. All the eddies and currents of this glittering whirlpool seemed to revolve exclusively around her. Was she Mrs Nie?

Staring at this rugby scrum it suddenly occurred to Hu Lan-shih that wearing a white blouse and black trousers to such an event, which she had, was probably not the right thing. But then she didn't have any other clothes.

Li Dequan was sat alone at the back. Even she had made some attempt to escape her peasant clothes. But she waved encouragingly at Hu and it was this alone which kept Hu to her task, smiling bravely, telling stories of plucky peasants and intelligent whores and fighting soldiers.

Suddenly the entire geography of the room shifted. A small, middle-aged woman in shabby peasant clothes, ugly and with horse's teeth, modestly entered the room and quietly sat down amid a row of less important women in the middle of the room. (The most important women in the room naturally sat – or sat when they felt like sitting – in the foremost rows at the front.) Anyhow, as soon as this unimportant woman sat down in the middle of these less important women the less important women immediately stood up en masse and found more appropriate seating for themselves elsewhere. The rather dowdy woman with horse's teeth sat surrounded by empty seats. This lady was Deng Yingchao, the wife of the Vice Chairman of the Chinese Communist Party, Chou En-lai. When the Nationalists and Communists had declared themselves united following the Japanese invasion the previous year, Chou became the chief Communist representative and minister in the government of Chiang Kai-shek. But the seniority of her husband's position within the government did not seem to grant Deng any recognition within the higher ranks of Wuhan society. Not that that bothered Deng in the least. Li Dequan, the only other peasant-dressed outcast in the room, went over and sat down beside her, gave Hu an encouraging wave, and then herself immediately started talking in an animated fashion to Deng – thus leaving Hu on her own to carry on ploughing her lonely furrow, relating the tragic tale of how nearly all the soldiers they had befriended and supported for so long had died heroically fighting the Japanese in the trenches they and the girls had all dug together. Hu never stopped smiling.

Once again the geography of the room dramatically re-crystallized. Two similar-looking ladies – one wearing dowdy but respectable clothes and the other wearing expensive but tasteful clothes – a patriotic blend of Chinese and Western styles – walked into the room and immediately sat down in the two empty seats on either side of Deng Yingchao and Li Dequan. The two ladies were Soong Chingling, the widow of Sun Yatsen, the father of the Chinese Revolution, and Soong Ailing, the wife of China's richest banker. They were sisters, and their third sister, the youngest (not present), was none other than Soong Meiling, Mrs Chiang Kai-shek. The chairs around these four ladies, deserted when the horse-toothed Deng Yingchao had sat down there, suddenly became the most valuable property in Wuhan. The women closest to them, those of middle-ranking importance who had just deserted them, immediately reoccupied them, but then, realizing that favours granted to more high-ranking women would be valuable capital in the future, quickly ceded their seats to the more important women. The rather large woman with the piercing voice – who Hu Lan-shih feared was Mrs Nie – sat down alongside Soong Ailing. There was now a seated scrum parked all around the four not particularly well-dressed women in the centre.

As everyone continued to shriek at each other Hu finally reached the end of her lonely speech. She stopped. No one noticed. She decided to descend from the rostrum. She descended from the rostrum. Suddenly Shi Liang emerged from the scrum and hurried towards her.

'Brilliant. Absolutely brilliant. Just what was needed,' she said. 'Now,' she said, turning, 'back to business.' As she disappeared into the throng she pointed off to the side. 'Help yourself to some food.'

To one side stood this enormous table covered in what Hu assumed was food. But she'd never seen any food like this before. Mountainous. All shapes and sizes and exotic cuts and colours and textures and finely curlicued tidbits and delicate morsels of – what? Hu finally recognized some dumplings. She took two and, partly to avoid Mrs Nie, walked out into the fresh air.

She spent the next two hours, while all those inside laid siege to the table, walking around the magnificent gardens, nibbling her lunch and admiring especially the strutting, wonderful peacocks – their lacquered iridescent wings and breast feathers, their imperious eye, their wonderful displays. Though mainly of course, being from good peasant stock, she was wondering what they tasted like.

Her role in this event seemed to have ended. What was she still doing here? Should she leave? She looked at her invitation again. It said she was invited from eleven til four. Another two hours? Should she go back inside?

At this moment Li Dequan hurried out of the French windows and came towards her. Hu smiled with relief. Li would know. Li apologized profusely for abandoning her during lunch. Hu said it didn't matter. Li congratulated Hu on her speech and said she thought it had gone down very well. Several women had spoken favourably to her about it.

'But nobody was listening,' said Hu.

'Don't believe that,' said Li. 'Mrs Nie came up to me at the end and mentioned several points you'd made.'

'Was that that large woman with the loud voice?'

'That's her.'

Hu's heart sank.

'Hu,' Li reassured her, 'society women have very sharp antennae. They can concentrate on many different things at the same time.'

Hu looked at Li. Li looked at Hu. They both laughed.

Li explained she'd been detained because she'd had to explain to the two Soong sisters before they left about the problems her husband Feng was having upstream in Chungking with building homes and factories for the refugees. They'd promised to speak to their husbands. She'd also been trying, without much success, to persuade all the society ladies here to donate generously to the Orphan Fostering Commission, which this event had been organized on behalf of. She was its vice chairman. 'It's hard work,' she said.

'Of course you should have been doing that,' said Hu supportively. 'Just passing all those starving, dying children on the street is terrible. It's a scandal.'

'Look,' said Li, 'I think you should stay this afternoon. Shi Liang has planned a bit of a show – to finally wrench the money out of these women. Someone you know will be there.'

Inside the ladies were being detached from their food and reassuring gossip and herded by a very determined Shi Laing out of another door into a large cobbled courtyard. Tall walls stood all around.

Before them, in the bitter winter cold, stood a line of half-starved youngsters, scruffy and wild, desperate for food and warmth. Some of them had runny noses. They smelt, they were scabby, most were probably diseased. The women in their couture dresses just gaped. Hu was amazed to see, of all people, Spider Girl stood in their midst. Her hair and clothing had been distressed and her face muddied. She looked furious. This must be Shi Laing's doing, thought Hu.

The ladies stared at the lost legion of hobbledehoys and derelicts and waifs. The lost legion stared back. Even Mrs Nie was silent.

Shi Liang, seasoned courtroom performer, seized the moment.

'Dear ladies,' stated short and bespectacled Shi, 'we earlier spent a very pleasant lunch talking about starving children and homeless and abandoned orphans. So I thought it would be good for you to actually see some – to meet children abandoned by their parents, children whose families have been butchered by the Japanese, homeless, starving children who we have taken off the streets of Wuhan this morning.'

'Ladies,' she said, 'I was at school with many of you. I studied at university with some of you. Look before you. Before you stands your problem, our nation's problem. Abandoned children. We fine ladies travel through the streets of Wuhan in our automobiles, our carriages, our fine rickshaws, and we do not even notice them, see them.

'Ladies, I will remind you of one thing. The Japanese are coming. Creatures who drive bayonets into the arms, the legs, the bodies, the eyes, the vaginas of all the Chinese women they meet.'

A ripple of fear passed through the ladies.

'What shall we do? Flee? To Hong Kong, to Singapore, to Paris? But all our wealth is centred here in China. If we flee abroad we will lose it, become paupers on the streets like these very children.'

By now her audience were definitely taking notice.

'Our wealth can only survive if we stay here in China. But that will require us to fight the Japanese – with bayonets and rifles and guns. And to do that we will have to organize ourselves, our whole Chinese nation, educate and train all its peoples in order to fight them. We will require factories and steel plants and armouries, skilled engineers and technicians, roads and railroads and airfields and guns so we can attack and defeat these uncivilized barbarians. To do that, to fight them, to defeat them, what will we require above all else…?'

The great performer looked questioningly about, then pointed dramatically at the line of bedraggled children.

'We will require these children – precisely these urchins and strays and delinquents and hoodlums – disciplined and fed and nurtured and trained and educated – to fill those factories, build those machines, forge that steel, man those trenches, plough those fields. Skilled people alone can win this war. Bring victory to China. If you wish to survive this war this nation requires your money.'

Shi cast a practised eye over her audience. They were moved, but not enough. She could see them calculating – 'All right, I will give them money – but not today. I'll give them money tomorrow – probably.' Good, thought Shi, just as I want them. Shi, the consummate courtroom general, smoothly switched to phase two of her campaign.

She clapped her hands. Another door onto the courtyard swung open and a discord of military music hit everyone's ears as, from the door, marched a line of tiny five- and six-year-old tots, banging on drums and heartily blowing on penny whistles. But unlike the filthy and ragged older children, these tots were clad in smart clean khaki uniforms, their skin glowed from regular scrubbing and washing, their bellies were visibly full of food, and their heads lice free because every last wisp of hair had been shaved off.

The line stopped dead in front of the ladies. The music stopped. There were some cooings and sighs from the ladies. Even Mrs Nie's visage softened. These children were cute, cuddlesome, clean – everything the desperadoes and urchins were not.

As if spontaneously they burst into a popular patriotic children's song written by none other than Lao Xiang, Lao She's pugnacious friend:

'The snow is dancing,
The lone crow is crying.
I am making a fur hat for the soldier.
Where can I find furs?
I ask help from a fox.

The fox runs into the grass.
Oh fox, oh fox, please don't run.
Can you lend me a big fur coat?
I won't wear it,
Nor will he,
We are sending it to the soldier at the front.
It feels so warm,
It looks so good,
We're sure to beat those Japanese.'

The song ended with a neat roll on the drums.

'You see, ladies,' Shi continued, 'this is what we can do for orphans. How we can transform ourselves. Two weeks ago these sweet young children were urchins and waifs wandering the cold streets of Wuhan. Starving. But we raised enough money to open a small temporary orphanage and this is what warmth, food and discipline can do. These twenty orphans are now ready to be shipped upstream to Chungking where they will start new and useful lives. But, as you know, there are thousands upon thousands of lost, homeless children – like those behind them – who are desperate. Desperate souls are a threat to us all. Those who are starving are forced to turn to crime which can endanger us all. Instead, through your generosity, your desire to be patriotic women serving your country, you can help turn our country around. Make us fight.'

There is nothing on this earth more difficult to do than appeal to the altruism of a wealthy person. Extracting money from their tightly clenched fingers. The crowd of rich women swayed backwards and forwards – slightly guiltily perhaps. Mrs Nie was checking her face in her mirror. Two or three perhaps walked back through the door to pay some small sum to assuage their consciences. The majority stayed put.

Now came Shi Liang's *coup de théâtre*. She turned and asked Spider Girl to step forwards.

'Ladies,' said Shi, 'I want to show you an example of outstanding courage.'

Spider Girl waddled up to her. Hu stared open-mouthed.

'This,' declared Shi Liang, 'this young girl, as you can see, cannot walk properly. She is partly crippled. And yet she undertook an extraordinary journey to get here to Wuhan. This young girl has rickets. It means that her legs and hips are wasted and bruised and feeble. It is extremely difficult and painful for her to walk. And yet, to join us free Chinese here in Wuhan, to do her bit, this young girl, with extraordinary courage, walked over one thousand miles to join us. To show her patriotism. I want you now to look at those twisted and tortured legs of hers so you can understand this girl's sublime courage.'

She turned to Spider Girl. Spider Girl stared grimly ahead.

'Wild Pear Blossom, please raise your skirts so that all these good ladies can see your terrible affliction.'

The women pushed forwards. (Let's be honest, we all love something really ghastly!)

Spider Girl – or to give her her formal name, Wild Pear Blossom – was naturally, like all ordinary Chinese girls, a deeply modest person. Nakedness was a taboo you never broke until your marriage night. She'd been greatly troubled by Shi's proposal. She did not raise her skirt.

'Wild Pear Blossom,' said Shi Liang, 'I can see you are a good and modest girl, and do not wish to do this in front of the other children.'

The other children were marched out. The ladies were now getting very involved in what would be revealed beneath the skirts.

'Wild Pear Blossom,' asked Shi, 'please raise your skirts.'

Spider Girl did not. The ladies were in a heat of expectation.

'Please raise your skirts,' requested Shi Liang. 'There are only women present. You have nothing to be ashamed of.'

It was at this point that Shi's carefully prearranged script came off the rails. Spider Girl, staring beadily ahead of her, did not raise her skirts. Just stood there.

It took a moment for Shi Liang to realize this. With slight uncertainty she moved closer to her – hissed in her ear.

'Wild Peach Blossom…?'

'Wild *Pear* Blossom!'

'Sorry, Wild Pear Blossom. Why aren't raising your skirts? As we agreed to?'

'Because I've decided not to.'

By now the ladies were in a frenzy.

'Do it.'

'No.'

Shi Liang looked her fully in the face.

'What do you want?' she hissed, desperately trying to soften her anger.

'Money,' Spider Girl hissed back.

'I'll pay you later.'

'Now.'

There was a pause. Things like this simply did not occur in courtrooms. Round the back of courtrooms, maybe. But never in an actual courtroom, in front of everyone.

'How much?'

A quick haggle ensued in which Spider Girl obviously held the superior hand. Very soon a considerable number of silver coins were surreptitiously showered into her purse and Spider Girl, still feeling the shame of it, raised her skirts.

The ladies darted forwards. They feasted their cultured eyes on the bruises and swellings and lacerations, the twisted bones and cartilage and thighs of Spider Girl's nether regions. And at their front, staring hardest at the red tortured flesh, was the face of Mrs Nie. It was as though, with this sight, all her profoundest feelings of anger and inadequacy and ugliness bathed and soothed and healed themselves in her intimacy with this horrible human suffering.

As the mob pressed ever closer, Spider Girl slowly raised her eyes to look at the skies. Indeed, as they became more excited, so she became calmer, more peaceful. In her hand she held the tiny stone bottle containing the last of her family's wild pear juice. She remembered another cold winter's day on the farm with the brave little wild pear tree holding out its branches which were drenched in creamy white blossoms and gentle green leaves soft as silk, standing resilient against the cold blue skies. It was far too early in the year for any bees to have ventured out to pollinate it. So her father, as she watched, climbed high in the fragile old tree and, leaning out precariously, held a long stick with a soft brush tied to its end with which he gently flustered, stroked every blossom so each was pollinated, so each would bear sweet fruit and the family would once again drink the juice from the earth in which her father's elder sister and the bones of all their other ancestors lay in.

Her father had been a great king bee at the centre of all her family, working incessantly to bring sustenance and shelter and harmony and blessing on them.

Spider Girl slowly realized the fine ladies were sated, were turning away, starting to make a beeline towards the room where at last they could make their – not particularly generous – donations. The day's entertainment was over. Shi Liang was herding the ladies indoors. Li Dequan had left in disgust before this highly lucrative pantomime had even started. Hu moved towards Spider Girl to offer her comfort.

It was at this moment, as the ladies were reaching the door, that the final and totally unrehearsed sensation occurred. From the door, despite the weather, stepped a slight lady immaculately dressed in a superb Mandarin dress with bright floral patterns slashing across a deep blue background – effortlessly combining Western and Chinese styles in one chic statement. Wearing high heels, her hair beautifully coiffured, an elegant cigarette dangled from her fingers. Every single wealthy lady stopped dead. All breathed in simultaneously.

'Ladies,' the lady stated, 'please continue indoors and contribute generously, extremely generously, to this wonderful charity for orphans. I myself have just contributed over ten thousand dollars.'

The entrance to the door suddenly became a scrum of upper-class women all desperate to be seen outspending each other. Shi Liang followed, smiling.

Superbly poised, the lady continued her way into the courtyard. Only Hu and Spider Girl still stood there.

Many strange and inexplicable things had happened to Hu Lan-shih today, ever since she'd walked through the iron gates of high society. She'd given a talk which no one had listened to but everyone had praised. She had seen a peacock spread its tail feathers. She'd watched while poor Spider Girl had been virtually forced to lift her skirts so that a whole lot of bizarre high-class ladies could stare at her crotch. But now – this topped it all. This lady was walking straight towards her and Spider Girl. Hu hastily looked behind them to see if there was someone else she might be walking towards – there wasn't!

'Good afternoon,' the lady said, holding out her hand to Hu, 'you must be Hu Lan-shih.'

Hu of course knew who this woman was. Her photograph was in every paper. Hu Lan-shih was shaking hands with, being addressed by none other than, Soong Meiling herself, the youngest of the Soong sisters, the cleverest, and China's First Lady. The wife of Generalissimo Chiang Kai-shek himself.

'I am delighted to meet you,' said Madame Chiang.

'Who's this?' asked a puzzled Spider Girl.

Hu looked at Spider Girl with a flicker of uncharacteristic irritation. 'Don't you know who this is? This is the wife of General Chiang Kai-shek.'

'Who's he?' asked Spider Girl.

Madame Chiang effortlessly took over the conversation. 'Hello,' she said to Spider Girl. 'I am told you are Wild Pear Blossom. I believe you have rickets. Please accept my sympathies, and I hope you will be able to get some treatment for it.'

She said this genuinely, without falseness or affectation.

She then turned and concentrated solely on Hu.

'I must apologize profusely for not being at your lecture, which I particularly wanted to hear. I'm afraid I was detained on other matters.'

'Of course,' said a still bewildered Hu.

'Shi Liang gave me a general idea of what you'd told her, but I really wanted to hear it from your own lips, so I sent a secretary of mine to copy down your speech word for word and I will read it this evening.'

'I am honoured,' said Hu.

'The biggest problem our country faces – and we will have to face it if we are going to survive – is that we ruling classes are so out of touch with ordinary people. There is a vast and terrifying gap between the rich and poor, and, unless it is bridged, it will mean the end of our civilization. We must have modern health services and education systems, modern industry and manufacturing, good social services and far more social equality. We must even try – chaotic as it always is – democracy. We either do these things, or we die.'

Madame Chiang had finished her cigarette. In one movement she flicked it away, snapped a gold cigarette case full of Wills's Gold Flake, offered them to Spider Girl, who took two and stuck them behind her ear, offered one to Hu, who refused because she did not smoke, took one herself, lit it, and continued, all without a break.

'Our great problem is not money, finance – though we don't have that much of it. It is essentially knowledge. We can make laws, we can pour money into projects, but we really have no way of knowing whether such actions will have practical effects. Whether they will actually result in building houses and factories and guns and wealth. Are they helping ordinary people to get on with their lives, get wealthier? Are they helping our soldiers on the battlefield? We don't know. Because we don't know how ordinary people work. How they think. What they feel. If they are going to do what we want them to do, or if they want to do it in a totally different way, and if so if we can reach a practical compromise. That's why we need you, Hu Lan-shih.'

'Me?'

'We have a committee in our government. An important committee. Where most of these progressive plans to get things moving, to reform things, are put forwards, discussed, and then passed if we think they will work. But the truth is that no one on this committee has the least idea how their plans and theories are going to go down with the very people who have to implement them, carry them out. The everyday people of China. That is where you come in. You will understand how people think, what their reaction is likely to be to what is being proposed. Whether they will carry it out? If not, why, and how can we modify them so that people *will* carry them out? You will be able to advise this committee on what is likely to be practical, and what isn't and why. From what I heard about you on your march, you were able to present workable solutions to problems, you were able to negotiate with all sorts of different people, you were able to conciliate – very rare skills in China today. I am asking you to become a member of this committee...'

'What?'

'...so that you can advise on what people will put up with and what they won't. How they can be favourably presented. And on what ideas you yourself have about what must be done and how they might be implemented.'

'Madame Chiang,' Hu interrupted, ' – and I apologize for interrupting you – but I do not think that I am in any way suited for this sort of work.'

'And I do not think,' rejoined the Generalissimo's wife, 'that you have the least idea how precisely dire this country's situation currently is.'

'I do,' said Hu, blushing, 'I certainly do. I know exactly how dire it is. Not only as far as the war is concerned, but in a thousand other ways. Having worked all my life in a Shanghai cotton mill I know precisely how dire things are.'

'Which is exactly why you are needed. I know how bad things are. You know how bad things are. But most of the people in our government haven't the slightest idea. They think it's all a game. "When things get really bad we'll do a deal with the Japanese," they say.'

Madame Chiang gave a snort. A ladylike snort, albeit, but definitely a snort.

'We will do a deal with the Japanese over my dead body. My and my sisters' dead bodies. I know, Hu, you are a socialist. I am not a socialist. You may well disapprove of my husband's government. But whatever our politics we are both Chinese. Chinese patriots. We need you.'

'But Madame Chiang,' stuttered Hu, 'I am not...'

Chiang interrupted her. 'I know exactly who you are. I looked you up in the files of my husband's secret police. You were a trade unionist. You are quite used to negotiating in a hostile environment...'

'A *very* hostile environment.'

'Committee life is not at all alien to you. And I'll bet, nice as you are, you know how to get your way.'

The two stared at each other.

'What do you want me to do?' cried Madame Chiang theatrically. 'Get down on my knees and beg you? I'd ladder my stockings. I have another very important meeting in' – she checked her watch – 'exactly twenty minutes. Are you expecting me to turn up to it in laddered stockings?'

The two women looked at each other. Then burst out laughing. Madame Chiang took that as assent.

'Hu, I apologize for addressing you in this brutal and manipulative fashion. In normal times we could have spoken to each other in a humane and courteous way.'

'In normal times,' said Hu, 'we would not have talked to each other at all.'

'That is true,' said Chiang. 'But this is a war. Hu, I would be very grateful if you could start work the day after tomorrow. I will brief the senior official of the committee that you are coming, that you are to be treated as a full equal, and if there are any difficulties he is to report them to me. He will fully brief you on the documents and policies coming before the committee. If you have any problems access me immediately through my office.'

She glanced at her watch again.

'I must be going.'

She shook Hu's hand.

'Thank you again,' she said, even though Hu had not assented.

She turned and shook Spider Girl's hand.

'It's a pleasure to have met you, Wild Pear Blossom,' she said.

She departed, trailing clouds of exotic Parisian perfume.

Spider Girl rubbed and smelt her hand. She'd never shaken hands before. She thought it rather indecent.

'What do you think?' asked Hu.

'I think you should have asked for a lot of money,' said Spider Girl.

Hu sighed. All this had happened because she'd met Li on the Bund and told her her story and Li had spoken to Shi Liang who'd talked to Madame Chiang.

'Cheer up,' said Spider Girl, 'the golden staircase opens before you.'

'No it doesn't,' said Hu.

Hu and Spider Girl walked slowly along the Bund back to their apartment.

One of the first acts of this new government of China – the new unity government of Nationalists and Communists – was the almost total abolition of press censorship. Each side wished to show how liberal and progressive it was. Only sensitive military information was censored.

The result was an efflorescence of news sheets and newspapers and pamphlets espousing every sort of weird and wonderful idea. Extreme Confucianists advocated a return to being ruled by an emperor – even though the present emperor was a Japanese puppet ruling in Manchukuo. Anarchists advocated being ruled by no one. There were free love newspapers, syndicalist newspapers, communist and nationalist and capitalist and socialist and Seventh Day Adventist newspapers – all being flogged vociferously on The Bund by their supporters. Newspapers were pasted on walls, and people read them aloud to those who couldn't read. Spontaneous debates and disagreements and shouting matches broke out, lifelong friendships were formed or broken in front of these walls, children picked pockets. In the first few weeks of press freedom the numbers of debaters were few, but by now whole crowds were forming, orators were orating, people flocking for entertainment and information and ideas. Policemen looked in the other direction – or listened keenly to debates while looking in the other direction. There was a hunger in the air. Suddenly everybody, Babel-like, had an opinion. People were even demanding elections!

Hu Lan-shih and Spider Girl ignored all this. Having just been steamrollered by Madame Chiang, Hu was feeling a bit disassociated.

'That woman's far too powerful,' opined the powerful Spider Girl. 'Her husband should beat her more often.'

'The trouble is,' said Hu, 'I liked it on the road, with all the soldiers. Meeting new people all the time, laughing, learning things, helping people, solving their problems. And I like being with you all here in Wuhan, in our apartment, coming out on the Bund, binding the poor soldiers' wounds, trying to comfort them. But sitting on a government committee? With all these high-class people, all educated, so they're really intelligent, talking about all these things I don't know the slightest thing about…?'

'Depends on what they're paying you,' said Spider Girl. 'I'd sit on it – no problem.'

Actually, Hu reflected, Spider Girl would probably be excellent on a committee. She'd put up with no nonsense, cut through waffle and double-talk, and get things done even if it meant holding a knife to the throat of some particularly irritating mandarin. Hu giggled. Her mood improved. Madame Chiang wanted her to do it. She'd give it a try!

Spider Girl was staring at a bookstall. The bookseller, who also sold newspapers, was shouting: 'I bring you news from all the war fronts, from Shantung and Hopeh, from northern Shansi, from Canton in the far south of our great China. I also sell books. Lots of books.'

Spider Girl was staring at the books. She and Old Man Chen were the only people in their village who could read, and they had read only newspapers.

'Hu,' she said, 'I've never read a book. What sort of book should I read?'

'What things interest you?'

'Well, I was thinking, all these high-class sorts of people we've been meeting lately, people who think and use long words, what sort of things do they read?'

'Oh,' said Hu, 'all sort of things.'

'Then what should I read?'

'Well…' said Hu.

Hu, thanks to her trade union library, was quite well read in progressive areas. She thought the Bible and Karl Marx might be a bit obscure for Spider Girl, but just before leaving Shanghai Hu had read Lao She's acclaimed new novel *Rickshaw Boy*. She bought it for Spider Girl.

That evening, as she lay in bed, Spider Girl started to read *Rickshaw Boy*. She didn't get very far. Somehow she couldn't arouse any enthusiasm for the hero's eternal laments and existential angst. It also had very long sentences. By the time you finished the end of a sentence you'd forgotten what the start of it was about. Spider Girl preferred action. So she put down Lao She and picked up a garish Shanghai detective novel she'd stolen off the bookstall while Hu was busy buying *Rickshaw Boy*. She'd been attracted by its wonderfully lurid cover – a glamorous scantily clad woman with a knife in her hand standing over a trilby-hatted man lying on the floor with large amounts of blood flowing out of him. Spider Girl licked her rather hairy upper lip and started to read.

For one night she did not think of her father.

8

When the Japanese invaded China in the late summer of 1937, in Sichuan – a remote mountainous province in the south-west of China – a warlord and his men were so incensed that all, officers and men, spontaneously swore an oath to drive the Japanese dogs out of their country.

This was their oath:

'We shall fight to the last drop of our blood to regain our lost territories. We shall survive if we succeed. We shall perish if we fail. If we die, we die for a righteous cause.'

The warlord promptly telegraphed Chiang Kai-shek to inform him that he and his men wished to fight the Japanese. Chiang Kai-shek was delighted. He immediately promoted the warlord to the rank of full general. His raggle-taggle band was overnight renamed the 22nd Chinese Army Group.

In truth these soldiers were in a terrible state – poorly armed, largely untrained, undisciplined. They either wore straw sandals or walked barefoot, instead of helmets they had large round straw hats and they carried paper umbrellas to ward off sun and rain and artillery shells. They were irregularly paid and poorly fed so many used opium to deaden their hunger. They were armed with a completely random collection of weapons. Some carried spears and broadswords, others 200-year-old blunderbusses and 100-year-old flintlocks. Their main weapon was the Type 79 rifle, a poor Sichuan copy of the Type 89 rifle, which was itself a poor Chinese copy of the fifty-year-old German Gewehr 88 rifle. The Type 79 rifles were made of inferior steel and their barrels would start to warp when heated by repeated firing. The ammunition was of low quality and unreliable and misfirings would often cause the breech to jam. The 22nds had no artillery, no anti-tank guns, only a few locally made inferior machine guns and some ancient pistols with a predilection for jamming when you pulled the trigger. Such weaponry was great for overawing peasants but useless against the Japanese.

So Chiang Kai-shek ordered that first the 22nd should march north to Xian, where they would be re-equipped with modern weapons and proper uniforms. Then they would be redeployed to the first battle front that needed them.

The intrepid 22nds set off for Xian with courage in their hearts and a spring to their sandal-clad feet. The only trouble was that Xian was 400 miles to the north and situated on the other side of several formidable mountain ranges. In addition, winter was setting in and they were wearing only paper-thin summer garments. Ignoring all this they marched through the mountains using the network of the 2,000-year-old Shu highways. As they approached Xian they suddenly saw some strange-looking troops deployed ahead of them. Since none of them, including their 'general', had ever set foot outside Sichuan, none of them had ever seen modern Chinese military uniforms and therefore assumed these troops ahead of them were the loathsome Japanese. They immediately attacked.

It was some time before they realized their mistake and the general of the opposing force descended upon our brave 22nds with hearty oaths and mighty threats, but before this misunderstanding could escalate any further the Japanese themselves turned up and started attacking both groups who, unable to immediately rally themselves, were together thrown back in confusion.

In this chaotic retreat the 22nd, quite fortuitously, lucked upon a very large and unguarded Chinese warehouse that happened to be jam-packed with the latest and best Chinese weaponry. What should they do? Well, they didn't spend too much time debating this particular moral quandary. The 22nd had originally been recruited from local bandits and criminals – both men and officers – so without too much prevaricating they took all they could carry and, because the Japanese were fast arriving, scarpered. Retreating at speed, they again by chance ran into the Chinese unit they had previously attacked. Their general again became apoplectic. That was *his* weaponry! But before things could once more get out of hand the Japanese arrived and the 22nd disappeared into the night.

But the outraged Chinese general did not leave things at that. He wrote an incensed letter about the appalling and unsoldierly behaviour of the Sichuan 'troops' to Chiang Kai-shek himself. 'These southern bandits and deplorables are besmirching the honour of our illustrious Chinese armed forces. They must be expelled immediately from our ranks.' To make matters worse, Chiang Kai-shek just happened to be a close friend of this particular general, who was one of the many incompetent generals Chiang Kai-shek kept about him to keep himself in power. So Chiang Kai-shek wrote a stinging letter to the general of the 22nd ordering him to march his rabble back to Sichuan and disband themselves.

Fortunately for the 22nd, the Generalissimo's order passed through the competent hands of General Bai Chongxi, who, since the execution of General Han Fuju, had gained control of running the war. Bai happened to know that while his friend General Li Zongren was busy assembling and organizing some of China's top troops to defend Taierzhuang, he was desperately in need of some stopgap troops to delay the swift advance of Japanese General Rensuke Isogai's 10th Division on Taierzhuang, even for a few hours.

These 'deplorable' Sichuan troops seemed to precisely fit the bill.

He phoned Li Zongren.

'Li, I have some Sichuan troops who might be of use to you. You could deploy them around Tengxian, hold up Rensuke for a day or two.'

'I need all the time I can get. What are they like?'

'Awful. Still wearing straw helmets and straw sandals.'

Both men guffawed.

'Men of straw, eh?' continued Li. 'Did not Zhuge Liang himself use straw dummies at the Battle of the Red Cliffs to fool the evil Cao Cao?'

'Indeed. And it worked.'

'Then I'll have these straw men. Send them to Tengxian. They will die, but they will die gloriously.'

And so was the fate of the 22nd decided.

These 'Deplorables' approached Wuhan from the west. They crossed the Han River on ferries and landed on the Bund. In a snowstorm they lay down on the cobbles and, finding shelter as they could, fell asleep.

It was here that Wei, the Shaanxi farmer who had lost all his family except for Spider Girl and wished to sacrifice his own life in fighting the Japanese, was recruited into the 22nd. Agnes Smedley – to whom Wei had sold Spider Girl – knew a medical orderly who was friends with an officer in the 22nd. The medical orderly took Wei to meet the officer. The officer accepted Wei and got him to swear what had by now become the Deplorables' official oath:

'I shall fight to the last drop of my blood to regain our lost territories. I shall survive if we succeed. I shall perish if we fail. If I die, I die for a righteous cause.'

He then ordered Wei to lie down on the cobbles and sleep. Wei covered himself with a discarded newspaper and lay down. The thought that he was now in the army and could fight comforted him and he fell swiftly into an easy sleep.

The next morning Wei awoke in the midst of the platoon in which the officer had placed him. The men grumbled and rubbed their cold limbs as they got up, went and pissed and shat over the edge of the quay into the river. Some lit their opium pipes to alleviate the cold or the shaking chills of malaria. Others set off to steal food from the market stalls, but by far their most successful food thief was a small dog named Greedy. The platoon would give him the instruction to steal food and with a lurcher-like leer he would slope off into the market to do his soldierly duty. If he was successful, and he invariably was, then Greedy was given the best cut and the rest was divvied up among the men. In a platoon full of thieves, Greedy was universally lauded as the greatest.

There was one difficulty with all this. As the platoon chatted and scratched and bitched among themselves, Wei came to realize that he hardly understood a word they were saying. They spoke an obscure Sichuan dialect that sounded like frail finches twittering in the bushes. He spoke in a deep Shaanxi accent. When they made comments or issued instructions to him he simply couldn't understand them. He became the butt of quite a lot of jokes and banter, but Wei ignored it and kept his counsel. An answer to this difficulty was finally reached when the corporal returned from his foray with a lot of fruit and nuts and some boiled rabbit. The corporal – known as Boss Eyes because he had boss eyes – had spent some time in Beijing working as a porter and thus had some understanding of northern dialects. As he was passing Wei some of the food he had stolen they discovered they had words which they mutually understood and this started a conversation. Wei told him the story of his family's retreat to Wuhan, and when Boss Eyes related this to the rest of the platoon it brought sympathetic murmurs and grunts. A soldier known as Creaky Door – because of his croaky throat – then related to Wei, through Boss Eyes the corporal, the story of the 22nd's patriotic outburst in Sichuan and their journey to Wuhan. Over the next few days Wei picked up some of the platoon's words and they learnt some of his, and within a week they were conversing easily.

There was still one problem, though. The matter of Wei's uniform. He was dressed in the traditional garb of a Shaanxi farmer. The lieutenant commanding Wei's platoon did not approve of it. He also did not approve of the semi-rags the rest of his platoon wore, but there was nothing he could do about that – they had not been issued with modern combat uniforms. But he wanted at least one member of his platoon to look smart and modern. So he ordered two members of his platoon – brothers named Dirty Rat and Fat Rat – to march with Wei to a high-class tailoring shop and there get him properly fitted out in a smartly tailored military uniform.

Dirty and Fat Rat licked their lips and marched into the crowds with Wei trying to keep step between them. Down a street they found a likely clothing emporium selling European-style outfits. Dirty and Fat Rat were both on the large size so they had no trouble with the guard standing at the doorway. They went into the hushed and tasteful interior. The proprietor was standing behind a long table covered in expensive and respectable looking fabrics and silks. He looked up and saw them approaching, then he looked behind them to see what the guard was doing. The guard didn't seem to be anywhere about. He looked at the three rough men beadily and drew himself up.

'What do you want?'

'We want a properly tailored soldier's uniform for our friend here from Shaanxi.'

The proprietor had obviously never had a peasant in his shop before. And the only soldiers he'd ever entertained here had been of the higher ranks.

'Get out of my shop,' he said, 'I don't serve ruffians.'

'Ruffians?' said Dirty Rat, placing his hands on the table and staring deep into the eyes of the now twitching proprietor. 'He's just called us ruffians.'

'I heard,' said Fat Rat, sitting down on one of the most expensive silks and blowing his nose on it.

'You call us ruffians? A civilian like you calls us soldiers, who are about to go out and die so that you might live, so that you can continue to make your sweet little profits and screw the whores down the road, you call us ruffians? We are patriots.'

Wei, the most law-abiding of men, had never found himself in a situation like this before.

'This man,' continued Dirty Rat, indicating Wei, 'he has lost almost every member of his family to the murdering Japanese dogs, and now, after all that, he is volunteering, he has sworn an oath to lay down his life, to die on the field of battle so that slugs and cozening worms such as yourself can continue to suck the life blood out of common people and ooze out your profits.'

Fat Rat had now set light to one of the proprietor's subtler textiles and was lighting his cigarette with it.

The proprietor stared desperately over Dirty Rat's shoulder. The guard was obviously long gone.

'All right,' said the shop owner, breathing out, 'what do you want?'

'As I've already told you,' said Dirty Rat, indicating Wei, 'I want a private's uniform for this northerner here, measured and fitted exactly to his body, made from the highest quality cloth, so that when he wears it he will bring splendour to our regiment and when he dies in it and passes into the afterlife it will be an honourable and fine shroud for him when he lies in the ground.'

'Do it now,' said Fat Rat, holding his burning rag close to a high pile of silks.

'If you come back this afternoon…' said the proprietor.

'Do it now,' said Dirty Rat, 'in twenty minutes, or we set fire to your shop.'

'Come in here,' shrieked the proprietor to his assistants, 'at once!'

The shop suddenly filled with fitters with measuring tapes and cutters with scissors and seamstresses with needles and pins and thread. The fitters ripped off Wei's farmer's clothes and started measuring him and screaming out numbers, the cutters measured out the olive brown cloth and sliced their scissors through it, throwing it to the seamstresses who with lightning fingers sewed and shaped the jacket and breeches and cap as all the while the proprietor screamed at all of them.

It had hardly started before it was finished. Wei stood before them in a full and magnificent private's uniform, tailored exactly to his body. The proprietor was on hands and knees before him fitting some smart black boots on him and winding puttees round his legs.

The proprietor arose and walked slowly around his employees' handiwork. He noticed some irregular stitching on the left shoulder of Wei's jacket.

'Nuan, you slut,' he hissed at a girl, 'look at this stitching.' He turned to Dirty Rat. 'Do you want it corrected?'

'Of course,' said Dirty Rat, who was scoffing some rather delicious sugared almonds laid out for customers on a side table, 'get on with it.'

Nuan scurried forwards, corrected her loose sewing and, with a cuff from her boss, scurried back to her position.

The proprietor bowed to the soldiers. Not returning his gesture, Dirty and Fat Rat started towards the door.

Wei had a dilemma. 'Thank you,' he muttered, half-bowing to the owner and then hurrying after the other two. The three of them marched out through the door. At least Dirty Rat and Fat Rat marched; Wei did his best to imitate them.

From then on, within the Deplorables, Wei, because of his uniform, was known affectionately as 'Posh Northerner'.

The 22nd set off on its march to Tengxian. They would march north-east through the mountains to Xuzhou then on to Taierzhuang – a distance of some three hundred miles – before turning north for a further fifty miles to Tengxian. At Tengxian they would face the full onslaught of the 10th Division of the Imperial Japanese Army under Rensuke Isogai. They would not retreat. They would fight until the last man.

Soldiers like marching. They comment on everything they pass. Pretty girls, ugly girls, self-important men, un-self-important men, swineherds, the swineherd's pigs, passing coolies and porters and carts and carriages. Children love to follow them, shouting out, waving, begging from them. The soldiers love answering back, laughing, giving as good as they get.

But above all they love singing.

Back in Wuhan a keen young student had been teaching the 22nd some gung-ho patriotic songs to proudly sing on the march. But, with his high Mandarin accent, they hadn't understood a word he'd said and he couldn't understand a word they said. Indeed, many of them hadn't even realized he was teaching them songs. So they didn't sing any of his songs. Instead as they marched they cheerfully sang songs about girls of low morals and what the whole regiment had done to them, popular drinking songs, a favourite song about a famous victory they'd won when they'd routed the army of a rival warlord who'd invaded Sichuan from the neighbouring state of Yunnan. But above all they sang children's songs, because everyone knew them and everyone liked them. Silly, nonsensical, fantastical doggerel.

At each halt Wei was given instruction by a sergeant – on cleanliness, orderliness, obedience, a list of punishments for major and minor crimes and misdemeanours, the chain of command, the orders expected on the battlefield and how they should be obeyed, how to avoid venereal diseases, and above all how to operate his rifle and the supreme importance of keeping it clean and ready for use at all times.

Wei was issued with a highly unusual rifle by the regiment's armourer. By now the armourer had run out of the rifles 'liberated' from the Chinese warehouse near Xian, and he was handing out weapons from the original Sichuan armoury which he had wisely kept in the back of his cart. So Wei was given a short Lee Enfield Mark 4 rifle. Instead of a normal bayonet it had a formidable nine-inch spike known as a pig-sticker. The weapon held ten rounds in its magazine with another up the spout and, with its superbly rifled barrel of finely forged steel, was extremely accurate and had a range of up to a mile. Because it was cased in wood from butt to barrel, it meant that rapid fire could be continued almost indefinitely without burning the soldiers' hands. It was extremely reliable if kept clean and oiled and fired .303 ammunition. Wei, who liked all well-made tools, admired it as it lay in his hand. On its casing it had stamped 'Made in the County of Middlesex'.

How had it suddenly turned up in remote Sichuan?

The Lee Enfield had been the standard issue rifle of the British Army for fifty years. Five years ago, a platoon of British soldiers had been ambushed in a remote mountain pass in Afghanistan by Pathan tribesmen and killed to a man. The Pathan stripped their bodies and took their rifles. Since .303 ammunition was scarce they sold them on across the Himalayas and this particular one had ended up in Sichuan. The armourer – who had a taste for fine weapons – brought it there at an arms bazaar but still had no ammunition for it. This problem was solved when, in Wuhan, he had visited the government arsenal and found a whole wooden box full of .303 ammunition. It had fallen off the back of a British Army lorry on the Bund.[2]

The armourer, during pauses on the march, because he admired this beautiful weapon, spent a great deal of time instructing Wei on how to fire it and how to clean and oil it. He emphasized again and again how clean it must be kept and how well oiled. Wei, the skilled farmer, knew all about maintaining fine tools and complex machinery.

The Deplorables marched on for Tengxian.

9

I have read my class's plays. They are awful. Totally unsuited to the job they are meant to do. Tian Boqi's is especially awful. One long Marxist rant with the chief character, an idealistic young student, screaming incessantly at a whole herd of peasants.

I decide the way to get them to understand what is needed, rather than holding long sterile debates in a classroom, is by letting them see first-hand some of the superb and wildly popular drama and drum singing which is performed each day on our streets. Let them see how ordinary Chinese flock to it, become enthralled in the story. How skilled writers and actors can bewitch and entrance their audiences – their techniques and tricks and artifices. How they can learn from this and serve their country.

So my class and I catch a morning ferry across the Yangtze to the Bund, where such a rich variety of drama is daily performed.

In fact, I'm not being exactly accurate when I describe all their scripts as worthless. There is one which is in fact quite useable, written, amazingly, by the perpetually smiling, perpetually childlike Chang Lee – he who was raised in rather sheltered circumstances by a rather over-controlling mother. His play is about a mischievous monkey who makes friends with a lonely child called Lian and comes to live with him in his house. This upsets Lian's mother because the monkey is often naughty and leaves terrible messes behind him. His mother tells Lian that the monkey must go. Lian is terribly upset. He talks with the monkey. The monkey is very sorry and explains he behaves this way because the Japanese came and set fire to the tree where he and his whole family lived and chased them all away so the monkey became lost and didn't know where to go. The monkey promises not to make any more messes. Lian and the monkey tell all this to Lian's mother and Lian's mother takes pity on the monkey, who stays and becomes a valued and beloved member of their household.

I can't see this story persuading many peasants to take up arms against the Japanese, but it will work beautifully with children. Especially children who have been scared witless by all the mayhem and fear they sense around them but don't understand why. This, in a gentle way, explains what is happening, gives reassurance.

I take the script down the corridor to my friend Lao Xiang – he who is so brusque and aggressive in his adult writing but maintains a soft spot for children and writes gentle truths for them in his poems and playlets. I explain to him some of Lee's more bizarre upper-class characteristics before suggesting the two of them might make a good children's writing team. Lao looks wolfish and licks his lips.

As our ferry departs from Wuchang I'm cheered to see large numbers of junks being loaded with the light industrial machinery and equipment of the worker cooperatives General Feng Yuxiang has been setting up in the refugee camps. The members of these co-ops carefully supervise the loading of their machinery while their families, laden with children and possessions, board the same junks for their long journey upstream to Chungking. We Chinese are starting to do that most un-Chinese thing – organize ourselves.

Our ferry is out on the waters. A dull throb starts to permeate the air. We look up. A large fleet of Japanese bombers are flying slowly, menacingly over Wuhan. This is the first time I have seen a large raid. The passengers chatter nervously among themselves. The planes are flying west over the Bund, crossing the Han River just before it joins the Yangtze, and are now starting to drop bombs over Hanyang, Wuhan's industrial area. It is packed with foundries and steel mills and armouries and factories and textile mills. Around them are packed the hovels of all the workers. The fattest and easiest of targets. The bombs rip into it – there are explosions, smoke, fires – our passengers gasp and cry out. My students shout angry slogans at the bombers. There is no anti-aircraft fire and the bombers fly slowly off, unharmed, towards the north.

Fires break out all over Hanyang. Much of our country's remaining industrial production is centred in that small area. The smoke from the fires combines with the smoke from Hanyang's factories and steel mills so that the whole area disappears beneath a pall of smog From within it issues a confused cacophony of ambulance sirens and fire engine bells. Finally, the Japanese bombers long since departed, three of our antiquated biplane fighters manage to rise into the air to fight them.

One thing cheers me, though. Down by the Hanyang riverside, despite the terror and chaos of the air raid, work continues uninterrupted around the docks and quays. Unflinchingly, coolies and dockers and cranes continue to load the freighters and junks tied up there with vital steel and machinery and lathes and generators and lorries to be transported upstream through the Three Gorges to the safety of South-West China where factories are even now being built to continue, indeed to increase our production. Whole foundries and factories are being systematically dismantled in Hanyang to be transported, piece by piece, upstream to their new sites. And all through the bombs and destruction the steamers and junks with their precious cargo keep backing out from the docks and steaming and sailing steadily upstream while other vessels nose in to take their places.

Quite sobered, we land on the Bund. The Bund is of course continuing in its usual frenzied manner, totally unaffected by life, death and Japanese bombers. We land amid the coffins and are met with a very stirring sight. A crocodile of very young children, orphans – heads shaven, uniforms neat and clean – make their way, hand in hand, down the gangplank onto a waiting steamer which will evacuate them upstream to Chungking and a new life. In the waters below churn the usual corpses (there has been a battle to the north and the bodies have floated down the Han River), so some kind soul has thoughtfully provided lots of kites streaming colourfully above the steamer – kites shaped like bright butterflies or castles or beautiful angelfish with streamers floating down from them – so the little children naturally stare upwards at them rather than down at the carnage below. They cheerfully pipe a popular children's song written by my friend Lao Xiang:

Fly away, fly away,
Fly away, birds.
Winter comes with frost and snow,
The cold chill comes, there is no food,
Fly away, fly away.
Fly back, fly back,
Fly back, birds.
Spring comes, the air is warm,
The trees are full of flowers and scent,
Fly back, fly back.

Let's hope when they get upstream they'll be able to watch a fine play by Chang Lee.

We pass from the world of coffins into the world of food and clothes markets. Then something unpleasant happens.

There is a part of the Bund where many beggars gather. Quite a few of them are children, because children attract the greatest pity and largest contributions from the public. The men – demons, more like – who run these children deliberately starve them so they look gaunt and pathetic. Some go even further. They deliberately and cruelly mutilate their limbs and faces – legs are removed, eyes are pulled out and faces cut about – 'This is what the barbarian Japanese have done to our poor children' shout their masters, 'come and see the horror' – so that, filled with pity, the crowds contribute even more. There is one tiny girl there with gouged-out eyes and a scar all across her face – those fiendish Japanese! She so upsets me – she reminds me of my own daughter who I deserted. She could herself now be living in such awful circumstances! I turn my head away. But one person in our company does not pass by on the other side.

Tian Boqi catches one sight of this girl and stops dead. His face turns white. Muscles swell and work up and down all through his throat and face. He is furious. Fists clenched he moves, staring towards the atrocity. I get between him and her.

'Tian Boqi There is nothing we can do for her.'

'Get out of my way, you cowardly Manchu worm,' he snarls,

brushing me aside, and pushing his way towards a guard who leans against a wall nonchalantly smoking a cigarette.

'You!' roars Tian. 'You!'

Tian Boqi is large and well formed. A formidable man. The guard half swallows his cigarette and shouts out 'Trouble!'

By the time Tian reaches the girl two muscular and extremely unpleasant thugs stand between him and her. One draws a knife. I get between them and him.

'Tian Boqi, there is nothing we can do. Do you want these gangsters to knife you? Your fists can do nothing against their knives. Get back.'

By now several of his classmates have gathered about him, urging him to be cautious.

He does not move.

'Tian Boqi,' I continue, 'there is nothing you can do about this now. It is only when we have real political power that we can deal with atrocities like this.'

Tian Boqi thinks for a moment. Then he looks round my head and at the two gangsters standing facing him. He points at them. In his finest and highest Han accent he pronounces:

'I tell you this. When the revolution comes, when the true and decent working people of China seize power from the rats and vermin such as yourselves who rule us now, this is what will happen. You will be the first to be hung before the people of China. Because of what you have done to these children you will be hung so high the birds of the air will build nests in your hair and peck out your eyes to feed their young.'

With that he pushes me away, turns around, and walks off. The rest of us follow obediently. The gangsters strike the distracted children to get them begging again. For the first time I realize there is something admirable in Tian Boqi. A decency and a real passion for righting wrongs. But why is he so angry?

I am taking them to a tent-like structure on the Bund where the famous Beijing drum singer Shanyaodan performs. I used to love his father's performances when I was a child on the streets of Beijing and have watched several of his plays here in Wuhan. His superb technique alternates between beating and gently tapping and brushing his drum – it almost sings! – and incanting and reciting a dramatic narrative, usually of a historical, mythological nature. His performance flows with strong rhythms and rich images. Audiences rush into the worlds he creates.

I speak sternly to my students before we go in. Say that this is one of China's greatest artists. (A few guffaws.) That they must show respect. This is the theatre the Chinese people love, and we must learn from it. Tian Boqi just looks at me.

We enter.

Packed, silent, dark.

Shanyaodan stands before us on a small stage. He holds a drum under one arm but does not look at it as he conjures all sort of sounds – from the harshest to the softest to the most subtle – from it. Instead he stares ahead of him, over the heads of his audience, into the distance., his face a mask of concentration, occasionally slipping into terror and tragedy or amusement.

He tells the story of how the mighty warrior Zhang Fei stood alone and held the crooked timber bridge at Changban against Cao Cao's whole army. China's greatest leader Liu Bei had been forced to retreat by Cao Cao's overwhelming numbers, but at Changban a sudden cavalry attack had split Liu Bei from his family, the civilians he had been protecting. Liu Bei was forced to retreat across the bridge, but first he sent his trusted lieutenant Zhao Yun to try and rescue his wife and only child. Until Zhao Yun returned, Zhang Fei, Liu Bei's greatest warrior, swore to hold the bridge against all comers.

Shanyaodan stares out beyond his audience. Face like stone, eyebrows raised, straight as arrows, eyes glaring.

A sudden pandemonium from his drum.

Silence.

'He, Zhang Fei, stands mighty on the rough and crooked
    timbers of the bridge.
The bridge sways and creaks. The wind sighs.

In the distance the cries of women and children being
    massacred,
defenceless people's blood flying red in the air.
In iron armour, handling his sword,
Zhang Fei impatiently treads from side to side.
No Zhao Yun, no wife or baby.
Soldiers approach.
Cavalrymen, archers, swordsman, spear men.
Zhang Fei lets them. He will not budge one inch from his
    narrow bridge.
Soldiers saunter up,
amused that only one man will fight.
Laugh, joke among themselves, call him out.
Zhang ignores this. Still no sign of Zhao Yun, mother and child.
One soldier, emboldened, brags before his fellows, swaggers up.
"Are you mighty Liu Bei's entire army?
The only soldier that will fight for him?
Scram!"
In Zhang Fei's red face, surrounded by black hair and black
    beard and black eyebrows,
furious demons spasm in his cheeks,
rage eats his soul...'

The drum thunders.

'...he roars as man has never roared before,
a roar so overpowering it sweeps all before it.
The single braggart and all his tittering friends and fellows are
    smashed off their feet, tumble, plummet back into a jumble
    of bodies fifty yards before the bridge.'

At this, cries break out among the audience, groans and sighs
and murmurs of wonderment. One of the student giggles.
    Shanyaodan speaks over them.

'Slowly the skittled terrified soldiers rise, reassemble
    themselves,

turn towards Zhang Fei.
Now they know they face a true opponent.
Still no sign of mother or baby or brave Zhao Yun.
His enemies murmur among themselves, take formation, as
    one charge.
Arrows, spears, swords axes arrows fly and smash and flash in
    the air,
arms and limbs and torsos fly in the air and scatter on the
    ground and into the water around the bridge,
screams and shouts and curses and groans.
Only Zhang Fei is unmoved,
silent and calm
he sheathes his sword,
hums his favourite tune
like a farmer scything his hay,
a baker pummeling his dough,
a shepherd counting his flock.
Then, in the distance, Zhang Fei sights brave Zhao Yun,
a baby tied to his back
but no mother,
galloping hard for the bridge.'

My ill-mannered students have started to talk among
themselves. Audience members look at them. Like the true
professional Shanyaodan raises his game.

'The soldiers turn,
see the approaching horseman,
turn to face and kill him.
But at this exact second – not having moved an inch from his
    position until now –
suddenly Zhang Fei launches himself from the crooked
    timbered bridge
and falls on the backs of his enemies
– cutting and slicing and severing and maiming
the enemies of China,
the enemies of justice and compassion and hope

– as across the bridge gallops Zhao Yun and his royal infant
followed by Zhang Fei
(unmolested by his shattered foes)
calmly retreating, always facing his enemy,
smashing one bridge timber after the next as he steps
    backwards.
On dry land he raises his sword and resounds in victory.
Brave Zhang Fei!'

There are shouts of joy. Screams of emotion and ecstasy and release from the audience.

Shanyaodan stands motionless, emotionless before them. Swiftly he bows and retreats behind a curtain.

I look at my students. Unmoved, dismissive of everything they have seen. Some gurn, others giggle. None do anything to hide their contempt. Which provokes angry comments from audience members who are leaving. One even accuses Tian Boqi of being a 'Japanese traitor!' Tian Boqi stares at him as if he's mad. Then shouts after him accusing him of being 'an ignorant peasant'.

I tell him to shut up.

He says he won't. 'Why did he accuse me of being a Japanese traitor?'

'Because, with your mockery and rudeness, you ridiculed an anti-Japanese play.'

'How was that load of feudal garbage and warlord posturing an anti-Japanese play?'

I look at them standing in the now empty theatre. They are all, in their youthful way, so literal, so intellectually muscle-bound, inbred in their thought.

'Didn't you think that when Zhang Fei held the bridge so heroically he was actually defending Wuhan against the Japanese? That the baby he was holding the bridge to rescue was in fact the infant China, the new China?'

'Don't be stupid.'

'Well, that's what the audience thought, however stupid. That was why there was such emotion. That's why your laughter and levity caused such upset.'

'They need plain undistorted truths and dialectics – not reactionary medieval gobbledygook.'

'Tian Boqi,' I ask him, 'have you ever wondered why in China there are more temples dedicated to Zhang Fei or Zhuge Liang than to Confucius himself?'

'No,' he said, 'I haven't! All temples should be burnt down!'

At this moment the curtain is drawn back again and Shanyaodan, his make-up removed, steps softly into the theatre.

'Gentlemen,' he addresses us, 'especially you young gentlemen,' he continues to my writers, bowing towards them, 'I am so honoured to have performed before you.'

Having attended several of his performances I had asked Shanyaodan if he would honour my students with a brief talk on the art of acting, of how to 'read' an audience as you perform before them so that you can adjust your performance and the script's meaning to please and intrigue and persuade them. Subtle skills vital to both acting and propaganda.

I address Shanyaodan.

'Revered master,' I say, 'thank you for the great performance we have just witnessed. I note that, since your previous performance, you have added more pointed barbs against our enemy and more patriotic pieces to please your audience.'

He bows to me, then turns to address my students. I stand behind him and glare at them. I so rarely glare that it seems, if only momentarily, to shock them into good behaviour. Perhaps I should glare more often.

'Yes,' he replies. 'I noticed, as I performed, that when my hero behaved selflessly – for the common good – or when he insulted or defeated his enemies – this led to greater involvement and emotion in my audience. So that I started to add to them. Be more flagrant in my contempt for the enemy, more daring and courageous in my hero's deeds and words. The audience reactions to this signalled to me they demanded even more. As an actor I am here to serve my audience. That is the actor's duty. The fact that I, as a Chinese man, fully share their anger at the Japanese and their emotions for my country are beside the point. I must express to them their feelings and desires.'

'Perhaps you could tell us more about how you read your audience?'

'As an actor, at every moment, you must watch, sense, ride your audience. Know precisely what they're thinking, what they're needing. You must continually trim and alter your performance, adapt your script, watch for every reaction and sigh. An audience controls, leads their actor.'

My class are not listening to him. Without being actually impolite they are looking elsewhere, scratching, even yawning. Of course Shanyaodan, the consummate actor, is immediately aware of this. His beautiful baritone starts to become a bit strained, nervous even. Partly it's the insecurity which all elder men feel when they are addressing youth. But also he senses that his mellifluous actorly voice is starting to feel insincere, superficial to them.

I see it is time to end this. I thank him heartily for his time, the wisdom of his talk, of the importance always of targeting your voice and your script towards your audiences' feelings and aspirations, so that, by engaging them, you can attract them to *your* meanings and *your* objectives. Shanyaodan bows and disappears once more behind his curtain. I herd my writers outside onto the Bund.

Coolies struggle past beneath their loads, mothers argue, market traders shout, a gaggle of students push past denouncing Germany's recent threats against Austria. All of this passes my group by. They are already huddled in deep ideological dissection.

Chou Taofen slides onto the dance floor first.

'Massification,' he pronounces, 'that play was total massification. A blind imitation of old forms. It capitulated to all the most reactionary social and political evils in China.'

Zou Feng follows seamlessly on.

'Our revolutionary drama must,' he demands, 'create mass revolutionary consciousness, form new art forms and contents, speak a new and pure language that all can understand.'

Tian Boqi turns directly at me. From his towering height glowers down on my insignificance and, ice in his immaculate Han accent, addresses me.

'You showed us your cowardly and grovelling reactionary

character earlier when you refused to allow me to beat the criminals who had so grievously wounded that poor little girl beggar.'

He continues.

'And now you bring us to this farce. We are serious writers. We have a revolution to engineer. Get out of our way, old man.'

Which leaves me, actually, with only one last card to play. I inform the group that I have decided that one of their plays must be performed. Publicly. Before an actual peasant audience. In an actual village. They have three days to prepare and rehearse it. Tian Boqi's play will be the one to be performed.

Hu Lan-shih had spent quite a lot of time worrying about what sort of clothes she should wear to her first meeting of the important government committee she'd so suddenly, so unexpectedly been appointed to. Not that she had that many different clothes to choose from. In fact she didn't have any. Just the ones she stood up in – her white blouse and black trousers. Spider Girl had very kindly washed them the night before and sewn up some tears in their fabric. But some of the blood stains Hu'd got from dressing the soldiers' wounds had proved impossible to remove. 'Well,' thought Hu to herself, 'I will present myself to these grand people as I am. And they can make of me what they want.'

She and Spider Girl were promenading slowly along the Bund – Spider Girl to do her daily shopping, Hu to attend her first meeting.

Hu was simultaneously fretting and trying to calm herself for the strange ritual she was about to undergo. A high government committee! She walked along in uncharacteristic self-absorption. Spider Girl took her silence to conclude she was in love. That she was probably going through a difficult phase with her lover. Spider Girl wanted to know all about it.

Hu denied she was in love.

This denial only confirmed Spider Girl's suspicions.

'If you're having difficulties with him I can recommend a really good witch. Just take her some hair or fingernail clippings and he'll be round your finger in an instant. And she's not expensive. I can introduce you to her.'

'Spider Girl, I am not in love. With anyone!'

Spider Girl could see Hu was too upset to talk about it so she recommended a pick-me-up potion that was on sale at a close-by stall and then went off to the food market to do her own shopping.

Hu returned to her preoccupations. If Agnes Smedley and Li Dequan, who Hu trusted implicitly, and Shi Liang and Madame Chiang, who Hu did not trust at all, all thought she could be of some use on this committee, if it could help people, lots of people, then she had to do it.

So she dutifully continued on her journey and arrived at the entrance to a great government building where the meeting was to be held.

She looked up at its many storeys towering above her. There were two guards on the door. She showed them her letter of introduction. They let her through. Into a great long corridor with high, high ceilings. A young official greeted her. He smiled, wasn't for a second taken aback by her primitive clothes, and shook her hand vigorously in a most un-Chinese fashion. He led her up staircases and down corridors until at last they arrived at the committee room. It was large enough to fit a farmhouse in.

The tables were set in a sort of square, with the chairs set outside the square so that the committee members all faced each other. Proceedings were overseen by a chairman who sat on an elevated dais surrounded by heraldic flags and carvings. The meeting looked as though it had been going on for several hundred years. One man was standing behind his table and speaking in a long, boring voice. No one was listening to him. A group had gathered at the foot of the chairman's dais and were laughing sycophantically at his jokes. Two other groups had assembled on opposite sides of the table square. Each was whispering conspiratorially among themselves and looking furtively over their shoulders at the group opposite. Every so often one member of the group standing on the inside of the tables would scurry quickly over to the other group and hostile whisperings and murmurs would be exchanged before the individual scurried back.

This was not a meeting as Hu remembered them from her trade union days in Shanghai. Then everyone was crammed into a tiny room around a small table with a few people sat down and everyone else jammed up against the walls. People spoke swiftly, curtly, to the point. Others stood outside guarding them against sudden and violent attacks from the secret police or company thugs. People were taken away from these meetings and shot.

The young official showed Hu to her seat – where sharpened pencils and writing paper had already been laid on the table before her – and was about to hurry off to join the lackeys at the feet of the chairman when Hu asked him what the meeting was about and to explain how she went about being recognized by the chair so she could speak? The young man said it was already arranged for her to speak and she would be called soon. He was just about to hurry off when Hu repeated – 'Yes, but what is this meeting about?'

'Ah,' said the clerk, looking momentarily flummoxed, 'someone said housing – I think.'

He was off. Hu sat there. The standing man continued his long, lonely speech in his monotonous voice. No one listened to him. Except Hu. Hu thought that by listening to him she might finally be able to discover what the meeting was about. Eventually she managed to work out it was indeed about the housing crisis.

Although it wasn't her subject – she had rather thought Madame Chiang had seconded her to this committee to speak about health issues, specifically soldiers' health – it didn't mean Hu did not have ideas about housing. Housing was one of the main subjects she and Agnes and Li Dequan discussed when Li visited the apartment.

While working with Agnes on the Bund, treating the wounded soldiers and refugees, Hu had noticed all the sampans moored to the quay. They had grown exponentially over the last few months. Now at least half a mile of the Bund had these tiny craft tied up to it. And to each moored sampan a whole string of more sampans were roped so they trailed out far into the river. Each boat was protected from the elements by a low-arched covering of bamboo mats under which thrived entire families – grandparents, parents, multitudinous children. The boats were linked by planks, so that these narrow highways – constantly in use – stretched far out into the waters. From nothing a miniature floating city had created itself, an anthill of human activity, replete with those eternal human constants – birth, marriage and death. The craft were hired for pennies by refugee families from the north and east, whose men now worked as coolies and porters and labourers on the docks. They carried endless goods in panniers slung from poles, they pushed wheelbarrows, shifted heavy stone or iron, with heavy ropes slung over shoulders they tugged at vast human-drawn carts while many more shoved and strained from behind. Homely smoke rose from chimneys on each craft as the food for every family was prepared.

But over the last few weeks, sharp-eyed Hu had noticed a change in this activity. Instead of the number of boats continuously expanding – there was plenty of spare dockside they could moor to – the constant growth of this city had mysteriously come to an end. But why? These homes were precisely what the refugees needed. Families who before had had to survive only on handouts and charity became independent, could fend for themselves, became a burden on no one.

Hu asked among the boatmen why this increase had ended. The answer was that this demand had caused such a shortage of boats in the Wuhan area that their price had shot up. But, Hu thought, further up the Yangtze, further up the Han and Xiang rivers, there were thousands of such craft, dead cheap. Why wasn't the government buying or hiring them, sailing them downstream, and then either giving them away or hiring them out and bringing down the prices?

What is more, reasoned the quick-witted Hu, with all these families now joined together by their wooden highways into a larger community, why not tow these living communities upstream with government-hired tugs to Chungking or Changsha, whose ports and industries were desperate for new labour? All that was required was some organization.

Hu sat there for a long time waiting to be called. Because health was her main area of expertise, she asked various people if they knew if there was a corresponding health committee she could contribute to, but no one seemed to know. A long lunch was held, for at least three hours, while Hu sat all alone in this cavernous room. Luckily she had brought a couple of dumplings which Spider Girl had given her. There was a bowl of water already on the table. The young orderly again passed – on his way back from lunch – and again reassured her that she would be heard soon. Daytime passed into evening, which turned into night. Soon there was only the chairman and his clerk and Hu left. Now at last I must be heard, thought Hu, but the chairman got up and walked out. After a while the clerk finished writing and looked up.

'You may speak now if you wish,' he said.

'But no one is here,' responded Hu.

'You may make your comments and I will write them down,' stated the clerk. 'So that anyone who is interested might read your contribution.'

Well, someone might see them, thought Hu. She also realized that, if Madame Chiang read the notes, she would assume that Hu had taken a full and meaningful part in the meeting. So Hu, all alone in the vast room, started to speak.

This was not how Hu had envisaged a committee working.

10

On what would be the battlefield of Taierzhuang the Sichuan troops of the 22nd Army Group – the Deplorables – and their commanding officer Wang Mingzhang, were given a banquet by General Li Zongren, commanding officer of the Fifth War Zone, the man given the responsibility of defending Wuhan and Central China from the Japanese. All around the diners were thousands of coolies and pioneer troops and engineers and officers frantically digging trenches and tunnels, building fortalices and machine gun nests and mortar and artillery emplacements and first aid posts, reinforcing command posts, stringing out telephone lines, piling up supplies and food and ammunition in cellars and fortified buildings, preparing the defences of Taierzhuang.

So that all this building and work could be completed and Li Zongren's finest troops arrive and be deployed within the city, it was the task of the 22nd to march fifty miles north to the town of Tengxian and there hold up the advance of Rensuke Isogai's crack 10th Division of the Imperial Japanese Army for as long as was possible. To the last man. The Deplorables knew that they were all going to die.

It was a simple banquet. Plain food and cheap wine laid out on tables.

Before it started, Wang Mingzhang, their commanding officer, addressed Li Zongren.

'Both the First and Second War Zones reject us, in the whole wide world there is no place for us, then you, Commander Li, accept us in the Fifth War Zone. We are indebted to your grace. Whatever you command we shall certainly do. Being soldiers it is our duty to sacrifice ourselves to protect the nation. Now we can only resolve to sacrifice everything to complete our mission, even if not a single one of us survives.'

This was met with a resounding cheer by the troops. The banquet started. Quite a lot of wine was necked.

Fat Rat was boasting that as they were from Chengdu, the capital town of Sichuan and once the capital city of the great warrior Liu Bei, hero of the *Romance of the Three Kingdoms*, this meant they were invincible.

Boss Eyes the corporal, a man with a broader knowledge of China than Fat Rat, pointed out that they were even more invincible than that because Linyi – a town only a few miles east of Tengxian (the town they were being sent to die in) – was the birthplace of Zhuge Liang, Liu Bei's political and military advisor and the greatest soldier China has ever known.

For some reason this caused a fight. Fat Rat hit Boss Eyes. Creaky Door with the croaky voice hit Fat Rat. Dirty Rat hit Creaky Door but then hit his brother Fat Rat because Fat Rat had stood on his foot. The fight quickly became general. The Deplorables specialized in this sort of thing.

Meanwhile Greedy the dog, oblivious to mere human animosities, gorged himself almost to death on all the food and wine that was spilling from the tables.

As evening arrived the Deplorables managed a muster, collected their kit, and, despite their bruises and hangovers, lined up ready for the march. At the command, straw hats on, teapots and opium pipes jangling from their belts, straw sandals swashing in the mud, they marched off north towards Tengxian.

Greedy the Dog was the most drunk of all, but, having four legs rather than two, managed to stay more upright than several members of his platoon.

Tengxian was an unpretentious market town surrounded by stone walls which were being frantically repaired. From the north came already the ominous growl of heavy artillery. Japanese reconnaissance planes overflew them constantly. To the west the

Jinpu Railway, from Jinan to Nanking, ran north–south. Hundreds of pioneer troops and farmers were busy tearing up the track and blowing up the bridges to slow the Japanese advance. Similar work was being done every night to the north, in Japanese-held territory, by thousands upon thousands of brave peasants.

The Deplorables swung proudly through the southern gate and into the town. Tengxian was largely built of stone and had narrow streets filled with homes and light industry and shops. The railway lines which the railway workers and local peasantry had been tearing up had been transported into the town and local blacksmiths were cutting them up and a spontaneous cooperative of some sixty blacksmiths and railway workers were melting them down and beating out crude broadswords, tempering and sharpening their blades and passing them out to those pioneer troops not armed with swords and to any local peasants who looked ready for a fight.[3]

Wang Mingzhang decided to make his headquarters in a light bulb factory by the west gate, and his forward command post in a salt merchant's shop. The troops were put to immediate work reinforcing the outside walls, constructing fortified strongholds on the walls, and digging trenches and tunnels within the town. Members of the local Red Spear Society helped them wherever they could, handing out free food from the local shops and laying telephone wires between all the command posts.

All around everyday life continued in the town. A market was open and thriving – Greedy, having walked off his hangover, was in dog heaven – priests and monks chanted prayers within the temples and mosques, farmers and corn merchants haggled with each other in the streets, a little girl gaily flew a kite. Wei gazed at her for quite a while. She reminded him so much of Cherry Blossom. Then with redoubled zeal he set to filling the sandbags. He knew now what he was going to defend.

Wei's platoon had been sent to reinforce some trenches that had been dug outside the north wall. Wei was sandbagging a machine gun emplacement in one of them while beyond him Creaky Door and Fat and Dirty Rat were driving stakes into the ground and winding coils of barbed wire around them and nailing them to the stakes. Wei was enjoying himself. For the first time in months he was using his body as it was meant to be used – for work. The swing of his arms, the crunch of his stomach muscles as the shovel drove into the sand and then the clench of his shoulders and twirl of his arms again as he swung the sand into the sack. The familiar, soothing rhythm of it all. Several of the soldiers congratulated him on the speed and deftness of his work.

Then came this sound. The drone of an approaching aircraft, the scream as it started to dive. Wei looked all around him, then directly up into the sky. There it was! Directly above him, falling precisely where he stood, its engine screaming with hunger and hatred. Wei remembered what one bomb had done to his family. Panic seized him. He ran. Ran anywhere, everywhere, in ever decreasing circles. Then came the whistle of a bomb falling, followed by a thump and crack as it fell onto empty ground some two hundred yards from Wei. Wei stood still. The other troops started jeering him from the trench where Wei had been working and where they had all immediately taken shelter.

Wei returned shamefaced to the trench. He was here to fight, not run. He was here to avenge his family, atone his ancestors, gain redress for all his crops lying wasted and dead in his fields. Boss Eyes took him to one side.

'When bullets start to fly, when shells start to land, when bombers start to bomb, always remember, there is only one safe place – the earth, a trench. You can't outrun a bomb.'

Wei apologized, said he felt disgrace. Boss Eyes continued kindly.

'Don't apologize. Don't feel ashamed. I ran three times when I was first bombed. Remember, Posh Northerner, a trench in the ground, deep in the soil, is always your best friend. Tudeh will protect you there, his earth will shelter you from all the bombs and bullets.'

Wei looked at Boss Eyes.

'You pray to the earth god Tudeh? You were a farmer once?'

'Many years ago,' said Boss Eyes sadly. 'Before all these unending wars started.'

After that both men felt close to each other.

On 15 March 1938, Wang Mingzhang ordered the four gates of Tengxian, north, south, east and west, to be sealed. No one was to leave. Civilians from the surrounding villages could still be allowed in to seek shelter. The trenches immediately surrounding the walls were still to be manned and the troops in them could gain access to the town by ladders set against the walls. At the last moment, at the railway station at the west gate, a train delivered a very large consignment of hand grenades. They were swiftly distributed to the troops throughout the town. Every soldier now had access to fifty grenades.

Three thousand Chinese troops, poorly armed, poorly trained, waited inside Tengxian Town. Ten thousand crack Japanese troops, the vanguard of the Imperial Japanese Army's 10th Division, approached and largely surrounded it.

At dawn on 16 March, twenty Japanese troops, disguised as civilians, approached the east gate and asked to be admitted as refugees from local villages. They were recognized and shot dead. Japanese artillery then fiercely bombarded the east gate for several hours while their troops approached under cover of the bombardment. Tengxian was bombed repeatedly from the air. It had no anti-aircraft defences.

A small breach was made in the eastern wall close to the gate. The Japanese prepared to assault it. Wei's platoon was withdrawn from their northern trench, climbed up their ladders, and ordered to reinforce the troops close to the breach in the eastern wall. They hurried through the town. Buildings were burning, they saw several dead and injured civilians. They saw the body of the young girl they'd earlier seen so merrily flying her kite. This stiffened their resolution. As they arrived at the breach sixty or so Japanese jumped into the dried-up moat beneath the breach in an attempt to storm it. Each member of Wei's platoon threw several grenades into the moat and all the Japanese died.

Wei and his platoon were ordered up onto the walls to join the other troops already there while pioneer troops and local volunteers worked to seal the breach. The breach was heavily bombarded by the Japanese artillery. As fast as the Chinese rebuilt the wall the artillery and aerial bombs demolished it. Many Chinese died but the breach was not widened. Some two hundred Japanese tried to storm it. Rifle fire and a shower of grenades from the soldiers on the walls killed almost all of them and the remnant were driven back. But more and more were coming up and taking cover behind a ridge on the other side of the moat.

To free themselves of the devastating fire from the Chinese troops on the wall the Japanese bombarded it with heavy artillery. They killed many of their own troops hiding in the moat, but also killed almost two hundred Chinese and blew another breach in the wall.

Before the Japanese troops in the moat could recover from their own bombardment, carts arrived from within the town laden with large sacks of corn and salt, taken from the warehouses and cellars of the town's merchants, and local people rushed to fill the breaches with them.

Wei was surprised to find himself quite calm. He admired the efficiency and practicality of his fellow soldiers. They cheered when the enemy was killed, gave out bloodcurdling screams as they drove them back. All the time they looked about them to see what was happening, what was about to happen. When a comrade was in difficulty. They stepped in to aid him. When a friend was killed, they cursed briefly but wasted no time in mourning. They thought as a group, they acted as a group. Wei started to see that fighting was as skilled a trade as farming.

With the Japanese concentrating their fire increasingly on the eastern gate and with more and more Chinese being killed, ever more Chinese reserves (of which there were few) were fed into the zone. Crude barricades had been thrown up back from the breach – made partly of the sacks of corn and salt and partly of the carts that brought them – so that the Chinese had a second line of defence if the troops holding the breach were driven back. A mass Japanese attack was expected imminently.

Covered by machine gun fire and a hail of grenades, hundreds of screaming Japanese stormed the breach. The Chinese holding the breach fought bravely but, bayoneted and shot, they were overcome and the Japanese, shrieking, charged through the smoke and flames at the barricade. In a second all was chaos and pandemonium – bayonet thrusts and parries and counter-thrusts, pistol shots, kicks, punches, fingers in eyes, fists through teeth, skulls against rifle butts – swaying back and forth, grappling for advantage, toppling, screaming – but in the end it was the broadswords of the surviving Chinese with their quick sweeps and counter-sweeps and thrusts which turned the tide and drove the few surviving Japanese back through the breach.

Dirty Rat would not hit Creaky Door again. Both were dead. Their bodies lay on the ground. Fat Rat mourned his dead brother. Several other members of their platoon were also dead or wounded. Orderlies carried their bodies away. The remaining members of the platoon drank water (or wine if they'd stolen some), ate their rations, and talked soberly among themselves about the recent engagement, discussing details, arguing technicalities. They consoled Fat Rat on his loss. Several come up to Wei and congratulated him on his calmness and fortitude in his first engagement. The member of the platoon who seemed to have enjoyed it most was Greedy the Dog. All the explosions and fires and collapsing masonry had loosed thousands of terrified rats into the town. Greedy, laying about himself left right and centre, was treating the whole place as a sumptuous rat buffet. Snapping a large rat's neck with a jerk of his teeth, Greedy sent it flying over his left shoulder and it landed smack in Boss Eyes' face. Everyone laughed. Boss Eyes wiped his face and mouth and delivered Greedy a sound kick.

Wei's platoon, quite badly depleted, was withdrawn from the breach and sent up to the relative safety of the walls. Another platoon from their company took their place.

It was now the late afternoon of 16 March. After a brief period of respite in which the platoon tried to rest an ominous rumbling was heard beyond the battlements, a clanking and squealing of iron machinery and the brutish roar of diesel engines. They peered over the wall. Tanks, squat on the ground, emitting clouds of diesel, advanced towards them.

For a second Wei froze, then below him, by the breach, he noticed something strange. Several soldiers he knew from the 22nd, all opium addicts, were having wreathes of explosives and grenades wound around them; an officer was attaching a plunger and detonator to each garland of high explosive. The men to which they were being attached looked calm, serene even.

Wei asked Boss Eyes what was happening.

'Suicide bombers,' said Boss Eyes. 'Some of them are opium addicts. They've been fairly heavily dosed, so they're happy. And they've been promised their families will be well imbursed and special prayers for them will be said on their ancestors' graves.' Boss Eyes paused. He spoke quietly and with respect. 'But most have volunteered. They believe it is good to die in a noble cause. Until now, with all our civil wars, it has been very difficult to die for a noble cause. Now we have that chance.'

The suicide bombers were ready to go. The officer bowed to each one. Each of them clambered down from the breach and as soon as all of them had reached the ground they fanned out in case any of them exploded prematurely. Laden with explosives they waddled towards the tanks.

Immediately the Japanese infantry sheltering behind the tanks opened fire on them. Wei and the others on the walls returned immediate and deadly fire on them. For the first time Wei appreciated what an accurate and formidable weapon his Lee Enfield rifle was. The soldiers crumpled but the machine gun fire from the tanks themselves hit and detonated two of the bombers. In response the bombers broke from a waddle into a top-heavy jog and lumbered unerringly in on the separate tanks. There were shouts, bangs, explosions. Everything was engulfed in smoke and screams. When the smoke finally cleared four of the tanks were ablaze, their ammunition exploding, and a couple of flaming figures visible inside them, flailing desperately to escape the infernos. The surviving tanks frantically reversed. Two ran into each other. One last bomber zeroed in on them and exploded.

So ended the first day of battle.

★ ★ ★

During the night the remnants of Wei's shattered company were withdrawn to a quieter section of the siege on the northern walls and in the trenches before them. Fresh troops took their place.

Of Wei's original platoon only Boss Eyes and Fat Rat were still alive. Greedy the Dog was also alive and when not chasing down the numerous rats was happy to enjoy their affection. The three survivors were amalgamated with those of three other platoons. Wei knew several of them because they'd marched close to each other on the road.

In the morning the Japanese forces, now deployed almost all around the town, launched a colossal attack on Tengxian. Sixty planes carpet-bombed the town, heavy artillery rained down shells on it, one hundred tanks and thousands of infantry closed in on its defenders. The main attack was again focused on the east gate. It was again breached and the tanks and infantry stormed inside. All along the south-east wall holes were being blown in the masonry through which poured the light-khaki uniforms of the Imperial Japanese Army. In bitter house-to-house fighting they started to take over the south-eastern quarter of the town.

In the trenches to the north of the town's walls, which they'd dug only two days before, Wei's company was bombed repeatedly and bombarded with heavy artillery shells. The ground shook continuously as he and his fellow troops hugged the earth in the bottom of their trenches, burrowing their faces into it, almost eating it – praying that, like moles, they could burrow deeper and deeper into it. Wei understood the wisdom of Boss Eyes' statement that the earth was their saviour, their protector. Wei thanked Tudeh the earth god with fervour.

Suddenly there was silence.

'Up,' roared Boss Eyes, who was now the corporal of their new platoon, 'Get up, They're coming!'

All the platoon jumped to their feet, wiped the dust out of their eyes, peered over the edge of their trench. The first Chinese trench was about fifty yards before them. They were in the second line of defence.

The silence continued for another second and then the air was split with scream of 'Banzai' and the bloodcurdling cries of the

Japanese infantry as they charged. They appeared ghostly through the smoke and dust still swirling from the bombardment. Wei and all his platoon in the second trench opened supporting fire on the Japanese infantry as they picked their way through the barbed wire. After two shots Wei got his eye in and saw a Japanese soldier he'd aimed at jerk over as he fired.

The Japanese arrived at the first trench. They fired down into the trench; Chinese troops fired up at them. An officer leapt in, sword flashing, and others followed. Screams and shouts of rage and terror rang out. A general melee ensued. Wei's platoon had no idea what was happening in the first trench. All they could hear were cries of anger and fear. Occasional helmets or bodies were seen rising and falling. If they were Japanese the platoon fired at them.

There was growing frustration in the second trench. Why weren't they joining in, why weren't they aiding their comrades? Their commanding officer, a very young lieutenant, had only joined them this morning (the previous one had died at the east gate) and obviously didn't know what he was doing. Suddenly Fat Rat raised his bayoneted rifle and shouted out.

'Why are we waiting? Why are we waiting? They need our help. Over, lads, over and at them.'

And the whole company cried out 'Over! over! over!' and they climbed over the top and charged towards the first trench. Wei climbed out with Fat Rat immediately before him. Suddenly Fat Rat jerked, and then fell backwards onto his considerable arse. His hands squeezed his stomach. Wei stopped by him.

'What is it, Fat Rat, what is it?'

Fat Rat was lying flat on his back, a cavernous wound opened in his chest, blood welling from a pit of broken bones and ruptured guts and organs.

'Oh,' he grunted, 'Oh the pain. Mother. Mother.'

He died. Wei stared at him. Suddenly he became aware of the shouting and the gunfire coming from in front of him, left Fat Rat and, grabbing his Lee Enfield, ran full tilt for the fight.

The first trench was a frenzy of limbs and bodies and bright steel. For a second Wei waited, weighing what was happening, who needed help, where he could be most effective, then he leapt in behind a Japanese officer and drove him through his back with his 'pig-sticker' bayonet. Blood fountained from the officer's back all across Wei's well-tailored uniform. The officer fell. Wei faced the Chinese soldier who was fighting the officer. Someone was screaming like a banshee. Behind the soldier a Japanese soldier started to thrust with a bayonet. Wei shot him and turned and became involved in a three-way fight between two Japanese – one wounded in the arm – and a Chinese. The wounded one managed to trip the Chinese soldier and the other Japanese soldier stabbed him. Greedy the Dog, fully involved in the fighting, sank his teeth into the Japanese soldier's hand. Wei advanced on them...

The fighting lasted all of four minutes. Four minutes of frenzied chaos. Every eye on stalks to read every motion of all around them. Japanese officers shouting at their men, Chinese soldiers all the time exchanging shouts and warnings to each other. Neither side gained a clear advantage til the Chinese, at Boss Eyes' shout, dropped their rifles and bayonets and drew their broadswords. Nothing as terrible as a broadsword, with its swift jabs and cuts and counter-cuts, in close-quarter combat. Bayonets were clumsy in comparison, guns needed constant reloading and attention.

Most of the Japanese were hacked to death and the rest fled to Chinese cheers and abuse. The surviving Chinese congratulated each other. Wei checked his work. The Japanese officer lay on his back, staring manically at heaven. A little way along the trench lay the Japanese private Wei had shot. He'd shot him in his face. Blood ran from one of his eyes through which Wei's bullet had entered. It clotted and encrusted as it oozed down his face. The force of the bullet had knocked the other eye clean out of its socket. It hung down upon his chest. Flies already clustered and feasted all along the trench. They found Japanese and Chinese equally appetizing. The Chinese were moving among the dead Japanese, removing and pocketing any cigarettes or valuables about their bodies. Japanese cigarettes were not popular but smokable. The Chinese troops were removing the same things from the pockets of those friends who had given them permission to take what they wanted if they died. Prayers were muttered. With a sudden self-preserving reflex Wei looked out over the top of the trench to check if any more Japanese were advancing. They weren't.

A messenger arrived from Wang Mingzhang's headquarters and reported to the young lieutenant. Because of the advance of the Japanese into the east of the town and the heavy Chinese casualties, he was having to shorten his lines. Their company was to withdraw from their trenches and man the walls behind them. The soldiers already there were being transferred to the east. This met with a certain amount of dissension. The victorious company felt it could take on the entire Japanese Army. But the young lieutenant was obeyed. He'd won respect in the eyes of his soldiers by his display of swordsmanship in the trench.

They started to withdraw to the walls. Wei helped a man with a wounded leg, the man's arm over his shoulder. As they hobbled along they passed the body of Fat Rat. Wei glanced down at him. It could only be thirty minutes since he'd died, but such was the intensity of what Wei had been involved in, he could hardly remember Fat Rat's death. It was as though it had all happened a hundred years ago.

As Wei climbed the ladder back onto the wall, as he almost reached the top, he felt a thump in his left shoulder. He lost his hold. He would have fallen if Boss Eyes, already on top of the wall, had not caught hold of him and dragged him over. He fell in a heap, back against the wall. There was blood. Wei had been shot by a Japanese sniper.

Wei had been moved by Boss Eyes to a cellar close to the wall. A family huddled along a wall opposite them.

'You have been shot in the shoulder by a Japanese sniper,' Boss Eyes explained to Wei. 'It's a flesh wound. It passed right through your shoulder without hitting any bones. Tudeh was looking out for you. But what you have to fear is infection. The wound festering internally, gangrene.'

The two men looked at each other closely. Boss Eyes smiled.

'Fortunately we have Greedy the Dog to help you.'

Greedy was summoned from the carcase of a particularly tasty rat. Boss Eyes took out his knife and cut away the expensive fabric of Wei's shirt from front and back of his shoulder.

'Sorry about your shirt,' he apologized.

He picked up the dog and held him to Wei's wound. Greedy started to lick it.

'Dog licking is a good way to cleanse a wound,' he explained. 'It slowly draws the infection out of the wound. Let him lick both sides for as long as he wants. He's a clever dog.'

Boss Eyes left. The defence of the wall needed organizing, men needed shouting at, weapons checked and cleaned.

Greedy the Dog licked gently and caringly. Wei was used to animals healing wounds. His family always used one of their cats if someone was cut or grazed. Dogs' tongues were softer than cats'.

From outside, all through the night came the crump of bombs and whistles of incoming shells. Distant shouts and screams and the sound of masonry collapsing. Still suffering from the shock of being wounded, Wei slept fitfully through it, but by morning the artillery bombardment had increased, and from just outside the cellar steps there were confused shouts and orders.

The Japanese were not only pushing northwards through the town from their east gate bastion, but they had also entered the town from the west. Now they were again attacking the north wall.

Wei hoisted himself onto his feet. Boss Eyes had left his ammunition pouch and Lee Enfield against the wall. Using his right hand, Wei looped first the pouch and then the rifle over his right shoulder. He went up the stairs. There were Chinese soldiers still on the north wall. His platoon. He climbed the steps onto the wall. The men were firing and swearing. Every so often one of them threw a grenade, shrieking at their enemy. Then there was a bang and the top of a ladder was thrown against the top of the battlement. Two Chinese soldiers immediately threw grenades, destroying both ladder and those climbing it.

Boss Eyes was still there and the two men exchanged weary nods.

Wei looked about him. What could he do with just one arm and hand? He couldn't use a bayonet. He could throw grenades, but that was already being done. He looked over the battlement.

There were Japanese advancing in the distance. Everyone was too busy dealing with those actually coming over the walls to bother about them. Wei knelt down by a crenellation in the wall. A shell exploded quite close by but he didn't notice. He placed his ammunition pouch by his right hand, then, with his rifle leant against the wall to his right, started feeding its chamber one by one with bullets. It was full. He lifted the rifle to rest on the top of the parapet then raised his left arm – it was largely useless – to rest on top of the rifle to keep it steady. He squinted through the sights and took aim, searching for a target. There was a small rather hunched figure about two hundred yards away shuffling forwards. Looked rather scared. Wei breathed out, took aim, then fired. He didn't bother to look to see if he'd hit but immediately started searching out someone new.

This process went on for some time. Firing all his bullets, refilling the breech, firing again. Gradually he improved his technique. He could prepare the rifle quicker, his aiming became more accurate. He could have sworn that he hit some green-uniformed officer shouting his men onward.

Then came another lull in the fighting. The few surviving men smoked and ate rations and grumbled among themselves. They drank wine they'd found in a destroyed shop to give them energy and concentration. Wei steadily continued his sniping.

There was a large explosion. A Japanese artillery shell had blown a gaping hole in the wall just to the left of the platoon's position. Japanese troops started pouring through the breach.

To avoid being cut off they were forced to immediately withdraw. They jumped and clambered off the wall and immediately started retreating, running down a street with the Japanese close behind. Boss Eyes must have fallen at this point for Wei never saw him again. It caused him no pain, there was no time to mourn.

They reached some sort of haphazard barricade someone had thrown up. The young lieutenant rallied them behind it. Chickens squawked, hysterical mothers ran hither and thither seeking children, machine gun fire cut down birds and people left and right.

There were only about ten of them. The Japanese attacked. A hail of those precious grenades drove them back. A lull. The young lieutenant looked frantically left, right. What should he do? They were in this street. They couldn't see anywhere outside this narrow street. Were there Chinese troops to the left and right of them, out of sight, holding their lines, or were they by themselves and being encircled this very moment by the Japanese? The young lieutenant decided to hold his line. But he needed information, he wanted instructions and orders from an officer senior to him who knew the whole situation. He looked around, swiftly assessing his men. He chose Wei as the man least capable of fighting, but still mobile.

'Wei.'

'Sir?'

'You know where General Wang's headquarters are? I think he recently moved them to the central crossroads in the town.'

'I know it, sir.'

'Explain to him what's happened, the situation we're in. Does he want us to hold our position or fall back? Are there any troops around us we can link up with?'

'Yes, sir.'

'Do you want me to write it down or can you remember it?'

'I can remember it, sir.'

'Good luck,' said the lieutenant, dismissing him.

Wei took his Lee Enfield, what ammunition remained. No one else in the platoon knew how to operate it. There wasn't anyone left in the platoon to say farewell to; he didn't know anyone else any longer. Except one. Greedy the Dog came up and gave his right hand a quick lick. Then, tail wagging, turned back to the fray. Every dog has its day.

Wei walked amid apocalyptic scenes. It was too painful to run.

Night had again fallen and the flames of the burning town lit a vision of hell. Explosions, flashes, tiny human screams, bewildered grandmothers, abandoned toddlers. In a house that was alight a mother suddenly appeared in an upper window screaming for someone to catch her baby. A man passing managed to catch it. Suddenly he had a child.

Wei made his way with difficulty, having to turn back here or there because he had lost his way or because there were Japanese troops ahead of him. At one stage, stampeding straight down the street at him, was a terrified herd of transport camels, one with its fur ablaze. Wei stepped quickly aside. Finally he arrived at the central crossroads. A soldier stood on guard outside a partially collapsed inn. It must be the headquarters. Wei went up to him.

'Is this HQ?'

'Yes.'

'I have a message for General Wang.'

The guard let him through.

Inside several senior officers were busy putting on their scabbards and swords. They were attired in full dress uniform.

'Yes?' one of the officers asked Wei.

'I have a message for General Wang.'

'General,' said the officer speaking to Wang, 'a message for you.'

'What is it?' Wang asked Wei.

'I have a message from Lieutenant Huang.'

'What company?'

'I don't know, sir, we have mixed up with so many other companies.'

'Where are you positioned?' asked the general, adjusting his regimental sash. Another officer was waxing his moustache.

'On the north wall, sir. Or retreating from it. It's been taken. He asks whether he should hold his ground or retreat?'

The general stopped and sighed. 'Tell him...' Then he had a thought and looked at Wei.

'Can you ride a bicycle? With that arm of yours?'

'Should think so, sir. I could balance well enough.'

'Just the man,' said General Wang, stepping back to his desk and picking up a pen. 'There's still a way out of Tengxian. The enemy haven't taken the south gate yet, but they will do very soon.

I want you to take this message south – you'll have to cut through the countryside, keep away from the main roads. It's for General Sun Zhen. He's positioned at Lincheng. We can't radio because our sets were destroyed and all the telegraph wires are down. Do you think you could get through – arm and all?'

'Yes, sir.'

Wang Mingzhang passed Wei his message.

Wei and the general and all the senior officers left the inn. Wei set off, wobbling a bit, southwards, with his rifle slung across his back. The staff officers, plus the guard outside, resplendent in full dress uniform, swords drawn, set off to meet the enemy and die.

Wei just made his escape. On occasion he had to hide in ditches and woods as Japanese patrols past. But even in total darkness he knew which direction to take. At his back, to the north, all the skies were filled with the flames of a burning Tengxian. Of his burning colleagues.

He arrived in Lincheng the next morning, exhausted, and delivered his message from General Wang to General Sun. It was a farewell.

General Sun looked at Private Wei for quite a while. Then he ordered him to see a medical orderly to get his wound disinfected and properly dressed. When that was over a junior officer handed Wei a railway pass to travel south to Taierzhuang, where he would be reassigned to a fresh regiment for training for the coming battle of Taierzhuang.

Wei saluted and, still with his rifle on his back, set off on his cycle for the station.

The Battle of Tengxian lasted for four days. For four days the 22nd Army Group, the Deplorables, had held up Rensuke Isogai's 10th Division in its march on Taierzhuang. Those four days were to prove vital to the upcoming battle.

Fifty miles to the east, at Linyi, the birthplace of China's greatest soldier, Zhuge Liang, a similar number of Chinese troops managed to successfully halt the Japanese 5th Division – the second part of the pincer that with the 10th Division was meant to encircle and crush Taierzhuang – and drive them back. Only 5 per cent of them survived.

There were no survivors of Tengxian – except for Wei, who is a fictional character. The defenders did not stop their attackers – they were just meant to hold them temporarily. So by the time General Rensuke got his army beyond them, he would be advancing on Taierzhuang alone.

11

General Feng has generously lent us one of his army lorries so that my students and I can travel fifty miles into the countryside to put on a play by Tian Boqi.

My students stand debating among themselves – working out and memorizing lines, arguing between each other on particular points of ideology and dialectic – while the driver and I load the backdrops and props into the back of the lorry.

We drive off, the students in the back still arguing ideology, the driver and I in the front. The driver spends the journey explaining to me precisely how much he hates rickshaw drivers, bicyclists, cart drivers and all other road users.

We arrive. Nobody seems to know anything about us. I locate the village stage and we start to set up our backdrops and curtains. The students are still arguing. A few curious children and two dogs turn out to watch them. The dogs start to fight. For the first time Tian Boqi looks nervous. I suggest that perhaps, in their costumes, they could go into the village and invite the people to attend their performance. Their costumes have been designed in the latest German expressionist style. George Grosz bankers, Kandinsky policemen and a landlord who looks like Nosferatu set off into the village. They certainly attract an audience. Tian Boqi, dressed as himself, gives me a triumphal look.

As a curious audience gathers I mix with them, chat with them. I put on my best Mandarin accent and am relieved that they at least understand what I am saying. Hopefully they will be able to understand the actors as well. I explain these young people are from the government.

'That's very kind of the emperor. I hope there's lots of dancing.'

On that inauspicious note the play starts.

It is about a youthful but rather shy peasant boy (played with some disassociation by the young anarchist with the interesting linguistic theories) who is in love with a beautiful young peasant girl, played by Shan Shuang, the revolutionary poetess. She has removed her glasses for the play and is consequently somewhat short-sighted. They want to marry but before they can the Nosferatu-like landlord turns up with a whip and a rich banker. The banker wants to sleep with the girl. The boy tries to explain he and the girl are in love. The landlord starts to whip the boy. The boy cringes and backs away.

This puzzles the audience.

'Why doesn't he fight back?'

'Punch him!'

'He should get out his sword.'

'He doesn't have one.'

The fact that he doesn't carry a sword clearly baffles the audience, who then start to ask further questions.

'Where is the king?'

'Why is there no king or emperor?'

'I hope there's going to be a princess who suffers terribly and then gets married. Or commits suicide.'

'Why is there no music?'

'Or dancing?'

'I think,' ventured one would-be expert, 'that this is a comedy. That's why they're all talking in such funny voices.'

A sigh of understanding goes up from the audience.

On stage the rich banker is trying to drag the young peasant girl away but she starts to fight back and refuses to go with him, while her peasant lad continues to cringe before his betters. The landlord starts to beat her with his whip. Most cruelly.

Which is met with roars of laughter from the audience. The more Nosferatu lashes the damsel and the more she suffers the louder they laugh.

Shan Shuang, the short-sighted revolutionary poetess playing the peasant girl, puts on her glasses to see what on earth is going on. More gales of laughter. She is not amused.

'Shut up, you ignorant fools. How dare you pollute this revolutionary drama with your coarse laughter. Sit down and learn something, you rural imbeciles.'

This only increases the laughter.

The actors are looking at each other in bewilderment. But the show must go on! The peasant girl, glasses removed, is being dragged offstage by the lascivious banker when suddenly onto the stage springs a Japanese officer of the Imperial Japanese Army, shouting threats that he will massacre every innocent Chinese civilian he finds and waving a large sword around his head.

'At last, a sword!'

'Let's hope the peasant has a sword and can kill him and win the girl.'

But the anarchist/linguist peasant boy continues to cringe. The banker and the landlord run away and the Japanese officer drags the young peasant girl off to do his worst.

'I shall defile your pure Han flesh with my foul imperialist blade.'

The young peasant, alone on stage, starts to bewail his lot.

There are shouts from the audience of 'Get after him,' 'Fight the bastard,' and 'Get your sword out and win back your girl.'

But suddenly onto the stage – he's obviously worried enough by the audience to have borrowed the Japanese officer's sword – leaps Tian Boqi, sword in hand, as a young militant revolutionary student dressed – well, dressed as himself.

A sigh of relief sweeps the audience. Another sword on stage. That obviously means there's going to be a sword fight.

Tian addresses the cringing peasant:

'Oh ignorant beast of burden, weighed down by the neo-feudal reactionary landlords and bankers of the imperialist and capitalist classes. Quit your craven lackeydom! Cast off your subservient shackles and stir your proud loins, stiffened by the resolve of pure Marxist-Leninist ideology and revolutionary materialism to smash the bourgeois fascist...'

This speech goes on for some time. The audience grows restless.

'What is all this rubbish?'

'Why aren't you running after your girl and saving her?'

'Who unlocked these lunatics?'

'Where's the dancing?'

Tian Boqi, looking more than a bit desperate, raises his voice above them, shouting full into the peasant boy's face.

'Break the foul bonds of your reactionary servitude and march with the proud steps of dialectical materialism into the promised land of revolutionary praxis!'

Suddenly the peasant boy leaps to his feet. Tian Boqi's words and arguments have convinced him at last.

'Yes, I will avenge myself against the Japanese imperialists, the Western capitalist bankers and the reactionary landlord clique!' he cries, thrusting his fist to the skies.

An elderly member of the audience has managed to clamber on stage. He starts to complain that the presence of a female actor on stage is a threat to public morals.

Meanwhile another villager has also climbed up and is shouting that these actors are foul Japanese propagandists sent secretly to destroy the morale of the noble Chinese people.

A third mildly tries to point out to everyone that the Japanese, like the Chinese, are a Buddhist people – therefore the ordinary Japanese soldier must be as equally gentle as the ordinary Chinese soldier. They are being driven to these atrocities by their evil Bushido officers.

The stage has become flooded with villagers expressing their various opinions and general outrage at the play and the young hooligans who dared put it on. One old lady particularly unloads her bile on Tian Boqi, who sits by himself on the stage staring manically ahead of himself. A man berates him.

'To think we wasted time on your stupid play. We could have been in the fields working!'

The other actors have retreated to the lorry.

Gradually the villagers, grumbling and gesticulating, climb down off the stage and, still complaining, walk back into the village, leaving the wrecked stage behind them.

Tian Boqi sits alone. Utterly alone. Utterly humiliated. I go up to him. Sit down beside him.

There is silence. Then Tian speaks.

'You know what always used to scare me more than anything? That I would never be accepted by the working classes because I was upper class.'

Silence.

I try to comfort him. 'Look, Tian…' I say.

'Fuck off,' he says.

'Why are you always so angry?' I ask him.

He stands up, starts to walk into the village. I follow. The other actors, still bewildered, climb down from the lorry and follow us.

It is when we reach the village square that everything changes.

There are still groups of villagers standing around, complaining about our play. Some are preparing to return to the fields. Old people drink tea in the tea house. Suddenly, into our midst, marches a troupe of young children. Half-starved, dirty-faced, dressed in rags, no more than seven, eight years old. One of the many bands of young parentless children roaming our country. They're led by a young girl of about ten years old. She has a determined, single-minded look to her.

The villagers make sympathetic noises as they see them.

The children walk to the centre of the square. The eldest steps forwards and addresses us all.

'All but one of us are from the village of Xiazhuang in Shandong Province. We do not have any parents any longer. They were all killed by the Japanese when they came to our village. We hope you will listen to our story, feel pity for us, and give us some alms so we can continue our journey to safety.'

Everyone falls silent. Gathers round. Stands or sits on walls or benches so they can follow and listen.

Six of the children, with the eldest, stand in a line before us. The seventh, the smallest, only three years old or so, wanders around as the others speak, staring directly at each member of the audience, smiling sweetly, then frowning and moving on to the next. All the six in the line suddenly speak.

'Listen to our story, dear people.
Listen to what happened to us, dear people.
Listen to what you must do, dear people, if you are to help us.'

The eldest girl steps forwards.

'Listen to my story, dear people. I am Su. My father was a
shepherd.
One night he was out in the fields tending a sick sheep while
the rest of us were all at home.
Suddenly, into the house, into the candlelight, he staggers in.
Blood is running from his head.
"Help me," he says, "these soldiers attacked me."
He falls. My mother and we children cry out. Neighbours rush
in to see what has happened. But as they do there are other
cries from elsewhere in the village.
Screams, shouts, the sounds of guns.'

She steps back. A young boy steps forwards.

'Listen to my story, dear people. My name is Park.
I am asleep. Suddenly my mother leaps up.
Someone has set light to our house. The thatch roof is burning.
Bits of burning straw fall upon us.
My father rushes to the door.
Standing outside – I can see him in the light of the flames – is a
Japanese soldier.
He forces his bayonet into my father.
All the rest the family are pressing out, scared of the flames. He
bayonets them all.
I escape through a hole in the back wall of the house.
I see flames all about me in the village. Hear screams. I run into
the darkness.'

He steps back. A girl slightly older than him, quite nervous,
moves forwards.

'Listen to my story, dear people. My name is Jiang.
Soldiers come into my house.
They are rough, shouting. They shoot my daddy.
Then grab all the rest of us, even my old gran, and pull and tug
    us towards the centre of the village.
All around us are the flames from all the burning houses.
    Shouts and screams.
And in the centre of the village I see all the villagers being
    herded,
surrounded by the soldiers with their swords and bayonets,
and just at that moment I trip, and the soldiers behind me tread
    over me without seeing me,
trample me.
My family walk on surrounded by soldiers.
Dear people, what do I do?
Do I run on to join my dear family,
my dear sisters and brothers and mother and gran,
or do I run into the darkness?'

For a second the girl hesitates. A stricken look comes over her
face.

'I leave them. I leave my family. I run away into darkness.'

Lost in the horror of the moment, Jiang hesitates, then
remembers herself, steps back into the line. A boy slightly older
than her steps forwards. He has a slight limp.

'Listen to my story, dear people. My name is Ma.
The soldiers drive my whole family out of our home, beat us with
    their rifle butts, then drive us towards the centre of the village
where like sheep we are driven into a group of all the villagers.
We are surrounded by soldiers aiming their guns and bayonets
    at us.
The soldiers are drinking.
Drunk and singing.

They see my eldest sister and drag her out
and before us all, dear people,
they defile and shame and then bayonet her.
They all start to fire their guns into us.
People started stumbling and pushing and falling and
    screaming
I fall over
then all sorts of people, people bleeding, people screaming,
    people writhing
start falling on me
and above me, through the bodies,
I hear the fire continuing until it stops
and there is silence,
and then I hear the soldiers start to walk among the people
    killing those still alive.
I am beneath three grown-ups and I lie very still and they miss
    me.
I lie there for hours, not moving, peoples' blood running all
    over me,
sticking and hardening all over me,
the bodies on top of me are very heavy but when I can hear no
    more,
when there is silence,
at last, very slowly dear people, I start to push my way out from
    underneath my village.
The last man I get out from underneath is my uncle. I can't see
    any soldiers. I run away.'

I stand there and listen to their stories. The hair on my head
rises. Though it is not warm I start to sweat. I breathe with
difficulty. All around me is that terrible silence which occurs in a
play when every single member of the audience is rapt, entrapped
in each syllable and word that is uttered.

But the most haunting, disorientating aspect of the children's
performance is the behaviour of the youngest child, the toddler.
She continues walking round and round the audience, looking
into the face of each adult, her face momentarily lighting with

recognition, smiling with delight, only for it to relapse into a frown, almost a scowl, as she turns and walks on to the next.

The children having finished their various stories, Su, the eldest, starts to speak. She tells us how they, the surviving children, hid in a cave they used to play in before the soldiers came. They wondered whether they should return to the village. They all thought that was too dangerous. So they had to set off. The soldiers came from where the sun rose so they set off to where it set. They walked and walked and when they came to villages they told their story and begged for food and shelter. They became travellers.

At this point Su, the eldest girl, walks forwards to where the young sweet-faced toddler is still searching from adult face to adult face. I note that Tian Boqi especially stares at the toddler with terrified fascination.

'And so, dear people, we come to the story of the last of us,' she says. 'This tiny infant came to us when we were in a forest. She just walked up to us. She smiles a lot but speaks very little, but when she came to us I asked her what her name was and she said she could not remember. So we called her Lim, which means "From the Woods". One night, when she and I were talking, she said she wanted to find her parents. She knew they were somewhere. So everywhere we go, every village we come into and speak to, she wanders among you, searching for her parents.'

The toddler is standing near me, looking into a farmer's face. I see something. Something terrible. Fear. Insecurity. She is doing what any lost child of that age would do – she is using the one tool of communication God has given her, her smile, to desperately win affection and nourishment and love. To somehow conjure up her forgotten, mysterious parents in the faces of those she looks so earnestly into. But always as she looks some distant ghost memory of her actual parents returns, her smile hesitates. and disappointed she turns smiling to the next.

Su picks her up and cuddles her. Su looks up.

'But now, dear people, she has her parents, her family again. She has us children.'

Su, carrying the toddler, returns to the line. They all speak.

'You all listened to us, dear people.

You all listened to what happened to us, dear people.

Listen now to what you must do if you are going to help us,
dear people.'

One by one the children speak.

'One day I want there to be a knock at the door. I am terrified. I
fear another soldier. I go to the door. I open it. It is a soldier.
But it is not a Japanese soldier with blood on his sword, it is
a Chinese soldier.

"Hello, little one," he says, "I have come to protect you."

He is strong. He is proud. He smiles at us.

He does not shout or rave. He has a gentle voice.

He leans down and he lifts me up with his strong hands and
hugs me. "Hello, dear Jiang," he says.

He says that he and all the other Chinese soldiers have come to
rescue us.

That they will take us back to our villages and we will be safe
and happy.'

'And so, dear people,' says Su, facing the people, 'we ask you all
to do what you can to support our brave Chinese soldiers so that
one day we can all return to our village.'

From the mouths of babes. They bow to us.

There is applause for this performance. Warm feelings for the
children are expressed by the villagers. An elderly man, obviously
the person used to speaking for the village, steps forwards. He
thanks them emotionally for what they have said. He says the
whole village has sympathy for their suffering. Congratulates
them on their courage and on the truths they have spoken. He says
all Chinese people must be patriots and fight for their country.

The villagers then take the children to the temple where they
have swiftly organized food for them and a place for them to spend
the night.

Which leaves my would-be playwrights. Each one has been
deeply moved by what they have just seen. The walls of class have

been torn down. Tian Boqi sits alone by himself, tears pouring down his face. Then he gets up and moves over to his classmates.

'We have all been fools,' he admits. 'We must talk among ourselves, debate, so that we too can write drama which can move and motivate people like those children moved us.'

They do talk among themselves. Not in the way they used to – with sharp tones of point scoring and egotism – but more quietly, more warmly and respectfully, listening to each other, starting to construct things together.

I have a sudden thought. It is obvious I am not needed any longer by my students. They will decide for themselves what they will do and how they will do it. I follow the villagers to the temple.

The children are seated around a table being served and feted by the villagers. It is a beautiful sight. I go up to the elderly man who had spoken for the village. I apologize to him for my behaviour, for the behaviour of my students. For inflicting that play on the village. I say that the children have taught us how we should write plays, that we have learnt our lesson.

He looks at me and smiles wryly.

'I watched your face while your students were making their play. I saw what you were about. You were using our village to teach your students a lesson.'

I smile. I think.

'Perhaps,' I say, 'perhaps my students could at some time come and talk with the villagers. That they could bring their new plays down here and perform them before the people and then listen to the peoples' comments. They are young, they need their advice.'

'I could discuss it with the people,' says the old man. 'Explain things.'

'I would be very grateful for that. But,' I say, 'that is not the real reason why I came to talk to you.'

'No?'

'It's about the children. I am from the government. Now I know that the government, among good people, is very often disliked. Distrusted. And quite rightly. It takes often, it rarely gives back. It can do very bad things.'

He again smiles wryly at me.

'Have you spoken to the children?' I ask.

'We have spoken to Su, their leader, yes,' he says.

'It is my job within the government to put on plays that will arouse, move the people towards supporting the government in their fight against the Japanese. That is why I want my students to write good plays. War is a horrible thing, but we must learn to defeat the Japanese. We, the Chinese people, must defeat the Japanese.'

He looks at me without expression. I continue.

'I know a man who writes poems and songs for children. He wrote the "Fox's Fur Coat" which a lot of children sing.'

'Ah, I've heard that song.'

'He also writes plays for children to perform. The thing is, these children perform a play. They perform a wonderful play. But my friend has wisdom and knowledge which will help them perform even better plays. He has money so that they can be safe and secure in their lives, so that they can buy costumes and swords, so that they can have time to develop more plays of their own, perhaps perform some of his. Do you know what these children are doing tomorrow, where they are going?'

'We have arranged with them to stay with us for several days while they go to nearby villages each day and perform their play. They can eat here each evening and sleep safely.'

'It's just that I think, instead of perpetually wandering, these children need some sort of permanent security, a home. We can give it to them.'

He looks at me and smiles.

'You need to talk to young Miss Su. She's the boss.'

I thank him.

After she's finished feasting I talk to Miss Su. She is sceptical. She likes the way they work now. Artistic freedom, eh! But she agrees to meet Lao Xiang, talk things over with him. I think Lao Xiang is exactly the right person for her to talk things over with.

I congratulate her on her performance and walk away.

★ ★ ★

One thing I have not explained to you is the anxiety I felt when I first saw that raggle-taggle string of children enter the village. How I minutely scanned each individual face. Any one of them might have been one of my children, all of my children, cast adrift, helpless on the tides of war. But none of them were my children.

I return to the students who are intensely debating future plays and productions. They are talking about writing their next play collectively – dividing up the scenes and speeches among themselves. The lorry is reloaded with the remnants of our props and backdrops. Still talking, the students pile into the back. Except one. Tian Boqi. He looks at me.

'I want to talk to you.'

We both climb into the cab with the driver and set off.

Tian turns and looks at me with that intensity he always stares at people with. I have learnt that he is not always trying to intimidate people when using it, it is his habitual look.

'You asked me why I am always so angry.'

'I did.'

'I will try to explain.

By the way, I apologize for the appalling way I have treated you in the past. Especially my comments on the Manchus. They were unforgiveable.'

'Let's deal with the present,' I say.

'My anger,' he says. 'I was brought up in Tianjin. A typical bourgeois merchant family. Wealthy. I had the best education. But I found the bourgeois life sterile, lifeless, squalid. I could not bear it. My whole country was falling to pieces – starvation, civil war, exploitation – while people lived like this! At university I became a Marxist-Leninist, joined the Communist Party. Various of my plays were performed in Shanghai, Beijing. They were praised. Probably, from what I know now, they were not very good.

'I largely lost contact with my family. They did not approve of me, I did not approve of them. Harsh words were spoken on occasion. Then came the war. As you know Tianjin was one of the first places to be invaded. When I heard I froze. My family! My blood! In danger! I jumped on a train. The train stopped several miles before Tianjin. The Japanese had bombed the track. I jumped off, started walking. I passed people fleeing who said "Do not go there! It is terrible." I ignored them. It was dark. I entered the city. Moved from doorpost to alleyway, keeping in the shadows. There was screaming, fires, drunkenness. I managed to avoid the Japanese. In the morning I reached my family's apartment block. I went in. Everything seemed normal. I ran up the large marble staircase to my parents' apartment. I walked to the door. It was open. I walked in. My family. My grandmother, my father, my mother, my three young sisters and my two younger brothers, several of the servants, all dead, lying there, soaked in blood – shot, bayoneted, their flesh shredded and hacked. Unspeakable obscenities done to my mother and three young sisters. And I had not been there. Why had I not been there? Why had I not been there? If an eldest son was not there to defend his family…? I was so angry. Angry with myself. Angry with everything. Angry with everyone except my family. Lao She, for a while I was so angry I could not think. Then I covered them up. What should I do? Above all I wanted revenge. Should I try and bury them? Give them honourable funerals? How?!? I'd be butchered in the streets. I must have revenge, even if it meant abandoning them. I knew I must think. Calmly, rationally. I must escape. Wait for night. Flee and join the army to kill the bastards. But then I had another thought. Money. My father had a safe. I knew the combination because I had spied on him once when I was a boy. I went to it. They had only been bent on murder and mayhem. It was untouched. So I opened it, took out the money.

'That evening, I slipped out of the city, made it to Shanghai. Went straight to the head of my Communist cell. Gave him the money. Said I wanted a gun. So I could join the fight. Join the guerrillas.

'"No," he said.

'"What?" I said. "What do you mean? I am going to fight like a devil. I'm going to kill every Japanese dog I meet. Make them pay for the murder of my poor family."

'"No," he said. "Tian Boqi, you are far too valuable to the party, the Chinese people, as a playwright, as a propagandist. Anyone can fight, anyone can die. You must write, you must set peoples' hearts alight. You must make them want to fight and die."

'I felt so disgusted with myself. Hiding behind my pen. But he was right. I had to write, no matter how angry I felt with myself. So that was what I did. But my anger remained – til today. We have decided – we, the writers in your class – that we must write as those children spoke. To the heart. With action and emotion. And with hope.'

'Don't forget the dancing,' I add.

'And the swords,' he adds.

'You could try sub-machine guns on occasion,' I add.

Silence falls. Our lorry arrives at Wuhan.

Feng Yuxiang is waiting for us. When I tell him what happened his eyes twinkle.

'I always knew you were the man for the job.'

He drives off with the lorry driver.

But someone else has also been awaiting our arrival. My companion and fellow writer Lao Xiang. I must tell him about the children, but first he has something to get off his chest.

He watches my students disembark from the lorry. Notes their quietness, their cooperation as they pick up their props and stage sets to carry them into the university. He addresses them in an unusually restrained manner.

'Had any of you fuckers ever met a peasant before today?'

They do not answer him.

'I'll tell you something. Something you must never forget. Just because you're an intellectual doesn't mean you're in any way intelligent. Most intellectuals are unbelievably stupid. I've met peasants who are way more intelligent than anyone here. And I include myself and Lao She in that. Do you know how much intelligence it takes to repair a water pump? The intricacy of the mechanism – all the parts of which you have to make yourself? The complexity of holding in your head the exact water levels of all the different water courses in your irrigation system, so that if you shut down the water wheel to repair the pump all the surrounding fields do not flood? Every single farmer has to hold that knowledge in his head. Could you ever fit a red-hot iron tyre around a wooden cartwheel? A cartwheel is a most fragile and complex construction of many pieces of wood, and you have to adjudge precisely when that iron tyre is hot enough to be placed around the wooden rim so that when it cools and contracts it snatches every part of that wooden wheel in on itself so it forms a rock-hard wheel. A farmer must be able to look at a field of growing corn and know precisely where it is flourishing, where it is failing, because he knows the precise history of that field – and know exactly what he must do to cultivate those parts which are failing. You try being a farmer sometime – wankers – you wouldn't even get past the first blade of grass.

'Always remember: poor people are smarter than rich people. They have to be smarter, because that is the only way they can survive. They don't have rich daddies to bail them out every time they fuck up.'

With that we all go home.

When I reach my room, with dawn breaking, I look out of my window. On a branch of the red persimmon tree growing in my courtyard I see a first scarlet blossom breaking.

12

Blood and flies clotted black on the Bund's flagstones as Hu and Agnes worked at the soldiers' dressing station, bandaging their wounds, sorting out which might possibly live from those who would definitely die. In the morning Hu always put in a couple of hours working here before going off to sit on her Very Important Committee. She found it kept her sane.

As they worked Hu unburdened upon Agnes all her doubts and frustrations about working on the committee.

'It doesn't do any good. It's like speaking into emptiness. No one listens to anything anyone else says. No one comments or criticizes or agrees with anything anyone else says. It's not as though there aren't a few people on it who know about the subject, have really good ideas about housing and what should be done. I talk with them out in the corridor. But they're the least listened to. The only people the minister listens to are those who fill his ears with flattery and, I suspect, money. Why should I be there instead of somewhere useful like this?'

Agnes's weather-beaten, prematurely aged face smiled gently.

'The only people being really effective in the housing crisis,' said Agnes, 'are General Feng and his wife Li Dequan with their refugee camps and training programmes, and they're completely free of the committee and the government – they work through the army and the Soong sisters.'

While Hu lifted the leg of a soldier on the table Agnes disinfected his wound and deftly wound a bandage round his leg.

'I sometimes think,' said Hu, 'that people in the government are being bribed by the landlords to stop any building programme because that keeps property scarce and profits sky high.' She blushed because she'd spoken ill of people.

Agnes gave her a wolfish grin.

'Governments are corrupt. Always corrupt. Even in countries like mine, so-called democracies. The businessmen, the financiers move in and bribe the politicians. The politicians pass laws to ensure the rich stay rich, the poor poor. Then, as soon as the politicians retire, they're given big fat jobs in the companies the rich men own.

'I distrust any top-down organization. Leave it to the people. Supply them with the tools and they'll do it. Like you in Shanghai. The Young Women's Christian Association gave you the tools – the introductions to each other, the education, the theory – and you and your friends organized the trade unions on the streets, behind the walls in the back alleys. People organize themselves.'

She looked into the empty eye socket of the next soldier.

'That was the beauty of the IWW, the Wobblies. Big Bill Heywood, Elizabeth Gurley Flynn, Joe Hill. Every year all up through the Midwest, starting in the south as the crops ripened, then following the harvest north over the Great Plains all the way up into Canada, there were these huge armies of hobos and bums and working stiffs, millions of them, hopping the railroad freight cars from job to casual job. Used to call themselves the Great Black Shadow. And the IWW took them on and helped to organize them so they won decent wages, permanent jobs. It was magnificent. There was violence – company thugs, railroad goons – but they won.'

'You think that could happen here?' asked Hu.

'It's why I spend so much time marching with and reporting on the Communist Eighth Route Army. Not because communism doesn't have its faults. Spent enough time in Russia to know that. But up there in the far north-west the Communist armies can't use regular bases – too many Japanese around – so instead they have to use guerilla tactics. Go out into the field in small groups, travel at night, attack and then skedaddle. The only way they can survive like that is through the support and knowledge of the country people. The country people fight side by side with them, feed them information and intelligence, help them understand the lie of the land, explain who is to be trusted among them and who not. So the communists, however indoctrinated and regimented they might have been to be the "vanguard", out in the field have to follow the advice and judgement and will of the people. It is a joy to behold! And peasants make such good, effective fighters. Peasants are the cleverest people on earth.'

Agnes's craggy face gave a sad smile.

'Of course, it won't last. In the end the Japs will win, or the Nationalists or the Communists. What we're living through here is only a moment. But what a moment! It's so wonderful just to be alive in it. Seeing human beings for once living up to what they can be.'

Hu looked at Agnes. She looked so worn, so old despite only being in her forties. That's what comes from a year's continual marching with the Eighth Route Army, endlessly reporting and working for the revolution and tirelessly caring for and bandaging the sick and wounded, especially the soldiers who no one else can be bothered with. But just look at her face, thought Hu! Lit by inner light, inner moral compulsion! She's like someone from the time of the saints!

Hu had to leave for her committee. She said farewell, washed her hands and hurried off along the Bund. As she was passing through the food markets she suddenly saw someone she hadn't seen since the march from Shanghai to Wuhan. The Intelligent Whore! They stopped and joyfully greeted each other. Intelligent Whore suggested they have a tea and catch up with each other. Hu sighed and excused herself, explaining that she didn't have time because she was sitting on this government committee and she was late. Intelligent Whore roared with laughter.

'You – on a government committee?'

'Yes,' said Hu, feeling ashamed, 'really.'

A thought suddenly struck Intelligent Whore.

'There's something you really must see.'

'But I have to get to work,' said Hu. 'I'm already late.'

'This is connected with your work. It will only take a minute. You simply must see it.'

So Hu went with her friend and saw what her friend wanted her to see. It was quite extraordinary. She knew immediately that Madame Chiang must see it too.

Madame Chiang sent an aide telling Hu she'd meet her by a certain fish stall in the market at three tomorrow afternoon. Hu said that if Madame Chiang met her at such a place she would attract a lot of attention and this would make it very difficult for her to see what Hu wanted her to see. The aide informed her that Madame Chiang would be absolutely discreet and Hu was to meet her at the fish stall at three o'clock precisely. Not a minute early. Not a minute late. He left.

The next day at precisely three o'clock, among the crowds and the women stall holders in their high sopranos singing the excellence of their fish and fruit and vegetables, in the midst of coolies labouring and sweating past with huge sacks of flour and boxes full of delicate duck eggs and baskets heaving with live threshing fish, amid mothers beating their children, Madame Chiang arrived at the fish stall. Totally discreetly. Hu stared at her. If there was one thing that Hu considered impossible it was that Madame Chiang could appear un-chic. But there she stood before her, totally un-chic. Hu's eyes searched her body, her clothing, her hair, and found not one single scintilla of chic. Madame Chiang looked boringly ordinary. Slightly drab even. Just like any other person you never notice.

'I often do this,' said Madame Chiang. 'Dress this way, walk about, listen to what the people are saying, see what they are doing, what they're feeling. Just the sort of information you need in government but can never get. And it keeps me sane.'

A swarm of students swept past, shouting and chanting. One was dressed up as Hitler. They were demanding that Hitler keep out of Czechoslovakia and that the Chinese people show complete solidarity with the Czech people.

'Now,' said Madame Chiang, moving off in a businesslike fashion, 'where is this thing which you wish me to see?'

'There are two things, actually,' said Hu. 'The first is about housing, which you asked me to keep you up to date with.'

'Good,' said Madame Chiang.

Hu led her to the part of the Bund where the city of tiny sampans had so suddenly sprung up. She explained briefly how practical these boats were for housing large numbers of refugees, how convenient they were for labourers working in the docks, how they kept families together.

Madame Chiang got her point.

Hu explained how there was space for mooring plenty more but that the price of the sampans had shot up since they'd become so popular. The owners of the sampans were reluctant to import more because that would lower their rents. Hu thought the government should intervene. There were thousands of cheap sampans upstream in the many little river ports and lakes to the west and south of Wuhan. The government should buy them and flotillas of them could be towed down the Yangtze by tugs for newly arrived families to use. Meanwhile, on the tugs' return voyage, they could tow established communities of sampans upstream to ports like Changsha and Chungking where, with all the new traffic and industries, there was a great demand for labourers.

'This is essentially what General Feng and Li Dequan are doing with their land-based refugees,' observed Madame Chiang, 'establishing communities and then taking them upstream to populate the new cities and farmlands.'

'It is,' agreed Hu.

'Excellent,' said Madame Chiang. 'I'll talk to my sister Soong Ailing, she can arrange the finances.'

As they were talking Hu became aware of a rather unpleasant smell. They were standing at the edge of the dock as slowly before them paraded a string of barges exuding a foul stench. Known locally as 'the honey barges', their job was to carry Wuhan's raw sewage from the city to be spread on the fields where most of Wuhan's fresh vegetables were grown. They made several trips a day.

Hu felt embarrassed about this. She suggested that perhaps

they should move on to the second thing she wished Madame to see. Madame sniffed the air vigorously.

'Ah,' she announced, 'the honey barges of Wuhan. I was talking to a French sanitary engineer only the other day and he told me that there are two grades of excrement they carry — Chinese and European. The European excrement fetches twice the price of the Chinese because Europeans have such rich diets. In fact this Frenchman went on boast to me that the French have the finest excrement in the world because they eat the finest food.'

Hu looked at Madame Chiang. Madame Chiang turned away.

'Now,' she said matter-of-factly, 'let's see your second secret. This is about health, isn't it, not housing?'

'It is. It's not far away.'

Hu was sure that Madame Chiang would not have come on this expedition without some security, but repeated furtive glances over her shoulder failed to reveal anyone following them.

Hu was leading Madame Chiang to a tea house.

'Tea houses' can mean many varying things in China. They can be houses where tea is served and drunk. Where old friends meet up. Where gossip is exchanged, pipes smoked, opium discreetly or indiscreetly taken, mahjong played, newspapers read, wine drunk. They can be labour exchanges, money exchanges, places where secret societies congregate, where crimes are planned, where learned societies meet. This tea house was richly furnished with carved blackwood from the south and filled with square wooden tables and chairs packed with customers. Music was being played quietly in a corner.

But this tea house was not quite how it seemed. From the centre of the room a large, ornately decorated staircase lead up to the first floor. Had Hu and Madame Chiang arrived here a few hours later the scene would have been very different. Raucous music would be playing, the customers would be drunk, everyone would be shouting at each other as down the stairway, into the brilliantly lit room would trail a procession of young girls. All very pretty and very youthful. Sheathed in silk or satin, adorned with jewellery, their faces heavy with paint and powder, they would wend their way between the tables around the floor as their Madam stopped at each table and drew the patrons' attention to the particular appeals and attractions of each girl. One by one the girls would be chosen and walk up the stairs, to the cheers of the crowd, with their clients.

Madam Chiang stopped as soon as she walked through the door. A woman of the world, she knew exactly where Hu had brought her. A brothel. Suddenly, miraculously, behind her materialized her til now invisible security detail. Two of them. Still very discreet.

'This is a brothel,' Madame Chiang quietly told Hu. 'If word got out that I have visited a brothel my reputation, more importantly my husband's reputation, would be ruined. Why have you brought me here, Hu Lan-shih?'

'Because I think it very important that you see what I am going to show you.'

Madame Chiang looked full into Hu's face. Took a step back.

'I trust you, Hu Lan-shih. Show me what you want me to see.'

'I apologize, Madame Chiang, but it is upstairs.'

'Then let us go up there,' said Madame Chiang.

Hu led the way up, followed by Madame Chiang and, at a discreet distance, the two bodyguards.

They passed through a door and stepped into a plushly decorated, dimly lit corridor. Some doors were open and the sounds of noisy springs and lusty intercourse were coming from almost every room. Hu thought she would die of embarrassment. Madame Chiang had a fixed expression on her face, and the two bodyguards exchanged unbelieving looks. In one room a naked girl sat on a large colourful bedspread and wept.

At last they reached the end of the corridor and two corridors led off it left and right. From the left-hand corridor Hu suddenly saw a naked man approaching them with an enormous erection followed by two fat naked ladies. She immediately turned Madame Chiang to the right – a short corridor with a door at the end. She hurried Madame Chiang through the door and her two bodyguards followed. She shut the door. This was a completely different corridor. It was quiet. Almost silent. It was painted white.

Hu indicated Madame Chiang should follow her. At the first door they looked in. There was a man in a bed there. A small bed with very white sheets. There were several other small beds in the room, all with white-faced men beneath white sheets. Many of the men were heavily bandaged, some with white bandages round their heads, some over their arms or chests, some entirely covered in bandages.

Hu and Madame Chiang and her two guards continued down the corridor. In each room it was the same. Bandaged men in beds, some being attended by nurses.

'It is a hospital,' said an awed Madame Chiang.

'Yes,' said Hu, 'at last a proper hospital has been found for some of our poor soldiers.'

'But it's in a brothel,' said a still gobsmacked First Lady.

'There's someone I want you to meet,' Hu said, and led Madame Chiang down the corridor to a small room set aside for visitors. It was empty. Hu ushered them in. 'I'll just fetch her,' she explained, shutting the door on them.

Madame Chiang paced up and down the room. She was quite upset by it. It had somehow moved her deeply, but she didn't understand why. She was chain smoking.

Into the room came Hu, followed by Intelligent Whore. Intelligent Whore was dressed in the colourful uniform of the brothel – which meant she wasn't wearing much – and perched on her hip she had a young boy of some three years. The boy stared boldly at everyone in the room. She let him down and he stood beside her, still inspecting these strangers.

'Mummy,' said the boy, 'I want to draw some pictures.'

'That's a good idea, little Aigou, I've brought some paper and crayons with me.'

She laid down the papers and the crayons on the ground before him.

'Mummy, what should I draw?'

'How about some dragons?'

Aigou thought for a second. 'I think I'll draw some dragons,' he said, and immediately became absorbed in his work.

Intelligent Whore looked at Madame Chiang. 'I apologize for

bringing my child with me, Madame Chiang,' she said without an ounce of regret in her voice, 'but, with my whoring and my work with the soldiers, I only have an hour a day together with him and I do not wish to waste it.'

'Of course,' said the still partially gobsmacked Madame Chiang. 'Do you mind if I smoke in front of him?'

'Of course not,' said Intelligent Whore. 'We're in a brothel. I smoke all the time.'

'Do you want one of mine?' asked Madame Chiang, proffering her a Wills's Gold Flake.

'Thank you, no,' said Intelligent Whore, 'I'll smoke my own.'

She lit a Chinese cigarette, inhaled it heavily.

'The reason I asked you to come here, Madame Chiang – you've seen the soldiers we've got…?'

'Yes,' said Madame Chiang.

'…is because we are having some problems at the moment—'

Madame Chiang interrupted her.

'First,' she said, 'I want to hear some of the background to this. How do wounded soldiers end up being treated – very well, from what I saw – in a brothel?'

'I'm sorry,' said Intelligent Whore, 'but I thought Hu would have explained this to you beforehand.'

'I didn't,' said Hu, 'because I thought if I said this was being done in a brothel Madame would not have come.' She blushed.

'All right,' said Intelligent Whore, 'some background…'

'Mummy,' said Little Aigou, 'what do you think of this dragon's eyes? I've painted them purple.'

Intelligent Whore looked down at her son's drawing. 'They look very nice. And I like those red claws.' Little Aigou became re-absorbed.

Madame Chiang took no offence at this interruption. She recognized another practical, business-like woman when she saw one.

'The background,' repeated Intelligent Whore. 'A group of us women – whores, taxi girls, mill workers – got very close in Shanghai and decided we would support the soldiers.'

'It's all right,' said Madame Chiang, 'I've already read a report on your march with the soldiers to Wuhan. I understand that. But why are soldiers being treated in a brothel?'

'Well,' said Intelligent Whore, 'when we got here we all went our separate ways. Most of us whores returned to our work because we needed to feed ourselves and our children. But we kept in touch and found we were all worried about the wounded soldiers being left to die on the Bund. We thought that was terrible. So we thought – how can we help them? And then we whores all thought – well, we all work in warm, waterproof rooms with lots of beds, why not take over parts of the brothels for the wounded soldiers?'

'This is happening in other brothels?'

'Yes.'

'But how do you persuade your bosses, the owners, to allow this? They are not, I would imagine, the kindest of men.'

Intelligent Whore smiled at her. She then leant down and put another sheet of paper before her son.

'Paint a boat on the river, little Aigou,' she said.

'I like ships,' said little Aigou. 'Especially the ones with guns.'

'Our pimps are often brutal men, yes. But they are also vulnerable. When we went to present our proposals we took with us newspaper reporters, photographers, suggested that if the soldiers did not get their beds, their nursing, then the newspapers would report this, name names, publicize addresses. We felt sure that patriotic, freedom-loving Chinese brothel owners would want to help our good boys who were nobly sacrificing themselves to save us all from the brutalities and mass murders of the Japanese. Would they want hordes of drunken murderous Japanese soldiers as their clients every night? We even hinted that perhaps the names of some of their more famous customers might appear in the newspapers.'

Little Aigou had got bored with drawing his ship and had embraced his mother's leg. He hugged her tight. She gently and reassuringly started to stroke his hair and he relaxed against her.

Intelligent Whore was about to continue when the door suddenly flew open and into the room stormed the naked man with the enormous erection last seen with the two fat whores in the corridor outside. He still had his enormous erection and he was furious. He stalked straight up to Intelligent Whore.

'There you are, you cunt. I fucking found you.'

Hu noticed that Intelligent Whore immediately started to massage deeply not only little Aigou's hair but also his neck, his shoulders, to reassure, to soothe him. She also moved so that Madame Chiang was behind him and that if she was hit by the lout she would not fall on her son. Simultaneously the two bodyguards moved to cover Madame Chiang, not only to stop any possible assault on her but to prevent the animal from recognizing her. Hu moved herself forwards, so that the man might have someone else to attack rather than Intelligent Whore.

The man grabbed Intelligent Whore behind her neck and pulled her forwards so their two faces jammed together.

'I asked for you and they sent me two ugly fat whores with the clap. I punched them both. Bruised them so their pimp won't be able to work them any time soon. I told him I want my prick up your cunt. Only you know how to squeeze and grind and tickle and suck it so I do not know who I am anymore and float off into heaven. So you come with me right now,' he hissed.

'I won't,' she said, quite calmly.

'What?'

'I am busy. This is what you will do. You will go to room number twenty-one. There Little Flower Petal will frot and floss and tug you so your prick gets even huger, so that when I come to you you can stuff it right up my cunt and we shall both go to heaven.'

'I can do that for you, get you to heaven, can't I?' he said eagerly.

Intelligent Whore ignored this. 'I will be with you in twenty minutes exactly. No sooner. No later,' she said.

The creature stepped back from her. His face collapsed. His fat body started to shake, losing all shape.

'You are so wonderful to me,' he said.

'Go,' she said.

He hurried from the room.

Intelligent Whore detached her son from her leg and sat him down on the ground. For a full ten minutes she gently coached and enticed him back into the world of drawing ships and clouds and gentle dragons. Then she stood up, brushed back her hair, and turned to Madame Chiang. One of Madame Chiang's bodyguards had meanwhile gone outside to prevent any further irruptions.

'Do you want to know anymore about how we got the soldiers into the brothels?' Intelligent Whore asked Madame Chiang.

'No,' replied Madame Chiang – likewise a woman of iron nerves. 'What is it you want from me?'

'Three things. Firstly, we need more medical supplies, and if possible trained medical staff.'

'Yes.'

'Secondly, we'd be grateful if you could help us with a problem. Our pimps and brothel owners are beginning to get a bit fed up with giving over their rooms to us. They are starting to threaten us. I wonder if you might intervene on this?'

'My husband and the Nationalist Party of China have no connections whatsoever with organized crime. Nevertheless, I will see what I can do.'

'Thank you. Finally, we need more space. We need more beds. Hu here works on the Bund every day, bandaging the wounded. She says their numbers have fallen a bit since we started these hospitals, but we still have a long way to go. As you probably know there are seven or eight floating brothels moored on the Bund. Full of beds. We wondered whether the government, for fully patriotic reasons, might commandeer three or four of them. They would make excellent and well-ventilated quarters for the wounded, and they could be used for transporting the wounded upstream to the safety of Changsha or Chungking so they can rest and recuperate.'

Madame Chiang laughed and clapped her hands. 'What an excellent idea. I will see to it immediately.'

Intelligent Whore smiled at Madame Chiang. Madame Chiang stared at Intelligent Whore. 'What an extraordinary woman you are.' She sighed. 'If only we had people like you in our government.'

She turned to go.

'I will leave you with the really important thing in your life – your child.'

They left. Intelligent Whore lay down with her son and re-entered his world of make-believe. She still had five minutes with him.

Once they were outside Hu and Madame Chiang walked for about a hundred yards and then stopped. Madame Chiang ordered one of her bodyguards to get her car. Within seconds a Rolls-Royce Silver Ghost whispered up. Her two bodyguards got into the front. Madame Chiang got in the back.

'Get in,' she said to Hu.

'But Madame,' said Hu, 'I have to attend my committee.'

'I'll deliver you there,' said Madame Chiang.

Hu got in.

Once inside Madame Chiang drew all the curtains, including the ones across the glass partition, so neither the public nor her bodyguards or driver could see them. She then switched off the intercom system to the driver so no one could overhear them. She looked at Hu.

'You are a good Christian.'

'Well...' said Hu.

'You took the pledge?'

'I did.'

'So did I,' said Madame Chiang, and took out a hip flask. She took three deep hits from it. She turned to Hu.

'I have never seen anyone so good as that woman. That whore. She was so in control, so powerful, yet never once did she show any anger or irritation. With her child, with me, with that madman, she was in perfect control, yet never once did she use her strength to manipulate, threaten, dominate. She must be like the saints of old.'

'I think she probably has to deal with problems quite often in a brothel – especially with men like that,' said Hu.

'No,' said Madame. 'Her first priority, her absolute priority, was that child. That child's being and peace of mind. At every single second she knew exactly what the child was thinking, where it was. Yet, simultaneously, she could mentally deal with all my questions and her complex, informed answers to them, and then with the violence and hysteria of that animal. How could she do it? It was a miracle. Her calmness, her control.

As I said to her, she should be running China. I meant it. No one could run this shithole like she could.'

Hu remembered the conversation she'd had with Agnes only two hours before.

'What I want to know is,' said Madame Chiang, lighting a new Gold Flake and taking another swig from her hip flask, 'what is this connection between soldiers and whores? I do not understand it. I mean, with the brains that woman has and the self-control she has she could be a powerful woman, a rich woman, running all sorts of things. But instead she lives penniless and devotes herself to caring for soldiers. Half the nurses in that "hospital" were whores.'

'Soldiers and whores have a lot in common, Madame,' said Hu. 'Whores are helpless. But not as helpless as soldiers. If whores are in brothels they'll survive for several years, til their looks wear out. If they are on the street they'll only live a few months. But soldiers only live for days, seconds, moments. Soldiers, with their lives, protect whores, protect all of us. So whores, who know death, admire them. They work for soldiers to bring them comfort, give them joy. And when the soldiers are happy, the whores are happy. Bringing joy to someone whose life is even shorter than yours brings you happiness. You talk about money, Madame Chiang, but which would you rather have – money or happiness?'

Madame Chiang burst into tears.

'I'm sorry, Madame Chiang, I'm sorry that I upset you.'

Madame touched her arm to show her it was not her fault.

Hu looked at her face. Had she been in full chic with expensive make-up and mascara, her face would now be a mess. But because her face was entirely unmade-up, even with the tears flowing down it, she looked natural and beautiful.

Madame Chiang stopped her crying, wiped her tears and blew her nose. Lighting another cigarette she pulled at it, took another swig, and stared grimly ahead of her. She made a decision. Still staring ahead she spoke.

'Hu, I live in a world where I can trust no one. But I trust you. Should I trust you?'

'Yes, Madame Chiang,' said Hu, 'you can trust me.' And she meant it.

'I am not going to complain about being a poor lonely girl all alone at the pinnacle of power. After all, I fought hard enough to get there. I want to tell you about my husband.'

'Madame Chiang…!' said Hu, but Chiang put a hand on her arm to shut her up. She still stared robotically ahead of her.

'Those who work for him in the government, his generals – perhaps even the population at large – see him as a dogged, wooden, rather unimaginative politician. A man not responsible for our situation, the attack by Japan, but doing his best, in his cautious, shy manner, to right it.'

He turned to Hu, her eyes flashing. Her voice was strangled, almost manic.

'He is not like that at all. People have got him completely wrong. My husband is not normal. My husband is incredible. Incredibly uncommunicative, incredibly rude in the way he blanks people, arguments, ideas. He's a blank. A blank so blank it screams. A vortex into which all things – ideas, people, projects, thoughts, enquiries, arguments, suggestions, recommendations, careers, real men and women, whole armies and cities and citizens – are sucked and disappear forever. People back him to the hilt and disappear. Warnings and pleadings are presented to him and he ignores them. He is a total nobody, a non-existence, a non-thing – and this perpetually shut, unopenable blank has absolute power, runs our country!'[4]

She stopped.

Hu didn't know what to say or where to look.

She started again.

'It's not just his teeth that are false. Every single part of him is false!'[5]

Another pause.

'And when it comes to it, he'll surrender us to the Japanese. Just hand us over. There, I've said it. At last.'

Madame Chiang continued staring stonily ahead, drawing heavily on her cigarette.

'But he's not going to. China's not going to surrender. We Soong sisters will not allow that. You will not allow that. Above all, Intelligent Whore will not allow it.'

Her Rolls-Royce had arrived outside the building where Hu's committee met. Madame Chiang thanked Hu profusely for all that she'd shown her today and said she'd do her best to help organize those things they had discussed. She'd stay in touch with Hu and hoped Hu would act as her go-between with Intelligent Whore. Hu assented to this and left the car.

Madame Chiang sighed, took out her make-up compact, evaluated her face in its mirror, and then set about repairing the damage.

Five minutes later, crisp, confident, impeccably chic, she stepped down from her limousine to greet a delegation of Texas businessmen.

Hu did not go into the committee. Instead she went straight home.

Back in the apartment she sat stunned. The most powerful woman in China had just confided to her facts about her husband, the President of China, which were shocking. Which were deeply dangerous to know. These facts – which anyone who had suffered for years in Shanghai from the thuggery and intimidation of Chiang Kai-shek's secret police and associated gangsters, as Hu had – came as no surprise. But the fact that it was his wife who had confirmed his incompetence and malice could make Hu a marked woman.

She sat there.

All she could do was trust in God. And, if what was going on in Wuhan was any sign, God was definitely on the side of change!

Spider Girl sat by her to keep her company, but she too was silent. She thought solely of her father. She had visited the temple on her way to the market this morning, lit candles, burnt incense, and prayed to her gods to protect him.

13

...bugles sounded and gongs clanged and the streets filled with people. I stood under the old town gate to watch long grey-blue columns of men and women march past. I have never been able to convey the impression they made upon me. They were grave, solemn. Not a breath of bravado was in them, yet they seemed dedicated to death – and to life. In them was a simple grandeur as fundamental and as undemonstrative as the earth.

They belonged to China, they were China. As I watched them, my own life seemed but chaos.

Agnes Smedley, Battle Hymn of China

General Li Zongren, commander in chief of China's Fifth War Zone, wrote to Chi Fengcheng, commander of the 2nd Army Group:

'It is your duty to repulse the Isogai Division. I have heard the Japs are nervous of broad-bladed sabres. Whether or not we can encircle and crush our enemy outside entirely depends on your ability to pin down our enemy inside the City of Taierzhuang. I expect, as you have said, your soldiers will be bold in slaying him to comfort our elders and brothers throughout the nation.'

Chi Fengcheng Commander of the Second Army Group addressed his troops:

'Let Taierzhuang be our grave. There is no retreat.'

On 25 March at 4 p.m. the Japanese opened a heavy bombardment on the northern wall of the city. The Battle of Taierzhuang had started. They bombarded especially the north and north-west gates. The Chinese defenders sustained a large number of casualties, and many were killed. The shells blew holes and breaches in the walls. Seven hundred Japanese infantry then charged the north gate and broke into the city. The Chinese surrounded them and drove them into the Chenghuang Mosque. Throwing incendiary bombs into the mosque they set fire to the interior. Only four Japanese soldiers survived. The Chinese regained control of the north gate.

The next day, angered by this display of defiance, Rensuke Isogai, commander of the Japanese 10th Division, ordered the whole of his 63rd Regiment to assault the north gate. Once more the Chinese drove them into the mosque, but this time, with nothing to burn, the Japanese survived. The mosque became their command post. The Chinese attacked it ferociously and, with hundreds of casualties on both sides, retook it but then in a counter-attack, with hundreds more dead on each side, the Japanese retook it. This back-and-forth warfare continued for several days. Thousands of dead and dying lay in mounds all around the building.

Eventually the Japanese managed to gain a foothold in the streets and alleyways in the north of the city. They made a considerable advance into the eastern city.

The Chinese battalion commander Zhang Jingbo was wounded and retreated from the fighting. He was immediately executed by his commanding officer Mie Zibin.

Wei lay sleeping amid his platoon. Around midnight, his face pressed hard into the soil, he awoke. There was a smell in the earth. It was not the nullness of winter, of frost, when the soil is dead and it has no smell. Tonight it held the scent of wetness and growth; he felt the earth stirring, roiling underground, roots and unformed plants rutting, twining in the earth, striking for the surface. As though a gigantic dragon rolled and shook beneath the earth.

In a second the whole lethargy and death of winter fell off him. He sat up, filled his lungs with the air – not dead and stale like winter air, but rank with dampness and life. It reminded him of the scents of his marriage bed on their wedding night. Spring had come once more to the earth. Winter was dead. He leapt up and danced the joyous dance his village always danced on the night of the vernal equinox.

The next morning his regiment, on its journey to Taierzhuang, marched through unending fields of fresh green wheat, waving and rippling in the wind like an unending ocean, the clouds in the sky shadowing alternative waves of light and dark across its surface. They passed four peasants, stood on a platform, working with their feet a treadmill to raise the water from a canal into their fields. As their legs pumped unendingly beneath them, above they leant languidly over a wooden bar and disputed learnedly among each other. Naked children rode on the backs of water buffalo as they ambled gently down to wallow in their pools.

Wei looked at it. It was beautiful to see. Buds on the trees starting to green the branches, birds in full song defending their nests, the crops breaking through the earth. But it was also terrible. Wei thought of his family's fields at home. The immaculate rows of burdock, gaoliang, cabbage planted out by him, his wife, Eldest Son, with Second Son helping and Cherry Blossom creating a scene and stamping her feet. The earth cultivated, nursed, tendered for a thousand years by his family, his ancestors. Now deserted, withering, rank with weed and thorn. The family pig that he'd slaughtered just before they left so that it would not starve. Would not be feasted on by the Japanese. Young saplings rooting, starting to build their kingdoms in the air. He felt outrage.

The regiment marched on.

Suddenly, from above, snowed a thousand sheets of white paper. Japanese propaganda pamphlets dropped by a passing aircraft floating down. A soldier who could read picked one up and read it aloud:

'Greetings, Chinese soldiers. The Greater East Asian Co-Prosperity Sphere of the Empire of Japan brings unlimited joy and bounty to all the people of China. We, the Imperial Japanese

Army, have always been invincible. Your resistance is stupid. The Empire of Japan is as eternal and mighty as the sun. To oppose the Imperial Japanese Army is stupid. Surrender at once!'

The Chinese ground their teeth and spat. But much as they hated these pamphlets they gathered them up. They could use them to light fires and wipe arses.

They marched over the brow of a hill. There before them lay the city of Taierzhuang. Built of black stone, ominous. A haze of smoke lay over the city and its surrounding plains were lit continuously by flashing explosions and burning fires. There was the distant rumble of artillery and exploding shells and bombs. The regiment cheered.

Between them and Taierzhuang were laid out a series of orchards. So the soldiers marched beneath boughs hung with spring blossom. Sweet-smelling petals of plum and orange and cherry and pear snowed on them, mantling their shoulders and heads with fragrance. They felt joyful. Marching beneath bright red pomegranate blossoms caused especial mirth because eating pomegranates was held to be the surest way of fathering innumerable children!

The mood became more serious. They were passing beneath the boughs of a giant peach orchard. Above myriads of bees and insects feasted on its sweet blossoms and flowers, their humming and buzzing turning the orchard into a great solemn cathedral of sound. Everyone understood the symbolism of the peach orchard. It had been in such a place, beneath its pink, fragrant blossoms, that the three great heroes of the *Romance of the Three Kingdoms* had first met and there sworn their immortal oath to always fight together to defend the Han emperor, to preserve the unity of China. One of the soldiers, who knew the passage by heart, recited it aloud:

"'When saying the names Liu Bei, Guan Yu and Zhang Fei,
   although the surnames are different,
yet we have come together as brothers.
From this day forward, we shall join forces for a common
      purpose: to save the troubled and to aid the endangered.

We shall avenge the nation above, and pacify the citizenry
    below. We seek not to be born on the same day, in the same
    month and in the same year.
We merely hope to die on the same day, in the same month and
    in the same year.
May the Gods of Heaven and Earth attest to what is in
    our hearts. If we should ever do anything to betray our
    friendship,
may heaven and the people of the earth both strike us dead."
Blossom fell like soft snow on them.
Then they marched like happy brides to their death.'

    Wei's regiment marched on in silence.

    The sound of battle grew.

    They passed a dead farmer with a dead goose he had been taking to market. A woman, blood dripping from her arm, her face white. Refugees leaving the city.

    They marched past the railway station. Middle-class families patiently waited for their train with their baggage. Soldiers frenziedly unloaded a freight train and a long line of coolies ported its contents – ammunition, food, supplies – straight into the city. On the ground by the train lay lines of wounded soldiers, ready to be loaded onto the train when it had been emptied.

    They passed a boy with a wheelbarrow full of matchboxes to be sold in the city.

    The regiment Wei was marching with were not like the raggle-taggle band of soldiers he'd first served with. These troops had smart uniforms and were extremely experienced and disciplined in fighting war. They'd first fought as members of General Feng Yuxiang's North-West Army. He had trained them especially in the techniques of broadsword and night fighting. Being a good Christian, Feng had also baptized them wholesale by directing fire hoses on them as they stood on parade in the open fields. When Feng was sent into internal exile in Jinan after he criticized Chiang Kai-shek's appeasement of Japan, the regiment was taken over by other generals, but they maintained the core skills that Feng had taught them.

As they marched across the pontoon bridge over the Grand Canal and entered Taierzhuang by its south-east gate they broke into spontaneous song. Being good Christians they chose for their bloodcurdling battle anthem Psalm 68:

Let God arise,
let his enemies be scattered:
let them also that hate him flee before him.
As smoke is driven away, so drive them away:
as wax melteth before the fire, so let the wicked perish at the
    presence of God.
O God, when thou goest forth before thy people,
when thou didst march through the wilderness; Selah:
The earth shook, the heavens also dropped at the presence of
    God,
The chariots of God are twenty thousand,
even thousands of angels:
the Lord is among them, as in Sinai, in the holy place.
The Lord said, I will bring again from Bashan,
I will bring my people again from the depths of the sea.
That thy foot may be dipped in the blood of thine enemies,
and the tongue of thy dogs in the same.[6]

Just as three centuries gone by Oliver's troops thundered out this psalm as they charged down upon and annihilated the royalist poraille at Naseby and Marston Moor, so China's troops thundered it out as they passed beneath the Moloch-like jaws of Taierzhuang's south-east gate and entered Armageddon.

Wei did not need to sing any Christian hymn – he just thought of his family and his farm. He thought of defending the life of his beloved Spider Girl.

The southern part of the city which the regiment entered, with its dark buildings and narrow streets, was still surprisingly full of life. Fresh patriotic posters plastered the walls. A cinema was showing *Shanghai Love Story*. Newsboys called out newspaper headlines, men with sandwich boards advertised concerts and haberdashers, students performed patriotic plays. They marched on. A fat soldier beside Wei, called, unsurprisingly, Grand Arse, scratched his arse. Huang, a soldier in the rank behind, observed, 'When the shells start to fly, even Grand Arse will forget his fleas.' They all laughed, even Grand Arse. He laughed loudest of all.

The city became darker and darker. The streets closer and closer. All the soldiers were peering hard ahead of them, trying to assess the situation, take in as much information as they could.

Civilians passed, distressed, fleeing. Some clutching belongings, others too bewildered to carry anything. A woman somehow carried three young children.

Soldiers passed. One cradled a shattered arm, talking to himself, trying to brace himself as blood poured down his hands. Men on stretchers were carried by coolies. Wei's company asked for information from those who were wounded and still conscious. The wounded replied variously:

'Hard fighting.'

'Watch out for snipers.'

'Japs don't like steel. Get in close to 'em.'

One wounded man spoke especially to Wei. 'Don't throw away your life. Take your time. Think. The longer you live the more Japanese you can kill.'

Wei's company digested these words. Exchanged opinions, guesses, fears, all the time craning their necks ahead. Grand Arse even ceased scratching.

They were being fed into the north-eastern corner of the city where the fighting, the devastation, was at its most brutal. As they advanced different detachments of them branched off, taking different routes and alleys towards the fighting. They no longer advanced at the march but slowly, carefully, picking their way from building to building, ruin to ruin. Heavy firing came from just ahead, great clouds of heavy oily smoke swirled around them, they choked, cursed. Dead and blown apart abandoned bodies – Chinese and Japanese – became common. In a narrow alley their platoon came to a halt. Between bursts of fire a young officer ran back down the alley to them, conferred with their officer, ran back up the alley. One by one they ducked along the alley, bullets spraying the wall to their right, then tumbled down into the cellar of a semi-destroyed building to their left. They were entering the Taierzhuang Underground.

They followed a maze of tunnels – some dug underneath the ground, others trenches covered with wooden doors or slats. Above them muffled explosions, cries. Sweat was on all their faces, their breathing became harder, sometimes choking on the dust, the smoke-laden air. Gripped their rifles even harder, checked their swords and grenades. Speech evaded them, they grunted at each other. In the darkness, lit only by a single candle, they saw a ladder. Their guide signalled they must be very quiet. With difficulty they quietened their breathing. One by one they climbed up into a lower room in a house. Four Chinese soldiers held it, they all looked to a wall to their right – the wall shared with the house next up the alleyway. Into the wall a cavity had been partly excavated. The guide signalled that four of their detail should relieve the soldiers in this room, the other five should follow him up to the next floor. Wei, three others, and their officer climbed ghostlike up the rungs of the ladder.

Another room, the top floor, with four soldiers lying flat on the floor, two of them with their ears jammed to the wall to their left, listening intently. They signalled for absolute silence, for them to remove their boots. Suddenly there was a hammering from next door, into their wall. One soldier signalled an exact spot. He and his mate took up positions on either side. One took out two grenades, checked them, while the other placed a wooden spigot on the floor and picked up a sledgehammer. They signalled for Wei's squad to move to either side of the room. They silently did so. Suddenly a crack, a crash, a hole appeared in the wall, and through it almost immediately was thrust a rifle barrel which, before it could be fired, the waiting soldier smashed with his sledgehammer, the barrel crumpled, the gun backfired, there was a scream of pain from the other side of the wall, the Chinese soldier dropped his sledgehammer and grabbed the flattened barrel, pulling it through. In the same moment the other soldier popped two primed grenades into the hole, then the spigot, and banged the spigot with the sledgehammer. Two quick muffled explosions were followed by some screams – the two soldiers pulled out the spigot and inserted a crowbar which they jerked up and down, pulling out masonry that was thrown behind for the rest to pile up. Another grenade followed the first two. The first stuck his head through the hole and looked around, signalled two dead Japanese to those behind him in the room, then withdrew his head. Wei wondered why he did not go through. The soldier signalled to Wei and another member of his section to pass him some pieces of the masonry. These he cast on the wooden floor next door. Immediately the whole floor exploded in sub-machine gun fire, fired from below and splintering and shattering the wood. The soldier grinned at his mate. His mate passed him a primed grenade. Taking careful aim he carefully threw it through a hole in the floor next door. Sounds of mass consternation, panic, a large bang. The soldier signalled to a comrade squatting by the ladder, who signalled downwards. This was followed by an outbreak of frantic hammering and crashing from the room below them as their comrades smashed through the rest of the cavity in their wall followed by two sharp cracks as their grenades exploded then lots of shouting and screaming as they rushed through the breached wall. Simultaneously all those upstairs wriggled through their hole, drew their broad sabres for battle, but there was no one still alive up there. Just the two already dead Japanese. The soldier shouted down a short sentence. A voice below answered in a broad Shanxi dialect. Cheering and shouting. The house was theirs. Those on the ground floor repaired the hole in the further wall through which the surviving Japanese had fled.

The four Chinese wished their successors, Wei and his detail, good luck and disappeared down the ladder. Downstairs they congratulated their fellow soldiers and all disappeared down the ladder into the tunnel. When it becomes time for them to run down sniper alley, there was noticeably less fire onto the right-hand side of the wall than when Wei's platoon detail had run up it.

Upstairs Wei's officer looked gingerly out through the window and up the alley. Not gingerly enough. He was shot through the throat and fell backwards. His detail watched him shake and bubble and convulse on the floor. He drowned in a welter of blood, slowly relaxing, prostrating, bleeding out.

The four soldiers in the room looked at each other. They whispered to those downstairs what had happened. Then carefully took a position out of line with the window. Wei and Grand Arse passed into the room just captured from the Japanese and took up positions on the new right-hand wall, listening for Japanese in the next house. After a while two coolies arrived with food, water and cigarettes and took away the officer's body to give him a respectful burial. The two coolies were cheerful because they'd haggled triple time. To show their gratitude and respect for the soldiers they left them an extra pack of cigarettes.

After they'd left Grand Arse remarked, 'Bet they nicked a whole lot more packs from which they gave us just one.' They all laughed. Except for Huang who, Wei was told, always fell asleep after intense combat. He snored peacefully.

The Japanese of course did not take this lying down. Their house and several more on the left-hand side of the alley had been taken by the Chinese. They called in an immediate airstrike. What's the point of having high-technology weapons if you don't use them? Unfortunately for them, just a few seconds before it was due to release its bombs the Japanese bomber called in was hit by a sudden gust of wind and was blown several yards off its course so that its bombs, targeted on the Chinese-held houses to the left of the alley, instead landed on the Japanese-held houses on the right of the alley. These houses collapsed into a slaughterhouse of tangled rubble, smashed bodies and smouldering wooden beams. A blinding tornado of yellow dust hurtled in through the window of Wei's room, choking them, followed by the sound of frantic whistles. Grand Arse grabbed Wei by his arms and stuffed him down the ladder while handing him his Lee Enfield (an officer had decided Wei should keep it as it could be useful for sniping). Wei slid down, followed by Grand Arse. The one following them down, Huang, just woken from profound sleep, was less lucky. He missed a rung, fell and sprained his ankle. All around there were frantic cries of 'fix bayonets', 'swords at the ready' as everyone bundled out of the houses on the left-hand side of the alley. Huang hobbled frantically behind them. His life depended on keeping up with everyone. The purpose of this panic was to seize control of the vantage points on the newly created rubble mounds on the right-hand side of the alley before the inevitable Japanese counter-attack.

About a hundred troops scrambled up the sides of the rubble – still enshrouded in dust and smoke rising from the burning timbers below – seized the natural vantage points on the mounds and, lying full length, started frantically re-piling masonry and furniture and bodies and body parts as parapets for cover and protection.

The Japanese counter-attack was delayed because they had expected to come from the west, attacking the demolished houses on the left-hand side of the alley. Instead they had to redeploy to the north to attack the whole wall of rubble their inaccurate bombing of the right-hand side of the alley had caused.

The dust was clearing, though the smoke was increasing, and before them the Chinese saw quite a lot of open ground before the next line of rubble and demolished homes held by the Japanese. In the middle sat a two-year-old child, bewildered by what had happened, paddling her arms desperately in the air and screaming her lungs out. The Chinese tried to ignore her. If they listened to her cries their emotions would get entangled, someone might rush out to try and save her and get cut down by machine gun fire. Instead, from some sort of cover to the east, her mother rushed out, shouting to her. A Japanese machine gun cut her down. A sniper took out the baby.

There was a roar from across the open space. Three Japanese tanks appeared and started waddling towards them, belching clouds of diesel, machine guns chattering. All the Chinese started cursing. Japanese infantry clustered behind the tanks. Wei didn't know how to deal with tanks – everyone was urging everyone else to keep lying low, to wait until the tanks reached the rubble – so instead, with his Lee Enfield, he concentrated on picking off the sheltering infantry. The more you concentrated in war, Wei was learning, the less you feared. Two he probably hit before the tanks reached their line of rubble. Their steel wheels and tracks screeched as they bit into the heaped rubble, their noses reared up, and suddenly their machine guns, pointing skyward, could no longer fire accurately. Two things happened simultaneously. Three Chinese soldiers wearing harnesses stuffed with grenades rose up screaming hideously 'Fuck your mums' and raced down the slope to throw themselves under the rearing snouts of the tanks, simultaneously detonating their grenades. Two of the tanks exploded, the third continued to grind up the slope because the suicide bomber had detonated his harness prematurely.

At the same time the rest of the Chinese rose from the rubble mountain screaming their terrifying battle cry 'Hit the Hard' and descended on the Japanese infantry waving their broad-bladed sabres above their heads. Wei, untrained in sword work, snapped his nine-inch spike bayonet into place. A wild melee enveloped the Japanese and Chinese – screams, thrusts, flashing bayonets, slashing swords severing arteries – kicking, bleeding, eye sockets gouged, even brawls with fists. Wei discovered at first hand why his spike bayonet was called a 'pig-sticker' and just how superior it was to the common broad-bladed bayonet. In a melee a Japanese had just bayoneted a Chinese through the ribs and, seeing Wei charging him, was frantically trying to dislodge its wide blade stuck between his ribs to parry Wei. Not in time. Wei punched his pig-sticker through his throat and slipped it out a second later. Meanwhile the surviving Japanese were starting to waver; the Chinese holding the high ground were still able to crash down on them with their swords while Wei and others went in under their raised arms with their bayonets. Just as the tank seemed to be regaining its equilibrium another Chinese suicide bomber threw himself successfully under it. Both violently exploded. This did it. The Japanese started to turn back, flee back across the open ground. Rather than follow them the Chinese turned and raced back to the shelter of their rubble. As soon as the Japanese regained their lines their machine guns would open up. Wei managed a shot or two at them but couldn't tell if any of them were hit before he turned and raced up the rubble himself, helping the limping Huang. Dying Chinese and Japanese lay indiscriminately among each other on the brief battlefield, their groans and screams mixing with the cries of crows and ravens and kites that wheeled and circled excitedly all over the battlefield of Taierzhuang.

Already their ridge of rubble was growing hot from the timbers burning beneath it. Several areas became impossible to stay on. While others kept watch above Wei and Grand Arse slipped down close to the alleyway. 'Well,' said Grand Arse, waving away the smoke, 'why don't you brew some tea and I'll bake some dumplings. No need to light a fire.' Everyone laughed except Huang, who had already fallen asleep. 'The longer you sleep,' he claimed continuously, 'the longer you live.'

Several more attacks happened that day and were beaten back.

After one Wei fell asleep. As he slept he did not dream of the terrifying flight from his home and the death of his family on their forced march, he did not see pictures of the mad slaughter he had just participated in. Instead he was back home on his farm. It was harvest and he was worrying deeply about a broken sickle which the blacksmith had not repaired yet. If it was not repaired by dawn only four men would be able to harvest his crop and he badly needed five. Everything would go wrong if…

He awoke in a sweat as Grand Arse shook him harshly.

'Hurry up – they're coming back.'

'How long did I sleep?'

'About a quarter of an hour. They're getting ready to charge again.'

14

My students, even Tian Boqi, are now happily writing, organizing, producing and acting in their own plays. Even better, they are cooperating with each other. Working as a team. When they have a production that is ready to go on the road out into the far-flung villages and towns of China, first they take it down to the village where Tian Boqi's original play had its disastrous premiere, and there play it in front of that village's hyper-critical audience. There are debates, discussions, suggestions – all of which they listen to and mostly incorporate. With suitable alterations made, the plays then go on the road. Several of the villagers from the original village have become so involved in the process they are starting to write their own plays or become actors themselves.

Feng Yuxiang has just handed me the list of my next batch of students. We're due to have our first meeting tomorrow. Mercifully my arch-nemesis, Guo Morou, is still not on the list. This is a bit of a mystery. Literary gossip has it that he has left Hong Kong where he was living and has reputedly arrived here in Wuhan – but no one seems to have seen anything of him. Perhaps, as 'China's Greatest Writer', he is refusing to be taught anything, especially by me.

Outside my window, and this is glorious, the red persimmon tree has burst into full flower. Vulvous scarlet blossoms race along the boughs like flames. Rich, gorgeous. My wife and my favourite blossom. We feel so close when...

I turn back to my desk. Empty my piled-high ashtray into the wastepaper basket. Up to three last night writing another bloody agitprop play – *The Daring River Pirates' Patriotic Victory*. It's actually quite good, despite its title. I've even managed to slip in some sly bits of humour and gentleness, though my popular writing still lacks the flow and naturalness of everyday street theatre. Someday I shall learn!

Also on my desk lies a rather cryptic piece of paper. A brief note from Feng Yuxiang informing me that a rickshaw will be calling for me at ten this morning and I am to go 'where the rickshaw driver takes me'. That's all. Having written a (rather successful) novel on rickshaw drivers, I consider myself a bit of an expert on them and usually like to choose my own, but Feng's note leaves me no choice. Knowing neither the address nor the person I'm meant to visit, I have to sit and await his arrival.

The man who arrives is young, straight-backed and brusque – I prefer them old, round-shouldered and loquacious – but he's a competent enough runner and avoids the potholes. It's a lovely morning. The first warmth of spring, with all its accompaniments of blossom, sweet scents, and animated birdsong. We are passing through some of Wuchang's most prosperous suburbs, gardeners out early cutting back the Westernized lawns, a few walls enclosing more traditional courtyards. Rickshaws bearing civil servants and merchants pass in the opposite direction, all off to their days work in the tri-city. But where am I going? The size of the houses is decreasing, the road is getting rougher. Finally the rickshaw man draws up outside a modest and secluded bungalow. I reach into my purse to pay him. The man grunts.

'No payment, comrade. No true proletarian accepts money in exchange for labour. It is demeaning.'

'I see.'

'It has been an honour providing transport for a writer of such socialist truths as *Rickshaw Boy*. Long live the revolution.'

With that he picks up his rickshaw and lopes off.

I think about this for a moment, then turn up the small pathway.

The garden is hung with peach and cherry trees in full bloom. Tulips, roses and peonies proliferate beneath them. Obviously the owner is a man of taste. And here is the owner himself, coming down the steps to greet me, a slight man in simple but tasteful trousers and shirt. I know him. I definitely know him. But I can't place him. Who *is* he?

'It is so kind of you to come, Mr Lao,' he says in an immaculate Han accent. 'I am so honoured that you have agreed to meet me.'

'This is a beautiful garden that you have.'

'Thank you, I am quite proud of my peach blossom.'

Both of us are of course far too astute to make any historical allusions.

Who is he, I think, *who*? Those eyebrows!

The stranger invites me into his modest living room. On the walls are a couple of contemporary German woodcut prints – very powerful – and three Li Hua woodcut prints of Chinese peasants and refugees. We sit down in two Western easy chairs. On the low wooden table between is a small vase holding a few delicately arranged orchids. This man is obviously Westernized, but still retains a real respect for China.

'Mr Lao,' says the man, 'let me first say what a great admirer I am of your work. I think your *Rickshaw Boy* speaks more immediately to the profound problems we Chinese face than any other novel I know.'

'Thank you.'

'A poor Manchu hero, struggling in the world, making mistakes, being beaten down and destroyed. And I understand how difficult this must be for you, Mr Lao, a Manchu, to have to sit and listen to me, a Han, pontificating and patronizing you in my immaculate East Coast accent – after all the brutality and violence we Han have visited on your people.'

I look mildly embarrassed. The man hurries on.

'But I want to say especially that the works of yours that I admire most are not *Rickshaw Boy* or your other novels but your short stories on women – 'The Crescent Moon' especially. It moves myself and my wife to tears. No one for me expresses the systematic repression and cruelty towards women of our present society more powerfully than you.'

This man is certainly a person of genuine feeling, I decide. And also a consummate actor. I look at him sharply. *Who is he?!?* The man takes my look to mean I am offended.

'Please, Mr Lao,' he says, leaning forwards and offering me some cigarettes, 'would you like Senior Service or Craven A?'

When I lived in London I always craved Senior Service, to savour their smooth cultivated taste, but could never afford them. Instead I smoked Player's Weights. Since my return to China I've always smoked Chinese cigarettes – fragrant as pig's droppings, but cheap. Trying not to be too eager, I take a Senior Service. The man leans forwards to light it. Suddenly I realize who he is. I can't believe it! The man lighting my cigarette is Chou En-lai. Chou En-lai! Vice Chairman of the Communist Party of China and number two to Mao Tse Tung himself. I drop my Senior Service.

'I'm so sorry for my clumsiness,' he apologizes. 'Please, have another one.'

This time I manage to light it. Chou En-lai! With the Japanese invasion, after years of war, the Nationalists and Communists have finally managed to form a unity government against them. Mao has sent Chou to Wuhan to sit as his representative in Chiang Kai-shek's War Cabinet. Chou is in control of the country's civilian war effort. Why has Feng sent me to meet him?

He looks at me. Beneath his languid, aristocratic appearance I see he has a lean, hard body. That's what marching 6,000 miles on the Long March gets you. I study his face to gain some clue as to what he wants from me, but all I see on it is confusion and embarrassment. What is going on?

He fiddles with his cigarette, then plunges in.

'I can't tell you how embarrassed I am about this whole affair. The thought that I should have to call upon a great writer such as yourself to intervene, waste your time, on a matter so trivial...'

Before I can intervene he ploughs on.

'Look, I understand that writers – and you yourself, a naturally modest and generous individual, are a shining exception to this rule...'

Not as modest or generous as you might think, I reflect.

'...but *most* writers tend to be badly behaved, egotistical, and often plain nasty.'

I stir uneasily.

'This unfortunate matter in which I wish you to be involved

concerns an extremely famous writer of ours who, not for the first time, considers himself to be madly, insanely in love with yet another woman. Narcissism bordering on the psychotic! He, unsurprisingly, considers himself to be the greatest Chinese writer alive. Amazingly, many Chinese agree with him.'

We both understand we are talking about Guo Morou. I groan inside.

'I personally,' Chou continues, 'would take every fucking European romantic poet – Shelley, Goethe, Byron – out behind a pigsty and happily shoot the lot of them for the calamitous effect they've had on our young revolutionary intellectuals. They read their Marx. They are convinced. They become sober and dedicated revolutionaries. Then suddenly they're reading fucking Goethe's fucking *The Sorrows of Young Werther* or some sob piece by Shelley and suddenly they're jumping off fucking cliffs or slashing their wrists or drowning themselves in a midnight pool with the moon reflected in it. They become insane. All for love! Half our female intellectuals have succumbed to "free love" pregnancies!'

There is a moment's silence in his tirade.

'I suppose you know who I am talking about?'

I smile vaguely. Chou sees I understand who he means, drags on his Craven A and plunges onward.

'Guo Morou was born into wealth, had a top-class education in China and Japan, became a rock-hard revolutionary, fell madly in love with a Japanese girl, stayed in Japan, married the poor girl and had four children by her while tirelessly sleeping with every other woman in Japan. All in the name of love. In 1927, with revolution breaking out here in China, Guo decided to help us out with it and came home, abandoning his wife, children, and various mistresses. Here, with his bad verse and histrionic speech making, he became an inspirational leader for many young Chinese intellectuals. Marx meets Goethe! The revolution was squashed by our present allies, many of us were executed, and Guo became part of a forced march south to escape the butchery. I will say, he did know how to march and carry a rifle and on occasion fire it. We escaped, he returned to Japan, where he decided to become not only our most famous poet but also our greatest intellectual and polymath, branching off into many areas of sociology, psychology, and even archaeology – Han archaeology, of course. He started an affair with Yu Lichun, *Dagong Bao*'s Japan correspondent. Then Japan invaded us. He obviously couldn't stay there, but instead of joining us here in our fight to the death he decided to flee to Hong Kong because he'd some particularly important Han archaeology to undertake. He again abandoned his wife and four children and Yu Lichun. Yu Lichun committed suicide. Another Goethean! While in Hong Kong Guo happened to be at an art show opening when he fell in love with an exquisitely beautiful young dancer, Yu Liqun. Yu Liqun just happens to be the sister of the late Yu Lichun. This family connection didn't appear to bother Mr Guo in the least, nor Miss Liqun, who never got on with her sister. But what did bother Miss Liqun was that she believes all true Chinese revolutionaries should be here in China fighting the Japanese. She had no time for the advances of an ageing semi-Japanese lothario lurking in Hong Kong rather than serving his country here in Wuhan. She told him this in no uncertain terms and got on the next flight to Wuhan, where she is a member of a modernist dance troupe performing in front of audiences of baffled peasants. I am sure you're well aware of this whole farrago from the literary grapevine.'

I try to look as though I never listened to literary gossip.

'This is our problem. In a nutshell. For reasons of national prestige and morale, we desperately want our "most famous writer" – apologies, Lao She – to become cabinet Minister for Cultural Affairs in our unity government, to give inspiring speeches in public all over the country and all over the world.'

'I'm still not certain why you want me involved in all this? Why not just offer him the post?'

'We did. Practically on our knees. But, he says, he is so much in love with young Miss Yu, he is so distraught at her callous rebuttal of his heartfelt offers of amour, that he cannot even think of getting involved in anything as mundane as politics. She is equally adamant. She will not marry him. When we suggest that as an idealistic young communist revolutionary she should be prepared to sacrifice herself for the revolutionary struggle, she looks at us coldly and asks us whether women's emancipation is not at the very top of our agenda.'

A long silence ensues. I say nothing, because I do not understand the situation. And because, instinctively, I understand that the less I understand about the complexity of this situation the less complicated my life is likely to become.

'What we want you to do,' says Chou, 'is this. And I am fully aware what an unpleasant task this is likely to be for you. As you probably know Guo Morou has agreed to come to Wuhan. He is due on the train tomorrow. But he is still adamant on his demands. No Yu Liqun, no revolutionary work. He would be rendered incapable.' Chou En-lai pauses. 'I've done a lot of soundings on this. Everyone, including Feng Yuxiang, has said that you, a natural conciliator, a natural bringer-together – you've succeeded so well already with persuading and cajoling so many of your fellow writers into working successfully for the war effort – a man who naturally empathizes and understands his fellow human beings, who implicitly sees the funny side of things, can smooth the way...'

Holy Moses! He wants me to be a matchmaker. A fucking matchmaker!

'Excuse me,' I interject, 'you are asking me to betray a young and decent and idealistic girl into what is essentially a forced marriage to an unscrupulous and uncaring old lecher? And you are the one who just now said how much you admire my "Crescent Moon" story about a young girl forced into prostitution. How it reduces you and your wife to tears!'

'This is a war. I do not wish to be melodramatic...'

I rise up, walk out of the front door, Chou follows, the two of us end up standing under the peach blossoms.

'Would you like another Senior Service?'

'No thank you. I'd prefer the rubbish brand of Chinese ones I normally smoke,' I say, taking out and lighting one and blowing the smoke in his face. Chou En-lai winces, then takes out another Craven A. By now he's consuming cigarettes like an express train on fire. A moment. Beneath the peach blossoms he speaks with emotion.

'I am aware of your terrible situation with your wife and family.

There can be nothing worse than not being able to communicate with your most dear ones. Not even knowing whether they live or die. I understand from your writings how deep your feelings for your wife must be.'

I do not respond.

'Have you heard from them?'

I glare at him.

'It might be possible for us, through our networks, to discover what is happening with them. I give you this offer whether you accept my proposal or not.'

What a consummate politician this fellow is.

'Let me tell you a story,' says Chou, 'about myself, my wife, on the Long March. The 6,000-mile Long March. She is not the prettiest of women. I did not marry her for her looks, I married her because I loved her. During the march she became pregnant. She realized that bearing a child would slow down the march. Without even telling me she was pregnant she had an abortion. Partly as a result of her resultant weakness she developed tuberculosis, she started spitting blood. But she would not leave the march. She marched on and on and on. She would not quit. She survived. People say to me she is ugly, she cannot bear you children, why not divorce her like other successful men do. I would never, ever leave my wife. I respect women. But we are at war. Young men die for our country. So do young women. Is it that wrong to ask Yu Liqun to lose her virtue? During the Rape of Nanking family women who were facing rape and assault asked prostitutes, who were more used to such things, to take their places to save them from violation. The prostitutes agreed to that. Is it wrong to ask you, a good and a humble man, a Christian and a socialist, to abase yourself before Guo Morou, to bow your head to his insecurities and empty boasts about his literary eminence, so that in the future we can build a world where such abominations and immoralities can never reoccur?'

There is silence beneath the peach blossoms. Finally I bow to him. He bows to me. My life has suddenly got a whole lot more difficult.

15

Wei cleaned his Lee Enfield with intense care. He oiled the bolt and firing mechanism, tried them again and again to check they were working smoothly, polished the wood casing and cleaned out and oiled the barrel with a rag. This ritual, which he performed many times a day, soothed him. Wei liked his machinery to work.

Grand Arse crawled up to him. A day later they were still holding the same ridge of demolished houses against repeated Japanese attacks. Grand Arse liked to soothe himself by talking. He told Wei a story from his childhood. One day in his village he'd come across a drunken farmer, slumped unconscious against a wall. He looked around to check no one was watching, then picked his pockets. In his bag he found a large bag of flour. He took it home to his mum. His mum beat him black and blue for stealing it. She then used it to make the most heavenly, scrumptious dumplings he had ever tasted. After they were all finished his mother gave them all a lecture on how stealing was wrong. This story really tickled Grand Arse. Huang, who was waking up, asked what the joke was. Before Grand Arse could tell him the whole story all over again whistles sounded. The Japanese were attacking again.

For the rest of this second day these attacks continued. The hand-to-hand fighting was scrappy, the tanks ineffective due to both suicide bombers and the unevenness of the ground. Casualties were heavy. Replacements arrived almost continuously.

After one attack Wei saw Grand Arse sitting in a doubled-up position and rocking backwards and forwards as though he desperately needed to shit but couldn't. He was crying in pain. Wei hurried to him, put his arms around him.

'Wei, I shall die. I shall die. I can't stick it. Its ripping me apart.'

It was terrible to watch him. Froth came from his mouth, sweat poured off his face. Thank the gods he'd soon be out of his pain. He had been shot from the side – the bullet going through both hip bones and his lower gut. With a groan and an agonized twist he died. Wei rifled his pockets and found six silver coins. They had reached an agreement early on in the fighting that if either died the other could have his money. His few other belongings – a billy can, a small knife, a lucky charm and some tobacco – Wei laid out on the ground for the rest of the company to take what they wanted.

Wei knew he'd never forget Grand Arse because of his mouthwatering description of eating those dumplings.

That night a strong wind sprang up from the east and the Japanese devised a new plan to destroy the stubborn defenders of Taierzhuang.

In their hurry to prepare the city as a battlefield the Chinese had forgotten to remove the wooden roofs from the central parts of Taierzhuang. Noting the strong wind from the east the Japanese decided to use incendiary shells and bombs to set alight the roofs and burn the defenders out of central Taierzhuang. The shells and incendiary bombs rained down and almost immediately flames started seizing hold and, in the wind, leaping from roof to roof, wooden buildings and temples exploding into flame, shops and warehouses containing oil or diesel detonating fireballs into the sky like red and yellow flowers. A firestorm raged throughout central Taierzhuang.

With the Chinese soldiers and civilians in the streets and houses, the flames streamed above their heads, roofs crackling, tiles exploding in the heat and raining down on their heads. Flames roared from the windows of houses, sweeping their flowerpots from their window ledges, their herbs and dahlias and orchids flaming like pennants as they hurtled into the streets below. Great multi-coloured flames leapt into the dark skies – yellow, orange, pale white and crimson, red, green and blue, twisting, blossoming above the city like giant tulips and peonies.

Trapped in the upper storeys of the houses and temples humans roasted as if they had been spitted before a good kitchen-fire. They were burnt quite brown, every stitch of clothing singed off, and as their bodies dried and crackled in the heat their tendons and muscles pulled their limbs tight and twisted like dried frogs.

Wakened by the sudden light and thinking it day and therefore time for more carrion, crows and kites left their roosts and started flying into central Taierzhuang. A whole raucous flock of rooks from a nearby park joined them. But soon the fire was so fierce that its huge thermals swept the bewildered birds tumbling upwards into the skies above, screeching and cawing in terror. In the intense heat of the air currents they started igniting spontaneously in clouds of burning feathers. Smoke was everywhere, billowing and swirling and revealing and concealing the flames like vast velvet curtains. Dragons lived above Taierzhuang.

And the inhabitants below? There were civilians down there, refusing to leave their homes – because they feared the loss of all their property and livelihoods, because they were too old or because they were too young, because they knew of nowhere else to go and couldn't conceive of living anywhere other than the place they'd always lived. And there were soldiers. A fire like this did not consume all oxygen. If the fire was to live it must suck in oxygen from below to feed it above. The streets and alleys beneath the fire became like tornadoes, hurricanes, with air being sucked in from all the surrounding countryside. Most people found shelter in cellars or in the tunnels. But there were still people in the streets. Doctors, nurses, firemen, fighting the almighty winds, dodging falling tiles and dead birds. And all the coolies shielded from the heat above by their great conical straw hats – bringing in ammunition, food, medicines, and above all water – cheerfully on their return journey taking out children and the elderly and the dead and wounded. Their hats smouldered, their clothing smouldered, but they mainly thought excitedly about all the money they were making on quadruple time. This war couldn't go on too long!

The Chinese commanders understood the Japanese would be waiting to the north, just on the edge of the flames, ready to envelop them the second the flames quietened. What could they do? From experience fighting in Shanghai, in Tengxian, and here in Taierzhuang, they knew that Japanese infantry preferred waiting at a distance while aircraft, artillery, tanks and poison gas did their work, and then sweeping in to mop up their already mainly destroyed, completely disorientated enemy. It was what they had been trained to do. And the Chinese commanders knew that what their enemy disliked above all else was close combat, face-to-face fighting, fighting at night. Anything that was intimate, personal, inescapable in the darkness.

So the Chinese troops sent forwards through the hurricanes and the heat had congregated even closer beneath the flames than the Japanese troops and then, as the Japanese shielded their faces and eyes against the heat, had charged them out of the flames and fallen upon them. Simultaneously, using the tunnel systems which they had dug and still used while the Japanese occupied the ground overhead, Chinese troops rose behind the Japanese troops and attacked them from the rear. Figures from hell. The sky thundered. The earth thundered. Soldiers thought their hearts would explode, the skin on their backs would burn up. The earth cracked, everything cracked, the skies roared. Everything swayed back and forth in crazy hallucination. Oaths, stabs, screams, sudden ambushes, frenzied stiflings, gougings and guttings. The only thing of value was water. Water to gulp down and water to drench your clothes with so they didn't burst into flames. Many soldiers, on both sides, spontaneously combusted in blazing torches.

Such resistance did not last, however. The Japanese simply brought forward their heavy artillery and, at point blank range, blasted all the fighters – Chinese AND Japanese.

How could the Japanese do this to their own people? Where did this obscene madness come from? It came from the science of Social Darwinism, of eugenics. All members of the master race were but pawns and ants, expendable in the struggle of the race for supremacy. And so this English disease of Herbert Spencer and Francis Galton, Darwin's cousin, and possibly even Darwin himself, was unleashed by the Japanese upon the Chinese, by the Germans upon the Russians and Poles and Jews and Gypsies. And all in the saintly name of science![7]

A few Chinese survived. They came out from beneath the flames, immediately drank all the water they could find. Amid the ashes of central Taierzhuang the Chinese lines held. They were swiftly reinforced.

With their advance through central Taierzhuang denied, the Japanese reverted to their southward attacks in the eastern city. Only three members of Wei's platoon were still alive. Even Huang was gone, taken out by a sniper. One second he was drawing deeply on a cigarette and complaining about having inherited Grand Arse's fleas, the next he was no more. Brains blown clean out of his head. Which went to show, Wei reflected, that sleeping long did not necessarily mean living long.

With troops continuously being killed and incapacitated and complete strangers arriving all the time to fill the ranks – all from different units and from different parts of China, trained in different ways to fight and speaking endless different (and often incomprehensible) dialects – how did the Chinese soldiers still manage to maintain cohesion and common understanding and cooperation between each other in the fighting? One thing certainly united them. In the continuous charging and counter-charging in this battle, their bloodcurdling battle cry 'Hit the Hard!!!' clearly not only terrified the Japanese (their 'Banzai' was small beer in comparison), but unloosed in the Chinese huge surges of euphoria and energy and togetherness just as they hit the enemy lines. It made them one.

But in the end the sheer firepower of the Japanese wore down the Chinese. After several more hours of to-and-fro insanity, with bodies banked all around, they were finally forced to retreat from the line of one row of demolished houses back fifty yards to the next line of demolished houses, holding them and their associated maze of trenches and tunnels as tenaciously as they had held their previous line.

As a result the Japanese tanks now had to advance slowly, cumbersomely, and vulnerably across even more mounds and pits of rubble to close on their enemy. Supplies of food and water and ammunition for them were likewise becoming more difficult to deliver. A modern army equipped with trucks could no longer access those areas they were meant to. Regular soldiers had to be withdrawn from the front line in order to transport food and ammunition for other troops in the front line. Fuel for the tanks also had to be carried by hand in large jerry cans. The Chinese had never bothered or been able to afford much mechanized transport. A coolie would go anywhere – provided you paid him enough (which was virtually nothing).

The waves of Japanese frontal assaults continued. The dead continued to pile up all around. In this frenzied fighting Wei developed a useful skill. Untrained in sword play, in fighting he tended to take a position in the second rank, picking off with his bayonet those Japanese who broke through. But he soon realized that simply shooting them with his rifle was more effective. Even back on his farm with an ancient musket, the crows and pigeons had quickly learnt to keep a respectful distance from him. But in this fighting the Lee Enfield proved a godsend. Its high-quality British-forged steel meant its barrel did not warp in the heat and it never jammed. No matter how much he fired and however hot the metal became, as the whole gun was encased in wood he could keep firing it for as long as he needed.

An officer noticed Wei standing there in the second rank blazing away. The accuracy of his fire. He immediately ordered him back behind the ridge to continue his firing. After all, why waste a good sniper in hand-to-hand fighting? Other officers noted his competence too.

In the next lull in the fighting Wei was ordered back to battalion HQ. He made his way back, having to ask directions all the time through a maze of alleys and tunnels. He passed soldiers being shaved by barbers and simultaneously dictating farewell letters to professional scribes, handymen repairing water and food canteens, cooks filling them, telephone lines being laid, the dead being stacked, the wounded moaning, cigarettes being bartered, even the odd whore plying her trade to those about to die. He found it amazing walking upright again instead of having to crouch and scuttle all the time.

In the solid black stone building in which the battalion had made its latest headquarters Wei passed commanding officers listening to reports, issuing orders, a radio operator frantically trying to contact regimental headquarters, a drunken sergeant being prepared for execution.

Wei was directed to the back of the building to some stables. The battalion armoury. He produced a note an officer had given him and the armourer, having admired Wei's Lee Enfield, read it. He walked back into his stores and came back holding a large and very clumsy-looking rifle. It was a crude Chinese copy of a Japanese Type 97 anti-tank rifle. The Russians had captured some from the Japanese in their border skirmishes with them in Siberia in 1936. They'd passed one on to the Nationalist Chinese who, not having any of their own, copied it. The specially trained detail that were due to fire it had been wiped out by a random shell before they managed to get to the front but their weapon was intact. The armourer gave Wei a hurried thirty-minute course on how to load and fire it, apologizing for its inaccuracy and general unreliability. He also handed him a satchel full of ammunition. He emphasized that it was necessary to get as close as possible to the enemy tank before firing this weapon at it and that reloading it could take a while. Finally he said that if the weapon cracked or fractured itself in any way when firing Wei was to bring it back so he could try to repair it. It was the only one they'd got. He gave Wei a note permitting him to retreat.

On his way back to rejoin his section Wei thought about this, all the time handling and balancing the weapon as he would a new-bought hoe or scythe, clicking and opening and closing the breech and firing chamber and pin. Back at the line his new anti-tank weapon prompted a lot of cheerful comments.

'That rubbish won't never work.'

'How do you get a punch out of a thing like that?'

'A suicide bomber's got better chances of living than you.'

One nervous young recruit ventured to ask:

'But how do you actually fire it?'

'That's the difficult part,' replied Wei. 'I've been thinking about it.'

'You'd better think about it fast,' replied one veteran of at least eight hours. 'That's fresh Japanese troops we've got in the line opposite us. They're readying for an attack. And they've got lots of tanks.'

From their observers stationed in their network of tunnels and trenches and positioned high and precariously in wrecked buildings, the Chinese were well aware of this gathering of heavy Japanese reinforcements. Originally intended for the expected offensive into central Taierzhuang following the devastating firestorm, when that enterprise failed this massed Japanese force was redeployed to the eastern side of the city. This took some time and losses. The streets were narrow, many of the interconnected houses continued to contain pockets of Chinese troops and suicide bombers, many Chinese fighters continued to lurk in the tunnels and trenches and even the primitive sewers, letting off mines and explosive devices beneath tanks, throwing grenades into troop carriers from high windows. But they finally made it.

When they arrived two companies of Japanese shock troops – fanatical followers of the emperor and the cult of Bushido – were positioned in the front line, along the ridge of demolished houses which the Chinese had once occupied but which had now been taken by the Japanese. These fanatical storm troopers had been ordered at dawn to charge directly at the Chinese line of defence. They were told that anyone retreating back to their own lines, unwounded or wounded, would be shot on sight. They would take the lines or die. These troops applauded enthusiastically when they heard of their fate.

That night, in the centre of the Japanese lines, other soldiers laboured to build clear gaps in the rubble of the line of ruined buildings they held so that their tanks could get a clean run at the Chinese defence line. This activity gave Chinese skirmishers an excellent opportunity, under cover of darkness, to sneak in among these toiling Japanese, knife them, throw grenades, assault them cheek by jowl, unnerve the whole Japanese line with bloodcurdling screams, play very loud music from loudspeakers – all the psychological tricks of night fighting that disorientate and demoralize your enemy, rob him of sleep and peace of mind before he attacks.

Meanwhile, armed with his anti-tank rifle, Wei used the confusion to sneak up to a burnt-out tank, positioned on the right-hand side of the gap out of which the Japanese tanks were due to emerge. He carefully slid underneath it and concealed himself beneath debris and stones. To the left of the gap a lot of partially destroyed dwellings reached from the Japanese lines up towards the Chinese lines. During the night a substantial number of Chinese troops – including the remnants of Wei's company – concealed themselves within these ruins and in the trenches and tunnels which still ran in the area.

Just before dawn the Chinese arose and emerged from these positions and attacked the left flank of the Japanese lines. The fighting was fierce. It distracted the Japanese storm troopers for a while and forced them to deal with the Chinese marauders. They did this fairly quickly and efficiently. Wei was now the last remaining survivor of his company. Twenty minutes later the Japanese storm troopers redeployed themselves in their original positions, the cries of 'Banzai' rang out and the suicide troops charged.

They charged straight past Wei, concealed beneath his burnt-out tank, and disappeared into the dust and smoke which concealed most of the battlefield. Shouts and screams and roars of 'Hit the Hard' were heard in the distance as they met the Chinese counter-charge. In murk and obscurity huge streams of humanity flowed back and forth in madness and slaughter.

Closer to Wei, from just beyond the Japanese line of rubble, came the familiar grumble of tanks being started and roaring as they warm up. Clouds of diesel plumed out from behind the lines and added to the murk and confusion. Wei understood he was likely to die very soon. He thought of his family and his ancestors. Then he set himself, calmed himself to fight.

The first tank waddled through the gap. Then another and

another. Wei pushed a grenade into the barrel of his gun and aimed. He waited and he waited. The tank waddled towards him. Two others behind it. Closer and closer. He must not fire too soon or the first one would shelter the other two. Or too late as the first one would be behind him. He was relying on the second two to hesitate when the first one was hit, so he had time to hit them too. The first one was almost beside him. He fired through the broken tracks of his tank into the wheels and tracks of the Japanese tank. There was a huge flash as his gun fired, his face seared with pain and he was temporarily blinded. Five seconds later, when he could see again, he pushed another grenade into his barrel, saw the first tank's tracks shearing off, flames spreading, and hears screams from inside as he turned and saw, as he'd hoped, the other two tanks stopped. He aimed at the second tank, at an angle to him because when it stopped it was positioned to pass his tank. He fired, a flash, pain, his grenade flew beneath the tank's hull and hit the tracks away from him on their inside. Again it twisted them off their wheels, flames, screams. But there were bangs and ricochets from above him. The third tank had spotted where his fire was coming from and was advancing on him, its machine gun raking his place of concealment. It was approaching from an angle so, withdrawing behind the shelter of his tank's twisted tracks, he hastily rammed another grenade down his barrel ready to fire. But how to get into a satisfactory firing position without being first shot down himself? The machine gun rounds continued to hammer into the body of his own tank. He waited for a pause. Any pause. It came. He stuck his head out, aimed and fired. This time his gun half exploded, the grenade flew out, his face was seared with flames, he was knocked on his back, the grenade hit its target. It took him thirty seconds to recover his wits, his eyesight. He looked. A track had come off the third tank and it was sheering round sideways, partly blocking the gap through which the rest of the tanks were meant to come. But Wei was not going to be able to stop them when they came. He couldn't even fire at them. His anti-tank rifle had split down most of its barrel. What should he do? He thought. As he thought about his situation, his options, Wei was completely calm. As calm and rational as when he had once surveyed his fields, deciding which crops should be planted where, which members of his family should plant them, on what day the family pig should be slaughtered and butchered into all its constituent parts, what the family's ancestors should be told and in what order they should be told it. Wei was always calm. Should he stay and fight? No. He had no effective weapon to fight with. Should he withdraw? The armourer had given him explicit instructions: if the weapon malfunctioned and could not be repaired, it must be brought back to him. It was too valuable to lose. He had given him a note to cover his retreat.

Wei picked up his weapon and headed into the dust cloud and smoke where the infantry were still fighting. He passed through a ghostly, silent place. Almost everyone was dead. Bodies piled everywhere. Silent, disassociated as the grave.

At the Chinese front line he was challenged. An officer recognized him. He gave him a brief report on his actions then said he must return his gun to the armourer for repairs. He walked back behind the rubble, unearthed his Lee Enfield which he had buried so, if he did not die, he could still fight with it, then made his way through the lines.

He was challenged at a Chinese military police checkpoint which was stopping and shooting deserters.

'You are a deserter,' they said.

Wei showed them his anti-tank rifle with its split barrel, explaining that the armourer had ordered him to return it if it misfired and needed repairing.

'You're lying.'

Wei showed them the note from the armourer.

None of them could read.

But, like most illiterate people, they maintained a superstitious fear of anything written down. The sergeant in command ordered his corporal to escort Wei back to the armourer. If he tried to run away – shoot him. If it was found that the paper was a lie – shoot him.

Wei and the corporal disappeared back into the gloom of the eastern part of the city. On the way they met officers marching men forwards to the front line. So desperate was the situation in the east they were commandeering clerks, cooks, orderlies, servants, jankers men, even criminals, rushing them forwards to plug the gaps. They commandeered the corporal. They read Wei's note and let him continue. Wei wished the corporal good luck. The corporal cursed Wei.

The Battle of Taierzhuang, at shocking human cost, was fulfilling the task the Chinese High Command had required of it. Like some gigantic insect Rensuke Isogai's 10th Division – the most brutal and destructive of all Japan's armies – had rushed headlong into the city and its head was now locked immovably into ten thousand different skirmishes and actions and feuds within Taierzhuang's black granite buildings and fortifications, unable to move or free itself. Meanwhile the flanks and rear of this colossal beast, tasked with supplying the head, were laid open to pincer attacks by other divisions of the Chinese Army. Like ants, all along the 150-mile length of the railway from Jinan, armies of country people blew up the trains and cut the tracks and roads, shutting off Isogai's supplies. But the arrogance and hubris of Rensuke Isogai, stung by the resistance of such untermenschen, howling for fame and glory in the eyes of his god-emperor, could focus his mind only on the crushing and utter destruction of Taierzhuang.

And who sacrificed themselves by their tens of thousands in Taierzhuang? Those who spoke so loudly about freedom and civilization and capitalism and equality and liberation and revolution? No! Ordinary people, poor people, uneducated people, inarticulate and modest people, the very dregs of society swept up off the floor and press-ganged into its armies and battalions where they so willingly and uncomplainingly and heroically died for a country in which they had no interest or standing or acclamation.

So is history made.

Wei found that the armoury to which he was making his way had been withdrawn several hundred yards. When he finally located it the armourer looked at the anti-tank rifle and shook his head.

'That'll take a time to repair,' he said. 'Was it any good?'

Wei nodded. 'Took out three tanks.'

'Good,' says the armourer. 'I've got new orders for you.'

He took out a piece of paper. Somewhere within the collective memory of the rapidly dying regiment someone had remembered Wei's prowess with his Lee Enfield. His potential as a sniper.

The armourer handed the paper to Wei.

'These are your orders. You are to be transferred to the western side of the city, where the western gate is coming under heavy attack. They desperately need snipers.'

'Oh,' said Wei.

'Ah,' said the armourer, suddenly remembering something. 'I've got a little present for you as well.' He passed back into the stores and re-emerged with something in his hand. 'Things being as they are we've been amalgamated with several other armouries since I last saw you.' (Which must have been at least twenty-four hours ago.) 'When checking their inventories I happened to see this. Thought, if you ever returned from the front, it would be just the thing for you.'

It was a brand new, immaculate sniper scope made specifically to fit a Lee Enfield .303 – gleaming and shiny.

Wei took it and gazed at it with admiration.

'Oh, and I found these too,' said the armourer.

He plonked two large pouches of .303 ammunition on the table. Wei grinned.

A large shell landed nearby.

'I'll show you how to operate the scope later,' said the armourer. 'But first, when did you last sleep and when did you last eat?'

Wei couldn't remember either.

The armourer gave him a wholesome meal then ordered him to sleep for two hours on the floor. Wei did so. The armourer woke him, instructed him on the use of the sniper scope, presented him with his written orders and sent him on his way.

Wei walked back through the streets, passing through several military police checkpoints, all of which fortunately contained soldiers who could read.

He passed out of the south-east gate, over the pontoon bridge, and then followed the south bank of the canal to the west. Suddenly he could see long distances again. He saw trees and hills and in the distance mountains. He walked on earth. Birds sang. Crickets chirped. He breathed more easily. Crossing the canal again on a bridge of single planks, he walked on grass up beside the western walls of the city. Ahead of him were the sounds of heavy fighting.

16

Guo Morou faced a bit of a dilemma. Normally life was so easy. But now? In Wuhan? He could address crowds with no problem – have them eating out of his mind. He could face the most arcane, abstruse of theoretical problems and his flawless Marxist dialectic would waltz through them without even hesitating. But now?

He was feeling restless and ill at ease. To Gou Morou the world just did not seem right. Why was it so much at odds with him? In the past it had always agreed with him. Echoed him. Congratulated him on his verbal fluency, his intellectual rigour, his dialectical brilliance. His selfless dedication to the cause of world revolution!

But now something was wrong. Was it being in Wuhan? Such a grimy, ugly place. Nowhere the slightest concession to beauty, enlightenment. The worst sort of industrial city. Just like Chicago. Of course, its workers were magnificent. Full of revolutionary fire and heroism! But that was back in 1927. Now Wuhan was ruled by that squalid little fascist Chiang Kai-shek. And the communists – the Communist Party of China, no less!!! – squatted subserviently beneath his throne and did whatever he ordered them to!

That was bad, dispiriting enough. But something else, something even worse, ate into him like a cancer. In a horribly ordinary hotel room, curtains drawn to keep out the stench and the smoke, poor Guo was stricken with lethargy and despair. Even his brain had stopped!

For why? For why should he be carrying all the sorrows of Young Werther? Why was this young dancer – why was she acting in such an irrational manner? A liberated feminist refusing his advances? He had never heard of such a thing. Here he was, China's most illustrious intellectual, litterateur, orator. Women had never been an obstacle in the past. They'd just fallen into bed with him. But this thing, this stripling of a girl – muscles of iron, mind of iron – was refusing him, point blank, without a trace of embarrassment or apology. Was it something they put in the water in Wuhan? Something in this filthy industrial air?

His mind, like a wounded hart – to think he was now the hunted, not the hunter – returned yet again, obsessively, to their first fateful meeting in Hong Kong.

He'd accepted an invitation to attend the opening of an exhibition of young Chinese artists in Hong Kong's most avant-garde art gallery. There he first set eyes on the young, the beautiful, the firmly muscled eighteen-year-old body of Yu Liqun, the Marxist dancer. The sun was setting dramatically across Victoria Harbour, great jagged black clouds reflected its yellows and reds and oranges, thunder rolled in across the bay. Groups of English and Chinese aesthetes debated Art in the dull monotones of English. (A recording of Arseny Avraamov's *Symphony of Factory Sirens, Artillery Guns and a Hydro Plane* played randomly in the background.) Suddenly there, before him, stood his fate. Set against the dramatic lighting of the bay. Indifferent to the chatterings in the rest of the room, alone and alienated like him, she danced. Quivered her arms, abruptly jerked her back and legs, imitating the harsh movements and rhythms of a piece of industrial machinery, she danced her Marxist dance to the groans and shrieks of Arseny Avraamov.

Entranced, he approached. He assumed he'd do what he always did. That what always happened would inevitably happen. He addressed her.

'I'm Guo Morou.'

This did not seem to impact on her in any way. She continued her mechanistic motions.

'The writer.'

'Of course you are. You had an affair with my sister, Yu Lichun,' she said, continuing her motions.

'Oh, er, yes, I did, most unfortunate.'

'It is of no importance to me,' she said, still continuing her exercises. 'The fact that she continually indulged herself in petit bourgeois Goethe-esque melodramatics and finally ended it all in an entirely frivolous and self-indulgent suicide is not of the slightest interest to me.' She stopped her machinations for a second. 'In an age of revolution, proletarian steel and sacrifice, she was a counter-revolutionary disgrace.' She resumed her articulations.

Guo was enraptured.

'So you're a dancer.'

Very slowly she slowed down, like a complex piece of machinery coming to rest. He looked down into her face. Every muscle fixed as iron, not a single etch of emotion or life or femininity.

'Of course I'm a fucking dancer.'

In the background someone in a monotonous voice was reciting Boris de Schloezer's treatise on *musique concrète*, while harsh squeals and grunts escaped the gramophone.

Like an implacable machine, like a gun turret swirling on a battleship, like a piston driving the mighty wheels of a locomotive ever onward, she resumed her motions. In her whole body there was not one touch of sympathy, warmth, sens- or sex-uality.

Guo's mouth was very dry. He could imagine her starting to melt like steel. Slowly meld and molten and consume in flame and tempest til all yielded and exploded like bombs.

Guo had never fallen in love so quickly or fatally before. He had an enormous erection – not that anyone of the mindless bourgeois in the art gallery were paying the least attention; they continued to chatter away in English about Picasso and Mondrian.

He moved in close to her.

'I would like to see you again.'

Nothing. Guo Morou coughed.

'I said, "I would like to see you again,"' he repeated.

'I am a revolutionary. In three days' time I am going to Wuhan with my revolutionary dancing to inspire the masses to repulse the Japanese attacks, overthrow the fascist Nationalist regime, and install the eternal dictatorship of the proletariat. Daddy has booked my ticket.'

'But I really must see you again.'

She shrugged her un-sexual shoulders.

'I rehearse in my studio every morning. If you insist you can come and watch.'

Guo Morou, pot belly and erection, did go and watch. But to no avail. On the third day the completely indifferent eighteen-year-old packed her bags and flew to Wuhan.

Guo had eventually followed her.

Now, hopeless, feeling sick, he drew back a curtain and stared from his hotel window out on to the madhouse of The Bund. It was as though he was twenty years old again, lost in deliriums of Shelleyan madness and emotion.

And, to cap it all, they were sending that worm, that dismal little hack Lao She round to try and entice him to write, to orate, to inspire once more. Apparently he was even going to try and persuade him to write as Lao She wrote. Him? Guo Morou?? Write like Lao She??? Just let him try!!!

For early April it is a very hot day.

I plod along the Bund. I pass the walls where the newspapers are pasted and political debates take place. Discussions which involved four or five people three months ago have now grown to billowing crowds of several hundreds, all vociferously debating each other, orators and would-be politicians and revolutionaries and fanatics from all parties and none precariously perched on soap boxes orating and aerating on future worlds. Their audiences love it. The government, feeling under pressure, has even announced there will be some sort of elections. Elections in China?!?!?

I plod up the concrete steps outside Guo Morou's plush hotel. The doorman inspects this scruffy human being. I have to open the door for myself. I ask the clerk at the desk the number of Guo Morou's room. He tells me to wait. I sit down on a sofa, which the label informs me was made in Swansea.

This whole business of being a pimp is exhausting. Ever since Chou En-lai dumped his patriotic blackmail on me I've been unable to think of anything else. I've continued writing, of course. Actually, I've discovered that writing soap opera while thinking of

something else actually improves the quality of the soap opera –
but I don't think that's a lesson I'll pass on to my students!

There is no escape from the fact that I am about to betray every
feeling and ideal I have ever held about women. Every time I see
a young girl or old woman tottering along the Bund, scarcely
able to keep her balance on the tips of her miniscule bound
feet. Every time I see girls and women being auctioned by their
fathers, husbands, owners on the street – that terrible blank look
on their faces. Every time I see wives being publicly whipped and
beaten by their husbands. Every time as a child I watched my poor
mother having to degrade herself as she fought to support our now
fatherless family. What has my writing been about, pretty much
from the start, but the trials and horrors Chinese women have to
daily face? And yet here I am now, pimping a girl into an arranged
marriage!

Of course, I know my beloved wife would have no scruples
about it. If it comes down to choosing between the fate of one single
girl or one single family and the fate of the whole of China, there is
no choice. The people of China come first! That's why Chiang Kai-
shek or Chou En-lai can send off millions to their deaths. That's
why soldiers lay down their lives without a murmur. Because they
have decided to. This is war. And you, Lao She, have no choice but
to fight it too.

I shake my head vigorously, trying to remove the rats from my
brain.

The clerk approaches and informs me that Mr Guo will now
see me. He gives me his room number. Shrewd Chou En-lai was
right. The pleas of party apparatchiks and outraged citizens could
be ignored. But the threat of a rival writer…?

I climb the well-carpeted stairs. But why does it have to be Gou
Morou, a writer who makes me incandescent with rage? Why must
I plead, grovel, ingratiate myself with this monster of egotism and
terrible prose…?

An ice-cold glance from my wife silences me. I *will* humiliate
myself, I *will* grovel before him. Agree with everything he says.
All the time, by effortless guile, slick-tongued flattery, guiding
him towards the deal, the horse trade, the final grand bargain.

'In exchange for being lionized, loved, deified by the Chinese intelligentsia for your high-flown glorious writings and crowd-inspiring oratories – for you are loved, Guo Morou, you alone are truly beloved above all writers in China – in exchange, in your big fat marriage bed, you will receive the staked-out, beaten, humiliated... the loving, keen and amorous young virgin, Miss Yu Liqun.' That is all I have to achieve. And will achieve.

I have arrived outside his door. I knock on it.

No answer.

I knock again.

Still no answer.

Eventually the door opens.

Guo Morou, pot-bellied, balding, in a dressing gown, looks down at me.

(Actually, he's considerably shorter than me, but he still looks down on me.)

'Ah, the Manchu scribbler.'

'Yes,' I say.

'Standing there like some cringing European Jew. Not of course that all Jews are like that. Marx and Lenin were both brilliant and noble.'

I smile at his correctness.

'What do you want?' he demands in his perfect Han accent.

'Can I say, Mr Guo,' I say, 'that I have always been a great admirer of your work. That in many ways you have been the greatest inspiration for all my own writings.'

Guo looks at me.

'And can I say, as chairman of the "Resist to the End" writers' collective, that all of us welcome such a great writer as you yourself here in Wuhan.'

'Shoddy hacks,' states Guo.

'Beside a writer such as yourself,' I say, 'we undoubtedly are.'

He ignores this and carries on.

'If you want to inspire the Chinese masses to greatness, to immortality, you do not speak to them in the mealy-mouthed street banter which you employ in your "novels", the argot which I hear you insist all your fellow writers here adopt for their street drama. The Han people of China have time and again evolved the highest, most enlightened civilizations in world history. And from these civilizations have crystallized the most divine, the most exquisite language mankind has ever heard. All that is needed is for someone who loves High Mandarin, who knows expertly how to use and play it like a musical instrument, to stand up in public and start to descant its beautiful notes and tones – and every Han there, whether peasant or scholar or factory worker or coolie, will be transported and transformed, reborn in action and industry and...'

He stops abruptly. Turns and walks to the window and stares moodily out of it, like a hero in some cheap Hollywood melodrama.

Guo Morou is being overwhelmed by images of the lissome young Miss Yu Liqun, alone with him in this room now. Naked. Dancing. Her limbs and nipples and wet places glowing and pulsing, leading him on, leaning over his sofa, enticing his hands to... Then he looks up and what does he see? This pathetic worm Lao She. He cannot bear it. He lights a Senior Service.

I meanwhile have been droning on about why speaking in dialect is necessary when addressing audiences of country people, of how much can be done in the popular imagination by using stereotypes and melodrama and constant surprises, but when he lights a Senior Service something within me snaps. I don't know whether it's class hatred, the thought of what an easy life this thing has had, how he's had everything handed to him on a plate, but in revenge I immediately take out one of my cheap-as-chips Chinese cigarettes and light it.

Clouds of foul smoke enshroud the room.

Guo Morou's nose puckers in disgust.

'What on earth is that you're smoking?'

'A cigarette. A proletarian Chinese cigarette,' I reply, heartily inhaling and blowing the smoke all round the room.

Oh God, I think, I hope I haven't gone too far...! I haven't. Rather than rising to my challenge he turns away.

Guo Morou is flooded with emotion. That it should come to this! Arguing with some literary rent boy in a tawdry hotel room. He is in utter despair! All Guo Morou's age, his eminence, his brilliance falls away from him. Again he is a twenty-year-old student. Flaming with desire and passion but turned away, denied the eternal burning beauty of a young female's flesh. The agony, the humiliation! There is only one way out. Guo Morou climbs onto the window sill.

What is he doing, I ask myself?

He opens the window.

'What are you doing?'

He steps out onto the sill.

Oh my God, I think, he's going to kill himself, go the full Goethe. I am going to be held responsible for the death of China's most eminent writer – all because I lit a Chinese cigarette. I'm never going to hear the end of this.

'Don't do it,' I cry, 'don't jump!'

Guo Morou is already having second thoughts about jumping. He's forgotten his room is only on the first floor and, looking down, he sees below him a large and very thorny rose bush into which he is likely to plummet.

I grab him round his legs in a sort of rugby tackle, which almost propels him out of the window. For a second we sway back and forth, he clinging on to my receding hair, before I manage to pull him back in.

'I'm sorry,' I say to him, 'I'm really sorry.'

He looks at me. Hostility, malevolence starts to gleam in his eye. Someone has to be blamed for his humiliation of himself. For a story that is now likely to be repeated in every literary salon for the rest of time.

'You worm. You interfering, snivelling little Manchu worm,' he states, in his immaculate Han accent. 'You couldn't write a decent line of prose if you worked a thousand years at it. You'd have more chance of writing a truthful, socialistic jot of truth if you threw dice or coins in the air and wrote down the results. I've read your shitty books from cover to cover with their boring, mundane characters, their crude language, their low humour. You are a disgrace to the high and honourable art of literature. Fuck off out of my room!'

Suddenly, completely unexpectedly, I find myself grasping

his throat. I appear to have lost every semblance of civilization, reverting to my barbarian Manchu past. I drag him over to an armchair and slam him down in it. I rest the two arms of my large, non-athletic body on its two armrests and stare down into the quivering visage of my pot-bellied opponent. I draw my face extremely close to his.

'Listen, you little cunt,' I hiss, 'I'm not some nancy-boy university-educated poseur, I'm a pimp. Your pimp. This is the deal. You want to fuck Yu Liqun? This is how. You work your fucking arse off on behalf of the government, you propagandize for them, you scream your head off for them at rallies, you scribble endless encomiums in praise of their greatness and the valour of the Chinese peoples, and, that done, I sign, seal and deliver to your bedroom one naked and willing, oh so willing, Yi Liqun. How about it?'

For two seconds Guo Morou hesitates. Those two seconds are enough to tell me I've won. Thank God for my childhood in the rougher backstreets of Beijing. After two seconds Guo manages to reassemble himself and starts angrily protesting, but those two seconds are enough. I've hooked my fish. I grin and leave.

I'm halfway down the stairs before it strikes me that I might have behaved in a slightly disgraceful manner. But mud wrestling with a moral dwarf like Guo Morou is hardly reprehensible. I realize the real moral squalor lies ahead.

17

Taierzhuang was a mass of ruin and rubble, choked with smoke and flame and clouds of dust, across and through which struggled and swirled huge torrents and gouts of humanity, shouting and screaming in slaughter and frenzy. Attack and counter-attack. Stab and backstab. Stagger and counter-stagger. Charging into curtains of machine gun fire, being cut down like corn. Two insatiable monsters feasting on each other.

Similar skirmishes and manoeuvres were taking place simultaneously all across the wide plains and hills around Taierzhuang as the Japanese fought to maintain their supplies to their troops inside the city and the Chinese fought to choke off those supplies. The black granite farmhouses and fortalices on the plain, which the Chinese had held from the start, were now starting to fall. Invulnerable to aerial bombing, artillery shells, tanks, poison gas, the Japanese at last found the strongholds, with their supporting network of trenches and tunnels, were vulnerable to up-close attacks by suicide troops aiming flame throwers accurately into the gun slits and ports from which the Chinese fired. Many Japanese exploded in flame when Chinese counter-fire hit the fuel pack they carried on their backs, but those who got close enough could direct a dragon of fire through the opening which devoured all within. Slowly the Japanese spread out across the plain.

Within the city the same pieces of land had been fought back and forth across so many times during the preceding three weeks that no one had been able to remove the bodies of the dead or dying. They just piled up, one on top of the next. Heaped bodies became barricades behind which the living could take cover, sneak up upon the enemy from behind. The smallest alleys and courtyards, even houses or single rooms within a house, were fought over ferociously time and again. They were choked with the dead. Mountains over which attacking and retreating troops must clamber. No one yielded an inch. New soldiers, arriving continuously to take the places of the dead, might recognize the uniforms and even faces of those on the topmost layer of a pile – their comrades who'd gone in immediately before them – but were they to delve deeper into the strata of the dead, even ignoring the Japanese ones, almost immediately they would find themselves among bodies and uniforms they knew nothing of, belonging to whole regiments and battalions long since slain. A whole archaeology of layered death lay all about them. Living soldiers hung clothing or their weapons upon the protruding arms and legs of the dead.

Crows and kites and ravens feasted. Flies sucked. Rats gorged. The whole city stank.

In some areas the dead paved the streets so thickly vehicles just drove over them; wheelbarrow-pushing coolies cursed them as they clogged up their wheels. Tanks crashed over them so flesh spurted out sideways from under their tracks like toothpaste from a tube. Whole families caught in the open by machine gun fire lay across the ground crusted in layers of dust and soot. As if they had lain there a thousand years. Flies feast, ants crawled in and out of snapped legs and opened brain pans, busy about their living. Beneath them black rafts of dried blood. An old woman went silently from body to body, peering intently at each. Their faces had been turned green by poison gas. She put out a hand to touch one, that she might see more clearly the face, and suddenly threw herself upon the ground beside it, kissing it in an abandonment of grief. 'That's enough now, grandmother, that's enough,' said a gentle soldier, trying to pull her to her feet, but the old woman cleaved to her daughter and he left her for more important matters. An old man had found his dead wife. He ran from soldier to soldier shouting, 'My old woman's dead, my old woman's dead!'

Taierzhuang entered its final week of battle.

Wei looked down on all this. Literally. As a sniper he spent his time finding vantage points, eyries, concealed positions from which he could scan the battlefield, pick his prey. But the battlefield was also, of course, scanned just as ardently by his enemies, their snipers. They looked for and picked off ordinary soldiers, but even more, they watched for enemy snipers. A sniper could spot preparations for a surprise attack, pick off senior officers from seven or eight hundred yards, cause madness in the minds of well-trained soldiers going about their daily routines. So snipers were prime targets for other snipers.

Wei examined the battlefield minutely. He'd chosen the wreckage of a bombed-out factory for his lair, about a hundred yards behind the front line. Part of its third floor still stood, sagging and creaking but still upright. Wei had picked his position on it behind a partly demolished window. The glass had shattered and part of the sill had been blown away, so, rather than presenting a recognizable silhouette above a straight window ledge, he concealed his head within the cavity and, hopefully, was invisible to an enemy sniper. He did not hold his rifle at this stage – too recognizable a shape. Instead he detached its scope and scanned the battlefield through it. Fortunately his enemy was to the north of him. This meant there was no chance of a glint of sunlight reflecting off his scope – and he'd already rubbed mud all over his rifle so there was no reflection off that. But his enemies, driving south through the city, all faced south. He watched and watched. With infinite patience. Never for a second did he lose concentration. He welcomed thirst and cramp because they kept him awake.

A gleam from atop some rubble 600 yards ahead of him suddenly momentarily winked at him. Extinguished almost immediately. As though the sniper was aware he'd revealed his position. Wei reattached his scope to his Lee Enfield and concentrated entirely on that one spot. He did not immediately fire. He aimed, carefully calibrating his scope so that his victim's most likely position was exactly within its crosshairs. He gently squeezed the trigger so it was within a hair's breadth of firing. But still he did not fire. He knew that with no clear target he would probably miss. And to fire would almost certainly expose his position to the enemy's snipers and call down artillery shells on his position within thirty seconds. A skilful sniper fires only when he is certain of a kill. And immediately after that skedaddles. So he waited.

What made Wei such a good sniper were qualities he'd inherited from his life as a farmer. He possessed infinite patience. Patience that once meant he could wait and wait until a crop was precisely ripe before he harvested it. That meant in late spring he could wait and wait til the price of wheat finally rose to its highest point – after all his fellow farmers had panicked and sold theirs at lower prices – and then and only then sell. He possessed deep calmness. When a violent row broke out within his family and everyone shouted – including his ancestors – he listened calmly to all the different opinions, then privately made his own decision (sometimes this could take months, even years), before politely presenting his decision to the whole family and his ancestors. He would not be pushed.

And finally – derived from his first two qualities – came his finest quality. His ability to concentrate on something. To control his mind so it did not wander. To control his body so that its pain and tiredness did not distract him. His ability to just watch and watch for hour after hour, holding his rifle totally still and on target, holding its trigger on a hair's breadth.

Suddenly movement. Almost simultaneously he fired. He'd seen through his sight a quick kerfuffle. His enemy convulsed, flopped, Wei withdrew his rifle, wriggled back across the floor, slithered down a heap of bricks, and was out through the back door of the factory as the first artillery shell landed on where he'd been.

He reported all this to his company commander. Said he'd worked out two other positions from which he could snipe at the enemy. His company commander was not interested in this. There was a far more imminent threat. A large group of Japanese troops had been spotted behind some ruined buildings to the north-west. They were about to launch an attack. Wei was to stay undercover just behind the front line and pick off as many attackers as possible. If the position became desperate he was to fix his bayonet and join in the hand-to-hand fighting. As he spoke to Wei he was also busy sharpening his sword with a whetstone. A sergeant came in and the officer handed his sword to Wei to finish sharpening while he talked intensely with the sergeant. The conversation finished and the sergeant hurried away. Wei handed the sharpened sword to his commanding officer and the two men hasten towards the front line.

Wei chose a line of rubble just behind and slightly above the Chinese lines. A friendly Japanese shell had blown a large hole in its crest which provided excellent cover. Wei quickly scrabbled together a screen of bricks and stone to protect him, and, looking out, immediately spotted the concentration of Japanese troops – only partly concealed by a semi-destroyed building – to the north-west. Their heads were bobbing up and down in an animated fashion, their officers obviously fomenting them into a fever for their charge. Wei removed his scope – they were too close for him to need it – and slipped it in his pocket. He immediately started firing at the sea of bobbing heads. Three popped – two certain hits because he saw their heads jerk or explode, the third uncertain – he might have tripped. They were charging.

As they charged he continued to fire, almost certainly bringing down three or four more. The Chinese troops – an unmilitary-looking bunch of reservists, cooks and telegraph clerks – jogged off to meet the Japanese. Not the most ferocious looking bunch, reflected Wei, but then the Japanese themselves hardly looked imperial – he had witnessed far more terrifying, suicidal assaults only a few days ago.

The charging Chinese finally hit their stride as they chanted their battle cry. 'Hit it hard. Hit it hard! Hit it haaaarrrrdddd!!!' Raised and energized, they struck the charging Japanese with strength and resolution. Hard and vicious fighting broke out, and Wei continued to pick off isolated and single Japanese in the melee. But the Chinese were starting to weaken, waver. Wei saw he should be joining them. He took his pig-sticker bayonet from his scabbard and rammed it into the iron clasps of his Lee Enfield.

He rose and was about to charge when something astonishing happened.

From nowhere suddenly appeared a swarm of angry children, Chinese children, armed with knives, homemade spears, hammers. They must have been hiding in a cellar or fox hole somewhere on the battlefield. They rose up like wasps from the ground, ferociously assaulting the charging Japanese. All the soldiers – from both sides – stopped in surprise. Taking advantage of this the children, dancing and weaving, emitting tiny screams, ran in, stabbing and slashing at the startled Japanese, fighting for the ground of what must once have been their homes and courtyards. The Japanese started to respond, but swift as horseflies the children ran in and out and around, stabbing, piercing. One ran between the legs of a slow-witted giant and stabbed upwards, ripping through his testicles and anus. He collapsed. Spears stuck into backs, hammers smashed kneecaps. Cheered by this, the Chinese charged again.

The Japanese wavered.

Retreated.

The skirmish faded away.

The feral children scurried back to their holes. The Chinese returned to their lines.

Wei lay stock still almost at the top of another pile of broken masonry and rubble. It was late afternoon but the sun was still hot. Wei had a thick layer of dust wedged in his throat and lungs but he did not cough or move. He was partly covered by some light-brown canvas for camouflage.

He watched the ruins of a temple nearly half a mile away with his scope. He had seen movements within its burnt-out timber frame, but they had been too momentary and sporadic to risk a shot.

He'd not slept for three days. During the day, as a sniper, he must not sleep. At night he joined the rest of his troop in harassing the enemy. They wriggled close to them, threw grenades, made short, sharp little forays into their trenches and dug-outs, shouted at them from their trenches and dug-outs, flung curses, sang songs (someone played a wind-up gramophone) – anything to keep the Japanese awake and terrified. They attacked them with knives, broadswords, entrenching spades – short, brutal scraps in almost complete darkness. One of the most effective ways to keep them nervous, fearful, was to loudly sharpen their knives and swords and spades with whetstones, scraping the stone back and forth across the blade, again and again, until it was razor sharp. The Japanese knew exactly what their enemy was doing.

The Chinese even had a young student in the front line with them who spoke Japanese. He would sneak right up to their lines and listen intently to their conversations, then wriggle back and, from his own lines, start telling the Japanese that with a certain sergeant whose cruelty they had been complaining about, they should stab him in the back one night and dump his body away from the trench. If the body was found they could blame it on a sudden Chinese attack. After that the young student started to get more personal. He listened on the most intimate discussions soldiers tend to have late at night about their families and their loved ones. One Japanese soldier had praised the wife he'd left behind him in Japan, praised her chastity, her faithfulness, her exquisite pristine beauty. The student started to inform the husband, in the most raucous terms, of how he'd spent all last week fucking his wife seven ways til Sunday and supplying every detail. This enraged the husband, who burst out of the trench. On this occasion the student had unwisely not retreated far enough from the Japanese trench and the husband caught him in open ground and cut him to pieces with his sword, before a Chinese soldier decapitated the gulled husband with one swipe of his broadsword.

So, as Wei lay out in his canvas-covered eyrie in the late afternoon sun, not having slept for three days, he became drowsy. He had the discipline to keep this doziness at arm's length for a while, but all the time it crept back on him, again and again, soothing him, crooning to him, trying to seduce him into its welcoming arms. He shook it off, readjusted his rifle scope, continued to scrutinize each detail of the wrecked wooden temple, but again it returned, a drowsy, a humming, bumbling sort of sound – 'Come into my arms. Rest in my arms,' it sang – again he jolted awake (a foolish thing for a sniper to do, had anyone seen his sudden movement?) but, strange thing, the buzzing sound had not ceased. It seemed to be all around him. What was it? Suddenly, a bee landed on his hand. Then another. Then they both took off. What was going on? He was not a flower. Bees only landed on flowers. Then he became aware of a more resonant sound, a high-pitched whine, gradually descending into a deep roar. What was it? A new Japanese weapon? He looked up out of his hiding hole. It had grown quite dark outside. A sort of cloud surrounded him. Not poison gas. Suddenly he saw what it was. Thousands and thousands of bees. Flying round him in a circle, a vortex. And immediately he knew what it was. A bee swarm. He was in the middle of a bee swarm. He grinned. He loved bees. But then he paused. A bee swarm in the middle of Taierzhuang? In the middle of a battle?!? The swarm was starting to settle on a lone post nearby, sticking up out of the rubble. Adhering, cohering together on top of it, forming a moving, flowing black ball, increasing in size and concentration all the time. The ordinary bees were flocking round the Emperor Bee to protect him from the world, forming chains and ropes of living bees around him for his defence. What were bees doing swarming here? In the midst of a battlefield? There must be a nest, a hive close by from which they had flown. But how were they still alive? This became a mystery to Wei. A fascinating mystery. But not one to be solved right now. Chiding himself for his indiscipline, Wei returned to his observation of the temple.

After dark Wei told his latest commanding officer – junior officers had an even higher death rate than non-commissioned soldiers – that he needed some sleep if he was going to perform effectively as a sniper. Since keeping Japanese troops awake and scared through the night was not the most skilled of tasks, his CO told him he could have two hours off.

For an hour Wei slept, then, taking an empty ammunition box, he disappeared into the night. Returned to his sniper eyrie. Got out his knife. Gently approached the swarm clinging to its post. It was contentedly humming to itself. The post stood at a considerable angle to the ground. If he was soft with his knife, brushed them gently with the side of the blade, he should be able to let them to quietly drop, transfer themselves into the wooden box. A nice, snug new home. Slowly, humming to them, he swept the drowsy bees into the box and closed its lid.

Now for the interesting part. Where was the nest from which they came? He'd had his eyes on a few mainly wrecked houses a couple of hundred yards behind the front line. He started to clamber from ruined building to ruined building. Suddenly in front of him, beneath him, lay a large black hole – some ten yards by ten yards. What was it? The moon came out from behind a cloud. He could not believe his eyes. Before him as laid out a tiny, immaculate courtyard, with potted herbs and tomato and aubergine plants in pots all round its walls, completely undamaged. In the midst of all this desolation and destruction it had survived. And beside it was a tiny shack with wisps of smoke emerging from a hole in its thatch. In the middle of the courtyard sat an old man on a stool. He was humming to himself and whittling a piece of wood.

'Old man,' said Wei softly, 'old man.'

Without fear the old man looked up.

'Yes?' he asked.

'Have you lost some bees?'

'I have,' said the old man. 'I was quite worried about them. In the midst of all this…'

He gestured around him.

'I found them,' said Wei. 'I have brought them back to you in this box.'

'You are a kind man indeed,' said the old man. 'I will get you a ladder so you can come down into my courtyard.'

He did, and Wei clambered down.

Wei handed the box to the old man and looked about. The courtyard was unharmed and immaculately maintained. By some miracle it had been spared the devastation all around.

'Come inside,' said the man, 'I will make you some tea.'

'Thank you,' said Wei.

They walked inside. It was dark. The man lit a candle. Wei

looked around. He saw where the bees lived. Long combs blackened by the smoke hung down from the ceiling – six, seven feet in length, stopping just a few inches above their heads. The bees drowsed quietly and contentedly to themselves. The smoke from the fire kept them relaxed. There was a small hole in the wall just above the door through which the bees would fly out during the day. Bees and humans living together in perfect harmony.

They sat down at the table and drank their tea. They talked about bees – their habits, their idiosyncrasies, their generosity.

'Where do the bees get their pollen and nectar from around here, with all this destruction?' asked Wei.

'They must fly a long distance,' replied the man. 'To the south-west of the city there are many fruit trees growing. They are in blossom now.'

'Ah, yes,' responded Wei, remembering the orchards they had marched through.

'Bees are very knowledgeable creatures,' said the old man.

As Wei was leaving to return to the world of the dying, the old man insisted that he take with him two small jars of orange blossom honey.

'It will be good for you. It will give you strength and power. The bees are thanking you for rescuing them and returning them home. I will build a separate hive for those you brought back.'

Wei thanked the old man, took them, left, and returned to his duty of scaring the heebie-jeebies out of the increasingly disorientated and sleepless Japanese.

By 5 April, the situation within Taierzhuang had become desperate. The Japanese held nearly 80 per cent of the city. Conditions were particularly dangerous within the south-east of the city where the Japanese had pushed the Chinese almost back to the city's southern wall. Beyond the wall lay only the waters of the Grand Canal. One wooden pontoon bridge over the canal was the only contact those inside the city had with those outside. Across it came all their vital supplies.

General Sun Lianzhong, commander of the 31st Division – the

unit holding Taierzhuang – phoned his commanding officer, General Li Zongren.

He pleaded that his men – those still surviving – be allowed to temporarily retreat across the canal for a short period of rest and regrouping. Li replied by saying that Chinese attacks on the Japanese supply lines to the north of the city had succeeded and the Japanese within the city were now cut off. Troops would shortly be available to reinforce General Sun. They would arrive by noon tomorrow.

'Don't retreat,' Li ordered him. 'As I told you when I first briefed you, this battle will be lost or won in its last five minutes. Possibly by the last five men. We know that General Rensuke Isogai is desperate. He intends to throw every last man of his into an attack tomorrow afternoon. It is his last throw of the dice. You will pre-empt that attack with an attack of your own. It is *our* last throw of the dice. First you will send in suicide squads to break up his troops, then you'll order a full general attack. Draft in porters, cooks, children, anyone who can fight. I am confident this will break the Japanese.'

One last time General Sun asked to be able to withdraw his shattered troops across the canal for temporary respite.

General Li Zongren replied:

'When your men have fought to the last man, go yourself to the front. When you have gone to the front, I will go there too to join you. Anyone who retreats across the canal commits an unpardonable sin and will be executed.'

He put down the phone.

Wei's company of men were stood down from the fighting on the western side of the city. Fighting there had become sporadic and it was obvious that the Japanese were withdrawing most of their men to concentrate on their big push on the eastern side of the city to storm the southern wall and then cross the Grand Canal.

General Rensuke Isogai, his forces in Taierzhuang now completely cut off from the outside world, desperate to somehow save his military reputation and win glory in the eyes of his beloved emperor, determined to grind these Chinese untermenschen and cockroaches finally into the dust, was gambling all on this one last attack. He was Japanese. He was superior. He would win.

Wei's company had been ordered to hand over their lines to some ghosts and relics of troops spirited up from somewhere. They marched down the western side of the walls, crossed over the bridge of a single plank. They walked to the east along the southern bank of the canal. As they did they passed the naked bodies of Chinese soldiers executed for desertion. Their pink bodies lay in rows on the ground, like radishes pulled fresh from the earth.

They reached the pontoon bridge and marched across it. They were the last troops into Taierzhuang. As soon as they had crossed, on the orders of General Sun Lianzhong, to show that from now on there would be no retreat whatsoever, the bridge was dynamited.

Wei's company entered the city by its south-eastern gate. It had greatly changed since Wei had last left it. No civilians. Very few buildings. The streets and houses reduced to rubble. The sound of gunfire and mayhem very close.

An armourer awaited them. Not the friendly armourer Wei had dealt with before. This one scowled at Wei's Lee Enfield and took it.

Wei tried to argue that as a sniper he needed his rifle.

'Only standard rifles to be issued,' replied the armourer. 'That's orders.'

Wei, though upset, could see the cold logic behind it. When he died, the soldier who inherited his Lee Enfield would have no idea how to operate it.

They marched on. Wei had not entirely abandoned his Lee Enfield. In his pocket he carried its sniper scope.

18

I look very closely into her face. Someone has quite deliberately drawn a razor blade straight across it and left a great gaping scar. Someone brutally and deliberately blinded the little girl in both eyes so the voids of two empty sockets stare back at me. She smiles sweetly in my general direction. 'Please sir. Alms, sweet sir.' Above her a notice reads *This awful atrocity to this beautiful Chinese child has been done by the murderous Japanese devils!*

I know this is a lie.

Beside her, against the wall, sit other warped, mutilated, mangled children. Their owner walks up and down before them, threatening those who do not cry out for alms piteously enough with a whip. They cry out enthusiastically. Some have been raised in tiny cages so their limbs are bent, their spines crooked, their shoulder blades stick out like delicate twigs.

Until now I have avoided this wall of child beggars – gravely wounded so they might attract the greatest sympathy and generosity from passing people. The blinded girl with the torn and ploughed face upsets me particularly. So normally, when I am on the Bund, except for the occasion when Tian Boqi made his brave stand against them, I avoid it. Those children could be mine!

But today, as I set off on my sordid quest to enslave young Yu Liqun, buy her as a sex slave to sell to the awful Guo Morou, I find my self-loathing and self-disgust reflected exactly in this child's ripped and ruptured face. I pay a particularly large sum into her bowl in the hope that her owner will treat her better – at least for a while. As I leave he starts to beat her. The more she suffers the more money she attracts!

I continue my journey. I locate the place on the Bund where Miss Yu and her idealistic young dancers are presenting a patriotic dance-and-speech spectacular entitled 'Sign Up for the Military!' A group of striking young ladies, attired in smart and alluring military uniforms, march and strut up and down before a stage, vigorously striking militaristic poses, saluting each other crisply, twirling their wooden rifles. They chant and sing patriotic slogans and songs. Miss Yu is by far the most gifted and eye-catching performer. Nobody juts her chin out like her, struts up and down like a clockwork doll like her. Meanwhile on the stage an earnest young East Coast male, with a striking Han accent, urges all and sundry to rush off and sign up for the military immediately.

The young ladies by themselves attract quite a large crowd, but as soon as the young man with the posh accent starts addressing them alone, the audience disappears.

The performance over the stage is quickly dismantled and the various participants go their separate ways. Feeling dirty and soiled I follow Miss Yu.

She enters a shabby apartment building.

I ring her doorbell.

It opens.

I look at her. She looks at me.

'Hello. My name is Lao She.'

'Yes?'

'I am a writer.'

'Oh,' replies the eighteen-year-old. 'I think I have heard your name.'

'I saw your military display just now. I thought it was very good.'

The ageing, slope-shouldered male stands before the spick-and-span young woman.

An edge enters her voice.

'What do you want?'

'I wondered if I could speak with you.'

'I do not sleep with men. All you middle-aged men – you come round here after I've finished performing, asking to sleep with me.'

'I'm not…' I stutter.

'I am dedicated to one thing,' she continues, 'one thing alone in this world. The revolution.'

Oh dear, I think, whatever I say, she will rightly refuse me.

I look at her.

'Excuse me. I've not come here to ask you to sleep with me, I've come to ask you to do something infinitely worse. I feel terrible coming to ask you this, but I too serve the revolution you serve, and believe me, it can demand you do things which are awful.'

'The revolution would never ask you to do something that is immoral. Revolution is the ultimate morality.'

I look down at the ground.

'Believe me, I come here in the name of the revolution to ask you to do something that is utterly immoral.'

'What do you do?'

'I am a propagandist for the revolution.'

'You'd better come in,' she says. 'No hands. I have to go out in five minutes for rehearsals at the theatre.'

We enter her small apartment, hung with revolutionary posters and half-read books. I sit on a chair. I ask her which theatre company she works for.

'The Anti-Japanese Drama Troupe. We are putting on a new play full of revolutionary zeal called *We Have Beaten Back the Enemy.*'

'Oh yes,' I say, 'I know the writer.'

She is now sitting opposite me. Waiting for me to speak. Enough flannelling, I get to the nub.

'I come from the very highest levels of the revolutionary party.'

'Yes? How high?'

'The highest.'

'What, from…?'

'The one just below him?'

She now looks straight at me.

'And what does he have to say?'

I look at her. She sits so straight-backed. The infinite confidence of the upper classes! The shield of their education, their breeding! Which is why they get me to do their dirty work for them. Because, a mere lower class Manchu, I'm used to grovelling and worming for a living. Get on with it!

I look directly at her.

'Revolutionary comrades are not always so – revolutionary – as you might think. Sometimes revolutionary machines need dirt, grit in their gears and wheels to make them bite, to make them turn.'

'What on earth are you talking about?'

'Our leaders are not always paragons of virtue. They demand prices. They cheat. They lie.'

'That is a lie. You are a liar.'

'Miss Yu, as I said, I've been sent by the highest of leaders in the party. Believe me, they would not request from you what I am about to request from you if they were not absolutely desperate, unable to resolve things in any other ways. The leaders of the party are of course highly moral people,' I lie.

By her expression I can see she is starting to become interested in what I am saying.

'But what do they want me to do?' she asks. 'Do they want me to die? I would die for the revolution, without a second thought!'

'No, they do not want you to die for the revolution. I am afraid what they want is far more ignoble, far more degrading, than that.'

There is a pause. I continue.

'There is a man vital to the success of the revolution. If he were to be freed so that he could stand up, speak out, write about our revolution, the struggle against the Japanese barbarians, he would speak in a voice which would encourage, inspire so many people, he would utter phrases which would stop people in their tracks, arouse them to perform heroic acts, to redouble their efforts to win this war. He is a man of the greatest integrity, already a hero of the people, and all he requires is...'

'Me?'

I can see how my words are starting to arouse her. Her eighteen-year-old imagination is beginning to catch alight with all sorts of girlish imaginings and simplicities. From my description, my lying description of 'him', she is doubtless imagining some dashing young star of the silver screen, some Shelleyan poet desperate to fall into her arms.

'I suppose this would involve…?'

'Yes, it would involve…'

She understands the undertaking. She thinks.

'Well, I suppose I am an actress.'

'Yes.'

'It is my job to imitate others, enter into their lives and emotions as if they were my own. And it would only be for a while…'

I do not correct her there.

'…and in my heart of hearts I would never betray my one pure love – the revolution. After all, I am a modern woman, a liberated woman, a feminist. To be intimate with a man one does not have to marry him.'

I swallow hard.

'Who is this man?'

Aye, there's the rub!

'As I said, he is a man of great integrity, a vital part of the revolution.'

'What is his name?'

'I'm afraid he might not be quite as young as you are imagining.'

'An older man? Does he possess some great secret or something, vital to the party, that I must somehow, like a spy, wheedle out of him? I would be good at that! Or must I carry secret messages to him?'

'No, it is nothing like that. The thing is, he wants to marry you. For you to carry his children. He is much older than you. He is vital to the success of the revolution.'

'Who is he?'

'You already know him.'

She looks at me, baffled.

'I am speaking of Guo Morou.'

Her mouth falls open. She slumps back onto the sofa. Oh you murderer, I think, you murderer! But I continue with my knife-wielding duties.

'He is vital to the success, the survival of the Chinese people. He is our greatest speech maker, our greatest polemicist, our greatest writer. If he were to speak publicly here in Wuhan it would unite the people, fire them, inspire them as no other speaker could.'

'But what does this have to do with me? Why must *I* marry *him*? The creepy little man. I despise him.'

'He says that he is paralyzed, he is devastated, he is unable to think or even move, such is the desolation he feels being unable to be united, as one with you. The leaders of the party have sent me here to plead with you, beg with you. They desperately need him to become the Guo Morou he once was, to unify the masses, to unite them against the barbarians, to send them forth to battle. They ask you to do your duty.'

Her face has become a great cavern of desolation. Suddenly she is no longer a sharp, confident young lady, she is a teenage child loose and abandoned in the world. Without home, without family, without love. I continue in my hollow way.

'He is a great man. When you see his greatness, you will come to love him. You will be proud to be the mother of his...'

I stop talking. She has risen up, she is looking straight at me.

'He is a worm and a traitor of the first order. You don't even like him, do you? In fact, I'd venture, you despise him every bit as much as I do.'

After that, there isn't much else to say. For the first time I look her straight in her eye. What a brave little girl! Honesty is the least she deserves.

'Yes. I do not like him very much.' I pause. 'But this is war we are in. One has to do what is necessary.'

There is a long pause. A wave of emotion overcomes me.

'Do you mind if I tell you about my wife?'

'Please do,' she says icily.

'I too was asked by the nationalists and by the communists to come here to write for them for the war effort. I was very torn. I too love China. I desire above all else to see China become once again a strong and a decent country, in which all citizens, especially the poorest, are treated with respect, are lifted out of their terrible poverty. And – and I know this will make you think I am the most despicable of hypocrites – I have always felt that those who need the most liberating are the women of China. Their slavery, their forced marriages, their bound feet.

'Myself and my family were living in Jinan, a long way from here. And the Japanese were advancing on us fast, and the telegrams kept arriving for me from Wuhan – "Come here! Come to Wuhan!" I am a Confucian, a Christian, a socialist – a terrible mess. In my writings I have continually attacked the Confucian morality of family above all things, said it was paralyzing China, holding it back. But in the moment of crisis I became totally a Confucian. I had a wife, three young children, an aged mother who could not be moved, had to be nursed all the time. So, as the father, the head of the family, the servant of every other member of the family, I could not abandon my mother. I decided I must stay. Do my best somehow to protect my family from Japanese bayonets. I would forget Wuhan.'

'And what happened?'

'My wife. My wife came to me and in the strongest possible terms told me that China needed me, that I was to get on the train, and she would defend and feed our family. She could quietly get work – she is a graphic designer – I must abandon her and my family, I must go and do my duty to the new China.'

'And so you did your duty? You came to Wuhan?'

'My wife did my duty.'

'Is your wife, your family safe?'

'I do not know.'

'And what is it like living here in Wuhan?'

'Hell. It is darkness and desolation.'

Now I am the one slumping back in my chair while she looks at me straight-backed.

'Your wife loves you?'

'I think so.'

'Good. Then I will follow your wife's judgement of you. And do what you ask me to do.'

I look at her. She gives me a saucy smile in return.

'Your wife's duty means she's got to live alone and defenceless in Japanese territory and somehow protect and support her family and nurse her mother-in-law. While I only have to marry an old roué. I think I've been very lucky.'

I do not know whether to sing Hosannah or vomit.

An unhostile silence follows. I move to reassure her.

'Your marriage will probably not be too onerous. I'm sure you will be able to pursue your career. He will require a certain amount of time away for work and – other interests.'

'I think I will have "other interests" too. I shall come and see you…'

I turn bright red.

'…and your wife, when she arrives.'

'I doubt if Guo Morou will come with you. He and I are not the best of friends.'

'Good. My visits will be an irritant for him and a joy for me.'

'And for us.'

19

And yet they split apart mountains and streams,
And carved up the empire,
How could a hundred myriad loyal troops
All at once discard their armour
To be moved away and chopped down
Like grass and trees?
…{How could Heaven have been so drunk?}

Yu Xin, 'The Lament for the South'

Wei slept deep inside the rock. Entombed, embedded within the comforting black granite of Taierzhuang.

He lay sleeping on a shelf of stone dug into the side of the trench in which his company was posted. Rock above him, rock beside him, rock beneath him. He was safe, guarded. Ever since he'd been driven off his land, all through the terrible loss of his family, Wei had felt estranged and abandoned by his god. Tudeh, god of earth, had given them no protection. But now, fighting in Taierzhuang, sheltering among the god of earth's rocks, shielded by his stone and rubble, sleeping in his earth, Wei once more felt sustained, guarded by his god.

He was roused and another soldier took his place. Evening was drawing in – though you could hardly tell it. Black smoke hung in the air, peoples' faces were black, everything was cast in gloom.

Some fifty yards behind them lay the south wall of the city. Behind it lay the waters of the Grand Canal – uncrossable since the wooden pontoon bridge linking Taierzhuang to the southern shore had been destroyed. These fighters were here til they were either killed by the Japanese or drove the Japanese northwards and out of the city.

The men snatched moments to eat, their strips of white pork fat immediately turning black in the dust and smoke. They were huddled only yards from the nearest Japanese dug-out and trenches. ('Get as close as you can to your enemy so he can't bomb and shell and gas you without also destroying his own troops! Be intimate with him – cheek by jowl. Don't let him sleep, keep him on edge at all times. Talk loudly to each other to let him know you're here, throw occasional grenades at him to keep him awake and shivering, sing coarse and vulgar songs to grate his nerves, always sound cheerful and positive.')

But tonight a strange, profound silence had fallen all across the battlefield. Both sides knew tomorrow would be the final bloodshed. Both sides rested, reflected upon it. At midday the Chinese were to charge, to pre-empt the Japanese attack at three in the afternoon.

Wei hardly knew the people he was wedged in among, who he would die with. Men from every part of China. Strangers. The sole survivors of a hundred different outfits and regiments from a hundred different armies Every one with a different accent, a different dialect. But the exigencies of battle had, of necessity, forged among the soldiers of Taierzhuang a common understanding – through looks, grunts, certain key words common to all dialects, new words they'd had to learn in double quick time in the chaos of battle. And those had, of necessity, grown and evolved into a common dialect, a universal tongue capable of expressing just not actions, but feelings and emotion.

They could understand each other, but they were still all as strangers to each other.

In the dark before their final battle they chatted among themselves. Started to talk about the villages they were brought up in. Where they were the local kids, the rascals and ne'er-do-wells before the wars snatched them away. Someone had found wine in a cellar. They passed it round. Someone else had found cartons of cigarettes the Japanese, desperate to resupply their troops, had parachuted into the city. The parachute had fallen among Chinese troops. They passed them around.

They began to reminisce about the celebrations, the festivals their villages had held every year.

One soldier was from the far north province of Heilongjiang.

'In our village, Fenjiatun, so we could bring down the gods from heaven to be among us, we would hire spirit masters to summon them. Six spirit masters there always were. On the first evening there'd be lots of drumming and the spirit masters would fall on the ground and go into trances. As a kid my hair used to stand on end when they did. They'd writhe about. Then they'd stand up, all strange, and they'd become like horses – neighing, stamping their feet, tossing their heads back and forth. They were the horses that come down from heaven with the gods riding on their backs! Oh what joy! What shouting! The gods were among us. Through the spirit masters the gods spoke to us, we told them how joyous we were to see them, the gods asked, through the spirit masters, for wine and cigarettes – we gave them to them and then had some ourselves. Then them and us, gods and people, all started dancing and dancing, singing songs. Then, the evening over, we helped each god to step into their statues, which we had put up on a platform. The gods were on their thrones – we could start our festival.'

Another soldier, from Shandong Province, took up the story.

'In my village we paraded our gods in their statues around the village. All around the neighbouring villages. Singing, shouting. As we passed people crowded up to the statues to thank the gods for having cured their illnesses, women prayed to them asking to bear male children, everyone they passed greeted them and begged them for good fortune in the coming year – plentiful crops, many children, few deaths. "May our pigs be as large as oxen!"

'People garlanded their statues with flowers and blossoms. Put out offerings to them of our finest food and choicest wines. Then – the food and wine tasted by the gods – we'd all carry it into the village temple and everyone feasted and drank. We ate the food of the gods. Then we danced. And danced. And danced. And then, the festival over, we burnt paper images of the gods to show that they had returned up to heaven. Because they had left we all wept and lamented.'

A strong voice from Gansu Province spoke out.

'Sometimes it wasn't as easy as that, though, was it? One year we had this terrible drought. It went on and on. Not a drop of rain. And the heat from the sun was terrible. So everyone in the village decided we should ask for help from our ancestors. We burnt them incense and paper money and offered them the choicest pork and chicken. But no rain. By now we were really suffering from the drought. Our old people were getting ill. Two children died. So, to show our rain god what a lousy job he was doing we dragged his statue out and dumped him in the middle of a parched field so he could feel what it was like to have that burning sun on his bald head all day.'

Everyone burst out laughing at this.

'But still no rain. Every field was yellow with dying crops. We would all starve to death. So we held this meeting. At it we all decided to behead the Drought Demon who was causing it. We built a straw body of the Drought Demon and made his head out of a large gourd. We cut the insides out of the gourd and put them in a large tub of water so all the water turned blood red. Then, bareheaded and barefoot, we dragged the Drought Demon out into the field – everyone striking and cursing him – and right in front of the statue of the rain god we cut off the head of the Drought Demon and poured all the red juice all over his body to stand for his blood and everyone cheered crazily and we laid his remains at the feet of the rain god and shouted at the god, 'Bring us our rain!!! Where is our rain???' Within half an hour it was raining, it was pouring with rain the like of which you're never seen. We left the rain god outside so he could enjoy it too and then afterwards, to thank him for his wonderful bounty, we put on an opera specially for him.'

Someone shouted out to the sleepless Japanese in their next-door trench that this proved Chinese rain gods were superior to Japanese rain gods. He followed it with a grenade, just to keep them nerve-wracked and fearful.

A voice from Anhui spoke next.

'I never liked festivals, because of all the dancing and noise,' he said – which met with some jeering. 'But I do like that you can meet up with all your family and relatives who you haven't seen for ages and catch up on things. Have a good chat. And also you can usually pick up cheap bargains in the market.'

'You tight-fisted Anhui bastard,' said another voice.

'I heard that, you Zhejiang bastard,' responded the Anhui bastard, to laughter.

Someone had rescued an ancient wind-up gramophone from a ruined house and a cracked recording of Marlene Dietrich's 'Lili Marleen' ground out across tomorrow's battlefield.

'I'm from Zhangzi in the province of Shanxi,' announced an older voice. 'One year I was elected to be the Grand Marshall of the parade at our festival.'

This announcement was met with some 'oohs' and 'aahs'. Being chosen as a Grand Marshall meant this soldier must once have been quite an important person.

'It's a real worry being the Grand Marshall, a real responsibility. Everything must be done exactly right. Once the gods have arrived down from heaven and stepped into their statues, then every god must be lifted gently and reverently into their sedan chairs. If a god were to fall out of their sedan chair then they could get really tetchy. Once they're in their sedan chairs and happy, you then have to get everyone else all lined up behind them and in precisely the right order and position, all the banners and flags and costumes must be bright and clean, all the music played at the right time, all the dancing done exactly and no steps missed out or muddled up or the gods would get upset. Finally, when everything is right, the sacred musket is fired and the procession can move off. Everything must be exactly right. I used to worry about it all the time.'

'Excuse me, father,' asked a polite voice with a Guanxi accent, 'but how could a man like you, who must have been quite prosperous to be Grand Marshall, why did you end up in the army?'

'In our civil wars,' said the older voice from Shanxi, 'two

warlords had a war and chose our village as their battlefield. It was totally destroyed. All my family was dead. I was penniless. So what could I do? I joined the army of the warlord who won.'

This story made the men sigh and shake their heads with distress. Wei particularly felt very sad.

The next voice did not cheer things up.

'I'm from a village in north Shaanxi,' he said. 'In our festival we had to dance a ritual dance which was very dangerous. Not joyful at all. If we did not dance it precisely correctly it could bring all sorts of misfortunes on our village.'

This caused great interest among everyone,

'What was it?'

'Why was it so dangerous?'

'Well, each year we had to build this maze. It was a very powerful maze. And we could only process through it on the darkest of nights. It was made from 367 lanterns. And as we, the whole village, went through it one by one, at every lantern, we had to remember which was the right way to go – left or right. And if we did not get it right, as soon as we made a wrong step, the gods would snatch our souls down into hell. The whole village, one by one, every year, had to get it exactly right.'

'No!' said some voices.

'That sounds terrible!'

'Did you all get through?'

'We spent months beforehand,' said the man from north Shaanxi, 'the whole village, learning the turnings one by one, rehearsing them. Over and over again. So we got this walk through the darkness correct.'

'Did you always get around safely?'

'While I was there, yes. We were guided by our elders – who knew the way. But I always remember looking out into that blackness, thinking it could snatch me away at any second. But it was worth it. If we did it properly it would bring us a year of fertility and blessings, being spared droughts and floods. And it always brought the village together. People who'd quarreled tended to make up after it, people helped each other out, everyone smiled at each other.'

But the listeners were not cheered by this. The whole group seemed downcast by the story. It reminded them too much of what they themselves were about to go through.

Wei stepped into the breach.

'What I always liked best about our village's festivals,' said Wei positively, 'was how they brought everyone together. The whole village. We all had to work as one. Decide which musicians we wanted, what dancers and spirit masters and actors would be best for our plays and operas and ceremonies. We'd work together as teams to build the stages, make the costumes and decorations, cook the food exactly so the gods would love it, prepare our finest wines. Everyone had something to do, problems to work out. We all had to reach agreements with each other and then keep them. People who didn't know each other had to work together, help each other out, and in doing that they became friends, it brought trust and fellowship into the village.

'And the dances and all the complex rituals and ceremonies? They were the most difficult thing we had to do – and the most joyful. When, after all the rehearsing our moves in which each member had to trust each other member to know exactly where they had to be, precisely what they had to be doing at precisely that moment – that was the moment when the whole village harmonized, meshed together, became as one in the sacred dance...'

There was silence. Each one remembering their own particular moment.

Their own brief festival now over, the Chinese soldiers threw all their empty wine bottles into the Japanese trench, followed by oaths and grenades. Then everyone fell asleep in the deep night except for Wei and a few others who were on guard.

Spider Girl was very worried about her father. She wanted to know what was happening to him.

Each morning she religiously read the newspapers pasted on the walls on the Bund, but they seemed to say less and less about the war, about who was fighting who and where. (This was because, very wisely, the military censors did not want news of the cataclysmic Battle of Taierzhuang to come out until its outcome was decided.)

So to find out what was happening in the world, rather than reading the newspapers, Spider Girl adopted the revolutionary technique of talking to people. And the even more revolutionary technique of listening to them. The Bund was awash with rumours of an almighty battle being fought near Xuzhou.

Spider Girl required more details.

So she tapped into the traditional network by which news had always been disseminated through China. Through the market traders. All sorts of stall holders hawked 'reliable news', gleaned from the travelling merchants they bought their wares from, to their customers. Buy three pounds of spuds and 'get the news free'. But such news was not always reliable.

The stall holders who always had the highest reputation for accuracy were the barbers. From seven o'clock onwards they received civil servants and merchants on their way to their offices. From them, as they shaved or trimmed their hair, they received the news these clients had gleaned from their telegraphs and telephones. Each client had a different area of expertise – stock markets prices, political or military information, sexual scandals and gossip – and the barber in turn was able to relay back to their clients the important news they'd gathered from other clients who had different areas of expertise. By nine o'clock the barbers were well enough informed from a lot of different sources to provide a comprehensive news service to their clients. These clients would, of course, be charged a premium price for the barber's services. And the barbers who charged the highest prices were those who had the reputation for the greatest accuracy.

So Spider Girl, who did not want either a shave or a haircut – being a practical working-class girl living with two other practical working-class girls, they all cut each others' hair – spent considerable amounts of her shopping time shuffling around one particular barber's stall (the most expensive), earwigging the conversations.

From this she learnt of a great battle being fought at Taierzhuang. There had been terrible casualties on both sides. This worried Spider Girl terribly.

Taierzhuang lay in almost complete ruin, a cemetery of rubble and broken stones and bodies rising above the surrounding plains, circled by a moat. The dead were piled beneath and above and protruding from the rubble. Over the dead walked the immortals, those still alive, shuffling awkwardly, murmuring to each other, awaiting their own particular deaths.

Knowing that the Chinese intended to attack in the morning, just before dawn the Japanese had withdrawn their harassed and exhausted troops in close proximity to the Chinese lines. They'd all retreated to the main line of Japanese troops several hundred yards back, where they would await the Chinese charge and then mount their own counter-charge.

Everyone had run out of food. Soldiers on both sides talked obsessively about imagined feasts, their lips lingering lovingly over evocations of rice and fish and flesh and sweet sauces and sharp chillies and oranges and apples and plums and peaches. Everyone had run out of water. As they talked they nostalgically remembered sitting by the waters of flowing rivers, drinking sweet water from a well, the icy freshness of a mountain stream.

Wei was slightly detached from all this. He stayed on watch. He'd moved so he lay on a slight rise above the trench. Removing his Lee Enfield's sniper scope from his pocket he viewed the large plains of desolation before him. There was very little movement among the Japanese. They seemed stricken by lethargy, indifference. Then he saw something. Movement behind the ruins of a bombed cinema. A large group of Japanese troops were being marshalled. Drawing themselves up for action. If only he still had his Lee Enfield!

They were being marshalled by a brute of an NCO. Ranting at them. The muscles in the back of his neck bulged out. He screamed at three men in particular. They had not joined the rest of the troops. They stood by themselves, heads hanging, refusing to respond to his taunts as he bawled in their faces. Suddenly he pushed one sprawling in the dust, stomped over to him, leant over the man, shrieked a question at him. The man slowly shook his head. The sergeant drew his revolver and shot him in the face.

The whole company of men who the sergeant has marshalled looked at each other, swayed.

The sergeant stalked over to the other two men who had refused to be marshalled and started bawling in the second man's face. As he was doing this Wei noted two or three of the marshalled Japanese sneaking away to hide among the seats of the shattered cinema. The sergeant continued to shriek at the man. Two more snuck off. The man shook his head. The sergeant shot him. He turned to the last man, screaming and waving his revolver in his face. The man's head dropped. He went to join the ranks of the already marshalled.

What was the difference between the Chinese troops waiting stoically, accepting of their deaths, and the Japanese being driven like terrified cattle towards theirs?

The Chinese had deep bonds of community, of fellow feeling, of trust. They were spiritual beings, well used to communing with their ancestors, their gods, continually trafficking back and forth between life and death. For them death was not the end so they had a reason to live.

The Japanese were the products of the theories of insane European and British and American scientists and materialists. Men had no souls. They were animals, machines who had no purpose or value but to operate until they were worn out and then were replaced or destroyed by another. Men were to be driven until they died and then to be replaced by others who were treated likewise.

But human beings cannot be treated as objects. A machine. A function. It is unsustainable. They have no reason to live.

Wei returned to his lines and reported what he had witnessed to his officer. His comrades were chatting among themselves.

The man from Shandong who'd stuck his bald god out in the field to get a suntan was looking on the bright side.

'Thank the gods we'll soon be fighting. It's the only way I can forget my hunger.'

The others chuckled.

A man from Sichuan told a dirty joke. Everyone roared with laughter. Death and sex are so closely intertwined.

Some prayed for the survival of their families – those who had them. A rough altar had been constructed from the rubble and joss sticks were burnt and requests made to gods and ancestors. Others just reflected quietly or gave rueful grins to their comrades.

The man from north Shaanxi who'd told the story about the lanterns took a shit.

'I want to die relaxed.'

Pet dogs wandered around or got into fights with each other. One man had found a blackbird in a cage and was encouraging it to sing.

Their ranks were strengthened all the time. The Chinese were withdrawing all possible troops from the western half of the city to face the Japanese, who themselves had been withdrawn from the rest of the city to fight and drive the Chinese in the south-east back into the waters of the Grand Canal. Everyone who could be drawn up had been drawn up.

General Rensuke Isogai was not giving up. No sharp disembowelling sword for his stomach!

Wei went to the altar and asked for the recognition and forgiveness of his ancestors. He thanked his god Tudeh for all the fertility and life he gave him on his farm. For his rocks and stones which had protected him here on the battlefield of Taierzhuang. He remembered his parents, his father's long stories, his wife with her fierce defence of his family, Eldest Son's slow smile, Cherry Blossom twirling her parasol, Second Son with his sharp eyes and intelligence, Baby Girl Wei with her happiness (which he murdered), Baby Boy Wei's staring eyes, and the child who was born and died on the march. Above all he thought of his beloved eldest daughter Spider Girl. He prayed for her well-being and survival.

Bayonets were fixed. Men exchanged last cigarettes, offered each other encouragement, wished each other good fortune. The man with the caged blackbird set it free. The whistles sounded. Officers shouted. Men shouted. They clambered out of their trench and started to lumber out across the rubbled plains of Taierzhuang. Artillery and mortar shells landed. They disappeared into a pandemonium of noise and smoke. Shells, explosions, detonations. They seemed to float through it.

'Hit it hard,' they started to chant. 'Hit it hard!' they chanted louder. 'Hit it haaaarrrrdddd!!!' they all roared.

They emerged into daylight. Out of the smoke. They had a long way to charge.

Desultory fire was coming in. A bit disorganized. The older man from Shanxi, the Grand Marshall of his festival, toppled backwards with a bullet through his head. A merciful death. His brain, keeper of all the intricacies and sanctities of those rituals and dances, whiffled into nothingness.

The machine guns opened up. Their bullets came at the men like crowded hailstones. Swept into them. Swish! Swish! Swish! People dropping, somersaulting, arms flailing, legs jerking. Wei looked around. Men just faded away on either side of him. The man from the far north of China, from Heilongjiang Province, he who had once smoked cigarettes and drunk wine with the gods, was sliced in two. The discontent from Anhui Province who never liked festivals fell when his left kneecap exploded. The Zhejiang bastard who he'd exchanged insults with caught a mortar in his chest and exploded. From somewhere in the midst of this surreal landscape Marlene Dietrich wearily lilted her way through 'Lili Marleen'.

Right in front of Wei suddenly appeared a terrified hare. He almost trampled it. Eyes bulging, it raced off, tracing wild geometries across the battlefield. An abandoned horse stood entirely subdued, limbs trembling, trying to stand upright. From nowhere the feral children who yesterday helped Wei's platoon now arose and joined the charge with banshee wails.

A shell exploded the horse and two kids.

The battle cry came again – 'Hit it hard. Hit it hard! Hit it haaaaaaarrrrrddddddddd!!!' This time it was ragged, ragged as the thinning ranks of the men, but it heartened those still alive.

Just keep going, thought Wei. All around me men are falling, but ignore them. If you aren't hit just keep going. But he was noticing things. The machine gun fire was not so regular. And on either side of him, in the distance, ahead of him, he glimpsed khaki uniforms – Japanese, not Chinese – starting to peel away, rise from their trenches and firing positions, scuttle, scurry, legging it for safety. As if there were safety on this battlefield? He looked about him. Just three of them left – the man from Shandong who'd enjoyed his festivals so much, one kid and the man from north Shaanxi who was terrified of losing his soul amid the lanterns. Wei looked further back – very few men trudging on, heads bent into the bullets, no signs of any officers to give orders or commands. All dead. Keep going. A large swish of bullets came in and the happy man from Shandong fell backwards, his knees and lower legs jiggering with frenzy as his soul escaped his body. The kid fell. A thunderclap – perhaps a mortar – and the Lantern Man who'd taken a shit to relax disintegrated and relaxed completely.

Ahead of him Wei saw men, Japanese men, their backs to him, fleeing. He noticed them to each side of him too. Well, if they were fleeing from him and he was the last person left alive on his side, he'd just have to keep charging to keep them fleeing.

'Hit them hard. Hit them hard! Hit them...'

A blow like a sledgehammer hit his chest.

Wei, a man who could scythe an acre of grass in a day, who could most delicately brush smut from a tiny child's eye, who could most competently organize all the complexities and diplomacies of his village festival, a good man, a modest man, a man of great generosity to his family and others – why should this man fall when other men – men without conscience, men utterly void of fear of the gods, men that would leave not a scrap for others huggering up fortune after fortune – greedy gulls, cormorants, cut-throats and thieves; yea, men that would devour all men and women and children for power and domination and profit – why should such devils have life and riches while the meek and innocent of this world have no life at all?

Wei fell to the ground as his sickle had once swept the golden corn to the ground. His eyes dissolved into a million blue stars...

He lay, face down. Through immense pain he climbed back into consciousness. He thought. His family had died because of his errors. He now hoped he had partially repaid his debts to them. And, by his actions, he hoped, with his last remaining strength, that he had given his beloved Spider Girl a chance of life.

With that he ceased thinking.

There are times in history when only the bravest will find the courage to stand alone against the most powerful in their attempts to erase our existence from our planet. We are all living through one of those times and we are witnessing a battle of two worlds. On one side is the world of imperialist oppression, violence, perpetual war, to benefit the predators of our world – on the other are those who wish to see the supremacy of international law and perpetual peace with benefits for all mankind.

Those who have taken the ultimate stand against these forces of subjugation are the Syrian Arab Army and their allies who have stood firm and proud against overwhelming military force and a terrifying apparatus of war. The Syrian Arab Army does not only fight for Syria and its people, it fights for all of us – in Palestine, in the UK, the EU, South America, Yemen, everywhere... Syria is not only the cradle of civilization, it is the cradle of resistance around which are circling those who would destroy it and those who would defend it. We stand with those who defend it.

21st Century Wire[8]

20

In Jincheng, music of silk and flutes mixes together all day,
Half goes to the river breeze, half goes to the clouds.
Music such as this should only go to heaven above,
In this human world, how many times can it be heard?

Du Fu

On the morning of 8 April 1937, the first swallows of the year were seen in the skies over Wuhan, flying high above the city, skittering madly across the blue waters of the Yangtze. Whether they'd arrived overnight or in the first light of dawn only the swallows themselves knew, but their joyous twittering exuberance warmed and spread happiness and hope in the hearts of all the city's citizens.

Spider Girl hurried, as fast as she could, back from the markets of the Bund to Hu and Agnes's apartment. She had some vital news. News she had overheard at the barber's stall. She was excited, she was very emotional, and she was terrified.

'There's been this incredible battle,' she announced to the breakfast table. 'Between the Chinese and the Japanese. And the Chinese have won. The Chinese have smashed the Japanese.'

Agnes looked at her sceptically.

'Where was this "great victory"?'

'A place called Taierzhuang.'

'Never heard of it. Where did you hear this news?'

'On the Bund. It's all over the marketplaces. People are rejoicing.'

Agnes's scepticism continued.

'I think, if there'd been a great Chinese victory, I'd have heard about it over the news wires, or from government sources.'

'It is. It's true. We have won.' She paused. 'And thousands and thousands of people have been killed on both sides.'

With that she burst into tears.

Hu moved over to comfort her. The Drab just stared. Agnes went over to the stove to make some tea for Spider Girl.

Just at this moment a runner burst in with a message for Agnes. She looked at it. Then she looked at Spider Girl.

Then she read out the message.

'From the official spokesman of the Peoples' United Republican Government of China, the Honourable Hollington Tong. "Dearest correspondents of China and of the Free World, you are humbly invited to attend a special news conference at 11 a.m. this morning, where I will make a highly important and auspicious announcement. Please attend."'

Agnes looked up at Spider Girl. She picked up the tea she had prepared and took it over to her. She touched her on the shoulder.

'Drink this. It will soothe you. You are a very clever girl, Spider Girl. A very clever and brave girl. Sometime I will talk to you about your news gathering sources. I wish mine were as good.'

She moved away and start to prepare to leave for the news conference. She had to get there quickly. The pre-conference gossip among the correspondents would be almost as juicy as the news itself.

She left the apartment with Hu still comforting Spider Girl.

When I hear the news it is inevitably Lao Xiang who tells me it.

I am still asleep in bed, having spent most of the night wrestling with *Seven Chinese Virgins Sink a Japanese Torpedo Boat*, when he bursts in.

'Fuck,' he says. 'Fuck fuck fuck fuck. And fuck again.'

'What?' I say, blearily fighting for consciousness.

'The news,' he says, 'the fucking news!'

'What fucking news?'

'We've only gone and fucking fucked them.'

'Who's gone and fucked what?' I ask. 'And can we please stop all this fucking fucking.'

'We've fucked them. The fucking Chinese have gone and fucked the fucking Japanese!'

Finally, through a blizzard of 'fucks', I am at last able to discern that the Chinese have managed to defeat the Japanese. In a major and devastating fashion. THE FUCKING CHINESE HAVE FUCKED THE FUCKING JAPANESE MAJORLY!!! Yes, really!'

I fall back onto the bed. Then get up again. And start to try and pull all my clothes on simultaneously while dancing round the bed with Lao Xiang and shouting obscenities out of the window. The ten thousand blossoms on the red persimmon tree outside my window riotously toss their claret-coloured heads in joyous dance. Reminds me greatly of the celebrations that used to take place on the Chicken Run terrace at West Ham after they'd scored a goal!

As soon as I've managed to organize my clothing into some semblance of order I give Lao Xiang a great comradely hug and rush down to the docks. There's only one place to be for the celebrations today – the Bund!

The large room for Hollington Tong's morning news conference was abuzz with Western and Chinese correspondents. Agnes moved from group to group, trying to glean any details about what the announcement was likely to be. Nobody had a clue. Agnes ventured to suggest that perhaps there might have been a great Chinese victory. Everyone immediately pooh-poohed it. They pooh-poohed it so much that the received wisdom of the room quickly became that there had been a great Chinese defeat, and some even opined that Hollington Tong was about to announce China's craven surrender.

On one thing only could everyone in the room unanimously agree. That the free coffee offered by the Chinese Ministry of Information tasted like old socks.

Most of the Western journalists present – mainly young, idealistic and penniless 'stringers' – were deeply sympathetic to the Chinese cause. Many had come to Wuhan directly from Spain, where the democratically elected Spanish government's heroic attempts to defend themselves against the fascist invasion were now on their last legs.

Jack Belden was there – an American college kid who hadn't been able to find work in Depression America, had worked his passage to China on a tramp steamer and then laboured for several year as a coolie in the Shanghai docks before becoming a journalist. So was George Hogg, a nervous young English Quaker. Izzy Epstein, a fervent communist and United Press reporter, was arguing with George Wang of Reuters over what were the precise colours of Madame Chiang's polka dot sweater. His boss in New York had sent him an imperative cable ordering him to uncover this vital information rather than endlessly rabbiting on about the terrible sufferings of the Chinese people under the Japanese boot. 'Give us a story with pizzazz,' he demanded.

'What colour is her fucking sweater, George?' demanded a desperate Izzy. 'You're fucking Chinese, you should know.'

'Hell,' responded George, 'just make it up.'

Izzy grinned wolfishly.

'Purple with pink dots!'

In a corner at the back sat two callow and rather clumsily dressed young Englishmen – Wystan Hugh Auden and Christopher Bradshaw Isherwood. Sporadically they tried to speak to a massive and muscular Chinese general who sat beside them. Feng Yuxiang would only respond to their questions with a grin as wide as the Yangtze. He was here to celebrate. Celebrate most especially the triumph of his two friends, Generals Bai Chongxi and Li Zongren, and, to a lesser extent, of himself. And to ensure that not one ounce of credit went to the charlatan General Chiang Kai-shek. The more Auden and Isherwood badgered him, the more he smiled.

'Inscrutable,' said Auden to Isherwood.

Feng's smile grew even wider. Auden and Isherwood reminded him of Laurel and Hardy.

Isherwood scratched the top of his head.

At the end of the row of seats, all by himself and perfectly self-composed, sat a youthful and dashingly attired Old Etonian,

Peter Fleming, the special correspondent for *The Times* and *The Spectator*. Peter Fleming was a man of many secrets, none of which we will go into at the moment.

There was a fluster up front and suddenly Hollington Tong's portly figure bowled through a door and bounced onto the podium.

'What's the colour of Madame Chiang's polka dot sweater, Hollington?' shouted Izzy Epstein. Everyone laughed, Hollington most.

Hollington was widely respected by the press corps. Ever since taking his position at the start of the Wuhan government he had adopted a revolutionary position as government press officer. He told the truth. Or almost told the truth. He had intelligently calculated that the Chinese nation's position was so dire that it was best to be honest about it. Since the government's position was that they wished for immediate economic and military aid from Britain and France and America, the worse the Chinese nation's position became and the more powerful the Japanese grew, the more likely it was that these nations would involve themselves in these wars. It was a slender hope, a very slender hope considering these countries were all lead by appeasers and isolationists, but still a hope. So Hollington almost entirely told the truth, and the press corps loved him for it. And they entirely understood that on certain matters – namely military ones – no government on earth in a war can afford to tell the truth about its military activities.

Hollington continued to grin, incontinently, then spoke.

'Gentlemen, the united government of China has very important, auspicious news for you. News which I hope and trust you will report faithfully and as loudly as you can. It is truly momentous news for your governments and peoples to hear.'

He paused.

'General Rensuke Isogai is the commanding officer of the Imperial Japanese Army's most formidable and powerful military force, its 10th Division. This is the news I bring you and the world. Military forces of the Chinese government and nation have for the last three weeks engaged the Imperial Japanese Army's 10th

Division under the command of General Rensuke in sustained and ferocious and unremitting combat in and outside the city of Taierzhuang in Shandong Province.'

Agnes reminded herself she really had to speak to Spider Girl.

'The Japanese 10th Army Division, I am pleased to announce, has been utterly and completely annihilated by our heroic Chinese forces. Only a few hundred members of the 10th Division have been able to escape to the north. The rest are dead or captured. This Taierzhuang victory ensures that, for a time, Wuhan, the capital of China, is safe from the Japanese invaders.'

There was a stunned silence, followed by riotous cheering and applause. The press corps were overwhelmingly young, leftist, and absolute supporters of China. Only one man in the room did not cheer or rave. Peter Fleming, Old Etonian, sighed, stood up and quietly exited. He was soon followed by a herd of screaming journalists stampeding for the phones.

News of Taierzhuang spreads swiftly upwards from the market-places on the Bund and downwards from those with radios and telephones and telegraphs. The news meets somewhere in the middle. I am later told that those who received the news simultaneously from below and above have never really recovered from the experience, such was the joy and relief which exploded within them.

Swallows and house martins and swifts tumble and somersault across the spring skies as slowly and methodically pairs of storks – great white elegant birds with black linings all along their wings and legs trailing behind – return from their winter migrations and reclaim once more their traditional nests. As the pairs land they excitedly clack their long bills together as though rejoicing at the great victory. Their nests are on temples and in trees.

The great trees themselves blow their blousy new leaves in the air, each green leaf trying to reach closer towards the sun than all its neighbours. A lively breeze breathes into them and their boughs sough up and down as though in celebration.

I walk beneath the trees on the Bund, the sun dappling

through their leaves onto my face. All around me are crowds. Individuals, lovers, families, crowds of even a hundred families – children, adults, grandparents – capering and jumping and parading. Chinese flags are being waved everywhere. Crowds peel off into the Chinese Big World Amusement Park – shoot up in the air on giant wheels, plummet to earth on helter skelters, amid gaudy flashing lights and raucous music. In the Good Fortune Roller Skating Dance Hall packed crowds suicidally career round and round, arms flailing, legs flying. I pass a cinema showing the latest Fred and Ginger musical. It inauspiciously belts out the sounds of 'Let's Face the Music and Dance'. The management has patriotically declared all performances for the day free, but wisely doubled the price of its refreshments.

Firecrackers fizzle and explode among our feet. Berserk groups of children rush around screaming and shouting, demanding of their parents that they add to their sugar rush by buying them yet another candy floss. I pass a marriage procession – a red-clothed bride in her red-painted carriage – followed almost immediately by a solemn funeral procession with red-robed Buddhist priests, bells, drums and candles round the red-draped coffin and professional mourners all around. The sounds and musics of wedding and funeral blend perfectly into one.

Up above us old men have released their pet doves into the air and have tied tiny flutes and whistles to their tail feathers so as they flutter and circle through the upper airs the sounds of sweet whistles and harmonies fill the skies. Amid them small children's and large adults' kites ride the wind – glittering, swooping and swirling in a thousand vibrant colours.

Acrobats. Yes, lots of acrobats. Contortionists, jugglers, dog and monkey shows, dog and pony shows, storytellers, street pedlars selling noodles, noodle dumplings stuffed with pork, soup with glutinous rice flour dumplings, sweet cakes, round flat wheat cakes.

It is still relatively early in the morning so blue-coated farmers with sturdy barefooted wives are still tramping in from the countryside to sell their produce, slung from poles between their two shoulders – great round baskets of dewy fresh vegetables, large bundles of dried hay for kindling, often trailed by a caravan of neat-footed little donkeys pattering past with enormous cylindrical bags of flour or rice crossed upon their backs.

The clatter of mahjong tablets in a cafe and the pipings of a flute player. Hawkers selling small wooden combs, packets of powder, pocket mirrors. A travelling dentist who sits his clients in a large wheelbarrow and tries to extort money from a large crowd of onlookers hungry to witness the next tooth extraction. On a side table he displays a large pile of decayed teeth to show his successful extractions, and he employs a drummer to drown out his customers' screams.

I am passing the walls where the newspaper pages are pasted up. A week ago there used to be quite large groups of people there hotly debating the news, arms flying, jaws hinging, everyone conversing and debating vital topics of politics, war, economics, governance, the foreign situation – with especial reference to Hitler's invasion of Austria and his new treaty with Japan – even going as far as to hint that perhaps we needed new leaders and, dare to whisper it, elections.

But the victory at Taierzhuang has changed everything.

There is an ocean, in fact there are several oceans, of packed people around the walls – a turmoil and roar of humanity as they all express their own different opinions and points of view and fervent beliefs. Socialism, Communism, Buddhist parties, Daoist parties, an Independence for Tibet Party, an All-Woman's Party, a No Tax Party, a Let's All be Ruled by Experts Party, even a Let's Get Back to the Good Old Days of the Emperor Party. Never before have I witnessed such release, such exuberance, such unleashing of opinion and intention and belief in public. Speaking your mind? It is bad manners! You might upset someone important! But now, it is as though a tsunami has been unleashed, the banks of the Yangtze River broken open. A universal unlocking of jaws! Great tides of humanity flow back and forth, orators cling to their soap boxes so they are not swept away. Everyone is insulting, disagreeing with, debating, agreeing with, cheering, booing everyone else.

And their greatest cries are for elections and for fighting the Japanese!

I walk among them open-mouthed. I listen in awe to the speakers, to the groups of people debating among themselves. I mean, what I love is the way in which ordinary people are suddenly speaking. With passion, with deadly humour, with great charity. They suddenly, mysteriously speak like angels – openly, beautifully, freely, dealing with the most complex subjects and ideas in the simplest, most concise language. I came to Wuhan to teach educated people how to write as common Chinese people speak. But when I hear these common people speak, these ordinary, everyday, modest people, they speak the most heavenly, the highest Chinese ever spoken.

It does an old socialist's heart good. I mean, you can sense, you can almost see the high and the mighty, the powerful – amid all this popular ferment and action, people carrying on as though they are their own masters, feeling their own power – you can sense the powerful flinching, for a second doubting, even foreseeing their own end.

John Milton's great words come to my mind:

Methinks I see in my mind a noble and puissant Nation rousing herself like a strong man after sleep, and shaking her invincible locks: Methinks I see her as an Eagle muing her mighty youth, and kindling her undazl'd eyes at the full midday beam; purging and unscaling her long abused sight at the fountain itself of heav'nly radiance.

A call for joyous prayer resonates from the minaret of a nearby mosque.

I am hit full in the face by a random egg. This really is a proper political meeting! It reminds me of my days in London's East End.

Wiping the yolk from my face, I suddenly recall I should be elsewhere. As the unofficial matchmaker between Yu Liqun and Guo Morou, at this very moment I should in fact be at a meeting between the 'happy' couple to help 'negotiate' their marriage. I hurry off.

★ ★ ★

Amid all these celebrations Hu had stayed to comfort the weeping Spider Girl. Spider Girl apologized for weeping. Weeping was a selfish and time-wasting thing to do! She had not done it since she was a tiny child. Hu assured her it was perfectly all right. She told The Drab, Spider Girl's assistant, to prepare another bowl of Oolong tea to soothe her.

Hu herself was likewise facing difficulties. It was getting time for her to go and attend her daily government committee. Hu increasingly harboured doubts not only about the usefulness of the committee – it never seemed to reach a decision about anything except for matters which favoured the already rich and powerful – but also of her own presence on it. No one ever listened to a thing she said.

What she had told Madame Chiang had had some effect. The hospitals which the whores had set up inside the brothels were no longer being harassed as much by the owners' goons and gangsters. Two of the floating brothels had been adapted into hospitals and wounded soldiers were now being transported upstream to Changsha and Chungking in them. And her ideas on getting many more sampans moored around Wuhan to provide homes to house the refugees had resulted in a few being towed downstream, but not many.

The main resistance to all these schemes was the opposition, the total opposition, of Wuhan's landlords. The scarcer property became the higher the rents they could charge. And the landlords wielded great influence within the government and within her own committee. Even Madame Chiang could not get far against such powerful vested interests. Brothels were definitely more profitable than hospitals, and the more sampans that were brought in the lower they would drive rents.

Hu was a rare and rather bizarre creature in human life. Her great desire was to be helpful. To serve others. To work for the greater good. She was as dedicated to her work as any medieval nun. While her committee work was of little use, her relationship with Madame Chiang was useful and did help some people. She did not want to upset Madame Chiang, who she thought of as a good person, by resigning from the committee. Even if she did resign, at the moment she did not have any other useful job or work to go to. She was in a quandary.

Then she had an idea to help Spider Girl.

'Spider Girl, I've decided not to go to my committee today. Instead of you being upset here in the apartment, why don't you come along with me and help us bind the soldiers' wounds on the Bund?'

Spider Girl looked at her. Spider Girl was always practical. No point letting your grief get in the way of doing something good.

'Yes,' she said. 'Good idea. I don't know anything about binding wounds, so you're going to have to show me.'

'We'll start with the easy stuff.'

'You never know,' pondered Spider Girl, 'my father might just turn up there. I could look after him.'

They got ready to go. Spider Girl's spirits were reviving. She gave The Drab a cuff to remind her she should prepare the vegetables ready for cooking before she and Hu returned, then they set off along the Bund.

The snows had been melting on the great mountains of Tibet so the Yangtze was now in full and glorious spate. The sun shone. Everywhere Chinese flags were flying – from the factory chimneys of Hanyang, the battlements of Wuchang and in all the Chinese areas of Hankou. Even the embassies in the foreign concessions flew flags and their warships anchored in the river were covered in bunting. At least on the British and French and American embassies and boats. The Italian ones remained stark and unfestooned.

Li Dequan and her husband Feng Yuxiang were working at the dressing station as they arrived. Hu introduced Spider Girl.

Feng looked Spider Girl up and down.

'You look like a good stout peasant girl,' he opined. 'Bet you could collar a good husband.'

Spider Girl had never blushed before but found herself doing so now. What a generous man! And he had a pretty fine figure himself!

Feng left to attend to several of his many duties and Spider Girl, instructed by Hu, started enthusiastically rolling up disinfected bandages. She fantasized about good fat husbands with lots of land.

As they bandaged and swabbed and staunched the bleeding and tried to set broken bones and lessen the pain and suffering, Li Dequan and Hu swapped news.

Two or three times different candidates came up to them and handed them their policy pamphlets for the upcoming elections. Spider Girl, who'd been following the news by reading the papers on the walls and listening in at various barbers' stalls, had several sharp questions for them.

Hu started to explain to Li Dequan her doubts about staying on the government committee. She didn't feel she was doing any good.

Li thought that Madame Chiang would be upset. She had great respect for Hu.

'But I'm not doing anything useful. Look at us here. We're helping these soldiers in their terrible pain. We might even be saying the lives of a few of them. But on that committee…!'

Li Dequan looked at her.

'What would you do instead?'

'I don't know. I don't know at the moment. And I don't want to upset Madame Chiang. I think she is a good person.'

'She is a good *powerful* person,' Li Dequan corrected her.

'If I was to do something else,' said Hu, 'I'd still think of good things to do, watch the world around me and hand any suggestions I had to Madame Chiang to help her – but what I should be doing in this terrible world we're in at the moment, with so much suffering, such injustice, is helping ordinary people. Just like Jesus tells us to.'

'Amen,' said Li. 'I will speak to Madame Chiang,' she continued. 'Explain to her that you do not like the committee work. And why. She won't like your decision. But do not worry, she is not a vindictive person.'

'Thank you, Li,' said Hu.

'And,' said Li, 'I have an idea what you could do afterwards, as a useful job.'

'Yes?' said Hu.

'You like talking to people, lots of different people, don't you?'

'Well, I suppose I do.'

'Just look at you on your march from Shanghai with the mill girls and whores and soldiers, you enjoyed that, didn't you?'

'Oh, I did, I loved that,' agreed Hu.

'Bet you never stopped talking,' said Li. 'Just look at you here, you never stop chattering and joking with the soldiers.'

'Oh, I love soldiers,' said Hu.

'I heard that,' said a soldier whose leg they were plastering.

'You behave yourself,' said Hu, and they all laughed.

'Well,' said Li, 'the thing is, Feng is soon going upriver, to Chungking, so he can properly organize all the cooperatives and businesses and industries they're starting up there. One job he will not be able to do – and he will miss it – is meeting all the refugees as they arrive at the camps, talking to them, vetting them, observing them. I think you'd be very good at that.'

'What?'

'You like meeting people. You are sharp, You're funny, you're humane. You have an instinct for people. The upset, the unusual, the good, the ungood. You could stand at the gate.'

'But...'

'I'll tell Madame Chiang about your decision. I suspect you will spot many things on the gate which could be helpful to her. I hope she'll still listen to you.'

Meanwhile a keen young politician had spent twenty minutes trying to persuade Spider Girl to support his party So far she was unconvinced. But she had got him helping to roll bandages.

Peter Fleming was pretending to write an article for *The Spectator* magazine on 'The Ancient and Honourable Sport of Chinese Duck Fighting', but mainly he was trying to eavesdrop on a conversation on the table to his left at the Last Ditch Press Club. The Last Ditch Club had been founded by journalists based in Wuhan. Journalists who all swore that they would be the last journalist to leave Wuhan before the Japanese arrived. It was rowdy, drunken and situated on the second floor above a popular restaurant, Rosie's.

Six days had passed since the announcement of China's victory at Taierzhuang.

At the bar to the left of Fleming, well into their drink, sat Agnes Smedley, Wystan Auden and Christopher Isherwood, all trying to pick up the youthful and nervous young Quaker George Hogg. Hogg was only interested in talking about cooperatives. Fortunately the New Zealander Rewi Alley, an expert on cooperatives, turned up at this moment and Hogg was able to have an intelligent conversation with him.

Peter Fleming, seated in an armchair in the centre of the room, sipped on a dry martini with a twist of lemon in it.

The conversation he was trying to listen in to, at the large table to his left, was being conducted raucously by two Russians and an American. The table was covered in maps of the Taierzhuang battlefield. They were poring over them; the American Colonel Evans Carlson was taking down notes of what Colonels Vasily Chuikov and Georgy Zhukov were telling him. They were all military observers.

Colonels Chuikov and Zhukov had just returned from the Taierzhuang battlefield where they had spent two days exhaustively debriefing an already exhausted Li Zongren on the extraordinary tactics and strategies he had improvised in the battle. As the Russians spoke Carlson kept on whistling and whispering 'Oh boy! Oh boy!'

Peter Fleming wished he could see the maps which they were discussing with such enthusiasm. Fleming didn't like Russians, but he disliked Americans even more. So he wasn't best pleased when Agnes Smedley, having given up in the chase for George Hogg, decided to hit on him.

'So Peter,' she slurred, 'what are *you* doing in Wuhan?'

Agnes had just written four different articles for the *Manchester Guardian*, the *News Chronicle*, *The Nation* and one for a *Chicago Daily News* friend who was sick, analyzing in detail not only the victory itself but an accurate and prescient forecast of just how it would alter the entire geo-strategic balance of the region (and even the world). Having finished this Herculean task she had now hit the bottle.

'I am writing a report for *The Times* on the military and political consequences of the Battle of Taierzhuang on China and its contiguous nations,' replied an icy Fleming.

'But you don't know anything about those sorts of things,' said Agnes, 'you're a travel writer.'

'I am *not* a travel writer. I know *all* about it,' replied a piqued Peter. 'As a member of the Fleming banking family, closely associated with Jardine Matheson, we've been in Hong Kong for a hundred years, so I know everything there is to know about China.'

'You know all about opium smuggling,' retorted Agnes, who was starting to enjoy the fisticuffs. 'Incidentally, how's that article you're writing on duck fighting coming on?'

'I'm not writing an article on duck fighting,' ground Fleming, surreptitiously hiding the article he was writing on duck fighting.

'I hear they hunt ducks on horseback in England.'

A couple of other hacks drifted over to enjoy the free entertainment.

'So is it the ducks on horseback or the hunters?'

Fleming was silently cursing Smedley, as she was drowning out the military information from the next table and he was instinctively repulsed by the uncouth advances of an American woman with the build of an ageing pugilist. He preferred fragile, delicately boned women like his wife Celia Johnson – star of the silver screen and BBC Home Service.

'Go away,' stated Fleming flatly.

'Who's going to make me, limey?' responded Agnes, advancing on him fists raised before tripping over the carpet and falling flat on her face.

Fleming turned his ear again to the table on his left, but by now the military attachés had finished their analyses and were rolling up their maps.

'Gee,' said Evans Carlson, 'wait til FDR hears of this. It's going to change his whole view of China.'

'Damn,' said Fleming to himself. 'Damn, damn, damn.'

Her two supporters were dragging Agnes back to the bar in the hopes of reviving her for Round Two.

The wedding negotiations have been concluded. They lasted quite some time and involved the presence of not only myself but a rather heavily built lawyer from the Chinese Communist Party.

This will be how the wedding proceeds.

Firstly, the happy couple are to be solemnly married. Since both parties to the marriage are ardent revolutionaries, the ceremony will be conducted in the offices of the Communist Party of China, with various officials, including Chou En-lai and the heavily built lawyer, present, as well as myself.

The bride, Mr Guo Morou, will then proceed with Mr Chou En-lai, myself and the heavily built lawyer to a Grand Unity political rally to be held on the Bund on the afternoon before the elections are due to be held, where Mr Guo Morou, in an 'extremely impassioned fashion', will address the crowds, will speak 'with inspiration and conviction' of supporting the Communist Party of China, the Nationalist Party of China, and all the other political parties standing in the next day's election. He must emphasize over and over again the importance of unity among the Chinese peoples, he must praise the glorious victory of our soldiers at Taierzhuang, and again and again he must state that the heroic Chinese people can only win this war if they selflessly sacrifice themselves and commit all their energies and intelligence towards the victory.

After this rally is concluded Mr Guo Morou will willingly attend a reception of influential citizens where, attended by Mr Chou En-lai of the Chinese Communist Party and a senior member of the Nationalist Party of China, yet to be appointed, he will spend at least three hours socializing with those present and repeatedly emphasizing the virtues of unity, self-sacrifice, a positive mental attitude in the nation's conflict with the barbarian Japanese, and the need for individuals to donate large sums of money towards the war effort.

Although at this stage of the wedding process Mr Guo would still be accompanied by Messrs Chou En-lai, a senior member of the Chinese Nationalist Party, yet to be appointed, and the heavily built lawyer, I had successfully managed to excuse myself from it by arguing that, with none of her family present, I should in fact be acting *in loco parentis* on behalf of Miss Yu, now Mrs Guo, and should accompany her to the lavish bridal suite hired by Mr Guo, where she and I would prepare for the arrival of Mr Guo. Once Mr Guo arrived, I would stay in a side room to the bridal suite, in case my presence be requested by either party at any time during the night.

The first part of the agreement, the actual wedding ceremony, works reasonably well. As the lengthy clauses and sub-clauses to the wedding contract are read aloud, Mr Guo stares with great intensity at Miss Yu while Miss Yu looks elsewhere.

But things get interesting as we walk towards the great rally upon the Bund.

All through the negotiations Guo Morou showed little or no interest in the rally, and it was with an air of indifference, if not downright hostility, that he agreed to all the clauses and sub-clauses enforcing him to speak with inspiration and conviction and passion to all those attending the rally.

But as we approach the back of the speakers' platform, it becomes obvious that the numbers of those attending the rally are enormous. They are greeting every statement and sentence of every speaker with roars and huzzahs of approval. Even the speaker for the 'Let's Get Back to the Good Old Days of the Emperor' party is receiving cheers.

Guo Morou starts to twitch like an aged warhorse hearing the sounds of distant battle. The muscles in his shoulders and arms pull and ripple as though preparing for much swinging and windmilling of his arms. The muscles in his jaws and face rictus in preparation.

'There are a lot of people here,' he whispers to Chou En-lai.

'There are indeed,' agrees Chou. 'They have come from everywhere to listen to you.'

'You think that's true?' answers Guo.

'I am certain of it,' says the deft Chou. 'No one can equal the great Guo Morou. All the people of China wait to hear you.'

'I can do it again,' says Guo, mainly to himself, 'just like in the old days. I can speak to the people. I can speak *for* the people.'

After that there is no holding him back. He positively bounds onto the stage. He looks at the audience. A small man, he suddenly grows big. He starts to speak. For a few seconds he stumbles and misfires, emits a few croaks, but then he remembers and his voice starts to soar, his body strengthen and relax, so that when he gets to sad bits it weakens and sags, when he gets to strong, fiery passages, like steel it stiffens and strikes. He defeats a thousand Japanese armies on stage. He rescues a million helpless refugees. His pure Han voice – commanding, arrogant, absolute – sings and spans out across all the silent ocean of peasants and sailors and civil servants and coolies from every province of China. They understand him! His flawless Han accent. Even in the most difficult, complex pieces of Marxist dialectic they all listen.

I watch and listen. Even though I know him to be a sham and a mountebank I start to get swept away in his floods of rhetoric. How I start to hate the Japanese! Well, I hate them anyhow. They've quite likely murdered my wife and mother and children. Look what they've done to my country! But now I *really* hate them! He allows me to feel good – really good – about hating them. I love myself for hating them. For feeling murderous. I could rise up right now and seize a bayonet and… The crowd has gone crazy. And now he starts to go on about the glories of China. Its poets, its artists, its soldiers and statesmen – the greatest civilization on earth, the greatest country on earth!!! There is nothing we cannot achieve! We are now going to go out there and…!!!! Everyone out there must sacrifice themself and…!!!!

And with that I think of little Yu Liqun, sitting there all alone in her hotel, her bridal suite, preparing herself…

As the wedding contract stipulates I attend Mr Guo and Chou En-lai and the now-appointed member of the Nationalist Party and the heavily built lawyer to the post-speech reception tent where Guo the oratorical sensation – I really must stop this snide literary bitchiness – disappears into a scrum of adoring and gobsmacked grandees bombarding him with drinks and flattery. Guo Morou has been reborn. Chou En-lai gives me a wry smile.

I hurry to the hotel.

Yu Liqun, or Guo Liqun as I must now call her, appears quite calm. She has prepared herself. She asks me about the meeting. I give a restrained description of it. She sees through me.

'You liked it, didn't you? He did some shameless rabble-rousing. He even got you all roused up.'

She laughs. We both laugh.

'That is good,' she says. 'If the Chinese people get all worked up to fight the barbarians, then it means my wedding is worthwhile.'

'Are you ready?' I ask.

'For tonight? Perfectly.'

There is a slight wobble to her voice.

'Perhaps you'd like to do something,' I say, 'before he arrives?'

'Do you play cards?' she asks.

'Yes, I do. Very badly.'

'Well I play them very badly too. So let's play cards.'

So we play cards. As neither of us really know how to play we both make up our own rules, and thus makes the game much more interesting and disputatious.

One hour passes. Two hours pass.

I order tea and, as it's a Western hotel, cake.

As I turn back from ordering the food on the phone, I see a small tear escape her eye.

'Oh,' I say, 'I'm terribly sorry. Look…'

'Please,' she says over me, 'I don't want any sympathy. That is the last thing I need. I am an adult. In fact, you helped me become an adult. We are at war. War and sacrifice go together. Someday, as a result, we will build a better world.'

The cards seem to have finished.

'What do you want to do?' I ask.

She thinks.

'You're a writer. Why don't you read me one of your books?'

My mind flips rapidly through my work. 'Crescent Moon' – the story of an innocent girl slowly forced into prostitution and an early death – no! *Rickshaw Boy* – a tale of a once optimistic hero similarly succumbing to fate – again inappropriate! I really must write more cheerful books! Then I realize I don't have any copies of them on me anyhow. I look around. The hotel, in order to flatter their guests that they are intelligent, sports a shelf of leather-bound

Western literary classics. I look at them. Jane Austen? No – she's far too hard-headed and aware of the sacrifices necessary to life. Charles Dickens? Yes! I've never been a great fan – far too sugary and sentimental – but for tonight...!

I choose *A Tale of Two Cities*, translating it as I read. We both sink into a sea of sentimentality.

Another hour passes.

Then another.

I look at her.

'I know,' she says. 'He's late. According to our contract he is at least two hours late.'

We talk in a desultory fashion for another hour, then another. All the time she is getting more and more upset.

'Perhaps...' I say.

Suddenly there is a crash. The door flies open.

Guo Morou stands there. Or at least he sags against the doorpost. He has a soppy beatific smile on his face. He looks at us.

'Hello,' he says, as though he's never seen us before. As though this isn't his bride...

'Do you know,' he says, 'they loved me. They really loved me. I thought I was old, past it, that they'd laugh at me, not listen to what I said. But I had them eating out of my hand. Out of my fucking hand. I am so happy.'

And with that he proceeds, very slowly, still smiling beatifically, to wander in a not particularly straight line through the room and out through the door into the bridal bedchamber.

There is silence.

We look at each other.

'I think,' I say hesitantly, 'I should be going. To my room.'

'You stay right there,' she says.

She walks over to the door and quietly enters the bridal chamber.

Another silence.

Equally quietly, she tiptoes out of the bridal chamber, shutting the door softly behind her.

She looks at me.

'Fast asleep. Flat out. Face down on the bridal bed.'

We look at each other.

'I don't know whether to scream or cheer.'

I start to move.

'Don't you dare go,' she says. 'If ever a bride needed a friend it is now.'

'Shall I order some food?' I ask.

'Brilliant. And order the best French wine. That old bastard can pay for it.'

I order it on the phone. I add in five packets of Senior Service.

'Well,' she says when I've put the phone down, 'I'm getting very bored with Dickens. How about some more card playing.'

And so, with the sated groom's snores echoing from next door, amid happy insults and name-calling, we resume our random games of cards.

It was Hu's third day on the gate. Already she was relaxing into the job. A steady flow of endlessly different people came towards her.

Some of them were distressed.

'My family needs food. Already three of them have died from starvation.'

'Over there, friend. See – there is a kitchen. You can eat what you want – but don't eat too much. It could upset your stomachs.'

'That is wise advice. Thank you.'

'And come back here when you have fed. I will direct you to your new homes.'

Some of them were irritated.

'Five times. Five times we have been misdirected in this damn city. Everyone who lives in cities are crooks. Where are these homes?'

'Ah, I believe you are from Jiangsu Province? You have had a long journey.'

'We cannot understand what people are saying here.'

'I too am from Jiangsu. My family and ancestors come from Kaixiangong Village...'

'Ah, that is a good village. My mother came from there.'

'You walk along this street here, and you take the third turning on the left. In that street everyone is from Jiangsu, so they will understand what you are saying and they will show you where you are to live.'

'You are a good woman. Thank you.'

Some of them were obviously criminals.

'Where is Wang?'

'Wang? There are many Wangs here.'

'He told me to come over here. He said many of his mates were here.'

'Did he say where they were staying?'

'He said the street where they lived was filled with people from Jilin Province who couldn't understand what they were saying so no one could snoop on them.'

Hu made a prearranged signal to the soldiers behind her.

'The street for people from Jilin is up that road and seventh on the right.'

The obviously criminal man walked off. He was followed by a soldier in plain clothes. If the house he went to on Jilin Street was full of thieves – which Hu suspected – they would all be arrested and taken to the military barracks.

And then there were the comic.

'I am drunk.'

'Yes, you are drunk.'

'I hadn't drunk anything on the march for five days, my whole throat was parched, and when we got here someone gave me a drink of wine. I was so thirsty I drank the whole bottle.'

'Why don't you lie down over there. And when you wake up I'll tell you where to go.'

'You'll make someone a good wife.'

The elections have been held. Various parties have been elected. The assembly in which they sit will not have any real powers – the government retains those – but they will be allowed to 'advise' the government. They will even be allowed to criticize the government. Free speech in China?! I have spent short bits of my life in prison and long bits of it in internal exile because of my enthusiasm for democracy, free speech, the right to say what you bloody well want to say. And now the day has at last arrived!

I hurry down to the large hall where the assembly – it is called the People's Political Council – is to be held.

The elected politicians are all sitting up on the stage. Some look like normal human beings, but most look distinctly grand. That's what being elected does for you. And there are actually ten elected women on the stage.

I find a seat towards the back of the hall. I sit down beside a stout young country girl who I partly recognize. We smile at each other in a half-knowing way and then set ourselves to listen to the debate.

We have to wait quite some time. First we have to wade through rather a lot of pleasantries and self-congratulations and general bloviations before they start. Then various votes and points of order and jockeying for position have to take place.

This goes on for about an hour. The audience grow a bit restless and start talking among themselves.

The girl next to me and I fall into conversation.

We agree that we've met before, on the Bund, by the dressing station for wounded soldiers.

'I was with Feng Yuxiang and his wife Li Dequan. They were helping Agnes Smedley, the American journalist, and her young Chinese friend, to bind the soldiers' wounds.'

'Yes. I work for Miss Smedley. I'm her cook.'

'Oh.'

'What do you do?'

'I'm a writer.'

'A writer? You write books?'

'Yes. Do you read books?'

'Yes. I read Shanghai detective books. I like stories with lots of blood and violence in them. And love.'

'Oh. Do you read any other sorts of books?'

'I once read part of a book by someone called Lao She. My friend Hu said I should read it. But I found it very boring.'

'Yes,' I say, 'indeed, Lao She can be very boring.'

'It was just this man pulling this rickshaw, going on and on about how bored and fed up he was with everything and how he didn't see the point of anything. As if anyone pulling around a rickshaw would have time to think about stuff like that.'

'Yes.'

'I like books, proper books, but mainly I read newspapers.'

'Newspapers? So you must be interested in politics.'

'No.'

'Why?'

'I am too poor to think about that. Most people don't have time to worry about what the world could be, they're too busy trying to survive in the world as it is.'

'You have a very novel way of looking at the world.'

'I have a very sensible way of looking at the world.'

'Then if you don't read the papers to follow politics, why do you read them?'

'I want to follow the war. What is happening in it. For example, have you heard, with the barbarians in retreat, our 85th and 52nd Corps have linked up at Taodan – well to the north of Taierzhuang – and 10th and 5th Japanese Divisions are in full retreat back up the railway line to Jinan?'

Suddenly I understand why she is so interested in the newspapers.

'Do you have a member of your family in the war?'

For the first time in our conversation she hesitates.

'Yes, I do,' she says. 'Do you have a member of your family in the war?'

For the first time in our conversation I hesitate.

'Yes,' I say, 'I do.'

The tone of our conversation changes after this. We are both gentler, more relaxed with each other.

Finally, after two hours of showboating, the politicians on the stage grace us with a debate. What we've all been waiting for. People in the audience stop talking and begin listening. Matters get lively. Politicians start shouting at each other. Members of the audience start shouting at each other. Fisticuffs break out.

'Ah,' says the girl, 'this is the sort of politics I like.'

I note she has some rather large eggs in her basket. Doubtless she will deploy them if things get boring again.

It is well past midnight.

Gou Liqun, the young bride, is all alone in the world again. Her husband, the wildly in demand orator and pamphleteer and litterateur and intellectual Guo Morou, is out once more away on vital government work – making speeches, holding debates, reading from his books. Next week he will leave by himself on a tour of China's southern and western cities to speak to and raise the morale of the whole Chinese nation.

There have been couplings between husband and wife. But brief and inconsequential. Instead of feasting his impassioned eyes upon Guo Liqun's naked and exquisitely toned body as they lie in bed it is obvious that his mind, his whole being, is elsewhere. He even mutters and rehearses bits of speeches and turns of phrase to himself while they intertwine. Sometimes he just stops dead and stares at the bedclothes. Then he laughs suddenly.

Guo Liqun is not the sort of girl to be beaten by such behaviour. She is still her own mistress.

In the darkness she dances. Naked. Moving, winding, twisting, revolving like machinery. Implacable machinery. She is the future. Resolute as steel.

Across the river in his university room Lao She lies in his bed in the darkness. From his pajama pocket he gently removes his wife's Indian silk scarf, given to her by their friend, Rabindranath Tagore, the revolutionary Indian poet. Lao smells it. Drinks in the scent of his wife. Remembers when they received the gift, when they were first married, before even the fruitfulness of their children. He weeps.

Spider Girl stands alone in her dark kitchen, thinking fiercely of her father. She always stands when she thinks of her father, ready and waiting to serve him. Against her heart she clutches the small stone bottle containing the last remnants of her family's wild pear juice. She will not allow darkness and bleakness to enter her soul.

1   Comfort ye, comfort ye my people, saith your God.

2   Speak ye comfortably to Jerusalem, and cry unto her, that her warfare is accomplished, that her iniquity is pardoned:

3   The voice of him that crieth in the wilderness, Prepare ye the way of the Lord, make straight in the desert a highway for our God.

4   Every valley shall be exalted, and every mountain and hill shall be made low: and the crooked shall be made straight, and the rough places plain:

5   And the glory of the Lord shall be revealed, and all flesh shall see it together:

Isaiah 40:1–5

BOOK THREE

THE ROAD FROM WUHAN

To Ruth, Ray, Stan, Freda and Margaret.

PRELUDE

A clear, hot day in late May, 1938. Brilliant Blue skies all across Hubei Province. Except over its capital city, Wuhan. Here smoke and dust from repeated air raids rose heavy above the tri-city, especially over the industrial city of Hanyang. Fires raged amid the closely packed hovels and shacks of the workers and throughout the docks. Two of its four great steel mills, despite the damage, continued proudly belching smoke and forging steel. No smoke arose from the other two – not from the first because it had been razed to the ground in a previous Japanese raid; not from the second because, in order to dismantle it and for all its many and often colossal sections to be transported up the Yangtze to build the new steel mills being constructed in Chongqing and Sichuan province, it had been deliberately shut down. Now vast armies of coolies and chargehands and engineers and labourers crawled all over its huge corpse, disincorporating and disembowelling it component by component, stripping out and bearing away small single and labelled components to be packed onto horse or mule or ox-drawn carts or placed on the backs of coolies for the long trek westward. Simultaneously, huge, supervised gangs worked incessantly to break apart its gargantuan machinery and furnaces and then heaved and shifted and hauled each mammoth part down to the river.

Among the largest and heaviest sections of a steel mill were its gigantic forging rolls – huge steel rolling pins – over which hissed molten strips of iron and steel gouting direct from the roaring furnace. There were hundreds of these spinning forging rolls, each weighing fifteen tons, which delivered the molten steel to the presses where the flaming steel was crunched and hammered and forged and squeezed into all the necessary shapes and thicknesses and qualities that customers required. And the huge forging rolls were only one part of this rolling mill, every component of which – work rolls, back-up rolls, the mill housing and the presses – had to be each individually extracted and one by one hauled down to the docks, hoisted aboard and then towed upstream. And that was only the rolling mill. The blast furnace, even when it was disassembled all to pieces, would be still more massive.

Each fifteen-ton forging roll had to be individually raised from its resting sockets, hurdled and hunted through the remnants of the mill, and then guided and braked down a steep cinder track to the dockside below. The only suitable and flexible enough source of energy and power to lift and shift these behemoths through and over such a twisted and uneven course were human beings. Great teams of experienced, specialist coolies, squads versed in levering up massive weights, propelling them forwards with sudden brute force, slewing and braking them expertly with immaculately timed counter-force. Each member of these expert teams moved as one, 'Hey Yah, Hai-yah,' synchronized to the split second by their rhythmic chants and cries and shanties, each moving simultaneously and in unison, flexible and experienced in changing their balance and throwing their body weight for or against a motion, using their muscles only when especial effort was needed, using great crowbars to lift out each huge forging roll from its cradle, large sledges and massive straw ropes to pull it forwards, increase its momentum, at crucial moments employing countersways, bunts and dunts to propel it precisely and blithely in another direction through the mill. They then used the ropes to brake it back when it moved too fast down the cinder slope, and bringing it exactly and gently to rest in the precise location on the dock where two great cranes, synchronized like twin flamingoes, swooped in and lifted each end simultaneously up and across and down into a waiting barge which suddenly floundered and lurched, its timbers squealing and protesting at the brute weight, before it regained its poise and was floated out obediently to join a string of other barges which then, hauled by a tug, were towed stately up the Yangtze to Chungking.

These teams of exquisitely skilled coolies shifted six such loads a day. There were twelve such teams working in Hanyang, amid the bombs and fires and slaughter and smoke and the ever-continuing industrial production. All the time, as they moved their great loads, amid and between them other lines of coolies wove in and out carrying panniers of coal to keep the remaining blast furnaces blazing, sacks of copper coins and lumps of scrap metal to be purified into industrial ingots, food and drink to fuel the workers and coolies, small children in carts, caged birds, family possessions, aeroplane parts, tank hulls and gun barrels, religious objects and statues, milking equipment for cows goats and sheep – everything nurtured and manufactured in Hanyang. All amid continual air raids.

1

Jack Belden was a large, gruff man. He'd been brought up in New York, went to college, but unable to find any work with the Wall Street Crash and America's descent into the Great Depression, he'd jumped on a steamer and worked his passage to China.

For several years he worked as a docker in Shanghai, tough manual labour, where he became a socialist and an alcoholic. A fully functioning alcoholic. He took up writing one-off articles for the thriving Shanghai press and by 1937 had worked his way up to being United Press International's chief correspondent in Wuhan.

Jack had worked in the docks. He'd worked in the streets and fields. He liked ordinary Chinese people. So when war broke out he was most comfortable as a correspondent reporting directly from the front line, living and talking with the soldiers in the trenches, the terrified civilians in the nearby villages. He shared this trait with Agnes Smedley. He lived and slept and marched with the troops.

He'd just returned from Taierzhuang, where he'd reported first-hand from the trenches. The man sat beside him in the Last Ditch Club had not only accompanied him all through the fighting, but had put himself in even greater danger than had Jack. While Jack sensibly kept his head down in the trenches, this man had leapt about, clambering onto vantage points and entering wrecked buildings visible to enemy snipers. This man, Jack's friend, was the Hungarian war photographer Robert Capa.

Robert was in tears.

'Here, Robert, have some of this tea, these sweet dumplings. They're very good. Have some of my bourbon if you want.'

Jack had an open bottle of bourbon, already half-empty, on the table before him.

'Anschluss is the death of my family.'

'You can't be sure of that,' said Jack gently.

'Fascism is winning everywhere.'

Robert had a copy of the airmail edition of *The Times* newspaper open on the table before him. The two of them had received no news of the outside world while in Taierzhuang and this newspaper report was the first Capa had heard of Hitler's invasion of Austria.

'Most of my family fled to Vienna to escape the Jewish pogroms in Hungary. Except for me. I argued with them. I told them that the Austrians would start their own pogroms. Persecutions, confiscations, executions. But they would not listen, they would not follow me to Paris. And now Hitler has invaded Austria. His storm troopers will be going berserk, smashing windows, beating up women, shooting...'

'You can't be certain that they've been arrested, Robert, they might have escaped.'

'My family are eternal Panglossians, Jack, eternal optimists. "This cannot happen to us! The apfelstrudels in Vienna are wonderful to taste! When are you coming to visit us?"'

Jack growled in sympathy.

The two of them had travelled back from Taierzhuang by overnight train and arrived in Wuhan very early in the morning. The club was empty except for the gloomy White Russian serving behind the bar. Robert returned to reading the article.

Jack felt deep pity for the man. Only months ago Robert had lost his young wife, Gerda. She, like him, was a war photographer and the couple had gone out to Spain to cover the war that had followed Franco's fascist invasion of the country. Robert's pictures of the fighting had made him famous around the world. His wife Gerda had gone to photograph the Battle of Brunete on the Madrid front. In the chaotic retreat afterwards she'd hitched a ride on the running board of a general's staff car. While they were at speed a Republican tank, amid the chaos, backed into the side of the roadster. Gerda was killed instantly.

Robert and Gerda regarded themselves as soldiers in the worldwide battle against fascism. Robert took her death as a soldier would, manfully. All through the fighting in Taierzhuang Jack had not discerned any grieving or lassitude in Robert. What mourning he did must have been done privately, in the rare moments he found himself alone.

Robert's pain as he imagined his family's fate in Austria turned almost immediately to anger.

'Look at this, look at this filthy piece of journalism,' he cried, pointing to the main leader in *The Times*. 'It makes me so angry.' He passed Jack the newspaper. 'Read this filth! Just read it aloud!'

Jack did so.

'"Herr Hitler enjoyed two days of triumphal progress from the Austrian Frontier. Our correspondent leaves no room for doubt about the public jubilation with which he and his army were greeted everywhere."'

'You see, Jack? Those words could have been written by Goebbels himself.'

'Knowing *The Times*, they probably were,' commented Jack.

'The Western press is so corrupt, so dishonest. Where's any mention of the trade unionists, socialists, Jews who'll all be being rounded up, kicked in the teeth, shot in the head?'

'All *Times* journalists are appeasement whores,' said Jack. 'And most of the British press too. Their proprietors spend half their time oiling up to the dictators, visiting the Berlin Olympics, hobnobbing with Himmler and Goering and the Führer. They've brainwashed the British people. Times are bad.'

Suddenly Robert smiled.

'When have they ever been anything else, comrade?'

He stood up and held out his hand.

'Jack, I've got to go. Catch the midday plane. I'm off to cover the last days of the Spanish Republic. Yet another fascist triumph to chalk up.'

'Don't get down, Robert,' said Jack, shaking his hand and staring intently into his friend's eyes. 'When the fascists get to you, remember Taierzhuang. We annihilated the cunts.'

Capa first bought two bottles of bourbon for Jack – it was

club tradition that any journalist deserting Wuhan and the Last Ditch Club had to buy all present a round – then collected his photographic equipment and departed. Jack emptied all three bottles and fell into a deep, deep slumber.[9]

Here is no continuing city.

It is a very strange thing to live in a city on the brink. In a place where you have experienced great joys, great comradeship, deep emotions, which you think of instinctively as home, and yet you know that very soon, almost immediately in fact, it will be brutally assaulted, sacked, brought to naught. That very soon it will lie cold, derelict, deserted as a bird's nest in January.

Following their defeat at Taierzhuang the Japanese have now, more cautiously than before, renewed their offensives. Up both banks of the Yangtze they are advancing slowly from Nanking west towards Wuhan. Their drive from the north has reached Zhengzhou, only 200 miles from Wuhan.

Those who walk the streets of London at least enjoy the illusion that their city is eternal, as do or did the citizens of Paris, Shanghai, Babylon, Persepolis, Balkh or Xanadu. Some cities – Rome, Constantinople, Damascus, Meshed, Hatra, Xian – actually are eternal.

But in Wuhan, before the barbarians arrive, we measure our city's life in months, days even.

Over the last few weeks I have become obsessed with one thing alone. Each day, as I wander along the Bund, I stare into the hideously mutilated face of the tiny beggar girl – the deep rips and gouges across her cheeks and mouth, the knife plunges into her eyes – who is coerced by the gangsters who mutilated her to cry ever more piteously to the crowds who pass her by: 'Look at me! Look at what these Japanese barbarians have done! Alms, I beg alms!'

How can anyone deliberately drag a knife across a tiny girl's face? Stab her tiny trusting eyes?

Of course, there is selfishness in my thoughts. She stands for what could have happened to my own tiny children. Cast out, abandoned by me. Defenceless in the world. My mother... My wife...

I turn off from the Bund and start to walk down a side street. It is at this point that I am seized by the secret police. A large black limousine hisses to a halt beside me, two burly young men, dressed in trench coats and dipped down fedoras – no cliche is left unobserved – spring out, grab me by the arms and in one fluid movement hoick me into its rear seat, climb in themselves, slam the door, rap twice on the dividing screen so the driver accelerates quickly away, and then sit heavily on either side of me. I do not even have time to say 'Oh.'

Pretty soon, though, I am reflecting on my situation.

'Who are you?' I ask.

No response.

'Are you police? Are you gangsters? Do you work for the government?'

No response.

The car melts through the streets – pedestrians, rickshaws, carts vanishing on either side of us – before we silkily draw to a halt beneath a vast building, oppressive and penitential in its appearance. I am bundled inside.

'Excuse me,' I say, desperately trying to maintain a scintilla of self-respect – 'but who are you, and what are you doing?'

I am bundled upstairs and into a small room in which a well-dressed man stares at me critically.

'He looks a total mess.'

'He's a writer, sir,' his assistant purrs.

'Haven't we got a halfway decent suit we can stick him into?'

A halfway decent suit is discovered and I am stuffed into it.

'And give him a shave.'

I am given a shave.

Thus en-wardrobed, I am pushed towards a large and rather grand-looking door.

'Look,' I say, starting to get seriously upset, 'will someone explain to me what the hell is going on?'

Me and the very well-dressed man are standing with our noses to the door.

'Just remember this,' he hisses at me, 'do not, do not in any way, not even remotely, do anything or say anything that might upset him. Do *not* upset him. Understood? Because if you do upset him, and he gets so upset he takes his false teeth out and throws them at you, then you are finished – understand me? – finished.'

Suddenly I understand who I am about to meet. I'd never given much credence to the rumours before, always dismissed them as too bizarre, but suddenly I realize they are true. I am about to be ushered into the presence of none other than the Chairman of the National Government of the Republic of China, the Supreme Commander-in-Chief of all the armed forces of the Republic of China, the Generalissimo *lui-même*, Mr Chiang Kai-shek!

Someone propels me from behind and we are suddenly in his presence.

'Good morning,' he says.

'Good morning,' I say.

'You are Mr Lao She,' he says.

'I am Mr Lao She,' I say.

There is a long silence.

'I don't know anything about plays,' he informs me, 'but my wife tells me that you are the best playwright in China.'

Now is not the time to quibble about being a novelist rather than a playwright. Besides, it's one in the eye for Gou Morou.

'I am a playwright,' I admit.

'Good,' he says.

Another long silence.

'The thing is, my wife, whose advice I greatly admire, has decided that it would be a good thing that a grand celebration and pageant sort of thing with speaking words and drama and lots of people marching around waving flags and shouting and singing with very moving and patriotic speeches and some dancing and laughter – a sort of entertainment thing but also a deadly serious piece entitled *Defend Wuhan!*, written by you – should be put on in front of thousands of citizens to improve the morale of the Chinese peoples. All right?'

I stare at him. I have literally been struck dumb.

'I said, is that all right?'

His face starts to discombobulate. His teeth work around inside his cheeks in a strangely sinister fashion. I suddenly remember the warning about his false teeth, their habit of escaping from his mouth, being violently propelled towards any object of his displeasure.

'Of course,' I almost shout. 'It is a brilliant, a wonderful idea. I will do it. I will immediately do it. I cannot wait to start doing it!'

Another long silence.

I clamp down on my own teeth, desperately hoping that their immobility will somehow placate his.

'Good,' he finally says, turning to his next business.

I disappear from the room.

Outside, excreted from the building and once more walking down the street as an average citizen (my halfway decent suit removed and my usual shabby attire restored), I ritually, methodically curse the name of Madame Chiang Kai-shek. I mean, I'm sure that in Britain, if Mr Neville Chamberlain the prime minister wishes to see Mrs Virginia Woolf to enquire of her if she would care to compose some popular all-singing all-dancing entertainment to bolster the morale of London's plucky East End cockneys, then he will not employ rough, surly men to snatch her off the pavements of Bloomsbury and bundle her post-haste into a back room in Downing Street.

But I live in China.

At the crowded bar of the Last Ditch Club the only topic of discussion was still Hitler's invasion of Austria. And where he was going to invade next.

First, to anchor themselves, they went through the long list of his and his fellow dictators' previous crimes.

'Manchuria in 1931, the Japanese invasion. That set the whole ball rolling.'

'Then there was Abyssinia in '35. That Italian bastard went and invaded.'

'Used mustard gas on the natives.'

'In '36 Adolf marches into the Rhineland. Do Britain, France, the League of Nations do anything?'

'Nothing.'

'And in the same year Franco invades Spain, overthrows the democratically elected government.'

'Britain and France look in the other direction.'

'And last year the fucking Japs go full banzai here in China. Twenty million dead.'

'Twenty million.'

The voices cataloguing this inventory of atrocities were not angry – despite the alcohol drunk – but rather weary and in despair.

Their anger only started to flicker when they started to read the *Times*'s apologia for Hitler's flattening of Austria.

Rewi Alley, the New Zealander, spoke first.

'The journalist who wrote this a disgrace. He leads with Hitler's triumphant arrival in Linz at the head of all his storm troopers. It's almost as though he's in love with all those blond, blue-eyed boys.'

'Flatulent bumboy!'

'No attempt to distance himself from them, objectify, give his readers some suggestion of what these thugs are getting up to in the backstreets – massacring socialists, gypsies, Jews.'

'It's not journalism, its propaganda.'

James Bertram, a young stringer for the *Telegraph*, took over the indictment.

'Then Hitler climbs out onto the balcony of some hotel in the marketplace and starts ranting on about blood and destiny and Aryan master races and the need to exterminate lesser races and beings – the full eugenics copy book – and the *Times* hack just scribbles it all down verbatim...'

'All the time creaming his pants.'

'...and the worst thing is *The Times* in London publishes it – verbatim. Not a single word of caution, reprimand, decency.'

'Hitler's just going to go on and on, isn't he,' stated Rewi Alley, 'and our leaders – Chamberlain, Daladier – aren't going to do a thing to stop him.'

'So where's the bastard going to invade next?'

'Czechoslovakia!' came the unanimous cry.

Only three people in the room – apart from the gloomy White Russian bartender – were uninvolved in this tribal denunciation. One was Jack Belden, who was still sleeping off his three bottles of bourbon. The second was the immaculately attired Old Etonian Peter Fleming, who sat in an armchair seemingly indifferent to it all. Surreptitiously, however, as the abuse of *The Times* (for which he wrote) heightened, he quietly folded away its airmail edition that he'd been reading and started perusing a dog-eared old copy of *Country Life*. The third silent individual was a rather nervous young English Quaker, fresh off the boat, named George Hogg. George had picked up a job as a 'stringer' with Reuters. He obviously had feelings about the discussion but did not dare enter it. Why, he wondered as a pacifist, were all his fellow journalists so keen on stopping this war in China, but couldn't wait to start a new one in Europe?

2

A prominent bow tie walked into the room followed by a man in a tweed suit. A very tall man with round tortoiseshell glasses. 'Gosh,' he said. He was carrying a shopping bag and was accompanied by Agnes Smedley, Wuhan's Patron Saint of Lost Causes. His shopping bag was filled with bicycle parts and he had a cheap Kodak camera slung round his neck. 'Gosh,' he said again, and took a quick snap of the table.

'I'd like you to meet Donald Hankey,' said Agnes, introducing him to the room, 'I found him wandering around on the Bund. He appeared to be lost.'

Spider Girl thought she had never seen anything so extra-ordinary in her life. She was particularly obsessed with his bow tie.

'Hello, Donald,' said Hu. 'Sit down.'

Donald sat his large frame down. Spider Girl continued to stare. She cuffed The Drab to keep her cutting the vegetables.

'And what are you doing in Wuhan?' asked the naturally polite Hu.

'Thought I ought to do my bit. See the enemy at close quarters, so to speak. So I came.'

'And what do you do?'

'I'm a surgeon.'

'A surgeon? What made you want to come here?'

'Gosh. Rather a long story,' said the naturally reticent Donald.

'Then tell us,' said Hu, smiling. 'In Wuhan conversation is our only enjoyment.'

Spider Girl brought him a bowl of tea and stayed by the table to hear his tale.

'Well, I'd just passed my finals at Barts and was tootling about London. I'd been thinking about coming out here to China – see the enemy at close quarters, so to speak – when who should I run into at some party at the Ritz but Bonkers Binkie, so I told him about my plan and he said "What a co-inky-dence! Pop's just given me this super aerothingy and I was thinking of flying it to China." So a couple of days later we took off to China – him in the front, me in the back – but we crashed just outside Paris. "Whoops," said Binkie, "pater's going to pop a piston." So that was air travel ruled out, so instead I hitched. Got to the Mediterranean, signed on as a stoker on some steamer. Lots of Chinese chaps shovelling with me so I soon picked up the lingo.'

'Your Chinese is very good,' said Hu, even though it was excruciating. Agnes had meanwhile drifted off to finish an article for the *Manchester Guardian*.

'Anyhow, it was very hot being a stoker in the Red Sea. And then we ran into a monsoon. But I was mainly worried that someone might steal my portmanteau, with all my surgical instruments in it. Vital for my work. But during the monsoon we ran into some rather rough weather and the captain's son was hit by some loose cargo in the hold. And it could have been serious for him, but I performed some emergency surgery and he was all right. The captain was very grateful to me and put my portmanteau and clothes chest in his own cabin, so that when we got to Shanghai he took me along to a junk captain he knew and in a rather rough manner told him to take me upriver to Wuhan and if he heard I'd been ill-treated in any way or had anything stolen he'd deal personally with the captain next time he saw him. So that's how I got here. A coolie's bringing my baggage up from the docks.'

He seemed relieved that his story was over and he could relapse into silence.

'Why is your shopping bag filled with bicycle parts and old bits of machinery?' demanded Spider Girl, still standing beside him.

'Oh,' said Donald, 'needs must, you know. When in Rome…'

'What's that mean?' asked Spider Girl.

'Well, in my training, I was always advised, if in foreign parts, to modify my surgery according to the technology of the country I was in. Well, since I got to China, I've seen an awful lot of bicycles.'

'Leave him alone,' ordered Agnes from next door, 'and make up a bed for him.' So Donald sipped his tea and ate some rice Spider Girl had prepared for him.

'You know,' he said to her, 'you have a bad condition of rickets – caused specifically by lack of vitamins and insufficient sunlight.' Unfortunately he didn't know the Chinese word for rickets and Spider Girl didn't know what 'rickets' was. So they just stared at each other. Spider Girl stared especially at his bow tie. What could it be? A religious object? A self-suicide mechanism? If you wound it up did the head fall off?

The next day, on her way to her own job, Hu showed Donald the way to the nearby hospital where he was to work. As he walked through the streets with his shopping bag, Donald continued to take random photos of random objects with his Kodak – holes in the ground, people with planks on their head, piles of abandoned ironmongery, the odd telegraph pole. Everything he saw fascinated him. 'Gosh,' he'd say, and snap away.

The hospital was a dingy building in an undistinguished street. Hu led him up its steps and into its main corridor. The first doorway on the right, without any discreet preliminaries, opened straight onto the main operating theatre. The floor was pitched in blood. Piles of assorted limbs lay stacked in every corner of the room. The wooden operating table at its centre was likewise covered in blood and had two young, wildly competitive Canadian doctors playing ping pong across it. The ball was stained bright red.

'Gotcha!'

'You ain't. At you!'

'Easy-peasy!'

'That? Huh! Result!'

'Jeez,' muttered the outwitted first doctor. 'We need more sawdust down.'

'Bad workmen...'

Suddenly Doctors Bob McClure, lead surgeon, and Dick Brown, second surgeon, became aware of Donald and Hu.

'Gee willikers,' said Bob.

'Who are you?' asked Dick.

'Name's Hankey, Donald Hankey,' said Donald, lumbering forwards and holding out a very large hand.

'A limey!' said Bob as they shook hands.

'Got any ping pong balls on you?' asked Dick.

'No, not actually.'

'Well, keep an eye out for 'em. They keep us sane.'

'And this is Hu,' added Donald.

'Hello,' said Hu.

She should have been getting on to her work but tarried because she found the place so fascinating.

'And what's your game, Donald?' asked Bob, who was agile and restless as a ferret.

'Rugby, I suppose,' replied Donald.

'No, I mean your trade?'

'Oh, er,' said the shy Hankey, 'I'm a surgeon, actually.'

'A surgeon!' said Bob.

'Indeed,' said Dick.

'Where did you graduate?'

'Barts, in fact.'

'Barts, indeed? Hey, fellas, we got a real live Barts guy here.'

He was addressing two young Indian trainee doctors sitting at a table by the far wall who were busy squabbling over some paperwork.

'Come over and meet Donald.'

The two Indians came over.

As they shook his hand the Indians did not look directly at him. There was a distinct chill to their greeting.

'This is Ahsan Bhattacharyya...'

'How do you do?'

'And Maninda Atwal.'

'How do you do.'

Ahsan and Maninda had every right to be reserved before this large and imposing Englishman. They were dark-skinned natives, members in India of the semi-banned Indian National Congress which was demanding independence from Britain. The chairman of the Congress, Jawaharlal Nehru, had sent these two, as a gesture of solidarity, to help out the Chinese, their fellow victims of imperialism. Following the Japanese invasion, the INC had immediately banned all its members from purchasing or dealing in any Japanese goods. This had seriously affected Britain's trade with Japan.

The English, as their colonial masters, were deeply suspicious of any INC members, especially if they were travelling abroad. So Bhattacharyya and Atwal had already experienced rough treatment and hostile interrogations from large red-faced English officials all the way from Bombay to Hong Kong.

The two quickly returned to their paperwork and resumed their argument. Almost immediately an ambulance bell rang outside.

'Customers,' shouted Bob.

'Bring on the bodies,' echoed Dick.

'Here we go!'

In seconds the room was transformed. A porter ran in and splashed a bucket of disinfectant all across the table and started vigorously scrubbing it. Two more attendants ran in with mops and brooms and started cleaning the floor. A series of nursing staff from the rooms nearby crowded in with sterilized needles and bone saws and scalpels and clamps and other operating paraphernalia.

'Better get your skates on, Donald,' advised Bob.

Donald hesitated a second, slightly flummoxed.

'Hand me your jacket, Donald,' ordered Hu, taking it and helping him roll up his sleeves. 'Shall I take your bow tie off?'

'No,' said Donald firmly. 'Helps me think.'

Five soldiers were stretchered in. Three had been shot in their legs, one in his arm. The fifth's left lung had been punctured by a bullet. He was set to one side, not expected to live.

Dick swiftly examined them.

'Four amputations,' he announced.

'Aren't those limbs saveable?' Donald asked Bob.

Ahsan started amputating the first leg – without anaesthetic – as two orderlies held the man down.

''Fraid not,' replied Bob. 'These guys are three or four days from the front. Some are already gangrenous, the others will get infected as soon as we open them up to try and set the splints across the bones.'

'But your instruments, splints are disinfected?'

'Yeah – though we'll be running out of disinfectant real soon. We're already clean out of formaldehyde. Had to resort to good old-fashioned brandy. Our biggest trouble is we can't get any proper sterilized splints. Amputations are their best chance.'

Bob and Dick's faces were drawn, their eyes starting to glaze. They'd been at the operating table for almost thirty hours. Most surgeons in such circumstances use amphetamines or booze to keep them going. Bob and Dick, being pious Methodists who had taken the pledge, relied on the power of prayer and vicious bouts of ping pong to keep going.

The limb was off, the table swiftly swilled with disinfectant and the next patient landed on its boards. Hu decided to leave, not because of the butchery – she'd had to treat wounded soldiers in even worse conditions on the Bund – but because she was by now very, very late for her work sifting the refugees as they arrived at the refugee camp.

The two trainees, Ahsan and Maninda conducted the remaining three amputations, with occasional quiet prompts from Bob, their surgical tutor. Dick, meanwhile, slept on a stretcher in the room next door.

The last patient, the one with the punctured lung, was hauled onto the table only for the doctors to discover he was already dead. He was about to be removed when Bob had an idea.

'Donald,' he said, 'how about a quick leg amputation? Have a looksee at your Barts skills.'

'Well,' said the ever-reticent Donald, 'I suppose I could.' He stepped nervously forwards and stood over his patient, briefly examined the leg, then with a few deft, decisive cuts severed the leg from the torso and neatly tied the arteries.

'Wow,' whistled Bob. 'Golly gee willikers!'

'Very good indeed,' murmured Ahsan Bhattacharyya.

'Most excellent,' echoed Maninda Atwal.

Bob clapped Donald on the back.

'Just to show that wasn't just limey luck, hows about his other peg?'

'If you insist,' said Donald.

'I do.'

'I'd rather be operating on live patients…'

'Don't worry. There are plenty more of them on the way.'

Donald went round the table to its other side, raised his arms, and excised the leg with the same sweet, effortless strokes.

'Praise the Lord!' said Bob.

A roar of diesel engines arrived outside, followed by a hubbub of noise. Three large lorries stuffed with wounded had just arrived and the patients, alive and screaming, were being carted into the theatre.

'OK, guys, skates on,' shouted Bob. 'And can someone get all these amputated limbs out the door. They're starting to stink the place out.'

The turnover rate on the table became intense. Bodies were hoicked up and then carried out, limbs again piling up on the floor. Screams, shouts, curses, swiftly swallowed bowls of tea, hurried instructions to nurses and orderlies, an occasional nutritious dumpling – hands having been washed before consumption. Puncture wounds, smashed femurs, broken limbs, head wounds, feet shot off. A complete charnel house. The floor was slippery with blood and had to be continually mopped. Two attendants were employed specially to swat the flies away. To begin with Bob led, with Maninda and Donald seconding him while Ahsan slept, but pretty soon Bob handed over the amputations to Donald – quick, deft slices and severances, neat tying of the arteries and veins lessening the pain – with Maninda and a reawoken Ahsan backing him up. Bob still led on wounds to the body and head.

Several times private patients, civilians, were slipped quickly in between the heavy traffic of wounded soldiers.

'A urovaginal fistula?' declared Donald enthusiastically. 'I love urovaginal fistulas! Can I do this one?'

'No,' said Dick. 'Go and sit down next door and take a few minutes' rest. You got another twenty hours ahead of you.'

The hours passed.

Several times as Donald swiftly examined the broken arms or legs of his patients before operating and amputating, he winced and hesitated. Finally Bob spoke to him.

'Donald, we're here to save lives, not limbs. If we had an afternoon, a half hour even, and the wound was clean and uninfected, then maybe you could do a proper splint insertion and we'd set the limb in casts and put them in traction. And even then most of the patients would die because our make-do splints are made of wood or steel and therefore infect the wound through either rotting or rusting and the limbs would still have to come off.'

'I know,' burst out Donald, 'but couldn't we get some proper stainless-steel splints?'

'Donald, the Orthopedic Frame Company of Kalamazoo, Michigan, which has a monopoly of such splints and sells them worldwide, charges two dollars a pop. We can't afford it – and besides, an order would take months to arrive. This is China. Lives before limbs.'

They returned to their work. More lorries arrived. Other casualties turned up in rickshaws or carried on people's backs. The frenzy was continuous. After a while Dick arose from his stretcher and Bob took his place. Ahsan and Maninda continued seconding Donald, since they'd only been working twenty-five hours so far.

But every time Donald came across a wound or a bone smashed in a limb which he knew he could have operated on and saved if he'd had proper equipment and conditions, he sighed. It caused him deep grief. As he worked amid the gore and the pain and the screams, he thought and he thought. He subconsciously tugged at his bow tie, getting it bloody.

Suddenly he had an idea. He looked towards the large shopping bag he'd brought with him. The large shopping bag filled with bicycle parts. Still carrying his scalpel, he hurried across and rummaged through it. Unfortunately it did not contain the parts he wanted.

I'll ask Spider Girl, he thought. Maybe she can pick some up down on the Bund.

3

I have a meeting to go to. A meeting I am really looking forward to. It is across the river from the university, at a tea house on the Bund.

On the way to the ferry I walk through my university campus. It is extraordinary how it has transformed. When you think of a university you think of hallowed groves of learning – silent libraries, scholars walking solemnly in long traditional robes down long corridors whispering erudite words to each other, paper scrolls of ancient learning tucked under their arm. Dust everywhere.

Now things are rather different. Loud, raucous, frenetic. Corridors crowded, jostling, people shouting out to each other, students running to their next class, discussions in crammed lecture halls breaking out into arguments, even fisticuffs in the passageways. Everyone has a point of view, everyone is desperate to find new truths, new knowledge, everyone *must* talk to everyone else.

All the time individuals and groups pour out from our campus. Expeditions set forth, one after another. Geography students are armed with theodolites, clinometers and compasses so they can accurately map out distant provinces where fighting might break out – and so our armies, using these highly accurate maps, can calculate the shortest and quickest routes our troops can march along to engage the enemy; so the roads our enemy use can be minutely studied for the best place to ambush them; so that our artillery can accurately bombard the enemy on the other side of a mountain without even seeing him.

Meanwhile groups of geology students are being despatched to those regions in the south-west we are most likely to hold on to so they can discover deposits of valuable metals, minerals, building materials. Coal, iron ore, limestone for steel, bauxite for aluminium, stone for constructing roads and railways and buildings.

Doctors and nurses, along with all available supplies and equipment, are being hurriedly despatched, trained or only partially trained, to the many fronts our troops are fighting on.

Engineers are being taught and deployed to build defences, bridges, weaponry, factories, hospitals, steel mills and airfields.

In the midst of death, everyone is very much alive.

Even our literature and drama department is crash coursing whole regiments of sensitive young poets and dramatists, turning them into blaring and totally unscrupulous brainwashing machines. They too march forth into the field.

Unscrupulous brainwashing machine I might be, but even I baulk at certain abominations. Such as the all-singing, all-marching, all-patriotic pileup entitled *Defend Wuhan!* which I am being forced to write for the delectation of General Chiang Kai-shek and his lovely lady wife. I ponder all this as my ferry chugs across the Yangtze towards Hankow.

Two weeks and I haven't had a single idea. A single tweak in my imagination. Popular culture? Popular culture! Popular culture?!? Why can't I write some unpopular culture? Something gentle, loving, about my wife and children and mother...

I step off the ferry and walk along the Bund towards my meeting. Only a few months ago this whole area was a towering necropolis of empty coffins and bodies being prepared for burial. All is changed. Money has changed hands, concepts explored. All the coffins serve the living before they serve the dead. A whole community has sprung up amid them. Coffins are used as ironing boards, cupboards, pantries. The big formal ones made of blackwood or camphor wood are used as temporary desks in temporary offices for lawyers and accountants and will writers, or as tables and chairs in cafes which serve passengers awaiting boats or rickshaw men and coolies taking a break. Whole families sleep in them, rolling them over on top of them as protection from the rain as they sleep. They are hired out during the day to anyone who needs a sleep, even to fornicators and worse. Mini-hotels. Apothecary shops have laid out counters of blue and white jars containing medicinal roots and herbs and seaweed and chalk and glass jars with snakes preserved in alcohol inside them or dried alligator skins. Dead ladybirds are considered efficacious for liver complaints; the alcohol drained from the dead snakes does wonders for your potency.

With deaths among the general population of Wuhan in decline, there is only one time when this now large community reverts to its roots. When there is an air raid. A bombing is immediately followed by a frenzied deconstruction of the community as coffins are sought en masse to be rushed to the stricken area. We Chinese like to be in the comfort of our coffins as soon as possible after our deaths.

As I emerge from the extraordinary integration and dis-integration, I notice a cinema to my left. It's running an old James Cagney musical – *Footlight Parade*. I'm not too fond of Cagney. Too wild haired, wild eyed for me. I prefer the softness and subtlety of Fred and Ginger. There's something so unassuming, so gentle about Fred, with Ginger effervescing away backwards before him, heels clacking, blond hair bobbing. And I love their emotional numbers, like 'Let's Face the Music and Dance'. Its loneliness, its dark desperation. With Europe in such danger, the Nazis marching, the two of them face the music – and dance!

Please excuse me – I'm being far too self-indulgent. I look again at the Cagney posters. Fred wouldn't be at all appropriate as my hero in *Defend Wuhan!* I need a fireball like Cagney, punching out haughty dames, rich tycoon types and the Japanese. A hero with swagger! A Chinese Cagney! Yangtze Doodle Dandy? Shanghai Li?

And of course we'd need some big Busby Berkeley-like numbers. Like that thundering finale to *42nd Street* with Ruby Keeler and Dick Powell tap dancing into the blackness of infinity.

The Yanks might be lousy at fighting fascism but they're great at putting on shows!

But then I start to doubt again. This is China. What I propose would be great in America, but who would understand it here? What Chinese person would like the aggressive dancing, the loud music, all the mugging and grimacing?

I am passing a puppet play with a crowd gathered tightly round it. What are they doing? What drama causes such 'oohs' and 'aahs?' I worm my way in. It's that old favourite, *Mulan Joins the Army*. What a shrewd choice by the manager! All about a young girl whose family is threatened by raiding nomads. Since there are no boys in the family she dresses as a soldier and volunteers. On the battlefield she is a brilliant warrior. All her comrades love her. None suspects she is a young girl. Together they drive out the Japanese – sorry, nomads – and then she returns to her farm as a pious daughter to serve her mother. What story could more deeply move the Chinese at this time? At this time of war? The play is at least two thousand years old!

It is so confusing being in Wuhan at the moment. Everything is a blur. All is changing. The people of Wuhan and I myself love the old, the familiar, the reassuring, but at the same moment we're starting to be seduced by, lured into the modern. Its movement, its endless restlessness – let's face it – its frenzy! Everyone loves the new for no other reason than that it's new. There's nothing more exciting than something new! A lamp stand, a cigarette holder, a light bulb, chewing gum. It's new! It's new! The second it's old everyone loses interest. Which do I choose – new or old? Which would my audience want to stir them and inspire them into fighting back against Japan? What is Wuhan? What is China?

I am almost at the tea house where I am due to meet my friend. I order my brain to remember in detail everything I've just been thinking – about Cagney, Busby Berkeley, *Mulan Joins the Army* – ancient vs modern – but like all writers I'm well aware of the holes which can suddenly appear in your brain the second you try to remember what you wanted to remember. OK, so I'll write it down with pencil and paper. Then I remember I've forgotten my pencil and paper. A writer must always remember to bring pencil and paper to write down what he wants to remember in case he forgets it. But in this case I've forgotten them.

I look around. A woman is selling onions on a stall beside me.

'Excuse me,' I say, 'I'm sorry to bother you, but could you briefly lend me some pencil and paper?'

'Of course,' she says. 'My boss has some.'

She picks them up off a back shelf and hands them to me, quite trusting I will return them. Ordinary people are so naturally helpful. She sees I need them, I'm not a thief, so she just hands them to me and lets me get on with the strange mysteries and rituals of writing on a piece of paper. She herself is clearly illiterate.

I finish my writing and pass her back the pencil, thanking her profusely. I feel immensely guilty that she has given me something for nothing and I cannot give anything in return. I buy a large bag of onions.

Jack Belden the American and Rewi Alley the New Zealander took the ferry across the Yangtze from the Bund to Wuchang on the south shore.

The tiny ferry steamed past the Western gunboats anchored in a line off the Bund, guns all pointed at the teaming onshore hordes.

Jack looked at the gunboats.

'What I can't figure,' he said, 'is the point of these fucking gunboats? Here they are, in Chinese waters, guns all pointing at the Chinese but never firing at them, and then a few hundred miles downstream in Shanghai there's an identical line of British and American and French gunboats, in Japanese waters, all pointing their guns at the Japanese but not firing at them. Pretty soon the Japs will take Wuhan and then they'll all be pointing their guns at the Japanese and not firing them. What's the fucking point of it?'

'Bloody obvious,' responded Rewi, pointing along the Bund. 'What's those bloody great buildings all along the waterfront?'

'Banks.'

'Banks. Western banks. That's what they're here to defend. All our governments care about is keeping our banks open. The

Japanese have killed, what, twenty million Chinese, but if the Japanese request a loan from one of these banks so they can slaughter even more – "Great! How much do you want?"'

'But what I can't figure,' continued Belden, 'is why? Why they're loaning the Japanese all this money so they buy steel and oil and chemicals to make arms, ammunition and poison gas? Can't the fucking banks, can't our fucking governments, see they're building a monster out here in Asia – just like in Europe, where they're financing the Nazis – which one day, pretty soon, will turn on us, devour us too?'

'Then the banks'll be able to finance our own war industries and armaments and make even bigger profits.'

'So, whether we live in democracies or dictatorships, the bankers are going to rule us forever?'

'That's what bankers think. But, whisper it, bankers are incredibly stupid, short-sighted, ill-informed creatures. They believe they shall rule us forever. They believe that the wolves can eat as many sheep as they want but that they will never develop a taste for fat, short-sighted bankers. And that even the sheep themselves might one day have had enough and start chomping their teeth.'

'Not with politicians like Chamberlain and Daladier around they won't.'

The ferry arrived in Wuchang.

The two had been invited by the Chinese government's press office to attend the site of a recent Japanese atrocity where the Japanese Imperial Army had used poison gas against Chinese troops and civilians. The attack had taken place about fifty miles east along the southern bank of the Yangtze River at Kiukiang.

The Japanese attack had not been entirely successful. They had fired chemical mortars and gas cylinders – containing mustard gas – into the Chinese lines and the village behind them. The gas was successful, killing many Chinese, but then suddenly the wind changed direction and the gas was driven billowing back into the faces of the advancing Japanese troops. It killed all of them too. The area where this atrocity had taken place was thus still in Chinese hands.

A smart young officer greeted them on the quayside and they drove off.

They passed through the familiar sights of an army in retreat. Civilians, carts, lorries, wounded soldiers walking, women and children.

They arrived at the village and the two men walked quietly amid the houses and surrounding fields. Corpses lay all over the place, strangely united in death. Japanese uniforms, Chinese uniforms, peasant smocks and shoes, tiny children with their playthings, ducks and pigs, even the odd rat and crow who'd turned up for a free bite. To die in a gas attack is particularly painful. Once the gas gets into your lungs you are stricken with fever and chills. Then you get a craving, a desperate thirst for water. Your throat is on fire. So you gulp it down, and as the liquid spreads through your body your face turns black and swells and bursts in pustules and blood pours from your mouth and nose and your lungs start fermenting and melting and the poison finally enters your bowels and guts so in your last agonies you squirm and writhe and give rictus grins which freeze in death.

Belden and Alley had both been on battlefields before so they were quiet, matter of fact and detached as they went round viewing the slaughter, noting down the details, searching for the correct words and phrases.

'Like to see *The New York Times* or the *Chicago Tribune* printing this,' murmured Jack.

Jobs done, the two returned to their car.

Rewi Alley was a short, straight-backed New Zealander. He sported a military moustache and black swept back hair. His liberal parents, of Scottish ancestry, named him after Rewi Maniapoto, the legendary Maori warrior who had fought back against the British invaders. In 1916 Rewi had volunteered for the Western Front and won the Military Medal. After the war he'd become a factory inspector in Shanghai and was so appalled by the conditions the mill workers were forced to work in he resigned and, with the help of several Chinese trade unions, had started organizing self-governing cooperatives where members could work in safe and sanitary conditions.

When the Japanese overran Shanghai, he and the cooperatives swiftly moved machinery, workforce and families upstream to Wuhan. Here in Wuhan, he worked with General Feng Yuxiang in funding and organizing further cooperatives and facilitating their movement upstream to Chungking.

Short of money, he also worked as a 'stringer' for various New Zealand and British papers.

Rewi sighed.

Jack passed him his flask of bourbon. Rewi drank from it.

Rewi sighed again.

'Got something to say?' enquired Jack.

Rewi paused.

A shadow passed over his face.

'I lost a brother, my older brother, in the Great War, in France. My parents have never recovered from it.

'You know why all we soldiers volunteered and set sail from New Zealand, on the other side of the world, travelled thousands of miles across the oceans to fight that bloody war in Europe?'

He paused.

'Because the bloody politicians told us, swore, it was the last war, the very last war, the war to end all wars. By fighting in this war, they promised us, we'd stop *all* future wars. Because when the war was won they, the politicians, would set up this League of Nations, a worldwide organization that would never allow another war. They swore it! Not one single war! Because any nation trying to start a war with any other nation would be immediately stopped by all the other nations, members of the League, sending all their troops and battleships to intervene and stop it. They told us this. The fucking governor general of fucking New Zealand himself stood on the verandah of our cricket pavilion in front of our whole school, lined up on the field, and fucking swore to our faces that the imperial British government in London had solemnly pledged that this is what would happen. The League of Nations would be set up. It was for this promise my brother died on the Western Front. It was for this promise millions of young men were butchered.

'Look at this slaughter here in China. Twenty million dead because our governments refused to allow the League of Nations to intervene. Intervene in Manchuria, in Abyssinia, in the Rhineland, in Spain, in China, in Austria…'

He paused.

'The thing I feel worst about, hurts me the most, is the shame, the bloody shame. That we have betrayed all those young men who laid down their lives fighting for a better world, for peace. All their families who have grieved their loss ever since. All the weak, defenceless nations we've allowed these fascists to devour.

'Above all – we've betrayed ourselves.'

There was a pause.

'Rewi?'

'Yeah?'

'How did your brother die?'

'In a bloody gas attack.'

I continue my stroll down the Bund, carrying my large bag of onions, and arrive at the tea house. My friend is sat outside. The sun has certainly got to him, his face is tanned. He looks fitter and healthier and more relaxed. Must be all that walking and fresh air. He looks about him, watching all the faces and people passing by him, then he sees me. His face breaks into a wide grin.

'Mr Lao,' he shouts.

'Tian Boqi,' I shout.

'It is so good to see you.'

'And you. You are looking so healthy.'

'All the walking, route marches. Putting up stages, taking them down, engaging in fierce sword fights, talking all hours of the night and day to all sorts of people.'

'And you are looking really happy. I am so glad.'

A shadow crosses his face.

'Compared to last time, you mean? My family?'

'No,' I hasten to tell him.

He thinks a second, then smiles.

'I love the countryside. And the people. The warmth, comradeship even more. And the going up into the mountains. They give me such strength.'

One piece of information I should give you before Tian Boqi and I get stuck into our conversation is that he is sporting a very prominent black eye. But I naturally ignore this. I order tea for us both – he might have more-than-full-time work but he is still paid virtually nothing. I put my bag of onions on the table, we sit down, and I demand to hear his story.

'Well, first we returned to the village where we had our disgraceful first show. We apologized over and over to the villagers for what we'd done and then talked a lot with them about drama. We told them of various ideas, they had their own ideas, so we worked on them together with the villagers and then played them out in front of the whole village. They had their comments and suggestions which we tried to incorporate – if they were practical – into the plays. People would come up to us and say – "He wouldn't say that in that circumstance. That sounds daft. You should have that woman saying it. She'd be much funnier." And we'd do it. And of course everywhere we travelled we heard: "We have to have more swords. We must have to have more fights. And more romances. Lots and lots of sighing and suffering!" Four or five villagers joined us in the troupe – a couple as actors, one as a writer (though technically he couldn't write, I wrote down his dialogue – which was incredibly good – and of course he always got the dialect dead right) and the other two using their carpentry skills to build our stages and sets.'

Sometimes it's difficult to follow Tian as he's speaking at such a gallop. He asks me what had happened to all those orphan children who had put on that extraordinary play that day?

I smile. 'They came back with us to the university and started to work with my colleague Lao Xiang on the play they were performing, then on other plays he wrote for them, and some which they wrote for themselves.'

'And they're off touring?'

'Yes. In a way. They were put into the government's orphans programme. But because they were already such a strong group, a family almost under their young leader Su, it was decided not to split them up but instead to give them an "aunty" and then send them all upstream to Chungking so they could start to work with all the other orphans there, helping them with their problems and fears, touring out into the countryside. I decided to put Chang Lee in charge of them. The student in your group who walked all the way from Shanghai?'

'I remember him,' says Tian.

'He is quite childish in his way. And he relates to children very well. Has their fantasies, knows how to express their feelings, their thoughts.'

Suddenly Tian Boqi is serious.

'I am such a horrible man,' he says. 'I treated him so badly, mocked him and bullied him. I was so stupid.'

'And you have learnt how not to be stupid. We have all had to learn how not to be stupid. Except the rich and powerful. You remember the little girl, the silent one, Lim From The Forest? The one who went from person to person in the audience, staring at them and trying to see her parents in them?'

'I still have nightmares about her.'

'She's started talking again. Only a little bit. She'll only talk within the group, to those she knows and trusts. But a doctor I spoke to is sure she'll change. That she'll soon be a non-stop chatterbox. And she's stopped looking for her family everywhere.'

Our tea and sweet dumplings have arrived. I'd ordered a double portion because Tian Boqi is looking quite gaunt. I still do not mention his black eye.

'So tell us about how you work in the countryside, sort out your plays?'

'Well, as we learn we adapt. We've developed different kinds of drama for different situations. There's a lot of sharp minds in our group.

'If there's a tea house in the village we warn them ahead of time, then we enter the tea house as customers, start mixing with the villagers, performing our prearranged play in a way that involves interacting with all the villagers, bits of comedy, bits of anger, improvising lines and actions, leaving them intrigued because they can't decide which bits are real, which are fantasy. We do slapstick (always clearing up afterwards), information bits, bits of traditional theatre while we're there drinking their tea.

Generally the audiences love it. If people are put off or scared we explain to them what is happening and once they understand they start joining in themselves.

'We do the same sort of improvised stuff in the streets. Sometimes, when a village festival is on, we – with the villagers' permission – take part in the procession, distributing propaganda leaflets, making the people laugh, then we put on a proper play on our stage. One of the problems is that in many places people know that there is a war on, are terrified of it, but don't have any idea what it's about. So we put on a play about when the Japanese first attacked us at Marco Polo Bridge, or one celebrating Taierzhuang or the communists' victory at Pingxingguan. People are very moved to see that we are fighting back. Even winning. It makes them want to join in. On other days and nights we do great patriotic plays from the legends and histories of China. You'd enjoy them,' he says, grinning at me.

I laugh back. It is wonderful to watch his enthusiasm.

'On occasions, if something important has happened in the war, like Taierzhuang, we work up an overnight improvisation on it to inform people about it immediately.

'And all the time we're travelling. On and on and on. Some of our audiences want to put on their own plays, pass the message on to other nearby villages we haven't been to. So we leave one of us behind to help them prepare it, then let them stand on their own two feet. We do some literacy work, especially among children, so they can go back to their parents and start teaching them how to read and write.

'And we travel so much – through beautiful country, amid all sorts of different cultures and peoples. In some areas people are prosperous, in other areas, especially in the mountains, with villages and terraces clinging to the mountainside, we pass through places where women will never leave their own homes because they're too poor to afford clothing.

'We do plays encouraging villages to set up their own committees and start trying to cooperate, govern themselves. We discovered that that was already happening in many places spontaneously. In Nationalist areas Chiang Kai-shek's officials and politicians would often be hostile to this. In the Communist areas they try to make them tow the party line. But the best places are behind the enemy lines.'

I was shocked. 'You've been behind enemy lines?'

'The Japanese have taken over vast areas. Far too large for their troops to properly control. In many places the lines between the Japanese and the Chinese are extremely fluid. Those areas, those villages and communities, are the best places to be. They're wonderful. The peasants have simply taken over. They run the landlords out and take over the government. They're organizing the resistance. And they're so knowledgeable. All the little details and jokes we put in our plays they get. And they suggest new ones.

'Everything is working fine, but then Nationalist agents and officials turn up. "You can't put stuff like that on. Say things like that. Be disrespectful to our great leaders." And the villagers simply stand up and throw them out. Some of the officials sneak back and watch the shows because they agree with them. And the communists are just as funny. They start to tell everyone what to do in these solemn Marxist voices and the villagers simply start to argue back, saying "That won't work. That's nonsense. If you want people organizing themselves effectively you've got to allow this and that and this." And when the Eighth Route Army turns up – the communist soldiers – the peasants have already worked out the best way of defeating the Japanese in their area, the best places to waylay and ambush them, the best ways to confuse and terrorize them. Because they know their own countryside, every hollow and copse and cave, and the soldiers don't. So the soldiers – the revolutionary vanguard – have to follow the orders of village peasants. It's wonderful!'

We both laugh. Seeing him makes me so happy. Seeing his metamorphosis.

Tian Boqi has come to Wuhan for three days so he can advise and train our current students on how to put on the most effective propaganda in the towns and villages. I can think of no one more inspiring to encourage and steer them.

I make a passing reference to his black eye. He grins.

'The perils of acting! In one town we were doing some

improvised street theatre. I was playing this villainous money lender. Playing it very well. Too well, in fact. This farmer comes round the corner, doesn't realize a play is going on, listens to all my foul deeds and love of other people's gold and wives, and promptly punches me straight in the face. One must suffer for one's art!'

'It's a credit to your acting,' I say. 'And it gives you a certain air of derring-do! You look a bit like Errol Flynn in one of his pirate movies.'

'My acting is a bit forceful,' agrees Tian. 'It's true, I do like to play villains.'

We finish our food and part. Since he is obviously living in straightened circumstances and has little to eat I offer him the only thing I have that might help him, my bag of onions. He gratefully accepts them.

What neither of us realizes, as we have sat there talking and laughing, is that, not six feet away, someone has been sitting at a nearby table and noting down every exact word we have spoken.

Before long I will be sitting somewhere else, listening and sweating while someone reads back to me every single word of our conversation.

'Why does Donald want these bicycle parts?' asked Spider Girl.

'Not sure,' replied Hu. 'It's to do with his surgery.'

'That's cutting people up?'

'That's cutting people up to make them whole again.'

'I want to come and see him cutting these people up and making them better. Sounds like a butcher's stall.'

'I'm sure you can come,' said Hu.

Spider Girl and Hu were pushing their way through the crowds on the Bund.

'He's a very strange man, Donald.'

'He seems a very nice man to me,' said Hu.

'He is very nice. But he is also strange. With his bow tie.'

'That is just a piece of dressing. Which Europeans wear.'

'That is maybe what they tell us. I was washing it last night.

It was covered in blood. I thought it could have many powerful magical spells woven into it. He looks so strong when he wears it.'

'Donald Hankey is not a magician.'

'Of course he is not. He is trying to save people's lives. And he needs great strength to do that. Which is why he wears his bow tie.'

Hu could see this conversation was going nowhere and so shut up. They pressed on through the Bund.

The Bund is an aggregation, a concretion, a huge amassal of created things. Vegetables, fruit, bowls, salt, spices, flowers, musical instruments, shoes, hats, chairs, barbers, mattresses, coffins, small machines (sometimes large machines), clothing, dead meat, live meat, entertainments, witches who could curse anyone you wanted them to curse, astrologers who could foretell the future, bedding and chamber pots and inkpots. All in their different ways created, made.

But it was also a mass assemblage of unmade things. Things dismantled, torn apart, disaggregated back into their constituent parts and pieces. These too could provide money and income by being traded with people who did not want the whole object but only one part of it. On sale in this area of the Bund were machine parts, clock parts, typewriter bits, wagon and rickshaw and motor car and cinema projector and electrical bits, wooden legs and arms and fingers and teeth. It was also an area which sold lots of worn-out tat and clothing and holey shoes and well-into-rottenness fruit and vegetables and meats. There is money to be made as much in de-creation and decomposition as in creation and aggregation.

It was into this graveyard of once complete aggregations that Spider Girl and Hu pushed in search of Donald Hankey's requested bicycle segments. Neither of them had ever visited this bit of the Bund before. All sorts of parts and offcuts and remnants were on sale.

'There!'

Quick-eyed Spider Girl had spotted it. A necropolis of dead, disincorporated bicycles. Once noble cycles split apart, butchered up, rendered into their meanest, tiniest parts. All lying in piles and mounds.

'And there's the parts he wants,' said Hu.

A bucket full of them stood like a quiver full of porcupine quills.

Hundreds of them.

Spider Girl looked at the proprietor, who returned her gaze. He was dirty, dodgy and devious. She licked her lips.

'How many does he want?'

'Fifty at least. But for what God alone knows.'

I do this for you, noble surgeon, thought Spider Girl. She eased into her haggle.

Donald nervously fiddled with his bow tie and set his large shopping basket down on the operating floor.

Hu had accompanied him to the hospital, partly to ensure he did not get lost, but also because she was becoming more and more fascinated by the work being done there. The deftness and expertise of the surgeons, the lives they saved, their dedication and sheer indefatigability. She also tarried there, of course, because she was fascinated by what Donald was actually going to do with the bits of bicycle she and Spider Girl had purchased.

Bob McClure was in conference with Ahsan Bhattacharyya and Maninda Atwal. Dick Brown had disappeared for food. Donald waited til the conference was over and then approached Bob.

'Hello,' he said.

'Howdy, Donald,' said Bob, 'what can I do you for?'

'Just wondering, and I don't want to be a pain, but if, later, we should happen to have a lull in the number of patients…?'

'Yes?'

'Well, I was wondering if I could try out a few tests on a broken-femur patient – if one should present and nothing else was going on. I swear it will be nothing in any way hazardous.'

Bob looked at him with a squint.

'Is this more of your saving limbs crusade, Donald?'

'Sort of. I think I have a solution. I've thought of something we could use as a splint which won't infect the patients. Do you have any traction equipment?'

'We have one set. It happens to be unused at the moment. The patient left last night.'

'And plaster?'

'We have plaster.'

Bob's squint was getting ever more gimlet.

'Then, if we have the time, and it should only take a few minutes, and if we have a suitable patient, I would like to attempt an operation to save their leg without infecting the wound.'

Bob thought.

'Well, *if* we have the time – and that's a big if – but *if* we have the time, yes, you can do it. We'd be very interested. And we can always have the leg off if it doesn't work.'

Donald sighed with relief. His newly washed and ironed bow tie positively glowed.

Late that afternoon a lull did occur. Donald's operation was possible. There were no more patients and they'd held back one, a young soldier, with a broken femur.

As he was being lifted onto the table Donald approached Hu, who was standing in a corner of the room to watch.

'I say, Hu, couldn't help me out in this operation, could you?'

'I don't have any skills, Donald.'

'That doesn't matter. I'll just need you to hand me some things while its going on.'

'All right.'

'First, go into the next-door room, roll up your sleeves and wash your hands and arms thoroughly.'

'Yes.'

'Then, by the sterilizing equipment you'll find a tray covered with a clean cloth. Just bring it in here to the operating table. You will stand by me during the operation and, when I ask you, just lift up the cloth and pass me one of the splints. OK?'

'OK.'

Hu went into the room next door, carefully picked up the tray, and brought it back into the operating theatre. The patient lay on a wooden board on top of the operating table. He had been quietened with brandy. Two strong orderlies pinned him by his shoulders, another held his unwounded leg. Hu stood beside Donald with her tray. The other surgeons stood behind her and on the other side of the patient.

Donald did two swift incisions to the soldier's upper leg – one above the break in the femur, the other below. He then delicately cut away the broken flesh between the two cuts, revealing the broken bone. He took a small surgical drill and drilled two small holes into the bone, one a few inches above the break, the other the same distance below. The patient tried to squirm. A strong nurse stopped him doing this by pinioning down his hips.

Donald moved away and carefully washed his hands in a bowl. He stepped back.

'A splint please, Hu.'

Hu lifted the cloth. Beneath it lay a whole array of bicycle spokes. She handed one to Donald.

'Bicycle spokes!' exclaimed Bob.

'Bicycle spokes?' asked Dick. 'They're made of steel. They'll rust and infect the patient just like any other splint.'

'They're not made from ordinary steel, Dick,' said Donald. 'In China, for some reason or other, they make bicycle spokes out of stainless steel.'

'*Stainless* steel?' said Bob.

'Stainless steel doesn't rust,' said Maninda.

'I noticed it,' said Donald, 'when I was taking a snap of a bike someone had parked on the Bund. It's always jolly important to observe things at close quarters,' he added, giving his bow tie a quick preen.

'Get on with the operation, Donald,' said Bob.

Donald held the spoke against the bone, measuring the distance between the two drill holes and, having calculated a slightly shorter length for when the bone had been reset, cut off the requisite length with some sterilized pliers which Hu handed him from the tray. Then, having bent back the two ends of the spoke with the pliers, he placed the crimp of one end of the spoke into the drilled hole above the break – it fitted perfectly – then gently manoeuvred the lower leg so that the two ends of the broken leg reformed and then popped the second crimp into the second hole. The two ends held. The bone was now aligned correctly, pinioned securely, and ready to start the slow process of re-forming.

Donald quickly swabbed the wound with a chloride solution and then sewed up the flesh he'd cut through, except he left a small hole over the break where the bone could be inspected and disinfected. He closed the hole with a swab dipped in chloride solution. Donald nodded and the patient was carried out for plastering and traction.

Bob looked at Donald for a long time. Then he spoke.

'Okelly-dokelly. The procedure works. We've got enough plaster and chloride solution and we got splints by the million. But – how do we get hold of sufficient traction units? There's the problem.'

Everyone turned and gazed at the bike Bob had ridden in on. He'd left it leaning against a wall in the operating theatre. All had suddenly become seized by a sudden faith in the humble bicycle's ability to solve all their surgical problems. What other miraculous singularities might it be imbued with?

'When I was very young,' said Ahsan, 'we used to go and visit our uncle in the countryside. I remember there was a man who came quite regularly on his bicycle. He was a knife grinder. When he got to the village all the wives would bring their kitchen knives out for him to sharpen. He would turn his bicycle upside down so it rested on its saddle and handlebars, then he unhooked its chain, detached its rear wheel, and then in its place put a circular grindstone. He reattached the chain and then, turning the pedal so that the grindstone spun round, he sharpened their knives on the whirling grindstone.'

Everyone approached Bob's unfortunate bike and turned it upside down. They then all stared at it. They studied it from various angles. Every so often someone would turn the pedals. They all reached a unanimous decision.

'Wowzer!' said Dick.

'But you're not using my bike,' stated Bob.

* * *

Spider Girl never had any doubt that Donald's operation would succeed. Not that she had any idea what an operation was. But Donald, she knew, was a man who would always succeed in life. And she admired him for that.

So that morning on the Bund, after she'd found and purchased Donald's bicycle spokes and Hu had left for her work, Spider Girl set off for the area of the market where the vegetables were sold. She was after one particular one. She was going to cook Donald a very special meal to celebrate his success. She searched out the vegetable very carefully – spring chives. She found four stalls selling them. She touched the spiked green stems very gently. Then she asked each stall holder the same question.

'When were these chives last rained on?'

The first three said something like 'last week' or 'I don't know'. Only the fourth one answered correctly. 'Last night.' She took a large handful.

Her mother had always told her that chives which had been rained on the night before tasted the most sweet and the most succulent. She also purchased some expensive rice and various special spices – all from her own savings.

She got home and started to prepare the meal for Donald all by herself and then cook it. The Drab for once had no work to do so sat down. To pass the time she started crooning. She was a very bad crooner. Every so often Spider Girl had to cuff her to shut her up.

It took a lot of slow cooking and delicate stirring and gradual commingling of the various spices and condiments and culminated finally with the stirring in of the chives.

It had to be eaten right now. Spider Girl had timed it for nine o'clock exactly because by then everyone had usually returned from their work. But no one had turned up. The dish had to be eaten within ten minutes of it having been cooked. Spider Girl's mother had always been adamant about this: if you don't eat it in ten minutes it loses all its flavour and succulence. Her family always did this and it was always followed by much smacking of lips and heartfelt burpings.

Ten minutes passed. Half an hour. The Drab started crooning

and stopped abruptly. Eventually, two hours later, Hu came in. She looked at Spider Girl.

'What's the matter?' she asked.

'I cooked this meal. This lovely meal for Donald. To celebrate his successful operation. It had chives in it which had been rained on last night…'

'Ah, my mother always said they tasted best.'

'…and no one turned up. The meal's ruined.'

'I dropped in on them. They're all busy arguing about bicycles.' Hu got out a piece of paper with a list on it. 'And they want you to buy a whole lot more bicycle parts at the market tomorrow.'

Spider Girl looked upset.

'Come on, Spider Girl,' said Hu. 'I'd really like to eat it. I'm sure it's wonderful. I used to love it when my mother cooked it for me when I was back home.'

So they all sat down at the table – including for the first time The Drab – and silently ate Spider Girl's excellent celebration meal.

4

It was mid-August. The heat was awesome. It pounded down from the skies. It thundered up from the earth, and sideways off the buildings. Human beings tried to survive betwixt and between.

Wuhan needed a new aerodrome – partly as a place to base fighter planes to defend the city from the almost continuous Japanese bombing, but it was also to be used as a civilian airport, a place where vital spare parts and machinery and weaponry could be flown in, and a place from which important civilian and military officials could be flown out. The fact that it would be in Japanese hands in three months was neither here nor there. It had to be done now!

American military contractors estimated that, employing all their heavy earth-moving machinery, it would take them one month to complete. The Chinese needed it in a week.

The aerodrome was to be built on ground raised above the paddy fields to the east of Hankou. Paddy fields filled with thousands of naked peasants harvesting and planting their rice.

The Chinese brought in 40,000 coolies.

They drained the chosen area. They shovelled and slopped out the worst of the silt and mud into panniers and baskets which were hoisted onto the backs and shoulders of black-clad Hakka women who set off in their crownless straw hats across the plains like busy columns of ants to dump the mud and fill their baskets with stony and flinty clay (dug out by more coolies) and then procession in black lines back to the aerodrome where the original coolies first dammed up the outer perimeter of the excavation with the clay to prevent the mud and water from morassing back in and then pounded it into the floor of the vast hole so that the water could not ooze back up. Horses, mules, camels and yaks were also used in this enormous operation, filling in the hole with the clay until it rested three yards above the surrounding rice paddies.

Then began the levelling, the pounding down. With thousands of trampling feet to begin with – including the hooves and pads of camels and horses and yaks and mules – and then with wooden hand paddles and bamboo tampers with flat stones lashed to their base. In the dust clouds row after row of coolies and black-clad Hakka women stamped and thumped and chanted. Finally a great grass roller, purloined from the English Cricket Club (whites only, with the occasional Pathan thrown in to float unfathomable googlies!), was brought in and dragged endlessly back and forth. All the time levelling out was being carried on, new loads of soil were being judiciously added and then in turn pounded down until at last it stood alone and, while far from perfect, presented a sufficiently flat and firm surface for even the heaviest approaching aircraft to land on. Which they started to do, amid clouds of swirling dust, immediately.

The whole operation had taken only ten days (and nights) to complete. So much for American know-how and heavy machinery! The Chinese calculated that it would survive two or three months of heavy usage, but that the rains of late autumn and winter would destroy it, rendering it unusable for the Japanese.

Within hours two squadrons of brand-new Soviet I-16 fighter aircraft were smartly lined up on the apron ready to scramble. They were manned by Chinese pilots and Russian 'volunteers'. American Vultee transports and passenger planes were coming in and taking off with Chinese and American pilots.

Among the first passenger planes to land was the daily flight from Hong Kong. Passengers on Imperial Airways could now fly from London, by way of Penang, to Hong Kong, and then take the short local flight on to Wuhan. The whole journey took only eight days.

The de Havilland DH-86 Dorado landed and taxied towards the awaiting officials, friends, rickshaw drivers and a small ambulance (a gift from the Chinese Laundryman's Association of

New York and commandeered to carry Very Important Persons directly into the city). No airport buildings had yet been built – nor indeed ever would be. There was a tent for the aircrews. The de Havilland's four engines arrived, churning up thick clouds of dust which immediately engulfed both plane and those awaiting it.

Freda Utley, an English reporter working for the *News Chronicle*, emerged with a handkerchief clamped to her face. The dust was not only thick but filled with dried particles of yak, camel and human excrement. It stank. Bewildered and disorientated, with her glasses too dirty to see through, Freda stumbled into the maelstrom.

Freda was a woman in conflict. She did not know where she was going. She did not know who she was. Her life had been and was disastrous. She'd only come to Wuhan because Agnes had assured her that it was a fascinating place, that all sorts of interesting things were going on there, and that uniquely in the world the country was standing up to fascism.

Agnes appeared out of the dust.

'Freda, hi.'

'Agnes,' Freda spluttered, 'oh my goodness.'

'Have a good flight?' asked Agnes.

'It was a nightmare. I haven't slept for eight days. I really need a bath.'

'Good luck with that,' said Agnes, leading Freda towards a rickshaw she'd booked. Agnes did not believe in pandering to the complaints of soft Westerners. China was China.

Spider Girl was having quite a difficult day. Not only did she have to buy and cook food for an ever-increasing colony of people who'd set up home in Agnes's apartment, but following Donald's request for more bicycle parts – not only more stainless steel spokes but now whole bicycle frames and chains and pedals and even brake cables to be used in constructing the traction frames – she had to haggle at even greater length with the scrapyard merchant and then organize the transport of all the various bicycle parts to the hospital.

Agnes had helped her out by quickly persuading the informal rickshaw drivers' collective she'd set up to ferry wounded soldiers to the hospital to also pick up all the bicycle parts Spider Girl had haggled for from the market and carry them to a new workshop that the hospital had rented nearby where the traction frames and pulleys and wires were to be constructed. Hu helped out too by speaking to General Feng Yuxiang and getting him to send two welders and some mechanics from one of his collectives to start assembling the traction units.

Then, just as Spider Girl was at last about to start cooking the meal – it would have to be hurried – this bizarre foreign lady suddenly turned up and started demanding that she get her a bathtub and some hot water for her to bathe in! She'd been in an aeroplane for eight days! Chop chop! What an extraordinary request, thought Spider Girl. Who would waste their money in Wuhan buying water to bathe in? Buying water fit to drink was expensive enough.

When Spider Girl appeared recalcitrant, Freda, who spoke awful Chinese, started making a scene. Agnes came out of her room, where she'd been writing chapter five of her new book, *Battle Hymn of China*, and calmed her down. Freda started sobbing and then explaining she was tired out, and this whole city smelt and was dirty, and why was this servant girl refusing to do what she told her to do and, as this same servant girl was about to start preparing their meal, why were her hands black with grease and oil and mud?

Spider Girl, though the conversation between Freda and Agnes was being conducted in a foreign language, stood there arms akimbo, staring at this bizarre foreign creature. Every so, often she cuffed The Drab just to relieve her feelings. She had never witnessed such a performance in her life. A grown woman in public behaving and carrying on like a tiny child. Where was her dignity, her self-respect, her self-control? Even Agnes seemed to be getting a bit short with her.

'All I want,' said Freda, 'is a bath. A nice warm bath. That'll settle me, calm me down.'

A silence followed. Agnes wanted positive journalists to write

positive stories out of Wuhan. Freda's readers in the liberal British
News Chronicle were precisely the people in the West that had to
be reached if China was ever going to be helped. As always it was
going to have to be the working classes that carried the burden.

'Spider Girl, get Freda here a bath – I don't care from where –
and warm water to fill it!'

Spider Girl stared at her. Agnes was standing a little behind
Freda and opened her hands, signalling to Spider Girl that she'd
appreciate her cooperation.

'Very well, Agnes,' said Spider Girl, 'for you,' and stumped off.

As she was walking – her hips and upper legs were killing her
– down to the Bund, again, Spider Girl reflected that this woman
was behaving as people said all Westerners behave – arrogantly,
selfishly, unfeelingly. But then she remembered that Agnes and
even more Donald were Westerners, and neither of them would
ever think of behaving like that.

By early evening a disgruntled Spider Girl had through her
contacts managed to appropriate a bathtub and sufficient water for
Freda to take her bath in and emerge fragrant and newborn from.
But the time needed to procure a bathtub and sufficient water for
Freda meant Spider Girl had no time left to cook the meal. The
Drab could cut vegetables but nothing else. Agnes had to abandon
chapter five of the *Battle Hymn of China*[10] and fangle up a meal.

Agnes, fag hanging from her lower lip, was not a natural cook.
In fact she wasn't really interested in food at all. She was quite
happy eating the iron rations that the many armies she'd marched
with had relied on. So the meal, when it eventually emerged, was
lumpy and only partly digestible.

Neither Hu nor Donald were there – they were both at the
hospital – so while she and Freda worked their slow way through
the meal, with Spider Girl muttering from the stove and cuffing
The Drab, Agnes tried to explain to Freda how one treated servants
in Wuhan.

'It's not the same in Wuhan as it is in most other places, Freda.
Here everyone is involved in the war effort – servants as well as

their employers. So service is not always guaranteed. Sometimes the servant is busy doing other, more important things. We're all fighting for survival.'

'I know, Agnes. I really know. But the thing is – perhaps it's the way I was brought up – but I do insist that servants must be clean. There's something deep within me that recoils when I see a dirty servant. I mean, when I was growing up our servants were always immaculately clean. My mother insisted on it.'

Agnes sighed. Spider Girl had spent half a day lugging around oily bicycle parts and the rest of it extracting Freda's bath from under a pile of scrap.

'You see,' continued Freda blithely, 'I've really been in the midst of all sorts of unpleasantness since I saw you last. My life is in turmoil, and it's taking me a bit of time to adjust.'

Agnes looked at her without too much patience and was about to say something sharp when mercifully, just as they were about to eat, a bicycle courier rushed in with a message from the Chinese Ministry of Information, saying the Chinese Minister of Information, the Honourable Hollington Tong, was about to hold a news conference where an important announcement was due to be made.

'Oh good,' said Freda. 'A government press conference. Gives me a chance to get a sense of the place.'

'The Chinese Ministry of Information will be the last place to get a sense of China,' replied Agnes. And then remembered Taierzhuang. 'Well, we'd better go,' she conceded, 'they do occasionally have interesting stuff.'

They departed, leaving Spider Girl.

Spider Girl carried the uneaten food back to the stove and started to cook it once more – this time slowly, properly, for her and The Drab. As she did so she had a thought. All that water she had had to buy out of the household budget for Freda was still in the bath. There was no commodity in Wuhan more expensive and more scarce than relatively clean water. Relatively safe water you could drink with some confidence that it would not poison you or infect you with dysentery or gastroenteritis. Typhoid even. Poor people could not afford to be too fussy about what they drank.

Spider Girl waddled to the bath and tasted Freda's bath water. It had quite a bouquet from the expensive Parisian soap Freda had been using. Spider Girl calculated she could sell it as European water. The secret water that Europeans drink to stay so much more fit and healthy than their Chinese counterparts.

And she knew where she could find a whole lot of empty bottles.

Agnes had not had enough money recently to pay her any wages – though, as Agnes's slave, she did not in fact have to pay Spider Girl any wages at all. But Spider Girl did not begrudge her this. She knew Agnes had been spending a lot of her money recently buying medical supplies for wounded soldiers on the Bund. Spider Girl thought this good and honourable behaviour. Besides, her own father was a serving soldier who she prayed for continually. But Spider Girl was herself in need of money. She was addicted to lurid Shanghai detective novels and the bookseller on the Bund was by now starting to suspect she stole books from him; his attentiveness whenever she picked up a book meant she now had to pay to read the latest thrilling and bloody adventures of Detective Wang, his glamorous (and dangerous) assistant the beautiful Liu Jingfei, and their supernatural and implacable enemy, the Ghost of the Evil Englishman.

Perhaps, she thought, with all this wheeling and dealing over bicycle parts, she herself might be able to make some money on the side.

5

I take my wife's scarf from its drawer in my cabinet. Slowly unfold it. Then hold its softness, its gentleness to my face. My head, my lungs, my whole body fills with the warmth and fragrance of my wife, my family.

And then, as I have taught myself, I fold it up again, place it gently back in its drawer, and shut my cabinet.

That is all the emotion I allow myself.

Although I usually return to my room to work, this morning I walk outside into the courtyard and the sunshine and sit on a bench set beneath the leafy canopy of the red persimmon tree. Its fruit, still small and green, slowly grows and ripens on its branches. I instruct myself to think about my play, *Defend Wuhan*, commissioned by our illustrious and worthy leader General Chiang Kai-shek. The difficulty is that the Generalissimo, as a commissioner of the arts, is hardly in the league of the Qianlong emperor or even Lorenzo the Magnificent. His commission to me was neither clear nor coherent.

I have two meetings today. The second is in the late morning with a government minister, the Minister for Education. It is a purely formal meeting – so that our part of the government machine can let his part of the government machine know what we are doing. I will also try to get from him some funding so that we can start organizing patriotic plays in our nation's schools. My first meeting is much more enjoyable. Tian Boqi has spent his three days coaching and advising and rousing our latest batch of agitprop students before they go out into the field. We are meeting here beneath the red persimmon tree so I can thank him for his work, wish him luck as he returns to the field, and, more deviously, pick his brains for any tips or help he can offer on writing my *Defend Wuhan!* masterpiece.

He approaches, we greet each other with delight (and emotion), sit down, pass through the formalities before getting down to the nitty gritty – *Defend Wuhan!* I explain the unorthodox commissioning process.

'Keep it simple,' he advises. 'It'll be about what all our stories are about. Average person, good clean-living bloke with a loving wife, realizes he must go and fight the Japanese. At first his wife says no but then, suddenly, she witnesses some Japanese atrocity or something, she is persuaded he must go, insists he must go. She will guard the home. He goes. The play is set here in Wuhan?'

'I think so,' I say.

'So it should be modern.'

'Ah, modern, yes, you're right.'

'You need lots of searchlights sweeping round the sky. Martial drums, musical instruments, military tunes, loud bangs, people marching up and down, stirring speeches and patriotic songs and dances.'

'Yes,' I say, but not in the most positive of tones.

Tian Boqi looks at me.

'Dear Lao, this is war. War is not the most subtle of phenomena. It is not Percy Bysshe fucking Shelley. War is nasty, brutish and degrading. But this one has to be fought. The basest human emotions must be unleashed, so that sometime, in the future, when we have destroyed this evil, as artists we can once more start to kindle and arouse the finest, the noblest, the most beautiful of human emotions and ideas. Just like Percy Bysshe fucking Shelley.'

We both contemplate this for a while. Tian continues.

'Look, this is set in Wuhan? So the bloke, the hero, is presumably from Wuhan?'

'I suppose so,' I say.

'And all the audience will be from Wuhan. Even if they've only been here a few weeks or months. Everyone in that audience will have experienced something uplifting, extraordinary, unique about living in Wuhan, because Wuhan, in these few short months, has been, *is* an extraordinary place to live. The whole audience will know that. So you need the hero – who can wax eloquent every so often even though he's an average down-to-earth bloke – to speak out with passion, with joy about all the special and wonderful qualities – which the audience will recognize and empathize with – of living in Wuhan. The spirit, the dedication, the inspiration, the change. Which he must now leave, and take some of it with him, to go and fight the Japanese. Cue tears. Farewell to his wife. Lots and lots of tears. And the audience all deciding they will live and fight even harder for their beloved China.'

That final bit, about Wuhan, its special qualities, I will definitely put in.

I pause.

'It's strange,' I say, 'here I am, putting on this play, about 'defending Wuhan', and yet everyone, every single person in that audience, will know, despite all the official statements, that we will be leaving extremely soon, that it will be falling within months to the Japanese.'

'So? When we get to Chungking, put on the same play renamed *Defend Chungking*. You are not talking about just Wuhan in this play. You are talking about China. China marching into the future.'

We part, I catch the ferry across the Yangtze and walk along the Bund to meet my government minister.

On the way I drop into the central post office to see if there has been a letter for a Mr Wu Lei, from my wife. Nothing.

I breathe out. Walk out on to the Bund again. Breathe in. Everyone is very busy. Everyone is moving with purpose. I move with purpose too, observing as I go. There are few destitute people, even fewer dying or dead. Ships – both passenger and freight – are bustling in and bustling out – always fuller when they depart than when they arrive. And people are looking cheerful!

This all makes me feel very positive, very progressive. Evolution and improvement are all about me. As Tian Boqi said – 'China is marching into the future!'

I am about to meet Mr Chen Lifu, the Minister of Education. He has a rather odd reputation. Originally a mining engineer, Chiang Kai-shek plucked him from obscurity (a bit like me) and, only a few weeks ago, appointed him his Minister for Education. A strict Confucian, Chen has the reputation of favouring a traditional and hierarchical form of society. His first act as Minister of Education was to order all China's universities and scholars to remove themselves to the remotest parts of the country in order to escape the Japanese. Quite a good idea in itself. But this was not to safeguard our scientific and technical expertise – vital to our war effort – but rather to preserve our venerable traditions of Chinese scholarship and culture from the pollutions and barbarisms of modern Japanese and Western 'thought'. Personally I have never had any doubt that our ancient intellectual and humanistic traditions – the oldest and finest in the world – would ever be seriously threatened by crude fascist 'thought' or crude Western 'culture'. We are too civilized and tolerant for that. But I have not come to challenge the minister, just to make contact and ask for some funding.

His room is simply and modestly furnished. He wears the plain blue robe and hat of a traditional Chinese scholar. It's as though the Revolution of 1911 has never taken place! He looks me sternly up and down. I must admit I have not dressed for this interview, I am my usual sloppy self.

I make my greetings. I explain what I and my department are trying to do at the university. I explain that I would like to extend our programme of education and promotion of fighting the Japanese to our schools and inform him we will require some funds for this.

He does not respond. Just stares at me.

I get a bit uneasy. I explain our work is vital for the war effort. For reforming our society so that we can better defeat the Japanese.

I stop. There is a silence. He speaks.

'I have read some of your books.'

Never a good sign.

'I found them disturbing and unpleasant,' he says. 'I do not think authors should write degrading books about prostitutes.

Women – and men – of loose morals should not be allowed in books.'

'Oh,' I say.

'But I liked that book about the rickshaw driver even less. It appealed to and celebrated the basest instincts in humanity – greed, ambitious social climbing, more loose women, humans who only care about money and power. That is not reforming a people, that is undermining and destroying the harmony and hierarchy and delicate balance of a healthy and functioning society. It brings in its place chaos and anarchy and intense human suffering.'

'I was not trying to put forward the merits of greed and capitalism, but rather...'

He speaks over me.

'Capitalism is the lowest and most base form of society possible,' he informs me. 'Even more debased than Marxism. The merchant classes are always the most treacherous and unstable elements in any society. Minds wholly preoccupied with personal material gain, with no interest in the stability or well-being of the society they live among. They constantly bring chaos and collapse to every society they infest. Just look at the destruction and decay caused to our China by the actions of the foreign imperialists and bankers. They have so undermined and impoverished our society they have made it impossible for us to defend ourselves.'

He rests a moment. I am not too sure what we are disagreeing about. We seem to agree on quite a lot of things. He continues:

'I always think the finest, most subtle solution to the natural mendacity and treachery of the merchant classes was that imposed by our greatest and wisest emperors. Firstly they imposed upon our country a stern and uncompromising social hierarchy. And they then composed that hierarchy in such a way that the merchant class was always placed just below that of hermits and ascetics. When, by greed and deviousness and rapacity, a merchant had risen to the top of his class, he was automatically promoted by the emperor to the next class – that of anchorites and eremites. Having first given away all his money and worldly possessions, he then had to spend the rest of his existence living off crusts of bread and rainwater in a remote cave atop an almost unscalable mountain. Any merchant who managed to survive the climb to the top was then strongly advised, if he valued his life, to never attempt to climb down again. That, I think, provides the finest antidote possible to the ambitions of the merchant classes.'

There is a comic short story in that. I must remember it. I think I am warming to him.

'Well, I think we agree about quite a lot there,' I say.

'We don't agree about anything,' he rejoins icily. 'You are a socialist. A wishy-washy progressive, and liberal who believes in a whole lot of inconstant and ever-changing values. You want to take away society's anchor and mainstay – a strong and organic hierarchy – and in its place install a vapid and vacuous personal morality of general equalness and do-goodery, a making-it-up-yourself philosophy in which no one knows where they are or what their place, meaning or function is, and in their disorientation allow the most immoral and rapacious among them – through demagoguery and bribery and violence – to seize control of all things and to rule like wolves!

'Can't you understand that you progressives cannot simply destroy everything and then, from the wasteland you have created, expect people to spontaneously resurrect and reorientate themselves as a living and healthy society? It takes years, centuries, of travail and disappointments and disasters to do that. To create a whole new pattern and system.'

He suddenly changes tack drastically.

'You have been in England, haven't you?' he asks.

'I have,' I confess.

'I myself would never go to such a barbaric nor anarchic place, but I do admire some of their authors.'

'Oh?'

'I'm not thinking of modern novelists like Virginia Woolf, with their pretentious and excruciating prose and self-indulgent twiddlings.'

Something else I could almost agree with.

'But have you ever read the poet and novelist G. K. Chesterton, a grounded man, often exquisitely imaginative?'

I admit I've read some of his Father Brown detective stories.

'Harrumph,' he says. 'A pity. He would help you become a better writer. He once wrote this delightful short story. About a man, a very progressive man, who goes around sweeping away the cobwebs of all these fusty old traditions, destroying ancient buildings and laws and habits, because he must have modernity, innovation, impactfulness. And one day he's walking around making decisions and doing destructions and he comes across this hedge. "Why is this hedge?" he asks. No one with him seems able to answer this question. "What is its purpose?" No one seems to know. "Then cut it down," this progressive orders. So it is cut down. And ten minutes later he is killed by a bull.'

That really is very good. I must remember to read more Chesterton.

'And yet you progressives don't see that's exactly what you're doing here. China has always essentially been a pacifist nation. And yet what are you doing? Tearing down its ancient customs and traditions and laws – which often have deep common sense and practicality and caution in them – simply because they are old. Don't you understand the violence and anarchy this nihilism will unleash? We won't need the Japanese any longer. In the future the Chinese will all be butchering and torturing and terrorizing each other. That's what it's going to be like,' he says.

Suddenly he's weary. Slumps back into his chair.

'You want some money?' he asks wearily.

'Well, er...'

'For this preposterous schools idea.'

'Yes.'

'Well, Chiang Kai-shek, or at least Mrs Chiang, seems to like you. And as I believe in and live in a hierarchical society and General Chiang is my boss, I suppose I must grant you his wish.'

'Thank you,' I say. 'That is very kind.'

I leave the Ministry of Education and walk along the Bund.

Wuhan is such a strange place. All sorts of tides and forces are pulling it in all sorts of directions. One minute I am giddily progressive with Tian Boqi, the next crushingly reactionary with Chen Lifu.[11]

It is all such fun!

6

George Hogg, the young Quaker from England, was a tad unsettled. The subject of Europe, the dictators, Britain's policy of appeasement, had been discussed frequently at the Last Ditch Club, and Mr Chamberlain's name had never been mentioned in favourable terms. Indeed, he was the subject of often vitriolic abuse. This upset George. As a Quaker, of course, he was a sincere and dedicated pacifist. He believed that war, all violence, was horribly wrong. One just had to look around in China to see the appalling, the devastating effect that war had – especially on children. George had been in Nanking and witnessed the appalling Rape of Nanking. For atonement, indeed, he spent some of his time in Wuhan working for free in an orphanage. So when Mr Chamberlain, rather than diving straight into a war, which most members of the Last Ditch Club seemed to think he should, announced that he would rather talk and would rather negotiate with Mr Hitler and the other dictators in order to first see if he could reach a peaceful and just settlement concerning all their various grievances, George was solidly in favour. Not being a drinker, George stood to one side of the bar sipping a lemonade. If the conversation turned to Czechoslovakia and the Runciman Mission he was determined to have his say.

In the centre of the bar, commanding the room, stood a new arrival from London whom everyone seemed to know.

'Vernon, so good to see you.'

'How's things in London, old chap? What's the latest?'

Vernon Bartlett was suave in manner and smartly dressed. He sported a fresh orchid in his buttonhole. When his plane had landed at the aerodrome a couple of hours earlier, he had been a seasoned enough traveller to wait in the aircraft until the dust clouds outside settled before exiting. Left wing in politics, he wrote for *Reynold's News*, a liberal Sunday newspaper, and, with his very reassuring voice, was the acknowledged master of the BBC's popular 'fireside chat' radio programmes.

Under his arm he carried a folded copy of the latest edition of *The Times* (now eight days old) which he had brought with him from London.

George Hogg wasn't sure he either liked or trusted 'Vernon.' Then instantly chastised himself for being so uncharitable.

James Belden looked at Vernon with a steady eye.

'Tell us what's really happening in Downing Street, Vern. The truth.'

'Yeah, tell us about the traitors,' added Izzy Epstein.

Peter Fleming sat on the opposite side of the room reading a Nancy Mitford novel.

'You've all read the latest edition of *The Times*?' enquired Bartlett.

It had arrived from the airport half an hour before Bartlett, being delivered by bicycle courier. They'd all pored over it.

'Yes,' said Rewi, 'Beneš and Henlein.'

'A bit of background,' said Vernon. 'We all know Hitler is going to seize Czechoslovakia. He's employing exactly the same tactics he applies everywhere. Thanks to the Treaty of Versailles Czechoslovakia is a ragbag of nationalities – Czech, Slovak, Poles, Hungarians, Rumanians, all crammed together. A province of German-speakers inside Czechoslovakia stretches all the way down the border with Germany – the Sudetenland.

'The leader of the Sudetens, Konrad Henlein, is a fascist, a Hitler bootlicker. So the Führer invites Mr Henlein to Berlin and orders him to start staging riots, demonstrations, demanding the right, as German-speakers, to secede from Czechoslovakia and join up with their brothers and sisters in the German Reich.'

George Hogg readied himself.

'I think you'll find,' he ventured, 'that in the Treaty of Versailles, the Sudeten Germans were treated especially harshly, and...'

A chorus of 'hushes' and 'shut ups' greeted his foray. Instinctively polite, he stopped.

'So,' continued Vernon, 'Henlein stages all sorts of riots and provocations and the German press goes into hysterics about the "brutality" of the Czech police...'

'The Czech police *were* brutal,' insisted George. Everyone ignored him. Vernon continued.

'...Hitler moves his army up to the Czech border and demands that, if the international community does not intervene and suppress these "massacres" immediately, he will be forced, much against his will, to invade Czechoslovakia. Which triggers panic inside Downing Street. That's not in the script! Herr Hitler's meant to be the victim, not the aggressor. He's going to start a war!

'I was *Reynolds News*'s lobby correspondent – for three whole days we didn't hear a dicky bird from them. Paralyzed! Finally they tell us some ancient relic from the House of Lords, Lord Runciman, has been dug up and is travelling "immediately" to Prague and Berlin to "consult."'

'Waste time. Prevaricate.'

'Exactly. He was to spend weeks travelling the capitals of Europe and would then write some enormous report which in the end would make no firm recommendations about anything, by which time Chamberlain obviously hoped the whole thing would have...'

'Blown over.'

'Journalists are no longer allowed to tell the truth in London. Proprietors threaten editors who threaten journalists to fall into line or be sacked. MI5 smears anyone who tells the truth. The BBC couldn't wait to click its heels.'

A silence.

'Just before I left London I learnt the truth – what was really going on. What Runciman's mission was really about.'

'Yeah...?' everyone chorused.

'Who told you? Name names!'

They all crowded round.

It was at this moment that George decided to make his last stand.

'This whole Sudetenland matter is being completely mis-represented,' he stated.

'Shut up,' everyone shouted, some quite aggressively.

For the first time in his life George felt anger licking within him. Since, as a good Quaker, he'd never been angry before, these feelings puzzled him, worried him even, and he stopped short.

Bartlett continued.

'The true situation, gentlemen, was personally told to me by a senior and impeccable source within the Foreign Office. To my face.'

'Yes…?'

'He told me that Lord Runciman had been sent by Chamberlain to President Beneš with precisely the opposite brief to the one that's been in all the newspapers. Chamberlain told Runciman to order Beneš to immediately secede the Sudetenland to Hitler – lock stock and barrel – or Britain and France would abandon Czechoslovakia. Hitler could invade Beneš's whole country and Britain and France wouldn't lift a finger.'

There was a long pause.

'And that, gentlemen, is what the Runciman Mission is all about.'

'Treason!'

'No wonder they've got MI5 strong-arming journalists!'

'Fact is,' concluded Bartlett, 'the government's panicked. Retreated into a bunker. They listen to no one but themselves. They've decided that if they don't appease Hitler the communists, the Russians, will take over the world. Doesn't matter what Churchill, what Eden, what Attlee tell them… Nothing will get them out of their funk hole. Beneš has no option but to yield the Sudetenland.'

George had suppressed the flickerings of anger within him and was determined to speak.

'This whole situation is being grossly misrepresented,' he shouted. 'Mr Chamberlain is a man of honour. He cares about peace. Lord Runciman is a man of honour. He too has been…'

'Shut the fuck up,' screamed Izzy Epstein, stepping towards George with his fists up. 'Shut the fuck up, you dirty little Jew hater…'

George stared at him.

'I have nothing against Jews,' he stuttered, 'I like Jews...'

'You fucking Nazi,' screamed Izzy.

Izzy was about to launch himself into the bewildered pacifist when suddenly the room was filled with the scream of a nearby air-raid siren. Bombs! Everyone instinctively ducked, then grabbed their glasses and stampeded down the stairs into the cellar.

Downstairs in the darkness, rather than debate the latest vagaries of Chamberlain's European policy, there was sombre silence. Even though it was a Europeans-only shelter they had always allowed the Chinese and White Russian staff from the club and the restaurant below, along with their customers, to enter with them. Everyone stood packed tight together, silent, stifling, sweating as the bombs began to fall and the ground shook around them. The Chinese were doubtless thinking and praying for their families and friends and property caught above ground. The Europeans, as they stood there, sank into ever deeper gloom as they analyzed over and again the desperate situation their own continent now found itself in. How many months or weeks even would it be before Europe too, indeed the whole world, was plunged into this chaos and slaughter? They thought of their dear ones and families at home suddenly having to cower in their cellars, or being enlisted to fight in unending wars. And they felt especial anger as they faced the pusillanimity, the duplicity, worst of all, the sheer stupidity of their leaders. Stupid as heifers standing patiently in line at the abattoir.

At least, the Europeans felt, as the ground shook around them, the Chinese are fighting back.

As George Hogg was leaving the air-raid shelter to return to his office, Peter Fleming of *The Times* slipped in beside him.

'Going back to your office, old chap?'

'Yes.'

'Why don't we share a rickshaw? My office is just down the road from yours.'

'Oh. All right.'

They both clambered into a rickshaw and the driver started off with his burden.

'George,' said Fleming, as if he'd known him all his life (they'd never actually spoken before), 'congratulations, I thought you were jolly brave in there – speaking up for the prime minister against all those awful lefties.'

'Oh,' said George. He actually considered himself rather 'lefty' – in favour of getting the government to support the poor, increasing employment, not getting involved in endless wars – but anyhow...

'You showed real courage.'

'Well,' said George modestly, 'it's just I feel that, if there's a discussion, both sides of the argument should be heard before a decision is made.'

'That's democracy.'

'Not that I know much about Chamberlain and so on,' George added diffidently.

'Don't run yourself down, old chap. Don't let yourself be intimidated by all those damned Bolshies. For years they've been running round demanding we end all wars and scrap all armies and navies. Everyone must sign the Peace Pledge. Every single weapon we have must be melted down and turned into ploughshares and baths for the poor.'

'I rather agree with that melting down into ploughshares bit,' suggested George.

'Yes, George, yes, but then suddenly, overnight, the lefties turn through 180 degrees and start shrieking that everyone must fight, we must all stand up against these dreadful fascists and pick up our weapons that we've just melted down and denounce the cowardly ruling classes for having melted them down and not having armed us properly. Two-faced twisters!'

Fleming turned and looked fully into George's face.

'It took a lot of pluck to say what you said in there, George. For me it was a real pleasure listening to a chap speaking a bit of common sense.'

'You're very kind,' said George gently, 'but it was only a political discussion. I hardly spoke a word.'

He looked away. The Old Etonian continued to study George's face. Hogg – awful name – hadn't actually agreed with anything he'd said, but so far he hadn't dismissed anything either. He would require a bit of work.

'And don't get upset with all those accusations of anti-Semitism,' he continued. 'Jews always use that trick when they're losing an argument.'

George turned a bit red.

'And on politics, let's face it, Woodrow Wilson, with all his silly idealism, created the most godawful mess at the Treaty of Versailles...'

George agreed with that 100 per cent, but didn't say so.

'...especially in Eastern Europe. All sorts of nationalities jumbled together. Why we should be forced to fight on behalf of a repressive government like Czechoslovakia I don't know. You have Germans on one side of a contiguous border living beside Germans on the other side – let the two of them join together. It's common sense!

'Personally, old chap, I don't think our ruling classes are in a funk. I think they're holding their nerve – unlike some of those lefties in there. Why's it suddenly in everyone's interest to have a war? The last war left us crippled, flat on our backs. Then, just as we were recovering, along came the Wall Street Crash and the Great Depression. Here we are, just picking ourselves up again from that, starting to regain our trade, our industry, starting to be able to provide jobs for everyone, and suddenly the lefties demand we get involved in yet another ruinous European war. Britain is a trading nation – we trade with the whole world. Let the Nazis fight the Bolsheviks and the Bolsheviks fight the Nazis and the Czechs sort themselves out. What's it to us? Once we were the world's number one trading nation – with all the jobs and prosperity that gave us. The strongest banking system in the world. We could be that all over again – provided we ignore these endless European entanglements.'

'll there was neither agreement nor disagreement from Hogg.
vou're playing a particularly shy fish, you must
'ime approach your bait.

'Where were you at school, old chap?'

'St George's, Harpenden.'

'St George's, Harpenden,' replied Fleming, implying he knew the place well, even though he'd never heard of it.

'You were at Eton, weren't you?'

'Yes. Did you go to university?'

'Oxford.'

'Really? Which college?'

'Wadham,' said George, with a slight fall to his voice. Wadham was Oxford's least illustrious college. 'And you?'

'The House,' replied Fleming with the aplomb only an Old Etonian can muster.

'You were in the Bullingdon, weren't you?' asked George, a note of disapproval in his voice.

'Oh,' said Fleming, caught out for a second. He covered rapidly. 'Yes. Hardly ever attended though. Spent most of my time out hunting and fishing. I love fishing.'

In fact Fleming had studied hard at Oxford and won a First in English. But appearances must be maintained.

This brief quadrille over English social standing ended swiftly with both parties knowing precisely where they stood, who was on top and who below. Fleming of course displayed no sign of his victory. With a grateful smile he turned to his companion as the rickshaw drew up at his office.

'Been a real pleasure talking to you, George. Can't tell you how refreshing it is in Wuhan to hear an informed person speak their mind, say exactly where they stand on a subject. Let's keep in touch.'

He left without paying and disappeared through his office doors.

In truth George didn't actually have the least idea where he stood or what he thought. Born in Harpenden, the son of a successful Quaker businessman who had ambitions for him, he'd gone to the local school and then, miraculously, won a scholarship to Oxford. On leaving Oxford his father declared George was to become a banker but for once George put his foot down. Or rather, as a Quaker, the spirit moved him. 'Before I do that, Father,' he said, 'I want to see the world. I want to work things out.' Not only a banker, thought his father, but an international banker! He promptly funded George for a year's trip round the world. For reasons unknown George had ended up in Wuhan.

The rickshaw pulled up outside his office. George paid the boy and was about to walk into his office when the air-raid siren sounded for the second time that day. There were distant crumps and thumps. They were bombing Hanyang again.

George's spirit decided he must go. Much as he hated seeing the aftermath of a raid – the slaughter, the suffering – George always painstakingly reported it in detail. So his readers would know what war was really like. So that they would do everything they could to avoid it.

On the ferry from the Bund to Hanyang, George found himself on the same boat as Freda Utley and Agnes Smedley. He didn't know Freda but recognized Agnes from the Last Ditch Club. They didn't speak.

They were met with a scene of utter devastation. They hurried in among the fires and ruins to get their stories, those images and phrases of war that would hopefully lodge themselves irremovably into their readers' minds and memories.

Freda suddenly became a different person. She ceased being an educated upper middle-class Englishwoman embroiled in emotional and neurotic passions and dilemmas. Suddenly she metamorphosed into a proper fit-for-purpose journalist. Calm. Icy almost. Concentrating hard on what she saw, calculating exactly how she would vividly capture that particular image or event in words, stepping amid the bodies and chaos as easily as she would have stepped among the guests at a picnic on Hampstead Heath. This is what she noted down:

Acres smouldering ruins, wounded being stretchered off, burnt bodies amid debris, wounded being dressed by first-aid workers on the spot. 100s of artisan shacks destroyed. In ruins horribly mutilated bodies. Near waterfront mangled mess of human limbs and sand where bomb had exploded on a primitive hut. Wounded children screaming, frightened children crying, women distraught.

Red column of flame rising to sky. Stumble over body of a man by waterside, entrails exposed. Still breathing. No one has time to attend him or he's regarded as a hopeless case. Pr'aps he's unconscious, can feel no pain. Pass gruesome sight after another. Wish above all things there was morphine for the wounded.

A woman, dead husband at her feet, at her breast a baby with its face blackened by the blast, a child about two screaming beside her. Man trying to do something for his wife – obviously beyond help but still breathing. Mutilated children, mothers, men. Most pathetic of all, small boy crying beside mother's horribly mangled body in remains of their one-roomed shack. 'Where is your father?' I ask through my companion. 'Killed in another bombing,' he cries. Nearby an old grandmother, her whole family killed, now herself doomed to die of starvation.

Further on. Mother wails unceasingly over the dead body of her baby, a small boy howls beside her. Houses blazing like matchwood, the heat so great I can't get close to them. Along the waterfront families with few pitiful possessions: mattresses, tables, wooden boxes, cooking vessels. Attempts being made to put out fire, men, women, and boys passing buckets and basins from hand to hand in long chain. When a primitive fire engine at last arrives can't get its pump working. Frantic. At last a hose-pipe draws water from the river, it spouts onto blazing buildings and fire is under control. All started by direct hit on a small paper factory, the burning papers falling on surrounding thatched hovels. Hundreds have lost homes/livelihoods.

Just the sort of reporting Agnes had been hoping would start to appear in the British *News Chronicle* when she'd invited Freda to Wuhan.

From another area of the carnage George Hogg was also reporting. He'd never seen anything this bad before. It should never have been allowed to happen. This was war. What war really was. He must report exactly what he saw so his readers would know and would never allow another war in Europe. He noted:

Men cry and scream digging frantically into disintegrating earth while fearful they might strike some dead or halfdead thing. Old woman silently from body to body, peering intently at each. Puts out a hand to touch one, that she may see more clearly the disfigured face, suddenly throws herself to ground beside it, kissing it in an abandonment of grief. 'That's enough now, old lady, that's enough,' says man in uniform, trying to pull her gently to feet; but she cleaves to her daughter so he leaves her to turn to other victims. Old man who's been digging half an hour discovers his wife was one of the first to be dug out dead and too mutilated for him to recognize. 'Aiya. What an affair. my old woman dead.' He throws down spade and runs up to me crazed. I sympathize and he hurries on. 'My old woman's dead,' he calls to the next man. Scurries on, white-faced, stopping everyone he meets. 'My old woman's dead.'[12]

Hogg scribbled faster and faster.

Huge conflagration, dense smoke, bursting flames, shrieks and children wailing, cries of wounded buried in rubble. Also kind voices, movement. Calm courageous people move beneath flames, extinguish fires, throw sand on incendiary bombs, rescue aged from ruins. Men/women soldiers/civilians in smouldering clothes, faces grim and black, fight for the city, its life. Miraculously they appear, walking out of the flames and inferno, beat out the live sparks and flames sprouting on their clothing, walk back in.

Chains of humans pass buckets hand to hand. Lines of people carry the wounded on stretchers, in their arms, drag them along. Stranger saving stranger. Chinaman saving Chinaman. Dead camel lying by side of street, horse screaming with broken legs. Mother runs screaming with body of dead child in arms, old men and women sit patiently on bundles surrounded by rescued household goods, poultry, favourite gods, flowerpots. The sun shines deadly and pale amid dust/smoke/crashing walls. Dogs and rats gnaw the dead. Quivering wounded people sob, pinned beneath fallen beams.

God, thought George, the next time we discuss war at the Last Ditch, if I do one thing in my life, I will speak out against this insanity, this foulness. Speak out for peace and reconciliation. Speak out for appeasement.

And all the time, amid the dead, moved the quick, the coolies. Deftly portering pans and brooms and cushions and piled cartons of matchboxes from the factories and huge machines and engineering equipment – components and segments from the dismantled steel mills and factories – stepping carefully amid the slaughter and the pity. Making their careful way down towards the dockside, piling what they carried into junks or steamers or carts or onto the backs of yet more coolies – so that all might be transported safe up the Yangtze to distant Sichuan, Yunnan.

7

I receive a letter. Not through the usual channels – a postman or academic dropping it into my pigeonhole in the college office. This message is slipped under my door. Late at night. I pick it up, open the door to see who left it, but the person has gone.

I open it. It is not addressed to me, it is unsigned. I take it to my desk and start to read it. It informs me that my friend and pupil Tian Boqi has been arrested while travelling in the countryside and brought to Wuhan. He is incarcerated in the police barracks, in the section of it occupied by the State Security Force – our secret police. The branch of our (very large) secret police that deals with internal subversion and counter-terrorism.

If they have him, he will be being tortured and all sorts of other things I do not wish to think about.

At first I am unsure whether this letter is true or not. It could be a deliberate provocation, to watch me, see what my reaction is, whether I contact anyone else they might consider disloyal. But then I see a familiar tic in certain characters in the letter. They belong to Tian's fellow student in our class, the revolutionary poetess Shan Shuang. I judge her to be a person of integrity. (albeit a terrible poet, but dead straight in her morality and integrity). I believe what she has written in the letter. Tian Boqi is in prison.

The letter continues. Shan Shuang (and probably others) beg me to intervene with the authorities. I am an influential novelist and writer. A public figure of standing and respect. If I were to intervene it might influence the authorities to release him – or at least not torture him. The letter implores me to do this and then ends.

I burn the letter so Shan Shuang cannot be traced. Then I think.

I too have been under arrest, for my writings which were – and doubtless still are – considered subversive. Three or four years ago I was interrogated and thrown into prison. I was not tortured or put on trial, I was beaten up a couple of times. I fared far better than some of my fellow writers who were tortured and two or three of them shot in some dark cell in the early hours of the morning.

Should I do what the letter asks me?

I think first of my family. If I have a family. If they are still alive. And if they are still alive, maybe they are at this very moment in the act of escaping from the Japanese-held north, trying to make their way south so they can join up with me here in Wuhan. If they arrive to find me in prison – or worse, purged, disappeared, dead – who will support them? They will be all alone in chaos. Then I think more rationally. If I were dead, my wife would support them, as she is doing now (if they are still alive). And what is more, if I had failed to support my fellow writers, she would have some rather stern words for me.

So should I stick my neck out, intervene?

Government repression has been getting worse over the last few weeks. Ever since the victory of Taierzhuang the authorities have been feeling more confident. Police and some of their gangster friends have been raiding leftist booksellers in Wuhan and Chungking, confiscating pamphlets and books, beating up anyone who objects.

But the thing is I hate politics. I despise it. The sort of people who get involved in politics are, by and large, the lowest forms of human life. I always felt the British cockneys had it about right. Insult politicians year in and year out and then, when at last it comes to an election, go out still insulting them and vote for them. In huge numbers.

I belong to no political party, but I am a socialist. And a Christian. (And these days even a bit of a Confucian!) I am not particularly fond of the communists, but then they're not as bad as the nationalists. By and large they are not corrupt, they are patriotic, they ban foot binding and give women the freedom to choose who they marry. They'd end debt slavery and curb our accursed landlords. But I still don't trust them. That's the Manchu in me. All those braying upper-class Han accents. But then the Nationalists are even more upper-class Han!

I feel my emotions are taking over control of my reason. Which is not a bad thing.

I mean, who needs the bloody secret police? They are of no use to anyone in China except the powerful. And the people of China are quite happily getting on with fighting and resisting the Japanese whether our leaders like it or not. (And quite a few of our milquetoast leaders don't like it. Our heroic leader Chiang Kai-shek himself had to be bullied into entering the war – even after the Japanese invasion.)

So somehow or other it would appear I've manoeuvred myself into a position where I've got to speak out, intervene, protest even, at the arrest of my friend and comrade Tian Boqi.

Who do I know who I can approach who is influential and powerful enough to help me in my intervention? In fact, virtually no one. One person, in effect – General Feng Yuxiang. And not only is he not here, but hundreds of miles upstream in Chungking – organizing its new heavy industries and factories and cooperatives – but in addition, since the victory at Taierzhuang, he and his fellow generals Bai Chongxi and Li Zongren have been demoted and despatched to unimportant posts far from the fighting.

It is something I will have to do by myself.

Being a writer, I decide to write a letter.

8

Red is, of course, the colour of luck. It's also the colour of blood. But if you display enough red on your clothing and in your home, then with any luck your luck will extend to you not having to shed any of your own actual blood. Your life will be prosperous and long and totally unbloody. Even if you lived in Wuhan in the late August of 1938.

Everyone was wearing red. If they were Chinese all their clothing, visible and invisible, was totally red. If they were English they were more surreptitious and wore only red undergarments. But they all wore at least some red. And they were all in a state of near frenzy.

The cause of this impaction of thousands of beetroot and scarlet-clad Westerners and Chinese in a state of near hysteria was the occasion of the last ever horse race to be held at Wuhan's rather grand Union Jack Racing Club. Wuhan had traditionally possessed two racetracks – one for the Chinese, the Big Win Happy Day Race Track, and the more sedate Union Jack Club for the English and Europeans. But the exigencies of war had caused the shutting down of the Chinese club several months previously and was now bringing about the closure of the English one. The English committee had sagely discerned that unlike the English and Chinese – who were both passionate about horses and betting – the Japanese held little interest in either. So this was the final meet. And in a noble gesture of solidarity – and a regard for the gate receipts – the English stewards had invited the Chinese for the first (and last) time ever to attend their meet. The race for the Wuhan Oaks Cup was always the climax to every season's racing.

The sun beat down. Low-flying aircraft stooged overhead on final approach to Wuhan's brand-new airport. The stands were packed. Almost everyone was drunk. The betting was insane.

The horses were, at best, nags. Fodder and grain being in such short supply and thus very expensive, many were indeed on their last legs. And their pragmatic owners, keen to get the last drop of profit out of their ailing nags, had arranged for butchers to attend the race so that as soon as it was over and money had been exchanged the horses could be slaughtered and cut up and their flesh sold to meat-starved citizens on the Bund.

'How very French,' observed a well-dressed lady.

Unsurprisingly a fair number of journalists were present. British and Chinese of course, but also an enthusiastic sprinkling of Australians and Yanks and the odd Frenchman and Indian.

Jack Belden was already seven sheets to the wind but perfectly lucid. He was observing the preliminaries through a large pair of binoculars borrowed from a naval captain.

'Jeez,' he said, 'most of these runners aren't going to make it to the starting line, let alone the finishing line.'

'Let me have a look, Jack. Let me have a look.'

The small Izzy Epstein was unsuccessfully wrestling the enormous Jack for his binoculars.

'Who're you backing?' asked Jack.

'Everyday Lettuce,' said Izzy.

Chinese racehorses have unusual names.

'Who are you on?'

'Print Bank Notes,' replied Jack. 'I know the trainer. And I got a side bet on Pineapple Bun With Butter.'

'Gimme a look, Jack, gimme a look.'

'Go on, call me an anti-Semite.'

'Anti-Semitic bastard.'

'You got money on that too?'

This being a horse race it meant for betting purposes, with eager punters all over the Far East hanging on the result of the race, that a telegraph had been installed so that the good or bad news could be instantly flashed around the world. But equally, being a telegraph, it also meant that news could as easily be signalled inwards. George Wang of Reuters was in control of it.

There were thirteen starters for the Wuhan Oaks Cup. The last Wuhan Oaks Cup ever. The last horse race ever. The jockeys were all imported from Mongolia. Their resplendent tops were woven from Shantung silk. The firm favourite in the race was Exotic Panda, the horse with the number '8' on its saddle cloth. But then all Number 8s are always firm favourites in China. Eight is the luckiest number in China.

The Sikh military band struck up a somewhat ragged version of 'Over the Hills and Far Away', a pistol exploded, and the horses, no spring chickens, leapt into a trot, then a canter, and finally – at least for some of them – the ghost of a gallop. All except unlucky Number 8, who promptly expired on the starting line to a universal Chinese groan. Immediate fighting broke out between bookies and punters, punters arguing, with some justice, that since it had never crossed the line it had in fact scratched.

The race continued oblivious.

'Come on Happy Dragon Go Go!' cried Vernon Bartlett.

He was sporting a splendid white lily in his buttonhole and drawing on an expensive-looking cigar. Bookies were doing a roaring trade.

'Get moving, you lazy bitch,' screamed Ralph Shaw at his punt Wine, Women, Poems and Perfume, who was still teetering on the starting line. Ralph was accompanied by his White Russian floozy Big Wanda.

As the horses began to lumber off round the circuit all their hooves started to stir up the dust. A whole lot of it. Pretty soon horses and riders were engulfed in clouds of the stuff, every so often emerging into the open and then disappearing inside again.

Through his binoculars Jack Belden caught sight of his side bet Pineapple Bun With Butter in a very favourable position before it again vanished into the cloud

'Come on,' roared Jack, 'come on you beauty.'

Izzy's Everyday Lettuce was visibly wilting. He was dancing in frustration.

It was in the midst of this insanity that the telegraph started to chatter. George Wang bent down to read it.

'Hey, guys, there's something about Czechoslovakia on the wires. President Beneš.'

A moment of silence from the journalists. Followed by a moment of indecision. Which was more important – the outbreak of a Europe-wide war or a horse race? Jack Belden solved the crisis. As a functioning alcoholic he could concentrate on two things at once. 'Let's hear the news,' he stated, simultaneously adding, 'Come on you dirty nag' as his main bet Print Bank Notes fell off the pace.

'It seems Herr Hitler and Herr Henlein may have made a mistake,' reported George. This caused instant attention and instant silence from everyone in the press box.

'What?' said James Bertram. 'What did you say?'

'Well,' said George, 'you know Konrad Henlein of the Sudetenland is a very stupid man, and Hitler ordered him to reject anything Beneš offered him?'

'So what did Beneš offer him?' asked Vernon.

'Ha,' said George. 'Beneš is a very clever fellow. He told Henlein he could have the Sudetenland.'

'And Henlein,' added the acute Jack Belden, 'what did he say?'

'Well, as a very stupid man, he did exactly what Herr Hitler had ordered him to do and turned down Beneš.'

'Turned down the Sudetenland?' cried Izzy.

'HAAAAAAAAA!' roared Belden in triumph, 'HE JANXED THEM!!!,' simultaneously noting that his side bet Pineapple Bun With Butter now appeared to be in the lead.

'Hitler must be eating the carpet,' cried Izzy, briefly reconciled to the faltering Everyday Lettuce.

'And what's the reaction elsewhere in Europe?' questioned Vernon.

A bookie was screaming his odds just below their box.

'Fuck off,' bellowed Belden at him. Jack was large and the bookie small. The bookie moved his pitch.

'It seems to have turned the whole situation on its head,' said George. 'Czechoslovakia used to be seen as the big unreasonable one, bullying its minorities; now it's Henlein and his master who are being unreasonable, belligerent. Everyone's seen through the ruse and is feeling sympathy for Czechoslovakia.'

'Poor little Czechoslovakia.'

'I can imagine what the reaction is in Downing Street,' said Vernon, smiling and drawing on his cigar. 'Chamberlain must be furious. His whole Runciman strategy is in ruins. What's the British press saying, George?'

'Don't know,' said George, 'but the Reuters wire is headed "Chamberlain backs the wrong horse".'

Talking of horses, Izzy's attention was suddenly snatched back by the race. His favourite, Everyday Lettuce, was now not only wilting but had actually expired. It lay on its back, legs in the air. Two butchers' carts approached at speed.

A low-flying aircraft with a misfiring engine passed overhead and spooked both Jack Belden's front runners – Print Bank Notes and Pineapple Bun With Butter. Both hared off towards Wuhan.

Which left Ralph Shaw's Wine, Women, Poems and Perfume and Vernon Bartlett's Happy Dragon Go Go as the only two left in contention. While Ralph leapt up and down in ecstatic frenzies his floozy Wanda calmly powdered her face in prospect of his finances being considerably more liquid in the next few days. Vernon, who wasn't really that interested in horse racing, calmly looked on, puffing his cigar.

At the last second Ralph's steed tripped and spilled his jockey all over the ground, Wanda ceased powdering her nose, and Vernon's nag rode on to triumph – and the butchers' knives.

'Yes,' said Vernon sagely, adjusting his buttonhole, 'I always back a horse whose name begins with H. And jolly good news from Czecho!'

Donald asked Hu if she'd work with him full time as his assistant, sterilizing and preparing his surgical instruments for theatre, aiding him in the actual operations. He admired her dexterity and intelligence and adaptability. Hu, fascinated by Donald's work, immediately spoke with Li Dequan, General Feng's wife, asking if she could give up her job vetting refugees arriving at the camps. Knowing Hu's keenness for nursing and healthcare Li agreed. Hu's assistant was almost as competent as she was. Refugees were still pouring into Wuhan as the Japanese drew ever closer, but many were now being quickly fed, clothed, medically checked, fumigated and then shipped straight upstream to Chungking to be sorted out there. Those who instead continued walking on the long trek westward – amid the streams of coolies and carters and soldiers also on the roads – were now being fed and watered and sheltered and medically checked at regular government way stations along the routes. Things were at last being organized.

The two women smiled, wished each other well and went their separate ways. Such swift meetings and partings had become part of the fabric of Wuhan.

With Spider Girl now being expected to provide various bicycle parts for the traction workshop close to the hospital, Hu helped her on her forays to the Bund in the mornings. Hu bought the food, Spider Girl haggled over bicycle parts, other mechanical detritus, and second-hand welding equipment. Having organized the transport, Spider Girl and Hu would then sit on the tailgate of the wagon chatting and laughing before it dropped Hu off at the hospital – plus spokes – and continued with Spider Girl to the workshop where the traction frames were being welded together. Being a highly intelligent country girl and sharing her father's passion for all things mechanical, Spider Girl soon got involved in the problems and pleasures of assembling the frames and traction pulleys and ratchets (adapted from bicycle chains and sprockets and cogs), and even picked up the rudiments of welding. Which meant that the actual process of cooking increasingly fell by the wayside. And the meals themselves, when she had time, were being prepared by someone whose oily hands and dirty clothing were less than hygienic.

But all these mighty complications are for the moment mercifully ahead of us.

Today Spider Girl was very excited. Because today was the day she'd been promised a visit to the hospital to see Donald at work.

She wasn't excited at the prospect of seeing the butchery – as we know, she was already well experienced in that side of life. What fascinated her was the chance to watch Donald at work.

All through her life she had been interested in watching skilful people working, seeing how they observed and calculated things, then practically applied that knowledge to the job at hand. Her mother running a complex family. Her father working on some machine or calculating the order of harvest, the timing of lifting and then drying and then storing the various crops. Fang the Builder staring at the stones lying in front of him, constructing in his mind where each individual stone would end up in the completed building. Or watching Agnes puzzling again and again over the wording in one small part of an article.

Nobody ever really realized how carefully Wild Pear Blossom watched them all.

She was standing in the operating theatre. The soldier, with an abdominal wound, was already lying on the table and his gut and wound was being cleansed as much as possible by Hu. Hu smiled at Spider Girl as she worked. Spider Girl watched fascinated. Then Donald came in, cleansed hands held upward to dry, bow tie immaculate. Hu washed her hands and brought Donald's sterilized equipment on a tray to his side. She sterilized the instruments next door in pressure cookers sat on Bunsen burners. Maninda joined Donald opposite him as his junior. Two burly attendants held down the patient's shoulders, another his legs.

It started.

The soldier's entrails were swiftly sewn together, the damaged gut excised, the wound being disinfected and bound up, the patient removed, table disinfected, hands washed, next patient on the table, sterilized instruments brought in as everyone washed their hands, wound disinfected, the whole process starting all over again. Pretty soon the arrival and departure of the patients merged into a blur.

It was not the wounds Spider Girl noticed, the pain, the groans, the blood. Instead she stared at Donald's concentration, his fluency and economy of movement, the skill and speed of his hands as he flicked and drew and sliced, the deftness and decision of his knife work, the swift dexterity of his sewing. And how all his movements were juxtaposed and orchestrated with the movements and actions of Maninda and Hu; the way the attendants understood and foresaw the rhythms and jags of the patients' pain and strongly but gently restrained them.

And above all Spider Girl stared at his bow tie, which she had scrupulously washed and dried and ironed the night before. It positively shone as with his scalpel and knife Donald Hankey – like Achilles on the plains of Ilium – waded his way through the blood and bodies and gore before him. But unlike Achilles, Donald's face was not wrathful, proud, arrogant, as any person with his skills and virtuosities would have every right to be. Instead it was quiet and modest and concerned, always showing his appreciation of his fellows' work with grunts and smiles and congratulations, listening continuously to them, their suggestions and point of view, making a joke when things got grim and a murmur of restraint when things turned silly. On the battlefields of the operating theatre Donald Hankey was the *verray parfit gentil knyght*.

Just like her father!

Spider Girl walked home. She was a mass and conflict of emotions. She did not really understand herself at this moment – a highly unusual state for her to be in. She had started getting these strange feelings in parts of her body she'd never really taken any notice of when she was a child. She had started to bleed – she'd asked Hu about that. And hair was starting to grow in places it had never been before. She really must remove the hair she'd felt growing on her upper lip. And whenever she saw Donald or was in his presence she'd started having thoughts and feeling feelings she'd never known existed.

Maybe it was the influence of all the Shanghai detective novels she was reading. Their most evil villains, to which she was always most strongly attracted, were invariably red-faced, sweaty Englishmen. Donald didn't have a red face, but he certainly sweated a lot!

★ ★ ★

Back home Spider Girl, already unsettled, walked straight into the midst of some full-blown domestic hysteria – concerning her!

Freda had discovered a whole stash of bottles, filled to the cap with her used bath water.

What was going on, she wanted to know? What was this servant girl daring to do, bottling her private bath water? This was outrageous! When was Agnes going to put her foot down?

Such behaviour was not likely to intimidate Spider Girl, who drew herself up to her inconsiderable height, straightened her back, and prepared for combat.

Agnes put a stop to that.

'Spider Girl,' she asked, 'why have you been bottling Freda's bath water?'

'Because it's valuable.'

'What do you mean, it's valuable?'

'What is she saying?' asked Freda, who still spoke very little Chinese.

Agnes ignored this.

'Why is it valuable?'

'You have not been paying me enough money recently to pay for our food or Miss Freda's bath water. I do not object to this. You use your money for worthy things like buying bandages for wounded soldiers.'

'I'm sorry I haven't paid your wages recently,' said Agnes, ever the punctilious socialist.

'That does not matter. You owe me no wages. I am your slave. But it is my responsibility. And sometimes I have to chip in money to help buy bicycle parts for Donald. No one has any money.'

'What is she saying?' demanded Freda.

Both of them ignored her.

'So,' continued Spider Girl, 'clean drinking water in Wuhan being so expensive, and fetching such a high price that many poor people cannot afford it, I thought that I could make some money by using Miss Freda's used bath water to sell drinking water at a cheap price.'

Agnes looked at Spider Girl. What a skilled negotiator she was. She knew several trade unions that could make use of her.

'In fact,' continued Spider Girl, 'with the taste of Miss Freda's perfumed soap in it, I am able to sell it at a slightly higher rate as a European water, whose perfume brings good luck and long life. I then buy our food from its profits.'

'You're a rogue,' said Agnes, and burst into laughter.

'I'm an honest girl,' rejoined Spider Girl. 'Look, I have brought you a bottle of wine out of my profits,' she added, taking one out of her basket.

'What on earth is going on?' demanded Freda.

Agnes described exactly what had been going on.

'This is outrageous,' said Freda. 'I feel personally violated. Servants should not be allowed to behave in this terrible manner. They need disciplining. They should wash their hands and clothing. I'm sorry that I am acting in such a bourgeois manner, but there must be standards! She's bought bottles of wine out of my bath water!'

For a second Freda thought about this.

Agnes looked at her very hard.

The bottle of wine stood on the table between them.

Then Freda's face started to wrinkle, crumble into a smile, followed by laughter, guffawing, and finally shrieks of laughter.

And after several bowls of wine that night Freda made the fateful decision to accompany Agnes to the Last Ditch Club.

Following President Beneš's swift-footed humiliation of Herr Henlein and Herr Hitler and especially of Mr Neville Chamberlain – the Runciman Mission had been abandoned tout court – the mood in the Last Ditch Club was extremely positive. Repeated toasts were drunk to the crafty Czech president, and headlines were triumphantly read aloud from newspapers from all four quarters of the earth which had somehow washed up in Wuhan.

Agnes, well raddled, had always – for reasons completely mysterious to her – fancied the ice-cold Peter Fleming. He attracted her as a cobra attracts a mongoose. So, when he refreshed his ice-cold martini at the bar, she tried a bit of gentle ribbing.

'Reckon that's one in the eye for your beloved prime minister, Peter. The Sudetenland is staying Czech.'

Fleming considered her.

'Germany and the Sudetenland are one nation – united by race, by a common language and contiguous borders. Nothing can stop them reuniting.'

'Yes, but...' continued Agnes.

Fleming cut her dead, returning to his chair with his martini, a neat twist of lemon on top.

George Hogg was made of sterner stuff – in his Quakerly way. Amid this raucous conviviality he'd attempted to put the opposing point of view. That what had happened was a bad, a dangerous thing. That whereas once Hitler was only going to take a small portion of Czechoslovakia, the Sudetenland, now he was so angry and humiliated that in his rage he would probably take the whole country, and then others after it, whether they had German populations in them or not. And after the behaviour of President Beneš Chamberlain would likewise feel so angry that he would refuse all help not only to Czechoslovakia but also to all those other countries. The very thing Chamberlain wanted – to rid his country of all these European entanglements through a deal with Herr Hitler so Britain could get back to its traditional job of trading with the rest of the world – was being offered him on a plate.

His repeated arguments were met with hostility, in some cases extreme hostility, but since everyone was in such good spirits because of the news (and the horse racing) no fisticuffs ensued.

George returned hurt and bewildered to his chair close to Fleming. Emotion was something he did not understand at all. As a child he'd been taught it was the most dangerous of all human qualities. It led all too often to violence. All things must be worked out and resolved through debate and pure reason. The pure reason of God.

'Hard luck,' said Fleming.

'They wouldn't listen,' said George.

'Halfwits.'

Once again George was feeling flickerings and darts of emotion, of anger within himself. He swallowed, but he could not stop them.

'They wouldn't listen. I tried and tried...'

'Arrogant fools. I mean, they all assume that Hitler wants war. The man spent four damn years in the trenches. A man who's seen the horrors of war like he has is the last person to go marching into another war. Stands to reason. All he wants is the return of all those German possessions and peoples stolen by the bloody Treaty of Versailles.'

'That Woodrow Wilson,' muttered George.

'George,' said Fleming, leaning closer, 'the reason all these bloody lefties here want a war is because that's what their boss Stalin wants. Stalin wants a war between Britain and Germany so that when both sides are exhausted he can march in and take the lot.'

George looked around the room. Fleming's right, he thought, a lot of these people are communists, or at least extreme lefties. Far more left than me. How do I stop them and their lust for war?

Fleming watched Hogg nibble at the bait he'd moulded so cunningly about his hook. All that was needed was one swift jerk.

'By the way, George...'

'Peter?'

'I'm off for a while. Got to take a quick trip to London. My editor wants a word at *The Times*...'

'I see,' said George.

'We two must stick together. You know, keep up the fight for peace and common sense. Sing from the same hymn sheet, so to speak.'

'I agree.'

'So I was wondering – just so I'm right up to date when I get back, understand who's been saying what in this little leftie hothouse – if you could maybe keep a few notes on who's saying what to whom about war, so the moment I'm back we'll be able to resume our little crusade against these damn warmongers. I'll know exactly the right arguments to deploy.'

George looked at Fleming. Fleming looked sincere and caring.

George still felt anger within himself. Would he be agreeing to this just because he was angry? George quietly suppressed his anger. He reconsidered Peter's request. He came to the same conclusion.

'I'll do it. For the cause of peace.'

And he meant it.

Agnes had left the club so that she could escort Freda to it and introduce her to the members. Freda had insisted on taking another bath, so Agnes had had to make the journey from apartment to club twice. As they were arriving Fleming was leaving. Fleming opened the door for them with a flourish of faux gallantry. Agnes ignored this and walked straight past him. Freda, on the other hand, more uncertain and insecure, mini-moued at him and bobbed a semi curtsey.

As Freda entered a brief silence fell. Good looking Western women, even if they were wearing glasses, were a rarity in Wuhan. Freda had taken some trouble with her appearance and make-up. She looked nervously around the room. Her eyes came to rest of the urbane and polished figure of Vernon Bartlett. His eyes fell on her.

9

Ilie in a cell. Curled up. I have just been heavily beaten by a man with a bamboo stick. My limbs and body ache and shoot with pain, my face is covered in blood which pours from my nose and mouth. I think I have lost two teeth. The man is now in the cell next to mine dishing out the same treatment to someone in there. From a distance come the screeches and yowls of something I'd rather not think about.

I start to weep. I stop weeping.

I lie in the darkness.

I must be in a cell of the State Security Force. I spoke with the man while he beat me. I tried to persuade him that they had got the wrong man, I was friends with Chiang Kai-shek himself, I was writing a play for him, that I was employed by his government. But I do not think he was the sort of man who even knew who Chiang Kai-shek was.

I assume this has happened because of the letter I wrote in support of my friend and fellow writer Tian Boqi. Tian is probably in here as well. Perhaps that is him being beaten in the next cell.

I stare into the stony darkness. What is my primary duty in life? To protect my family. I have *not* protected them. Firstly I deserted them, abandoned them to the invading Japanese. I was a coward. Secondly, by writing that letter to defend Tian Boqi I have put them at even greater risk. Say two of my children do survive, turn up here in Wuhan looking for me? I, their father, will not be there, to protect, to shelter, to comfort them. They shall be homeless. They shall be orphans. They will... I refuse to think of that poor scarred girl on the Bund.

Should I have written that letter to Tian Boqi? I know my wife holds very strong views on this, but even my wife is wrong – on occasions.

What can I do?

Wait til I am 'interrogated' by someone who actually knows who Chiang Kai-shek is? Even more importantly, who his wife is? But then I think that if the people who arrested me knew anything about my connections with Chiang, then they wouldn't have arrested me in the first place. Our security forces are notorious for their incoherence, their overstaffing, their corruption. No one knows, or worse, cares, what anyone else is doing within them. But then the main purpose of any security service is not to arrest and stop plotters, spies, mad bombers – it's to terrify, intimidate the people themselves. The more incompetent, the more random they become, the better they're doing their job!

I must hope that somehow I meet an official that believes my story about my knowing the Generalissimo.

I mean, this is not the first time our security services and I have met face to face. A light beating here, some quite powerful interrogations there. But, unlike several of my fellow writers, I am still alive.

I pray. I remember that others are in far worse situations than me. I think of the thousands of our soldiers giving their lives that we might live. I think of Our Lord Jesus Christ standing before Herod and Pilate, then hanging on his cross deserted by all the world, by his own father.

The door opens.

The man returns for my next beating.

Peter Fleming's family had originally made its fortune in Dundee. It owned several large jute mills there.

Pretty soon they owned their own jute plantations and warehouses around Calcutta in British India.

These widespread interests involved large-scale movements of capital, so pretty soon they founded a family bank, Robert Fleming & Co., which quickly became even more profitable than the jute business.

The bank specialized in Indian and Far Eastern trading.

Thus, when Fleming arrived at Croydon Airport – eight days out from Wuhan – the bank's Rolls-Royce met him and whisked him off to its headquarters in the City where he was bathed, his hair trimmed, and while a valet dressed him, he caught up on the latest news from Europe flicking through a copy of today's *Times*. Hitler had not been amused by President Beneš' antics. He'd moved his army to the Czech border. Either Czechoslovakia yielded the Sudetenland or it was war.

Fleming sighed.

The valet made a final adjustment to his buttonhole.

The Rolls whisked him down to Printing House Square, from where *The Times* was published.

The doorman saluted him and he walked up the stately carpeted stairs to the editor's office on the first floor, where he was greeted by the editor's secretary, Mr Greaves.

'Good evening, Mr Fleming,' said Greaves.

'Greaves.'

'Mr Dawson will see you straight away. Just go in.'

Fleming placed his hat and umbrella on the hat stand and walked through.

Dawson, the editor of *The Times*, sat behind his desk, squinting at an early blatt of tomorrow's leader page. As Fleming entered he removed his glasses.

'Ah, Peter,' he said with affection.

'Geoffrey!'

Ever since he was a little boy Peter, when meeting famous people, had invariably addressed them by their first name. Such familiarity would normally be frowned on – especially as Peter frequently met very pompous famous people – but somehow – perhaps it was that magic Etonian mixture of cheek and charm – no one was ever offended. To everyone else at *The Times* Mr Dawson was Mr Dawson. To Peter he'd always been Geoffrey.

'You've come over to see "our friends", I take it?'

'Yes.'

'Suppose you're seeing them tonight?'

'Tomorrow night, actually.'

'Well, that *is* good news.'

'Good news?'

'Peter, I'm having a bit of trouble composing tonight's editorial. It needs precise, yet elliptical diction, reassuring ambiguity...' Dawson searched for the right words.

'Honest duplicity?'

'No, Peter,' said Dawson somewhat sternly, 'that's not what I mean. I have to express what our prime minister is actually thinking. It must be authoritative. Trustworthy. But also suggest novel, perhaps even startling thoughts and possibilities. He is being flexible, as a statesman should, but not inconsistent.'

Dawson paused. Fleming knew what was coming next.

'Thing is, Peter, no one can write editorials like you. Both solid and fluid. Only got two hours before we go to press.'

'You want me to write it?'

'I do.'

'Then you'd better tell me precisely what the thinking is in Downing Street.'

Dawson looked at Fleming.

'Might take some time. Do you have any other appointments tonight?'

'I was due to meet my wife at the Savoy for dinner after her performance at the St James.'

'Ah,' said Geoffrey, 'what an actress! The best Elizabeth Bennet I have ever seen. Such understatement, such intelligence.'

'Celia's a good girl,' said Peter.

'Sit down,' said Geoffrey, 'sit down.' Fleming sat down on the sofa.

Geoffrey instructed Greaves to ring the St James Theatre and convey the message to Miss Johnson. He then came and sat beside Peter.

'Thing is, Peter, Neville's really in a pickle. Completely undecided. Just take the economy. At the moment its nicely under control. Unemployment holding down wages. But what happens if there's a sudden war scare? We'll have to declare full-scale rearmament. Heavy industry, armaments factories will boom. Workers, their unions demand huge wage rises – which we'll be forced to concede. The City and the bankers will panic, the pound will plummet, the empire will…'

'Not pleasant.'

'No. And foreign policy… This is Neville's difficulty – he can't allow himself to look weak in front of the dictators. But simultaneously we can't afford another European war. And while he finds himself in this terrible bind we must simply back him up.'

'Never desert your friends on a battlefield.'

'Exactly. But it's precisely at this moment that many in the press – normally his most loyal supporters – have used the excuse of Beneš's outrageous behaviour to criticize the prime minister. Whinge about "poor little Czechoslovakia!"'

Peter grimaced.

'Where to start?' said Geoffrey, opening his hands. 'The prime minister needs to inform President Beneš that he is on his own, France and Britain will do nothing to aid him, while simultaneously signalling to the British public and all our other friends in Europe upset by Henlein's – and, as they see it, Mr Hitler's – threats…'

'Supposed threats.'

'Indeed… that we will not allow the dictators to triumph.'

'Is the prime minister considering any ways of extricating us?'

'I've spoken to both Neville and Halifax at the Foreign Office. There's talk of Neville, in the name of peace – and we should never forget how strong the wish for peace is among the British people, despite all this leftist agitation – of Neville perhaps calling a big meeting or conference for peace, possibly in Central Europe – with all the leaders of the area discussing and then reaching a decision on what is to happen.'

'I presume that Beneš will not be invited?'

'Of course not.'

'Good. Yappy hounds need the whip.'

'But all this is in the future. They're still planning, feeling it all out. In the meantime…'

'We need reassurance. A smoothing of the ways. Make the alarming look harmless.'

'Precisely.'

Two men watch me.

At first they just peer at me through the spyhole in my cell door. Draw back the latch, peer in – one face followed by the other – then slam it shut.

They do this for several days.

Then one day the two men do not just stare at me through the spyhole, they actually open the door. Stand in the corridor staring at me.

'See you soon,' they say. They saunter off down the corridor. A warder slams the door shut in my face. Soon afterwards terrible cries come from a room further down the corridor.

This goes on for three more days.

I wonder to myself if anyone out there even knows I'm in prison? If there's anyone who will enquire after me? Tell other people, dare to kick up a fuss? What can I do myself? I've tried shouting out: 'I am a friend of General Chiang Kai-shek and his wife, and they have commissioned me to write a play which I should be writing.' They ignore this. Probably half the prisoners in here spend their time exhaustively explaining they have powerful, influential friends outside who will be really angry when they hear about this. I try to think of any other influential people I know. There's really only General Feng Yuxiang, but he's out of favour with the government, and besides he's presently up in Chungking.

The door opens. The two men stare at me.

'Hello,' they say. And guffaw. They wear cheap grey suits. Both have their hair slicked back. One has glasses. 'Today you're coming with us. Down the corridor. Follow us.'

Shaking, I walk to my doorway. No one else is in the corridor. They look back.

'Follow us,' they state. They walk down the corridor.

I follow them, trying to stop my shaking.

They get to another door. I stop. They open the door.

'Come on in,' they say.

I cannot move.

'Come on in,' they say. 'We're not going to harm you. Just walk in.'

They make way so I can walk between them through the door.

I don't want to go into that room.

'Please,' they say. And smile.

Well, I conclude, I can go in by myself, or someone will roughly push me in. Then follow me in and be a whole lot rougher.

I walk between them. Into the room. I expected blood and gore and bits of hair and skin to be decorating its walls and floor. Instead there's a table. A single chair on one side of the table, with its back to the door. On the other side of the table two chairs. There is a single file on the table.

'Sit down,' they say, indicating the single chair. I do so. They sit on the two chairs opposite me. The door behind me stays open.

I hear footsteps. Boots. They march down the corridor, stop at our door, enter, and come to a halt just behind me. I do not look around.

The one with the glasses opens the file, takes out its papers, places them neatly on the table. He looks at the papers. For a whole he reads them. Then he looks at me.

'You are Mr Lao She? An author?'

I cannot answer him.

He repeats the questions.

I am acutely aware of the man behind me.

'Yes,' I croak.

He starts reading again. I cannot bear this.

'Look,' I say. 'I think there must have been some mistake. You're confusing me with another Mr Lao She? I am a friend of General Chiang Kai-shek. And his wife Madame Chiang. He asked me to write a play for them…'

The other man speaks.

'Shut up,' he says. 'We're not interested in your made-up tales. You speak out of turn once more and you will be hurt.'

I shut up.

The man with glasses continues his leisurely read. He stops.

'On the third of June, 1938, in a corridor of a building on the campus of the University of Wuchang you were seen to have an altercation with a Professor Liang...'

'Did I? I don't remember...'

Professor Liang? Professor Liang? Then I remember him. I thought we were quite good friends.

'I don't remember any disagreement with him?'

'That's strange. Several reliable people noticed you arguing and reported it. Professor Liang is a firm patriot and strong supporter of our government.'

'Well, so am I.'

'Then why were you arguing in such a violent way with him?'

'I wasn't. I don't remember.'

I wrack my brains to recall the incident. My brain doesn't work that fast in such circumstances. Then I remember.

'I remember,' I say. 'I remember. Professor Liang and I were discussing a poem by the poet Du Fu. A favourite of us both. The poem is in the form of an argument. We were each reciting the opposite side of the argument. So we probably sounded as though we were arguing.'

'The people who observed you said you were arguing. And you were not reciting poetry.'

Suddenly I remember that in this encounter, after the poem recital, we had had some disagreement about a certain line in the poem. Not unfriendly or anything.

I explain this.

'So you admit you were arguing.'

'We were disagreeing. He thought this way about a line, I the other.'

'You were arguing.'

'That's what academics do. We have disagreements with each other. It's how we earn our living.'

Without waiting a moment he continues smoothly.

'On the fourteenth of July, 1938, you were observed upon the Bund in the company of the known Marxist agitator Mr Tian

587

Boqi at the Happy Sunshine Tea House. Your conversation with him was overheard by several patriotic citizens who immediately considered it their duty to report what they had heard to the authorities.'

Now we are arriving at the difficult part. The part I knew was coming.

'Mr Tian Boqi is my pupil. I was employed by the government to teach him how to write propaganda plays to encourage the country people and working people of China to fight more diligently against the Japanese invaders, to defend our country. I did not choose him as my pupil. He was selected by others and sent to me for me to instruct. He and I never spoke a single disloyal word to each other in all the time we worked together.'

The man facing me without glasses flickers his eyes and I feel a horrendous pain in my back. I scream. For a moment my eyes blur. I bite my tongue savagely to stop my scream. My eyes refocus. I cower forwards in my chair. There is blood in my mouth.

This, I tell myself, is what comes from helping your friends. Then feel immediately guilty.

The man with glasses continues in his monotonous voice.

'Your whole conversation was overheard by several people. So dismayed were they at the disloyalty and treachery that you were expressing that they wrote down what you were saying, word for word.'

'Neither of us said anything disloyal or treacherous about the government. We are both patriots...'

Again, I am hit heavily in the back.

'Please,' I say, 'please do not hit me again.'

'Did you not speak positively of the communist terrorists as they forced the local peasantry to pay them money and give them their sons as recruits?'

This told me that they had indeed overheard our foolish conversation. Missing the subtlety of it as we were criticizing the communist guerrillas in the field and praising the behaviour of the peasants, but damning none the less.

I was an idiot!

'Do you want to be hit again?'

'No. No. Please.'

'Then you will tell us precisely what Mr Tian Boqi told you about his travels and who he met in the countryside and what they discussed.'

Two things. Firstly, they obviously want to break Tian Boqi – he is their main target. Maybe they want to turn him. That happened to several of my writer friends in the early thirties. My 'confession' could do that. And secondly, they obviously didn't record our entire conversation, or they wouldn't be asking who his contacts in the countryside are. A subject we had not discussed.

I swallow some blood.

'Tian Boqi and I did not discuss who he met in the countryside.'

A crack in my back.

'Tell us!' shouted the man without glasses.

'I can't,' I say, 'we didn't discuss it.'

I flinch just before the man behind me hits me. His blow sends me sprawling across the table. It knocks my glasses flying. I am near sighted. I can focus on things close to my eyes but not on anything any further away. As I sprawl on the table my head comes into contact with the file and, right next to my eyes, I see the list of people who have requested and presumably read my file. Two names jump out. The men behind the table have obviously not bothered to read it themselves. Perhaps they just assumed they were other low-grade civil servants, torturers like themselves. But on this list, through my short-sighted eyes, I clearly see the initials SML and CKS. Soong Meiling and Chiang Kai-shek. The most powerful man in China and his even more powerful wife. I raise my head slightly. Stare directly into the face of the man with glasses. Admittedly I can't see him that well, because I've lost my own glasses.

'You obviously have not checked the list of people who have read my file. Or you would not be treating me like this.'

I continue to stare. Even with my blurry vision I can see he is hesitating, calculating whether he will lose some power over me if he gives in to my request and reads the list, but simultaneously worrying about the chance of there having been some cock-up. Some really important person, or people, might be on that list – people who could, on hearing a friend of theirs had been tortured, be in a position to wrathfully descend upon him and annihilate him forever.

'You do not dare to read it,' I say.

Interrogations like this are all about power.

He is still hesitating when the man without glasses snatches the file from him and runs his eye down the list. And stops. And blanches.

'Shall I hit him, boss?' enquires the unseen man behind me.

'No,' says the man, slight panic in his voice.

A series of rapid calculations are obviously spinning through his mind.

'Get out,' he orders the man behind me.

'Yes, boss,' says the man. He marches away and down the corridor. I will never see my assailant's face.

By this time the man with glasses has read the list on the file and his face has turned deepest grey. The man without glasses is meanwhile still sunk in desperate calculation.

'Could you pass me back my glasses?' I ask with quiet authority.

They scramble to return them. Suddenly start howling out apologies. Deluge me with grovels and pleas for forgiveness, each offering the other as sacrificial victim.

Within twenty minutes, my wounds doctored, my clothing brushed and restored, I am standing – just about – on the street outside. Beside me stands Tian Boqi – just about. This time he has got more than a black eye.

Celia Johnson was about the only stable thing in her husband Peter Fleming's life. The next evening he watched her as she patiently removed her make-up from her face in her dressing room in the St James. She did it in that slow, thorough way in which she approached life. She specialized in playing ordinary, sensible, uncomplaining people on stage. Which was what made her Elizabeth Bennet so interesting. A serious, feeling woman, sometimes aghast at her own flippancy and malice, slowly, painfully working her way towards becoming a worthy woman and wife to a man himself going through similar ordeals.

In everyday life she was exactly the same – intelligent, reserved, kind, with infinite patience. She'd once trekked over the Himalayas with him. Not one single complaint. Fleming wondered what he would do without her. She was his rock. Of course, he couldn't wait to get away. More from London, from England, than from her. He found London a prison. But then abroad was not much better. The wilder, the more primitive it was the better he could cling on.

'Got to go, old girl,' he told her.

'You're going straight to the airfield after your meeting?' she asked.

'Yes.'

She didn't rise to kiss him farewell because she didn't want any of her make-up to smear his face or his immaculate evening dress.

'You're a good girl,' he told her, his voice thickening slightly with emotion.

'You look after yourself,' she told him, as she knew that was what he wanted to hear.

He left. She did not drop a tear because, however sad she felt, that would help no one. She continued patiently removing her make-up.

Fleming was soon in the garish light of Piccadilly. A tart trolled past looking for custom. A negro leant against a shop front picking his bright white teeth with a toothpick. Fleming's car, black and sleek, swept up to the curb. He stepped in and was whisked into the night.

In 1938 MI6 was ruled by an unstable quadvirate of rivals – its ailing head, Admiral Sir Hugh Sinclair; his soon-to-be successor, Major General Sir Stewart Menzies (Sir Hugh having died at his desk); Colonel Valentine Vivian, known as 'Vee-Vee', ex-Indian Police officer with a monocle to match; and Colonel Sir Claude Dansey, who, he liked to tell people, could think in nine directions at once.

MI6 inhabited a bizarre and dilapidated block of flats. Peter Fleming was visiting Major General Sir Stewart Menzies, whose office was perched on top of the roof. An assistant guided Fleming though a rabbit warren of passageways, corridors, nooks and alcoves. At the end of all this he was led up a flight of stairs so narrow a stout man would become irretrievably wedged. Finally, on the roof, they crossed an iron bridge and Fleming was ushered into Sir Stewart Menzies's private office, a cramped shed measuring ten feet by ten.[13]

Sir Stewart Menzies's chief claim to fame was that during the 1924 general election he had helped forge the notorious Zinoviev letter, which 'proved' that the Labour Party, which was poised to win the general election, was directly under the control of the Kremlin. Published in the ever-cooperative *Daily Mail*, this document immediately destroyed Labour's election chances.

'Peter,' said the major general.

'Stewart,' said Peter.

'Good flight?'

'Yes. And you, how are you?'

'Not bad.'

'Any good hunting?'

'Went out with the Beaufort a couple of times in the spring, with Henry Somerset.'

'How's he keeping?'

'Not too bad. Asked to be remembered to you.'

'I could do with a good gallop sometime.'

'Henry said there'll always be a horse for you.'

Slight pause.

'I asked you to fly over for two reasons, Peter. Firstly, to brief you on what's happening here. Big moves ahead on the European front. PM's due to fly to Germany to meet the corporal and smooth out an agreement on the Sudetenland.'

'Beneš will be ignored?'

'Not permitted within a hundred miles of it. But deals on the Sudetenland are not the main purpose of the conference. While there, Chamberlain intends to work out a far more general arrangement, a solemn and binding agreement on the future of the whole of Europe. Hitler must keep his hands off the rest of Czechoslovakia and France, the Low Countries and Scandinavia...'

'The civilized bits.'

'...and he can do what he damn well wants with the East. The sooner he lays into those Bolshevik animals in Russia the happier we'll all be.'

'Agreed.'

'Which means that, a New European Deal signed, we can at last be rid of the place and all its perpetual squabbles and Britain can once again rule the empire and the world. Resume our rightful position as the world's leading trading nation.'

'What about Eden and Churchill and their rabble?'

Menzies sighed.

'Don't those imbeciles realize that another European war will destroy our Empire, Britain's financial and military strength in the world? Because of our obsession with Europe we see increasing demands for independence in India, the Americans stealing our markets in China and Japan and South America…'

There was a pause.

'I called you in, Peter, because we want someone out there who can keep his head – so in case things go pear-shaped here in Europe, you can step in with the Chinese government and reassure them there's no cause for alarm. Do you have contacts with the Japanese intelligence services in Wuhan?'

'Yes.'

'Then you must convey the same message to them. Business as usual.'

'You can rely on me.'

'Of course I can, Peter.'

Menzies admired Peter. His endless treks and expeditions through wild and remote places. His taste for the dangerous and exotic. He reminded him of Buchan's Richard Hannay, forever playing the Great Game, guarding the outposts of Empire.

'Recruited any useful agents in Wuhan? Got any insights into what our enemy's intentions are over there?'

'The Bolsheviks are there in force. They've got communists in the government. Chou En-lai and so on.'

'Not good.'

'The press corps is almost entirely Bolshie, or at best socialists.'

'You've got names?'

'Well, there's the well-known ones like Agnes Smedley,

probably a lesbian, or the Snows, or Jack Belden, an alcoholic. But they're Americans, so there's little we can do about them.'

'I know a couple of chaps in Washington who'd be interested in their names.'

'And you can tell them Evans Carlson, their so-called military attaché, talks openly and in depth every day with his Russian counterparts. And he spends as much time in the north-west plotting with the communists as he does in Wuhan.'

'Useful. He's Roosevelt's man, isn't he?'

'Yes. In the British press there's Vernon Bartlett...'

'That creepy little parlour socialist. Have to switch the wireless off every time he comes on.'

'James Bertram of the *Telegraph* – he's pretty red. The Kiwi Rewi Alley, out and out communist. And there's someone who's just turned up, from the *News Chronicle*, a woman called Freda Utley. Looks a bit of a mess. According to gossip she spent quite a lot of time in Moscow. They all work little bits of socialist propaganda into their reports – the changes in Chinese society, social medicine, educational reform, the "fight" against fascism...'

'Good,' said Menzies, having noted down all their names and the papers they wrote for. 'I'll get in touch with their proprietors and editors. Either get them sacked outright or get someone in head office to rewrite their stories before publication. Recruited any agents?'

'One likely candidate – a George Hogg – Quaker, works for UPI. Not exactly top drawer. Went to some school in Harpenden, then Wadham.'

Menzies raised an eyebrow.

'Earnest, not bright,' continued Fleming. 'I managed to turn him, as a pacifist, against all the lefties perpetually screaming for war. I've impressed on him the prime minister's desire for peace.'

'I'll run a check on him. What's his politics?'

'Liberal. But I've tutored him to see lefties as the enemy. Before I left I got him to note down while I was away what other journalists were saying, conversations he'd overheard. I'll send you a copy. I'll have him signed up within a month.'

'Splendid.'

Then Menzies pulled a face.

'Not going to cost us a lot of money, is he? Our budget's pretty tight.'

'He won't cost us a penny. He'll spy for us out of pure idealism.'

'The best sort of spy,' opined Major-General Sir Stewart Menzies.[14]

It is a fact rarely acknowledged by writers that in fact they themselves have very little to do with the actual act of writing. Of course, after the fact, it is great to claim credit for one's wonderful creation – gorgeous prose, deeply memorable characters, thrilling plot etc. etc. – but, in truth, while in the substantive act of creation, one has virtually no control whatever over the actual process or its results. It just sort of occurs.

Of course, one does one's research for such things. The background. Draw up sketchy versions of the final characters. Have a rough idea of the plot and the tone and the 'what it's all about'. But then you enter a period of complete blankness. You wander around listlessly doing nothing in particular like some broody duck. Then miraculously, spontaneously, without any conscious actions or decisions on your part, it breaks forth, starts pouring out of you, in uncontrolled and uncontrollable gushes. Walms up from nowhere, nothingness, and pours forth onto your page. In all this you are but a mere medium, a duct of the downpour. It writes itself without any intercession or deliberation or consciousness from you. And then, suddenly one day, miraculously, it all ends. You mysteriously regain your normality and become once again just an ordinary person. And no one is more ordinary than a writer.

But I am not here to reveal to you the embarrassing and hidden truths about writing. Let the mystery of brooding genius remain! I am exposing these soiled trade secrets because they help explain to you precisely how it was that I managed to write my embarrassingly successful entertainment *Defend Wuhan!*

As I have previously explained, I had for some time been fiddling with ideas and themes and characters and tones and styles. All with absolutely no result. My mind remained a complete blank. My creative constipation was so obvious it became an embarrassment. But then suddenly...! Well, you know what happened. I was arrested. Yes, arrested. And this is where it becomes deeply embarrassing, and why I haven't told you about this until now. Because, whatever your circumstances, however dire your situation, nothing can stop the arrival of creativity. So while I lay quivering in my cell, while enormous men were raining lusty blows on me, while afterwards I lay inert and silent upon the stone floor, then, then the words commenced. At first in dribs and drabbles. Then with sudden spurts, finally in torrents. I became like an incontinent baby. Words, words, words! Words immeasurable as stars in the midnight sky. And as a writer, a proper professional writer, I knew that unless I caught them then, in spate, in full roar, remembered them, every single one exactly and in place, then they would have gone, emptied forever into the void. So all the time I was being beaten, interrogated, humiliated, shouted at, simultaneously I found it necessary, unavoidable, that I MUST record and exactly memorialize obsessively each and every word that evacuated into my consciousness. And, believe it or not, somehow or other, I managed it. Such are the abnormalities of writers.

Which was why when I met Tian Boqi on the pavement outside the prison I was in such a hurry to leave him. Because I had all these words bursting within me. I had to write them down. And judging by the look on his face and the gait of his body he found himself in a similar circumstance.

So when I get home I immediately seize my pen and start writing. It flows from me. My play has to start in a prison. A single man in a prison cell. Where can I have got that idea from? And of course it has to be a Japanese prison cell, not a Chinese one! And he of course, with great courage and physical daring, has to escape. And because of his courage and all-out patriotism, under the leadership of the heroic Chiang Kai-shek, he quickly becomes a great commander of men and leads innumerable armies of China onto the fields of battle and there defeats sub-human Japanese at every turn. And now he stands here in Wuhan, sworn to defend it to the very death! (Even though, of course, everyone in the audience will know that within days Wuhan will fall to the horrors of the Japanese.) But that is the very purpose of art. To dream the impossible dream!

We'll need lots of marching people – so through Chiang Kai-shek's office I contact the army. The Boy Scouts and Girl Guides are added for more marching. We get the anti-aircraft corps to contribute various searchlights (provided there isn't an air raid that night) and a military band for martial music. I request my old friend and comrade Yu Liqun – or Guo Liqun, as she now is – if she and her theatrical troupe can provide some stirring military dancing for us. It's what they specialize in. For emotional music I contact my old friend Shanyaodan, who does the great drum song epics in his tented theatre down on the Bund. His orchestra can provide the music, and I also ask him to play our hero. He may be a bit old but no one can deliver lines with the strength and conviction and emotion he can. He'll transform my feeble and unconvincing hero into a second Zhang Fei holding the bridge at Changban, and everyone will understand and feel the parallel.

But I still have one problem. I really need in my torrid extravaganza to show a bit of what the Americans call 'leg'. A bit of pizzazz and flapdoodle. Something that is simultaneously exotic but also exceedingly modest. General Chiang Kai-shek and his wife are both stern Christians. And so am I.

Where on earth am I going to find that in Wuhan?

10

This afternoon George Hogg was doing what he enjoyed doing more than anything else in Wuhan. He was in a shed. A very small, cramped shed.

In this shed lived the orphans George had volunteered to look after – nearly fifty boys – where, for several extremely frantic hours, he tried to organize them into team games, stop them fighting each other, keep an eye on the violent ones and stop them from attacking the vulnerable ones, get them all singing cheery patriotic songs and trying to teach them the rudiments of reading and writing.

Since George's skills in writing and reading Chinese were only slightly more advanced than theirs, however, this was an uphill process.

Overall it was bedlam, but slowly, through the screaming and punching and howling and laughter – because they did like this big, chunky and not very sharp Englishman, or at any rate feared his size and strength – very gradually George was able to discern at least some improvement, some calming of their behaviour. They were the survivors of blown-apart families, kids who'd had to resort to violence and thieving and even murder to survive. Deeply disturbed and grieving children, some of whom had had to invent entirely new imaginary worlds and personas to escape into in order to survive. But amid this cacophony George noticed individuals starting slowly to abandon their extreme isolation, to explore new ways of relating to each other, beginning to realize that on occasions cooperation and trust might be a more effective way of surviving in the midst of such violence and insanity.

All this took place in the shed where they also lived. Sometimes they went for walks, but at least two adults were required to keep under control the strays and berserkers. George often wished that they had some sort of play area, or even better playing fields – like he'd had at St George's School, Harpenden – where they could roam and explode their energies and angers.

Liang got on well with Hua, but always quarreled with Chin. Chin was scared of the bigger Heng and used to descend into gibbering terror whenever Heng knocked roughly into him – which was often. But Heng, surprisingly, got on well with Bojing, the weakest of the group, whenever anyone tried to bully him. Bojing reminded Heng of his younger brother, who'd been killed outright before Heng's eyes. Three of them – Cong, Xingfu and Wen – refused to speak to anyone else but were slowly learning to communicate with – George wouldn't put it as high as talking to – each other. They watched each other all the time and went everywhere together.

Strangely, the flames of anger and irritation which so often licked about him when he was in the Last Ditch Club didn't trouble him in the least when he was in the midst of this bedlam. Indeed, their shouts and blows and tantrums were like balm to his soul.

Anyhow, this afternoon George was taking them all for a walk along the Bund. He was able to do this by himself because he had promised them that if they behaved and stayed together, at the end of their walk they would visit a cinema. None of them had ever been to a cinema before. They were going to see a Walt Disney film, *Snow White and the Seven Dwarfs*. No one had any idea who Walt Disney was or even what a film was, but it sounded great. They spoke to each other in hushed tones about it, and by and large they even stayed in line. The one exception was Guang, who rather fancied himself as a ladies' man – even though he was only ten – and made various pert comments to passing ladies which led to quite a few 'incidents'. But Heng kept Guang in some semblance of order with hard cuffs. Heng was anxious to see this 'film'.

They managed to get into the packed cinema, fifteen wedged into a row of five seats. It was here that George's problems started.

Problems not with the boys – because the entire audience was behaving as wildly – but with George himself.

The difficulty for George was that before the Disney film started a newsreel was being played of various events, both inside China itself (with lots of footage of the war), and of the outside world. Although the event in question had taken place at the end of June, nearly two months previously, film of it had only finally arrived in Wuhan the day before.

It was a newsreel of the momentous boxing match held on 22 June 1938 in Madison Square Garden, New York to decide the heavyweight championship of the world. It was fought between Max Schmeling, from Germany – Nazi Germany – and Joe Louis, the American champion, a negro. Max Schmeling had in fact already fought an off-form Joe Louis back in 1936 and beaten the previously unbeaten Louis in a surprise upset. Back in Germany, Hitler had gone wild. The Aryan Nazi superhero had knocked out the 'champion' of the decadent West – and a sub-human negro to boot! In fact, in real life Max Schmeling and Joe Louis were the best of friends – Max wasn't a Nazi at all – and the two of them remained close up to their deaths, with Max helping out Joe when he ran into financial difficulties. But never allow truth – or subtlety – to get in the way of a fantastic story!

Anyhow, Joe Louis, all-American hero – though I somehow doubt that he was the hero of 'all' of America – stepped out into a blaze of lights to fight the Nazi Beast and the whole of Madison Square Garden – which contained a large Jewish contingent – went berserk. The Chinese cinema audience – or perhaps mob would be a more exact word – likewise went berserk. They too had had more than enough of fascism and racial prejudice recently and saw the whole thing in black and white terms – so to speak.

The fight itself turned out to be the shortest bout in world heavyweight boxing history – before or since. It lasted for all of two minutes and four seconds, including three floorings before the final knockout.

George the Quaker, entirely opposed to violence in any form, just stared with his mouth open, while all around him the cinema went ape.

Louis, the Brown Bomber, came out of his corner fast. Two lefts to Schmeling's face and a crack to his left jaw. Schmeling feebly patted Joe's grim face. Joe countered with a barrage of rights and lefts to the head which drove the German smack into the ropes where he could not raise his arms to defend himself against the ceaseless onslaught. The referee stepped between them and the fight resumed in the middle of the ring.

Louis cracked a right into Schmeling's jaw and Schmeling was down for a count of three. He raised himself on shaky feet to be pummeled non-stop in his gut and chest with crushing pile-drivers before Louis drove a sharp left hook into Schmeling's jaw followed by a right to the chin which felled Schmeling to the floor again.

George was fervently hoping that *Snow White* would start soon. Very soon.

Glassy-eyed and rubber-legged, the stupefied non-Nazi Schmeling arose and tried in vain to hold off his on-fire opponent, but his torso and gut were again pummeled with Louis's Götterdämmerung blows before a sharp left hook to his jaw followed by a missile of a punch dead on the end of his chin felled Schmeling yet again onto his back. Somehow or other he managed to roll over onto all fours but then could not move and stayed there motionless, panting, head down like a poleaxed ox.

On the count of three Schmeling's frantic trainer threw his towel into the ring, but this token of surrender was then unrecognized in American boxing codes and the referee turned away from the trainer, scrutinized the German, and on the count of five signalled the fight was over. In less than a single round. Two minutes and four seconds.

The problem was that such was the Chinese audience's reaction to this newsreel that the manager decided it would be a popular move to repeat it – to wild approbation from the packed cinema – and then repeat it again. And then twice more. And this became a real problem for George. The problem for George the Quaker was not that this atrocious act was being shown again and again before all these people. Or even that it was being rerun again and again before the eyes of his traumatized boys (all of whom were shrieking louder than anyone else for it to be reshown. They'd all decided they really liked 'films'.) No, the real problem was in George himself. Somewhere deep and horrifying within himself. To his eternal shame, in a part of himself he hadn't even known existed before, George Hogg was starting to enjoy, deeply enjoy, exult in this barbarism. Each bone-crunching blood-spurting hammer and blow.

George Hogg, Quaker, pacifist, stood there, baying like a wild animal. Partly it was because George was a decent middle-class liberal and the sight of a poor negro, the descendant of slaves, now battering nine bells out of a racist white supremacist was deeply, if shamefully, satisfying to him. But it went deeper than that. In the shadows, the deep shadows Joe Louis was smashing through, lurked the faces of all those damned warmongers at the Last Ditch Club who were continually humiliating him and shouting him down, perpetually demanding the whole world lay down and be slaughtered by unending war and suffering. Next time he was going to stand up and start smashing…

George suddenly sat down. Overcome with shame. Remorse. Where on earth had that animal leapt from? Where was his reason, his civilization, his pacifism? Fortunately everyone else in the cinema was in an even worse state than him so no one noticed his fall, his expulsion from Eden.

Eventually everyone calmed down. The bloodcurdling newsreel was followed by the anodyne waffles and cutesiness of *Snow White*. The audience thought it pretty poor fare after the wonders of Joe Louis.

George sat demanding of himself what that beast was? Where it had come from? And worrying above all about when it might return?

11

As the Japanese imperial armies drew closer and closer to Wuhan their bombing raids became more and more frequent. Raids would take place at all times of the day and night, and a single day could see several raids.

This raid started early one afternoon and was heralded by the heavy throb of bombers approaching from a distance, then their appearance high in the clear sky, the sun glinting menacingly off their wings and fuselages. Their fighter escorts flew above them in flawless, invincible formations. On the ground the bark of anti-aircraft guns opened up followed by the explosions of small white smoke balls in the skies far above. On this occasion the Chinese and Allied air forces actually succeeded in scrambling in time. Russian fighters and their pilots – 'volunteers' from the Soviet Union – and hired American mercenaries in obsolete British fighters, plus two or three actual Chinese planes, managed to wobble erratically into the skies like fragile gnats to combat the solid steel phalanxes of the Japanese armada. In attempting to climb above the Japanese bombers they were swooped down on by an angry swarm of Japanese fighters. Dog fights broke out all over. Furious as wasps, fighters circled, fired, wheeled and manoeuvred. Anti-aircraft shells burst indiscriminately among friend and foe, seldom hitting either. Strings of bombs were starting to explode across Hanyang and the government and university offices south of the river in Wuchang, slicing through the air like screaming knives. Three Soviet fighters, dancing and swerving, managed to find a path between the Japanese fighters and fell upon the large cumbersome bombers. Sounds of screaming engines trying desperately to gain height, the deep groan of the fighters diving for a kill, a Japanese bomber exploding in a great flash – triggered frenzied applause from the crowds of Chinese civilians spectating from the streets below as the bomber's wings disintegrated and the tail section fell in lazy cartwheels and loops down towards the city. Another bomber, its engines afire and out of control, trailing a tail of black smoke, streaked earthward in a long slanting death dive, finally blowing up in a shattering burst of flame and smoke. Two fighters collided in midair in a great splash of fire.

Long red banners of fire and crimson smoke furled up into the sky amid the confused sounds of ambulance and fire engine bells. Lorries tore up and down streets carrying volunteers and first aid workers to help dig out the victims. They were helped by troops of Boy Scouts. Even George Hogg's orphans were there with George, digging away. The dead lay on the ground, their skins tattooed with gravel and sand and shrapnel.

There was method in this murder. By the evening, knowing that all the casualties and wounded from their earlier raids over Hanyang and Wuchang would by now have been transported to Wuhan's only hospital in Hankou, knowing that the hospital itself would be crammed with desperately wounded patients, that night they deliberately switched their targeting precisely to the hospital and its immediate area. The same hospital where Donald and Hu and the Canadian and Indian surgeons now worked with such ferocity and exhaustion.

One of those clever little Social Darwinist, eugenicist tricks the Japanese had learnt from Britain and Europe and America. Lesser races beneath the bombs.

Various unforeseen problems had resulted from the decision by Dr Bob McClure, chief surgeon of Wuhan's hospital, to abandon his previous policy of amputating the limbs of wounded servicemen and adopting Donald Hankey's novel technique of using bicycle spokes to knit together broken bones and then place the patients in traction. You cannot really move patients in traction. Or you can, but only very slowly and with great care. This meant that the hospital itself, as well as all those patients recovering from other surgery, was now silting up with hundreds of tractioned soldiers unable to be moved far. Indeed, so many of them were there and so successful had Donald's surgical innovations proved, that the two wards allocated to them were already brimming and the patients and their beds and traction equipment had spilled out into the hospital's gardens and lawns. Thanks to the warm weather they were quite comfortable through the days and nights. And thanks to Hu's connections with Intelligent Whore and Madame Chiang, many more girls had been successfully recruited from the brothels to nurse the extra patients.

Up until now, with all this extra help, it had been possible to carefully and painstakingly manoeuvre the tractioned patients back into the hospital during air raids aimed at other parts of Wuhan. The corridors were crammed, and in the two specialist wards it was almost impossible to move, but it just about worked.

But tonight was going to be different. Very different.

Twenty minutes before the raid started, Japanese aircraft dropped flares to designate the exact location of the hospital so that their bombers, following behind, would know precisely where to drop their bombs. The Japanese had already used this flare technique in other parts of the city, so the inhabitants of both the hospital and the surrounding area knew exactly what was in store for them as the flares floated down among them.

Pandemonium broke out, but within the hospital was quickly suppressed. The staff were by and large dedicated and disciplined people. They were used to emergencies and panic and pain. All the patients were successfully and swiftly transported back into the hospital. The place was jam-packed. And then they started to hear the thrum-thrum of the bombers' engines as they approached. Now came the difficult part. It was hospital policy, and a very wise if cold-blooded policy, for the staff at this time in a raid to abandon their patients to fortune and, along with those patients who were capable of moving, leave the hospital for the nearby shelters. If these abandoned patients did not survive then they did not survive. If the doctors and staff did not survive, however, then no future patients, thousands and thousands of them, could survive either. The roar of the bombers' engines was almost overhead. So the staff, including all the doctors and nurses and assistants and orderlies and Hu, rushed to the safety of the shelters.

But at this moment, in the darkness of the blackout, with patients moaning and stirring around him, Donald decided he could not leave.

He made a medical, a surgical decision. The fact was that with bombs likely falling all around and indiscriminately, his patients in traction would almost certainly panic, start writhing and moving and twisting about in their terror, rupturing their traction, breaking open their wounds and shattering their mending bones and flesh, destroying their chances of once again living a normal, proper, human life. He must stay. He must, somehow, calm them.

Donald didn't know anything about how to calm people, how to adopt a strong, gentle, reassuring voice. Besides, he hardly spoke any Chinese. He was a lousy singer. He stood alone in the midst of two darkened wards, the corridors crammed fast with patients.

'Crikey,' thought Donald. 'What can I do?'

He carried a single candle. The bombs started to scream and plummet down all around the hospital. Into the gardens, the surrounding buildings.

'I must be able to do something!'

He felt in the pocket of his tweed jacket. He found a piece of paper.

When Donald had so suddenly made his surprise decision to come to China after meeting with his long-term chum Bonkers Binkie at the Ritz, he had telegraphed his parents in Wiltshire to tell them he was leaving for China the next day and could they please send up some of his clothes and necessities to London posthaste. His mother, being a farmer's wife, did not immediately panic, but instead stoically started packing a suitcase. Since she did not have any tissue paper to stuff Donald's pockets with – as was the custom in those days – and it was three days before she was due to catch the bus into Wincanton to do her weekly shop, she instead took an old copy of *The West Wilts and Trowbridge Advertiser* off a pile of them in the kitchen, cut it up into strips and lined his suitcase and stuffed his pockets with them. She then cycled to the station with the suitcase on her handlebars and sent it up to London. Donald picked it up the next morning at the left luggage office at Waterloo Station.

So it was a strip of paper from *The West Wilts and Trowbridge Advertiser* that Donald now found in his hand in the darkened hospital in Wuhan. It turned out to be a long list of the market prices fetched for sheep at the previous week's livestock auction in Westbury. All around the hospital the bombs were falling, the ground shaking, Donald's patients were starting to moan and shriek and writhe in their beds. All their wounds and healing would be soon torn apart. Donald's mind remained a complete blank. He could remember not a single poem or prayer. And, as already noted, he was a lousy singer. All he could think to do was read aloud from this months-old report of the prices sheep were fetching at Westbury market.

He started nervously.

'Sheep and lamb and hogge prices. Fifteen sheep heavy. One shilling two pence per pound. Thirty-eight hoggets light. Ten pence per pound. Twenty-eight lambs standard, one shilling and six pence per pound.'

At least the patients were quietening a bit. What on earth was this crazy Englishman doing?

His voice was deepening. There started to be an element of empathy, concern in his tone.

'Forty-two hoggets medium. One shilling and four and a half pence per pound. Twenty-four lambs heavy, one shilling eight pence per pound.'

His voice was starting to croon, to sing almost. Donald in his tweed jacket with his spectacles glinting in the candlelight slowly picked his way amid their beds and traction equipment, through the wards, down corridors, piece of paper in hand, candle before him, thunderous explosions, bomb concussions just outside, Donald's voice carrying through, working over, calming, creating softness and gentleness and peace amid bedlam. Maybe his voice might keep everyone safe?

'Unweaned lambs, eight pence per pound. Old rams, four pence per pound. Ewes medium, one shilling one pence per pound.'

As Donald gained confidence, slowly his repertoire started

to widen. Suddenly he remembered the words to his favourite hunting song, and the runes of 'D'ye Ken John Peel' started to sound out in Wuhan.

> D'ye ken John Peel with his coat so
>   gay,
> D'ye ken John Peel at the break of
>   day,
> D'ye ken John Peel when he's far away,
> With his hounds and his horn in the
>   morning.

Donald remembered the days when he had been happiest. When he'd been a boy on his pony, streaming in the early morning winter sunshine across the great green open downs of Salisbury Plain, with the hounds of the South and West Wilts Hunt in full cry before him, the sound of the horn, the whole field in a flat-out gallop around him, scarlet-coated and black-coated hunters and boys and girls and farmers in tweeds all in full halloo, the vicar on his grey, the red, red coat of Reynard far, far ahead. Oh those skies full of blue. Those days! Those glory days! The days before he'd been sent off to that awful public school!

His voice had become soft and gentle and full of feeling.

> 'Twas the sound of his horn
> Brought me from my bed
> And the cry of his hounds
> Has me ofttimes led
> For Peel's view holloa
> Would awaken the dead
> Or a fox from his lair
> In the morning.
> Do ye ken that hound
> Whose voice is death?
> Do ye ken her sons
> Of peerless faith
> Do ye ken that a fox

With his last last breath
Cursed them all as he died
In the morning?
Yes, I ken John Peel
And auld Ruby, too
Ranter and Royal
And Bellman so true
From the drag to the chase,
From the chase to the view
From the view to the death
In the morning.

There was total silence all about him. The bombing had ended. His patients were all alive and were all calm.

Every window was broken, splinters were embedded in the walls and pillars. The end wall of one ward was split wide open. The plaster had all come down from the ceiling, landing indiscriminately upon floor and patient. In the middle of the room stood Donald. He had plaster on his head and on his shoulders, even a couple of specks of it on his bow tie. And, although Donald spoke awful Chinese, he was chatting to the patients, and the patients, speaking no English, were happily chatting back to him. Not one patient had moved or torn themselves free. There had not been a single dislocation or rupture among any of them.

From that day on Donald was known among the Chinese as 'Noble Soul'.[15]

Hu was hurrying to the air-raid shelter as the first bombs started to fall. Usually the most level-headed and unflappable of human souls, Hu was terrified by bombs. They just fell. At random. Out of nowhere, into your midst. By and large Hu could face with equanimity living in a war zone, sharing risks with everyone else, dealing with disaster when it occurred, even if it occurred to her. But bombs! Bombs were chaotic, bombs came from nowhere, bombs blew you unknowing into nothingness.

So as the bombs started falling Hu panicked and ran straight to the shelter, forgetting she should have called in at the apartment to check that Spider Girl and The Drab were coming. As soon as she entered the shelter she remembered what she should have done and would have returned, bombs or no bombs, but the warden would not allow her to leave. Besides, the entrance was being blocked by a farmer trying to drive his cows into the shelter for safety. Hu looked all around in the darkness for Spider Girl and The Drab but could see nothing.

The shelter was packed. Hundreds and hundreds of people jammed together in close damp darkness. Some were moaning, others coughing. Tuberculosis was rife in the city and the disease was easily passed on in these fetid conditions. Hu decided not to think about such depressing things.

The bombs increased. The earth shook.

Then even more fell. The whole earth was shaking and heaving.

A deep fatalistic despair fell in the shelter. The darkest, most deadly depression. Like cattle awaiting slaughter. Like the prisoner awaiting the executioner's sword upon his neck.

There was a thunderous crunch, like a punch which knocks out your breath, great sucking sounds as the explosion snatched all the air and structure from surrounding buildings, the crashes as they fell to the ground, all but the building above the shelter. There was no movement from it.

All instinctively looked upward. Hu, crushed and cramped, close to the steps to the entrance, after a moment of outright panic, started to realize the building above was not moving, a moment of pure rapture seized her – I am alive! It is over and I have survived! Then there was a creak, a groan, and suddenly the building above them sagged, started to topple, cave in, fear flooded all over her, her mouth and throat were full of dust, bodies squirmed all around her, threshing about in darkness as earth and masonry vomited down. Hu fought to keep some inner reason, some sense of goodness, Christian peace, of God. They were all drowning in a sea of their fellow men. There was no air.

In the remains of the street above there were frantic attempts by the emergency services to locate the shelter, but so much rubble had been thrown about and so many surrounding buildings collapsed that they were completely unable to identify it. People were digging frantically here and there. Teams of men and women and children everywhere tore away the stones and bricks. But no one knew where to look, where to dig.

It was like being gripped hard in some great squirming, agonized beast, hundreds of bodies twisting and turning and crying and slowly suffocating through lack of oxygen. The remaining oxygen was filled with the stench of panicked urine and faeces. Children screamed bewildered. Adults cried out for loved ones, lost in the charnel tomb. Hu, modest as ever, prepared herself for death. Asked Jesus to guard her family, the people of Wuhan, especially those doing good like the medical corps, and China itself. Her brain started to fail. She asked for God's mercy. Perhaps she was here, perhaps she was there. Hallucinations, dreams entered her brain, she started to relax as all those around her, dying, started to relax, floated in calmness, peace. No more terrors.

Suddenly there was a bang. A sudden rush of coldness. Was this death? Her soul being transported? Something grabbed her wrists. Hands grabbed her wrists. As though in a dream she was dragged from comfort and darkness like a baby pulled from the womb into sudden light. Left lying helpless, new-formed upon the earth. Her lungs exploded as she started to breathe again. All around her there was busynesse, frantic endeavour. Dumped on the ground half-conscious, from clear black air she voraciously sucked in oxygen to her lungs. All around her other bodies – some alive, most dead – were being dragged out from the shelter, and then slowly, her eyes gradually refocusing, she saw leaning over her, staring at her with a look of deep concern, Spider Girl.

'Am I in heaven? Were you killed too – because of me?'

'No,' said Spider Girl prosaically, 'you are alive.'

Hu was still struggling for reason.

'What happened?'

'Your shelter collapsed. No one could find the entrance among all the new rubble. So I, who'd come out to look for you, told them where it was.'

'How did you know?'

'Rickets. Each step I take is painful. So, on any new journey, I count my footsteps so the next time I make that journey I will know how many steps I still have to take. The steps from our apartment to the shelter entrance are exactly 141. I paced out the steps and they dug you out.'

Hu, lying on her back, stared up at Spider Girl. In the past Spider Girl had been an acquaintance, a friend. Nothing special. Sometimes irritating, sometimes funny. You took what you got. But now Hu saw Spider Girl as she was. Her gentleness. Beneath all the roughness and bluster she saw the kindness and concern. In her still semi-conscious state she watched Spider Girl's face shape-shift from the unwashed physical to the luminous spiritual and back to hairy upper-lipped physical. Where before there'd only been something temporal, now she saw the eternal. She was about to say something, probably something completely meaningless, when there was a commotion behind Spider Girl. Agnes Smedley's white, shocked face appeared over Spider Girl's shoulder.

'Spider Girl,' she said urgently, 'you must come with me to the hospital. Now. Something has happened.'

Spider Girl did not move.

'Now,' commanded Agnes, with a harshness in her voice. 'It's most important.'

Spider Girl sighed, touched Hu's arm, raised herself with difficulty to her feet, and she and Agnes disappeared. Hu continued to lie pleasantly on the ground. Then the word 'hospital' ground into her. Hospital! Duties!! Responsibilities!!! Somehow she got to her feet. In a landscape bereft of any familiar buildings or landmarks she was momentarily lost, but a fireman pointed her in the right direction. She staggered off, dreaming, following a winding procession of stretcher bearers and grieving relatives. All the time around her she saw not only the living, but also the souls of the dead and dying arising from their bodies, from out of the rubble piled above the air-raid shelter.

As she regained focus and concentration Hu walked faster and faster, though her consciousness of the intermingling of physical and spiritual did not leave her. It seemed such a calm, natural process.

Because Agnes and Spider Girl could only walk at Spider Girl's pace, in the end Hu arrived in the still largely intact hospital only moments behind them.

Covered in white dust and ashes, looking like a ghost, Hu was hurrying down the main corridor when she heard an almighty cawing ahead of her, a clamouring, like a great bird in pain. She hastened into the main operating theatre and there, Donald and Agnes watching, stood Spider Girl, almost clawing at a soldier lying on his back on the operating table, groaning and croaking above him.

'Father,' she was crying, 'Father! You are alive! You are alive!'

Wei lay on his back on the table, a great wound open in his chest. He was barely conscious, staring up at his daughter in confusion and wonderment.

'Donald,' cried Spider Girl with great force, turning to Donald, who was standing there ready to operate, 'Donald,' she cried, advancing on him and grabbing him, 'this is my father, my father, you must save him,' she cried desperately, 'you must!!!'

Agnes moved in to separate them and simultaneously translate for them.

'Donald, he is alive, alive, you *must* save him!'

Agnes separated them but Donald moved back, close to Spider Girl, putting his hands gently on her shoulders, looking intently into her eyes.

'Spider Girl,' he said, 'I will do everything I can to save your father, because I can see how much you love him. But...' he added.

Agnes indicated he should soften what he said, but Donald ignored her. Donald understood Spider Girl.

'But,' Donald continued, 'I must tell you now that his chances of recovery are slim and, as you can see' – the room around them and the corridor outside were crammed with those wounded in the air raid – 'we have many other patients it is my duty to help. Now if you go and stand by that wall over there and wait, I will examine your father and tell you what I find.'

Spider Girl controlled herself. She looked at Donald.

'Donald,' she said, 'I know you will do your best.'

With that she softly brushed the dust from his bow tie and she and Agnes and Hu retreated to the wall. Donald checked Hu.

'Hu,' he said, 'I need you. Go and wash and scrub up.'

'Of course, Donald,' said Hu, immediately recollecting herself and hurrying off.

Donald looked at Hu. Dirt and dust all over her.

'Wish I had my camera,' he joked before turning to Wei's wounds.

He still had plaster sticking out of his hair.

'How did you find my father?' Spider Girl asked Agnes.

'I was dressing wounds on the Bund. He was lifted on the table and I recognized him immediately. From the time he sold you as a slave.'

This being wartime, Donald's inspection was quick but thorough.

Such was the number of badly wounded patients presenting that a second table had been set up alongside Donald's and Maninda and Dick were operating on it.

Donald asked Hu to cleanse Wei's wound with some chloride solution and then bind it. Meanwhile he walked over to Spider Girl and Agnes to show them some of the fragments he'd removed from Wei's body and report on his condition. Ahsan took Donald's place at the table and started on the next patient.

Agnes translated as Donald spoke to Spider Girl.

'Your father was hit by a Japanese rifle round.' He showed Spider Girl the bullet. 'Lucky it was a Japanese bullet and not a Chinese one, as Japanese bullets have steel cases and are far cleaner.' He dropped the bullet in a bucket. 'It also luckily hit a rib bone. The bone fragmented but it slowed the bullet's path and it did not penetrate the chest much further. There were fragments of bone deeper in the chest which I removed.' He showed a couple of fragments and threw them in the bucket. 'Normally, with a chest wound such as this, infection, sepsis sets in within the vital organs in hours and the patient is very soon dead. But something else simultaneously entered with the bullet. A miracle, I'd say.'

Donald held up a couple of small china shards.

'What are they?' asked Spider Girl.

'Pottery fragments. Apparently your father was carrying a small jar in his top pocket where the bullet entered. The bullet smashed through the jar and its contents entered the wound simultaneously with the bullet.'

'What was in the jar?' asked Agnes.

Donald took a small jar out of his pocket. He showed it to them.

'We also found this in another pocket. An identical jar. It is almost empty.'

Spider Girl snatched it and smelt it.

'Honey?'

'Yes, honey. It has well known antiseptic qualities,' continued Donald in a rather technical tone. 'It attacks and kills bacteria. So the tissue that was torn open by the bullet and bone fragments was simultaneously cleansed and disinfected by the honey.'

It was the honey, the two small jars of honey the old man on the battlefield of Taierzhuang had presented Wei with when he had kindly returned the old man's swarm.

But Spider Girl was thinking of another exchange. Remembering the day when the family, in panic, had been leaving their farm, their home. And her father had ordered her to kill the bees so she could get their honey quicker. But Spider Girl had not done this and had undergone the pain of their stings because she admired bees and they were powerful in the spiritual world. She had helped them; now they had helped her. Her father's life for their lives. She thanked them with quick fervent prayer.

Hu had returned from the corridor.

Donald continued:

'Most of the honey from the second jar has been used, so I presume the patient, sorry, your father, has been cleansing his wound with it since then, keeping the infection at bay.'

Spider Girl looked directly at Donald.

'Then you mean my father might…?'

Donald reached out immediately and held her wrists. He spoke to her gently but strongly.

'No, Spider Girl, I'm afraid your father will not grow better.

The condition is known as osteomyelitis.' Agnes had some difficulty translating this. 'Despite the honey an inflammation has set in within your father's bones and their marrows caused by pus-forming bacteria and mycobacteria. That is spreading. Honey is only slowing down its progress. Your father only has a few weeks to live.'

Hu watched Spider Girl's body convulse as for a second her soul was seized with a condition she'd never known before. Despair. Black, black despair. She sent out a great howl. But then Hu watched as Spider Girl's extraordinary self-control reasserted itself. Her ability to deal with what was in front of her.

Donald was in front of her. She looked at him. She saw a man of kindness and great gentleness. A man with extraordinary gifts that he devoted entirely to helping others, saving the lives of many, many men. Spider Girl greatly admired him for this. Donald looked out for everybody – except for Donald. That was Spider Girl's job. Spider Girl looked out for Donald. She washed and patched and ironed his often ragged clothes. She always gave him the best of the food, the most nutritious parts. Some she cooked for him specially, mixing in herbs and other beneficial ingredients to give him strength and intelligence. Sometimes, indeed, she even added certain love potions, though in her heart she knew Donald would never be interested in women – or men, for that matter. Donald's sole interests were surgery, bicycle parts, and taking photos of random objects.

The wonderful arrival of her father, however short his remaining life, now meant she had two good men to love and look after and, if necessary, murder for. She thanked her gods for their generosity.

She looked directly and formally at Donald.

'Thank you, Donald, for telling me what will happen. For fighting for my father, but also telling me the truth. Every single extra second I have with my father I will value. Thank you for your gift. In return, is there any service I can do for you?'

'Golly,' said Donald. And thought for a moment. 'Well, actually, I'm feeling a tad peckish. But first, Spider Girl, I want to show you something which will help your father live longer and which you have played a very big part in acquiring. Come here.'

He led her to the operating table. By now Hu had finished dressing and binding the wound, but a hole, a tiny entrance in the flesh remained. Hu stood beside the patient, holding the sterilizing tray. On it lay a tiny rubber valve used to inflate bicycle tyres. Spider Girl had bought it only this morning on the Bund. Donald picked up this sliver of sterilized rubber and neatly inserted it into the hole in the flesh, then plugged it.

He looked at her.

'It will seal your father's wound off from outside infection. It will also be used every few hours to drain the poison from your father's wound and to feed chloride solution in to sterilize it. By your own actions you have made your father live a bit longer.'

Spider Girl felt very emotional again. Then stopped herself.

'What is it you want me to do for you, Donald?'

'Cripes,' he said, thinking. 'Love a Spam sandwich, if poss, and a cup of jolly old char.'

Donald had brought several mysterious tins of 'Spam' with him from England. Spider Girl had tasted it once and thought it pointless, without any taste or texture whatsoever. But that was none of her business. So she waddled back to the apartment to fetch Donald his Spam sandwich and tea. Wei had meanwhile been given opium and was sleeping like a baby on a mattress on the floor of a hospital corridor.

Before Spider Girl made Donald his sandwich, she felt inside her smock pocket. There rested the tiny, nearly empty stone bottle of wild pear juice. The Wei family lived.

12

Spider Girl held her father's hand. She sat beside him as he lay unconscious – still in an opium dream – on a bed.

He breathed and he breathed. Slow and steady. Like a great river flowing.

Spider Girl gently moved a damp, warm cloth across his slightly feverish forehead. He sighed. Then he stirred, he moved a bit restlessly. Perhaps it was a bad dream, a memory of battle? His body tensed and bowed, his head turned from side to side. The great river had undercurrents and turmoils within it.

Very gently Spider Girl took from her clothing the tiny bottle of wild pear juice and carefully smeared a few drops across his lips. He stirred again, but this time differently, as though some memory, some familiarity moved deep within him, and again he settled, he lay, his breathing once again resumed its calm, its powerful progress.

Spider Girl waited a few minutes, then quietly withdrew.

She washed the bowls and pans – The Drab was too clumsy to be trusted with the china – while The Drab scrubbed the floor.

Spider Girl dusted and cleaned Agnes and Hu's rooms and filled three crates of Freda's bottled bath juice, got The Drab to carry the crates downstairs to the street door where Spider Girl hailed a rickshaw and paid him to transport the crates to a market stall on the Bund (where they were wildly popular!).

Instructing The Drab on which vegetables to chop for the meal, Spider Girl returned to her father's side and took his hand in hers.

Just to touch him, just to feel him, just to smell him was all she wanted.

It was the morning after Agnes had rescued Wei. Donald and Hu, after they'd finished their shift, had carried him back to the apartment on a stretcher. Agnes insisted Wei, as a soldier, be given the place of honour so he lay on Freda's bed and Freda had had to move in and share Agnes's bed. Spider Girl slept on the floor beside her father's bed, The Drab continued to sleep under the sink and Donald lived in the pokey little attic where he was perfectly content.

One matter which has not been much covered in this chronicle is the flowering relationship between Freda Utley and Vernon Bartlett. This is probably because they were both very discreet about it – Vernon because he was a gentleman, Freda because she was still horribly undecided on whether to commit herself or not.

She was in turmoil. While Spider Girl sat with her father in Freda's ex-bedroom, Freda explained her many problems and difficulties to Agnes in the kitchen.

'He is a very attractive man.'

'He is, if you like that sort thing. I prefer them rougher.'

'We talk an awful lot, discuss all sorts of things. We agree on a lot.'

'I agree on a lot of things with you. It doesn't mean I want to go to bed with you. If you want to go to bed with him, why don't you go to bed with him?'

Agnes had chapter ten of her book to finish.

'It's not that simple. I have a child.'

'And...?'

There was a pause. Freda continued:

'You and I haven't seen each other in a long time – ten years at least. A lot's happened since then.'

Agnes forgot about chapter ten.

'Tell me, Freda...'

'Well, you knew me when I was married to Arcadi Berdichevsky, the Russian who used to work at Arcos, the Soviet Trade Mission in London. Before MI5 got them thrown out in '27 on trumped-up charges of spying.'

'Yes. We met just after that in '28, I think, in Berlin, when I was working for the Indian Nationalist Movement.'

'Well, Arcadi did various jobs for Russia around the world. He was a wonderful man. We had a baby, the beautiful Jon Basil. We were both committed communists. But in 1936 we were summoned back to the Soviet Union. On April the fourteenth of that year, Arcadi was arrested. He disappeared. I was left alone with my baby in this tiny, damp, dirty little flat in Moscow. I hardly had any money. Jon Basil had the most awful croup. I didn't know what to do. I went to the police station. They said they didn't know anything about it. I went to the central prison. They wouldn't say anything about him. Not even say they'd arrested him. I said I had no money, a baby who was sick, they shrugged.'

'They were probably using you and your baby as a lever,' said Agnes matter-of-factly, 'to get Arcadi to talk. That's how secret services work.'

'I asked if he was going to be put on trial, if I could go. They shrugged. I returned to our flat. My neighbours wouldn't speak to me. For a while I traipsed back and forth to the prison, demanding to know what had happened to my husband, trying to push them into letting him go. Nothing. In desperation I tried to write to my parents, begging to send me money so I could leave. The police visited me, threatened me with a beating.'

Agnes listened to all this in a fairly dispassionate manner. She'd been beaten up by the Chinese Nationalists when she'd returned from communist areas of the country, by the Japanese as she was covering their invasion of Manchuria, by MI6 in Berlin and New York while she working for Indian independence, and when only a child she'd watched miners being shot dead in the street before her by Pinkerton men in Nevada and Colorado. Violence and murder, as she saw it, was an everyday part of the revolutionary process.

'This was happening while all the show trials were going on in Moscow,' Agnes observed.

'Yes,' said Freda very quietly. Then she continued. 'Eventually my parents managed to arrange for me and Jon Basil to return to England. But I still don't know whether Arcadi is alive or dead.'

Agnes offered Freda a cigarette, lit it, lit one for herself. For a while they smoked in gentle companionship.

'In England my parents took over raising Jon Basil. I thought I should get a job so I could support us, put some money aside for Jon Basil's education. I knew quite a lot about China, Japan – did my PhD on them, their trade issues – so I became a journalist and came out here. Mind you, I'm still slanting my articles with a pro-Soviet angle. I'm scared stiff if I write anything hostile they'll take it out on poor Arcadi.'

There was a pause.

'So what exactly is the problem you have with sleeping with Vernon Bartlett?' asked Agnes.

Freda ignored this and continued with her own train of thought.

'There are an awful lot of communists out here in Wuhan, in the press corps. I find it quite intimidating moving among them, listening to their loud voices and sloganizing – when I know what I know. And how do I know they're not spying on me?'

'Well, I'm a communist,' said Agnes. 'Not the Russian sort, more the Chinese variety – with lots of syndicalism thrown in from my wonderful days in the IWW. And I'm not spying on anyone.'[16]

'You're different,' said Freda.

'And Vernon isn't a communist, he's a wishy-washy sort of socialist-cum-liberal – so what's the problem?'

Freda paused. Then continued.

'The difficulty I have with sleeping with Vernon is that I'm still in love with Arcadi – deeply, completely – whether he's alive or dead. I love him with every fibre in my being. But I am a woman. I like a man to look at me as Vernon looks at me. With admiration, with arousal. I expect Vernon's a bit of a roué, a bit too smooth. All those radio shows he does...' She paused. Then with emotion: 'The thing is, I don't want to be abandoned again.'

Agnes sighed. She could never fathom how upper middle-class Englishwomen could be so utterly self-obsessed while surrounded by millions of people starving to death.[17]

★ ★ ★

That evening, as Spider Girl tended him, her father, still unconscious from the opium, seemed more restive, more sentient. As though just below the surface he was quickening, pushing to break from the depths and stick his head above the water so he could be reborn into this world.

Ah, she thought, the wild pear juice works within him.

His hands were moving restlessly, as though searching for an implement or tool he needed. His legs flexed, unflexed, as if he was walking, searching. His face was pursing, grimacing like a man working out a problem, trying to reach a decision.

Spider Girl knew where he was. He was back on their farm. He was always restless, pacing like this early in the morning when, having inspected his fields, he was deciding who in the family should do what tasks that day, always bearing in mind who could do particular jobs best and who was feeling ill or incapable that day.

She gripped his hand. (Only gently, so that she did not wake him.) Her love was without end.

13

I meet her at the Methodist chapel. We've just had a particularly rousing sermon from our fiery young preacher about all the hopes for us, for China, that lie ahead, despite the fact that this will be probably one of our last services in Wuhan before most of us flee to escape the Japanese. But he sees only good things ahead for China. And it is cheering for us all to hear him.

After the service, as always, we reassemble in the hall next door for tea and biscuits. Everyone sits in a large circle and we all chatter away nineteen to the dozen. I find myself next to a vivacious and funny young lady. She introduces herself as Miss Hu Lan-shih. She runs what appears to be a professional eye over the various cuts and bruises on my face, which I received while in prison. I ignore this and introduce myself.

'My name is Lao She.'

'Oh,' she says, 'Lao She? The writer? I have read several of your books. I really enjoyed them!'

A writer always like to hear this sort of thing, especially from non-literary people. Literary people tend to read complicated theories and psychologies into your books which you never intended in the first place. It turns out she's read *Rickshaw Boy* (inevitably), *Cat Country*, and my early comic novel *Mr Ma and Son* about my experiences in London in the 1920s. She's also read my short story 'Crescent Moon', which, as a woman, she likes.

I find out a bit about her – her life in a Shanghai cotton mill, her escape from there to Wuhan, the varied and interesting jobs she's done since getting here. Wuhan is such an extraordinary place!

It's so invigorating! Instead of everyone being stuck endlessly in the same unchanging, repetitive lives which most people in most places in the world inhabit, Wuhan is filled with extraordinary people adapting themselves continuously to doing different and challenging work and getting great satisfaction from doing so.

She asks me about my bruises. She is a nurse, after all. I make a few dismissive remarks. As a bright and perceptive young girl she doesn't ask me more. Instead she asks what I am writing at the moment.

Ah, well, there's a question. I embark on an odyssey of explanations and descriptions of *Defend Wuhan!* – what it's all about, its themes, its characters. She is very interested. She gets the detail into her head very quickly and laughs at the jokes and hopes all the marching will work. The people of Wuhan deserve a bit of enjoyment in their lives, she observes. After all, I add, we're not going to be here much longer. We both laugh.

Then I get on to the sort of stuff which writers love to talk about at length with willing listeners – the difficult bits which aren't working.

I point out I've pretty much got the main bits – strong patriotic speeches, a young hero (played by a middle-aged actor) breaking out of jail and leading the resistance, young women dressed as soldiers doing superbly choreographed marching, lots of music and songs and choruses. But the thing I haven't got really, yet…

'Yes?' she asks.

'Well,' I say, 'this isn't really the thing to say in a Methodist church hall, but we need a bit of…'

'Sauce?' she says. 'Sensuality?'

'What the Americans call "leg".' I blush, look around me. 'Sexy,' I say, sotto voce. 'Traditional Chinese dancing can be very charming, alluring, but…'

'Ah,' she says, and thinks. Such an innocent young lady. 'I think there's someone you should meet,' she announces.

We leave the Methodist hall. In our Sunday best we pass down the Bund – fewer people around because all the time its population is vanishing upstream. Until we arrive at a tea house. Not just any tea house, but 'that sort of' tea house.

'Do not be worried,' says Hu, smiling gently. 'But you really must meet this woman.'

This nice Methodist girl leads me in through the door, up the stairs. No one bats an eyelid. We are passing down this corridor, girls and boys and patrons parading up and down in various states of undress, some completely naked. I am not embarrassed by this. As a boy, scraping a living off the streets of Beijing along with the rest of my family, I had often carried messages and letters in and out of brothels at all times of the day and night. None of it surprises or upsets me. But the sight of this pristine and delightful young Methodist girl, clothes carefully washed and pressed, leading me confidently through this gruesome bacchanal, appeals to me. It's the sort of scene that might appear in one of my novels.

We go through a door. Suddenly the atmosphere changes completely. It is quiet, clean. Amazingly, in the rooms off the corridor, men, what appear to be patients, are lying in beds.

'I hope she's not working,' observes Hu, as we pass two nurses carrying bandaging.

I am in some state of astonishment.

'Is this a hospital?' I ask.

'Yes,' she replies.

Hu knocks on a door. There's a voice from inside.

'Good,' she says, 'she's here.'

We walk in. A lady, wearing very little and with a young child on her hip, is talking to two similarly clad whores. There is obviously some dispute over who gets more money for servicing the same customer. The woman with the child reaches a decision, gives it, and the two accept it without demur and exit.

'Hu,' says the lady.

'Intelligent Whore,' says Hu. 'I have a gentleman who needs your help.'

'Will this take some time?' asks 'Intelligent Whore'.

'Yes,' says Hu.

'Intelligent Whore' turns to her child and says:

'Little Aigou. How is your book coming on?'

'Well, Mummy. I am drawing aeroplanes in it. Like the ones I want us to fly in.'

'That is very good,' says Intelligent Whore, letting her child slip to the ground. 'Why don't you paint a picture of the ship we are going to sail up the river in? With sails and people and you and me standing in it?'

'I want to do that,' says Little Aigou, obviously her son, and hurries over to a corner of the room where a book and a box of crayons lie. He plonks down and starts drawing.

Hu introduces me to Intelligent Whore.

'Ah,' she says, 'you are Lao She. I've read some of your short stories – that one about the girl being forced into prostitution.'

'Oh,' I say, '"Crescent Moon".'

'Much too sentimental. Now, what do you want from me?'

Hu explains, briefly, concisely – time is obviously of the essence with Intelligent Whore – about my project *Defend Wuhan!* What it's about, what it's trying to achieve, the problem I face. Hu, I feel, would make a first-rate aide to some high-powered business tycoon.

'What Mr Lao wants is a dancer, a traditional dancer, sensual but also modest – fully dressed – who will lure and win the hearts of all the audience – women as well as men – and display the spirit of Wuhan. I thought of you.'

Little Aigou has wandered back to his mother, holding his book.

'Mummy?'

'Little Aigou?'

'This boat?'

'Yes?'

'I've drawn it, and now I'm drawing you and me standing in it.'

'Yes?'

I am standing there, witnessing this, and having to force myself not to weep, so much does it remind me of my own youngest child and her constant requests of me.

'Well, Mummy, what coloured dress should I draw you wearing?'

'How about you painting my yellow one? It's my favourite dress'

'No,' says Little Aigou quite decisively, 'I'm going to paint you in your green one. That's the one I like best.'

With that he hurries back to his crayons to continue his creation.

Intelligent Whore continues the conversation as though there has been no interruption whatsoever. She looks directly at me.

'So you want me to dance a dance which expresses the soul of Wuhan. This dance must be alluring but not sexual.'

'Yes.'

'Do you want me to sing?'

'Yes. That would be good. If I can find the right words. But first I need to hear you sing and see you dance.'

'Of course. Just wait a minute.'

Intelligent Whore tells her son she'll just be gone a moment, exits from the room, and returns almost immediately with two musicians, one with a two-stringed fiddle, the other with a zither. Brothels always have musicians on call in case any clients like musical accompaniment to their various grunts and thrusts.

'What would you like me to sing?' she asks.

'Something moving,' I suggest, 'noble.'

She has a brief confab with her musicians, then sings.

She has a beautiful voice. Firm, strong even, but also able to suggest emotion, vulnerability. She stands there and belts out a patriotic song and I see China in all her glory, all her majesty, all her suffering. Wow! I am not going to have any difficulty finding the right words for such a singer. We can work out the music later.

But now we have got to the tricky bit. The dancing.

'How much of my body do you want me to show? Do you want something risqué?'

'No,' I say, quite firmly, 'not risqué.'

But what *do* I want?

'The thing is, you've got to be feminine, of great beauty, lithe and supple...'

'Yes?'

'But it's also quite important...'

This is getting quite embarrassing. After all, I am talking to a whore.

'The thing is, I want you to project – well – purity.'

'Purity. Why d'you think I can't project purity?'

'Well, er...'

'Believe me, whores are good at nothing so much as projecting purity. It's what every client wants. The thought that this girl is so innocent and so pure and that this is the very first time they have ever, ever fucked. Or even known what fucking is. I can do purity so well I make Hu here look like a tuppenny up-against-the-wall whore.'

Hu dissolves into giggles. I look a bit embarrassed. Intelligent Whore deals briefly with an aesthetic question from her son then confers with her musicians.

She starts to dance. It is noble dancing. Striking. Heroic, even. But it is also feminine. The hips sway. There's a liquid flow to her body. As a woman, as China, she's unafraid, unapologetic, all-conquering.

I take some time to recover. I remember myself. Panic slightly.

'You will of course be paid,' I assure her.

'Of course I will. And handsomely.'

'Intelligent Whore,' I say, stepping forwards to shake her hand, 'I really look forward to working with you, and can I say...'

She cuts across me.

'There is one other condition to my working with you.'

'Yes?'

'I want my son to be on stage with me. I want him to be part of my act. He and I will arrange between ourselves what he is going to do.'

It is an extraordinary thing – life. You sort of come from nowhere, nothingness, and suddenly you are here, in motion, in momentum, crashing through. You don't know what you are, who you are, where you came from, where you're going – but you're going, have impetus, things come at you, people, situations, events, and it's amazing, terrifying, far beyond any sort of analysis. And then, suddenly, you are no more.

George Hogg wasn't thinking about any of this kind of stuff.

Even though he was in the midst of it all. In fact he was so in the midst of it all that he had absolutely no time to think about it.

He had still not managed to deal with his anger. It was still there – simmering within him, likely to erupt into flames at any moment like a fire on a peat moor. He still, poor torn Quaker, had visions and fantasies of doing to the Last Ditch warmongers what Joe Louis did to poor Max Schmeling.

He so much missed the quiet provincial life of Harpenden where every Sunday the whole community gathered in the Friends Meeting House where they could discuss things like this. State your problem and they would gently and wisely counsel you, point you to the path of righteousness – the steady, calm light of God's reason, which would enable you to sit through all the taunts and dishonesties and lies of the Last Ditch Club without a smoulder of anger.

But Harpenden was Harpenden and Wuhan was Wuhan, and in Wuhan George had a problem to solve. It concerned the children, the orphans he worked with and had come to know and care for. Deeply. He needed a solution.

He checked in with his boss at the news agency, who told him there weren't any important stories at the moment. George asked for the day off – a very rare event for the conscientious Quaker – and his boss said that if he kept in touch during the day in case any big stories broke or there was a major air raid, then he could have it off.

George spent the whole day scurrying from government office to government office, speaking to responsible official after responsible official, trying to discover what plans they had to evacuate his orphans to a place of safety before the Japanese arrived. Everyone knew that Wuhan was about to fall. Already in the distance artillery fire could sporadically be heard.

Ever since the temporary government had been set up in Wuhan nearly a year ago it had implemented a large scale and generally successful evacuation of orphans – of whom there had been so many – upstream to safety in the far-off provinces of South-West China. He saw the crocodile processions of neat and shorn and fumigated orphans, hand in hand, singing their patriotic songs, wending their way every day along the Bund to their awaiting ships. Why not his?

He asked this question again and again to the ever fewer civil servants he could access – they too were being filtered away upstream. Who was going to rescue his orphans? Who was going to take care and responsibility for them?

And gradually it dawned on him that no one was. That his orphans were probably too crazy and unhinged and wild for anyone to want to take care of in these circumstances. The few nurses and assistants who were still present in Wuhan were probably far better employed looking after and organizing better-behaved and more docile children than his own, who would take many staff to control and manage. He at last realized that his orphans were going to be left for the Japanese to take care of. With bullets.

Who would look out for Chin, who was always whining? Liang, who protected Hua? Would anyone be able to stop Heng and his bullying? Perhaps talk to him long enough so that one day Heng would understand why he did it and stop? And what about the mysterious, silent trio – Cong and Xingfu and Wen – would they ever talk again? Or Bojing? Each in their own private world of torment.

Spider Girl had settled into a routine of nursing her father. She watched him during the day and woke every two hours to check him during the night. Donald and Hu, when they returned exhausted from work and just before they returned for their next shift, would inspect him and advise Spider Girl on how he should be treated while they were away.

Three times each day Spider Girl swabbed and disinfected his wound and changed his bandages and when it was necessary gently replaced his soiled sheets and bedclothes and bathed him with a sponge. All the time cawing to him and crooning in a low, loving voice.

She boiled his bandages and clothing to disinfect them.

Gradually, bit by bit, Wei started responding to her cradling and coddling. To her gurning and gaping and clucking – like a mother trying to coax a smile from her baby – he'd grunt and moue his mouth, his eyes would flicker, and then suddenly his eyes opened and he looked.

She looked.

He recognized her. From profound depths he attempted to dredge up her name.

'Wild... Wild... Wild Pear Blossom.'

'Father.'

Then he looked away and would not look at her again. For he remembered not just her but everything else that had happened.

14

Freda Utley didn't dress like some glamorous Hollywood star. She had no furs nor diamonds. She wasn't that sort of upper middle-class girl. After all, she'd been a member of the Communist Party of Great Britain until very recently. But appearances did matter to her. Especially tonight.

Vernon Bartlett had invited her to dine with him alone in his hotel room.

She'd taken a bath. Which involved all the usual unpleasantness of having to think of that servant girl greedily bottling all her bath water, her intimate bath water, then selling it to...

She'd taken the bath in her shared room. (Agnes was away attending the opening of a soldiers' rehabilitation centre.) She washed herself as thoroughly as she could. She'd earlier had her hair set, quite expensively, in a hair salon in a Western hotel and had wrapped it carefully in a towel while she bathed. She arose from her bath and softly dried her body. She slipped quickly into her clothes. Freda was not a great dresser. She wrote books and was a bit of an intellectual. On occasions her dress could be described as almost dowdy, and she wore spectacles. But she did have one outfit which she wore when she wanted to – well – draw attention to herself. It emphasized her figure – still good – and suggested, especially in candlelight, what might lie beneath.

She had made no decisions, absolutely no decisions, on what might or might not occur later that evening. She was a married woman.

It was time to put on her make-up.

Mirrors were not that common in China and were particularly

expensive in Wuhan, so most people didn't really bother with them. Agnes and Hu certainly didn't! But Freda had managed to purchase a very small one on the Bund and it was now balanced precariously above a small table she was using as her dressing table.

There's another thing. Women with glasses have quite some difficulty when it comes to applying make up. Glasses cover a fair amount of your face, especially those areas which require the most detailed and delicate attention. So the glasses have to be removed. But then you can't clearly make out the areas you are having to pay the closest attention to. Short-sighted women have to get very close to the mirror in order to make sure everything is being done correctly.

Freda muttered to herself, and then started her make-up.

She applied vanishing cream – not too much – to all her face. She then lightly dusted white powder over this foundation. She decided not to use red rouge – too healthy outdoor – but added a soft topping of apricot rouge to highlight her cheekbones.

Should she wear her glasses?

Men seldom make passes at girls who wear glasses.

But did she want men making passes at her?

And if she *didn't* wear glasses she might walk into furniture or knock over wine glasses.

She decided to leave the glasses decision til later.

Freda had never had her eyebrows tweezed – far too bourgeois. But they *were* a bit wild – she wished she could. But she didn't have any tweezers.

She did have her eyeliner pencil. Should she go for the full Harlow half-moon? Decisions, decisions. She went for a half Harlow quarter-moon. It looked quite good.

She dabbed petroleum jelly on her eyelids for the shine. And a twizzle of henna across her eyelashes to draw attention to herself when she blinked – Freda would never flutter.

The lipstick.

Not too red.

But red enough to hint at...

She applied it.

Why do women have to go through indignities like this?

Freda stopped still.

She now faced the really big decision of the night. Not whether to wear glasses or how much red lipstick she should or should not apply.

She had to decide on her perfume.

The special bottle of 'Irresistible' perfume stood on the table before her. She had bought it in Paris. She had bought it for the night that she and her husband Arcadi would somehow or other be reunited. Her husband, the father of her child, who had been dragged away from their flat in Moscow one night and had never been heard of again. She shuddered. Who had quite probably been shot by Stalin's secret police. And if he was, by some miracle, still alive, might now be slaving in one of Stalin's rumoured Siberian death camps. It was for him she had been saving her 'Irresistible' perfume. Their ecstatic night of reunion when...

But that was then. And now is now. Two years had gone by. She had to start making her own life. She had a young child she was responsible for. And she really did like Vernon Bartlett. He might have a white patch on his finger where he'd removed his wedding ring, but she had almost forgotten what the intimacy of two people in a bed was like. And Vernon had a paternalism and gentle manner that soothed and smoothed her eternal fretfulness. And he was intelligent!

She dabbed the perfume quickly behind her ears and inside her elbows and then in more intimate places. She hid the bottle behind Agnes's bookshelf – just to hide her shame from herself – then squinted at herself in the mirror. She didn't look that bad.

Freda Utley was armed and ready to go. Glasses and all. She marched through the door.

Wei continued in his mood of shame, of depression. Spider Girl knew that if she did not cheer him, lighten him up, he would die even sooner.

As she sat beside him on his bed, his face still averted, she reached a decision.

She spoke to him straightforwardly, matter-of-factly.

'Father, do you remember Fat Yao?

No response.

She continued confidently, as though he'd answered.

'Yes, the really fat farmer in our village. The one who fell down the well and couldn't get out? Just stuck there fast? So they tied rope under his arms and tried to pull him out – six or seven of them – but he wouldn't budge an inch. They tried everything. Nothing. So in the end they had to starve him to get him up.

'He'd always been fat, which was why they called him Fat. But now when Fat Yao walked around the village he was so thin no one recognized him. And even when it was explained who he was no one knew what to call him, since you couldn't call a thin man fat. He was so thin his wife started to complain, saying that her parents had married her to a fat man because that meant he was healthy and strong and would likely grow rich, but now instead she had a thin and wasting husband who sat around all day lamenting and was good for nothing. So she left him.

'Fat Yao became so desperate he started to eat again, enormous amounts, cooked with love by his mother. And started to put weight on. Pretty soon all his old weight returned. So his wife returned to him and villagers knew how to address him. But ever after Fat-Then-Thin-Then-Fat Yao never went anywhere near his well and employed a young boy to draw all his water.'

Wei stopped himself from laughing. But he could not contain a swift rictus grin splitting his face.

Spider Girl saw it was working. She continued her determined wooing.

'Father, remember old farmer Gao, who owned so much land but had no relatives to leave it to? And those two young ambitious farmers – Tang and Dong – both with large hungry families but without the money to purchase Gao's land?

'So one day Tang goes to his rival Dung and says, "Neither of us can afford that land that Old Gao will sell."

'"You're right," said Dung.

'"You and I will grow old and our children will starve if we do not get more land."

'"You're right there," said Dung.

'Tang was smart and Dung was not.

'"But," said Tang, "because we've both known each other a long, long time and two of our sisters have married into the same family, this means we are good men and can trust each other…"

'"Indeed," said Dung.

'"…So if we were to put our money together, as one, we would have enough money together to buy Old Gao's land and then, when we'd bought it, we could divide it up between ourselves fifty-fifty and we'd both have got what we want."

'"I agree," said Dung. "You are a good man."

'"But don't tell anyone," added Tang, "or Old Gao will put the price up."

'So Dung gave the good Tang most of his money and Tang went to Old Gao and purchased the land and paid him the money for it and after all the official documents and everything had been drawn up and signed and so on Dung went to his friend Tang and said "Well, how are we going to divide up this land?" and Tang replied "We aren't. I don't think it's a good idea anymore."'

This time Wei exploded at this old village tale. In fact he laughed so much his daughter worried about him and decided her next story should be sad.

Wei looked at her.

'Daughter,' he said.

And thus was Wei, by his daughter's craft, slowly drawn from his shell.

Freda and Vernon were dining *intime*. In his hotel suite. From the balcony there was a wonderful view across the vast Yangtze, moonlight dancing off its waves. The room was lit by only two candles on their small dining table. Freda was still wearing her glasses but wasn't quite sure about this.

The conversation had started with a discussion of her book *Japan's Feet of Clay*, which had caused quite a stir when it was first published. It was a Marxist analysis of the Japanese class structure. She had argued it was antique and inflexible. The book, researched with great diligence, exposed the terrible exploitation of workers in Japanese textile mills, especially those in Shanghai, and argued that this revealed the essential flimsiness of Japan's whole economic structure. Stable and enduring economies and societies require a sharing of their wealth among all classes.

The book had caused outrage in Japan and interest throughout the rest of the world, especially in China. Vernon had not read it but intended to do so. So Freda filled him in on its details. Vernon listened fascinated.

Then the conversation turned to mutual friends. It happened they both knew George Bernard Shaw, Harold Laski and Bertrand Russell. Bertie had given Freda quite a lot of help in trying to find out what had happened to Arcadi by writing repeated letters to the Russian ambassador in London.

This reassured Freda. It meant that Vernon was liked and respected by people she too was close to.

Finally they got on to the really big subject of the day. Chamberlain's flight to Munich. What was likely to happen there? Both Hitler and Mussolini were present. Would Chamberlain betray Britain again? Freda hadn't really been keeping up with the whole crisis – Eden's resignation, the Anschluss, the Sudetenland. In London she'd been totally preoccupied with the campaign to free her husband. So Vernon now briefed her on what was actually going on. As lobby correspondent for *Reynold's News* he'd been at the very centre of the battles within parliament and in Fleet Street.

He refilled her glass.

'Truth is, Freda, our country's utterly divided. There's this tiny elite in London, centred round the City, Downing Street, Fleet Street, the BBC, who are determined, absolutely adamant, they'll appease Hitler at all costs. And then there's everyone outside. The provinces, the working classes especially, who are dead set against giving way to him. Who think the appeasers are criminals betraying their country. We've never been so divided.

'I'll give you an example,' he said as Freda watched him through the candlelight. 'Ran into Harold Nicolson just before I left. He said he'd been dining at his club the night before and at the next table sat three young peers of the realm all declaring, in the loudest possible voices, that rather than having a socialist government in power they'd prefer to see Adolf Hitler sat in Downing Street.'

Freda muttered.

'Poor Harold was so upset he ran out of the dining room and was sick in the toilet. Next day he was up in Leicester – his constituency – addressing a meeting in a working men's club. And he told me his audience, the whole audience of working men, were boiling in fury at the impudence and treachery of Chamberlain, of appeasement. Shouting out and cheering every time he criticized the government. Provincial journalists I know say this is the norm throughout the country. Everywhere dissent and outrage, except London.

'But they're not allowed to report it. Chamberlain has the proprietors on his side and they control the editors, who censor the journalists. Journalists are writing articles describing the public's feelings, refusing to alter them, and being sacked. The night Eden resigned huge crowds gathered outside his home cheering him on. Not a word in the papers or on the BBC. When Attlee was interviewed supporting Eden on a newsreel, all the copies of the newsreel were recalled and the interview cut out. Only the provincial papers like the *Manchester Guardian* and the *Yorkshire Post* and my *Reynold's News*, are still standing up to Chamberlain. British newspapers make *Pravda* look honest.'

Freda smiled at this. He'd criticized the Soviet Union. It made her feel safer. He continued.

'It's something when the most ordinary people in the provinces and dominions can understand the sheer stupidity of a policy, yet the elite continue to blindly bulldoze it through. And it's wonderful that ordinary people, despite the unending propaganda and lies, see straight through them and know what has to be done. I tell you, somehow or other the English regions are going to engineer a revolt.'

Freda felt very warmly towards Vernon. Whether it's communist dictatorships you hate or a brutal capitalist oligarchy, it's so good to hear a radical and a socialist standing out for the truth.

At some time during the evening Vernon had briefly withdrawn to his bedroom and now wore a dressing gown rather than his clothes. He looked at her so gently.

'And so…' said Vernon. He stood up.

There was only one thing Freda wanted to do. Amid all this chaos and hatred. She stood up. Vernon moved towards her and smiled. He gently removed her scarf, button after button he slowly undid her clothes button by button so in the end they fell from her rather than having to be removed. Finally he removed her glasses. Freda stood naked before him, dressed only in her make-up and perfume.

And splendid was the night.

15

Tonight in Fuzhou the moon shines.
In her chamber, my wife must watch alone.
I pity my distant boy and girl
who don't know why she remembers Chang'an,
her cloud-like hair coiled and fragrant with mist,
jade-like arms cold in the moonlight.
When shall we lean in the open window,
together without tears in moonlight?

Du Fu

*

Mournful moonlight, symbol of sorrow for a thousand years,
venerable Du Fu's sad thoughts, then and now we feel the same;
jade-like arms shining bright, cloud-like hair coiled and
    fragrant with mist,
heartless autumn moon, shining again on parting and
    upheaval.

Lao She

It is 10 October. The day of the Mid-Autumn Festival of the Moon.
The day when families reunite (if any of us have any families left
to reunite with) to celebrate the bringing home of the harvest and
to thank the gods of the soil and vegetation for their generosity –
provided they have been generous.

It is the day, like every other day, that I visit the central post office to see if there is any letter for a Mr Wu Lei from my wife and family. There isn't.

But today, the day of the Mid-Autumn Festival, is also the day, or rather the night, of the one and only performance of my Chiang Kai-shek-commanded extravaganza – *Defend Wuhan*. With an exclamation mark after it. '!' That exclamation mark reminds us that we are all determined to stay in Wuhan and fight to the very last drop of our blood – even though the majority of us Wuhanites are all busy shutting up shop and getting ready to flee for the hills.

I apologize if I have started this chapter sounding rather ill tempered, not to say cynical, but I will do my best as it proceeds to cheer you and myself up.

All the frenzied business of script writing, of script rewriting, of meeting actors, of read-throughs and rehearsals and set building and lighting and choreography and everyone rushing around screaming at everyone else – with Yu Liqun reassuring me at all times that everything is going just fine – is at last over and complete, and now we face only one more cliff edge to fall over – the first (and last) night.

I feel awful. My play is meant to rouse people's patriotic and human spirits. Inspire and transform them. Will it?

It is a calm beautiful night. On the waters of the Yangtze the moon's reflection floats supreme. In the heavens above it sails majestic through silvery flakes of cloud like the scales of a fish. The crowds, chattering and relaxed, move towards the arena. There are drums and flutes and trumpets and marching bands. Amid the approaching crowds march schoolchildren with lanterns and torches. Scouts and Youth Corps members shout slogans – 'Resist to the last! Defend Wuhan! Down with the invaders!' Through the streets, along the Bund, they come in their thousands. The businesses, all the trade guilds of Wuhan – each brandishing the tools of their trade – come marching up the wide Kianghan thoroughfare – carpenters with their hammers and saws, masons with their chisels and trowels, merchants with their abaci. Everyone is cheering everyone else on, shouting their jokes back and forth.

This is cheering me up.

Just before it dies, Wuhan lives.

We arrive at the amphitheatre. There are stands all around the arena, row after row of them, rising to the skies. The crowds start to seat themselves, though many stay on their feet to cheer and applaud. They have brought their food and drink with them. Tugboats and ferries hoot on the river. Insects and moths flutter all around the floodlights and stage lights like angels' haloes. Children shout and scream and stagger around drunkenly on too much sugar.

Into the arena, having been paraded through the streets, come enormous, illuminated floats of giant aeroplanes, powerful tanks, great battleships – but also goddesses of peace, gods and goddesses of harvest and plenty and wisdom and hope. And finally, and most triumphantly – victory.

The audience roars and cheers. I wipe a tear from my eye. But now comes the bit I've been dreading. My play.

We discover our young hero (played by my ageing friend Shanyaodan) in prison. Alone in chains. But he cries out his support, his love for the people of China in their united fight against the forces of darkness and degeneration. Then, to much booing, his Japanese guards run on stage and start beating him for his patriotic views. Somehow or other our hero – not unlike Zhang Fei on the bridge at Changban – manages to free himself from his chains and sets upon his torturers and kills them. Every single one of them. The audience roars. He escapes into the night.

Then a clown comes on. And clowns a lot. Audiences – especially children – always love this sort of thing.

Then there is some dancing by some pretty girls (including Yu Liqun). Audiences love this sort of thing too.

The next time we see our hero, he is behind enemy lines, leading a cadre of young guerrillas against the enemy and encouraging the peasants to join in the fight. At first they are reluctant, but under blasts of our young hero's patriotic rhetoric – which the audience loves – they are won over and bravely arming themselves they set off for a vital battle which they resoundingly win.

(This is getting more and more like an early Tian Boqi play!)

Meanwhile Yu Liqun and her troupe – whatever happened to all their modernistic dancing *concrète*? – have undergone a swift costume change. They now re-emerge as smartly dressed young soldiers strutting up and down in immaculate formations and manoeuvres, faces resolute and then smiling, resolute and then smiling – attracting quite a few ribald comments – before marching off with a final defiant, and rather sexy, kick.

(Tian Boqi would never have done that!)

But at the battle's very final climax – at the very point of victory – with bangs and flashing lights and heroic gestures all around, our young hero is suddenly snatched away by Japanese desperadoes, who lead him off to torture and execution!

The audience is in despair!

More clowns.

This is not, I admit, the Peking Opera. I see quite a few well-dressed, more refined members of the audience wincing as street patois and coarse jokes and hoary platitudes splatter the air. But the audience as a whole roars them on.

General Chiang Kai-shek, sat on his special illuminated victory plinth on a high platform, looks down blankly and with complete indifference to all the proceedings. But Madame Chiang, by his side, watches everything with intense interest.

(Interestingly, at the foot of their plinth, I see the two men who tortured me. The one with glasses, the one without glasses. They are not watching me, they are not watching the play. With avid interest they study every single expression and gesture of Chiang Kai-shek up above them, as if their lives depend on them. Which they probably do.)

Anyhow, after some more dancing the arena darkens and we see our young (but balding) hero being led to the scaffold. His mother pleads with the officer in charge not to execute him. As he is led out onto the scaffold he shouts out patriotic slogans for China to fight on to final victory. He is forced down on his knees, his neck is stretched out, the executioner raises his sword...

Suddenly there is a bang. The peasants, now fully armed and skilled guerrillas, rush on stage and free our hero and kill all the disgusting Japanese. Celebrations, explosions, rows of marching

Boy Scouts and chorus girls and singing choirs, etc., etc. Victory! The whole audience starts chanting 'Defend Wuhan! Defend China!'

But the play is not over.

Once again the stage darkens. The audience quietens. What is about to start is what I have been waiting for. Intelligent Whore and her son Little Aigou. What on earth are they going to do?

Sombre music.

Intelligent Whore enters with solemnity. Her apparel is both erotic and modest, her dancing both arousing and pure. There is great melancholy in her movement. For the dead. Her motions embody, sanctify, memorialize the dead of China. Everyone is entirely sunk in this melancholic moment.

But suddenly, onto the stage, runs her son, Little Aigou, clutching a drawing book and some crayons.

'Mum,' he says, 'I'm going to do some drawing!'

Intelligent Whore has stopped her dancing entirely.

'What are you going to draw?' asks Intelligent Whore, in her normal voice.

'I'm going to draw China,' says Little Aigou.

'Then go and draw China.'

Little Aigou runs down the stage and throws himself on the ground. He starts to draw in his drawing book.

Intelligent Whore smiles at him and then smiles at the audience. She starts to dance like a proud mum. With hope, with optimism about what her son will do, what he will become.

All the time Little Aigou concentrates on his book, cramming in colour after colour, great blazes and zigzags of red and yellow and purple and green and blue.

And as Little Aigou scribbles with his crayons all the different colours and shapes and visions and possibilities of the new China, so his mum's dance becomes ever more vital and delightful and awe-inspiring, twisting and spiralling and weaving, lifting with her the entire audience who cheer and stamp and choke with emotion until Little Aigou suddenly jumps up and, with raised arms, displays his riotous colour-filled tapestry of the future of China to all the audience.

Tumultuous, heartfelt, ecstatic applause.

It is over.

Intelligent Whore and Little Aigou do not bow and scrape before the audience. They look straight out at the audience and the audience looks straight back at them. They are one and the same.

Well, that didn't turn out as bad as I thought it was going to. At least the audience haven't lynched me. People are singing some of the songs out loud, little children are marching up and down like toy soldiers and shouting military orders to each other. Young men and women are eagerly arguing over how best to mobilize the peasantry.

Amazing as it might seem quite a lot of people are actually coming up to me and congratulating me. I bow to them. I smile. This is all quite pleasant.

The pale silvery clouds have entirely drifted away. The yellow moon lies huge and beneficent across the heavens.

Young Hu Lan-shih arrives giggling and saying she was right to tell me Intelligent Whore would do us proud. She was very right, and I thank her for it. Beside her is that rather formidable young country girl with the peculiar walk who I met at our parliament's grand opening. The one who brought a basket full of eggs. She tells me my play was quite good – but it would have been better if it had been done as a proper puppet play. She is entirely right. I thank her for her criticism. When I get to Chungking I must do precisely that.

Yu Liqun – all these pretty girls! – comes and laughingly tells me that us two serious revolutionaries should never have allowed ourselves to get dragged into such bourgeois frivolities.

(Thank God her husband Guo Morou isn't here. He's presently involved in a monster lecture tour of the entire Soviet Union. Had he attended I'd never have heard the last of it.)

She asks me if I have heard from my wife. I say no. She squeezes my hand.

I go up to Intelligent Whore and thank her and Little Aigou for their beautiful and profound contribution. I look at her. What a formidable woman! I tell her she was correct to criticize my short story 'Crescent Moon' – the story of the young woman driven to prostitution – for its sentimentality. She smiles.

'I'm sure you have much better work inside you,' she said. 'You are a good writer. You listen.'

As they walk away I see the many admiring looks being cast in her direction by prosperous-looking gentlemen. I smile. I'm sure that by the time she reaches Chungking she'll have been the object of proposals from many wealthy men. She will doubtless marry a multi-millionaire. And as he gets poorer the number of hospitals in Chungking and its surrounding areas will increase.

Then something completely unexpected happens. I suddenly see Madame Chiang Kai-shek sailing down on me with her husband in tow.

'Mr Lao,' she says, shaking my hand and holding on to it, 'let me congratulate you on such an invigorating play. Both my sisters were here and all their friends and they all thought it was the best play they had ever seen!'

One of the worst aspects of being involved in theatrical productions is having to endure the post-first night party, when unbelievable insincerities and untruths are pronounced by all and sundry with sickening gusto.

But at the same time I remember that when everyone is in Chungking, myself and my fellow writers may be desperately in need of all the allies and supporters we can muster. I notice that just behind her and her husband, among their entourage, lurk the two men who tortured and beat me in prison. They are watching myself and General and Madame very closely.

Suddenly, everything gets worse.

The Generalissimo himself steps forwards and addresses me. For several minutes he speaks. I am unable to discern a single moment of meaning or coherence in his entire speech. Nothing! He rambles and rambles then finishes. I naturally reply in similar terms. His wife smiles at me – she is wearing a purple polka dot cardigan with pink dots – and they walk away.

But the two torturers – the one with glasses, the one without glasses – stay. They are all over me. Congratulating. Oleaginous.

Flattering. Obsequious. This is indeed the worst first night party I have ever attended! My gorge is rising unstoppably in my throat and is about to come projecting violently out of my mouth!

But I stop myself.

Tonight has shown my power over them. They have seen my closeness to their capos – especially Madame Chiang. That will give me power in Chungking when the knockings on writers' doors start to come again. It will give me a formidable card to play in defence of them. And myself.

So instead I am incredibly nice – if a little condescending – to them. I oleagenate every bit as much as they oleagenate – though my oleagination is slightly more robust than theirs. We are old friends, comrades, the best of fellows, laughing and joking – with always that slight edge from me. That gleam in the eye. At last, sufficiently reassured, but still unsure, they skitter off after their fellow sycophants and courtiers.

I am exhausted. I thank the director, the actors and dancers, the stagehands and technicians, then I catch the ferry home, collapse on my bed, fall into oblivion.[18]

16

Chamberlain's betrayal of Czechoslovakia burst upon the Last Ditch Club mid-afternoon.

They first heard it over a crackly shortwave radio where voices thousands of miles away randomly wobbled into earshot and equally randomly dissolved back into blizzards of electronic squeals and shrieks. The crowd packed densely round the radio with their ears pressed hard to the speaker managed to discern something about 'peace for our time'.

A universal groan arose. Big glasses containing beer and fashionable glasses containing cocktails were jettisoned. There was a sudden universal demand for small glasses holding very hard liquors. The White Russian barkeeper was besieged with orders.

More detailed and reliable information hurried through on the wires. Of grim-faced dictators. Of Chamberlain and Daladier, the French prime minister, signing a document. Of President Beneš of Czechoslovakia, who commanded a modern and efficient army, being humiliatingly forced by Britain and France to cede his country's Sudetenland. Of Chamberlain flying home to Heston Aerodrome and waving a small piece of paper around, cheerfully announcing 'peace for our time' and then driving 'triumphantly' through cheering London crowds all the way home to Downing Street.

Vernon Bartlett lowered his head and muttered to himself. (Freda was happily ensconced in his hotel room taking a series of baths and typing an article for the *New Statesman*.)

Rewi Alley, with blank, staring eyes, stamped his foot. All

those comrades of his, lying beneath Flanders fields, soon to be joined by a new generation!

Agnes Smedley went away into a corner and wept. For the first time in her life since she had been a tiny child, Agnes permitted herself the luxury of tears.

Jack Belden alone forswore hard liquor. He wished to face this catastrophe (relatively) sober.

They all knew that treachery was afoot. The distortions, the relentless lies pushed by the newspapers and broadcasting organizations that most of them worked for.

Then, into the midst of this black gloom, hurried the bicycle courier from the airport, carrying the airmail edition of *The Times*. Of course this edition was now eight days old, but they fell on it like hungry dogs because they were seeking out treachery, treachery planned many days, many weeks, in advance. The government had been softening up the British and the Empire's citizens to accept and shrug away this betrayal.

Vernon Bartlett, so recently a member of the parliamentary lobby and thus an expert on which journalist rimmed which politician's anus in Westminster, was given the document to decipher. Almost immediately he came across a passage which throbbed. He read from it.

'If the Sudeten Germans now ask for more than the Czech Government are apparently ready to give in their latest set of proposals, it can only be inferred that the Sudetens are going beyond the mere removal of disabilities and do not find themselves at ease within the Czechoslovak Republic.'

'At ease,' murmured Jack Belden, 'at ease.'
'Shit and treachery,' stated Rewi Alley.
Bartlett continued.

'In that case it might be worth while for the Czechoslovak Government to consider whether they should exclude altogether the project, which has found favour in some quarters, of making Czechoslovakia a more homogeneous

State by the secession of that fringe of alien populations who are contiguous to the nation with which they are united by race.'

'The "sheep must apologize to the wolf for any unpleasantness" gambit,' observed James Bertram.

'Makes you bloody ashamed to be British,' shouted out a voice.

Peter Fleming, immaculately dressed, walked into the room, detached as the proverbial cucumber.

'Gentlemen,' he said. And then, noticing Agnes in the corner, 'And ladies.'

He walked to the bar and ordered his habitual iced martini with a twist of lemon.

Suddenly James Bertram walked over to him.

'Have you been reading the shit your paper's been peddling about the Munich crisis?'

'My paper does not write shit,' replied Fleming curtly.

'It writes shit and lies,' said Bertram. 'It disgraces the whole bloody English race.'

Fleming raised his eyebrows and walked away just as George Hogg came in. George had already read the news about Munich on the wires and, after a day of futile frustration trying to find help for his orphans, was really cheered by the opportunities for peace Munich offered.

'Peter,' he said, 'so good to see you back.'

'It's really good to see you too, George,' said Fleming, with more enthusiasm than was his wont.

George noticed the rather hostile group of journalists staring at Fleming.

'Anything wrong?' he asked.

'Absolutely nothing,' responded Peter, and started to tell him of his adventures in London – with certain omissions, of course.

Vernon Bartlett had been studying the editorial in some detail. He opined.

'Reads like *The Times*'s usual well-oiled cant. I'd say it was written either by their deputy editor, Barrington-Ward, or Dawson himself. Dawson after all spends more time in Chamberlain's office than he does in his own. He obviously knew that Chamberlain was going to sell the Czechs out eight days before he actually signed the agreement. And where *The Times* leads all the British and imperial press follow. This piece is deliberately smoothing the way for the treachery to come.'

Agnes, standing in the corner, dried her eyes, blew her nose. She'd been listening intently to everything that was being said in the room. Suddenly, decisively, she walked over to Vernon Bartlett and took the paper from him.

'Barrington-Ward, that creepy little cunt, didn't write this editorial,' she stated. 'Neither did Geoffrey Dawson.'

She read out a part of the article.

'In that case it might be worth while for the Czechoslovak Government to consider whether they should exclude altogether the project, which has found favour in some quarters, of making Czechoslovakia a more homogeneous State by the secession of that fringe of alien populations who are contiguous to the nation with which they are united by race.'

Then she walked over to Fleming and George. She held the paper up to Fleming.

'You wrote this editorial, didn't you, Peter?'

'Don't talk nonsense,' responded Fleming. 'What are you blithering about, you stupid woman?'

'You've just flown back from London. This paper was in the aircraft's hold. You'd have read the editorial before you even left London.'

'So?' asked Fleming.

This so far quiet confrontation was causing interest in the rest of the room. The other journalists moved towards Agnes and Fleming. George instinctively moved to block them off.

Remember you're a Quaker, he thought to himself, remember you're a Quaker.

'Educated upper-class people like you like to use long, little-known words in order to impress the rest of us with just how clever and superior you are. You don't use language to communicate, like ordinary people do, you use it to block off and distance yourself from the rest of us. This editorial uses the word "contiguous".'

'So,' said Fleming, dancing on his toes slightly.

'You've used the word "contiguous" at least twice in my presence here in Wuhan. It was such a rare word that I had to look it up in a dictionary. The full Oxford English twelve-volume dictionary at the British Embassy, because no other dictionary mentioned it. The OED stated that the word had last been used in 1856. "Contiguous" is your word, Peter. You must have stumbled across it in some dusty Oxford library and used it and treasured it ever since to show how much more educated and superior you are to the rest of us.'

There was a pause. Agnes, speaking for the world, continued.

'What your superior education failed to teach you, Peter, is that just because someone has not received an education does not mean they're not intelligent.'

Fleming's upper lip was squirming with a life all of its own. The other journalists were moving quite steadily in on him. George Hogg had forgotten all about being a Quaker as the flames of war – in the cause of peace – licked all around him.

Jack Belden, an ex-docker, muscular and heavy, spoke very softly.

'Just before this all descends into fisticuffs, Fleming,' he said, 'and by the way, that editorial was written in the most excruciating English – I'd like to ask you something – we all being in China as we are? I'd like to ask you, as someone who's obviously just been talking intimately with the most powerful men in Britain, what – if the policies of the British and French governments towards Europe are ones of wholesale abandonment of defenceless peoples to barbarism – what precisely are the policies of the British and French governments towards the peoples of China? You know, all these folk who are so generously allowing us to live among them? Are they to be allowed to be butchered wholesale by the barbarous Japanese?'

'China,' expostulated Fleming, 'what the hell does China have to do with anything?'

'Answer the fucking question! What is Britain and France's position on the Japanese–Chinese War?'

Fleming, faced by this mountain of muscle, with only George between him and Belden, could not control his face, his patrician contempt for the leftist poraille all around him. Could not control his Etonian instinct to show himself the intellectual superior of all other men. Besides, George would bear the brunt of the assault, and the door was nearby.

'What is China to us?' he laughed. 'You really want to know? Though you won't have the intellectual capacity to understand it. I asked when I was in London.'

'Well?' asked Agnes.

'It is blindingly obvious. Let the dogs fight – in Europe, in Asia. Chamberlain backs Japan. Why? Because, if Japan beats China – which it will – then Japan will be free to attack Russia – just as it's tried to do twice in the last two years – and with German troops pouring from the west (all fear of English or French opposition now removed) – the Soviet Union will be completely smashed between the two. The Bolshevik virus will be exterminated – forever. And the war over, all the peace treaties signed, an exhausted Japan will be permitted to keep China as a reward.'

There was a silence. This statement required quite a lot of digesting. Especially by George, who stood as Peter's line of defence against the ring of journalists.

So Britain is going to allow Japan to seize control of China, thought George, butcher its inhabitants, including my orphans, all so Britain and France can utterly destroy the Soviet Union? All this for that, thought George? And in Eastern Europe too, he thought, slightly guiltily.

He half-looked back at Peter. Peter gave him a swift reassuring smirk, that swift reassuring old Etonian smirk which says, 'Don't worry, old chap, I know exactly what I'm doing and if you ordinary folk do exactly what I tell you then everything will turn out just tickety-boo!'

George was not the quickest of thinkers, but on this occasion he did himself credit. Into his mind came the image of a cold winter's night in Oxford when he had been making his way back from a meeting to help Ethiopian refugees after Mussolini's invasion of their country. In a backstreet he had suddenly run into a pack of Bullingdon boys, all in white tie and tails, surrounding an aged and defenceless tramp lying in the gutter. And they were kicking and punching him and laughing hysterically. And then they stopped. It was what happened next that really sickened him. The leader of the feral pack leant down and, with an immaculate drawl, offered the old tramp a five-pound note. And the tramp took the note gratefully and in the most fawning tones thanked the Bullingdon boys most profusely and assured them that they were gents and if they ever wanted to beat him up again he would be most eternally grateful. Both sides then went their separate ways.

In one second George transmuted. In an instant the flames which had been licking greedily within him to lay into these warmongering journalists switched 180 degrees and now, engulfed in blood-red fire, George the Quaker turned and smote Fleming the old Etonian a dolorous blow upon his nose.

Peter Fleming fell to the ground. Then stared upwards.

He had never been punched by a Quaker before. In fact he had rarely been punched by anyone before. There were strict rules within the Bullingdon Club about who smote whom. A non-Etonian was not allowed to punch an Etonian. Only Etonians were allowed to punch fellow Etonians. And then only if they had been a member of the club longer than their opponent. So this blow by a mere Quaker from some place called Harpenden came as a profound shock to him. His sangfroid positively bled.

Everyone stared at George.

George, smote with shame, immediately apologized to the surrounding journalists.

'I'm sorry. I shouldn't have done that!'

'You should, you should,' they all assured him.

Jack Belden and Agnes patted George on his back.

'That was a great punch,' Agnes whispered to him.

Lots of his fellow journalists wanted to buy him drinks, then remembered he was a Quaker.

Fleming crept from the room.

As he left the room a bicycle courier came in with a telegram from the central post office for Vernon Bartlett. It was from Somerset in England.[19]

That same evening Spider Girl was alone with her father in the apartment – except for The Drab, who was crooning to herself somewhere. Donald and Hu were working at the hospital. Agnes, having left the Last Ditch Club and all its excitements, had gone on to a meeting with a communist friend and Freda was lying in bed in Vernon's hotel room smothered in 'Irresistible' perfume awaiting his return.

Spider Girl's father had greatly improved since she had related those various comic events which had become part of village lore. In fact they talked mainly of their life on the farm – incidents and happenings which had made them merry.

It lightened his heart.

But Spider Girl wanted to say something. Her father was a modest man. He would not approve of her saying it. He could even be offended. But such was the strength of her emotion, her need to express it, that even Spider Girl's legendary quantities of common sense and realism were thrown to the winds.

'Father,' she said, 'I just want to say how grateful I am, how proud I am of you, that when you could have turned your back and fled, instead you volunteered for the army, gloriously stood upon the battlefield, and fought so heroically, so courageously for us our family, for your country. I am so proud of you. Thank you for your valour.'

There, she'd said it.

Wei stared at her.

He spoke icily in reply.

'There is no valour in war. You become a bandit. You think like a bandit, you fight like a bandit, you die like a bandit. There is no valour. War is a slurry pit.'

He thought. Then coldly continued.

'Everything you know, everything you love in people, is destroyed in war. All those things that have brought you together in this world – raising families, working with your fellow men, working as one in the fields, at our precious ceremonies and festivals – if you fight, if you go to war you take knives and bullets and slice and rip all those good things apart. The precious tendons and hands and fingers and sinews of people, of communities which draw us all together – which drew together our Japanese foes in their communities just as much…'

He paused.

'I mean – you remember that barn that Fang the Builder made for us…?'

'Yes.'

'…and how we, the whole family, went inside it when he had finally finished it (he always took so long finishing things) – and we looked around and saw what he had created – his beautiful stonework, his wooden beams and posts so beautifully carved. When I went in I just stood and stared, ran my hands and fingers over his joinery and beams so smoothly and beautifully crafted by him – and all that work, all that incredible skill which he had shown in creating that barn, in one moment, in one moment of war, was ripped part, destroyed in a frenzy of madness… There is no valour in war.'

He looked away from her. Her heart sank. Then he looked back. He addressed her.

'Daughter, as you and I both know, I will soon die.'

Spider Girl hung her head.

'But until then let us remain friends. And no mention of valour.'

17

Wuhan was in a state of evacuation. Mass evacuation. The evacuation was being organized by the military.

First to go, by river, were the large majority of wounded soldiers. All those at the hospital and in the surrounding grounds had been transported by stretcher or by cart or in buses if they could walk to the docksides on the Bund or to the railway station across the river in Wuchang where special trains awaited them. Every floating brothel had been commandeered and many of the whores – male and female – had been re-employed as nurses and orderlies. They gently helped the stricken soldiers up the gangways and then tended to them once they were in their bunks. Those with broken limbs who were suspended in the bicycle tractions were smoothly lifted and carried with great care by coolies who specialized in moving delicate porcelain and intricate pieces of machinery and art.

This proved a disaster for the wealthy, who were in the midst of evacuating themselves and all their extremely rare and valuable works of art and antique porcelain. They needed precisely the same highly skilled coolies. They offered them stupendous sums to work for them. Army officers stepped in.

Whole universities and factories sailed upstream – pupils, workers, machinery and equipment – often as one.

The famous Hing Fu-tsai restaurant, which claims an unbroken history from the Ming Dynasty and was patronized by fifteenth-century emperors, having been first removed from Nanking, was now removed again – chefs, waiters, kitchen boys, pots and pans, maître d's and sauciers and sommeliers and the entire contents of its legendary wine cellar – all the way upstream to Chungking.

The indefatigable Madame Chiang saved hundreds of cases of art treasures and priceless manuscripts from the golden ages of Chinese culture and had them shipped upstream.

Those whores who did not go upstream as nurses were left with a dilemma. Unlike in Nanking, the population of Wuhan was well aware of what the Japanese probably intended for them, with the result that the majority of whores – who in Nanking had so heroically and patriotically offered themselves for rape (and worse) at the hands of Japanese soldiers to sate them and save the purity and virtue of upper-class ladies (a gruesome and heroic sacrifice for which they were never thanked or received any compensation) – in Wuhan instead clambered aboard the steamers and junks side by side with the fine ladies and sailed away together into the western sunset. This left just a few of the whores, who calculated that with so few remaining for their enemies to choose from, the Japanese would be forced to pay them extra-high rates and treat them with less ferocity.

It was early autumn. White mists settled on the river and over its ever quieter streets as a majority of Wuhan's inhabitants bled away.

As Hu walked to the hospital she was preoccupied and just a little worried.

Ever since Spider Girl had rescued Hu from the collapsed air-raid shelter, Hu had watched Spider Girl very closely. As a friend monitors a friend. She was aware that every so often Spider Girl quietly suffered black moments, dark moments of despair – a most un-Spider Girl-like condition. She also understood that Spider Girl was faced with a terrible dilemma, the dilemma so many had faced in this war. In the face of the murderous Japanese advance – did you stay with your infirm relatives who could not be moved, or did you abandon them? Of course, Hu understood that Spider Girl would never abandon her father. Under any circumstances. But if she had some contingency plan to move her father, Spider Girl had not confided in Hu about it, despite attempts by Hu to raise the subject. There was also the question of what would happen to The

Drab. Hu watched Spider Girl as she stoically hobbled around the apartment and then off down the street to do her shopping. Pain was written across her face as she waddled on her rickets-crippled joints. How could she help?

Agnes had her own plans for the future and had offered Spider Girl her freedom and a substantial sum of money so that she could arrange her – and presumably her father's – exit from Wuhan. Provided her father was still alive. But Spider Girl turned her down. Quite decisively. Agnes needed her money to spend on the good things she spent it on and Spider Girl would look after herself.

Donald had volunteered to stay in Wuhan operating until almost the end. As an invaluable – and innovative – surgeon he had been allotted a seat on one of the last planes leaving Wuhan for Chungking. He had also been told that there would be a spare seat on it for his most valued assistant. Donald had privately offered Hu the seat. Hu had thought about this a lot – all the lives she could help save – but turned him down. She felt her loyalties must be with Spider Girl. Spider Girl, who had rescued her from the air-raid shelter. She should be ready to do the same. But Spider Girl had given no sign of what she intended to do.

While Hu worried Spider Girl scoured the markets on the Bund, searching for the most nourishing and antiseptic honeys in China to treat her father's wounds. She went from stall to stall, comparing different honeys, talking to the stall owners. Eventually she settled on two. A rare, pure honey from China's far northern province, Jehol – renowned for its nourishing properties when fed to the patient – and a honey from Mangshi in the far south-west, gathered off the sides of mountainous cliffs by men clinging precariously to long ladders, which, blended with white peony roots, liquorice, cinnamon and dried ginger and when smeared on the patient, could provide relief from abdominal pains. Spider Girl would feed it into his wound, alternating with the chloride solution, through the rubber bicycle valve.

These rare honeys were not cheap. Much of the money that she spent on them was money obtained by less than honest dealings. But that was why Spider Girl was dishonest. So that honest people would not have to be dishonest.

At the moment she had a lot on her plate. In addition to nursing her father and keeping Donald's bow tie in a state of perky immediacy and visiting a nearby temple to pray for things and cooking and doing the housework for an ever-changing menagerie of visitors, she also had to buy the food and other household necessities in the market as well as all the bicycle parts demanded by Donald's surgery. She also still put in stints at the workshop producing traction units for the hospital – though the workmen were slowly being sent away to work in a new prosthetics factory opening upstream in Chungking.

Within the apartment, because of all Spider Girl's extra activity, The Drab was being slowly promoted – although she was unaware of this herself. Now not only did she have to prepare all the vegetables, but she also had to do some of the cooking and housework – none of which tasks she did well. Agnes and Hu and even Donald helped her out when they had time, though Donald was even more clumsy than The Drab.

I pay my daily visit to the central post office to once more to ask if there is any letter from my wife and family. The answer is, as always, no.

I wander distractedly along the Bund. There are fewer and fewer people in the city. I sit down at an outside table of my usual tea house. Attempting to look cheerful, the average boulevardier, I sip my tea and watch the passers-by pass by. At least *Defend Wuhan!* is finished. Now I can return to more exalted pursuits, such as rewriting *Seven Chinese Virgins Sink a Japanese Torpedo Boat*. Lao Xiang's advice on the subject – 'Fuck 'em' – has not proved helpful.

As I gaze around I notice the only other figure sat outside the tea house, a rather strained English gentleman sitting at a table quite close to me. He is of course immaculately attired. He has that common English air of self-sufficient aloofness. Except that suddenly he winces. And suddenly in his face I glimpse an ocean of pain, before he wriggles and almost immediately manages to reassert his mask of indifference.

What private agony is that poor soul passing through?

Peter Fleming was all facade. What else can an upper-class old Etonian be but that? That is all he had.

He was brought up in a vast and vulgar banker's mansion in the Chilterns. (With a quick train connection to central London to get away from it all.) The bathrooms were as big as tennis courts and you could set up home in the fireplaces. His father, thanks to the nearby station, spent most of his time in London. His very beautiful mother in her colour-clashing discordant clothes wandered like a lost soul through the endless halls ignoring her children.

Then came the First World War. His father suddenly reappeared in immaculate officers' uniform tailored by Turnbull & Asser of Jermyn Street. He looked very tall and very brilliant and very distant as he puffed on his Davidoff cigars. Peter stood as close to him as he dared with a very straight back and tried to look military.

His father went away to war and was killed in May 1917. Winston Churchill wrote his obituary in *The Times*.

His mother broke the news to her nine-year-old son, informed him he was now head of the family, then totally ignored him.

Peter took long walks, wandering alone through the nearby hills and woods. He became a keen ornithologist and observer of nature. He loved to be alone, in the Chilterns or on family holidays in the Highlands. He became an excellent shot and hunter.

Meanwhile his mother took a lover. Not just any lover. The ageing lecher and daubist Augustus John. Naked sketches of his mother with her legs open soon started to adorn the soulless mansion. Peter got sent away to school, then to Eton.

Eton is based on bullying. From the day you arrive, you are bullied. Fagging, flogging, buggery. Your education consists of learning how to avoid bullying. Excellent preparation for surviving and then thriving within the London elite. You can evade bullying by blaming others, inventing influential friends, toadying, clowning, superb and multi-layered lying, criminality, treachery, or, best of all, by becoming a bully yourself – while all the time exuding smooth-as-silk charm.

The fact that his mother insisted on turning up for sports day dressed in garish emerald and purple or yellow and magenta dresses did not help matters. Nor did the fact that, by Augustus John, she produced a child, Amaryllis, the noted cellist.

Peter went through Oxford, served in the Bullingdon, then stepped into *The Spectator* magazine with its faux rural airs set plumb in the middle of London's greasiest fleshpots. From which he needed to escape very quickly. He embarked on an eccentric voyage into the Amazonian jungle, followed by a 5,000-mile trek across the tundras and deserts of Central Asia, followed by a hike over the Himalayas, after which, he announced, his buttocks were 'taut enough to crack a walnut!' He wrote nonchalant bestselling travel books about his frolics. Englishman meets lots of funny foreigners!

And then he got mixed up in all this nonsense. In an odd sort of way he actually supported those animals back at the Last Ditch. Appeasement was almost certainly a fraud. A gamble. What would happen when Hitler had swallowed Western Russia and Hirohito Eastern Russia? Would they then say, 'Thank you so very much for allowing us to fight these wars on your behalf, now you can go back to ruling us all?' Or would they – armed with all Russia's vast natural resources and industries – then turn their guns roaring and blazing on us? But, he reflected, the game must be played – spying on colleagues, writing editorials – to its bitter end. Duty is duty.

The only thing that kept him going, kept him sane and functioning, was his beloved wife Celia. And, thug that he was, he could not bear to be anywhere near such a good and natural person.

Floreat Etona!

This strange Englishman sitting near me on the Bund suddenly convulses into tears and then even more suddenly convulses out of them and, hastily wiping away all trace of them, sets his face, straightens his back, arises, glares at me – a mere Chinese – and marches off.

Oh the horrors and burdens of empire!

I too must go. I promised the director of my Wuhan cavalcade that I would pop in to thank everyone in the production before they all disperse. Yu Liqun will almost certainly give me one of her saucy winks. Which reminds me so painfully of my wife.

At the hospital Donald Hankey and Bob McClure were the last surgeons in Wuhan. As the fighting steadily got closer and closer soldiers in all states of disfigurement and pain continued to present at the hospital, but most were being sent immediately upstream. Surgeons and doctors and skilled staff and nurses were similarly being transported to Chungking. Unskilled staff, including Hu, were being given ever-greater responsibilities.

One morning Donald and Bob and Hu were sitting in the side room. There was a lull in the arrival of patients. One of the Bunsen burners which had been used to heat the pressure cookers in order to sterilize their instruments was now being used to brew tea.

Hu turned the conversation to Spider Girl.

'Donald, Bob, I've been thinking,' said Hu.

'Gee!'

'What about?'

'Spider Girl. I'm worried about her.'

'Is she all right?' asked a surprised Donald.

Hu decided not to mention Spider Girl's black moments. There was nothing Donald could do about them, anyhow. So she concentrated on the things that could be done.

'Well – she doesn't show it of course, but she is worried about how she's going to get out of Wuhan. With her father – if he is still alive. I've said I will go with her. But if she's going to get away then she's going to have to be able to walk more easily. Even the shortest distances cause her pain with her rickets.'

'You're right,' said Donald, 'I should have thought about that.'

'Yep,' said Bob, 'we should.'

'I was just wondering if there was anything you two could do for her. To help her walk better.'

There was a silence, which went on for quite a not inconsiderable time. Hu, who'd been thinking deeply on this, prompted them.

'Perhaps it could involve bicycles?'

'Ah ha,' said Donald. 'Yes.'

'See what you mean,' said Bob.

They all turned to look at Bob's bicycle leaning against the wall. Bob felt a bit perturbed by this. He was very fond of his bicycle.

'Holy moly, when's all this cannibalism of innocent bicycles going to stop?' he lamented. 'Seems that more and more we're replacing vital bits of the human body with bicycle parts. Handlebars for shoulders, tubes for arms, legs for wheels! Half man, half bicycle!'

Donald walked over to the bicycle, looking upon it vulturously, especially its forks.

18

Spider Girl's father had been awake and fretting for most of the night. Spider Girl had just managed to get him asleep and was doing some cooking. Hu was reading her Bible, Agnes was in her room quietly working on the fifteenth chapter of the *Battle Hymn of China* and Donald was sitting at the table feverishly doing calculations on the backs of several envelopes, when suddenly, into their midst, strode a near-hysterical Freda.

Spider Girl ground her teeth.

'He's left me! He's left me! He's abandoned me! Again I've been abandoned by a man! A damned man!'

She exploded into fountains of tears.

'What is the matter, Freda?' Agnes enquired from her room in a rather commanding voice.

'He's betrayed me. That smarmy Vernon Bartlett. He asked for everything I could give him and then ran away. I'm alone again. With a three-year-old child!'

Donald was from a rural background and so was not accustomed to sudden hysterical outbursts such as this. Such disturbing phenomena seemed to occur mainly in cities, especially among women, and at that dreadful public school he'd had to attend. Furtively folding the envelopes into his jacket pocket he sidled out of the door to continue his work in some quiet tea house. In doing so he forgot to put on his bow tie, which Spider Girl had spent a considerable amount of last night primping for him.

This put Spider Girl in an even worse mood. Not only was this Freda woman likely to waken her father when he needed to sleep, but now she'd robbed Donald of his bow tie. She banged several pots and pans.

Agnes emerged from her room. She'd been struggling to pin down the exact date of the Battle of Pingxingguan (25 September 1937) and had only just located it.

'Freda,' she said, 'what is the matter?'

'Well...' sobbed Freda.

'Sit down,' Agnes ordered her. 'And Spider Girl, get her some soothing tea. Now,' said Agnes, sitting down beside Freda, 'tell us precisely what has happened.'

Everyone still in the room earwigged in – Hu, Spider Girl (as she banged around looking for the pu-ehr soothing tea) and even The Drab. Hu quietly provided a translation for them all.

'Suddenly he appeared. In the hotel room. I didn't have a stitch on. He had had a telegram. From some vicar in Somerset. On Exmoor! The Reverend Cresswell someone or other – what a name! And this vicar – who Vernon had been in the trenches with – was the chairman of the Minehead Labour Party. Somehow this priest had managed to wangle a by-election in his constituency, Bridgwater. But instead of candidates from all the different parties – Labour, the Liberals, the Communists – all standing against each other against the appeasement-supporting Tory candidate, he had somehow managed to wangle it so that only one candidate would stand against the appeaser candidate. They call themselves the Popular Front candidate. And this vicar on top of Exmoor wanted Vernon to be that candidate. And Vernon agreed, shouting, "At last the provinces have a chance to strike back!" Then he jumped on a plane and was gone. I stood there without any clothes on. Abandoned!'

'Well,' said a slightly flummoxed Agnes, 'well...'

Meanwhile Spider Girl, unable to locate the pu-ehr tea to soothe Freda's nerves – probably because The Drab in her attempts at cooking had misplaced it somewhere – relieved her own fury by giving The Drab a stout cuff round the ears.

Seeing this Freda leapt to her feet and redirected all her pent-up fury at Spider Girl.

'This is what I mean,' she screamed. 'This what I mean! This peasant girl, dirty, scruffy, striking innocent halfwits, stealing my bath water and selling it to God knows who... Sack her. Agnes, you've got to sack her!'

Everyone stared at Agnes.

Slightly bemused, Agnes rose to her feet. Bloody upper middle-class Englishwomen!

She was about to speak when something quite extraordinary happened.

Someone else spoke.

Usually totally incoherent, mumbling, talking to herself, crooning annoyingly on occasions, The Drab spoke. Spoke almost quite clearly, almost quite coherently. She addressed Freda.

'Excuse me,' she said, 'I am not very bright, and I don't usually talk at all, but I want to speak about Spider Girl.'

Agnes was so amazed at this intervention – like everyone else – that she started translating The Drab's words so Freda could understand.

'I want to say,' said The Drab, 'that I am alive because of Spider Girl. Without Spider Girl I would be dead. She picked me up off the street, where I was dying. If I lost Spider Girl and went back on the street I would die very soon. Because no one would need me. I am not very clever. In fact I can understand very little. And I forget things. Very easily. But Spider Girl helps me remember things. When I forget something she cuffs me and it hurts so that that thing I am meant to remember I remember because of the pain before I forget it again and Spider Girl has to cuff me again to make me remember it again. I am so grateful to her for this. She makes it possible for me to work, to be useful. If I lost Spider Girl – which I fear above all else – I would be back on the streets and would die very soon.'

There was a silence.

Spider Girl found the black pu-ehr tea and decided to make a bowl for everyone to calm them – except for The Drab, who might get so calm she'd fall asleep.

Agnes looked quite sternly at Freda, who'd sat down again.

'Freda,' she said, 'you're an upper middle-class Englishwoman. Isn't it about time you started behaving like an upper middle-class Englishwoman and *pulled yourself together*!'

Freda meekly pulled herself together. She even apologized to Spider Girl.

'And Freda,' continued Agnes, 'a bit of advice. You're a foreign correspondent. Here today and on the other side of the world tomorrow. If you're offered sex and want it, then have it. Enjoy it while it lasts – which won't be long. Then get on with the next bit of your life.'

Next morning, before Hu left for work, she asked Spider Girl if she could call in at the hospital at about eleven. Spider Girl assumed it was likely to be a request for yet another bicycle part, agreed and thought no more of it.

She bathed her father, changed his bandages and his bed clothing and put them to boil in the pot she used for sterilizing them. She dosed him with some opium and then chatted with him until he fell asleep. She then asked Agnes, who was working at her book, if she could keep an eye on her father while she was out and left.

She did her shopping on the Bund – food and bicycle parts – dropped the food off at the apartment (telling The Drab which vegetables to cut) and then carried on with the bicycle parts to the hospital.

On arrival she was greeted by Donald and Hu – Spider Girl had managed to get Donald's bow tie on him this morning and he looked resplendent – but rather than taking Spider Girl into the main operating theatre as usual instead they ushered her into a small side room. There were bits of bicycles leaning against the wall and some leather strapping. In the middle of the room stood a pair of parallel bars taken from a gym.

Donald immediately started fiddling with the bicycle bits and leather strapping. Hu shut the windows and drew the blinds. Something was obviously about to happen.

Hu turned to face Spider Girl.

'Spider Girl,' she said, 'Donald and I and all the doctors here have been thinking about your condition. Your "rickets".'

'Yes?'

'We think we might have come up with a system which might help your walking.'

Spider Girl took a step back.

'It will give you strength in your legs. It will let other parts of your body support your upper legs – it will strengthen them.'

Spider Girl swallowed.

'What do you want me to do?' she asked.

'This is the difficult part,' said Hu. 'I will be here to reassure and protect you. Donald will fit this system, this harness to you, but you will have to take your clothes off so he can do it.'

Spider Girl looked at Donald. Donald was far too deep into the process of organizing the harness, getting all its various straps and bicycle forks cohesing and conjoining, to bother about listening to what was being said.

Spider Girl rarely found herself in a quandary, but did now. Of course she did not want a man who was not married to her seeing her without clothes and naked. But at the same time it was Donald, the very subject of various early pubescent stirrings and strange dreamings within her. His eyes would be on her most secret, her most shameful parts – close up. But on the other hand, it would just be Donald. A good and most moral man. The man who was sustaining her father in life. Besides – as she watched Donald wrestling and puzzling his way into assembling his harness – Spider Girl, with more than a touch of sadness, accepted that as he handled and felt her body he would be far more engrossed and interested in organizing his contraption than he ever would be with her and her nakedness. Or anyone's nakedness. He was such a good man.

Spider Girl sighed and assented.

Donald continued to wrestle and finesse his harness as she stripped and stood there naked before him.

Hu led her to the parallel bars and stood her in the middle, placing her two hands on the two bars.

Suddenly it seemed as though Donald had solved his riddle. It was ready. He looked up at Spider Girl and grinned.

'Ready, Spider Girl?'

Spider Girl swallowed.

'Yes.'

'Super! This is an experiment, but I'm convinced it's going to work.'

He advanced on her, the harness of bicycle parts and leather held out before him, then sank down out of her sight. Spider Girl heard various jangles and clanks, but resolutely did not look down. She stared hard at the blinds ahead of her.

The harness that Donald was fitting for Spider girl consisted of four pairs of bicycle forks. Two long, two short. The two long ones, upside down, ran from her waist down to her knees along the outside of her thighs. The two shorter ones, the right way up, stretched from just below her crotch, inside her thighs, to her knees. The two longer forks were attached at their tops to a leather strap which formed a belt around her waist. The two shorter forks were attached at their tops to each other and by straps around each thigh to the longer fork on the outside of the thigh. The short forks were again joined by straps at the knees, to their respective longer fork.

While all this was going on Spider Girl stared dead ahead of herself. Like a scared rabbit. Stared at those blinds. But as she did so she was also feeling his fumblings and expeditions all around her intimate parts. She imagined him looking there, examining and detailing and calculating her most secret places. She started to get feelings, feel heats. Suddenly a picture of his bow tie sprang vividly into her mind...

'Spider Girl!'

Spider Girl awoke. Hu was standing before her, smiling.

'Everything all right?' she asked.

'Yes, of course,' replied Spider Girl in a slightly strangulated fashion.

'Jolly good,' said Donald. 'I think that's it. I think it's in place,' he added with a slight note of triumph to his voice. He rose up from her nether regions and stared directly in her face. 'I think, Spider Girl,' he said earnestly, 'you could try to walk forwards. Let's see if it works. And don't let go of the bars.'

Spider Girl did this, gingerly. Then a bit faster. It was amazing. The weight of her body, which had once ground down on her weak, twisted thighs, was now being partially carried by the exoskeleton of the bicycle forks.

'It works, Donald, it works!'

Hu chirruped with joy. Donald grinned broadly at her. Spider Girl started to walk slowly, triumphantly around the room – entirely forgetting that she was naked.

19

Wuhan was in its last few hours. Of survival. Of freedom. Of meaning. Already Japanese artillery was bombarding the eastern suburbs of Hankou on the north side of the river and Wuchang on its southern bank. Small arms fire could be heard crackling in the distance.

At the apartment everyone was to depart the next morning.

Freda had been offered a lecture tour in the States on the Japanese and Chinese economies. They all agreed it would calm her down.

Donald was to fly to Chungking early next morning.

Agnes had signed up with the Chinese Red Cross and was setting off on the long foot trek to the barren lands south of the Yangtze where the Communist Fourth Army guerrillas were deployed. She'd continue to contribute occasional articles to the *Manchester Guardian* and her book *Battle Hymn of China* had been safely despatched to her publishers.

Spider Girl and Hu weren't quite sure what they would be doing next, but that didn't bother Spider Girl (at least openly). But they would be going out to the aerodrome to wish Donald a safe journey.

That evening a farewell feast was held for the apartment's members to commemorate and celebrate their time together. It was quite solemn.

This meal over – and Spider Girl and The Drab duly congratulated and a few tears shed – Agnes suggested that to cheer everyone up they should all repair to the Last Ditch Club where a great wake was being held in memory and celebration of Wuhan's heroic stand against fascism and barbarism. And she included Spider Girl in that invitation (but not The Drab).

Spider Girl immediately objected on the grounds that she could not leave her father (and she didn't want to spend an evening with a whole lot of drunken Westerners, even if it did include Donald).

'No,' said Agnes, 'you are definitely coming. Nobody embodies the spirit of Wuhan like you.'

Donald (who didn't himself really want to go either, socializing wasn't at all his thing) suggested that he could stay behind and perhaps look after Wei while Spider Girl went.

Spider Girl glared at him.

'You are definitely attending,' commanded Agnes.

Hu thought 'why not?' and 'anything for a laugh' and agreed.

Freda announced she would not be coming. The Last Ditch Club would remind her too much of Vernon.

Agnes, rather than risk a histrionic row with Freda, acceded to this and stated that Freda could look after Spider Girl's father. Donald had after all had just dosed him with opium.

Spider Girl did not trust Freda enough to look after her father. But before she could think up a suitably diplomatic way of frustrating this plan – and Spider Girl could do diplomatic – suddenly through the door appeared Dr Bob McClure, chief surgeon at Wuhan's hospital. He was real sorry, he'd been bombed out of his house in East Hankou and could he please have a floor for the night? He and Donald were due to fly out on the same flight to Chungking tomorrow, so they could travel to the aerodrome together.

Spider Girl was neatly checkmated. Bob McClure was perfectly qualified to keep a professional eye on her father. And, as a pious Methodist and teetotaler, he was the last person to want to attend a pagan bacchanal at the Last Ditch.

Still, she refused.

'You can dance, Spider Girl,' Hu suggested, 'in your new harness Donald made for you.'

Spider Girl grimaced, but then looked at Donald, who appeared worried and disorientated at the prospect of some drunken party. She knew she should support him.

They set off.

* * *

The Last Ditch's final party did not so much resemble the Duchess of Richmond's ball on the eve of Waterloo as the Battle of Waterloo itself.

It was driven by black, crushing nihilism.

There was shouting, fighting and the ominous sound of artillery shells landing nearby. In toast after drunken toast the name of Neville Chamberlain was ritually cursed. He had betrayed his country. He had betrayed the world into darkness and perpetual war. Everyone was frighteningly drunk.

Agnes sat down at the ancient and discordant piano and started belting out 'The Daring Young Man on the Flying Trapeze' with Jack Belden standing beside her roaring out the verses and everyone joining in the chorus – followed by 'Lydia the Tattooed Lady' in all its cartographic glory and 'Mademoiselle from Armentières' in all its gynaecological glory. Agnes shared Jack's bottles of bourbon.

Hu, being a Methodist and so teetotal, set about enjoying herself.

Rewi Alley, standing on top of the piano, gave a long encomium in praise of honourable, decent blokes everywhere and how they were shortly to be exterminated off the face of the earth. He then fell off the piano and ended up under a table.

Spider Girl knew immediately she should not have come.

Donald likewise stared aghast. For several days now he had been feeling emotional. Of course he hadn't realized he was feeling emotional. He didn't know what emotions were. For him life revolved entirely around surgery, random photo snappings, and bicycles. That was pretty much it. He'd been so happy just being in Wuhan. Doing his surgery. Doing it and doing it and doing it. All the time thinking, working up new surgical skills, shortcuts, refinements – helping people. He had not been so happy since he was a boy on Salisbury Plain galloping across the green, green grass with raised head staring into the blue, blue heavens.

But in these last hours, as the time for their departure grew ever closer, all these strange, slightly ugly things started moving around inside his body. What *were* they? He was distinctly nervous. And so it was tonight that his 'emotions' finally burst from out of him.

A tray of drinks was passing by. He grabbed a large glass of scotch and swallowed it. He grabbed another large glass and swallowed it. Then another.

Spider Girl stared.

Izzy Epstein was in high spirits. Having attended the performance of *Defend Wuhan!* he'd actually seen Madame Chiang Kai-shek in the flesh and been able, with his own two eyes, to ascertain, irrefutably, that her polka dot sweater was in fact purple with pink dots. This would finally shut up his irascible editor in New York so that he could now write meaningful stories about the terrible sufferings of the heroic Chinese people.

James Bertram was somewhere on hands and knees.

George Wang punched his opposite number at AFP.

George Hogg had more important matters on his hands.

Peter Fleming was not present.

Agnes, having gone through 'Roll Out the Barrel' and 'Land of My Fathers' (for some reason or other), belted out 'The Internationale'.

By popular request 'Roses of Picardy' was sung by Ralph Shaw who possessed a particularly fine baritone.

Everyone wept.

Ralph then followed it with a long and maudlin anamnesis of all the many women he had slept with. Big Wanda, his White Russian squeeze, stared at him icily.

It was at this point that Donald suddenly remembered he could play the piano.

To Spider Girl's horror he was already three quarters of a bottle of scotch to the worse (he never drank), and his bow tie lay torn and bedraggled across his breast.

Donald approached the piano. Agnes saw he was going to play and made way for him. He bowed to her, nearly fell over, then unsteadily took his seat. He straightened his back, adjusted his cuffs, breathed in and then with hammer blows and shrieking chords set about Chopin's 'Heroic' Polonaise celebrating the

Parisian proletariat's valiant 1848 uprising against the brutal bourgeoisie. Occasionally he hit the right note.

The piano stood up to this assault for a commendable while but then started disintegrating under his hammer blows.

Spider Girl was aghast. She had never heard such ugly discordant sounds. It sounded like a hundred sawmills. Everything appeared black to her. She panicked and fled the club.

Donald was finally dragged from the by now largely demolished piano and was violently sick all over the floor.

There was a darkness, a desperation to the whole frenzied night. Wuhan was falling. They were all stumbling out into a deep dark world which could only get darker every day. Mr Chamberlain had won. Fascism had won.[20]

George Hogg made a decision. The authorities would not take responsibility for the orphans he had been working with. They were too traumatized, smashed about by life. With their violence and psychotic behaviour they were simply too dangerous to move. Leave them to the Japanese.

George examined his Quaker conscience. He understood he, and he alone, was now responsible for them. He was not going to be a banker. He was not going to be a journalist. He was certainly *not* going to be a spy. He was going to have to look after them.

He went to his bank and took out all his meagre savings.

At three in the morning he and his young wards sat crammed into their tiny hut. George addressed them.

'You have got me. I have got you. We are all we have in this world.'

He looked around at them – Liang, Hua, Chin, Heng, Bojing, Cong, Xingfu, Wen, the rest.

By now they understood that the Japanese were coming. Immediately. Each one of them was terrified – including George.

'We have to be together, as one. If we are not together, as one, we die. The Japanese are nearly upon us.'

He looked at them. They stared back at him like rabbits.

'You all fight each other. Your...' George remembered his own striking of Peter Fleming, corrected himself, '...our only chance of surviving, escaping the Japanese, is by working for each other, helping each other, protecting each other. Heng, if you bully Chin – the Japanese will kill us. Bojing, if you whine about Hua – the Japanese will kill us. If I lose my temper and shout at one of you – the Japanese will kill us. Everyone here must help each other, protect each other. Otherwise we will all die, be shot by the Japanese. Do you understand me?'

They all nodded.

'Where are we going?' asked Liang.

'West,' replied George, 'where the Japanese are not.'

'How are we going to get there?' asked the smallest, Chin.

'We will walk. A long, long walk. Day after day. Week after week. Month after month. And all that time we will help each other, protect each other, brothers, and when we get there, I promise you, when we finally get there you will have a proper life. You will have a garden. A very large garden. Where you can all grow our food – as you once grew your food on the farms you came from. We will be able to play games. And we will have a school room where we can all learn things and sleep at night.

'We will get there because we will not hit each other, all the time we will help each other, all the time. Otherwise we will all die.'

He looked around him at their dirty faces.

'Do we agree?'

A pause.

'Yes,' they all said solemnly, 'we agree.'

So they set off through the dark city. As each one left the hut George handed them a raw potato from a sack he'd bought on the Bund. They rubbed the dirt off on their clothes and started chewing the potatoes. He slung the rest of the sack over his shoulder and they walked westward, towards the ferry which would take them across the Han River to Hanyang, and then to the world beyond.[21]

***

Spider Girl walked alone through the dark cold streets of Wuhan. They were deserted. Shadows and figures flitted from door to door or into dark alleys. She ignored them.

She felt very emotional. In fact she was at the mercy of a whole conflict of emotions.

The two central conflicts were between Donald and her father. She did not want to lose either of them. But her father was dying and Donald was flying off to Chungking. Which was good. Donald was a good man and he was going to do good things. But…

By now Spider Girl realized she was in love with Donald. This feeling – entirely novel to her – was both enchanting and terrifying. She kept having these dreams. The two of them with no clothes on – she not even wearing the exoskeleton he had made for her. Of him sitting on a chair and she sitting astraddle him, facing him, as she had once seen her parents doing. But she didn't have the least idea what happened next except that Donald's bow tie – his only garment – glowed resplendently.

And besides all this strange stuff with Donald there was her father. The Japanese were arriving, in hours. Donald said it would be safe to move her father. Spider Girl certainly wasn't going to abandon him to the Japanese. But she needed a cart on which to lay her father, and everyone was buying carts, so the prices of both carts and the horses and donkeys to draw them had shot up, beyond what Spider Girl could possibly afford. And Hu had had complicated everything by refusing to leave for Chungking with Donald but instead insisting she stay with Spider Girl and her father and help them. Hu was a moral person; Spider Girl was not a moral person. Hu was likely to vigorously oppose certain steps Spider Girl might take in order to ensure they all survived. And then there was The Drab. Spider Girl would not abandon her – poor bewildered creature – to the Japanese.

But it was this rift in her loyalties and loves which split Spider Girl right down the middle. Wounded her. And it was through this wound that that most un-Spider Girl-like of all emotions entered her spirit – despair.

Blackness. Blackness.

She shook herself vigorously. She must do something decisive soon. But what? Characteristically, she was waiting for that moment, that chink in the armour of Fate to offer itself. And as soon as she spotted it she would charge through it. But until then...?

A cold wind blew through the darkness. Shadowy figures darted past her but she ignored them. She carried her pistol.

It was the emptiness, the eeriness, the desolation of this city which unnerved her. The moans and wails of the first winds of winter keening through its streets.

It was as though the ghosts and spirits of all those millions who had so recently and so desperately attempted to journey to Wuhan and had perished on the way, often horribly, it was as though now, as the living left, evacuated the city, these same lost ghosts and spirits of the dead were invading, sweeping into this city, occupying every last deserted cranny and crevice and nook of each human home and habitation. The city seemed filled with the restless souls and creeping shadows of the dead – including the many dead of her own family who she had failed to save – shivering and whining, edging, easing their way in. The dead uncles and aunts and children and grandparents and parents. Whole families and villages of the dead. Their spirits even in death still desperately trying to mingle with, warm themselves, chatter among the living.

But then cities, even with the living in them, were such strange places. All that hurrying, scurrying about, everyone rushing nowhere, no one knowing anyone, all that blankness and anonymity. In the country, in a village, you knew everyone – every single person, their family history, their parents and grandparents, children and grandchildren – you saw things directly, in straight lines, things starting, things being done, things being created and finished. You saw distances, perspectives, futures.

But in this new world. Here.

Without realizing it Spider Girl had stopped. Suddenly, vividly, before her, she saw her father in his prime, returning from the fields in the evening, being consulted by the family, reaching decisions and making judgements, then relaxing on the verandah beneath the eaves, sipping his goat's milk, singing a funny song.

In the dark Spider Girl ate bitterness.

But the old ways were the best. She shook herself, set herself again to her tasks, and walked on to the apartment.

20

It is about three in the morning. I cannot sleep. I sit out in the courtyard beneath my university window. I gaze up at the stars. Wuhan will fall today.

I sit on the bench beneath the boughs of the red persimmon tree. It is cold, but I do not need a coat. The tree's boughs are heavy with its fruit. I have reached up and tasted some of them but for once their taste does not ensnare me. Too sweet, too cloying!

Again and again I ask myself the question, 'What should I do?' and get no answer. An equally nice university bedroom and study awaits me in Chungking. Jump on the next boat – I've already cancelled two reservations – or hang on here, to the last moment, hoping that a letter might appear from my wife at the post office?

I decide there is only one place to be on Wuhan's last day. The Bund. The throbbing, inexhaustible, magical Bund. There I will make my decision. (And besides, I'm due to meet a friend there at midday.)

I climb back up to my apartment and gather my few belongings in a small suitcase, say farewell to the halls of my university, scuttle down to the ferry. The never-ending, ever-bustling ferries. How will their crews fare under the Japanese? With two robust hoots we set sail upon the black waters of the Yangtze, lights from either bank reflecting and bouncing up into my eyes.

We seem like a fragile saucer afloat on its vast, turmoiling energies and currents.

It is no easy matter leaving Wuhan. Why? A dirty, blackened industrial city filled with corrupt politicians and wretched bankers. But, in my time here...

I cry. Then stop when I see a fellow passenger look at me curiously.

I have never lived in such a place. The change, the constant flux. The joy – yes indeed, the exultation of living here. Not even the streets of Beijing when I was a penniless urchin nor the streets of London when I was a penniless scholar have given me such excitement as the wild streets of wild Wuhan. Round every corner lurks a new idea, a new invention, a new adventure waiting to attack you. Where the least likely thing to happen to you on earth will invariably happen to you sometime within the next six seconds.

I mean, who on earth would choose to live in London under the leaden spirit of Neville Chamberlain? In Europe under Daladier, Hitler, Mussolini or Franco? In the United States, with its squalor and corruption and gangsters? Who would leave this Chinese Athens or Florence or Manchester? A single precious beacon of light in a lightless world.

I really must stop being so enthusiastic. This is a terrible time, I face a terrible dilemma. Death is indeed everywhere here in Wuhan... But life is *even more* terrifyingly and extraordinarily alive here!

Somehow or other I, an artist, someday, am going to have – should I live – to distill, recreate this spirit, this fire, this insanity. Not just what is happening here but throughout China. Flattened under a century of civil war and foreign invasion, but once again its corpse, as so often before in history, is rising from its grave. How can I create art to match, to celebrate, immortalize this moment we have together lived through?

Just at this moment, suddenly, all the lights of Wuhan go out. We are pitched into deepest darkness.

How Wuhan!

Our ferry approaches the Bund, its lights illuminating a chaos and frenzy of escaping refugees.

There is no place like it.

21

Freda Utley and Agnes left first thing in the morning, Freda to catch the ferry to Shanghai – foreign nationals were still allowed to travel through Japanese-occupied China – and Agnes to catch the ferry to Wuchang, where she would commence her journey southwards.

Agnes said farewell to Donald and Hu and The Drab – insofar as you could say goodbye to The Drab – and lastly to Spider Girl.

Both being practical women their conversation was brief and to the point.

'You don't want any money?'

'No. You need it yourself.'

'If I was to give the money to The Drab?'

'She would not know what to do with it.'

'Look after yourself, Spider Girl.'

'You too, Agnes. You do not take care of yourself nearly enough. You eat too much rice. Eat more vegetables – ones which will cleanse you, ones which will nourish you.'

'Thank you, Spider Girl,' said Agnes, 'that is very helpful.' (Though she didn't have the least intention of doing it – she couldn't wait to get back on the iron rations of a route march.) 'You would make an excellent trade union negotiator,' she added.

'What's a trade union?'

'Stop stealing cheap detective novels from booksellers and start stealing socialist pamphlets.'

Agnes went. Everyone else (except The Drab) then travelled together to the aerodrome to wish Donald and Bob McClure a fond farewell. Before Spider Girl left Donald gave Wei a strong dose of opium. He also reassured Spider Girl that she was doing the best she could for him.

They drove in the ambulance that the Chinese Laundryman's Association of New York had presented to the Chinese people. The sombreness and quietness of the vehicle reminded Spider Girl of the special carts she used to sit in when the family were going to a funeral. Spider Girl still did not know how they would get out of Wuhan, but she refused to allow herself to feel down to ensure she would be alert enough to exploit any opportunity to escape.

At the aerodrome they climbed out. A cold and misty morning. The savage clump of artillery shells fell quite close. There were bomb craters the length of the runway but an adventurous pilot could still wind his way around them as he took off.

Bob's and most of Donald's baggage had been sent ahead by steamer. Donald still clutched his surgeon's portmanteau. He was harbouring a hangover and was minus his bow tie, which had unfortunately parted company with him during last night's bacchanal.

They looked dumbly at each other – all except for Donald, who looked at the ground as he was ashamed of last night's drunkenness.

'Remember, Hu,' said Bob, 'there will always be a place for you in any hospital I or Donald work in.'

'Here, here,' mumbled Donald.

'If you come to Chungking, look us up.'

'I will,' said Hu.

At last Donald looked up at Spider Girl.

'And if you want work, there'll always be a place for you as my housekeeper and helper, and plenty of space for your father, if he is…'

'Thank you, Donald,' said Spider Girl, looking at him, 'that is very kind of you. We will try to get there.'

Donald looked in his surgeon's bag.

'Spider Girl,' he said, 'thing is, I've got something for you.'

He took out a small empty bottle and a larger one filled with red liquid, then placed the portmanteau back on the ground.

'Been a bit short of money recently. Haven't we all? But there's this new really good anti-bacterial drug on the market. Antiseptic sulfonamide. It releases a process of bioactivation inside the body, especially against streptococci infections. I didn't have the money but I telegraphed my rugger chums in Wiltshire – decent chaps, all farmers – and they held a whip-round at the local pub and airmailed it to me.'

Spider Girl looked at him.

'Thing is,' he continued, 'I can't give you all of it. I must take it to Chungking for the many patients who will need it there.'

He started to carefully decant a small amount of the liquid into the small bottle.

'And, Spider Girl,' he said looking directly at her, 'it will not save your father's life. The infection, and other infections, are too deep set into him.'

Spider Girl looked at him.

'But he will revive for a short while. You must give him three drops through the rubber bicycle valve into his chest three times a day. Here you are.'

He handed her the small bottle. She continued to look straight at him.

'Thank you, Donald,' she said. 'You are a noble soul. Please thank your friends in England for this wonderful gift. I understand entirely why you can only give me some of it. It is noble that you will use it to save all sorts of other peoples' lives.'

Silence.

The aircraft was getting ready for take-off.

'And I've got something for you, Donald,' said Spider Girl. She took from her pocket his bow tie. She'd rescued it from the floor of the Last Ditch Club as she left. Never had it been so astoundingly laundered, so skilfully ironed, so lovingly folded. Its colours gleamed and glowed. It had blossomed.

'My lucky mascot,' murmured Donald. 'Well done, old girl.'

Spider Girl stepped forwards and tied it around his neck as a military general might pin a medal on a gallant soldier.

Donald touched her arm.

'Thank you, Donald,' said Spider Girl.

The pilots were starting the aircraft's engines. Time to leave.

Donald and Bob turned towards the plane.

It was at this moment that everything changed.

A bicycle courier (they must have passed him on their drive out to the aerodrome) puffed up with a message for Dr Robert McClure. He started waving it, shouting 'Dr McClure, message for Dr McClure.'

Bob indicated who he was. The messenger brought the telegram towards him. This interested Spider Girl. She asked Hu to translate for her what was being said.

Bob read the telegram.

'Damn,' he said. Then, as a pious Methodist, corrected himself. 'Jumping Jehoshaphat!'

'What is it, Bob?' asked Donald, slightly alarmed.

Hu and Spider Girl leant in to listen.

'That iron lung we ordered from America. It should have gone straight to Chungking. Instead it's just been delivered to the hospital workshop. They want to know what to do with it.'

Bob signalled to the pilot of the plane to hold on.

Donald and Bob stared at each other.

'We can't let it fall into the hands of the Japanese,' said Donald.

'If they could get it down to the Bund,' said Bob, 'there's a warehouse there for emergency freight. But there's only two of them at the workshop and one of them's just leaving.'

'I suppose it should be destroyed.'

Spider Girl's eyes glinted. She stepped forwards.

'Is the donkey and cart that brought it to the workshop still there?'

'Must be,' replied Bob. 'They won't unload it til they hear from us.'

'If me and Hu take it from the hospital to the warehouse, can we keep the donkey and cart?'

'The hospital won't have any further use for them. Why not?'

'We'll do it.'

After that it was only a matter of seconds while Bob scribbled instructions to the workshop staff, the address of the warehouse for Spider Girl and Wei, and a brief letter to the warehouse staff emphasizing to them the importance that the iron lung reached Chungking.

The airport staff were meanwhile frantically trying to herd Donald and Bob towards the plane, whose engines were roaring.

They went.

They leapt into the plane.

Spider Girl and Hu waved wildly.

The greatly overloaded aeroplane wobbled and staggered on a zigzag course down the runway, finally lurching into the air and almost immediately disappearing into the mist.

Spider Girl turned to Hu.

'We'll get the ambulance to drop us off at the hospital workshop.'

By midday it's turned into quite a nice day in Wuhan. The mist has lifted from the river and the swallows, zithering joyfully across the waters, do their final dances and pirouettes and death dives before heading off south for the winter.

I've paid my daily visit to the central post office to see if there is any post from my wife. Nothing.

In the river the imperial warships hold their usual smart line in the water, each with the flag of their respective nation painted on their deck so the Japanese hopefully do not bomb them. Past them hurry some of the last ships of the evacuation – jam-packed with families and soldiers, merchandise and heavy machinery.

Within hours Japanese warships will slip silently between the foreign warships, their wakes jostling and unsettling them, the new menace succeeding the old.

I sit outside a tea house on the Bund, smoking a cigarette and sipping my tea.

I see him coming from a distance, surprisingly light on his feet for such a heavy man.

'Lao She!'

'Feng Yuxiang!'

He is wearing his customary peasant clothes.

'How are you?'

'Alive.'

'Not many people can say that these days.'

It is really good to see him. He radiates *bon courage*.

'The wife sends her regards. She's in Chungking, setting up new schools.'

'Good for her.'

He orders tea and sits down. Looks about.

'You know the people who've done really well out of this war?'

'Japanese, American arms manufacturers?'

'No. Coolies. The Bund's still swarming with them. I mean look at them. How well they're dressed compared to the wretches they used to be. Strong, expensive fabrics, solid sandals. See that line of women over there, queuing for the boat?'

He points over to a line of quite prosperous-looking young women, some with babies and infant children.

'Yes?'

'I went up and talked to them. Know who they are?'

'Young bourgeois?'

He laughs.

'Coolies' wives. The wretches are doing so well they can even afford wives. And to dress them.'

'That's progress, comrade.'

We laugh.

'How's the war going?' I ask.

'Not the person to ask. I'm totally excluded from any sort of access to high command or decision-making. As are Generals Bai Chongxi and Li Zongren. They served their purpose, holding the Japanese at Taierzhuang, and afterwards they were immediately demoted. So they can't in any way threaten our great Generalissimo.'

I look swiftly around but can see no men with glasses or without glasses trying to listen in on our conversation. People are too disturbed and in a hurry to linger over their teas.

'Our leader is again promoting mediocrities?'

'Makes him feel safe. And at least we achieved our objectives. To check the Japanese. Give them a bloody nose. So in future they treat us with more respect, caution. Taierzhuang gave us the time to withdraw in good order, move our factories and steel mills upstream, rebuild them and modernize and expand them where they are safe, where our people are safe. Our leaders had little to do with it. Our people had everything to do with it.'

His tea arrives. He smells it and congratulates the tea boy just to encourage him. Tomorrow he will be serving Japanese officers. Or dead.

'Sorry I missed your great open-air play,' says Feng. 'I was in Chungking. But I'm sure it was adequately appalling.'

We both smile mordantly.

'You're probably the bastard who recommended I write it.'

He ignores this.

'Everyone thinks you've made a great success of your teaching. Our country is now filled with patriotic actors persuading the ordinary folk to rise up and murder the enemy.'

'Someday I will write decent novels again.'

'Someday we will all do good things again.'

'You think so? Chiang Kai-shek doesn't seem at all eager to win this war.'

'We all know that the man has an aversion to competent generals. We retreat to the south-west and other mountain fastnesses and then wait it out until stronger countries defeat the Axis powers.'

'The democracies aren't going to fight fascism. Chamberlain's just signed his surrender to it.'

'Chamberlain does not represent the people of the democracies. They will not allow fascism to triumph. The Soviet Union will not allow it. Chiang Kai-shek is waiting for them to enter the struggle, which will be worldwide, which the people will win. You read the papers? The Battle of Lake Khasan – back in August?'

'Of course.'

'For a second time the Japanese invade the Russians from Manchukuo, get utterly routed. They're stuck here in China, can't get out, even more desperate for raw materials than before they invaded. If they can't plunder them from Russia – and they can't – there's only one way they can go, south – for Dutch oil in the East Indies and British rubber in Malaya.'

'But Britain and France will drive them back.'

'They won't. By that time they'll be engulfed in their own life-and-death struggle in Europe.'

'So who…?'

'To get to the East Indies and Malaysia they'll have to go through the Philippines. The American Philippines. That means war. You do not take on the Russians AND the Americans. That will mean we survive. Terrible, disgusting war, I know – millions dead – but we will survive.'

A silence. He smiles.

'And how are you, dear friend?'

I pause and then answer, more emotionally than I intended.

'I don't know what to do,' I say. 'Whether I should leave or not.'

'Of course you must leave. The Japanese will be here today or at latest tomorrow.'

'But my wife and I had an agreement that if she and the family were well she would write to me care of Wuhan Central Post Office. I have not yet heard from her, but I know it is very difficult to get a letter through, and if I am not here I may never hear from them, know that they still live.'

'Your dear wife is a highly intelligent woman. She will know that Wuhan has fallen. It will be on every Japanese radio station and billboard. She will know to write to Chungking – the post office there.'

'She could have already posted it – to Wuhan.'

'Have you booked a berth on the steamer to Chungking yet?'

'No. I want to keep checking. The last post arrives at nine this evening.'

'The last boat leaves at midnight. You will be on it!' His voice has risen. 'I am your friend! Your wife is my friend! Your children are my friends! You pain me with your indecision!'

'I want to know whether my family is alive or dead.'

'You will be on that boat. Hu Jieqing could simply have decided not to write to you as it was too dangerous.'

'I have to know!'

Feng clicks his fingers. A young adjutant who's been quietly reading a newspaper at the next table comes over immediately. I recognize him as the young soldier Feng sent to Jinan to give me the letter summoning me to Wuhan.

'Hello,' I say. 'It is good to see you.' I remember him as a nice young man. He played with my children.

'Good morning, Mr Lao,' he says, clicking his heels. 'It is an honour to meet you again.'

'Yang,' says Feng. 'The last steamer to leave Wuhan is *Prometheus* – at midnight. I want you to write an executive order and take it to the captain immediately. He is to reserve a place for Mr Lao on it.'

He turns to me. Continues in the clipped military manner.

'When you arrive at the ship *before* midnight, you will not try to board at the passenger gangway, which will be jam-packed. You will go to the crew's gangway and board there. They will be expecting you. You have already sent your writings and books ahead of you upstream to Chungking?'

'Yes,' I admit in a surly voice, as if my doing so indicates some weakness in my character.

Feng sighs. He leans over and speaks gently.

'Dear Lao, my dear, dear friend. You are a wise man. A good man. It is right that you are upset about your family. You are deeply worried about what might have happened to them. But you staying on here in Wuhan will not help them in any way. Say you stay here and a letter arrives from your wife. They open and read it. You go, from wherever you are hiding, and get it – and immediately the Japanese arrest you. The famous Lao She! And they shoot you. Which they will. How, if your family is still alive, does that help them? They have lost a husband and a father. Their protector. And worse, the Japanese will now know, by the postmark, that you have a family, and in what district they live. Please, please get on that boat. *Prometheus*. Midnight.'

He gets up and he and his adjutant quietly leave.

I have not been won over by his arguments – but he certainly knows how to argue.

I set off for the post office. My letter might have arrived.

★ ★ ★

The ambulance dropped off Hu and Spider Girl at the hospital workshop. The workshop had been entirely cleared and all its valuable if antiquated engineering and welding equipment efficiently transported upstream. A single man awaited them, standing beside a donkey and a cart bearing a large iron lung. Spider Girl passed the man Bob McClure's note. He read it and handed over responsibility for the cart and the iron lung to the two women. Wishing them luck, he hurried off. He had a family to save.

'First we'll go to the apartment,' said Spider Girl, 'pick up my father and The Drab and supplies.'

Hu looked at her.

'You know what you're doing, Spider Girl?'

'Not yet. But I will,' said a now confident Spider Girl.

Hu had been pulled from the collapsed air-raid shelter and her life had been saved because of Spider Girl's cleverness. She trusted her now.

They arrived at the apartment. With infinite care Hu and Spider Girl and The Drab lifted Wei, still sleeping, down the stairs and laid him on cushions in the cart beside the iron lung. Spider Girl and The Drab had pre-packed the food and supplies in baskets and they quickly loaded the cart. Following her previous experience of long marches, Spider Girl understood the importance of water. Several crates of bottles containing Freda's fragrant bath water were hoisted onto the cart.

'There's posh,' said Hu.

They both laughed.

Hu tethered The Drab to the rear of the cart so she wouldn't wander. They set off, Hu leading the donkey and Spider Girl riding on the rear tailgate.

Following Bob's instructions Hu navigated their way to the warehouse for emergency freight. She showed the guard the letter from Bob McClure and he let them in.

The foreman led them to a space on the floor and a team of coolies arrived, and, having gently rested a still sleeping Wei upon the floor, removed the iron lung and secured it to a pallet, they then gently lifted Wei back on the cart as carefully as if he had been exquisite porcelain. Spider Girl thanked them.

Then something really bizarre happened.

Suddenly round a stack of crates containing invaluable works of art and priceless ancient manuscripts, immaculate as a diamond hatpin, strode Madame Chiang.

Not a perfectly painted eyelid batted as she saw them. With that flawless memory for names which so many influential people seem to possess, she immediately hailed them.

'Ah, Hu Lan-shih and Wild Pear Blossom, it is so long since I saw you. How are you both?'

Hu was a bit at sixes and sevens.

'We are well, thank you,' said Spider Girl.

Madame Chiang held out her hand. Hu went forwards to shake it. Then Spider Girl moved forwards to shake it too. As she did so, Madame Ching studied her.

'Excuse me for saying so, Wild Pear Blossom, but last time I saw you, I seem to remember you were suffering from rickets? You seem to be walking quite well now. What has happened?'

Now it was Spider Girl's turn to be a bit flummoxed. Hu leapt enthusiastically into the breach.

'Oh, Madame Chiang,' she said, 'this wonderful surgeon I went to work for...'

'Yes, I remember that,' said Madame Chiang, somewhat icily.

'Well, using bicycle parts – and he uses bicycle parts in quite a lot of his operations, because there are so many bicycles in China – he used these bicycle forks to support Wild Pear Blossom's legs so that she can now walk much more easily.'

'What is this surgeon's name?' asked Madame Chiang.

'Donald Hankey,' said Hu. 'He is very good.'

'Walk up and down again, Wild Pear Blossom,' instructed Madame Chiang.

Spider Girl rankled slightly at this. Hu gave her a meaningful stare. Spider Girl walked up and down a bit.

'Stand still,' ordered Madame Chiang. 'Bicycle parts he uses, you say?'

Hu smiled broadly at this. Spider Girl even allowed herself a silent whoopee.

But things took a turn for the worse.

'Lift your skirts, Wild Pear Blossom,' said Madame Chiang, 'I wish to examine his work more closely.'

What is it with upper-class women, thought Spider Girl, that they're always wanting to stare at my private parts?

She did not budge an inch.

Hu gave her a meaningful glare. Spider Girl gave Hu a meaningful glare. Then Hu gave Spider Girl a really meaningful glare. Spider Girl sighed and raised her skirts.

Madame Chiang croopied down and started thoroughly exploring all the various bicycle parts and leather strap parts festooning Spider Girl's private parts. At one stage she poked Spider Girl rather too vigorously. Spider Girl swayed and stopped herself from falling forwards by resting her hands briefly on Madame Chiang's back. She regained her equilibrium. Madame Chiang re-arose.

'Hankey,' she said. 'Donald Hankey. Where is he?'

'He's just flown to Chungking, Madame Chiang.'

'Just the sort of surgery this country needs. Cheap. Lots of easily available braces and supports. When I'm in Chungking I'll look him up.'

She looked at Hu.

'I suppose you left working on my committee so you could work with him?'

'Yes, Madame Chiang, that was the reason.'

'Good for you. But if you ever want your old job back…'

'Yes, Madame Chiang.'

'And thank you too for introducing me to Intelligent Whore. It has transformed our nursing services.'

'Madame.'

'Good luck to both of you,' said Madame Chiang, turning away. 'I've got all these artistic relics to get together for Chungking.'

And she strode briskly away.

Spider Girl and Hu, leading the donkey, walked on out of the warehouse and onto the Bund, with Wei still asleep in the cart and The Drab tethered behind.

'Spider Girl,' asked Hu, 'what are we going to do next?'

'I want to buy a coffin for my father,' said Spider Girl.

'Do you think this is the time for that?' asked Hu. 'We should be getting out of Wuhan. Besides, we don't have the money to buy one.'

Spider Girl stopped the cart.

'My father is going to have the very best coffin money can buy,' she stated bluntly. 'I've got my eye on a particular one.'

'But we don't have any money!'

Spider Girl looked at her.

'You didn't see what happened back there, did you?'

'What happened back there?' said Hu, perplexed.

'You are so innocent, Hu. We've got all the money we want.'

'What are you saying, Spider Girl?'

'You should have watched more carefully at the warehouse. Then you'd have seen me picking Madame Chiang's purse.'

'WHAT?!?'

Hu stared at her.

'While she was poking in her disgusting way around all my private parts, I fell forwards a bit. So I had to rest my hands on her.'

'Yes…?'

'That's when I did it. Picked it.'

'You can't have picked Madame Chiang Kai-shek's purse!?!'

Spider Girl put her hand in her smock pocket and surreptitiously displayed some rather large silver coins to Hu.

Hu stared at her. And stared at her. And then started to laugh. Laugh and laugh and laugh. People stopped and stared. Then Hu looked at Spider Girl, her eyes dancing.

'You are a wicked woman!'

'No, I am not. I am a practical woman. It would help you to be a practical woman too. That way you'd have got on that aeroplane and would now be helping Donald.'

Hu stared at her some more.

'But she's the most powerful woman in China. When she finds out she'll hunt us down.'

'What, in all this chaos?' asked Spider Girl, indicating the fleeing crowds all around them. 'She probably won't even look in her purse for a couple of weeks. Rich people never pay for anything. And even if when she finds out she decides it's us I doubt she'll do anything. Rich women like her quite like being stolen from.'

Hu looked at Spider Girl steadily, then they resumed their passage along the Bund.

The Bund was a sad sight.

Fewer people, ever more frantic.

The sounds of small arms fire could now be heard popping in the distance. Artillery shells were landing. The Japanese, against tooth and nail opposition from the Chinese Army, were grinding their way into the city's eastern suburbs.

Wuhan was falling.

But some Chinese people were still entering the city. Poor farmers and smallholders were arriving in their thousands. All year in the countryside outside they had been tending and cultivating and nourishing their precious fruit trees and bushes, coddling them like newborn babes, unable in all that time to earn a raw penny from them, having to gamble their existence on these few short weeks when their trees stood ripe and bearing. Whatever the circumstances, whether they had to face plagues, floods, Japanese bayonets, they would still bring their crops to market to earn the only money they would make for the whole of that year.

They came with their carts and fruit-laden baskets under their arms and slung from poles and bundled in blankets on their heads and they laid on the cobbles of the Bund their fruits in great long lines and piles and profusion. All of them crying out for custom.

Hu and Spider Girl passed silently between lines of the most wondrous, ripened fruits spilling out across the cobbles.

Every variety and size of grape – blue, green, black and purple – every kind and shape of pear, each variety of apple. Those beautiful, fragrant, sweet, crisp little pears; crab apples as big as harvest apples; and for fragrance only, the small apple-sized quinces; light orange-coloured, honey-flavoured Fuyu persimmons, heart-shaped Hachiya persimmons bitter in their taste, and the ancient red persimmons, heavy and succulent in flavour; enormous peaches with white flesh, tiny peaches with blood-red flesh; Beijing apples, covered with little gold stars, which decorated rooms and added fragrance to the air (how on earth had they got through the war zones?); tiny red dates with smiling faces; green apricots in little rush baskets the size of a fist which were sold with a dash of syrup to passing children; long apricots – half red, half green – others big and deep yellow, small and light yellow, or the tiny red ones; by themselves the famous white apricots. Fruit used in the worship of the moon – pillow-shaped watermelons decorated with strips of gold paper and displayed lying on red and yellow coxcomb blossoms. Chestnuts big and fat, being roasted over little sidewalk furnaces, drowned in molasses when eaten.[22]

The fruits of Wuhan.

The cries of the sellers, desperate that there were so few customers, went up to the skies, as all this abundance and fecundity lay ignored around them.

On the stalls of the wine pedlars lay great earthen jars of wine beside soft slices of mutton amid snow-white onions. Fresh water crabs, fed and fattened on grain, hung in baskets of matting from poles. Honey from all over China was being sold.

Hu and Spider Girl and The Drab stared open-mouthed at the profusion as they passed by. Even an awakened Wei struggled and raised himself to look over the cart's sides to gape at all the abundance. Spider Girl bought him a bag of Fuyu persimmons because they were his favourites, and two white-fleshed peaches. They might encourage him to eat.

For the first and only time in her life Spider Girl, purchasing the market traders' fruits and food, refused to haggle with the sellers and paid them whatever price they demanded. She also bought milk. There was a man who milked a cow on the Bund, milking it straight into his customers' containers. Spider Girl thought about buying some for her father – cow's milk is very nourishing – but he had never liked it as much as the thinner, less nutritious goat's milk. Back home Eldest Son had milked the goat and then, in the evenings, when he had finished in the fields, her father would sit and drink some and then sing songs. It was a family custom that when the songs finished Grandfather would tell a story and then they would all go to bed except Wei, who stayed up to repair his machinery. Spider Girl found the stall which sold goat's milk. Her father sipped and enjoyed it. He even smacked his lips.

Spider Girl bought honey to restore her father and winter clothing as they would be travelling through December mountains. She also purchased incense and joss sticks, a sheaf of paper money and a spade.

They passed through the flower markets. Although it was autumn there were camellias large as a girl's face, cascades and fountains of anemones, asters, astilbes, early plum blossoms, peonies, lilies, roses, magnolias, and a few chrysanthemums.

The blossoms of Wuhan.

There were only a few chrysanthemums because the sellers knew that the chrysanthemum was for the Japanese the most dazzling and emotional of all blooms. They were, for the time being, concealing them so that when the Japanese arrived they could display them in all their glory and the Japanese would be so overcome with emotion and joy they would be unable to bayonet their creators. They prayed.

Finally, at the far eastern end of the Bund, they entered coffin world. It had shrunk greatly since its days of pomp when coffins piled to the heavens and citizens colonized and plied their trades and slept within and between its wares. A huge row had broken out among the coffin-mongers. Most, calculating that the Japanese did not bother to put their victims in coffins but just left them where they killed them or rolled them into the Yangtze, had taken their coffins – piled high – upstream to Chungking, where people still respected the elaborate and profitable rituals of death.

But one old man had hung on. And Spider Girl had had her eye for a long time on one particular coffin of his. It did not look exactly distinguished. Its wood was deep pinkish, almost fulvous orange. It was unvarnished and rough and hard as teak, its surface ancient, gnarled and full of knotholes. But it was precisely what Spider Girl wanted. And when he peeked over the side of the cart, Wei wanted it too.

Spider Girl approached the coffin seller. She had no scruples about haggling with a coffin-monger.

'You have never sold this coffin. It has been here for months. No one wants it.'

'Anyone of taste wants it.'

'Look at the roughness of its side. The person buried in it will never be able to lie still because of all the splinters in it.'

'Look at the beauty of that red and orange. They will enjoy it.' He banged its side. 'Feel the quality of that wood, its hardness, its steadfastness. The human that lies in this coffin will lie in it forever as it sails into the eternal afterlife – his body will be safe within!'

Spider Girl was moving in for the deal.

'What's it made of?'

'Wild pear tree. The hardest wood ever.'

Spider Girl wasn't impressed.

'Never heard of it. Sounds like a weed.'

She offered a very low price. The salesman offered a very high price. Etc., etc.

As soon as it was bought Wei wanted to lie in it. He had known the wood immediately. The wood of his ancestors, the wood of the bones of his beloved sister. They laid him gently into it. He made little chirrups and squeaks of joy and touched its sides and ran his fingers up and down its rough, hard grain.

'It is mine. It is mine forever.'

They turned the donkey's head towards where the ferries for Hanyang and the west sailed.

On the ferry, as all the world fell apart, Spider Girl carefully dosed her father with three drops of the sulfonamide drug in his chest then dripped a few drops of wild pear juice and some of Freda's bath water down his throat. This revived him. As they crossed the Han River they dined on fat lamb and plump peaches and sweet chestnuts. The donkey munched contentedly on dried sorghum leaves and herbs, with some thistles and blackberry leaves thrown in. They felt like emperors.

The sun was setting over Wuhan. All the western skies were gloriously alight with the yellow of peaches and the purples of plum and grape.

All the time as they ate Spider Girl held her father's hand. She fed him tiny morsels of the delicacies they had brought, choosing each individual scrap scrupulously, cawing and clicking like a mother crow feeding her young.

'Oh Father. Oh Father.'

The Bund is filled with families carrying their bedding and furniture – pots and pans and food and keepsakes in panniers slung at either ends of poles – making their way to the final boats or ferries. The crackle of small arms fire comes distinctly from the eastern suburbs. The Chinese Army is making its last stand there. Well-to-do families with enormous female servants carry several babies and infants, poor peoples' children follow their parents through the chaos tied on a string so they will not be lost.

All the electric lights in the city have gone out.

Towards the ships people have stuck up violet-white arc lights and lit yellow flares. The ships themselves have trained their own lights on the chaos below. People flit past holding flaming torches or the better-off electric ones. Stray dogs, bewildered sheep absolved from execution, parents berserk – they've lost their children, old women clutching Pekinese. Everyone is shouting at everyone else.

I stand in the midst of all this. Indecisive, panicking. Which way to go – the ship or the post office? I went to the post office at nine and they said that in all the confusion the post from the north – which has been routed in from Ichang because of the fighting – would not arrive until twelve thirty. Thirty minutes after my boat sails. The last boat.

I find out why the lights have gone out. Amid this bedlam, like some immaculate ballet troupe, suddenly glides this flawless mechanism of coolies, grunting and chirruping messages and instructions back and forth to each other to maintain their perfect equilibrium of motion and support. Smooth as cream, an eighteen-ton circular turbine from the electricity-generating station – its whole steel mass intricately tressed and rigged with a whole spider's web of ropes and poles to evenly distribute its weight among the coolies – glides like a ghost through our midst and then disappears into the darkness where, at the dockside, the cranes are waiting to load it upon its ship.

So that was why all the power to the city was cut off early this morning. The city's electricity-generating plant is being shipped lock stock and light bulb to Chungking!

I make my decision. I will not be going up the Yangtze like Wuhan's electricity-generating plant. I *have* to know if my family still exists. I *must* know.

It is now eleven thirty. I turn towards the post office. Walk straight into the torrent of humanity hurtling in the opposite direction. Buffet, fight my way through. I am almost there when I hear a voice behind me calling out my name.

'Mr Lao! Mr Lao!'

I turn. See a young man looking at me, shouting my name. Straight-backed, open-faced. I sort of know him.

'Mr Lao,' he cries.

He is pulling a rickshaw.

'I have a message for you. A letter.'

I realize who he is. The young communist rickshaw man who took me out to see their deputy leader, Chou En-lai, in his bungalow. Months ago. It had started all that wretched Yu Liqun business.

I had liked him. I start to walk towards him.

'What is it?'

'Mr Lao, I have a message for you. It is from your family in the north. The comrades managed to get it south.'

He hands me a letter. I rip it open. From my wife. I race through the first bit. They are alive!

I stare at him with my mouth open.

'Are you all right, Mr Lao?'

'Yes,' I croak.

Then I think. If they are alive, I must stay alive. I must catch that boat.

'I must catch that boat. I must catch it.'

'It's almost midnight already. I'll give you a lift.'

I leap into his rickshaw.

He runs, avoiding pedestrians and carts like a deer in flight avoids trees in a forest.

I think back. At my meeting with Chou En-lai beneath the peach blossoms, about Yu Liqun's marriage to Guo Morou, Chou, in exchange for my help, had offered to use the resources of the Communist Party to find out whether my family was still alive.

Chou En-lai – a politician – had kept his word.

We arrive as close to my boat as we can get. It is still there.

I thank him.

'It is a great honour to help a great writer like you. Please keep writing.'

'I will.'

I pause.

'But what is happening to you? I am sure I could wangle a passage for you.'

'Thank you. I stay here.'

'But the Japanese...'

'It is my duty to stay. I will stay here and fight the Japanese.'

'But surely you'll be found?'

'I will. And they will shoot me. But someone else will take my place, and then someone will take his place – on and on til the people finally triumph. I am proud to serve.'

I am humbled. I touch his arm.

'Thank you.'

'Keep writing good books.'

He goes. I make my way up the crew's gangway. I get onto the deck, sit down, read my wife's letter in full. She and all the children are all alive but, sorrowfully, my mother has died. She did not survive her broken leg. My wife, with the children and with the help of a pious Japanese, took her body back to Beijing where my mother was buried among her ancestors. My wife now works quietly within our community – she is a Manchu like me – as a teacher and graphic designer. She is making plans to escape with the children and rejoin me in Wuhan – or Chungking.

I cover my face and weep.

The boat does not leave until one o'clock. On time. Feng Yuxiang tricked me. Once again.

22

The next morning Imperial Japanese warships anchored off the Bund. The warships of the other imperial powers, also anchored there, ignored them. As did their ambassadors and embassy officials.

Except the Italian consul-general who, as the Japanese naval officers stepped ashore on the Bund, was standing there in full plumaged regalia to greet them. He shook their hands heartily and congratulated them on their victory, then made a florid and very lengthy speech.

As Japanese troops marched into the city, Italian soldiers posted in the Italian Embassy deployed on either side of the street and as the Japanese marched between them they snapped their heels and gave the full fascist salute. White Russian dancing girls and prostitutes and bartenders, including Ralph Shaw's ex-squeeze Big Wanda, stood cheering them on the street and handing out free cigarettes to them.

There were not as many atrocities in Wuhan as there had been in Nanking or Shanghai. This was partly because the worldwide condemnation of these massacres had startled the Japanese. (Isn't this how imperial powers always behave?) But it was also because the Japanese High Command had realized that now, being in the middle of China instead of on its fringes, involved in what was going to be at best a protracted war and being surrounded by hostile countryside, they were going to have to treat the Chinese with a certain, albeit very low, level of humanity.

So there was comparatively little killing of civilians within Wuhan.

The defeated soldiers were a different matter. Several thousands were captured as the city was taken. Wounded ones were despatched immediately.

The rest were marched to the Bund's quayside. There some were used for bayonet practice, but most were driven out onto the long wooden pontoons floating in the river where they stood and were used as target practice and machine-gunned down until they were all dead. Their corpses floated downstream til they started to bob and knock against the hulls of the other nations' warships moored downstream.

'Look,' they seemed to say. 'Today it is us. Tomorrow it will be you.'

All the warships' crews had been sent below and the hatches battened down.

One junior officer was left on the bridge of each ship.

Aboard the British gunboat, HMS *Ladybird*, was a young British squaddie, Howard Andrews, posted to the British Embassy but sent on an errand to the *Ladybird* and caught there when the Japanese started machine-gunning their prisoners. He was sent below with the naval crew. They were able to witness the butchery through a porthole.

Howard, who was quite political, did not like fascism. He didn't like the Japanese – but he liked Hitler and Himmler and Goebbels even less, they being closer to his home and family. So, being a spirited lad, he started to think what he himself, post-Munich, might do to fight back now that his government had proved so passive and cowardly. He had a sudden idea. To rally people – not with political speeches, but with songs.

Even though the Sikh military band attached to the embassy was pretty rubbish, he enjoyed marching to 'Colonel Bogey'. It had swing, swagger. It made you feel good.

Howard liked words. Liked using them, liked writing them down. He started to compose a ditty.

How do you hit fascism below the belt? Where it really hurts? In

the short and curlies? Then the magical words started to arrive...
About Hitler. And his testicular shortcomings.

23

The little swallow, brightly dressed,
Comes every spring to visit us.
I ask the swallow: 'Why do you come here?'
She replies: 'Spring is the most beautiful here!'
Little swallow, let me tell you,
This year things here are prettier still,
We've built large factories,
With new machines.
Welcome,
And please stay for a long time.

'Little Swallow', Chinese children's song, 1953

The sun shines as *Prometheus* makes its stately progress up the great Yangtze River. Flat countryside on either side. Hills in the distance. Mountains beyond.

The coppery brown of the eternal river. Slipping, sliding on either side of us. The pale feathery green of bamboo groves beside white farm compounds and the flat jade green of rice fields and the glossy dark green of camphor and pomelo trees.

Men fishing from boats with tame cormorants. The cormorants perch all round the gunwales of the boat, squawking and flapping their wings. They have short strings attached to their legs and rings round their necks so they cannot swallow their prey. A kite tries to rob a cormorant of its catch, dancing and sliding in the air above it.

In some places whole banks are strewn with pink and white

autumn flowers and the breeze off them comes fresh and scented across our decks. A red line of hills grow more prominent as they approach us, with red orange patches of early autumn leaves and the dark green of camphor on their slopes, the lighter green of tea groves and bamboos, red soil and whitish rocks. The hills break upon the river in cliffs. Red cliffs.

Here, commanded by the great Zhuge Liang himself, Liu Bei's army defeated the forces of the evil Cao Cao – bent on conquering all China – at the mighty Battle of Red Cliffs. As we pass the passengers cheer and applaud. I, rather pathetically, cry.

My children are alive. My wife is alive. My mother has died. A sloping line of wild geese fly by.

As we sail, in parallel to us, on either bank, run roads and trackways along which travel patient lines of refugees, soldiers, civilians, farmers – all trekking steadily west. Lorries, buses, camels, cars, yaks, peasants driving livestock, carts piled high with belongings or farm implements, large groups of children, whole schools marching west, many singing songs. Coolies bearing equipment and parts of machinery and babies and old ladies and fat uncles in bathchairs or slung from poles or on their backs. The tracks and roads they travel on weave back and forth, so sometimes they are close to us and wave, sometimes they are far away and disappear. But there are regular food and fodder stations, where they can stop and rest. A whole nation on the trek.

On board there's just as much variety. Farmers with stock. Missionaries with Bibles. Farmers' wives with chickens and geese and ducks. In the saloon, with velvet upholstery and on glossy teak tabletops, twenty-four-hour gambling and chatter in a haze of cigarette and opium smoke, children squirming under the tables and women squatting on the floor breastfeeding, arguing, knitting, screaming at their children. A universal clack-magg!

On deck people parade. Or rather squeeze between each other. A university professor holds a seminar among his youthful students, all jammed together. A young couple in love conveniently crushed up against each other. Lots of people fast asleep on the deck. An anti-aircraft gun lonely on its platform with no one to man it. Someone has hung their washing over its barrel. The officer and seamen on the bridge ignore all we mere mortals. And up in the bows a flock of young, blind orphans chatter and bubble among themselves. They've been put in the bows because the blind love to smell things, and the beautiful scents and perfumes of the countryside we're passing through can best be savoured unsoiled by the smoke from the funnel and the stink of tobacco. A rather stern-looking woman with glasses commands them.

We sail on. Out into the flat countryside once more. On both banks are paddy fields, where the year's last crop of rice has a silver frosty bloom to its tips. Patchwork grass meadows rippling in the breeze like greensilver pools.

At night, beneath the heavens, we look down on the dots of light which dance upon the river – fishing sampans, shrimp trappers, passing steamships and junks. I lie on my back and look up into the depths of the Milky Way. A great estuary of light spread across heaven.

Praise to you, Lord Jesus Christ.

The next morning we steadily approach a line of mountains, its peaks like an army on the march. The Yangtze flows down, fast, impetuously amid these mountains. We must sail up through these fast, fierce waters before we can pass out on the other side into the broad fertile plains of South-West China.

We are approaching the famous, fearsome Three Gorges.

On either side the travellers on foot and on the road who have accompanied us thus far from Wuhan peel away to follow their own vertiginous routes through the mountains to Sichuan. On either side of the river – now narrower and much more fast-flowing – where freighters can unload their really heavy cargoes of machinery and steel, which will be hiked and hauled up through the passes by chained-together tractors, teams of horses, or long long lines of coolies. Junks also stop at these quays and unload their passengers, who will have to walk up through the mountains. Junks with just sails cannot make it through the gorges.

But our steamer will steam up through the great gorges. *Prometheus* is tough. *Prometheus* was built on the Tyne by boat builders Palmers of Jarrow. But even it has to pause at a quay while we load more coal and attach giant six-inch rice straw ropes around our bows while 300 coolies set off ahead of us up a track.

At the start of our voyage they do not have to take any weight because our boilers are at full cry, the smoke and steam roaring out, and we make progress against the flood.

But then we enter the gorge, the first gorge, and the coolies start to chant 'Hey Yah, Hai-yah' and take the weight, swinging into their work, swaying as one from foot to foot, drawing us forwards inch by inch, foot by foot, yard by yard, up into the high gorges.

Rolling waves sweep down the gorge which towers above us like a whale's jaws hugely opening – stone cliffs for lips, mountain after mountain high above like layers of serrated teeth, as around us, through its throat, roars the river's rage, spouting spray, gulping with hunger at our frail craft, making small ships and skiffs travelling down spin and skip and drop like feathers over rapids amid the surf and turmoil.

In case you are concerned, we make it through the first gorge.

Where the rock is hard-wearing limestone, the water has taken time to eat through it and the river is narrow and crowded by cliffs. These are the gorges. Where the rock is softer sandstone, the banks are more eaten away and the river has space to flow more gracefully.

In the comparative calm of the waters between the first and second gorges we make some headway and the coolies can rest as we slowly progress, but then we arrive at the second limestone gorge.

The coolies chant ahead of us. Our boiler incenses, fit to explode. Its pistons race and squeal.

The great cliffs are sheer on either side and smooth, as if they have been hewn and polished. The coolies toil upon a walkway chiselled into the rock. This dark dismal gorge is so narrow and the cliffs towering above it so close and high that the sun can only be glimpsed shining down for a few minutes at midday, and the moon will merely be glimpsed in all her godly serenity for a few seconds at midnight.

We toil amid the gloom.

Because limestone rocks often contain deep vertical fissures, over centuries the water has fingered its way deep down, slowly undercutting the precipitous cliffs above so that suddenly, without any warning, whole cliffsides can collapse and guillotine down into the water and liquidate all beneath. Ships, armies, emperors are known to have been annihilated beneath these monsters.

We tiptoe between them, cautious as mice. Finally we emerge into sunlight.

We moor to a quay and for half an hour we can walk and inspect some shops and market stalls. Most of us pray at an altar for a safe journey through the final gorge, the famous, infamous Qutang Gorge.

The view ahead of us is spectacular. A giant row of peaks stampede towards us like charging bulls, culminating in a mighty mountain which towers over us tiny frail mortals as we toil up through the gorge.

A new team of coolies are harnessed up for this final journey. We start. 'Hey Yah, Hai-yah.' Start up through the hungry waters.

We enter a very different sort of gorge. Silent, mysterious, almost magical.

As previously there are cliffs on either side, but these are lower, breaking off into great slopes covered in pine and vegetation. And above them, in their balconies, the great mountains – row upon row upon row of serrated peaks stretching into infinity.

We pass beneath cliffs where ancient runes and letterings have been engraved in the rocks. How did the Ancients manage, perched precarious and clinging to the cliff faces just above the merciless waters, to carve out their archaic characters? Most of these poems and runes have been washed away by time but a few are still legible. It is said they were carved by the great sage Zhuge Liang himself, welcoming travellers to the Kingdom of Shu Han.

Above us these great banks and cleavages of forest, rank after rank of serried pine trees, the mists moving slowly, mysteriously through their boughs. The towers and buttresses of rock like stately castles and fortresses. Sweeping upward and upward, vegetation spilling wildly from every available ledge however small. And above them mountain and sky.

It is so silent, so solemn. Like some giant European cathedral. Except for one sound. Apes live among these forests and cliffs. Their mournful, haunting cries and shrieks ring across its vast emptiness from bank to bank, over our heads. Holding us in thrall.

I look down into the waters. The violent turbid yellow snatching at us. Bounding and bouncing over rocks and boulders. And then suddenly, from the water's depths – leaping like salmon in spate, lambs in a spring meadow, calves in a spring orchard – dance, arc, dive, leap a steadfast line of Baiji, white-finned Yangtze dolphins – powerful, indefatigable, unyielding to the flood – shepherding, guiding, guarding us from all harm and all evil.

And they are gone. Our little guardians. And we are out into the wide waters of the upper Yangtze.[23]

At the top of the Three Gorges, on a bank, is conveniently situated the great and ancient Zhang Fei Temple. Convenient because all those who have just travelled up through the Three Gorges will, shaken and terrified, want to immediately thank all their various gods and goddesses for having spared their lives, while all those about to descend on their hair-raising, helter-skelter ride will, full of doom and despair, likewise want to demand their gods and goddesses protect them from all harm and disaster. So all in all Zhang Fei's ancient temple does a roaring trade.

Zhang Fei was the faithful lieutenant of Liu Bei (who is buried only a few miles away), the heroic first king of the Kingdom of Shu Han. Zhang Fei was his greatest warrior, Zhuge Liang his great counsellor and strategist. We are entering this lofty kingdom.

Within the temple is a huge and ancient statue of Zhang Fei, and a pavilion in honour of my favourite poet Du Fu, who sheltered here peacefully for three years in his war-torn, dislocated times.

I go to one of the altars, burn incense, say my prayers. As a Christian, a socialist, and a recent flirter with the ideas of Confucius, my prayers are general rather than particular, and spoken to all and every deity who will listen. I pray especially to the spirits of Zhang Fei, Liu Bei, and Zhuge Liang to protect our country in the years ahead.

I thank the Lord Jesus for having spared my family. I pray I am swiftly reunited with them. I pray for the soul and spirit of my dearest mother and that she is now, buried amid her ancestors, fully accepted into their ranks and is a garland and joy to their community.

It is at this point that I become aware of the blind orphans who are travelling in the bow of our ship. In a line, hands on the shoulders of the child ahead of them, they pass me by and then stop. I look down at them. First I see the officious and quite short lady with large glasses who is matter-of-factly in charge of them as they wind through the temple. She tells them of the wonderful statues of all the heroes and gods they are surrounded by. They are all savouring the smell of incense.

I suddenly recognize the woman. She is quite famous. Her name is Shi Liang. A lawyer known for her ferocity in court. I saw her at the opening meeting of our elected parliament when she had a lot to say about the rights of women – which I am greatly in favour of – and even more about the rights and well-being of children.

I wonder about whether to introduce myself to her but decide not to. She is ordering one child to stop picking his nose. But then, quite by chance, my glance falls upon the face of one particular child. I stand poleaxed. The child is smiling. Well, smiling as much as a child with her face cut half away and her eyes gouged out can smile.

It is the girl defaced, cut about, set to begging by the criminals on the Bund. Who Tian Boqi acted so bravely to defend. I continue to stare at the blinded child as she passes me by. This earns me a glare from Shi Liang. But before the child has passed me completely I hear her tell her companion that she loves blue parasols. She loves blue parasols.

On the way out of the temple there are some stalls selling tat to tourists. One of them sells cheap paper parasols – including blue ones. I buy one.

We rejoin our steamer and set off once more up the calm waters of the Yangtze towards Chungking.

I stand on the upper deck with the folded paper parasol beneath my arm looking down on the clustered blind orphans in the bow. She is chattering with animation in her twisted, devastated face. Blithely chattering away to her friends and comrades who she has never seen. Who have never seen her.

I walk down the steps and approach the stern Shi Liang.

'Excuse me,' I say.

'Yes?' she barks at me.

After the way I stared in the temple she's obviously already got me marked as a wrong 'un.

'Who are you? What do you want?'

'Well,' I say, 'my name is Lao She. I'm a novelist.'

'Don't read novels. Haven't got time.'

'The thing is, that girl with the horribly gouged face, I recognize her, from when she was on the Bund, back in Wuhan, being forced by those terrible criminals to beg.'

'And...?'

'Well, I overheard her back at the temple saying that she really loved parasols, blue parasols, so I thought I would buy her one so she could have it, play with it.'

'We get men like you coming up all the time, saying you just want to help these poor, defenceless children. You feel so sorry for them. Could you just meet them? And when you get hold of them you do all sorts of horrific, appalling things to them. You know the scum who held her on the Bund used to farm her out, at extreme prices, to people who wanted to do the sort of thing you want to do to her.'

'I do not in any way want to harm that poor child. Please let me explain.'

She grunts.

'I have children.'

I stop for a second. Carry on.

'When I used to see her on the Bund I did not know whether my own family, my own children, were alive or dead. We had become – separated. And I used to look at her because – because I feared, I feared that she might be one of my children...'

'Have you found out since whether your family is still alive?'

'I have. Thank God, they are still alive. But the whole ugliness, the whole shame I felt for abandoning my children, my family, was reflected in her poor, defenceless face. I want to give her something that she says she wants because it will make her happy.'

'I have heard her go on about blue parasols too,' says Shi Liang.

She looks at me without affection.

'You can take her the parasol. Talk to her for a while. But if I see anything, the slightest suggestion of malfeasance, I'll have the captain take you out and shoot you. And I have the powers to do that.'

I don't doubt her. She is a very senior lawyer with many high connections in the government. And good for her for not taking a plane to Chungking and staying behind in person to guard these tiny children.

Somewhat gingerly I step forwards, step between the children, make my way up to the little girl, sit down beside her.

'Hello,' I say.

'Who are you?' asks the little girl.

'I am Lao,' I say. 'What is your name?'

'I do not know,' she says.

'When you went to see that temple back there,' I said, 'you and all your friends walked past me, and I heard you say you liked blue parasols.'

'I love blue parasols,' she said. 'My sister Cherry Blossom once had one. She looked so pretty twirling it around that I have always wanted one. Once she let me hold it.'

'Where is your sister Cherry Blossom?' I ask.

'I do not know,' she said. 'We were going on this long walk. But then my father, who was a very evil man, would not let me walk with them anymore. He was very nasty with his spade. And he drove me away from my family and I was lost and had no food or water and I was crying and then I fell down and I could not walk anymore and I was very scared and then started to fall asleep I was so tired but then suddenly these kind men found me and took me up and gave me food and water and then they asked what had happened to me and I told them about my father and his spade and they said he was a very evil man and then they said they were very poor and had no money and no food to eat or water to drink that they could give me but I could help them to get that so that we could all eat and all drink and they said it would hurt a lot but that I was a brave and kind little girl, which I am, and they said could they do it and because they were good people, unlike my evil father, I said yes, and it did hurt a lot, a whole lot, and I could not see anymore, but they were still kind to me and fed me even though they beat me sometimes because I was a bad girl and did not cry out enough and I was a good girl and I always tried to cry out a lot and I was happy, even though they beat me sometimes, but then these rough men came up and beat my kind friends and drove them away and they took me and I was very sad and crying but they brought me to this place where there were lots of other children like me who could not see and then we started to know each other and talk to each other and feel and smell each other and tell each other stories – which is very nice – and now I have lots of friends and sing songs and hold everyone's hands and dance dances and then we got on this boat and we are going to a very happy place and we will always be together and never depart from each other and that will be very nice.'

She finishes.

'But why do you want a parasol?' I ask.

'Because my sister Cherry Blossom had one and I miss her.'

'Here,' I say, 'this is a blue parasol for you.' I hand it to her.

She holds it. Feels it.

'Is this a blue parasol?' she asks, wonderingly.

'Yes,' I say, 'this is a blue parasol.'

She looks straight into my face. And somehow or other I do not see the scars. All I see is the beauty and the wonder in her face.

'Thank you,' she says, 'thank you.'

'Shall I open it for you?' I ask.

'Please,' she says, 'yes!'

I take it back and carefully open it. It's one of those parasols with tiny fluted vents in each segment, so that when you twirl it it make a sweet hum.

'Here you are,' I say, handing it carefully to her.

'Oh,' she says, holding it before her. She gives it a slight twirl and it gives a low hum.

'Oh,' she cries. 'It's one that sings. I really wanted one that sings. Look, Huiliang,' she cries to the boy beside her, 'I've got a parasol. A blue parasol.'

Of course he can't look, but that's not the point.

I make my way back to the unsmiling Shi Liang and thank her. She grunts.

'What will happen to them when they get to Chungking?'

'We will keep them together. That is vital. Because they know and understand each other. They do not know what it is like to see so it does not bother them. A special school is being built for them, where they will be taught how to do things through feel. Practical things mainly. And when they are older they will be sent to a factory for the blind. All together still. Where they can work on simple tasks like folding cardboard boxes, making simple clothes, winding rope. So they can be useful. Like all of us.'

She turns away from me and resumes her gimlet watch upon her flock. Our conversation is obviously over.

What a formidable woman! How admirable! A mother hen looking out for her chicks. If she ever stands for election I will definitely vote for her.

I walk away. Stop. Suddenly I realize that the little nameless girl's gouged face and blinded eyes do not matter anymore. She is among, she will always be, among people that cannot see her. Do not care about what she looks like, because they do not know what looks are. They will judge her, value her, by the beauty in her voice, the smell of her body, her soul. She will not be weighed down like the rest of us, stuck in the deadweight of our flesh and its looks. She will fly.

I walk up the steps again to the top deck. Look forwards. To the sun setting fire to the west as it sets. To the beauty of the plains and woods we sail amid. To the hopes I have of reuniting with my family again. And especially I look at the little girl, sitting in the bow, parasol hoisted aloft, twirling proudly round and round, all a-chatter with her friends.

Blessings to you, Lord Jesus.

24

Old men and women are dead, as well as craftsmen and professional people: tailors, shoemakers, tinsmiths, jewellers, house painters, ironmongers, bookbinders, workers, porters, carpenters, stove makers, jokers, cabinetmakers, water carriers, millers, bakers, and cooks; also dead are physicians, prothesists, surgeons, gynaecologists, scientists – bacteriologists, biochemists, directors of university clinics – teachers of history, algebra, trigonometry. Professors, lecturers, doctors of science, engineers, architects. Dead are agronomists, field workers, accountants, clerks, shop assistants, supply agents, secretaries, night watchmen, dead are teachers, dead are babushkas who could knit stockings and make tasty buns, cook bouillon and make strudel with apples and nuts, dead are women who have been faithful to their husbands and frivolous women are dead, too, beautiful girls, and learned students and cheerful schoolgirls, dead are ugly girls, silly girls, women with hunches, dead are singers, dead are blind and deaf mutes, dead are violinists and pianists, dead are two-year-olds and three-year-olds, eighty-year-old men and women with cataracts on hazy eyes, with cold and transparent fingers and hair that rustled quietly like white paper, dead are newly born babies who had sucked their mothers' breast greedily until their last minute. All these skills, this knowledge, this intention, are now sleeping in the ground.

Vasily Grossman

Lux aeterna luceat eis, Domine,
cum sanctis mis in aeternum,
quia pius es.
Requiem aeternam dona eis, Domine,
et lux perpetua luceat eis,
cum sanctis tuis in aeternum,
quia plus es.

As the cart came to the crest of the hill after a long and weary climb, Hu and Spider Girl saw it was another false summit and yet another long, long climb through the midday sun lay ahead of them. This had already happened several times.

Spider Girl said something dark and Hu laughed.

The Drab was leading the donkey. As she just had to follow the road it wasn't too difficult for her. Except when she reached a fork in the road, when she would stop until Spider Girl told her which way to go.

Hu sat on the tailgate of the cart and swung her feet.

Spider Girl sat in the well of the cart beside the coffin holding her father's hand. Holding it and holding it. Wei stared up at the blue skies. All the time she sat beside his coffin and held his hand, a darkness was welling inside her, the darkness of despair, but always she managed to fight it down.

As The Drab plodded along beside the donkey she and the donkey struck up a relationship. Every so often The Drab would start gently crooning to it. The donkey would respond with quiet hew-haws. But gradually the two, setting each other off, would get louder and louder, more and more raucous, til Spider Girl would have to sharply tell The Drab to shut up. The Drab would remember to remain silent but then, after a while, she would forget and she would start her soft crooning again.

The blackness came again. Spider Girl fought it off.

Spider Girl fed her father some of the goat's milk. She spilled drops on his mouth and his feeble lips licked them. She spilled more. He licked them again. He drank a little and this seemed to revive him.

Spider Girl thought desperately for a cheering subject. She thought of one.

'Father, do you remember how once you and I were sitting in the courtyard under the verandah eaves?'

Wei answered haltingly, with a croak, but as the conversation proceeded he spoke more fluently.

'You and I used to sit under the verandah eaves often in the evenings, after I'd finished work in the fields.'

'Indeed, and once we'd settled down and you'd sung some songs, we'd talk and we'd talk. But on one particular evening it was growing dark and the bats were flying low...'

'They always flew low, flittering in to catch the insects and moths around the lamps.'

'...and suddenly an old thrush flew into the courtyard with a snail in its beak.'

'That old thrush was always flying in with a snail.'

'Yes. And it started banging the snail on a flagstone to separate the meat from the shell. And it went on and on because that night it was a really stubborn snail...'

'Bang, bang, bang.'

'Yes. Bang, bang, bang. Then you, Father, you turned to me and said, "Just look at that old thrush. He's doing exactly what we do."

"And what's that, Father?" I ask.

"Why, he's doing his winnowing," you replied.

And I laughed and I laughed. I thought that was the funniest thing I ever heard.'

And the two of them, father and daughter, looked at each other and laughed. Out loud. Just as they'd laughed that night back on the farm.

And for a while the darkness in her lifted.

All around them streamed and turmoiled the busy life of the highway, an artery of the country. The road, with all the associated pathways and tracks which accompanied and threaded in and out of it as it crossed the land, hummed with life. People and lorries and carts and buses and bathchairs all progressed steadily but at different speeds westward. A line of sick soldiers judged fit to walk the 300 miles to Chungking stepped slowly and carefully along a trackway, some helping each other, others singing, others arguing. Teams of sturdy mules carried packs of fitted metal boxes with

4,000 rounds of ammunition in them. Unending columns of refugees. Lines of coolies, chanting their work shanties and songs, paid at one cent per mile, swinging along with fifty-pound loads hanging from each end of long wooden poles or on their backs. They portered their 100-pound loads twenty-five miles a day and dreamt of the sweet bodies and cooking of their young wives back home in Chungking. A white-uniformed army officer wearing slippers sat neatly on his mule, his wife with her permanent-waved hairdo perched on a donkey behind.

But this was not at all like the death marches which had crossed China only one year previously. Now every five miles a government way station had been set up to feed all travellers and their livestock, irrespective of class or age or race, with fresh water for drinking and washing. The travellers were offered canvas shelters and fresh bedding to sleep on – night and day. Doctors checked their temperatures and breathing and health and nurses cured little infants' sore throats with cough syrup and rubbed coolies' aching limbs and joints with liniment.

The great road went on and on and on.

And if some huge lorry or a very important general officer's staff car or a millionaire's Rolls-Royce or some gangster's gaudy roadster broke down right in the very middle of it, blocking everything, with great patience and resource the lines of coolies and refugees and soldiers and mules and asses and donkeys and carts simply wove their way around it, smooth as silk, along the side paths and trackways, flowing ever onwards, a great unstoppable flood. And the staff officers, millionaires or gangsters simply had to get out and walk like everyone else.

Wei suddenly became ill at ease, agitated, waving his arms to and fro. He raised his head and stared about him at the countryside. Spider Girl had been treating him with the medicine Donald had given her and drops of wild pear juice. Donald had warned her that his medicine would revive Wei only for a short while. Perhaps that time was now over?

'Father, are you all right?'

He looked at her. Straight in her eyes. He even worked his way up onto one elbow. A frenzy seemed to seize him.

'There is no good in killing people, Wild Pear Blossom,' he stated vehemently and with effort. 'You kill something which will never be on this earth again. It is not a good thing. That person will never be on the earth again and you have killed him. Just as I killed Baby Girl Wei…'

'You did not kill her.'

'I did.'

'You killed her that we might live. That Eldest Son might live.'

A silence. Her father thought about this. Then he looked at her.

'You live, Spider Girl,' he said with pain.

'Thanks to you, Father, you gave me life.'

'I cast you out.'

'And in return I gave you life.'

He considered the wonder of this. Then with an effort he said:

'You cannot stop life, can you?'

You can, thought Spider Girl bitterly, you can.

Wei must have had the same thought, because he thought and spoke again.

'Well, for a while you can't.'

Spider Girl looked softly at him.

He continued to her, painfully animated.

'Children will be running round your feet before you know it, Spider Girl. Can't stop life. By the time you die there will be grandchildren, too.'

There was a pause.

'Will you have children, Wild Pear Blossom?'

'Well…'

Spider Girl was suddenly overwhelmed by visions of her and Donald Hankey surrounded by swarms of tiny bow-legged bow-tied children running round and round them. For a second there was light all around her.

'…That depends.'

'Do,' said Wei emphatically, 'do. Because without children life is nothing.'

A pause. He spoke quietly.

'You know you are now head of the family, Spider Girl?'

'I cannot be head of a family, Father, I am a woman.'

'*You* can be. You should be in charge of everything. You will be as great a head of our family as the very first Wei who carved our land out of woodland and dug it and planted the first crops.'

For a second he reflected. Then he started to wilt and slumped backwards onto his back. Spider Girl moved to help him but he pushed her away and struggled back up by himself.

'Father, you should rest.'

He ignored this.

'Never forget, Spider Girl. Now you are head of our family, Spider Girl, never forget – as I did – how fast, how treacherously the world can change. One moment on the farm everything was certain, everything never-changed, season followed season, year year, then suddenly, in a second, in the twinkling of an eye, everything was in change, continual and terrifying turmoil. The whole world turned itself upside down. Everything that had been was no more, everything that could never have been was. What was right became wrong, what was wise became stupid, what seemed eternal was now dead and in ruins before us. That is life. Never forget. People who have been your sweetest friends all your life have become bitter enemies. Family members who have loved you turn into monsters that kill you. Life!'

His voice weakened. It became more loving.

'But you understand that, Spider Girl. You have lived through it and by your guile and intelligence and goodness you have survived it. You help others to survive it, even though you know they might do you harm. You can fight life and you can win.'

'You fought it too, Father.'

Suddenly the spirit went out of Wei. He slumped backwards into his coffin.

The darkness returned to Spider Girl. She grabbed his hand. She stroked it, she tickled his cheek, she tried to revive him. Caressed his arm, spoke of times past – when Cherry Blossom fell into a barrel of teazels and had a tantrum, when she, Spider Girl, tried to juggle two hedgehogs, when Grandpa had fallen into the latrine pit.

Ancient stories of legendary family events. Hallowed by repetition down the ages. Causes of laughter and tears around the kitchen table. Now, Spider Girl realized, being rehearsed within the family for the very last time.

But no response from her father. One of his hands slowly rubbed the side of the wild pear tree coffin, gaining comfort from its knotted strength. Spider Girl clung to his other hand. All her love, all her support, all her strength flowed from her hand into his hand, from her flesh into his flesh, just as he, when she had been a tiny child, had held her hand and supported and guided her as she hobbled along.

She gently stroked his arm. She sang him family songs and ditties, softly beating out their tunes and rhythms on his forearm as his own mother had once sung and soothed him when he himself had been a child. And as Spider Girl stroked and touched his hand and forearm it became as though their two spirits – father and daughter – dissolved and their flesh swam and washed gently into each other so they became one.

This love between Spider Girl and her father is not a commodity, not something you can break up, slice or dice, divvy up into chunks of wealth and money or fine clothes or exotic mansions. It has no value in this world. No recognition. It is not listed on any stock exchange. But as it unfurls itself in life, it is the only thing which lives on after death, is immortal, eternal, without end. At death its light becomes quite delicate – things dance in a haze rather than are, golds and silvers transcend mere greens and blues and blacks – what was intangible becomes touchable, explorable – what was tangible melts away and becomes nothingness.

Her father's hand died. One moment it was everything. The next nothing.

She let out a great cry.

'He is gone! He is gone!'

It echoed off the hills, up into the mountains. People stared. The Drab stopped the cart in terror. Spider Girl nearly fell over with the jolt. This sudden movement recalled her to her duties. She must not allow the great black figure of Despair standing at her shoulder to take her over. She shrugged it away. She had proper and pious funeral duties to perform as a dutiful daughter for the spirit of her father.

She smiled at The Drab to show her she was not upset by her sudden stop of the cart. She looked at Hu. She picked up the lid of the coffin, looked at her father one last time, placed the rough wood over his face and body and closed it.

At this time in China long seven-day traditional funerals had become rare, one hundred-day ones even rarer. In a world of continual movement and turmoil and change, people did not have the time or means for such things.

Spider Girl got down from the cart.

Hu, sensing she should help her stricken friend, removed Spider Girl's red scarf from her head and replaced it with one of her own white ones. She removed her own red jacket. The Drab was not wearing any red so she left her alone.

Spider Girl hired a passing coolie to dig the grave with the spade she had purchased on the Bund. He dug it swiftly and efficiently as he had another job further down the valley. In an hour he had removed the ton of earth and piled it neatly to one side. He and Hu, helped by Spider Girl, then carefully lowered the coffin down into the grave. The Drab looked on in bewilderment.

The fake bank notes were passed to any passing travellers, who burnt them and wished his spirit well. Some food and bottles of Freda Utley's bath water were passed around and drunk.

All this time Hu saw and sensed the tensions and furies and blackness growing within her friend.

Joss paper and incense was burnt. A squad of soldiers passing by, on learning Wei had been a soldier, gave him a rousing huzzah to cheer his spirit on its way.

Then Spider Girl, with the help of Hu and the coolie, was lowered down into the grave and stood upon the coffin. She knelt on it and prayed. She prayed with bitterness to the gods who Wei had worshipped and given offerings to in life. Who were meant to protect him. She prayed fervently that her father would find rest and enrichment in the afterlife, that he would not become a restless wandering ghost. She swore that after her death she would seek him out and become his companion – as she had been in life. She removed the small stone bottle from her smock, wet her lips with a few remaining drops of the wild pear juice within it, and then, standing with her two legs on either side of the coffin, lifted its lid and placed the bottle with its final few drops by his hand for his refreshment. She closed the lid and Hu and the coolie lifted her from the grave. Spider Girl looked at the coolie. The coolie swiftly and expertly refilled the grave, was paid in full by her and hurried off.

Stood by his grave Spider Girl gave a brief and angrily ironic funeral oration. She praised her father's lack of wisdom, his foolishness, which had been such a great gift to the family as he carried them on his broad shoulders for so many years. She spoke of how unwise he had been in loving his elder sister and his eldest daughter – her – and how his foolishness had ensured her survival, and thus the survival of the family. And she spoke of his foolishness in becoming a soldier and fighting the Japanese and being killed. But in being killed he had given her and so many other Chinese the gift of life. Finally her irony, her bitterness softened, her voice became gentle and loving, she thanked her father for his modesty and self-effacement, which had given her so much to be proud of.

Then the three of them restarted their journey into the high mountains – The Drab leading the donkey, Hu following the cart, Spider Girl sitting alone and upright in the cart.

And the tide of blackness and despair now took over Spider Girl completely.

Hu looked on in distress. She'd never seen her dear friend like this. Gone was her liveliness and humour, her insights and intelligence. Her inexhaustible ability to adapt and improvise in even the most extreme circumstances. She sat crushed in the cart.

Bitterness had not just eaten part of Spider Girl's soul. It had devoured it all. Hu touched Spider Girl's arm. Spider Girl pulled it away.

When The Drab reached a parting in the road and stopped because she did not know which way to go, this time it was Hu who indicated which way to go.

All around them the mountains grew taller and steeper. People lived in their heights. Colourful temples and monasteries clung to cliffsides and vertiginous slopes like fabulous jewelled insects. Villages likewise precariously clutched the mountainsides, each house or shack built on the roof and walls of the house beneath it. Lean out of your window too far and you could tumble a thousand feet. And from these villages snaked out, like necklaces around the mountain's sides, sinuous terraces cradling precious soil and growing green vegetables and crops, with farmers and their wives far above garnering in the last of the summer wheat or ploughing the soil ready for early sowing and next year's rich crops. Every so often the wind carried their chants and singing and laughter down on the heads of those far below.

As the road wound higher and higher the surrounding villages and cultivated terraces slowly disappeared, their places taken by slopes of dark, foreboding pine and conifer. Eagles and buzzards screamed from the heights. Their road became ever more precarious, so the donkey laboured and Hu helped it by pushing the cart. Spider Girl sat unmoved in the cart.

They passed up through layer after layer of cloud. As they entered the clouds all around them became dark and claustrophobic. Hu noted that Spider Girl seemed to welcome this, sucking their darkness into her lungs to make her even more angry and furious.

What could Hu do? How could she help her friend? How could she break through to her?

Their track at last reached a small plateau. Upon it rested various empty carts and wagons. In its midst there was a hut – an official government hut.

Here they were confronted by one of China's most ancient forms of transport. Already we have met them in Book 1 – the sailed wheelbarrow. After the fall of the Han Dynasty around AD 200, China's superb highway system fell into desuetude (like the similar Roman one) and Zhuge Liang was faced with the problem of maintaining trade and communications across this vast country. He invented the sailed wheel-barrow with its wheel in the middle so, balanced and steered, it could reach high speeds and carry heavy loads. But the trackways they operated on had poor and uneven surfaces. Then someone else – whose name we do not know – thought of building narrow stone pathways, eighteen inches wide and engineered with mild gradients – so travelling along them the wheelbarrows could reach high speeds.[24]

These ancient trade arteries were still in use. As the even more ancient footpath up over the mountains – involving thousands and thousands of vertiginous steps – was too steep for the freight and the luggage the refugees were carrying, travellers were selling their carts to the government – the man in the hut – and then walking the laddered steps up over the mountain (a shorter route) while the eighteen-inch wheelbarrow trackway, precariously carved into the side of the mountains, was sailed by skilled coolies who carried their luggage on their wind-powered wheelbarrows. When the two routes met again on a similar plateau on the other side of the mountain, the travellers would reclaim their baggage, the carts from travellers going in the other direction would be bought back from the government at a reasonable price, and they would continue their journey.

Our three travellers now stood on one of these plateaus.

Above them, stretching into the clouds, stood a ladder of sheer stone steps – a thousand of them. Above which stood another thousand steps, then another, then another.

Spider Girl, the natural haggler, was too preoccupied and self-absorbed, so the far-from-ideal Hu had to sell the cart and consequently got a poor price.

Spider Girl was completely unmoved by this.

Instead she stood staring ahead as the black, gaunt figure of Despair, of Fate, stood at her shoulder. She was equally indifferent to him. Instead she thought fiercely, concentrated solely on one single thought. She thought of Second Son. Her younger five-year-old brother who had been decapitated by the unexploded Japanese bomb. She remembered his courage, his quick-witted intelligence, his resilience. Only five years old, he had immediately volunteered to walk ahead of the cart in the darkness when they thought bandits might waylay them. Second Son had fearlessly run out into the refugee crowds to search for her when she had disappeared from the family. What courage! What a brave, caring child!

A fury was building inside her.

During the family's long, catastrophic march, a bit of Spider Girl was monitoring Second Son – his problems, his state of mind – as she monitored everyone in the family. From almost the beginning he had had problems. When they'd taken water from that stream and father had ordered them all to look in the opposite direction so they would not see the butchered family, as she had peeked behind her to see them, she'd seen Second Son peeking as well. What an awful effect that would have had on him. Why hadn't she quietly counselled, comforted him? When he led the donkey through the carnage and the bodies on the march, what fear must have entered his tiny soul. But she had done nothing. She was too busy dealing with her mother and her aching limbs and looking for an escape route for herself!

And now she turned and stared blackly into Fate's very face. But still she thought of Second Son.

From almost his earliest days in the family it had become obvious that sometime in the future there would be big problems between Second Son – fiery, shrewd, intelligent, all excellent qualities for a farmer – and Eldest Son – dreamy, gentle, passive, which would have made him a useless farmer. There would be endless rows between the two, with Second Son constantly challenging Eldest Son's authority and judgement. Her father, she realized, was already aware of this problem and would act to reconcile them, to subtly steer decisions in Second Son's favour without upsetting Eldest Son's self-esteem. And when Father died the responsibility for handling that problem, resolving it with endless subtle diplomacy, would have been hers. And she could have achieved it, worked it through. That is what family is. Service. Patience. Foresight. Reconciliation.

A family is an extraordinary, rare thing. Fast and changing as a chameleon, vivid, vital, eternal, centipeding relentlessly through generations – endless in its quicksilver variety. Each one is unique unto itself. The family is the root, the foundation on which we build all things, on which we flower and flourish. And what lies at its very heart, its very core? Wisdom. Patience. Understanding. And above all service. Duty.

Had that not been her family? And yet...

Her father – dead! Her grandfather – dead! Her mother – dead! Eldest Son – dead! Cherry Blossom – dead! Second Son – dead! Baby Girl Wei – dead! Baby Boy Wei – dead! That baby born under the cart – dead!

Spider Girl studied the black figure of Fate as he stood before her. His callous eyes, his greedy mouth, his shocking ugliness. And her fury boiled over. She strode straight at him, into him, through him as though he was not there and out the other side. Which is not the sort of action a god appreciates!

Hu was still handing over their baggage to the wheelbarrow coolie as suddenly Spider Girl set off up the ancient stone steps at a ferocious pace. Despite her ricket-ridden legs, which were only partially helped by Donald's bicycle harness, using her anger and despair as an engine, she shot up the steps. Her pain must have been agonizing.

'Spider Girl,' shouted out Hu, 'Spider Girl!'

But Spider Girl took no notice, storming up the steps.

Hu grabbed the donkey and a bag of food and, shouting to The Drab, who was very scared, started to hare up the steep steps, with precipitous drops to either side of them.

'Spider Girl,' shouted Hu, 'Spider Girl!'

Spider Girl was not going as fast as she had been, but she was still holding her own over the other two and the donkey.

'Stop,' panted Hu, 'stop.'

Finally Spider Girl did stop. She had reached a small resting place before the next towering ladder of a thousand ancient hollowed-out steps. Panting and bewildered and exhausted Hu and The Drab and the donkey finally caught up.

'What is the meaning of this, Spider Girl? What is the point of this?'

But Spider Girl was ignoring them. She was concentrating, tensing herself for the next climb. And she set off on it.

'What is it, Hu?' asked a bewildered Drab, 'What is Spider Girl doing?'

'I don't know,' panted Hu, 'I don't know. But we must follow her. Make sure she comes to no harm.'

So they did. Up the next ladder. Through a layer of cloud. Up the next. Through another layer of cloud, with only their laboured and desperate breathing for company. Finally the final ladder. How Spider Girl was finding the strength, the fury to do this, Hu did not know, but find it she did.

Eventually, almost at the top, Spider Girl did slow. In fact she almost fell over. But clawed herself back upright, tried to continue but couldn't, and sat down.

The Drab was weeping with incomprehension and fear at these events. Hu kept her and the donkey going and finally they drew parallel with Spider Girl, who had sat down on a patch of grass beside the steps. A mountain stream brawled past her feet and above her stood this ancient pine, arthritic and twisted with age. Spider Girl sat, staring straight ahead, full of rage and anger.

'What is this, Spider Girl? Do not do this. You are frightening us all. Stop it!'

Spider Girl took no notice of them.

And then it happened.

The valley between them and the next mountain – heavily veiled by layers of cloud – as so often in mountains suddenly cleared. An ominous roll of thunder, the welkin roared, and there, hanging above them, loomed an immense hammerhead thundercloud like some huge fire-scarred anvil black in the sky, descending on them, threatening to engulf them like some ancient man-of-war, broadsides of thunder and lightning shooting out from either flank, sheet lightning flickering and boiling within its black belly, bolts of pure darkness stabbing, daggering straight at them.

The three of them stood tiny, defenceless.

Hu's hair stood on end. She dived for the ground. The Drab and the donkey, scared out of their wits, sank on the grass attempting to clutch each other.

Spider Girl alone glared straight back into the blackness, anger and contempt firing from her eyes, standing there defiant as it swallowed them. She licked her lips in anticipation.

'Lie down, Spider Girl, lie down,' shrieked Hu. 'The lightning will strike you!'

Spider Girl remained where she was, her face boiling and twisting black with fury.

'Spider Girl—' screamed Hu, but could not finish, because suddenly an almighty crash of thunder and a huge, brilliant sword of lightning plunged down towards them, and in her terror Hu, glimpsing Spider Girl still defiant, hid her eyes.

Oh, Spider Girl. Dear Spider Girl, she thought, she mourned.

The lightning crashed. Hu hid her eyes and hid her eyes and then finally opened them. Spider Girl still stood there defiant. And then above them, a hundred feet further up the mountain, there was a creaking and a groaning. Hu looked up and saw the huge and ancient pine above, struck by the lightning, split its base so that the great and gnarled trunk trembled and then slowly pitched forwards and plunged down straight towards them. It struck the mountainside only yards above them and then somersaulted over their cowering faces and bodies – Spider Girl still standing – and then hammered and crashed on down the sheer mountainside, bouncing and vaulting and cracking over the cliffs and slopes, booming at each strike, til finally it was swallowed into the clouded depths deep below them. Still they could hear its screams and groans as it ricocheted and cannonaded down into the very belly of the valley and the river that ran through it.

There was silence. A long, long silence.

Then Spider Girl turned and looked at the staring Hu. Saw her horror, her concern, her love. And she started to understand things. Saw that as she, Spider Girl, had served others, so now Hu was serving her. She could have got on that aeroplane to Chungking, but instead she had stayed at Spider Girl's side to support and protect her. Always in the past Spider Girl had supported, sustained others – her father, her mother, Donald – but now, she realized, someone was doing it for her – nursing, comforting her in her weakness, her frailty, her fear. And this understanding entered her body as a mother's gentle milk enters and warms a baby's. From that day on she formed a deep bond with Hu, such as she had only ever formed before with her father and with Donald.

She looked at the terror-stricken Drab and her donkey and realized that she, Spider Girl, in her rage, in her foolishness, had left the poor witless woman unprotected. She who should have been serving The Drab had deserted her and had served only herself. She had even deserted the donkey, which seemed to have somehow wound itself into their fellowship.

And she knew that this was not now the end – of her, of her family. In the afterlife she would seek out her father. And then she would take him back to his family and she would give their ears such a banging and a battering they would be forced to accept him back into their ranks – and grant him a place of honour, what's more! She knew there would be no place for her – the ugly, meddling cripple. Her mother would never allow it (quite rightly!). But she could found her own family (with Donald, even!), get a nice, responsible, honourable husband. And she would make certain their family did not lack. A whole new family. She might even take back the family farm. That would set up a din among her ancestors!

She looked at Hu.

Hu approached her and gently touched her arm.

'Spider Girl, are you all right?'

'I am sorry I did that. Acted so badly.'

'You did not act badly. You acted in grief.'

'Spider Girl,' asked The Drab, seeing both the storms had passed, 'are you all right?'

'Yes, I am,' said Spider Girl.

'You scared me so much,' said The Drab. 'You were running away. I thought I should lose you.'

'I will never leave you again. I swear it.'

Even the donkey seemed a bit cheered by this.

Hu suggested they sit on the grass and have some food and drink the cold, clear water from the mountain stream. And they did.

There is no liquid on earth more invigorating, more uplifting, more exalting than the water from a high mountain stream.

And as they sat there, eating and reflecting, a miracle occurred.

The clouds disappeared. Every single cloud in high heaven, in all the heavens, simply vanished before their eyes, revealing row after row of majestic mountain tops in serried ranks and regiments, marching away into infinity.

And these were the colours of these eternal mountains

– jacinth and topaz and sapphire and ruby and coral and onyx and pearl and emerald and jasper and chrysolite and beryl and amethyst and cinnabar and gold and silver.

And then they gazed up into the very highest peaks around them, into the thinnest, most rarified airs, where earth finally meets heaven, matter meets spirit, where tiny wisps and slivers of cloud tangle and dance and dream about and between the highest peaks, where you can no longer discern where earth stops and heaven begins, and there Hu witnessed Jacob's Ladder, with its unending traffic of humans and angels passing up and down between earth and heaven, and Spider Girl witnessed the heights where ancient emperors once made love with the angels and created man.

Hu saw a Christian heaven and Spider Girl saw a pagan heaven and both saw the same heaven.

Piety, peace, justice, compassion, equality.

An end to war, an end to the suffering of children, an end to poverty, disease, starvation and ignorance (including their own)…

They sat for a while upon the grass, contemplating this.

The storm over, the stream of refugees threading their way over the mountain had restarted. Spider Girl, Hu and The Drab stood up. Because she had exhausted herself on the way up, Hu and The Drab helped Spider Girl onto the back of the donkey, and then the three of them set off, carefully picking their way step by step down the other side of the mountain on the road to Chungking.

Hu with her Bible, Spider Girl packing her pistol and The Drab leading her donkey.

1 The wilderness and the dry land shall be glad,
   the desert shall rejoice and blossom; like the crocus

2 it shall blossom abundantly and rejoice with joy and singing.
   The glory of Lebanon shall be given to it,
   the majesty of Carmel and Sharon.
   They shall see the glory of the Lord,
   the majesty of our God.

3 Strengthen the weak hands and make firm the feeble knees.

4 Say to those who are of a fearful heart, 'Be strong, fear not!
   Behold, your God will come with vengeance,
   with the recompense of God.
   He will come and save you.'

5 Then the eyes of the blind shall be opened and the ears of
   the deaf unstopped;

6 then shall the lame man leap like a hart and the tongue of
   the dumb sing for joy.
   For waters shall break forth in the wilderness and streams in
   the desert;

10 And the ransomed of the Lord shall return and come to
   Zion
   with singing;
   everlasting joy shall be upon their heads;
   they shall obtain joy and gladness,
   and sorrow and sighing shall flee away.

                                            Isaiah 35:1–6, 10

*

I finished this book – its second draft – on the very day that Wuhan declared itself free of coronavirus and the lights came on again in a spectacular light show.

Wuhan lives!
Let's hope we all do!
Hallelujah!

History of the Non-Fictional
Characters after 1938

General Feng Yuxiang

Feng became increasingly estranged from Chiang Kai-shek's Nationalist government, with its corruption and repression. Although he was a socialist and remained one, he grew closer to the communists.

At the end of the Second World War he openly split with the Nationalists and travelled to America, where he became an impassioned opponent of that country's increasing support for Chiang and hostility to the Chinese Communist Party.

In 1946, he lobbied his old friend General Joseph Stilwell to help stop President Truman's increasing Cold War belligerence towards China. Stilwell died before Feng arrived.

> A few days after her husband's death, Mrs Stilwell was upstairs at her home in Carmel, California when a visitor was announced with some confusion as 'the Christian'. Mystified, she went down to find in the hall the huge figure and cannonball head of Feng Yuxiang, who said, 'I have come to mourn with you for Shih Ti-wei, my friend.[25]

In 1948 Feng was travelling to the Soviet Union. While crossing the Black Sea by steamer with one of his daughters the cabin they were travelling in caught fire and they both died. There were rumours that it was foul play and that the cabin's door was locked from the outside. He had certainly become close to the communists and as a relatively well-known and popular figure in America since the 1920s, the CIA or MI6 might have thought him a suitable figure for elimination. With the usual Cold War distortions surrounding the event, it is not really possible at the moment to know the truth.

He was an honourable man and a patriot. In 1953 his remains were returned to China and he was buried with honours on the slopes of the sacred Mount Tai, where his wife Li Dequan had founded fifteen schools for the poor in the early 1930s and where they and their friends –Lao She and his family – used to take picnics.

General Li Zongren

General Chiang Kai-shek continued to keep Li Zongren in a very junior position throughout the Second World War and for the ensuing Chinese Civil War. Following several decisive victories by the Communists over the Nationalists in late 1948 and 1949 Chiang Kai-shek was removed from office and Li took his place. A four-month truce followed. Horrified by Li's moves towards peace Chiang again resumed power and Li resigned and went to America. Chiang was defeated and withdrew to Taiwan.

In 1965, with Chou En-lai's support, Li returned to China, where he was greeted and treated as a national hero. He stayed and died in 1969. He is buried in the Babaoshan Revolutionary Cemetery, Beijing's main resting place for the highest-ranking revolutionary heroes.

In the 1920s Li and Bai Chongxi had been mainly fascist in their politics. They led Chiang Kai-Shek's butchery of communists in his suppression of the Wuhan Uprising in 1927. It is rumoured that Chou En-lai was spared by them on the intercession of the Soong sisters.

His favourite book was Gibbon's *Decline and Fall of the Roman Empire*.

Donald Hankey

Donald Hankey did not serve in Wuhan at this time – he worked in Zhengzhou (north of Wuhan) with the Canadian missionary doctors McClure and Brown. All of them visited Wuhan, however, and McClure held an important government medical position there. The two Indian doctors are fictional, but the Indian National Congress did send doctors to China at this time.

I relocated them because all three of them were extraordinary characters who lived amazing lives. The Canadian playwright Munroe Scott has written an excellent play celebrating their work – *McClure* – and McClure's biography: *McClure: The China Years*. McClure served in the Red Cross in China throughout the Second World War and then was head of the United Nations medical relief team for Palestinian refugees. He was also on the staff of the Church Missionary Society Hospital at Gaza.

A formidable man.

After 1938 Donald Hankey falls off the radar, though he remained working in China through the war, until his reappearance in 1944 in the extreme south-west of China, in Yunnan Province. He was working with the British Red Cross but was seconded to the Friends' Ambulance Unit, a Quaker outfit.

This is from a Quaker memoir:

The three teams formed under the scheme adopted by the Staff Meeting of May 1943 for work under the Chinese Red Cross, one with the help of the British Red Cross Unit, were to operate behind the Chinese forces in Yunnan that were facing the Japanese on the Salween front in readiness for the drive into Burma. In fact, the offensive did not begin until April 1944, and the three teams had some months of waiting, filled in with medical work before military activity began. M.T.3 was in Hsiakwan, already familiar to the Unit, M.T.4 towards Yenshan on the Indo-China border, and the mixed M.T.5 for a time in Tsiao Chien, which they reached on horseback after a grim ride in pouring rain along ravines, precipices and watercourses. Here the hospital consisted of three temples, 'two used as wards and one as administrative centre – and all still used as temples. The wards have some very fearsome deities in them, and it has been found necessary to cover them up for the sake of the peace of mind of some of the patients.'

A New Life Movement team, which handed the premises over to them, had set up a laboratory and diet kitchen and had maintained a high standard of cleanliness throughout the hospital. The work was mainly surgical; there was a predominance of ulcers due largely to the paucity of Army diet. In the medical ward were typhus, relapsing fever, malignant malaria, hookworm, dysentery and other diseases. A delousing plant which the team set up was in great demand by the troops. That was the beginning of M.T.5's work.

It was while working with this team in Tengch'uan that Dr. Donald Hankey, of the British Red Cross, died of typhus in January 1944. To the F.A.U. the losing of so close a friend was no less a blow than the loss of one of its own members.

Apparently, with the rapid Japanese advance, typhus broke out in a Chinese unit facing the Japanese. Donald rushed to the front and somehow or other managed to inoculate the 10,000 soldiers in one day. He only forgot to inoculate one person: himself. He died a few days later and was buried beside a lake.

His name is on the war memorial of his home village of Semley in Wiltshire. It is also on a plaque inside the church which lists those of the parish who died in the Second World War. I go there sometimes to commune with his soul. I've read him a couple of the chapters in which he appears. There's a very nice pub across the green to which we afterwards repair.

In his adventures in Yunnan, I do not know whether or not he was accompanied by a fictional Chinese housekeeper.

This is a poem written by a member of the Quaker ambulance unit, Rita Dangerfield, while she was in Yunnan. It is not dedicated to Donald, but is relevant to the beauty of the place where he was buried.

'To a Yunnan Waterfall'
This offspring of the hills and rain,
This shimmering cloud of billowy train
Twisting, twirling, foam – unfurling
Dancing, prancing, light enhancing
Leaping, sweeping, ever seeking

Further heights to torrent down
O vision joyous and abandoned,
O rhythmic harmony unbounded
By man's creative rules and standards,
Go swiftly, charge your gleaming masses
Onward, onward through the mountains
Till your bright transcendent smile
Greet some other land awhile.

As the Chinese called him, Noble Soul.

Lao She

Lao She was never one of life's lucky people. But it never stopped him trying.

His wife Hu Jieqing and their three children made the perilous journey out of Japanese-occupied China and joined him in Chungking.

Life in Chungking became increasingly repressive there under the rule of Chiang Kai-shek, especially for writers and left-wingers. While there Lao wrote his novel *The Drum Singers* on the life of a popular theatre troupe – based on his collaboration with Shanyaodan – and his real-life success in preventing the leading girl being sold into concubinage.

After his wife joined him, he wrote his great novel *Four Generations under One Roof*, based on his wife's experiences of living under Japanese occupation.

With the end of the world war and the restart of the Chinese Civil War between Nationalists and Communists in 1946, Lao moved to the US, tired to death of war and its tyrannies and hoping to become a serious international writer. One of the many perils of being a writer during wartime (apart from political repression and bombs falling) is the repeated loss of completed manuscripts through bombing of publishers, collapse of postal services, etc. etc., all of which Lao She suffered.

There he and his friend Ida Pruitt (daughter of Southern Baptist missionaries and born and raised in rural China) decided together to rewrite – from memory (I think) – *Four Generations Under One Roof* in English, renaming it *The Yellow Storm*. In doing so they produced a book which I consider to be the greatest novel of the twentieth century.

It was published and received rave reviews in the *New York Times* etc. Bestseller, Hollywood films etc. etc. Then something catastrophic happened – as so often in Lao She's life. The communists won the civil war. Lao She considered it is his duty, as a socialist, as a patriot, to return to the new China and do his bit. And did so.

Overnight, thanks to the CIA etc., he became a 'communist collaborator' and non-person in the West. He was dropped tout court by anyone influential or 'artistic'. *The Yellow Storm* disappeared from the shelves and became, almost overnight, impossible for freedom-loving Westerners to read. It is currently unavailable on Amazon. I managed three years ago to finally purchase a copy for £70, remaindered from Ilkley Public Library. (God bless independent-minded freedom-loving Yorkshiremen!)

The Lao family set up home in their birthplace, Beijing. Lao's first act on moving in to their new home was to plant a red persimmon tree in their courtyard. He was invited to write articles and plays, and he wrote *Teahouse*, his gentle comedy about censorship in China from the time of the last Qing emperor all the way through to the last days of Chiang Kai-shek. When first produced in 1957 it was a great success, but its popularity slowly waned and under the youthful Red Guards it became one of the symbols of 'reaction'. Lao was targeted by the Red Guards, beaten up, imprisoned, and then released. This happened several times. His death remains mysterious. He either was killed by drowning or deliberately committed suicide as a protest.

His play *Teahouse* is now considered a classic of Chinese theatre and is performed widely and regularly throughout China to great acclaim.

What a great man!

His wife Hu Jieqing went on to become a famous contemporary artist in China. She died aged ninety-six.

Peter Fleming

Peter Fleming, though he wrote pro-appeasement editorials for *The Times*, probably did not write the notorious 7 September 1938 one quoted in this novel. According to Richard Cockett,[26] that editorial was most likely written by the paper's chief editorial writer on foreign affairs, Aubrey Leo Kennedy, with Dawson adding the fatal passages quoted in this novel.

During the war, like many other young appeasers including Quintin Hogg and Patrick Heathcoat-Amory, loser of the Bridgwater by-election, he joined the armed forces. He was involved in a commando group in the Norway campaign, then he organized small groups of commandos in Kent who would fight behind the German lines after an invasion. He then joined Special Operations Executive (SOE) – which is generally now regarded as having been more leftish and effective than MI6 – and went to India and the Far East to organize disinformation campaigns against the Japanese.

MI6 continued with its anti-communist obsessions throughout the war (while blindly allowing itself to be infiltrated by communists like Philby and Burgess because they went to the right schools). This meant that it frequently fell prey to right-wing anti-communists (who also happened to be Nazi double agents). Writers like Malcolm Muggeridge and Graham Greene served in MI6 and later mocked its incompetence.

After the war Peter Fleming left SOE, returned to his banker's mansion at Nettlebed and played the country squire, with lots of hunting and shooting, but still spent most of his time in London contributing to *The Spectator*. He died in 1971.

He was partly the inspiration for his brother Ian's James Bond.

Celia Johnson

Peter Fleming's wife (best known for her performance in *Brief Encounter*) continued her acting career until her death in 1982.

It is one of my great regrets that I never saw her as Elizabeth Bennet (though I'm a proud owner of her reading of *Pride and Prejudice*). She gives intelligence and reflection and suffering to the role, unlike modern dramatizations, where it's all about female wit and superiority to all the troglodytic males.

Freda Utley

In the interests of writing entertaining fiction, I have probably been cruelest to Freda Utley. She was an extraordinary woman and I apologize to her and her spirit.

As far as I'm aware she did not have an affair with Vernon Bartlett. Paul French's *Through the Looking Glass: China's Foreign Journalists from Opium Wars to Mao* gives a portrait of her in Wuhan, her writing and the Last Ditch Club.

Freda went on to have a fascinating odyssey of a career after China. She never lost her horror of war and her opposition to it after her spell in China. This should be remembered.

After her experiences in China she settled in the United States, where she moved strongly to 'the right' – and by 'right' I mean McCarthyism. After the end of the Chinese Civil War and the defeat of Chiang Kai-shek and the triumph of communism, with her experiences in Wuhan she became an 'expert' at naming the Americans in China responsible for 'the loss of China'.

It should be remembered that although McCarthyism is now portrayed as a far-right-wing wave of deliberately induced hysteria and repression (like the recent anti-Corbyn and American Russiagate hysterias), many of its roots were in the pre-war isolationist movement. McCarthyites were the Americans who wanted no war with the rest of the world and no interventions or foreign military adventures. McCarthyism was in many ways their revenge on the leftist and liberal East Coast internationalists and interventionists, who they saw as being responsible for dragging an unwilling America into the war and the subsequent growth of the worldwide American 'empire' post 1945 and its endless interventions and wars.

The right wing in America has always had anti-war and

isolationist elements in it. Today they are represented by such individuals as Ron Paul and his son Rand and to an extent figures like Ronald Reagan, Donald Trump and Tulsi Gabbard.

Freda Utley and, after her death, her son Jon Basil Utley, have been central to continuing to support anti-war causes. Jon Basil was a founder of the strongly anti-war *American Conservative* magazine, a tireless journalist, and was central to the setting up of the website antiwar.com with its extraordinary editor Justin Raimondo who, until his recent death, analyzed with uncanny precision every lying word and shameful military and political aggression of the Western War Party – neo-conservatives, Israel Firsters, and members of the Military Industrial Complex. Years before I knew anything about the Utley family, antiwar.com, with its digest of news reports and articles on wars all around the world, was and is the first thing I read in the morning when I blurrily go online.

And Freda, however bad her actions in the McCarthy hearings were against certain China hands with communist sympathies, never lost her love nor profound respect for the leading communist there, Agnes Smedley. In 1970 she was fair-minded enough to write:

> Agnes was one of the few people of whom one can truly say that her character had given beauty to her face, which was both boyish and feminine, rugged and yet attractive. She was one of the few spiritually great people I have ever met, with that burning sympathy for the misery and wrongs of mankind which some of the saints and some of the revolutionaries have possessed. For her the wounded soldiers of China, the starving peasants and the overworked coolies, were brothers in a real sense. She was acutely, vividly aware of their misery and could not rest for trying to alleviate it. Unlike those doctrinaire revolutionaries who love the masses in the abstract but are cold to the sufferings of individuals, Agnes Smedley spent much of her time, energy, and scant earnings in helping a multitude of individuals. My first sight of her had been on the Bund of Hankou, where she was

putting into rickshaws and transporting to the hospital, at her own expense, some of those wretched wounded soldiers, the sight of whom was so common in Hankou, but whom others never thought of helping. Such was her influence over 'simple' men as well as over intellectuals that she soon had a group of rickshaw coolies who would perform this service for the wounded without payment.

To add further praise to a woman I have not treated well in my fiction, I would say that this short description she gave of refugees arriving on the Bund in 1938 became my central inspiration for this novel – or at least book one:

Many families had been on the march for weeks, some for months. Families which had set out with five or six children had reached Hankou with only one or two. Small girl children were scarce; when the mother and father have no more strength to carry the little children, and when the small children are too exhausted to move another step, some have to be left on the road to die. With what agony of mind must some children have been abandoned so others can be saved! Who can even imagine the infinite number of small individual tragedies amongst the millions who have been driven from their homes by the Japanese?*

Although I cannot remember now definitely, I am almost certain I read this passage first in Stephen MacKinnon's magnificent *Wuhan, 1938: War, Refugees, and the Making of Modern China*.

Hu Lan-shih

There is only one reference I have come across to Hu Lan-shih. It is in a particularly vivid and intelligent interview she gave to the American communist writer and journalist Anna Louise Strong

---

* Freda Utley, *China at War*

on the Bund when she arrived after her trek from Shanghai with the cotton mill girls and the army. She probably wasn't an actual mill worker but a writer who had worked closely with the workers for years. Strong describes her as 'a well-poised young woman, with a vivid sense of humor and superlatively straightforward and honest.' I have found no trace of her apart from this one interview:

A group of Shanghai textile workers, among those present, had just arrived in Hankow, coming on foot by a thousand-mile zigzag course, helping wounded soldiers and doing propaganda work in villages along the way.

They told me the highest wages ever known in the textile industry had been ten to fifteen dollars (American money) a month in 1926–27, when the trade-unions were strong. The biggest drop in wages came in 1932 after the Japanese invasion of Shanghai, especially through the uncontrolled wage-cutting in Japanese-owned factories. When the war broke (out), most of the girls had been getting only three to six dollars (American) monthly, and had been without trade-union protection.

But they were not illiterate or ignorant of world affairs. During the years when trade-union activities were not permitted, the Y.W.C.A.'s industrial courses had provided extensive education for Shanghai's working-class girls. The girls said, 'The freeing of workers and of women must be worked out in connection with the freeing of the Chinese people as a whole. Workers and women suffer the most from Japanese oppression. The Japanese mills are the worst; they often made us work sixteen to eighteen hours, and until noon on Sunday without extra pay. Now the Japanese have destroyed all our homes and factories. So the working women are strongest to help the army. We go in the very front lines.'

The most amazing account of the work of women behind the lines was given by Hu Lan-shih, (a well-known woman writer who organized a group of Shanghai working girls in the earliest days of the war). Most of the girls came originally from farming families; Miss Hu herself had an almost uncannily shrewd knowledge of the Chinese farmer mind. A quiet, well-poised young woman, with a vivid sense of humor and superlatively straightforward and honest, she went with her uniformed but unarmed group among the soldiers and villagers of the Yangtze delta. Though the spectacle of women organizing a war startled the Chinese villagers, the women often got better results than either army officers or college students. They induced Chinese farmers to harvest at night between battle lines, reclaimed dozens of 'child-traitors' and halted demoralized, retreating soldiers. Lived on red pepper, tou-fu, and turnips dug from fields.

'In August at the beginning of the war,' related Miss Hu, 'we offered our services to the commander to whom we were sent. He told us that his first difficulty was lack of food for the soldiers since the nearby farmers had all fled, leaving their crops unharvested. We followed the farmers to the places to which they had fled and urged them to return, at least as long as the soldiers were there. We said, 'A new day has come to China. The army no longer exploits the people but wants to be their friend. They will help you harvest, and you must give them hot water and help the wounded/ At first they would not believe us, but we gave them our word and we also held the general to his promise. Thus a large section of territory behind Shanghai was repopulated; the people gave housing and food to the soldiers, and the soldiers helped get in the crops.'

Later, the harvest on one of the fronts was dangerously located in a zone of fire and no one had succeeded in persuading the farmers to harvest it. By visiting the families and promising to go with them, the girls got 130 volunteers who harvested all one night and got eighty loads of crops. With keen intuition the girls worked with soldiers who had violated the 'new spirit' by paying too little for farm products. 'Suppose a farmer complains that a soldier took a pig that was worth ten dollars and gave only four dollars. We would not humiliate the soldier by reproving him. We would rather congratulate him because he did not take pigs for nothing, but believed in the new spirit between people and army.'*

---

* Anna Louise Strong, *One-fifth of Mankind. New York 1938. Available free on the internet.*

I also owe descriptions of the working conditions and life of girls working in the Shanghai mills to Emily Hong's book *Sisters and Strangers: Women in the Shanghai Cotton Mills, 1919–1949*.

Soong Ching-Ling, Li Dequan & Shi Liang

All three of these women were socialists and practising Christians.

Soong Chingling, widow of Sun Yat-sen and sister of Madame Chiang, served in various communist governments from 1949 until 1981. She was Vice President of China from 1949 until 1975.

Li Dequan, wife of General Feng Yuxiang, became the first Minister of Health in 1949 and continued in senior government positions almost until her death in 1972. She only joined the Communist Party in 1958.

Shi Liang, the ferocious lawyer and ferocious defender of children, was the first Minister of Justice of the People's Republic of China from 1949 to 1959.

Agnes Smedley

Much of Agnes's life has been covered in the book.

At one stage (Book 3, Chapter 12) I have Agnes denying she is spying on Freda but in fact she probably was for the Soviet Union – though this might be mere Cold War propaganda. If she was, she was working for her ex-lover Richard Sorge, the twentieth century's greatest and most successful spy.

In 1941 he had embedded himself as a German officer in the Japanese intelligence agencies in Tokyo. There he learnt that the Japanese were to attack Pearl Harbor, not to go westwards into Russia. This news reached Russia as Hitler arrived at the gates of Moscow and enabled Stalin, now certain he would not be attacked by the Japanese, to transfer all his crack troops from the Far East to turn back the Nazi attack on Moscow. This event won the war for the Allies, saved democracy in Western Europe and probably in the rest of the world. Such is war!

Sorge was discovered by the Japanese and later executed.

There is, however, no likelihood that Agnes (if she spied for the Soviet Union) ever reported to Moscow on Freda. Freda – who became virulently anti-communist later in life – continued always to speak in the highest possible terms of Agnes, even after the (probably true) stories about Agnes and Sorge came out.

After the Second World War – during which she spent most of her time marching with and reporting on the communist armies – Agnes returned to the US to fight the growing McCarthyite witch-hunt against those who had 'lost China' to the communists. Unwell, and under enormous pressure, she then fled to England where she died in 1951, aged fifty-eight, after an ulcer operation.

Brave heart.

Freda Utley's heartfelt encomium to her is published in the Freda Utley section of these notes. It was written after Freda would have known the accusations of Agnes being a spy.

Avoid the Wikipedia article on Agnes. It drips its usual neo-McCarthyite, neo-Cold War liberal poison against her.

Rewi Alley

Following George Hogg's death in 1945, Rewi Alley took over running his school.

With the end of the civil war in 1949 he settled in Beijing but continued to tour the world, espousing especially nuclear disarmament. He was honoured by the New Zealand government in 1985, being made a Companion of the Queen's Service Order. The award ceremony finished, the prime minister turned to him and said: 'New Zealand has had many great sons, but you, Sir, are our greatest son.'

He died, aged ninety, in Beijing in 1987.

Fang the Builder

Fang's method of work is partly built on the similar working methods of a friend I have in my village. He spends hours just staring at the stones before building a stone wall which is always delightful to see with his subtle colour plays between all the different stones and the fossils placed so cleverly within it. He also lays a mean hedge. He once did an exquisite long winding hedge right next to – two or three feet from – a very busy road. A dangerous place to work. When finished, with all the splinted wood in it, it twisted and turned like a white snake.

He is the sort of person that deserves an Arts Council grant. A large Arts Council grant. Except he's never heard of the Arts Council and the Arts Council is far too stupid and out-of-touch to have ever heard of him.

He has had a variety of cider named after him.

Evans Carlson

In 1933 Evans Carlson, of the US Marine Corps, was in charge of President Roosevelt's military guard. He and FDR became close friends.

While in Wuhan as a military observer Carlson wrote many letters to FDR about the situation in China. Fascinated by the way the Chinese communist guerrilla forces in North-West China related to and cooperated with the peasantry, he spent many months marching with and observing the Communist Eighth Route Army's guerrilla tactics.

A man of strong socialist principles, in 1942 he founded 'Carlson's Raiders' within the US Marine Corps. Abolishing the normal caste divisions between different ranks, he developed tactics which he copied from the Chinese communist guerrillas. He led the famous Makin Raid and then 'the Long Raid' behind the Japanese lines in Guadalcanal in 1942, adopting the phrase 'gung ho', used by the communists to describe their soldiers positive attitudes, for use within the US Marine Corps. The phrase has since developed an ironic life of its own.

Carlson, relieved of his command for his political beliefs, and worn out by his intensely active military life and by various tropical diseases, died at the early age of fifty-one in 1947.

He is generally credited with being the founder of American special forces.

Colonels Vasily Chuikov and Georgy Zhukov

Colonels Vasily Chuikov and Georgy Zhukov went on to command Russian forces at the Battle of Stalingrad. It is obvious that they employed there many of the strategies and tactics thought out and improvised by the Chinese generals at Taierzhuang.

Georgy Zhukov was the single most important individual in the overthrow of European Nazism.

In August 1945 US General Eisenhower visited Moscow and became friends with Zhukov. He stated: 'To no one man does the United Nations owe a greater debt than to Marshal Zhukov [...] one day [...] there is certain to be another Order of the Soviet Union. It will be the Order of Zhukov, and that order will be prized by every man who admires courage, vision, fortitude, and determination in a soldier.'

Zhukov had always had a very difficult relationship with Stalin, who had been on the verge of executing him on several occasions. Zhukov fell into obscurity in the Soviet Union after the war. His role was only fully recognized in 1995.

Any individuals in the book I have not included in this list can, probably, be looked up online. With the exception of the Wei family and The Drab, of course, who are entirely fictional.

The American Firebombing of Wuhan, December 1944

One sad footnote to the sufferings of Wuhan should be added. Having survived the horrors of Japanese occupation, the citizens of Wuhan had to go through one more horror before the war finally ended for them.

In the autumn of 1944 General Curtis LeMay was put in charge of the strategic bombing of Chinese and Japanese cities. With ninety-four brand-new B-29 Superfortress bombers, LeMay used the new techniques of low-level incendiary bombing – first developed in Europe by the RAF – to bomb Wuhan in preparation for the later firebombing of Tokyo and Japan.

Forty thousand Wuhan citizens died in this bombardment.

ACKNOWLEDGMENTS

My thanks go to:

Liz MacLeod, executive producer, Meridian Line Films (China projects); Stephen Griffiths. Liu Yamin; Dr Joanne Ferguson for her medical advice on the text; Freda; Ruth and daughters and grandchildren; Candace. Janet Rundle and the other excellent staff at the brilliant and indispensable Shepton Mallet Library who've helped me so much, finding me the books I have needed over the years. 'Use it!'; Stan and Wendy for tea, sympathy, wine, magnificent Italian cooking and advice on my text. My literary agents Oliver and Mic Cheetham. My editor Clare Gordon. My publisher Nic Cheetham. My TV and radio agent Norman North. Robert Temple, Somerset's resident sinologist, friend of Lao She's family. Eddie Donnelly and Michael Simpson for comradeship (except when it comes to Catholicism). Dr Chunyun Li for her very kind translation of some Lao She. Dave Chapple for his powerful and emotional speeches and endless trade union work, and him and Glen for their friendship. Father Dom Bede Rowe for his counselling and homilies; Our Vicar, Gawd bless 'er, for continuing to think when everyone else has given up. Des and Di. My son, partner, and rather vigorous granddaughter; my parents and two sisters and numerous offcuts; Rory Meek; Diana Howard and Rose Batty; Cadi; Ros Henderson; Rosie Edwards for the long and extremely helpful conversation I had with her about her experiences of treating traumatized refugee children on the Greek island of Lesbos (they're still stuck there!); Misha Graham Patel; Suzanne Collins.

ENDNOTES

1. Although I've given these 'poems' to a fictional character, in fact these poems are by the now forgotten American communist poet Joseph Freeman. He published much of his revolutionary verse in *The New Masses*, a journal of the interwar American literary left.

2. This enthusiastic evocation of the Lee Enfield Mark 4 owes much to George MacDonald Fraser's encomium to it in his superb memoir of his service in the Burma campaign, Quartered Safe Out Here.

3. Agnes Smedley witnessed one such railway workers/blacksmith cooperative and reported on it and photographed it.
   http://www.chinaww2.com/2014/07/16/a-social-and-visual-history-of-the-dadao-chinas-military-big-saber-ii/

4. This description of Chiang Kai-shek was not uninfluenced by the columnist Matthew Parris's brilliant description of Theresa May in *The Times*.

5. Chiang Kai-shek had false teeth. In moments of great rage with a subordinate he was known to remove his false teeth and throw them at him. Madame Chiang was said to keep spare sets of his dentures in her handbag for him.

6. Such is the potency and potential for destruction that this psalm is said to contain, until recently it was banned in several African countries.

7. Extraordinarily the evil and destructive theories of eugenics were not buried for ever after the barbarisms of World War II, but even now are making a comeback in alt-right circles around the world, not least in the unscientific and disastrous theories of 'herd immunity' being applied to the fight against Covid-19.

8. http://21stcenturywire.com/2018/05/02/in-honour-of-the-syrian-arab-army-and-allies-war-on-terror/

9. Amazingly, Robert Capa survived as a war photographer, including taking famous photographs of the D-Day landings on Omaha Beach, until he was killed covering the 1954 First Indochina War in Vietnam.

10. Still an excellent read – still available for free online and all good bookshops!

11   Chen Lifu lived to 100 and died in 2001 on his chicken farm in New Jersey. Although he disliked Chiang Kai-shek's slickness and lack of morality, as a Confucian believer in traditional hierarches and faithfulness to one's emperor he continued to serve him through the Second World War and the Chinese Civil War, not leaving his service until the Nationalist government had been evacuated to Taiwan in 1949.

Dismissing all governments as corrupt and self-serving, he bought his chicken farm in America. As he wrote: 'From now on, I will never serve anybody and will never have this kind of feeling again when looking after the chickens.' He attributed his longevity to: 'The ability to fall asleep quickly, a good temper, good memory, a healthy diet with mostly vegetables and drinking only boiled water.'

I owe the story of how the ancient emperors dealt with the merchant classes to my old friend John Michell (now unfortunately dead) – Platonist, radical traditionalist, visionary, wit and rediscoverer of ley lines.

12   The descriptions of this air raid are taken almost verbatim from Freda Utley's own description of it in *China at War*, George Hogg's writings including from his book *I See a New China*, and Vasily Grossman's superb wartime novel *The People Immortal* – now almost unobtainable in the West because it is not anti-Soviet – in which Grossman graphically describes a German air raid on a Soviet city.

13   Page, Bruce, Leitch, David, Knightley, Phillip, *The Philby Conspiracy*, Doubleday (1968).

14   It was Major General Sir Stewart Menzies who, later in his career, recruited into MI6 that ultimate unpaid spy, working for his masters 'out of pure idealism' – Kim Philby. Others included, notably, Guy Burgess.

If the point of being in MI6 during the war was killing Nazis, Menzies certainly got his money's worth with Kim Philby. While most of MI6 couldn't decide whether it hated communists or Nazis more, Philby – citizens of his beloved Soviet Union being slaughtered in their millions by the Nazis – set about silently and efficiently killing Germans in large numbers, while his fellow officers wavered to and fro.

15   The description of this extraordinary event involving Donald Hankey, especially my final paragraph, is taken from Munroe Scott's wonderful biography of Dr Robert McClure, *McClure: The China Years*, published in 1977.

See 'Jian Bei Pian: Lao She's Forgotten Wartime Epic Poem' by Janette Briggs:

https://researcharchive.vuw.ac.nz/xmlui/bitstream/handle/10063/6168/thesis.pdf?sequence=1/

This lengthy poem has interesting parallels (and differences) with Louis MacNeice's similar and almost contemporaneous epic poem *Autumn Journal*.

24 http://www.lowtechmagazine.com/2011/12/the-chinese-wheelbarrow.html/

25 Tuchman, Barbara W., *Stilwell and the American Experience in China 1911–1945*, Macmillan Publishers (1971).

26 Cockett, Richard, *Twilight of Truth: Chamberlain, Appeasement, and the Manipulation of the Press*, Weidenfeld and Nicolson (1989).

ABOUT THE AUTHOR

JOHN FLETCHER is a Neoplatonist, a syndicalist and a Catholic. Over the course of his life he has been many things, including a construction worker, a shepherd, a white van driver, a gravedigger, a steelworker, a cleaner, a teacher, a broadcast journalist, and a writer. *Wuhan* is his first novel.

FEAST DAY OF FOOLS

JAMES LEE BURKE

WHEELER
WINDSOR
PARAGON

This Large Print edition is published by Thorndike Press, Waterville, Maine USA and by AudioGo Ltd, Bath, England.
Copyright © 2011 by James Lee Burke.
The moral right of the author has been asserted.
Wheeler Publishing, a part of Gale, Cengage Learning.

Wheeler Publishing Large Print Hardcover.
The text of this Large Print edition is unabridged.
Other aspects of the book may vary from the original edition.
Set in 16 pt. Plantin.

LIBRARY OF CONGRESS CATALOGING-IN-PUBLICATION DATA

Burke, James Lee, 1936–
    Feast day of fools / by James Lee Burke.
        p. cm.
    ISBN-13: 978-1-4104-4214-7 (hardcover)
    ISBN-10: 1-4104-4214-4 (hardcover)
    1. Texas—Fiction. 2. Large type books. I. Title.
PS3552.U723F43 2011b
813'.54—dc23   2011033664

BRITISH LIBRARY CATALOGUING-IN-PUBLICATION DATA AVAILABLE
Published in the U.S. in 2011 by arrangement with Simon & Schuster, Inc.
Published in the U.K. in 2012 by arrangement with The Orion Publishing Group Ltd.
U.K. Hardcover: 978 1 445 87325 1 (Windsor Large Print)
U.K. Softcover: 978 1 445 87326 8 (Paragon Large Print)

Printed and bound in the United Kingdom by MPG Books Ltd.
1 2 3 4 5 6 7 15 14 13 12 11

For Dora, Mike, and Alicia Liu

The wild beasts will honor me, the jackals and the ostriches, for I give water in the wilderness, rivers in the desert, to give drink to my chosen people.

— Isaiah 43:20

CHAPTER ONE

Some people said Danny Boy Lorca's visions came from the mescal that had fried his brains, or the horse-quirt whippings he took around the ears when he served time on Sugar Land Farm, or the fact he'd been a middleweight club fighter through a string of dust-blown sinkholes where the locals were given a chance to beat up what was called a tomato can, a fighter who leaked blood every place he was hit, in this case a rumdum Indian who ate his pain and never flinched when his opponents broke their hands on his face.

Danny Boy's black hair was cut in bangs and fitted his head like a helmet. His physique was as square as a door, his clothes always smelling of smoke from the outdoor fires he cooked his food on, his complexion as dark and coarsened by the sun and wind as the skin on a shrunken head. In summer, he wore long-sleeve cotton work shirts buttoned at the throat and wrists to keep the heat out, and in winter, a canvas coat and an Australian flop hat tied down over his ears with a scarf. He fought his hangovers in a sweat lodge, bathed in ice water, planted by the moon, cast demons out of his body into sand paintings that he flung at the sky, prayed in a loincloth on a mesa in the midst of electric storms, and sometimes experienced either seizures or trances during which he spoke a language that was neither Apache nor Navajo, although he claimed it was both.

Sometimes he slept in the county jail. Other nights he slept behind the saloon or in the stucco house where he lived on the cusp of a wide alluvial floodplain bordered on the southern horizon by purple mountains that in the late-afternoon warp of heat seemed to take on the ragged irregularity of sharks' teeth.

The sheriff who allowed Danny Boy to sleep at the jail was an elderly six-feet-five widower by the name of Hackberry Holland, whose bad back and chiseled profile and Stetson hat and thumb-buster .45 revolver and history as a drunk and a whoremonger were the sum total of his political cachet, if not his life. To most people in the area, Danny Boy was an object of pity and ridicule and contempt. His solipsistic behavior and his barroom harangues were certainly characteristic of a wet brain, they said. But Sheriff Holland, who had been a prisoner of war for almost three years in a place in North Korea called No Name Valley, wasn't so sure. The sheriff had arrived at an age when he no longer speculated on the validity of a madman's visions or, in general, the foibles of human behavior. Instead, Hackberry Holland's greatest fear was his fellow man's propensity to act collectively, in militaristic lockstep, under the banner of God and country. Mobs did not rush across town to do good deeds, and in Hackberry's view, there was no more odious taint on any social or political endeavor than universal approval. To Hackberry, Danny Boy's alcoholic madness was a respite from a far greater form of delusion.

It was late on a Wednesday night in April when Danny Boy walked out into the desert with an empty duffel bag and an army-surplus entrenching tool, the sky as black as soot, the southern horizon pulsing with electricity that resembled gold wires, the softness of the ground crumbling under his cowboy boots, as though he were treading across the baked shell of an enormous riparian environment that had been layered and beveled and smoothed with a sculptor's knife. At the base of a mesa, he folded the entrenching tool into the shape of a hoe and knelt down and began digging in the ground, scraping through the remains of fossilized leaves and fish and birds that others said were millions of years old. In the distance, an igne-

11

ous flash spread silently through the clouds, flaring in great yellow pools, lighting the desert floor and the cactus and mesquite and the greenery that was trying to bloom along a riverbed that never held water except during the monsoon season. Just before the light died, Danny Boy saw six men advancing across the plain toward him, like figures caught inside the chemical mix of a half-developed photograph, their torsos slung with rifles.

He scraped harder in the dirt, trenching a circle around what appeared to be two tapered soft-nosed rocks protruding from the incline below the mesa. Then his e-tool broke through an armadillo's burrow. He inverted the handle and stuck it down the hole and wedged the earth upward until the burrow split across the top and he could work his hand deep into the hole, up to the elbow, and feel the shapes of the clustered objects that were as pointed and hard as calcified dugs.

The night air was dense with an undefined feral odor, like cougar scat and a sun-bleached carcass and burnt animal hair and water that had gone stagnant in a sandy drainage traced with the crawl lines of reptiles. The wind blew between the hills in the south, and he felt its coolness and the dampness of the rain mist on his face. He saw the leaves on the mesquite ripple like green lace, the mesas and buttes shimmering whitely against the clouds, then disappearing into the darkness again. He smelled the piñon and juniper and the scent of delicate flowers that bloomed only at night and whose petals dropped off and clung to the rocks at sunrise like translucent pieces of colored rice paper. He stared at the southern horizon but saw no sign of the six men carrying rifles. He wiped his mouth on his sleeve and went back to work, scooping out a big hole around the stonelike objects that were welded together as tightly as concrete.

The first shot was a tiny *pop,* like a wet firecracker exploding. He stared into the fine mist swirling through the hills. Then the lightning flared again, and he saw the armed men stenciled against the horizon and the silhouettes of two other figures who had broken from cover and were running toward the north, toward Danny Boy, toward a place that should have been safe from the criminality and violence that he believed was threading its way out of Mexico into his life.

He lifted the nest of stony egg-shaped artifacts from the earth and slid them into the duffel bag and pulled the cord tight through the brass eyelets at the top. He headed back toward his house, staying close to the bottom of the mesa, avoiding the tracks he had made earlier, which he knew the armed men would eventually see and follow. Then a bolt of lightning exploded on top of the mesa, lighting the floodplain and the willows along the dry streambed and the arroyos and crevices and caves in the hillsides as brightly as the sun.

He plunged down a ravine, holding the duffel bag and e-tool at his sides for balance. He crouched behind a rock, hunching against it, his face turned toward the ground so it would not reflect light. He heard someone running past him in the darkness, someone whose breath was not only labored but desperate and used up and driven by fear rather than a need for oxygen.

When he thought that perhaps his wait was over, that the pursuers of the fleeing man had given up and gone away, allowing him to return to his house with the treasure he had dug out of the desert floor, he heard a sound he knew only too well. It was the pleading lament of someone who had no hope, not unlike that of an animal caught in a steel trap or a new inmate, a fish, just off the bus at Sugar Land Pen, going into his first night of lockdown with four or five mainline cons waiting for him in the shower room.

The pursuers had dragged the second fleeing man from behind a tangle of deadwood and tumbleweed that had wedged in a collapsed corral that dog-food contractors had once used to pen mustangs. The fugitive was barefoot and blood-streaked and terrified, his shirt hanging in rags on the pencil lines that

14

were his ribs, a manacle on one wrist, a brief length of cable swinging loosely from it.

"*¿Dónde está?*" a voice said.

"*No sé.*"

"What you mean you don't know? *Tú sabes.*"

"*No, hombre. No sé nada.*"

"*¿Para dónde se fue?*"

"He didn't tell me where he went."

"*¿Es la verdad?*"

"*Claro que sí.*"

"You don't know if you speak Spanish or English, you've sold out to so many people. You are a very bad policeman."

"*No, señor.*"

"*Estás mintiendo, chico. Pobrecito.*"

"*Tengo familia, señor. Por favor. Soy un obrero, como usted.* I'm just like you, a worker. I got to take care of my family. Hear me, man. I know people who can make you rich."

For the next fifteen minutes, Danny Boy Lorca tried to shut out the sounds that came from the mouth of the man who wore the manacle and length of severed cable on one wrist. He tried to shrink himself inside his own skin, to squeeze all light and sensation and awareness from his mind, to become a black dot that could drift away on the wind and re-form later as a shadow that would eventually become flesh and blood again.

15

Maybe one day he would forget the fear that caused him to stop being who he was; maybe he would meet the man he chose not to help and be forgiven by him and hence become capable of forgiving himself. When all those things happened, he might even forget what his fellow human beings were capable of doing.

When the screams of the tormented man finally softened and died and were swallowed by the wind, Danny Boy raised his head above a rock and gazed down the incline where the tangle of tumbleweed and deadwood partially obscured the handiwork of the armed men. The wind was laced with grit and rain that looked like splinters of glass. When lightning rippled across the sky, Danny Boy saw the armed men in detail.

Five of them could have been pulled at random from any jail across the border. But it was the leader who made a cold vapor wrap itself around Danny Boy's heart. He was taller than the others and stood out for many reasons; in fact, the incongruities in his appearance only added to the darkness of his persona. His body was not stitched with scars or chained with Gothic-letter and swastika and death's-head tats. Nor was his head shaved into a bullet or his mouth surrounded by a circle of carefully trimmed beard. Nor did he wear lizard-skin boots that were plated on the heels and tips. His running shoes

16

looked fresh out of the box; his navy blue sweatpants had a red stripe down each leg, similar to a design a nineteenth-century Mexican cavalry officer might wear. His skin was clean, his chest flat, the nipples no bigger than dimes, his shoulders wide, his arms like pipe stems, his pubic hair showing just above the white cord that held up his pants. An inverted M16 was cross-strapped across his bare back; a canteen hung at his side from a web belt, and a hatchet and a long thin knife of the kind that was used to dress wild game. The man leaned over and speared something with the tip of the knife and lifted it in the air, examining it against the lights flashing in the clouds. He cinched the object with a lanyard and tied it to his belt, letting it drip down his leg.

Then Danny Boy saw the leader freeze, as though he had just smelled an invasive odor on the wind. He turned toward Danny Boy's hiding place and stared up the incline. *"¿Quién está en la oscuridad?"* he said.

Danny Boy shrank down onto the ground, the rocks cutting into his knees and the heels of his hands.

"You see something up there?" one of the other men said.

But the leader did not speak, in either Spanish or English.

"It's just the wind. There's nothing out

17

here. The wind plays tricks," the first man said.

"*¿Ahora para dónde vamos?*" another man said.

The leader waited a long time to answer. "*¿Dónde vive La Magdalena?*" he asked.

"Don't fuck with that woman, Krill. Bad luck, man."

But the leader, whose nickname was Krill, did not reply. A moment that could have been a thousand years passed; then Danny Boy heard the six men begin walking back down through the riverbed toward the distant mountains from which they had come, their tracks cracking the clay and braiding together in long serpentine lines. After they were out of sight, Danny Boy stood up and looked down at their bloody handiwork, scattered across the ground in pieces, glimmering in the rain.

Pam Tibbs was Hackberry's chief deputy. Her mahogany-colored hair was sunburned white at the tips, and it hung on her cheeks in the indifferent way it might have on a teenage girl. She wore wide-ass jeans and half-topped boots and a polished gun belt and a khaki shirt with an American flag sewn on one sleeve. Her moods were mercurial, her words often confrontational. Her potential for violence seldom registered on her adversaries until things happened that should not have

18

happened. When she was angry, she sucked in her cheeks, accentuating a mole by her mouth, turning her lips into a button. Men often thought she was trying to be cute. They were mistaken.

At noon she was drinking a cup of coffee at her office window when she saw Danny Boy Lorca stumbling down the street toward the department, bent at the torso as though waging war against invisible forces, a piece of newspaper matting against his chest before it flapped loose and scudded across the intersection. When Danny Boy tripped on the curb and fell hard on one knee, then fell again when he tried to pick himself up, Pam Tibbs set down her coffee cup and went outside, the wind blowing lines in her hair. She bent down, her breasts hanging heavy against her shirt, and lifted him to his feet and walked him inside.

"I messed myself. I got to get in the shower," he said.

"You know where it is," she said.

"They killed a man."

She didn't seem to hear what he had said. She glanced at the cast-iron spiral of steps that led upstairs to the jail. "Can you make it by yourself?"

"I ain't drunk. I was this morning, but I ain't now. The guy in charge, I remember his name." Danny Boy closed his eyes and opened them again. "I think I do."

19

"I'll be upstairs in a minute and open the cell."

"I hid all the time they was doing it."

"Say again."

"I hid behind a big rock. Maybe for fifteen minutes. He was screaming all the while."

She nodded, her expression neutral. Danny Boy's eyes were scorched with hangover, his mouth white at the corners with dried mucus, his breath dense and sedimentary, like a load of fruit that had been dumped down a stone well. He waited, although she didn't know for what. Was it absolution? "Don't slip on the steps," she said.

She tapped on Hackberry's door but opened it without waiting for him to answer. He was on the phone, his eyes drifting to hers. "Thanks for the alert, Ethan. We'll get back to you if we hear anything," he said into the receiver. He hung up and seemed to think about the conversation he'd just had, his gaze not actually taking her in. "What's up?" he said.

"Danny Boy Lorca just came in drunk. He says he saw a man killed."

"Where?"

"I didn't get that far. He's in the shower."

Hackberry scratched at his cheek. Outside, the American flag was snapping on its pole against a gray sky, the fabric washed so thin that the light showed through the threads. "That was Ethan Riser at the FBI. They're

20

looking for a federal employee who might have been grabbed by some Mexican drug mules and taken to a prison across the border. An informant said the federal employee could have gotten loose and headed for home."

"I've heard Danny Boy has been digging up dinosaur eggs south of his property."

"I didn't know there were any around here," Hackberry said.

"If they're out there, he'd be the guy to find them."

"How's that?" he said, although he wasn't really listening.

"A guy who believes he can see the navel of the world from his back window? He says all power comes out of this hole in the ground. Down inside the hole is another world. That's where the rain and the corn gods live. Compared to a belief system like that, hunting for dinosaur eggs seems like bland stuff."

"That's interesting."

She waited, as though examining his words. "Try this: He says the killing took fifteen minutes to transpire. He says he heard it all. You think this might be the guy the feds are looking for?"

Hackberry bounced his knuckles lightly up and down on the desk blotter and stood up, straightening his back, trying to hide the pain that crept into his face, his outline massive against the window. "Bring your recorder and a pot of coffee, will you?" he said.

The report Danny Boy gave of the murder he had witnessed was not one that lent itself to credulity. "You were drinking before you went digging for dinosaur eggs?" Hackberry said.

"No, sir, I hadn't had a drop in two days."

"Two days?" Hackberry said.

"Yes, sir, every bit of it. I got eighty-sixed. I didn't have no more money, anyway."

"Well, you must have seen what you saw," Hackberry said. "Want to take a ride?"

Danny Boy didn't answer. He was sitting on the iron bunk of his cell, wearing lace-up boots without socks and clean jailhouse jeans and a denim shirt, his hair wet from his shower and his skin as dark as smoke. His hands were folded in his lap, his shoulders slumped.

"What's the problem?" Hackberry said.

"I'm ashamed of what I done."

"Not helping this guy out?"

"Yes, sir. They was talking about La Magdalena."

"Who?"

"A holy woman."

"Don't feel so down about this, partner. They would have killed you, too. If they had, you wouldn't be helping us in the investigation, would you?" Hackberry said.

Danny Boy's eyes were focused on a spot

22

ten inches in front of him. "You didn't see it."

"No, I didn't," Hackberry replied. He started to say something about his own experience in No Name Valley many years ago but thought better of it. "Let's get this behind us, partner."

Pam Tibbs drove the three of them down the main street of the town in the department's Jeep Cherokee, the traffic light over the intersection bouncing on its cable in the wind. The newer buildings on the street were constructed of cinder blocks; some of the older ones were built out of fieldstones that had been cemented together and sheathed with plaster or stucco that had fallen off in chunks, leaving patterns that resembled a contagious skin disease. Pam followed a winding two-lane state highway southward through hills that looked like big brown ant piles or a sepia-tinted photograph taken on the surface of Mars. Then she drove across Danny Boy's property, past his stucco house and his barn that was plated from the bottom to the eaves with hubcaps, onto the geological fault that bled into Old Mexico and a strip of terrain that always seemed to ring with distant bugles echoing off the hills. For Hackberry Holland, these were not the horns blowing along the road to Roncevaux.

Pam shifted down and kept the Jeep on the high ground above the riverbed that Danny

23

had walked the previous night, the hard-packed gravel vibrating through the frame. "There," Danny said, pointing.

"Under the buzzards?" Hackberry said.

"Yes, sir."

"Where are your dinosaur eggs?"

"At the house."

"You sure those aren't rocks?" Hackberry said, his eyes crinkling at the corners.

But his attempt to relieve Danny Boy of depression and fear was to no avail. The guilt and sorrow Danny Boy had taken with him from the previous night would probably come aborning in his dreams for many years, and all the beer in all the beer joints in Texas would not make one dent in it, Hackberry thought. "Get upwind from it," he said to Pam.

She crossed a slough chained with red pools and layered with clusters of black butterflies sucking moisture from the sand, their wings shuddering as though they were ingesting toxin. She parked on the incline, above the collapsed rails of the corral that had been used by a one-eyed man who killed and sold mustangs for dog food. When Hackberry stepped out on the passenger side, his eyes roved over the tangles of tumbleweed and bleached wood and the remains of the man whose death may have been the most merciful moment in his life. "You ever see anything

24

like this?" Pam said, her words clotting in her throat.

"Not exactly. Maybe close, but not exactly," Hackberry replied.

"What are we dealing with?" she said.

"Call the coroner's office, then get Felix and R.C. down here. I want photos of this from every angle. String as much tape as you can around the crime scene. Make sure nobody disturbs those tracks going south."

She went to the Jeep and made the calls, then walked back down the incline, pulling on a pair of latex gloves, her upper arms ridging with muscle. Danny Boy remained in the vehicle, his head lowered. "What did he say the leader's name was? Krill?" she said to Hackberry.

"I think that was it."

"I've heard that before. It's Spanish?"

"It's a shrimplike creature that whales eat."

"Funny name for a killer with an M16 strapped on his back." When he didn't answer, she looked at him. "You okay, boss?"

He nodded at the slope above where the victim had died.

"Jesus Christ," she said.

"He was scalped, too."

Then the wind changed, and a sickening gray odor blew into their faces. It was like fish roe that had dried on warm stone and the putrescence of offal and the liquid wastes poured from a bucket into a ditch behind a brothel on a Saturday night, and it made Pam Tibbs hold her wrist to her mouth and walk back up the incline, fighting to hold back the bilious surge in her stomach.

Hackberry stepped back from the site and repositioned himself so he was upwind again. But that did not change the nature of the scene or its significance. Often he wondered, as an anthropologist might, what the historical environment of the human race actually was. It wasn't a subdivision of sprinkled lawns and three-bedroom houses inside of which the television set had become the cool fire of modern man. Could it be a vast sun-baked plain broken by mesas and parched riverbeds where the simian and the mud-slathered and the unredeemed hunted one another with sharpened sticks, where the only mercy meted out was the kind that came as a result of satiation and exhaustion?

The compulsion to kill was in the gene pool, he thought. Those who denied it were the same ones who killed through proxy. Every professional executioner, every professional soldier, knew that one of his chief duties was to protect those he served from knowledge about themselves. Or at least those were the perceptions that governed Hackberry's judgments about societal behavior, even though he shared them with no one.

He looked to the south. Dust or rain had smudged out the mountains, and the plain

26

seemed to stretch endlessly into the distance, the way a snowfield could extend itself into the bottom of a blue winter sky, dipping over the edge of the earth into nothingness. Hackberry found himself swallowing, a nameless fear clutching at his viscera.

The coroner was Darl Wingate, an enigmatic single man who had been a forensic pathologist with the United States Army and CID before he retired back to the place of his birth. He was laconic, with sunken cheeks and a pencil mustache, and he often had liquor on his breath by ten A.M. He also had degrees from Johns Hopkins and Stanford. No one had ever been quite sure why he chose to spend his twilight years in a desolate place on the edge of the Great American Desert. It was certainly not because he was filled with compassion for the poor and the oppressed, although he was not a callous man. Hackberry believed that Darl Wingate was simply a pragmatist who saw no separation or difference between the various categories of the human family. In Darl's mind, they all belonged to one long daisy chain: They were creatures who came out of the womb's darkness and briefly saw light before their mouths were stopped with dust and their eyes sealed six feet down. As a consequence of his beliefs, he remained a witness and not a participant.

Darl placed a breath mint on his tongue

and put on latex gloves and a surgeon's mask before he approached the remains of the dead man. The day had grown warmer, the sky more gray, like the color of greasewood smoke, and gnats were rising from the sand.

"What do you think?" Hackberry asked.

"About what?" Darl said.

"What you're looking at," Hackberry replied, trying to repress his impatience.

"The fingers scattered up on the slope went one at a time. The toes were next. My guess is he died from shock. He was probably dead when he was scalped and taken apart, but I can't say for sure."

"You ever work one like this?"

"On a couple of backstreets in Bangkok. The guy who did it was a church missionary."

"So the human race is rotten?"

"Say again?" Darl said.

"You're not giving me a lot of help."

"What else can I provide you with?"

"Anything of specific value. I don't need the history of man's inhumanity to man."

"From the appearance of the victim — his nails, his emaciated condition, the infection on his manacled wrist, the scabs on his knees, and the lice eggs in the remnant of his hair — I'd say he was held prisoner in primitive and abusive conditions for at least several weeks. The scarring on his face and neck suggests smallpox, which tells me he's probably

Mexican, not American. What doesn't fit is his dental care."

"I don't follow you."

"It's first-rate."

"How would you explain the discrepancy?"

"My guess is he came from humble origins but did something good with his life," Darl said.

"Successful criminals don't see dentists?"

"Only when the pain makes it imperative. The rest of the time they're getting laid or huffing flake up their nose. I think this guy took care of himself. So far, I see no tattoos, no signs of intravenous use, no scars on his hands. I think we might be looking at the remains of a cop."

"Not bad."

"What happened here says more about the killer than the victim," Darl said.

"Pardon?"

"Whatever information he had, he shouted it to the heavens early on. But his tormentor took it to the finish line anyway. You got any idea what he wanted?"

"You ever hear of somebody called La Magdalena?" Hackberry asked.

Darl nodded. "Superstitious wets call her that."

"Darl, would you please just spit it out?"

The coroner screwed a cigarette into his cigarette holder and put it between his teeth. "Sometimes they call her *la china.* Her real name is Anton Ling. She's Indo-Chinese or French-Chinese. She looks like an actress in a Graham Greene film. Ring any bells?"

Hackberry blinked.

"Yeah, that one," Darl said. He lit his cigarette and breathed a stream of smoke into the air. "I remember something you once said. It was 'Wars of enormous importance are fought in places nobody cares about.' "

"Meaning?"

"Deal me out of this one," Darl said. "It stinks from the jump. I think you're going to be splashing through pig flop up to your ankles."

CHAPTER TWO

Six hours later, Pam Tibbs and Hackberry Holland drove down a long dirt track, twenty miles southwest of the county seat, to a paintless gingerbread house that had a wide gallery with a swing on it and baskets of petunias and impatiens hung from the eaves. The landscape looked particularly strange in the sunset, like terrain that might have been used in a 1940s movie, hard-packed and rolling and biscuit-colored and notched with ravines, marbled by thunderheads and the reddening of the sky and dissected by lines of cedar fence posts that had no wire on them.

Lightning rods flanged each end of the house's roof, and a windmill in back was ginning furiously, pumping a jet of water into an aluminum tank where three spavined horses were drinking. A white-over brick wall surrounded the house a hundred feet out, like the walls at the Alamo, the top festooned with razor wire and spiked with broken glass. The wood gates on three of the walls had been removed and pulled apart and the planks used to frame up two big vegetable gardens humped with compost, creating the effect of a legionnaire's outpost whose defense system had been rendered worthless.

"What's the deal with this place?" Pam asked.

"Miss Anton bought the house from a secessionist who took over the courthouse about twenty years ago. After she moved in, I think the Rangers were sorry they locked up the secessionist."

"Miss?" Pam said.

Hackberry was sitting in the passenger seat, his Stetson over his eyes. "It's a courtesy," he said.

They parked the Jeep outside the wall, and got out and studied the southern horizon through a pair of binoculars. "Take a look at this," she said.

Hackberry rolled a folder filled with eight-by-ten photos into a cone and stuck it in the side pocket of his trousers, then focused the binoculars on a rocky flume rimmed by mesquite and scrub oak and willow trees. The sky above the hills looked like green gas, the air glistening with heat and humidity, the shell of an automobile half buried in the bleached-out earth, the metal wind-polished as bright as foil. But the contemporary story of this particular place was written across the bottom of the flume. It was layered with moldy clothes, scraps of plastic tarp, tennis shoes split at the seams, smeared toilet paper, spoiled food, empty water bottles, discarded sanitary napkins, and plastic diapers slathered with feces. A circle of turkey buzzards floated just above the hills, the edges of their wings feathering in the wind.

"She used to be part of that Underground Railroad or whatever?" Pam said.

"Up in Kansas, I think," Hackberry said. "But I wouldn't put it in the past tense."

"You call the feds yet?"

"I haven't gotten to it."

He could feel her staring at the side of his face.

"If I can make a suggestion —" she began.

"Don't," he said.

"You were a lawyer for the ACLU. That name has the status of whale shit around here. Why add to your problems?"

"Can you stop using that language on the job? I think both you and Maydeen have an incurable speech defect."

He had stepped into it again, allying his dispatcher Maydeen Stoltz with Pam; they were undefeatable when they joined forces against him, to the extent that he sometimes had to lock his office door and pretend he was gone from the building.

"You don't know how to cover your ass," Pam said. "So others have to do it for you. Ask anybody in the department. Your con-

33

stituency might tell you they love Jesus, but the truth is, they want you to grease the bad guys and not bother them with details."

"I can't believe I'm the sheriff of this county and I have to listen to this. And I mean listen to it every day."

"That's the problem. Your heart is too big. You need to be more assertive. Ask Maydeen." Pam took the binoculars from his hand and replaced them in the leather case and dropped the case on the driver's seat. "I say too much?"

"No, why would you possibly think that?" he replied.

But Pam's hands were on her hips, and she was obviously thinking about something else. "This woman is supposed to perform miracles? She's Our Lady of Lourdes out on the plains?"

"No," he said. "No, I mean I don't know. I can't keep up with your conversation. I can't track your thoughts, Pam. You're impossible to talk with."

"What you're not hearing is that other people know your weak spot. Don't let this Chinese broad jerk you around. Too many people around here already hate your guts. Wake up. You're kind to the wrong people."

"I don't see it that way. Not at all."

"That's exactly what I'm talking about."

Hackberry fitted on his Stetson and widened his eyes, letting the moment pass, his

34

face tight in the wind. "When we talk with this lady, we remember who we are. We treat people with respect, particularly when they've paid their share of dues."

"People with causes have a way of letting others do their time on the cross. Tell me I'm full of shit. I double-dare you."

Hackberry felt as if someone had set a small nail between his eyes and slowly tapped it into his head with a tack hammer.

It was hard to estimate the age of the Asian woman who came to the door. She had a compact figure, and wore dark glasses and a white dress with black ribbon threaded through the top of the bodice, and looked no older than a woman in her early forties. But Darl Wingate, the coroner, had told Hackberry that she had lived through Japanese incendiary raids and the massacre of Chinese civilians by Japanese troops, and perhaps had worked for Claire Chennault's Civil Air Transport. The latter had overtones Hackberry didn't want to think about.

He removed his hat when he stepped inside and let his eyes adjust to the poorly lit interior of her home. The furniture looked second-hand, the couch and chairs covered with cheap fabric, the rugs threadbare, an ancient glass wall case stuffed with books probably bought at yard sales. "We're looking for a man who may have been an intended victim in a homicide, Ms. Ling," he said.

"Why do you think he's here?" she asked.

Through the back window he could see a stucco cottage by a slat-wall barn, alongside a flat-roofed, oblong building that once could have been a bunkhouse. "Because you live in the middle of an unofficial international highway?" he said.

"What's this man's name?" she asked.

"We don't know. The FBI does, but we don't," he answered.

"I see. Well, I don't think he's here."

"He might have a manacle on one wrist, but we can't be sure of that. I suspect he's terrified and desperate," Hackberry said. "The man he may have been manacled to was tortured to death by six men carrying rifles. They probably came out of Mexico."

"If this man is desperate, why wouldn't he come to you?" the Asian woman said.

"My guess is he doesn't trust the authorities."

"But he would trust me?"

"We're not with ICE or the Border Patrol, ma'am," Pam said.

"I gathered that from your uniform and your badge."

"The point is, we're not worried about somebody feeding or sheltering wets," Pam said. "They've been with us a long time."

"Yes, they have, haven't they?"

Pam seemed to think about the implication of the statement, plainly wondering if the barb was intentional or imaginary. "I was admiring your side room there. Is that a statue of the Virgin Mary in front of all those burning candles?"

"Yes, it is."

"It doesn't weep blood, does it?" Pam asked.

"Ms. Ling, if you don't feel you can confide in us, talk with the FBI. The man we're looking for barely escaped a terrible fate," Hackberry said.

If his suggestion had any viability at all, it did not show in the Asian woman's face. "I'll keep in mind what you've said," she replied.

Pam Tibbs's arms were folded on her chest. She gave Hackberry a look, waiting for him to speak, the fingers of her right hand opening and closing, her breath audible.

Hackberry took the manila folder from his side pocket and removed the sheaf of eight-by-ten photos. "These were taken today at a crime scene no more than a half hour from your house. What you see here was done by men who have no parameters, Miss Anton. We have a witness who indicates the victim gave up the name La Magdalena before he died. We think the torture death of the victim was conducted by a man called Krill. That's why we're here now. We don't want these men to hurt you or anyone to whom you may have given shelter. Have you heard of a man named Krill?"

Her eyes held on his. They were dark, unblinking, perhaps containing memories or knowledge she seldom shared with others. "Yes," she replied. "Three or four years ago, there was a coyote by that name. He robbed the people who paid him to take them across. Some say he raped the women."

"Where is he now?"

"He disappeared."

"Do you know how he came by his name?"

"He was a machine-gunner somewhere in Central America. His nickname came from the food of the whale. He ate the 'krill' in large numbers."

It was silent in the room. Hackberry glanced through the door of the side room, which must have served as a chapel of some kind. Perhaps thirty or forty candles were burning in red and blue and purple vessels, the light of the flames flickering on the base of the statue. "You Catholic, Miss Anton?" he said.

"That depends on whom you talk to."

"Expecting some visitors tonight?" When she didn't reply, he said, "Can we look out back?"

"Why do you ask me? You'll do it whether I like it or not."

"No, that's not correct," Pam replied. "We don't have a search warrant. We'll do it with your permission, or we can get a warrant and come back."

"Do whatever you wish."

"Excuse me, ma'am, but what if we just leave you alone here?" Pam said. "Would you prefer that? Then you can deal with Mr. Krill and his friends on your own."

"We'll wander out back, if you don't mind," Hackberry said, placing a business card on the coffee table. Then he smiled. "Is it true you worked for Civil Air Transport, Claire Chennault's old airline?"

"I did."

"It's an honor to meet you."

Minutes later, outside in the wind, Pam Tibbs's throat was still bladed with color, her back stiff with anger. " 'An honor to meet you'?" she said. "What the hell is that? She's a horse's ass."

"Look at it from her point of view."

"She doesn't have one."

"She stands up for people who have no power. Why not give the devil her due?"

Pam went inside the stucco cottage, then came back out, letting the screen slam behind her. "Check it out. There's a mattress in there soaked in blood, and bandages are scattered all over the floor. The blood is still sticky. I bet that guy was here while we were talking in the house. What was that stuff about Claire Chennault's airline?"

"It was a CIA front that became Air America. They supplied the Laotian resistance and flew in and out of the Golden

Triangle."

"They transported opium?"

Hackberry removed his hat and knocked a dent out of the crown and put it back on. He felt old in the way people feel old when they have more knowledge of the world than they need. In the south the sky was blackening in the sunset, and dust was rising off the hills. "I think it's fixing to blow," he said.

Krill squatted on the edge of the butte and looked out at the desert and at the red sun cooling on the horizon. The sky had turned green when the wind drove the rain from the west, and dust devils were spinning across the landscape below, the air blooming with a smell that was like wet flowers and chalk. He had washed his body with a rag and canteen water, and now his skin felt cool in the breeze and the layer of warm air that had risen from the desert and broken apart in the evening sky. His eyes were a milky blue, his expression composed, his skin dusky and dry and smooth and clean inside his wind-puffed shirt. As often happened in these solitary moments, Krill thought about a village in a country far to the south, its perimeter sealed by jungle, a dead volcano in the distance. Across the road from the house where he had lived, three children played in a dirt yard in front of the clinic that had been constructed by East Germans and burned by the army. In

40

Krill's reverie, the children turned to look at him, their faces lighting with recognition. Then their faces disappeared, as though airbrushed from his life.

"What we gonna do now, *jefe?*" Negrito said, squatting down next to him. He wore a greasy leather flop hat pushed back on his head, his hair curling like flames from under it.

Because Negrito was of mixed blood and his first language was bastardized English, he believed he and Krill were brothers in arms. But Krill neither liked nor trusted Negrito, whose facial features resembled those of an orange baboon that had fallen into a tub of bleach.

Krill continued to gaze at the desert and the way the light pooled in the clouds even though the sun had already set.

"Don't believe that stuff about La Magdalena. She ain't got no power, man," Negrito said. "You know what they say about *puta* from over there. It's sideways. That's the only difference."

Krill's expression never changed, as though Negrito's words were confetti falling on a flat stone. Out of the corner of his eye, he could see Negrito leaning forward, dangerously close to the edge of the bluff, trying to earn his attention.

"Why's this guy so important?" Negrito asked. "He got a lot of dope hid someplace?"

"See down there below?" Krill said. "That's a coyote den. See in that creek bed? Those are cougar tracks. The cougar has to kill fifty fawns to feed just one kitten. Except there aren't fifty fawns around here. That means the coyote's pups have to die instead."

Negrito's eyes went back and forth as he tried to puzzle through Krill's statement. In the fading spark of sun on the horizon, his face was as rosy as a drunkard's, his jutting forehead knurled, his mouth ringed with whiskers. "I'll get it out of her. You say the word, *jefe*. She'll be asking for knee pads," he said.

Krill stared into Negrito's face. "I'm not your chief. I'm nobody's chief. You follow me or you don't follow me."

Negrito brushed one hand on top of the other, the horned edges of his palms rasping like sandpaper, his gaze avoiding Krill's. He rocked on his heels, the points of his cowboy boots inches from the edge of the bluff. "You need a woman. It ain't natural to be out here long without a woman. We all need a woman. Maybe we ought to go back to Durango for a while."

Krill stood up and looked at the other men, all of whom were cooking pieces of jackrabbits they had killed and dressed and speared on sticks above a fire they had built inside a circle of stones. He picked up his rifle and put it across his shoulders and draped his

42

arms over either end of it, creating a silhouette like that of a crucified man. "In the morning," he said.

"We get out of here in the morning?" Negrito said. "Maybe to Durango?"

"You heard me, *hombre.*"

"Where you going now?"

"You'll hear one shot. It'll be for the cougar. You hear more than one shot, that means I found some real pissed-off gringos out there."

"Because of what we done to that cop?"

"He worked for the DEA."

"Man, you didn't tell us that."

"You still want to go after La Magdalena?"

Negrito's eyes contained no emotion, as though they were prosthetic and had been inserted into his face by an indifferent thumb. He stared emptily at the desert, his eyelids fluttering when a cloud of bats lifted from a cave opening down below. Then he looked into the darkness, perhaps considering options, entertaining thoughts he hid by rubbing his forehead, shielding his eyes.

"You think too much, Negrito," Krill said. "When a man thinks too much, he's tempted to go beyond his limitations."

Negrito stood up and took off his hat. "Watch this," he said. He flipped his hat in the air, then scooted under it, catching it squarely on his head, his face splitting into an ape's grin. He wobbled slightly, his arms straight out for balance, rocks spilling from

43

under his boots over the edge of the bluff. "*Chingado,* that scared me. Don't worry, *jefe.* I'll always back you up. I don't care about no pissed-off gringos or Chinese *puta* that thinks her shit don't stink, either. You're my *jefe* whether you like it or not. I love you, *hermano.*"

Hackberry Holland had come to believe that age was a separate country you did not try to explain to younger people, primarily because they had already made up their minds about it and any lessons you had learned from your life were not the kind many people were interested in hearing about. If age brought gifts, he didn't know what they were. It had brought him neither wisdom nor peace of mind. His level of desire was the same, the lust of his youth glowing hot among the ashes each morning he woke. He could say with a degree of satisfaction that he didn't suffer fools and drove from his company anyone who tried to waste his time, but otherwise his dreams and his waking day were defined by the same values and frame of reference that came with his birthright. If age had marked a change in him, it lay in his acceptance that loneliness and an abiding sense of loss were the only companions some people would ever have.

The most influential event in Hackberry's life had been his marriage to Rie Velasquez, a labor organizer for the United Farm Workers of America. When she died of uterine cancer, Hackberry had sold his ranch on the Guadalupe River and moved down to the border, leaving behind all memory of the idyllic life they'd shared, ridding himself of the things she had touched that made him so lonely he wanted to drink again, embracing the aridity of a parched land and its prehistoric ambience and its violent sunsets, the way a Bedouin enters the emptiness of the desert and is subsumed and made insignificant by it. Then bit by bit the horse farm he bought became a hologram, a place that fused past and present and re-created his childhood and adolescence and his life with Rie and their twin sons in one shimmering, timeless vision. It was a place where a man could see his beginning and his end, an island that was governed by reason and stewardship and the natural ebb and flow of the seasons, a place where a man no longer had to fear death.

He had two good wells on his land, and a four-stall barn and two railed pastures where he grazed his quarter horses and registered Missouri foxtrotters. He was also the unofficial owner of three dogs, a one-eyed cat, and two raccoons, none of whom had names but whom he fed outside the barn every morning and night.

His house was painted battleship gray and had a wide gallery and a breezy screened

45

porch in back and a rock garden and a deep-green lawn he watered with soak hoses and flower beds planted with roses he entered each summer in the competition at the county fair. A china-berry tree grew in his backyard, and a slender palm tree grew at the base of the hill behind the house. He built a brooder house on the side of the barn, and his chickens laid eggs all over the property, under his tractor and in his tack room. On each of his horse tanks he had constructed small ladders out of chicken wire that he wrapped over the lip of the tank, so small creatures that fell into the water could find their way out again. In one way or another, every day that he spent on his ranch became part of an ongoing benediction.

The two gun cases in his office held a Henry repeater, an 1873 Winchester, a .45–70 trapdoor of the kind the Seventh Cavalry carried into the Little Big Horn, an '03 Springfield, a German Luger, a nine-millimeter Beretta, a Ruger Buntline .22 Magnum, and the converted .44 Navy Colt his grandfather, Old Hack, had carried the morning he knocked John Wesley Hardin from his saddle and kicked him cross-eyed and nailed him down with chains in a wagon bed before transporting him to the Cuero jail.

Hackberry loved the place he lived, and he loved waking inside its soft radiance in the morning, and he loved following his grand-

46

father's admonition to feed his animals before he fed himself. He loved the smell of his roses inside the coolness of the dawn and the smell of well water bursting into the horse tank when he released the chain on the windmill. He loved the warm odor of grass on the breath of his horses and the vinegary smell of their coats, and the powdery green cloud of hay particles that rose around him when he pulled a bale apart and scattered it on the concrete pad in the barn.

All of these things were part of the Texas in which he had grown up, and they were unsoiled by political charlatans and avaricious corporations and neocolonial wars being waged under the banner of God. He did not tell others about the bugles blowing in the hills, less out of fear that they would suspect him of experiencing auditory delusions than out of his own conviction that the bugles were real and that from the time of Cortés to the present, a martial and savage spirit had ruled these hills and it was no coincidence that a sunset in this fine place looked like the electrified blood of Christ.

Early on the morning after he and Pam Tibbs had interviewed the Asian woman known by the Mexicans as La Magdalena, Hackberry looked out his bathroom window and saw Ethan Riser park his government motor-pool car by the front gate and walk up the flagstones to the front entrance, holding

47

two Styrofoam containers on top of each other, pausing briefly to admire the flowers in the bed. Hackberry rinsed the shaving cream off his face and stepped out on the veranda. "This can't wait till eight o'clock?" he said.

"It could. Or maybe I could come back another day, when you're not tied up with something important, like shaving," Riser said.

"I have to feed my animals."

"I'll help you."

Ethan Riser's hair was as white as cotton and had all the symmetry of meringue. His nose and cheeks were threaded with tiny blue and red capillaries, and his stomach and hips protruded over the narrow hand-tooled western belt he wore with a conventional business suit and tie. He had been with the FBI almost forty years.

"Fix some coffee while I'm down at the barn," Hackberry said.

Twenty minutes later, he returned to the house through the back door and washed his hands in the kitchen sink.

"You got a reason for always making it hard?" Riser said.

"None I can think of."

"Why didn't you call me about the homicide south of that Indian's property?"

"It's not a federal case. It's not y'all's damn business, either."

48

"You're wrong about that, my friend. The victim was a DEA informant."

"It's still our case. Stay out of it."

"Beg your pardon?"

"I've been on a need-to-know basis with y'all before. I always had the feeling I was a hangnail."

"The informant's name was Hector Lopez. He was a dirty cop from Mexico City who worked both sides of the fence. Our people weren't entirely comfortable with him. Lopez and a physician once tortured a DEA agent to death."

"I remember that case. The physician went down for it. Why not the dirty cop?"

"That's the way it is. I'm sharing this with you because we can help each other."

The microwave made a dinging sound. Ethan Riser took out the two Styrofoam containers and opened them on the breakfast table. They contained scrambled eggs and hash browns and sausage patties smothered with milk gravy. He took the coffeepot off the stove and set cups and silverware on the table. Hackberry watched him. "Does everything meet the standard here? My house tidy enough, that sort of thing?" he said.

"We talked to Danny Boy Lorca already," Riser said. "He gave us the name of this guy Krill. Have any idea who he is?"

Hackberry hung his hat on the back of his chair and sat down to eat. "Nothing real

49

specific other than the fact he's a killer."

"We think he takes hostages and sells them," Riser said. "The guy we want is the guy who was on the other end of the cable locked on the dead man's wrist. We think he's the federal employee we've been looking for."

"What kind of federal employee is he?"

Riser went silent. Hackberry put down his fork and knife. "Tell you what, Ethan," he said. "This is my home. People can be rude whenever and wherever they want. But not in my kitchen and not at my table."

"He's a Quaker who should have been screened out of the job he was assigned to. It's the government's fault."

"I guess Jefferson should have gotten rid of Benjamin Franklin at first opportunity."

"Franklin was a Quaker?" When Hackberry didn't answer, Riser said, "Your flowers are lovely. I told you my father was a botanist, didn't I? He grew every kind of flower mentioned in Shakespeare's plays."

Hackberry got up from the table and poured his breakfast into the trash can and wiped his hands on a piece of paper towel. "I'm running late. Can you let yourself out?" he said.

"I've tried to put you in the loop."

"Is that what y'all call snake oil?" Hackberry said.

Through her windshield Pam Tibbs saw the

oversize pickup on a winding stretch of isolated two-lane road that was spiderwebbed with heat cracks and broken so badly in places that it was hardly passable. The road went nowhere and had little utilitarian value. The sedimentary formations protruding in layers from the hillsides had been spray-painted by high school kids, and the areas under the mesas where the kids parked their cars at night were often littered with beer cans and used condoms. The road dipped over a rise and ended at the entrance to a cattle ranch that had gone out of business with the importation of Argentine beef in the 1960s.

Through the cruiser's windshield, Pam saw the pickup weave off the road, skidding gravel down a wash. Then the driver overcorrected and continued haphazardly down the center-line, ignoring the possibility of another vehicle coming around a bend, as though he were studying a map or texting on a cell phone or steering with his knees. Pam switched on her light bar and closed the distance between her cruiser and the truck. Through the pickup's back window, she saw the driver's eyes lock on hers in the rearview mirror.

When the driver pulled to the shoulder, Pam parked behind him and got out on the asphalt, slipping her baton into the ring on her belt. The truck was brand-new, its hand-buffed waxed yellow finish as smooth and glowing as warm butter, a single star-spangled patriotic sticker glued on the bumper. The driver opened his door and started to get out.

"Stay in your vehicle, sir," Pam said.

The driver drew his leg back inside the truck and closed the door, snugging it tight. Pam could see his face in the outside mirror, his eyes studying her. She heard his glove compartment drop open.

Pam unsnapped the strap on her .357 Magnum. "Put your hands on the steering wheel, sir. Do not touch anything in your glove box." She moved forward but at an angle, away from the driver's window, her palm and thumb cupped over the grips of her holstered revolver. "Did you hear me? You put your hands where I can see them."

"I was getting my registration," the driver said.

"Do not turn away from me. Keep your hands on the wheel."

His hair was gold and cut short, his sideburns long, his eyes a liquid green. She moved closer to the cab. "What are you doing out here?" she asked.

"Taking a drive. Looking through my binoculars."

"Turn off your engine and step out of your vehicle."

"That's what I was trying to do when you told me to get back inside. Which is it?"

"You need to do what I say, sir."

"It's Reverend, if you want to be formal."

"You will step out of the vehicle and do it now, sir," she said.

"I have a pistol on the seat. I use it for rabbits. I'm no threat to you."

She pulled her revolver from its holster and aimed it with both hands at his face. "Put your right hand behind your head, open the door, and get down on the ground."

"Have you heard of the Cowboy Chapel? Don't point that at me." He looked straight into the muzzle of her gun. "I respect the law. You're not going to threaten me with a firearm. My name is Reverend Cody Daniels. Ask anybody."

She jerked the door open with one hand and stepped back. "Down on the ground."

"I will not do that. I will not tolerate your abuse, either. I did nothing to deserve this."

She was holding her .357 with both hands again, the checkered grips biting into her palms. "This is your last chance to avoid a very bad experience, sir."

"Do not call me 'sir.' You're deliberately being disrespectful in order to provoke me. I know your kind, missy."

She was gripping the pistol so tightly, she could feel the barrel tremble. Her temples were pounding, her scalp tight, her eyes stinging with perspiration. She stared at the driver in the silence. The skin around his mouth

53

was bloodless, his gaze iniquitous, dissecting her face, dropping to her throat and her breasts rising and falling inside her shirt. When she didn't move or speak, his eyes seemed to sweep the entirety of her person, noting the loops of sweat under her arms, a lock of her hair stuck on her damp forehead, the width of her hips, the way her stomach strained against her gun belt and the button on her jeans, the fact that her upper arms were as thick as a man's. She saw a smile wrinkle at the corner of his mouth. "You seem a mite unsettled, missy," he said. "Maybe you should be in another line of work."

"Thank you for saying that," she replied. She pulled her can of Mace from her belt and sprayed it in his face and jerked him out of the cab, then sprayed him again. He flailed his arms blindly, his eyes streaming tears, then he slapped at her hands as a child might, as though he were being violated. She threw him against the side of the truck, kicking his feet apart, stiff-arming him in the back of the neck, the tensions of his body coursing like an electric current through her palm.

When he continued to struggle, she slipped her baton from the ring on her belt and whipped it behind his calves. He dropped straight to his knees, as though his tendons had been cut, his mouth open wide, a cry breaking from his throat.

She pushed him facedown on the ground and cuffed his wrists behind him. His left cheek was printed with gravel, his mouth quivering with shock. He wrenched up his head so he could see her. "No hot coal will redeem your tongue, woman. You're a curse on the race. A pox on you and all your kind," he said.

She called in her location. "I've got a lulu here. Ask Hack to pull all the reports we have on somebody who was shooting at illegals," she said.

CHAPTER THREE

Hackberry Holland sat behind his desk and listened to Pam Tibbs's account of the arrest. Outside the window, the American flag was straightening and popping in the wind, the chain rattling on the pole. "What's our minister friend doing now?" he asked.

"Yelling for his phone call," she replied. "How do you read that stuff about a hot coal on my tongue?"

"It's from Isaiah in the Old Testament. Isaiah believed he was a man of unclean lips who dwelled in an unclean land. But an angel placed a burning coal on his tongue and removed his iniquity."

"I'm iniquitous for not letting him kill himself and others in an auto accident?"

"The sheriff in Jim Hogg told me about this guy a couple of months ago. Cody Daniels was a suspect in the bombing of an abortion clinic on the East Coast. He might not have done it himself, but he was at least one of the cheerleaders. He roams around the country and tends to headquarter in places where there's not much money for law enforcement. I didn't know he was here."

She waited for him to continue, but he didn't. "You think he could be the guy taking potshots at the illegals coming across the border?" she said.

"Him or a hundred others like him." Hackberry took off his reading glasses and rubbed his eyes. "Did he threaten you in a specific way?"

"On the way in, he told me I was going to hell."

"Did he say he was going to put you there or see you there?"

"No."

"Did he touch the gun on the seat?"

"Not that I saw."

"Did he make a threatening gesture of any kind?"

"He refused to get out of the vehicle while telling me he was armed."

"He told R.C. you hit him in the head after you cuffed him."

"He fell down against the cruiser. What are you trying to say, Hack?"

"We don't need a lawsuit."

"I don't know if I'm more pissed off by this nutcase or what I'm hearing now."

"It's the kind of lawsuit that could cost us fifty thousand dollars in order to be right."

Hackberry looked up at her in the silence.

57

Pam's eyes were brown, with a reddish tint, and they became charged with light when she was either angry or hurt. She hooked her thumbs in her gun belt and fixed her attention outside the window, her cheeks spotted with color.

"I'm proud of the way you handled it," he said. "You did all the right things. Let's see if our man likes his accommodations."

Hackberry and Pam Tibbs climbed the steel spiral steps in the rear of the building and walked down a corridor of barred cells, past the old drunk tank, to a barred holding unit that contained nothing but a wood bench and a commode with no seat. The man who had identified himself as Reverend Cody Daniels was standing at the window, silhouetted against a sky that had turned yellow with dust.

"I understand you were potting jackrabbits from your pickup truck," Hackberry said.

"I did no such thing," Cody Daniels replied. "It's not against the law, anyway, is it?"

"So you were cruising down the road surveilling the countryside through your binoculars for no particular reason?" Hackberry said.

"What I was looking for is the illegal immigrants and drug transporters who come through here every night."

"You're not trying to steal my job, are you?"

"I go where I've a mind to. When I got up

58

this morning, this was still a free country."

"You bet. But you gave my chief deputy a hard time because she made a simple procedural request of you."

"Check the video camera in your squad car. Truth will out, Sheriff."

"It's broken."

"Pretty much like everything in this town. Mighty convenient, if you ask me."

"What are you doing in my county?"

"Your county?"

"You'd better believe it."

"I'm doing the Lord's work."

"I heard about your activities on the East Coast. We don't have any abortion clinics here, Reverend, but that doesn't mean we'll put up with your ilk."

Cody Daniels approached the bars and rested one hand on the cast-iron plate that formed an apron on the bottom of the food slot. The veins in his wrists were green and as thick as night crawlers, his knuckles pronounced, the back of each finger scarred where a tattoo had been removed. He held Hackberry's gaze. "I have the ability to see into people's thoughts," he said. "Right now you got more problems than your department can handle. That's why you select the likes of me as the target of your wrath. People like me are easy. We pay our taxes and obey the law and try to do what's right. How many drug dealers do you have locked up here?"

"There's a kernel of truth in what you say, Reverend, but I'd like to get this issue out of the way so you can go back to your job and we can go back to ours."

"I think the real problem is you got a romantic relationship going with this woman here."

"Deputy Tibbs, would you get the reverend's possessions envelope out of the locker, please?"

Pam gave Hackberry a look but didn't move.

"I think Reverend Daniels is a reasonable man and is willing to put this behind him," Hackberry said. "I think he'll be more mindful of his driving habits and the next time out not object to the requests of a well-meaning deputy sheriff. Is that a fair statement, Reverend?"

"I'm not given to making promises, particularly when I'm not the source of the problem," Cody Daniels said.

Hackberry drummed his fingers on the apron of the food slot. "Deputy Tibbs, would you get the paperwork started on Reverend Daniels's release?" he said.

"Yes, sir," she replied.

Cody Daniels's eyes followed her down the corridor, his gaze slipping down her back to her wide-ass jeans and the thickness of her thighs. "I guess it's each to his own," he said.

"Pardon?" Hackberry said.

"No offense meant, but I think I'd rather belly up to a spool of barbed wire. That's kind of coarse, but you get the picture."

"I hope you'll accept this in the right spirit, Reverend. If you ever sass one of my deputies or speak disrespectfully of Chief Deputy Tibbs again, I'm going to hunt around in that pile of scrap wood behind the jail until I find a long two-by-four, one with sixteen-penny nails sticking out of it, then I'm going to kick it so far up your ass you'll be spitting splinters. Get the picture? Have a nice day. And stay the hell out of my sight."

Anton Ling heard the man in the yard before she saw him. He had released the chain on the windmill and cupped water out of the spout, drinking it from his hand, while the blades spun and clattered above his head. He was gaunt and wore a short-sleeve shirt with no buttons; his hair hung on his shoulders and looked like it had been barbered with a knife.

"*¿Qué quieres?*" she said.

"*Comida,*" the man replied.

He was wearing tennis shoes. In the moonlight she could see his ribs stenciled against his sides, his trousers flattening in the wind against his legs. She stepped out on the back porch. The shadows of the windmill's blades were spinning on his face. "You didn't come out of Mexico," she said.

61

"How do you know?" he replied in English.

"The patrols are out. They would have stopped you if you came out of the south."

"I hid in the hills during the day. I have no food."

"What is your name?"

"Antonio."

"You are a worker?"

"Only for myself. I am a hunter. Will you feed me?"

She went into her kitchen and put a wedge of cheese and three tortillas on a paper plate, then covered them with chili and beans that she ladled out of a pot that was still warm on the stove. When she went back outside, the visitor was squatted in the middle of the dirt lot, staring at the moon and the lines of cedar posts with no wire. He took the paper plate from her hand and ignored the plastic spoon and instead removed a metal spoon from his back pocket and began eating. A knife in a long thin scabbard protruded at an angle from his belt. "You are very kind, *señora*."

"Where did you learn English?"

"My father was a British sailor."

"What do you hunt, Antonio?"

"In this case, a man."

"Has this man harmed you?"

"No, he has done nothing to me."

"Then why do you hunt him?"

"He's a valuable man, and I am poor."

"You'll not find him here."

62

He stopped eating and pointed at the side of his head with his spoon. "You're very intelligent. People say you have supernatural gifts. But maybe they just don't understand that you are simply much more intelligent than they are."

"The man you are looking for was here, but he's gone now. He will not be back. You must leave him alone."

"Your property is a puzzle. It has fences all over it, but they hold nothing in and nothing out."

"This was a great cattle ranch at one time."

"Now it is a place where the wind lives, one that has no beginning and no end. It's a place like you, *china*. You come from the other side of the earth to do work no one understands. You don't have national frontiers."

"Don't speak familiarly of people you know nothing about."

The man who called himself Antonio lifted the paper plate and pushed the beans and chili and cheese and pieces of tortilla into his mouth. He dropped the empty plate in the dirt and wiped his lips and chin on a bandanna and stood up and washed his spoon in the horse tank and slipped it into his back pocket. "They say you can do the same things a priest can, except you have more power."

"I have none."

"I had three children. They died without baptism." He looked toward the west and the

63

heat lightning pulsing in the sky just above the hills. "Sometimes I think their souls are out there, outside their bodies, lost in the darkness, not knowing where they're supposed to go. You think that's what happens after we're dead? We don't know where to go until someone tells us?"

"How did your children die?"

"They were killed by a helicopter in front of the clinic where they were playing."

"I'm sorry for your loss."

"You can baptize them, *china.*"

"Do not call me that."

"It wasn't their fault they weren't baptized. They call you La Magdalena. You can reach back in time before they were dead and baptize them."

"You should talk to a priest. He will tell you the same thing I do. Your children committed no offense against God. You mustn't worry about them."

"I can't see a priest."

"Why not?"

"I killed one. I think he was French, maybe a Jesuit. I'm not sure. We were told he was a Communist. I machine-gunned him."

Her eyes left his face. She remained motionless inside the pattern of shadow and light created by the moon. "Whom do you work for?" she asked.

"Myself."

"No, you don't. You're paid by others. They

64

use you."

"*Conejo,* you are much woman."

"You will not speak to me like that."

"You didn't let me finish. You are much woman, but you've lied to me. You've given Communion to the people who come here, just like a priest. But you turn me away."

"I think you're a tormented man. But you won't find peace until you give up your violent ways. You tortured and killed the man down south of us, didn't you? You're the one called Krill."

His eyes held hers. They were pale blue, the pupils like cinders. In silhouette, with his long knife-cut hair and torso shaped like an inverted pyramid, he resembled a creature from an earlier time, a warrior suckled in an outworn creed. "The man I killed in the south did very cruel things to my brother. He had a chance to redeem himself by being brave. But he was a coward to the end."

"Others are with you, aren't they? Out there in the hills."

"Others follow me. They are not with me. They can come and go as they wish. Given the chance, some of them would eat me like dogs."

"When you were a coyote, you raped the women who paid you to take them across?"

"A man has needs, *china.* But it wasn't rape. I was invited to their beds."

"Because they had no water to drink or

65

food to eat? Do not come here again, even if you're badly hurt or starving."

The man watched the heat lightning, his hair lying as black as ink on his shoulders. "I can hear my children talking inside the trees," he said. "You have to baptize them, *señora*. It doesn't matter if you want to or not."

"Be gone."

He raised a cautionary finger in the air, the shadow of the windmill blades slicing across his face and body. "Do not treat me with contempt, Magdalena. Think about my request. I'll be back."

Three days later, on Saturday, Hackberry rose at dawn and fixed coffee in a tin pot and made a sandwich out of two slices of sourdough bread and a deboned pork chop he took from the icebox. Then he carried the pot and sandwich and tin cup down to the barn and the railed pasture where he kept his two Missouri foxtrotters, a chestnut and a palomino named Missy's Playboy and Love That Santa Fe. He spread their hay on the concrete pad that ran through the center of the barn, and then he sat down in a wood chair from the tack room and ate his sandwich and drank his coffee while he watched his horses eat. Then he walked out to their tank and filled it to the rim from a frost-proof spigot, using his bare hand to skim bugs and dust and bits of hay from the surface. The

66

water had come from a deep well on his property and was like ice on his fingers and wrist, and he wondered if the coldness hidden under the baked hardpan wasn't a reminder of the event waiting for him just beyond the edge of his vision — an unexpected softening of the light, an autumnal smell of gas pooled in the trees, a bugle echoing off stone in the hills.

No, I will not think about that today, he told himself. The sunrise was pink in the east, the sky blue. His quarter horses were grazing in his south pasture, the irrigated grass riffling in the breeze, and he could see a doe with three yearlings among a grove of shade trees at the bottom of his property. The world was a grand place, a cathedral in its own right, he thought. How had Robert Frost put it? What place could be better suited for love? Hackberry couldn't remember the line.

He slipped a halter on each of the foxtrotters and wormed them by holding their head up with the lead while he worked the disposable syringe into the corner of their mouth and squirted the ivermectin over their tongue and down their throat. Both of them were still colts and liked to provoke him by mashing down on the syringe, holding on until he had to drop the lead and use both hands to pry the flattened plastic cylinder loose from their teeth.

Just when he thought he was done, the

chestnut, Missy's Playboy, grabbed his straw hat and threw it on the branch of a tree, then thundered down the pasture, trailing the lead between his legs, kicking at the air with his hind feet. Hackberry did not hear the woman come up behind him. "I let myself in the gate. I hope you don't mind," she said.

She was wearing khakis and sandals and a white shirt with flowers on it and a white baseball cap with a purple bill. When he didn't answer, she looked around her, uncertain. "You have a beautiful place."

"What can I do for you, Miss Anton?"

"Two nights ago a man came to my house. He said his name was Antonio. But I think he's the man called Krill."

"What did this fellow want?"

"He said he was a hunter. He said he was hunting a man for pay. I told him the man he was looking for had been at my house, but he had gone and wouldn't be there again."

"Why did you wait to report this?"

There was a beat. "I'm not sure."

"You thought you would be violating a confidence?"

"This man is deeply troubled. In part, I think he came to me for help. Why are you shaking your head?"

"Don't be disingenuous about these guys. You know what the conversion rate is on death row? Try a hundred percent. Turn them loose and see what happens."

68

"You believe the state has the right to kill people?"

"No."

"Why not?"

"Who cares?"

"Sheriff, I came here as an act of conscience. This man probably won't harm me, but eventually, he'll kill others. So I had to come here."

"You don't think he'll hurt you? Why should you get an exemption?"

"Three of his children were killed by a helicopter gunship. He believes their spirits will wander until they're baptized. He thinks somehow I can baptize them retroactively. He says he can't take his problem to a priest because he murdered a French Jesuit."

"I think you're dealing with someone who's morally insane, Miss Anton. I think it's both naive and dangerous to pretend otherwise. Who's he working for?"

"I asked him that. He wouldn't say."

"Who's the guy you gave refuge to?"

"A man of peace. A man who became involved in a military program that kills innocent people."

"Has the FBI interviewed you?"

"No."

"When they do, I suggest you give them a better answer than the one you just gave me. You were in the employ of Air America in Indochina, Miss Anton. People who have a lot of guilt have a way of showing up under one flag or another."

She took a Ziploc bag from her pocket. In it was a dirty paper plate. "Antonio ate from this. I suspect it will be of some help to you."

"Why are both the FBI and Krill after the same man?"

"Ask them. Before I go, I need to straighten out something. My work has nothing to do with guilt. We live in a country that has created a huge serving class of illegals who work for low pay at jobs Americans won't do. We get along very well with these people during prosperous times. But as soon as the economy goes down, they're treated like dirt. You're obviously an intelligent and educated man. Why don't you act like it?"

She turned and began walking back toward the gate. Then she stopped and faced him again. For some reason, her baseball cap and her tight-fitting flowered shirt made her look younger and smaller than she was. "One other thing, sir," she said. "Why do you look at me so strangely? It's quite rude."

Because you remind me of my beloved wife, he thought.

The Reverend Cody Daniels had carpentered his house to resemble the forecastle of a ship, up on a bluff that overlooked a wide arid bowl flanked by hills that contained layers of both red and chalk-colored stone, giving them in the sunset the striped appearance of a freshly sliced strawberry cake. A sandstone bluff rose straight into the air behind the house, and on it he had painted a huge American flag, one that was of greater dimension than the roof itself. In the evening, Cody Daniels liked to walk back and forth on his front deck, surveying the valley below, sometimes gazing at the southern horizon through the telescope mounted on the deck rail, sometimes simply taking pleasure in the presence of his possessions — his canary-yellow pickup, his horse trailer, his cistern up on the hill, his silver propane tanks that ensured he would never be cold, the smell of the game he had shot or beef he had butchered dripping into the ash inside his smokehouse, the wood shell of a church that came with the property down on the hardpan, a building he had given a second life by putting pews inside it and a blue-white neon cross above the front door.

Some evenings, after the last wash of gold light on the eastern side of the valley had risen into the sky and disappeared like smoke breaking apart in the wind, he would focus his telescope on a gingerbread house far to the south and watch the events that seemed to unfold there two or three times a week.

When the evening star rose above the hills, Cody Daniels could see small groups of people moving out of the haze that constituted the Mexican border — like lice fleeing a flame, he thought, carrying their possessions in backpacks and knotted blankets, their children stringing behind them, not unlike nits.

He had heard about the woman who lived in the gingerbread house. The wets coming across the border knelt before her altar and believed the glow of votive candles burning at the base of a statue somehow signaled they had reached a safe harbor. Not true, Cody Daniels thought. Not as long as he had the power to send them back where they came from. Not as long as there were still patriots willing to act independently of a government that had been taken over by mud people who were giving away American jobs to the beaners.

Cody could have tapped just three digits into his phone console and brought the authorities down on the Asian woman's head. The fact that he didn't made him swell with a sense of power and control that was rare in his life. The Asian woman, without even knowing it, was in his debt. Sometimes she passed him on the sidewalk in town, or pushing a basket in the grocery store, her eyes aimed straight ahead, ignoring his tip of his hat. He wondered what she would say if she knew what he could do to her. He wondered how she would enjoy her first cavity search in a federal facility. He wondered if she would

72

be so regal in a shower room full of bull dykes.

On the deck this evening, with the wind cool on his face, he should have felt at peace. But the memory of his treatment by the deputy sheriff, the one named Tibbs, was like a thumbtack pressed into his scalp. His eyes had the cupped look of an owl's from the Mace she had squirted into them. The baton stroke she had laid across the back of his calves flared to life each time he took a step. Then, for reasons he didn't understand, the thought of her slamming him against the truck, of forcing him on his face and kneeing him in the spine and hooking him up, brought about a weakening in his throat, a stiffening in his loins, and fantasies in which he and the woman were in a soundproof room that had no windows.

But Cody did not like to pursue fantasies of this kind, because they contained images and guilty sensations that made no sense to him. It was not unlike watching two or three frames of a film — an image of her hand flying out at his face, a fingernail cutting his cheek — and refusing to see what was on the rest of the spool.

Unconsciously, he rubbed the dime-sized pieces of scar tissue on the back of his fingers. Long ago, when he was hardly more than a boy riding freight trains across the American West, he had learned lessons he would take

73

to the grave: You didn't sass a railroad bull; you didn't sass a hack on a county penal farm; and you didn't put tattoos on your body that told people you were nobody and deserving of whatever they did to you. You rinsed their abuse off your skin and out of your soul; you became somebody else, and once you did, you no longer had to feel shame about the person who somehow had brought degradation upon himself.

Then you did to others what had been done to you, freeing yourself forever of the role of victim. Or at least that was what some people did. But he hadn't done that, he told himself. He was a minister. He had an associate of arts degree. Truckers talked about him on their CBs. He handed out pocket Bibles to rodeo cowboys behind the bucking chutes. Attractive waitresses warmed up his coffee for free and called him Reverend. He wrote letters of recommendation for parolees. He had baptized drunkards and meth addicts by submersion in a sandy pool by the river that was as red as the blood of Christ. How many men with his background could say the same? And he had done it all without therapists or psychiatrists or titty-baby twelve-step groups.

But his self-manufactured accolades brought him no solace. He had been bested by Sheriff Holland's chief deputy and, in a perverse way, had enjoyed it. He had been threatened with bodily harm by the sheriff, as though he were white trash. And while all this was happening, an Oriental woman was openly aiding the wets and getting christened for her efforts as La Magdalena. Anything wrong with this picture?

Maybe it was time to let Miss Chop Suey 1969 know who her neighbors were.

In the fading twilight he drove in his pickup down the long, tire-worn dirt track that traversed the valley from his house to the county road that eventually led to the southern end of the Asian woman's property. He passed two abandoned oil storage tanks that had turned to rust, a burned-out shack where a deranged tramp sometimes stayed, and a private airstrip blown with tumbleweed, the air sock bleached of color. He turned onto the Asian woman's property and passed a paint-skinned gas-guzzler driven by two men who were sitting on a hillside, staring north at the Asian woman's compound. They were smoking hand-rolled cigarettes and wore new straw hats and boots that were curled up at the toes. One of them pulled on a bottle that had no label, and gargled with whatever was inside before he swallowed. The other man, the taller of the two, had a pair of binoculars hanging from his neck. His shirt was open on his chest, and his skin looked as brown and smooth as clay from a riverbank. Cody Daniels nodded at him but didn't know why. The man either ignored or took no notice of

Cody's gesture.

If you want to live in this country, why don't you show some manners? Cody thought.

He drove between the gateless walls of the Asian woman's compound and was surprised by what he saw. Mexicans were eating from paper plates on the gallery and the front steps and at a picnic table under a willow in the middle of the yard. Obviously, no effort was being made to conceal their presence. He got down from his truck and immediately saw the Asian woman staring at him from the gallery. She was the only person among all the people there who looked directly at him. She stepped into the yard and walked toward him, her eyes never losing contact with his. He felt himself clear his throat involuntarily.

"What are you doing here?" she asked.

"Introducing myself. I live up yonder, in the bluffs. I'm Reverend Cody Daniels, pastor of the Cowboy Chapel."

"I know who you are. You're a nativist and not here on a good errand."

"A what?"

"State your business."

"Who are all these people?"

"Friends of mine."

"Got their papers, do they?"

"Why don't you ask them?"

"I don't speak Spanish."

"You have a cell phone?"

"Yeah, I do, but the service isn't real good

76

here. Want to borrow it?" He felt the open door of his truck hit him in the back.

"Either call 911 or leave."

"I didn't come here to cause trouble."

"I think you did."

"I try to save souls, just like you. I saw y'all from my deck up there, that's all. I got a telescope. I'm an amateur astronomer."

She stepped closer to him. "Let me see your hands."

"Ma'am?"

"I won't hurt you."

"I know that," he said, half laughing.

"Then let me see your hands."

He held them out, palms up, in front of her. But then she turned them over and moved her thumbs across the scar tissue on the back of his fingers. "You were in prison, weren't you?" she said.

"I don't know if I'd call it prison." He paused. "I was on a county farm in New Mexico when I was a boy."

"You had your tattoos removed when you came out?"

"I did it myself. Burned them off with acid and took out the leftover flesh with nail clippers." He started to pull his hands away from her, but she held on to them. He grinned. "I know what you're gonna say. You're gonna tell me I had 'love' and 'hate' on my fingers, aren't you? Well, I didn't. I guess that shows how much you know."

77

"No, you had the letters B-O-R-N tattooed on your left hand, the letter T on your left thumb, the letter O on your right thumb, and L-O-S-E on your right hand. Who taught you such a terrible concept about yourself?"

"I had no such thing on there."

"Why do you feel guilty over things that weren't your fault? You were just a boy. People hurt you and tried to rob you of your innocence. You don't have to be ashamed of what happened to you. You don't have to be afraid of people who look different or speak a different language."

He felt himself swallowing. Through the wetness in his eyes, he saw the people in the yard and on the steps and gallery shimmer and go in and out of focus. "I'm not afraid of anything. If I ever catch up with the sonsof-bitches who did what they did, you'll see how afraid I am."

She squeezed both of his hands tightly in hers. "You have to forgive them."

He tried to pull away from her again, but she held on. He said, "I hope those men go to hell. I hope they burn from the top down and the bottom up. I hope Satan himself pours liquid fire down their throats."

"Would you drink poison in order to get even with others?"

"Sell that Dr. Phil douche rinse to some-body else. They draped me across a sawhorse. I was seventeen. You ever been raped? You wouldn't be so damn quick to advise if you had."

"Stay and eat with us."

"Are you out of your mind, woman? Let go of me."

But she didn't. She squeezed his hands tighter, her face staring intently up into his. He freed one of his hands and used it to pull her other hand off his and fling it from him. He got into his truck and started the engine and rammed the transmission into reverse. He steered by glancing over his shoulder, the pedal to the floor, scouring dirt out of the yard, so he would not have to look into the Asian woman's face again.

How had she gotten into his head? How did she know his history with such accuracy? He had always claimed he could read people's thoughts. But that wasn't true. He could read personalities, character traits, and especially secret designs that hid in the eyes of a manipulator. Every survivor could. That was how you became a survivor. But she was the real thing. She had seen into his past in a way no one ever had, and that thought made him grind his molars.

The purple haze he had seen earlier had spread across the valley floor, and he had to turn on his headlights to see his way down the dirt track to the county road. He had forgotten about the two Mexicans who had been smoking on the hillside earlier; he had even temporarily forgotten the rudeness one of them had shown Cody when he tried to say hello. The two men had gotten back into the gas-guzzler, and evidently had decided to stop and urinate at a spot where the dirt track was pinched on either side by big piles of rock.

He slowed his pickup and hit his high beams, drenching the two figures with an electric brilliance, carving their rounded spines, their splayed knees, the cupping of their phalluses, the amber arc of their urination out of the darkened landscape.

The license plate on the gas-guzzler was dented and filmed with a patina of dried mud and attached to the bumper with coat-hanger wire. Cody could see COAHUILA at the bottom of the plate. He mashed on his horn, holding the button down, clicking his high beams on and off, while the two men stuffed their phalluses back in their pants, their eyes glinting like glass.

The shorter of the two men walked toward Cody's truck, shielding his eyes from the glare with one hand. His jaw was as heavy-looking as a mule's shoe, his forehead ridged like a washboard, his hair and chin stubble the color of rust. "You got a problem, *chico?*" he said.

"*Chico?*" Cody said.

"That means 'boy,' " the man with orange hair said. "You got a problem, *chico* boy?"

80

"Yeah, how about getting your shitbox off the road? Also, find a public restroom and stop polluting the countryside. There's one at the truck stop up on the four-lane. It's got a dispenser of toilet-seat covers on the wall. The sign on the dispenser says MEXICAN PLACE MATS. That's how you'll know you're in the restroom."

"This is a funny guy here," the man called back to his friend. "Come up here and listen. He is very funny."

Cody looked in his rearview mirror and could see only a dim glow from the compound of the Asian woman. The stars seemed to arch overhead and stretch beyond the horizon and curve over the earth's rim. "I need to get about my business. How about it?" He lifted his finger to indicate their vehicle, but his hand felt disconnected from his wrist, lighter than it should.

"What is your business, *señor?*" said the man with a jaw like a mule's shoe, leaning in the window, his breath rife with onions and mescal, the whites of his eyes a watery red.

"I'm a preacher."

"Hey, *jefe,* the funny gringo is a preacher. That's why he called my car a shitbox and shone his headlights on us while we were relieving ourselves."

The second man approached Cody's window, touching his friend on the shoulder, indicating he should move aside. "That's

81

right? You're a preacher?" he said.

"Reverend Cody Daniels. But I got to be getting on my way."

"You work with La Magdalena?"

"I'm just a neighbor making a neighborly visit. I live up yonder, in the bluffs. I got people waiting on me."

The tall man's shoulders seemed unnaturally wide for his thin waist. His profile made Cody think of an ax blade. "Why are you so nervous?" the man asked. "I do something to make you nervous? You have never seen somebody relieve himself on a road in the dark?"

"You got a pistol stuck down in your belt. That's what some might call carrying a concealed weapon. In this county I wouldn't mess with the law."

The tall man fingered his cheek, then pointed at Cody. "I think I know you."

"No, sir, I don't think that's the case."

The tall man jiggled his finger playfully. "You are like me, a hunter. I've seen you down on the border. You hunt coyotes. Except these are coyotes with two feet."

"Not me. No, sir."

"No? You're not the man who likes to look through a telescope?"

"I just want to be on my way."

"What did you see up there at the house of *la china*?"

"Of *la* what?"

82

"You seem like one stupid gringo, my friend. Do I have to say it again?"

"If you're talking about the Chinese woman, I saw the same thing you saw through your binoculars — a bunch of people stuffing food in their faces."

"You were watching us?"

"No, sir, I passed you on the road here, that's all. I wasn't paying y'all any mind."

"You're one big liar, gringo."

"That woman up yonder is your problem, not me."

"You're a *cobarde,* too."

"I don't know what that means."

"You're a coward. You stink of fear. I think maybe you're a *cobarde* that shot at me once. A man up in the rocks with a rifle. You were far away, safe from somebody shooting back at you."

"No, sir," Cody said, shaking his head.

"What we going to do with you, man?"

"I'm gonna turn out on the hardpan and drive around those rocks and let y'all be. You're right, sir, none of this is my business."

"That's not what's going to happen, man. You see Negrito over there? He drinks too much. He's a *marijuanista,* too. When he drinks and smokes all that dope, you know what he likes to do? It's because he was in jail too long in Jalisco, where he was provided young boys by his fellow criminals. Now when he drinks and smokes marijuana, Negrito thinks he's back in Jalisco. If you try to drive out of here before I tell you, you will learn a lot more about your feminine side than you want to know."

"Don't be talking to me like that. No, sir."

The shorter man, the one called Negrito, opened the passenger door and sat down heavily in the seat. He smiled and touched the side of Cody's head and ran one finger behind his ear. "You got gold hair," he said. He touched Cody's cheek and tried to insert the tip of his finger in his mouth. "Mexican place mats, huh? That's really funny, gringo."

"You get him out of here," Cody said to the tall man.

"*La china* is hiding a friend of ours, a man who has gone insane and is wandering in the desert and needs his family. You need to find out where *la china* is hiding our friend. Then you need to build a fire and pour motor oil on it so the smoke climbs straight up in the sky. If you call anybody, if you make trouble for us, we're going to get you, man."

"I won't do it," Cody said.

"Oh, you're going to do it. Show him, Negrito."

The man named Negrito fitted his hand over the top of Cody's head, his fingers splaying like the points of a starfish. When he tightened his fingers, the pressure was instantaneous, as though cracks were forming in Cody's skull.

"I crushed bricks with my hands in a carnival," Negrito said. "I ate lightbulbs, too. I could blow fire out of my mouth with kerosene. I snapped a bull's neck. I can punch my fingers through your stomach and take out your liver, man. Don't pull on my wrist. I'm just gonna squeeze tighter."

"Please stop," Cody said.

When Negrito released his grip, Cody's eyes were bulging from his head, tears running down his cheeks, his ears thundering.

"When I see the smoke climbing up from the bluffs, I'll know you'll have something good to report," the tall man said. "If I don't see any smoke, I will be disappointed in you. Negrito is going to stake you out on the ground in the hot sun. Your voice is going to speak to the birds high up in the sky. Maybe for two or three days. You will learn to yodel, man."

"I was just driving down the road. All I did was blow my horn," Cody said.

"Yes, I have to say you're a very unlucky gringo," the tall man said.

They were both laughing at him, their work done, Cody's self-respect in tatters, the person he used to think of as the Reverend Daniels gone from inside the truck.

"What you done to have this kind of luck, man?" Negrito asked, caressing Cody's cheek with the back of his wrist. "Maybe you just act like you're a funny man. Maybe you've done some things you want to tell me and Krill about. Things that make you feel real bad. You're a nice boy. We're gonna be good friends." He leaned close to Cody's ear and whispered, his breath like a feather on Cody's skin. Then he withdrew his mouth and smiled. "You gringos call it pulling a train. But in your case, I'm gonna be the train, the big choo-choo in your life, man."

CHAPTER FOUR

Hackberry Holland had given the paper plate used by Krill to the FBI. That was on a Monday. The next day he heard nothing but marked it off to the workload that beset all law enforcement agencies. On Wednesday he began making calls, none of which were returned. Nor were they returned on Thursday. Late Friday afternoon Maydeen Stoltz came into his office. She had fat arms and wore too much lipstick and smelled of cigarettes and took a pagan joy in her own irreverence. Hackberry had been reading a book he had checked out of the public library. He closed it and let his arm rest on the cover. "That fed was on the phone," Maydeen said.

"Which fed?"

"The one who uses the department to wipe his ass on."

"Good heavens, Maydeen —"

"If it was me, I'd slap him upside the head, I don't care how old he is."

"Would you kindly tell me who we're talking about?"

"Ethan Riser, who'd you think?"

Hackberry rubbed his temples, his gaze fixed on neutral space. "What did Agent Riser have to say?"

"That's the point. He didn't say anything, except you should call him. I told him you were in your office. He said he didn't have time to talk with you right now. He said you can call him back later on his cell phone."

Hackberry tried to process what he had just heard, then gave up. "Thanks, Maydeen."

"Want me for anything else?"

"Nope, but I'll tell you when I do."

"I'm just passing on the conversation."

"Got it," he said.

A half hour later, Ethan Riser called again. "Why wouldn't you talk to me a while ago?" Hackberry asked.

"I had an incoming call from Washington. I thought I explained that to your dispatcher."

"Evidently not. Did your lab get some prints for us?"

"Come down to the saloon. I'll buy you a drink."

"You're in town?"

"Yeah, I have to be over in Brewster tonight. But I like the saloon and café you have here. It's quite a spot."

"I'm glad you were able to find time to visit.

You have a reason for not coming to my office?"

"Can't do it, partner. That's the way it is," Riser said.

"I see. My dispatcher is named Maydeen Stoltz. If you run into her, just keep going."

"Care to explain that?"

"You'll figure it out." Hackberry hung up the telephone without saying good-bye. He got up from his desk and went into Pam Tibbs's office. "Let's take a walk," he said.

When they entered the saloon, Riser was eating a hamburger and drinking beer from a frosted mug in a back booth. His gaze slipped from Hackberry's face to Pam's, then back to Hackberry's. "Order up. It's on the G," he said.

Pam Tibbs and Hackberry sat down across from him. The saloon was dark and cool and smelled of beer and pickled sausage and ground meat frying in the kitchen. The floor was built from railroad ties that had been treated with creosote and blackened by soot from prairie fires, the heads of the rusty steel spikes worn the color of old nickels. The mirror behind the bar had a long fissure across it, shaped like a lightning bolt, so that the person looking into it saw a severed image of himself, one that was normal, one that was distorted, like a face staring up from the bottom of a frozen lake. Riser drank from his beer, a shell of ice sliding down his fingers. "I like this place. I always stop here when I'm in the area," he said.

"Yeah, it's five stars, all right. How about losing the charade?" Hackberry said.

"I do what I have to do, Sheriff."

"I'm not sympathetic."

"Okay," Riser said, setting down his beer, pushing away his food. "The guy who ate off that paper plate doesn't have prints on file in the conventional system. But you knew that or you wouldn't have given it to us. You were trying to use us, Sheriff."

"I gave you the paper plate because I had a professional obligation to give it to you," Hackberry said.

"Deputy Tibbs, can you go up to the bar and get whatever you and Sheriff Holland are having and bring another beer for me?" Riser said.

"No, I can't," she replied.

Riser looked at her out of the corner of his eye. He finished his beer and wiped his mouth with a paper napkin. "This guy Krill is in the computer at Langley. Before 9/11 we didn't have access to certain kinds of information. Now we do. A couple of decades back, our administration had some nasty characters working for us in Central America. Krill was one of them. He was of low-level importance in the big scheme of things but quite valuable in the bush."

"What's his real name?" Pam asked.

90

"Sorry?" Riser said.

"Are you hard of hearing?" she asked.

"Sheriff, we have a problem here," Riser said.

"No, *we* don't have a problem," Pam said. "The problem is you treat us like we're welfare cases you keep at bay with table scraps. Sheriff Holland has treated you and the Bureau with respect. Why don't you and your colleagues pull your heads out of your asses?"

"I had hoped we might establish some goodwill here," Riser said.

"I think Pam has a point," Hackberry said.

"I don't make the rules. I don't make our foreign policy, either," Riser said. "Nobody likes to admit we've done business with crab lice. Our friend Krill's real name is Antonio Vargas. We don't know that much about him, except he was on the payroll for a while, and now he's off the leash and seems to have a special hatred toward the United States."

"Why?" Hackberry asked.

"Maybe the CIA paid him in Enron stock. How would I know?"

"You need to stop lying, Mr. Riser," Pam said.

"Ma'am, you're way out of line," Riser said.

"No, you are," she said. "We bagged up that guy's dirty work. You ever pick up human fingers with your hands? Anybody who could do what he did has a furnace inside him instead of a brain. For us, these guys are not an abstraction. We live on the border, in their midst, and you're denying us information we're entitled to have."

Riser picked up his hamburger and bit into it. He chewed a long time before he spoke, his face looking older, more fatigued, perhaps more resigned to serving masters and causes he didn't respect. "This saloon reminds me of a photograph or a place I saw on vacation once," he said.

"The Oriental in Tombstone," Hackberry said. "It was run by the Earp brothers. That was just before the Earps and Doc Holliday blew three of the Clanton gang out of their socks at the O.K. Corral, then hunted down the rest and killed them one by one all the way to Trinidad."

"You guys must have a different frame of reference, because I'm never quite sure what you're talking about," Riser said.

"The message is we don't like getting dumped on," Pam said.

"This has really been an interesting meeting," Riser said. He got up from the booth and studied the check. He wore a brown suit with a thin western belt and no tie and a cowboy shirt that shone like tin. He didn't raise his eyes from the check when he spoke. "I love this country. I've served it most of my life. I honor other people who have served it, particularly someone who was a recipient of

92

the Navy Cross. I also honor those who work with a man of that caliber. I'm sorry I don't convey that impression to others. I hope both of you have a fine weekend."

Pam and Hackberry said little on the way back to the department. Rain and dust were blowing out of the hills against the sunset, a green nimbus rising from the land as though the day were beginning rather than ending. Hackberry took down the flag and folded it in a military tuck and put it in his desk drawer. He started to pick up the book he had left on his desk blotter. He was not aware Pam was standing behind him. "Don't buy into it," she said.

"Into what?"

"Riser is putting the slide on us."

"He isn't a bad man. He just takes orders. Consider how things would be if the Risers of the world hung it up and let others take their place." There was silence in the room. "I say something wrong?" he asked.

"Your goodness is your weakness. Others know it, and they use it against you," she replied.

"You need to stop talking like that to me, Pam."

She glanced at the title of the book on his desk blotter. "You reading about Air America?" she said.

"I thought it wouldn't hurt."

"Is the Asian lady's name in there?"

"In fact, it is."

"You like her?"

"I don't think about her one way or the other."

Pam gazed out the window. Down the street, a neon beer sign had just lighted in a barroom window. The pink glow of the sunset shone on the old buildings and high sidewalks. Pickup trucks and cars were parked at an angle in front of a Mexican restaurant that had a neon-scrolled green cactus above its front entrance. It was Friday evening, and as always in the American Southwest, it came with a sense of both expectation and completion, perhaps with the smell of open-air meat fires or rain on warm concrete. "Hack?" she said.

Don't say it. Don't think about it, he heard a voice say inside him. But he didn't know if the voice was directed at Pam or him. "What?" he asked.

"It's pretty here in the evening, isn't it?"

"Sure."

"I didn't mean to embarrass you in front of Riser."

"You didn't."

She looked out the window again. "We're off the clock now. Can I ask you a question?"

No, that's not a good idea, he thought.

"Hack?" she said, waiting for his response.

"Go ahead." In his mind's eye, he saw the

94

motel room in the crossroads settlement north of the Big Bend; he even felt the primal need that had caused him to break all his resolutions about involvement with a woman who was far too young for him and perhaps interested only because he had become a paternal figure in her life.

"Do you think about it?" she asked. "At all?"

"Of course."

"With regret?"

He took his hat off the rack, glancing into the outer offices. "No, but I have to remind myself that an old man is an old man. A young woman deserves better, no matter how good her heart is."

"Why is it that I don't get to make the decision, that you have to make it for me?" she asked.

Because you're looking for your father, he thought.

"Answer me," she said.

"I'm still your administrative supervisor. You have to remember that. It's not up for debate. This conversation is over."

"I've seen your wife's picture."

He felt a tic close to his eye. "What are you trying to tell me?"

"The Asian woman. She looks like her, that's all."

"I think I'd better head for the house."

He started to put on his hat, although he

95

never did so unless he was going out a door. She stepped close to him, her thumbs hooked in the sides of her belt. He could smell her hair, a hint of her perfume, the heat in her skin. There was a glaze on her eyes. "What's wrong, Pam?" he asked.

"Nothing."

"Tell me."

"Nothing. Like you say, you'd better go to your house. It's the kind of evening when most people want to celebrate the sunset, have dinner, dance, hear music. But you'd better go to your house."

"That's just the way it is," he replied. Then he remembered those were the words Ethan Riser had used to defend behavior that Hackberry considered morally indefensible. As he walked away, he heard her draw in a deep breath. He kept his eyes straight ahead so he did not have to look at her face and feel the hole in his heart.

Hackberry seldom slept well and never liked the coming of darkness, although he spent many hours sitting alone inside of it. Sometimes he fell asleep in his den, his head on his chest, and awoke at two or three in the morning, feeling he had achieved a victory by getting half the night behind him. Sometimes he believed he saw the red digital face on his desk clock through his eyelids. But quickly, the haze inside his head became the dust on a road north of Pyongyang and a molten sun that hung above hills that resembled women's breasts.

Sometimes as he dozed in the black leather swivel chair at his desk, he heard an airplane or a helicopter fly low overhead, the reverberations of the motors shaking his roof. But he did not identify the sound of the aircraft with a law enforcement agency patrolling the border or a local rancher approaching a private airstrip. Instead, Hackberry saw a lone American F-80 chasing a MiG across the Yalu River, then turning in a wide arc just as the MiG streaked into the safety of Chinese airspace. The American pilot did an aileron roll over the POW camp, signaling the GIs inside the wire that they were not forgotten.

When Hackberry slept in his bed, he kept his holstered blue-black white-handled custom-made .45 revolver on his nightstand. When he dozed in his office, he kept the revolver on top of his desk, the handles sometimes glowing in the moonlight like white fire. It was a foolish way to be, he used to tell himself, the mark of either a paranoid or someone who had never addressed his fears. Then he read that Audie Murphy, for the last two decades of his life, had slept every night with a .45 auto under his pillow, in a bed he had to move into the garage because his wife could not sleep with him.

Sometimes Hackberry heard the wind in

the trees or the clattering of rocks when deer came down the arroyo on their way to his horse tanks. Sometimes he thought he heard a messianic homeless man by the name of Preacher Jack Collins knocking through the underbrush and the deadfalls, a mass killer who had eluded capture by both Hackberry and the FBI.

Hackberry tried to convince himself that Collins was dead, his body long ago eaten by coyotes or lost inside the bowels of the earth. Regardless, Hackberry told himself, Collins belonged in the past or the place in the collective unconscious where most demons had their origins. If evil was actually a separate and self-sustaining entity, he thought, its manifestation was in the nationalistic wars that not only produced the greatest suffering but always became lionized as patriotic events.

At 2:41 Saturday morning, his head jerked up from his chest. Outside, he heard a heavy rock bounce down the arroyo, the breaking of a branch, a whisper of voices, then the sound of feet moving along the base of the hill. He unsnapped the strap on his revolver and got up from his desk and went to the back door.

A dozen or more people were following his fence line toward his north pasture. One woman was carrying a suitcase and clutching an infant against her shoulder. The men were all short and wore baseball caps and multiple shirts and, in the moonlight, had the snubbed profiles of figures on Mayan sculptures. So these were the people who had been made into the new enemy, Hackberry thought. Campesinos who sometimes had to drink one another's urine to survive the desert. They were hungry, frightened, in total thrall to the coyotes who led them across, their only immediate goal a place where they could light a fire and cook their food without being seen. But as John Steinbeck had said long ago, we had come to fear a man with a hole in his shoe.

Hackberry stepped outside with his hat on his head and walked into the grass in his sock feet. In the quiet, he could hear the wind blowing through the trees on the hillside, scattering leaves that had been there since winter. *"No tengan miedo. Hay enlatados en la granja,"* he called out. *"Llenen sus cantimploras de la llave de agua. No dejen la reja abierta. No quiero que me dañen la cerca, por favor."*

There was no response. The people he had seen with enough clarity to count individually now seemed as transitory and without dimension as the shadows in which they hid. "My Spanish is not very good," he called. "Take the canned goods out of the barn and fill your containers with water from the faucet by the horse tank. Just don't break my fences or leave the gates open."

There was still no response or movement at the base of the hill. But what did he expect? Gratitude, an expression of trust from people sometimes hunted like animals by nativist militia? He sat down on the steps and rested his back against a wood post and closed his eyes. Minutes later, he heard feet moving down the fence line, a squeak of wire against a fence clip, then a rush of water from the faucet by the horse tank. No one had opened a gate to access or exit the lot; otherwise, he would have heard a latch chain clank against the metal. He waited a few more minutes before he walked down to the barn. The boxed canned goods were still in the tack room. His two foxtrotters stood three feet from the tank, staring at him curiously. "How you doin', boys? Make any new friends tonight?" he asked.

No reply.

Hackberry went back inside the house. He dropped his hat on the bedpost and laid his pistol on the nightstand. Still wearing his clothes, he lay down on top of the covers, one arm across his eyes, and fell asleep, his thoughts about war and the irreparable loss of his wife temporarily sealed inside a cave at the bottom of a wine-dark sea.

Hackberry knew what he was going to do that

morning even before he got up. Saturday had always been the day he and his wife attended afternoon Mass at a church where the homily was in Spanish, then later, ate fish sandwiches at Burger King and went to see a movie, no matter what was playing. After her death, he had an excuse to drink, but he didn't. Instead, he lived inside his loneliness and his silent house from Friday night to Monday morning, his only companion a form of celibacy that he had come to think of as the iron maiden.

Today was going to be different, he told himself with a tug at his heart and perhaps a touch of self-deception. He fed his animals and drank one cup of coffee and shaved and showered and shined his boots and put on a new pair of western-cut gray trousers and a wide belt and a navy blue shirt. He strapped on his revolver and removed his dove-colored Stetson from the bedpost and went out to his pickup truck. The sun was below the hills, the north and south pastures damp and streaked with shadow, the stars and the moon just starting to fade back into the sky. *You're too old to act like this,* a voice told him.

"Who cares?" he said.

Don't use your legal office for your personal agenda or to make a fool of yourself.

"I'm not," he said.

If there was any reply in his debate with himself, he refused to acknowledge it.

When he cut his engine in front of the Asian woman's house, he could hear metallic scraping sounds in back. He walked around the side of the house and saw her scrubbing out the corrugated tank by the windmill with a long-handled brush. She wore oversize jeans that were rolled up in big cuffs, and a long-sleeve denim shirt spotted with water. She pushed a strand of hair out of her eye with the back of her wrist and looked at him.

"I need to ask you a question or two about the fellow who got loose from our man Krill," Hackberry said.

"I can't help you," she said.

"You gave assistance to this fellow when he was hurt. I saw the bloody bandages and the mattress in the bunkhouse. You didn't trust me enough to tell me that. Then you told Krill something to the effect that this fellow wouldn't be at your house again. Not at your *house,* right? But he might be somewhere in the vicinity. I think you don't want to tell a lie, Miss Anton, but for various reasons, you're not telling the truth, either."

She held his gaze for a moment and seemed about to speak, but instead, she bent to her work again. He took the brush from her hand. "You're doing it the hard way," he said. He lifted the tank on its rim and dumped out all the water lying below the level of the drain plug. Then he righted the tank, released the chain that locked the windmill blades, and

102

began filling the tank again while scrubbing a viscous red layer of sediment from the sides and bottom. "This stuff forms from a mixture of water and leaves or dust or both, I've never figured it out. It's like most things around here. Little of what happens is reasonable. It's the kind of place people move to after they've been eighty-sixed from Needles, California."

"What do you expect me to tell you?" she asked.

"You don't need to, Miss Anton. I think I know the truth."

With a spot of dirt on one cheek and the wind dividing her hair on her scalp, she waited for him to go on. When he didn't speak, she placed her hands on her hips and stared at the horse tank. "Sheriff Holland, don't play games with me."

"The federal employee who was taken hostage by Krill is probably a single man with no family; otherwise, they would be down here looking for him or making lots of noise in the media. The fact that he sought sanctuary with you indicates he's either on his own or he thinks you can provide him with a network of pacifists like himself. It also means he's probably somewhere close by, up in those hills or in a cave. From what little you've said, and from what the FBI hasn't said, this fellow was probably working in a defense program of some kind, one that presented him with problems of conscience. Maybe I can sympathize with his beliefs and also with yours. But Krill tortured a man to death in my county. Your friend the federal employee probably has information that can help me find Krill. Also, I think your friend is in grave jeopardy. I need your cooperation, Miss Anton. You've seen war in the most personal way. Don't let your silence contribute to this man's death."

"You'll turn him over to the FBI," she said.

"What would be the harm in that?"

"He has information the government doesn't want people to hear."

"The government doesn't operate that way. Politicians might, but politicians and the government are separate entities," Hackberry said.

"I heard you were once an attorney for the American Civil Liberties Union. You hide your credentials well."

He didn't reply and used his palm to deflect the water jetting from the well pipe in order to clean the scrub brush. He could feel her eyes peeling the skin off his face.

"I make you smile? There's something amusing about my speech?" she said.

"Somebody else once told me the same thing. Sometimes she'd tell me that every day."

She looked at him for a long time. "Are you a widower?"

104

"Yes, ma'am."

"Very long?"

"Eleven years."

"I'm sorry."

"She was a great woman. She was never afraid, not of anything, not in her whole life. She never wanted people to feel sorry for her, either, no matter how much she suffered."

"I see," she said, obviously trying to conceal her awkwardness.

He flicked the drops off the end of the brush onto the ground. He glanced up at the salmon-colored tint in the sky and looked at the hills and could almost smell the greening of the countryside and the feral odor that hung in its pockets and cracked riverbeds. He wondered how a land so vast and stark and self-defining could be marked simultaneously by both dust storms and acreage that was probably as verdant as the fields in ancient Mesopotamia. He wondered if the writer in the Bible had been describing this very place when he said the sun was made to shine and the rain to fall upon both the wicked and the just. He wondered if the beginnings of creation lay just beyond the tips of his fingers. "Have breakfast with me," Hackberry said.

"Sir?"

"You heard me."

"I don't know if that would be appropriate."

"Who's to say it's not?"

"You think I'm hiding a fugitive from the FBI. You virtually accused me of it."

"No, you're not hiding him, but you're probably feeding him and treating his wounds."

"And you want to take me to breakfast?"

"Look at me, Miss Anton. You think I'd try to trick you in some way? Ferret out information from you under the guise of friendship? Look me in the eye and tell me that."

"No, you're not that kind of man."

He let the water tank fill to the halfway mark, then notched the windmill chain and shut off the inflow valve. "I know this spot on the four-lane that serves huevos rancheros and frijoles that can break your heart," he said.

Cody Daniels felt he was not only the captain of a ship but the captain of his soul as he peered through the telescope mounted on the deck rail of his house. The valley was spread before him, the American flag painted on the cliff wall behind him, the wind blowing inside his shirt. As he watched the arrival of the sheriff at the Oriental woman's compound, his loins tingled with a surge of power and a sense of control that was so intense it made him wet his bottom lip; it even made him forget, if only briefly, his humiliation at the hands of the Hispanics named Krill and Neg-

106

rito. He was fascinated by the body language of the sheriff and the woman, she with her demure posturing, he pretending he was John Wayne, scrubbing red glop off the sides of the horse tank like nobody else knew how to do it. Maybe the sheriff was not only pumping his deputy, the woman who'd stuck a .357 in Cody's face, but also trying to scarf some egg roll on the side. *Yeah, look at her,* Cody told himself, she was eating it up. These were the people who'd treated him like butt crust, a guy who had founded the Cowboy Chapel? They were the elite, and he was a member of the herd? What a joke.

With one eye squinted and the other glued to the telescope, Cody was so enamored with his ability to dissect fraudulence and self-serving behavior in others that he didn't notice the two dark Town Cars coming up the dirt track on the hardpan. The cars rumbled across Cody's cattle guard and parked by his church house, their dust floating up in a cinnamon-colored cloud that broke apart on his deck. Seven men wearing either suits or expensive casual clothes and shades and jewelry and shined shoes or boots got out and walked up the wood stairs. Their faces had no expression. When they neared the top step, they looked at him with the nonchalance of people entering a public restroom.

One man in the middle of the group was

obviously not cut out of the same cloth as the others. He removed his shades and pinched the bridge of his nose. Then he extended his hand and smiled good-naturedly, with the authority of a man who was comfortable in any environment. "It's Temple Dowling, Reverend. I'm pleased we could meet," he said. "You have a fine place here. You're not afraid to display the flag, either."

The other men walked past Cody as though he were not there. "Where are they going?" he asked.

"Don't worry. They're professionals," Temple Dowling said.

"They're going into my house."

"Concentrate on me, Reverend. We're on the same side. This country is in danger. You agree with that, don't you?"

"What's that got to do with those guys creeping my house?"

" 'Creeping' your house?"

"Yeah, breaking into it. That's what it's called. Like burglary."

"I could tell you I'm CIA. I could tell you I'm NSA. I could tell you I'm with the FBI." Temple Dowling's hair was silver and black, thick and freshly clipped, the part as straight as a taut piece of twine. His face wore the fixed expression of a happy cartoon, the skin pink and creamy, his lips too large for his mouth. He reached out and took Cody's hand again, except this time he squeezed hard, his gaze locked on Cody's. Cody felt a ribbon of pain slide up his wrist to his armpit. "What are you doing?" he said.

"Congratulating you. I love to fly the flag. I love the people who fly it, too."

"But you're with the government, aren't —" Cody began, opening and closing his bruised hand, his words catching in his throat.

"No, I'm like you, a citizen soldier. We're looking for a man by the name of Noie Barnum. He's a misguided idealist who can do great harm to our country. A man such as yourself has many eyes and ears working for him. You can be of great assistance to us, Reverend."

"I don't have anybody working for me. What are you talking about?"

"You have a church house full of them."

"People in my congregation got their own mind and go their own way."

"We both know better than that. You put the right kind of fear in them, they'll do whatever you say."

"I don't want any part in this. You get those guys out of my house," Cody said.

"Reverend, let's be frank. You've stumbled into a world of hurt. Would you rather deal with people of your own race and background or Mr. Krill?"

"How do you know about him?"

"We watched you talk with him. Mr. Krill is the man who wants to sell Noie Barnum to Al Qaeda. Would you like that to happen?"

"You were spying on me?"

"What does it matter? You're working for us now."

"No, sir, I work for the Lord."

"You're saying I don't?"

The other men reemerged from Cody's house. "It's clean," one of them said.

"Answer my question," Temple Dowling said to Cody. "You're telling me to my face I'm not on the side of our Lord?"

"No, sir, I didn't say that. What's he mean, it's clean?"

"It means you're not hiding the man we're looking for. It means your computer doesn't indicate you're in touch with the wrong people. It means you just passed a big test. I'm going to give you a business card, Reverend, and I want you to call me when you find out where Mr. Barnum is. I also want you to keep me updated on what that Chinese woman is doing. That means I want to know about everything that happens down there on her property. You're going to be my pipeline into Mr. Krill's little group. Whatever he does, whatever he tells you, you'll report it directly to me."

"You're going too fast," Cody said.

"You're doing all this out of your own volition. That's because you're a patriot. I know

110

about that clinic bombing. You're a man willing to take risks. That's why I'm making you part of our team."

"I didn't have anything to do with that clinic business. No, sir."

Temple Dowling set his hand on Cody's shoulder. "We're going to take care of you. There'll be a chunk of cash in it for you, too. You've got my word. Give me a big hug."

"What?"

"Just kidding. I had you going, didn't I?"

Cody's head was swimming, a smell like soiled cat litter rising from his armpits. "No, sir," he said.

"No, sir, what?" Temple Dowling said.

"I'm not working for y'all. I'm not having any part of this."

"I have two affidavits that say you bought the oven timer that detonated the bomb at the clinic. It blinded and disfigured a nurse. I have pictures of her if you'd like to see them. I have a videotape of you in the crowd across the street. You couldn't stay away from your own handiwork, could you, sir? That's what I mean when I say you're a man who lives on the edge. You're not a suck-up, kick-down kind of guy. You know how to rip ass, Reverend. That woman won't be in the baby-killing business anymore, that's for sure." He glanced at his men and was no longer able to contain his laughter. All of the men had a merry expression in their eyes and were

111

clearly enjoying themselves. "Reverend Daniels, you're a special kind of shepherd," Dowling said.

When his visitors had driven away, Cody could hear kettle drums pounding inside his head. He sat down on a wood bench, his spine bowed, his eyelids fluttering, his muscles as flaccid as if his bones had been surgically removed from his body. The only other time he had felt this level of despair was when two county-prison gunbulls had finished with him and lifted him off a sawhorse and dropped him on a workroom floor like a slab of sweaty beef. He wondered why people thought they had to die in order to go to hell.

CHAPTER FIVE

Late Sunday afternoon Pam Tibbs parked the department's Jeep Cherokee at Hackberry's front gate and walked up the flagstone steps to his gallery and knocked on the door. He answered in his sock feet, his reading glasses on his nose. "I called twice and you didn't answer, so I thought I'd drive out," she said.

"I was in the pasture," he said.

"Maydeen got a report on an illegal dumping and another one on a break-in at a hunting camp. Both instances involved two guys. The dumping turned out not to be a dumping."

"I'm not following you."

"Last night a motorist saw two guys prowling in a creek bed and thought they were dumping trash. It turned out they were rifling the back of a camper. They stole some clothes and shoes and sleeping bags and a propane stove and a first-aid kit. This morning a guy with a long, pointy beard, wearing a tattered suit coat, was seen busting the lock on the back door of a hunting camp. He sounds like the same homeless guy who's been getting into people's garbage by Chapala Crossing. Except this time he had someone with him. They cleaned about forty pounds of venison out of the game locker. The witness said the guy in the tattered coat looked like he belted his trousers with a piece of clothesline. Sound familiar?"

"Jack Collins is dead," Hackberry said.

"You're convinced of that?"

"He either died of his wounds underground or was eaten by coyotes or cougars. He wasn't a supernatural entity. He was a psychopath and misogynist who probably couldn't tie his shoes without a diagram."

"Then who's the guy who keeps showing up around here?"

"Another lunatic. We're not in short supply of them."

"The guy with the tramp was limping. Like maybe a guy who ran a long distance with no shoes on."

"The man who escaped from Krill?"

"You know that burned-out shack where the tramp with the beard was probably living?"

"What about it?"

"I checked it out. It was soaked with an accelerant. Who would go to that much trouble to burn a shack?"

"You really think Collins is alive?"

114

"I'm not sure. But I'm bothered that you won't accept the possibility. I think you want to believe that evil dies."

She couldn't tell if he was thinking about what she had said or if he had lost interest. The sun had gone behind a hill, darkening the inside of his house, and she couldn't see past him into the shadows. "Did I disturb you?" she said.

"Pardon?"

"You didn't invite me in. Are you with someone?"

"Do I look like it?"

"You tell me. Did you enjoy your Mexican dinner with China's answer to Mary Magdalene?" She didn't wait for him to reply. "It's a small town. Why don't you at least spend the gas money to go into another county?"

"You need to concentrate on other matters, Pam."

"You're eating out with a woman who's part of a homicide investigation. Maybe someone who's aiding and abetting."

"Come in."

"No."

"Don't be resentful toward her."

"I'm resentful toward you. You're letting her jerk you around. You're acting like a damn fool."

"You mean an old fool."

"Don't put words in my mouth. Don't you dare act like I've ever been disloyal to you."

He held his eyes on hers, refusing to concede an inch. She picked up his hand and pressed it against her left breast, clenching down on his wrist so he couldn't remove it. "Feel my heart."

"Don't do this, Pam."

"Don't you ever accuse me of disloyalty."

"I wouldn't do that, Pam. Never."

"Then why the hell do you hurt me?"

"I don't mean to."

"That's all you're going to say?"

"Yes, ma'am, that's about it."

"I want to hit you. With my fists. As hard as I can. I want to break the bones in your face."

"Go ahead."

Her eyes went in and out of focus, a nest of blue veins pulsing by her temple. "What do you want me to do now?" she said.

"About what?"

"About Preacher Jack Collins or whoever this tramp and his friend are. About doing my goddamn job."

"We start at the hunting camp. Later, I'd like to buy you dinner."

"In your dreams," she said. "I'll wait for you in the Jeep."

Inside a ravine snaking back through a collection of sandstone formations that resembled pillars in an ancient church, a man wearing a soiled panama hat tipped down over his brow and a pin-striped suit coat that

116

was frayed white on the tips of the sleeves squatted at the opening to a cave. He stared into a cook fire that he had built inside a ring of stones, and he fed the fire incrementally, stick by stick, as though fascinated with either his power over the flames or an image he saw inside them. In the firelight, his face seemed dotted with lumps of proud flesh, his cheeks and throat streaked with the irregular stubble of a man who had shaved with a dry razor.

"Why are you grinning?" asked the man on the opposite side of the fire ring.

"No reason," the man in the suit coat replied.

But he was not telling the truth. Inside the flames, he saw a woman's hair and the paleness of her face and the redness of her mouth. He saw the wantonness of her smile, the lewdness in her eyes, the flash of an incisor tooth as she glanced at him from behind a blanket she had hung on the wash line dividing the boxcar where she and her son lived. He heard the heavy weight of a Mexican gandy dancer settling between her thighs.

"You're a mysterious fellow," said the man on the far side of the fire ring.

"How's that?"

"You have little to share, but you befriend a stranger who has nothing. You're willing to break the law to find food for a man you owe nothing."

"Maybe I stole it for myself."

"A man as poor as you is not a thief."

"Maybe I like your name."

"It's hardly original," said the man on the opposite side of the fire. His face was long and homely, his ears too large, his nose shaped like a big teardrop, his shoulders knobbed as though they had been turned on a lathe. His name was Noie Barnum.

"Noie restarted the human race," the man in the suit coat said. "Noie watched Yahweh hang the archer's bow in the sky. 'God gave Noie the rainbow sign / It's not by water, it's the fire next time.' You know that song?"

"I haven't heard it."

"Yahweh made a contract. He stopped the rain and stilled the water and brought Noie and the ark to land. Before the flood, man was not supposed to break the skin of an animal with a knife. After the flood, the lion was supposed to lie down with the lamb. But it didn't work out that way. That's why the land is cursed."

"You're either a closet college professor or you've spent a lot of time in the public library," Noie Barnum said.

"You wouldn't mock a fellow, would you?" the man in the suit coat replied. His teeth shone at the corner of his mouth when he spoke, but there was no rancor in his voice.

"No, sir, I think you're a good man. You and the Asian lady saved my life."

"Which Asian lady?"

"The one the Mexicans call La Magdalena."

"The papist?"

"I'm not sure what she is. I know she's brave and she's kind. I think she's a lot like you, Jack."

"I doubt that." Jack flipped a twig into the fire, fascinated with its fate. He pried open the blade from his pocketknife and stripped the bark from a mesquite branch and sharpened the end into a point, then speared four chunks of venison and watched them curl and brown over the campfire. His fingernails were rimmed with dirt, his shapeless trousers stuffed inside the tops of his cowboy boots. As he squatted on his heels, his buttocks looked as thin as barrel slats. He opened a can of beans and stuck them down in the coals. He poured water from a canteen into two aluminum cups and handed one of them to Noie. "You hear that sound?" he asked.

"What sound?"

"Out yonder, to the southwest, just below the evening star."

"I don't hear or see anything," Noie said.

"It's a helicopter. When it flies over, don't look up. The light always reflects off your face. Even starlight does. Ever see ducks or geese change their flight pattern when you glance up at them? They read the propensities down below a lot better than we do."

"Shouldn't we put out the fire?"

119

"These hills and canyons and dry washes are full of fires. The people in that helicopter are looking for white men. They're looking for us."

"Who are you, Jack?"

"You don't want to know."

From his belt loops, Jack pulled the piece of rope he had been using to hold up his trousers. He dropped it in the fire and watched it spark and then dissolve on the coals like a snake blackening and curling back on itself. He uncoiled a belt he had taken from the camper shell of the parked pickup and threaded it through the loops on his trousers, working the point around his skinny hips to the buckle, totally absorbed with the task.

"I didn't mean to offend you," Noie said.

"Why study on a wretch like me?" Jack said. The thropping sounds of a helicopter passed overhead, the airframe silhouetting briefly against the moon like a giant predator. Jack sat motionlessly on a rock, smiling crookedly from under the brim of his panama hat, until the helicopter and the downdraft of its blades had disappeared in the darkness. He tossed Noie a tin plate. "Eat up. White-tailed venison cooked on a mesquite fire with a little pepper and salt is about as good as it gets."

Pam and Hackberry's investigation into the theft at the hunting camp and from the

120

camper shell of the pickup truck went nowhere. There were no recoverable prints and no witnesses who could provide any additional information or descriptive detail about the two men who had committed the break-ins. Early Monday morning Hackberry drove by himself to the burned shack where the tramp had occasionally been seen. But he was not the first to arrive there.

Ethan Riser was standing among several men holding a conversation between two parked SUVs. Even though the morning air was soft, the sun hardly above the hills, the ground moist with night damp, all of the men were in shirtsleeves and wore shades, as though the sun were blazing in the center of the sky. Only Riser bothered to look at Hackberry when he got out of the cruiser and approached the SUVs. "Be with you in a minute, Sheriff," Riser said.

"No, sir, I need to talk with you now," Hackberry said.

Riser separated himself from the group and walked beside Hackberry toward the pile of ash and charcoal that had once been a shack where a nameless tramp sometimes lived. "Are you here for the same reasons I am?" Hackberry said.

"What would that be?" Riser asked.

"Don't try to take me over the hurdles, Ethan."

"The federal employee we're looking for is

named Noie Barnum. If this guy falls into the wrong hands, he can do enormous injury to this country. Believe me, you cannot imagine the extent of the damage. I need your cooperation, and by 'cooperation' I mean you have to stop intervening in our affairs."

"Noie?"

"Yeah, like the spelling in the King James Bible," Riser said. "People in the southern mountains pronounce it 'No-ee.' "

"This is my county and my jurisdiction. You guys are our guests," Hackberry said.

"That's outrageous."

"So is federal arrogance."

"I have to get back to work."

"No, you don't," Hackberry said. "What's your interest in a burned-down shack?"

"That's not your concern."

"You think Jack Collins might have given refuge to Barnum?"

"If you've figured everything out, why bother asking the FBI?"

"I'm not asking the FBI. I'm asking you, man to man."

"We never found Collins's body. His case is still open."

"You think he burned his shack to get rid of his prints?"

"We haven't come to any conclusions about any of this, at least not that we can pass on."

"*We?* I asked you for an opinion about the

torching of the shack. It's not a difficult question."

"I think you should take your mind off world events. Do that for us, and we'll do our best to stay out of your hair."

Hackberry gazed at the gray and black humps of ash and charcoal and scorched boards and cans of food that had exploded in the heat and the strips of rusted corrugated tin protruding from the pile. A charred Bible had been raked out on the grass. The pages, all of them burned as black as carbon paper along the outer margins, were flipping in the wind. Hackberry turned his attention back to Riser.

"You didn't bag the Bible," Hackberry said.

"Why should I?"

"To see if Collins's prints are on it."

Riser removed a ballpoint from his shirt pocket. He seemed to study it a moment; then he started clicking it. "I can never get these things to work right."

"You already know whose Bible that is. It belongs to Collins, doesn't it?" Hackberry said.

Riser stuck the ballpoint back in his pocket and glanced at his watch and at his colleagues by the SUVs. "I hope all this works out for everybody. Be seeing you, Sheriff," he said.

"Something else happened here. Collins didn't burn the shack, did he?"

"How do you know that?"

"He's a religious fanatic. He wouldn't burn his Bible."

"You're too smart for your own good. I mean that in a kindly way."

"You guys did it."

"No, *we* did not do it."

"Or somebody from ICE or the Border Patrol or the DEA. But one of y'all did it. Tell me I'm wrong. I want you to."

"So maybe you're not wrong," Riser said. "Maybe a hothead got pissed off and wanted to send Collins a message. Maybe unlike you, not everybody is always in control of his emotions."

"You're telling me one of your people soaked private property with an accelerant and put a match to it, and you're telling me lawmen do this with regularity?"

"The U.S. Forest Service used to burn out squatters all the time."

"Nobody can be this dumb. Do you realize what y'all have done?"

"The Department of Justice isn't exactly Pee-wee Herman. We don't quake in our shoes because we have to hunt down a self-anointed messiah who probably hasn't changed his underwear since World War Two."

Hackberry walked over to the group of federal agents, still gathered between the two SUVs. "Which one of you guys torched the shack?" he asked.

They stared at him blankly from behind

their shades. "What shack?" one of them said.

"I dug up nine of Jack Collins's victims, all of them Asian, all female, some of them hardly more than children. He used a Thompson submachine gun, a full drum, fifty rounds, at almost point-blank range. Then they were bulldozed over behind the ruins of a church. One of them may have been still alive when she went into the ground. A Phoenix mobster sent three California bikers to pop him. Jack bribed their chippies to set them up and then turned the three of them into wallpaper."

"Sounds like the right guy might have got his house burned down," one of the agents said.

Hackberry walked back toward his cruiser, his face tight, his temples knotted with veins. Behind him, he heard one of the agents make a remark the others laughed at. But Hackberry didn't look back. Instead, he kept his eyes focused on Ethan Riser. "That bunch of Ivy League pissants back yonder?" he said.

"What about them?" Riser said.

Hackberry opened the door to his cruiser. "I thought you were different, that's all," he said.

"You should have stayed with the ACLU, Sheriff. At least they have an understanding of procedure and protocol," Riser said. "They try to think twice before they put their own agenda ahead of their country's security.

Where do you get off lecturing other people? Who died and made you God?"

"Nobody. And that's the problem every one of y'all has, Ethan. You wrap your lies in the flag and put the onus on others. Shame on every one of you," Hackberry said.

When he drove away, the back tires of his cruiser ripped two long lines out of the grass.

That evening Hackberry was about to relearn that the past wasn't necessarily a decaying memory and that its tentacles had the power to reach through the decades and fasten themselves onto whatever prey they could slither their suction cups around. When he returned home from work, he found an envelope stuck in his doorjamb. Inside was a silver-edged sheet of stationery folded crisply through the center. The note on it was written in bright blue ink, in a flowing calligraphy, the curlicues fading into wispy threads. It read:

Dear Sheriff Holland,

Congratulations on all your political success. My father always spoke fondly of you and I'm sure he would be very proud of you. Forgive me for dropping by without calling first, but your number was unlisted. Call my car phone if you can have drinks or dinner, or I'll try to drop by later or at your office.

With kindest regards,
Temple Dowling

Unconsciously, Hackberry glanced over his shoulder after reading the note, as though an old adversary lay just beyond the perimeter of his vision. Then he went into the house and tore the note and envelope into four pieces, then tore them again and dropped them in the kitchen waste can and washed his hands in the sink.

It was easier to cleanse his skin than rinse his memory of Temple's father, United States Senator Samuel Dowling. And Hackberry's thoughts about the senator were uncomfortable not because the senator had been mean-spirited and corrupt to the core, but because Hackberry, when he ran for Congress, had, of his own choosing, fallen under the senator's control.

The 1960s had been a transitional time in Texas's political history. Hispanic farmworkers were unionizing, and huge numbers of black people had been empowered by the Voting Rights Act of 1965. Hackberry had watched the changes take place from a distance, at least when he wasn't driving across the river to the brothels in Coahuila or Nuevo León, or staining the shaved ice in a tall glass one jigger at a time, with four inches of Jack Daniel's, adding a sprig of mint and a teaspoon of sugar, just before taking the first drink of the day, one that rushed through his body with the intensity of an orgasm. Both the Democratic ticket and Hackberry's first wife, Verisa, were delighted at the prospect of a handsome, towering war hero representing their district. Hackberry soon discovered that his addiction to whiskey and the embrace of a Mexican girl's thighs didn't hold a candle to the allure of celebrity and political power.

The attraction was not entirely meretricious in nature. Couched inside the vulgarity and the crassness of the new rich who surrounded him, and the attempts at manipulation of the sycophants, were moments that made him feel he was genuinely part of history. For good or bad, he had become a player in the Jeffersonian dream, a decorated former navy corpsman from a small Texas town about to take up residence at the center of the republic. Maybe Jefferson's dream had been tarnished, but that did not mean it was lost, he had told himself. Even George Orwell, describing a Spanish troop train leaving a station on its way to the front while brass bands were blaring and peasant girls were throwing flowers, had said that maybe there was something glorious about war after all.

Hackberry remembered one balmy summer night of the campaign in particular. He had been standing on a balcony at the Shamrock Hotel in Houston, wearing only a bathrobe, a

128

tumbler of whiskey and ice in one hand. Far below, columns of electric light glowed beneath the surface of a swimming pool built in the shape of a four-leaf clover. Across the boulevard, in a strange blend of the rural South and the New American Empire, oil wells pumped up and down — *clink, clank, clink, clank* — like the steady and predictable rhythm of lovers copulating, while cattle grazed nearby in belly-deep grass and thunder leaked from banks of black- and plum-colored rain clouds overhead.

The hotel had been built by a notorious wildcatter who sometimes came into the Shamrock Room and got into brawls with his own patrons, wrecking the premises and adding to a mythos that told all of its adherents they, too, could become denizens of the magic kingdom, if only the dice toppled out of the cup in the right fashion. In forty-five minutes Hackberry was to address a banquet hall filled with campaign donors who could buy third-world countries with their credit cards. When he was in their midst, he sometimes had glimpses in his mind of a high school baseball pitcher who resembled him and who took a Mexican girl to a drive-in theater in 1947, knowing that as soon as he went into the restroom, he would be beaten senseless. But Hackberry did not like to remember the person he used to be. Instead, he had made a religion out of self-destruction and surrounded himself with people he secretly loathed.

On that balcony high above the pool, he had not heard the senator walk up behind him. The senator had cupped his palm around the back of Hackberry's neck, massaging the muscles as a father might do to his son. "Are you nervous?" the senator had said.

"Should I be?"

"Only if you plan to tell them the truth."

"What *is* the truth, Senator?"

"That the world we live in is a sweet, sweet sewer. That most of them would drink out of a spittoon rather than give up their access to the wealth and power you see across the boulevard. That they want to own you now so they don't have to rent you later."

Hackberry had drunk from the tumbler, the ice cubes clattering against the glass, the palm fronds moving in the breeze down below, the warmth of the whiskey slowing his heart like an old friend reassuring him that the race was not to the swift. "Telling the truth would be my greatest sin? That's an odd way of looking at public service, don't you think?"

"There's a far graver sin."

"What would that be?"

"You already know the answer to that one, Hack."

"A worse sin would be disloyalty to someone who has reached out and anointed me with a single touch of his finger on my brow?" Hackberry had said.

"That's beautifully put. Your wife said you bedded a Mexican whore in Uvalde last night."

"That's not true. It was in San Antonio."

"Oh, that's good. I have to remember that one. But no more local excursions. There will be time enough for that when you get to Washington. Believe it or not, it will be there in such abundance that you'll eventually grow bored with it, if you haven't already. Usually, when a man of your background screws down, he's not seriously committed to infidelity. It's usually an act of anger rather than lust. A bit of trouble at home, that sort of thing. It beats getting drunk. Is that the case with the girl in San Antonio?"

Hackberry had not answered.

"Fair enough. There's no shame in having a vice. It's what makes us human," the senator had said. Then he had patted Hackberry gingerly on the back of the head, after first leaning over the rail and spitting, even though people were eating at poolside tables directly below.

Those moments on the balcony and the touch of the senator's hand on his head had remained with Hackberry like a perverted form of stigmata for over four decades.

An hour after tearing up the message left by Temple Dowling, Hackberry glanced

131

through the front window and saw a man park a BMW at the gate and walk up the flagstones to the gallery. The visitor had thick silver-and-black hair and lips that were too large for his mouth. He was carrying an ice bucket with a dark green bottle inserted in it. Hackberry opened the door before his uninvited guest could ring the bell.

"Hello, Sheriff. Did you find my note?"

"Yes, sir, you're Mr. Dowling. Leave the bucket and the bottle on the gallery and come in."

"Excuse me?"

"Guests in my home drink what I have or they don't drink at all."

"I was supposed to meet a lady friend, but she stood me up. I hate to see a good bottle of wine go to waste. My father said you used to have quite a taste for it."

"You want to come in, sir?"

"Thank you. And I'll leave my bucket behind." Dowling stepped inside and sat down in a deep maroon leather chair and gazed through the picture window, patting the tops of his thighs, a thick gold University of Texas class ring on his left hand. He wore a gray suit and a tie that was as bright as a halved pomegranate. But it was the composition of his face that caught the eye — the large lips, the pink cheeks and complexion that looked as though they had been dipped out of a cosmetics jar, the heavy eyelids that seemed translucent and were flecked with tiny vessels. "What a lovely view. The hills in front of your house remind me of —"

"Of what?"

"A Tahitian painting. What was his name? Gauguin? He was big on topless native women."

"I haven't studied on it."

Temple Dowling smiled, his fingers knitting together.

"Do I amuse you, sir?" Hackberry said.

"I was thinking of something my father said. He admired your élan. I told him I'd heard you'd had a lot of girlfriends. My father replied, 'Mr. Holland is a great lover of humanity, son. But let's remember that half the human race is female.' "

"I think maybe the senator misrepresented the nature of our relationship. We were not friends. We used each other. That's a reflection on me, not him."

"Call me Temple."

"I was a drunkard and a whoremonger, not a man who simply had girlfriends. I used the bodies of poor peasant girls across the river without thinking about the misery that constituted their lives. When I met Senator Dowling, I was arrogant and willful and thought I could play chess with the devil. Then the day came when I realized I had gravely underestimated Senator Dowling's potential. After I mentioned my father's political principles and his friendship with Franklin Roosevelt, the senator explained why my father had shot and killed himself. My father had taken a bribe. The people who bribed and later tried to blackmail him were friends of Senator Dowling. The senator took great pleasure in telling me that story."

"I'm not my father, Sheriff."

"No, sir, you're not. But you're not here out of goodwill, either."

"How much money do you think it would take to shut down the city of New York?"

"I wouldn't know, and I'm not interested."

"I don't mean to just disrupt it, like the 9/11 attacks. I mean to flood the tunnels and destroy the bridges and hospitals and poison the water supply and to spread fire and plague and anthrax and suffering all over the five boroughs. What if I told you that fifty thousand dollars spent in the right place by the wrong guys could turn New York into Dante's ninth circle?"

"What business are you in, sir?"

"The defense of our nation."

"Would you answer the question, please?"

"Unmanned aerial vehicles."

"Drones that fire missiles?"

"Sometimes. Other times they're observation vehicles. The cost to manufacture a Patriot missile is three million dollars. The cost of drones is nickels and dimes in comparison. A small drone can be powered with batteries and is invulnerable to heat-seeking missiles. They can fly so slowly that jet interceptors can't lock down on them. Hezbollah has used them inside Israeli airspace."

"What do you want from me?"

"Nothing. I'm here to offer my services."

"They're not needed, and they're not wanted."

"Somewhere out there in those hills is a man named Noie Barnum. He's an idealistic idiot who believes that sharing knowledge about our weapons will make for a safer world."

"My impression is that he was kidnapped and about to be sold to Al Qaeda when he escaped. He doesn't sound like a willing participant in any of this."

"So why doesn't he come in?" Dowling said.

"That's a good question."

"Barnum has told others he has 'problems of conscience.' His 'problem' is the fact that UAVs can cause collateral damage. I wonder what he thinks about the collateral influences of napalm and bombs dropped from B-52s. Or maybe he'd like more of our soldiers killed while digging ragheads out of their caves."

"Why are you here, sir?" Hackberry said.

"I want Noie Barnum in a cage. I don't want him in front of a microphone or a camera. I'd like to see him buried under concrete at Guantánamo, after his head was wrapped in a towel and half the Atlantic was poured into it."

"I'll pass on your remarks to the FBI the first opportunity I have."

"Sheriff, who do you think runs this country?"

"You tell me."

"Lyndon was put into office by Brown and Root. Lyndon is moldering in the grave, but Brown and Root merged with Halliburton and is still alive and well. You think our current president is going to rescind their contracts at almost every United States military base in the world?"

"I wouldn't know."

Temple Dowling stood up from his chair and removed a strand of cat hair from his sleeve. "My father said you were never a listener."

"You ever hear of Preacher Jack Collins?"

"No, who is he?"

"The most dangerous man I've ever met," Hackberry said.

"What does that have to do with Noie Barnum?"

"Jack may be feeding and protecting him. I'm not sure why. Maybe because the feds burned Jack's shack. Keep hanging around this area, and you might get a chance to meet him. If he chats you up, try to get it on tape."

"Why would I want to do that?"

"Because it's the only record people will have of your death. Thanks for coming by."

Chapter Six

Using only starlight, Jack Collins and Noie Barnum made their way up a deer trail along the side of a bluff and into a narrow canyon that was threaded by a creek and strewn with chertlike yellow rock that had toppled from the ridges. Jack was in the lead, a nylon pack on his back, the straps pinching his suit coat tightly into his armpits, his body straining forward. Noie was limping badly, barely able to keep up, one arm tucked against his rib cage. There was a layer of fertile soil on the ground that sloped from the base of the cliffs down to the creek, and grass and wildflowers grew on it.

Jack paused and wiped his face and took his companion's measure. "You want to sit down, bud?" he asked.

"No, sir, I'm fine."

"You're a tough *hombre*."

"I'm not in your class, Jack. You're a mountain goat."

Jack walked back down the trail to where

his companion was leaning on the twisted remains of a cedar tree, breathing through his nose. "It gets steep up yonder. Put your arm on my shoulder. If you hear a rattler, hold still and give him time to get out of your way."

"What if he doesn't?"

"Throw a rock at him."

"For real?"

"I have the feeling people didn't tell a lot of jokes where you're from."

A cabin stood at the head of the canyon. Next to it was a loading chute that had turned gray with dry rot. In back were a barn with a sliding door and, farther up the hillside, an aluminum cistern supported on steel stanchions. Jack helped Noie the rest of the way up the trail, then slung his pack on the cabin's porch and eased Noie down on the steps. "I'll open up and fire the stove and get some food started," he said.

"Who owns this?" Noie asked.

"Me."

"You own property?"

"A mess of it."

"You're quite a kidder, Jack."

"That's me."

Jack removed the door key from behind a wallboard, unlocked the cabin, and went inside. He stuffed newspaper and kindling and three chunks of firewood in the cook-stove and set them ablaze, then went outside and started the gasoline motor that powered the water pump and the electric lights. He slid open the barn door and gazed at an unpainted Trans Am that had lines of rust around the fenders, though it was mounted with four Michelin tires that looked fresh from the dealership. Then he returned to the cabin and opened two cabinets lined with canned goods and boxes of cereal and jars of preserves. He filled a skillet with corned beef and hash and dumped a can of spinach into a pan and set them on the stove. He went back on the porch and helped Noie to his feet. "I think your ribs are fractured," he said. "The pain will probably be with you six weeks at the inside. You take the bunk, and I'll make a pallet on the floor."

"Jack, I have no idea what's going on. Is this really your camp?"

"You haven't figured out who I am?"

"No, sir, I'm pretty confused."

"I was a longtime exterminator for Orkin. I still have my license. That's a fact."

"You're a pest exterminator?"

"That says it all," Jack replied.

"Why are you doing all this for me?"

"I like your accent. I never met a Quaker from Alabama."

In the early morning, Jack rose from his pallet and slipped on his boots and retrieved a flashlight and a shovel from the barn. The sky was bursting with stars as he labored up a path to a cave entrance that was not much wider than his hips. He squeezed through the opening, then stood up slowly, in a crouch, and flicked on the flashlight. The interior of the cave was as orange and pale as the inside of a pumpkin, the roof jagged and blackened by the cook fires of hunters and gatherers who may have been there before the Indians. On one wall, petroglyphs and images cut with stone tools depicted the slayings of both animals and people. Jack sometimes wondered if the battle in the stone mural had been fought over food or if the animals had been slain to ensure that the survivors would starve. There was another artifact in the cave that seemed to answer the question for him. A hole used to grind corn had been augered into a slab of table rock that ran the length of one wall. Jack believed the grinding hole proved the battle was not over game. In Jack's opinion, man killed because he had lost Eden. The bitterness was obviously so great that nothing short of mass fratricide could assuage it. Why else did people enjoy it so? Killing over food? Who was kidding whom? The throngs who attended blood sports weren't worried about the quality of the hot dogs.

The air inside the cave was cool and smelled of guano and damp clay and the field mice that nested on the ledges. Jack worked his way to the rear of the shaft, then set his light

141

on the table rock and went to work, his dirty panama pulled down on his brow, his unshaved cheeks as lined as old parchment. The mixture of sand and clay and charcoal curdled up like old skin on the shovel's blade as he pushed the handle toward the rear wall, peeling the ground away in layers, tossing each shovel load to one side. When he was down less than a foot, he glimpsed a piece of black vinyl in the dirt. He got to his knees and began scraping the dirt out of the hole with his fingers, brushing off the vinyl, pushing his hands sideways into the dirt to find purchase on the outer edges of the bag, feeling the hard, familiar contours inside it. He dug faster, his heart beating, his throat tingling with anticipation, his breath loud inside the confines of the cave. He sculpted the bag free of dirt from head to foot, then fitted both hands under it and lifted it from the ground. A damp odor that was as cool and pungent as bruised nightshade rose into his face.

In his haste, he knocked the flashlight off the table rock, and the inside of the cave went black. He groped in the dirt until he felt the aluminum cylinder with his fingers, but when he pushed the switch on and off, nothing happened. The inside of the cave contained a level of darkness that only a blind man would understand. Jack felt as though his eyes had been scooped out of his head with a spoon.

He stared up the shaft, hoping to see a glimmer of starlight through the opening, but there was both a bend and a drop in the floor, and the darkness was so absolute that it seemed to flow like liquid through his eyes into his skull.

It was not unlike the inside of a cargo trunk his mother had kept in the boxcar where they had lived. "You cost me the trick, Jack. That's the only way Ma and you can get by," she would say. "It hurts me to do this. Why are you such a headstrong little boy? Why do you force Ma to do this to her only begotten?"

He dragged the bag behind him, feeling above with one hand to protect his head, the weight inside the bag slapping across the cave floor. Then he rounded the bend and saw the stars in the sky and felt a sense of release that was like an infusion of pure oxygen into his soul. He climbed through the cave opening into the breeze and the smell of creek water and wet grass and desert bloom, then pulled the bag through the hole after him. When he sat down on the incline, sweat was leaking out of his hat and drying on his face. He waited until he had caught his breath, then tore the garbage bag away from the hard outline. His hands were shaking when he unsnapped the series of latches on the top of the guitar case and pried the top up on its hinges. Set inside the velvet pink liner, just as he had left them one year ago, were his

Thompson .45 submachine gun, a box magazine, two fifty-round ammunition pans, and six boxes of cartridges. He touched the cold blue oiled smoothness of the frame and saw the vaporous whorls of his fingertips clouding on the steel and evaporating, like the melting of dry ice or hailstones. Did the ancient gods give power with the touch of a finger? he asked himself. Or did they absorb it from the beings they touched? Didn't Death depend on his victims in order to sustain his own existence? Jack wondered what Ma would think if she saw him now. He wondered if she would smile in awe when the electric arc leaped from the muzzle of his Thompson, when he cut down his enemies like a harvester ripping a scythe through wheat. Would she believe her son had become the left hand of God and be proud of him? Or would she run squeaking and skittering like a dormouse squeezing through its hidey-hole?

He entered the back of the cabin and removed fresh underwear and socks from a dresser, and a white dress shirt and an unpressed clean brown suit from the closet. He stripped off his soiled clothes and let them drop to the floor and wrapped his body in a quilt. Then he carried the guitar case and his razor and a bar of soap and the change of clothes down to the creek. He laid out his suit and underwear on a rock and sat

144

down in the center of the creek, the current frothing around his chest, a cluster of deer watching him from an arroyo. He washed his hair and face and body and lathered his throat and cheeks and shaved by touch. Even though he climbed dripping wet onto the bank and dressed without drying off, his skin was as warm as a heated lampshade. The light had started to go out of the sky, but the evening star still hung low in the west, just above the hills, twinkling like a harbinger of a fine day.

He slipped on his boots and lay down on the quilt, the Thompson at his side, his head cushioned on his arm. The ground was patinaed with tiny wildflowers, and as he breathed their fragrance, he thought he could hear the wind whispering through the grass. The whispering grew in volume until it sounded like bees buzzing in a hive, or the whisperings of desperate girls and young women who had been trapped unfairly underground long before their time, all of them Asian girls whose sloe eyes pleaded for mercy and whose voices asked, *Why did you do this to us?*

I freed you from a life of degradation, he replied.

But his words were like the weighted tips of a flagrum whipped across his soul.

Early the next morning, Maydeen Stoltz

walked into Hackberry's office. She had a pink memo slip in her hand. "That was Bedford at the firehouse. He said he had a call maybe we should know about."

"Concerning what?"

Maydeen looked at the memo slip. "The caller gave his name as Garland Roark. He said he was an arson investigator with the Texas Department of Public Safety. He said he was compiling information about the incidence of arson along the border."

"Say that name again."

"Garland Roark."

Hackberry wrote it on a legal pad.

"So Bedford told him about the shack burning down, the one maybe Collins was living in," Maydeen said.

"Go on."

"The caller wanted to know how Bedford knew it was arson. Bedford told him the whole place stunk of kerosene. Then the caller asked if Bedford had any suspects in mind. Bedford goes, 'Not unless you count the FBI.' "

"Wait a minute," Hackberry said. "When did Bedford get this call?"

"A week ago, right after the fire."

"Bedford suspected the feds did it but didn't tell us?"

"Hold your water two seconds and I'll try to finish," Maydeen said.

"Excuse me."

146

"I asked Bedford the same question. He said a trucker saw a car with a government tag parked by the shack just before the flames went up. Bedford figured if the feds set fire to it, there was a reason. He thought maybe it was a stopover place for illegals."

"So why is Bedford calling us now?"

"He started wondering why this guy Roark didn't ask about the arson incidents involving wildfires. Like what was the big deal with a shack? This morning he called Austin and was told nobody by the name of Garland Roark worked at the Department of Public Safety."

"That's because he's dead," Hackberry said.

"You knew him?"

"Garland Roark was the author of *Wake of the Red Witch*. Jack Collins likes to appropriate the names of famous writers. He used the name of B. Traven, the author of *The Treasure of the Sierra Madre*, on several legal documents. Jack is quite the jokester when he's not murdering people."

"You want me to get Bedford on the phone?"

"Forget Bedford. Call Ethan Riser and fill him in. If he's not in, leave the information on his voice mail."

"Shouldn't you do that?"

"I'm done pulling Ethan's biscuits out of

147

the fire," Hackberry replied. "Ask Pam to come in here, please."

"Yes, sir."

A moment later, Pam Tibbs tapped on the doorjamb.

"Jack Collins knows the feds burned him out," Hackberry said.

"Is Riser aware of this?"

"He will be. You have any suggestions?"

She shrugged. "Not really. Collins is going to square it."

"You and I know that. But we're the only law enforcement personnel around here who have dealt with him head-on."

"So maybe Riser will learn a lesson and not be such a smart-ass."

"We're not going to let Collins make this county his personal killing ground."

She took a box of Altoids out of her shirt pocket and put one on her tongue. "Why did you want to talk to me, Hack?"

"You know how Collins thinks."

"You're asking me what his next move will be?" she said.

"I thought you might have an opinion, since he tried to machine-gun you."

"That's not a subject I'm flippant about."

"Neither am I," he said.

"Collins hunts like a cougar," she said. "He'll go to the water hole and wait for his prey."

"Where's the water hole?"

148

"Wherever he thinks the feds will show up," Pam replied.

"Where would that be?"

"You already know where."

"Tell me."

"The Asian woman gave refuge to Noie Barnum. The feds are probably watching her. One way or another, Collins will find that out."

"Want to take a ride?" Hackberry said.

She looked out the window at the flag popping on the silver pole in front of the building. In the north a line of rain mixed with dust was moving across the hills, but to the south the sky was blue, the early sun already hot and as yellow as egg yolk. "Why ask me? You're the boss man, aren't you?" she replied.

Two men driving a black SUV had parked their vehicle behind a knoll and set up a high-powered telescope with a camera attached to it on a flat spot that overlooked the valley where the Asian woman lived. They were both dressed in stonewashed jeans and alpine shoes with lug soles and short-sleeve shirts with many pockets. They were both tan and wore shades and had the body tone of men who swam or ran long distances or trained at martial arts or followed a military discipline in their personal lives. One of them opened a lunch box on a rock and removed a thermos of hot coffee and two ham sandwiches. Both men carried Glocks in black nylon holsters on their belts.

Ten minutes later, a rock bounced down from the knoll. The men turned around but saw nothing out of the ordinary. After they finished their sandwiches and poured themselves a second cup of coffee, they heard the pinging of a guitar string. They turned around and saw a solitary figure sitting on the bleached trunk of an uprooted tree, thirty yards up a wash, his face darkened by the brim of a panama hat stained with soot or grime, a guitar propped on one thigh. He picked at a treble string with his thumbnail while he twisted a tuning peg on the guitar's head. "Howdy," he said without looking up.

"Where the hell did you come from?" one of the men in shades said.

"Up yonder, past those boulders," the seated man replied.

"Mind telling us who you are?"

"Just another pilgrim."

"Where's your car, pilgrim?"

"Who says I have one?"

The men in shades looked at each other. "He teleported," one said.

"You cain't ever tell. I get around. You ever hear that song by the Beach Boys? It's called 'I Get Around,' " the seated man replied.

"I get it. You've been shooting the curl off Malibu."

"There aren't many places I haven't been."

"I dig your threads."

"This?" the seated man said, pinching his suit coat with two fingers.

"Yeah, I thought it might be an Armani."

"Could be. You fellows are FBI, aren't you? Or maybe DEA?"

The two men in shades and stonewashed jeans glanced at each other. "Looks like we've been made," one said.

"I can tell because you're wearing Glocks."

"What's your name, asshole?"

The seated man laid his guitar flatly across both thighs, his gaze focused on neutral space, the bumps and knots in his complexion like tan-colored papier-mâché. A closed tortoiseshell guitar case lay on the ground by his foot. It was of expensive manufacture, the kind of case that might contain a Martin or vintage Gibson. "I disturb y'all?" the seated man said.

"That guitar looks like a piece of junk."

"It is," the seated man replied. "It's got rust on the strings. They sound like baling wire."

"So how about playing it somewhere else?"

"Y'all think the government has the right of eminent domain?"

"Of *what?*"

"The right to burn down someone's house just because the government takes a mind to."

"I've got an extra sandwich here. You can have it. But you need to eat it downwind."

151

"You haven't answered my question. Somebody gave y'all the right to burn a man's house and his books and clothes and even his Bible?"

"What's it take, pal? You want me to bust your guitar over a rock? Do we have to walk you over the hill and put you in your car?"

The seated man set down his guitar, the bottom of the sound box grating in the sand. He rubbed his palms up and down on his thighs, the focus gone from his eyes, his lips compressed, downturned at the corners. The knees of his trousers were shiny from wear. "You boys aren't much of a challenge."

"Repeat that?"

The seated man lifted his face, the sunlight shining clearly on it. "You don't recognize me?"

"Why should we? Who are you supposed to be? Somebody from *America's Most Wanted?*"

"How'd you know?"

The two men stared silently at the seated man and the somber expression on his face and the uncut hair on the back of his neck lifting in the wind. Their irritability was obviously growing, but the seated man seemed to pay no attention to it. He grinned, his teeth as tiny as pearls. "Got you, didn't I? They say that Chinese woman down yonder works miracles. Y'all believe that?"

"Buddy, you just don't listen, do you?"

"You reckon she can mix her spit with dirt

152

and touch the eyelids of a blind man and give him back his sight? Because that's the kind of he'p both of y'all need. Like all benighted men, you're arrogant. You walk upon the precipice and never glance at your feet."

"In about ten seconds, I'll be forced to hurt you."

"You wouldn't be the first."

One of the men removed his shades and slipped them in a leather case, then began picking up rocks from the ground.

"If you'd read the Bible you burned, you would have learned how Joshua took Canaan for the Hebrews," the seated man said. "He always attacked at daybreak, with the sun rising on his back. His enemies had to look into the glare while he was killing them."

The man who had taken off his shades flung a rock at the seated man and struck the side of his face. The rock was sharp-edged and triangle-shaped and left a one-inch cut as thin as thread just below the seated man's eye, one that seeped blood like tears on ceramic.

"You get the message?" the rock thrower said. "Do I have to do it again?"

"Well, it's been nice talking to you," the seated man said. He stood up, silhouetted against the sun, the brim of his panama hat riffling in the wind. He lifted his guitar case from the ground and set it on the hard, barkless worm-scrolled apex of the tree trunk and began unsnapping the latches. When he turned around again, the two men he had mistakenly identified as federal agents stared at him openmouthed, their hands wooden at their sides, their expressions frozen like those of statues.

"It's a beaut, isn't it? I paid eighteen thousand for it. Same model you see John Dillinger carrying in that famous photograph."

"We can talk this out, pal," the rock thrower said.

"My biggest problem with you boys is your lack of respect. But maybe the devil can teach y'all manners."

Against the brilliance of the sun, the spray of rounds from the Thompson seemed like an eruption of lightning bolts from a black cutout. The few rounds that missed their target whanged off the rocks and ricocheted into the distance with a sound like the tremolo in a flopping saw blade. Then the man in the panama hat pulled the ammunition drum from the Thompson's frame and laid the Thompson and the fifty-round drum inside the guitar case and shut and latched the top. Before leaving, he took the remaining ham sandwich from the lunch box on the rock and unwrapped it from the wax paper and let the paper blow across the landscape. He ate the sandwich with one hand while he walked back to his vehicle, the guitar case

154

knocking against his leg, the soles of his boots clopping on a series of flat stones like the feet of a hoofed animal.

When Hackberry and Pam arrived at the Asian woman's house, the air was dense and sparkling with humidity, coating every surface in sight, clinging to the skin like damp cotton, as though the sunrise were a source not of light but of ignition. The morning itself seemed divided between darkness and shadow, the clouds overhead roiling and black and crackling with electricity against an otherwise blue and tranquil sky. In the north Hackberry could see a great brown plume of dust lifting out of the hills, and he thought he could smell an odor like baitfish that had been trapped in seaweed and left stranded along the edge of a receding ocean, although he was hundreds of miles from salt water. His eyes burned with his own sweat as he watched the Asian woman approach from the backyard, wearing a white dress and a necklace of black stones.

"Here comes *Teahouse of the August Moon,*" Pam said.

"Don't start," Hackberry said.

"I can't help it. This woman is a fraud."

"Time to be quiet, Pam," he said.

She turned and stared at the side of his face, her nostrils dilating. He stepped forward into the breeze, removing her from the

155

periphery of his vision. He tipped the brim of his hat. "How you doin', Miss Anton?" he said. "Sorry to bother you, but we've got a problem with a guy by the name of Jack Collins."

"I don't recall the name," she replied.

"Collins is a mass killer. Some federal people burned a shack he was using. I think Jack aims to do some serious payback. Your place is probably under surveillance by the feds. I suspect Jack knows that. My bet is he'll be coming around."

"Why should this man know I'm under surveillance?"

"Krill knew to come here. Krill is a lamebrain compared to Collins. The Mexicans say he can walk through walls. Collins has killed people for years but has never been arrested or spent one day in jail. He murdered nine Thai girls down by Chapala Crossing. I dug them up."

"He's the one who did that?" Anton Ling said, her face frozen as though painted on the air, her eyes elongated and lidless.

"He tried to kill my chief deputy in her cruiser. He executed one of his own men in a cave we had cornered him in. He blew three outlaw bikers all over a motel room. He pushed a corrupt PI off a cliff up in the Glass Mountains. A little earlier in the day, he wiped out a whole collection of gangsters in a hunting lodge. He dressed as a cleaning

156

woman in a San Antonio motel and murdered an ICE agent. Nobody knows his body count across the border."

Anton Ling seemed to listen less with shock or horror than with the fixed attention of someone revisiting a tape seen before. "You think he's a threat to the people who come to my house?"

"Probably not. They don't have anything he wants," Hackberry said.

"But he could be a threat to me?"

"Possibly."

"Well, I appreciate your telling me this. But I can't control what this man does or doesn't do."

"It's not all about you, Ms. Ling. Believe it or not, we'd like to get this guy in custody," Pam said. "Collins wears suits and fedoras he buys from the Goodwill. His face looks like it was stung by bumblebees. See anybody like that around?"

"No, I haven't. Otherwise I would have told you."

"Sure? So far you haven't been very forthcoming," Pam said.

"Madam, what did I just say?"

"You can call me Chief Deputy Tibbs, thank you."

"I'd like to invite you in," Anton Ling said to Hackberry. "But I have to go to San Antonio. Some of our people are in jail."

"Your people?" Pam said.

157

"Yes, that's what I call them. They're destitute, cheated out of their money by coyotes, hunted by nativist snipers, and generally treated as though they're subhuman. The particular woman I'm going to try to bail out watched her two-year-old daughter die of a rattlesnake bite in the desert."

"I think Pam was just asking a question, Miss Anton," Hackberry said.

"No, she was making a statement. She's done it several times now."

"Why is it we have to keep coming out here to protect you from yourself? To be honest, it's getting to be a drag," Pam said.

"Then your problem can be easily solved. Just leave and don't bother to come back."

"I think that's a good idea," Pam said.

Hackberry was not listening. The thunderheads had blotted out the sun, dropping the countryside into shadow. He had turned his head toward the southeast, where the wind was whipping dust off the hilltops and riffling the mesquite that grew down the slopes. His eyes fixed on a spot where rain had started to tumble out of the sky and a muted sound like crackling foil seemed to leak from the clouds. Hackberry opened and closed his mouth to clear his ears and listen to the sound that had started and now had stopped.

"What is it?" Pam said.

"Somebody was firing a machine gun," he replied.

"I didn't hear it," she said.

Because you were too busy talking, he thought. But he didn't say it. "You drive. Good-bye, Miss Anton. Thank you for your time."

"I'll follow you," she said.

"That's not a good idea," he said.

"My property line goes right through the hills. I have a right to know who's on my land."

"In this case, you don't. Stay here, please. Don't make me ask you again," he said.

He got in the passenger side of the cruiser and closed the door, not looking back, then glanced in the outside mirror. Anton Ling was already getting into a skinned-up pale blue truck seamed with rust, the front bumper secured by baling wire. "This stuff has to stop, Pam," he said.

"Tell *her,*" Pam said.

"You two are more alike than you think."

"Which two?"

"You and Miss Anton. Who else?"

"Yeah?" she said, giving him a look. "We'll talk more about that later."

"No, we won't. You'll drive and not speak for me to others when we're conducting an investigation."

"Maybe I should turn in my badge, Hack. That's how you make me feel. No, I take that back. I can't even describe how you make me feel," she said. "You treated me like I was a fence post." She started the engine, then had to stop and concentrate on what she was doing.

"You're one of the best cops I've ever known," he said.

"Save it. You hide behind your years. It's a sorry excuse."

"My wife died on this date, Pam. I don't want to participate in this kind of conversation today. We're on the job. We need to give this nonsense a rest."

"I went out to the grave this morning. I thought you might be there."

He looked at her blankly. "Why did you go there?"

"I thought you might need somebody. I put flowers on her grave."

"You did that?"

She stared at the hills, her hands tight on the steering wheel, rain striking on the glass. Her expression was wan, her eyes dead. "I think you heard thunder," she said. "I don't believe anything is out there."

"You put flowers on Rie's grave?"

She would not speak the rest of the way to the place in the hills where Hackberry believed he had heard the staccato firing of a submachine gun. He took a bottle of aspirin from his shirt pocket and ate two of them and gazed out the window, his thoughts poor consolation for the spiritual fatigue that

160

seemed to eat through all his connective tissue.

Pam drove off the main road and up an incline dotted with cactus and small rocks and mesquite and yucca plants whose leaves were darkening in the rain. She squinted at a flat place between two knolls, the sky sealed with black clouds all the way to the southern horizon.

"There's a telescope on a tripod. It looks like it has a camera on it," she said.

"Stop here. You go to the left. I'll come around from the right," Hackberry said.

She braked the Jeep and turned off the ignition. "Hack?" she said.

"Yes?"

"Nothing," she said.

"Say it."

"I've got your back."

"You always do. That's why I wouldn't partner with anyone else," he said.

She looked directly into his face, her lips slightly parted, her teeth white. She made him think of a young girl outside a prom, her face tilted up, waiting to be kissed. Then she opened the door and stepped out into the rain, unsnapping the strap on her .357, her arms pumped and brown and glistening. She looked beyond him, down the incline, and lifted her chin as though pointing. He turned around and saw Anton Ling's pickup truck approaching from the dirt road, clattering across the rocks, the cactus raking under the bumper and oil pan. "Get down there and stop her," he said.

"Gladly," Pam said.

As soon as Pam began walking down the incline, Hackberry headed uphill between the two knolls toward the telescope and camera. He pulled his .45 revolver from its holster and let it hang loosely against his leg, his back straight so the pain that lived in his lower spine would not flare like an electric burn across his back and wrap around his thighs. He glanced once over his shoulder, then continued straight on toward the telescope, knowing already what he would find, knowing also that his nemesis, Jack Collins, had once again written his signature across the landscape with a dirty finger and had disappeared into the elements.

When Hackberry was little more than a teenage boy, in a battalion aid station at Inchon and later on the firing line at the Chosin Reservoir and even later in a giant POW enclosure the prisoners called the Bean Camp, he had acquired an enormous amount of unwanted knowledge about the moribund and the dead and the rites of passage from the world of the living into the land of the great shade. The opalescence in the skin, the wounds that had the glassy brightness of roses frozen inside ice, and the bodies stuffed in sleeping bags and stacked as hard as

162

concrete in the backs of six-bys were the images a war poet might focus on. But the real story resided in the eyes. The marines and soldiers and navy corpsmen who were mortally wounded or dying of disease or starvation had stared up at him with a luminosity that was like ground diamonds, the pupils tiny dots, so small they could not have recorded an image on the brain. Then, in a blink, the light was gone, and the eyes became as opaque and devoid of meaning as fish scale. That was when he had come to believe that the dying indeed saw through the curtain but took their secrets with them.

The two men on the ground, dressed as casual hikers, must have thought they had walked into a Gatling gun. Their clothes were punched with holes from their shoes to their shirt collars. The spray of ejected shell casings showed no pattern, indicating the shooter had probably shifted his position and fired several bursts from different angles, as though enjoying his work. The fact that one man's hand was twitching at his side seemed almost miraculous, as though the hand were disembodied and the only part of the victim that was still alive.

"Pam! Call for the paramedics and the coroner and tell Felix and R.C. to get out here!" Hackberry shouted down the incline.

He holstered his revolver and walked past a downed tree, the root-ball impacted with dirt.

A worthless guitar, the strings coated with rust, lay on the ground. He gazed down a series of flat yellow rocks that descended like stair steps into a wide flume where an SUV was parked and a second vehicle had left a curlicue of tire tracks in the dirt. He strained his eyes against the distance and thought he saw a speck on the horizon that might have been a car, but he couldn't be sure. Then the speck was lost inside the bolts of lightning that leaped from the earth to the clouds like gold thread.

"Collins?" Pam said behind him.

"Who else kills like this?" he said.

"I think one of them is still alive."

"He's brain-dead. The twitching hand doesn't mean anything."

"Better tell her that," Pam replied.

He turned and saw Anton Ling on her knees next to the dying man, trying to resuscitate him, forcing her breath inside his mouth and down his windpipe, mashing on his chest with the heel of her hand. Her dress and hair and chin and cheeks were speckled with his blood. She turned his head to one side and drained his mouth, then bent over him and tried again.

"Miss Anton?" Hackberry said.

She didn't speak or even look up.

"This fellow is gone, Miss Anton," he said.

She stared up into Hackberry's face. Her mouth was smeared, her eyes slightly crossed.

164

"You gave it your best," he said, putting his hands under her elbows, lifting her up.

"Who did this?" she said.

"The man who calls himself the left hand of God."

"That's an insult to God," she said.

"Jack Collins is an insult to the planet," Hackberry said. "But Pam and I need to get to work."

"Are these federal agents?" Anton Ling asked.

"Maybe," he said. His knees popping, he squatted down, wincing at the pain in his lower back. He slipped the wallet from the back pocket of the man Anton Ling had tried to resuscitate. The leather was warm and sticky, and he had to wipe his fingers on a handkerchief before he opened it. Hackberry sorted through the credit cards, driver's license, and celluloid photo holders, then set the wallet down by the dead man's foot. He recovered the wallet from the second victim and did the same. He got to his feet, slightly off balance. "If Collins was trying to do payback on the feds, he screwed up."

"How?" Pam said.

"These guys worked for a security service out of Houston. My bet is they were doing scut work for Temple Dowling. He's a defense contractor and the son of a United States senator I was a hump for."

"I didn't catch that."

"I got politically ambitious back in the sixties."

"Everybody makes mistakes," Pam said.

"A mistake is something you do when you don't know better."

"What's the guitar doing here?" she said.

"Who knows? Collins is a harlequin. He has contempt for most of the people he kills."

Pam gazed down the incline. While Hackberry looked through the wallets of the two dead men, Anton Ling had gone back to her truck and was now walking back up the slope with a small silver bottle in her hand. She unscrewed the top and knelt by the man whose life she had tried to save. She put a drop of oil on her finger and drew the sign of the cross on his forehead.

"Miss Anton?" Pam said. "We shouldn't mess too much with the bodies until the coroner gets here."

"If you don't want me to, I won't," Anton Ling said.

Pam looked at Hackberry and waited.

"It won't hurt anything," he said.

Pam watched Anton Ling kneel by the second man and make the sign of the cross on his forehead with her thumb. Then Pam went back to the Jeep and returned with an oversize United States Forest Service canteen and a roll of paper towels. She poured water on a clutch of paper sections and squatted down by Anton Ling and began to wipe her

166

hands and her face and then her hair.

"You don't need to do that," Anton Ling said.

"I know I don't," Pam said.

"I'm quite all right," Anton Ling said.

"Yeah, you are, ma'am. That's exactly what you are," Pam replied. "You're damn straight you're all right."

Anton Ling looked at her quizzically.

Hackberry walked down the slope to the Jeep. He scratched idly at his cheek with three fingers and wondered why men tried to puzzle through the mysteries of heaven when they couldn't even resolve the ones that lived in the human heart. He picked up the hand-held radio from the seat of the cruiser and called R.C. and Felix and asked for their ETA. When a tree of lightning burst on the horizon, he thought he saw a solitary figure standing as starkly as an exclamation point on the deck of a house high up on a plateau. But the raindrops were striking his hat as hard as marbles, and he had to concentrate on his call to Felix and R.C., and he paid no more attention to the solitary figure or the house that resembled the forecastle of a ship, a huge American flag painted on the sandstone bluff behind it.

CHAPTER SEVEN

The Reverend Cody Daniels did not like sleep. During the waking day, he could deal with the past by constantly rebuilding his mental fortifications, alternately suppressing uncomfortable shards of memory or re-creating them so they didn't detract from his image of himself as the pastor of the Cowboy Chapel. Sleep was another matter. Sleep was a stone jail cell without windows or light, where any number of malformed creatures could reach out of the darkness and touch him at will, their fingers as gelatinous and clinging as giant worms. Sometimes the creatures in the dream pressed their faces to his and ran their tongues along his skin, their breathing labored in his ear, the invasion of his person so complete that he felt his entrails would burst, his pelvis would split apart.

When he woke, he would have tears in his eyes and would sit on the side of the bed in the dark and beat his fists on his thighs.

Almost twenty-four hours had passed since

he had looked through his telescope and had witnessed the machine-gunning of two men by a man wearing a rumpled suit and a panama hat. At first he had not believed what he was watching. The efficiency of the killer, the way he methodically hosed down his victims, blowing them all over the rocks and sand, had made Cody numb with fear and horror but at the same time had left him in awe of the shooter, a man with cheeks like emery paper and whose clothes and hat looked as though they had been stripped from a scarecrow.

Then Cody had watched the arrival of the sheriff, and the female deputy with the wide ass and big shoulders, and the Asian woman who had held his hands in hers and looked into his eyes and read his most private thoughts. But they were not witnesses. *He*, Cody Daniels, was. He had seen it all and could describe how the victims had raised their arms in front of their faces, their mouths pleading, their eyes squeezing shut, their coffee spilling to the ground. It was Cody Daniels who had experienced an almost omniscient oversight of events that others would have to guess at and reconstruct and debate and analyze in a laboratory. All he had to do was make one phone call, and the sheriff who had threatened to kick a nail-studded two-by-four up his hole would be treating him as a friend of the court, hanging on his words, the female deputy reduced to nothing but an insignificant functionary in the background.

Except Cody didn't make the call.

Why?

He knew all too well the answer. It was fear, the succubus that had fed at his heart all his life.

Temple Dowling had given him a business card and had told him to report whatever happened on the Asian woman's property. Krill and the degenerate named Negrito had weighted him with the same obligation, telling him to build a signal fire and pour motor oil on it, like he was an Indian in a loincloth in a John Wayne movie. Dowling claimed to have evidence that could send Cody to prison for the clinic bombing. Krill and Negrito's potential was even worse. No matter which course of action Cody chose, he had become a human piñata for people he despised, the rich and powerful on one side and a pair of pepper-belly sadists on the other.

Why had all this befallen him? He had bought the oven timer; he didn't set it. The others had said the bomb would go off in the middle of the night, that no one would be hurt, that the object was to scare the shit out of people who were killing the unborn. It was a noble cause, wasn't it?

But why had he gone to the scene immediately afterward, hiding in the crowd,

170

fascinated, his head reeling with both exhilaration and guilt? Unfortunately, Cody got to see more than he had planned. He had watched dry-mouthed while the firemen and the paramedics pried the nurse from the rubble. Then he saw the glass and brick that had embedded in her face and eyes, and the blood that had fried in a black veil on one side of her head. He had tried to push his way back through the crowd, away from the paramedics loading the nurse into an ambulance only a few feet away. A fat white woman had blocked his way, virtually shoving him, her face blazing with anger. "Watch it, buster," she said. "I'll punch you in the mouth. I've seen you around here before."

She had terrified him. That night he had bought a bus ticket to San Antonio and since then had never picked up the phone when the caller ID indicated the call had originated in the East. But this particular dawn, Cody was strangely at peace. The air was cool, the sun still below the earth's rim, his bedroom filled with a softness that he associated with the promise of rain and the bloom of desert flowers. He had not done the bidding of either Temple Dowling or the blue-eyed half-breed Krill, and now almost twenty-four hours had passed without incident since he had witnessed the killings in the foothills below his house. Maybe these guys were all bluster, he told himself. Cody had dealt with meth-head bikers and gangbangers and perverts of every stripe on a county prison farm, including the two Hispanic hacks who had walked him out to the work shed where a solitary sawhorse waited for him under a naked lightbulb. What could Krill or Dowling do to him that hadn't been done to him before? Cody was a survivor. *Screw these guys,* he thought.

He rolled over in bed and let the soft blue coolness of the dawn seep inside his eyelids and lull him back to sleep. That was when he heard a sound that made no sense. Someone was brushing his teeth in Cody's bathroom. He sat up in bed and stared in disbelief at a man who was bent over the lavatory, jerking Cody's toothbrush like a ragged stick in his mouth, toothpaste and saliva running down his fingers and wrist.

The figure looked like a half-formed ape wearing a vest and striped trousers without a shirt or belt, his skin streaked with tufts of orange hair. A knife in a scabbard was tied flatly along his upper right arm with leather thongs. He stopped brushing and cupped water into his mouth and spat into the lavatory. "How you doin', man?" he asked.

"You're using my toothbrush."

"Yeah, it's a good one, man."

"How'd you get in?"

"You were supposed to make a signal fire.

How come you didn't do that? Krill is pissed at you."

"Signal fire for what?"

"About that crazy man who killed those two guys down below. He had a machine gun. You can hear it a long way, man. You didn't hear nothing?"

"I was gone. I didn't hear or see anything. All I know is what was on the news. Get out of here."

"A friend of ours says your truck was parked here all day yesterday. You calling our friend a liar?"

"Where's Krill?"

"Outside, looking through your telescope at *la china*. He's got a fascination with her. Know why that is?"

"No. I mean I don't care. I just want you guys out of my life."

"Krill's children were killed by a U.S. Army helicopter. They wasn't baptized. He thinks *la china* can do it for him. At least he's been thinking that up till now. Guess why Krill likes you?"

"Likes me?"

"Yeah, man, you're lucky. He likes you a lot, even when he's pissed at you. He needs you to do him a favor. You got a lot of luck."

"What kind of favor?"

"He wants you to baptize his kids."

"You said they're dead."

"Yeah, man, they're dead. They're gonna

173

be that way a long time."

"I cain't baptize dead people. Nobody can."

"Why not? They're the ones that need it most. I was baptized when I was born. It didn't do me no good. Maybe it's better to get baptized after you die. Then you can't fuck things up anymore."

"How long have his kids been dead?"

"A lot of years, man."

"Then they're buried, right? In Nicaragua or El Salvador or Guatemala or one of those other shitholes, right?"

"Not exactly."

Cody waited for Negrito to go on, his heart dilating with fear for reasons he didn't understand. Negrito was grinning at him, his eyes lit with a lunatic shine. "They're in a box," Negrito said. "He carried it around a long time, then buried it in the desert."

"They're what?"

"He's got them in a wood box. Their bones look like sticks inside skin that's all shriveled up. Like little mummies. When you shake the box, you can hear them rattle."

"That's sick."

"Say that to Krill and see what happens. He talks to them, man. Krill's brain is a couple of quarts down sometimes. That's why he's out here in a place that's like a big skillet. That's why all of you are here. It's a place for losers, man. You ain't figured that out?"

"Figured out what?"

174

"Why you live here. You, *la china,* the crazy man they call Preacher Jack. Krill understands. But you can't figure it out? You're saying you're not as smart as Krill?"

"Smart about what?"

"About who you are, man. About where you live. Krill says you're in the belly of God. That's what Krill thinks the desert is. You thought I was scary, huh? What you think now, man? Look at Krill. He takes scalps 'cause he's more Indian than white. You gonna tell him you ain't gonna baptize his kids 'cause they already turned into mummies? You got that kind of guts? I sure ain't."

"That's what it will take to get shut of y'all?"

"No, man. That's just a small part of it."

Negrito removed the knife from the scabbard tied down on his upper arm and began cleaning his nails as though he had forgotten the point of the conversation. His hand slipped, and the tip of the knife sliced open the ball of his index finger. He watched a thick drop of blood well from the proud tissue, then inserted his finger in his mouth and sucked the wound clean.

"Go on with what you were saying. What does Krill want?" Cody said.

"Your soul, man. What'd you think?" Negrito replied. "He collects souls that he wants to take with him into the next world. Why are you so stupid, my little gringo friend?"

■ ■ ■ ■

That same morning, Maydeen Stoltz walked into Hackberry's office without knocking, her mouth glossy with lipstick. She waited as though gathering her thoughts, her love handles protruding over her belt. "A guy who refuses to give his name has called twice on the business line and demands I put you on the phone," she said.

"Demands?"

"I think he said, 'Get to it, woman.' "

"What's on his mind?"

"He wouldn't say. He claims you two go back." She looked at him blankly.

"What are you not telling me?"

"His voice isn't one you forget. I think I talked to him once last year."

"Collins?"

"How many sexist pricks call in on the business line?"

"If he calls again, put him through."

"I put him on hold. I also told him if I get my hands on him, his brains are gonna be running out his nose."

"You said that to Jack Collins?"

"If that's who he is."

"I'm going to pick up now. See if you can get a trace."

"Watch yourself, Hack."

He winked at her and lifted the receiver to

his ear. Oddly, it gave off a sound like a high wind blowing through the holes in the earpiece. "This is Sheriff Holland. Can I help you?" he said.

"I thought I ought to check in. We haven't talked in a while."

The accent was what a linguist would call southern midlands, a dialect common on the plains west of Fort Worth and up through Oklahoma, the pronunciations attenuated, as though the speaker doesn't have enough oxygen in his blood. This speaker sounded like he had put a teaspoon of metal filings in his morning coffee.

"It's good to hear from you, Mr. Collins. I had you figured for dead," Hackberry said.

"In a way, I was."

"Can you clarify that? I'm not that fast."

"I did penance for one year. I ate from people's garbage and slept in caves and wore rags and washed myself with wet ash. I think you know why."

"I dug those girls up. I wish you could have shared the experience with me. I think you'd find your role as penitent a little absurd."

"Judge me as you will."

"Oh, I will."

"How about those two federal agents? Do you think they were innocent victims?"

"The two guys you capped? I've got news for you. They were PIs out of Houston, not feds. They didn't have squat to do with burning up your shack and your Bible."

"I'm sorry to hear that."

"Tell that to their families."

"No, I mean I'm sorry I wasted all that ammunition. There's been a right smart jump in the price of bullets since the election of our new president."

"You made a mistake coming back here, bub."

"I address you by your title, Sheriff Holland. I'd appreciate your showing me the same level of respect."

"In your way, you're an intelligent man. But you're also a narcissist. Like most narcissists, you're probably a self-loathing failure whose mother wished she had thrown her son away and raised the afterbirth. All of your power is dependent on the Thompson you use to overwhelm your victims, some of whom were Thai girls hardly older than children. How's that feel, Mr. Collins? You think authors such as Garland Roark or B. Traven would break bread with you?"

"I don't make claims for myself or impose myself on others."

"How about Noie Barnum? Does he know you're a mass killer?"

"Who says I know such a person?"

"You were seen with him while robbing food and camping gear from other people. I hate to disillusion you about your criminal abilities, but you have a tendency to leave fecal prints on whatever you touch."

"Noie is a decent man untainted by the enterprises you serve, Sheriff."

"That could be, but you're *not* a decent man, Mr. Collins. You bring misery and death into the lives of others and quote Scripture while you do it. I'm not a theologian, but if the Prince of Darkness has acolytes, I think you've made the cut."

"You're a damn liar."

"No, sir, you're the dissembler, but the only person you deceive is yourself. This time out, I'm going to burn your kite and expose you for the cheap titty-sucking fraud that you are."

"You won't talk to me that way."

"I just did. Don't call here again. You're an embarrassment to talk with." Hackberry eased the receiver back into the phone cradle. Maydeen appeared at the doorway and studied his face. "Get it?" he asked.

"Nope. He's using some kind of relay system."

"I was afraid of that. No matter. We'll see him directly, one way or another."

"I have a feeling you made sure of that," she said.

He leaned back in his swivel chair and put his boots on the cusp of the wastebasket and stretched his arms. "You got to do something for kicks," he said. "Can I buy you and Pam lunch?"

Anton Ling had just pushed her grocery cart around a pyramid of pork and beans when another shopper wheeled his cart straight out of the aisle and crashed into her basket so hard that her hands flew in the air as though they had received an electric shock. A bag of tomatoes she had just sacked spilled over the top of the basket and rolled across the floor.

"Sorry, I didn't see you there," Cody Daniels said.

"You did that on purpose," she replied.

"No, ma'am, I certainly did not. I was looking for the Vi-ennas and soda crackers, and there you were."

"The what?"

"Vi-enna sausages. They don't have those in China?"

"Have you been drinking?"

"I have a diabetic condition. It causes my breath to smell like chemicals." He grinned at her stupidly, his face dilated and shiny. "It's colder than a well digger's ass in here."

"Why are you acting like this?"

"Here, I'll pick up your 'maters. Want to get a snack over at the Dog 'n' Shake? It's on me."

"Sir, you can hardly stand."

"Drunk on the love of the Lord, is what I call it."

180

"Don't touch my tomatoes. Don't touch anything in my basket. Just get away from me," she said.

She picked up her tomatoes from the floor and replaced them in her cart and got in line at the cash register. But when she went into the parking lot, Cody Daniels was waiting by her pickup truck. "We're both clergy, Miss Anton. We've got us a mutual problem, and we need to put our heads together and work out a solution."

"I'm not a cleric, Reverend Daniels. I think you're very confused and should go home."

"Easy for you to say 'should go home.' Krill was at my house. Krill wants me to baptize some dead children he's got buried out in the desert. He gave me the feeling you won't do it, and so it's getting put on me."

"Of course I won't do it."

"So why should it fall on me?"

"I don't know. Talk to Sheriff Holland."

Cody Daniels swayed slightly, obviously trying to concentrate. "Sheriff Holland threatened me. I'm not one of his big fans."

"Look at me."

"Ma'am?"

"I said look at me."

"What the hell you think I'm doing?"

"Why are you so angry at yourself and others?"

The sky was gray, and the wind was blowing in the parking lot, and pieces of news-

181

paper were flapping and twisting through the air. Cody Daniels's eyes seemed to search the sky as though he saw meaning in the wind and the clouds and the flying scraps of paper imprinted with tracks of car tires. "I'm not angry at anybody. I just want to go about my ministry. I want to be let alone."

"No, you carry a terrible guilt with you, something you won't tell anybody about. It's what gives other people power over you, Reverend Daniels. It's why you're drunk. It's why you're blaming everybody else for your problems."

"I was saved a long time ago. I don't have to listen to anything you say."

She dropped the tailgate on the back of her truck and loaded her groceries in the bed, hoping he would be gone when she turned around again. She closed the tailgate and latched it with the chain, her gaze focused on a blue-collar family getting in their automobile, the children trying to pull inside the stringed balloons they had gotten at a street carnival. Cody Daniels had not budged. "Let me get by, please," she said.

"I could have dropped the dime on you any time I wanted and had you arrested," he said.

"For what?"

"Smuggling wets, aiding and abetting dope mules, maybe hiding out a fellow name of Noie Barnum, a guy who might end up in the hands of Al Qaeda."

182

She tried to walk around him, but he stepped in front of her. His breath made her wince. "I saw the man with the machine gun kill those two men down below your place," he said. "It was Preacher Jack Collins."

"So what?"

"If you ask me, not everything he's done is all bad."

"Say that again."

"Nits make lice."

"Excuse me, sir, but you're disgusting."

"Those Thai women didn't have any business in this country. Just like those Mexicans you're bringing in. Every one of them is a breeder, wanting to have their babies here so they can be U.S. citizens."

Anton Ling's eyes were burning, her jaw clenched. She held her gaze on him as though watching a zoo creature behind a pane of glass. He stepped back, a twitch in his face. "Why you staring at me like that?"

"It had to do with a woman, didn't it?" she said.

"What?"

"You hurt a woman very badly. Maybe even killed her. That's it, isn't it?"

"You spread lies about me, I'll come down there and —"

"You'll what?"

His face was contorted, his eyes hot and small and unfocused. "I just wanted to be your friend," he said. "You're putting Krill

183

and that man Negrito on me while you're walking around with your nose in the air like you're some kind of female pope. La Magdalena, my cotton-picking ass."

She got in the cab of her pickup and started the engine. "Don't come around my home again. Don't presume about whom you're dealing with, either."

"*Presume?* What's that supposed to mean?" he asked. "You gonna call the Chinese army down on me?"

She drove away without replying, her truck rattling and leaking smoke at every rusted seam.

"*Presume* what?" he shouted after her.

Hackberry worked late that evening, and at dusk he removed his hat from the peg on his office wall and put it on and hung his gun belt and holstered white-handled revolver from his shoulder and drove out to the site where Jack Collins had machine-gunned the two PIs. The crime-scene tape that had been wrapped around the mesquite and yucca had been broken by wild animals, the brass cartridges from Collins's gun picked up from the ground, the blood splatter washed from the rocks by the previous night's rain, even the sandwich crumbs eaten by ants and the ants in all probability eaten by armadillos. Other than the broken yellow tape, impaled and fluttering among the creosote bush and agaves and prickly pear, there was little to indicate in the reddish-blue melt of the sunset that two men had pleaded for their lives on this spot less than thirty-six hours ago, their sphincters failing them, their courage draining through the soles of their feet, all their assumptions about their time on earth leached from their hearts, their last glimpse of the earth dissolving in a bloody mist.

What good purpose could lie in his visit to the site of an execution? he asked himself. Perhaps none. In reality, he knew why he was there, and the reason had little to do with the two gunshot victims. Hackberry had come to learn that wars did not end with a soldier's discharge. The ordeal, if that was not too strong a word, was open-ended, an alpha without an omega, a surreal landscape lit by trip flares that could burst unexpectedly to life in the time it took to shut one's eyes.

Hackberry had many memories left over from the war: the human-wave assaults; the .30-caliber machine-gun barrels that had to be changed out with bare hands; the Chinese dead frozen in the snow as far as the eye could see; the constant blowing of bugles in the hills and the wind furrowing across the ice fields under a sky in which the sun was never more than a gaseous smudge. But none of these memories compared to a strip of film that he could not rip from his unconscious, or kill with alcohol or drugs or sex or born-again religion or psychotherapy or good works or sackcloth and ashes. He did not see the filmstrip every night, but he knew it was always on the projector, waiting to play whenever it wished, and when that happened, he would be forced to watch every inch of it, as though his eyelids were stitched to his forehead.

In the filmstrip, Sergeant Kwong would finish urinating through a sewer grate on Hackberry's head, then extract him from the hole where, for six weeks, Hackberry had learned how to defecate in a GI helmet and survive on a diet of fish heads and weevil-infested rice. In the next few frames of the strip, Hackberry would stand woodenly in the cold, his body trembling, his eyelashes crusted with snow, while Kwong lifted his burp gun on its strap and fired point-blank into the faces of two prisoners from Hackberry's shack, their bodies jackknifing backward into an open latrine.

They died and Hackberry lived. The other prisoners in his shack were also spared. But all of them were made to believe their comrades' deaths were caused by them and their willingness to confess to imaginary conspiracies in order to free themselves from the holes in the ground where they shivered nightly.

If Hackberry had to face Sergeant Kwong's burp gun again, would he be less fearful than the morning he had watched his fellow POWs executed, their hands lifting helplessly in front of their faces? If he met Kwong on a street, would he let the past remain in the past? Or would he call him out, as would his grandfather Old Hack, pistol-whipping Kwong to his knees?

Hackberry would never know the answer to those questions. Kwong had probably gone back home after the war and repaired bicycles or worked on a communal rice farm. With regularity, he had probably battered and impregnated a peasant girl he bought from a neighbor. He had probably treated his children with both fondness and cruelty while he watched them grow into imitations of himself. If he ever thought at all about the crimes he had committed in the Bean Camp, it was probably only to ask himself if he had been too lenient on the foreigners who had caused him to leave his home and serve in the frozen wastes of North Korea. He would probably be amazed that a lawman on the South Texas border did not go through one day or night in his life without thinking of him.

Hackberry walked to the top of the incline where the two PIs had died, his binoculars hanging from his neck. He gazed through the lenses at Anton Ling's house and at the lightning rods on the peaked roof and at the gables and the wide gallery and the paintless weathered severity of the wood in the walls. The house reminded him of Old Hack's place, a displaced piece of Victorian design dropped by happenstance on the Texas Plains, as though its picket fence and latticework and baroque cornices could end tornadoes and prairie fires and ice storms that froze a man to the saddle, or stop rogue Indians from rope-dragging white families through cactus or hanging them upside down over a slow flame.

He moved the lenses across Anton Ling's gallery and the hanging baskets of impatiens and coffee cans planted with violets and petunias. Children were sitting on the wood steps, playing with a whirligig. A meat fire was smoking in the backyard, the windmill's blades ginning, and Mexican families were sitting at the plank tables under the fruit trees by the barn. Then he saw her emerge from the back door, a straw basket on her arm, and begin setting the table with plastic forks and knives and paper plates and jelly glasses. She wore cowboy boots and a navy blue dress with a long brocaded hem and silver trim at the neck, one like his dead wife, Rie, would wear, adding to the effect of her dark features and the highlights in her hair. Then he saw the Mexicans bringing colored glass vessels from the chapel to the tables, candles flickering. The Mexicans were singing songs, the words rising and falling in the wind, their work-seamed faces exactly like those of the people who had always surrounded Rie. He

188

had to take the binoculars from his eyes and sit down on a rock, a pang not unlike a sharp stone piercing his heart.

Was he so foolish that he would try to re-create his wife inside the skin of the Asian woman? Would he never learn to accept the world for what it was, a place where the sunlight blinded us to the figures beckoning to us from the shade?

In that moment he wished Preacher Jack Collins would once again appear in the middle of his life, his cheeks unshaved, his fingernails half-mooned with dirt, his rumpled suit coat and sweat-stained dress shirt like those of a drunkard out to spoil a party, the Thompson pointed dead center at Hackberry's chest. You feared whiskey in your dreams or in a store window or behind a bar, not when you drank it, Hackberry thought. You feared death only as long as you held on to life. Mr. Death lost his dominion as soon as you faced and engaged him and dared him to do his worst.

None of these thoughts brought comfort to Hackberry Holland. The unalterable reality that governed every moment of his waking day was simple: The love of his life was dead, and he would never see her again.

CHAPTER EIGHT

Danny Boy Lorca's home was not so much a house as a collection of buildings and shacks and pole sheds in or under which he cooked his food or ate or slept or worked or got drunk. He smoked his own meat and grew his own vegetables, did his own repairs on his army-surplus flatbed truck, and washed his clothes in an outdoor bathtub and dried them on a smooth-wire fence. He seldom locked his doors, except on a shed whose walls were layered like armor plate from the roof to the ground with chrome hubcaps. The interior of the shed had nothing to do with mechanized vehicles. It was there that he kept the cases of Corona and the gallon bottles of Bacardi and Oso Negro he bought in Mexico and brought back into the States through a ravine where seventeenth-century Spaniards had carved Christian crosses on the rocks to commemorate a battle in which they had slain dozens of Indians.

When Danny Boy drank, he did it methodically and with dedication, his time frame open-ended, his progress from the first drink to the last as steady and unrelenting and disciplined as anyone's can be while he is systematically sawing himself apart. His benders lasted from a few days to a few weeks, and they always commenced when a clock inside him would go off without warning and a voice would whisper, *It's time.* Danny Boy never argued with the voice. He would fill a bucket with crushed ice he bought from a filling station down the road, unlock the shed where he kept his beer and liquor, and stuff a dozen bottles of Corona into the ice. Then he would sit down at a plank table that overlooked the miles of ancient topography to the south, pour three inches of Bacardi into a jelly glass, and snap the cap off a Corona, the foam sliding down the bottle neck and wrapping around his wrist like a white snake.

The first drink produced the second, then the third, and eventually he would lose count of his consumption and slip into a blackout in which his motor control still functioned but his soul went somewhere else. When his supply in the shed was gone, he would panhandle on the streets or swamp out bars in exchange for alcohol, sleeping in alleys or on the floor of a jail cell. The pattern never changed. The first two days of his bender were memorable. The rest of it was a void that he learned about later from police officers and bailiffs.

It was four A.M. when he began his current bender at the plank table behind his house. The sky was spangled with stars, the desert floor silvery and pale green and rustling with forms of life that no one saw in the daytime. The visions he had of the land and its great alluvial vastness were always a puzzle to him. Sometimes he thought he saw dinosaurs rearing their long necks out of a marshy bog, great tendrils of vegetation and root systems hanging from their mouths, while people wearing animal skins squatted by campfires up in the rocks. Someone had told him that his visions were nonsense, that dinosaurs were extinct long before man appeared on the planet. Danny Boy did not argue with his detractors. How could he? Even though he had once claimed the powers of a shaman, he had hidden, as a coward would, while a defenseless man was tortured to death. Any powers he had possessed had been taken from him and surely given to someone else. Danny Boy did not contend with his fate. He had failed. A shaman did not fear either this world or the next. But if his power was gone, why was he experiencing another vision, in this instance a figure walking up the long alluvial plain toward him, a man who seemed made of sticks? The figure was wearing a pale wide-brimmed hat and a shapeless business

192

suit, the cuffs of his trousers stuffed inside the tops of his cowboy boots, an old-style holster slung at an angle on his hip, brass cartridges inserted in the leather ammunition loops.

Danny Boy watched the figure draw nearer, the toes of his boots cracking through the shell of baked clay along the streambed, the sky behind him a royal purple, the mesquite and piñon trees on the hillsides alive with birds that only minutes ago had been sleeping. Danny Boy drank the rum from his jelly glass and lifted the Corona bottle and swallowed until he could no longer taste the rum in his mouth, until his tongue was dead and his chest was warm and empty of fear. He rubbed at his eyes with the back of his wrist, hoping that when he stared back down the slope, the figure would be gone, just another gargoyle that took up temporary residence in Danny Boy's dreams and went away.

"Some people say insomnia is a disorder. I say it's not," the man said, the wind ruffling the brim of his hat and fanning open his coat over his flat stomach. "I say it's a mark of somebody who sees things as they are."

Danny Boy remained silent, his face as square and expressionless as a stone carving, his shoulders slumped, his hands resting palms down on the table, like animal paws.

"You know who I am?" the man asked.

Danny Boy seemed to think about the question. "Maybe," he replied. "But probably not. I get things mixed up in my head sometimes."

"It doesn't make any difference. I'm here. That's all that counts. It's a fine spot to stand on, too. What a vista."

"Where'd you come from?"

"Out yonder." The man looked over his shoulder and pointed at a distant spot on the horizon.

"Where you're pointing at is Mexico."

"I get around."

"Why you carrying a pistol?"

"For snakes and such. You getting a jump on the morning or tapering off from last night? You look like you got rode hard and put away wet."

Danny Boy thought about what the man had said. "I reckon some people's ways ain't the best," he replied. He looked without focus at the tops of his hands and at the grain in the table's planks. He kept waiting for the visitor to speak, but he didn't. "You want a drink?"

"I'm not keen on alcohol. Can I sit down?"

This time it was Danny who didn't speak. He felt the visitor's eyes roving over his face in the silence. "You spend some time in the prize ring?" the visitor asked.

"I was a club fighter."

"You took some hits."

"Not from fighting other pugs. We traveled from town to town, like wrestlers do. The

194

owner wheeled the fights any way he wanted. We all knew each other and slept at the same motel."

"So what happened to your face?"

"For a hundred bucks, locals could go three rounds with me. I got half of the hundred to let them go the full three. I got sixty-five if I let them work me over." He tried to smile when he spoke, the scar tissue in his eyebrows stretching his eyes into the shape of a China-man's. "They'd knock my mouthpiece into the seats. All the time I was holding them up, and they'd be hitting me with everything they had. Their gloves would be shiny with my blood, and all the time they'd be thinking how they busted up a pro."

"What you did back then isn't important. You're not an ordinary guy." The visitor turned and looked behind him, down the slope, his gaze lifting into the stars. Then he looked at Danny Boy again. "What do you see out yonder?"

"Rocks and sand. A desert. Sometimes bad people bringing dope through the ravines."

"I'm not an ordinary fellow, either, so don't talk down to me. I came a long way to see you. I'm going to sit down now. But don't you disrespect me again."

"I don't know why you're talking to me like this," Danny Boy said.

"Because you just lied to me."

Danny Boy watched his visitor raise one

foot over the plank seat and sit down at the table, his body all angles, like coat hangers, his holstered pistol binding against his belt and thigh, the leather creaking. "I see an ocean sometimes," Danny Boy said. "I can hear the waves in the wind. Or maybe it's just the sound the wind makes in the trees. It sounds like water rushing through a canyon."

When the visitor made no reply, Danny Boy lifted his arm and pointed. "The turtle eggs used to hatch in the sand, right at the base of those cliffs. If they hatched in the sunlight, the baby turtles would try to run to the surf before the birds got them. Sometimes I hear the sounds the turtles make when the birds have got them in their beaks. Or maybe it's the birds squeaking."

"Is that what you see now?"

"Not no more. I see sand and cactus. I ain't got no power now. You're him, ain't you?"

"Depends on who you mean."

"Him."

"You lost me. Some folks get around, but I get around a lot. Is that what you mean, a guy who gets around?"

"There ain't anything here you want."

"I'll decide that."

Danny Boy watched his visitor's eyes and hands in the starlight. "I'm gonna put my jacket on. It's cold. At least for this time of year," he said.

"Why should I care what you do?"

"I just thought I'd say."

"Your name was in the newspaper. You saw a man tortured to death. He was a corrupt Mexican cop. The man who killed him was named Krill. I aim to find him."

Danny Boy lowered his eyes.

"Did you hear me?"

"I don't know where he's at."

"Are you afraid of him?"

Danny Boy felt his fingers curl up and touch the heels of his hands. His mouth and throat went dry, and he could feel a stone drop in his chest and settle in the bottom of his stomach.

"Cat got your tongue?" the visitor said.

"I hid in a ravine while he killed that fellow."

Danny Boy pulled the sleeve of his denim jacket up on one arm, then forgot what he was doing and stared emptily at his visitor. There were lumps on the visitor's face, as though insects had fed on it.

"Is that why you're a drunk, or were you a drunk before you hid in the ravine?"

"I don't make no claims about myself. I am what I am."

"So what are you?"

"What you're looking at, I reckon."

"A drunk Indian?"

Danny Boy felt a pain in one temple; it ran down through his eye like an electric current, obscuring his vision, as though a cataract had suddenly formed on the lens. "This is my place. Everything you see here, it's mine. It's where I grew up."

"What's that mean?"

Danny Boy couldn't formulate an adequate answer to the question, but he tried. "My daddy drilled a deep-water well with an old Ford engine and grew corn and squash and melons. We sold them at the farmers' market every Saturday. We'd go to the picture show in the afternoon and sneak in our own popcorn and Kool-Aid in a quart jar. My mother was alive back then. We all went into town together in our truck, with us kids sitting on the flatbed."

"If there's some kind of allegorical meaning, it eludes me."

"You ain't welcome here."

"I want the man named Krill. Most of the illegals in this county come through your land or the Asian woman's. So get used to me being around. Krill hurt a friend of mine. His name is Noie Barnum."

"The guy named Krill ain't your problem."

"Explain that to me."

Danny Boy reached for his bottle of Corona, but the visitor pulled it from his hand. "You shouldn't drink any more," the visitor said.

"Look out yonder."

"At *what?*"

"Them."

The visitor turned and gazed down the slope at the scrub brush and yuccas and mesquite trees rustling in the breeze. Then he stared at the mauve tint in the darkness of the sky and at the silhouettes of the mesas and hills and at the stars disappearing into the false dawn. "You see turtles out there?" the visitor said.

"No, I see the women and girls who been following you."

"What'd you say?"

"All them Asian women and girls you killed. They're standing just yonder. The Ghost Trail runs right through here. My people keep them safe now. After I hid from the man named Krill, I couldn't see the Ghost Trail no more. But now I can."

"I'd think twice before I ran my mouth to the wrong fellow."

"They're pointing at you. There's nine of them. They want to know why you stole their lives. You didn't have nothing to gain. They were begging when you did it. They had their fingers knitted together like they were in church. They were crying."

The visitor reached out and tapped Danny Boy on the cheek with the flat of his hand. "I can hurt you, fellow."

"Put a bullet in me. I was on Sugar Land Farm. You cain't do no worse than has already been done to me."

"You know the line 'Don't tempt the Lord

thy God'?"

"But you ain't Him."

The visitor rose to his feet. The flap of his coat was hooked back on the butt of his revolver. He was breathing hard through his nose, his gaze wandering from one object to the next, as though his thoughts were of no avail to him. He stared at Danny Boy. "Sheriff Holland spat on me once. Did you know that?"

"No, sir."

"You know what it feels like when another man spits on you? I'm not talking about a woman, because they do that sort of thing when a man offends their vanity. I'm talking about a man doing it. You know what that feels like?"

"No, sir."

"Sheriff Holland did that to me. I could have shot him then, but I didn't. Know why?"

"No, sir."

"Because I'm a merciful man. Because when I deliver Sheriff Holland up to judgment, it won't be the result of an emotional reaction. It will be under circumstances of my choosing."

Danny Boy nodded, his gaze turned inward.

"Tell the sheriff I was here," the visitor said. "Tell him I keep my word. Tell him he'll know when it's my ring. Can you keep all that in your head?"

"Yes, sir, I can," Danny Boy said.

"That's good. You're a good listener." Then the visitor poured the jelly glass half full of rum and picked it up from the table and threw it into Danny Boy's face.

That same morning, Hackberry went to the office early, his mind clear after a good night's sleep, the wind cool out of the north, the broken sidewalks dark with night damp, the hills outside town a soft green against an ink-wash sky. He could smell food cooking at the Eat Café down the street. Pam Tibbs met him at the back entrance of the department. "Danny Boy Lorca just came in half drunk and asked me to lock him up," she said.

"You mean he wants to sleep it off?"

"No, he wants to be locked up. He says he had a visitor this morning."

Hackberry walked through the hallway and hung his hat on a wood peg in his office. "I hate to ask," he said.

"The guy didn't give his name. Danny Boy said he was carrying a pistol. He was wearing a suit and a hat and beat-up needle-nose boots. He said he'd be looking you up and you'd know when it was his ring."

"Why is Collins pestering Danny Boy?"

"That's not all that happened this morning. I was down at the café, and two SUVs loaded with some cowboy cutie-pies came in. Stonewashed jeans, mustaches, two or three days of beard, stylized haircuts. They looked

201

like porn actors."

"Like the two guys Collins popped?"

"The guy in charge knew the waitress. He had on a blue suit and a silver western shirt without a tie, like he was one of the boys. After they left, I asked her who he was. She said that was Temple Dowling."

"Forget about Dowling."

She closed the office door and approached his desk. "It didn't quite end there. I heard him talking in the booth. I heard him use your name."

"We need to get to the point, Pam."

"He called you a drunk."

"That's what I used to be."

"That's not all of it. I heard him whispering, then all of them laughed."

"Blow it off. These guys aren't worth talking about."

"Then one guy said, 'He brought clap home to his wife?' Dowling said something I couldn't hear, and they all laughed again, loud enough that everybody in the café turned around and looked at them."

"What that man said isn't true. But I don't care whether he says it or not. If he does it in my presence, I'll do something about it. In the meantime, let's forget it and talk to Danny Boy." Hackberry took the ring of cell keys off a peg next to his hat.

"I followed them into the parking lot," Pam said.

"Did you hit somebody?"

"No."

"All right, then let it go."

"I took the motormouth aside, the one who said something about clap. He was the driver of one of the SUVs. I told him I wasn't going to cite him for his broken taillights, but if I ever heard him slander your name again, I was going to beat the living shit out of him."

"He had two broken taillights?"

"He did after I broke them."

"Pam?"

"What?"

"What can I say?"

"I don't know."

He stepped closer to her, towering over her, and cupped his hand around the back of her neck. Her skin felt hot against his palm. He could smell the shampoo in her hair and the heat in her body and feel the hardness of the muscles in her neck. "You have to stop protecting me," he said.

"You're my boss, and I won't allow white trash to tell lies about you."

"You really know how to jump-start a man's day," he said.

She lifted her eyes to his. Her mouth looked like a flower that had crumpled in on itself in the shade. "Think so?" she said.

He removed his hand from the back of her neck and tried not to swallow. There was a thickness in his throat, a tightness in his chest, and a weakness in his loins that he did not want to recognize. "Why would Collins bother Danny Boy?" he said hoarsely.

"He wants to hurt you."

"It's that simple?"

"You bet your ass," she replied.

They climbed up the spiral steel stairs in the back of the building and walked down the corridor to a cell whose outer wall was a checkerboard pattern of steel bands and cast-iron plates that had been painted white and were now crosshatched with scratch marks and stained by orange rust around the rivets. Danny Boy was looking out the window when they approached the cell. When he turned around, his head and neck were framed against the window, his body enveloped in shadow, so that his head seemed to rest, decapitated, upon a plate. "I don't want out," he said.

"Can't lock up a man who hasn't committed a crime," Hackberry said.

"I'll drink if I'm back on the street," Danny Boy said.

"Incarceration is not the best way to find sobriety," Hackberry said.

"I'm not like you. There's still liquor at my house. I'll drink it if I can get back to it. In a few days, I can go without it."

"Was Preacher Jack Collins at your house?"

"If that's his name."

"Who'd he say he was?"

"He didn't. I said 'You're him.' "

"What did he say to that?"

"Nothing. Like it wasn't important. Or it wasn't important that a guy like me knew. When I told him the girls he'd killed were out there in the desert pointing at him, he told me to watch my mouth."

"What else did he say?"

"He's after the guy named Krill. He thought I might know where he was at."

"What'd you tell him?"

"That I hid when that fellow was murdered."

"You listen to me," Hackberry said. "You think I should feel guilty because I hid from the Chinese soldiers who were trying to kill me? You remember the name of General Patton?"

"No, who is he?"

"He was a famous military leader. He said you don't win wars by giving your life for your country. You win them by making the other son of a bitch give *his* life." Hackberry tried to smile and lift Danny Boy's spirits, but it did no good. "What else did your visitor say?" he asked.

"He'd be looking you up."

"What else?"

"Nothing. He threw a glass of rum in my face."

Pam Tibbs tapped her ring on the steel door in order to direct Danny Boy's attention to

205

her. "Jack Collins has a way of showing up in people's lives when they're unarmed and vulnerable," she said. "He wants to rob people of their self-respect because he has none for himself. Don't be his victim."

"Listen to her," Hackberry said. "You're a fine man. You have an illness in you that's not your fault. One day you'll wake up and decide you don't want any more of the old life. That's when you'll start getting rid of all the problems that kept you drunk. In the meantime, you're going to take a shower and put on some fresh jeans and a sport shirt I have in my closet, and then you and I are going to have a steak-and-egg breakfast down at the café."

"I saw the Oriental girls standing in the desert. There was nine of them. They're waiting for him," Danny Boy said.

"You saw them when you were drinking?"

"It don't matter what I was doing. They were there. Collins knew about my visions. He knew what was in them. No, that's not exactly right. He knows things don't happen in order, like past, present, and future. He knows things happen all at the same time, all around us, people we cain't see are still living out their lives right next to us. Not many people know that."

"Collins is a fraud. Don't pay attention to what he says," Hackberry said.

"If he's a fraud, who's he pretending to be?

You ever know anybody like him?"

Pam Tibbs looked at Hackberry and raised her eyebrows. She took the ring of keys from his hand, unlocked the cell, and swung the door back heavily on its hinges, the bottom scraping the concrete. "Time to hit the shower and get something to eat, Danny," she said.

By eleven A.M. the sun was bright and hot outside Hackberry's office window, the block-like sandstone courthouse on the square stark against a blue sky, the courthouse lawn green and cool-looking under the shade trees. A church group had opened a secondhand sale on the sidewalk in front of the Luna Theater, and people were going in and out of the courthouse and the old bank on the corner much as they had in an era when the town was supported by a viable agrarian economy. It was a good day, the kind when boys used to cut school to go bobber-fishing or tubing down a river. It was not a day when he wanted to deal with the unpleasant realities of his job or the vestiges of his past. But when a black SUV pulled to the curb in front of his office and Temple Dowling got out, followed by three of his men, Hackberry knew exactly how the rest of the morning would go.

There was a class of people who always supported law and order. They believed that police officers and sheriff's deputies and the law enforcement agencies of the United States government constituted a vast servile army with the same raison d'être as insurance carriers, tax accountants, medical providers, and gardeners — namely, to take care of problems that busy and productive people shouldn't be concerned with.

Hackberry watched Temple Dowling stride toward the front door of the building, coatless, his silver shirt crinkling like tin, a martial glint in his eyes, his creamy complexion moist in the heat. But it was the man's lips that Hackberry couldn't get out of his mind. They seemed to have the coloration and texture of the rubber in a pencil eraser. They belonged on the mouth of a man who was cruel, whose sentiments were manufactured, whose physical appetites were visceral and base and infantile all at the same time. Watching him stride up the walk, Hackberry decided he had been too kind in assigning Dowling and his peers to that innocent and insular group who treated police officers as they would loyal servants. Temple Dowling, like his father, the senator, was a man who knew the value of the whip and how to turn the screw in order to bend others to his will. The fates may have given Temple Dowling a face that would never allow him to ascend to the throne. But Hackberry guessed that in Dowling's view, the power behind the throne was gift enough.

Hackberry got up from his chair and met Dowling at the entrance to the building. "What's your problem?" he said.

"I have a grocery list of them," Dowling said.

The three men standing behind him had come to a stop. They wore western hats and sunglasses and had the physiques of men who worked out regularly in health clubs. They wore mustaches and a growth of beard that Hackberry guessed was deliberately maintained rather than shaved entirely off. Their hands were folded in front of them, their faces turned at a deferential angle so Hackberry would take note that they were not staring at him from behind their shades. One man had a puncture in his cheek that looked like a hole someone had made by inserting his thumb into putty. One man wore a tattoo inside the growth of beard on his throat. The third man had facial skin that was as dark as saddle leather and flecked with scars that resembled tiny pieces of brown string.

"Lose the entourage and come in," Hackberry said.

"These men go wherever I go."

"Not here they don't."

"Why do I continue to have trouble with you, Sheriff?"

"Because you asked for it."

"I had to replace both the brake lights on my vehicle this morning."

"Yeah, I heard about that. That's too bad."

"You're aware your deputy broke them?"

"Be advised I support my deputy in whatever she does. I'm pretty busy. You want to stand out here in the sun or come inside?"

"Here will be just fine," Dowling said. He wiped his forehead and upper lip with a handkerchief, then shook it out and wiped the back of his neck. He gazed down the street at the courthouse, a slick of sweat on one cheek, his eyes intense with the words he was preparing to speak. Hackberry realized Dowling's next remarks would be part of a performance that was not for him but for his employees. "I've lost two good men to a psychopath who should have been mulch the first time you saw him. This same man has murdered an untold number of people in this county, *your* county, but you don't seem to have a clue where he is, nor do you seem bothered by your ignorance. Instead of conducting an investigation, your personnel are vandalizing people's SUVs. I understand that mediocrity is a way of life in a place like this, but I won't abide incompetence when it comes to the welfare of my people or the security of my country. We'll do your work for you, but you need to stay out of our way."

"If you interfere in a homicide investigation, you're going to find yourself in handcuffs, Mr. Dowling."

"My father said something about you,

210

Sheriff, that maybe you should hear. He said you were one of those rare politicians to whom nobody had to pay money in order to corrupt. All they needed to do was appeal to your Don Quixote complex. He said the only payment you required was a chance to play the role of the knight-errant so you could self-destruct and absolve yourself of your petty sins. I think my father read you like a book."

"Tell you what, I changed my mind about something I told my chief deputy this morning. I said I couldn't care less if you tried to slander my name. But on second thought, some might think the elements in your lies refer to my dead wife, Rie, and the nature of my relationship with her. You did make those remarks, didn't you?"

"I didn't have to make them. Everyone who knew you already has."

"I don't like to humiliate a man in front of his employees, but for you, I'm going to make an exception. I'm probably in the top of the eighth inning or the bottom of the ninth, which means I don't have a lot to lose. You ever play much baseball, Mr. Dowling? If you crowd the plate with the wrong pitcher, you can bet the next pitch will be a forkball at the head, the kind that hits you like a dull-bladed guillotine." Hackberry smiled pleasantly and winked at him. "What do you think about that?"

"Considering the source? Not very damn much," Dowling said.

Hackberry went back inside his office, sat down at his desk, and did not look outside the window until he heard the SUV drive down the street. But the anger that had bloomed in his chest would not go away. A half hour later, the phone on his desk rang. He looked at the caller ID and answered. *"¿Qué tal?"*

"¿Qué tal?" Ethan Riser repeated.

"Yeah, what's up?"

"I know what it means."

"Say what's on your mind."

"This is a personal call and off the record."

"I'm the sheriff of this county. I'm sitting at my office desk, on the job, in my official capacity. Nothing that occurs here is off the record."

"You sound a little short."

"What do you want, Ethan?"

"I'm taking early retirement. I wanted to tell you that. Plus a couple of other things."

"Like what?"

"You're in the way."

"Say again?"

"This guy Noie Barnum is the Holy Grail. We want him, Krill and his people want him, Al Qaeda wants him, Temple Dowling wants him, and now Josef Sholokoff wants him."

"Why would a Russian porn dealer risk his immigration status by going into espionage?"

212

"Josef Sholokoff has been spreading drug and porn addiction around the country since he arrived in Brighton Beach. Why should doing business with third-world bedbugs bother him?"

"You said I was in the way."

"Guys like you are not team players. You're a hardhead, you don't chug pud, and you cause major amounts of trouble. Government agencies might say otherwise, but they don't care for guys like you."

"What difference should that make to me?"

"They won't have your back, bud."

"Have you been drinking?"

"I'm at a driving range. I wish I'd done more of this a long time ago."

"When do you retire?"

"Three months, more or less. Yeah, about three months."

"You're retiring but you're not sure when?"

"I'm terminal."

Hackberry leaned forward on his desk. Before he could speak, Riser cut him off. "I used to smoke three packs a day. Five years ago I quit and thought I'd gotten a free pass. I went in for a blister on my nose last week, and the doc said it was already in my liver and pancreas and had reached the brain."

"I'm sorry, Ethan."

"There's something I never told you about my history with the Bureau. You remember right after 9/11 when a planeload of bin

213

Laden's relatives was allowed to leave the country without being detained, except for the fifteen minutes we were allowed to interview them on the tarmac? I was one of the agents who went on board the plane. I should have resigned in protest then. But I didn't. I've always regretted that. Take this for a fact. When you get to the end of the track, you don't regret the things you did. You regret the things you didn't do. You're a good man, Hack. But good men are usually admired in retrospect, after they're safely dead."

After he had hung up, Hackberry sat for a long time in his chair, the right side of his face numb, a sound like an electrical short humming in his ear.

CHAPTER NINE

Anton Ling woke in the darkness to the flicker of dry lightning and a rumble of thunder that shook the walls of her house in the same way that the reverberations of aerial bombs could travel through the earth and cause a house to rattle miles away. She went to the kitchen and sat at the table in the dark and drank a glass of warm milk and tried not to think about the images reawakened in her unconscious by the thunder and the yellow ignition in the clouds.

The night was unseasonably cold, the sky churning with clouds that looked filled with soot. She thought she heard a coyote's wail inside the wind, or perhaps the shriek of a rusty hinge twisting violently back on itself. An empty apple basket bounced crazily past the water tank in the backyard. The tank was overflowing, the blades of the windmill ginning, the stanchions vibrating with tension. Had she been so absentminded that she had forgotten to notch down the shutoff chain on the crankshaft?

She put on a canvas coat and went outside and was immediately struck by the severity of the wind and a smell that was like creosote and wet sulfur and the stench off a smokestack in a rendering plant. She hooked the chain on the windmill and realized the doors were slamming on all her sheds, a loose section of the tin roof on the barn clanging against the joists, as though things were coming apart and indeed the center could not hold. Was the odor coming from across the border, where industry did as it wished? The clouds were black and billowing and lighted from the inside, like giant curds of smoke rising from wet straw set ablaze by a chemical starter.

When would she be freed of her dreams and the sensations and shards of memory that followed her into the day and fouled her blood and made her wonder if her entire mission wasn't that of a hypocrite? Why could she not accept the fact that amnesia did not necessarily accompany absolution?

Don't think about it, she told herself. *Pray for the maimed and the dead and ask nothing more from life than another sunrise, and maybe along the way do a good deed or two.* She couldn't change the past. Why did she have to revisit the same slide show over and over?

Gasoline and diesel, drums of it, with Tide detergent poured into the mix so that the

216

liquid adhered to every surface it touched, a homemade form of napalm dropped end over end from a few hundred feet while tiny figures below raced from their huts into the trees or sometimes rolled burning in the rice paddies to smother the fire on their skin.

From a great distance, she had witnessed the B-52 raids in Cambodia and had heard the thump of the bombs and had felt the explosions through the soles of her shoes and had seen the surface of rice paddies wrinkle, but the tremolo that spread invisibly through the floor of a rain forest was little different from the vibration of a subway train passing under the streets of a metropolitan city. The fifty-gallon drums filled with diesel or gasoline or both were different; they were up close and personal, their effect unforgettable. She had helped slide them off the tailgate of a Chinook, had cupped her hands around their hard rims, had watched them suddenly detach themselves from the plane and drop as heavily as woodstoves through the air into a landscape of elephant grass and tropical trees and fields of poppies that bloomed pink and red against a backdrop of blue mountains. Then she had seen them explode in a village that was a resupply depot for the Pathet Lao, but also a home to people who ate monkeys and dogs and harvested rice with their hands, and who knew nothing of the global powers that had decided to use their country as a battlefield.

She went back inside the house and hung her canvas coat on a peg and checked the locks on the doors, then sat down on the side of her bed, her head bent forward, the images and sounds from her dream gradually disappearing. The wind gusted under the house, causing the floor and the walls to creak and a tin cup to topple into the kitchen sink. She got up from the bed to pull the curtain on the window just as a net of lightning bloomed in the clouds. By the corner of the old bunkhouse, she saw a shadow. No, it was more than a shadow. It not only moved; light reflected off it. She stared into the darkness, waiting for the electricity to jump in the clouds again. Instead, drops of rain began to patter on the roof and in the dust around the windmill and in the nubbed-down grass near the barn, and all she could see through her bedroom window was darkness and the sheen of rain on the bunkhouse and an empty dark space where she thought she had seen the outline of a man.

She opened the bottom drawer of her dresser and reached inside it and groped under a pile of folded clothes for an object she hadn't touched or even thought about in many months. She went into the kitchen and pulled open a drawer, and from a collection of screwdrivers and hammers and pliers and duct tape and wrenches and scattered nails, she removed a flashlight. Then she put on a baseball cap and unlocked the back door and went outside, this time without her coat.

She moved the beam of the flashlight along the side of the bunkhouse and the stucco cottage, then shone it on the railed horse lot and through the open door of the barn, the light sweeping against the stalls and wood posts inside. She crossed the yard and looked inside the bunkhouse, then inside the cottage. She searched behind the bunkhouse and worked her way back to the corner where she thought she had seen the figure.

The rain was ticking on her cap and her shoulders, spotting her clothes and running down the back of her neck. She walked toward the barn, the flashlight beam spearing the darkness and bouncing off the tools and dust-covered tack inside. She took a deep breath, oxygenating her blood, and stepped through the door into the heady odor of horse sweat and decayed manure and pounded-down clay that was green with mold.

"What are *you* doing here?" she said.

"Nothing," said the figure in the shadows, raising his arm against the glare of the flashlight.

"You were looking through my windows."

"I was not. I just wanted to talk. I didn't understand what you said there at the grocery store."

"About what?"

"You said I shouldn't presume. You said I didn't know who I was messing with. You thought I was threatening you? I wouldn't do that. You made me feel bad, like I was a bully or a freak or something. Ma'am, is that a pistol in your hand?"

"What does it look like?"

"We're kindred spirits."

"No, we're not. How long have you been out here?"

"Just a few minutes. Maybe I was gonna knock on your door. I know you stay up. I've seen those candles glowing in your chapel late at night."

"How did you see them?"

"I got a telescope on my deck. I do stargazing sometimes. It's a hobby I got."

"Where's your vehicle?"

"Down the road a mite."

"You're a voyeur, Reverend Cody. Get off my property. If you ever come on it again, I'll shoot you."

"Don't talk like that. You got me all wrong, ma'am."

"No, I don't. I think you're haunted by a terrible deed you did to a woman or a group of women. It's something so bad you can't talk about it to anyone. But that's your problem, not mine. Get out of here and never come back. You understand?"

"Yes, ma'am, if that's what you say."

She lowered the pistol and stepped aside.

When he ran past her, his face was disjointed with fear and humiliation, like that of a child caught in a shameful act. She went back inside the house and locked the door behind her and replaced the small-caliber pistol in the bottom drawer of her dresser. She took off her damp clothes and dried herself with a towel and put on a pair of pajamas and lay down on the bed, a pillow over her face. She was surprised at how quickly and easily she fell asleep. Outside, a bolt of lightning struck the top of a hill and turned a pine tree into a crisp red fingerprint against the unrelieved blackness of the sky.

Cody Daniels's waxed canary-yellow pickup was parked off the side of the dirt road, down by a creek bed whose banks were bordered by gravelly soil and cottonwood and willow trees. The rain had beaded on the wax, and when electricity leaped between the clouds, his truck looked like a bejeweled artwork, a thing of beauty and power and comfort that had always given him an enormous sense of pleasure and pride and control. But now Cody Daniels took no joy in anything — not his truck, nor his Cowboy Chapel, nor his title of Reverend, nor the house he had built up in the cliffs, where he had strode the deck like the captain of a sailing vessel.

He had not only been caught hiding in the Chinese woman's barn, he had been accused

221

of voyeurism and driven from her property as a degenerate might. Worse, he could not explain to himself, much less to Anton Ling, why he had gone there. To tell her he was sorry for approaching her in the grocery store while he was drunk? Maybe. To tell her that no matter what he might have done in the past, he would not try to harm her? Maybe. To look through her windows?

He wanted to say no to his last question but found himself hesitating. Of course he wouldn't do something like that, he told himself. Never in his life had he ever entertained thoughts like that. Why would she think that of him? Why would he doubt himself now?

Because there was no question he had become obsessed with her. While he set out his prayer books in the Cowboy Chapel or tried to prepare a sermon, he wondered what kind of services she conducted inside that little room where racks of candles burned in rows of blue and red vessels. He wondered why none of the Hispanics, at least the legal ones, ever came to his church. What did he ever do to them? He wondered if Anton Ling possessed powers that would never be given to him. What was the line in Scripture? Many are called but few are chosen? That seemed like saying there was a collection of real losers out there and Cody Daniels was probably one of them.

Was that his lot? To have the calling but never feel the hot finger of destiny on his forehead? Was he cursed with the worst state of mind that could befall a man, envy of a woman, in this case an Oriental whose features and figure and grace turned his loins to water?

He turned his face toward the sky. *Why have you done this to me?* he asked.

If there was any reply, he didn't hear it. The only sound he heard was that of a heavy vehicle, one with a diesel-powered engine, grinding its way down a dirt track between two hills on the north side of the Chinese woman's property. He could see the headlights in the rain and the outline of the extended cab and the large bed in back. It was an expensive vehicle that could seat a driver and five passengers easily. What was it doing in these hills at this time of night? It was now dipping off the road, proceeding down a long incline that fed into flatland and a string of cedar fence posts with no wire.

Cody got into his pickup and rolled down the passenger window so he could watch the diesel-powered truck as it approached the back of Anton Ling's house, its headlights turned off.

Maybe they're part of her Underground Railroad or whatever the hell they call it, he told himself.

But he knew better. He opened his cell

phone and looked at the screen. No service. *Well, that's the breaks,* he thought. What had she told him? To get out, to never come back? Something like that. So, sayonara, see you tomorrow, or whatever they said over there. *Maybe next time you'll appreciate it when a good man comes around. Voyeur, my dad-burned foot,* he thought.

He clicked on his headlights, dropped his transmission into gear, and drove south into the rain, away from Anton Ling's property, the clouds crackling like cellophane behind him.

It was still dark when she woke and realized that the four men standing around her bed were not part of a dream. She could smell the mud on their boots and the rain and leaves on their hooded slickers. She could hear their weight shift on the boards in the floor. She could see their gloved hands and the heavy dimensions of their torsos and arms. The sense of physicality in the three men who stood closest to her was overwhelming, as palpable as a soiled hand violating one's person. The fourth man, who stood in the background, did not seem to belong there. He was much shorter, his physical proportions lost inside his raincoat. The only thing she couldn't see were their faces, which were covered with a camouflage-patterned fabric that had been drawn tight against the

224

skin, the material creased with lines like a prune might have.

She sat up in bed, the sheet pulled to her waist, her heart beating high up in her chest. She waited for one of them to speak. But none of them did. The luminous clock on her dresser said 4:54 A.M. Another hour until sunrise. "The doors were dead-bolted," she said.

"Not anymore they're not," one man said. He was taller than the others, maybe wearing cowboy boots, a military-style wristwatch with no reflective surfaces strapped just above the glove on his left hand.

"I'm of no value to you," she said.

"What makes you think this is about you?" the man asked.

"The man you're looking for stayed here briefly. I gave him food and dressed his wounds. But he's not here anymore, and I don't know where he has gone. So I'm in possession of nothing you want."

"You never can tell," the man said.

She tried to look straight into his eyes and confront his sexual innuendo. But she could see nothing behind the holes in his mask. "How many of you are outside?" she asked.

"What makes you think anyone is outside?"

"There are at least two. One in front, one in back. Because you used four men to confront one woman inside the house, you have personnel to spare. So there are at least

225

two outside."

"You're a smart lady," the tall man said. "But we knew that when we came here."

"Then you know I'm not trying to deceive you. It wouldn't be in my interest or in the interest of the work I do. I have no personal agenda and nothing I need to hide from you."

"Maybe *I* know that. But others may not. You were in Laos and Cambodia. You were in Tibet, too. You did airdrops to the Tibetan resistance. Not many people have a history like that."

"More than you think."

"The Communists had their hands on you for a while. Where did that happen?"

"In Tibet."

"What was that like?"

"Not very pleasant."

"Your record indicates you gave them nothing and lived to tell about it. So others might take that to mean we shouldn't believe anything you say unless it withstands the test of ordeal. Don't make us go through that, ma'am."

"Do you think politeness in language excuses you from what you're doing? You break in to my home and wake me from my sleep and suggest you might torture or rape me, then address me as 'ma'am'? What kind of men are you? Does it bother you that you mask your faces in order to bully a woman?"

She realized she was saying too much, that

226

she was taking the exchange over the edge and ignoring the fact that her intruders wore masks because they did not plan to kill her. She tried to keep her face empty of expression, to not signal them in any way that she understood their thought processes or the methods they were considering using against her. It was time to distract them by giving them information they probably already had that would indicate she was telling the truth but be of no help to them. "The man you're searching for is probably with a homicidal lunatic by the name of Jack Collins."

"You have any idea where Collins might be?"

"Are you serious?" she replied.

In the silence, she could hear the tall man breathing and see the camouflaged fabric ruffling around his mouth. Why was he breathing through his mouth? In anticipation of what he was about to do? Was he about to make a decision that would take him and her across a personal Rubicon she did not want to think about?

"Collins is a religious head case. He seems to have obsessions with women in the Bible," the tall man said. "You might fit the bill. What's your opinion on that?"

Don't let him know you're afraid, a voice inside her said. "I think you're an idiot."

The short man standing behind the others peered through the corner of the window shade into the yard. He wore heavy boots that looked like they had elevated soles and heels. She saw his head tilt upward and guessed that he was checking for the first glow of dawn beyond the ridgeline. Then she realized that the tall man was watching the man at the window shade. The tall man was not in charge. He was waiting on the man at the window to tell him what to do.

The man at the window did not speak but made a rotating motion with his index finger, as though saying either "continue" or "wrap it up."

But which?

The tall man went to the closet and threw a robe on Anton Ling's bed. "Put it on," he said.

"What for?" she asked.

"Certain things have to be done. Don't make them harder than they already are."

"Who do you work for?"

"The country. The people who want it to remain free. You think protecting a traitor like Noie Barnum is a noble act?"

"I won't put a robe on. I won't move. I have no control over what you're about to do. But I won't cooperate with it."

The tall man leaned down and took her wrist in his hand. His fingers went easily all the way around it, as though he were compressing a stick in his palm. "Get up."

"No."

"You're making this personal, Ms. Ling. It's unwise."

"Don't use my name. I don't know you and have no intention of knowing you. Don't you dare address me as though you know me."

"I heard you were arrogant, a Mandarin princess or something." He jerked her up from the bed and knotted her hair in his fist, twisting it hard, pulling her head back until her mouth fell open. "We used to call this cooling out a gook. Is that what you want? Tell me. Tell me now." He twisted her hair tighter. "I don't like to do this. This is all on you. I can make it worse and worse and worse, to the point I start to enjoy it. Don't make me do that."

When he released her hair so she could speak, she gathered all the saliva in her mouth and spat it full in his face. Then he hit her so hard with his fist that two picture frames fell to the floor when she crashed against the wall. Two of the other men picked her up and shoved her toward the doorway. She thought she heard the sound of water running in the kitchen sink.

Cody Daniels kept his truck pointed south, slamming over the ruts, water splashing up on the hood and across the windshield. He had his radio tuned full-blast to an English-language station that broadcast from across the border to avoid FCC regulations, its signal reaching all the way to Canada. Twenty-four hours a day, it provided a steady stream of country music, evangelical harangues that left the preacher gasping into the microphone, and promotions for baby chicks, tulip bulbs, bat guano, aphrodisiacs, glow-in-the-dark tablecloths painted with the Last Supper, and miracle photographs of Jesus. Late at night it was the refuge for the insomniac and the ufologist and the sexually driven and those who loved the prospect of the Rapture. But right now, for Cody Daniels, it was a source of maximum electronic noise that he hoped would pound the name of Anton Ling out of his head.

He was pastor of the Cowboy Chapel, not the overseer for Asian females in Southwest Texas. Why didn't she go back where she came from? She had told him to get lost. All right, that's what he was doing. Live and let live. Besides, maybe the truck with the extended cab wasn't going to Anton Ling's. Maybe it was the Border Patrol rounding up stray wets. The wets traveled by night. Wasn't it reasonable for Cody to at least conclude the oversize pickup was on a government mission?

Except the Border Patrol usually operated by the numbers and didn't use pickup trucks to round up wets or drive down hillsides through private property in the dark.

Why did his mind always set traps for him?

His own thoughts were more intelligent and wily than he was. Again and again, his thoughts knew how to corner and bait him, as though a separate personality were constantly probing at him with a sharp stick.

Without thinking, without planning, as though his motor control had disconnected itself from his instincts, he removed his foot from the accelerator and depressed the brake pedal. He felt the truck slowing, the vibration in the frame diminishing as though of its own accord. Then the truck stopped as rigidly as a stone in the road. He switched off the radio and listened to the windshield wipers beating in the silence. He opened his cell phone, praying that this time the screen would show at least one bar.

No service.

Where was the sheriff? Where was the female deputy who had thrown him in the can? This was their job, not his. Who had dumped all this responsibility on Cody Daniels? He looked through the windshield at a long white streak of lightning that leaped from the hills into the clouds.

You? he asked.

No, God had more to do than concern Himself with the likes of Cody Daniels.

How do you know? a voice said, either inside or outside his head.

Cody put his truck into reverse and turned around in the middle of the road, wondering if the tattoo BORN TO LOSE that he had removed from his skin should have read BORN TO BE STUPID.

Two men held Anton Ling's arms while a third plunged her head into the water brimming over the sides of the sink. She clenched her mouth and held her breath and tried to twist away from the hand that pushed her head deeper into the water. She kicked sideways with her feet and pushed against the cabinets with her knees. All she accomplished was to drain herself of the energy and oxygen she needed to survive. After what was surely a minute, her lungs were bursting and air was bubbling out of her mouth and she knew she was only seconds away from both swallowing water and breathing it through her nostrils. Then the hand went away from the back of her neck and she reared her head above the level of the sink, gasping for air.

"Noie Barnum must know other people around here besides you. Who would he contact?" the tall man said. His gloved right hand and sleeve were dark with water. She realized it was he who had held her head down in the sink.

"He's a Quaker. Other Quakers."

"Where do they live?"

"There're none around here."

"Wrong answer."

232

"He's with Collins."

"Where's Collins?"

"I don't know anything about Collins."

"Hold her arms tighter," the tall man said.

"No, wait," she said.

"Your time is running out, Ms. Ling."

"Noie has no ties here. He is wherever Collins is. How could I know where Collins is when the FBI doesn't? You're making me do the impossible. I can't prove to you what I don't know."

"I got to admit I wouldn't want to be in your shoes. But you created this situation, not us. This is the way it stands: You went down the first time for exactly one minute and ten seconds. The second time you're going down for two minutes and twenty seconds. Think you can hold your breath for two minutes and twenty seconds?"

"I can't."

"Then you're going to die. Maybe you'll have a heart attack before you drown, so it won't be that bad. I'll let you fill up with air first. Nod when you're ready."

"My father flew with the original Flying Tigers. He was a friend of Claire Chennault."

"Who cares?"

"If he were here, you'd have to hide."

He plunged her face into the water and leaned his weight heavily on his hand, driving her forehead to the bottom of the sink, his gloved fingers spreading like banana peels on

233

the back of her head. Her skin broke against the porcelain, and blood curled around her face and rose in a smoky string to the surface. The more she struggled, the weaker she became. Her lungs burned as though someone had poured acid in them. She dug her knees into the cabinets and pushed herself backward with all her remaining strength. Then she realized that the incendiary raids she had lived through as a child, the pancake air crash she had survived on a Laotian airstrip, the ordeal she had endured at the hands of Chinese Communists, had been illusions, flirtations with a chimera who was a poseur. Death did not appear with a broad flapping of leathery wings; death came in the form of a stoppered silvery-green drain hole at the bottom of a flooded sink, while three men snapped her sinew and bones with their hands.

But something had just happened that neither she nor her adversaries could have anticipated. Her upper body was soaking wet, and the man on her left let his grip slip for just a second. When he tried to reposition his hands, she jerked free of him and fell backward to the floor, sucking air as raggedly into her windpipe as she would a razor blade.

The tall man reached down and grabbed the front of her shirt and pulled her to her feet. She could feel the sourness of his breath on her face. "Now, you listen," he said.

"You're making us waste time that we don't have. You're vain from your hairline to the bottoms of your feet, and you know it. You've turned your pride into a religion and convinced a bunch of ignorant peons you're a Catholic saint. Be assured, if you want to be a martyr, we'll arrange that. But in the meantime, you're going to tell us where Barnum is or prove to us you're as unknowledgeable as you claim. If you don't know where he is, give us the name of somebody who does. That will get you off the hook, *that* and nothing else.

"If you doubt me, tell me how you feel one hour from now, after I let my associates take you back in the hills. Maybe you saw ugly things in the Orient, the kinds of things my associates are capable of doing, but you *saw* them, they didn't happen to you. If they had happened to you, you wouldn't be here today. You would be either dead or in an asylum, unable to deal with your own memories of what was done to you. My associates have insatiable appetites. When they start in on you, you will renounce everything you ever believed in just to make them stop what they're doing for only one minute. You'll give up your lover, your family, your religion. I've seen them at work. I don't judge them for what they do. They are only satisfying the desires that to them are natural. But I never want to witness human behavior like that again. You don't know how kind I have been to you, Ms. Ling.

"There's another notion I want to dispel here. People in your situation convince themselves that a miracle is going to happen, that their pain will be taken away, that angels will protect them in their last agonizing moments. But it doesn't work that way. No God will help you, no plastic Madonna, no hallelujah choir will arrive singing the praises of Anton Ling. You'll die a miserable death, and no one will ever know where you're buried. Tell me what you want to do."

Her hair formed a tangled skein in front of her eyes and dripped water and blood on her face and shirtfront. Her eyes were crossed from shock and trauma, her bare feet slippery on the wet floor, her pajamas sticking like wet Kleenex to her skin. Her chest was still laboring with shortage of breath, her heart swollen as big and hard as a cantaloupe. "I know nothing," she said.

"Then enjoy your time in hell, bitch."

His hand reached out and settled almost lovingly on the nape of her neck. Then she twisted her body and back-kicked him with more strength and force than she thought she had.

He wasn't ready for it, and his upper body jacked forward with the blow, both of his hands grabbing his genitalia, a cry rising involuntarily from his throat. The man to her right tried to grab her, but she ripped her elbow into his rib cage, then kicked the tall man again, this time in the face. The third man grabbed her pajama top, tearing it down the back, but she pulled loose from him and got past the tall man and the man who had been holding her left arm. The inside of her head was roaring with noise, her hair matted with blood, her feet slipping on the floor. She felt a hand grab her neck, then fingers trying to find purchase inside the religious chain she wore.

The drawer holding the collection of tools and wire and duct tape was half open. She got her hand inside the drawer and picked up a screwdriver, a short one with a thick stub of a handle and a wide blade and perhaps a two-inch shank. She whirled and plunged it into the face of the man whose hand was tangled in her chain. The blade pierced the fabric of his mask right below his left eye, the shank sinking all the way to the handle, the wood and fabric pressing into the wound. The man screamed once, then touched the screwdriver's handle, his hand trembling, and began screaming again, this time without stop.

"You shut up! You eat your pain and shut your mouth!" the tall man said.

"I'm blind!"

"No, you're not. You're in shock. Shut your fucking mouth," the tall man said. Then he whirled around. "Get her!"

Anton Ling ran through the enclosed back porch and crashed through the screen into the yard, falling once, getting up, then plunging across the yard toward the barn, where her pickup was parked with the keys in the ashtray.

That was when another hooded man, even bigger than the others, a man whose breath smelled like snuff and spearmint, picked her up in the air, crushing her against his chest with his huge arms. "What do we got here?" he said, his lips brushing against her cheek through his mask. "A flopping goldfish, I'd say. We better slow you down a little bit. How about some hair of the dog that bit you?"

He carried her kicking to the horse tank by the windmill, his big hands and wrists notched into her rib cage.

Cody Daniels had turned the truck around in the middle of the road, his stomach churning with fear, his sweat as cold as ice water. He slowly depressed the accelerator, his right hand trembling on the gearshift, each jolt in a chuckhole like a piece of glass in his entrails. He wiped the sweat out of his eyes with his sleeve and swerved wildly around the pools of water in the road, wishing he would break an axle or tip off the shoulder's edge into a gulley. He prayed for the dawn to come, for lightning to strike Anton Ling's house and set it ablaze, for the FBI to descend from the sky in a helicopter. He had never been this afraid in his entire life. But why? Just because an oversize diesel-powered truck had come grinding down a hill? It was irrational.

No, it was not. Cody knew he had a talent, and it was not one to be proud of. He was con-wise. He knew how to read iniquity in others because it resided in him. He also had a tuning fork that vibrated when he was around dangerous people. And he understood that cruelty was not an occasional vice. If it existed in an individual, it was systemic and pervasive and always looking for a new prospect. Cody knew the oversize truck was coming for Anton Ling, and inside it were men in the employ of Temple Dowling, or maybe even Dowling himself.

The lessons he had learned in prison were simple. There were two kinds of people in the slams: screwups like himself and those who had not only gone over to the dark side but enjoyed being there and had no plans to return. The joke was the latter category was not confined to convicts. The worst people he had ever known had worn uniforms or used ballpoint pens to do damage that no burglar could ever equal. How did you recognize the Temple Dowlings of the world? That one was easy. They always mocked. It was in their voice, their use of difficult words, the way they twisted whatever came out of your mouth. They stole other people's dignity and made them resent themselves. He and his men had invaded Cody's home and treated him as though he were sewage, then had driven away as indifferently as if they had run over a bug.

Where did that leave him in the mix, a man who had helped blind and disfigure a nurse in an abortion clinic? He didn't like to think about that. His one serious fall was on a forgery charge. He had never deliberately hurt anyone. Why had he gotten mixed up with the people who had set off the bomb at the clinic? That one, too, was easy. They knew a useful loser when they saw one.

Maybe what was waiting for him under the thunderclouds up ahead wasn't a totally undesirable fate. Maybe this was as good a place as any to cash in. He had spent most of his life waking up with a headful of spiders, then spending the rest of the day pretending they weren't there. He had shot over the heads of Mexicans coming out of the desert, scaring the hell out of women with infants hanging in slings from their chests and backs. He had painted the American flag on the cliff above his house but had never been in the service. He was a religious hypocrite and a peckerwood bully. His mother took off with a trucker when he was three, and his father, whom he had loved, had placed him in an orphanage when he was nine, promising to return after working a pipeline job in Alaska. But he never saw his father again or heard what happened to him, if anything. Was everything a conspiracy against Cody Daniels? Or wasn't it more probable that he was simply unwanted and, worse, unwanted for a legitimate reason? Gravity sucked, and shit always slid down the pipe, not up.

He felt his foot pressing on the accelerator. He had never thought so clearly about his life. The thunder rolling through the hills, the smell of the ozone, the cold tannic odor of the rain and dust, the branches of the mesquite and scrub oak bending almost to the ground all seemed like the pages of a book flipping before his eyes, defining the world and his role in it in a way he had never thought possible. Let Temple Dowling and his men do their worst. What was so bad about ending here, inside an electric storm, inside a clap of thunder that was as loud as God slapping His palms together?

Cody had all of these thoughts and was almost free of his fear when he drove into Anton Ling's yard and his headlights lit up the scene taking place by the windmill. Then he remembered why he had been so afraid.

CHAPTER TEN

Two men were holding Anton Ling by her arms. Her bare feet were bloody, her wrists duct-taped behind her. They had just lifted her out of the tank. Four other men stood close by, watching. All of the men were masked and had shifted their attention from Anton Ling to Cody. The only person not staring at him was Anton Ling, whose head hung on her chest, her wet hair wrapped around her cheeks. Cody Daniels braked and stared back at the men staring at him. He felt he had walked into someone else's nightmare and would not be leaving it any time soon.

He opened the door and stepped out of his vehicle, the engine still running. The ground seemed to shake with thunder, pools of quicksilver rippling through the clouds. "Howdy, fellows," he said.

No one answered him. Why did they look so surprised? Hadn't they heard or seen his truck coming? Maybe the sound of the engine had gotten lost in the thunder. Or maybe

Temple Dowling's people had recognized his truck and had already dismissed his presence as insignificant. "It's me. Cody Daniels. What's going on?" he said.

"Turn off your engine and lights and get over here," a tall man said.

"I was just doing like y'all told me. Keeping an eye on the place and all. I don't think y'all should be doing this to Miss Anton."

"Did you hear me?"

"Yes, sir."

"Then cut your engine and your lights."

"Yes, sir, I'm on it," Cody said. He reached back in the cab and turned off the ignition and headlights. He looked at the sky in the east and the wind flattening the trees on the hillcrests and the darkness that seemed to extend to the edges of the earth. "Boy, this has been a frog-stringer, hasn't it? Where's Mr. Dowling at?"

"What are you doing here?"

"Motoring around and such."

"Motoring around?"

"Yes, sir."

"Take out your wallet and put it on the hood of your vehicle."

"You don't know me?"

The tall man approached him. "Don't make me repeat myself."

"See, I thought y'all might be the cops I called earlier. I saw the lights on down here, which didn't seem right, so I did a nine-one-

one and figured y'all were with Sheriff Holland. I expect he ought to be showing up any time now."

"You're a damn poor liar, boy."

"I'd appreciate it if you wouldn't call me that."

"Get on your knees and put your hands behind your head."

"That woman hasn't done anything to y'all. Why don't you leave her alone?"

The tall man drove his fist into Cody's stomach, burying it to his wrist. Cody doubled over, his breath exploding from his chest, his knees collapsing in the dirt. The tall man shoved him over with his boot, then stepped on the side of his face. "Who are you?"

"A guy who lives up in the cliffs."

"Who'd you call?"

"Nobody. I didn't call anybody. You cain't get service out here."

"You know a man name of Noie Barnum?" The tall man pushed his boot tighter into the side of Cody's face.

"I've heard of him. I don't know him."

"Where did you hear about Barnum?"

"From a man name of Dowling. I thought that's who y'all were."

"What did you see here this morning?"

"Nothing," Cody replied, his mouth mashed against his teeth.

"Sure about that?"

244

"I know better than to mess with the wrong folks."

The tall man did not release his foot from Cody's face. He seemed to be looking at a diminutive man in the background, perhaps waiting for instructions. Cody could feel the lugs and grit on the bottom of the tall man's boot biting into his cheek and jawbone. He could smell the soiled odor of the man's foot and sock and the oil that had been rubbed into the boot's leather. The pressure on Cody's skull and jaw was unrelenting, as though the tall man were on the edge of cracking Cody's facial bones apart.

Cody was not seeing the tall man now. He saw two prison-farm gunbulls walking him from the trusty dormitory to the shed with the sawhorse standing under a bare lightbulb. They were both drunk and laughing, as though the three of them were only having fun, not unlike kids putting a friend through a harmless initiation ritual. Maybe at first that was all they had intended to do — just scare him and knock him around for sassing one of them that afternoon, what did they call it, making a Christian out of a hardhead? He knew the reality was otherwise. These were men for whom cruelty was as natural a part of their lives as eating breakfast. Their only task had been to hide their intentions from themselves, to set up the situation, then to simply follow their instincts, not unlike flinging gasoline on a fire and stepping back to watch the results. Cody would never forget the lustful cry of release in the throat of the first gunbull who mounted him. He would also never forgive himself for being their victim, accepting what they did to him as though somehow he had deserved his fate.

"I didn't see anything here except six men tormenting a he'pless woman," he said.

There was a pause. "You saw what?" the tall man asked, twisting the sole of his boot on Cody's cheek.

"Saw a tall man that's got so much chewing tobacco in his mouth, he cain't swallow. Saw a li'l bitty fellow over yonder by the horse tank. Saw one man that's bleeding through a hole in his mask, like somebody seriously fucked up his face. Saw a big gray truck with a diesel engine and a stack on it. Saw a bunch of men that dress like they been in the military. Saw a bunch of men that wouldn't believe me when I said I called Sheriff Holland. I'm here to tell you the sheriff of this county is one mean motor scooter. He'll flat kick a two-by-four up your ass. I know. I've been in his jailhouse."

Cody thought the torque in his neck was going to snap his spinal cord. He could hear the windmill's blades spinning, a loose door banging in the barn, the thunder in the clouds retreating in the hills. Through the dirt and sweat and rain mist in his eyes, he could see a pale band of cold light appear beyond the hills in the east, as though the season were winter rather than spring. He heard someone snapping his fingers, as though trying to get the attention of the tall man. Then the boot went away from Cody's face.

"You're a lucky fellow," the tall man said, lifting Cody to his feet by his shirtfront. "But let me leave you this little reminder of what happens when you wise off to the wrong people." He drove Cody's head into the truck fender and dropped him to the ground.

Cody felt himself descending into a deep well, one that was cool and damp and colored by a sunrise that had the texture and pinkness of cotton candy. As though from a great distance, he could hear glass breaking, furniture being overturned, a telephone crashing through a window into the yard, a computer being smashed into junk. These things were not his business any longer. Somehow Cody Daniels had faced down and bested the men who had raped him when he was seventeen. That an event of that magnitude could take place in his life seemed impossible. All he knew was that after a few minutes at the bottom of the well, the truck with the diesel-powered engine drove away, and he found himself cutting the duct tape on Anton Ling's wrists and ankles, wondering if she was still alive.

■ ■ ■ ■

The 911 call came in to the department at 6:47 A.M. The caller said he was an emergency electrical worker who had been sent out to find a downed power line in the neighborhood and had been flagged down by a man claiming to be a minister. "Y'all better get out here. This guy isn't making much sense," the caller said.

"Neither are you. What's the nature of your emergency?" Maydeen said.

"The guy says there's a Chinese woman inside that almost drowned. The place looks torn to hell. There're two pickup trucks in the yard with the wiring ripped out of the dashboards. Maybe a bunch of those Mexicans went crazy."

"Which Mexicans?"

"The ones that come through here every night. Maybe now y'all can get off your asses and do something about it."

"What's your name?"

"Marvin."

"What's your last name, Marvin?"

"I didn't give it."

"Well, Marvin I-Didn't-Give-It, you keep yourself and your smart-aleck mouth there till a deputy sheriff arrives. You also keep this line open. You copy that, Marvin?"

"Yes, ma'am," he said. "Ma'am?"

"What?"

"I'm standing in the yard by the horse tank. There's blood in the water and on the side of the tank. There's something else, too. Hang on."

"Are you still there?"

"There's a car, maybe a Trans Am, driving up from the back of the property. It doesn't have any paint. A guy is getting out."

"What about him?"

"I don't know. A guy in a suit and a hat. A guy in a dress shirt. I don't know where he came from. There's no road back there."

"Have you seen him before?"

"I waved at him, but he's just standing there. His engine is running."

"Can you get the tag?"

"No, ma'am. He's got his door open and he's staring at me. He hasn't shaved in a while. His shirt is yellow-looking, like there's dried soap in it."

Then the caller went silent.

"Are you there? Stay with me, Marvin," Maydeen said.

"I don't know what he wants. He's just staring at me. His pants are stuck down inside the tops of his boots. Are y'all on your way yet?"

"Can you ask the driver who he is?"

"No, ma'am."

"Why not?"

"I'm not sure why not. This isn't a reg'lar

sort of guy."

"What do you mean by that?"

"The way he's staring at me. He's got a shoulder rig on."

"He's carrying a weapon?"

"Yes, ma'am, a big revolver in a shoulder rig. I can see it against his chest."

"Go to your vehicle, Marvin."

"I don't think he wants me to do that."

"Listen to me, Marvin. Take your cell phone from your ear and walk to your vehicle with it. But don't break the connection. Are you listening?"

"He's walking up to me, ma'am."

"Drive away, Marvin."

"No, ma'am. This is not the time to go anywhere. Jesus Christ, lady, get out here." There was a pause, then: "I'm from the power company. I'm not sure what's going on. The place is a wreck, isn't it? I think a lady in there might be hurt real bad. Sir, you cain't take the keys out of my truck. That's a company vehicle. They don't allow unauthorized personnel inside their vehicles. Sir, don't throw my keys up there. I'm gonna be in a heck of a lot of trouble."

The connection went dead.

Maydeen dispatched the paramedics and two deputies to the house, then called Hackberry at his home and told him of the 911 call. "The guy from the power company didn't

250

say who the minister was?" he asked.

"No clue."

"And nothing else about the guy in the Trans Am?"

"Just what I told you."

"Collins?"

"I've tried to call Marvin twice, but I go to voice mail."

"Call the power company and ask them to call the radio in his truck."

"Yes, sir."

"There was blood in the horse tank?"

"That's what the caller said."

"I'm on my way. Get Pam out there."

"She just walked in."

"Put her on, please."

"It's Collins, isn't it?" Maydeen said.

"That's my guess."

"You'll probably beat the ambulance there. Wait till I get R.C. and Felix out there for backup."

"Do what you're told, Maydeen."

"You're too goddamn old and stubborn for your own good, Hack. You're gonna get yourself killed."

Pam picked up the extension. "What's going on?" she said.

"We ROA at Anton Ling's place. Maydeen will fill you in. Get ahold of Ethan Riser and tell him Jack Collins is probably in the neighborhood. Put out an APB on a Trans Am with no paint on it. Include Collins's physical description."

"Copy that," she replied. "Hack?"

"What?"

"If you see Collins, forget the rules."

"We never forget the rules."

"Haven't you figured it out? That's exactly what Collins counts on."

Maydeen was right. Because Hackberry was driving from his ranch, he arrived at Anton Ling's property before the ambulance or the deputies from his department. The rain had stopped, and the great boundless baked emptiness of the land that was not unlike the floor of an ancient ocean seemed to have risen cool and green and washed from the storm, a blue and pink and turquoise rainbow arching over the hills, anchoring itself and its promise somewhere beyond the clouds.

Cody Daniels's truck was parked in front of the house, the ignition wires ripped out. The lineman's truck was parked close by, the driver's door open, the keys gone from the ignition. There was no movement either inside or outside the house. Hackberry walked to the barn and the bunkhouse and the stucco cottage and looked inside. There was no one there, and the Trans Am was nowhere to be seen. He pulled his revolver from its holster and entered the house through the kitchen door, the pistol hanging heavily from his hand. The contents of the

252

cupboards and the pantry had been raked on the floor. Through a side door, he could see into the room that served as a chapel. The statue of the Virgin Mary had been broken in half, and the tiered rack of votive candles had been flipped over and the candles and glass holders smashed and ground into the floor. The small altar had been flung into the folding chairs, the white altar cloth grimed with footprints.

The only sound he heard was the wind flapping the curtains on the windows. Through a doorway, he could see the dining and living rooms. The pictures had been stripped from the walls and the dining table turned over, as though someone had been looking for something taped under it, the fabric on the stuffed chairs sliced open.

"This is Sheriff Holland! Who's in here?" he called.

"Sheriff?" a familiar voice said.

"That's what I said."

"It's Cody Daniels."

"Walk out here where I can see you, Reverend."

"Did you bring the ambulance?"

"Do what I say, please."

"Yes, sir, I'm coming," Daniels said, walking into the dining room. "They beat up Miss Anton and almost drowned her. We got to get her to the hospital. Sometimes people get pneumonia when they almost drown."

Hackberry still held his revolver, his eyes roving around the house's interior, searching over Cody Daniels's shoulder. "Where's Collins?"

"Is that his name?"

"Will you answer the question?"

"You're talking about the guy who killed all those Thai women, right? He didn't give us his name. He just asked who did this to Miss Anton. I told him I didn't have a clue."

Hackberry holstered his revolver and went into the bedroom. Anton Ling lay on a mattress that had been pulled off the bedsprings. Her dresser drawers had been dumped and her clothes pulled from the hangers in the closet. There was blood on her pillow, her clothes were drenched, and her eyes had the lack of focus that accompanies brain concussion. He knelt beside her. "Who did this to you, Miss Anton?"

"They all wore camouflage masks. Only one man spoke."

"What was Jack Collins doing here?"

"The man in the suit?"

"Yes, what did he say to you?"

"He wanted to know who the men were. He said he and I were on the same side. He touched my face with his hand. Cody told him not to do that, and for a minute I was afraid for Cody's life."

Cody?

"If it weren't for him, I'd be dead."

254

Hackberry looked over his shoulder at Cody Daniels and said, "Where's the guy from the power company, the one named Marvin?"

"The guy in the suit threw his keys on the roof and told him to hoof it. So that's what he did," Cody Daniels replied.

"The ambulance will be here in a few minutes, Miss Anton," Hackberry said. "I need to talk with the reverend, but I'll be right outside."

"I think I heard someone speak in Russian," she said. "But I can't be sure."

"You're pretty sure of that?" Hackberry said.

"Yes, I'd almost swear it was Russian, or at least East European."

As Hackberry got to his feet, tentacles of pain wrapped around his lower back and his buttocks, sinking into his viscera and then disappearing. He walked Cody Daniels toward the kitchen. "What were you doing out here?" he said.

"I wanted to see if she was all right. Then I left. That's when I saw this gray truck with an extended cab come down from the hills behind her fence line. It had a smokestack on it, one sticking up by the cab. The only guy I talked to had a mouth full of chewing tobacco and smelled like it, too."

"What time did you arrive on her property?"

"It was dark. I didn't note the time."

"You were looking in her windows?"

"I don't do things like that."

"You just drive out to other people's property in the middle of the night?"

"Yeah, in this case, that's what I did. I got a better question for you. When's that dadburn ambulance coming?"

"Why were you suspicious of the truck?" Hackberry said.

" 'Cause I thought they might be working for Temple Dowling."

"You know Dowling?"

"Dowling was at my house. He said he wanted me to spy on Miss Anton."

"Why would he select you for such a noble enterprise, Reverend?"

"Ask him."

"Don't worry, I will."

"You got the right to think anything you want of me, Sheriff. But I told you the truth. If you don't like it, that's —"

"Who were those guys?" Hackberry said.

"It wasn't Dowling or his people."

"If they wore masks, how can you be sure?"

"Dowling and his thugs invaded my house and threatened me on my deck. They would have recognized me. These guys didn't know who I was. What's so hard to understand about that?"

"Did Dowling offer you money?"

"He mentioned it."

"What else did he mention?"

"Sir?"

"I know the Dowling family. I know how they work. Is Temple Dowling blackmailing you?"

Cody Daniels's hand was resting on the kitchen drainboard. His fingers twitched slightly, then became motionless. "I guess you could call it that. No, it's not up for debate, that's exactly what he was doing." His gaze drifted from the side window to the yard. "There're your deputies and the ambulance coming. Can I talk to your chief deputy a minute?"

"No, you can't. Did you have a gun or a weapon of any kind when you came back to help Ms. Ling?"

"No, sir."

"You just did it?"

"Not exactly. My teeth were rattling like Chiclets."

"What does Dowling have on you, partner?"

"You've pulled my sheet. Take your choice."

"You went down for forgery, but that's not it, is it?"

"I got no more to say on the subject."

"It's the bombing at the abortion clinic, isn't it?"

"I need to talk to your deputy. It's important. At least it is to me."

"Go sit on the gallery and let your mind think cool thoughts. You know who said that?

257

Satchel Paige. He said the key to longevity was to have cool thoughts and not to eat fried food. Why don't you try that?"

"Why you got it in for me, Sheriff?"

"Because I think you helped blind and mutilate a defenseless woman. Because I think anyone who plants a bomb among unsuspecting people should be stuffed feet-first into a tree shredder."

The skin of Cody Daniels's throat prickled, as though it had just been windburned. "You really mean that?" he said quietly.

"Probably not," Hackberry said. "But I mean something right close to it."

"You're not one given to mercy, Sheriff. I don't think it's right to talk to people like that, even the likes of me," Cody Daniels said. He went outside and sat by himself on the front steps, his face wan, his gaze fixed on the apron of bare earth at his feet.

Hackberry helped the paramedics place Anton Ling on the gurney and take her out to the ambulance. Before they put her inside, she touched his wrist. "I could hear you in the kitchen," she said. "Don't be too hard on Reverend Daniels."

"He has no explanation for being at your house."

"It was his pride. I shamed and demeaned him in the parking lot at the grocery store. I treated him like human refuse."

"To my mind, that's not an unfair description of a clinic bomber."

"You're wrong about him," she said.

"We'll straighten up your house and lock the doors. I'll be up to see you at the hospital. In the meantime, I don't want you to worry about anything. We'll get the guys who did this."

"Maybe," she replied.

"What were they after, Miss Anton?"

"Noie Barnum."

"No, in the house. What were they looking for?"

"My guess is they're looking for technical material about the Predator drone."

"Is it there?"

She shook her head.

"Did Barnum have it on him?"

"To my knowledge, all he brought to this house were his wounds. He stayed in the cottage. I forgot to tell you something. I hurt one of the men who was holding me at the sink. I stabbed him just below the eye with a screwdriver. He'll have to go to a hospital or see a doctor."

"You're a tough lady, Miss Anton."

"You won't catch them."

"Pardon?"

"The men who did this to me have been with us a long time. They're in our midst every day. We just don't acknowledge their presence," she said.

A paramedic closed the back door of the

ambulance. Hackberry watched the ambulance drive away, then walked back to the windmill and watched Pam Tibbs and R.C. stringing crime-scene tape from the barn to the front of the house. R.C. was over six feet and had a skeletal frame that looked tacked together from the staves in an apple box, his stomach and buttocks flat, his waist twenty-eight inches, his face perpetually young, his mouth small like a girl's, his eyes always bright with surprise. He was chewing gum, snapping it in his jaw, his coned-up white straw deputy's hat slanted down over his brow. "Found a bloody screwdriver that somebody kicked under the counter in the kitchen, Sheriff," he said.

"Did you bag it?" Hackberry said.

"Yes, sir."

"Good. That must be the one Ms. Ling put in a guy's face."

"You want to make casts of those tire tracks?"

"That's a good idea."

"See the tracks on top of the truck tires? Those are Michelins."

"How do you know?"

"I can tell by the width and the tread. They're brand-new, too. Want to start checking the dealerships?"

"You can identify a Michelin tire just by looking at the tread marks?"

"I only mounted about five hunnerd of them."

Hackberry glanced at Pam. She brushed at her nose with her wrist, her eyes smiling.

"What are y'all laughing at?" R.C. asked.

"Nothing," Hackberry said.

"I say something wrong?" R.C. asked.

"No, not at all," Hackberry said.

"I was just making an observation," R.C. said, his cheeks reddening.

"We were laughing because you were two jumps ahead of us, R.C.," Hackberry said. "Don't tell the voters I said that, or they might take my star away."

"No, sir, they're not going to do that," R.C. said. "They think you're one of them bleeding-heart liberals, but they trust you to do the right thing more than they trust themselves. How's that for smarts?"

"On the subject of smarts, what's with shit-for-brains over there on the steps?" Pam asked, glancing in Cody Daniels's direction. The sun had broken through the clouds, and her bare arms looked brown and big in the sunlight as she unrolled and tightened the crime-scene tape, her dark mahogany hair that was either sunburned or white on the tips curled against her cheeks, her breasts as firm-looking as softballs against her khaki shirt.

"He says he wants to talk with you about something," Hackberry replied.

"I think I can forgo the pleasure," Pam replied.

"Anton Ling says he saved her life."

"If he did, it was by accident."

Pam went back to work, stringing the tape behind the barn and around the back of the stucco cottage and the bunkhouse. She secured it to a fence post on the far side of the main house and returned to the windmill, her hair moving in the wind, strands touching her mouth. In moments like these, when she was totally unguarded and unmindful of herself, Hackberry knew in a private place in the back of his mind that Pam Tibbs belonged in that category of exceptional women whose beauty radiated outward through their skin and had little to do with the physical attributes of their birth. In these moments he felt an undefined longing in his heart that he refused to recognize.

"Mind if I see what he wants?" Pam asked.

"Suit yourself," Hackberry replied.

"Come with me."

"What for?"

"This is the same guy who claimed I assaulted him. I don't want him telling lies about anything I say to him now."

"Then I'd leave him alone."

"Jesus Christ, Hack, first you tell me the guy wants to talk to me, then you tell me not to talk with him. In between, you tell me he saved someone's life."

"What are you laughing at, R.C.?" Hackberry said.

"Not a thing, Sheriff. I was just enjoying the breeze and the freshness of the morning. This cool wind is special. Lordy, what a fine day," R.C. said, folding his arms over his chest, gazing at the sunlit greenness and clarity of the hills, puffing out his cheeks, sucking his teeth.

"I'll talk to you later," Hackberry said.

"Yes, sir," R.C. said.

Hackberry walked with Pam to the gallery, where Cody Daniels was sitting on the steps in the shadow of the house, staring into space, a bandage taped to his forehead. "You wanted to say something to Chief Deputy Tibbs, Reverend?" Hackberry said.

"I'd like to do it in private, if you don't object," Cody Daniels replied.

"Say what's on your mind. We have work to do," Pam said.

Cody Daniels looked back and forth, his mouth a tight seam. He fiddled with his shirt buttons and made lines in the dirt with the heel of his shoe. Strands of his hair were stuck inside the tape on his bandage, which gave him the appearance of a disorganized and hapless child. "I apologize for the way I acted when you arrested me. I deliberately provoked you," he said to Pam.

She touched a nostril with one knuckle and huffed air out her nose. "Is that it?" she said.

"I also made some smart-ass remarks when I was in the holding cell. I'm sorry I did that."

"What smart-ass remarks?" Pam said.

"I said something to the sheriff. I don't remember it real clear. I should have kept my mouth shut, that's all."

"What remarks?" Pam said.

Cody Daniels wiped a piece of dirt off his face and looked at it. "Just idle, disrespectful stuff that doesn't mean anything. The kind of things an uneducated and angry man might say. No, 'angry man' doesn't cut it. The kind of thing a half-baked mean-spirited pissant might say. That's me I'm talking about."

"What did you say?"

"Sheriff?" Cody Daniels said, raising his eyes to Hackberry's.

"The man said he was sorry. Why not let it slide?" Hackberry said to Pam.

"Reverend, you've got about five seconds to get your head on right," Pam said.

"Cain't recall."

She pulled a braided slapjack from her side pocket and let it hang from her right hand.

"I said I'd rather belly up to a spool of barbed wire," Cody Daniels said. He knitted his fingers together and twisted them in and out of one another, his teeth clenched, breathing through the side of his mouth as though he had just eaten scalding food, patting the soles of his shoes up and down in the dirt. Hackberry could hear the blades of

264

the windmill rattle to life as R.C. unchained the crankshaft and cupped a drink of water from the pipe.

"What did Sheriff Holland have to say about your remark?" Pam asked.

"He said something about kicking a two-by-four with nails in it up my ass till I'd be spitting splinters. Or something to that effect."

Pam brushed at her nose again, pushing the slapjack back into her pocket. "What do you think we ought to do with you?"

"You got me," he replied, shaking his head, his eyes lowered.

"Look at me and answer my question."

"Shoot me?"

"It's a possibility," she said.

"She's not serious, is she?" Cody Daniels said to Hackberry.

"You'd better believe it, bud," Hackberry said.

Pam and Hackberry went inside the house and, with two other deputies, began picking up the furniture and sweeping up the glass in the kitchen and the chapel. "Are we doing this because you're a Catholic?" Pam asked.

Hackberry reset the altar at the front of the chapel and picked up the broken pieces of the statue of the Virgin Mary and laid them on top of the altar. "We're doing this because it's the right thing to do," he said.

"Just thought I'd ask," she said.

"We protect and serve. We treat everybody the same. If others don't like the way we do things, they can run us off. End of discussion."

"Who spat in your Cheerios this morning?"

"Stop and consider the image that conjures up. Why don't you and Maydeen develop a small degree of sensitivity about the language you use? Just once, try a little professionalism." He propped his broom against the wall, knocking it into the wood.

"My uncle said I put him in mind of a cow with the red scours downloading into a window fan," she said.

Hackberry gave up. Through the window, he saw Cody Daniels rise from the steps and begin walking down the road toward the highway. Pam saw him, too, and seemed to lose her concentration. She stopped sweeping and blew out her breath. "Is there a shortcut to his place?" she asked.

"No, on foot it's four miles, most of it uphill," Hackberry replied.

"The sheriff in Jim Hogg told you Daniels was dirty on a clinic bombing back east?"

"He said Daniels was at least a cheerleader in the group. Maybe worse, who knows? He acts like he's dirty, though. If I had to bet, I'd say he was a player."

She propped her broom against the scrolled-iron candle rack and bit a piece of skin on her thumb. "Like you say, we treat everyone the same, right?"

"That's the rule."

"The guy stood up. It's not right to pretend he didn't."

"I wouldn't say he stood up completely, but he made an effort."

"You mind? I'll make him sit behind the grille."

"No, I don't mind at all," Hackberry replied.

He watched Pam go out the front door and get in her cruiser and drive down the dirt road. She braked to a stop by Cody Daniels, rolling down her window and speaking to him over the sound of the engine. Daniels got in the backseat, ducking his head, like a man coming out of a storm into an unexpected safe harbor.

Go figure, Hackberry thought.

Chapter Eleven

Hackberry had never considered himself prescient, but he had little doubt about who would be calling him that evening. As the sun set behind his house, he sat down in a spacious cushioned swaybacked straw chair on his back porch, his Stetson tilted down over his brow, his cordless phone and a glass of iced tea and his holstered .45 on the table beside him. He propped his feet up on another chair and sipped from his tea and crunched ice and mint leaves between his teeth and then dozed while waiting for the call that he knew he would receive, in the same way you know that a dishonorable man to whom you were unwisely courteous will eventually appear uninvited at your front door.

He could hear animals walking through the thickness of the scrub brush on the hillside and, in his half-waking state, see a palm tree on the crest framed against a thin red wafer of sun imprinted on the blue sky. For just a moment he felt himself slip into a dream about his father, the University of Texas history professor who had been a congressman and a friend of Franklin Roosevelt. In the dream there was nothing about President Roosevelt or his father's political or teaching career or his father's death, only the time when Hackberry and his father rode horses into the badlands down by the border to hunt for Indian arrowheads. It was 1943, and they had tied their horses outside a beer joint and café built of gray fieldstones that resembled bread loaves. The land dipped away into the distance as though all the sedimentary rock under the earth's crust had collapsed and created a giant sandy bowl rimmed by mesas that were as red in the sunset as freshly excised molars.

The sun was finally subsumed by clouds that were low and thick and churning and the color of burnt pewter. In the cooling of the day and the pulsation of electricity in the clouds, dust devils began to swirl and wobble and break apart on top of the hardpan. For reasons he was too young to understand, Hackberry was frightened by the drop in barometric pressure and the great shadow that seemed to darken the land, as though a shade were being drawn across it by an invisible hand.

His father had gone inside the café to buy two bottles of cream soda. When he came

back out and handed Hack one, the ice sliding down the neck, he saw the expression on
his son's face and said, still hanging on to the
bottle, "Something happen out here, son?"

"The land, it looks strange. It makes me
feel strange," Hackberry said.

"In what way?"

"Like everything has died. Like the sun has
gone away forever, like we're the only two
people left on earth."

"Psychiatrists call that a world-destruction
fantasy. But the earth will always be here.
Hundreds of millions of years ago, out in that
great vastness, there was an ocean where fish
as big as boxcars swam. Now it's a desert,
but maybe one day it will be an ocean again.
Did you know there were probably whales
that swam out there?"

"No, sir."

"It's true. Mythic creatures, too. See those
pale horizontal lines in the mesas? That's
where the edge of the sea was. You see those
flat rocks up a little bit higher? That's where
the mermaids used to sun themselves."

"Mermaids in Texas?"

"One hundred million years ago, you bet."

"How do you know that, Daddy?"

"I was there. Your dad is a pretty old fellow." Then he rubbed his hand on top of
Hackberry's head. "Nothing is worth worrying about, Hack," he said. "Just remember
how long this place has been here and all the

270

people who've lived on it and maybe are still out there, in one form or another, maybe as spirits watching over us. That's what the Indians believe. Our job is to enjoy the earth and to take care of it. Worry robs us of our faith and our joy and gives us nothing in return. How about you and I go inside and play the pinball machine and order up a couple of those barbecue-chicken dinners? When we come back outside, one of those mermaids might be up there in the rocks winking at you."

That was the way Hackberry always wanted to remember his father — good-natured and protective and knowledgeable about every situation in the world that a man might face. And that was the way he had thought of him without exception every day of his young life, up until the morning his father had taken a revolver from his desk drawer and oiled and cleaned it and loaded each chamber with a copper-jacketed hollow-point round, then placed a pillow behind his head and cocked the hammer and fitted the barrel into his mouth, easing the sight behind his teeth, just before he blew the top of his skull onto the ceiling.

The sun had gone behind the hill when Hackberry's cordless phone rang and woke him from his dream. He checked the caller ID and saw the words "wireless" and "unknown." He clicked the "on" button and said,

"What's the haps, Mr. Collins?"

"I declare. You're on it from the gate, Sheriff."

"It's not much of a trick when you deal with certain kinds of people."

"Such as me?"

"Yeah, I think you definitely qualify as a man with his own zip code and time zone."

"Maybe I'll surprise you."

"Hardly."

"How's the Oriental woman doing?"

"Call the hospital and see."

"I would, but hospitals don't give out patient information over the telephone."

"Ms. Ling has had a bad time, but she's going to be all right. What were you doing at her place? Just happened to be in the neighborhood?"

"I have people watching it for me. Which is what you should have been doing."

"Thank you. I'll make a note of that. Are you done?"

"Pretty near but not quite."

"No, you're done, sir. And I'm done being your echo chamber. You're not Lucifer descending upon Eden in a Miltonic poem, Mr. Collins. You were a bug sprayer for Orkin. You probably skipped toilet training and have lived most of your life with skid marks in your underwear. I know of no instance when you've fought your fight on a level playing field. You consider yourself educated, but you understand nothing of the books you read. You're a grandiose idiot, sir. You'll end on the injection table at Huntsville or with a bullet in your head. I'm telling you these things for only one reason. Last year you invaded my home and tried to murder my chief deputy. I'm going to get you for that, partner, and for all the other things you've done to innocent people in the name of God."

"You need to be quiet and listen for a minute, Sheriff Holland. You probably have all kinds of theories about who hurt the Oriental woman and tore up her house. This defense contractor Temple Dowling has been looking for Noie Barnum all over the countryside, but I doubt it was him. There was a little man among that bunch in the truck. From what I could gather, he didn't have a lot to say, but he was the one giving orders. I suspect that's Josef Sholokoff. Do you call that name to mind?"

"Not offhand," Hackberry lied.

"I once worked for Josef Sholokoff. He tried to have me killed. He sent three degenerates on motorcycles to do the job. Some poor Hispanic maid had to scrub them off the wallpaper in a motel room. I always felt bad about that. I mean leaving her to clean up such a mess."

"Yes, you surely know how to write your name in big red letters, Mr. Collins. I don't think Ted Bundy or Dennis Rader or Gary

Ridgway or any of our other contemporary psychopaths quite meet your standards."

"There are different kinds of killers in the world, Sheriff Holland. Some do it out of meanness. Some do it for hire. Some do it because they're schizophrenic and attack imaginary enemies. Politicians have the military do it to increase the financial gain of corporations. Sholokoff takes it a step further. Ask yourself what kind of man would allow his people to vandalize a chapel and torture a female minister."

"Sholokoff has declared war on the Creator?"

"You could say that. He's a procurer. Is there anything lower than a man who lives off the earnings of a whore?"

"I don't think you have a lot of moral authority in that area, Mr. Collins. You're a murderer of innocent girls and women, which means you're a moral and physical coward."

"Could it be you who's wanting in courage, Sheriff, and not me? Did you sit with a weapon by your hand while you waited on my call? Were you that fearful of a homeless man?"

Hackberry's eyes swept the hillside, searching in the shadows that the trees and underbrush made on the slope. Then he examined the ridgeline and the trees growing up an arroyo and the outcroppings of sandstone and layers of table rock exposed by erosion, all the places that a man with binoculars could hide in the setting sun.

"You used a generic term. You said 'weapon.' What kind of weapon would that be, Mr. Collins?" Hackberry said.

"Maybe I was just trying to give you a start."

"I always said you were quite a jokester."

"That's not what you just called me. You said I was a coward. I'm many things. But 'coward' isn't among them. A coward fears death. But Death is my friend, Sheriff Holland. You remember the poem by e. e. cummings? How does it go? 'How do you like your blue-eyed boy now, Mr. Death?' The poet was talking of Buffalo Bill. Will you be corrupted by the grave like Buffalo Bill? Or will you be freed by it? Can you say you have no fear of the black hole that awaits you?"

"Rhetoric is cheap stuff."

"Is it, now?"

"I'm going to sign off and ask that you not call again. I'll be seeing you down the pike. This time out, there won't be any warning."

"You're a judgmental man, Sheriff. As such, you may be the orchestrator of your own undoing."

"I don't think it's going to play out that way."

"Maybe you'll rethink your attitude."

The red dot of a laser sight appeared on the back of Hackberry's left wrist and traveled up his arm and across his chest. Hackberry sucked in his breath involuntarily, as though a black widow or tarantula had crawled across his body. He tried to get to his feet as the red dot paused on his heart, but he fell back in the chair, knocking over the iced tea, his back aflame. The red dot dropped to his loins and touched his scrotum and then was gone, all in under two seconds, so fast he wondered if he had imagined the event. He stared into the black-green shadows on the hillside while rocks clacked and spilled from somewhere near the ridgeline and the dial tone of his cordless phone buzzed like an electrified horsefly in his hand.

He lay sleepless in his bed most of the night, furious that he had let himself be bested by a messianic poseur and mass killer like Preacher Jack Collins, then doubly furious that, in his anger, he was giving away power to Collins and letting Collins rob him of sleep and peace of mind and, finally, self-respect. He had known reformers and Bible-thumpers all his life, and not one of them, in his opinion, ever proved the exception when it came to obsession about sexuality: To a man, they feared their own desires and knew after waking from certain kinds of dreams what they would be capable of doing if the right situation presented itself. Every one of them was filled not with longing but with rage, and their rage always expressed itself in the same fashion: They wanted control of other people, and if they could not have control over them, they wanted them destroyed.

The legacy of Salem did not go away easily. Vigilantism, the Klan, the acolytes of Senator McCarthy and others of his stripe formed a continuous thread from 1692 to the present, Hackberry thought. But that did not change the fact that Hackberry had failed miserably in dealing with Jack Collins, who killed people whenever and wherever he wished and seemed to walk through walls or leave no indicators of his presence except the funnel-shaped tracks of an animal.

The next morning did not go well, either. The previous day Ethan Riser had shown little interest in the events at Anton Ling's house, explaining that the break-in and the assault on her person did not constitute federal crimes and that Jack Collins's appearance and departure from Anton Ling's home provided no information or clue as to where he and Noie Barnum were hiding. "Let me call you back early tomorrow," Riser had said. "I'll try to find out where Josef Sholokoff is right now. If he's here, we can probably step into things and leave a lot heavier footprint."

"Why the sudden due diligence with Sholokoff and not our local residents?" Hackberry had said.

"Jack Collins is an aberration who will

probably self-destruct. Sholokoff is a contagious disease. If he can get his hands on a working model of a Predator drone or its design, Al Qaeda will have it in twenty-four hours."

"How would Sholokoff even know about Noie Barnum?"

"Temple Dowling used to be a silent business partner of his. We've had our eye on Dowling for a long time. He just doesn't know it. Or care. Weren't you associated politically with Dowling's father?"

"Yeah, I was, much to my regret. I'll expect your call early in the morning, Ethan," Hackberry had replied.

But Riser did not call back, and Hackberry's messages went unanswered. That afternoon another agent called Hackberry's office and told him that Ethan Riser had gone back to Washington.

"What for?" Hackberry asked.

"Ask him when he gets back," the agent said, and hung up.

Hackberry visited Anton Ling in the hospital but otherwise spent the rest of the day unproductively, still resenting himself for allowing Jack Collins to get inside his head. Or was something else bothering him as well?

That evening he drove to Pam Tibbs's house with a gallon of vanilla ice cream and a six-pack of A&W root beer packed in his cooler. He rang the doorbell, then sat on the front steps, staring into a street lined with bungalows and two-story frame houses that had been built during the 1920s, the porches hung with swings, the flower beds blooming, American flags hanging from staffs inserted into metal sockets on many of the wood pillars. It was a neighborhood that belonged to another era, one for which most Americans are nostalgic, but the people who lived in the neighborhood did not recognize it as such.

Hackberry heard the back screen slam, then a moment later, a man backed a waxed red convertible into the street and drove away, his attention concentrated on the traffic. Pam opened the front door. "Hi, Hack," she said.

He turned around and looked at her. She was wearing blue-jean shorts and a pink blouse and earrings and Roman sandals. "Hi," he replied.

"You want to come in?"

"Who was the guy in the convertible?"

"My cousin."

"I've never seen him. Does he live around here?"

"No."

"So where does he live?"

"He's a sales rep for a computer company. He travels a lot."

"People who travel a lot don't have addresses?"

"It's none of your business, Hack."

"You're right, it isn't."

She looked at the six-pack of root beer next to Hack's leg. The vapor on top of the cans was contracting, the beaded moisture on the sides running onto the porch. "What's in the sack?"

"Vanilla ice cream."

"You want to come in?"

"I should have called first."

"What's going on?"

"Nothing is going on. I thought you might like a root-beer float. It's that kind of evening."

"What kind?"

"When I was a kid, it was a treat to go to the A&W root-beer drive-in. We thought that was big stuff. Later-spring and summer evenings are the best moments in the year."

"Come inside."

"Another time."

"Come inside or I'm going to kick you in the small of the back as hard as I can."

He looked at the street in the gloaming of the day and at the darkness of the lawns in the shade, and he knew what had been bothering him since early that morning. A teenage boy on a bicycle was riding down the sidewalk, sailing a folded newspaper with the accuracy of a marksman onto each porch, whapping it solidly against the front door, the canvas bags slamming hard on his racks each time he banged over a peak in the sidewalk. The boy reminded Hackberry of

280

himself, or maybe he reminded Hackberry of most boys of years ago, winsome in a way that was not calculated, full of expectation, full of innocent pride in their skill at lofting a tightly rolled, string-wrapped newspaper onto a front porch. But why was the boy throwing his route so late? Hackberry wondered. Why was the light so peculiar in tone — sepia-tinted, golden inside the branches of the trees, a smell like chrysanthemums pooling in the flower beds, more like autumn than spring?

"Hack?" Pam said.

"Yeah?"

"I'd really like some ice cream and root beer. It's very thoughtful of you to bring some by. Come in, won't you?"

Her mouth was red, her voice infused with a protective emotion that she rarely allowed anyone to see.

"Sure. That's what I was about to do," he replied.

She held the screen door open for him while he walked inside. He could feel her eyes slide across the side of his face when she latched the screen behind them. Then he heard her close the inside door and push the dead bolt into place.

"Why'd you do that?" he asked.

"Do what?"

"Lock the door."

"I didn't think about it."

281

"You think Collins will come around?"

"I hope he does. Except I don't think he's interested in me," she said.

"Then why did you lock the door?"

"Maybe I don't want to be disturbed by a couple of my busybody neighbors. You're acting a little strange, Hack."

"It goes with my persona. The VA gave me a D-minus on normalcy fifty years ago."

He went into the kitchen and set the root beer on the counter and put the ice cream in the freezer. His lower back felt like a junkyard that had fallen down a flight of stairs. He propped his hands on the edge of the sink and extended his legs behind him and leaned heavily on his arms, the pain slowly draining out of his spine and disappearing down the backs of his thighs into the floor. She placed her palm against the small of his back. "I hate to see you like this," she said. "I wish it was me instead of you."

"Like what?"

"In pain, depressed, unhappy. What did Collins say to you when he called your house?"

"It's not what he said. It's what he is. He loves death. That's his edge."

"So he'll have a smile on his face when we blow his head off."

"I met Jim Harrison once. He's a novelist. He made a remark in passing that I never forgot. He said, 'We love the earth but we don't get to stay.' On an evening like this, an irrefutable truth sometimes has a way of invading your soul. As a nihilist, Collins doesn't bear that burden. He seeks the dark hole in the ground that the rest of us fear. For that reason, we have no power over him. Even in killing him, we do his will. For that reason alone, I never believed in capital punishment. You said it when we first started dealing with Collins. He wants me to be his executioner."

She stretched her arm across his back and hooked her hand on his right shoulder and laid her face against his arm. "You were actually mad because my cousin was here?"

"No," he lied.

"He came to borrow money. His wife left him. He's a philanderer. No one else in the family will have anything to do with him." She exhaled and slipped her hand under his arm and squeezed it. "You and I were born by accident in different generations, Hack. But we're opposite sides of the same coin. Why do you keep thinking of yourself as old? You're handsome and youthful, and your principles have never changed. Why do you think people around here respect you? It's because from day to day you're always the same good man, one who never goes with fashion."

"There is no worse fate than for a young woman to marry a drunkard or an old man who is about to fall apart on the installment plan."

"Boy, do you know how to rain on a parade." She brushed her forehead back and forth on his shoulder. "What are we going to do, Hack?"

"About what?"

"Us."

"You want a root-beer float?" he asked.

"I feel like running off with my cousin. I probably would if he wasn't my cousin. I think right now I'd run off with Attila the Hun."

"You're the best, Pam."

"Best what?"

"The best of everything."

"I can't tell you how depressed that makes me feel."

The silence that followed seemed to envelop them, as though the inadequacy of the language they used in speaking to each other had come to define in an unalterable way the impossibility of their relationship. His cell phone vibrated in his pocket. It was R.C. "Maydeen told me to call you direct, Sheriff," he said. "I'm down in Coahuila in kind of a cantina."

"What are you doing in Coahuila?"

"I got a girlfriend in El Cibolo. On the way back, I blew out a tire and found out somebody had stolen my spare. I bummed a ride to this beer joint, except it's not exactly just a

284

beer joint. There's some cribs in back, and up the street there's some reg'lar hot-pillow joints that need turnstiles on the doors. There was an *hombre malo* in here earlier, one I couldn't get a good look at, but he looked like he had a dent in his face. After these guys left, I asked this mulatto shooting pool who they were, and he said they were guys I shouldn't be asking about unless I was interested in guns that went south and cocaine that went north. He also said the guy they worked for was getting his ashes hauled up the street, a joint that specializes in girls in their early teens."

"Could the guy with the dent in his face be the one Anton Ling put a screwdriver in?"

"Maybe. He was back in the shadows, shooting pool on the edge of the light. All I could tell was that one side of his face looked caved in."

"Are there any Mexican cops around?"

"Not unless you count the two who're getting blow jobs out back."

Hackberry took a notepad and a ballpoint pen from his shirt pocket. "What's the name of this place?" he said.

R.C. was having a hard time focusing on the face of the mulatto drinking next to him at the bar, not only because of the mescal he'd knocked back a shot glass at a time and chased with Corona but because the light

285

outside and inside the cantina was unnatural and seemed out of sync with the hour of the day and the geography of the countryside. The sun had gone down inside the clouds west of the mountains but had not died. Instead, a dull silver luminescence had pooled like smelted nickel in the clouds, accentuating the darkness of the valley and the poplar trees along the broken highway and the red-lit stucco houses along the street where the prostitutes sat in the windows, wearing flip-flops and loose dresses and no underwear because of the heat and the summerlike deadness in the air.

Though a big window fan sucked the cigarette smoke out of the cantina, the drain holes in the concrete floor smelled of stagnant water and spilled beer. R.C. could also smell the ammonia-like reek of the long stone trough in the *baño,* which had the words SOLO PARA URINAR painted over the open door. Most of the electrical lighting in the cantina came from the neon Dos Equis and Carta Blanca signs above the bar; but there was a purple stain to it, from either the gathering of the dusk in the streets or the tarnished glow inside the clouds west of the mountains, and the faces of the men drinking at the bar had the garish characteristics of cartoon figures. For R.C., the drinks the mulatto had bought him were coming at a high cost. His head was ringing, his heart was beating faster than it should, and the atmosphere around him had become as warm and damp and suffocating as a wool cloak.

Why was he having these thoughts and mental associations and seeing these images? he wondered.

The mulatto wore a smoke-stained, greasy wide-brimmed leather hat with a leather cord that flopped under his chin, and a leather vest without a shirt and striped suit pants without a belt and boots that had roweled spurs on the heels. Locks of his orange hair were flattened on his forehead; his eyebrows formed a solid line; his square teeth and the bones in his face and the thickness of his lips made R.C. think of a hard, compact gorilla. The mulatto filled his mouth with mescal and gargled with it before he swallowed, then pulled a bandanna from his back pocket and wiped his chin. "What'd you say you was doing here, man?"

"Trying to get my tire fixed," R.C. said.

"Yeah, me, too, man. That's how I ended up on a street full of *puta.* Getting my tire fixed. That's good, man. You ain't been in back yet?"

"I'm here 'cause a guy gave me a ride here."

"You want a ride, there's a *chica* out back will buck you to the ceiling." The bartender set a plate of sizzling onions and sliced green peppers and skillet grease and tortillas in front of the mulatto and went away. The mulatto rolled a tortilla full of onions and peppers and started eating. "Put something in your stomach, man. But don't drink no more mescal. You look like you been on board a ship in a bad storm. Hey, Bernicio, give my friend some coffee."

The bartender filled a cup from a tin pot that sat on a hot plate by the line of liquor bottles on the back counter. R.C. lifted the cup to his mouth, blowing on it, hardly able to swallow because it was so hot.

"What kind of work you do, man, besides drive around in Mexico and have flat tires?" the mulatto asked.

"I buy and sell livestock."

"Wild horses, huh?"

"Sometimes."

"For dog food?"

"I don't know what happens to them."

"You guys have shot most of them, *hombre*. There ain't many left. Where do you go to shoot them now? On the street of *puta?*"

"I'm just the middleman."

"You're wearing ironed blue jeans and a clean cowboy shirt with flowers printed on it. You got Tony Lamas on your feet. You got a shave and a new haircut, too. You're down here for *puta,* man. You ain't been buying no horses."

"I've got me a girlfriend here'bouts, but I don't call her what you just said."

"When you're in the sack with a woman,

288

hombre, it's for one reason, and the reason has got one name. Don't feel guilty about it. It ain't natural for a man to go against his desires."

R.C. drank again from the coffee cup, then set it down on the bar. His throat felt clotted, as though he had swallowed a handful of needles and could not blow them from his windpipe.

"Here, eat a tortilla," the mulatto said. "You ever have your throat blessed by the crossing of the candles on St. Blaise's Day? See, the priest puts the candles in an X on your throat, and for the next year you don't got to worry about choking on a bone or a piece of glass somebody put in your food. You okay, *rubio?*"

"Why you calling me that?"

" 'Cause you're *rubio* and macho, man. You're blond and strong and got cojones and can kick ass, I bet. Here, drink your coffee, then we'll go out back. It won't cost you nothing. I got a tab here. The best thing about my tab is I ain't got to pay it. You know why that is, man?"

R.C. could feel the skin on his face shrinking and growing hot, the beer signs and long bar and cuspidors streaked with tobacco juice slipping out of focus, the colors in the plastic casing on the jukebox dissolving and fusing together, the grin on the mulatto's face as red and wet as a split in a watermelon.

"I'll tell you why I ain't got to pay. I'm friends with La Familia Michoacána. You know who them guys are? They're religious crazies who cut off people's heads when they ain't transporting meth up to your country. We got your country by the balls, man. You need our dope, and you like to screw our women. But I'm gonna take care of you. Hang on to my arm. I'm gonna introduce you to a *chica* out back you gonna love. You can use my spurs on her, man."

R.C. felt himself falling to the floor, but the mulatto and a second man grabbed him and fitted each of his arms across their shoulders and carried him through the back of the bar, past a small dance floor and the stone urinal that was shielded only by a bead curtain, and into the alleyway between the cantina and the row of cribs that had canvas flaps on the doorways.

R.C. heard himself speaking as though his voice existed outside his body and he had no control over it.

"What's that you say?" the mulatto asked. "I couldn't hear. My ears are stopped up, and my mind is slow. It's 'cause of the way I grew up, working on a gringo ranch for a few pesos a day and eating beans that never had no meat in them. Getting slapped on the ear didn't help none, either. Okay, go ahead, I'm listening real good now."

R.C. heard himself speaking and then

laughing like he had never laughed in his life, his legs as weak as tendrils hanging from the bottom of his torso.

"Oh, that's good, *hombre,*" the mulatto said, having listened carefully to R.C.'s words. " 'Mexico would make a great golf course if it was run by Texans.' But you're a narc, man, so guess who we gonna sell you to? You get to meet La Familia Michoacána. They don't mess around. When they catch informers or narcs pretending to be down here for *puta,* they put their heads out on the sidewalk with the blindfolds still on and sometimes a cigarette in their mouths. Believe me, man, when I tell you this. What's gonna happen to you ain't gonna be like life on no golf course."

CHAPTER TWELVE

When Hackberry came through the front door of the cantina, he saw the bartender take note of him and Pam, then continue eating from a bowl of tripe, blowing gently on each spoonful before he placed it in his mouth. The bartender was seated on a stool, a napkin tucked inside the top of his shirt, his throat skin as coarse and wrinkled as a turkey's, his eyes like big brown buttons in a pie-plate face, his head shaved bald and a large black swastika, with red feathers for appendages, tattooed on the crown of his skull. He told Hackberry that he was sorry, but no, he had not seen anyone in the bar resembling Hackberry's young friend. His hands were big and square and looked like those of a bricklayer rather than those of a bartender. He continued eating, leaning forward over the bowl of tripe, careful not to spill any on top of his stomach.

"How long have you been on duty here?" Hackberry said.

"A few hours," the bartender replied. "But sometimes I got to serve food and drinks in the back. Maybe your friend was here but I didn't see him."

"In back?" Hackberry said.

"That's right, *señor.* We rent rooms to people who have traveled from far away. Sometimes they drink too much and want to rest before they drive home again."

"That's a very intelligent service you provide. How long does it take for you to carry a service tray to the back and return to the bar where your customers are waiting?"

"That depends, *señor.* Sometimes my customers take care of themselves. They are poor but honest, and they leave the money on the bar for whatever they drink."

"What's your name?" Hackberry asked.

"Bernicio."

"You have maybe a half-dozen customers in here. You can see everyone in the cantina from the front door to the back. My friend called me from here. He gave me the name of the cantina and directions to it. My friend is tall and looks very much like an Anglo. Don't offend me by pretending you were not aware of his presence."

"*Claro* that maybe he was here, but I didn't see him. I wish I had. Then I could be helpful. Then I could finish my supper."

Hackberry found himself trying to think through a peculiar manifestation of dishonesty that is considered normal in the third world and is totally antithetical to the average North American's point of view. The individual simply makes up his own reality and states that black is white and white is black and never flutters an eyelash. Appearance and denial always take precedence over substance and fact, and the application of logic or reason will never sway the individual from his self-manufactured convictions.

"Did you see a man with a wound in his face playing pool?" Hackberry asked.

"No, *señor.*"

"You were already shaking your head before I finished my question," Hackberry said.

"Because I have no information that can help you. The people who come here are not criminals. Look at those by the pool table. They're campesinos. Do they have the wary look of dishonest men?"

"I'm an officer of the law in the United States, Bernicio. I have friends who are officials here in Coahuila. If you have deceived us and put my friend in harm's way, you will have to answer both to them and to the United States government."

"Will you join me, you and the *señorita?* I can put onions and extra tortillas in the tripe, and we will have enough for three. I would like very much for you to be my guests and to accept my word about what I have said. I also hope you find your young friend. The

294

Americans who come here are not on a good errand, *señor*. I hope your friend is not one of these. I worked in Tijuana. Marines would be arrested by our police and moved from jail to jail in the interior and never seen again. Your government could do nothing for them. I served time in one of your prisons. It was a very nice place compared to the prisons here in Mexico. Fortunately, I am a Christian today, and I no longer think about these kinds of things."

Hackberry studied the swastika that was tattooed as large as a hand and clamped down on the bartender's shaved scalp. "Do you have to wear a hat when you attend church?" he asked.

Bernicio leaned forward, lifting the spoon to his mouth, his eyes focused close together, as though he were staring at a fly three inches from the bridge of his nose. *"Buena suerte, señor,"* he said.

Hackberry and Pam went back out onto the street. The dusk had settled on the countryside, and the sky was traced with shooting stars that fell and disappeared beyond the mountains in the south. Farther up the street, a band was playing in a cantina, and prostitutes were sitting on the steps of the brothels, some of them smoking cigarettes that glowed in the shadows and sparked brightly when the girls flipped them into the gutters. Across from where Hackberry and

Pam had parked their unmarked Cherokee was a squat one-story building constructed of rough stone with steel bars on the windows and a single tin-shaded yellow bulb over the entrance. Through the main window, Hackberry could see a beetle-browed man in a khaki uniform wearing a khaki cap with a lacquered black brim. The man was absorbed in the comic book he was reading, the pages folded back tightly in one hand.

"You want to check in with the locals?" Pam asked.

"Waste of time," Hackberry replied.

"It's like prayer. What's to lose?"

"It's not like prayer. The cops run the cathouses."

She was chewing gum, looking up and down the street, her hands propped on her hips. "This is what hell must look like."

"It is hell," he replied.

She glanced at him, then concentrated her attention on the police station across the street. He could hear her gum snapping in her jaw.

"I was a frequent visitor," he said. "Not to this place in particular but seven or eight like it. I was educated and had money and power and a Cadillac to drive. The prostitutes were hardly more than girls. Some of them were the sole support for their families."

"How many people were in a North Korean POW camp? How many of them spent months under a sewer grate in a dirt hole in winter?" When he didn't answer, she glanced at him again, still chewing her gum, shifting it from one side of her jaw to the other. "Let's stomp some ass, Hack. R.C. said the guy with the hole in his face worked for somebody who was visiting a cathouse?"

"Yeah, one that features teenage girls," Hackberry replied.

Krill was furious. He paced back and forth in the last silver glimmering of sunlight inside the clouds, staring at the open trunk of the gas-guzzler Negrito had parked behind the ruined adobe house where they were staying. In his right hand, he clenched a braided wallet, the shape as curved as his palm and pocket-worn the color of browned butter. "You smoked some bad weed?" he said to Negrito. "Something with angel dust or herbicide sprinkled on it? *¡Estúpido!* Ignorant man!"

"Why you say that, Krill? It hurts my feelings," Negrito said.

"You kidnapped a Texas deputy sheriff!"

"I thought he was valuable, *jefe.*"

"I'm not your *jefe.* Don't you call me that. I am not the *jefe* of *estúpidos.*"

"It's clear that he's a narc. Or maybe worse. Maybe he came down here because of us and the DEA informer we killed. We can sell the Tejano to La Familia Michoacána. They'll cut his tongue out. He ain't gonna talk to nobody if he ain't got a tongue."

Krill ripped Negrito's leather hat off his head and slapped him with it, raking it down hard on his face. Negrito stared at Krill blankly, the orange bristles around his mouth and along his jaw and on his throat as stiff as wire, his lips parted, his emotions buried in a stonelike expression that seemed impervious to pain. Krill whipped the hat down on his head again and again, his teeth clenched. "Are you listening to me, *estúpido?*" he said. "Who gave you permission to act on your own? When did you become this brilliant man with a master plan for the rest of us?"

"You keep saying you're not my *jefe*. You keep saying we follow or we don't follow, that you don't care about these small matters. But when I use my perceptions to make a decision, you become enraged. I am a loyal soldier, Krill."

"You are a Judas waiting for your moment to act." Krill hit Negrito once more, and this time the leather chin cord with the tiny wooden acorn on it struck Negrito in the eye, causing it to tear.

"Why you treat me like this? You think I'm an animal and this is your barnyard and you can do whatever you want with me because I'm one of your animals?" Negrito said.

"No, an animal has brains. It has survival instincts. It doesn't always think with its penis. Who saw you leave the house of *puta* with the deputy sheriff?"

"It wasn't a house of *puta*. I don't got to go to houses of *puta*. It was a cantina. Bernicio the bartender drugged his coffee. We took the boy out the back. Bernicio is a member of La Familia and ain't gonna tell nobody about it. You worry about all the wrong things. Now you're taking out your anger on your only friend, someone who has been with you from the beginning."

The dirt yard where they stood was blown with tumbleweeds and chicken feathers and lint from a grove of cottonwood trees. A hatchet was embedded in a stump by an empty hog lot, and on the ground around the stump were at least two dozen heads of chickens, their beaks wide, their eyes filmed with dust. Someone had lit a kerosene lamp inside the ruined adobe house, and through the back window, Krill could see five of his men playing cards and drinking at a table, their silhouettes as black as carbon inside the window glass. He tried to clear his mind of anger and think about what he should do next. He gazed at the bound and gagged figure lying in an embryonic position inside the trunk of the gas-guzzler. *It is not smart to abuse Negrito anymore,* he told himself. *Negrito's stupidity is incurable and cannot be addressed effectively except by a bullet in the head. There will always be time for that, but not now. The others admire Negrito for his muscular strength and his ability to endure pain and the great reservoir of cruelty that he willingly expends on their behalf. Keep this Judas in full view and never let him get behind you,* Krill told himself, *but do not abuse or demean him anymore, particularly in front of the others.*

When Krill had finished this long thought process, he was about to speak in a less reproving way. But Negrito, being the man he was, began talking again. "See, everybody has been worried about you, man. Bringing that box out here with your children's bones in it, it's like you're putting a curse on us. The dead got to be covered up, Krill. You got to place heavy stones on their graves so their spirits don't fly around and mess up your head. The dead can do that, man. Even your kids. Baptism can't do them no good now. They're dead and they ain't coming back. That's why the earth is there, to hide the body's decay and to make clean the odors it creates. What you're doing goes against nature. It ain't just me that says it. You call me a Judas? I'm the only one who tells you the truth to your face. Those inside are not your friends. When you ain't around, they talk among themselves."

Krill squatted in the dirt and began pulling the photos and credit cards and the driver's license and Social Security card and the various forms of personal identification, including a membership card in a state law enforcement fraternity, from the wallet of the Texan who lay bound in the trunk of the car, his mouth wrapped with duct tape, his forehead popping with sweat. Krill took a penlight from his shirt pocket and shone it on a photo of a girl standing in front of a church. The girl was wearing a sundress and a red hibiscus flower in her hair and was smiling at the camera. The church had three bell towers and a tile roof and looked like a church Krill had seen in Monterrey. Krill focused the penlight's beam on the driver's license and studied the photo and then shone the penlight on the Texan's face. Still squatting, he let the contents of the wallet spill to the ground and draped his hands on his thighs.

"What are you thinking, *jefe?*" Negrito asked.

Krill started to correct him for calling him *jefe* again, but what was the use? Negrito was unteachable. "Where is the Texan's money?" he asked.

"He must have spent it all."

Krill nodded and thought, *Yes, that's why it now resides in your pocket.* He stared at the Texan in the trunk and at the dust rising off the hills into the sky and at the chicken heads lying in the dirt. He could hear a sound inside his head like someone grinding a piece of iron unrelentingly against an emery wheel. He squeezed his temples and stared at Negrito.

"You know the dirt road that goes into the desert?"

"Of course."

"You have been there and can drive it in the dark, through the washouts and past the mountains where it becomes flat and no one lives?"

"I've done all these things many times, on horseback and in cars and trucks. But why are you talking about the desert? We don't need no desert. You know the place I use for certain activities. I'm telling you, this is a valuable man. Don't throw good fortune away. Make good things come out of bad."

"Do not speak for a while, Negrito. Practice discipline and be silent and listen to the wind blowing and the sounds the cottonwoods make when their limbs knock against each other. If you listen in a reverent and quiet fashion, dead people will speak to you, and you will not be so quick to dismiss them. But you must stop speaking. Do not speak unless you can improve the silence. *¿Entiendes?* Do not speak for a very long time."

"If you hear dead people talking to you, it's 'cause you're dead, too," Negrito said, his mouth gaping broadly at his own humor.

Krill gathered up the contents of the Texan's wallet and began sticking them back in the compartments and plastic windows. He closed the wallet in his palm and walked to the trunk of the car and tossed it inside.

While he did these things, he could feel the eyes of Negrito boring into his neck. He stared into the sweating face of the Texan. He could see the indentation in the tape where it covered the Texan's mouth. He thought he heard the Texan try to cry out when he slammed the trunk shut.

"This is what you need to do, Negrito," Krill said. "First, you —"

"You don't got to tell me. I'll get the shovel and take care of it. But it's a big waste of opportunity, man. And going out in the desert is a double waste of time and gas and effort. The others ain't gonna like this. We ain't been making no money, Krill. Everything we do is about your dead kids and getting even with the Americans 'cause their helicopter killed them. But how about us, man? We have needs and families, too."

Krill waited for Negrito to finish before he spoke, his face neutral, his white cotton shirt filling with air in the wind. "See, what you don't understand, my brother in arms, is that the Texan hasn't done anything to us. You fill the big wood canteen with water and put it in the car, and you put a sack of food with it. Then you drive the Tejano at least fifty kilometers into the desert and turn him loose. Later, you meet us in La Babia. With luck, all this will pass. If you hurt or sell the Texan, we will have no peace. Do you understand that now, my brother?"

303

"If that's what you say," Negrito replied.

"Good."

"And after La Babia?"

"Who knows? The Quaker belongs to us. We have to get him back. If you want to get paid, that's how we will all get paid. Then you can entertain all the *chicas* in Durango and Piedras Negras and Chihuahua. You will be famous among them for your generosity."

"You'll sell the Quaker to the Arabs but not the Texan to our own people?"

"The man Barnum has made machines that kill from the air, no matter what kind of conversion he claims to have gone through. All the gringos are makers of war and the killers of our people. Let them lie together in their own waste and eat it, too."

"I ain't never gonna understand you."

Krill watched Negrito enter the back of the farmhouse, the rowels on his spurs tinkling, the pad of orange hair on his arms and shoulders glowing against the light that fell from the kitchen. Unconsciously, Krill rested his palm against the car trunk and felt the exhaust heat in the metal soak into his skin and leave his hand feeling scorched and dirty.

The brothel where two SUVs with Texas plates were parked did not look like a brothel. Or at least it did not resemble the adobe houses or clusters of cribs on the far end of town where the street bled into the darkness

304

of the desert and drunks sometimes wandered away from their copulations to bust beer bottles with their firearms out on the hard-pan. The brothel frequented by the Texans was located at the end of a gravel lane and was actually an enclave of buildings that had once made up a ranch. The main house was built of stone quarried out of the mountains and had a wide terrazzo porch with large glazed ceramic urns that were planted with Spanish daggers and flowers that opened only at night. The colonnade over the porch was supported by cedar posts and covered with Spanish tile and tilted downward to direct rainwater during the monsoon season away from the house.

There was no lighting outside the building, which helped preserve the anonymity of the patrons. The night air smelled of flowers and warm sand and water that had pooled and gone stagnant and was auraed by clouds of gnats. Pam Tibbs pulled the Cherokee to a stop and cut the ignition. "How do you want to play it?" she said.

"We wear our badges and carry our weapons in full view," Hackberry replied.

"I've seen that purple SUV before."

"Where?"

"When I broke both of its taillights in front of the café."

"*That's* Temple Dowling's vehicle?" he said.

"It was when I broke his taillights. You're

surprised Dowling would be here?"

"Nothing about Dowling surprises me. But I thought the man with the hole in his face might have been working for the Russian, this guy Sholokoff."

"Let's find out."

"You feel comfortable going in there?" he asked.

She rested her hands on top of the steering wheel. Even in the starlight, he could see the shine on her upper arms and the sunburned tips of her hair. He could also see the pity in her eyes. "It's not me who's uncomfortable," she said. "When are you going to accept your own goodness and the fact that you've paid for what you might have done wrong when you were young?"

"When the mermaids come back to Texas," he said.

"Pardon?"

"It was a private joke between my father and me. Ready to make life interesting for the shitbags?"

"Always," she replied.

They got out on either side of the Cherokee and went inside the brothel. The living room was furnished with a red velvet settee and deep leather chairs and a cloth sofa and a coffee table set with wineglasses and dark bottles of burgundy and a bottle of Scotch and a bucket of ice. There was also a bowl of guacamole and a bowl of tortilla chips on the

306

table. The only light came from two floor lamps with shades that were hung with pink tassels. Two mustached men Hackberry had seen before sat on the sofa, dipping chips into the guacamole and drinking Scotch on the rocks. A Mexican girl not over fifteen, in a spangled blue dress, was sitting on the settee. She wore white moccasins on her feet and purple glass beads around her neck. Her skin was dusky, her nose beaked, her Indian eyes as elongated as an Asian's. Her lipstick and rouge could not disguise the melancholy in her face.

"How are you gentlemen tonight?" Hackberry said.

"Pretty good, Sheriff. I didn't think you'd remember us," one of them said.

"You came to my office with Mr. Dowling," Hackberry said.

"Yes, sir, that's us. What might you be doing here?" the man said.

"Not a lot. Just driving around the countryside trying to find a deputy of mine who got himself kidnapped. Do you boys know anything about a kidnapped deputy sheriff by the name of R. C. Bevins?"

The two men looked at each other, then back at Hackberry. "No, sir," the first man said.

Hackberry could hear the clatter of pool balls in a side room. "Is that more of your crowd in there?"

"Yes, sir, they're with us. We'd help you if we could, Sheriff, but I think you've come to the wrong place."

"This is the wrong place, all right, but for reasons you evidently haven't thought about," Hackberry said.

"Sir?"

"How old do you reckon that girl is?"

"We don't make the rules down here. Nobody does," the second man said.

Both men were wearing skintight jeans and snap-button shirts and belts with big silver-and-gold-plated buckles, and they both had the styled haircuts and carefully maintained unshaved look of male models in a liquor ad or on a calendar aimed at homosexuals rather than at women. The second man had a deeper and more regional voice than the first, and a formless blue tattoo, like a smear, inside the whiskers that grew on his throat.

"Were any of y'all in a cantina earlier?" Hackberry said.

"Not us," the second man said.

"We're looking for a guy with a hole in his face. You know anybody like that?"

"No, sir," the first man said.

"I see," Hackberry said. "Is Mr. Dowling in back?"

Neither of the men spoke. The second man glanced at Pam Tibbs, then filled a taco chip with guacamole and stuck it in his mouth and chewed it while he took her inventory.

308

"What's in back?" Hackberry said.

"The whole menu," the first man said.

"You two guys go outside," Hackberry said.

"You've got no jurisdiction down here, Sheriff," the second man said.

"Who cares? I'm bigger than you are. You guys want trouble? I'll give it to you in spades."

The two men looked at each other again, then got up from the settee. "We'll honor your request, Sheriff Holland. We do that out of respect for you and our employer," the first man said.

"No, you'll do it because if I catch one of y'all putting your hands on this little girl, I'm going to kick your sorry asses all the way to Mexico City. And if I find out you're involved with the kidnapping of my deputy, I'm going to blow your fucking heads off."

Hackberry did not wait for their reaction. He walked into the side room, where two men were shooting pool inside a cone of light created by a tin-shaded bulb that hung from the ceiling. The pool table was covered with red velvet, the pockets hung with netted black leather, the mahogany trim polished to a soft glow. "You!" he said, pointing at the man about to break the rack. "Yeah, you! Put your cue down and look at me."

"*¿Hay algún problema?*"

"Yeah, you. Remember me?"

"Yes, sir, you're the sheriff."

"You were shooting pool at a cantina tonight."

"Maybe I was. Maybe not. So what?" There was a deep indentation below the pool shooter's left eye, as though a piece of the cheekbone had been removed and the skin under the eye had collapsed and formed a hole a person could insert his thumb in. But the injury was an old one. It was the same wound that Hackberry had seen in the face of one of Temple Dowling's employees when they came to his office.

"There's no maybe in this," Hackberry said. "You were in the Cantina del Cazador. You were shooting pool there. My deputy saw you in there and described you to me. In very few words, you need to tell me what happened to my deputy."

The pool shooter's shirt was open on his chest, exposing his chest hair and nipples and a gold chain he wore around his neck. *"¿Quién sabe, hombre?"*

"You *sabes*, bud. Or you'd better."

"I was in the cantina. I didn't see anybody who looked like a deputy sheriff. What else can I say?"

"Why'd your friends out front say you weren't there?"

"Maybe I didn't tell them."

"I can see you're a man who likes to keep it simple. So how about this?" Hackberry said. He pulled his white-handled blue-black .45

310

revolver from his holster and swung it back-handed across the pool shooter's mouth. The blow made a clacking sound when the heavy cylinder and frame and the barrel broke the man's lips against his teeth. The pool shooter dropped his cue and cupped both of his hands to his mouth, his face trembling with shock behind his fingers. He removed his hands and looked at the blood on them, then spat a tooth into his palm.

"*Chingado,* what the fuck, man!" he said.

"You *sabes* now?"

"What's going on here?" said a voice behind Hackberry.

Temple Dowling had come out of a bedroom down the hall. He wore slippers and a towel robe cinched around his waist. Lipstick was smeared on his robe, and his exposed chest looked pink and blubbery and his breasts effeminate. Two young girls were leaning out of the doorway behind him, trying to see what was happening at the front of the house. Hackberry could see a large man in a long-sleeve white cotton shirt and bradded jeans coming out of an office in back, a wood baton gripped in one hand.

Hackberry put his revolver in the holster and raised his left hand, palm out, at the man with the baton. "My business is with Mr. Dowling and his associates. Mix in it and you'll take their weight," he said.

"*¿Qué dice?*" the man with the baton asked

311

one of the girls who had stepped out of the bedroom.

"No sé," she replied.

"Está bien. It's all right, Hector," Dowling said to the Mexican with the baton.

"One of my deputies was kidnapped out of a cantina where your hired piece of shit with the bloody mouth was shooting pool," Hackberry said. "He denies seeing my deputy, even though my deputy described your man to me over his cell phone."

"Why would one of my employees have any interest in your deputy, Sheriff Holland?" Dowling said. "Are you down here about Jack Collins?"

"No."

"You're not?" Dowling said, looking confused.

"Why would I be looking for Collins on a street full of Mexican cathouses?"

"He's everywhere," Dowling replied.

"You've become a believer?"

"I haven't done anything to this man. I didn't say anything about him."

The register in Dowling's voice had changed, the vowels and consonants not quite holding together. The skin twitched under one eye as though a fly had settled on his skin. Hackberry wondered how many young girls had paid the price for the fear that Dowling had probably spent a lifetime trying to hide from others.

312

"Have you had an encounter with Collins?" Hackberry asked.

"I thought you knew."

"Knew what?"

"I put a reward on him. He killed two of my men. That's why I put the reward on him."

"You put a reward on Jack Collins?"

"For arrest and conviction. That's all the statement says. I didn't tell people to go out and kill him. It's what any employer or family member would do if their employees or family members were murdered."

"Have you seen him?"

"Last night there was a man outside my motel. My men tried to catch him, but he disappeared. He was wearing a dirty hat of some kind. He was in the shadows on the other side of the parking lot, under a sodium lamp. What do you call that kind of hat? A panama? It's made of straw and has a brim that dips down over the eyes."

Dowling seemed to wait, hoping that Hackberry would dispel his fears and tell him that the shadowy figure, for whatever reason, could not have been Collins.

"That sounds like Jack, all right," Hackberry said. "Congratulations, you've brought down perhaps the most dangerous man in America on your head. Jack's a real cutup. I've been trying to punch his ticket for over a year. Maybe you'll be more successful. You

313

guys have any armored vests in your vehicles?"

"You're enjoying this."

"I guess it beats hanging in an upscale cathouse that provides services for pedophiles."

"Don't you dare talk to me like that."

"I was a whoremonger, Mr. Dowling. When I see a man like you, I want to shoot myself. I don't know if some of the girls I slept with were under the legal age or not. Most of the times I went across the river, I was too drunk to know what universe I was in."

Dowling was not listening. "Did you see anyone down here who looked like him?"

"Like Jack?"

"Who do you think I'm talking about, you idiot?" Dowling said.

"He paid a visit to my ranch just yesterday. He put a laser sight on me, but he didn't pull the trigger. That tells me he has something else planned for me. In your case, I doubt you'll see that red dot crawl across your skin. You'll see his Thompson for a few seconds, then you won't see anything at all."

A hulking Mexican woman appeared out of the back office and placed a highball in Temple Dowling's hand. Dowling looked at the drink as though he couldn't understand how it had gotten there. The two girls he had been in bed with were whispering under their breath, one translating to the other the conversation of the gringos, both of them trying not to giggle. *"Señor, este es muy malo para los negocios,"* the Mexican woman said.

Her words of concern about her business realities had no effect on Temple Dowling. Instead, his eyes remained fixed on Hackberry's, a lump of fear sliding down his throat so audibly that his lips parted and his mouth involuntarily made a clicking sound.

"I don't have any authority down here, Mr. Dowling," Hackberry said. "But when I get back to Texas, I'll make sure the appropriate agencies hear about your sexual inclinations."

"You're a bastard, Holland."

"You don't know the half of it," Hackberry replied.

CHAPTER THIRTEEN

Enclosure of any kind had always been R. C. Bevins's worst fear, the kind that is so great you never willingly confront it or discuss it with anyone else. Inside the darkness of the car trunk, while the gas-guzzler continued down a dirt or rock road of some kind, he tried to work his way forward and push his knees against the hatch and spring the lock. His wrists were taped together behind him, and the tape was wound around his ankles, forcing him to lie on his side, so he could not find purchase against a hard surface. There was a hole in the muffler, the engine's deep-throated sound rising into the trunk, the smell of the exhaust mixing with the dirty odor of the spare tire that R.C. could feel against the back of his head. He was finally able to touch the hatch with the points of his boots, but he was not able to exert any viable degree of pressure. The man named Negrito had done his job well. He had probably done it well many times before, R.C. thought.

He felt the car dip off the edge of the road and bounce heavily down an incline until it was on a flat surface again. Then he heard scrub brush raking thickly under the car frame, small rocks pinging under the fenders. R.C. strained against the duct tape, trying to stretch it to the point where he could slip one wrist free or work it over a boot heel so he could extend his legs and tear the tape off his wrists, even if he had to strip the skin from his thumbs.

Negrito was playing the radio, listening to a Mexican station that blared with horns and mariachi guitars. The car veered sharply, thudding off what was probably an embankment into a dry riverbed, jolting R.C. into the air, knocking his head against the spare tire. The gas-guzzler rumbled over rocks and tangles of brush while tree branches scraped against the fenders and doors and oil smoke from the broken muffler leaked through the trunk floor. The car swerved again, fishtailing this time, and came to a stop that caused the car body to rock on the springs.

Negrito waited until the song had ended, then turned off the radio and cut the engine. The night was completely silent except for the ticking of the heat in the car's metal. The driver's door opened with a screech like fingernails on a blackboard, and R.C. heard the tinkling of Negrito's roweled spurs approaching the trunk.

When Negrito popped the hatch, the sweet, cool, nocturnal smell of the desert flooded the inside of the trunk. But R.C.'s sense of relief was short-lived. Negrito's outline was silhouetted against the stars, a .45 auto strapped on his hip. "You okay, Tejano boy?" he asked. "I was worried about the way you was bouncing around in there. Here, I'm gonna get you out and explain our situation."

Negrito grabbed R.C. by one arm and the back of his belt and slid him over the bumper, letting him drop to the ground. "See, my friend Krill has got his head up his ass about a lot of things and don't know what's good for himself and others lots of the time. So I got to make decisions for him."

For no apparent reason, Negrito stopped talking and looked over his shoulder. From where he lay on the ground, R.C. could see that the car had ended up in a sandy wash, like a cul-de-sac, at the bottom of a giant hill that looked compacted of waste from a foundry. Negrito was staring into the darkness, turning his head from one side to the other. He picked up a rock and flung it up the incline and listened to it clatter back through the thinly spaced mesquite. "Maybe we got a cougar up there," he said to R.C. "But more likely a coyote. They come around, I'm gonna shoot them. They eat carrion and carry diseases. Like some of my girlfriends in Durango. What you think of that?"

Between Negrito's booted feet, R.C. saw an image that made his heart sink. On a level spot at the edge of the wash were at least five depressions, each of them roughly six feet long and three feet wide, the top of the depressions composed of a mixture of soil and dirt and sand and charcoal from old wildfires, all of it obviously spaded up and shaped and packed down by the blade of a shovel.

"See, I got to leave you here for a while and make some contacts," Negrito said. "You're gonna be safe till I get back. I like you, Tejano boy, but I got to make money and take care of my family. There's only one question I got to ask you. When I was a little boy working on this *turista* ranch in Jalisco, there was a gringo there who looked just like you. After he shot pigeons all day, he made me pick them up and clean them for his supper. While I did that, he screwed my sister. You think maybe that was your father?"

For a second, R.C. thought Negrito was going to pull the tape from his mouth so he could answer. Instead, Negrito's head jerked around and he stared again into the darkness, his nostrils flaring as though he had caught a scent on the wind, the thumb of his right hand hooking over the butt of his holstered .45. He walked up to the flat place and stood among the row of depressions, looking from one side of the hill to the other.

"¿*Quién está ahí?* Somebody out there want to talk to me?" he said to the wind.

He waited in the silence, then returned to the rear of the car, glancing once behind him. He squatted down and ripped the tape from R.C.'s mouth. "I'm gonna ask you this question once, no second chances," he said. "Be honest with me, I'm gonna be honest with you. You had somebody with you tonight? Or maybe you had somebody following you? 'Cause that's the feeling I been having all night."

R.C. tried to think. What was the right answer? "No," he said.

"That's the problem you gringos got. You're always trying to figure out what kind of lie is gonna work, like right now you're wondering how stupid is this Mexican man you got to deal with. I'm gonna be honest with you even if you ain't been honest with me. You're gonna have a bad night, man. You can cry, you can beg, you can pray, but only one thing is gonna happen to you, and there ain't no way to change that. Don't try to fight it. Tonight is gonna be a son of a bitch. Tomorrow, who knows? Maybe you're gonna catch a break."

"I'm not a narc," R.C. said.

"Maybe, maybe not. But the people I sell you to are gonna find out." Negrito stood up and opened one of the back doors of the car and returned with a shovel and a gas mask

320

that had an extra-long breathing hose. "See this?" he said. "It's your chance to live. You just got to have a lot of self-control and not let your thoughts take over your body."

"Don't do this to me."

"It's out of my hands, Tejano boy. I was just having a drink in the cantina. You came into the wrong place and put your nose in the wrong people's business. Now you got to pay the price."

"The other guy said to turn me loose."

"You talking about Krill? He ain't never gonna know what happened to you. Krill thinks he's smart, but most of the time, his thoughts are in the next world, where he thinks his dead kids are." Negrito brushed a piece of dirt off R.C.'s cheek with his thumb and smiled. "You're a gringo cop who has a flat tire and ends up drinking in a whorehouse that has a bartender who works for La Familia? I hope in the morning you get a chance to tell these other guys that story. It's a very good one, man. You got to tell them the joke about the golf course, too. They're gonna really laugh."

After Hackberry and Pam Tibbs left the bordello and got in the Cherokee, Pam remained silent for a long time. Then she started the engine and looked at him. "Where to?" she asked.

"Back to the cantina. That bartender was

lying," he said.

"I was a little worried in there."

"About what?"

"When you cracked that guy in the mouth."

"He'll get over it."

"I've never seen you like that."

"I don't like child molesters."

"You told those two guys in the living room you'd blow their heads off. I could hear you breathing when you said it."

"That's because I meant it."

"That's what bothers me."

"Let's get on it, Pam," he said.

On the way back to the cantina, Hackberry lowered the brim of his Stetson and shut his eyes, wanting to sleep for an eternity and forget the violence and cruelty and sordid behavior and human exploitation that seemed to become more and more visible in the world as he aged. According to the makers of myth and those who trafficked in cheap lies about human wisdom, the elderly saw goodness in the world that they had not been allowed to see in their youth. But Hackberry had found that the world was the world and it did not change because one happened to age. The same players were always there, regardless of the historical era, he thought, and the ones we heeded most were those who despoiled the earth and led us into wars and provided us with justification whenever we felt compelled to commit unconscionable acts against our fellow man. Maybe this wasn't a good way to think, he told himself, but when you heard the clock ticking in your life, there was no worse disservice you could do to yourself than to entertain a lie. Death was bad only when you had to face it knowing that you had failed to live during the time allotted you, or that you had lied to yourself about the realities of the world or willingly listened to the lies of others.

He felt his body rock forward when Pam touched the brake in front of the cantina.

"Take it easy in there, okay?" she said.

"I wonder what kind of night R.C. is having," Hackberry replied.

"You can really drive the nails."

"If we mess up here, R.C. dies. Inside that stone building on the corner are men in uniform who would gladly work in an Iranian torture chamber for minimum wage. The meth being funneled through this town probably originates with a bunch down in the state of Michoacán. These are guys who make the cops in the stone building look like the College of Cardinals."

She turned off the ignition and stared straight ahead, her hands resting on the wheel. "I wasn't criticizing you back there. I just worry about you sometimes. You don't handle regret very well."

"The person who does is dead from the neck up."

"One of these days I'll learn to keep my counsel."

"Watch my back. I don't want those *rurales* coming through the front door and planting one in my ear."

"R.C. is a tough kid. Give him some credit," she said.

"What's that mean?"

"Put it in neutral, Hack."

"Cover my back and lose the bromides."

"You got it."

Hackberry had already gotten out of the Jeep and crossed the sidewalk and entered the cantina before Pam had reached the curb. The bartender with the enormous swastika was stacking chairs on a table by the small dance floor in back. He grinned when he saw Hackberry. "Hey, amigo, you decided to come back and have dinner with me! Welcome once again. You brought the lady, too."

"Who wouldn't love a place like this? Excuse me just a second," Hackberry said.

"What are you doin', *señor?*"

"Not much. When I played baseball, I was a switch-hitter. I sometimes wonder if I still have it," Hackberry said. He pulled a pool cue off the wall rack and grasped the thinly tapered end with both hands and whipped the heavy end across the bartender's face. The cue splintered with the same hand-stinging *crack* as a baseball bat when it catches a ninety-mile-an-hour pitch at the wrong angle. The weighted end of the cue rocketed into the wall, and the bartender crashed over the table into the plastic-cased jukebox, blood pouring from his nose.

The bartender placed the flats of his hands on the floor and tried to straighten himself against the jukebox. Hackberry raised his right boot fifteen inches into the air and stomped it down into the bartender's face. The man's head pocked a hole the size of a grapefruit in the jukebox. "Where's my deputy?" Hackberry said.

"I don't know," the bartender said.

"You want another one?" Hackberry said.

Three men at a table by the dance floor got up quickly and went out the back door. A fourth man emerged from the bathroom and looked at the scene taking place by the jukebox and followed them outside. Hackberry could hear a whirring sound in his head and behind him the sound of Pam Tibbs chewing gum rapidly, snapping it, her mouth open. "Hack, dial it down," she said.

"No, Bernicio here wants to tell us where R.C. is. He just wants the appropriate motivation. Right, Bernicio? You have to explain to your friends why you cooperated with your gringo dinner guests." He brought his boot down again.

"Oh, shit," Pam said, her voice changing.

Hackberry turned and saw two Mexican policemen in unpressed green uniforms come through the front door and walk the length of the bar. Both of them wore lacquered-billed caps and were short and dark-skinned. Both wore brass badges and shiny black name tags on their shirt pockets and semiautomatic pistols on their hips. One of them wore thick-soled military boots that were spit-shined into mirrors, the laces starched white. He had tucked the cuffs of his trousers into the boots, as a paratrooper might.

"*¿Qué pasa,* gringo?" asked the policeman with the shined boots.

Hackberry opened his badge holder and held it up for both policemen to see. "My deputy was kidnapped from this cantina. We were having a discussion with Bernicio as to my friend's whereabouts. Thank you for your assistance."

"*Chinga tu madre. Tus credenciales valen mierda, hombre,*" the policeman in shined boots said.

"My badge is worth shit? I should fuck my mother?" Hackberry said. "I'm not sure how I should interpret that."

"*Venga,*" the policeman said, crooking two fingers.

"With respect, we're not going anywhere with y'all except maybe to find my friend," Hackberry said. He repeated himself in Spanish and then said in English and Spanish, "Right now we're wasting time that we don't have. My friend's life is in jeopardy. The man on the floor is a criminal. You know that and so do I. We are all officers of the law, separated only by a few miles of geography. I ask your cooperation, and I say all these things to you out of respect for your office and the importance of your legal position in the community."

"We are not interested in your evaluations of our community. You're coming with me, gringo," the policeman replied, this time in English, once again crooking two fingers. "You have no authority here, and you have assaulted an innocent man."

"How's this for authority, dickhead?" Pam Tibbs said, pulling her .357 Magnum from her holster and aiming it with both hands at the policeman's face.

"You are very unwise," the policeman said.

"That's right," Pam replied. She cocked the hammer on her revolver with her thumb. "I have little judgment. That's why I'm two seconds from flushing your grits."

"Flushing? What do you mean, 'flushing'?"

"Don't test her, partner," Hackberry said, surprised at the level of caution in his voice.

"No entiendo," the policeman said.

Hackberry could feel a band of tension spreading along one side of his head. It was of a kind that he had experienced only a few times in his life. It stretched the blood veins along the scalp into knotted twine. You felt it seconds after hearing the spatter of small-arms fire, a sound that was as thin and sporadic and innocuous as the popping of Chinese firecrackers. Or you felt it when someone shouted out the word "Incoming!" Or when it wrapped itself around your head like piano wire as a monstrosity of a human being in a quilted coat slathered with mud on the front and mucus on the sleeves pulled back the bolt on a Soviet-manufactured burp gun and lifted the muzzle into your face.

Hackberry could smell the stagnant water and expectorated tobacco juice under the drain covers in the concrete floor, and the stale cigarette smoke in the air and the residual odor of dried sweat that seemed layered on every surface of the cantina. From the cribs in back, he could smell a stench that was like fish roe in the sun and human waste leaching from an open ditch. He could hear a drunk singing in one of the cribs in the alleyway. He could hear his own heartbeat starting to crescendo in his ears.

"She'll kill you, buddy. Don't lose your life over a man who wears the tattoo of a self-important fool on top of his head," Hackberry said.

What followed was a phenomenon that Hackberry had seen perhaps no more than a dozen times in war and during his career as a lawman. Perhaps it could be called a vision of mortality. Or a moment when a person simply calculated his risk and evaluated what was to be lost or gained and then made his bet with full knowledge that his foot rested on the edge of the great precipice. Sometimes the heart-stopping pause that took place before the die was cast, when the filmstrip seemed to freeze inside the projector, dissolved into what Hackberry called "the blink." The blink was not in the eyes but deep down in the soul, and the effect was immediate and as real as the brief twitch, like a rubber band snapping, that shuddered through the person's face.

"I see nothing either exceptional or of value here," the policeman with shined boots said. "This is not worthy of official attention. Serious men do not waste their time on situations such as this. Good evening to you, *señor* and *señorita*."

With that, he and his companion walked out of the cantina and into the street.

Hackberry heard Pam release her breath and ease down the hammer on her revolver and return it to its holster. "I don't want to ever relive that moment or even discuss it," she said.

"Neither does Bernicio," Hackberry said, looking down at the bartender. "Right?"

"Fuck you, man," the bartender said.

Hackberry knelt on one knee, the splintered felt-tipped end of the pool cue still in his hand. He glanced at the front door to ensure that the policemen had not returned. He

329

knew at some point they would try to back-shoot him and Pam in the street or call their friends to devise a means to get even for having their faces put in it by a woman. You didn't shame a Mexican cop without running up a tab.

"You know where my deputy has been taken," Hackberry said. "Not approximately but *exactly.* If you claim to not have this information, I will not believe you. The continuation of your life depends entirely upon your ability to convince me that you know where my friend is. Do you understand the implications of what I have told you?"

"No, I do not understand these things. Your words are mysterious and confusing. Why are you doing this to me?" the bartender said, blood glistening on his upper lip.

"Because you're an evil man."

"No, *hombre,* I am not evil. I'm a worker. I am part of the revolution."

Hackberry placed his knee against the bartender's chest and leaned forward and forced the shattered end of the pool cue over his teeth and into his mouth. "In five seconds I'm going to push this down your windpipe and out the side of your neck. Look into my face and tell me I won't do it."

He could feel Pam Tibbs's hand clasp the top of his shoulder and squeeze. "Hack," she said softly.

He paid no attention.

■ ■ ■ ■

R.C. massaged his wrists, then picked up the shovel by his foot, as the man named Negrito had told him to do. The sky was black and hazed with dust, and the shooting stars above the hills looked like chips of dry ice that were melting into nothingness. R.C thought he heard a train whistle in the distance and the sound of boxcars with their brakes on sliding down an incline, the wheels shrieking against the rails.

"What are you waiting for, Tejano boy? Start digging," Negrito said.

R.C.'s hands were propped on the shaft of the shovel, the worn, rounded, silvery tip an inch into the dirt. Strips of severed duct tape hung from his boots. He could feel his heart beating against his ribs and a line of sweat starting to run from each of his armpits. Negrito was squatted on a rise fifteen feet away, his 1911-model United States Army .45 gripped casually on one knee, his fingers loose around the trigger guard, completely confident about the situation he had created. His leather hat hung on the back of his neck, the chin cord taut against his throat. He picked up a dirt clod and threw it at R.C.'s head.

"I've been kind to you," he said. "Don't abuse my charity. I'm not a nice man when

I'm provoked."

"I cain't do it," R.C. said.

"Sí, puedes."

"I ain't. That's what I meant to say." Even to himself, R.C.'s voice seemed full of broken glass, his words thick, the worst fate he could imagine about to be realized only a few inches from where he stood.

"Meant to say what, Tejano boy?"

"I meant to say I ain't gonna dig my own grave," R.C. replied. "And I ain't no boy."

"It don't matter what I call you, man. You're gonna dig."

"No matter how it plays out, I ain't gonna he'p you. No, sir, I won't do it."

"That's what they all say. They buy a little time that way, and it makes them feel less bad about themselves. They want to believe their friends are gonna come over the rise and kill Negrito and take them home to their mothers and fathers and wives and husbands, but finally, they dig. You don't got to feel bad about it."

R.C. raised one foot and rested it on the top of the shovel blade, still gripping the shaft with both hands, his eyes stinging with sweat, a vinegary stench rising from his armpits. His heart felt as though it had been invaded by threadworms and was slowly being reduced to the point where it could no longer pump his blood.

"I make twenty-six thousand dollars a year.

332

I break up domestic fights and run in drunks and wets and nickel-and-dime meth mules."

"So?"

"Your friends won't pay money for me."

"You want me to shoot you, man?" Negrito raised the .45 and pointed it at R.C. and playfully sighted down the barrel. "Ever see one of these hit a kneecap? Or a guy's foot? I use hollow-points."

R.C. swallowed. Each time the gun's muzzle swung across his person, his colon constricted and his entrails turned to water.

"I'm gonna shoot you in a place that hurts like a son of a bitch, man," Negrito said. "Then you're going in the ground with all that pain while you try to breathe through the gas mask. Why you want to do that to yourself?"

R.C.'s head was spinning, bile rising from his stomach, his fear so great and his anger at himself and his despair so intense that he could feel himself walking through a door into a place where nothing mattered anymore. "I just remembered what you look like. I couldn't think of it. But it's real clear in my head now," he said, breathing hard through his mouth.

"Why you always got to talk, man? You are like a woman, always talking, filling the air with sounds that grate on the ear."

"I couldn't remember what you remind me of. At the cantina I was thinking about it, but

I couldn't get it straight in my head because I drank too much."

"What I remind you of?"

"An orange Brillo pad. Those steel-wool pads women use to clean grease and fish skins and fried crud out of skillets. After a while, the pads turn orange and blue with soap and rust and all the glop that's glommed up inside them."

"That's what I look like?"

"Yes, sir, I'd call it a match."

"Be quiet," Negrito said, rising to his feet.

"Like my mother says, looks is only skin deep."

"*Silencio,* foolish boy who does not hear or listen."

R.C. realized his tormentor was not interested in deflecting insults and that he had heard something out in the darkness. Negrito walked up the incline, away from the dry wash and the row of graves and the greasewood and the stunted willows along the bank and the tortoise-shaped sandstone boulders that were weathered through with holes the length of a man's arm. "Is that you out there, Mr. Crazy Man?" he said. "You want to fight Negrito? Come down and fight. I don't fear you."

R.C. watched, stupefied.

"The gringos fear you! But I don't! *¡Me cago en la puta de tu madre!* I take a shit in your mother's womb. How you like that?"

Negrito said.

"Who you talking to?"

Negrito said nothing in answer to R.C. He was standing on a slab of stone that was tilted upward on the slope, one pointy cowboy boot stationed in front of the other, his shoulders humped, his .45 hanging from his right hand. In profile, his right eye seemed to watch both the hillside and R.C. simultaneously, the way a shark's eye views everything in its ken, both enemy and prey, revealing no more emotionality than a flat coat button.

"Hey, *sacerdote* of the garbage dump and eater of your own feces! You think we treated your little Quaker friend bad?" he called out. "What if I bring you down here and make you suck my dick? I can do that to you, man, with great pleasure."

There was no reply from the hillside, and R.C. could see no movement among the shadows and mesquite and rocks and the dead juniper trees that looked like gnarled and polished bone. Negrito continued to stare into the darkness, his nostrils swelling, his profile as snubbed as a piranha's. He squeezed his scrotum with his left hand. "Come take it, *cabrón!*" he yelled.

The moon broke from behind a cloud and turned the hillside gray, the scrub brush pooling with shadows. "No? You prefer shooting women and people who ain't got no guns? You're a sorry Christian, Mr. Preacher. A

Christian without cojones."

"You know Preacher Collins?" R.C. said.

"The crazy man up there ain't gonna help you. So give that up," Negrito replied, backing down the slope, his gaze still concentrated on the hillside. "He's the hunter, the left hand of God. He don't have interest in a boy like you."

"But he's interested in you?" R.C. said.

"Of course. He knows we're brothers. Under our skin, we're no different."

"Brothers?"

"That's right, Tejano boy. Preacher and I are both dead. Our souls died many years ago. What do you see in my eyes?"

"Nothing."

"That's right. Nothing. And that's why you're gonna start to dig. Or maybe I'm gonna start shooting you in various places that will hurt more than you can believe."

"I done told you, I ain't gonna do it. So you'd better kill me, 'cause somewhere down the road, I'm gonna catch up with you. You damn betcha I will."

Negrito's eyes were rheumy, his face dull with fatigue, his mouth caked. He made a snuffing sound and rubbed his nose with the back of his wrist. "Release the shovel and get in the trunk of the car."

"What are you gonna do?"

"I got to dig your hole. That makes me very mad. You are lucky I am a merciful man."

R.C. let the shovel fall to the ground and started toward the gas-guzzler, glancing warily over his shoulder, then tripping and stumbling. He heard Negrito pick up the shovel.

"Look up there," Negrito said.

"At what?"

"The preacher up there in the rocks. See, against the moon. He wants to be your friend. The *sacerdote* who eats his own *mierda* has come to your rescue. Or maybe it's the sheriff you work for. Maybe this is your lucky day."

R.C. stared at the clumps of brush in the arroyos and at the layers of rock exposed by erosion in the hillside and at the tailings of a mine that spilled like rust down to the wash. He saw a shadow move across the moon. "That's a coyote," he said.

He turned around just as Negrito whipped the shovel with both hands through the air and almost flattened the concave steel blade on the back of R.C.'s head.

"I think you was right. It was just a coyote," Negrito said, staring up the hill.

Jack Collins lay below the crest of the hill, his belly and loins and legs stretched out on a flat rock that had ripples in it like water, his hat beside him, his eyes raised just above a pile of crumbling stone. Behind him, the two Mexican informers, cousins who did murders for hire, were talking quietly to each other, sometimes glancing up in his direction. They were restless men and did not like either indecision or complexity and often found themselves caught between their own self-protective instincts and their hesitancy to challenge the strange ways of the gringo *loco* whose lethality was a legend in Coahuila and Chihuahua. Finally, the one named Eladio approached the unshaved and unwashed American who dressed in rags and wore a heavy revolver on his hip, squatting down so as not to silhouette against the sky. "Señor Jack?" he said.

"Be patient," Jack said, peering down the opposite slope.

"Why don't we just go down there in the streambed and kill Negrito? I'll do it without no charge."

Jack looked back over his shoulder and grinned. "You boys were supposed to give me the man named Krill. We didn't come out here to hunt an orange ape."

"I thought Krill would be at the farmhouse. He's a very hard man to catch, boss. This is the place Negrito sometimes uses to bury his victims. It is fortunate that I knew that."

"So we're saved from your incompetence by the intervention of the fates, and that should make me feel good?"

"You talk too fast for me to understand sometimes, boss."

Jack worked his way backward on the rock

until he was well under the level of the hill-crest, then got to his feet. He dusted off his knees and the elbows of his suit coat and fitted on his hat, glancing at the strips of black cloud across the moon. He gestured for the other cousin to join him and Eladio. But minutes seemed to pass before he spoke. In the silence, he glanced at one man, then the other, and then into space, as though viewing two different screens in his head. "I pay you boys enough?" he asked.

"*Sí*," both of them said, nodding.

"Krill has done great injury to a friend of mine. The one down the slope, the ape, isn't even a cipher."

"What is this 'cipher'? These kinds of words don't mean nozzing to us, boss," Eladio said.

"The fact you boys were raised up poor and ignorant isn't your fault. Most of y'all's mothers would have had you aborted if they'd had the money. But today there's no excuse for ignorance in an adult. People in mud huts watch CNN. The Internet is available in a street-corner café. You boys have access to the same knowledge a university professor does. I suggest y'all start showing a little more initiative regarding your self-improvement."

"We seek to please you, not to upset you, Señor Jack," Eladio said.

"You did very well following Temple Dowling for me. You did well learning of the machinations of Negrito with the young law-

339

man. But you haven't given me Krill. Krill is the objective, not his monkey. Are y'all listening?"

"We ain't perfect, boss," the cousin said. His name was Jaime, and of the two Mexican killers, he was the less intelligent and the more recalcitrant.

Eladio looked angrily at his cousin, then turned his attention back to Jack, trying to undo any damage his cousin might have caused. "We can take Negrito alive and entertain him in ways he'll understand," Eladio said.

"Is he the kind of man who gives up reliable information when he's in pain?" Jack said. "Or does he lie and tell you what you want to hear?"

"You are very intelligent, Señor Jack," Eladio said. "Negrito has the strength of a mule and the brain of a snake. Pain means nothing to him. As a boy, he blew flaming kerosene from his mouth in a carnival. His *putas* say they can still smell it on him."

Jaime chewed on a weed and took a watch with a broken strap from his shirt pocket and looked at it. "Eladio is right. If Negrito ain't of no value, maybe it's time we took care of him and also the American you don't like at the whorehouse and get some sleep. What is of more importance? The cost of a bullet or the time we waste speaking of these men you say are worthless? Constantly talking of these men makes me resentful of myself."

Jack's face registered no emotion. It seemed as serene as a layer of plastic that had melted and cooled and dried in dirty lumps. He watched the lights in the sky and the dust that swirled off the desert floor and buttoned the top of his shirt with one hand as though expecting rain or cold. The Mexicans who worked for him were a mystery, an improbable genetic combination of Indian bloodlust and the cruelty of the Inquisition. The angular severity of their features, the way their skin stretched tautly on their bones, the greasy black shine in their uncut hair, the obsidian glint in their eyes at the mention of violence or pain made him wonder if they were remnants of a lost tribe from biblical times, perhaps an unredeemed race that had floated on the Flood far away from where Noah had landed on Mount Ararat. It would make sense. They were unteachable and killed one another with the dispassion and moral vacuity of someone who idly watches his children wander onto a freeway.

What was Jaime saying now? His lips were still moving, though no sound seemed to come from his mouth. Jack disengaged from his reverie and stared at him. "Repeat that?" he said.

"How come we ain't at least killed the *abusador de niños?* He was at the whorehouse. We could have done it easy. Not even the *policía* would object to our killing such a man."

"I don't go in whorehouses," Jack said. "Also, don't speak to me of your policemen's virtue. They're jackals and will steal the coins off a dead man's eyes. What none of you seems to recognize is that your country is ungovernable. Your national heroes are peons who decorated trees with the bodies of their fellow peons. Do not tell me what I should do and not do."

"Señor Jack is very wise. We need to listen to him, Jaime," Eladio said.

"But we keep playing games with gringos who should be food for worms," Jaime said. "This man Holland is the enemy of Señor Jack, but we don't do nozzing about him. Why not kill Holland? It would give me great pleasure to do this for Señor Jack. What is so special about this man?"

Jack pulled the weed from Jaime's mouth and tossed it to one side. "Do not refer to Sheriff Holland by his last name only. His name is Mr. Holland or Sheriff Holland. Do you understand that?" he said.

Jaime started to speak, but Eladio squeezed his arm. "You are a man of honor. We will always follow you and do as you tell us," Eladio said.

"You wouldn't josh a fellow, would you?" Jack said.

"We are hurt deeply when you talk like that

to us, Señor Jack," Eladio said.

"Really?" Jack said. He gazed out at the desert and the nighttime glow of a distant town in the clouds. "That flatters and humbles me. I declare, you boys are full of surprises."

The two cousins waited for him to continue, neither of them meeting his eyes, Eladio's hand still locked on Jaime's forearm. "You didn't develop laryngitis on me, did you?" Jack asked.

"We are simple men, boss," Eladio said.

"That's why I like you. That's why I consider you not just friends but family. I wouldn't offend either of you for the world."

"Is true what you say?" Eladio asked.

"Cross my heart," Jack replied, his teeth showing in the moonlight. "But right now I want to see what this *hombre malo* Negrito is doing. He's a pistol, isn't he? A man that keeps his own private burying ground. Y'all surely grow some strange critters down here."

Jack walked back up the slope, then shook out a handkerchief and placed it on the ground and knelt on one knee so he could look down the far side of the hill without silhouetting. While he studied the scene down below, his right hand played with his revolver, lifting it partially out of the holster, reversing the butt, then reversing it again, dropping it back into the hardened leather with a dry *plop.*

"Come on up here and check this out," he said, motioning at the cousins.

The two Mexicans approached him, bent over, gravel rilling from under their cowboy boots, each of them attentive to the motion or lack of motion in Jack's right hand. Out on the hardpan, the gas-guzzler was driving away, its headlights lighting the scrub brush and cactus. "What is it?" Eladio said.

"I was just talking about strange critters," Jack said. He stood up and pointed down the slope. "Look yonder at that new grave. What's that sticking out of the dirt?"

Both cousins stared down into the moonlit wash, their foreheads knitted with thought. "An elephant's trunk?" Eladio said.

"It's the hose and filter on a World War Two gas mask. What do you boys think we ought to do about that?" Jack said.

R. C. Bevins had been raised in a fundamentalist church where the minister went to great lengths to instruct his congregation in the details of Jesus' crucifixion. His dedication to the macabre seemed equaled only by his dedication to busing as many congregants as possible to the local theater's showing of *The Passion of the Christ*. In his presentation, the minister included descriptions of long square-headed spikes that had pierced the victim's wrists — not his hands, the minister said, because the hands would have torn loose

344

from the fastenings; not so the spikes through the wrists. The bones and tendons in the wrist were much sturdier and up to the task of supporting the victim's weight. Also, he pointed out, the spikes were not driven through the tops of the feet, as is often depicted. The knees were folded sideways on the perpendicular shaft, the ankles placed one on top of the other. A single long spike was adequate to pinion the two appendages together.

The minister also explained that death came by asphyxiation as a result of the tendons in the upper torso constricting the lungs and forcing the air back up the victim's windpipe. But for R.C., the worst detail was the minister's speculation that the trauma of being nailed to the cross and the cross being dropped heavily into a hole caused the victim to go into shock only to become conscious a few minutes later and discover that he was not waking from a nightmare but instead was anchored hand and foot to a cruciform of pain from which there was no escape.

That was how R.C. had woken under the ground, with the vague sense that something was wrong with his arms and legs, that he had heard a sifting sound of dirt and gravel sliding off a shovel blade, followed by a thump of stones being dropped heavily on top of him. His eyes were unable to see, his throat raw, as though he had not had water in days. When he tried to raise his head, he realized he was not only impaled by the earth but locked solidly inside it, the air that he breathed coming to him through a tube that smelled of rubber and canvas. The level of panic that occurred in him was like a violent electric surge throughout his body, except the electricity had no place to go.

The inside of the mask was soggy and foul with his sweat and his own breath, and no light at all came through the plastic eyepieces. He stretched out his fingers and for just a moment thought he might be able to work his hands through the dirt toward the surface an inch at a time. Then he discovered that by straightening his hands, he had allowed the overburden of the grave to press down on him more firmly, like an octopus tightening its tentacles on its prey.

Who were the fools who constantly taught about man's harmony with the earth? he asked himself. An uncle who had once worked in a Kentucky coal mine had told R.C. that the earth was not man's friend, that it was unnatural to enter the ground before one's time, and that if a man listened carefully, he would hear the earth creak in warning to those who thought they could tunnel through its substructure without consequence.

He could feel his fear going out of control and his breath beginning to rasp inside the mask, the weight of the earth and stones like

346

knives around his heart. He tried to turn his thoughts into wings that could lift his soul above the ground and allow him to revisit scenes and moments he had associated with the best parts of his life: floating down the Comal River on a burning July afternoon, his wrists trailing in water that was ice-cold, the soap-rock bottom gray and smooth and pooled with shadows from the overhang of the cottonwood trees; dancing with a Mexican girl in a beer garden in Monterrey where Indians sold ears of corn they roasted on charcoal braziers, backdropped by mountains that were hazy and magenta-colored against the sunset; throwing a slider on the edge of the plate for the third strike and third out in the bottom of the ninth at a state championship game in San Marcos, the grass of the diamond iridescent under the electric lights, the evening breeze cool on his skin, a high school girl waiting for him by the bleacher seats, her hands balled into fists as she jumped up and down with love and pride at the perfect game he had just pitched.

His fondest memory was of his twelfth birthday, when his widowed mother took him on the Greyhound all the way from Del Rio to the state fair in Dallas. That evening he stared in awe at the strings of colored lights of the Ferris wheel and the Kamikaze printed against a blue sky puffed with pink clouds. High school kids screamed inside the grinding roar of the Tilt-A-Whirl and the Super Loops, and the air was filled with music from the carousel and the popping of balloons and target guns on the fairways. He could smell the aerial fireworks spidering in a purple and pink froth above the rodeo grounds, and the caramel corn and fry bread and candied apples and tater pigs in the food concessions. His mother bought cotton candy for him and watched him ride the mechanical bull, holding the cotton candy in her hand, smiling even though she was exhausted from the long day on the bus, her wash-faded dress hanging as limp as a flag on her thin body.

R.C. tried to fix the fairground in his mind so he could stay safe inside it, free of the grave and the weight on his heart, wrapped in the calliope's music and the shouts of children and teenage kids, his mother's smile on the edge of his vision, the electric glow of the amusement rides rising into an ethereal sky that was testimony to everything that was good and beautiful in the world.

If there was a way, Sheriff Holland would find him, he told himself. He had given the sheriff his location. It was only a matter of time before the sheriff found the bar and forced the bartender to tell him where R.C. had been taken. All R.C. had to do was hold on, to breathe in and out, to not let go of the fairgrounds and the best day of his life. The soul could go where it wanted, he told himself. It existed, didn't it? If it could fly from you at death, why couldn't it leave you while you were alive? He didn't have to abide the condition he had found himself in. Or at least he didn't have to cooperate with it.

When he swallowed, his saliva was bilious, and his eyes watered at the fate that had been imposed on him. In his impotence and rage and fear, he cursed himself for his self-pity.

He heard a shovel sink deep into the dirt and felt it graze his side, not unlike the tip of a Roman spear teasing the rib cage of an impaled man.

A moment later, the hands of two men began scraping the dirt away from his face and shoulders and arms and sides, lifting his head free, slipping the mask from his face, allowing him to breathe air that was as clean and pure as bottled oxygen. He could see the silhouette of a third man against the moon, a holstered thumb-buster revolver on his hip, his fingernails like the claws on an animal. He wore a sun-bleached panama hat that was grimed with finger smears on the front brim.

"Who are you?" R.C. said, unsure if he should have even asked the question, his face cold with sweat.

CHAPTER FOURTEEN

Hackberry looked through the front windshield at the long, flat, sunbaked rawness of the land and at the purple haze that seemed to rise from the creosote brush and the greasewood and the patches of alkali along streambeds that were hardly more than sand. In the distance, he could see hills in the moonlight and stovepipe cactus in the yard of an adobe house whose roof had collapsed. He looked through his binoculars at the hills and at the house and thought he could see a dirt road behind it that switchbacked up the side of the hill, but he couldn't be sure.

The bartender with the swastika tattooed on his scalp had given him and Pam Tibbs directions to the place where he believed Negrito was taking the young Texas lawman. When Hackberry had asked whether he was sure, the bartender had replied, staring at the broken pool cue Hackberry had almost stuffed down his throat, "It's where Negrito always disposes of people he has no more use for. It's the underground prison he likes to stand on top of. Maybe he comes back for them. Maybe that's where you will end up seriously *jodido,* that's what I hope."

Hackberry's cell phone vibrated on the Jeep's dashboard. He picked it up and put it to his ear. "Sheriff Holland," he said.

"It's Maydeen. Did you find R.C.?"

"Not yet."

"Let me try to get you some backup."

"There's nobody down here I trust."

"Hack, I called because I'm at the hospital. Anton Ling says she saw the guy she put a screwdriver in. He and another guy were in the hallway right outside her room."

"How did she know it was the guy she hurt? He was wearing a mask when she put the screwdriver in his face."

"She said she recognized the guy with him. She said she was mixed up in an intelligence operation of some kind years ago, and this guy was part of it. Felix and I are in her room now. She wants to talk with you."

"Put her on."

Hackberry heard Maydeen speaking to Anton Ling, then Maydeen got back on the cell. "She wants us to leave the room. When y'all get finished, I'll come back in. Felix will stay here the rest of the night."

"Tell Anton Ling that anything she wants to tell me, she can say in front of you."

"Don't worry about it, Hack. I need a cup

351

of coffee," Maydeen said.

A moment later, Anton Ling got on the cell. "I'm sorry to bother you with this, Sheriff Holland, but I needed to get something off my chest," she said.

"Miss Anton, in my department, we don't have private conversations, and we don't keep secrets from one another," Hackberry said. "I'm making an exception in this instance because your life may be in jeopardy."

"I didn't want your deputies to hear our conversation for the same reason. I have knowledge that can get people killed."

"Knowledge about what?"

"There was a political scandal years ago that flared and died. A reporter broke a story that the Contras were introducing cocaine into American cities to pay for the guns that were being shipped to Nicaragua. A couple of newspapers in the East debunked the story, and later, the reporter committed suicide. But the story was true. The guns were AK-47s and came from China. They were assembled in California and shipped south. The dope went to the West Coast first, then other places later. I was involved in it."

"Why didn't you tell someone about this?"

"No one cares. They didn't care then, they don't care now. It was *The Washington Post* and *The New York Times* that debunked the story."

"Do you know the names of the guys you

352

saw outside your room?"

"No, but I think they were here to wipe the slate clean. The man I recognized was a connection between the Contras and some dope mules in California."

"Do you know the name Josef Sholokoff?"

"I do. He was part of the drug deal with the Contras. There's no end to this," she said.

"To what?"

"To the grief I've caused others."

"People like us don't make the wars, Miss Anton. We just get to fight in them," he said. "I've lost a deputy sheriff down here in Mexico. For all I know, he's dead now. When I catch the guys who did this, I'm going to cool them out proper and not feel any qualms about it."

"I think you're not served well by your rhetoric."

"I've got a flash for you, Miss Anton. The only real pacifists are dead Quakers. Ambrose Bierce said that when reflecting on his experience at Shiloh."

"It's also cheap stuff. Good-bye." She broke the connection.

"Look up ahead," Pam said, steering down into the streambed. "There're tire tracks in the sand. They go through the backyard of that adobe house. This has to be the hill the bartender was talking about."

Hackberry turned on the spotlight mounted on the passenger side of the Jeep and shone it through the darkness. A yellow dog with mange on its face and neck, its sides skeletal, its dugs distended, emerged from the shell of the house and stared into the brilliance of the beam before loping away.

"You want to try the switchback up the hill or go around?" Pam asked.

"We take the high ground. Park behind the house. We'll walk over the hill and come down on top of them."

"Back there in the cantina, I saw a side of you that bothers me, Hack," she said.

"I don't have another side, Pam. You stand behind your people or you don't stand behind your people. It's that simple. We get R.C. back from this collection of cretins. When I was at Inchon, I was very frightened. But a line sergeant told me something I never forgot. 'Don't think about it before it happens, and don't think about it when it's over.' We bring R.C. home. You with me on that?"

"I'm with you in everything. But my words mean little to you," she replied. "And that bothers me more than you seem able to understand."

He didn't speak again until they had parked the Jeep behind the adobe house, and then it was only to tell her to walk behind him when they went over the crest of the hill.

The man wearing the hat and holstered thumb-buster squatted on his haunches, eye level with R.C. His breath was as dense and tannic as sewer gas. Two Mexicans wearing jeans that looked stitched to their skins stood stiffly on either side of him, like bookends fashioned from wire. "You have a bad moment or two down there?" the man asked.

R.C. nodded, meeting the strange man's eyes briefly.

"Enough to make you wet your britches?" the man asked.

"No, sir, I didn't do that."

The man lifted his chin and pinched the loose flesh under his throat. He was unshaved, and his whiskers looked as stiff as pig bristles. "What's it like under the ground, with a mask on your face and a lifeline anyone can pinch off with the sole of his boot?"

"Dark."

"Like the inside of a turnip sack, I bet."

"That comes right close to it."

"Your heart start twisting and your breath start coming out of your windpipe like you swallowed a piece of glass?"

"That pert' near says it," R.C. replied.

"I can sympathize."

"You been buried alive?"

"Not in the way you have."

"You either have or you haven't."

"When I was a little boy, my mother would stick me eight or nine hours inside a footlocker. I'd pretend I was on the spine of a

355

boxcar, flying across the countryside under the stars. Did you have fanciful notions like that? Then you opened your eyes and thought somebody had poured an inkwell inside your head."

"Maybe your soul can go somewhere else. That's the way I figure it. That's how come people don't go crazy sometimes," R.C. said. Then he added, as though he were in the presence of a confidant, "I got wrapped up in a rubber sheet when I was a little baby and almost suffocated. My mother was in the yard and looked through the window and said I'd already turned blue. She ran inside and saved my life."

"You saying you had a real mother but mine was cut out of different cloth, maybe burlap?"

"No, sir, I didn't say that," R.C. replied, looking away.

"I wouldn't care if you did. Do you think I care about your opinion of my mother?"

"No, sir."

"What's the nature of your relationship with Sheriff Holland?"

"Sir?"

"You deaf?"

"I'm his deputy. My name is R. C. Bevins. I grew up in Ozona and Del Rio and Marathon. My daddy was a tool pusher in the oil field. My mother was a cashier at the IGA till the day she died. She went to work one day and never came home."

"Why should I care what your parents did or didn't do?"

" 'Cause I know who you are. 'Cause I know what happens to people when you get your hands on them. So if you do the same to me, I want you to know who I am, or who I was."

"Who do you think I am?"

"A stone killer who don't take prisoners."

"For somebody who was just dug up from a grave, maybe you should take your transmission out of overdrive."

"Maybe you should have practiced a little self-inventory before you murdered all them Asian girls."

"You're ahead of the game, boy. Best respect your elders."

"I ain't the one trying to get inside somebody else's thoughts, like some kind of pervert."

"You were in the whorehouse to play the piano?"

"If that's what it was, I was there because I blew out my tire. So don't go belittling me."

The man in the hat glanced up at the two Mexicans, his eyes amused, the soles of his boots grating on the gravel. "You thirsty?"

R.C. swallowed but didn't reply.

"You ever kill a man?"

"I never had to," R.C. said.

"Maybe that's waiting for you down the pike."

"If I got choices, it ain't gonna happen."

"You want a drink of water or not?"

R.C. sat erect and pulled his knees up before him, the dirt and pea gravel shaling off his clothes. "I wouldn't mind," he said.

The man with yellow fingernails that were as thick as horn signaled for one of the Mexicans to pass R.C. a canteen that was attached to a looped GI web belt.

"Does Sheriff Holland treat you all right?"

"We share commonalities. That's what he calls them, 'commonalities.' "

"In what way?"

"We both pitched baseball. I pitched all the way through high school. He pitched in high school and three years at Baylor. He got an invitation to the Cardinals' training camp. I wasn't as good as him, though."

"I declare."

"He has the Navy Cross and a Purple Heart. He treats everybody the same, black or Mexican or Indian or illegal, it don't matter. That's the kind of man he is."

"He sounds like a father figure."

"If he is, it's nobody else's business."

"The sheriff is a widower and doesn't have family close by. It must be a comfort for him to have a young fellow like you around. Someone he thinks of as a son."

"I got to use the restroom."

The man found a more comfortable position by easing his weight down on one knee.

"You might be hard put to find one out here," he said. He gazed into the distance, his eyes dulled over, seemingly devoid of thought. The collar of his white shirt was yellow with dried soap. "What if I gave you a choice, one that would he'p you define your loyalties in a way you wouldn't forget? That nobody would forget?"

R.C. had taken one sip from the canteen and had started to take another. But he stopped and set the canteen down on the edge of the grave and stared at it, his hand still cupped on the canvas snap-button pouch that held it. He waited, his eyes fixed in empty space, the wind flattening the mesquite along the banks of the streambed. He knew what was coming.

"Here's the situation as I see it," the strange man said. "The sheriff tried to kill me by firing a whole magazine down a mine shaft. He has also insulted me several times on a personal level without provocation, even though I have always treated him with respect. So principle requires that I do something in kind to him, otherwise I'll be guilty of what's called a sin of omission. Are you following me?"

"You're Preacher Jack Collins. Around here, that translates into 'crazy.' I don't have conversations with crazy people."

Collins shifted his weight and pulled his revolver from its holster and fitted his thumb over the hammer. "You'd better listen up, boy." He pulled back the hammer to full cock and touched the muzzle to R.C.'s temple. "With one soft squeeze, I can scatter your buckwheats all over that streambed. There will be a flash of light and a loud roar in your ears, then you'll be with your dead mother. I'll make sure the sheriff understands I did this as payback for what he's done to me. In that way, I'll rob him of any peace of mind for the rest of his life. But there's a problem with that choice. Other than not knowing how to stay out of a hot-pillow joint, you're an innocent boy and shouldn't have to pay the price for the sheriff's actions. So I'm going to create a choice for you that most people in your situation don't have."

Collins lowered the hammer and released the lock on the cylinder and tipped it sideways from the revolver's frame. He shucked the six brass cartridges into his palm. "Are you a gambling man?" he said.

"Whatever it is you're thinking about, I'm not interested."

"Believe me, you will be."

"Sheriff Holland is gonna hunt you down in every rat hole in Coahuila. Don't be talking down to me about no whorehouses, either. You got whores working for you as informants, and I suspect that ain't all they're doing for you, provided they're not choosy."

Collins stood up. "I'm going to put one in

360

the chamber and spin the cylinder. When I hand you the revolver, I'm going to cover the cylinder so you cain't see where the load is. If you'll hold the muzzle to your head and pull the trigger twice without coming down on the wrong chamber, I'll turn you loose. If you refuse, I'll pop you here and now."

"Why you doing this to me?"

"Boy, you just don't listen, do you?"

"Let me think it over. Okay, I have. Kiss my ass. And when you're done doing that, kiss my ass again."

"Why don't you have another sip of water and rethink that statement?"

"I don't need no more of y'all's mouth germs."

"Get up."

"What for?"

Jack Collins laughed to himself. "You're fixing to find out."

"I'm tired of all this."

"Tired?"

"Yeah, of being treated like a sack of shit. Just like I told that guy who took me out here, go on and do what you're gonna do. Fuck you, I couldn't care less. Hackberry Holland is gonna turn you into the deadest bucket of shit that was ever poured in the ground."

Jack Collins let the revolver hang loosely at his side, outside the holster. "Stand up and look me in the face."

R.C. got to his feet, his knees popping. He wiped the sweat and beaded rings of dirt from his neck and looked at his hand. His eyes drifted to the revolver in Preacher Jack's right hand. He closed his eyes and opened them again, forcing them wide, refusing to blink. On the edge of his vision, he thought he saw his mother watching him, a cone of cotton candy clutched in her hand.

"Just to set the record straight, the breed who buried you wasn't coming back. He's in Durango now, drunk out of his senses," Jack Collins said. "You would have died underground of thirst and starvation. If I had my druthers, I'd take a bullet anytime."

"I'll take a bullet just so I don't have to listen to you no more," R.C. said.

Jack Collins laughed again and picked up the canteen and looped the web belt over R.C.'s head, easing it down so as not to clip his ear. "Stay on the edge of the hillside and go due north for about three miles, and you'll hit a dirt road. Follow it eastward, and you'll intersect an asphalt two-lane that'll take you to the border."

R.C. stared at him dumbly, the backs of his legs shaking. He tried to think about what Collins had just said. The words made no sense. He felt as though the horizon were tilting sideways, the mountains going in and out of focus.

"You really thought I was going to cap

362

you?" Collins said.

R.C. didn't answer. He glanced sideways at the spot where his mother had been standing, but she had disappeared.

"I wouldn't do that to you, kid. You've got sand," Collins said.

With that, he and his friends walked away like Halloween trick-or-treaters who had lost interest in their own pranks.

A few minutes later, Hackberry Holland and Pam Tibbs came over the crest of the hill and looked down on the riparian landscape and the empty streambed that resembled a pale scar cutting across it, and the graves where the half-breed named Negrito had buried his victims, some of whom may have been alive when they went into the ground.

There was no one down below. Pam swept the area with her binoculars and then pointed at the north, handing the binoculars to Hackberry. In the moonlight, he saw a solitary figure walking alongside the streambed, a canteen slung from his shoulder, his shirttail hanging out, his shadow as sharp as a fence post on the ground. "R.C.," he said.

"How'd he get loose from the guy who kidnapped him?" Pam said.

"I don't know," Hackberry said. He focused the lenses on the southern horizon and thought he saw headlights dip over a rise and briefly reflect off a sandstone bluff and then

363

disappear. "Let's find out."

They climbed back down the opposite side of the hill and drove north in the Jeep until they were out on the flats again and could drive past the hill and intersect the streambed R.C. was following. As they drove toward him, their high beams suddenly defining him among the pale greenery that grew out of the sand, burning the shadows away from the youthful angularity of his face, Hackberry experienced one of those moments doctors at the navy hospital in Houston defined as post-traumatic stress disorder but that Hackberry thought of as the natural entwining of events and people, past and present, that seemed to take place as one reached the end of his life.

The totality of a man's days eventually became a circle rather than a sum, and one way or another, he always ended up at the place where he had begun. Or at least that was what Hackberry believed.

As he looked through the windshield at R.C., he saw himself in the late summer of 1953, crossing the wooden pedestrian bridge at Panmunjom, the last man in a column of prisoners being returned from the camps south of the Manchurian border. He had been emaciated, barely able to walk and control his dysentery, his marine utilities stiff with salt and faded almost colorless. A photographer from *Stars and Stripes* took his picture with a big Speed Graphic camera, and later, the photo was picked up by the wire services and published all over the country above a cutline that began, "The last American soldier to cross Freedom Bridge . . ."

But he had not been the last man across Freedom Bridge. Others would follow and others would be left behind, perhaps four hundred of them who were moved by their captors across the Yalu River into Communist China and forgotten by the rest of the world.

Was it worth it? The great irony was that no one cared enough to even ask the question. The dates, the battles, the strafing of civilian refugees by American F-80s, the misery of the Chosin Reservoir, the red-hot thirty-caliber barrels they unscrewed with their bare hands, leaving their flesh on the steel, the systematic cruelty inside the gulag of prison camps in the north, Hackberry's time in a place called Pak's Palace, which had been housed in an abandoned brick factory where the North Koreans refined a method of torture known as Pak's Swing, all these things were smudged entries in a tragedy that had become little more than an inconvenient memory. But the participants never forgot the details of their experience, and like the Wandering Jew, they were condemned to remain their own history books, each containing a story they could not pass on to others and from which no one would learn anything of value.

Hackberry could see himself in R.C., walking down the flume of an ancient riverbed, staring back into the Jeep's headlights, his mouth cut with a grin, the soft white baked clay cracking under his weight. Youth was its own anodyne, Hackberry thought. For R.C., the world was still a fine place, his faith in his fellow man renewed by the arrival of his friends, his life unfolding before him as though it had been charted with the same divine hand that had placed our progenitors in an Edenic paradise. For just a second, Hackberry wanted to take all the experience out of his own life and give it to R.C. and pray that he would do better with it than Hackberry had.

He rolled down the passenger window. "Miss your turnoff to San Antone?" he said.

"I knew y'all would be along," R.C. said, grinning broadly, getting in the back. "What kept you? I was starting to get a little antsy."

"Bad traffic jam. What kept *us?* What the hell happened out here?" Hackberry said.

"This half-breed Negrito buried me after he almost took my head off with a shovel, that's what happened. Then Jack Collins and two Mexicans dug me up."

Pam put her foot on the brake. "Collins is down here?"

"He *was.*"

"Where?" she asked.

"Him and the two Mexicans walked over a rise and just went *poof,* gone, just like that."

"Did they have a car?" Hackberry said.

"I didn't hear one. But the wind was blowing out of the north. Maybe I just didn't hear them start it up."

"What did Collins say to you?" Hackberry said.

"He said I had a choice. I could play Russian roulette or he'd pop me. When I told him I wouldn't do it, he gave me directions to the highway. I cain't figure it out. Maybe everything people say about him ain't altogether true."

"Don't fool yourself," Hackberry said.

"So why'd he cut me loose?"

"He told you to tell me something, didn't he?"

"He's got you on his mind, that's for sure, but he didn't send no message. No, sir."

Hackberry looked straight ahead at the countryside and at the stars that were going out of the sky.

"Did I miss something back there?" R.C. asked.

Collins wants me in his debt, Hackberry thought. But that was not what he said. "You did just fine, R.C. Who cares what goes on in the head of a madman?"

"I do. He's a scary guy."

"He is. He kills people."

"No, in a different way. His breath. It smells

367

like gas. His skin, too. It doesn't smell like sweat. He doesn't smell human."

The Mexicans say he walks through walls, Hackberry thought.

"Sir?"

"There's a town not far away. You hungry?"

"A twenty-ounce steak and five pounds of fries and a gallon of ice cream would probably get me through till breakfast," R.C. replied.

"You got it, bub," Hackberry said.

By dawn Hackberry was back home. He called Ethan Riser's cell phone and left a message, then slept four hours and showered and called Riser again. This time Riser answered. "I need you here, partner," Hackberry said.

"I got your message about Collins. We've contacted all the authorities in Coahuila."

"That's like telling me you just masturbated."

"Why do you go out of your way to be offensive?"

"Anton Ling told me she was involved in an arms-for-dope operation. The dope went into American ghettos, the guns went to Nicaragua. She says Josef Sholokoff was a player in the deal."

"I've heard all that stuff before."

"Is it true?"

"Maybe on some level it is. But it's yesterday's box score. Sholokoff is our worry, Sheriff. You worry about Collins and this guy Krill. It's clear they're both operating in your jurisdiction. Sholokoff is a separate issue."

Hackberry could feel his hand clenching and unclenching on the phone receiver. Through his window, he could see his horses running in the pasture and yellow dust rising off the hills, plum-colored rain clouds bunching across the sun. *He has cancer. He's at the end of his row. Don't insult him,* he heard a voice say.

"I'm against the wall," he said. "My deputy was drugged and buried alive. Federal agencies and their minions, people like Temple Dowling, are wiping their ass on my county, and I can't do anything about it. I'm throwing away the rule book on this one, Ethan."

"That's always the temptation. But when it's over, the result is always the same. You end up with shit on your nose."

"You coming down here or not?"

There was a long silence. "I'm tied up. I can't do it. Listen to me, Hack. Stay out of events that happened years ago. Stay away from this Anton Ling woman, too. She's an idealist who's full of guilt, and like all idealists, she'd incinerate one half of the earth to save the other half. She had a chance to return Noie Barnum to his own people — that's us, the good guys, we're not Al Qaeda. Instead, she chose to hide and feed him and

369

dress his wounds and let him end up in the hands of Jack Collins. Are you going to put your bet on somebody like that? Use your head for a change."

That evening Danny Boy Lorca entered a saloon off a two-lane highway that wound through hills that resembled industrial waste more than compacted earth. The saloon was built of shaved and lacquered pine logs and had a peaked green roof that, along with the Christmas-tree lights stapled around the window frames, gave it a cheerful appearance in a landscape that seemed suitable only for lizards and scorpions and carrion birds. The saloon's name was spelled out in a big orange neon sign set on the roof's apex, the cursive words LA ROSA BLANCA glowing vaporously against the sky. The owner went by the name Joe Tex, although he had no relationship to the musician by the same name. When patrons asked Joe Tex where he had gotten the name for his saloon, he would tell them of his ex-wife, a big-breasted stripper from Dallas who had a heart of gold and a voice that could break windows and a thirst for chilled vodka that the Gulf of Mexico couldn't quench. The truth was, Joe Tex had never been married and had been a mercenary in Cambodia, operating out of Phnom Penh, where he had been close friends with the owners of a brothel that specialized in

370

oral sex. The name of the brothel had been the White Rose.

Danny Boy had parked his deuce-and-a-half army-surplus flatbed and walked unsteadily across the gravel to the entrance, the drawstring of a duffel bag corded around his forearm, the weight in the bottom of the bag bumping against his hip as he scraped against the doorframe and headed for the bar.

Next door was a 1950s-style motel bordered with red and yellow neon tubing whose circular porte cochere and angular facade and signs gave it the appearance of a parked spaceship. The customers in the saloon were long-haul truckers staying in the motel; women who carried spangled purses and wore eyeliner and lip gloss and had mousse in their hair and whose voices seemed slightly deranged; locals who had been in Huntsville and were probably dangerous and not welcome at other clubs; and college boys looking to get laid or get in trouble, whichever came first.

Joe Tex dressed like a Latino, his cowboy boots plated on the toes and heels, his black cowboy shirt stitched with red roses. He smiled constantly, regardless of the situation, his teeth as solid as tombstones, the black hair on his forearms a signal to others of the power and virility wrapped inside his muscular body, one that pulsed with veins when he lifted weights in nothing but a jockstrap out back in 110-degree heat.

Danny Boy skirted the dance floor, walking as carefully as a man aboard a pitching ship. He set the duffel bag on the bar, the canvas collapsing on the hard objects inside.

"A beer and a shot?" Joe Tex said.

"I want to pay my tab," Danny Boy said.

Joe Tex took a frosted schooner out of the cooler and drew a beer from a spigot and set it in front of Danny Boy, then poured a shot glass up to the brim with Jim Beam and set it on a napkin next to the schooner. His expression made Danny Boy think of a profile carved on the handle of a Mexican walking cane — fixed, slightly worn, the paint chipping away. Joe Texas opened a drawer below the bar and looked in a metal box and removed a slip of paper columned with penciled sums. "Call it seventy-five even," he said.

"I got some dinosaur eggs. I want to sell them."

"If I was in the dinosaur business, wouldn't I have to be worried about something called the Antiquities Act?" Joe Tex's teeth were white against the deep leathery tan of his face when he smiled.

"These come from the back of my property. The government don't care what I dig up on my own land. I got two eggs, big ones." He raised the bag slightly by the drawstring, tightening the canvas against the shapes

372

inside. "They're worth five thousand apiece. You can have them both for four thousand."

"That's how you're gonna pay your tab?"

"I saw a killing. It was done by a guy named Krill. I'm gonna put a bounty on this guy. I'm gonna put a reward on a guy named Noie Barnum, too, and maybe get him some he'p."

Joe Tex propped his hands on the bar. He seemed to gaze at the college boys and women and truck drivers sitting at the tables and the couples dancing by the jukebox without actually seeing any of them. He seemed to look at all the illusions that defined the lives of his clientele and maybe think about them briefly and then return to the realities and deceptions that made up his own life. "What are you doing this for, Danny Boy?"

" 'Cause I seen a murder and I didn't do nothing to stop it. 'Cause maybe I can make up for it by he'ping a guy name of Noie Barnum. He got away from this fellow Krill. He run right past me. Maybe he's hiding out with the one called the Preacher."

Joe Tex studied the tops of his fingers and the hair that grew from the backs of his hands along his wrists and under the metal band of his watch and the snap-button cuffs of his embroidered shirt. "This isn't the place to square a personal beef. The shot and the beer are on the house. Let's eighty-six the eggs. This isn't a souvenir shop."

Joe Tex walked away, his metal-plated boots making dull sounds on the duckboards. Danny Boy's eyes closed and opened as he tried to think his way through the haze and confusion that Joe Tex's words had caused in his head. He drank from the shot glass, a small sip at a time, chasing it with the beer, slumping forward for balance, one work-booted foot on the bar rail, his facial muscles oily and uncoordinated, the row of bottles on the back counter sparkling with light. The shot glass and the schooner seemed to go empty by themselves, his foot slipping off the rail as he stared wanly at them. "Hit me again," he said when Joe Tex walked past him to wait on a customer at the far end of the bar.

Danny Boy waited for his schooner and shot glass to be refilled, as though his level of desire were enough to make a reality out of a wish. But Joe Tex remained at the far end of the bar, talking to some college kids who were asking him about Big Bend National Park, and Danny Boy's shot glass and schooner did not get refilled. "Give me another one," he said to Joe Tex's back.

He rested his hand on top of the heavy, solid, thick shapes of the fossilized eggs and stared at the way Joe Tex's shirt stretched tightly across his shoulders, the tendon and sinew that tapered down to a thirty-two-inch waist, the wide belt he wore and the tight

374

western-cut gray trousers and the polished Tony Lama boots. Couldn't Joe hear him? Danny Boy knocked on the bar with his knuckles. "Give me a beer and a sandwich," he said. "One of them ham and onion ones. Give me a shot, too."

But no one was listening to him. Not Joe Tex or the college kids or the dancers or the people drinking and eating at the tables. Didn't others understand the value of what he had found? The eggs proved a great antediluvian world was still out there, inhabited by stubby-legged creatures with reptilian necks. All you had to do was believe and you could see through time into the past and maybe even touch it with your hand. That's what happened when you went inside the desert and were absorbed by the rocks and the layers of warm air rising off the sand. You became part of a place where there was no past or future and where all things happened at the same time. "Hey, Joe, why you talking to them people?" he said. "I want a drink. Forget them kids. I want a fucking drink."

Did he just say that?

Joe Tex walked slowly toward him on the duckboards, a pocket of air forming in one cheek. He picked up the shot glass and schooner and set them in an aluminum sink filled with dirty water. The glass and the schooner sank down through the film of soap and grease and disappeared. "Time to go home, Danny," he said.

"I come here to pay my tab. I come here to drink like anybody else."

"Another time."

"I'll pay my tab tomorrow. I'll find somebody to buy the eggs."

Joe Tex lifted his hands and set them on the bar again. "I can get someone to drive you home, or you can sleep it off in back," he said. "That's it. We're done."

When Joe Tex walked away, Danny Boy felt like he was standing on a street corner by himself, watching a city bus lumber away from the curb, his reflection on the windows sliding past him, the passengers inside reading newspapers or talking to one another or listening to music through earphones as though he didn't exist. His lips were caked, his throat clotted, the veins tightening in his scalp, the bottles of rum and bourbon and tequila and vodka as mysterious and alluring as the radiance in a rainbow. "I been a good customer. I been your friend," he heard himself say.

Then he felt instantly ashamed at his plaintive tone, the pathetic role of victim once again his public mantle.

"Want a drink, chief?" a voice said.

When Danny Boy turned around, he saw a tall, clean-shaven man with wavy brown hair standing behind him. Three other men were sitting at a table behind the tall man, smoking cigarettes, drinking beer from the bottle. The tall man could have been a cowboy or a buyer of rough stock for a rodeo, but in reality, he probably did something else, Danny Boy thought, like manage a big-game ranch up in the Glass Mountains or cater to the needs of a rich man who hired others to do his work for him. He wore mirrored sunglasses and a sky-blue silk shirt and Wrangler jeans belted high up on his flat stomach. He had an easy smile and big hands with knuckles that looked like walnuts. Maybe he was a cowboy after all, Danny Boy thought, a regular guy who didn't mean anything by the word "chief."

"I'm tapped out," Danny Boy said.

"That's not just booze talking. You got some dino eggs in there?"

Danny Boy tried not to acknowledge the first part. "They come from the back of my place. I dug them up." He glanced at the bottles on the back counter and wiped his nose with a handkerchief. He watched the cowboy drink from the bottle of Mexican beer, his throat working smoothly, his cheeks glistening with aftershave, the label on the bottle gold and red and translucent and somehow beautiful. Danny Boy waited for the cowboy to offer him a drink.

"Maybe I could help you out," the cowboy said.

Danny waited, trying not to let his gaze

settle on the bottles of whiskey and rum and gin and vodka.

"Can I look at them?" the cowboy said, cupping his hand on the outline of the eggs.

"Maybe this ain't the place."

"I don't see any problem." The cowboy slipped a wallet from his back pocket and set it on the bar. The edges of a thick sheaf of crisp bills protruded from the braided edge of the wallet.

Danny Boy loosened the drawstring on the duffel bag and stuck his arm inside and slowly removed each dinosaur egg and placed it carefully on the bar. When he looked back into the cowboy's mirrored sunglasses, he saw the reflected image of a dark-skinned, truncated man in a dirty olive-colored T-shirt and canvas trousers he had probably pissed in without remembering.

"How much you want for them?" the cowboy asked.

"Two thousand for each."

"They look like a pair of petrified titties to me, and not very good ones, at that."

Danny Boy made a snuffing sound down in his nose and looked at the far wall and at the people on the dance floor and at the layers of smoke that flattened and sometimes swirled under the ceiling. "I could go eighteen hunnerd for each."

"And you're gonna use this money to round up a fellow name of Noie Barnum? You're kind of a specialist in solving big-picture problems? Tell you what, before you answer that question, how about one-fifty for both your busted titties here, and then you take yourself and your stink out of here? Have you noticed that your britches look like somebody shoved a wet towel in your crotch?"

Danny Boy stared at his reflection of the man trapped inside the cowboy's sunglasses. The trapped man's hair was cut in bangs, his skin so dark it looked as though it had been smoked on a fire; his emotionless expression was like that of a retarded man who absorbed insults without understanding the words; the scar tissue in his eyebrows and the gaps in his teeth and the rounded mass of his shoulders were those of a man who had been pounded into the ground for a lifetime, a hod carrier working under the scaffolding of a cathedral while stone dust filtered down on his head. He stared into the cowboy's sunglasses until the image of himself seemed to break into gold needles.

"I dug them up on my place," he said. "I'm gonna use the money to he'p this fellow Noie Barnum. I think you know who he is or you wouldn't be talking down to me."

The cowboy gripped Danny Boy's upper arm tightly with one hand, leaning over to whisper in his ear, his words wet with the smokeless tobacco tucked inside his lip. "I'm gonna walk you outside, boy, then we're gonna have a talk. In the meantime, you keep your mouth shut."

"I was a middleweight. I fought at the Olympia in L.A. I knew Tami Mauriello. He give me some pointers once. He sat in my corner and said I was as good as him. Tami almost nailed Joe Louis."

"You get your goddamn worthless stink-ass Indian carcass out front. You hear me, boy? You know what no God or law west of the Pecos means? It means this is still a white man's country."

The cowboy's teeth were clenched, his anger telegraphing through his grip, his breath wet against the side of Danny Boy's face.

Maybe it was the use of the word "boy" or the ferocity of his grip. Or maybe it was the years of contempt and ridicule and insult that Danny Boy had come to accept as a way of life, part of the tab that came with being a drunk and a swamper of saloons and bathrooms where people vomited in the lavatory and threw their paper towels on the floor and shit on the edge of the bowl. Or maybe it was none of these things. Maybe he just wanted to be seventeen again, fresh out of the Golden Gloves, lean and hard, his left as quick as a snake's head, his right hook under the heart enough to make a grown man's eyes beg.

This time Danny Boy's right didn't hook in to an opponent's rib cage; it went straight

380

into the cowboy's mouth, breaking his lips against his teeth, knocking his mirrored shades off his face. The shock and pain in the cowboy's eyes could be compared to that of a man stepping out of a car and being hit by a bus. Before the man could raise his hands to protect himself, Danny Boy threw the whole factory at him: two left jabs, one in the eye, one high up on the cheekbone and the bridge of the nose, then a right delivered straight from the shoulder with his weight solidly behind it, his fist driving into the bloody hole he had already created in the bottom of the cowboy's face, breaking off his teeth at the gums, knocking a wad of blood and phlegm and smokeless tobacco down his throat.

All sound in the saloon stopped except for the voice of Willie Nelson on the jukebox. He was singing "Blue Eyes Crying in the Rain," his voice like a long strand of baling wire being pulled through a hole in a tin can. Danny Boy replaced the dinosaur eggs in the duffel bag and wrapped the drawstring around his forearm and started toward the door. The fight should have been over. The cowboy was sprawled backward on the floor, his nose and mouth dripping blood on his sky-blue shirt. Even Joe Tex, who usually broke up fights immediately, was observing silently from behind the bar, indicating that it was over, that all Danny Boy had to do now was walk out of the saloon.

That was how it should have gone. But it didn't. Danny Boy had taken only three steps when he heard the cowboy coming hard behind him. He turned, the duffel hanging from his left forearm, automatically setting himself, ready to unload with his right and this time click off the cowboy's switch.

Except the cowboy came in under the swing, gripping an antler-handled knife with a four-inch blade, the blade protruding from the heel of the hand and the fingers, his forearm and elbow raised in front of his face to absorb Danny Boy's next blow. Danny Boy tried to jump backward but tripped against a chair. He felt the knife go into his thigh like an icicle, all the way to the bone, thudding dully against it, a pocket of pain and nausea spreading out of the wound into his groin and stomach. He remembered hearing about an artery the heart depended on, and then he was outside himself, watching Danny Boy Lorca labor toward the door, his duffel bag swinging from his arm, his right leg as stiff as wood, the knife driven all the way to the hilt against his canvas trousers. Outside, bathed in the orange glow of a neon sign that advertised a Texas saloon and a Cambodian brothel, the entire world and the stars above it were draining down his leg into shale that creatures with long serpentine necks had probably once walked upon. It was a funny way to catch the elevator going south, he thought, just as the parking lot rose up and hit him between the eyes with the impact of a fist.

CHAPTER FIFTEEN

The attendant who stayed in the back of the ambulance with Danny Boy during the ride to the county hospital had acne on his forehead and on the bridge of his nose and on the point of his chin, so that his profile looked like it had been sawed out of a shingle with a dull knife. His skin and clothes were rife with the smell of nicotine, his hair flecked with dandruff, his arms as thin as sticks inside his shirtsleeves. The asphalt road was badly cracked, and Danny Boy's gurney and the equipment inside the ambulance were vibrating loudly, but the attendant seemed to take little notice.

"What do you call that artery in the thigh?" Danny Boy asked. "The one you don't want to get cut?"

"The femoral," the attendant said.

"Is that where he got me?"

"Guess."

"He didn't?"

The attendant untwisted the cellophane on

a piece of peppermint. "I got dry mouth," he said. "I'd offer you one, but you're not supposed to have anything right now."

"The artery is okay?"

"Jesus, buddy, what do you think?"

"I think I used to know you. Your nickname was Stoner or something like that."

"That doesn't sound familiar."

Danny Boy continued to stare at the attendant's profile. "I worked at a carnival in Marathon. I saw you at the free clinic. You were trying to get clean."

"Yeah, that could have been me. You were in a program there?"

"I went to the clinic 'cause of my headaches."

"The guy you decked, he's a private detective. He works for Temple Dowling." The attendant waited. Danny Boy stared at him without replying, the inside of the ambulance rattling each time the tires thudded across a tar-patched crack in the road. "You don't know who Temple Dowling is?"

"No."

"His father was a senator."

"Of what?"

The attendant shook his head. "The bartender told the cops you wanted to put a reward on a guy named Barnum. You know, same name as the circus?" He blew his nose on a tissue and stuck the tissue in his shirt pocket, sniffing, his gaze shifting sideways

385

onto Danny Boy. "Maybe I know where he is. Or who he's with. You following me?"

"Tell the sheriff."

"Were you ever in N.A.?"

"What's that?"

The attendant sniffed again. "I sold some medical supplies to a guy. A guy I don't like to think about. He had me meet him at night out in the desert. You know who I'm talking about?"

"Maybe. What's his name?"

"If you meet this guy, you don't use his name."

"The one they call Preacher?"

"You said it, I didn't."

Through the back window, Danny Boy could see the reflection of the emergency lights racing along the sides of the highway. "That guy's a killer," he said. "You were selling him dope you stole?"

"Maybe I don't feel good about it."

"My leg hurts. I don't want to listen to this no more."

"I want to go to California and get clean and start over. Give me one of the eggs. I got the information you want."

Danny Boy looked at the attendant for a long time, his eyes going dull with fatigue. "My duffel bag is on the floor."

"You're doing the right thing, man. But I got to ask you something. Why you want to help this guy Barnum?"

" 'Cause I got to make up for something."

"Like what?"

"I was there when Barnum escaped from some killers. I saw the killers torture a man to death."

"For real?"

"Where's Noie Barnum?"

"I don't know the exact place, but when I gave the man in the desert the medical supplies, he looked at the north and said, 'It's fixing to rain snakes and frogs up yonder.' I go, 'Where up yonder?' He says, 'In the Glass Mountains. You ought to come up there and stand in front of a gully washer. It'd flat hydrate all that dope out of your system, make a man out of you.' " The attendant looked into space. "He's got a special way of making people feel small."

Danny Boy didn't reply.

"He made you feel the same way, didn't he?" the attendant said.

"Not no more he cain't," Danny Boy said.

It rained that night. To the south, a tropical storm had blown ashore on the Mexican coast, and the air smelled as dense and cool and laden with salt as seawater, almost as if a great displaced ocean lay just beyond the hills that ringed the town. Before Hackberry Holland and Pam Tibbs arrived at the hospital to interview Danny Boy, a bolt of lightning knocked out the power all over the county.

Flashes of white electricity flickered inside the clouds, and Hackberry thought he could smell tropical flowers and dried kelp in the wind and gas inside the trees on the hospital lawn. He was sure these were the musings of a self-absorbed old man, one who could not stop thinking about the past and the ephemerality of his life.

He and Pam Tibbs interviewed Danny Boy before he went into surgery, then tried unsuccessfully to find the ambulance attendant. Hackberry and Pam and their deputies and the surgeons and the other hospital personnel all did their jobs throughout the power outage, not thinking, just doing, never taking the time to wonder if any of it mattered or not. You did your job and you let the score take care of itself. How many times a day did Hackberry offer that same tired workhorse counsel to himself? Was that how one ended his days? Probably, he thought. No, there was no "probably" about it. If you thought about mortality in any other fashion, you'd go insane or put a gun in your mouth.

After the power came back on, he and Pam drove two blocks to a café on the courthouse square and had coffee and a piece of pie. Through the window, Hackberry could see the trees on the courthouse lawn and the mist blowing across the lawn and the streetlights shining on a bronze statue of a World War I doughboy, his '03 Springfield gripped in one hand, his other hand raised above his head as though he were rallying his comrades.

"You look tired," Pam said.

"You mean I look old."

"No, I don't mean that at all."

"I'm fine. I've never been better."

"Pray that liars aren't kept a long time in purgatory."

"Pam, you should have been a low-overhead dentist, someone who does fillings and extractions without the extra cost of Novocain."

She gazed out the window at the rain and at the drops of water beaded on the glass. Her eyelashes were reddish brown against the glow of the streetlamp; a wet strand of hair curved against her cheek. He couldn't tell if she was thinking about the two of them or all the events of the past few days. She seemed to read his thoughts. "Why does a mass killer make himself vulnerable to arrest by buying stolen medicine from a junkie in order to take care of a stranger?" she said.

"That's what every one of them does."

"Every one of who does what?" she said.

"All sociopaths. They do good deeds as a tribute to their own power and to convince others they're like the rest of us."

"You don't think Collins has any feelings about Noie Barnum?"

"I think the only genuine emotion he's capable of is self-pity."

"I don't like to see you bitter."

He placed his fork on the side of his plate and poured cream from a small pitcher on top of his half-eaten wedge of blueberry pie. He picked up his fork and then hesitated and set it down again. "By the seventh-inning stretch, this is what you learn. Evil people are different from the rest of us. Redneck cops, Klansmen, predators who rape and murder children, ChiCom prison guards, and messianic head cases like Jack Collins, all of them want us to think they're complex or they're patriots or they're ideologues. But the simple truth is, they do what they do because it makes them feel good."

"Would you have put that broken pool cue down that bartender's throat?"

"The bartender thought so. That's all that counts."

"Don't stop being who you are because of these guys. You've always said it yourself: Don't give them that kind of power."

Hackberry stared out the window at the electricity trembling on the tree above the bronze figure of the doughboy. The statue's head was turned slightly to one side, the mouth open, as though the doughboy were yelling an encouraging word over his shoulder to those following him across no-man's-land. Did they know what awaited them? Did they know the Maxim machine guns that would turn them into chaff were the creation of a British inventor?

Hackberry wondered who had erected the monument. He wanted to call them idiots or flag-wavers or members of the unteachable herd. But words such as those were as inaccurate as they were jaundiced and hateful, he thought. In our impotence to rescind all the decisions that led to war, we erected monuments to assuage the wandering spirits whose lives had been stolen, and to somehow compensate the family members whose loss they would carry to the grave. Who were the greater victims? Those who gave their lives or those who made the war?

He said none of these things and instead watched a man in a wilted hat park his car in front of the café and come inside.

"Ethan Riser is here," Hackberry said. "There's something I didn't tell you about him. He found out recently he has terminal cancer. No matter what he says tonight, he gets a free pass."

"Why didn't you tell me?"

"I don't think he wants other people to know. He's one of those guys who never shows his hole card, even when the game is over."

She pinched her eyes with her thumb and index finger, then widened them, the lines in her face flattening. "I'm not to be trusted?" she said.

"Don't do that."

"You treat me like I'm some kind of burden

391

you have to put up with, someone you have to instruct regarding decent behavior."

"Come on, Pam, stop it."

"You have no sense at all of the pain your words cause, particularly to someone who cares about you. Goddammit, Hack."

He let out his breath and tried to keep his face empty when he waved at Ethan Riser.

"Just go fuck yourself," she said.

"Did I walk in on anything?" Ethan said, not looking directly at either one of them, his smile awkward.

"How you doin'?" Hackberry said.

"Pretty good. Can I join you?"

"Yes, sir," Hackberry said.

"You sure?"

"Sit down, Ethan," Hackberry said, moving over, not looking at Pam.

"Lorca is out of surgery," Riser said. "It's nice to see you, Chief Deputy."

"You, too," Pam replied.

"Lorca told me about the ambulance attendant and the possibility of Jack Collins and Noie Barnum being in the Glass Mountains. I have the feeling you might be headed up there, Sheriff."

"I can't say I've given it any thought," Hackberry replied.

"I have trouble believing that," Riser said. "This time out, you and Chief Deputy Tibbs need to stay in your own bailiwick. I can't order you to do that, but I can ask you."

"Whatever we decide to do, we'll coordinate with the Bureau," Hackberry said.

"Ever hear how Pretty Boy Floyd died?"

"Shot down while running from some federal agents on a farm in Ohio?"

"Something like that. Except there's an unofficial account to the effect that he didn't die right away. He was wounded and lying on his back when the agents got to him. One agent asked him if he was Pretty Boy Floyd. Floyd answered, 'I'm Charles Arthur Floyd.' Then somebody gave the order to finish him off, and that's what they did."

"Why are you telling us this?" Hackberry said.

"It makes for a good story, that's all."

"It's not your style."

"Probably not," Riser said. "I'd sure like some of that pie."

"Ethan, did you hear me? That's not your style."

"I'm all talk. You know that. Miss, could I have a piece of that blueberry pie with some ice cream on it and a cup of coffee?"

"It's on us," Pam said.

"I appreciate it."

"Listen to Hack, Agent Riser."

"Of course."

The waitress brought the pie and ice cream and coffee, and Pam and Hackberry watched Ethan Riser eat. They also watched the way his eyes crinkled and the way his gaze seemed to probe the darkness outside the window, and each sensed in the other the embarrassment they felt while they watched a brave man try to mask the fact that he was under a death sentence.

"This area has never been quite real to me," Riser said. "It's a place where nothing is what it seems. A piece of moonscape where improbable people live and lunatics can hide in plain sight."

"All empires have their dustbins," Hackberry said. "It's the place we bury our sins."

"That's too deep for me."

"What do I know?" Hackberry said.

"A lot more than the Bureau wants to concede," Riser said. "They consider you a pain in the ass. Stay out of the Glass Mountains, my friend."

Pam drove Hackberry home in the rain. The fields were sodden on either side of the road, the sky black, the long lines of cedar fence posts and barbed wire glistening in the cruiser's headlights. "He's going to cool out Collins?" she said.

"I think that was all rhetoric. He's angry because he has to die. Ethan's a straight arrow. People like him make a pact with themselves and never violate it."

"I told you to go fuck yourself earlier."

"Forget it."

"No, I meant it. I just shouldn't have put it

394

that way."

"I see."

"Do you?"

"I'm old, Pam. You think it's honorable for an old man to take advantage of a young woman's affections? You want to become romantically involved with a man who would use a young and attractive woman, knowing eventually he would be a burden to her?"

"I think age doesn't have crap to do with any of it. With you, it's all about pride. You've never forgiven yourself for the mistakes of your youth, so you have to create a standard that's superior to everyone else's. It's not a lot different from the bad guys who are always trying to convince themselves of their own humanity."

"That's a rotten thing to say."

"Too bad."

He could feel his left temple throbbing again, and he knew that in the next few seconds, a sliver of pain as cold and hard as a stalactite would slide through his eye and the muscles of his left cheek. Up ahead, he saw his house suddenly illuminated by a bolt of lightning that struck in the trees behind his office, the same trees where Jack Collins had hidden and trained a laser sight on him. "You don't have to pull into the drive. Just drop me on the road," he said.

"You like walking in an electric storm?"

"In this case, I do."

"Too bad again," she said.

She drove across a wood bridge that spanned a creek running high with rainwater, the wild roses along the bank trailing in the current; then she turned in to his driveway and stopped at the picket fence that enclosed the front yard. "You think I'm unfair?" she said.

"I don't think anything," he said, getting out of the cruiser.

"There's an umbrella in the backseat."

"I've got my hat," he said, closing the passenger door.

She reached into the backseat and gathered up the umbrella and stepped out into the rain. She tried to pop it open, but the catch was jammed.

"Get back in the cruiser," he said.

But she didn't. She followed him up the flagstones to the gallery. She was wearing a department-issue campaign hat, and the rain was beating on the crown and the brim, rolling in rivulets down her shoulders and shirt-front. "I think I should resign, Hack. I think I should go back to Houston," she said.

"That's not going to happen."

"Who the hell are you to tell me anything?"

"I'm your boss, that's who."

"I can't tell you how bad you piss me off."

He walked back down the flagstones and took the umbrella from her hand and popped it open above both their heads. He could hear the rain thudding as hard as marbles on the nylon. "You're the most stubborn woman I have ever met. Why do you act like this?"

"Why do you think?"

"Come in."

"For what?"

"Just come in."

He put his arm over her shoulders and walked her up the steps and unlocked the door and held it open for her. The living room was unlit and smelled of the couch and the carpet and the drapes and the wallpaper and the polished hardwood floors; it smelled like a home; it smelled like a fine place to be while lightning flashed on the hillsides and the wind and rain blew against the window-panes and whipped an unfastened door on the barn and bent the trees and scattered the lawn with leaves and broken flowers. He dropped the umbrella on the rug and touched her face with his fingers, and in seconds felt her against him, her feet standing on top of his boots, her loins and breasts tight against his body, her hair wet against his cheek, her arms clenched around his back, all his personal resolve and his concerns about age and mortality and honor draining like water through the bottom of a paper bag.

"Oh, Hack," she said. "Oh, Hack, Hack, Hack."

From his deck Cody Daniels watched the

storm move out of the south and seal the sky, trapping the light between a blue-black layer of clouds and the desert floor and mesas that were pink and talc-colored and that made him think of pictures of ancient Phoenician ships he had seen. When the power outage spread across the county, he saw the reflected glow of the town flatten against the clouds and die, a surge of cool air rising from the valley floor into his face. Hailstones clattered on the hardpan and on the deck, dancing in a white haze, and in the smell of ozone and the drop of temperature, he felt as though the world were fresh and clean, as though every bad memory of his life were being washed away, every failure and personal affliction slipping over the edges of the earth.

If only things were that easy.

Cody started up his gas-powered generator and went back in the house to resume the most difficult task in his life — writing a letter to the FBI. He had attempted a half-dozen versions on his computer and had been unhappy with all of them. His language was either stilted and sounded self-serving, or it became so confused it was almost unintelligible. The last attempt was two double-spaced pages long and gave details about his recruitment into a small group of anti-abortion activists in northern Virginia. It wasn't a bad statement, except it indiscriminately included the names of his fellow travelers, some of whom may have been unaware of the group's ultimate goal.

He had gone out on the deck without saving the letter on his hard drive, and the power outage had wiped his screen clean. When he reentered the house, the lights burning dimly on the low wattage produced by his generator, he sat down at his desk and picked up a felt-tip pen and addressed an envelope to the Federal Bureau of Investigation in Washington, D.C., no zip code. He put his return address in the upper-left-hand corner of the envelope. Then he wrote the following letter on a yellow legal pad:

Dear Sirs,

I am the pitiful son of a bitch who bought the oven timer for the bomb that blew up the abortion clinic outside Baltimore three years back. I thought the bomb would go off in the middle of the night. But that doesn't help the woman who got her face blown off. I can't give you the names of any of the other people involved. This letter is about the evil deed done by one son of a bitch and one son of a bitch only, and as I have stated, that son of a bitch is yours truly,

Sincerely,
Rev. Cody Daniels

From outside, he heard the hiss of air

brakes and the sound of a tractor-trailer shifting down. He looked through the window and, in the rain-streaked fading of the twilight, saw an eighteen-wheeler parked by the Cowboy Chapel, its high beams on, the engine still hammering, and what appeared to be a lead car parked in front of it. Cody had seen the lead car before, without the clamped-on brace of yellow lights on the roof; it belonged to a musician, a man who stopped by on occasion at the Cowboy Chapel and drank coffee and ate doughnuts in the hospitality room Cody left open for truckers or travelers on their way to the Big Bend country.

Cody draped a slicker over his head and went down the wood steps to the coffee room in the back of the chapel. "Getting out of the storm?" he said to a small tight-bodied man sitting at the long table in the middle of the room, a chrome-plated guitar across his thighs.

"Hey, Reverend, I didn't see you, so I just come inside," the man said. "Hope you don't mind."

"That's what it's for. The name is Rector, isn't it?"

"Dennis Rector, that's me," the man replied. "I saw your nail gun there. You've been doing some carpentering."

"You play a Dobro?"

"You know your instruments. That's what it

is, resonator and all." The small man had the dark skin of a field hand and hair that looked like it had been cut with fingernail clippers. He wore lace-up boots and a tie-dyed T-shirt and denim work pants. His upper torso was bent like a question mark. "It's a Fender, built on the old National model. It feels like a Coca-Cola box packed with ice hanging from your neck."

Dennis Rector ran a steel bar up and down the neck of the Dobro and began playing a tune with the steel picks on the thumb and index and middle fingers of his right hand. "Recognize that piece? That's 'The Great Speckled Bird.' Same tune as 'The Wild Side of Life.' Same tune as 'It Wasn't God Who Made Honky-Tonk Angels.' "

Through the window, Cody could see two men sitting in the cab of the eighteen-wheeler. "What are y'all carrying?" he asked.

"Exotic animals. Want one?"

"You work for a zoo?"

"I guess you could call it that." Dennis Rector was smiling as though he possessed private knowledge that he might or might not share. "We supply a wild-game ranch up in Pecos County."

Cody nodded and didn't reply.

"You're not keen on them kind of places?"

"Live and let live."

"That's the way I figure it. Their misfortune and none of my own. You know you got some beaners parked down yonder on your road?"

"Pardon?"

"Some pepper-bellies in a beat-up old car with a busted headlight."

"Who are they?"

"Maybe a couple of people fucking. How should I know? I couldn't see them that good." The small man was still smiling.

"This is a church house, even if it's just the coffee room," Cody said.

"Sorry."

"Did you catch the tag?"

"I wasn't paying them much mind. They looked away from our lights when we passed. That's why I figure they were people making out. Mexicans tend to breed in the spring and domino in the winter."

Cody studied Dennis Rector from behind his eyelashes. "You from here'bouts?"

"Wherever I hang my hat. Jobs are kind of thin these days. Seems like there's less and less work for a white man. What's your feeling about that?"

"I never lost a job 'cause of my skin color."

"That sounds different from a couple of your sermons."

"Could I he'p y'all with something?"

"No, I just wanted to show my friends your church and get out of the storm."

Cody nodded again, looking out the door at the truck and the animals he could see behind the ventilation slots in the sides. "You

402

mind locking up when you leave? I've got some work to do in the house."

The small man filled his mouth with a jelly doughnut, pushing the overflow back into his mouth with his wrist. His chrome-plated instrument swam with an oily blue light. "No problem, Reverend," he said.

Cody walked back up the stairs and across his deck into the house, forcing himself not to look back over his shoulder. He felt a sense of ill ease that he couldn't define. Was it the rawness of Dennis Rector's language? Or the fact that Cody had helped encourage the role of victim in many of his congregants? Or did he see a reflection of his former self in the lewdness of mind that characterized men like Rector? Why was a man like that playing "The Great Speckled Bird," a spiritual that was as deep-seated in southern religion as "The Old Rugged Cross"? Something wasn't a right fit.

There was also the business about the Hispanics parked on the road. He should have pumped Rector about them. Could the car have contained Krill and Negrito? It couldn't be them, could it? They were professional criminals, hunted by the local sheriff and the FBI and probably the Texas Rangers. Why would Krill and Negrito invest their lives in persecuting Cody Daniels, a mail-order minister who was awakened at two each morning by a blind woman with a disfigured face rattling his bedroom windows?

Just as the power went back on, Cody saw the eighteen-wheeler turn in a wide circle, led by Dennis Rector's car, and head south down the road, the edges of the trailer etched with chains of gold running lights. He folded the confessional letter he had written to the FBI and placed it in the envelope and licked the seal, his stomach churning, his head as light as a helium balloon. Then he sat at his desk, his head in his hands, and wondered how he had made such a catastrophe out of his life.

The wind was swirling out of the desert, the rain driving hard on the roof, dancing on the handrails of his deck, blowing in the blue-white radiance of the neon cross he had mounted above the entrance to the Cowboy Chapel. Maybe it was time to pile a few belongings into the cab of his truck, drop his letter to the FBI in a mailbox, and disappear inside the vast anonymity of the American West.

He could sell his truck in California and pick fruit in the San Joaquin, harvest beets up in Oregon and Washington, maybe lumberjack in Montana or get on a fishing boat in Alaska. If the law caught up with him, fine. If it didn't, that would be fine, too. Why not just roll the dice and stay out of the consequences? In the United States a person could get a new identity and start a new life as easily as acquiring a library card. He had to wonder at the irony of it all. In his fantasy, he was joining the ranks of the migrant workers he had railed against.

He went into his bedroom and began stuffing the clothes from his dresser and closet into a duffel bag. That was when he felt the air decompress around him and the cold smell of rain surge through the house, the joists and wood floors creaking as the temperature dropped inside. He turned around and stared into the faces of two men whose hats were wilted on their heads, their brown skin shiny with water, their clothes smelling like horses and wood smoke and sweat that had dried inside flannel.

"Why won't y'all leave me alone?" Cody said.

"You know," Krill said.

"I don't know anything."

"Yes, you know. Do not pretend you don't know. Do not make an insignificance of my children."

"I'm worthless as a minister. I'm no different from you. I he'ped put together a bomb that was used on an abortion clinic. I ruined a woman's life. I'm not worth shooting."

Krill was already shaking his head, indicating Cody's wishes had little to do with what was about to occur. Negrito was smiling broadly. "We told you we'd be back, man. But you don't listen," he said. "You got anything to eat? I'm really hungry. What was that about a bombing?"

"You got a hearing defect?" Cody said.

"End this silly talk and come with me," Krill said.

"Where?"

"Out into the rain, *hombre*."

"I'm no count as a pastor, no count as a man. That's not humility talking, either. It's the truth."

"*Venga conmigo.* Now. No more talking."

"You don't have to point a gun at me. I'm plumb worn out with people pointing guns at me."

"It's necessary, *hombre.* Your ears are wood, your thinking processes like cane syrup. It is clear you're of low intelligence."

"You want to hold a gun on me? Here, I'll he'p you."

"Let go of my wrist."

"Put one through my heart. I'm tired of y'all pestering me."

"Show him," Negrito said.

"Don't underestimate me," Krill said to Cody. "I have taken many lives. I have machine-gunned a priest."

"Then pull the trigger," Cody said.

Cody's hand remained clenched tightly on Krill's wrist. He could feel Krill's pulse beating against his palm. Krill's eyes were inches from his, the onions and wine and fried meat on Krill's breath as damp as a moist cloth on

406

Cody's face. "Are you going to help me?" Krill asked.

"Maybe, if you put the gun away," Cody said.

Krill's eyes were black and as flat as paint on a piece of cardboard. "It is as you request," he said, lowering his pistol. A curtain of rain slapped against the window and across the top of the church. "My car is parked behind your church."

"Let me put on my coat," Cody said.

"You will not try to deceive us?" Krill said.

"Why should I deceive you?"

"We know of your message to your flock. You have not been our friend. You make them feel comfortable with their hatred of us."

"I think maybe you aim to kill me when this is over."

"Would that be a great loss to the world?"

"Maybe not. But that doesn't mean I'd necessarily enjoy it."

"You are a very funny man," Krill said.

They went out the door and into the rain and down the stairs to the back of the Cowboy Chapel, where Krill's gas-guzzler was parked in the lee of the building. Krill opened the trunk and lifted out a large wood box tied with rope. Cody stared at the box and wiped his mouth. "They're in there?"

"Of course."

"I've always baptized by immersion," Cody said, the rain beating on his bare head.

"What does 'immersion' mean?"

"I take people down by the creek and put them under. If the water is low, I have to dam up the creek. If everything is completely dried out, we go to the river. The creek is probably running pretty good now."

"No, we aren't going to a creek."

"Then come inside," Cody said.

They walked through the lighted coffee room and into the chapel, both of Krill's hands cupped under the rope that bound the box, the weight hitting against his knees and sides. Cody removed his coat and wiped his face on his sleeve. He noticed that Negrito never touched the box, even though it was apparent that Krill was struggling with it. Krill set the box down heavily by the altar and untied the rope and let it snake to the floor.

The only light in the room came from a small stage hung with a blue velvet curtain. The interior of the chapel was immaculate, the pews gleaming, the floors polished. For some reason, as though for the first time, Cody realized what good care he had taken of the building. He had just installed new support beams under the peaked roof, heightening the effect of a cathedral ceiling, and had reframed the windows and painted birds and flowers on the panes. He had built a stage out of freshly planed pine in hopes that next year he could put on an Easter pageant and attract more children to his Bible-study classes. The air around the stage was as sweet-smelling as a green woods in spring, not unlike a deferred promise of better things to come.

"You have a very nice church here," Krill said.

"I'm going to get a pitcher of water out of the coffee room. I'm not gonna call anybody or give y'all any trouble. What I'm doing here might not be right, but I'm gonna do it just the same."

"What do you mean, 'not right'?"

"The papists anoint at death. We baptize at birth."

"These are considerations that are of no importance to me. Go get the water. Do not let me hear you talking on a telephone."

"Don't trust him, *jefe*. He's a capon, the friend of whoever he needs to please at the moment," Negrito said.

"No, our friend here has no fear. He has no reason to lie. Look at his eyes. I think he doesn't want to live. He's a sadder man than even you, Negrito."

"Don't talk of me that way, *jefe*."

"Then don't call others a capon, you who are afraid to touch the box in which my children sleep."

Cody went into the coffee room and filled a small pitcher with tap water. His head was pounding, his breath short, but he didn't know why. Was it just fear? Krill may have been a killer, but he was no threat to him. Krill was totally absorbed with the status of his children in the afterlife. What about Negrito? No, Negrito was not a threat, either, not as long as he was under Krill's control. So what was it that caused Cody's heart to race and the scalp to shrink on his head?

This was the first time he had ever done anything of a serious nature as a minister. And he was doing it at a time when he was about to flee his church and home and become a fugitive, just like the road kid who had forged checks and ended up on a county prison farm. He walked back into the chapel, knocking against a worktable he had fashioned from two planks and sawhorses, spilling a nail gun and a claw hammer to the floor.

Krill had opened the top of the wood box and was standing expectantly beside it, his gaze fixed on Cody. "How do you want to do it?" he asked.

Cody hadn't thought about it. The images that went through his mind were too bizarre to keep straight in his head. He looked into the box and swallowed. "Put them on the edge of the stage," he said.

"They're watching," Krill said.

"They're watching?"

"From limbo. They want to be turned loose. That's what you're going to do."

"Listen, I don't know about those kinds of

things," Cody said. "Don't make me out something I'm not."

"You have cojones, *hombre*. I misjudged you." Krill placed his children, one after another, on the apron of the stage. The oldest child could not have been over four when he died. The younger ones might have been three or two. All three were wrapped tightly in cloth and duct tape. Only their faces were exposed. Their eyes were little more than slits, their skin gray, their tiny cheekbones as pronounced as wire. There was no odor of decomposition. Instead, they smelled like freshly turned dirt in a garden, or like damp shade in woods carpeted with mushrooms.

"What are you waiting for?" Krill said.

"I feel like I'm doing something that's dishonest," Cody said.

"Your words make no sense. They are the words of a man with thorns in his head instead of thoughts."

"Your children are innocent. They never hurt anybody."

"Do not make me lose my patience, *hombre*. Do what you need to do."

Cody poured water from the pitcher on the thumb and the tips of his fingers and made the sign of the cross on each child's forehead. "I baptize these children in the name of the Father, the Son, and the Holy Spirit."

"That's good. I'm proud of you, man," Krill said.

"But it's me and these two men who need absolution, Lord. These children didn't commit any sin," Cody said. "I left a woman blinded and maimed for the rest of her life, and the two men standing beside me are covered with blood splatter. We're not worthy to touch the hem of Your garment. We're not worthy to baptize these children, either, particularly the likes of me. But You're probably used to hypocrites offering up their prayers, so I doubt if two or three more liars in Your midst is gonna make a lot of difference in the outcome of things."

"You better shut your mouth, gringo," Negrito said.

"I'm done. I'm sorry for what happened to your children, Krill. If y'all are fixing to kill me, I reckon now is the time."

He walked into the coffee room, his back twitching. Out the window, he could see the deck of his house glimmer in a bolt of lightning, like the bow of an ark sliding out of a black wave. He sat down in a folding chair, his back to the doorway that gave onto the chapel. A phone was on the counter by the sink, and for a moment he thought about picking it up and dialing 911. But what for? If Krill planned to kill him, he would do it before a sheriff's cruiser could arrive. Also, Cody would eventually have to tell the sheriff or one of his deputies about the clinic bombing, and Cody had no intention of going back to jail, or at least no intention to actively aid and abet his own imprisonment.

One minute clicked on the clock mounted on the wall, then two, then three. He heard Krill's and Negrito's boots walking across the chapel floor. He closed his eyes and clasped his hands between his thighs. He could hear his breath rasping in his throat. His fingers were trembling, his sphincter constricting. Then he heard the front door of the chapel swing open and felt a rush of air sweep through the pews. A moment later, he heard the gas-guzzler start up and drive away.

Cody opened his eyes and got up from the chair and began stacking dirty cups and saucers and plates in the sink and wiping down the long table in the center of the room. He had never thought the act of cleaning up a coffee room could be so pleasurable. Why had he spent so much of his life concentrating on every problem in the world rather than simply enjoying the small pleasures that an orderly life provided? Why did wisdom come only when it was too late to make use of it?

He poured a cup of coffee and put a small teaspoon of sugar in it and gazed out the window at the rain blowing off the hills and mesas in the west. Tumbleweed was bouncing as high as a barn, smacking his church, skipping through the yard, embedding under the stairs that led to his deck. A storm was a fine and cleansing thing, he thought, not to be feared or avoided but welcomed as one would a cool finger touching one's brow.

He heard the front door open a second time, and the wind cut through the chapel and blew a stack of hymnal sheets fluttering in the air. He set down his coffee cup but remained seated at the table. "I told y'all we were done," he called into the chapel.

A small, muscular man appeared in the doorway. "Brought some friends with me," Dennis Rector said. "You met them before, but they had masks on. Look, I'm just making a buck. Don't take this as personal."

CHAPTER SIXTEEN

Anton Ling opened the back door of her house to let in her cat and smelled the smoke inside the rain. She looked up into the bluffs and, in the blackness of the storm, saw a fire burning as bright and clean as the red point of flame on an acetylene torch. She dialed 911 and reported the fire, then got into her truck and headed down the dirt road for Cody Daniels's house, a fire extinguisher bouncing on the passenger seat.

Cody Daniels knew his fate was not up for discussion when he saw that the men who had followed Dennis Rector into the chapel had not bothered to mask their faces. What he had not anticipated was the severity of design they were about to impose on his person. They pulled back the velvet curtain on the stage in the chapel and lifted him above their heads, as college kids might at a fraternity celebration, trundling him on their extended arms and hands to the wood cross he had constructed for a passion play that had never become a reality. They were smiling as though Cody were in on the joke, as though it were a harmless affair after which they would all have a drink.

The man actually in charge was not Rector but a diminutive man who spoke in an accent that sounded like Russian. His chin was V-shaped, his teeth the color of fish scale, his nose beaked, his cheeks and neck unshaved, his maroon silk shirt unbuttoned on a chest that looked almost skeletal. He wore three gold chains on his neck and a felt hat cocked jauntily on his head. He had the face of either a goat or a pixie, although the purple feather in his hatband suggested a bit of the satyr as well.

"Have you seen my good friend the Preacher lately?" he asked.

The men had set down Cody on the stage so he could face the man in the cocked hat. "The killer? I saw him once at Miss Ling's house. But I don't know him," Cody said.

"I need to find my friend the Preacher and his companion Noie Barnum. I think Ms. Ling has probably told you where they are."

"No, sir, she didn't do that."

"Why should I believe you?"

"Why shouldn't you? I don't know anything about Barnum. I wish I had never heard of him."

"But you do know Temple Dowling."

416

"I wish I'd never heard of him, either."

"Did you know he was a pedophile?"

"No."

"When you went to work for him, he didn't ask you to find young girls for him?"

"I'm not gonna even talk about stuff like that."

"Before this is over, you'll talk about many things. We have all night."

Cody felt himself swallow. The man with the Russian accent sat down in the front pew and smiled and made a gesture to his men with his right hand. His men picked up the cross that had been propped against the back wall and laid it down on the stage, then spread Cody Daniels on top of it and removed his shoes. Cody had constructed the cross out of railroad ties, and he could smell the musky odor of the creosote and oil and cinders in the grain and feel the great hardness of the wood against his head and back and buttocks and thighs.

They're only going to scare me. They won't do this, a voice inside him said.

Then he heard the *pop* of the nail gun and felt a pain explode through the top and bottom of his foot. He tried to pull himself erect, but a man on either side of him held his arms fast against the cross's horizontal beam. He closed his eyes and then opened them and stared upward into the cathedral ceiling. For the first time in his life, Cody Daniels had a

417

sense of finality from which he knew there was no escape. "I shot over the heads of poor Mexicans coming into the country," he said. "When I was a boy, I made a fifteen-year-old colored girl go to bed with me. I wrote a bad check to some old people who let me charge groceries at their store. I stole a woman's purse in the bus depot in Denver. I took a watch off a drunk man in an alley behind the Midnight Mission in Los Angeles. I almost killed a woman outside Baltimore."

"What is he saying?" said the man with the Russian accent.

"He's sorry he's on the planet," said a man holding one of Cody's arms.

"See what else he has to say," said the man with the Russian accent.

Cody heard the nail gun again and felt his other foot flatten against the vertical shaft of the cross and try to constrict against the nail that had pinioned it to the wood. This time he thought he screamed, but he couldn't be sure, because the voice he heard did not seem like his own. The popping of the nail gun continued, the muzzle working its way along the tops of his feet and his palms and finally the small bones in his wrists. He felt himself being lifted up, the top of the cross thudding against the wall behind him, his weight coming down on the nails, the tendons in his chest crushing the air from his lungs. Through a red haze, he could see the faces of his executioners looking up at him, as though they had been frozen in time or lifted out of an ancient event whose significance had eluded them. He heard himself whispering, his words barely audible, his eyes rolling up into his head.

"What'd he say?" one man asked.

" 'I'm proud my name is on her book,' " another man said.

"What the fuck does that mean?" the first man asked.

"It's from the song 'The Great Speckled Bird,' " Dennis Rector said.

"What is this speckled bird?" asked the man with the Russian accent, standing at the foot of the stage.

"In the song, it's supposed to mean the Bible," Dennis Rector replied.

The man with the Russian accent gazed through the side window at the rain striking the glass.

"What do you want us to do, Mr. Sholokoff?" Rector asked.

"Is he alive?"

"I think he is."

"You think?" Sholokoff said.

"Just tell me what you'd like me to do, sir," Rector said.

"Do I have to write it down?"

"No, sir."

"Don't come into this county again."

"I come through here to deliver the animals

to your game ranches."

"You need to take a vacation, Dennis. Maybe go out into the desert for a while. Here, I have some money for you. I'll call you when it's time to come back to work."

Sholokoff began walking down the aisle toward the front of the church.

"I did what you wanted," Rector said. "You shouldn't treat me like this. I ain't somebody you can just use and throw away."

Sholokoff continued out the front of the church into the night without replying or looking back. Dennis Rector pinched his mouth with his hand and stared at Cody Daniels and the blood running from his feet and hands and wrists and down his forearms. He stuck Sholokoff's wad of bills into his jeans. "I'm gonna get the gas can out of my car," he said. "Did you guys hear me? Don't just stand there. Take care of business."

None of the other men spoke or would look directly at him.

A local rancher flying over the church saw the flames burst through the roof of the Cowboy Chapel and reported the fire before Anton Ling did. By the time she had headed up the road to the church, the volunteer fire department truck and Pam Tibbs and Hackberry Holland and another cruiser driven by R. C. Bevins were right behind her.

"Jesus Christ, look at it," Pam said.

420

The building was etched with flames that seemed to have gone up all four walls almost simultaneously and had been fed by cold air blowing through all the windows, which probably had been systematically smashed out. The fire had gathered under the ceiling and punched a hole through the roof that was now streaming sparks and curds of black smoke into the wind.

"Somebody used an accelerant," Hackberry said.

"You think it's the same guys who broke into Anton Ling's house?"

"Or Temple Dowling's people."

"You believe in karma? I mean for a guy like Cody Daniels."

"You mean is this happening to him because he was mixed up in the bombing of an abortion clinic? No, I don't believe in karma, at least not that kind."

"I thought maybe you did," Pam said.

"Who gets the rougher deal in life? Beggars on the streets of Calcutta or international-arms merchants?"

Pam's attention was no longer focused on their conversation. "Hack, Anton Ling is getting out of her truck with a fire extinguisher."

Hackberry saw Anton Ling run from her truck directly through the front door of the church, a ropy cloud of blue-black smoke funneling from under the top of the door-frame. Pam braked the cruiser behind the

421

pickup, and she and Hackberry and R. C. Bevins and two volunteer firemen ran up the steps behind Anton Ling.

When Hackberry went inside the church, the intensity of the heat was like someone kicking open the door on a blast furnace. The walls were blackening and starting to buckle where they were not already burning, the sap in the cathedral beams igniting and dripping in flaming beads onto the pews below. Hackberry could hardly breathe in the smoke. Anton Ling went down the main aisle toward the stage, the fire extinguisher raised in front of her. Through the smoke, Hackberry could see a man crucified on a large wooden cross at the rear of the stage, his face and skin and bloodied feet lit by stage curtains that had turned into candles.

Hackberry caught up with Anton Ling, his arm raised in front of his face to protect his eyes from the heat. "Give it to me," he said.

"Take your hand off me," she said.

"Your dress is on fire, for God's sake," he said.

He tore the fire extinguisher from her hands and pulled the pin from the release lever and sprayed foam on her clothing. Then he mounted the stairs at the foot of the stage, the heat blistering his skin and cooking his head even though he was wearing his Stetson. He sprayed the area around the man on the cross while the volunteer firemen, all of them wearing ventilators, sprayed the walls with their backpacks and other firemen pulling a hose came through the front door and horse-tailed the ceiling with a pressurized jet of water pumped from the truck.

"Let's get the cross down on the stage and carry it through the door," Hackberry said. "He's going to die in this smoke."

But when Hackberry grabbed the shaft of the cross, he recoiled from the heat in the wood.

"Sheriff?" R.C. said.

"What?"

"He's gone."

"No, the wounds aren't mortal."

"Look above his rib cage. Somebody wanted to make sure he was dead. Somebody shot nails into his heart," R.C. said.

The flashlights of the firemen jittered and cut angles through the darkness and smoke, the rain spinning down through the hole in the ceiling. "Nobody from around here could do something like this," one of the firemen said.

"Not a chance, huh?" Hackberry said.

"No, this kind of thing don't happen here," the fireman said. "It took somebody doped out of his mind to do this. Like some of those smugglers coming through Miss Ling's place every night."

"Shut up," Anton Ling said.

"If they didn't do it, who did? 'Cause it

wasn't nobody from around here," the fireman said.

"Give us a hand on this, bud. We need to get Reverend Daniels off these nails and onto a gurney. You with me on that?" Hackberry said to the fireman.

Outside, fifteen minutes later, Hackberry watched two paramedics zip a black body bag over Cody Daniels's face. The coroner, Darl Wingate, was standing two feet away. The rain had almost quit, and Darl was smoking a cigarette in a holder, his face thoughtful, his smoke mixing in the mist blowing up from the valley.

"How do you read it?" Hackberry said.

"If it's any consolation, the victim was probably dead when the nails were fired into his rib cage. Death probably occurred from cardiac arrest. The main reason crucifixion was practiced throughout the ancient world was that it was not only painful and humiliating but the tendons would tighten across the lungs and slowly asphyxiate the victim. The only way he could prolong his life was to lift himself on the nails that had been driven through his feet or ankles. Of course, this caused him to increase his own torment a hundredfold. It would be hard to invent a more agonizing death."

"I'd like to believe this poor devil didn't go through all that, that he died early," Hackberry said.

"Maybe that's the way it went down, Hack," Darl said, his eyes averted. "Did you know I got a degree in psychology before I went to med school?"

"No, I didn't."

"I wanted to be a forensic psychologist. Know why I went into medicine instead?"

"No, I don't," Hackberry said, his attention starting to wander.

"Because I don't like to put myself into the minds of people who do things like this. I don't believe this was done by a group. I think it was ordered by one guy and a bunch of other guys did what they were told," Darl said.

"Go on."

"The guy behind this feels compelled to smear his shit on a wall."

"Are you thinking about Krill?"

"No. The perp on this one has a hard-on about religion."

"How about Temple Dowling?"

"Stop it. You don't believe that yourself."

"Why not?"

"Dowling is inside the system. He's not a criminal."

"That's what you think."

"No, the problem is the way *you* think, Hack. You'd rather turn the key on a slumlord than a guy who boosts banks. You've also got a grudge against Dowling's father."

"Say that again about religion."

"I have to give you an audiovisual presentation? We're talking about a murder inside a church, on a cross. It was done by a believer."

"A believer?"

"Yeah, and he's really pissed."

"How about Jack Collins?"

"Collins is a messianic killer, not a sadist."

"You should have been a cop, Darl."

"That's what I did in the army. It sucked then and sucks now."

"Why?"

"Because arresting these bastards is a waste of time," Darl said.

Hackberry walked toward his cruiser, where Pam and R.C. were waiting. The hair was singed on the backs of his arms, and the side of his face was streaked with soot. The churchyard was filled with emergency vehicles, the red and blue and white flashers pulsing in the mist.

"Wrap it up here," he said to Pam.

"You tried to save him, Hack. When you went inside, you didn't know if the roof was coming down or not," she said.

"Call Ethan Riser."

"Riser is no help," she said.

"She's right, Sheriff. Them FBI people wouldn't take time to spit in our mouths if we were dying of thirst," R.C. said.

Hackberry opened his cell phone and found Riser's number and punched it in, then walked off into the darkness and waited for

426

the call to go to voice mail. Surprisingly, the agent picked up.

"Ethan?" Hack said.

"Yeah, who'd you expect?"

Hackberry told him what had happened. "I need everything you can get me on Josef Sholokoff. I need it by noon tomorrow."

"Can't do it, partner."

"Cut this crap out, Ethan. I'm not going to put up with it."

"There're probably fifty agents in half a dozen agencies trying to shut down this guy. If you screw things up for the government, they're going to drop a brick shithouse on your head."

"Where are you?"

"In the Glass Mountains."

"Who's with you?"

"A friend or two."

"I think you're trying to take on Collins by yourself."

"Collins is long overdue for retirement."

"You don't know him. I do. Let me help you."

"I wish you'd been with me when we had bin Laden's family on the tarmac. But this one is all mine," Riser said.

"That's a dumb way to think."

"Did you ever hear of this black boxer who went up against an Australian who was called 'the thinking man's fighter'? The black guy scrambled his eggs. When a newsman asked

427

how he did it, the black guy said, 'While he was thinking, I was hitting him.' "

"Don't hang up."

"See you around, Hack. I've been wrong about almost everything in my life. Don't make my mistakes."

Early the next morning, as Jack Collins listened to Noie Barnum talk at the breakfast table in the back of the cabin, he wondered if Noie suffered from a thinking disorder.

"So repeat that for me, will you? You met the hikers on the trail and you did what?" Jack said.

"I wanted to try out that walking cane you gave me, and I made it down the hill just fine and along the edge of the creek out to the cottonwoods on the flat. That's when my breath gave out and I had to sit down on a big rock and I saw the hikers. They were a very nice couple."

"I expect they were. But what was that about the Instamatic?"

"At least I think it was an Instamatic. It was one of those cheap cameras tourists buy. They said they belonged to a bird-watching club and were taking pictures of birds along the hiking trail. They asked me to take a snapshot of them in front of the cottonwoods. It was right at sunset, and the wind was blowing and the leaves were flying in the air, and the sky was red all the way across the horizon.

So I snapped a shot, and then they asked if they could take my picture, too."

"But you've left something out of the repeat, Noie."

"What's that?"

"The first time around, you mentioned this fellow's line of work."

"He said he was a Parks and Wildlife man. He didn't look to be over twenty-five, though. He said he and his wife were on their honeymoon. She had this warm glow in her face. They put me in mind of some folks I know back home."

"And where do they live?"

"He said Austin. I think. Yeah, that was it. Austin."

"Austin. That's interesting."

Jack got up from the table and lifted a coffeepot off the woodstove with a dishrag and poured into his cup. The coffee was scalding, but he drank it without noticing the heat, his eyes fastened on Noie. "You like those eggs and sausage?"

"You know how to cook them," Noie replied. "What my grandmother would call 'gooder than grits.' "

"You're a card, Noie. So this fellow was from a law enforcement agency?"

"I don't know if I'd call Parks and Wildlife that."

"And he lives in the state capital?"

"Yep, that's what he said."

"And you let him take your photograph? Does that come right close to it?"

Noie seemed to reflect upon Jack's question. "Yeah, I'd say that was pretty much it."

In the early-morning shadows, Noie's nose made Jack think of a banana lying in an empty gravy bowl. His long-sleeve plaid shirt was buttoned at the collar, even though it was too tight for him, and his suspenders were notched into the knobs of his shoulders like a farmer of years ago might have worn them. He was freshly shaved, his sideburns etched, his face happy, but his jug-shaped head and big ears would probably drive the bride of Frankenstein from his bed, Jack thought. Noie preoccupied himself with whittling checker pieces he kept in a shoe box, and he had the conversational talents of a tree stump. Plus, Noie had another problem, one for which there seemed to be no remedy. Even though he bathed every night in an iron tub by the barn, his body constantly gave off an odor similar to sour milk. Jack decided that Noie Barnum was probably the homeliest and most single man he had ever met.

"Did it strike you as unusual that this couple would want to photograph a man they'd known for only a few minutes?"

"My grandmother used to say people who are rank strangers one minute can turn out the next minute to be your best friends."

430

"Except we're not rank strangers to the law, Noie."

"That brings me to another topic," Noie said. "I know the government wants to get their hands on me, but for the life of me, I can't figure why you're running from them."

"You've got it turned around, pard. I stay to myself and go my own way. If people bear me malice, I let them find me. Then we straighten things out."

"I bet you give them a piece of your mind, too."

"You could call it that."

"You ever take your guitar out and play it?"

"My guitar?"

"You keep the case under your bed, but you never take your guitar out and play it."

"It sounds like it was tuned to a snare drum. That's because I tuned it."

Noie's expression had turned melancholy. He set down his fork and studied his plate. "That couple I met on the trail don't mean us any harm, Jack. Particularly toward a fellow like you. I don't know why you choose to be a hermit, but you're the kindest man I've ever known, and I've known some mighty good ones."

"I believe you have, Noie."

"I worry about you because I think you're bothered about something in your past, something you probably shouldn't be fretting yourself about."

431

Through the back window, Jack could see the rain from last night's storm still dripping off the barn roof and dew shining on the windmill and steam rising off the horse tank. The blueness of the morning was so perfect, he didn't want to see the sunlight break over the hill. "We've got us a fine spot here," he said. "Sometimes if you listen, you can hear the earth stop, like it's waiting for you to catch up with it. Like it's your friend and it wants you to be at peace with it. That's why I live alone and go my own way. If you don't have any truck with the rest of the world, it cain't mess you up."

Noie seemed to study the content of Jack's words, then he stared at his plate again and put his arms below the table. "I got blood on my hands," he said.

"From what?"

"Those Predator drones."

"It's not your doing."

"Those things have killed innocent people, Stone Age peasants who don't have any stake in our wars."

"That's just the way it is sometimes."

"My grandmother used to say there're two kinds of men never to associate with. One is the man who'll shed the blood of the innocent, and the other is a man who'll raise his hand to a woman. She always said they're cut out of the same cloth. They're of Cain's seed, not Abel's." Noie picked up his fork

432

and waited for Jack to speak. Then he said, "Go ahead."

"Go ahead what?" Jack asked.

"You looked like you were fixing to say something."

"If you see that Parks and Wildlife guy again, don't be in a hurry to have your picture taken," Jack said.

"Where you headed?" Noie asked.

"I thought I might tune my guitar. I'll be up yonder in the rocks."

"Why are you taking your binoculars?"

"After a storm, there're all kinds of critters walking around, armadillos and lizards and such. They're a sight to watch."

That same morning Anton Ling received the most bizarre phone call of her life. "This is Special Agent Riser, Ms. Ling," the voice said. "You remember me?"

"I'm not sure," she replied. "You're with the FBI?"

"I was the supervising agent who talked to you after your home was invaded."

"I'd like to believe you're calling to tell me you have someone in custody."

"You don't think much of us, do you?"

"No, I don't."

"I don't blame you. I want to tell you a couple of things, Ms. Ling. We have a file on you that's three inches thick. I've tapped your phones and photographed you from a distance and looked with binoculars through your windows and invaded every other imaginable aspect of your privacy. Some of my colleagues have a genuine dislike of you and think you should have been deported years ago. The irony is you worked for the CIA before a lot of them were born. But my issue is not with them, it's with myself.

"I want to apologize for the way I and my colleagues have treated you. I think you're a patriot and a humanitarian, and I wish there were a million more like you in our midst. I think Josef Sholokoff was behind the invasion of your home. I also think we've failed miserably in putting his kind away. In the meantime, we've often concentrated our efforts on giving a bad time to people such as yourself."

"Maybe you're too hard on yourself, Mr. Riser."

"One other thing: Be a friend to Sheriff Holland. He's a lot like you, Ms. Ling. He doesn't watch out for himself."

"Sir, are you all right?"

"You might hear from me down the track. If you do, that'll mean I'm doing just fine," Riser said.

Ethan Riser closed his cell phone and continued up a deer trail that wound along the base of a butte with the soft pink contours of a decayed tooth. He passed the rusted shell of an automobile that was pocked with small-caliber bullet holes and beside which turkey buzzards were feeding on the carcass of a calf. The calf's ribs were exposed and its eyes pecked out, its tongue extended like a strip of leather from the side of its mouth. The air was still cool from the storm, the scrub brush and mesquite a darker green in the shadow of the butte, the imprints of claw-footed animals fresh in the damp sand along the banks of a tiny stream. Ethan was sweating inside his clothes, his breath coming short in his chest, and he had to sit down on a rock and rest. Behind him was a young man dressed in pressed jeans and a white shirt with pockets all over it and canvas lug-soled shoes. He wore an unpretentious black-banded straw hat with the brim turned down and a western belt with a big, dull-colored metal buckle that fit flat against his stomach.

When the young man reached the rock where Ethan was sitting, he unslung a canteen from his shoulder and unscrewed the cap and offered Ethan a drink before drinking himself. "I got to be honest with you. I think this is a snipe hunt," he said.

"Hard to say," Ethan said, blotting his face with a handkerchief.

"That fellow was standing in the shade and wearing a hat when I took his picture. He could be anybody."

"That's why I want you to go back now. I've wasted enough of your time."

"You shouldn't be out here by yourself."

"It beats twiddling my thumbs in a motel."

"Let me treat you to lunch."

"What's farther up?"

"Jackrabbits and open space and some more hills. A game ranch or two, maybe one guy running cows. A gun club has a couple of leases where some oil-and-natural-gas guys bust skeet and drink whiskey. I think there might be a cabin that somebody uses during deer season."

"Who might that be?"

"Not somebody anyone ever paid much mind to. Ethan, you don't look well. Let's go back."

"I got no reason to. You're the one on his honeymoon."

"I shouldn't have ever told you about that fellow we ran into. On the homely scale, he was just this side of a mud fence. About as harmless-looking, too. If this guy is a threat to national security, we're all in deep doo-doo."

"You also said he talked like he had a mouthful of molasses. Noie Barnum is from northern Alabama."

"A Quaker from Alabama?"

"I grant you he's a strange duck. But compared to Jack Collins, he's as normal as it gets."

"My folks have always lived here'bouts, and they haven't heard any talk about hermits

436

wandering around with Thompson machine guns."

A single-engine plane passed overhead, its shadow racing across the treetops and boulders on the sunny side of a hill.

"It's a fine day to be out and about, isn't it?" Ethan said.

"I cain't argue that."

"Help me up, will you?"

Ethan Riser's friend remained motionless.

"What are you looking at?" Ethan asked.

"I thought I saw a reflection of some kind up there on that hill." The young man removed a small pair of binoculars from a leather case on his belt and adjusted them to his eyes. "I declare, it's a book."

"A what?"

"Yeah, its pages are fluttering on top of a rock. Cain't anybody say people in Southwest Texas aren't literary. Stop looking at me like that, Ethan. There's nobody there. It's just a book somebody left on a rock."

Preacher Jack Collins was reading in the Book of Kings, the wind and sun on his face, when he glanced up long enough to see the single-engine plane coming out of the southeast, its wings tilting in the updrafts, its engine sputtering as though it were low on gas. He stepped backward into some piñon trees growing out of the rocks, his body motionless, his face pointed at the ground, his thumb inserted as a bookmark in the pages of his Bible. He heard the plane pass overhead, then the engine caught again, and when he climbed to the crest of the hill and looked between two boulders, he saw the plane disappearing over a long stretch of flat-land, its wings level and parallel with the horizon.

Feds? Maybe. Probably a rancher who was burning the valves out of his engine with ethanol. Jack resumed reading in his comfort-able spot among the rocks, the pages of the Bible as white as snow in the sunlight, the print on them as clear and sharp and defin-ing as the lettering that Yahweh had seared with a burning finger in the Mosaic tablets. For Jack, there was no such thing as "inter-pretation" of the Scripture; there was also no such thing as "metaphor." These were devices that allowed the profligate and the libertine to consecrate behavior that made Jack's stomach curdle.

Homosexuality? Sodomy? Not exactly. It was a type of behavior that somehow re-mained nameless. It was more like a memory or the shadow of a person or an event that hid behind a corner on a long street he was forced to walk in his sleep. The street was uniformly gray, as though all the color had been leached out of the concrete and asphalt and stone. There were no people on the sidewalks or in the buildings, and when he crossed an intersection, he hoped to hear a roar of traffic or at least the footsteps of other pedestrians on a side street, but instead, he heard no sound except the pounding of blood in his ears.

In his dream, he would try to wake himself before he reached the last block on the street, but his willpower had no influence on his dream. At the corner of a building on the end of the street, a figure was moving into full view on the sidewalk. The figure wore a hooded workout jacket and a print dress and pink tennis shoes and a sequined belt, as though she had dressed randomly off the rack at a Goodwill store. Everything about her was in some fashion a frightening contradiction. She looked too young and pretty for the damage the world had probably done her. Her mouth was down-hooked at the corners, her brow dimpled with anger, her eyes lit with a quiet scorn that showed she was not only privy to Jack's most private thoughts but disgusted by them. Her meanness of spirit and the depth of her disdain for him did not seem to fit with the youthfulness of her face. How could he possibly understand the physiological riddle that she presented to him?

She beckoned to him, confident he would come to her, even as she removed her belt and wrapped one end around her palm.

When he would wake from the dream, he would sit on the side of his bed, his hands clenched between his knees, filled with self-loathing that seemed to have no cause.

The degradation that invaded his soul in his sleep never left him during his daylight hours, unless he could transfer its origins onto someone else. It might have seemed a twisted way to think, Jack told himself, but he did not invent the world, nor did he create the people who had bedeviled him without cause for a lifetime or gone out of their way to reject him.

It was the latter category that bothered him most. He did not subscribe to the belief that woman was man's downfall. Nor did he blame women for their vanity or the fact that guile was sometimes their only defense against man's exploitation of their bodies. No, it was the strange light in their eyes when they looked upon his person that caused a match to flare on the lining of his stomach. They not only feared him, they were viscerally repelled by him, a man who, in his entire life, had never referred to a woman in a profane or unseemly manner.

So he had found another kind of woman, one he could trust and who was worthy of a man people on both sides of the border referred to as the left hand of God. She lived inside the Scripture and was always waiting on the attention of his eyes when he turned to the thumb-creased pages where her story began but never ended. This woman did not have one name; she had many. She was Esther, who told Xerxes he would have to walk in her blood before she would allow him to harm her people; she was Rebecca, with the water jug on her shoulder, the strong-willed, intelligent wife of Abraham's son; she was the Samaritan woman with whom Jesus had the longest conversation in the New Testament; and ultimately, she was Mary of Magdala, who subsidized Jesus' ministry and stayed with him at the cross and became the first apostle of the new religion when she announced on Easter morning, "He is risen."

The figure who hid behind the wall at the end of the street could lay no claim upon Preacher Jack as long as he had his Testament.

He heard the plane again. This time it was coming out of the northwest, retracing its earlier flight path. He crouched inside the shade of the piñon trees and removed his panama hat and focused his binoculars on the side of the plane as it passed dangerously low over the crest with at least three men inside the cabin. Jack doubted they were feds. Feds didn't take unnecessary risks; self-important corporate douchebags who paid large sums of money to shoot captured animals on a game farm did. Just for fun, Jack picked up his submachine gun and aimed through the iron sights at the tail of the plane. "Pow," he whispered as softly as smoke.

Then he realized the distraction of the plane and his idle thoughts about game farms and douchebags had just cost him. Across the flatland to the southwest, two figures had emerged from a rocky basin and were headed in his direction. In fact, if they stayed on course, they would follow the creek up into the buttes to the natural fort where he had built his cabin.

He lay on his stomach, his elbows propped on grit, his binoculars aimed through the piñon branches. Both of the figures were men. One was young and athletic-looking, a canteen slung on his shoulder, wearing a hat that a tourist or rock collector would wear. The other man had meringue hair and a flushed face and was sweating and obviously slowing the younger man. The sun was white in the sky and had robbed the morning of all its redemptive qualities. These two men, particularly the older one, were not here to enjoy the Texas landscape.

What to do? Jack asked himself.

CHAPTER SEVENTEEN

Ethan Riser got up from the place where he had been resting and followed Caleb, his young friend from Austin, across the stretch of flatland that was streaked with alkali and dotted with green brush and that was now turning into a mirror under the hot sun. Ahead, he could see hills that gave shade and the promise of a cool alcove where the stone still smelled of predawn hours and flowers that opened only at night.

"What the hell?" Caleb said.

A group of at least five dirt-bike riders were headed across the hardpan, their engines whining like dentist drills, their deeply grooved tire treads scissoring the topsoil and weaving trails of dust and smoke in the air. Sometimes a biker roared over a knoll and became airborne, or gunned his engine and deliberately lifted his front wheel off the ground, scouring a long trench with his back tire. The collective cacophony the bikers created was like broken glass inside the eardrum.

Worse, at least to Ethan and his friend, the smells of exhaust and burnt rubber were the industrial footprint of modern Visigoths determined to prove that no pristine scrap of an earlier time was safe from their presence.

"This is one bunch that needs to get closed down in a hurry," Caleb said. He opened his badge holder and held it up in front of him so the sun would reflect off it. But the bikers either ignored his attempt to identify himself or were so committed to recontouring the area that they never saw him at all.

Just as Caleb took out his cell phone, the bikers were gone, as quickly as they had arrived, disappearing over a rise, their bandannas flapping, the roar of their exhausts echoing off a butte where piñon trees grew in the rocks.

"I'll make a deal with you," Caleb said.

"What might that be?" Ethan said. The armpits of his long-sleeve blue shirt were looped with sweat, his khaki pants hanging low on his stomach, his eyes squinting in the glare, even though he was wearing a bill cap. In spite of the semiautomatic on his hip, he looked like an old man who would not concede that disease had already taken him into a country from which no amount of pretense would ever allow him to return.

"We'll go one more mile, up into the shady spot," Caleb said. "We can sit by a little creek there. The Indians carved turkey tracks on some of the rocks thereabouts. They always point due north and south. That's how they marked their route, using the stars, never one degree off. You can set a compass on them. It's just a real fine place to cool our heels."

"Then what do we do?"

"We go back. It ain't up for grabs, either," Caleb said.

"I'll sit down with you a minute, but then I'm going on."

"Sometimes we have to accept realities, Ethan."

"That I'm worn out and can't make it?"

Caleb looked at the mottled discoloration in his friend's face. "I don't think Jack Collins is out here. If he is, we'll hear about it and come back and nail his hide to a cottonwood. In the meantime, it's not reasonable to wander around under a white sun."

"I spent seven months in a bamboo cage. The man next to me had a broken back and was in there longer than I was," Ethan said.

"In Vietnam?"

"Who cares where it was?" Ethan said.

In the distance, they heard the sound of a solitary dirt bike, the engine screaming as though the back tire had lost traction and the RPMs had revved off the scale. Then there was silence.

"Collins is here," Ethan said.

"How do you know?"

Ethan looked to the north, where turkey

buzzards were turning in a wide circle against a cloudless blue sky. "Know what death smells like?"

"Yeah, like some dead critter up there. Don't let your imagination start feeding on loco weed."

"Do you smell anything?"

"No, I don't."

"I can. It's Collins. It's Collins who smells like death. He's here. When you've got death in you, you can smell it on others."

Jack did not like what he was watching. Where did this bunch get off, invading a place that was *his,* one that could have been sawed loose from the edges of Canaan and glued onto the southwestern rim of the United States? Why was the government worried about working-class people crossing the border when a bunch like this were given licenses and machines to destroy public lands? Jack knelt on a sandstone ledge, the butt of his Thompson resting by his knee, the drum magazine packed with fifty .45 rounds, the clean steel surfaces of his weapon smelling slightly of the oilcloth he had used to wipe down and polish it last night. He longed to raise the stock to his shoulder and lead the bikers with iron sights and squeeze off three or four short bursts and blow them into a tangle of machines and spinning tires and disjointed faces, not unlike the images in the

Picasso painting depicting the fascist bombing of Guernica.

One of the bikers, as though he had read Jack's thoughts, veered away from his companions and roared up the hillside toward Jack's position, his goggles clamped like a tanker's on his face, one booted foot coming down hard on the dirt to keep his machine erect, his jeans stiff with body grease, his black leather vest faded brown and yellow under his naked armpits.

The biker throttled back his engine and swerved to a stop just twenty feet below Jack's position, smoke and dust rising behind him in a dirty halo. His teeth looked feral inside his beard, his chest hair glistening with sweat. Jack laid his Thompson on a clean, flat rock and stood up in full view. "How do, pilgrim?" he said.

"Were you flashing a mirror at me?" the biker asked.

"Not me."

"I think it *was* you. You got one of those steel signal mirrors? You being cute or something?"

"You probably saw the reflection off my field glasses."

"So you want to tell me what the hell you're doing?"

"Not much. Studying on the general state of mediocrity that seems to characterize the country these days. Did you know the United

States has the highest rate of functional illiteracy in the Western world, even though we have the most libraries? What's your thought on that?"

"My thought is, I'm getting a crick in my neck looking up at you. Who the fuck you think you are?"

"The worst mistake you ever made."

The biker put a pinch of snuff under his lip. "It's been good talking to you. Keep your flopper oiled and cocked. The right girl is out there waiting for you somewhere."

"Maybe you can he'p me with a theory I have. It has to do with atavistic behavior. That means a throwback to the way things were when people hunted each other with rocks and sharp sticks. Did you ever notice that most of the fellows in biker gangs are strange-looking? By that I mean way overweight, with double hernias and beetle brows and pig noses and bulging scrotums and hair growing out of their ears. You'd think it would dawn on them."

The biker pushed his goggles up on his forehead with his thumb. There were white circles around his eyes. "What would dawn on them?"

"That ugly and stupid people find each other."

The biker twisted the gas feed with his right hand, revving his engine, making a decision. "I hate to tell you this, pal, but I don't think your opinion carries a lot of weight. If you haven't noticed, your suit looks like Sasquatch wiped his ass with it. You've got pecker tracks on your fly and enough dirt under your fingernails to grow tomatoes. If the wind turns around, I expect I'll have to put on a respirator."

Jack gazed across the flats into the distance. With his naked eye, he could not see the two hikers. The wind was up, out of the south, the piñon trees bending. The sound of a short burst might be mistaken for the backfire of a dirt bike or be lost altogether inside the wind. Yes, maybe this was an opportune moment. "You like tearing up the countryside, making lots of noise with your machines, smearing your scat on the morning? Look at me."

"What for?"

"The man who snuffs your wick is always the one you least suspect. You're tooling along, and you shoot off your mouth to the wrong fellow in the middle of a desert, and somebody stuffs a cactus plant up your ass. That's what the crossroads is all about."

"*You're* the wick snuffer?"

"Close your eyes and count to three and open them again. I have a surprise for you."

"Screw you," the biker said.

He turned his bike around and rode back down the slope, shooting Jack the finger just before heading across the flats, a fountain of gravel and silt flying from under his back wheel.

Jack let out his breath with a sigh. *Just two more seconds,* he thought. Oh well, maybe it was better that he kept his priorities straight. But before Jack could turn his attention to the hikers, the goggled, head-wrapped dirt biker had reconsidered and nullified his wise choice and spun his machine in a circle. He was headed back full-bore to the hillside, his thighs spread, his knees high, his shoulders humped, a simian throwback determined to teach a lesson to an unwashed, ignorant old man.

He veered north of Jack's position and bounced onto a narrow trail that would take him to where Jack was standing behind a boulder. Jack temporarily lost sight of him, then heard the biker gun his engine and mount a steep grade, gravel splintering off his back wheel.

Jack waited, his Thompson hanging from his right hand, his coat fluttering open in the wind, a half-smile on his face. The biker had reached the top of the grade and was bouncing up and down with the roughness of the trail as he approached Jack's position. Thirty feet below was a gully strewn with chunks of yellow chert and the dried and polished limbs of dead trees. Jack stepped out from behind the boulder and raised the muzzle of the Thompson at the biker's chest.

"I cain't blame you, pilgrim. Pride is my undoing, too," he said.

He never got a chance to squeeze the trigger. The biker saw the Thompson and threw his hands in front of his face, then plummeted off the trail straight into the gully, upside down, his machine crashing on top of him.

Jack walked to the edge of the trail and peered down at the biker and the wrecked bike, its front tire still spinning. "Ouch," he said.

The sun was blinding when Caleb approached the butte where he thought he had seen one of the bikers split off from the pack and power up the hillside. His eyes were stinging with salt, his mouth dry, and he wanted to stop and take a drink from his canteen, but he felt a cautionary sense he couldn't dispel. Why had the biker left his comrades? Who or what was up in the rocks where Caleb had seen book pages flipping in the wind? And why hadn't the biker come back down the hill? He cupped his hands around the sides of his mouth. "Hello up there!" he yelled. "I've got an injured man on the trail and need some help!"

He heard his voice echo in an arroyo that twisted toward the crest and opened into a saddle green with trees. "I don't have cellphone service," he called out. "I need somebody with a vehicle to go for help!"

Caleb began walking up the slope toward the boulder where he had seen the book. He heard slag sliding down the hill and clacking into a gully. A man appeared on a sandy patch of ground between a boulder and two piñon trees. He was wearing dark goggles and a bandanna on his head and a black leather vest that was discolored a sickly yellow under the armpits. The sun was shining in Caleb's eyes, but he could see that the man's face and arms and chest hair were streaked with blood.

"Did you spill your bike?" Caleb asked.

"I went off into the gully and busted my head. You say you got a hurt man with you?"

"He twisted his ankle."

"Let's take a look at him."

"Where's your dirt bike?"

"At the bottom of the gully."

"You cain't drive it?"

"No, it's finished."

"What's wrong with it?"

"It's broken."

"Maybe we can fix it. I'm a fair mechanic."

"I'm not?"

"We need your vehicle. I have to get my friend out of here. He's not well, and the heat has been pretty hard on him."

"That's what I said. Let's take a look at him."

"Maybe you should sit down. You've got

blood all over you."

"It's no problem. What's your friend doing out here?"

"He's an FBI agent."

"Is that a fact?"

"Where are the guys you were riding with?"

"Gone."

"They deserted you?"

"Are you a law dog, too, pilgrim?"

"Parks and Wildlife. I'm not sure I like the way you're talking to me."

"Don't Parks and Wildlife people carry weapons? I would. This area is full of rattlers."

"Where's the cut on your head? I don't see it."

"You're pretty damn inquisitive for a man asking other people's he'p. How far back is your FBI friend?"

"Not far. Are the other bikers coming back or not?"

"You cain't tell about a bunch like that. Y'all should know. They tear up the countryside wherever and whenever they want, and y'all don't do squat about it."

"They?"

The man in goggles pressed the back of his wrist to his mouth, as though his lip were split or his teeth had been broken or knocked out. Then Caleb realized there was nothing wrong with his mouth or teeth and that he was making a decision, one that would probably have irreversible implications for both of them.

"This is my neighborhood. You made your bed when you came into it," the man in goggles said.

"This is public land. It belongs to the people of Texas. We'll go wherever we please in it."

"Don't pretend you don't know who I am."

Caleb wet his lips and closed and opened his hands at his sides. "Give yourself up, Mr. Collins."

"You're honeymooning here?"

"What's it to you?"

"Answer me."

"I was recently married, if it's any of your business."

"Oh, it's my business, all right. You should have stayed with your woman. You've spat in the soup, fellow."

"I'm going to walk out of here now. When I come back, I hope you're gone. If you're not, you're going to be in custody."

Jack Collins thumbed the goggles off his face and threw them aside. He reached behind the boulder and lifted up the Thompson and pointed it at Caleb's midsection. "Why'd you wander in here, boy? Why'd you let the FBI use you?"

Caleb felt the muscles in his face flex, but no words came out of his mouth.

"You have cuffs or ligatures on you?" Jack

454

Collins said.

"No."

"Where's the agent?"

"In a cool place out of the sun. Let him be."

"What's his name?"

"Riser."

"Ethan Riser?"

"You know Ethan?" When Collins didn't answer, Caleb said, "You killed the biker?"

The bumps and knots and sallow skin and unshaved jowls that constituted the face of Jack Collins seemed to harden into a mask, as though his breathing and all the motors in his head had come to a stop. His eyes became lidded, without heat or anger or emotion of any kind. Then his chest began to rise and fall. "Sorry to do this to you, kid," he said.

"Buddy, before you —"

"Don't talk." Jack Collins's eyes closed, and his mouth formed into a cone, as though he were devolving into a blowfish at the bottom of a dark aquarium, a place where he was surrounded by water that was so cold he had no feeling at all.

Ethan was sitting on a flat rock inside an alcove that had a sandy floor and was protected on the north side by a big sandstone boulder. He heard an abrupt sound inside the wind, like a burst of dirty thunder, and for a moment thought the plane with the sputtering engine had returned or the dirt biker had cranked up his machine and was gunning across the hardpan. Riser stood up and stepped from behind the boulder. Out of the white haze, he saw a figure walking toward him, a man wearing a leather vest with a panama hat slanted on his head, his face swollen with lumps that looked like infected insect bites, his trousers stuffed into the tops of his cowboy boots. The man was holding a Thompson submachine gun with his right hand. "Need to talk," he said.

Riser stepped back quickly behind the boulder and pulled his semiautomatic from the holster on his hip.

"You hear me? It doesn't have to end the way you think," the man called out.

Ethan inched forward and looked around the edge of the boulder. The man with the Thompson was gone, probably up in the rocks from which he could follow a deer trail over the top of the alcove or remain where he was and wait for Ethan to come out in the open.

"You sick down there?" the man said from somewhere up in the piñon trees.

"Come down here and find out," Ethan said.

"You're not calling the shots, Mr. Riser."

"Other people know where I am."

"No, I think you're out here on your own hook."

"Where's Caleb?" Ethan said.

"He's not here."

"Where is he?"

"He's somewhere else."

"You killed him?"

"I'm going to ask you a question. You need to think carefully before you answer. If you lie, I'll know it. Are you the agent who burned me out?"

"No. What did you do to Caleb?"

"Did you *order* my house burned?"

"That wasn't a house. It was a shack. You were squatting in it."

"Did you order it burned? Did you burn my Bible?"

"No, I had nothing to do with it. Where's Caleb?"

"Who told you where I was?"

"No one."

"It was your buddy Caleb, wasn't it? He and his wife took a picture of Noie Barnum and showed it to you."

"You've got your facts turned around, Collins. We received reports on you from the Border Patrol. They'd rounded up some illegals who'd seen you up here."

"Why would wetbacks take note of a fellow like me?"

"It's your BO. As soon as they mentioned it, we knew who they were talking about."

"Throw your piece out on the sand. Throw your cuffs out, too."

"You're a public fool, Collins. You're not a religious warrior or an existentialist hero. You're a basket case who probably killed his mother. You murder young girls and pose as a political assassin. Let me tell you a story. You know what the Feast Day of Fools was in medieval times? It was a day when all the lower-level dysfunctional people in the church were allowed to do whatever they wanted. They got sodden drunk, fist-fought in front of the altar, farted to hymnal music, buggered each other and each other's wives and sodomized animals or anything with a heartbeat, and had a glorious time. They got it out of their system, and the next day they all came to church hungover and were forgiven.

"Five hundred years ago there was a place for a pitiful fuck like you, but now there isn't. So you trail your BO around the desert and terrorize unarmed people and pretend you're the scourge of God. You need to sew bells on your suit, Collins. Maybe you can get a job as a jester in a medieval reenactment."

Ethan waited for Collins's response. The only sound he heard was the wind.

"I rumpled your feelings?" Ethan said. "Hypersensitivity usually goes back to a person's problems with his mother. Sexual abuse or constant criticism, that kind of thing. If so, we've got a special titty-baby unit we can get you into."

Ethan waited, his palm perspiring on the

458

grips of his semiauto. A gust of wind blew a cloud of alkali dust into his face. He wiped his eyes clear and tried to see above the top of the alcove without exposing himself to a burst of submachine-gun fire. He stepped back into the shade, letting his eyes readjust. Then he knew something was wrong. The alkali dust had not dissipated but had grown thicker. Above, he heard footsteps inside dry brush and the sound of tree branches being broken and dragged over a stone surface. He smelled an odor like greasewood burning and realized he had not been looking at alkali dust but at smoke from a fire, one that was being stoked into a blaze that was so hot, it immediately consumed whatever was dropped into it.

"You burn a man out of his house and excuse yourself by calling it a shack?" Collins said. "Now it's your turn, Agent Riser. See how you like it."

A rain of burning grass and tree limbs and trash scraped out of a deadfall showered down on the opening to the alcove, filling the air with smoke and soot and red-hot cinders. Then Collins pushed another load of dry fuel down on top of it.

"I can keep doing it all day, Mr. Riser," Collins said. "Or you can throw your weapon on the far side of the fire and walk out after it. I won't shoot."

"You were the right age for Vietnam. Where

were you when the rest of us went?" Ethan said.

"Those were your enemies, not mine. I never injured a man who didn't ask for it."

"How about Caleb?"

"Maybe he's still breathing. Come out of your hiding place and we'll go see."

Ethan charged through the flames, his clothes catching fire, his eyebrows and hair singeing. He whirled about, raising his semi-auto, hoping for a clear shot at Preacher Jack. But the black silhouette he saw imprinted against the sky was armed with a magic wand that burst with light brighter than the sun, brighter than the fire eating Ethan's skin, even brighter than the untarnished shield to which he had dedicated most of his adult life. The Thompson seemed to make no sound, but its bullets struck his body with the impact of an entire hillside falling on top of him.

Jack Collins climbed down the slope, careful not to scrape the wood or the steel surfaces of his submachine gun on the rocks, and removed the semiautomatic from Ethan's hand and the cell phone from the pocket of his khakis. He flipped open the phone and idly reviewed the most recently dialed numbers. The first name to appear on the list was not one he was expecting to see.

Riser had been in touch with *her* only that morning. Why?

He tossed the cell phone into the fire, and for just a moment he thought he saw the face of the Chinese woman called La Magdalena rise from the flames.

CHAPTER EIGHTEEN

Six hours later, Hackberry Holland sat numbly in his office chair, his forehead propped on his fingers, and listened to the sheriff of Brewster County read from the notes he had made at the crime scene. As in all crime-scene reports, the factual nature of the language served only to further depersonalize and degrade the humanity of the victims: The bodies had been discovered by the friends of the missing dirt biker; Ethan Riser was DOA; Riser's companion on the trail, Caleb Fry, was in a coma and barely alive; the dirt biker had died of either a broken neck or massive head trauma; the wounds to Ethan Riser indicated that he had been shot many times after mortality had occurred, to the degree that he had to be identified by his possessions.

"Are there any witnesses at all?" Hackberry asked. "Did anyone see Collins in the vicinity?"

"No, we've got no visuals on anything," the

sheriff in Brewster County said.

"Have you talked to the other bikers?"

"Yeah, they say their bud saw somebody flashing something at them from the rocks. Their bud was a lone wolf and liked to get into it with other people. By the way, we found his vest not far from where the agent died. Collins is here, isn't he? In my county?"

"That'd be my guess. Is the FBI there yet?"

"Like flies on shit. There's another detail I ought to pass on. There was a melted cell phone in the ashes of the fire. I suspect it was the FBI agent's. It was too deep inside the burn ring to have fallen there. Why would the shooter throw the guy's cell phone in the fire?"

"Fingerprints?"

"Maybe, but he didn't bother to pick up the brass."

"The day you understand Jack Collins is the day you check yourself in to rehab for the rest of your life," Hackberry said.

"Where do you think he's hid out?"

"The Unabomber lived in Lincoln, Montana, for ten years. He had no plumbing or electricity in his cabin. Forest Service personnel think he shot at their planes. The locals considered him a regular guy. Maybe Collins isn't hiding. Maybe he's out there in full view. It's a sign of the times. The standards for normalcy find a new low with each passing day."

"That's not funny."

"Who said it was?"

After Hackberry hung up, he called R. C. Bevins and Pam Tibbs into his office and told them of the conversation he'd just had.

"I'm sorry, Hack," Pam said.

"There is nothing for us to feel sorry about. We honor Ethan's memory by nailing the bastard who killed him," Hackberry said. "R.C., I want you to go up to Brewster and get a topography map and look up the land records of every piece of property within five miles of the crime scene."

"What am I looking for?" R.C. asked.

"Collins likes to take on the personae of obscure writers. Google the names on the land titles and see what pops up. Pam, you and I need to do something about Josef Sholokoff. For two years his name has been coming up in our investigation of Collins's background. Sholokoff used Collins as a hit man, and he was also the business partner of Temple Dowling. Plus, Anton Ling says Sholokoff was mixed up with shipping arms to the Contras in the 1980s. He's gotten a free pass for over twenty years, I think in part because he was a useful tool for some guys in the government."

"What do you want to do about him?" she asked.

"He's a Russian criminal. Maybe he needs a reminder of what life in Russia can be like,"

Hackberry said.

After Pam and R.C. had left his office, he felt no better for his rhetoric and could not rid himself of the words the sheriff in Brewster had used to describe the wounds to Ethan Riser's body. What had Ethan said to Collins that had filled him with such animus? Collins had always been cold-blooded and methodical when he killed, not driven by emotion or impetuosity. Before dying, Ethan had gotten to him. A remark about his mother? Maybe, but not likely. Collins had no illusions about the woman who had raised him. It was something else. Something that had to do with his image of himself. What greater bane was there for a narcissist than deflation of his ego? In his mind, Collins believed himself a Titan, a warrior-angel with a wingspan that could blot out the moon. Ethan had been well read, intelligent, and con-wise and had thought of Collins as a noisy, misogynistic nuisance who would eventually be greased off the planet. Somehow, before he died, he told Collins that in the great scheme of things, Collins had the wingspan of a moth and was hardly worth the effort of swatting with a rolled magazine. With luck, Hackberry might have a chance to deliver the same insult.

Something else was bothering him. Historians wrote of battles as epic events involving thousands of soldiers acting in concert, all of them directed by a brilliant strategist such as Alexander or Napoleon or Stonewall Jackson. But for the grunts on the line, the reality was otherwise. They took home a limited perspective, a few shards of memory, flashes of light, a name being called out, the whirring sound of a projectile flying past one's ear. In the larger context of the battle, the individual's perspective was little more than a sketch on the back of one's thumbnail. The invasion at Inchon saved United Nations troops from being pushed into the sea. But Hackberry remembered only one detail from it. A group of marines under the command of a young naval lieutenant had captured a lighthouse. They were aided by Korean civilians. Had they not held the lighthouse, the peninsula would have been lost. In retaliation, the North Koreans began executing civilians. Some of the civilians armed themselves with captured weapons and fought back at a railway station, where they filled suitcases from the baggage room with dirt and barricaded themselves inside. They should have survived, but they didn't. A shell from either a railroad gun or an offshore battery hit the depot and killed everyone inside. The shell must have contained phosphorus, because the bodies of the dead were burned uniformly black, as though they had been roasted on a slow fire, the skin swelling until it burst.

Hackberry had never forgotten the image of the dead Koreans and their frozen posture inside the ruins of the building. Nor would he ever forget the image of Ethan Riser dying in a spray of .45-caliber bullets fired into his face by Jack Collins. People said time healed. If it did, Hackberry thought, the pocket watch he had inherited from his father must have been defective.

"Pam?" he said through the open door without getting up.

"Yes, sir?" she answered.

"See if Anton Ling is home. If she is, tell her we're on our way out."

"What's up?" Pam said, standing in the doorway.

"It's time for Miss Anton to get honest about her past."

"You talking about that Air America bullshit?"

"No, arms to northern Nicaragua, courtesy of Josef Sholokoff. Would you stop using that language?"

Pam looked out the window at a woman coming up the sidewalk. "She must be psychic," Pam said.

Hackberry wasn't sure whether there was a thread of resentment or jealousy in Pam's voice. He had given up dealing with the mysteries of eros and was sure that at some linguistic juncture in ancient times, the words "error" and "erotic" had sprung from the same root. The truth was, he could not define his own feelings about either Anton Ling or Pam Tibbs. One reminded him of his dead wife, Rie, who would always remain the love of his life. The other woman, Pam Tibbs, was as brave as Rie had been and equally protective of him, even to the point of causing him public embarrassment, and the look in her eyes always told him that she saw the young man inside him and not the man who was almost eighty. Also, she gave no quarter in either love or war, and her level of loyalty was ferocious. No man could have a better companion as a lover or friend. He could have worse problems, he thought. But damn it to hell, an old fool was still an old fool.

Anton Ling walked past Maydeen and R.C. and Felix and a bail bondsman and Pam Tibbs and a drunk cuffed to a D-ring as though they were not there. "I just heard about Ethan Riser on the radio," she said.

"Chief Deputy Tibbs and I were just about to come out to your place," Hackberry said.

"Agent Riser called me this morning on his cell phone. I wish I'd gotten ahold of you."

"Called you about what?"

"He apologized for invading my privacy. He told me to be a friend to you. He sounded like a man making his peace. I asked him if he was all right. He said if I heard from him again, that would mean he was doing just

468

fine. Why are all these people standing around here?"

"We work here," Pam said.

"Do you want to sit down, Miss Anton?" Hackberry said.

"No."

"How do you know Ethan was on a cell phone?" Hackberry asked.

"He was breaking up. Jack Collins just called me."

"Wait a minute. I don't understand. Collins called to tell you Ethan was dead?"

"No. He didn't mention anything about Mr. Riser. He asked me if I had given the FBI his location. I told him I didn't have any idea what he was talking about. He asked if I had learned of his whereabouts from the illegals who come to my house. When I told him I had no interest in either him or the FBI, he told me I was a Jezebel. On the way into town, I heard the news report about Agent Riser on the radio."

"Sit down," Hackberry said.

"No. I have to go."

"Where?"

"Home. Collins is insane. I have people coming tonight. He'll take his revenge on them."

"I doubt it. Come in and close the door, Deputy Tibbs."

"You're holding me?" Anton Ling said.

"The sheriff in Brewster County found

469

Ethan's cell phone inside the ashes of a bonfire that Collins set. Collins probably threw the phone there after he recovered the list of calls Ethan had made in the last few days. That's why Collins associated you with Ethan discovering his whereabouts. He also has a way of blaming women for most of his problems."

"Why were you coming out to my house?"

"We want Josef Sholokoff in a cage," he said.

"Then talk to the government agencies that have let him run loose all these years," Anton said.

"You recognized a man outside your hospital room. He was connected with smuggling guns into Nicaragua and introducing cocaine into the United States. He was with the guy whose face you put a screwdriver in. You've worked intimately with Sholokoff's people, and you have information about them that we don't. You have to give us some leads, Miss Anton."

"I don't have any."

"What you mean is you don't want to give us any," Pam said.

"Do I look like a professional informant?" Illogically, Anton said, "Most of the people I knew years ago are probably dead."

"This isn't Cambodia. We're sick of people working out their problems at our expense," Pam said. "It's time to get your head out of

470

your ass, Ms. Ling."

"Why don't you get your head out of yours?" Anton said. "The electorate in this area puts people in office who belong on chain gangs."

"I guess that includes the sheriff," Pam said.

"You know what I mean," Anton said.

"No, I don't," Pam said. "We know you're sheltering illegals. We also know you were part of an Underground Railroad that hid them in Kansas back in the eighties. But we look the other way. Maybe you should decide who your real friends are."

Hackberry felt a pain spreading through his head as though someone were tightening a vise on his temples. "This isn't solving our problem," he said.

"The man I recognized outside my hospital room was a handler of animals," Anton said. "Exotic animals of some kind. I didn't like him. But I was part of the gun-smuggling operation, Sheriff Holland. I'm responsible for the deaths of innocent people."

"Did this guy supply exotic animals to game farms?" Hackberry asked.

"Maybe. He talked about it. I remember his complaining about driving a truckload of them into West Texas," Anton said.

"Where in West Texas?" Hackberry asked.

"This was twenty-five years ago."

"Where?" he said.

She shook her head. "I don't remember.

He probably didn't say. Wait a minute. He made a nasty joke once about a brothel in Phnom Penh. It specialized in . . . I don't care to talk about what it specialized in."

"Oral sex?" Hackberry said.

"Yes," she replied. "He said he had a friend in Texas who used to hang out in this particular brothel. The friend owned a nightclub in Texas."

"*La Rosa Blanca?* The White Rose?" Hackberry said.

"Pardon?" she said.

"Bingo," Pam said.

The orange neon sign on the roof of Joe Tex's saloon glowed against a turquoise sky that was bottom-rimmed in the west by strips of red and black clouds. The evening could not have been more beautiful. The wind was balmy and out of the south and smelled of distant rain. An obsolete windmill was clattering by an abandoned loading pen on the hardpan, like a beneficent reminder of a grand tradition as well as the potential the land held for all those who lived humbly upon it. Even the tractor-trailers wending their way down the two-lane through compacted hills that resembled ant mounds seemed like a testimony to the industrial success of a new nation rather than harbingers of pollution and the loss of Jefferson's agrarian vision.

There were few patrons in the saloon when Hackberry and Pam entered through the front door. Joe Tex was stocking his beer cooler behind the bar; Rosanne Cash was singing on the jukebox; the lacquered pine logs in the walls seemed to exude a golden light like warm honey. Joe Tex was smiling when he lifted his head from his work, his hair as shiny and black as a raven's feathers, his rolled shirtsleeves exposing his vascular arms. "My favorite sheriff and lady deputy," he said. "What are y'all having?" He propped his arms on the bar, waiting. The top of his white cowboy shirt was unsnapped, and his chest hair was fanned out on his skin like the points of a star. His eyes were so lidless in their intensity that he seemed incapable of blinking.

"Your name has come up in an investigation, Joe," Hackberry said, setting his hat crown-down on the bar. "Not that you did anything wrong. We just thought you could help us figure out a thing or two."

"Who was the shooter on the grassy knoll?" Joe Tex said.

"No, it has to do with the name of your saloon," Hackberry said.

"I remember now. Lime and soda and ice, right?" Joe Tex said. "How about you, Miss Pam?"

"Who was the White Rose?" she asked.

"My wife. She was a stripper in Big D. She

actually worked in Jack Ruby's old joint."

"We did some checking on that, Joe," Hackberry said. "Nobody can find any record of your being married."

"I guess that's their problem. My wife and I got hitched at a drive-by window in Matamoros."

"I heard you might have done some quasi-governmental work in Cambodia," Hackberry said.

"I'm not big on revisiting the past, Sheriff. I was a GI on the Mekong River. It took me to lots of places, most of them better forgotten."

"You fly in and out of the Golden Triangle at all?" Hackberry asked.

"I don't remember. I have a bunch of big blank holes in my memory when it comes to Indochina. I'll tell you one thing, though. I'm not ashamed of anything I did over there."

"I'm not questioning your service to your country," Hackberry said. "I'm interested in a man by the name of Josef Sholokoff. A man who works for him helped torture a local woman and maybe crucify Cody Daniels. That man was in the company of a guy who knows you, Joe. He used the name of your saloon. He used to deliver exotic animals to game farms. Does that ring any bells?"

"I guess I'm tone-deaf on that one."

"The White Rose was a whorehouse in Phnom Penh, right?" Hackberry said.

"Could be. Cherry Alley wasn't an open-air fruit market in Tokyo. But that doesn't mean I went there to find out. I got to get back to work."

"What you need to do is take the shit out of your mouth," Pam said. "I pulled Cody Daniels's feet and hands off the nails someone used to hang him on a cross inside a burning building. He was alive when his killers started the fire. With good luck, he died of smoke inhalation."

"I saw it on the news. You think something like that is lost on me? Years ago I knew some intelligence people. But I don't remember anything about some guy who hauled exotic animals around. Unless y'all got a warrant, get out of my establishment."

"You got a meth problem, Joe?" Hackberry said.

Joe Texas leaned across the bar. His skin was so dark that in the shadows, it looked like it had been removed from a tannery and kneaded and softened and fitted on his bones; his eyes stared out of the sockets like those of a man living inside a costume. "You don't have a clue about what you're dealing with," he said. "You want to end up a bump out there in the desert? Just keep fucking with the wrong people. You'll wish you were still drunk and humping underage Mexican whores, Sheriff. Y'all aren't the only people with access to security files. Get a warrant. In

475

the meantime, I'm D-D-D. That stands for 'deaf, dumb, and don't know.' "

That night Hackberry went out to his barn and clicked on the interior lights. The row of bulbs on the ceiling glowed with a chemical-like iridescence inside the humidity. Bales of green hay bound with red twine were scattered on the concrete pad that extended between the stalls located on either side of the building, and a speed bag and an Everlast rebound board were mounted on the back wall of the rear stall. Hackberry's barn was not a bad refuge from the cares of the world. He began hitting the bag with a rotating motion, landing each blow on the heel of his fist, thudding the bag up into the circular rebound board before it could swing full-out on its cable, increasing his velocity until the bag became a blur, the rhythm as steady and loud as a drumroll.

But he could not clean Joe Tex's words out of his head. Hackberry had made no secret of his life as a drunk and an adulterer and a frequenter of brothels in northern Mexico. The age of the prostitutes had seemed insignificant at the time, as callous as that sounded. In daylight he would not have recognized most of them. Sometimes he went into a blackout, and when he woke sick and hungover in the morning, the only knowledge he had of the previous night came from his empty wallet and the mileage on his odometer. He suspected that the women or teenage girls who touched his body had done so with indifference if not with revulsion. The odium was his, not theirs. The man with a sprawling ranch and a Navy Cross and a Purple Heart hidden away in a seabag, the man who drove a Cadillac with fins and who had a law degree from Baylor, was the sybaritic visitor to a row of shanties built along an open sewage canal. Shame and dishonor were his flags, and self-loathing was his constant companion. His presence or his absence in the life of these girls or women was as significant as a hangnail they might clip off and drop outside into a waste bucket.

Even knowing these things, he had repeated the same behavior over and over and hadn't bothered to question himself about a form of immorality that went far beyond his unfaithfulness to Verisa, who'd had at least two affairs that he knew of, one with a banker in Victoria and one with an airline pilot who'd flown an F-86 in Korea. In Hackberry's mind, his greater sin was his sexual exploitation of girls and women who had no choice in the world. There was no way to excuse or rationalize his callousness toward the deprivation and sadness that constituted their lives. The fact that his behavior was documented in a security file was of no concern to him. The fact that a man like Joe Tex could have access to it and taunt him with it was.

He hit the bag one last time with the back of his fist and walked to the front of the barn and flicked on the outside flood lamp. His two foxtrotters were watching him from the far side of their water tank. "What are you guys up to?" he said.

Love That Santa Fe blew air through his lips, and Missy's Playboy whipped his tail back and forth across his hind legs.

Hackberry had nailed an apple basket against the side of the barn, roughly approximating the heart of the strike zone for a six-foot batter. He took a fielder's glove and a canvas bag of baseballs out of the tack room and carried them to the improvised mound he had constructed sixty feet from the apple basket. "Watch this," he said to the horses. "The batter is crowding the plate and staking out territory he hasn't earned. We're going to serve up a forkball to help him in his search for humility."

Hackberry spread two fingers on the ball, notching the stitches, hiding the pitch in his glove, then let fly at the basket, whipping the pitch overhand, throwing his shoulder and butt into it. The ball smacked into the wood, just wide of the apple basket, and the two horses whirled and plunged out of the light and into the darkness, making a wide circle and returning, their tails flagging.

"Okay, you got that out of your system?"

Hackberry said to the horses. "Now watch. This next one is a changeup, to be followed by a slider and then my favorite."

For the changeup, he held the ball in the back of his palm and floated it into the basket and then buzzed the slider wide and knocked a slat out of the basket.

"All right, forget the slider," he said. "The ball is getting thrown around the infield. The last guy to touch it before it comes back to me is the shortstop. This guy has no ethics at all. He's cut a hole in the pocket of his glove, and between his palm and the pocket is a wet sponge. When the ball comes back to me, it feels like it's been through a car wash."

Hackberry put two fingers in his mouth, then fired an in-shoot into the basket that sounded like silk ripping.

"What do you think of that, fellows?" he said.

He realized he had lost the attention of his foxtrotters and that they were looking at something out in the darkness, something just on the edge of the floodlight's glare.

"I didn't mean to give you a start," a voice said.

"Who are you?" Hackberry asked.

"Dennis Rector is my name. You're Sheriff Holland, right?"

"I was when I woke up this morning. What are you doing on my property?"

"I got a couple of hypotheticals to ask you."

"Where's your vehicle?"

"Out yonder, on the road, just about out of gas."

Dennis Rector walked farther into the floodlight. He was a small man whose head was shaved and whose skin was white and whose body looked molded from plastic. His jeans were too large for him and were rolled in big cuffs above his work boots. His shirt was torn and the side of his face scraped.

"You carrying a weapon, Mr. Rector?"

"No, sir. I'm not a violent man. But I know men who are. Men you're looking for."

"You're looking right into a flood lamp, Mr. Rector. But the pupils of your eyes are as big as inkwells. Can you tell me why that is?"

"I'm a truck driver, sir. I've pulled Monarch and Wolf Creek Pass when it was ten below, and I've gone sliding sideways on ice at forty miles an hour through Pagosa Springs. I've driven from Manhattan to Los Angeles in one haul, and I mean not ever shutting it down, either. I used to do whites on the half-shell, then I got into black beauties and have never quite got rid of their appeal. Those babies will flat cook your mush, I'm here to testify. Know a man name of Josef Sholokoff?"

"What about him?" Hackberry said.

"What about him, he asks," Dennis Rector said, as though a third party were there. "What this is about is I ain't no Judas Iscariot. I don't like getting treated as one, either. I don't like getting run through brambles and chased across the countryside like a fugitive from a chain gang is what I'm talking about. I shaved my head to disguise myself. I do not like this way of life."

"That's interesting. I think you might like our detox unit, Mr. Rector. You can get some medication and therapy and maybe enter a program. Let's take a walk up to the house, and I'll arrange some transportation, and in the meantime you can tell me about Josef Sholokoff."

"You can keep your detox and three hots and a cot, Sheriff, 'cause that ain't why we're having this meeting of the minds. I did what I was asked and got involved in something that just ain't my way. I know how things work. A bunch decides to do something really awful, and I mean awful, as bad as it gets, something that's worse than any nightmare, and one man gets blamed for it and becomes the stink on horse pucky."

"You have a point," Hackberry said. "There's a chair by the tack room. Take a load off, and I'll be right back with a couple of sodas. How's that sound?"

"I could use it, yes, sir."

Hackberry walked up to the house and called for a cruiser. Then he took two cans of ginger ale from the icebox and dropped two pieces of fried chicken in a paper bag and walked back down to the barn. He saw no

481

sign of Dennis Rector. The moon was brilliant over the hills, the wind sweeping in the trees, his horses blowing in the pasture. The lights were still on inside the barn, and he heard a sound like the speed bag thumping irregularly against the rebound board in the rear stall, as though it were being struck by someone who did not know how to use it.

Then he noticed that the chair he kept on the concrete pad was gone and that the tack room door was ajar. He dropped the two cans of soda and the bag of fried chicken into the dirt and ran inside the barn and threw open the tack room door. The chair lay on its side. Above it, Dennis was still swinging from the impact of the drop, his throat wrapped tightly with horse reins, his arms twitching, his neck broken.

CHAPTER NINETEEN

Preacher Jack Collins was not in a good mood. Since the long drive from the cabin on the creek, he had said little to Noie Barnum. Also, he had offered no explanation for his and Noie's sudden departure, scowling whenever Noie asked a question, brooding and moving his lips without sound as though sorting out his thoughts with a hay fork. The decrepit stucco house they had moved into had been a home for bats and field mice and smelled of the damp earth under the floors. The toilet and sink and bathtub were streaked with orange rust and filled with the shells of dead roaches. In the back of the house was a butte that resembled a row of giant clay columns eroding side by side, creating an effect that was both phallic and effete. The front windows gave onto a long sloping plain and a junkyard that was surrounded by a twelve-foot fence with spools of razor wire on top. In the late-afternoon sun, the compacted and polished metal in the junkyard and the razor wire protecting it took on the sharpened brilliance of hundreds of heliographs.

Jack had flung his suitcase on a bunk bed, then brought his guitar case inside and set it on the kitchen table and unsnapped the top.

"What's that?" Noie asked.

"They were called trench sweepers in the Great War," Jack replied, setting the Thompson and two ammunition pans and box upon box of cartridges on an oily cloth. "They were manufactured too late to be used in the trenches, though. That's how guys like John Dillinger and Baby Face Nelson ended up with them."

"What are *you* doing with one, Jack?"

"Home protection."

"I don't get it."

"Get what?"

"Anything we're doing."

"There're people out there who want to hurt me. It's not a difficult concept."

"Hurt you why?"

"I'm hiding you, boy." Noie's adenoidal accent was starting to wear on him. Jack threaded a cleaning patch through the tip of a metal pod and dripped three drops of oil on the patch and pushed it down the muzzle of the Thompson. He worked the rod up and down, then inserted a piece of white paper in the chamber and looked down the inside of the barrel at the whorls of reflected light spinning through the rifling. "Did you ever take classes in speech or diction?"

"I was an engineering major."

"It shows."

"Pardon?"

Jack's eyes wrinkled at the corners. "Don't let my tone bother you. I got to stop fretting myself about our enemies. Some people aren't made for the world. That's the likes of us. That's why we're hunted."

"A man deals his own play. The world doesn't have much to do with it," Noie replied. "That's the way I look at it."

With his fingertips, Jack began loading one of the ammunition pans, lifting each .45 cartridge from its individual hole in a Styrofoam block and lowering it into a pod inside the circular magazine, as though he took more pleasure in the ritual than its purpose. "All I ever wanted from people was to be let alone. Learn it soon or learn it late, a man doesn't have peace unless he's willing to make war."

"Have you shot somebody with that thing?"

"They shot themselves."

"How so?" Noie asked, his throat clotting.

"They line up to do it. They cain't wait."

"That doesn't answer the question."

How was Jack to explain that he had two optical screens in his head? On one screen were people who caused him trouble or threatened his life. On the other screen was the backdrop against which they had originally appeared, but they were airbrushed from it. *Poof,* just like that. The alteration of the images had little to do with him. One side of his brain spoke to the other side. One side defined the problem; the other side took care of it. The people who disappeared from the screen designed their own fate and were responsible for their own diminution.

"Look out the front window," Jack said.

"At the two-lane?"

"I'm talking about the junkyard. You think anything inside it is of any real value?"

"Not unless you're keen on junk."

"But the man who owns the junkyard has razor wire on top of all his fences. That wire probably cost a lot more than anything anybody might steal off those rusted-out or compacted cars. The whole place is the automotive equivalent of a warthog. The wire deflates the value of the property around it and makes Nebraska look like the French Riviera. But nine out of ten people in this county would defend the guy's right to build a huge eyesore on the highway they paid to have poured."

"What's that have to do with your machine gun?"

"Not every asylum has walls."

"They're out to get us?"

"The government has been trying to put me out of business for twenty years. So has a guy by the name of Josef Sholokoff. His ex–

486

business partner, Temple Dowling, would like to see you dead, and Sholokoff would like to see you in a cage so he can sell you to Al Qaeda and screw Dowling. In the meantime, the likes of us are considered criminals. Am I getting through to you?"

"There's gunpowder residue on your cleaning patch."

"That's right."

"You fired your Thompson recently?"

Jack snapped the top back on the metal drum and began twisting the winding key. "The Oriental woman gave up our location to the FBI. At least that's my belief until I find out different."

"Miss Anton? She dressed my wounds. She wouldn't inform on me."

"How about on me?"

"You didn't harm her, did you?"

"No, I did not. But a couple of other guys paid her tab."

"What are you telling me?"

"You want to be back in Krill's custody? Time to take the scales from your eyes, son. Who do you think Krill used to work for? The United States government is who."

"What have you done, Jack?"

"Nothing. I told you that at the outset. Moses slew two hundred of his people for erecting the golden calf. He killed, but he didn't murder. His followers got what they deserved."

487

"Tell me if you killed somebody. Just say it."

Jack exhaled and stared into space, the lumps in his face spiked with unshaved whiskers. "Years ago I did something that still disturbs me, but you can make up your own mind about it. My mother was a prostitute. Most of her clients were gandy walkers or brakemen off a freight line that went past the boxcar we lived in. One guy in particular would come by every two weeks or so. He had a family in Oklahoma City, but that didn't stop him from topping my mother when he was on a bender. I'd have to wait outside, which I had more or less gotten used to, but on one occasion it was about fifteen above and snowing, and I spent an hour wrapped in a piece of canvas, crouched down out of the wind behind his car, which he kept locked because he didn't want a smelly little boy sitting on his leather seats.

"The next summer I was working as a dishwasher in town, and this same fellow came in and ordered the beef-stew special. He looked like he was just coming off a drunk and could have eaten a whole cow between two slices of white bread. That morning I'd swept up some broken glass off the back step and put it in the trash can. The glass was as fine as needles, but I mashed it up even finer and put it in his stew with a lot of potatoes. About thirty minutes later, he went down on the sidewalk like he swallowed a handful of fishhooks. I heard he died, but I didn't go around asking questions about it."

Jack snapped the ammunition drum onto his submachine gun and laid the gun lopsidedly inside the guitar case. He wiped the oil off his fingers with a paper towel and gazed somberly into Noie's face, his eyes melancholy and shiny. Then as though he had been holding his breath underwater to the point where his lungs were bursting, his mouth fell open and his lips creased back in a broad smile. "Got you, boy! I had you convinced you were bunking with Jack the Ripper. My mother was an elementary teacher in Okemah, Oklahoma, and died of Huntington's chorea. My last job was at a Pee-wee Herman theme park. I couldn't hurt a fly."

"What about the submachine gun?"

"I've got a whole collection of rare firearms in Rio de Janeiro. One day I'll show them to you. You don't believe I'm a rich man, do you?"

"I don't know what to believe, Jack."

"That's because you're a good kid. Get out your checker set, and let's put on a pot of coffee and play a game or two."

The information that came in from the National Crime Information Center on Dennis Rector was of little value, other than to indicate that he had been arrested twice for DWI and once for domestic battery, and the United States Navy had given him a general discharge for the convenience of the service. His wallet contained an Arizona driver's license, a Social Security card, fourteen dollars, a condom, a GI can opener, a coupon for a box of cereal, a speeding citation that was four months old, a torn ticket to a concert in Branson, Missouri, and a photograph of the deceased in a navy uniform standing next to an Asian girl wearing a shift and flip-flops. Written in pencil on the back of the photograph were the words "With Luz, Mindanao, Aug. 6, 1982."

In his right-hand pocket Rector had been carrying seventy-three cents in change, three metal finger picks, and a half stick of gum wrapped in tinfoil.

Hackberry placed Rector's possessions in a manila envelope and gazed out the window at a pallid and sultry sky and hills that barely contained enough moisture to go with the greening of the season. What was the sum total of a man's life? Scraps of paper issued by the state? A photo taken with a peasant girl on the rim of the New American Empire on the anniversary of Hiroshima's bombing? A ticket to a country-music event at which the stage performers wore tasseled red, white, and blue costumes and offered up a meretricious tribute to a culture that celebrated its own vulgarity? A half stick of chewing gum?

Who was Dennis Rector, and what had he come to confess? How could a man who had acquired so little and left such a microscopic trace on the planet be so serious about himself that he would take his own life? What could he have done that was that bad? Hackberry picked up his desk phone. "Would you come in here, Maydeen?" he said.

Ten seconds later, she was standing in his doorway, pear-shaped, wearing a flowery western shirt with her department-issue trousers and a stitched belt and too much lipstick, her perfume flooding the room. "Are you gonna just stare at me or tell me what you want?" she said.

"If someone said to you 'I ain't no Judas Iscariot,' what would you say was on his mind?"

"Did you call him a Judas?"

"*I* didn't. To my knowledge, no one did."

"I'd say he sold out someone who trusted him, and his guilt was eating his lunch. Are we talking about the guy who hanged himself?"

"That's the guy."

"It seems like he had biblical stories on his mind. Like the crucifixion in particular."

"I believe you're right."

"You think he knew Cody Daniels?" she asked.

"He knew Josef Sholokoff, that's for sure."

"You think Sholokoff crucified Daniels?"

491

"I think it was either Sholokoff or Krill. Except a guy like Dennis Rector wouldn't have occasion to be mixed up with someone like Krill. So that leaves Sholokoff. Is Pam still at lunch?"

"She got a call from the Blue Bonnet Six. A guy skipped on his bill and stole the television set out of the room. Before he skipped, he tried to sell the owner something called a Dobro. What's a Dobro?"

"A guitar with a resonator in it. It's played with metal picks, like the ones I just put in this manila envelope."

"The guy who hanged himself played a musical instrument?"

"Evidently. Why?"

"Musicians make poor criminals. Outside of wrecking hotel rooms, they're amateurs when it comes to serious criminality," Maydeen said. When Hackberry didn't reply, she said, "Know why that is?"

"I think you're fixing to tell me."

"You'll figure it out," she said.

"Has R.C. called in yet?"

"No, sir."

"Let me know when he does. Tell me why musicians make poor criminals."

"They believe they have a gift, so they feel less inclined to steal. They also think they're special and they don't have to prove anything."

"I never thought of it that way," he said.

492

"My first husband was hung like a hamster. But after he recorded once with Stevie Ray Vaughan, you'd think he was driving a fire truck up my leg."

"I can't believe you just said that."

"Said what?"

"Out, Maydeen. And close the door behind you, please."

Hackberry walked to the saloon and ate lunch in the darkness of a back booth and tried to forget the image of Dennis Rector hanging from a barn rafter. But a larger issue than the suicide was bothering him. Hackberry believed that most crimes, particularly homicide, were committed for reasons of sex, money, power, or any combination of the three. Beginning with the murder of the DEA informant by Krill, the homicides Hackberry had investigated recently seemed to defy normal patterns. Supposedly, the central issue was national security and the sale of Noie Barnum to Al Qaeda and the compromise of the Predator drone. But that just didn't wash. The players were all people driven by ideology or religious obsession or personal rage that was rooted in the id. It was too easy to dismiss Preacher Jack Collins as a psychopath. It was also too easy to categorize Josef Sholokoff as a Russian criminal who slithered through a hole in the immigration process during the Cold War. Something much worse seemed to have come into the lives of this small-town society down here on the border, like a spiritual malignancy irradiating the land with its poisonous substance, remaking the people in its image.

Is that too dark and grandiose an extrapolation from the daily ebb and flow of a rural sheriff's department? Hackberry wondered. *Ask those medieval peasants who were visited in their villages by the representatives of the Inquisition,* he said to himself in reply.

He stared at the diamondback rattlesnake that the saloon owner kept in a gallon jar of yellow formaldehyde on the bar. The snake's body was coiled thickly upon itself, its mouth spread wide against the glass, its eyes like chips of stone, the venom holes visible in its fangs. The rattlesnake had been in the jar at least three years; its color had begun to fade, and pieces of its body were starting to dissolve in dirty strings inside the preservative. Why leave something that ugly if not perverse on top of a bar for that long?

Because the owner was making a statement, Hackberry thought. Evil was outside of us, not in the human breast, and could be contained and made harmless and placed on exhibit. Wasn't the serpent condemned to crawl on its belly in the dust and to strike at man's heel and be beaten to death with a stick? What more fitting testimony to that fact than a diamondback yawning open its mouth impotently six inches from the tattooed arm of a trucker knocking back shots of Jack and chasing them with a frosted mug of Lone Star?

Hackberry made a mental note to talk with the bartender. Then his cell phone vibrated on the tabletop. He opened it and placed it to his ear. "Sheriff Holland," he said.

"I called the office, Sheriff, but Maydeen said you were eating lunch," a voice said. "Hope I'm not bothering you."

Hackberry looked down at his plate of enchiladas and Spanish rice and frijoles that were growing cold. "Go ahead, R.C."

"I did what you said. I got a range-and-township map and looked up the title of every piece of land in a five-mile radius from the spot where that FBI man was killed. I Googled all their names and got a hit on one guy, but he's not a writer."

"What's the name?"

"W. W. Guthrie. Google took me to a folksinger by the name of Woodrow Wilson Guthrie."

"That's Woody Guthrie, R.C. He didn't just write folk songs. He published two books. One was *Bound for Glory*. It was made into a film. I think you just found the hideout of Preacher Jack."

"I'm on my way out there right now. I'll call you back as soon as I find out anything."

"What kind of help are you getting from the feds?"

"At the courthouse, one of them told me where the men's room was. Another one said he thought it might rain directly. That's the word he used — 'directly.' Like he was talking to somebody on *Hee Haw.* Are they as bright as they're supposed to be?"

"Probably."

"They sure know how to hide it," R.C. said.

Hackberry finished eating and left thirteen dollars on the table and used the restroom and dried his hands and picked up his hat from the booth and started toward the front door. Then he paused. "I almost forgot," he said to the bartender.

"Forgot what?" the bartender said. He was a big, dark-haired man with a deeply creased brow who wore a white dress shirt with the sleeves rolled up high on his arms.

"Can you put a bag over that snake jar the next time I come here?"

"Any reason?"

"Yeah, so I don't have to look at it while I'm eating."

"Who lit your fuse?"

"Did you read the paper this morning?"

"Something happen?"

"If I come in here again, refuse to serve me," Hackberry said. "I'd really appreciate that."

Halfway to the office, his cell phone vibrated again. "Sheriff Holland," he said.

"It's me, Sheriff."

496

"Yeah, I thought it might be you, R.C."

"How you doin'?"

"Fine."

"I'm parked at this cabin that's between a creek and a bluff. You cain't see it except from the air. Feds are all over the place, but I found something they missed. It's a checker. They didn't know what it was."

"I'm not quite tracking you."

"It's a homemade checker, one somebody carved out of wood. I'm not explaining myself real good. The property is in the name of W. W. Guthrie, but nobody around here seems to know what he looks like or where he's from. When the feds got here, the cabin and the house were clean. I went out to the barn and saw the same Michelin tire tracks we saw at Anton Ling's place. Then I went inside, and this fed was looking at a little round wood button that he found behind the kitchen door. You following me?"

"Not really."

"I'll try again. On the bottom of it were the initials N.B. For 'Noie Barnum.' On the top was a K. The fed didn't know what that meant. I told him it was K for 'king.' So he says, 'Yeah, it must have rolled behind the door.' So I went into the bedroom and found another one, except this one was wedged in the side of the dresser. That whole place was broom-sweep clean, Sheriff. The second checker, the one stuck in the dresser, wasn't

497

left there by mistake. When I showed the fed what I'd found, he looked pretty confused."

"Noie Barnum isn't a willing companion of Jack Collins?" Hackberry said.

"Or he's covering his ass," R.C. replied.

Or he has his own agenda, Hackberry thought. "You did a fine job, bud. Come on in," he said.

Minutes later, he called both Maydeen and Pam into his office.

"Is this about my language?" Maydeen said. "If it is, I'm sor—"

"Forget your language. The feds have treated us like dipshits. Find out everything you can about Noie Barnum," he said.

Krill squatted down on a bare piece of ground a few feet from the common grave where he had buried his three children. The grave was marked by a Styrofoam cross wrapped with a string of multicolored plastic flowers. He upended an unlabeled bottle of mescal and drank from it against the sunset, the light turning to fire inside the glass. A copy of the *San Antonio Express-News* was weighted down on the ground with rocks he had placed on each corner of the front page, the paper riffling with wind. Krill drank again from the bottle, then pressed a cork into the neck with his thumb and gazed at the sun descending into a red blaze behind the hills.

Negrito squatted next to him, his greasy

leather hat flattening the hair on his forehead. "Don't pay no attention to what's in that newspaper," he said.

"They're gonna put it on us, *hombre*. It means trouble."

"*That* means trouble? What do you call killing a DEA agent?"

"He wasn't an agent. He was an informant and a corrupt Mexican cop. Nobody cares what we did to him. Reverend Cody was a minister."

"We didn't do it to him, man."

"But our prints are there, *estúpido*."

"That ain't what's bothering you, Krill. It's something else, ain't it?"

"He baptized my children. Nobody else would do that. Not even La Magdalena. To treat him with disrespect now is to treat my children with disrespect."

"That don't make sense."

"Where's your brain? He had the power to set my children free from limbo. Should I tell them I care nothing for the man who did this for them? Can't you think? What is wrong with you?"

"You are making me confused. It makes my head hurt."

"Because you are stupid and self-centered. Go get the others and meet me at the car."

"Where are we going?"

"To get the men who did this to the minister."

"No, no, this is a bad idea. Listen to me, Krill. I'm your friend, the only one you got."

"Then follow me or go into the desert. Or to your whores in Durango."

"You're going after Noie Barnum. Some of the others might think you're gonna sell him and maybe forget to share the money."

Krill stood up to his full height and pulled Negrito's hat off his head. Then he slapped him with it, hard, the leather chin cord biting into the scalp. He waited a few seconds and hit him again. "We're going after the Russian. He should have been killed a long time ago. Don't ever accuse me of treachery again."

"How you know he did it?" Negrito asked, his eyes watering, his nostrils widening as he ate his pain and humiliation at being whipped by Krill.

"Because he hates God, stupid one."

"I hear this from the killer of a Jesuit priest?"

"They told us he and the others were Communists. There were five of them. I shot one, and the others shot the rest. It was in a garden outside the house where they lived. We killed the housekeeper, too. I dream of them often."

"Everybody dies. Why feel guilt over what has to happen to all of us?"

"You say these things because you are incapable of thought. So I don't hold your words or deeds against you."

"You hit me, *jefe.* You would not do that to an animal, but you would do it to me? You hurt me deep inside."

"I'm sorry. You are a handicapped man, and I must treat you as such."

"I do not like what is happening here. All this makes my head throb, like I have a great sickness inside it. Why do you make me feel like this, *jefe?*"

"It is not me. You are one of the benighted, Negrito. Your problems are in your confused blood and your tangled thoughts. For that reason I must be kind to you."

"I will forget you said that to me, 'cause you are a mestizo, just like me. I say we return to Durango. I say we get drunk and bathe in *puta* and be the friends we used to be."

"Then you must go and pursue your lower nature."

"No, I'll never leave you, man," Negrito said. "What does 'benighted' mean?"

Krill gestured toward the hills in the west, where the sun had become a red melt below the horizon and the darkness was spreading up into the sky. "It means the dying of the light," he said. "The benighted place is out there where the coyotes and carrion birds and Gila monsters live and the spirits wander without hope of ever seeing the light."

■ ■ ■ ■

At ten the next morning Pam Tibbs tapped on the doorjamb of Hackberry's office. She had a yellow legal pad in her hand. "This is what we've found out about Noie Barnum so far," she said. "There're a couple of holes in it. You want to hear it now or wait till Maydeen gets off the phone?"

"Who's she talking to?"

"The state attorney's office in Alabama."

"Sit down," Hackberry said.

"Barnum grew up in a small town on the Tennessee line and was an honor student in high school. His father died when he was three, and his mother worked at a hardware store and raised him and his half sister by herself. He was never an athlete or a class officer or a joiner of any kind. He won a scholarship to MIT and went to work for the government when he graduated. As far as anybody knew, he was always religious. When it came to girls and social activities, he was as plain as white bread and just about as forgettable. The exception came when he was seventeen. A three-year-old boy wandered away from the neighborhood, and the whole town organized search parties and went looking for him. Barnum found him in a well. He crawled in after him and got bitten in the face by a copperhead but carried the kid on his back four miles to a highway. By all odds, he should have died."

"What happened to the mother and the half sister?"

"The mother passed away while Barnum was at MIT. The half sister moved to New York and went to work for a catering service. Some stories came back about her, but no one is sure of the truth. She wasn't looked upon favorably in her hometown. She had been arrested in high school for possession of marijuana and was believed to sleep around. This is where it becomes cloudy."

"What does?"

"She used her father's last name when she moved to New York. Hang on," Pam said. She got up from the chair and went to the door. "Maydeen's off the phone."

When Maydeen walked into Hackberry's office, her expression was blank, as though she were looking at an image behind her eyes that she did not want to assimilate.

"What is it?" Hackberry said.

"The Alabama state attorney did some hands-on work for us," she replied. "He found a guy in a state rehab center who was the half sister's boyfriend. She died in the Twin Towers. She was called in to work on her day off because somebody else was sick. She was in the restaurant on the top floor. She was one of the people who held hands with a friend and jumped."

503

his back four miles to a halfway. By all odds, he should have died."

"What happened to the mother and the half sister?"

"The mother passed away, while Hatsum was in 1917. The half sister moved to New York and

CHAPTER TWENTY

At the bottom of Danny Boy Lorca's land was a ravine that few people knew about or chose to travel. It led from Mexico into the United States, but the entrance was overgrown with thornbushes that could scrape the skin off a man or the paint from an automobile. The sides of the ravine went straight up into the sky and had been marked in four places by the lances of mounted Spaniards who littered the bottom of the ravine with the bones of Indians whose most sophisticated weapons had been the sharpened sticks they used to plant corn. The few illegals who used the ravine and even the coyotes who guided them swore they had seen Indians standing on ledges in the darkness, their faces as dry and bloodless and withered as deer hide stretched on lodge poles. The specters on the ledges did not speak or show any recognition of the nocturnal wayfarers passing between the walls. Their eyes were empty circles that contained only darkness, their clothes sewn from the burlap given them by their conquerors. No one who saw the specters ever wanted to return to the area, except Danny Boy Lorca.

He woke to the grinding noise of a car in low gear laboring up a grade and a brittle screeching that was like someone scratching a stylus slowly down a blackboard. When he went to his back door, he saw a gas-guzzler bounce loose from the ravine, its lights burning in the fog, strings of smoke rising from the rust in its hood. He saw the silhouettes of perhaps four men inside the vehicle.

He pulled on his boots and lifted his twenty-gauge from the antler rack on the wall and limped out onto the back porch. The fog smelled of dust and herbicide and a pond strung with green feces and someone burning raw garbage. The gas-guzzler was traversing his property, its engine rods knocking, its low beams swimming with dust particles and candle moths.

He walked toward it, a pain flaring in his thigh each time his foot came down on the ground, the shotgun cradled across the crook of his left arm. His twenty-gauge was called a dogleg, a one-barrel one-shot breechloader he had used to hunt quail and doves and rabbits when he was a boy. It was a fine gun that had served him well. There was a problem, though: He had not bought shells for it in years. He was carrying an unloaded weapon.

He limped through the chicken yard and past the three-sided shed where his firewood was stacked and through one end of his barn and out the other until he stood squarely in the headlights of the gas-guzzler. The driver touched his brakes and stuck his head out the window. "We got a little lost, amigo. Know where the highway is at?"

Danny Boy moved out of the headlights' glare so he could see the driver more clearly. "You got dope in that car?" he said.

"We're workers, *hombre*," the driver said. "We don't got no dope. We are lost. That canyon was a pile of shit. You got a cast on your leg."

"Yeah, and you got a bullet hole in your window," Danny Boy said.

"These are dangerous times," the driver said. "You have an accident?"

"No, a guy put a shank in me. Did you see the Indians in the ravine?"

"A shank? That ain't good. You said Indians? What is with you, man?" the driver said. He turned to the others. "The guy is talking about Indians. Anybody here see Indians?"

The other men shook their heads.

"See, ain't nobody seen no fucking Indians," the driver said. "We're going to Alpine. Come on, man, you need to stand aside with that gun and let us pass."

Danny Boy's gaze had been fixed on the driver's orange hair and whiskers and the gorilla-like bone structure of his face, so he had not paid attention to the man sitting in the passenger seat. At first the passenger's sharp profile and unnaturally wide shoulders and slit of a mouth were like parts of a bad dream returning in daylight. When Danny Boy realized who the passenger was, he felt his breath catch in his throat. He stepped back from the car window, gripping the shotgun tightly. "I seen you before," he said.

"You talking to me?" the passenger said.

It ain't too late. Don't say no more, a voice inside Danny Boy said. *They will disappear and it will be like they were never here.* "I remember your trousers."

"What about them?"

"Dark blue, with a red stripe down each leg. Like trousers a soldier might wear, or a marine."

"These are exercise pants. But why should you care about my clothes? Why are they of such consequence?"

Danny Boy had to wet his lips before he spoke. "I watched you from the arroyo. I heard that man screaming while you did those things to him."

"You're mixed up, man," the driver said. "We ain't from around here. You ain't never seen us."

"Let him talk," said the passenger.

"You tied the man's scalp on your belt," Danny Boy said. "You heard a sound up in

507

the rocks and looked up at where I was hiding. I acted like a coward and hid instead of he'ping that guy you killed."

"Many of our people use this place to enter Texas. We are workers trying to feed our families," the man said. "Why make an issue with us? It is not in your interest."

"Listen to him, *indio*," the driver said. "You can get that shotgun kicked up your ass."

"This is my land. That house is my home," Danny Boy said.

"So we're going off your land now," the driver said. "So get out of our way. So stop being a hardheaded dumb fuck who don't know not to mess with the wrong guys."

"You ain't gonna talk to me like that on my land," Danny Boy said.

"What I'm gonna do is spit on you, *indio*. I don't give a shit if you got a gun or not."

Danny Boy reversed the twenty-gauge in his hands and drove the stock into the driver's mouth, snapping back his head, whipping spittle and blood onto the dashboard and steering wheel.

"*¡Mátelo!*" a man in the backseat said. "Kill that motherfucker, Negrito."

"No!" the passenger in the front seat shouted, getting out of the car. "You!" he said, pointing across the top of the roof. "Put your gun away. We are no threat to you."

The driver was still holding his mouth, trying to talk. "Let me, Krill," he said. "This one deserves to die."

"No!" the passenger said. "*You,* Indian man, listen to me. You are right. This is your land, and we have violated it. But we mean you no harm. You must let us pass and forget we were here. I saw no Indians in the canyon, but I know they're there. I'm a believer, like you. We are brothers. Like you, I know our ancestors' spirits are everywhere. They don't want us to kill one another."

The passenger had walked through the headlights and was standing four feet from Danny Boy, his eyes roving over Danny Boy's face, waiting for him to speak.

"I was in Sugar Land with guys like you. You're a killer. You ain't like me, and we ain't brothers," Danny Boy said.

"Have it as you wish. But you're putting us in a bad position, my friend. Your fear is taking away all our alternatives."

"Fear? Not of you. Not no more." Danny Boy pushed the release lever on the top of the shotgun's stock and broke the breech and exposed the empty chamber. "See, I ain't got a shell in it. I ain't afraid of you. I ain't afraid of them guys in the car, either."

"*Está loco,* Krill," one of the men inside the car said.

The passenger folded his arms and stared into the darkness as though considering his options. "You got some real cojones, man," he said. "But I don't know what we're going to do with you. Are you going to turn us in?"

"When I can get to a phone."

"Where's your cell phone?"

"I ain't got one."

"You got a regular phone in your house?"

"No, I ain't got no phone."

"You don't have a telephone? Not of any kind?"

"You see a pole line going to my house?"

Krill stared at the house and at the barn and at the truck parked next to the barn. "The man you saw me kill out there in the desert? He was a corrupt Mexican cop who tortured my brother to death."

"Then you ain't no different from the Mexican cop."

"You are fortunate to have this fine place to live on. I had a farm once, and children and a wife. Now I have nothing. Don't judge me, *hombre.*"

Krill pulled a long game-dressing knife from a scabbard on his side and walked to Danny Boy's truck and sliced the air stems off all four tires. *"Buenas noches,"* he said as he got back in the automobile. "Maybe one day you will understand men like us. Maybe one day the Indians who live in the canyon will tell you who your real brothers are."

"They ain't you!" Danny Boy shouted at the car's taillights.

In the gloaming of the day, Preacher Jack

510

Collins and Noie Barnum pulled into the drive-in restaurant on the state four-lane and parked under the shed and ordered hamburgers and fries and onion rings and frosted mugs of root beer. The evening was warm, the wind blowing steadily across the rolling countryside, the storm clouds in the south bursting with brilliant patterns of white electricity that made Jack think of barbed wire. He had not spoken since they had left the cottage on the hillside above the junkyard.

"You're not letting me in on where we're going?" Noie said.

Jack chewed on his food, his expression thoughtful. "You give much thought to the papists?"

"The Catholics?"

"That's what I just said."

"Not particularly."

"That Chinese woman, the one who dressed your wounds, is a puzzle to me."

"She's just a woman with a big heart."

"Maybe she's spread her big heart around a little more than she should have."

"If you read Saint Paul, there's no such thing as being too charitable."

"She may have been acting as a friend to the FBI. If that's true, she's no friend to us."

"You saying she's a turncoat?"

"I'd like to talk to her about it. Here's a question for you." From the side, Jack's eyes

511

looked like glass marbles pushed into dough that had turned moldy and then hardened. The amber reflection in them was as sharp as broken beer glass but without complexity or meaning. In fact, the light in his eyes was neutral, if not benign. "You put a lot of work into whittling out that checker set. Each one of those little buttons was a hand-carved masterpiece. But two pieces were missing from your poke, and you didn't seem to give that fact any thought."

"I guess I dropped them somewhere."

"When you counted the checkers out, you didn't notice that two were gone?"

"Guess not."

"Too bad to lose your pieces. You're an artisan. For a fellow like you, your craft is an extension of your soul. That's what an artisan is. His thoughts travel through his arm and his hand into the object he creates."

"That's an interesting way to look at it."

"Think they might have fallen out in the trunk when we were moving?"

"I'll look first chance."

"You like your hamburger?"

"You'd better believe it."

"Does it bother you that an animal has to give up its life so we can eat types of food we probably could do without?"

"You know how to hang crepe, Jack."

"Think we'd be welcomed by the papist woman?"

512

"You know what I would really like, more than anything else in the world? I mean, if I could have one wish, a wish that would make my whole life complete? That would make me so happy I would never ask for anything else as long as I live?"

"I cain't figure what that might be, Noie."

"I'd like to make peace with the men who held me hostage and killed the Mexican man I was handcuffed to. I'd like to make peace with the Al Qaeda guys they were going to sell me to. I'd like to apologize to them for the innocent people I helped kill with the drones I helped develop. Most of all, Jack, I'd like to repay you for everything you've done. When they made you, they busted the mold."

Jack worked a piece of food out of his jaw with his tongue and swallowed, his gaze straight ahead. He sipped from his mug, grains of ice clinging to his bottom lip. An attractive waitress in a rayon uniform roller-skated past the front of the Trans Am on the walkway under the shed, but he didn't seem to notice. "Who's 'they'?" he asked.

"Pardon?"

"You said 'when they made you.' You didn't use God's name. Like it would be irreverent. Is that just a quirk, or are you saying I wasn't created by the hand of God?"

"I said it without thinking, that's all. It was just a joke."

"Not to me it isn't. Know why people use

passive voice?"

"I know that it has something to do with grammar, but I'm an engineer, Jack, not much on the literary arts."

"Passive voice involves sentence structure that hides the identity of the doer. It's a form of linguistic deception. Pronouns that have no referents are also used to confuse and conceal. A linguist can spot a lie faster than any polygraph can."

"You never went to college?"

"I never went to high school."

"You're amazing."

"That's a word used by members of the herd. Everything is either 'amazing' or 'awesome.' You're not a member of the herd. Don't act like you are."

"Jack, eating supper with you is like trying to digest carpet tacks. I've never seen the like of it. My food hasn't even hit my stomach, and I'm already constipated."

"Look at me and don't turn around."

"What is it?" Noie said.

"A highway patrol cruiser just pulled in five slots down. There're two cops in it."

The waitress came to the window and picked up the five-dollar tip and lifted the tray off the door and smiled. "Thank you, sir," she said.

"My pleasure," Jack said. He watched her walk away, his eyes slipping off her onto the side of the cruiser.

"We got to back out and drive right past them," Noie said. "Or wait for them to leave."

"I'd say that sums it up." Jack bit down on his lip, his face shadowed by the brim of his hat. He removed it and set it on the dashboard and combed his hair in the rearview mirror.

"What are you doing?" Noie said.

Jack got out of the car, yawning, rubbing his face, a weary traveler about to hit the road again. "Ask the cops for directions to the cutoff to I-10," he replied. He gazed up at the sky and at the network of lightning that was as spiked as barbed wire inside the clouds. "You can almost smell the salt and coconut palms on the wind. Mexico is waiting for us, son. Soon as we tidy up a few things. Yes, indeedy, a man's work is never done."

When Hackberry arrived at work early the next morning, Danny Boy Lorca was sleeping on a flattened cardboard carton in the alleyway behind the rear entrance, one arm over his eyes.

"Want to come in or sleep late and let the sun dry the dew on your clothes?" Hackberry said.

Danny Boy sat up, searching in the shadows as though unsure where he was. "I ain't drunk."

"Where's your truck?"

"At the house. Krill cut all my tires. I hitched a ride into town."

"Krill was at your house?"

"I busted his driver in the mouth. There was four of them together. They come up the ravine behind my property."

"You sure it was Krill, Danny? You haven't been knocking back a few shots, have you?"

"I'm going up to the café now and have breakfast. I told you what I seen and what I done."

"Come inside."

Danny Boy scratched at a place on his scalp and let out his breath and watched a shaft of sunlight shine on a dog at the end of the alley. The dog had open sores on its skin. "You ought to call the Humane Society and get some he'p for that critter. It ain't right to leave a sick animal on the street like that."

"You're a good man, Danny Boy. I meant you no offense," Hackberry said.

Danny Boy went inside and sat down by the small gas stove and waited, his work-seamed hands folded between his knees, his ruined face without expression, while Hackberry called Animal Control and fixed coffee and attached the flag to the chain on the metal pole out front and ran it up the pole, the flag suddenly filling with wind and popping against the sky.

"The guy named Krill said I don't know who my real brothers are," Danny Boy said.

516

"He did, huh?"

"His eyes are blue. But his hair and his skin are like mine."

"I see," Hackberry said, not understanding.

"He ain't got no family or home or country. Somebody took all that away from him. That's why he kills. It ain't for money. He thinks it is, but it ain't. He'd pay to do it."

"Why are you telling me this?"

"He believes the dead are more real than the living. That's the most dangerous kind of man there is," Danny Boy said.

An hour later, Hackberry called R.C. and Pam Tibbs into his office. "Here's the lay of the land," he said. "I've made six calls so far this morning and have been stonewalled by every fed I've talked to. My best guess is that Noie Barnum deliberately got himself kidnapped by Krill so he could infiltrate Al Qaeda's connections in Latin America. I'm not sure the FBI was in on it. Maybe Barnum is working for an intelligence group inside the NSA or the Pentagon or the CIA. Or maybe he's working on his own. Frankly, I don't care. We've been lied to over and over while serious crimes were being committed in our county. If any fed obstructs or jerks us around again, we throw his bureaucratic ass in jail."

"You sure you want to do that, Hack?" Pam said.

"Watch me."

517

"I don't get your reasoning, Sheriff. If Barnum wanted Krill to sell him to these Al Qaeda guys, how come he escaped?" R.C. said.

"Maybe Krill was going to piece off the action and sell him to a narco gang and wash his hands of the matter. So Barnum decided it was time to boogie."

"He wants to do all this to get even for what happened to his sister in the Towers?" R.C. said.

"Wouldn't you?" Hackberry asked.

"I'd do a whole sight more," R.C. replied.

"Right now we don't have eyes or ears out there. We need to find a weak link in the chain," Hackberry said.

"These guys are pros, Sheriff. They don't have weak links," R.C. said.

"We'll create one."

"Who?" R.C. asked.

"I saw Temple Dowling busting skeet by the Ninth Hole last night," Pam said.

It wasn't hard to find him. In the county there was only one country club and private golf course and gated community that offered rental cottages. All of it was located on a palm-dotted watered green stretch of rolling landscape that had all the attributes of an Arizona resort, the rentals constructed of adobe and cedar, the walks bordered with flower beds, the lawns flooded daily by soak hoses at sunset, the evening breeze tinged with smoke from meat fires and the astringent smell of charcoal lighter. The swimming pool glowed with a blue radiance under the stars, and sometimes on summer nights, a 1950s-type orchestra performed on the outdoor dance floor; the buffet-style fried-chicken-and-potato-salad dinners were legendary.

The club not only offered upscale insularity, it also allowed its members to feel comfortable with who they were and gave them sanction to say things they would not say anywhere else. Political correctness ended at the arched entranceway. On the links or in the lounge known as the Ninth Hole, no racial joke was too coarse, no humorous remark about liberals and environmentalists unappreciated. In the evening, against a backdrop of palm trees and golf balls flying under the lights on the driving range, in the dull popping of shotguns and clay pigeons bursting into puffs of colored smoke against a pastel sky, one had the sense that the club was a place where no one died, where all the rewards promised by a benevolent capitalistic deity were handed out in this world rather than the next.

The irony was that most of the members came from the Dallas–Fort Worth area or Houston. The other irony was the fact that the environs on which the club was built were part of the old Outlaw Trail, which had run from the Hole in the Wall Country in Wyoming all the way to the Mexican border. Butch Cassidy and the Sundance Kid and Kid Curry and Black Jack Ketchum and Sam Bass and the Dalton Gang had probably all ridden it. Thirty years before, wagon tracks that had been cut into the mire of clay and mud and livestock feces during the days of the Chisholm and Goodnight-Loving trails were still visible in the hardpan. When the topography was reconfigured by the builders of the club, the hardpan was ground up by earth-graders and layered with trucked-in sod and turned into fairways and putting greens and sand traps and ponds, for the pleasure of people who had never heard of Charles Goodnight or Oliver Loving or Jesse Chisholm and couldn't have cared less about who they were.

Deputy Sheriff Felix Chavez was twenty-seven years old and had four children and a wife he had married when she was sixteen and he was twenty. He was devoted to his family and loved playing golf and remodeling and improving his three-bedroom house. He was also a master car mechanic and a collector of historical artifacts and military ordnance. Because he often swung his cruiser off the main road and patrolled the country-club parking lot without being asked to do so, the management allowed him to use the driving range free whenever he wished, although the gesture did not extend to the links or access to the Ninth Hole. The consequence was that no one paid particular attention to him on the cloudy afternoon when he parked his cruiser by the clubhouse and got out and watched the golfers teeing off or practicing on the putting green. Nor did they think it unusual that Felix strolled through the lot, either checking on a security matter or enjoying a breezy, cool break in the weather. The drama at the club came later in the day, and Felix Chavez seemed to have no connection to it.

Temple Dowling was on the driving range with three friends, *whock*ing balls in a high arc, his form perfect, the power in his shoulders and thick arms and strong hands a surprise to those who noted only the creamy pinkness of his complexion and the baby fat under his chin and his lips that were too large for his mouth. The coordination of his swing and the whip of his wrists and the twist of his hips and buttocks seemed almost an erotic exercise, one that was not lost on others. "Temp, you're the only golf player I ever saw whose swing could make the right girl cream her jeans," one of his companions said.

They all roared, then sipped from their old-fashioneds and gin gimlets and turned their attention to the two-inch-thick bloodred steaks Temple had just forked onto the barbecue grill.

"What was that?" said one of the friends, a man with hair like an albino ape's on the backs of his wrists and arms.

"What was what?" Dowling said. He looked around, confused.

"I don't know," his friend said. "I thought I saw something. A red bug."

"Where?"

The friend rubbed at one eye with his wrist. "I probably looked into the sun. I think I need new contacts."

"It looked like it was fixing to crawl in your collar," another man said.

Temple Dowling pulled his shirt loose from his slacks and shook it. "Did I get it?"

"Nothing fell out."

"It wasn't a centipede, was it?"

"It was a little round bug," said the man with white hair on his arms.

Temple Dowling straightened his collar. "Screw it. If it bites me, I'll bite it back," he said. His friends grinned. He picked up a fork and turned the steaks, squinting in the smoke. "Right on this spot, before this was a country club, my father had a deer stand where he used to take his friends. I wasn't supposed to be there, but I snuck off to it and shot a nine-point buck with my twenty-two. Except I gut-shot him. He took off running, just about where that water trap is now. I had to hit him four more times before he went down. I was so excited I pissed my pants. I showed my father what I'd done, and he dipped his hand in the deer's blood and smeared it on my face and said, 'Damn if I don't think you've turned into a man. But we got to get you a thirty-thirty, son, before you shoot up half the county.' "

"Were you and your father pretty close, Temp?"

"Close as ice water can be to a drinking glass, I guess."

Dowling's companions nodded vaguely as though they understood when in fact they did not.

"My father had his own way of doing things," he said. "There was his way, and then there was his way. If that didn't work out, we did it his way over and over until his way worked. No man could ride a horse into the ground or a woman into an asylum like my old man."

The others let their eyes slip away to their drinks, the steaks browning and dripping on the fire, the golfers lifting their drives high into the sunset, a skeet shooter powdering a clay pigeon into a pink cloud against the sky. At the club, candor about one's life was not always considered a virtue.

"On your shirt, Temp," said the man with white hair on his wrists and arms. "There. *Jesus.*"

Dowling looked down at his clothes. "Where?"

One man dropped his gimlet glass and stepped away, his eyebrows raised, his hands lifted in front of him, as though disengaging from an invisible entanglement that should not have been part of his life. The two other men were not as subtle. They backed away hurriedly, then ran toward the Ninth Hole, coins and keys jingling in their pockets, their spiked shoes clicking on the walkway, their faces disjointed as they looked back fearfully over their shoulders.

Out on the county road, one hundred yards away, Felix Chavez walked from an abandoned mechanic's shed to an unmarked car, threw a rifle on the backseat, and drove home to eat dinner with his family.

Hackberry was dozing in his chair, his hat tilted down on his face, his feet on his desk, when the 911 call came in. Maydeen and Pam and R.C. had stayed late that afternoon. Maydeen tapped on Hackberry's doorjamb. "Temple Dowling says somebody put a laser sight on him at the country club," she said.

"No kidding," Hackberry said, opening his eyes. "What would Mr. Dowling like us to do about it?"

"Probably bring him some toilet paper. He sounds like he just downloaded in his britches," she replied.

"Maydeen —"

"Sorry," she said.

"Is Mr. Dowling still at the club?"

"He's in his cottage. He says you warned him about Jack Collins." She looked at a notepad in her hand. "He said, 'That crazy son of a bitch Collins is out there, and you all had better do something about it. I pay my goddamn taxes.' "

"Is there any coffee left?" Hackberry asked.

"I just made a fresh pot."

"Let's all have a cup and a doughnut or two, then R.C. and Pam and I can motor on out," Hackberry said. He stretched his arms, his feet still on his desk, and tossed his hat on the polished tip of one boot. "I'd better take down the flag before we go, too. It looks like rain."

"You want me to call Dowling back?"

"What for?"

"To tell him y'all are on your way."

"He knows our hearts are in the right place," Hackberry replied.

Forty minutes later, it was misting and the clouds were hanging like frozen steam on the hills when Hackberry and Pam arrived at the club in one cruiser and R.C. in another. Temple Dowling met them at the door of his cottage, a drink in his hand, his face splotched, his eyes looking past them at the fairways and trees and the shadows that the trees and buildings and electric lights made on the grass. The wind toppled a table on the flagstones by the swimming pool, and Temple

Dowling's face jumped. "What kept y'all?" he said. "Who's this woman Maydeen?"

"What about her?"

"She told me to fuck myself, is what's about her."

Hackberry stared at him without replying.

"Come inside. Don't just stand there," Dowling said.

"This is fine."

"It's raining. I don't want to get wet," Dowling said, his gaze focusing on a man stacking chairs behind the Ninth Hole.

"R.C., go up to the clubhouse and see what you can find out. We'll be here with Mr. Dowling. Let's wrap this up as soon as we can."

"Wrap this up?" Dowling said. "Somebody is trying to kill me, and you say 'wrap this up'?"

Pam and Hackberry stepped inside the cottage and closed the door behind them. "You say somebody locked down on you with a sniper's rifle?"

"Yeah. Why do you think I called?"

"And Maydeen told you to fuck yourself? That doesn't sound like her."

Dowling's eyes were jumping in their sockets. "Are you listening? I know a laser sight when I see one. Who cares about Maydeen?"

"Did your security guys see it?"

"If they had, Collins would be turning on a rotisserie."

"The last time a couple of your guys ran into Jack, they didn't do too well," Hackberry said. "The coroner had to blot them up with flypaper and a sponge. Did you call the feds?"

"You listen," Dowling said, his voice trembling with either anger or fear or both. He set down his drink on a bare mahogany table, trying to regain control of his emotions. The velvet drapes were pulled on the windows, the dark carpets and wood furniture and black leather chairs contributing somehow to the coldness pumping out of the air-conditioning ducts. "Collins has killed at least two federal agents. Nobody can do anything about him. Even Josef Sholokoff is afraid of him. But you have a personal relationship with him. If you didn't, you'd be dead. I think you're leaving him out there purposely."

"Jack Collins tried to kill Chief Deputy Tibbs. He knows what I'll do to him if I get the chance, Mr. Dowling. In the meantime, I'm not sure anything happened here. If Jack had wanted to pop you, your brains would be on your shirt."

Even in the air-conditioning, the armpits of Dowling's golf shirt were damp, his face lit with a greasy shine. He picked up his drink, then set it down again, clearing a clot out of his voice box. "I want to talk to you alone," he said.

"What for?"

"You'll see."

"Pam, would you wait up at the club?"

"I love your decor, Mr. Dowling," she said. "We busted some metalheads and satanists who were growing mushrooms inside a place that looked just like it."

Dowling went into the bedroom and returned with a cardboard file folder secured by a thin bungee cord. He removed the cord and laid the folder flat side down on a dining room table, his chest rising and falling, as though wondering if he were about to take a wrong turn into the bad side of town. "I was going to give you this anyway," he said. "So I'm not giving it to you as a bribe or a form of extortion or anything like that."

"I have no idea what you're talking about," Hackberry said.

Dowling lifted his glass and drank and set the glass down again, his words steadying in his throat. "Years ago, when you were going across the border, my father had you surveilled and photographed. And buddy, did he get you photographed. Through windows and doorways, in every position and compromising moment a man and woman can put themselves in. You used three cathouses and three cathouses only. Am I right?"

"I don't know. I had blackouts back then."

"Trust me, if my father said you did, you did. Nobody in the history of the planet was better at cooking up a witches' brew to destroy people than he was. He drove my

528

mother mad and ruined his enemies financially and politically. In your case, he planned to blackmail you after you went to Congress. Except you married the union lady and got reborn with the proletariat and left the campaign."

"Why give me the photos?"

"I wanted to show you we're on the same side."

"We're not."

Dowling drank the rest of the whiskey in his glass, his cheeks blooming as though his soul had taken on new life. "Look, I don't have illusions about your feelings toward me. You think I'm a degenerate, and maybe I am. But I'm going to do something for you that nobody else can. You've made statements to people about your trips to Mexican whorehouses and the possibility that you screwed some underage girls. You were a whoremonger, all right, but not with young girls. If you had been, the photos would be in that file." Dowling pushed the folder toward Hackberry. "They're yours," he said.

"What about the negatives?"

"They're in there."

"And how about other prints?"

"There aren't any. I don't have any reason to lie. You may not like me, but I'm not my father."

"No, you're not," Hackberry said ambiguously.

"There's a barbecue grill on the patio out back. A little charcoal lighter and one match, and you can feed your mistakes to the flames."

"I tell you what," Hackberry said, sliding the folder back toward Dowling. "I'll provide you several phone numbers. You can give these photos to the San Antonio newspapers and my political opponents or ship them off to *Screw* magazine. Or you can thumbtack them to corkboards in Laundromats around town or glue them on the walls of washrooms and the sides of trucks. The Internet is another possibility."

"I thought I was doing the decent thing. I thought I'd put my own indiscretions in Mexico behind us. I thought you might hold me in a little higher regard."

"You profit off of war and people's misery, Mr. Dowling. My opinion about you has no weight in the matter. You're a maker of orphans and widows, just as your father was. You send others to fight wars that you yourselves will never serve in. Like a slug, your kind stays under a log, white and corpulent, and fears the sunlight and the cawing of jays. You have many peers, so don't take my comments on too personal a basis."

Dowling sat down in a straight-back chair, his hands cupped like dough balls. He was breathing through his mouth, looking upward, as though all the blood had drained out of his head. "You're a cruel, unforgiving man," he said.

"No, just a guy who has a long memory and doesn't allow himself to get bit by the same snake twice."

Pam Tibbs opened the front door without knocking and leaned inside. "Better come out here, Hack," she said. "R.C. talked to a caddie who saw a guy prowling around Mr. Dowling's SUV. R.C. is getting under it now."

The rain had stopped and the sky had started to clear and water was dripping off the fronds of the banana plants and palm trees and the roof of the shed on the driving range as they walked to the parking lot, Dowling's security men trailing behind them. In the waning of the sunset, they saw R.C. emerge from under the SUV, his uniform streaked with mud, one hand holding a serrated steel object. "It's either Chicom or Russian-made," he said. "The pin was wired to the wheel. One revolution would have pulled the pin and released the spoon."

"Where was it?" Dowling asked.

"This one was under the front seat," R.C. said.

"This one?" Dowling repeated.

"I thought I saw something back by the gas tank. I'll get a better light and check," R.C. said.

CHAPTER TWENTY-ONE

It took only two hours of worry and fear and the darker processes of the imagination to put Temple Dowling at Hackberry's front door.

"It's a little late," Hackberry said, a book in his hand.

"I'll tell you what I know, and you can do what you please with it. But you will not accuse me of being a murderer again."

"I didn't say that. I said you profited from it."

"Same thing."

"Do you want to come in or get off my property?"

Dowling sat in a chair by the front wall, away from the window, hands on the armrests like a man awaiting electrocution. He had showered and shaved and put on fresh clothes, but his face looked parboiled, his jaw disjointed, as though his mouth could not form the words he had to say. "I was a business partner with Josef Sholokoff," he said.

"In making and vending porn?"

"In entertainment. I didn't ask for details. It's a two-hundred-billion-dollar industry."

"What is?"

"Pornography. It's big business."

"You just said . . . Never mind. What about weapons?"

"I'm a defense contractor, but no, I don't work with Sholokoff. He does things off the computer with agencies that want anonymity. He's not the only one."

"Why does Sholokoff have it in for you?"

"He stiffed me on a deal, and I initiated an IRS investigation into his taxes. That's why he wants to get his hands on Noie Barnum. Josef will turn him over to Al Qaeda."

"What does he have to gain?"

"I hired Barnum. I thought he was a brilliant young engineer with a great future in weapons design. If Josef can compromise our drone program, I'll never get a defense contract again."

"You think Barnum would give military secrets to Islamic terrorists?"

"Of course. He's a pacifist and a flake or a bleeding heart, I don't know which. You don't think his kind want to flush this country down the drain? They want to feel good about themselves at somebody else's expense. What do you know about Barnum, anyway?"

Hackberry was sitting on the couch, half of his face lit by the reading lamp. He kept his expression blank, his eyes empty. "I don't know anything about him."

"No, you're hiding something," Dowling said.

"Like what?"

"I'm not sure." Dowling leaned forward. "You set me up."

"In what way?"

"At the country club. My father always said your best pitch was a slider. Son of a bitch. You took me good, didn't you?"

Hackberry shook his head. "You've lost me, Mr. Dowling."

"The grenade under my vehicle, the laser dot on my clothes. I must be the dumbest white person I ever met." Dowling waited. "You just gonna sit there and not say anything?"

Through the front window, Hackberry could see the hills and the stars and the arid coarseness of the land and the wispy intangibility of the trees in the arroyos and the glow of the town in the clouds. For what purpose had a divine hand or the long evolutionary patterns of ancient seas and volcanic eruption and the gradual wearing away of sedimentary rock created this strange and special place on the earth? Was it meant to be a magical playground for nomadic Indians who camped on its streams and viewed its buttes and mesas as altars on which they stood and stared at the western sun until they were almost blind? Or a blood-soaked expanse where colonials and their descendants had slain one another for four hundred years, where narco-armies waited on the other side of the Rio Grande, armed with weapons shipped from the United States, the same country that provided the market for the weed and coke and skag that went north on a daily basis? As Hackberry stared out the window, he thought he heard the rattle of distant machine-gun fire, a tank with a busted tread trying to dislodge itself from a ditch, the boiling sound napalm made when it danced across a snowfield. What did soldiers call it now? Snake and nape? What was the language of the killing fields today?

"You zoning out on me?" Dowling said.

"No, not at all. I was thinking about you and what you represent."

"Yes?" Dowling said, lifting his hands inquisitively.

"That's all, I was just having an idle thought or two. Good-bye, Mr. Dowling. There's no need for you to drop by again. I think your appointment in Samarra isn't far down the track. But maybe I'm wrong."

"My appointment *where?*"

Noie Barnum had experienced a recurrent dream for years that was more a memory than a dream. He would see himself as a boy again, hunting pheasants on his grandfather's farm in eastern Colorado. Noie had no memory of his father, who had died when he was three, but he would never forget his grandfather or the love he'd had for him. His grandfather had been a giant of a man, and a jolly one at that, who dressed every day in pressed bib overalls and, even though he was a Quaker, wore a big square beard like many of his Mennonite neighbors. When Noie was eleven, his grandfather had taken him pheasant hunting in a field of wild oats. The plains rolled away as far as Noie could see, golden and gray and white in the sunshine, backdropped by an indigo sky and the misty blue snowcapped outline of the Rocky Mountains. He remembered telling his grandfather he never wanted to leave the farm and never wanted to go back to the little town where his half sister was not allowed to bring her female date to the high school prom.

His grandfather had replied, "It doesn't matter where we live or go, Noie. The likes of us will always be sojourners."

"What are sojourners?"

"Folks like me and you and your mother and sister. We're the descendants of John Brown. We have no home in this world except the one we create inside us."

Just then two pheasants had burst from the stubble, rising fat and magnificent and thickly feathered and multicolored into the air, their wings whirring, their strength and aerial agility like a denial of their size and the laws of gravity.

"Shoot, little fellow! They're yours!" his grandfather had said.

When Noie let off the twelve-gauge, the recoil almost knocked him down. Unbelievably, the pattern hit both birds; they seemed to become broken in midair, dysfunctional, their wings crumpling, their necks flopping, their feet trying to hook the air as they tumbled into the stubble.

That night Noie had cried, then the sun rose in the morning as though he had wakened from a bad dream, and for years he did not think about the birds he had killed.

But after 9/11, the dream came back in a mutated form, one in which he no longer saw himself or his grandfather. Instead, he saw curds of yellow smoke angling at forty degrees across an autumnal blue sky and two giant birds on a window ledge entwining their broken wings and then plunging into a concrete canyon where fire trucks swarmed far below.

Noie woke from the dream, raising his head off his chest, unsure where he was, staring down the long dirt road that led to an unpainted gingerbread house.

"Who's Amelia?" Jack asked.

"My half sister. I must have dozed off. Where are we?" Noie said.

"Right up from the Chinese woman's place.

Does your sister live in Alabama?"

"No, she died nine years ago."

"Sorry to hear that. I was an only child. It must warp something inside you to see your sibling taken in an untimely way."

"I don't like to talk about it."

"That's the way I figure it. We all get to the same barn. Why study on it?" When Noie didn't reply, Jack said, "You scared of it?"

"Of what?"

"Dying."

"There are worse things."

"Cite one."

"Letting evil men harm the innocent. Not doing the right thing when honor is at stake. Why are we parked here?"

"Since we're wanted all over the state of Texas, I thought it might be a good idea to wait until it was dark before we drove into the yard of somebody who knows us."

"I don't think this is smart, Jack."

"Many a man has tried to put me in jail, but I've yet to spend my first day there."

Jack got out of the car and unlocked the trunk and came back with a suitcase that he set on the hood.

"What are you doing?" Noie asked.

"Changing clothes."

"On a dirt road in the dark?"

Jack began stripping off his soiled white shirt and unbuckling his trousers and slipping his feet from his battered cowboy boots, not replying, intent upon the project at hand, whatever it was. His chest and shoulders and arms and legs were white in the moonlight, and scars were crosshatched on his back from his ribs to his shoulder blades. He buttoned on a soft white shirt and pulled on a pair of tan slacks and slipped a pair of two-tone shoes on his feet, then unfolded a western-cut sport coat from the suitcase and pushed his arms into the sleeves. He sailed his wilted panama hat up an arroyo and knotted on a tie with a rearing horse painted on it and fitted a blocked short-brim Stetson on his head. He turned toward Noie for approval. "You know the mark of a man? It's his hat and his shoes," he said.

"You look like the best-dressed man of 1945," Noie said. "But what in God's name is on your mind, Jack?"

"Options."

"Can you translate that?"

"An intelligent man creates choices. A stupid man lets others deal the hand for him."

"You're not going to hurt that woman, are you?"

"You must think pretty low of me."

"Not true. But I got to have your word."

"That's what my mother used to say, right before she made me cut my own switch and skinned me into next week," Jack said.

The front porch light was on when they parked in the yard of the gingerbread house and knocked on the screen door. "Just an advanced warning, Noie," Jack said. "I think some lies are being told about me. So don't necessarily believe everything this lady says."

"What lies?"

"If people faced the truth about how governments work, there would be revolutions all over the earth. So they blame the misdeeds of the government on individuals. I happen to be one of those individuals. You never read Machiavelli up there at MIT?"

"*¡Venga!*" someone called from the kitchen.

"You heard her," Jack said.

They went inside and sat on the couch. A heavyset Mexican woman with a wooden spoon in her hand and her hair tressed up in braids came into the living room. Jack's Stetson was propped on his knee. He rose from the couch, his hat hooked on one finger. "Where's Ms. Ling?" he said.

"She went to the store. She'll be right back. I'm Isabel," the woman said.

"Mind if we wait?" Jack asked.

"The people are coming. If you don't mind them, they won't mind you," Isabel said.

"What people?"

"*La gente.* The people."

"Yeah, I got that. But what people?"

"The people who always come. You can sit at the tables in back if you want. I already put Kool-Aid out there. You can help me carry out the food," Isabel said.

"We don't mind in the least," Noie said. "Do we, Jack?"

Jack's expression made Noie think of a large yellow squash someone had just twisted out of shape.

They carried out lidded pots of beans and fried hamburger meat and plates of hot tortillas smeared with margarine. They set them on the plank tables under the trees and helped light the candles affixed to the bottoms of jelly jars. In the distance, they could see the headlights of several vehicles headed up the dirt road toward them.

"You have a bunch of wets coming through here?" Jack said.

"No, no wets," Isabel said, wagging a finger. "These are not wets, and 'wets' is not a term we use. You understand that, *hombre?*"

"When is the lady of the house due back?" he asked.

"Any time now. Sit down. We have plenty of food for everyone."

"We're not here to eat," Jack said.

"You should. You look like a scarecrow," Isabel said.

Jack stared at her back as she walked away.

"What are you thinking?" Noie asked.

"That woman has a figure like a garbage can with a pair of bowling pins under it."

"What lies would Miss Anton be telling about you, Jack?"

"Eat up and don't worry about it."

A caravan of cars and pickup trucks pulled into the yard, and Mexican working people filed around the sides of the house and through the front door without knocking and out the back door and sat at the tables and began filling their plates, talking incessantly, paying no attention to either Jack or Noie. Through the window of the chapel, Noie could see several of them placing their hands on the base of a wooden statue. "Why do they do that?" he asked.

"They're ignorant pagans is why. Didn't you ever read Ernest Hemingway?"

"I don't think so."

"You don't *think* so? What do you people read in college? Hemingway said Spain was a Catholic country but not a Christian one. Same with this bunch."

Noie hoped the people sitting near them did not know too much English.

Several children began battering a piñata with a broom handle, tearing apart the papier-mâché and colored crepe paper and stringing pieces of wrapped candy over the dirt apron under the tree. Several girls and young women sat down across from Noie and Jack, their backs turned, watching the children, sometimes reaching behind them to pick up a jar of Kool-Aid or a rolled tortilla. Jack was eating frijoles with a spoon, watching the women and girls, a smear of tomato sauce on his chin, the lumps in his face as swollen and hard-looking as cysts. The hair of the women and girls was so black it had a purple tint in it, like satin under a black light. Their skin was sun-browned, their teeth tiny, their eyes elongated, more Indian than Mexican. Their faces and throats were fine-boned, their features free of cosmetics; they looked like girls and young women from the Asian rim who might have just arrived in a new land where they would bear children and be cared for and loved by husbands who considered them a treasure and not simply a helpmate or a commodity.

Jack tore a section of paper towel off a roll on the table and wiped his mouth with it and balled it up in his hand. His eyes seemed to go in and out of focus; he pressed a thumb into his temple as though someone had shot an iron bolt into it.

"You have a migraine?" Noie said.

Jack didn't answer. He seemed to be counting the number of girls and women sitting on the other side of the plank table. There were nine of them. The wind had come up, fluttering the candles inside the jelly jars, blowing the hair of the women and girls into strands, like brushstrokes in an Oriental painting. The piñata finally exploded from the blows of the broom handle, showering candy on the ground, filling the air with the excited screams of the children. Jack's eyes were hollow, his mouth gray, his hands like talons on the tabletop.

"You don't look too good," Noie said.

"Are you saying something is wrong with me?" Jack said, glaring into Noie's face. "You saying I got a problem?"

"No, I was wondering if you were sick. Your eyes are shiny, like you've got a fever, like you're coming down with something." Noie tried to touch Jack's forehead.

"Mind your damn business, boy."

"That's what I'm doing. If you live with someone who's sick, you ask about him."

"It's the dust and the insect repellent and the stink coming out of that pot of tripe. I told you to eat up."

Jack kept huffing air out his nose, then leaned over and spat into the dust. But he didn't raise his eyes again and kept his gaze focused on his plate. "Where's that Amerasian or Chinese woman or whatever she is?"

"Don't speak rudely of Miss Anton. She's a fine woman. What's gotten into you?" Noie said.

"We have to go."

"It was your idea to come here. It's a grand night. Look at the stars. Look at the children playing. You should have a family, Jack. You'd see things different."

"Best shut your mouth, son."

"Sticks and stones."

"I cain't believe I've become a warder for a moron."

Jack stared at the women and girls again and pressed his fist under his chin to keep his hand from shaking. Now Noie had no doubt about the origins of Jack's discomfort. He lowered his voice when he spoke. "These are poor and desperate people, Jack. Why are you upset by them? Their kind are the salt of the earth. Come on, you're a better man than the one you're acting like."

Jack rose from the bench and picked up Noie's paper plate and their uneaten food and threw it in the garbage can. "You can get in the car or walk, I don't care which," he said.

"There's Miss Anton now," Noie said. "Why don't you talk with her? I'm like these others, I think she's a holy woman. We're already here. What's to lose? It's just like giving witness at a prayer meeting."

"You like to quote Saint Paul, do you? 'I put no woman in authority over a man.' Did he say that or not? He understood the treachery that's inherent in their nature. Tell me he didn't say that?"

"Paul was talking about cultists in Corinth who belonged to a temple dedicated to the worship of Diana. They were courtesans and were behaving as such in the church. Stop acting like you're unlettered."

"A pox on you," Jack replied.

Noie stood up and smiled as Anton Ling headed for their table, but she didn't ac-

545

knowledge him. She had parked her truck by the barn and was coming hard across the horse lot, past the windmill and the water tank, amid the tables and the seated diners and the children who were still hunting for the pieces of candy they had scattered on the ground. She paused only long enough to pick up the broom handle the children had used to burst the piñata.

"What are you doing here?" she said to Jack.

The women and the girls at the table scattered.

"To determine if you betrayed me to an FBI agent by the name of Ethan Riser," Jack said.

"Betrayed *you?* Are you insane?"

"Agent Riser tried to kill me. With no provocation."

"You murdered him. You also shot a man from Parks and Wildlife."

"I defended myself against them."

"Listen to me, Mr. Barnum," Anton said. "I don't know why you're with this man, but he's a mass murderer. He killed nine Thai girls with a submachine gun. He's a coward and a bully and mean to the bone. Stand up, Mr. Collins."

"I tried to be your friend, woman. I came to your house when Josef Sholokoff's men attacked you."

"Don't you ever address me as 'woman.' "

"How dare you sass me?"

"How dare you be on the planet?" she said,

546

and swung the broom handle down on the crown of his head just as he was rising from the bench. Then she attacked in serious mode, gripping the bottom of the handle to get maximum torque in her swings, slashing the blows on his ears and shoulders and forearms and forehead, any place that was exposed, cracking him once so hard on the temple that Noie thought the blow might be fatal.

"Miss Anton!" he said. "Miss Anton! Ease up! Please! You're fixing to kill him!"

Jack stumbled away from the table, blood leaking out of his hair, one arm crooked to protect his face. She followed after him, hitting him in the spine and ribs, finally breaking the broom handle with a murderous swing across the back of his neck. "Go into the darkness that spawned you, you vile man," she said. "Find the poor woman who bore you and apologize for the fact of your birth."

Jack fell to one knee. He had left his hat behind him, on the table, crown down. He seemed to look at it with longing, as though he had left behind the better part of him. Noie picked him up and helped him to the Trans Am, staring back over his shoulder at Miss Anton and the Mexicans standing in the backyard, their faces lit by the porch light and the candles flickering on the tables. Noie pushed Jack into the passenger seat. "I'll drive," he said.

"You're going with me?"

"What's it look like?"

Jack was smiling, his face threaded with blood running from his forehead. "You're a good kid."

"The hell I am." Noie started the engine and headed south down the dirt road, the headlights bouncing off mesquite that grew on the hillsides.

"I know a stand-up young guy when I see one," Jack said.

Noie accelerated, aiming over his knuckles at the road in front of him.

"Did you hear me?" Jack asked.

"Yeah, I heard you. Everything you've said. Night and day. I hear you. Boy, do I hear you. You killed an FBI agent and shot somebody from Parks and Wildlife?"

"They dealt the play. I didn't go looking for them."

Noie's jawbone tensed against his cheek in the dash light, but he said nothing in reply.

"You picked me up out of the dirt back there even though your ribs haven't mended. I know how much broken ribs hurt. There're not many kinds of pain I haven't experienced. But pain can be a blessing. It gives you fire in the belly you can draw on when need be, and it allows you to understand others, for good or bad. You hearing me on this, son?"

"I'm not your damn son."

"Have it your way."

"You have to help me find Krill."

"Why rent space in your head to a half-breed rodent?"

"I want Krill in leg irons," Noie said, looking away from the road into Jack's face. "That's the only reason I'm on board. You got that?"

"You believe I killed those Thai women?"

Noie's hands tightened on the wheel, and he looked at the road again. "Did you?"

"What's the deal with Krill?"

"He can take me to Al Qaeda. He was going to sell me to them. Then he decided to sell me to some narco-gangsters because it was easier."

"I think I'm seeing the landscape a little more clearly. Your sister died on 9/11?"

"In the Towers."

"If I he'p you find Krill and maybe even these asswipes from Al Qaeda?"

"I'll stay with you. I'll be your friend. I won't let you down."

"Turn east at the highway. We're not going back to our place. I'll show you a road through a ranch into Coahuila. Only a few wets know about it."

"But we leave everybody else here alone? Right? We find Krill but that's it?"

"You're preaching to the choir," Jack said. "All I've ever wanted was to be left alone. I never stole, and I never went looking for trouble. How many people can say that?"

Noie looked back at him. "I know you've done some dark deeds, but I can't believe you mowed down a bunch of innocent women. I just can't believe that."

"Believe whomever you want. I'm tired of talking. I've tired of everything out there."

"Out where?"

"There, in the dark, the voices in the wind, the people hunting and killing each other while they scowl at the likes of me. If I study on it, I have moments when I want to write my name on the sky in ways nobody will ever forget. That's the burden you carry when you're born different. You told me once your sister grew up bisexual or whatever in that small southern town y'all come from. Did she have a good time of it there? I think you've got more of me inside you than you're willing to admit, Noie."

"You're wrong."

Jack gazed silently through the front window, his forehead crosshatched with lesions, his thoughts, if any, known only to himself.

CHAPTER TWENTY-TWO

Anton Ling called in the report on Noie Barnum and Jack Collins's visit to her property five minutes after the two men had left. Maydeen Stoltz immediately called Hackberry at his home.

"Which way did they head?" he said.

"South, toward the four-lane."

"Get out traffic stops ten miles on either side of where they would enter the four-lane. Then call the FBI and the Border Patrol. Did Noie Barnum seem coerced?"

"Not according to Ms. Ling. She says Barnum heard her accuse Collins of murdering Ethan Riser and the Thai women, and Barnum left with him voluntarily. You think this is Stockholm syndrome or whatever they call it?"

"I doubt it."

"No matter how you cut it, Barnum isn't a victim?" Maydeen said.

"Not to us, he isn't," Hackberry replied.

"Ms. Ling says she beat the shit out of

551

Collins with a broom handle. You want me to check the hospitals?"

"Waste of time," Hackberry said. "I'll see you tomorrow."

"What do you think his next move is, Hack?"

"He's going to call either the department or my house."

"What for?"

"He made a public fool of himself at Anton Ling's," Hackberry replied.

"I don't get it."

"We're the only family he has."

"Yuck," she said.

The next morning Hackberry went to his office early and dug out the three-inch-thick file on Jack Collins and began thumbing through only a small indicator of the paperwork that one man had been able to string across an entire continent. The paperwork on Collins, who had never spent one day in jail, included faxes from Interpol and Mexico City, NCIC printouts, FBI transmissions, analytical speculations made by a forensic psychologist at Quantico, crime-scene photos that no competent defense attorney would allow a jury to see, autopsy summations written by coroners who were barely able to deal with the magnitude of the job Collins had dropped on them, witness interviews, crime-lab ballistic matches from Matamoros to San Antonio, and the most fitting inclusion in the file, a handwritten memo by a retired Texas Ranger in Presidio County who wrote, "This man seems about as complex as a derelict begging food at your back door and I suspect he smells about the same. I think the trick is to make him hold still long enough to put a bullet in him. But we've yet to figure out a way to do it."

What did it all mean? For Hackberry, the answer was simple. The system couldn't handle Jack Collins because he didn't follow the rules or conform to patterns that are associated with criminal behavior. He wasn't addicted to drugs or alcohol, didn't frequent prostitutes, and showed little or no interest in money. There was no way to estimate the number of people he had murdered, since many of his homicides were committed across the border, but he was not a serial killer. Nor could he be shoved easily into that great catchall category known as psychopaths, since he obviously had attachments, even though the figures to whom he was attached lived in his imagination.

Preacher Jack was every psychiatrist's nightmare. His level of intelligence and his wide reading experience allowed him to create a construct in which he shared dominion with the Olympians. His narcissism was so deeply rooted in his soul that he did not fear death because he thought the universe could not continue without his presence. He was messianic and believed he could see through a hole in the dimension and watch events play out in the lives of people who were not yet born.

With gifts like these, why should Preacher Jack fear a law enforcement agency? Like the cockroach and the common cold, he was in the fight for the long haul.

The irony was that in spite of his success in eluding the law for almost two decades, Collins shared a common denominator with his fellow miscreants: He needed law enforcement to validate who he was. Intuitively, he knew his own kind were by and large worthless and would sell him out for a pack of cigarettes if they thought they could get away with it. All career criminals wanted the respect of the cops, jailers, social workers, correctional officers, and prison psychologists whose attention gave them the dimensions they possessed in no other environment.

There was another consideration in regard to what went on in the mind of a man like Preacher Jack. His visit last night at Anton Ling's home reminded Hackberry of a similar event that had taken place in Jack's life the previous year, in San Antonio. Jack had become obsessed with a Jewish woman by the name of Esther Dolan and had invaded her home and indicated to her that he had chosen her as his queen. When she had recovered from the shock of his presumption, she called him a dog turd off the sidewalk and picked up a stainless-steel oatmeal pot and almost beat him to death with it.

Pam Tibbs leaned inside his door. "Guess who's on the phone," she said.

"Texas's answer to B.O. Plenty."

"Who?" she said.

"Collins?"

"I've already started the trace," she said.

"Have the feds called back this morning?"

"Nope."

Hackberry gazed at the blinking light on his telephone, then picked up the receiver. "What's the haps, Jack?" he said.

"I thought I'd check in."

"We figured we'd be hearing from you."

"You omniscient, Mr. Holland?"

"It's Sheriff Holland to you."

"I like to keep abreast of your activities, since you seem intent on doing me harm and forgetting I saved the life of your young deputy, what's-his-name, Bevins."

"No, I think you're calling because you became a human piñata out at Anton Ling's place, in front of dozens of poor Mexicans who are now convinced there's a serious problem in the Anglo gene pool. Just before you called, I was thinking about a pattern that seems to follow you around, Jack. Remember Esther Dolan in San Antone? She's the lady who drove you from her house with knots all over your head. Then there was that

555

good-looking gal, the country singer, Vikki Gaddis. She sprayed wasp killer in your eyes and took your pistol away from you and shot you through the foot. Why is it you keep getting into it with women who kick your ass? Do they remind you of your mother?"

"Good try, Sheriff. But I'm afraid you don't know much about my upbringing."

"You like to read novels. I've got a story for you, better than any fiction. Did you know that when Ma Barker and her son Fred were surrounded by the FBI, they executed each other with submachine guns? They sat across from each other in straight-back chairs down by the Everglades and blew each other all over the walls. How about that for a tight mother-son relationship? They were even buried in the same casket."

"You fear a woman's wrath, Sheriff Holland? The man who does will surround himself with manipulators and prostitutes and will never have a real woman in his life. The level of his anger hides the degree of his need. I thought you were wise in the ways of the world, but I'm starting to have my doubts."

"Ethan Riser was my friend, you arrogant son of a bitch."

"Ah, now we get down to the real issue."

"You emptied your magazine into him after he was dead. His face was unidentifiable. He said something to you before he died, some-

556

thing you couldn't abide, didn't he? What was it, Collins? That you were despised inside the womb?"

"To be honest, I couldn't quite make out Agent Riser's words in all that shooting. The Thompson makes a heck of a racket."

Hackberry could feel his hand gripping the phone receiver tighter and tighter, a bilious taste welling up in his throat. "No, it wasn't about your mother. It wasn't about your pathetic sex life, either. It had something to do with your vision of yourself, the Orkin man posing as Jesus. Ethan was a student of both history and Shakespeare. He reached back into his own reference and used it on you, didn't he? What made it doubly injurious was the fact that you acquired your literary background the hard way, and he used it to make you look like a fool. He called you a clown, didn't he? A collection of tattered rags flapping in the wind, a stick figure with a carved pumpkin for a head. That's you, Collins. Everyone knows it except you, you moron. Even the dead people who follow you around know it. You're an object of pity. You think women like Gaddis and Dolan and Ling would be in a room with you unless you were holding a gun on them? Don't call here again, even to surrender yourself. A phone conversation with you is like someone putting spittle in my ear. I don't know how else to describe it. You have that effect on people."

Hackberry replaced the receiver in the phone cradle and stared at it, his hand shaking on the desk blotter.

"That was a beaut," Pam said from the doorway. "Think you got to him?"

Hackberry shook his head. "There're no handles on Collins. I had no design in mind."

"You could have fooled me."

He looked at her for a long time. "Be careful," he said.

"Of Collins?"

"Of everything. We can't lose our good people."

"Nothing is going to happen to me," she said.

"Don't say that. It's bad luck."

She came into his office and closed the door behind her. "The minister from my church dropped by. He said he wanted to warn me about a rumor he'd heard."

"What did you tell him?"

"That whatever it was, it was probably true, and I wasn't interested in hearing it."

He folded his hands behind his head and put one boot on the corner of the desk. "You're heck on wheels, kiddo."

"Call me that after quitting time and I'll hit you."

"I believe it," he replied.

In the darkness the game ranch was a surreal place that seemed more like African dry land drenched in moonlight and shadowed by an enormous mountain that was over six thousand feet in elevation. The sand in the streambeds was white, the rocky sides of the declivities as sharp as knives, the land rustling with desert greenery and tabled with slabs of sedimentary rock that looked like the marbled backs of albino whales. The steel fence that enclosed the ranch seemed to roll for miles across the countryside, and the mesh was so thick that it took Krill's men twenty minutes to scissor an opening in it with the bolt cutters. Out in the darkness, they could hear large animals banging around in the brush, hooves clattering on rocks, and they wondered if the noise would give warning to Josef Sholokoff and his entourage at the big stone house in the valley.

Krill led his men single-file through the slit in the fence, his M16 now equipped with a bipod and slung on his right shoulder, his eyes locked on the lighted compound down below. The wind was up, bending the trees and the tall grasses, which was not good for men threading their way through trees and foliage. When the wind blew, everything in the environment moved, even the shadows, everything except Krill and his men. But bad luck was an element to which a man adjusted and did not allow himself to be overcome by. Negrito was another matter. Suddenly, he had become an expert on all matters of importance and would not shut up: "This place has got rattlesnakes and Gila monsters in it . . . Those big animals you hear snuffing, that's rhinos. One wrong step and *squish* . . . A *puta* for one of the Russian's men told you where he was at? How dependable is that? What if he ain't there? What if we kill a bunch of guys and don't get the Russian? We got to wipe the slate clean, Krill. We turn the house down there into a cemetery."

"Once again you have shown your great wisdom," Krill said. "But now you must be quiet."

"I am operating as your loyal lieutenant and adviser, my *jefe.*"

"Yes, yes, I know. But you talk like a bat flapping its wings in a cave, filling the air with sound that means nothing. You must cease this constant talking. It's like glass in my ears."

Negrito's BB eyes seemed to grow closer to the bridge of his nose. "I'm here to serve you, nothing more. I worry about this mission. We are killing the Russian because he killed the minister who baptized your children. But this all has it origins with La Magdalena. If she had baptized them as you asked, we would not be having these problems. The Russians are dangerous. If you kill one of them, you kill them all. They come out of prisons worse than Mexico's. They fuck their mothers and kill their children. Many of them were in

560

insane asylums."

"Where do you get these ideas, *hombre?*"

"You don't listen to the new music, the *narcocorridas*. The *narcocorridas* tell us all about these guys. That's why our people have to be vicious and show no mercy."

"Look up there on the hillsides, above the stone house. Those two men are Sholokoff's guards. Let your actions replace your words, Negrito. Take Lupa and Mimo with you and do your job."

"Stay here and I'll bring you back their ears. I don't need Mimo and Lupa to do it, either."

Krill waved a finger back and forth. "No, you don't bring back ears."

"You took the scalp of the DEA agent."

"Because he killed my brother. Because I had to bring an offering to my brother's grave so he could rest. You do not bring back trophies from these men. They are only doing what they are told."

"Wait and see," Negrito said.

"Everything with you is an argument." Krill pulled Negrito's leather hat off his head and started to hit him with it but instead simply shook his head and handed the hat back. He waited several seconds before he spoke, the heat dying in his chest. "The moon is going behind the mountain. As soon as the shadow falls on the house, kill Sholokoff's guards and come back to me. You are very good at what you do, Negrito. Do not fail me."

"I will never fail you. When the rooster crows and the sun rises, you will see me at your side and know I have been your loyal servant and follower."

The moon slipped behind the crest of the mountain, dropping the valley into black shadow. Negrito and the two other men filed down a game trail and climbed silently over a table rock and disappeared into a thicket that was rife with thorns, never hanging their clothes on one of them, never rustling a branch. Krill unslung his assault rifle and knelt in the grass and waited, his gaze roaming over the lighted stone house and the swimming pool steaming behind it and a children's swing set whose chains made a tinkling sound in the wind.

His M16 had been stolen from an armory in Mexico, along with crates of ammunition and United States Army .45 automatics and bayonets and grenades and flak vests and other forms of military ordnance that Krill considered of no value. But the M16 was indeed a wondrous product of American manufacturing genius. It was lightweight, simple in design, easy to disassemble, rapid-firing, and soft on the shoulder. In semiauto mode, it could snap off shots individually with lethal accuracy or, on auto mode, hose down an entire room in seconds. The newer ones seldom jammed, and in the dark, the shooter could easily drop an empty magazine and replace it with a fresh one. Krill had jungle-clipped a twenty-round and thirty-round magazine together, so when his bolt locked open on an empty chamber, he could invert the two magazines and jam the full one into the loading slot without ever missing a beat.

Argentinean and American advisers had taught him how to shoot and care for the M16 and how to aim in the dark and not silhouette on a hill and how to crawl through wire on his stomach and sink mines in the trails used by the Sandinistas. They had also taught him the use of the M60 machine gun, a weapon whose murderous effectiveness had never ceased to amaze him. What his advisers had not taught him was how to live with the virus the guns had given him, because that was what it was, he told himself, a virus, one that produced an insatiable bloodlust that was like walking around in a warm pink mist and always wanting more of it.

He looked at the luminescent numbers on his wristwatch. Seventeen minutes had passed. He wondered what was keeping Negrito and the others. Lupa and Mimo were not killers by nature, but they would do as they were told and would not question the morality of the orders, as was almost always the case with poor men who became soldiers. Lupa had earned his nickname, "the magnifying glass," because of the cheap spectacles he wore in order to read and his attention to details that were of no importance. Like Lupa, Mimo had been a farmer in Oaxaca before the prices for corn had gone to virtually nothing, but he was also a drunkard who drank huge amounts of liquor, made from sugarcane, that could be bought for a few cents a bottle. Neither man was dangerous or violent in himself, and both men together did not form another personality that was necessarily dangerous. But under the direction of Negrito, they would commit any number of heinous acts as long as they believed they were committing them in the interest of their families. Mexico was not a country, Krill thought. It was a revolution that had never stopped. The only things in it that stayed the same were the killings and the river of narcotics flowing to the north. The poor suffered and worked in sweatshops and lived in hovels and abandoned their children to live on the streets of Mexico City. Why did they not all rise up and kill their masters? Krill had no answer. Could it be that they were holy in their passivity? As with Negrito, these were ideas he could not fathom, at least not adequately. Maybe that was why Negrito had become his companion and lieutenant. This last conclusion was a disturbing one, and he did not want to dwell further on it.

He saw Mimo and Lupa coming through

the trees and tall grass, bent down, their un-shaved faces as severe as those of men staring into an ice storm.

"*¿Qué pasa?*" Krill asked.

Their eyes avoided his. Lupa looked over his shoulder.

"*¡Dígame!*" Krill said.

"*Muerto,*" Lupa said.

"*¿Quiene?*" Krill asked.

"*Ellos,*" Mimo replied.

"Do you think I am stupid? What did you do out there?" Krill said in English.

Neither man replied. They squatted and kneaded their thighs as though they had run a long distance. They wiped their noses on their hands and felt in their pockets for tobacco or chewing gum, then looked with relief over their shoulders when they heard Negrito coming through the brush, bent low, a button-down shirt wadded in his hand.

"What happened out there?" Krill said.

"We took care of them guys. Like you told me. The second guy fought," Negrito replied.

"What is in your hand?"

"Nothing anybody's gonna miss. At least them guys ain't."

"Do not play games with me, Negrito."

"Krill, we are doing these things out of loyalty to you. We ain't getting paid. Why are you on my case, man?"

"Put the shirt on the ground and open it."

"I am at your orders. But you make a big

thing out of nothing. You didn't want no ears. So I took their noses. They were dead. What does a dead man care about a nose? What's he gonna smell? There ain't no flowers in a grave, at least the graves these guys are gonna have."

"The second man? You said he fought. He alerted others?"

"He couldn't talk, know what I mean?" Negrito drew a finger across his throat. "But he fought hard just the same. I think he was Russian. The Russians got cojones like baseballs. You got to kill them guys really dead. Krill?"

"*¿Qué pasa?*" Krill answered, overwhelmed by the processes of Negrito's mind.

Negrito seemed to stare at the stone house and the light falling out of the windows on the patio and the windmill palms and umbrella trees and the dark surface of the swimming pool. The wind gusted, wrinkling the water, rustling the limp chains on the swing set. His brow furrowed. "Me and Lupa and Mimo was talking," he said. "The inside of that house is like a bank. There's got to be cash all over it. Maybe cocaine, too. We do everybody in there, man, then take what we want."

"No."

"What do you mean 'no'? Come on, *cabrón*. We suppose to work for nothing? It ain't fair. We're amigos. We have always shared. But

566

you can't share nothing."

"Go back on your own if you don't like our mission."

"I will never leave you."

"Then do as I say."

"And what is that? To let the Russian's friends hunt us down? We're gonna kill them all, right? If we kill them all, why not take what should be ours? All of this land belonged to our ancestors. Now it is owned by everybody except us."

"You are a logical man. But we do not have an issue with anyone but Josef Sholokoff. I do not want his possessions. We avenge Minister Cody. We made fun of his manhood, but it was he who set the souls of my children free. For that I honor his memory. Do not intrude upon my purpose here."

Negrito raised his big hands and turned in a circle like a baboon attempting a pirouette. "Then let's kill the Russian and be gone. I am tired of this place. Do you want me to do it? I would do it with great pleasure. I am tired of talking about baptism and souls while we don't get paid for the work we do. I am not a mystic. I believe in the knife and gun and dealing seriously with my enemies."

"You also believe in the shovel."

"You speak of my cemetery? I signal our adversaries of our potential."

"You keep a museum under the ground for your pleasure. As a ghoul would. *Vámonos*,"

Krill said. He slung his rifle over his shoulder and walked off through the brush and started down the incline, Negrito's close-set pig eyes slipping off the side of his face.

As Krill approached the stone house, he forgot about Negrito and began to think about the challenge at hand. When the two guards Negrito had killed did not report in, others would be sent outside to find them. In the meantime, Krill had to find a spot that would allow him a clean shot through the front window. He thought he could hear the sound of a television coming from the front of the house, but in the wind he couldn't be sure. His informant had told him that Sholokoff was staying at the house with no more than four men. Two of those were already taken care of. If Krill could get a clear shot at Sholokoff and kill him instantly, he might not have to kill his men, too. Few hired killers were willing to risk their lives for a dead employer. But if they chose to avenge their employer's death, they would share the fate of their comrades on the hillside, Krill thought, and the choice would be theirs, not his.

He stayed in the shadow of the mountain and found a flat place up on a bench behind a rock, perhaps thirty yards from the front of the house, with an unobstructed view through the picture-glass living room window. He removed a small pair of binoculars from a pouch on his web belt and focused them through the glass. A diminutive, gray-headed, wizen-faced man in a belted scarlet robe was watching television from a reclining chair. His wiry beard and angular features made Krill think of a ferret or a toy constructed of Popsicle sticks and glue. How could one so small possess so much wealth and exert so much power over others? Krill wondered. Why did the gringos allow this tiny man to do so much damage in their country? The narcotics he sold were the poor man's hydrogen bomb. But that was their business and not his. Krill wrapped his left forearm in the rifle sling, fitted his right hand in the pistol grip, and looked through the iron sights. Behind him, he could hear Negrito breathing in the darkness, an aura of dried sweat and tobacco and wood smoke emanating from his body.

"*¡Qué bueno, hombre!*" Negrito said.

"Do not talk," Krill said, shifting the bipod on the rock, depressing the barrel slightly so the hood on the front sight formed a perfect circle around Sholokoff's tiny head. He tightened his finger on the trigger, letting out his breath, his cheek flush against the dull black finish of the rifle stock.

"*Chingado,* go ahead!" Negrito said. "Burn the whole magazine. It's time we got out of here. I want to fuck my woman tonight."

Krill had released his finger from the trigger and was staring numbly down the incline at the window. Two little girls and a little boy had just run from a side room and climbed into Sholokoff's lap. Negrito leaned over Krill's shoulder to see better, his loins brushing against Krill's buttocks, his body odor and the smell of onions and garlic and fried meat on his breath enveloping Krill in a toxic cloud.

"Fuck, man, do it," Negrito said. "I hear a plane. Them hunters come in and out of here all the time. They got a landing strip on the other side of the house."

"Shut your mouth," Krill said.

"You ain't thinking straight. We already killed two guys. You got to finish the job, man. Sholokoff has many friends. We cannot have this man hunting us. Do it now, *jefe*."

"Take your hand off my shoulder."

"Then shoot."

"You will not give me orders."

"Then give me the rifle."

"Remove your hand and take your odor out of my face."

"Look at the plane. It's dipping out of the sky. You have to choose between our families and these worthless people. You worry about my odor? What is wrong with you, man?"

"You are like an empty wagon rattling across a bridge," Krill said. "You speak craziness and nonsense. You are like the demoniac babbling among the swine. We do not kill children. Have you learned nothing? Do you understand nothing except killing?"

"We did not put the children here. This is not our fault. Lupa and Mimo and me will do everything that is necessary inside the house. You will not have to see or hear anything that happens down there. One day you will be right in the head, but now you are not. So we will do these things for you and forget the bad words that you have spoken."

"You will do nothing without my permission."

"Take the shot, Krill. Please. You can do it. I've seen you shoot the head off a dove at a hundred meters. Concentrate on the Russian and don't worry about the children. They will be all right. But we cannot leave this man alive."

Krill's head was pounding, his ears filled with whirring sounds that were louder than either the wind or Negrito's incessant talking. Had it been like this for the soldiers in the helicopter who had machine-gunned the clinic built by the East Germans? Had they seen Krill's children playing in the yard and wondered if they should not abort their mission? Had they fired on the building in hopes that they would not hit the children? Or had they given no thought at all to what they were doing? Did they simply murder his children and fly back to their base and eat lunch and drink warm beer under a palm-shaded table, staring idly at a smokeless blue volcano in the distance? Was that what happened when they slew the innocent children he had loved from the first breath they had drawn?

He bent over the rifle again, feeling the sling tighten on his left arm, his mouth filled with a taste like pennies, a brass band thundering in his head. The little boy was seated firmly in Sholokoff's lap, watching the television. Krill raised the rifle barrel until the hood on the front sight circled Sholokoff's head like the frame on a miniature photograph. He took a breath and waited a split second and then exhaled slowly, slowly, slowly, his left eye squinted shut, his right eye bulging like a child's marble, his index finger tightening as though it had a life of its own.

Suddenly, he stood erect, pulling his hand from the trigger guard as though it had been shocked with a cattle prod. His teeth were chattering, his breath catching in his throat. *Murderer,* he thought he heard a voice say. *Assassin! Man who brought death to his own children.* He stared wide-eyed at Negrito.

"You look sick, *cabrón.* You look like your mind has flown into the darkness," Negrito said.

"We go back through the grass and out the fence," Krill said. "We are through with this. We will deal with Sholokoff at another time."

"I cannot believe what you are doing," Negrito said. "You're letting us down, man. You are making a great mistake that each of us will pay for. It ain't fair. You are betraying us, Krill."

Krill was already walking deep into the mountain's shadow, his M16 reslung on his shoulder, his eyes empty, like those of a man who has looked into a mirror and is unable to recognize the image staring back at him.

CHAPTER TWENTY-THREE

Hackberry Holland did not learn of the killings near the Santiago Mountains from another law enforcement agency, because they were not reported the night they occurred or the following morning, either. He learned of them from a questionable source, one in whom he had already induced a sizable dose of paranoia. In fact, he had a hard time concentrating on the telephone conversation. It was raining, and he had forgotten to take down the flag outside his office window. The flag, soggy as a towel, hung twisted and forlorn against a gray sky, its chain vibrating against the pole like a damaged nerve. "Mr. Dowling, I've heard nothing about a shooting in this county or anywhere around here," he said. "It's been surprisingly quiet."

"Of course you didn't. Josef doesn't want cops crawling all over his property," Temple Dowling replied.

"You say two men were killed?"

"Right. Two security guys. Somebody cut their noses out of their faces."

"Sounds a bit strange, doesn't it? I mean, why is it you know about this but nobody else does?"

"Because maybe I got one or two people inside Josef's organization."

"What do you want me to do about this unreported homicide that only you seem to know about?"

"Go out to the game ranch. Investigate the crime. Stuff a hand grenade up his ass. What do I care? Why not just do your fucking job?"

"Because somehow you're at risk?"

"Josef believes I put a hit on him."

"Listen to what you're saying, Mr. Dowling. Two guys got killed outside Sholokoff's house, but no attempt was made to harm anybody inside the house. Does that seem like a rational scenario to you?"

"That's because a bunch of hunters had just flown in. Look, my source says Josef went apeshit. He had his grandchildren in the house." There was a pause. "His guys are coming after me."

Hackberry could hear the tremor in Dowling's voice, the frightened boy no longer able to hide behind arrogance and cruelty. "First, you have your own security service, Mr. Dowling. Why not make use of it? If a crime occurred in the place you describe, it's out of my jurisdiction. Second, maybe it's time for you to grow up."

"Time for me to —"

"Everybody dies. Why not go down with the decks awash and the guns blazing? You've probably made millions profiteering off of war. Get a taste of the real deal and scorch your name on the wall before you check out. It's not a bad way to go."

"You're a son of a bitch."

Hackberry rubbed his forehead and started to hang up, then placed the receiver against his ear again. "If you think you're in danger, get out of town."

"I'm already out of town. It doesn't matter. Sholokoff has a network all over the country."

"I think you're imagining things."

"You don't understand Josef. He doesn't just do evil. He loves it. That's the difference between him and the rest of us. Jack Collins is probably a lunatic. Josef isn't. He creates object lessons nobody ever forgets. He has people taken apart."

"He does what?"

Perhaps due to his fundamentalist upbringing, R. C. Bevins was not a believer in either luck or coincidence but saw every event in his life as one that required attention. The consequence was that he never dismissed any form of human behavior as implausible and never thought of bizarre events in terms of their improbability. The sheriff had once told

R.C. that if a UFO landed on the prairie, two things were guaranteed to happen: Everyone who witnessed the landing would grab his cell phone to dial 911, and R.C. would knock on the spaceship door and introduce himself.

R.C. had pulled into a convenience store and gas station on a county road just south of the east-west four-lane that paralleled the Mexican border, and had gone inside and bought a chili dog and a load of nachos and jalapeño peppers and a Dr Pepper and had just started eating lunch at a table by the front window when he saw a pickup stop and let out a passenger. The passenger limped slightly, as though he had a stitch in his side. He wore shades and an unlacquered wide-brim straw hat, like one a gardener might wear. His nose was a giant teardrop, his jeans hiked up too high on his hips, his suspenders notched into his shoulders, the way a much older man might wear them. The man went into the back of the store and took a bottle of orange juice and a ham-and-cheese sandwich from the cooler and a package of Ding Dongs from the counter. He paid, sat down, and began eating at a table not far from R.C.'s, never removing his shades. R.C. nodded at him, but the man did not look up from his food.

"Bet you could fry an egg out there," R.C. said.

"That about says it," the man replied, chewing slowly, his mouth closed, his gaze seemingly fixed on nothing.

"My uncle says that during the drought of 1953, it got so dry here he saw a catfish walking down a dirt road carrying its own canteen."

"That's dry."

"You looking for a ride? 'Cause the bread-delivery man is fixing to head back to town."

"No, I'm visiting down the road there. South a piece." The man drank from his orange juice and wiped his mouth with a paper napkin and began eating his sandwich again.

"Did you see any salt and pepper up there at the counter?" R.C. asked.

"I think I did. Where the ketchup and such are. In that little tray."

"You want some?"

"No, sir, I'm fine."

R.C. went to the counter by the coffee and cold-drink dispensers and began sorting through the condiments. "Do y'all have any hot sauce?" he said to the cashier.

"It's there somewhere," the cashier replied.

"I sure cain't find it."

The cashier walked over and picked up the hot sauce and handed it to R.C. He was a short man with a sloping girth who always showed up at work in a dress shirt and an outrageous tie and with polished shoes. He had a tiny black mustache that expanded like grease pencil when he grinned. "Glad it wasn't a snake."

"Keep looking straight at me," R.C. said.

The cashier's face clouded, but he kept his eyes locked on R.C.'s.

"You know that old boy over yonder?" R.C. said.

"I think he was in yesterday. He bought some Ding Dongs and a newspaper."

"He was by himself?"

"He came here with another man. The other fellow stayed in the car."

"What'd the other guy look like?"

"I didn't pay him much mind."

"What kind of car?"

The cashier looked into space and shook his head. "It was skinned up. It didn't have much paint on it. I don't know what kind it was."

"You ever see it before?"

The cashier rubbed his eye. "No, sir," he said. "Are we fixing to have some trouble here? 'Cause that's something I really don't need."

"No. Did the guy in the car buy gas with a credit card?"

"If he did, I didn't see it. He got air."

"What?"

"He went to the air pump. I remember that 'cause he was the last to use it. Somebody ran over the hose, and I had to put an out-of-order sign on it. Ain't nobody used it since."

R.C. went back to his table and set the bottle of hot sauce down, then snapped his fingers as though he had forgotten something. He went outside to his cruiser and picked up a clipboard off the seat, then walked past the air pump. The concrete slab around it was covered with a film of mud and dust that had dried into a delicate crust. A set of familiar tire tracks was stenciled across it. "Michelins," R.C. said under his breath.

R.C. went back to his table with the clipboard. "I got to do these dadburn time logs," he said to the man at the next table.

"I bet that's what we'll all be doing when somebody drops a nuclear missile on us," the man said.

"I never thought of it like that. I think you got your hand on it."

"Hope we get some rain. This is about the hottest place I've ever been," the man said.

"You know what General Sherman said when he was stationed here? He said if he owned both Texas and hell, he'd rent out Texas and live in hell," R.C. said.

The man tilted up his orange juice and drank it empty, swallowing smoothly, never letting a drop run off the side of his mouth. R.C. went back to eating, his long legs barely fitting under the table, his jaw filled with food, one eye on his clipboard. "This stuff is a royal pain in the ass," he said. "I'm going back on patrol. If they want my time logs filled out, they can fill them out their own self."

"If I were you, I'd put the times in there somebody wants and not worry about it. That's how organizations are run. You just got to make things look right. Why beat yourself up over it?"

"You sound like a guy who's been around."

"Not really."

"Where you staying at, exactly?"

"A little vacation spot a buddy of mine has got rented. It's just a place to go hunting for rocks and arrowheads and such."

"Look, is somebody coming to pick you up? You looked like you were limping."

"I'll hitch a ride. People here'bouts are pretty nice."

"I don't mind driving you home. That's part of the job sometimes."

"No, I was in an accident a while back. I don't like to start depending on other people. It gets to be a habit too easy."

R.C. picked up the remnants of his nachos and chili dog and threw them in the trash, then sat down at the table with the man, who was now feeding a Ding Dong into his mouth. "You seem like a right good fellow," he said. "The kind of guy who don't want to hurt nobody but who might get into something that's way to shit and gone over his head."

"I wouldn't say that."

"I always figured if a guy makes a mistake,

he ought to get shut of it as quick as he can and keep on being the fellow he always was."

"That could be true, but I think you've got somebody else in mind."

"You're not from Texas, but you're from down South somewhere, right?"

"Me and a few million others."

"But you weren't raised up to keep company with criminals. It's got to grate on you. I reckon that's why you hitched a ride here today."

"You want a Ding Dong?"

"Not right now," R.C. said, and fitted one end of his handcuffs onto the man's left wrist and snicked the ratchet into the locking mechanism. "Mind if I call you Noie?"

"I've answered to worse."

"You have a friend who drives a Trans Am that has Michelin tires on it?"

"Can't say as I do."

"Where's Preacher Collins at, Noie?"

The man squinted thoughtfully and scratched at an insect bite on the back of his neck with his free hand. "Who?" he said.

"You're not going to believe this," Maydeen said, standing in Hackberry's doorway.

He looked up from his desk and waited.

"R.C. says he's got Noie Barnum hooked up in the back of his cruiser," she said.

Hackberry stared at her blankly.

"He says Barnum walked into a conve-

582

nience store down by the four-lane," she said. "He'd hitched a ride to have lunch there."

"How does R.C. know it's Barnum?"

"He says the guy looks just like his photo, except he's a little leaner. He's got a limp and maybe has some broken ribs."

"The guy admits he's Noie Barnum?"

"R.C. didn't say. He just says it's him."

"What about Jack Collins?"

"R.C. said there were Michelin tire tracks where Collins's car was parked yesterday. I didn't get it all, Hack. Want me to notify the FBI?"

"No."

"You don't?"

"Did you hear me?"

"Yeah, I did. How about losing the tone?"

He stood up from his desk, staring out the window into the brilliance of the day, at the wind whipping the flag on the pole, at the hard blueness of the sky above the hills. His right hand opened and closed at his side. "Tell R.C. to bring him through the back."

"Hack?"

"What is it?"

"You always say we do it by the numbers."

"What about it?"

"Pam told me about you almost shoving a broken pool cue down a bartender's throat in that Mexican cantina."

"R.C.'s life was hanging in the balance. Why are you bringing this up?"

"I could have done the same thing to the bartender, maybe worse, and so could Pam or Felix and a few others in the department. We wouldn't be bothered about it later, either. But we're not you. All of us know that, even though you don't. You go against your own nature."

"Where's Pam?"

"In the restroom, the last time I saw her."

"Believe it or not, Maydeen, sometimes I have my reasons for doing the things I do. We're not the only people who want to get their hands on Noie Barnum. The less anyone knows about his whereabouts, the safer he is. You got me?"

"Yes, sir, I expect so."

Hackberry looked down the street to see if R.C.'s cruiser had turned into the intersection yet. He tried to clear his head, to think straight, to keep the lines simple before he gave up his one certifiable chance to nail Jack Collins. "Fill in Pam and get the trusties out of the downstairs area. I want the prisoners in the cells at the end of the upstairs corridor moved to the tank. Barnum goes into total isolation. No contact with anyone. His food is brought to him by a deputy. No trusty gets near him. We're in total blackout mode regarding his presence. Simply said, he doesn't exist. You copy that?"

"I guess that means no phone call."

He gave her a look.

"Got it, got it, got it," she said.

Hackberry went out the back door and waited for R.C. The alleyway was empty in both directions. *Think,* he told himself. *Don't blow this one.* Why would Barnum be in a convenience store by himself? Collins wouldn't allow him to go wandering about on his own. They either had a fight or Barnum got sick of Collins's egomaniacal rhetoric and decided to take a stroll down the road and find some other company. But why had he stayed with Collins in the first place? To find Krill? To find some Al Qaeda operatives in Latin America and even the score for the death of his half sister? That made more sense than anything else.

R.C.'s cruiser turned in to the alleyway, the flasher off. Hackberry looked at all the rear windows of the building. He saw a face at one of the windows in the upstairs corridor. A deputy or a trusty? R.C. helped his prisoner out of the backseat of the cruiser, and the face went away. The prisoner's wrists were cuffed behind him, the tendons in his neck corded with either embarrassment or anger. In the sunlight, there were pinpoints of sweat on his forehead.

"I'm Sheriff Holland, Mr. Barnum," Hackberry said. "You *are* Noie Barnum?"

"Your deputy called me Noie. But I didn't tell him that was my name."

"Have it any way you like, sir. You're in

protective custody, but you're not under arrest. Do you understand the difference?"

"Yes, you're saying I don't have the constitutional right to a phone call or a lawyer."

"No, I'm saying this is a safe place for you."

"I think I'd just rather hike down to that café we passed and have a piece of pie and a cup of coffee and be on my way, if you don't mind."

"That's not an option, Mr. Barnum. I also need to advise you that you're starting to piss me off."

"I don't see why."

"I'll explain. You're one skip and a jump from being charged as an accessory in several homicides, all of them involving your companion Jack Collins. I dug up nine of his female victims. When we get time, I'll show you their postmortem photographs. The photos don't do justice to the realities of an exhumation — the stench of decomposition and the eight-ball stare and that sort of thing — but you'll have some sense of what a spray of forty-five-caliber bullets can do to human tissue."

"It's true?" the prisoner asked.

"What?"

"What you just said. Jack did that?"

Pam Tibbs had just come out the back door. "Who the hell you think did it, son?" she asked.

The prisoner tried to hold his eyes on hers,

586

but his stare broke, and he sucked the moisture out of his cheeks and swallowed.

Pam and Hackberry took the handcuffed man up the steel spiral stairs to the second floor and walked him down the row of cells to the end of the corridor. Pam whanged her baton against a cell door when two men came to the bars. Hackberry unhooked the prisoner, and he and Pam Tibbs stepped inside the room with him.

"You have a lavatory and a toilet and a bed and a chair and a window that lets you see the street," Hackberry said. "I apologize for all the graffiti and drawings of genitalia on the walls. We repaint every six months, but our clientele are a determined bunch."

"The other cells have bars. Why am I in this one?"

"The only people you're going to talk to are us, Mr. Barnum," Hackberry said. "I have a feeling you and Preacher were holed up down by the border or just on the other side of it. But chances are he's taken off. Is that right? He's way down in Coahuila by now?"

"You call him Preacher?"

"I don't call him anything. Others do," Hackberry said. "You're a Quaker, right?"

"A man's religion is a private matter."

"You deny your faith?" Hackberry said.

"No, sir, I don't. As you say, I'm a Quaker."

"And your namesake sailed out on the Flood?"

"Yes, sir, my christened name is Noie. Same spelling as in the King James."

"Can you tell me, with your background, why in the name of suffering God you hooked up with a man like Jack Collins?"

"Because he befriended me when nobody else did. Because he bound up my wounds and fed and protected me when others passed me by."

"Do you know how many innocent people have been hurt or killed because they think you have the design for the Predator drone?" Hackberry said.

"I escaped from a bunch of Mexican killers. They'd held me prisoner for weeks. How could I be carrying the design to a Predator drone? How could anyone have ideas that are that stupid?"

"An FBI agent by the name of Ethan Riser called you the modern equivalent of the Holy Grail," Hackberry said. "The design is in your head. You're a very valuable man, Mr. Barnum. Ethan Riser could probably explain that to you better than I, except he's dead. He's dead because Jack Collins blew his face and skull apart with a Thompson submachine gun. Ethan Riser was a good man and a friend of mine. Have you ever seen anybody machine-gunned, Mr. Barnum?"

"I found out about your friend when it was too late to do anything about it."

"Are you a deep-plant, sir?" Hackberry said.

"A what?"

"You know what I mean."

"No, I was about to go public with some information about the numbers of innocent people we've killed in the drone program, but I went into the desert first to think about it. That's when I got kidnapped by Krill and his friends. They found my government ID and a letter from a minister about my concerns over the Predator program, and they thought they'd sell me to Al Qaeda. Then they decided that was too much trouble and they'd sell me to some Mexican gangsters. That was when another fellow and I broke loose."

"You thought you were going to bring down Al Qaeda by yourself?"

"I was aiming to get some of them, that's for sure. But I was done helping kill third-world people. I got to say something here. I don't know everything that goes on in Jack's head, but somewhere inside him, there's a better man than the one you see."

"Keep telling yourself that crap," Pam said.

"Chief Deputy Tibbs isn't very objective about Jack, Noie. That's because he tried to machine-gun her," Hackberry said.

Noie Barnum looked at her blankly.

"What do you know about Josef Sholokoff?" Hackberry asked.

"I don't recall anybody by that name."

"He's a Russian criminal who wants to sell

589

you to the highest bidder," Hackberry said. "We think he may have crucified a minister by the name of Cody Daniels. You ever hear of him?"

"No, I haven't," Noie said. "A fellow was crucified?"

"You seem blissfully ignorant of all the wreckage swirling around you. Does that bother you at all?" Hackberry said.

"You're damn right it does. You stop talking to me like that."

"There's a ranch about six miles below the four-lane. The south end of the property bleeds into Mexico. I think that's where y'all were hiding out. Jack is probably long gone, and he's not driving that Trans Am anymore, either. But I need to know. Is that where y'all were holed up?"

"Ask Jack when you catch him."

"We don't abuse prisoners here," Pam said, stepping closer to Barnum, one finger barely touching his sternum.

"Ma'am?" he said.

"I just wanted you to take note of that fact," she said. "It's why I'm not pounding you into marmalade. But you open your mouth like that one more time, and I promise you, all bets are off."

Downstairs, five minutes later, Pam came into Hackberry's office and closed the door behind her. "I'm backing your play, Hack, whatever it is. But I think you're taking an awful risk here," she said.

"We don't owe the feds diddly-squat," he replied. "We apprehended Barnum. They didn't. As far as I'm concerned, they're on a need-to-know basis. Right now I don't figure they need to know anything."

"This is a national security issue. They're going to eat you alive. If they don't, your enemies around here will."

"That's the breaks."

"God, you're stubborn."

"I got a call from Temple Dowling. He says Josef Sholokoff believes Dowling put a hit on him."

"Why's he think that?"

"Because somebody killed a couple of Sholokoff's men at his game farm."

"Why didn't we hear anything about it?"

"Sholokoff didn't report it."

"What did you tell Dowling?"

"To get out of town. That he was on his own," Hackberry said.

"What's the problem?"

"I was pretty hard-nosed with him. Maybe I took satisfaction in his discomfort."

"Dowling is a pedophile and deserves anything that happens to him."

"He said Sholokoff takes people apart."

"In what way?"

"Physically, piece by piece," Hackberry said. He realized her attention was focused outside the window. A man in rumpled slacks, wearing canvas boat shoes without socks and his shirttail hanging out, was crossing the street hurriedly, a brown paper bag folded under his arm. "What's wrong?" Hackberry asked.

"That guy out there. He was just released."

"What about him?"

"He's a check writer. Loving and Jeff Davis counties have bench warrants on him, but they didn't want to pay the costs for getting him back."

"I'm still not following you."

"He was waiting to be taken downstairs when R.C. brought Barnum in. I remember he was watching us move everybody down to the tank. He was at the window, too, looking down in the alley."

"He probably wouldn't know who Barnum is."

"No, I saw his jacket. He was in Huntsville. He got clemency on a five-bit for sending his cell partner to the injection table. He's a professional snitch."

Hackberry thought about it. "Leave him alone. If he has any suspicions, we don't want to confirm them."

"Sorry, I had my hands full up there."

"Forget it," he said.

She looked at him for a long time before she spoke. "You want them to come after Barnum, don't you?"

"I haven't thought about it. I'm not that smart," he said. "You think I made a target out of Temple Dowling?"

"You're in the wrong business, *kemo sabe,* but I love you just the same," she replied.

What a difference a day and a change of topography could make, Temple Dowling told himself as he gazed through the lounge window of the Santa Fe hotel he and three of his men had checked in to. The evening sky was turquoise and ribbed with pink clouds, a rainbow arching across a canyon in the west, the sun an orange ball behind the mountains. The bartender brought him another vodka Collins packed with shaved ice and cherries and lemon and lime slices, and when Temple lifted it to his lips, the coldness slid down his throat like balm to his soul. Somehow his feelings of failure and humiliation at the hands of that clown Holland had evaporated during the flight to New Mexico. In fact, Temple was confident enough to smile at his foibles, as though someone else had temporarily occupied his skin and admitted his fear of Josef Sholokoff. It was nothing more than a silly lapse, Temple told himself. He had been tired, worn out by worry, beset on all sides by an army of incompetent employees and government bureaucrats and hayseed cops, Holland in particular. Why had Temple's father ever thought that idiot could be a congressman, a man who probably couldn't find his dork unless he tied a string on it? Temple sipped from his Collins and dipped a taco chip in a bowl of guacamole and chewed on it. Then an image he didn't want to remember floated before his eyes — being discovered by Holland and his chief deputy in the Mexican brothel with two underage girls.

He quickly transformed his emotion into one of righteous outrage. Temple Dowling didn't turn them into prostitutes. Poverty and hunger did. Was that his fault? Should they starve? Would that make the world a better place? What gave Holland the right to look down on him? Wasn't he intelligent enough to understand that most men who are attracted to children seek innocence in their lives?

He stopped, his mind seizing up as though he had experienced a brain freeze. He shouldn't have used the word "children." He was never attracted to children. He was not a pedophile. He just wanted to be with teenage girls while they were blooming into women. What finer creation was there than a young girl? What greater tragedy was there than seeing them left to the mercies of America's street culture? Or seeing them turned over to degenerates like Sholokoff, who made addicts of them and used them in porn films? Why was Temple Dowling the scapegoat? He had never treated a woman or girl badly in his life.

He drank his glass empty. The sky had darkened over the mountains, as though a lavender rain were starting to fall where the sun had just set. Where were his men?

"Would you like another, sir?" the bartender asked. He wore a white jacket and a red bow tie and black pants. His face had no color, not even the shadow of a beard, but his hair was as black and liquid in appearance as melted plastic.

"Yeah, hit me again," Temple replied. "What's all that noise next door?"

"It's a young people's organization of some kind." The bartender's cheeks were sunken, his mouth like a button.

"Listen to it. That's a lot of kids."

"Can I order you something from the grill?"

"They seem to be having fun," Temple said, still distracted by the celebratory mood next door.

"The hotel gives them the space for their meetings one night a week."

"That's pretty nice." Temple gazed out the door at the teenagers going in and out of the lobby, the shadows of the potted palms sliding off their skin and hair and the flowers some of the girls were wearing.

"It's called Alla-something," the bartender said.

"Can you order me a steak?"

"Yes, sir. Right away."

"I like it pink in the middle," Temple said.

He worked on his vodka and waited for his food and listened to the pianist play "Claire de Lune." The pianist was dressed in a summer tux with a red boutonniere, his long fingers floating above the keys in a cone of blue light. Santa Fe was a grand place to be. The Spanish ambience, the wooden colonnades and earthen jars on the terrazzo entrances to the shops along the street, the stars twinkling above the vastness of the mountains — why should a man be afraid in a country as wonderful as this? Or why should a man be ashamed of what he was? He agreed with the liberals and libertines on this one. A man didn't choose his sexual inclinations. They chose him. Didn't Jesus say there are those who are made different in the womb?

The girl who came into the lounge from the lobby and sat down next to him at the bar had the face of a pixie, with a pug nose and an uplifted chin and thick dark red hair that was tied in back. She wore a sequined cowboy shirt and tight stonewashed jeans tucked into boots that came almost to her knee. "Hi," she said.

"Hi," Temple said.

"Can you help me out?"

"You kill anybody?"

"I'd like to. At least if I have to go back in there."

"Where?" he asked.

"To the Alateen meeting."

"What's Alateen?"

"A meeting that's a guaranteed cure for insomnia. I got sentenced to it by the court."

"Why'd the judge send you there?"

"My boyfriend totaled his car and left me unconscious inside it. My boyfriend is not only a needle-dick but a lying shit. I told the judge if he believed my boyfriend, he was a shitbird, too, but I wasn't sure whether he qualified as a needle-dick. What's that music?"

"Debussy, I think. You know, Claude Debussy?"

"Who's that?"

"He was a great composer."

She was chewing gum, her eyes rolling, her mouth indolent and somehow vulnerable. The sound of her gum wet and smacking in her cheek made him swallow. She smiled lazily, one eye crinkling at the corner. "Will you buy me a drink?"

"Are you legal age?"

"Why do you think I asked you to buy me one?"

"What are you having?"

"I don't care. Something with candied cherries in it. Something that's cold and warm at the same time."

When the bartender served the steak, Temple ordered another Collins for himself

597

and an old-fashioned for the girl. The bartender lowered his eyes with his hands folded, not unlike an undertaker who doesn't want to broach a difficult subject.

"She's my niece," Temple said. "Nobody would believe she's twenty-two."

"Very well, sir," the bartender said, and went to the end of the bar and took a tumbler from a rack on the back counter.

"That was impressive," the girl said. "I had an uncle like that. He could get people to do things for him and make them feel like they were doing themselves a favor. You know how he'd do that?"

"Tell me."

"He already knew what they wanted to do. They only needed permission from someone. It was usually about money. Or maybe sex. But one way or another, they were coming across for him. He used to say, 'Put a smile on their faces, and they'll follow you over a cliff.' "

"What happened to him?"

"Nothing. He owns a bunch of massage parlors in Los Angeles. Is that a Rolex?"

Temple looked at his watch, then realized how long he had been in the lounge. Where were his men? They had been acting strangely ever since two of them had been dumb enough to get themselves popped by Preacher Jack. "I never noticed. I have about a dozen watches I wear. Do you ride horses?"

"Sometimes. I barrel-raced when I was in Four-H. I was a hot-walker at Ruidoso Downs. Talk about a horny bunch. You ought to be in the bar after the seventh race."

"Yeah, but that's not your crowd. I bet you go to college."

"If that's what you call working at the McDonald's inside Wal-mart. How about that for being a two-time loser? Your steak is getting cold."

"You want one?"

"I'm a vegan. My whole life changed after I gave up meat and milk products. I thought my needle-dick boyfriend was the problem, but I think it was my diet."

"What problem?"

"My organisms were messed up."

"Beg your pardon?"

"Meat and cheese and barnyard shit like that are toxic to your erogenous development." The waiter placed a coaster in front of her and set down her old-fashioned. She wrapped her gum in her napkin. "Anyway, thanks for the drink. I can't take that group next door. You know their problem?"

"No," he replied.

She took a drink from her glass and her eyes brightened and her cheeks filled with color, in the same way a thirsty plant might respond immediately to water. He could feel the coldness of her breath when she exhaled. "They feel unloved," she said.

"You have a lot of insight for such a young woman."

"Yeah, that's why I'm in charge of the french-fry basket."

"You smell like orange blossoms."

"Maybe that's because I'm chewing an orange rind." She turned on the stool toward him, her knee hitting his. She let her eyes hold on his. "I bummed a ride here with a friend, but he's gonna stay at the meeting for another hour. I live six miles away, and I don't have money for a cab. I'd like a ride, but when I get home, I go in by myself."

"You're the captain of your soul?"

"No, I'm just not somebody's backseat fuck."

He picked up a small cooked tomato on the tines of his fork and placed it in his mouth and chewed slowly. "I wouldn't ever say or even think something like that about you," he said.

"So you're gonna give me a ride?"

"If you'll do one thing for me."

Her eyes shifted sideways with a level of dependence that made his heart drop. "What's that?" she said.

"Walk through the open-air jewelry market with me. I'm a sucker for Indian junk. I need an expert hand to guide me."

"You have a daughter?"

"No."

"I thought that's what you were gonna tell me."

"Why?"

"Most of the time they say I remind them of their daughter. They can't do enough for you."

"Who?"

"The kind of guys who like to grope young girls in the back of the church bus," she replied, picking up her purse. "Think I'm kidding? Ask yourself why any middle-aged man wants to make a career out of being a youth minister or a park director or a guy who teaches leather craft to rug rats. Because he likes the way the restroom smells after little kids have pissed all over the bowl? Give me a break."

"How *old* are you?"

"Buy me a veggie burger and I'll tell you. Let's go, I won't bite," she said, squeezing his arm.

CHAPTER TWENTY-FOUR

Krill had parked the car in a grove of dead fruit trees no more than fifty yards behind the house of the woman Negrito kept referring to as *la china*. After the setting of the sun, the wind had dropped, and the sky had turned as stark as an ink wash. The gingerbread house and trees and windmill and barn and horse tank, even the hills, seemed drained of color and movement of any kind. The horses and chickens were gone from the yard, and there was no birdsong in the trees. The only sound Krill could hear as he and Negrito approached the house was water ticking from a rusted pipe that extended over the surface of the horse tank. A nimbus of dust hung above the house like a great cloud of gnats.

Krill stopped and knelt on one knee behind a car that had no wheels or glass in the windows and whose metal was still hot from baking in the sun all day. He stared at the house and the absence of electric lights or movement inside. Negrito knelt beside him, the leather cord of his hat swinging under his chin, the heavy gray fog of his odor puffing out of his clothes. "Krill, you got to tell me," he said.

"Tell you what?"

"Why we are here. I don't see no percentage, man."

"There isn't one. Not for you, anyway, my old friend."

"The others have deserted you, but still you talk down to me like I'm the enemy and not the *maricones* who ran away."

Krill placed his hand on Negrito's shoulder, which felt like a flannel sack filled with rocks. "Like me, you are a killer. But killing is not a problem for you. You sleep without dreaming and rise each morning into a new day. But I relive all the times I watched the light go out of my victims' eyes. My thoughts have become my enemies."

"That's why there are whores and tequila in Durango. A trip there will ease your problems, *jefe.*"

"I have to talk to La Magdalena."

"You want to sleep with her? That's what's going on? You think there's something special about a Chinese woman in bed? They ain't no different from our women. You love them at night, and in the morning they make your life awful."

"Poor Negrito. Why do you always think

with the head of your penis?"

" 'Cause it ain't never let me down, man," said Negrito, and cupped his hand on Krill's shoulder. "Come on, tell me the truth. Why you got to talk to this woman if you ain't looking to poke her?"

"To confess my sins, *hombre*. To rid myself of the faces I see in my sleep."

"It ain't a sin to kill people in a war. We were farmers and cattle workers until the war came. The people we killed had it coming. What is the big loss when a Communist is killed?"

"My children died because of me."

"That don't make no sense, Krill."

"I used to blame the army and the Americans and those from Argentina who first gave us our guns. But I took the pay of corrupt political men and did what they told me. I killed the Jesuit and the leftists. You know these things are true, Negrito, because you were there. The helicopter machine-gunned the clinic, but I was their brother in arms. I helped bring a curse on our land."

"No, your head is screwed up, Krill. That woman ain't no priest. Whatever you confess to her, she's gonna tell the cops. Then they're gonna hunt us down. They don't want nobody to know what we done down there."

"There's something strange going on in that house," Krill said.

"What's strange is your head. It glows in

the dark. I think you got too many chemicals in it. Remember those nights in Juárez?"

"The woman's truck is by the barn, but there is no one moving in the house, and no electric light is turned on. But look through the window of the chapel. The candles are burning in front of the Virgin's statue."

"Of course. She burns candles all the time. That's what people like her do. They burn candles. The rest of us work and sweat and sometimes take bullets, but *they* burn candles."

"No, this one has been to war, Negrito. She is not one to go off somewhere or take a nap while an open flame burns in her house."

"You make a complexity of everything," Negrito said. "You are a man who cannot bear to have a quiet and simple thought. You constantly construct spiderwebs so you can walk through them."

"Look on the far side of the fence, beyond the barn, where the grass is tall."

"It's grass. So what is the great mystery about grass?"

"There is a channel through it. The wind is not making the channel. Somebody walked through there."

"Animals did. Deer or horses. They cross the field by walking on it. It took you a long time to figure that out?"

"No horses are in that field. And deer do not make paths on flat land, only on hillsides, where their feet have to find the same spot every day."

"See what I mean? A simple visit to the home of this pretender *sacerdote* becomes a torture of the brain."

"The back door is ajar, Negrito. There is something wrong in that house. You stay here and guard my back. You keep the rifle, but do not use it unless absolutely necessary. If everything is normal, I will come to the door and wave to you with my right hand, not my left."

"*Claro,* man. My head is starting to hurt again with all your cautions. I cannot stand this. We were never afraid before. I told you from the beginning, this woman who wears men's trousers was bad luck. But your obsession has no bounds."

"Then leave. Go to Durango. Bathe in the diseased fluids of your whores," Krill said.

Negrito was breathing heavily, the whiskers around his mouth as thick as a badger's. His pupils were no bigger than pinheads, the skin around his eyes wrinkled and flecked with scales. "You make me want to do something that's very bad."

"You want to be me, Negrito, to leave your own body and live inside mine. And because you are a killer by nature, you believe a bullet can give you my heart and brain."

"I am a loyal servant and follower and brother, not an assassin. I want you to be you

606

and the leader you used to be, Krill, not a self-hating fool ruminating on his sins."

"If I wave with my left hand from the door, rather than my right, what message will I be sending you?"

"I see only one message in any of this: that of a man being led with a ring through his nose by the Chinese *puta*."

"You are brave in ways that few men are, Negrito. But do not try to think anymore. For some men, thinking is a dangerous vanity. You must accept that about yourself."

Krill stood and walked toward the back entrance of the house, a holstered .357 Magnum hanging from the right side of his web belt, his skinning knife in a scabbard on his left. He stepped up on the back porch and listened, then felt a breeze on the back of his neck and heard the windmill come to life and water running into the horse tank. But where were the horses? Or the illegals who came almost every evening for food or benediction at the house of La Magdalena?

He paused at the back door and listened again. The windmill was stenciled against the black and gray patterns in the sky, and tumbleweed was bouncing through the yard, hanging in the fences, skipping by the junked car where Negrito was crouched with the M16. Krill pushed open the door and stepped inside.

Through the hallway, he could see her sitting very still in a straight-back chair, her hands resting on her knees, her hair tied in a bun. In the gloom, he could hardly make out her features. Her face was so still that in profile, it looked like it had been painted on the air. He eased his .357 from its holster and waited, his left foot in front of his right, breathing slowly through his mouth, the checkered grips of his revolver hard inside his palm.

He stepped backward, never taking his eyes off the Chinese woman, his left arm extended out the door. He opened and closed his hand so the fading light would reflect off it, then moved his arm up and down so Negrito could plainly see that he was signaling with his left hand and not his right. *Please remember what I told you,* he thought. *This is the moment I have to count on you, Negrito. This is when your skills will be of the greatest necessity.*

Krill went down the hallway and could see the woman watching him from the corner of her eye.

"Magdalena?" he said, his voice hardly audible.

She continued to stare straight ahead, her hands absolutely still.

"*¿Qué pasa?*" he said. He glanced over his shoulder. Where was Negrito? "*Señora,* look at me," he said. "It's Krill. I want to make

608

confession. I murdered a Jesuit priest. I must have absolution. You can give it to me."

He stepped into the room and felt the barrel of a gun touch the back of his head. "Bad timing, greaseball," a voice said.

There were four men inside the room, all of them wearing beige-colored gauzy masks with slits for the nose and mouth and eyes. One man stood against the far wall, his left hand on the shoulder of a girl not over ten years old. With the other hand, he held the stainless-steel four-inch blade of a clasp knife under the girl's throat. The girl's eyes were wide with terror and confusion, and her bottom lip was trembling.

The man holding the gun to the back of Krill's head removed the .357 from his grip. "Who's with you?" he said.

"A shit pile of people. They're going to cook you in a pot, too," Krill said.

"That's why you came in by yourself?"

"Who are you guys?" Krill said.

"Your worst nightmare, fuckhead."

"In my nightmares there are no guys like you. I don't have space in my head for guys in Halloween masks or guys who frighten little girls with knives. These are not the guys of nightmares. These are clowns and eunuchs who were born with penises but no cojones. Why would guys like these be in anybody's nightmares? That would be a great mystery to me."

"Antonio, don't speak to these men," the woman said.

"I was just clarifying my thoughts to myself, Magdalena. These men and their cleverness are a great mystery to me," he said. The yard was empty, the light dying in the trees, the windmill spinning against a horizon that looked as though the clouds were dissolving and running down the sides of the sky. Then he saw Negrito moving from behind the barn and around the front of the house, bent low, his greasy leather hat pulled down tight on his head, the M16 gripped with both hands, his heavy, truncated body moving with the fluidity of an animal's. In the distance, he thought he heard the thropping sound of a helicopter's blades.

"Take me but leave the child," the woman said to the man holding the gun to Krill's head.

"That's not a problem," the man replied. "But this guy is. Who is he?"

"A man seeking forgiveness. He's no threat to you," she said.

"You a coyote, buddy?" the man with the gun asked.

"No, *hombre*. I'm a Texas Ranger. I've been shooting the shit out of guys like you for many years."

"You're a real wit, all right. So smart you came in here and stuck your head in a mousetrap."

610

Then Krill heard banging and shuffling noises at the front of the house, booted feet coming down hard on the gallery, and a door flying back against a wall. Krill felt his heart drop. Two more men, each wearing the same masks worn by the men inside the house, were pulling and shoving Negrito into the living room. Blood leaked in a broken line from under the brim of Negrito's leather hat, running through one eyebrow, streaking the stubble on his cheek. His face was lit with a grin as wide as a jack-o'-lantern's. "*¡Qué bueno!* Everybody is here!" he said. Then Negrito saw the expression on Krill's face, and his grin faded. "These *cobardes* come up behind me. I'm sorry, Krill," he said.

"So you're the one they call Krill. We've heard about you," the man behind Krill said.

The helicopter passed overhead and circled over a field and began to descend on the rear of the property, the downdraft flattening the grass, blowing dust and desiccated cow manure in the air.

"Hey, Krill, I know who these guys are. They're Sholokoff's people," Negrito said.

"No, we have no interest in these people or the business they conduct," Krill said.

"Ain't that right?" Negrito said to his captors. "You work for that Russian prick. We know all about you. I hear a couple of your guys are missing their noses. Be nice to me, and maybe I'll tell you where their noses are

611

and you can glue them back on."

Negrito, Negrito, Negrito, Krill thought.

The man behind Krill stepped back and looked at both Krill and Negrito like a photographer arranging a studio portrait. "This is quite a pair," he said.

"What do you want to do?" said the man holding the knife to the little girl's throat.

"Take the girl in the kitchen."

"And?"

"What do you think?"

"I don't know, man. I don't know if this gig has parameters or not."

"There's a key sticking out of the lock in the pantry door. What does that tell you?"

"Lock her inside?"

"Brilliant," the man with the gun said. "Then take the woman to the chopper."

"What about these two?"

"That's a good question," the man with the gun said.

"I've got a question for you," Negrito said.

"*You've* got a question? Wonderful. What is it, greaseball?" the man with the gun said.

"If you're born without cojones, does that mean you're automatically a queer, or is it something you learn? 'Cause I believe every guy who ever called me a greaseball was probably a *maricón.* Know why I think that? 'Cause when I was in jail in Arizona and Texas, it was always the Aryan Brotherhood guys who were trying to get me in the sack.

612

That's right, man. Macho gringos like you was the main yard bitches in every joint I was in. I tell you what, man. 'Cause you look like a nice guy, I'm gonna do something for you. You surrender to me and Krill, I'll fix you up with some punks that ain't got a feather on them. You gonna dig it, man."

"We're wasting time here, Frank. What's it gonna be?" one of the other men said to the man with the gun.

"We split the difference," Frank replied. "Krill is the guy who kidnapped the Quaker. Josef will want to talk to him. The ape seems to have a death wish."

"Listen to me, *hombre,*" Krill said. "Negrito is a good soldier. He can be of value to you. He will never give up information to the FBI. Pain means nothing to him. His only defect is he runs his mouth when he shouldn't. But he can be a valuable man to your employer."

"I see your point," the man with the gun said. "We're all just making a buck. We shouldn't let it get personal. I totally understand where you're coming from."

No one in the room moved. In the silence, Krill could hear the little girl whimpering. The man who had been holding a semi-automatic on Negrito put it away and looked at the .357 he had taken from Krill. It was nickel-plated and had black checkered grips, and each chamber in the cylinder was loaded with a hollow-point round. "Your name is Negrito?" he said.

"That's my nickname. It's 'cause I'm mestizo."

"Do you mind riding in a helicopter?" the man asked.

Negrito shrugged and gazed out the window, his eyes dulling over, his mouth downturned at the corners.

"Because we don't want you to be uncomfortable. Can you handle heights? You don't get airsick or anything like that?"

Negrito looked at Krill. "We had some fun, didn't we, amigo? They're gonna remember us for a long time. Don't let this guy get to you. We're better than any of them. We're stronger and smarter and tougher. Guys like us come back from the dead and piss in their mouths and shit in their mothers' wombs."

Krill stood frozen, the sound of the helicopter blades growing louder and louder in his head, the dust swirling in the downdraft, the rain clouds forming into blue horsetails, the windmill shuddering against the sky, all of these things happening simultaneously as the man with the .357 lifted the barrel and fired a solitary round through one side of Negrito's head and out the other.

Hackberry Holland was reading a biography of T. E. Lawrence under a lamp by his front window when he heard thunder rolling in the

614

clouds far to the south, reverberating in the hills, where occasionally a flash of dry lightning would flicker and then die like a wet match. The book was written by Michael Korda and dealt with the dissolution of empires and a new type of warfare, what came to be known as "wars of insurgency," all of which had their model among the sand dunes and date palms of Arabia. As Hackberry read the lines describing the white glare of the Arabian desert, he thought of the snow that had blanketed the hills south of the Yalu the first morning he had seen Chinese troops in their quilted uniforms, tens of thousands of them, many of them wearing tennis shoes, marching out of the white brilliance of the snowfield, heedless of the automatic-weapons fire that danced across the fields and the artillery rounds that blew geysers of snow and ice and dirt and rock in their midst.

He closed the book and placed it on his knee and stared out the window. Not far down the road, he could see a tree limb that had fallen across the telephone line that led to his house. Just as he got up to check the phone, he saw a cruiser turn off the road into his drive, its emergency bar rippling, its siren off. Hackberry stepped out on the front porch and watched R. C. Bevins get out of the cruiser and walk toward him on the flagstones, his face somber. "You tried to call?" Hackberry said.

"Yes, sir, your phone's out. Your cell must be off, too."

"It's in my truck. What is it, R.C.?"

"We've got a homicide at the Ling place. The victim appears to be Hispanic. From the exit wound in his head, I'd say somebody used a hollow-point. A ten-year-old girl had been left in Ms. Ling's care and saw it all. When her mother came for her, she found the girl locked in a pantry. Ms. Ling is gone."

"What do you mean, gone?"

"From what the little girl said, there were six guys in masks. They took Ms. Ling and a friend of the dead man on a helicopter."

"How long ago?"

"A couple of hours."

"Did you print the victim?"

"Yes, sir."

"Get a priority with AFIS."

"Pam is already on it. Who do you reckon are the guys with the chopper?"

"Josef Sholokoff's people."

"The little girl said the dead man and his friend spoke Spanish. She also said the friend had a pistol on one hip and a long knife on the other."

"What else did she say about him?"

"She said he was tall and that he had funny shoulders. She said they were too wide, like he had a stick pushed sideways inside his shirt."

"That's Krill."

616

"What would he be doing at Ms. Ling's place?"

"I don't have any idea, none at all."

"You okay, Sheriff?"

"How long have you been trying to get me?"

"About fifteen minutes. There wasn't no way you could know the line was down."

"Was Ms. Ling hurt?"

"The little girl said a guy shoved her down. The same guy held a knife at the little girl's throat. She said they all had gloves on, and the shooter called the dead man a greaseball. You think these are the same guys who crucified Cody Daniels?"

"What's your opinion?"

R.C. scratched at his eyebrow. "I think we got a special breed on our hands," he said. "I think all this is related to that Barnum boy we got locked in our jail. I'm not sure if we done the right thing on that."

Pam Tibbs was waiting for Hackberry when he arrived at the jail. She was not wearing makeup, and there were circles under her eyes. "What do you want to do?" she asked.

"About what?" he said.

"Everything."

"Did you talk to the FBI yet?"

"I reported the homicide and the kidnapping. I didn't mention our boy in isolation," she said.

"You're uncomfortable with that?"

617

"I don't know what you're doing, Hack. I don't know what the plan is."

"They're going to call."

"The abductors are?"

"You bet."

"Then what?"

"We've got what they want. As long as Barnum stays in our hands, Anton Ling will be kept alive."

"Hack, they wouldn't have grabbed her if we hadn't locked up Barnum."

"You don't have to tell me."

"Where are you going?"

"To take a nap," he said.

He went up the spiral stairs and pulled a mattress from a supply locker into an alcove off the corridor and lay down on his side with his head cushioned on his arm and fell asleep with far more ease than he would have guessed, knowing that his dreams would take him to a place that was as much a part of his future as it was his past. He remembered the words of the writer Paul Fussell, who had said he joined the army to fight the war for its duration and had discovered that he would have to fight it every day and every night for the rest of his life. In his dream, Hackberry returned once again to Camp Five in No Name Valley and the brick factory called Pak's Palace outside Pyongyang. The dream was not about deprivation or the harshness of the weather or the mistreatment visited upon him by his captors. It was about isolation and abandonment and the belief that one was totally alone and lost and without hope. It was the worst feeling that anyone could ever experience.

In the dream, the landscape changed, and he saw himself standing on a precipice in Southwest Texas, staring out at a valley that looked like an enormous seabed gone dry. The valley floor was covered with great round white rocks that resembled the serrated, coral-encrusted backs of sea tortoises, stranded and alone, dying under an unmerciful sun. In the dream, he was not a navy corpsman but a little boy whose father had said that one day the mermaids would return to Texas and wink at him from somewhere up in the rocks. All he saw in the dream was his own silent witness to the suffering of the sea creatures.

"Jesus Christ, wake up, Hack," he heard Pam Tibbs say, shaking his arm.

"*What?* What is it?" he said, his eyes filmed with sleep.

"You must have been having a terrible dream."

"What'd I say?"

"Just the stuff people yell out in dreams. Forget it."

"Pam, tell me what I said."

" 'He takes people apart.' That's what you said."

The telephone call came in one hour later.

CHAPTER TWENTY-FIVE

From his office window, he could see flecks of rain blowing in the glow of the streetlights, the traffic signal at the intersection bouncing on its support cables, the electrical flashes in the clouds that ringed the town. "Don't try tracing this," the voice said.

"You're too slick for us?" Hackberry replied.

"You know what we want. Deliver him up and there won't be any problem."

"By now you've probably figured out I'm a bit slow on the uptake. What is it you think I have?"

" 'It' is a Quaker with a hush-puppy accent who by all rights is our property."

"Somebody snitched us off, huh?"

"Spying on you hasn't been a big challenge, Sheriff. You seem to leave your shit prints everywhere you go."

"Should we decide to deliver up our Quaker friend, what are y'all going to do for us?"

"Give you your Chinese girlfriend back, for

621

one. For two, you'll get her back looking just the way she did the last time you saw her. Are you getting the picture?"

"I don't know if it's the electrical storm or that peckerwood speech defect, but you're a little hard to understand."

"We have another guest here, a guy whose father you did scut work for. We're gonna let him be a kind of audiovisual aid for you. Hang on just a second. You're gonna like this."

The caller seemed to remove the phone from his ear and hold it away from him. In the background, Hackberry could hear voices and echoes inside a large room, probably one with stone or brick walls. "Turn up the volume for Sheriff Holland," the caller said.

Then Hackberry heard a sound that he never wanted to hear again, a cry that burst from the throat and reverberated off every surface in the room and died with a series of sobs and a whimper that the listener could associate only with hopelessness and despair.

"That's Mr. Dowling, Sheriff," the caller said. "As you've probably gathered, he's not having a good morning."

"You abducted Temple Dowling?"

"It's more like he abducted himself. All we had to do was get a little girl to perch her twat on a bar stool, and Mr. Dowling was in the net. Want to talk to Ms. Ling?"

Hackberry could hear his own breath

against the surface of the receiver. "Yes, I would," he said.

"You'd like that?"

"If you want to negotiate, I need to know she's there."

"She was with Civil Air Transport, wasn't she? What they called the Flying Tiger Airline?"

"If that's what she told you."

"She didn't tell me anything. She didn't have to. She has a tattoo of the Flying Tiger emblem on her ass. Have you ever had an opportunity to see it — I mean her ass?"

Hackberry's mouth was dry, his heart hammering, his breath coming hard in his throat. "No matter how this plays out, I'll be seeing you down the track. You know that, don't you?"

"You still think I sound like a peckerwood? I'd like to hear you say that one more time."

Hackberry swallowed, a taste like diesel oil sliding down his throat.

"No?" the voice said. "We'll give you a little time to think over your options. Noie Barnum belongs to us, Sheriff. Want to throw away Ms. Ling's life for an empty-headed government pissant? Do the smart thing."

"Why does he belong to you?"

"Mr. Dowling cost my employer a great deal of money. Barnum is the payback. Tell you what. I'm gonna send you a package. Check it out and we'll talk again. In the meantime, I'm gonna take personal care of Ms. Ling. Don't worry, I won't touch a hair on her head. Promise."

The line went dead.

Anton Ling's captors had placed her in a subterranean room that was cool and damp and smelled of lichen and the river stones out of which it was made. Three ground-level barred windows that resembled slits in a machine-gun bunker gave onto a scene that seemed out of place and time: a sunrise that had the bluish-red color of a bruise, a meandering milky-brown river from which the fields had been irrigated an emerald green, livestock that could have been water buffalo grazing in riparian grasses. But the people tending animals or working in the fields were not Indo-Chinese peasants; they were Mexicans who had probably eaten breakfast in the dark and gone to work with the singleness of purpose that characterized all workers whose aspirations consisted of little more than getting through the day and returning home in the evening without involving themselves in the political considerations of those who owned the land.

The floor was concrete, once covered with a carpet that had molded into a mat of black thread. Against one wall was a wooden bed with a tick mattress on it, and a toilet in the corner with a partition that partially shielded it from view. The bars in the door were sheathed in flaking orange rust, and the stones in the wall had turned black and oily with the seepage of groundwater. Someone had scratched a Christian cross on one stone; on another was a woman's name; on another were the words *Ayúdame, Dios.*

The screaming that had come from another part of the subterranean area had stopped about two hours ago. Briefly, Anton had seen a tall, mustached man in a suit and a soiled white shirt carrying a medical bag. He had studiously avoided looking at her, his shoulders rounded, the back of his head turned to her, his uncut hair hanging over his collar like a tangle of twigs. To someone else, he had said, "I have left you the hypodermics. That is all I will do. I have seen nothing here. I am going back to my bed."

She heard an upstairs door open and feet descending the steps. So far, her captors had not spoken to her without their masks. The man who was approaching her did not wear a mask; he wore elevated shoes, a white sport coat, a monogrammed lavender shirt unbuttoned below the collar, and black slacks. His nose was hooked, the nostrils thick with hair, his cheeks slathered with whiskers, the exposed top of his chest gnarled with tiny bones. He unlocked the cell door with an iron key and pulled it open and came inside the room, wiping the rust off his fingers with a handkerchief. His breath smelled of decay and seemed to reach out and touch her face like wet cobweb. "Frank doesn't like you," he said. "He says you spat on him. He says that's the second time you've done it."

"He tried to take my clothes off."

"He shouldn't have done that. I'll talk to him about it. Sit down." When she didn't respond, he beamed and said, "Please. Don't make everything unpleasant. You remember me?"

"No," she said, sitting down.

"I helped provide the AK-47s you and your friends shipped to Nicaragua."

"I dealt with many undesirables. I suspect you were among them."

"I've always wanted to talk with you on a personal level. You are quite famous. Do you want something to eat?"

"Yes."

"I knew we could be friends."

"You're Josef Sholokoff. You were at my house when your men almost drowned me."

"Maybe."

"You killed Cody Daniels in the cruelest way a man can die."

"The cowboy minister? He was of no importance. Why are you worried about him? You should be thinking about yourself. We're going to put you on the phone with Sheriff Holland." He was still grinning, his eyes so bright and intense and merry that they were

626

impossible to read. "One way or another, you'll get on the phone. Or you will be heard on the phone. You know what I mean, don't you?"

"No," she replied, looking straight ahead.

"You heard the man screaming earlier this morning. He was talking on the phone to Sheriff Holland. He just didn't know it."

"Is he still alive?"

"He might be, if his heart didn't give out. I'll check and see. Do you want to meet him?"

"Where is Krill?"

"These are insignificant people. Why do you keep dwelling on them?"

"I think you're evil. You're not just a man who does evil. You love evil for its own sake. I've known a few like you. Not many, but some."

"With the Khmer Rouge?"

"No, the Khmer Rouge were uneducated peasants who were bombed by B-52s. You're different. I suspect your cruelty is your means to hide your cowardice."

"And you? You didn't rain fire on people who lived in grass huts?"

"I did."

"But *I'm* evil?"

"You don't plan for me to leave here, not alive, at least. Take your lies and your deceit from the room. You're odious in the sight of God and man, Mr. Sholokoff. I suspect your role as a pornographer allows you to feel

627

powerful about women. But in any woman's eyes, you would be looked upon with pity. Your fetid breath and your physical repulsiveness are simply an extension of the blackness in your heart. Any woman who is not of diminished capacity would immediately be aware of that and want to flee your presence, no matter what she might tell you. Ask the people around you and see what their response is."

He was clearly fighting to retain the merry light in his eyes and to keep his grin in place, but his mouth twitched slightly, and his nostrils were dilating. "Do you like my farm?"

"Why should I care one way or another about your farm?" she asked.

"Because it's yours. Your permanent home. You will be among the people, part of the soil, fertilizer for their vegetables," he replied. "What finer fate for a martyr of your stature?"

Preacher Jack Collins didn't like to be pushed. Nor did he like losing control of things or, worse, having control taken from him. Not only had Noie Barnum, ingrate extraordinaire, strolled off from their safe house, he had managed to get himself arrested in a convenience store and put in a county bag that usually housed drunks and check writers and wife beaters. When Noie did not return from his stroll down the highway, Jack had gotten on his cell phone

628

and begun making calls to an informational network that he had created and maintained for two decades, a network that no one would ordinarily associate with a man who dressed in beggar's rags and wandered the desert like a Bedouin. It included hookers from El Paso to Austin, button men from both sides of the border, Murphy artists, street dips and stalls, shylocks, coyotes, second-story creeps, drug mules, corrupt Mexican cops, safecrackers, car boosters, money washers, fences of every stripe, and a morphine-addicted retired librarian in Houston who could probably find Jimmy Hoffa's body if the FBI would take time to retain her.

It didn't take long to discover what had happened. Noie had gotten pinched in the convenience store by the same deputy Preacher Jack had dug up from a premature burial. How about that for ingratitude? Then a snitch just getting out of the bag had spotted Noie in custody and dropped the dime on him with Josef Sholokoff's people. Now several Mexicans were saying that a bunch of guys in camouflage masks had landed a helicopter at the Chinese woman's place, murdered a man in front of a child, and abducted the Chinese woman and a half-breed.

Jack had no doubt who was behind the abduction. Josef Sholokoff wanted Noie Barnum in his possession. The quickest way to him was through the sheriff, and the quickest way to the sheriff was through Anton Ling.

At four A.M. the morning after the abduction, a man who was part albino and part black and who had pink eyes and hairless skin that resembled different shades of white rubber that had been stitched together delivered a new Toyota to Preacher Jack at a café just north of Ojinaga. "There's another registration and another set of plates under the seat. I got you two driver's licenses, too," he said. He put the keys in Jack's hand, his eyes holding steady on Jack's.

"Anyone ever tell you it's rude to stare into somebody's face?" Jack said.

"You're hot."

"You know a time when I wasn't?"

"Not like this. I had a hard time on the driver's licenses. Word is you popped an FBI agent."

"He popped himself."

"A photo guy I use says you're the stink on shit and for me not to come back again."

"You wouldn't try to put the slide on me, would you, Billy?"

"Just telling you like it is."

"You want more money?"

"I was thinking about visiting Baja. Maybe lie on the beach and cool out for a while."

"What do you use for suntan lotion — ninety-weight motor oil?"

"I was speaking metaphorically."

630

Jack took three hundred dollars from his wallet and folded the bills between his fingers and stuffed them in the man's shirt pocket. "A metaphor means comparing one thing in terms of another without using the words 'like' or 'as.' 'To lie on a beach' is not a metaphor. If I said to you, 'Tell your parents to buy a better quality of condoms,' I would be making an implication, but I would not be speaking metaphorically. Do you understand what I'm saying to you?"

"Grammar was never my strong suit."

"Literary terms have nothing to do with grammar," Jack said. "If you're going to speak your native language, why don't you invest some time in the public library? It's free. In the meantime, don't go around using terms you don't know the meaning of." Jack stuffed the keys to his Trans Am into the man's pocket, on top of the bills. "Drive it to San Antone and park it at the airport. Wear gloves, but don't wipe it down. Leave the keys on the dashboard and the parking stub in the ashtray."

"Somebody will boost it."

"Nobody slips one past you."

"The guy who boosts it will get pinched, and the cops won't know if he's lying to them or not — about where he got it, I mean. You're doing a mind-fuck on them?"

"Don't use that kind of language in my presence," Jack said.

631

"I'll never figure you out, Preacher."

"Get out of my sight."

An hour later, he drove his new car to within one block of Sheriff Holland's jail and, wearing a hat and round steel-rimmed sunglasses that were as black as welder's goggles, went into a café and ordered a to-go box of scrambled eggs, ham, grits, and toast and a cup of scalding black coffee. He returned to his car and spread his food on the dashboard and ate with a plastic fork and spoon without seasoning of any kind or even seeming to taste it, as though consuming chaff swept up from a granary floor. His windows were down, and the air was cool and smelled of rain, and the storm clouds above the hills were so thick and swollen that he could not tell when the sun broke the horizon. In moments like these, Jack felt a strange sense of peace, as though the travels of the sun and moon had been set into abeyance, as though time had stopped and the denouement of his life, one that he secretly feared, had been postponed indefinitely.

Jack picked up his coffee. It was still so hot, the steam rose into his hat brim and scorched his forehead. But his gaze, which was fastened on the jail, never wavered, nor did his mouth twitch when he drank the cup to the bottom.

The electric light was burning in the sheriff's office. When the front door opened, Jack saw the sheriff walk to the silver pole by the sidewalk and clip the American flag to the chain and raise it flapping in the wind. At the same moment, Jack's cell phone vibrated on the seat. The call was from the morphine-addicted reference librarian in Houston.

"I may have found your Russian," she said. "He owns a place down in Mexico, one with a helipad on it. It's a horse breeding farm. A French magazine did an article on it about five years back."

"Can you find out if he's there?"

"I'll work on it. I found three game farms he owns in Texas and a place in Phoenix. You want me to check them out, too?"

"No, concentrate on Mexico."

"I found something else. Sholokoff's name came up a couple of times with a guy by the name of Temple Dowling. You know him?"

"Dowling was running whores with Sholokoff."

"I did a search on Dowling and found the name of a security service he uses. I hacked into it and discovered Dowling just went missing in Santa Fe. You think there's a connection?"

Jack stared at the front of the jail and at the flag ballooning and popping against the charcoal-blue darkness of the sky. "You there, Preacher?" she asked.

"Yeah, Sholokoff's people probably grabbed him. No one else would have motivation."

"You doing all this to get the Chinese

woman back?"

"What difference does it make?"

"Because there's this story I don't believe. About these Thai prostitutes who were murdered. They had heroin balloons in their stomachs. Sholokoff was using them as hookers and mules at the same time. Some people say you did the hit. At some place called Chapala Crossing. But I never believed that."

Jack could hear the wind blowing in the street, the traffic light at the intersection swinging on its support cables, the tin roof on a mechanic's shed swelling against the joists.

"You're serious about your work, but you'd never hurt a woman," she said. "That's what I told them. That's right, isn't it, Preacher?"

He closed the cell phone in his palm, his hand shaking, his throat as dry and thick as rust.

Krill had never given much thought to the mercenaries he had known. To him, they existed in a separate world, one in which men did not serve a cause or even fight out of necessity. They were simply uniformed employees without depth or ideology, with no desire to know either the enemies they were paid to kill or the civilians they were paid to defend or the countrymen like Krill they were paid to fight alongside.

When Krill thought about them at all, it

was in terms of their physicality and their access to North American goods and to fine weapons of international manufacture. Mercenaries were almost always barbered and clean. When they sweated, they smelled of deodorant rather than the glands. They were inoculated against all the diseases of the third world. Their bodies were hard, their stomachs flat, their shoulders and arms of the kind that could carry ninety pounds of supplies and weapons and take the shock of a parachute opening, sometimes crashing through a jungle canopy in the dark, jolting inside their harnesses with enough force to break the back of a cow.

He mostly thought of them in terms of what they were not. They were not haunted by the specters that trailed behind Krill everywhere he went. They did not fear their sleep or need to drink themselves into a stupor when the light went out of the sky and the wind was filled with the sounds of people crying in a village while their huts burned and belts of cached ammunition began popping in the heat. The mercenaries opened their tinned food with a tiny can opener they called a P-38, their eyes fixed on the task with the quiet intensity of a watchmaker at his craft. The deeds they had just committed, no more than a kilometer away, had already disappeared from their lives. Why should it be otherwise? They were not moralists; they were advisers and oversight personnel and not makers of policy. They came and went, as shadows did. Empires fell apart and died and new nations were born. A footprint in a jungle was as transient as the life span of an insect. The porous stone altars of the Mayans still contained the blood of the innocents who had been sacrificed by pagan priests centuries ago. What were the lives of a few more Indians? Krill believed this was how the mercenaries thought when they thought at all. In truth, he had never really cared about these men one way or another. Not until now.

His cell had a domed ceiling and seemed to bloom with a cool, fecund odor that was like water in the bottom of a dark well or mouse droppings inside a cave that dripped with moisture. There was another odor, too, one that was like mushrooms someone had trodden upon in a forest that never saw sunlight. It was like the smell in the disinterred bodies of his children. It was an odor that only a grave produced.

Krill propped his arms against the bars on the door and watched the mercenary the others called Frank. "You took off your mask," Krill said.

"We're all family here," Frank said.

"You're a nice-looking guy, man. Why are you a hump for a man like the Russian?"

"Sometime we'll have a beer and I'll fill you in."

"I don't have illusions about my situation. But I think you do," Krill said.

Frank grinned. He was wearing a yellow T-shirt scissored off just below the nipples and a pair of black cargo trousers with big snap pockets stitched on the thighs. He had the clean, chiseled features and freshly scrubbed look of a 1930s leading man. "Just out of curiosity, what were you doing with the zip?" he asked. "Don't give me that seeking-forgiveness crap, either."

"What does 'zip' mean?"

"As in 'zipper-head.' I'm talking about the Chinese broad."

"She can absolve sins."

"Did you know your ancestors never invented the wheel?"

"Before the Spaniards came, there were no draft animals. Why would my ancestors want a wheel when they had no animals to hitch it to? They did not spend their time on non-utile pursuits."

"You said I'm operating under some illusions."

"When you killed Negrito, you freed his spirit. You don't know it yet, but you got some serious problems, man."

"You're inside a prison cell and I'm outside of it. But I'm in trouble? You got to clue me in here. I'm fascinated by Indian mumbo jumbo."

"Negrito wanted to be me, to live inside

my skin. The way an assassin wants to become his victim. But he was too loyal to hurt his friend. So you did it for him and let his spirit leave his body and go inside mine. Now, no matter what you do to me, Negrito is going to be waiting for you. That is very bad for you, man. You haven't figured that out yet, but you will."

"Can your friend's spirit rise out of concrete? Because you're gonna be part of the foundation in Josef's new barn."

"*Me cago en tu puta madre.* Or are you already standing in line for that?"

"What did you say?"

" 'I defecate in your mother's womb.' That was Negrito's favorite expression. See, I told you, Negrito is on the loose."

"See my friend there, carrying that bucket out? Know what's in the bucket?"

"The waste your mother usually makes you carry out?"

"Take another guess."

A thick-bodied man, stripped to the waist, with a buzz haircut, was walking up the cellar stairs, a bucket swinging from his left hand. The muscles in his back looked like oiled rope. In the yellow glow of the bare bulb that hung above the steps, Krill could see string-like tendrils of blood on the man's skin.

"The item in that bucket was donated by one of our other guests," Frank said. "Those two guys you whacked and mutilated at

638

Josef's place were friends of mine. Keep shooting off your mouth, greaseball. I'll make sure you're a donor, too."

At nine A.M. of the same day, an independent taxi operator parked his vehicle in front of Hackberry's office and came inside with a package under his arm. The package was wrapped in twine and thick brown paper. "Got a delivery for you from the airport, Sheriff," he said.

"Who's it from?" Hackberry asked, looking up from his desk.

"I don't know. There's nothing written on it except your name. I got a call telling me to pick it up at the ticket counter and to keep the fifty dollars in the envelope tucked under the twine."

"Where's the envelope?"

"In the trash. I didn't think it was important. What, you reckon it's a bomb or something?"

"Leave it there."

"It's cold. Maybe it's some food."

After the taxi driver had gone, Hackberry went into the outer office. "Pam, tell Felix to go to the airport and see what he can find out about a package that was left for me at the ticket counter. Then come into my office, please."

He pulled on a pair of latex gloves and removed a pocketknife from his desk drawer and opened the long blade on it. He placed the flat of his hand on the wrapping paper. He could feel the coldness in the box through his glove.

"Put on a vest and a face shield, Hack," Pam said.

"Step back," he replied, and cut the twine. He inserted his fingers under the paper and peeled it away in sections from the top of a corrugated cardboard box.

"Hack, call the FBI," Pam said.

He pulled back a strip of tape holding the flaps on the box's top in place and folded the flaps back against the sides. He looked down at a carefully packed layer of Ziploc bags containing dry ice. One of the bags had broken open, and the ice had slid down deeper into the box and was vaporizing against a round, compacted lump of matter wrapped inside a sheet of clear plastic. There were whorls of color pressed against the plastic that made him think of an uncured ham that had been freezer-burned in a meat locker.

"What is it?" Pam said, staring at the blankness of his expression.

He stepped back from the box, his hands at his sides. He shook his head. She stepped closer and looked down into the box. "Oh, boy," she said.

"Yeah," he said.

"It was flown here?"

He nodded and cleared his throat. "Get the key to Barnum's cell," he said.

They went up the stairs together, Hackberry holding the box, Pam walking in front of him. She turned the key in the cell door and pulled it open. Noie Barnum was lying on his bunk, reading a magazine. He put the magazine on the floor but didn't get up.

"Come in and close the door behind you," Hackberry said to Pam.

"Something going on?" Barnum said.

"Yeah, sit up," Hackberry said. "See this?"

"Yeah, a box."

"Look inside it."

"What for?"

Hackberry set the box on the foot of the bunk and picked up the magazine from the floor. He rolled it into a cone and slapped Barnum across the head. Then he slapped him a second time and a third. "I want to tear you up, Mr. Barnum. I don't mean that figuratively. I want to throw you down those stairs. That's how I feel about you."

Barnum's eyes were filming, his face blotched. "You don't have the right to treat me like this."

"Look inside that box."

"Somebody's head is in there?" Barnum said, his expression defiant, his eyes lifted to Hackberry's.

Hackberry hit him again, this time tearing the cover loose from the magazine. Barnum

641

lifted his hand to protect himself, then looked down into the box. The blood drained from his face. "Oh God," he said.

"Tell me what you see."

"It's a hand and a foot."

"Are they male or female?"

"Sir?"

"Answer the question."

"There's hair on the ankle. It must be a man's."

"Look at the hand."

"What about it?"

"Look closer. There's a ring on it. Look at it."

"I'm not responsible for this."

"That's a University of Texas class ring. The hand and the ring belong to Temple Dowling. The people who did this to him will probably start on Anton Ling next. Right now I'd like to rip you apart. Instead of doing that, I'm going to ask you a couple of questions, and you're going to answer them. Got that?"

"Yes, sir."

"Where were you and Jack Collins hiding?"

"Just like you said earlier, right south of the border. But Jack's gone by now."

"Gone where?"

"That's anybody's guess. You see him and then he's gone. He's standing in one place, then in another, without seeming to move. I've never known anybody like him."

"You're just catching on to the fact that

642

there's something a little unusual about him?"

"I don't know where Jack is. I don't know where Miss Anton is, either. I feel awful about what's happened. My sister died in the Towers. I wanted to get even with the people who killed her. I didn't want any of these other things to happen."

Hackberry let out his breath and felt the heat rise out of his chest like ash off a dead fire. "I want you out of here," he said.

"Say again?"

"You heard me. Hit the road."

"I don't get it."

"You don't have to. You just got eighty-sixed from my jail. It's a first. Burn a candle the next time you're in church."

"Maybe I don't want to leave."

"Son, you'd better get a lot of gone between you and this jailhouse," Pam said.

"Well, you're gonna see me again," Barnum said.

Pam raised her eyebrows threateningly.

"Yes, ma'am, I'm gone," he said.

Downstairs, ten minutes later, Pam said, "Hack, what in the hell are you doing?"

"Fixing to call the FBI," he replied.

But it wasn't for the reasons she thought.

CHAPTER TWENTY-SIX

Pam was still staring at him when he got off the phone. "You told the feds about Dowling's mutilation but not about Barnum?"

"That's right," he replied.

"Why does Barnum get a pass?"

"Because if the feds get him into custody, they'll probably lose interest in Anton Ling. Second, Barnum isn't a bad kid and, in my opinion, deserves another chance."

"You have a funny way of looking at the world, Hack."

"My father used to say, 'The name of the game is five-card draw. You never have to play the hand you're dealt.' He believed everything we see around us now was once part of the Atlantic Ocean, with mermaids sitting up on the rocks, and that one day I would see the mermaids return."

"We'd better get some breakfast, *kemo sabe*."

"I told you that's what Rie called me, didn't I?"

"Yeah, I'm sorry, I forgot," she said.

"Don't say you're sorry. You didn't know Rie. She'd like for you to call me that. She'd like you."

She looked at him in a strange way, her mouth slightly parted, her face suddenly vulnerable, but he did not see it. Maydeen had just come out of the dispatcher's cage, her anger palpable. "He's on the line, Hack," she said.

"Who is *he?*"

"He just told me, 'Put the sheriff on the line, woman.' "

"Collins?"

"I say we hang up on him. Don't let him jerk you around like this, Hack."

"No, I think this is the call we've been waiting on," Hackberry said.

Jack Collins was sitting at a small table under a canvas tarp propped on poles next to an airplane hangar, a corked green bottle of seltzer and a glass and a saucer of salted lime slices by his hand. A clutch of banana plants grew tightly against the hangar wall, beads of moisture the size of BBs sliding down the leaves. The wind was hot, the canvas riffling above his head, the desert lidded from horizon to horizon with a layer of solid blue-black clouds that seemed to force the heat and humidity radiating from the desert floor back into the earth. The clouds crackled with electricity but offered no real promise of rain or even a moment of relief from the grit and alkali in the wind and the smell of salt and decomposition that whirled with the dust devils out of the streambeds. Jack decided there was nothing wrong with Mexico that a half-dozen hydrogen bombs and a lot of topsoil couldn't cure.

Jack's pilot and two hired killers, the cousins Eladio and Jaime, were waiting for him by the two-engine Beechcraft on the airstrip. The pilot was on retainer, at Jack's beck and call on a twenty-four-hour basis. Eladio and Jaime were available for any activity that put money in their pockets, night or day; if there were any lines they would not cross, any deeds they would not perform, including a drive-by for La Familia Michoacána on a teenage birthday party in Juárez, Jack had not seen it. Their greatest problem, in his view, was the impaired thought processes that seemed to live behind the indolence in their faces. The inside of Jaime's head could only be described as a tangled web of cruelty that was linked somehow to his stupidity and sullen nature. The more intelligent of the two, Eladio, thought that his transparent childlike deceit and attempts at manipulation were signs of sophistication. During a rare loss of restraint with the two cousins, Jack had asked Eladio if his mother had been impregnated by a bowling pin.

Eladio had responded, "You are a man of knowledge, Señor Jack. But you must not misjudge simple men. We think and feel deeply about our mothers. They are the center of our lives."

"Then why do you say *chinga tu madre* to each other at every opportunity?" Jack had said.

"I am not equipped to discuss abstractions with a man of your intelligence," Eladio had said. "But my mother is eighty and still tells stories of her mother, who was a concubine of Pancho Villa and one of those who helped hide his severed head in the Van Horn Mountains. That is the level of respect we have for the women in our family."

Jack had made a mental note about the level of stability in his employees.

At this particular moment, he was irritated with the weather, the clouds of black flies buzzing over a calf's carcass in a nearby streambed, and the fact that the two cousins seemed incapable of doing anything right except killing people. The man who owned the airstrip and the hangar and the improvised café outside it had installed a jukebox just inside the hangar door, one loaded with gangsta-rap recordings that blasted through the speakers so loudly that the side of the tin hangar shook. Jack had told Eladio and Jaime to talk with the jukebox's owner, but either the owner had ignored the warning or they

647

had not bothered. So while he was trying to make notes in preparation for his conversation with the sheriff, his eardrums were being assailed by a level of electronic percussion that was like having a studded snow tire driven over his head.

Jack capped his pen, stuck it between the pages of his notebook, and went inside the hangar, where the owner was cleaning the concrete pad with a push broom. "Can I help you, *señor?*" he said.

Jack pointed to his ear, indicating he couldn't hear.

"You got a problem with your ear?" the owner shouted.

Jack pulled the plug on the jukebox, cut the electric cord in two with his pocketknife, and set the plug on top of the casing. "No, I'm fine now. Thanks," he said.

Then he sat down at his table under the canvas flap and drank a glass of seltzer and chewed on a lime slice, staring into space, each eye like a glass orb with a dead insect frozen inside it. He dialed his cell phone with his thumb and lifted the phone to his ear and waited, his body heat increasing inside his clothes, his pulse quickening. Why would his metabolism react to calling the sheriff? It could be anything, he told himself. Why dwell on it? Maybe it was because he had finally found a worthy opponent.

Or maybe it was something else.

What?

Don't think about it, he told himself.

Why not? I'm supposed to be afraid of my own thoughts? he asked himself.

Maybe Holland is the father you never had. Maybe you want him to like you.

Like hell I do.

You could have taken him off the board a couple of times. Why didn't you do it, Jackie Boy?

The situation was one-sided. There's no honor in that. Don't call me that name.

There was honor in the shooting of the nine Thai women?

I don't want to talk about that. It's over. I did my penance in the desert.

He thought he heard the hysterical laughter of a woman, someone who always hung just on the edge of his vision, ridiculing him, waiting for him to slip up, her smile as cruel as an open cut in living tissue.

When the female deputy answered, Jack said, "Put the sheriff on the line, woman."

Whatever she said in response never registered. Instead, he heard the voice of the woman who lived in his dreams and his unconscious and his idle daytime moments and his futile attempts at joy. He heard her incessant, piercing laughter, louder and louder, and he knew that eventually, he would once again resort to the release that never failed him, an eruption of gunfire that rever-

649

berated through his hands and arms like a jackhammer and made his teeth rattle and cleansed his thoughts and deadened his ears to all sound, both outside and inside his head.

"What do you need, Mr. Collins?" the sheriff's voice said.

"I know where the Asian woman is. I can take you there," he replied.

"Where might that be?"

"Down in Mexico, way to heck and gone by car, not so far by air."

"She's with Sholokoff?"

"She and Temple Dowling and the 'breed known as Krill. How's Noie doing?"

"I don't know. I kicked him loose."

"You did what?"

"Last time I saw him, he was walking toward the city-limits sign, whistling a song."

"The feds aren't going to be happy with you."

"I'll try to live with it. Where can we meet, Mr. Collins?"

"You ever lie?"

"No."

"Not ever?"

"You heard me the first time," Hackberry said.

"I'm trusting you. I don't do that with most people."

"Do whatever you want, sir. But don't expect me to feel flattered."

"I'll give you some coordinates and see you

no later than four hours from now. I suppose you'll bring the female deputy with you?"

"Count on it. Why are you doing this, Mr. Collins?"

"Sholokoff shouldn't have taken the Asian woman. She's not a player."

"There's another reason."

"Sholokoff tried to have me capped. I owe him one."

"There's another reason."

"When you find out what it is, tell me so we'll both know. Don't bring anybody besides the female deputy and your pilot. A couple of my men will pick you up. If you violate any aspect of our arrangement, the deal is off and you won't hear from me again. The Asian woman's fate will be on your conscience."

"If you try to harm me or my deputy, I'm going to cool you out on the spot. I'm like you, Jack — over-the-hill and out of place and time, with not a lot to lose."

"Then keep your damn word, and we'll get along just fine."

Jack clicked off his cell phone. Unbelievably, the jukebox sprang to life and began blaring rap music out the door. He remembered that the cord he'd cut had both a female and a male plug and was detachable from the box. The owner of the hangar had probably replaced it and decided to prove he could be as assertive and unpleasant as an imperious gringo from Texas who thought he

651

could come to Mexico and wipe his ass on the place.

Jack went to the plane and removed his guitar case and set it on top of the table. The wind was blowing harder, the heat and dust swirling under the canopy as Jack unfastened the top of the case and inserted plugs in his ears and removed his Thompson and snapped a thirty-round box magazine into the bottom of the receiver and went inside the hangar. The owner took one look at him and dropped his push broom and began running for the back door. Jack raised the Thompson's barrel and squeezed the trigger, ripping apart the jukebox, scattering plastic shards and electronic components all over the concrete pad, stitching the tin wall with holes the size of nickels.

"*Señor,* what the fuck you doin'?" Eladio said behind him.

Jack still had the plugs stoppered in his ears and could not hear him. The only sound he heard was his mother's laughter — maniacal, forever taunting, a paean of ridicule aimed at a driven man who would never escape the black box in which a little boy had been locked.

Krill did not know a great deal about the complexities of politics. A man owned land or he did not own land. Either he was allowed to keep the product of his labor or he was

652

not allowed to keep it. The abstractions of ideology seemed the stuff that fools and radicals and drunkards argued about in late-hour bars because they had nothing else to occupy their time. Though Krill did not understand the abstruse terms of social science or economics, he understood jails. He had learned about them in El Salvador and Nicaragua, and he knew how you survived or didn't survive inside them. Men in confinement all behaved and thought in a predictable fashion. And so did their warders.

Krill had a very strong suspicion that his captors did not understand how jails worked. The gringo Frank was a good example of what American convicts called a "fish." He had not only baited a prisoner but had informed the prisoner of his ultimate fate, which in this case was death and burial in concrete, telling the prisoner in effect that he had nothing to lose. Frank had made another mistake. He had not bothered to note that when Krill was placed in the cell, he was wearing running shoes, not pull-on boots.

Krill had slept three hours on the floor, his head cushioned on a piece of burlap he had found in the corner. As the early glow of morning appeared through the window on the far side of the cellar, a man came down the stairs carrying two bowls filled with rice and beans. He was a strange-looking man, with dirty-blond hair and a duckbilled upper lip and eyes that were set too far apart and skin that had the grainy texture of pig hide. He took one bowl to the cell where Krill believed La Magdalena was being held, then squatted in front of Krill's cell and pushed the second bowl through the gap between the concrete floor and the bottom of the door.

"I need something to eat with," Krill said.

"This isn't a hotel," the man said.

"We cannot eat our food with our fingers."

"Eat out of the bowl. Just tip it up and you can eat."

"*Hombre,* we are not animals. You must give us utensils to eat."

"I'll see what I can find," the man said.

"Bring me a spoon. I cannot eat rice with a fork. Bring us water, too."

"Want anything else?"

"Yes, to use a real toilet, one that flushes with water. Using a chemical toilet is unsanitary and degrading."

When the man had gone upstairs, Krill lowered his voice and said, "Magdalena, can you hear me?"

"Yes," the woman said.

"Did they hurt you?"

"No."

"Where is Dowling?"

"I think he's dead."

"Did they mutilate him?"

"Yes, very badly."

"Listen to me. I must say this in a hurry. I

654

have killed many men. I have also killed a Jesuit priest. I tortured and murdered a DEA informant. I need your absolution for these sins and others that are too many to name."

"I don't have that power. Only God does. If you're sorry for what you did and you renounce your violent ways, your sins are forgiven. God doesn't forgive incrementally or partially. He forgives absolutely, Antonio. That's what 'absolution' means. God makes all things new."

"You remembered my name."

"Of course. Why wouldn't I?"

"Because everyone calls me Krill."

"It's a name you earned in war. You shouldn't go by that name anymore."

"Maybe I'll stop using it later, Magdalena. But right now I got to get us out of here. We need a fork from the man who brought us our bowls."

"Why?"

"There are only two ways we're going to get out of here. I have to open the lock on my door or get a man in my cell. We need a fork."

"I heard you ask for a spoon."

"This man is stubborn and slow in the head. He will do the opposite of what he is asked."

The upstairs door opened, and the man with the duckbilled mouth came down the stairs. There were two dull metallic objects in

655

his right hand. "I got you what you wanted," he said. "Put your bowls outside the door when you're finished."

Krill stuck his hand through the bars and curved his palm around the utensil the man gave him. *A spoon,* he thought bitterly.

"Disappointed? I was jailing when I was sixteen," the man said. "Better eat up. You got a rough day ahead of you."

The single-engine department plane dropped down over a ridge and followed a milky-brown river that had spread out onto the floodplain and was dotted with sandy islands that had willow trees on them. Above the plane, Hackberry could see the long blue-black layer of clouds that seemed to extend like curds of industrial smoke from the Big Bend all the way across northern Mexico. Down below, the willow trees stiffened in the wind, the surface of the river wrinkling in jagged V-shaped lines. On the southern horizon, the cloud layer seemed to end and looked like strips of torn black cotton churning against a band of perfectly blue sky.

The wings of the plane yawed suddenly, the airframe shuddering. "We're fine," the pilot said above the engine noise. He was a crop duster named Toad Fowler who worked on and off for the sheriff's department. "Those are just updrafts."

Nonetheless, he kept tapping the glass on

656

his instruments.

"What's the problem?" Hackberry asked.

"The oil pressure is a little low," the pilot said. "We're okay. We'll be there in ten minutes."

"How low?" Hackberry said.

"It's probably not a line, just a leaky gasket," the pilot said. "I'll check everything out after we get down. Hang on. We might bounce around a little bit."

"You didn't check everything out before we left?" Hackberry asked.

"It's an old plane. What do you want? Shit happens," the pilot said.

When the plane dipped down toward the river, Hackberry felt Pam place her hand on top of his shoulder, her breath coming hard against the back of his neck.

"We're okay," Hackberry said.

"How do you know?" she asked.

"Toad just told me."

"Tell him I'm going to shoot him after we land."

Down below, Hackberry could see great squares of both cultivated and pasture land and bare hills that looked molded out of white clay that had hardened and cracked. The pilot made a wide turn, the wings buffeting, and came in low over the river, the islands sweeping by, then Hackberry saw a feeder lot and hog farm whose holding pens were churned a chocolate color and buildings with tin roofs and houses constructed of cinder block and then a short pale green landing strip that had been recently mowed out of a field, a red wind sock straining against its tether at the far end. They landed hard, rainwater splashing under the tires. A flatbed truck with two men lounging near it was parked by the side of the strip.

"You ever see them before?" Pam said.

"No," Hackberry replied. "You okay?"

She didn't reply until Toad had cut the engine and gotten out of the plane and lit a cigarette by the wing. "I'm backing your play, Hack, but the idea of getting involved with Jack Collins makes my stomach churn," she said.

"I wouldn't blame you if you stayed with Toad. I can handle it by myself."

"That's not going to happen," she said.

"I have to get Miss Anton back, Pam. If I don't, I'll never rest."

"We're making a deal with the devil, and you know it."

"That's the breaks."

"You mean after this is over, you're going to let that bastard slide?"

"Jack Collins isn't planning to leave Mexico," he said.

Her eyes went back and forth. "How do you know that?"

"Collins brought us here as his executioners," he said.

"Or maybe he plans on being ours," she said.

Hackberry and Pam pulled a duffel bag and a backpack off the plane and walked toward the flatbed truck. The Mexicans standing next to it introduced themselves as Eladio and Jaime. They were unshaved and wore slouch-brim straw hats and unpressed long-sleeve cotton shirts buttoned at the wrists. Their eyes wandered over Pam's body without seeming to see her, the laziness in their expressions as much mask as indicator of their thoughts.

"Where's Collins?" Hackberry said.

"He ain't here," Jaime said.

"That's why I asked you where he is," Hackberry said.

"We'll take you where he's at," Jaime said. "You two can ride in front with Eladio. I'll ride in back."

"Where are we going?" Pam asked.

"You'll know when we get there, *chica*," Jaime said.

"Call me that again and see what happens," she said.

"We are sorry. We do not mean to offend," Eladio said. "Can we look in your canvas bag and your pack? It would be good if we can look at your cell phones, too."

"Why would you want to do that?" Pam said.

"Among friends, there is no need of GPS

locators," Eladio said. "It is good to have things of that nature out of our discussions about the liberation of your friend. That is the only reason I raise this question."

"Look all you want," Hackberry said.

"Thank you," Eladio said. "What fine guns you have in your bag. What is in this metal box?"

"Cookies and fruitcake," Hackberry said.

"You carry such items with you when you go on a serious mission?" Eladio said.

"I have a sugar deficiency. I also thought you might like some. Take them if you like," Hackberry said.

"That is very kind of you," Eladio said. "I have children who will love these."

"When do we see Preacher?" Hackberry asked.

"Very soon. He looks forward to seeing you with great anticipation," Eladio said.

"You come all the way down here 'cause of *la china?*" Jaime said.

"You could say that," Hackberry replied.

"She must be some broad, *hombre*," Jaime said. "It's true what they say about Chinese women?"

"Do not speak further," Eladio said, raising his finger to his cousin's lips.

"It's just a question. I do not need to be censored," Jaime said. "These are gringos in our country. We do not suppress ourselves to please gringos in our own country."

660

"It's time for us to see Mr. Collins," Hackberry said.

He and Pam rode in the cab while Eladio drove and Jaime sat on the flatbed. They proceeded in a southerly direction down dirt roads through irrigated farmland for almost an hour. The colors and configuration and flora in the land were like none that Hack could remember. Wild grapefruit and hibiscus and pink camellias and palm trees with long, slender trunks grew in the turn rows. The soil was loamy and tinted a reddish-brown, as though it had been mixed with rust, but the hills were white and bare and gray-backed, like sea creatures that had died and fossilized. The topography made Hack think of imaginative paintings of ancient Egypt that depicted an era when the earth was still recovering from the Flood and deserts bloomed and gatherers filled date baskets with their hands. Why would a man like Josef Sholokoff locate himself in such a place? To re-create the introduction of the serpent into Eden?

No, nothing so grandiose, Hackberry thought. For Sholokoff, Mexico was probably nothing more than a good tax dodge.

The truck rolled down a long embanked road made of crushed stone, the rocks *ting*ing steadily under the fenders, the wind stream warm and sultry, the sky lidded with clouds that emitted no sunlight. Ahead, at a crossroads, Hackberry could see a small, paintless wood-frame store with a single gas pump in front and a screened side porch. Behind the store, the terrain seemed to stretch away endlessly, glazed with salt, cracked and sunken in places, as though a lake had once covered the area but had drained through a hole in its center. Eladio parked the truck and cut the engine. "Señor Collins awaits you on the porch," he said. "Do not take your guns inside. That would cause alarm for the owner of the store. Also, it is a very serious offense to bring guns into Mexico."

"That's like saying it's a serious offense to bring insanity into a lunatic asylum," Pam said.

"I am not educated and do not understand the comparisons you make, *señorita*," Eladio said.

Hackberry looked through the back window of the cab. "Your cousin is eating the cookies you were going to give your children," he said.

"Jaime, what are you doin', man?" Eladio yelled out the window.

Jaime replaced the tin lid on the container and wiped the crumbs off his fingers. Pam and Hackberry got out of the cab and followed Eladio to the screen door on the store's side porch. She glanced over her shoulder at Jaime, who had remained on the truck bed. "I don't guess these guys are students of Homer," she said.

"Shut up," Hackberry said under his breath. He opened the screen door and stepped inside, removing his Stetson hat. Inside the gloom, against the back wall, he saw a man eating refried beans and strips of steak and sliced peppers from a tin plate with a fork. The man wore a blocked hat and a seersucker coat and a gray dress shirt with no buttons on the collar and trousers that were tucked into the tops of his boots. A guitar case was propped on its side against the wall behind him. For Hackberry, Jack Collins was like a figure out of a dream, not quite flesh and blood, vaporous in its dimensions, waiting like an incubus to attach itself to the fear in its victim, in the way a leech attaches itself to living tissue in order to survive.

"Have a good flight?" Collins said.

"Not really," Hackberry said.

"Sit down. You, too, Deputy Tibbs."

"I think I'll stand. You don't mind, do you?" Pam said.

"I owe you an apology," Collins said, chewing while he spoke.

"For trying to kill me?" she said.

"If y'all had your way, you would have split me open and salted my innards and tacked me to a fence post. I figure what I did was just fair play."

"We didn't come here to talk past history, Mr. Collins. How far are we from our target?" Hackberry said.

Collins pushed two chairs out from the table with his boot. He was wearing a holstered thumb-buster revolver, the bluing rubbed bare around the cylinder, the cartridge loops stuffed with copper-jacketed .45 rounds. "Sit down. Have a Pepsi. The beans and meat aren't bad. We go in at sunset. Once inside that compound, we don't negotiate."

"Listen to me, Collins. You don't make the rules. I do," Hackberry said. "We're down here for one reason only, and that's to save the life of an innocent woman. We don't turn people into wallpaper. If you want to settle a personal score with Sholokoff, you find another time and place to do it."

Collins motioned at the waiter, then looked up at Hackberry. "I bought a big bottle of Pepsi and had him put it in the icebox for y'all. Now sit down and take your nose out of the air. You, too, Deputy Tibbs." He placed his fork on his plate and removed a folded piece of paper from inside his coat. "I've drawn a diagram of the compound and the entrances to it. Are y'all going to sit down or not?"

Pam Tibbs pulled back a chair and sat down, her eyes on his.

"You want to tell me something?" he asked.

"I'd like to park one in your brisket, you arrogant white trash," she replied.

Collins looked across the table at Hackberry. "I'm not going to have this, Sheriff."

"Show us the entrances to the compound," Hackberry said.

"No, you need to correct the mouth on this woman."

The waiter brought a tall plastic bottle of Pepsi and two glasses, then went away.

"We came a long way, Jack," Hackberry said. "You've done a lot of harm to a lot of people, some of them friends of ours. Don't expect too much of us."

"You say I've done harm? Right now the Asian woman and the fellow named Krill are learning what harm is all about. Josef Sholokoff doesn't know Noie is on the street. He thinks he's still in your jail, and he's mad as hell and sweating Ms. Ling and the half-breed because of it."

"You've got someone inside?" Hackberry said.

"What do you think?" Collins asked. "They started in on Krill about four hours ago. If I know Josef, he'll take a special interest in the woman. Why do you think he crucified Cody Daniels and set fire to his church with him hanging on the cross?"

"You tell me."

"It wasn't for money. It wasn't for sheer meanness, either."

Hackberry remained silent.

"Josef was born with the brain of a rodent and the face of a ferret, and he blames God for the pitiful little toothpick that he is,"

Collins said. "For formally educated people, neither of y'all seems real bright, Mr. Holland. But I guess overestimating the intelligence of my fellow man has always been my greatest character defect." He pushed the diagram toward Hackberry and resumed eating, his fork scraping in the grease at the bottom of the plate, his eyes as empty as glass.

CHAPTER TWENTY-SEVEN

They had beaten Krill in his cell and hung him from a rafter in the center of the cellar, where the Asian woman could see him hanging, and then had beaten him again. When they dropped him to the floor, his wrists roped together behind him, he had begun to slip in and out of consciousness and into a place where his children were waiting for him. They were standing outside a traveling carnival, their cheeks smeared with Popsicle juice, the carved wooden horses of a merry-go-round spinning behind them, the music of the calliope rising into the evening sky.

Frank or the man standing next to Frank poured water from a canteen on Krill's face. Josef Sholokoff was sitting on a chair two feet away, one knee folded over the other, smoking a perfumed cigarette that was gold-tipped and wrapped with lavender paper. "Noie Barnum remained for weeks in your custody, but you never made him draw the design of the drone? You're a businessman who kidnaps and sells valuable people, but you never try to extract information from them? You think I'm a stupid man, Mr. Krill?"

"My name is Antonio."

"You came to see the woman for religious reasons? You didn't know she helped transport arms to your country? It's just coincidence that we found you at her house while you were on a spiritual mission? You are a very entertaining man, I think."

"My women have always told me that."

"You worked for the Americans in your country?"

"Of course. Everyone does."

"But you planned to help Al Qaeda?"

"An American helicopter killed my children. But I know now that I am responsible for their deaths, not others."

"Oh, I see. Because you have discovered you are powerless against the killers of your children, you blame yourself and, in so doing, become a saint. So, in our way, we are helping you with your saintliness?"

"You taunt an uneducated man whose hands are bound after you have tortured him?" the Asian woman said from her cell. "You are a very small man, Mr. Sholokoff."

"Frank, take care of that," Sholokoff said.

"Sir?" Frank said.

"Ms. Ling. Take care of her."

"The only way to shut her up is to pour concrete in her mouth," Frank said.

"Then do it," Sholokoff said.

"Sir, we need to finish with the greaser one way or another," Frank said.

"All I get from you are admonitions but never results. In the last forty-eight hours, we have had in our possession a defense contractor, a notorious kidnapper and coyote, and an ex–CIA operative who flew with Air America. We get nothing out of any of them. Are you successful only with a worthless man like Cody Daniels? You certainly seemed to rise to the occasion when you turned him into a living passion play. I wonder about you, Frank."

"That was your doing, sir," Frank said. He was standing behind Sholokoff, wearing tight leather gloves like a race-car driver might wear, his flat stomach exposed by his scissored-off T-shirt.

Sholokoff turned in his chair. "You need to explain yourself, Frank."

"We shouldn't have been wasting our time on the minister. It wasn't me that had the hard-on about him. That's all I was saying."

Sholokoff puffed on his cigarette, his eyes warm and shiny, exhaling the smoke from his nostrils. He put out the cigarette under his foot, then picked up the butt and handed it to one of his men to dispose of. "Frank, tell me this. Why is it that Sheriff Holland is not responding to our calls? Even after we sent part of Temple Dowling to his office. Why is a man like Holland, a personal friend of Ms. Ling, seemingly detached from her fate?"

"I don't know, sir," Frank said.

"Could it be that he no longer has Noie Barnum in his possession? Or that he's closer to us now than he was this morning?"

"You mean he's coming here?" Frank said.

"Put Antonio back in his cell. I have to use the bathroom," Sholokoff said. "While I'm gone, I want you to devise something special for Ms. Ling. I also don't want to have to correct you again. Do you understand me, Frank?"

"Loud and clear, Mr. S.," Frank said.

"*Señor,* you got a minute for me?" Krill said from the floor, staring through the legs of the men who surrounded him.

"You want me to be your friend now, Antonio? To take you out of all this unhappiness?" Sholokoff said.

"Yes, sir. I am very tired of it."

"I'm glad to hear that."

"I don't want to be here when the next bad thing happens."

"With Ms. Ling?"

"No, with you and your friends, *señor.*"

"I think you have become delusional, my Hispanic friend."

"You didn't see what Negrito just did. Negrito was living inside my skin, but he just left my body and went up on the ceiling. Now he's standing right behind you. You are in deep shit, *señor.*"

"Who's Negrito?" Sholokoff asked Frank.

"The guy who's gonna fuck you with a garden rake," Krill said. Then he began laughing on the floor, his long hair hanging in a sweaty web over his face.

Sholokoff seemed more bemused than offended and went upstairs to use the bathroom. Two men picked Krill up by his arms and carried him to his cell and threw him inside. "Hey, Frank," one of them said. "There're scratches around the keyhole."

"What?" Frank said.

"His food bowl is here, but there's no utensil. The guy must have been using a fork on the lock."

"Somebody gave the greaser a fork?"

"Frank, I gave him a spoon," said the man who had brought Krill his food.

"Then where is it?"

"I don't know, man."

"We should tell Mr. Sholokoff," said the man who had discovered the scratches.

"Shut up. Both you guys shut up," Frank said. He stepped inside the cell and kicked Krill in the base of the spine. "Where's the spoon, greaseball?"

"That hurts, boss. It makes my mind go blank," Krill said. "Somebody gave me a spoon? I must have lost it. I am very sorry."

"Frank," one of the other men whispered.

"What?"

"Mr. Sholokoff just flushed the toilet."

Jack Collins had led the way in a Ford Explorer through a winding series of low-topped white hills on which no grass or trees or even scrub brush grew. The road through the hills was narrow and rock-strewn and dusty, the wind as hot as a blowtorch, smelling of creosote and alkali and dry stone under the layer of blue-black clouds that gave no rain.

He had seen white hills like these only one other time in his life, when he was marching with a column of marines in the same kind of dust and heat through terrain that was more like Central Africa than the Korean peninsula. The marines wore utilities that were stiff with salt, the armpits dark with sweat, the backs of their necks tanned and oily and glistening under the rims of their steel pots, their boots gray with dust. In the midst of it all, the ambulances and six-bys and tanks and towed field pieces kept grinding endlessly up the road, the dust from their wheels blowing back into the faces of the men. Ahead, Hackberry could see the white hills that made him think of giant wind-scrubbed, calcified slugs on which no vegetation grew and whose sides were sometimes pocked with caves in which the Japanese prior to World War II had installed railroad tracks and mobile howitzers.

That was the day Hackberry had an

epiphany about death that had always remained with him and that he called upon
whenever he was afraid. He had reached a
point of exhaustion and dehydration that had
taken him past the edges of endurance into
personal surrender, a calm letting go of his
fatigue and the blisters inside his boots and
the sweat crawling down his sides and the
fear that at any moment he would hear the
popping of small-arms fire in the hills. When
the column fell out, he looked at the red haze
of dust floating across the sun and on the
hills and on a long flat plateau dotted with
freshly turned earth that resembled anthills,
and he wondered why any of it should be of
any concern to him or his comrades or even
to the nations that warred over it. In a short
span of time, nothing that happened here
would be of any significance to anyone.
Ultimately, every cloak rolled in blood would
be used as fuel for flames, and the sun would
continue to shine and the rain to fall upon
both the just and the unjust, and this piece of
worthless land would remain exactly what it
was, a worthless piece of land of no importance to anyone except those who lost their
lives because of it.

Just as he had experienced these thoughts,
someone had shouted, "Incoming!" and
Hackberry had heard first one, then two, then
three artillery rounds arching out of the sky,
like a train engine screeching down a track

and then exploding, striking the earth in such rapid succession that he'd had no time to react. From where he was sitting on top of a ditch, he saw the barrage intensify and march across the plateau, blowing geysers of dirt and buried pots of kimchi into the air.

The North Koreans were laying waste to a field filled with buried earthen jars of pickled cabbage. Hackberry continued to stare at the rain of destruction on the most ignoble of targets, bemused as much by the madness of his fellow man's obsession as by the bizarre nature of the event. When clouds of pulverized dirt blew into his face, he never blinked. Nor did he blink when a piece of artillery shell spun toward him like a heliograph, its twisted steel surfaces flashing with light, whipping past his ear with a whirring sound like that of a tiny propeller. He felt neither fear nor self-recrimination at his recklessness, and he did not know why, since he did not consider himself either brave or exceptional.

His lack of fear and his whimsical attitude toward his own death stayed with him all the way to the Chosin Reservoir and his imprisonment in No Name Valley, and up until the present, he was not sure why his fear had temporarily disappeared or why it had returned. With time and age, he had come to think of mortality as the price of admission to the ballpark; but why had this road in Mexico taken him back to Korea? Was he finally about to step through the door into the place we all fear? Would his legs and his mettle be up to that dry-throated, heart-pounding, blood-draining moment that no words can adequately describe? Or would his courage fail him, as it had when he dropped a litter with a wounded marine on it and ran from a Chinese enlisted man who stood on a pile of frozen sandbags and sprayed Hackberry's ditch with a burp gun and shot him three times through the calves and left him with years of guilt and self-abasement that he came to accept as a natural way of life?

The flatbed truck followed the Explorer between the hills, then emerged into a green valley where a paved road lined with eucalyptus trees led due south through meadowland and cornfields and farmhouses that were built of stone or stucco or both. Finally, the Explorer turned off the road and crossed a cattle guard and passed a burned-out house and pulled into a two-story barn that was filled with wind and the sounds of rattling tin in the roof.

Jack Collins cut his engine and got out of the Explorer and pulled his guitar case after him, then shut the driver's door. "The sun will dip behind that mountain yonder in about four hours. If you want, you can rest up," he said.

"What is this place?" Hackberry asked.

"It used to belong to a friend of mine. At

least it did until the army burned him out."

"You've spent time around here before?"

"Now and then."

"Working for Sholokoff?"

"I did some contract stuff for him. I work for myself. I never 'worked' for Josef Sholokoff."

"Why the wait?" Hackberry asked. Through a side window, he could see Eladio urinating inside a grove of citrus trees.

"You want to attack a houseful of armed men in daylight?"

"I don't know if Ms. Ling can afford to write off the next four hours."

"She hit me with a piñata stick, but I'm risking my life to save hers," Collins said. "I don't think she's got any kick coming. Maybe Sholokoff will take some of the starch out of her."

Hackberry kept his face turned away so Collins would not see the emotion he was trying to suppress. Through the window, Hackberry saw Eladio turn his back to the barn and zip his fly, then remove a cell phone from his pants pocket. "What's your plan?" Hackberry said.

"I've arranged to have the cellar door and the French doors left unlocked on the patio. Three of us go through the French doors, and two go straight down the steps into the cellar. In the confusion, we'll pop two or three of them before they'll know what's happening. The others will cut bait."

"How do you know that?"

"They're for hire. They go whichever way the wind vane turns. How do you think revolutions get won? You get the religious fanatics and idealists on your side, people with no monetary interest. What kind of weapons did you bring?"

"An AR15, a cut-down twelve, a Beretta nine-millimeter, and our revolvers."

"Y'all didn't end up with any of that Homeland Security money?"

"Worry about your own ordnance, Mr. Collins. How far is Sholokoff's place?" Hackberry said, his gaze wandering out the window, where Eladio was walking back toward the front of the barn.

"Three miles, more or less," Collins said.

"We go in now."

"Impetuosity might be your undoing, Mr. Holland."

"It's Sheriff Holland to you."

"Not here it isn't. The only title that counts down here is the one you pay for."

"Is there any reason one of your men would be using his cell phone while he's hosing down a lime tree?"

Collins's eyes sharpened, but they did not leave Hackberry's face nor glance in the direction of Eladio, who had just walked through the barn's entrance.

"You saw that?" Collins said.

"Ms. Ling's life is hanging in the balance. Why would I try to throw you a slider?"

Collins's mouth flexed, exposing his teeth, his eyes staring at the straw scattered on the dirt floor of the barn. "You're sure about what you saw?" he said.

Hackberry didn't reply.

"All right," Collins said, his eyelids fluttering. "We go in now. Later, I'll clean up the problem you just mentioned. How about the woman?"

"You mean my chief deputy?"

"Yeah, that's what I just said. Can she take the heat in the kitchen?"

"You're really a test of Christian charity, Jack."

"Don't patronize me. I won't abide it."

"When this is over —" Hackberry began.

"You'll what?"

"Find out a way to get you into a clinical study. I think you'll be invaluable to researchers everywhere. We've always wondered where the gene pool got screwed up. Some think it's because the Neanderthal gene got mixed in with the Homo sapiens's, but no one is sure. Your DNA may contain the answer."

Collins's eyes were lifted to Hackberry's as Hackberry spoke. "Once inside, you'll see what the wrath of God is all about. Don't stand in its way or you'll feel it, too," he said. "You listening to me, boy?"

"Count your blessings, you piece of shit,"

Hackberry said.

Krill's plan to get one of his warders into the cell had not worked, and now he was being forced to witness the acts they were perpetrating upon the body of the Asian woman called La Magdalena. He had not been able to pick the lock with the shaft of the spoon, so he had deliberately scratched the metal around the keyhole, hoping the scratches would be detected and a man would enter the cell in order to search for the spoon. But none of them, particularly Frank, had so far been willing to admit to Josef Sholokoff the nature of their blunder, so Krill stood at the bars, staring impotently at the silhouette of La Magdalena, who had been strung from a rafter by her wrists, the soles of her feet barely touching the floor.

"I was mistaken about you, Señor Sholokoff," Krill said. "I thought I had been captured by the kind of mercenaries I knew in my homeland. But this is not so. As Negrito said, you are all *cobardes*. A nest of cowards. You smoke your purple cigarette with the gold tip and blow smoke through your nostrils like a dragon would, but you are a small, wasted goat of a man, I suspect one that has a very small penis and cojones the size of smoked oysters. Do you torture the woman because she rejected you? I have a feeling that may well be the case. A man like you was never intended to touch a woman of quality. Look at her, then look at yourself. She is beautiful and pure, but the people who smuggle your dope and know you say your whores call you a human tampon. These are not my words but Negrito's. He has a terrible fate designed for the *comunista* with the perfumed cigarette. That is what Negrito calls you, Señor Goat Man."

Five men stood in a circle around the woman. Two of them had taken off their shirts; they both had hair on their backs and large hands and jugheads and ears, the light from the bare bulb over the stairs yellow on their shoulders. Sholokoff stood directly in front of the woman, seemingly oblivious to Krill's taunting, sucking on his cigarette, blowing the smoke on the ash so the tip glowed a bright orange in the gloom.

"Noie Barnum made sketches of the drone," Krill said. "I have them hidden in Durango. I can take you to them."

"You missed the bus, greaseball," Frank said.

"Don't abuse the woman further, Señor Sholokoff," Krill said. "I am the one you want. I am the one who can increase your riches."

"How'd you like a can of Drano poured down your throat?" Frank said.

Through the ground-level window on the far side of the cellar, Krill could see a dirt road winding through the fields and rain starting to fall on a line of white hills and a flatbed truck and another vehicle coming down the road toward the compound, a rooster tail of dust rising behind each, the electricity in the clouds flicking like snakes' tongues, forked and sharp, without sound.

"Señor Sholokoff, your employees have been screwing you behind your back, conspiring against you in order to hide their incompetence," Krill said.

"What's he saying?" Sholokoff said to Frank.

"Mike let the half-breed have a spoon to eat with and didn't get it back," Frank said. "The guy was probably working on the lock with it."

"Where is the spoon now?" Sholokoff said, lowering his cigarette from his mouth.

"I don't know, sir. He isn't going anywhere," Frank said.

"You've decided that, have you?"

"It's not a big deal, sir. I'm taking care of it."

"Not only do you make decisions for me, you also decide whether or not I should know about them?"

Krill could see the rain sweeping across the fields in a gray line, dimming the hills in the background, the flatbed and an SUV behind it turning off the road into an unfenced pasture, the drivers circling behind a pecan orchard.

"You hear something?" Mike said.

"No," Frank said.

"I thought I heard a car," Mike said.

"It's thundering in the hills," Frank said.

"Señor Sholokoff, listen to me when I tell you I have the plans for the drone," Krill said. "I can be a very valuable employee to you. Your men are worthless. Look at them. They cannot think. They hide like children from their responsibilities. I retract my insults, *señor*. They were said in hot blood. We are both businessmen and need to behave as such, without rancor, without pissants like these to obstruct us."

"You shut the fuck up," Frank said.

"No, it's you who needs to be silent, Frank," Sholokoff said, glancing over his shoulder at the ground-level window. "I heard a car or truck. Look out the window, Craig."

One of the men standing closest to the far wall rose on his tiptoes to see outside. "There's a flatbed truck out by the pecan trees," he said. "It's probably some of your field hands."

"They're not supposed to be there," Sholokoff said.

"It's some peons, sir. I can see one of them," Craig said.

"Mike, you get the spoon back from the man in the cell," Sholokoff said. "The rest of you come upstairs with me."

682

"Sir, the woman is about to break," Frank said. "I got everything under control. I'll check around outside if you want, but don't ease up now."

"You received a phone call earlier. Who was that from?"

"A gal I met in the cantina," Frank replied. "I told her not to call while I was working."

"A girl from the cantina? You are always thinking about your appetites, Frank. Do you never think about the man who took you off a porn set and made a soldier out of you? Do you have no gratitude for the life I've given you — the women, the power, the money?"

"Sir, I got on the cantina gal's case. I want to prove myself to you. Leave me with the Chinese broad. Trust me, you'll have everything you need when you come back downstairs."

"You have a great problem, Frank. You have never been able to hide your lean and hungry look," Sholokoff said. "That's because a black heart has no loyalty. You can only think in terms of your own needs. I do not believe your story about the girl in the cantina. Have you done something you shouldn't? Do you want to confess to La Magdalena?"

"Why do you mock me, sir? I've done everything you wanted, including hanging up that cowboy preacher on a cross." Frank's features sharpened with resentment, his cheeks sinking and pooling with shadow. "I'm

683

surprised you didn't have us throw dice for his clothes."

One of the men on the first floor opened the door that gave onto the stairwell. "Mr. Sholokoff, there's a truck and an SUV out by them trees," he called down the stairs. "The maid hauled freight like somebody stuck a cattle prod up her ass. I sent Toy Boy out."

Hackberry and Pam Tibbs and Jack Collins and Eladio and Jaime fanned out in the pecan trees as soon as they had exited their vehicles. The rain was blowing in a fine mist against a barn that stood between them, dimming out Sholokoff's compound. Hackberry held the cut-down twelve-gauge with one hand, the barrel resting against his shoulder, and studied the main house through his binoculars. Pam was to his right, carrying the AR15 with her left forearm partially wrapped in the sling, a thirty-round magazine inserted in the frame. She had strung two pairs of handcuffs through the back of her cartridge belt and had stuffed a twenty-round magazine in the back pocket of her jeans.

The house was massive, the walls two feet thick, built of stucco that had been painted a mauve color, the flower beds bordered with bricks and packed with soil that was as dark as wet coffee grounds, the yellow and red hibiscus and climbing roses and Hong Kong orchids trembling with rain that dripped off the roof.

The position was bad; the angle of approach was bad; and there was too much light in the sky.

The back door opened, and an overweight Mexican woman came into the yard and walked toward a hogpen with a heavy bucket in her hand. Then she looked once over her shoulder and dropped the bucket, full of slops, onto the grass and ran past the barn into a cornfield.

"I think Jack's inside contact just blew Dodge," Hackberry said.

"Hack, this sucks," Pam said.

"There's nothing for it. We believe in what we're doing," he replied. "Those guys inside don't."

"You and I stay together. I don't want any one of these bastards behind me," she said. "They're planning to kill us. I know it."

Before Hackberry could answer, the back door opened a second time, and one of the biggest men he had ever seen came into the yard. His long-sleeve shirt looked like it was filled with concrete; his neck looked as stiff and hard as a fireplug; his hands were the size of skillets. But his face didn't match the rest of him. It was too small for his head, as though it had been painted in miniature on his skin, his hair cut like a little boy's. A MAC-10 hung from his right hand.

The man looked at the slop bucket on the

grass and walked toward the barn, looking neither to the right or left, entering the open front doors and walking steadily toward the open rear doors that gave onto the pecan orchard.

Before he emerged from the barn, Pam Tibbs moved quickly out of the trees, throwing the AR15 to her shoulder, aiming it at the center of the large man's face. "Drop your weapon," she said. "If you don't, I will kill you where you stand. Do it now. No, it's not up for discussion. Do not have the thoughts you've having. Drop the weapon. No, don't look at the others. Look at me and only me, and tell me I won't kill you. I'm the only person on the planet preventing you from going straight to hell in the next five seconds. The first round will be in the mouth, the second one between your eyes. You will not know what hit you. Indicate what you want me to do."

The man with the miniaturized face stared woodenly at her, his skin slick with rain, his chest rising and falling, the blood draining from his cheeks, mist blowing in his face. Pam closed her left eye and lifted her right elbow, her finger tightening inside the trigger guard. "Good-bye," she said.

"I was just checking the yard. I got no beef with y'all," the man said, letting the MAC-10 fall to the barn's dirt floor.

"Thattaboy. Now on your face. Come on,

handsome, do it. You're making the smart choice," she said.

As soon as he was on the ground, she handed her rifle to Hackberry and stripped a pair of handcuffs from the back of her belt and hooked up the man's wrists, snicking the ratchets into the locking mechanisms. When she straightened up, she was breathing hard, her cheeks pooled with color. "They must know we're here. What now?"

"We go through the cellar door. Let Collins and the Mexicans handle the upstairs," Hackberry said.

She took the assault rifle from Hackberry's hands and wet her lips. She looked over her shoulder to see where Collins and the two Mexicans were. Collins was talking to the Mexicans, all three of their heads bent together. Her breath was still coming short in her chest. "Hack, don't let those guys get behind us. Listen to me on this," she said.

"We're going to be all right."

"Saying it doesn't make it true."

"The way you took that guy down was beautiful. You're my champ, kid."

"Yeah, and this whole deal still sucks, and you'd better not call me kid again," she said.

Not only had the two visual screens inside Jack's head gone on autopilot and red alert, they had also gone out of control. On one screen, Jack had watched the female deputy disarm, take down, and cuff a giant of a man without breaking a sweat, patronizing him while she did it. *That* was more than impressive. Six like her could probably wipe out the Taliban, he thought. In fact, he felt a stirring in his loins that made him uncomfortable, not unlike a wind blowing on a dead fire and fanning to life a couple of hot coals hiding among the ashes. *Rid yourself of impure thoughts,* he told himself. *Do not be beguiled by a painted mouth at a time like this.* In spite of his self-admonition, he could not completely take his eyes off the female deputy.

Conversely, on the other screen were images that continued to disturb and anger him, namely Eladio and Jaime trading glances whenever they thought he wasn't looking, both of them as transparent as errant children, both of them armed with Uzis.

"Through the kitchen, boss?" Eladio said.

"No, we're going in through the patio," Jack said.

"The kitchen is wide-open, boss," Eladio said. "The big man with a child's face left it open."

"No, the French doors take us into the dining room, then down the stairs to the cellar," Jack said. "You two will go ahead of me."

"That's not your usual method, Señor Jack," Eladio said. "You are always our leader. No weapon does damage like your Thompson loaded with a full drum. It is magnificent to behold."

"We're involved in a military action here. We're splitting our forces and catching our enemy in a pincer movement," Jack said. "You know what that is, don't you?"

"No, what is it?" Eladio asked.

"The Germans learned it from Stonewall Jackson. They put their panzers on their flanks, just like Jackson put Jeb Stuart's cavalry on his. You boys are family. You think Stonewall Jackson wouldn't take care of his boys?"

"What is this about Germans and rock walls? This sounds like bullshit," Jaime said.

"Come on, boys, let's have some fun. While the sheriff and his deputy draw everybody into the cellar, we're going to put hair on the walls."

"The gringos are not to be trusted, Señor Jack," Eladio said. "The old one dotes on his *puta.* She has a foul mouth and looks at us with contempt. When they get what they want, they will dispose of us."

"The sheriff is a straight shooter. But that's also his great weakness," Jack said.

"He shoots straight? Shooting straight doesn't have nozzing to do with this discussion. You speak in nozzing but riddles," Jaime said.

" 'Nozzing'? Son, you obviously have a speech defect," Jack said. "When we get back to the States, I'm going to take you to a speech therapist, and we'll cure this problem once and for all. In the meantime, Eladio, could I see your cell phone?"

"What you want it for, boss?"

"To make sure we have service here. It's always good to be prepared," Jack replied.

CHAPTER TWENTY-EIGHT

Through the bars in his cell, Krill could see the rain blowing on the fields and the side of the house, and the hills that looked like giant white caterpillars disappearing inside it. Mike stood in the middle of the room next to the Asian woman, who was still suspended from a rafter. Mike was opening and closing his hands, his wide-set eyes turned upward at the sound of feet overhead.

"I am sorry I caused you this trouble, *hombre*," Krill said. "I have been a soldier in the service of others, just as you are. We take orders from little men who never have to kill or die in battle themselves."

"You talk too much," Mike said.

"Give the woman some water. She's done nothing to deserve what has been done to her."

Mike's attention was fixed on the sound of boots moving back and forth on the floor upstairs, and he could not be distracted. His blond hair was long and oiled and hung in strings over the tops of his ears. His eyes were so widely spaced, they looked as though they had been removed from his face and stitched back in the wrong place. He was a man to whom the fates had not been kind, Krill thought.

"Give the woman some water, and I'll give you back the spoon," Krill said. "Then Frank will not be able to use you as his scapegoat any longer."

"Where is it?" Mike asked.

"In the chemical toilet. Where else?"

"Get it out."

"You have to give the woman some water."

Mike walked toward the bars. "You're going to pay a big price if I have to come inside that cell."

"I am not putting my hand in a toilet for you. I am sorry, *señor*."

"Where are your shoes?"

"They hurt my feet. I took them off."

"Get back against the wall."

"What for, *señor*? I am not a threat to you."

Mike stepped closer to the bars. "Get back against the wall, turn around, and lean on it. I'm coming in." With a flick of his right hand, he whipped a telescopic steel baton to its full length.

"*Señor,* you're not going to use that on me, are you?" Krill said.

"Get back against the wall!"

The woman, still hanging by her arms,

lifted her head from her chest and parted her lips. "Give me some water," she said.

Mike looked over his shoulder at her. "Be quiet," he said.

"I need some water," she said.

"You did this to yourself, lady. I tried to be nice to y'all, and this is what I got. Now close your mouth." Mike turned back to Krill. "You move your ass to the back of the cell. Spread your legs and lean on your hands. Don't tell me you don't know the drill."

"Please give me water," the woman said.

Mike turned around again, his hand gripped tightly on the foam-wrapped handle of the expandable baton. "I've had it with you, lady. You open your mouth one more —"

From the back of his waistband, Krill pulled loose the shoestrings that he had removed from his running shoes and braided into a garrote. He flipped the garrote over Mike's head and jerked it tight around his throat and squeezed Mike's head between the bars, pulling backward with all his weight, the garrote sinking deep into the neck, closing the windpipe and carotid artery and shutting off the flow of blood to the brain. Mike tried to work his nails under the garrote while veins bloomed all over his neck, not unlike cracks in pottery. Krill pulled tighter as Mike slipped down the bars to the floor. Krill grabbed Mike by the back of his shirt so he would not roll away from the cell once he was on the floor.

Krill got down on his knees and reached through the bars and slipped his fingers into the dead man's shirt pockets but found nothing. With two hands, he turned him over so that the dead man faced the cell, his eyes half-lidded as though he had been shaken from a deep sleep. Krill got his hand into the man's left pocket and found a folding single-bladed knife and a wad of Mexican currency and a penlight and a betting receipt from a racetrack. In the other pocket was a three-inch iron key.

Krill was trembling as he rose to his feet and extended his arm through the bars and inverted the key and inserted it into the lock. The key was an old one, and he twisted it slowly so as not to break it off inside the mechanism. He felt the tumblers turn and click into place and the tongue of the lock recede into the door and scrape free of the jamb. He shoved the door open, pushing aside Mike's body.

"Hold on, Magdalena," Krill said. "You are a great woman, a master of distraction, the greatest woman I have ever known. I will get you down right now. I never could have done this without you. You were magnificent."

"Don't talk," she said, her lips caked, her voice hoarse. "His right ankle. You must hurry."

"What about his ankle?"

The color was gone from her face. "He has a gun," she said. "They're moving around upstairs. Hurry."

"No, we get you down first," Krill said. He fitted his left arm around her waist and lifted her weight against him, then sawed through the pieces of clothesline that held her wrists to the rafter. When she fell against him, her cheek and hair touched his face, and he thought he smelled an odor like seawater on her skin.

"The holster is Velcro-strapped to his right ankle," she said. "Take the pistol from the holster and give it to me."

"You are a woman of peace, Magdalena," he said. "You have no business with guns."

"Don't talk in an unctuous and foolish manner," she replied. "A shadow just went past the window. Please do not waste time talking. The men upstairs will show us no mercy."

Krill pulled up the right pant leg of the dead man and removed an Airweight .38 from the black holster strapped to his ankle. The woman took it from Krill's hand just as he heard an upstairs door crash open and glass breaking and a burst of machine-gun fire ripping through walls and doors.

"You have to live for your children, Antonio," the woman said. "You have to tell others what happened to them. From this point, you live among the children of light. You become one with them. Do you understand me?"

"I think I do," Krill said.

"No, say it."

"I understand, Magdalena. And I will keep my word and do as you have said," he replied.

Jack Collins pushed Eladio and Jaime ahead of him, through the patio door and into the dining room, both of them resisting and looking back at him anxiously. "Get to it, the pair of you," Jack said. "You look back at me again, you'll discover another side to my nature. You kill everything that moves on this floor."

"We are campesinos, Señor Jack," Eladio said. "We do not know tactics. We do not even know what we are doing here. What is the profit in rescuing a Chinese woman who teaches superstition to our people?"

Jack stiff-armed him between the shoulder blades, pushing him forward through the dining room, knocking over a heavy antique chair, breaking the crystal ware on a serving table. The first of Sholokoff's men to come out of the hallway was bare-chested, his shoulders and lats stippled with body hair, an automatic in his left hand. He raised the automatic straight out in front of him, his face averted, as though staring into a cold wind and a magic wand could protect him from its influence. At the same time, Eladio shouted out, "Not me, *hombre!* Do not shoot. I am not one of them! This is a great mistake."

Jack fired on Sholokoff's man, a burst of no more than seven or eight rounds that blew away the man's fingers from his grip on the automatic and stitched his chest and destroyed his jaw.

Eladio stared in horror at the man crashed against the wall and fell to the floor. Then he stared at Jack, his eyes seeming to search in space for the right words to use. "I froze. You saved my life, Señor Jack. We must prepare to attack the others," he said. "They're hiding back in the hallway. I can hear them."

"Your fear got the best of you, Eladio," Jack said. "This isn't like gunning down a bunch of teenagers at a birthday party, is it?"

"Yes, I was very afraid. I was speaking insane words."

"I wouldn't say that. You always knew how to cover your bets."

"Let us now go forward, Señor Jack. Tell me what you want me to do."

"Just rest easy a second," Jack said. With one hand holding the Thompson and the other holding Eladio's cell phone, Jack pressed the redial number with his thumb. In the back of the house, a cell phone rang.

"You would think your bud would have enough sense to silence his phone," Jack said. "That's the trouble with treacherous people.

Most of them cain't think their way out of a paper sack. Your man in there sold out Sholokoff, just like you sold out me."

"I don't understand," Eladio said.

"Your bud in there didn't tell Sholokoff we were coming. Otherwise, Sholokoff would have set up an ambush. Oh, here's your phone back."

Jack tossed the cell phone to Eladio. When Eladio raised his free hand to catch it, Jack lowered the barrel of the Thompson and fired directly into Eladio's chest, the shell casings bouncing off the furniture and rolling across the hardwood floor.

"Señor Collins, I do not know what is happening here," Jaime said. "Why are you killing my cousin? Why are you turning your gun on your own people? We came here to fight your enemies."

"You're not my people, son," Jack said. "Turn around and walk into the hallway."

"No, I cannot do that."

"Why is that, Jaime? You don't trust your compadres in there?"

"These are not my friends. You are a deranged man. You've killed Eladio. You speak craziness all the time, and now your craziness has killed my cousin."

"Pick up the cell phone and hit redial again. I want you to give somebody a message."

"What message? That you're killing your own people?"

698

"I want to tell Josef Sholokoff I'm just getting started. Can you do that for me, Jaime?"

"No, I will not do this. I didn't have nozzing to do with Eladio's transactions. I don't know nobody in there. I am not responsible for what Eladio may have done."

" 'Nozzing' again," Jack said. "I changed my mind about taking you to a speech therapist, Jaime. There's no cure for certain kinds of stupidity. It's kind of like laminitis in a horse. Instead of the hoof curling up, your kind of stupidity shrinks the brain into a walnut. We put horses down, don't we?"

Jaime was breathing through his mouth, staring at the muzzle of the Thompson, his nose crinkling, as though he had no place to put the fear and tension coursing through his body.

"You still have your Uzi," Jack said.

"I want to go back home."

"That's what everybody wants, Jaime. Even if home is just a place they made up in their minds. You know what home is? It's a black hole in the ground where somebody shovels dirt in your face."

Jaime swallowed. "Like Eladio, I took money from the gringo to betray you. My family lives in Monterrey. Get word to them that I am buried someplace and that my spirit will not wander, even if this is not true."

Jack sighed and gazed out the window at the rain sweeping across the fields and the wind troweling green and gold swaths through the corn. "Damn if you guys don't always make it hard. Leave the piece," he said.

"You will let me go? You will not harm me when my back is turned?" Jaime said.

"Did I ever lie to you?"

"I will never tell anybody what has happened here. I will always praise your name when I hear it mentioned."

"Time to haul freight, Jaime. I got my hands full. If I see you on the street somewhere, keep on going."

"I do not know what that means."

"It means some people are hopeless. Come on, there's the door, pilgrim," Jack said, and made a snicking sound in his cheek.

Jaime went out the French doors into the rain and crossed the patio and began running through the backyard, his head bent low. He ran past the slop bucket the maid had dropped on the lawn, past the barn and the cornfield, his clothes darkening in the rain, and was almost to the pecan orchard before he looked back at the house. His face was white and round and small inside the grayness of the afternoon. Jack watched all this from the window, simultaneously looking at the empty hallway, listening to the creaking of the house and the drumming of the rain, waiting to hear the whisper of voices or the sound of footsteps moving across the hardwood floors or perhaps a door slamming or an order being shouted. All he heard were the sounds of the wind and rain.

Jaime, maybe you're a whole lot luckier than I thought, he said to himself.

That was when someone from a back window zeroed in on Jaime with what sounded like a fifty-caliber sniper's rifle and squeezed off a single round and sent him crashing headlong into a tree trunk, dead before his knees struck the earth.

Hackberry had led the way from the barn and across the yard, the rain wilting his hat, driving as hard as ice crystals into his face. He could no longer see the patio and could barely make out the stairs that led down to the cellar door. When he reached the lee of the house, his clothes were wrapped around his body like wet Kleenex. Then he heard the first burst of machine-gun fire. He dropped down inside the stairwell and pulled Pam Tibbs after him.

He wiped the water off the dial of his watch. "That idiot went in early," he said.

"I told you he has his own agenda," she said.

He couldn't argue with her. Trying to put himself inside the thoughts of a man like Jack Collins had been insane. Collins had a Mixmaster in his head instead of a brain.

The door on the cellar was made of metal and had no windows. Hackberry placed his hand on the knob and twisted slowly. The knob rotated less than a quarter of an inch and then locked solid. "So much for Collins's intel," he said.

"Was that the Thompson firing?"

"Yeah, there's no mistaking it." He pressed his ear against the metal door but could hear nothing inside. He propped the cut-down Remington pump against the side of the stairwell and took out his Swiss Army knife and opened the long blade and worked it into the doorjamb, hoping to get it over the tongue of the lock. He heard a second burst from the Thompson.

"Sholokoff's people aren't firing back," Pam said.

"They've pulled back into the house. They're going to make Collins come after them," Hackberry said.

"I think something else is going on. I think he might be shooting his own people."

"Because I told him I saw Eladio making a phone call?"

"That or maybe he found the GPS locator we hid under the cookies and fruitcake and blamed them. It doesn't take much to set him off. He stubs a toe, and somebody has to die for it."

Hackberry pushed on the handle of the knife and felt the blade break off in the jamb. "Darn it," he said under his breath. Just then he heard a solitary shot from what sounded like a high-powered rifle. He picked up his shotgun and went to the top of the steps and looked out into the rain. He could see the cornstalks thrashing in the wind and the gray barn against the pecan orchard and lightning striking in the hills, but he could see nothing of Jack Collins or Eladio and Jaime. Why would the shooter of the high-powered rifle fire only one round? The submachine-gun fire had sounded like it was coming from within the house. Why would someone be using a sniper rifle at close quarters against men armed with automatic weapons?

Unless one of the men with an automatic weapon had bailed and started running and someone had tried to pot him from a door or window?

It was foolish to waste more time trying to figure out the madness of Jack Collins. "Pam, any element of surprise is gone," he said. "So this is the way we're going to do it. I'm going in first. Anybody who's not a friendly dies on the spot. Temple Dowling is probably already dead. The only two friendlies we know about are the hostages, Anton Ling and Krill. The servants are probably gone. That means everybody else is fair game. If I go down, don't worry about me. You blow up their shit, and we'll worry about me later. You got all that?"

"Stop playing the hero. You kick open the door and I go in first," she said. "You're big-

703

ger than I am, and you can shoot over and around me. I can't do that with you. I can't even see around you."

"You always argue, no matter what the issue is, no matter what I say, you always argue," he said. "I've never seen anything like it. You're unrelenting. It's like having a conversation with the side of an aircraft carrier."

She wasn't listening. She had tied a blue kerchief around her forehead to keep her hair and the rain out of her eyes. Her white cowboy shirt was drenched and split in back, her jeans and boots splattered with mud, and her eyes were charged with light, the way they became when she was either angry or hurt. He knew that in this instance, neither of those emotions was the cause of the intensity in her eyes. She moistened her lips.

"If we don't get out of this one, it's been a great ride," she said.

"It wasn't just a great ride, kiddo. You're a gift, Pam, the kind a fortunate man receives only once or twice in a life span. But you've got to make it out of here, you understand? I've been on borrowed time since the Chosin Reservoir, and at this point in my life, I don't want somebody else paying my tab. I'm going in first, and you're going to cover my back. If I go down, you stand on my dead body and waste every one of these guys, then pop Collins, no matter what he says or does.

But you get back home to tell the story. You got it?"

"What am I supposed to say? You're pig-headed," she replied. "If we weren't in this spot, I'd shoot you myself."

"You and Rie will always remain the best people I ever knew," he replied. "And both of you became a permanent part of my life. How many guys can have that kind of luck?"

He held his shotgun with one hand and the railing attached to the brick side wall of the stairwell with the other. Then he raised his right leg and drove the bottom of his boot into the metal door. The reverberation shook the lock and the jamb and the knob, but the door held fast. He raised his foot and smashed his boot into the door again, then again and again, each time bending the lock's tongue inside the jamb, until the door flew back on its hinges.

He heard the Thompson begin firing again and empty casings bouncing on the hardwood floors and feet running down a hallway. Then he was inside the cellar, inside the damp-smelling coolness that was not unlike a tomb's, inside the reek of sweat that had dried on the bodies of people who had been tortured, inside the dirty glow of a yellow lightbulb that shone on the faces of Anton Ling and Krill, which seemed as wizened as prunes, as though they had already entered a realm from which no one returned.

The first man to come down the stairs from the hallway may or may not have been armed. Hackberry could remember no details about him other than he was not wearing a shirt, that his head was shaved and his mouth was ringed with whiskers, that there was blood splatter on his chest and arms, that his boots sounded like they had lugs on them as they struck the wood stairs, that his cargo pants were buttoned under his navel, that his mouth dropped open and his face seemed to turn into a bowl of pudding when Hackberry pulled the trigger on the twelve-gauge and watched him buckle over as though he had swallowed a piece of angle iron.

The man who had been first down the cellar stairs had not suffered in vain. As he clutched himself and stumbled and fell down the stairs, three more men followed, shooting over their comrade's head, filling the cellar with a deafening roar of gunfire that echoed off the walls, the ejected casings shuddering in the electric light, the ricochets sparking off the stone walls and the bars and iron plating of the cells.

Hackberry worked the pump on his twelve-gauge and got another shell into the chamber and fired a second time at the top of the stairs. He saw the lightbulb hanging from the ceiling explode and buckshot cut a pattern across the wooden door that opened onto the hallway, but his adversaries were already into the cellar, firing blindly, breaking the glass in the far window, hitting the body of a man who lay on the floor by one of the cells, driving him and Pam Tibbs back toward the outside stairwell.

"Hack! The guy behind the post!" Pam shouted. Then she began firing the semiauto AR15 into a dark corner of the cellar, pulling the trigger as fast as she could, ignoring a bullet crease on her cheek and a blood-flecked rip in her shirt at the top of her shoulder.

Hackberry felt a blow strike him just above the hip, hard, a pain that punched through tissue and spread deep into the bone the way a dull headache might. He pressed his palm against the wound and saw blood well through his fingers, then something vital inside him seemed to fold in upon itself and melt into gelatin and cause him to lose balance and topple sideways toward a pile of cardboard boxes. All the while Pam kept firing, advancing toward the dark place in the corner, positioning herself between the shooter and Hackberry, shouting, "Suck on this, you motherfucker! How does it feel? Did you like that? Take it, take it, take it!"

Hackberry could not see the man she was shooting at. When Hackberry fell into the boxes, he saw Anton Ling and Krill and the silhouettes of two men who had made it to the bottom of the stairs without being hit.

Mostly, he saw the cellar turning sideways and the cardboard boxes coming up to meet him and his shotgun falling from his grasp as the boxes collapsed on top of him, all of this inside a roar of sound that was like a locomotive engine blowing apart, like an artillery barrage marching across a frozen rice paddy south of the Yalu River.

The shooting stopped as quickly as it had begun. The air was filled with smoke and lint and dust and tiny pieces of fiberboard. In the light from the hallway door, he could see two of Sholokoff's men standing in the drift of smoke, one with a revolver, the other with a semiautomatic carbine that was fitted with a skeleton stock. He realized that Pam Tibbs was down, somewhere behind several crates of wine bottles that were broken and draining onto the floor. He could not see either Krill or Anton Ling. He found his shotgun among the cardboard boxes and propped the butt against the floor and used it to raise himself to one knee, his side and back on fire.

He saw the silhouette of a small man go across the doorway at the head of the stairs. "Frank?" a voice with a Russian accent said. "What's happening down there?"

"We nailed the sheriff and his deputy," Frank said. "I've got everything under control."

"Are they dead?" the man with the Russian accent said.

708

"I'm not sure, sir."

"Then *be* sure. Kill them. I want to see their heads."

"You want to see their —"

"I want you to bring me their heads," the man with the Russian accent said.

"Where's Collins, sir?" Frank asked.

"Somewhere in the house. You finish down there and come around behind him. This is your opportunity to redeem yourself. Do not disappoint me, Frank."

Frank raised the carbine with the wire stock to his shoulder and began firing at random all over the cellar, the bullets notching the stone walls, whanging off the cell doors, splintering the cases of wine that were bleeding pools of burgundy on the floor. With one knee for support, Hackberry raised the twelve-gauge and fired at the two men who stood at the bottom of the stairs. Most of the pattern struck a wood post, and the rest of the load flattened harmlessly against a wall behind the stairs.

Hackberry tried to work the pump and hold the shotgun with one hand, but instead of ejecting the spent shell, the mechanism jammed, and the spent shell was crimped sideways between the bolt and the chamber. In the gloom, he saw Pam sitting flatly on her buttocks behind a stack of rubber tires, her legs stretched out straight in front of her. There was a bullet wound in her back and what appeared to be an exit wound in the top of her left arm. She was trying to free her .357 from her holster, but her hand kept fluttering on the grips and the leather strap fastened at the base of the hammer.

"Throw out your piece, Sheriff Holland," Frank said. "I'll talk with Mr. Sholokoff. He's a businessman. This doesn't have to end badly. Our common enemy up there is that smelly son of a bitch Jack Collins. Why take his weight?"

Hackberry's side was throbbing, his face breaking with sweat. He could hear glass crunching under the boots of Sholokoff's men as they began working their way carefully toward the pile of tires behind which Pam Tibbs had taken cover.

"Think about it, Sheriff," Frank said. "The people you're trying to rescue down here are killers. They murdered a guy who tried to treat them in a kindly way. Yeah, that's right. Mike was his name. He was a good guy. He's lying dead on the floor now, with shoestrings wrapped around his throat. How about it, Sheriff? How many guys get a second chance like this?"

Frank had grown cavalier about Krill and the Asian woman. When Anton Ling gathered herself up from the floor with the Airweight .38 five-round Smith & Wesson in her hand, Frank's expression seemed amused, taking her inventory, his eyes sliding over her blood-streaked shift, the bruises on her face and arms and shoulders, the gash in her lower lip.

"I had a Chinese bitch of my own once," Frank said. "Play your cards right and I might keep you around."

Her first shot hit him an inch above the groin; the second one entered his mouth and exited an inch above the neatly etched hairline on the back of his neck.

His friend dropped his semiautomatic to the floor and lifted his hands in the air just before Anton Ling shot him in the heart.

Upstairs, the Thompson began firing again without letup, the rounds thudding into walls all over the house, the casings dancing on the floors, as though Jack Collins had declared war on all things that were level or square or plumb or that possessed any degree of geometric integrity.

CHAPTER TWENTY-NINE

Nobody could say Preacher Jack Collins wasn't a fan of Woody Guthrie. "*Adiós* to you Juan, *adiós* Rosalito, *adiós mi amigo* Jesus and Maria," he sang above the roar of the Thompson as he burned the entire ammo drum, hosing down the house from one end to the other, the barrel so hot that it scalded his hands when he reloaded.

He hunted down Sholokoff's men in closets, crawl spaces, and behind and under the furniture and kitchen counters, blowing them apart as they cowered or tried to break and run.

These were the dreaded transplants from Russia and Brighton Beach or their surrogates in Phoenix? What a laugh.

Jack was having a fine time. He even enjoyed the rain blowing through the broken windows. It filled the house with a soft mist and the wet smell of grass and cornstalks and freshly plowed fields. The smell reminded him of rural Oklahoma during a summer rain, when the rivers and buttes were red and the plains green. His mother took him once to an Easter-egg roll behind a church where she had decided to get reborn. For whatever reason, Jack thought, it sure didn't take. In fact, he'd always had the feeling that his mother had seduced the preacher.

No matter. When Jack's Thompson was deconstructing the environment and people around him, he was no longer troubled by thoughts of his mother's cruelty and the strange form of catatonic trance that seemed to take control of her metabolism and cause her to slip from one personality into another. Well, she got hers when she took a fall off the rocks on the property that eventually became his. It was an accident, of course. More or less. Yes, "accident" was a good word for it, he thought. Even though he had been in his late thirties when it happened, the details had never quite come together for him. How had the chain of events started? She had tried to grab his hand, right? Yes, he was sure about that, although he was a little hazy on what caused her to trip and start slipping backward off the ledge. But he definitely remembered her reaching out, her fingers clutching at his shirt, then at his wrist, then at the ends of his fingers. So he was not really a player in any of it, just a witness. Maybe that was her way of airbrushing herself out of his life. One second she was there; a second later, she was receding into the ground, growing smaller and smaller as she fell, looking back at him as if she had just spread herself out on a mattress for a brief nap.

When anybody got up the nerve to ask Jack how his mother had died, he always gave the same reply: "As she had lived. On her back. All the way down."

Jack loved crime novels and film noir but could never understand the film critics' laudatory attitude toward James Cagney's portrayal of Cody Jarrett in *White Heat*. Would a mainline con like Jarrett crawl into his mother's lap? Yuck, Jack thought. The image made his phallus shrivel up and want to hide. And how about that last scene, when Jarrett stands on the huge propane tank outside a refinery, shouting at the sky? Here's a guy about to be burned to a crisp, and what does he say? "Made it, Ma! Top of the world!"

What a douchebag. Didn't Cagney know better? The real Jarrett would have had his mother stuffed and used as a hat rack or doorstop.

Jack stood in the middle of the kitchen and gazed at the house's interior and the level of destruction he had visited upon it. No one could accuse him of leaving the wounded on the field. Everyone he had shot was not only dead but dead several times over. He turned in a circle, the Thompson cradled across his chest, a tongue of smoke curling out of the barrel. The rain and wind were cool blowing on his skin through the shattered windows. On the lawn, he could see the slop bucket the maid had dropped when she was high-balling for the cornfield. Where oh where was little Josef?

"Can you hear me, little fellow?" Jack called out. "Let's fix a cup of tea and have a chat. Did you ever read *And Quiet Flows the Don?* It was written by a guy named Sholokoff. Are y'all related?"

There was no reply from the devastated interior of the house. Jack felt a terrible thirst but did not want to set down the Thompson to pour himself a glass of water. "It's pretty quiet downstairs, Josef. I have a feeling Frank lost out to Sheriff Holland and his deputy. What do you think?"

In the silence, he walked across the linoleum, bits of glass and china crackling under the soles of his cowboy boots. "I checked the upstairs and the attic, but you weren't there. That means you've got yourself scrunched under the floor or up a chimney. I cain't think of any other possibility. Unless you've already hauled ass. No, I would have seen you. Tell me, do y'all have a volunteer fire department in these parts?"

Jack lifted the Thompson to a vertical position and gazed at the ceiling and then out the window. He went through a mudroom onto the back porch and opened the screen door

715

and looked up at the window in the attic area and at a roof below the window. The roof was peaked, and Jack could not see on the far side of it. However, if anyone ran from the house, he would not find cover except in the barn, the cornfield, or the pecan orchard, where the flatbed truck and Jack's Ford Explorer were parked.

"Josef, I think you might have outsmarted me," Jack said to the wind. He walked to the hallway door that opened onto the cellar stairs. "You down there, Mr. Holland?"

"What do you want, Collins?" the sheriff's voice replied.

"You sound like you might have sprung a leak."

"We've got several dead people down here. You can join them in case you're having any bright ideas," the sheriff said.

"You never give me any credit, Sheriff. What have I done to you that's so bad?"

"Tried to kill me and my chief deputy?" the sheriff said.

"Y'all dealt the play on that one. Regardless, I think I squared the deal when I dug up that young fellow Bevins from his grave out in the desert."

"You're talking too much, Collins. That's the sign of either a guilty or a frightened man."

"It's *Mr.* Collins. What does it take for you to use formal address? In the civilized world, men do not refer to one another by their last names. Is that totally lost on you, Sheriff? If it is, I've sorely misjudged you. I'm coming down."

"We need medical help, Mr. Collins."

"Every one of the locals is on a pad for Sholokoff. They'd have you and your friends in a wood chipper by sunset."

Jack stepped into the doorway, silhouetting against the hallway light, then began walking down the stairs, his eyes trying to adjust to the gloom. His left hand was on the stair rail, his right holding the Thompson at an upward angle. Then he saw the Asian woman and the man named Krill and the sheriff and his chief deputy. "Looks like y'all got shot up proper," he said.

The sheriff had stood up but was bracing himself against a wood post, the heel of his hand pressed into his side. "Where's Sholokoff?" he asked.

Jack didn't answer. He crossed the cellar and scraped back the metal door to the outside stairwell and walked up the concrete steps into the rain and gazed at the yard and the barn and the pecan orchard and the cornfield, then at the roof that traversed the area under the attic window. He stepped back into the cellar, rainwater running off the brim of his hat.

"You planning on taking me out, Mr. Holland?" he said.

"Could be."

"But you won't."

"I wouldn't be so sure about that."

"You won't gun me unless I give you cause."

"What brought you to that conclusion?" the sheriff said.

"Your father was a history professor and a congressman. You were born with the burden of gentility, Sheriff: You either obey the restraints that are imposed on a gentleman or you accept the role of a hypocrite. The great gift of being born white trash is that no matter what you do, it's always a step up."

"You're referring to yourself, Mr. Collins?"

"I'd wager I have more education than anybody in this room, but I never spent a complete year in a schoolhouse. What do you think about that?"

"I don't," the sheriff replied.

Jack ignored the slight and glanced out the cellar window at the yard and the barn and the pecan orchard. Then he took a bottle of burgundy from a shattered crate and broke the neck off against the wall. The glass was black and thick and had a red wax seal on the label. He poured from the bottom of the broken bottle into his mouth, as though using a cup, not touching the sharp edges. "You want one?" he asked.

"I don't drink," the sheriff said.

"You ought to start. In my opinion, it'd be an improvement. Who popped the two guys by the stairs?"

"I did," the Asian woman said. She was sitting on a wood chair, the Airweight .38 in her lap, strands of her hair hanging straight down in her face. "You have something to say about it?"

"You decide you're not a pacifist anymore?"

"You murdered nine innocent girls, Mr. Collins," she replied. "I don't think you have the right to look down your nose at me or anybody else."

"If you ask me, your true colors are out, Ms. Ling. You're a self-hating feminist who tries to infect others with her poison. I've been entirely too generous in my estimation and treatment of your gender. The serpent didn't make Adam eat the apple. Your progenitor did. You're the seed of our undoing, and I won't put up with any more of your insolence."

"I warned you once before about addressing me in that fashion," she said.

"Mr. Collins?" the sheriff said softly.

"Enough of you, Sheriff," Jack said, his eyes burning into the woman's face, his hand flexing on the pistol grip of the Thompson.

"Ease up on the batter," the sheriff said.

"I said you stay out of this."

"We all fought the good fight, didn't we?" the sheriff said. "I appreciate the help you gave us. I appreciate your saving the life of my deputy R. C. Bevins. No one here should judge you, sir."

"You should have stayed in politics."

"I *am* in politics. I hold an elective office. How about it, partner?" the sheriff said. "A time comes when you have to lay down your sword and shield."

Jack could feel the fingers of his right hand tightening on the pistol grip and the Thompson's trigger. The rain was sliding down the cellar window and swirling through the door that opened onto the outside stairwell. Inside the steady drumming of the rain and the coldness seeping into his back, he realized the mistake he had just made and the price he would pay for his anger and pride.

He had forgotten about the chief deputy, the one called Pam Tibbs. In spite of her wounds, she had eased her .357 Magnum from her holster and stepped behind him and pointed the muzzle into a spot one inch above his hairline. He heard her cock the hammer into place.

"Put your weapon on the floor," she said.

"What if I don't?" he said.

"I'll cut all your motors," she replied.

"Do as she asks, Jack," the sheriff said.

"He already has," Pam said, ripping the Thompson from Jack's grasp with her bad arm. A surge of pain twisted her mouth out of shape, and she let the Thompson clatter to the floor.

"Y'all don't know who your friends are,"

Jack said. "I'm fixing to torch the place and fry Josef's bacon. He's hiding up there on the roof someplace. If it hadn't been for me, your heads would be on a pike."

"You're done. Get out," Pam said.

Jack turned and looked at her numbly. "Do *what?*" he said.

"Be gone. Into the darkness, where you belong," she said.

He continued to stare at her and at the smear of blood on her cheek and at the wounds in her arm that had painted her shirtsleeve red and at the steady rise and fall of her breasts and at the loathing in her eyes.

"I he'ped y'all," he said. "I made up for —"

"For what?" Pam said.

"The past. All of it. I ate out of Dumpsters and bathed with ash and sand. I wore the rags I pulled off a scarecrow."

"Lose your revolver and turn out all your pockets," she said.

"Why?"

"I collect car keys," she replied.

"That's all you have to say, you fat bitch?" he said.

She pulled his revolver from its holster and slung it into the pile of empty cartons. "Don't go near any uncapped tubes of roach paste," she said.

Hackberry and Pam watched Jack Collins walk into the rain, glancing back at them like

721

an errant child being driven from the school yard. "Where to now, boss?" Pam said.

"We blow Dodge and head for the plane," he replied. "I have a first-aid kit in my duffel. How are you doing?"

"I think the bullet that exited my shoulder didn't hit any bone. Anyway, it's numb now. Hack, you don't look good."

"I never do."

"Is the round still in you?"

"No."

"How can you tell?"

"I can't. But it's time to go home."

"I think you're bleeding inside. Maybe we ought to wait it out. R.C. must have a fix on us. He and Felix and the others might be coming any minute."

"I think the Mexicans found the GPS," Hackberry said.

"Why?"

"Because Collins has contempt for the Mexicans. He never would have relied solely on them. Had they not found a GPS, he would have searched us and our gear himself."

"Look," she said, pointing into the rain.

Hackberry realized he was about to witness one of those moments when evil reveals itself for what it is — insane in its fury and self-hatred and its animus at whatever reminds it of itself. In this instance, the medieval morality play had a cast of only two characters:

Josef Sholokoff running through the rain for the safety of the barn or the cornfield or the pecan orchard, and Preacher Jack Collins in pursuit, driven from the light by his fellow man.

The two of them came together in the yard, sheets of rain sweeping across them at they struck and clawed at each other. Then Jack Collins picked up a stone and swung it hard into Sholokoff's head. When Sholokoff fell backward and got up and tried to run toward the cornfield, Collins hit him twice more in the back of the head, then dragged him, fighting, past the slop bucket that still lay on the grass. In the roll of thunder that sounded like cannons firing in diminishing sequence, Hackberry watched Collins strike Sholokoff again and again with the stone, then lift him up and throw him over the top slat of the hogpen.

The squealing and snuffing sounds of the hogs in the pen were instantaneous.

"Holy God," Pam said.

"They may not have been fed in days," Hackberry said. "Let's get everybody together. I'm going to carry the Thompson. It's not a good idea for Krill to have access to any weapons. He still has a capital charge hanging over him in Texas."

"What do you want to do with him?"

"That's up to him. If he wants to take off, let him go."

"You don't want to hook him up?"

"We'll probably never see Noie Barnum again — the guy who started all this. Why lay all our grief on this poor bastard?"

"Look at me."

"What's wrong?"

"Your eyes are out of focus."

"No, I see fine."

"Your face is white, Hack. You can hardly stand up. Grab hold of my arm."

"I'm right as rain," he replied, the horizon shifting sideways.

The four of them walked out into the storm, the soaked countryside trembling whitely each time a tree of lightning printed itself against the clouds. The hogs had all moved into a corner of the lot in a half circle and were snuffing loudly, their heads down, their hooves churning in the liquescence around them, the bristles of their snouts coated with their work. Hackberry held his forearm tightly against the hole in his side and tried to keep his eyes on the horizon and put one foot after another, because the gyroscope inside him was starting to sway from side to side and was about to topple over.

He had learned to march in the infantry and sometimes even to sleep while he did. It was easy. You kept your eyes half-lidded and swung your legs from the hip and never struggled against the weight of your pack or your weapons. You just got in step and dozed and let the momentum of the column carry you forward, and somehow you knew, out there on the edge of your vision, there was always one to count cadence. *You had a good home when you left, you're right. Jody was there when you left, you're right. Sound off, one, two, three-four! You're right, you're right, you're right! Reep! Reep! Reep! Sound off! One, two, three-four!*

It was a breeze.

"Hack, hold on to me. Please," Pam said.

"Miss Anton is walking barefoot. You don't think I can cut it?" he replied.

"I should have popped him," she said.

He didn't know what she meant. They had entered the barn and should have been grateful for the warmth and dryness it offered them. Then he saw the firelight flickering in the midst of the pecan orchard. He set down the Thompson and the shotgun and walked to the open doors and stared at the flames swirling up from the interior of the Ford Explorer and the cab of the flatbed truck.

So this was both the reality and the legacy of Jack Collins, Hackberry thought. He wasn't the light bearer who fell like a shooting star from the heavens. He was the canker in the rose, the worm that flies through the howling storm, a vain and petty and mean-spirited man who left a dirty smudge on all that he touched. He had no power of his own;

he was assigned it by others whose personal fears were so great, they would abandon all they believed in and surrender themselves to a self-manufactured caricature who had hijacked their religion.

But Hackberry knew that if there was any lesson or wisdom in his thoughts, he would not be able to pass it on. The only wisdom an old man learns in this world is that his life experience is ultimately his sole possession. It is also the measure of his worth as a human being, the sum of his offering to whatever hand created him, and the ticket he carries with him into eternity. But if a man tries to put all the lessons he has learned on a road map for others, he might as well dip his pen into invisible ink.

They walked miles in the rain, into the hills and through ravines and across flooded creek beds, the sky growing blacker and blacker. Pam stumbled and dropped the AR15. Krill picked it up and then pulled the shotgun from Hackberry's hand and placed both weapons across his shoulders, draping one hand on the barrels and the other on the stocks, his head hanging forward.

"Give them back," Hackberry said.

"I am all right, *señor,*" Krill said. "I would not harm you. You are very good people. I like you very much."

"You're wanted for a capital crime," Hackberry said.

726

"I know. But that has nothing to do with us. This is Mexico," Krill said. "It is a place where everything is crazy. I told that to La Magdalena when I cut her down from the beam in the cellar. I told her she smelled like seawater. I told her she was probably a Chinese mermaid and didn't know it. She thought that was very funny."

"Say that again?" Hackberry asked.

"I'm very tired. We must go on," Krill said.

That was what they did. On and on, through rocks and brambles and thorns and deadfalls and cactus and dry washes and tree branches that lashed back into their faces and cut their skin like whips. The sky was as black as oil smoke, the explosions of lightning deafening inside the canyons. But when the four of them ascended a trail that led to a bare knoll, a peculiar event happened. They found themselves in front of two telegraph poles that had no wires attached to the crosspieces; to the west of the knoll was an infinite plain that seemed to extend beyond the edge of the storm into a band of blue sky on the earth's rim. The wind was bitter and filled with grit, the telegraph poles trembling in the holes where they were sunk, a twisted piece of metal roof bouncing and clanging across the knoll's surface. Krill stood at the top of the knoll, his arms hanging over the rifle and shotgun stretched across his shoulders.

"It's stopped raining," he said. "Look, you can see it blowing like crystal behind us and out on the plain and down in the canyon, but here there is no rain. *Qué bueno.* I think I will stay right here."

"Come with us," Anton said.

"No, this is my place. I am content here," he replied. "Good-bye to you, Chinese mermaid. And thank you, Sheriff Holland and Señorita Pam. All of you are very nice."

So this is how it ends, Hackberry thought. A man under a capital sentence stands impaled in a grandiose fashion against a blackened sky, ignoring the fact that he has become a human lightning rod, while two women and another man gaze up at him, all of them stenciled like figures on a triptych, all of them caught in roles they did not choose for themselves.

Maybe the mermaids have not made it to Texas yet, but give them time, and in the meanwhile blessed be God for all dappled things, wherever they occur, Hackberry said to himself, his eyes fixed on the band of blue light in the west.

ABOUT THE AUTHOR

James Lee Burke was born in Houston, Texas, in 1936 and grew up on the Texas-Louisiana Gulf Coast. He attended Southwestern Louisiana Institute and later received a BA and an MA in English from the University of Missouri in 1958 and 1960, respectively. Over the years, he worked as a landman for the Sinclair Oil Company, pipe liner, land surveyor, newspaper reporter, college English professor, social worker on skid row in Los Angeles, clerk for the Louisiana Employment Service, and instructor in the U.S. Job Corps. He and his wife, Pearl, met in graduate school and have been married fifty-one years; they have four children.

Burke's work has twice been awarded an Edgar for Best Crime Novel of the Year; in 2009 the Mystery Writers of America named him a Grand Master. He has also been a recipient of Bread Loaf and Guggenheim fellowships and an NEA grant. Three of his novels (*Heaven's Prisoners, Two for Texas,* and

In the Electric Mist with Confederate Dead) have been made into motion pictures. His short stories have been published in *The Atlantic Monthly, New Stories from the South, Best American Short Stories, Antioch Review, Southern Review,* and *The Kenyon Review.* His novel *The Lost Get-Back Boogie* was rejected 111 times over a period of nine years and, upon its publication by Louisiana State University Press in 1986, was nominated for a Pulitzer Prize.

He and Pearl live in Missoula, Montana.

We hope you have enjoyed this Large Print book. Other Thorndike, Wheeler, Kennebec, and Chivers Press Large Print books are available at your library or directly from the publishers.

For information about current and upcoming titles, please call or write, without obligation, to:

Publisher
Thorndike Press
10 Water St., Suite 310
Waterville, ME 04901
Tel. (800) 223-1244

or visit our Web site at:

http://gale.cengage.com/thorndike

OR

Chivers Large Print
published by AudioGO Ltd
St James House, The Square
Lower Bristol Road
Bath BA2 3SB
England
Tel. +44(0) 800 136919
email: info@audiogo.co.uk
www.audiogo.co.uk

All our Large Print titles are designed for easy reading, and all our books are made to last.